Agatha Christie

Postern of Fate

HarperCollins*Publishers*

HarperCollins*Publishers*
77–85 Fulham Palace Road
Hammersmith, London W6 8JB
www.**fire**and**water**.com

This *Agatha Christie Signature Edition* published 2001
3 5 7 9 8 6 4 2

First published in Great Britain by
Collins 1973

ISBN 0 00 711148 7

Typeset by Palimpsest Book Production Limited,
Polmont, Stirlingshire

Printed and bound in Great Britain by
Omnia Books Limited, Glasgow

Postern of Fate

Agatha Christie is known throughout the world as the Queen of Crime. Her books have sold over a billion copies in English with another billion in 100 foreign languages. She is the most widely published author of all time and in any language, outsold only by the Bible and Shakespeare. She is the author of 80 crime novels and short story collections, 19 plays, and six novels written under the name of Mary Westmacott.

Agatha Christie's first novel, *The Mysterious Affair at Styles*, was written towards the end of the First World War, in which she served as a VAD. In it she created Hercule Poirot, the little Belgian detective who was destined to become the most popular detective in crime fiction since Sherlock Holmes. It was eventually published by The Bodley Head in 1920.

In 1926, after averaging a book a year, Agatha Christie wrote her masterpiece. *The Murder of Roger Ackroyd* was the first of her books to be published by Collins and marked the beginning of an author-publisher relationship which lasted for 50 years and well over 70 books. *The Murder of Roger Ackroyd* was also the first of Agatha Christie's books to be dramatized – under the name *Alibi* – and to have a successful run in London's West End. *The Mousetrap*, her most famous play of all, opened in 1952 and is the longest-running play in history.

Agatha Christie was made a Dame in 1971. She died in 1976, since when a number of books have been published posthumously: the bestselling novel *Sleeping Murder* appeared later that year, followed by her autobiography and the short story collections *Miss Marple's Final Cases*, *Problem at Pollensa Bay* and *While the Light Lasts*. In 1998 *Black Coffee* was the first of her plays to be novelized by another author, Charles Osborne.

The Agatha Christie Collection

The Man In The Brown Suit
The Secret of Chimneys
The Seven Dials Mystery
The Mysterious Mr Quin
The Sittaford Mystery
The Hound of Death
The Listerdale Mystery
Why Didn't They Ask Evans?
Parker Pyne Investigates
Murder Is Easy
And Then There Were None
Towards Zero
Death Comes as the End
Sparkling Cyanide
Crooked House
They Came to Baghdad
Destination Unknown
Spider's Web *
The Unexpected Guest *
Ordeal by Innocence
The Pale Horse
Endless Night
Passenger To Frankfurt
Problem at Pollensa Bay
While the Light Lasts

Poirot

The Mysterious Affair at Styles
The Murder on the Links
Poirot Investigates
The Murder of Roger Ackroyd
The Big Four
The Mystery of the Blue Train
Black Coffee *
Peril at End House
Lord Edgware Dies
Murder on the Orient Express
Three-Act Tragedy
Death in the Clouds
The ABC Murders
Murder in Mesopotamia
Cards on the Table
Murder in the Mews
Dumb Witness
Death on the Nile
Appointment With Death
Hercule Poirot's Christmas
Sad Cypress
One, Two, Buckle My Shoe
Evil Under the Sun
Five Little Pigs
The Hollow
The Labours of Hercules
Taken at the Flood
Mrs McGinty's Dead
After the Funeral
Hickory Dickory Dock
Dead Man's Folly
Cat Among the Pigeons
The Adventure of the Christmas Pudding
The Clocks
Third Girl
Hallowe'en Party
Elephants Can Remember
Poirot's Early Cases
Curtain: Poirot's Last Case

Marple

The Murder at the Vicarage
The Thirteen Problems
The Body in the Library
The Moving Finger
A Murder is Announced
They Do It With Mirrors
A Pocket Full of Rye
The 4.50 from Paddington
The Mirror Crack'd from Side to Side
A Caribbean Mystery
At Bertram's Hotel
Nemesis
Sleeping Murder
Miss Marple's Final Cases

Tommy & Tuppence

The Secret Adversary
Partners in Crime
N or M?
By the Pricking of My Thumbs
Postern of Fate

Published as Mary Westmacott

Giant's Bread
Unfinished Portrait
Absent in the Spring
The Rose and the Yew Tree
A Daughter's a Daughter
The Burden

Memoirs

An Autobiography
Come, Tell Me How You Live

Play Collections

The Mousetrap and Selected Plays
Witness for the Prosecution and Selected Plays

* novelised by Charles Osborne

For Hannibal and his master

Contents

Book I

Book II

Book III

Four great gates has the city of Damascus . . .
Postern of Fate, the Desert Gate, Disaster's Cavern,
  Fort of Fear . . .
Pass not beneath, O Caravan, or pass not singing.
  Have you heard
That silence where the birds are dead, yet something
  pipeth like a bird?

from *Gates of Damascus* by James Elroy Flecker

Book I

Chapter 1

Mainly Concerning Books

'Books!' said Tuppence.

She produced the word rather with the effect of a bad-tempered explosion.

'What did you say?' said Tommy.

Tuppence looked across the room at him.

'I said "books",' she said.

'I see what you mean,' said Thomas Beresford.

In front of Tuppence were three large packing cases. From each of them various books had been extracted. The larger part of them were still filled with books.

'It's incredible,' said Tuppence.

'You mean the room they take up?'

'Yes.'

'Are you trying to put them all on the shelves?'

'I don't know what I'm trying to do,' said Tuppence. 'That's the awkward part of it. One doesn't know ever, exactly, what one wants to do. Oh dear,' she sighed.

'Really,' said her husband, 'I should have thought that that was not at all characteristic of you. The trouble with you has always been that you knew much too well what you *do* want to do.'

'What I mean is,' said Tuppence, 'that here we are, getting older, getting a bit – well, let's face it – definitely rheumatic, especially when one is stretching; you know, stretching putting in books or lifting things down from shelves or kneeling down to look at the bottom shelves for something, then finding it a bit difficult to get up again.'

'Yes, yes,' said Tommy, 'that's an account of our general disabilities. Is that what you started to say?'

'No, it isn't what I started to say. What I started to say was, it was lovely to be able to buy a new home and find just the place we wanted to go and live in, and just the house there we'd always dreamt of having – with a little alteration, of course.'

'Knocking one or two rooms into each other,' said Tommy, 'and adding to it what you call a veranda and your builder calls a lodger, though I prefer to call it a loggia.'

'And it's going to be very nice,' said Tuppence firmly.

'When you've done it I shan't know it! Is that the answer?' said Tommy.

'Not at all. All I said was that when you see it finished

you're going to be delighted and say what an ingenious and clever and artistic wife you have.'

'All right,' said Tommy. 'I'll remember the right thing to say.'

'You won't need to remember,' said Tuppence. 'It will burst upon you.'

'What's that got to do with books?' said Tommy.

'Well, we brought two or three cases of books with us. I mean, we sold off the books we didn't much care about. We brought the ones we really couldn't bear to part with, and then, of course, the what-you-call-'ems – I can't remember their name now, but the people who were selling us this house – they didn't want to take a lot of their own things with them, and they said if we'd like to make an offer they would leave things including books, and we came and looked at things –'

'And we made some offers,' said Tommy.

'Yes. Not as many as they hoped we would make, I expect. Some of the furniture and ornaments were too horrible. Well, fortunately we didn't have to take those, but when I came and saw the various books – there were some nursery ones, you know, some down in the sitting-room – and there are one or two old favourites. I mean, there still are. There are one or two of my own special favourites. And so I thought it'd be such fun to have them. You know, the story of Androcles and the

Lion,' she said. 'I remember reading that when I was eight years old. Andrew Lang.'

'Tell me, Tuppence, were you clever enough to read at eight years old?'

'Yes,' said Tuppence, 'I read at five years old. Everybody could, when I was young. I didn't know one even had to sort of learn. I mean, somebody would read stories aloud, and you liked them very much and you remembered where the book went back on the shelf and you were always allowed to take it out and have a look at it yourself, and so you found you were reading it too, without bothering to learn to spell or anything like that. It wasn't so good later,' she said, 'because I've never been able to spell very well. And if somebody had taught me to spell when I was about four years old I can see it would have been very good indeed. My father did teach me to do addition and subtraction and multiplication, of course, because he said the multiplication table was the most useful thing you could learn in life, and I learnt long division too.'

'What a clever man he must have been!'

'I don't think he was specially clever,' said Tuppence, 'but he was just very, very nice.'

'Aren't we getting away from the point?'

'Yes, we are,' said Tuppence. 'Well, as I said, when I thought of reading Androcles and the Lion again – it came in a book of stories about animals, I think, by Andrew Lang – oh, I loved that. And there was a story about "a day in my life at Eton" by an Eton schoolboy. I can't think why I wanted to read that, but I did. It was one of my favourite books. And there were some stories from the classics, and there was Mrs Molesworth, *The Cuckoo Clock, Four Winds Farm* –'

'Well, that's all right,' said Tommy. 'No need to give me a whole account of your literary triumphs in early youth.'

'What I mean is,' said Tuppence, 'that you can't get them nowadays. I mean, sometimes you get reprints of them, but they've usually been altered and have different pictures in them. Really, the other day I couldn't recognize *Alice in Wonderland* when I saw it. Everything looks so peculiar in it. There are the books I really could get still. Mrs Molesworth, one or two of the old fairy books – Pink, Blue and Yellow – and then, of course, lots of later ones which I'd enjoyed. Lots of Stanley Weymans and things like that. There are quite a lot here, left behind.'

'All right,' said Tommy. 'You were tempted. You felt it was a good buy.'

'Yes. At least – what d'you mean a "goodbye"?'

'I mean b-u-y,' said Tommy.

'Oh. I thought you were going to leave the room and were saying goodbye to me.'

'Not at all,' said Tommy, 'I was deeply interested. Anyway, it *was* a good b-u-y.'

'And I got them very cheap, as I tell you. And – and here they all are among our own books and others. Only, we've got such a terrible lot now of books, and the shelves we had made I don't think are going to be nearly enough. What about your special sanctum? Is there room there for more books?'

'No, there isn't,' said Tommy. 'There's not going to be enough for my own.'

'Oh dear, oh dear,' said Tuppence, 'that's so like us. Do you think we might have to build on an extra room?'

'No,' said Tommy, 'we're going to economize. We said so the day before yesterday. Do you remember?'

'That was the day before yesterday,' said Tuppence. 'Time alters. What I am going to do now is put in these shelves all the books I really can't bear to part with. And then – and then we can look at the others and – well, there might be a children's hospital somewhere and there might, anyway, be places which would like books.'

'Or we could sell them,' said Tommy.

'I don't suppose they're the sort of books people would want to buy very much. I don't think there are any books of rare value or anything like that.'

'You never know your luck,' said Tommy. 'Let's

hope something out of print will fulfil some bookseller's long-felt want.'

'In the meantime,' said Tuppence, 'we have to put them into the shelves, and look inside them, of course, each time to see whether it's a book I do really want and I can really remember. I'm trying to get them roughly – well, you know what I mean, sort of sorted. I mean, adventure stories, fairy stories, children's stories and those stories about schools, where the children were always very rich – L. T. Meade, I think. And some of the books we used to read to Deborah when she was small, too. How we all used to love *Winnie the Pooh.* And there was *The Little Grey Hen* too, but I didn't care very much for that.'

'I think you're tiring yourself,' said Tommy. 'I think I should leave off what you're doing now.'

'Well, perhaps I will,' said Tuppence, 'but I think if I could just finish this side of the room, just get the books in here . . .'

'Well, I'll help you,' said Tommy.

He came over, tilted the case so that the books fell out, gathered up armfuls of them and went to the shelves and shoved them in.

'I'm putting the same sized ones together, it looks neater,' he said.

'Oh, I don't call that sorting,' said Tuppence.

'Sorting enough to get on with. We can do more

of that later. You know, make everything really nice. We'll sort it on some wet day when we can't think of anything else to do.'

'The trouble is we always can think of something else to do.'

'Well now, there's another seven in there. Now then, there's only this top corner. Just bring me that wooden chair over there, will you? Are its legs strong enough for me to stand on it? Then I can put some on the top shelf.'

With some care he climbed on the chair. Tuppence lifted up to him an armful of books. He insinuated them with some care on to the top shelf. Disaster only happened with the last three which cascaded to the floor, narrowly missing Tuppence.

'Oh,' said Tuppence, 'that was painful.'

'Well, I can't help it. You handed me up too many at once.'

'Oh well, that does look wonderful,' said Tuppence, standing back a little. 'Now then, if you'll just put these in the second shelf from the bottom, there's a gap there, that will finish up this particular caseful anyway. It's a good thing too. These ones I'm doing this morning aren't really ours, they're the ones we bought. We may find treasures.'

'We may,' said Tommy.

'I think we shall find treasures. I think I really shall

find something. Something that's worth a lot of money, perhaps.'

'What do we do then? Sell it?'

'I expect we'll have to sell it, yes,' said Tuppence. 'Of course we might just keep it and show it to people. You know, not exactly boasting, but just say, you know: "Oh yes, we've got really one or two interesting finds." I think we shall make an interesting find, too.'

'What – one old favourite you've forgotten about?'

'Not exactly that. I meant something startling, surprising. Something that'll make all the difference to our lives.'

'Oh Tuppence,' said Tommy, 'what a wonderful mind you've got. Much more likely to find something that's an absolute disaster.'

'Nonsense,' said Tuppence. 'One must have hope. It's the great thing you have to have in life. Hope. Remember? I'm always full of hope.'

'I know you are,' said Tommy. He sighed. 'I've often regretted it.'

Chapter 2

The Black Arrow

Mrs Thomas Beresford replaced *The Cuckoo Clock*, by Mrs Molesworth, choosing a vacant place on the third shelf from the bottom. The Mrs Molesworths were congregated here together. Tuppence drew out *The Tapestry Room* and held it thoughtfully in her fingers. Or she might read *Four Winds Farm*. She couldn't remember *Four Winds Farm* as well as she could remember *The Cuckoo Clock* and *The Tapestry Room*. Her fingers wandered . . . Tommy would be back soon.

She was getting on. Yes, surely she was getting on. If only she didn't stop and pull out old favourites and read them. Very agreeable but it took a lot of time. And when Tommy asked her in the evening when he came home how things were going and she said, 'Oh very well now,' she had to employ a great deal of tact and finesse to prevent him from going upstairs and having a real look at how the bookshelves were progressing. It all took a long time. Getting into a house always took a long time, much longer than one thought. And so many irritating people. Electricians, for instance, who came and appeared to be displeased with what they had done the last time they came and took up more large areas in the floor and, with cheerful faces, produced more pitfalls for the unwary housewife to walk along and put a foot wrong and be rescued just in time by the unseen electrician who was groping beneath the floor.

'Sometimes,' said Tuppence, 'I really wish we hadn't left Bartons Acre.'

'Remember the dining-room,' Tommy had said, 'and remember those attics, and remember what happened to the garage. Nearly wrecked the car, you know it did.'

'I suppose we could have had it patched up,' said Tuppence.

'No,' said Tommy, 'we'd have had to practically replace the damaged building, or else we had to move. This is going to be a very nice house some day. I'm quite sure of that. Anyway, there's going to be room in it for all the things we want to do.'

'When you say the things we want to do,' Tuppence had said, 'you mean the things we want to find places for and to keep.'

'I know,' said Tommy. 'One keeps far too much. I couldn't agree with you more.'

At that moment Tuppence considered something – whether they ever were going to do anything with this house, that is to say, beyond getting into it. It sounded simple but had turned out complex. Partly, of course, all these books.

'If I'd been a nice ordinary child of nowadays,' said Tuppence, 'I wouldn't have learned to read so easily when I was young. Children nowadays who are four, or five, or six, don't seem to be able to read when they get to ten or eleven. I can't think why it was so easy for all of us. We could all read. Me and Martin next door and Jennifer down the road and Cyril and Winifred. All of us. I don't mean we could all spell very well but we could read anything we wanted to. I don't know how we learnt. Asking people, I suppose. Things about posters and Carter's Little Liver Pills. We used to read all about them in the fields when trains got near London. It was very exciting. I always wondered what they were. Oh dear, I must think of what I'm doing.'

She removed some more books. Three-quarters of an hour passed with her absorbed first in *Alice Through the Looking-Glass*, then with Charlotte Yonge's *Unknown to History*. Her hands lingered over the fat shabbiness of *The Daisy Chain*.

'Oh, I must read that again,' said Tuppence. 'To think of the years and years and years it is since I did read it. Oh dear, how exciting it was, wondering, you know, whether Norman was going to be allowed to be confirmed or not. And Ethel and – what was the name of the place? Coxwell or something like – and Flora who was worldly. I wonder why everyone was "worldly" in those days, and how poorly it was thought of, being worldly. I wonder what we are now. Do you think we're all worldly or not?'

'I beg yer pardon, ma'am?'

'Oh nothing,' said Tuppence, looking round at her devoted henchman, Albert, who had just appeared in the doorway.

'I thought you called for something, madam. And you rang the bell, didn't you?'

'Not really,' said Tuppence. 'I just leant on it getting up on a chair to take a book out.'

'Is there anything I can take down for you?'

'Well, I wish you would,' said Tuppence. 'I'm falling off those chairs. Some of their legs are very wobbly, some of them rather slippery.'

'Any book in particular?'

'Well, I haven't got on very far with the third shelf up. Two shelves down from the top, you know. I don't know what books are there.'

Albert mounted on a chair and banging each book in

turn to dislodge such dust as it had managed to gather on it, handed things down. Tuppence received them with a good deal of rapture.

'Oh, fancy! All these. I really have forgotten a lot of these. Oh, here's *The Amulet* and here's *The Psamayad*. Here's *The New Treasure Seekers*. Oh, I love all those. No, don't put them in shelves yet, Albert. I think I'll have to read them first. Well, I mean, one or two of them first, perhaps. Now, what's this one? Let me see. *The Red Cockade*. Oh yes, that was one of the historical ones. That was very exciting. And there's *Under the Red Robe*, too. Lots of Stanley Weyman. Lots and lots. Of course I used to read those when I was about ten or eleven. I shouldn't be surprised if I don't come across *The Prisoner of Zenda*.' She sighed with enormous pleasure at the remembrance. '*The Prisoner of Zenda*. One's first introduction, really, to the romantic novel. The romance of Princess Flavia. The King of Ruritania. Rudolph Rassendyll, some name like that, whom one dreamt of at night.'

Albert handed down another selection.

'Oh yes,' said Tuppence, 'That's better, really. That's earlier again. I must put the early ones all together. Now, let me see. What have we got here? *Treasure Island*. Well, that's nice but of course I have read *Treasure Island* again, and I've seen, I think, two films of it. I don't like seeing it on films, it never seems right. Oh – and here's *Kidnapped*. Yes, I always liked that.'

Albert stretched up, overdid his armful, and *Catriona* fell more or less on Tuppence's head.

'Oh, sorry, madam. Very sorry.'

'It's quite all right,' said Tuppence, 'it doesn't matter. *Catriona*. Yes. Any more Stevensons up there?'

Albert handed the books down now more gingerly. Tuppence uttered a cry of excessive delight.

'*The Black Arrow* I declare! *The Black Arrow*! Now that's one of the first books really I ever got hold of and read. Yes. I don't suppose you ever did, Albert. I mean, you wouldn't have been born, would you? Now let me think. Let me think. *The Black Arrow*. Yes, of course, it was that picture on the wall with eyes – real eyes – looking through the eyes of the picture. It was splendid. So frightening, just that. Oh yes. *The Black Arrow*. What was it? It was all about – oh yes, the cat, the dog? No. *The cat, the rat, and Lovell, the dog, Rule all England under the hog*. That's it. The hog was Richard the Third, of course. Though nowadays they all write books saying he was really wonderful. Not a villain at all. But I don't believe that. Shakespeare didn't either. After all, he started his play by making Richard say: "I am determined so to prove a villain." Ah yes. *The Black Arrow*.'

'Some more, madam?'

'No, thank you, Albert. I think I'm rather too tired to go on now.'

'That's all right. By the way, the master rang and said he'd be half an hour late.'

'Never mind,' said Tuppence.

She sat down in the chair, took *The Black Arrow*, opened the pages and engrossed herself.

'Oh dear,' she said, 'how wonderful this is. I've really forgotten it quite enough to enjoy reading it all over again. It was so exciting.'

Silence fell. Albert returned to the kitchen. Tuppence leaned back in the chair. Time passed. Curled up in the rather shabby armchair, Mrs Thomas Beresford sought the joys of the past by applying herself to the perusal of Robert Louis Stevenson's *The Black Arrow*.

In the kitchen time also passed. Albert applied himself to the various manoeuvres with the stove. A car drove up. Albert went to the side door.

'Shall I put it in the garage, sir?'

'No,' said Tommy, 'I'll do that. I expect you're busy with dinner. Am I very late?'

'Not really, sir, just about when you said. A little early, in fact.'

'Oh.' Tommy disposed of the car and then came into the kitchen, rubbing his hands. 'Cold out. Where's Tuppence?'

'Oh, missus, she's upstairs with the books.'

'What, still those miserable books?'

'Yes. She's done a good many more today and she's spent most of the time reading.'

'Oh dear,' said Tommy. 'All right, Albert. What are we having?'

'Fillets of lemon sole, sir. It won't take long to do.'

'All right. Well, make it about quarter of an hour or so anyway. I want to wash first.'

Upstairs, on the top floor Tuppence was still sitting in the somewhat shabby armchair, engrossed in *The Black Arrow*. Her forehead was slightly wrinkled. She had come across what seemed to her a somewhat curious phenomenon. There seemed to be what she could only call a kind of interference. The particular page she had got to – she gave it a brief glance, 64 or was it 65? She couldn't see – anyway, apparently somebody had underlined some of the words on the page. Tuppence had spent the last quarter of an hour studying this phenomenon. She didn't see why the words had been underlined. They were not in sequence, they were not a quotation, therefore, in the book. They seemed to be words that had been singled out and had then been underlined in red ink. She read under her breath: 'Matcham could not restrain a little cry. Dick started with surprise and dropped the windac from his fingers. They were all afoot, loosing sword and dagger in the sheath. Ellis held up his hand. The white of his eyes shone. Let, large –' Tuppence shook her head. It didn't make sense. None of it did.

She went over to the table where she kept her writing things, picked out a few sheets recently sent by a firm of note-paper printers for the Beresfords to make a choice of the paper to be stamped with their new address: The Laurels.

'Silly name,' said Tuppence, 'but if you go changing names all the time, then all your letters go astray.'

She copied things down. Now she realized something she hadn't realized before.

'That makes all the difference,' said Tuppence.

She traced letters on the page.

'So there you are,' said Tommy's voice, suddenly. 'Dinner's practically in. How are the books going?'

'This lot's terribly puzzling,' said Tuppence. 'Dreadfully puzzling.'

'What's puzzling?'

'Well, this is *The Black Arrow* of Stevenson's and I wanted to read it again and I began. It was all right, and then suddenly – all the pages were rather queer because I mean a lot of the words had been underlined in red ink.'

'Oh well, one does that,' said Tommy. 'I don't mean solely in red ink, but I mean one does underline things. You know, something you want to remember, or a quotation of something. Well, you know what I mean.'

'I know what you mean,' said Tuppence, 'but it doesn't go like that. And it's letters, you see.'

'What do you mean by letters?'

'Come here,' said Tuppence.

Tommy came and sat on the arm of the chair. Tommy read: '"Matcham could not restrain a little cry and even died starter started with surprise and dropped the window from his fingers the two big fellows on the – something I can't read – shell was an expected signal. They were all afoot together tightening loosing sword and dagger." It's mad,' he said.

'Yes,' said Tuppence, 'that's what I thought at first. It was mad. But it isn't mad, Tommy.'

Some cowbells rang from downstairs.

'That's supper in.'

'Never mind,' said Tuppence, 'I've got to tell you this first. We can get down to things about it later but it's really so extraordinary. I've got to tell you this straight away.'

'Oh, all right. Have you got one of your mare's nests?

'No, I haven't. It's just that I took out the letters, you see. Well – on this page, you see, well – the M of "Matcham" which is the first word, the M is underlined and the A and after that there are three more, three or four more words. They don't come in sequence in the book. They've just been picked out, I think, and they've been underlined – the letters in them – because they wanted the right letters and the next one, you see, is the R from "restrain" underlined and the Y of "cry", and then there's J from "Jack", O from "shot", R from "ruin", D from "death" and A from "death" again, N from "murrain" –'

'For goodness' sake,' said Tommy, 'do stop.'

'Wait,' said Tuppence. 'I've got to find out. Now you see because I've written out these, do you see what this is? I mean if you take those letters out and write them in order on this piece of paper, do you see what you get with the ones I've done first? M-A-R-Y. Those four were underlined.'

'What does that make?'

'It makes Mary.'

'All right,' said Tommy, 'it makes Mary. Somebody called Mary. A child with an inventive nature, I expect, who is trying to point out that this was her book. People are always writing their names in books and things like that.'

'All right. Mary,' said Tuppence. 'And the next thing that comes underlined makes the word J-o-r-d-a-n.'

'You see? Mary Jordan,' said Tommy. 'It's quite natural. Now you know her whole name. Her name was Mary Jordan.'

'Well, this book didn't belong to her. In the beginning it says in a rather silly, childish-looking writing, it says "Alexander", Alexander Parkinson, I think.'

'Oh well. Does it really matter?'

'Of course it matters,' said Tuppence.

'Come on, I'm hungry,' said Tommy.

'Restrain yourself,' said Tuppence, 'I'm only going to read you the next bit until the writing stops – or at any rate stops in the next four pages. The letters are picked from odd places on various pages. They don't run in sequence – there can't be anything in the words that matters – it's just the letters. Now then. We've got M-a-r-y J-o-r-d-a-n. That's right. Now do you know what the next four words are? D-i-d n-o-t, not, d-i-e n-a-t-u-r-a-l-y. That's meant to be "naturally", but they didn't know it had two "*l*s". Now then, what's that? *Mary Jordan did not die naturally*. There you are,' said Tuppence. 'Now the next sentence made is: *It was one of us. I think I know which one.* That's all. Can't find anything else. But it is rather exciting, isn't it?'

'Look here, Tuppence,' said Tommy, 'you're not going to get a thing about this, are you?'

'What do you mean, a thing, about this?'

'Well, I mean working up a sort of mystery.'

'Well, it's a mystery to me,' said Tuppence. '*Mary Jordan did not die naturally. It was one of us. I think I know which.* Oh, Tommy, you must say that it is very intriguing.'

Chapter 3

Visit to the Cemetery

'Tuppence!' Tommy called, as he came into the house.

There was no answer. With some annoyance, he ran up the stairs and along the passage on the first floor. As he hastened along it, he nearly put his foot through a gaping hole, and swore promptly.

'Some other bloody careless electrician,' he said.

Some days before he had had the same kind of trouble. Electricians arriving in a kindly tangle of optimism and efficiency had started work. 'Coming along fine now, not much more to do,' they said. 'We'll be back this afternoon.' But they hadn't been back that afternoon; Tommy was not precisely surprised. He was used, now, to the general pattern of labour in the building trade, electrical trade, gas employees and others. They came, they showed efficiency, they made optimistic remarks, they went away to fetch something. They didn't come back. One rang up numbers on the telephone but they always seemed to be the wrong numbers. If they were the right numbers, the right man was not working at this particular branch of the trade, whatever it was. All one had to do was to be careful to not rick an ankle, fall through a hole, damage yourself in some way or another. He was far more afraid of Tuppence damaging herself than he was of doing the damage to himself. He had had more experience than Tuppence. Tuppence, he thought, was more at risk from scalding herself from kettles or disasters with the heat of the stove. But where was Tuppence now? He called again.

'Tuppence! Tuppence!'

He worried about Tuppence. Tuppence was one of those people you had to worry about. If you left the house, you gave her last words of wisdom and she gave you last promises of doing exactly what you counselled her to do: No she would not be going out except just to buy half a pound of butter, and after all you couldn't call that dangerous, could you?

'It could be dangerous if *you* went out to buy half a pound of butter,' said Tommy.

'Oh,' said Tuppence, 'don't be an idiot.'

'I'm not being an idiot,' Tommy had said. 'I am just being a wise and careful husband, looking after something which is one of my favourite possessions. I don't know why it is –'

'Because,' said Tuppence, 'I am so charming, so good-looking, such a good companion and because I take so much care of you.'

'That also, maybe,' said Tommy, 'but I could give you another list.'

'I don't feel I should like that,' said Tuppence. 'No, I don't think so. I think you have several saved-up grievances. But don't worry. Everything will be quite all right. You've only got to come back and call me when you get in.'

But now where was Tuppence?

'The little devil,' said Tommy. 'She's gone out somewhere.'

He went on into the room upstairs where he had found her before. Looking at another child's book, he supposed. Getting excited again about some silly words that a silly child had underlined in red ink. On the trail of Mary Jordan, whoever she was. Mary Jordan, who hadn't died a natural death. He couldn't help wondering. A long time ago, presumably, the people who'd had the house and sold it to them had been named Jones. They hadn't been there very long, only three or four years. No, this child of the Robert Louis Stevenson book dated from further back than that. Anyway, Tuppence wasn't here in this room. There seemed to be no loose books lying about with signs of having had interest shown in them.

'Ah, where the hell can she be?' said Thomas.

He went downstairs again, shouting once or twice. There was no answer. Hc cxamined one of the pegs in the hall. No signs of Tuppence's mackintosh. Then she'd gone out. Where had she gone? And where was Hannibal? Tommy varied the use of his vocal cords and called out for Hannibal.

'Hannibal – Hannibal – Hanny-boy. Come on, Hannibal.'

No Hannibal.

Well, at any rate, she's got Hannibal with her, thought Tommy.

He didn't know if it was worse or better that Tuppence should have Hannibal. Hannibal would certainly allow no harm to come to Tuppence. The question was, might Hannibal do some damage to other people? He was friendly when taken visiting people, but people who wished to visit Hannibal, to enter any house in which he lived, were always definitely suspect in Hannibal's mind. He was ready at all risks to both bark and bite if he considered it necessary. Anyway, where was everybody?

He walked a little way along the street, could see no signs of any small black dog with a medium-sized woman in a bright red mackintosh walking in the distance. Finally, rather angrily, he came back to the house.

Rather an appetizing smell met him. He went quickly to the kitchen, where Tuppence turned from the stove and gave him a smile of welcome.

'You're ever so late,' she said. 'This is a casserole. Smells rather good, don't you think? I put some rather unusual things in it this time. There were some herbs in the garden, at least I hope they were herbs.'

'If they weren't herbs,' said Tommy, 'I suppose they were Deadly Nightshade, or Digitalis leaves pretending to be something else but really foxglove. Where on earth have you been?'

'I took Hannibal for a walk.'

Hannibal, at this moment, made his own presence felt. He rushed at Tommy and gave him such a rapturous welcome as nearly to fell him to the ground. Hannibal was a small black dog, very glossy, with interesting tan patches on his behind and each side of his cheeks. He was a Manchester terrier of very pure pedigree and he considered himself to be on a much higher level of sophistication and aristocracy than any other dog he met.

'Oh, good gracious. I took a look round. Where've you been? It wasn't very nice weather.'

'No, it wasn't. It was very sort of foggy and misty. Ah – I'm quite tired, too.'

'Where did you go? Just down the street for the shops?'

'No, it's early closing day for the shops. No . . . Oh no, I went to the cemetery.'

'Sounds gloomy,' said Tommy. 'What did you want to go to the cemetery for?'

'I went to look at some of the graves.'

'It still sounds rather gloomy,' said Tommy. 'Did Hannibal enjoy himself?'

'Well, I had to put Hannibal on the lead. There was something that looked like a verger who kept coming out of the church and I thought he wouldn't like Hannibal because – well, you never know, Hannibal mightn't like him and I didn't want to prejudice people against us the moment we'd arrived.'

'What did you want to look in the cemetery for?'

'Oh, to see what sort of people were buried there. Lots of people, I mean it's very, very full up. It goes back a long way. It goes back well in the eighteen hundreds and I think one or two older than that, only the stone's so rubbed away you can't really see.'

'I still don't see why you wanted to go to the cemetery.'

'I was making my investigations,' said Tuppence.

'Investigations about what?'

'I wanted to see if there were any Jordans buried there.'

'Good gracious,' said Tommy. 'Are you still on that? Were you looking for –'

'Well, Mary Jordan died. We know she died. We know because we had a book that said she didn't die a natural death, but she'd still have to be buried somewhere, wouldn't she?'

'Undeniably,' said Tommy, 'unless she was buried in this garden.'

'I don't think that's very likely,' said Tuppence, 'because I think that it was only this boy or girl – it must have been a boy, I think – of course it was a boy, his name was Alexander – and he obviously thought he'd been rather clever in knowing that she'd not died a natural death. But if he was the only person who'd made up his mind about that or who'd discovered it – well, I mean, nobody else had, I suppose. I mean, she just died and was buried and nobody said . . .'

'Nobody said there had been foul play,' suggested Tommy.

'That sort of thing, yes. Poisoned or knocked on the head or pushed off a cliff or run over by a car or – oh, lots of ways I can think of.'

'I'm sure you can,' said Tommy. 'Only good thing about you, Tuppence, is that at least you have a kindly heart. You wouldn't put them into execution just for fun.'

'But there wasn't any Mary Jordan in the cemetery. There weren't any Jordans.'

'Disappointing for you,' said Tommy. 'Is that thing

you're cooking ready yet, because I'm pretty hungry. It smells rather good.'

'It's absolutely done *à point*,' said Tuppence. 'So, as soon as you've washed, we eat.'

Chapter 4

Lots of Parkinsons

'Lots of Parkinsons,' said Tuppence as they ate. 'A long way back but an amazing lot of them. Old ones, young ones and married ones. Bursting with Parkinsons. And Capes, and Griffins and Underwoods and Overwoods. Curious to have both of them, isn't it?'

'I had a friend called George Underwood,' said Tommy.

'Yes, I've known Underwoods, too. But not Overwoods.'

'Male or female?' said Thomas, with slight interest.

'A girl, I think it was. Rose Overwood.'

'Rose Overwood,' said Tommy, listening to the sound of it. 'I don't think somehow it goes awfully well together.' He added, 'I must ring up those electricians after lunch. Be very careful, Tuppence, or you'll put your foot through the landing upstairs.'

'Then I shall be a natural death, or an unnatural death, one of the two.'

'A curiosity death,' said Tommy. 'Curiosity killed the cat.'

'Aren't you at all curious?' asked Tuppence.

'I can't see any earthly reason for being curious. What have we got for pudding?'

'Treacle tart.'

'Well, I must say, Tuppence, it was a delicious meal.'

'I'm very glad you liked it,' said Tuppence.

'What is that parcel outside the back door? Is it that wine we ordered?'

'No,' said Tuppence, 'it's bulbs.'

'Oh,' said Tommy, 'bulbs.'

'Tulips,' said Tuppence. 'I'll go and talk to old Isaac about them.'

'Where are you going to put them?'

'I think along the centre path in the garden.'

'Poor old fellow, he looks as if he might drop dead any minute,' said Tommy.

'Not at all,' said Tuppence. 'He's enormously tough, is Isaac. I've discovered, you know, that gardeners are like that. If they're very good gardeners they seem to come to their prime when they're over eighty, but if you get a strong, hefty-looking young man about thirty-five who says, "I've always wanted to work in a garden," you may be quite sure that he's probably no good at all. They're just prepared to brush up a few leaves now and again and anything you want them to do they always say it's the wrong time of year, and as one never knows oneself when the right time of year is, at least I don't, well then, you see, they always get the better of you. But Isaac's wonderful. He knows about everything.' Tuppence added, 'There ought to be some crocuses as well. I wonder if they're in the parcel, too. Well, I'll go out and see. It's his day for coming and he'll tell me all about it.'

'All right,' said Tommy, 'I'll come out and join you presently.'

Tuppence and Isaac had a pleasant reunion. The bulbs were unpacked, discussions were held as to where things would show to best advantage. First the early tulips, which were expected to rejoice the heart at the end of February, then a consideration of the handsome fringed parrot tulips, and some tulips called, as far as Tuppence could make out, *viridiflora*, which would be exceptionally beautiful with long stems in the month of May and early June. As these were of an interesting green pastel colour, they agreed to plant them as a collection in a quiet part of the garden where they could be picked and arranged in interesting floral arrangements in the drawing-room, or by the short approach to the house through the front gate where they would arouse envy and jealousy among callers. They must even rejoice the artistic feelings of tradesmen delivering joints of meat and crates of grocery.

At four o'clock Tuppence produced a brown teapot full of good strong tea in the kitchen, placed a sugar basin full of lumps of sugar and a milk jug by it, and called Isaac in to refresh himself before departing. She went in search of Tommy.

I suppose he's asleep somewhere, thought Tuppence to herself as she looked from one room into another. She was glad to see a head sticking up on the landing out of the sinister pit in the floor.

'It's all right now, ma'am,' said the electrician, 'no need to be careful any more. It's all fixed.' He added that he was starting work on a different portion of the house on the following morning.

'I do hope,' said Tuppence, 'that you will really come.' She added, 'Have you seen Mr Beresford anywhere?'

'Aye, your husband, you mean? Yes, he's up on an upper floor, I think. Dropping things, he was. Yes, rather heavy things, too. Must have been some books, I think.'

'Books!' said Tuppence. 'Well I never!'

The electrician retreated down into his own personal

underworld in the passage and Tuppence went up to the attic converted to the extra book library at present devoted to children's books.

Tommy was sitting on the top of a pair of steps. Several books were around him on the floor and there were noticeable gaps in the shelves.

'So there you are,' said Tuppence, 'after pretending you weren't interested or anything. You've been looking at lots of books, haven't you? You've disarranged a lot of the things that I put away so neatly.'

'Well, I'm sorry about that,' said Tommy, 'but, well I thought I'd perhaps just have a look round.'

'Did you find any other books that have got any underlined things in them in red ink?'

'No. Nothing else.'

'How annoying,' said Tuppence.

'I think it must have been Alexander's work, Master Alexander Parkinson,' said Tommy.

'That's right,' said Tuppence. 'One of the Parkinsons, the numerous Parkinsons.'

'Well, I think he must have been rather a lazy boy, although of course, it must have been rather a bother doing that underlining and all. But there's no more information re Jordan,' said Tommy.

'I asked old Isaac. He knows a lot of people round here. He says he doesn't remember any Jordans.'

'What are you doing with that brass lamp you've

got by the front door?' asked Tommy, as he came downstairs.

'I'm taking it to the White Elephant Sale,' said Tuppence.

'Why?'

'Oh, because it's always been a thorough nuisance. We bought it somewhere abroad, didn't we?'

'Yes, I think we must have been mad. You never liked it. You said you hated it. Well, I agree. And it's awfully heavy too, very heavy.'

'But Miss Sanderson was terribly pleased when I said that they could have it. She offered to fetch it but I said I'd run it down to them in the car. It's today we take the thing.'

'I'll run down with it if you like.'

'No, I'd rather like to go.'

'All right,' said Tommy. 'Perhaps I'd better come with you and just carry it in for you.'

'Oh, I think I'll find someone who'll carry it in for me,' said Tuppence.

'Well, you might or you might not. Don't go and strain yourself.'

'All right,' said Tuppence.

'You've got some other reason for wanting to go, haven't you?'

'Well, I just thought I'd like to chat a bit with people,' said Tuppence.

'I never know what you're up to, Tuppence, but I know the look in your eye when you *are* up to something.'

'You take Hannibal for a walk,' said Tuppence. 'I can't take him to the White Elephant Sale. I don't want to get into a dog-fight.'

'All right. Want to go for a walk, Hannibal?'

Hannibal, as was his habit, immediately replied in the affirmative. His affirmatives and his negatives were always quite impossible to miss. He wriggled his body, wagged his tail, raised one paw, put it down again and came and rubbed his head hard against Tommy's leg.

'That's right,' he obviously said, 'that's what you exist for, my dear slave. We're going out for a lovely walk down the street. Lots of smells, I hope.'

'Come on,' said Tommy. 'I'll take the lead with me, and don't run into the road as you did the last time. One of those awful great "long vehicles" was nearly the end of you.'

Hannibal looked at him with the expression of 'I'm always a very good dog who'll do exactly what I am told.' False as the statement was, it often succeeded in deceiving even those people who were in closest contact with Hannibal.

Tommy put the brass lamp into the car, murmuring it was rather heavy. Tuppence drove off in the car. Having seen her turn the corner, Tommy attached the lead to Hannibal's collar and took him down the street. Then he turned up the lane towards the church, and removed Hannibal's lead since very little traffic came up this particular road. Hannibal acknowledged the privilege by grunting and sniffing in various tufts of grass with which the pavement next to the wall was adorned. If he could have used human language it was clear that what he would have said was: 'Delicious! Very rich. Big dog here. Believe it's that beastly Alsatian.' Low growl. 'I don't like Alsatians. If I see the one again that bit me once I'll bite him. Ah! Delicious, delicious. Very nice little bitch here. Yes – yes – I'd like to meet her. I wonder if she lives far away. Expect she comes out of this house. I wonder now.'

'Come out of that gate, now,' said Tommy. 'Don't go into a house that isn't yours.'

Hannibal pretended not to hear.

'Hannibal!'

Hannibal redoubled his speed and turned a corner which led towards the kitchen.

'Hannibal!' shouted Tommy. 'Do you hear me?'

'Hear you, Master?' said Hannibal. 'Were you calling me? Oh yes, of course.'

A sharp bark from inside the kitchen caught his ear. He scampered out to join Tommy. Hannibal walked a few inches behind Tommy's heel.

'Good boy,' said Tommy.

'I am a good boy, aren't I?' said Hannibal. 'Any moment you need me to defend you, here I am less than a foot away.'

They had arrived at a side gate which led into the churchyard. Hannibal, who in some way had an extraordinary knack of altering his size when he wanted to, instead of appearing somewhat broad-shouldered, possibly a somewhat too plump dog, he could at any moment make himself like a thin black thread. He now squeezed himself through the bars of the gate with no difficulty at all.

'Come back, Hannibal,' called Tommy. 'You can't go into the churchyard.'

Hannibal's answer to that, if there had been any, would have been, 'I am in the churchyard already, Master.' He was scampering gaily round the churchyard with the air of a dog who has been let out in a singularly pleasant garden.

'You awful dog!' said Tommy.

He unlatched the gate, walked in and chased Hannibal, lead in hand. Hannibal was now at the far corner of the churchyard, and seemed to have every intention of trying to gain access through the door of the church, which was slightly ajar. Tommy, however, reached him in time and attached the lead. Hannibal looked up with the air of one who had intended this to happen all along. 'Putting me on the lead, are you?' he said. 'Yes, of course, I know it's a kind of prestige. It shows that I am a very valuable dog.' He wagged his tail. Since there seemed nobody to oppose Hannibal walking in the churchyard with his master, suitably secured as he was by a stalwart lead, Tommy wandered round, checking perhaps Tuppence's researches of a former day.

He looked first at a worn stone monument more or less behind a little side door into the church. It was, he thought, probably one of the oldest. There were several of them there, most of them bearing dates in the eighteen-hundreds. There was one, however, that Tommy looked at longest.

'Odd,' he said, 'damned odd.'

Hannibal looked up at him. He did not understand this piece of Master's conversation. He saw nothing about the gravestone to interest a dog. He sat down, looked up at his master enquiringly.

Chapter 5

The White Elephant Sale

Tuppence was pleasurably surprised to find the brass lamp which she and Tommy now regarded with such repulsion welcomed with the utmost warmth.

'How very good of you, Mrs Beresford, to bring us something as nice as that. Most interesting, most interesting. I suppose it must have come from abroad on your travels once.'

'Yes. We bought it in Egypt,' said Tuppence.

She was quite doubtful by this time, a period of eight to ten years having passed, as to where she had bought it. It might have been Damascus, she thought, and it might equally well have been Baghdad or possibly Tehran. But Egypt, she thought, since Egypt was doubtless in the news at this moment, would be far more interesting. Besides, it looked rather Egyptian. Clearly, if she had got it from any other country, it dated from some period when they had been copying Egyptian work.

'Really,' she said, 'it's rather big for our house, so I thought –'

'Oh, I think really we ought to raffle it,' said Miss Little.

Miss Little was more or less in charge of things. Her local nickname was 'The Parish Pump', mainly because she was so well informed about all things that happened in the parish. Her surname was misleading. She was a large woman of ample proportions. Her Christian name was Dorothy, but she was always called Dotty.

'I hope you're coming to the sale, Mrs Beresford?'

Tuppence assured her that she was coming.

'I can hardly wait to buy,' she said chattily.

'Oh, I'm so glad you feel like that.'

'I think it's a very good thing,' said Tuppence. 'I mean, the White Elephant idea, because it's – well, it is so true, isn't it? I mean, what's one person's white elephant is somebody else's pearl beyond price.'

'Ah, really we *must* tell that to the vicar,' said Miss Price-Ridley, an angular lady with a lot of teeth. 'Oh yes, I'm sure he would be very much amused.'

'That papier-mâché basin, for instance,' said Tuppence, raising this particular trophy up.

'Oh really, do you think anyone will buy that?'

'I shall buy it myself if it's for sale when I come here tomorrow,' said Tuppence.

'But nowadays, they have such pretty plastic washing-up bowls.'

'I'm not very fond of plastic,' said Tuppence. 'That's a really good papier-mâché bowl that you've got there. I mean if you put things down in that, lots of china together, they wouldn't break. And there's an old-fashioned tin-opener too. The kind with a bull's head that one never sees nowadays.'

'Oh, but it's such hard work, that. Don't you think the ones that you put on an electric thing are much better?'

Conversation on these lines went on for a short time and then Tuppence asked if there were any services that she could render.

'Ah, dear Mrs Beresford, perhaps you would arrange the curio stall. I'm sure you're very artistic.'

'Not really artistic at all,' said Tuppence, 'but I would love to arrange the stall for you. You must tell me if I'm doing it wrong,' she added.

'Oh, it's so nice to have some extra help. We are so pleased to meet you, too. I suppose you're nearly settled into your house by now?'

'I thought we should be settled by now,' said Tuppence, 'but it seems as though there's a long time to go still. It's so very hard with electricians and then carpenters and people. They're always coming back.'

A slight dispute arose with people near her supporting

the claims of electricians and the Gas Board.

'Gas people are the worst,' said Miss Little, with firmness, 'because, you see, they come all the way over from Lower Stamford. The electricity people only have to come from Wellbank.'

The arrival of the vicar to say a few words of encouragement and good cheer to the helpers changed the subject. He also expressed himself very pleased to meet his new parishioner, Mrs Beresford.

'We know all about you,' he said. 'Oh yes indeed. And your husband. A most interesting talk I had the other day about you both. What an interesting life you must have had. I dare say it's not supposed to be spoken of, so I won't. I mean, in the last war. A wonderful performance on your and your husband's part.'

'Oh, do tell us, Vicar,' said one of the ladies, detaching herself from the stall where she was setting up jars of jam.

'I was told in strict confidence,' said the vicar. 'I think I saw you walking round the churchyard yesterday, Mrs Beresford.'

'Yes,' said Tuppence. 'I looked into the church first. I see you have one or two very attractive windows.'

'Yes, yes, they date back to the fourteenth century. That is, the one in the north aisle does. But of course most of them are Victorian.'

'Walking round the churchyard,' said Tuppence, 'it

seemed to me there were a great many Parkinsons buried there.'

'Yes, yes, indeed. There've always been big contingents of Parkinsons in this part of the world, though of course I don't remember any of them myself, but you do, I think, Mrs Lupton.'

Mrs Lupton, an elderly lady who was supporting herself on two sticks, looked pleased.

'Yes, yes,' she said. 'I remember when Mrs Parkinson was alive – you know, old Mrs Parkinson, *the* Mrs Parkinson who lived in the Manor House, wonderful old lady she was. Quite wonderful.'

'And there were some Somers I saw, and the Chattertons.'

'Ah, I see you're getting up well with our local geography of the past.'

'I think I heard something about a Jordan – Annie or Mary Jordan, was it?'

Tuppence looked round her in an enquiring fashion. The name of Jordan seemed to cause no particular interest.

'Somebody had a cook called Jordan. I think, Mrs Blackwell. Susan Jordan I think it was. She only stayed six months, I think. Quite unsatisfactory in many ways.'

'Was that a long time ago?'

'Oh no. Just about eight or ten years ago I think. Not more than that.'

'Are there any Parkinsons living here now?'

'Oh no. They're all gone long ago. One of them married a first cousin and went to live in Kenya, I believe.'

'I wonder,' said Tuppence, managing to attach herself to Mrs Lupton, who she knew had something to do with the local children's hospital, 'I wonder if you want any extra children's books. They're all old ones, I mean. I got them in an odd lot when we were bidding for some of the furniture that was for sale in our house.'

'Well, that's very kind of you, I'm sure, Mrs Beresford. Of course we do have some very good ones, given to us you know. Special editions for children nowadays. One does feel it's a pity they should have to read all those old-fashioned books.'

'Oh, do you think so?' said Tuppence. 'I loved the books that I had as a child. Some of them,' she said, 'had been my grandmother's when she was a child. I believe I liked those best of all. I shall never forget reading *Treasure Island*, Mrs Molesworth's *Four Winds Farm* and some of Stanley Weyman's.'

She looked round her enquiringly – then, resigning herself, she looked at her wrist-watch, exclaimed at finding how late it was and took her leave.

II

Tuppence, having got home, put the car away in the garage and walked round the house to the front door. The door was open, so she walked in. Albert then came from the back premises and bowed to greet her.

'Like some tea, madam? You must be very tired.'

'I don't think so,' said Tuppence. 'I've had tea. They gave me tea down at the Institute. Quite good cake, but very nasty buns.'

'Buns is difficult. Buns is nearly as difficult as doughnuts. Ah,' he sighed. 'Lovely doughnuts Amy used to make.'

'I know. Nobody's were like them,' said Tuppence.

Amy had been Albert's wife, now some years deceased. In Tuppence's opinion, Amy had made wonderful treacle tart but had never been very good with doughnuts.

'I think doughnuts are dreadfully difficult,' said Tuppence, 'I've never been able to do them myself.'

'Well, it's a knack.'

'Where's Mr Beresford? Is he out?'

'Oh no, he's upstairs. In that room. You know. The book-room or whatever you like to call it. I can't get out of the way of calling it the attic still, myself.'

'What's he doing up there?' said Tuppence, slightly surprised.

'Well, he's still looking at the books, I think. I suppose he's still arranging them, getting them finished as you might say.'

'Still seems to me very surprising,' said Tuppence. 'He's really been very rude to us about those books.'

'Ah well,' said Albert, 'gentlemen are like that, aren't they? They likes big books mostly, you know, don't they? Something scientific that they can get their teeth into.'

'I shall go up and rout him out,' said Tuppence. 'Where's Hannibal?'

'I think he's up there with the master.'

But at that moment Hannibal made his appearance. Having barked with the ferocious fury he considered necessary for a good guard dog, he had correctly assumed that it was his beloved mistress who had returned and not someone who had come to steal the teaspoons or to assault his master and mistress. He came wriggling down the stairs, his pink tongue hanging out, his tail wagging.

'Ah,' said Tuppence, 'pleased to see your mother?'

Hannibal said he was very pleased to see his mother. He leapt upon her with such force that he nearly knocked her to the ground.

'Gently,' said Tuppence, 'gently. You don't want to kill me, do you?'

Hannibal made it clear that the only thing he wanted

to do was to eat her because he loved her so much.

'Where's Master? Where's Father? Is he upstairs?'

Hannibal understood. He ran up a flight, turned his head over his shoulder and waited for Tuppence to join him.

'Well, I never,' said Tuppence as, slightly out of breath, she entered the book-room to see Tommy astride a pair of steps, taking books in and out. 'Whatever are you doing? I thought you were going to take Hannibal for a walk.'

'We have been for a walk,' said Tommy. 'We went to the churchyard.'

'Why on earth did you take Hannibal into the churchyard? I'm sure they wouldn't like dogs there.'

'He was on the lead,' said Tommy, 'and anyway I didn't take him. He took me. He seemed to like the churchyard.'

'I hope he hasn't got a thing about it,' said Tuppence. 'You know what Hannibal is like. He likes arranging a routine always. If he's going to have a routine of going to the churchyard every day, it will really be very difficult for us.'

'He's really been very intelligent about the whole thing,' said Tommy.

'When you say intelligent, you just mean he's self-willed,' said Tuppence.

Hannibal turned his head and came and rubbed his

nose against the calf of her leg.

'He's telling you,' said Tommy, 'that he is a very clever dog. Cleverer than you or I have been so far.'

'And what do you mean by that?' asked Tuppence.

'Have you been enjoying yourself?' asked Tommy, changing the subject.

'Well, I wouldn't go as far as that,' said Tuppence. 'People were very kind to me and nice to me and I think soon I shan't get them mixed up so much as I do at present. It's awfully difficult at first, you know, because people look rather alike and wear the same sort of clothes and you don't know at first which is which. I mean, unless somebody is very beautiful or very ugly. And that doesn't seem to happen so noticeably in the country, does it?'

'I'm telling you,' said Tommy, 'that Hannibal and I have been extremely clever.'

'I thought you said it was Hannibal?'

Tommy reached out his hand and took a book from the shelf in front of him.

'*Kidnapped*,' he remarked. 'Oh yes, another Robert Louis Stevenson. Somebody must have been very fond of Robert Louis Stevenson. *The Black Arrow*, *Kidnapped*, *Catriona* and two others, I think. All given to Alexander Parkinson by a fond grandmother and one from a generous aunt.'

'Well,' said Tuppence, 'what about it?'

'And I've found his grave,' said Tommy.

'Found what?'

'Well, Hannibal did. It's right in the corner against one of the small doors into the church. I suppose it's the other door to the vestry, something like that. It's very rubbed and not well kept up, but that's it. He was fourteen when he died. Alexander Richard Parkinson. Hannibal was nosing about there. I got him away from it and managed to make out the inscription, in spite of its being so rubbed.'

'Fourteen,' said Tuppence. 'Poor little boy.'

'Yes,' said Tommy, 'it's sad and –'

'You've got something in your head,' said Tuppence. 'I don't understand.'

'Well, I wondered. I suppose, Tuppence, you've infected me. That's the worst of you. When you get keen on something, you don't go on with it by yourself, you get somebody else to take an interest in it too.'

'I don't quite know what you mean,' said Tuppence.

'I wondered if it was a case of cause and effect.'

'What do you mean, Tommy?'

'I was wondering about Alexander Parkinson who took a lot of trouble, though no doubt he enjoyed himself doing it, making a kind of code, a secret message in a book. "*Mary Jordan did not die naturally.*" Supposing that was true? Supposing Mary Jordan, whoever she was, didn't die naturally? Well then, don't you see, perhaps the next thing that happened was that Alexander Parkinson died.'

'You don't mean – you don't think –'

'Well, one wonders,' said Tommy. 'It started me wondering – fourteen years old. There was no mention of what he died of. I suppose there wouldn't be on a gravestone. There was just a text: *In thy presence is the fullness of joy*. Something like that. But – it might have been because he knew something that was dangerous to somebody else. And so – and so he died.'

'You mean he was killed? You're just imagining things,' said Tuppence.

'Well you started it. Imagining things, or wondering. It's much the same thing, isn't it?'

'We shall go on wondering, I suppose,' said Tuppence, 'and we shan't be able to find out anything because it was all such years and years and years ago.'

They looked at each other.

'Round about the time we were trying to investigate the Jane Finn business,' said Tommy.

The looked at each other again; their minds going back to the past.

Chapter 6

Problems

Moving house is often thought of beforehand as an agreeable exercise which the movers are going to enjoy, but it does not always turn out as expected.

Relations have to be reopened or adjusted with electricians, with builders, with carpenters, with painters, with wall-paperers, with providers of refrigerators, gas stoves, electric appliances, with upholsterers, makers of curtains, hangers-up of curtains, those who lay linoleum, those who supply carpets. Every day has not only its appointed task but usually something between four and twelve extra callers, either long expected or those whose coming was quite forgotten.

But there were moments when Tuppence with sighs of relief announced various finalities in different fields.

'I really think our kitchen is almost perfect by now,' she said. 'Only I can't find the proper kind of flour bin yet.'

'Oh,' said Tommy, 'does it matter very much?'

'Well, it does rather. I mean, you buy flour very often in three-pound bags and it won't go into these kinds of containers. They're all so dainty. You know, one has a pretty rose on it and the other's got a sunflower and they'll not take more than a pound. It's all so silly.'

At intervals, Tuppence made other suggestions.

'The Laurels,' she said. 'Silly name for a house, I think. I don't see why it's called The Laurels. It hasn't got any laurels. They could have called it The Plane Trees much better. Plane trees are very nice,' said Tuppence.

'Before The Laurels it was called Long Scofield, so they told me,' said Tommy.

'That name doesn't seem to mean anything either,' said Tuppence.

'What is a Scofield, and who lived in it then?'

'I think it was the Waddingtons.'

'One gets so mixed,' said Tuppence. 'Waddingtons and then the Joneses, the people who sold it to us. And before that the Blackmores? And once, I suppose the Parkinsons. Lots of Parkinsons. I'm always running into more Parkinsons.'

'What way do you mean?'

'Well, I suppose it's that I'm always asking,' said Tuppence. 'I mean, if I could find out something about the Parkinsons, we could get on with our – well, with our problem.'

'That's what one always seems to call everything nowadays. The problem of Mary Jordan, is that it?'

'Well, it's not just that. There's the problem of the Parkinsons and the problem of Mary Jordan and there must be a lot of other problems too. Mary Jordan didn't die naturally, then the next thing the message said was, "It was one of us." Now did that mean one of the Parkinson family or did it mean just someone who lived in the house? Say there were two or three Parkinsons, and some older Parkinsons, and people with different names but who were aunts to the Parkinsons or nephews and nieces to the Parkinsons, and I suppose something like a housemaid and a parlour maid and a cook and perhaps a governess and perhaps – well, not an *au pair* girl, it would be too long ago for an *au pair* girl – but "one of us" must mean a householdful. Households were fuller then than they are now. Well, Mary Jordan could have been a housemaid or a parlour maid or even the cook. And why should someone want her to die, and not die naturally? I mean, somebody must have wanted her to die or else her death would have been natural, wouldn't it? – I'm going to another coffee morning the day after tomorrow,' said Tuppence.

'You seem to be always going to coffee mornings.'

'Well, it's a very good way of getting to know one's neighbours and all the people who live in the same village. After all, it's not very big, this village. And people are always talking about their old aunts or people they knew. I shall try and start on Mrs Griffin, who was evidently a great character in the neighbourhood. I should say she ruled everyone with a rod of iron. You know. She bullied the vicar and she bullied the doctor and I think she bullied the district nurse and all the rest of it.'

'Wouldn't the district nurse be helpful?'

'I don't think so. She's dead. I mean, the one who would have been here in the Parkinsons' time is dead, and the one who is here now hasn't been here very long. No sort of interest in the place. I don't think she even knew a Parkinson.'

'I wish,' said Tommy desperately, 'oh, how I wish that we could forget *all* the Parkinsons.'

'You mean, then we shouldn't have a problem?'

'Oh dear,' said Tommy. 'Problems again.'

'It's Beatrice,' said Tuppence.

'What's Beatrice?'

'Who introduced problems. Really, it's Elizabeth. The cleaning help we had before Beatrice. She was always coming to me and saying, "Oh madam, could I speak to you a minute? You see, I've got a problem," and then Beatrice began coming on Thursdays and she must have caught it, I suppose. So she had problems too. It's just a way of saying something – but you always call it a problem.'

'All right,' said Tommy. 'We'll admit that's so. You've got a problem – I've got a problem – We've both got problems.'

He sighed, and departed.

Tuppence came down the stairs slowly, shaking her head. Hannibal came up to her hopefully, wagging his tail and wriggling in hopes of favours to come.

'No, Hannibal,' said Tuppence. 'You've had a walk. You've had your morning walk.'

Hannibal intimated that she was quite mistaken, he hadn't had a walk.

'You are one of the worst liars among dogs I have ever known,' said Tuppence. 'You've been for a walk with Father.'

Hannibal made his second attempt, which was to endeavour to show by various attitudes that any dog would have a second walk if only he had an owner who could see things in that light. Disappointed in this effort, he went down the stairs and proceeded to bark loudly and make every pretence of being about to make a sharp snap bite at a tousled-haired girl who was wielding a Hoover. He did not like the Hoover, and he objected to Tuppence having a lengthy conversation with Beatrice.

'Oh, don't let him bite me,' said Beatrice.

'He won't bite you,' said Tuppence. 'He only pretends he's going to.'

'Well, I think he'll really do it one day,' said Beatrice. 'By the way, madam, I wonder if I could speak to you for a moment.'

'Oh,' said Tuppence. 'You mean –'

'Well, you see, madam, I've got a problem.'

'I thought that was it,' said Tuppence. 'What sort of problem is it? And, by the way, do you know any family here or anyone who lived here at one time called Jordan?'

'Jordan now. Well, I can't really say. There was the Johnsons, of course, and there was – ah yes, one of the constables was a Johnson. And so was one of the postmen. George Johnson. He was a friend of mine.' She giggled.

'You never heard of a Mary Jordan who died?'

Beatrice merely looked bewildered – and she shook her head and went back to the assault.

'About this problem, madam?'

'Oh yes, your problem.'

'I hope you don't mind my asking you, madam, but it's put me in a queer position, you see, and I don't like –'

'Well, if you can tell me quickly,' said Tuppence. 'I've got to go out to a coffee morning.'

'Oh yes. At Mrs Barber's isn't it?'

'That's right,' said Tuppence. 'Now what's the problem?'

'Well, it's a coat. Ever such a nice coat it was. At Simmonds it was, and I went in and tried it on and it seemed to me very nice, it did. Well, there was one little spot on the skirt, you know, just round near the hem but that didn't seem to me would matter much. Anyway, well, it – er –'

'Yes,' said Tuppence, 'it what?'

'It made me see why it was so inexpensive, you see. So I got it. And so that was all right. But when I got home I found there was a label on it and instead of saying £3.70 it was labelled £6. Well, ma'am, I didn't like to do that, so I didn't know what to do. I went back to the shop and I took the coat with me – I thought I'd better take it back and explain, you see, that I hadn't meant to take it away like that and then you see the girl who sold it to me – very nice girl she is, her name is Gladys, yes, I don't know what her other name is – but anyway she was ever so upset, she was, and I said, "Well, that's all right, I'll pay extra," and she said, "No, you can't do that because it's all entered up." You see – you do see what I mean?'

'Yes, I think I see what you mean,' said Tuppence.

'And so she said, "Oh you can't do that, it will get *me* into trouble."'

'Why should it get her into trouble?'

'Well, that's what I felt. I mean to say, well, I mean it'd been sold to me for less and I'd brought it back and I didn't see why it could put *her* in trouble. She said if there was any carelessness like that and they hadn't noticed the right ticket and they'd charged me the wrong price, as likely as not she'd get the sack for it.'

'Oh, I shouldn't think that would happen,' said Tuppence. 'I think you were quite right. I don't see what else you could do.'

'Well, but there it is, you see. She made such a fuss and she was beginning to cry and everything, so I took the coat away again and now I don't know whether I've cheated the shop or whether – I don't really know what to do.'

'Well,' said Tuppence, 'I really think I'm too old to know what one ought to do nowadays because everything is so odd in shops. The prices are odd and everything is difficult. But if I were you and you want to pay something extra, well perhaps you'd better give the money to what's-her-name – Gladys something. She can put the money in the till or somewhere.'

'Oh well, I don't know as I'd like to do that because she might keep it, you see. I mean, if she kept the money, oh well, I mean it wouldn't be difficult would it, because I suppose I've stolen the money and I wouldn't have stolen it really. I mean then it would have been

Gladys who stole it, wouldn't it, and I don't know that I trust her all that much. Oh dear.'

'Yes,' said Tuppence, 'life is very difficult, isn't it? I'm terribly sorry, Beatrice, but I really think you've got to make up your own mind about this. If you can't trust your friend –'

'Oh, she's not exactly a friend. I only buy things there. And she's ever so nice to talk to. But I mean, well, she's not exactly a friend, you know. I think she had a little trouble once before the last place she was in. You know, they said she kept back money on something she'd sold.'

'Well in that case,' said Tuppence, in slight desperation, 'I shouldn't do anything.'

The firmness of her tone was such that Hannibal came into the consultation. He barked loudly at Beatrice and took a running leap at the Hoover which he considered one of his principal enemies. 'I don't trust that Hoover,' said Hannibal. 'I'd like to bite it up.'

'Oh, be quiet, Hannibal. Stop barking. Don't bite anything or anyone,' said Tuppence. 'I'm going to be awfully late.'

She rushed out of the house.

II

'Problems,' said Tuppence, as she went down the hill and along Orchard Road. Going along there, she wondered as she'd done before if there'd ever been an orchard attached to any of the houses. It seemed unlikely nowadays.

Mrs Barber received her with great pleasure. She brought forward some very delicious-looking éclairs.

'What lovely things,' said Tuppence. 'Did you get them at Betterby's?'

Betterby's was the local confectionery shop.

'Oh no, my aunt made them. She's wonderful, you know. She does wonderful things.'

'Éclairs are very difficult things to make,' said Tuppence. 'I could never succeed with them.'

'Well, you have to get a particular kind of flour. I believe that's the secret of it.'

The ladies drank coffee and talked about the difficulties of certain kinds of home cookery.

'Miss Bolland was talking about you the other day, Mrs Beresford.'

'Oh?' said Tuppence. 'Really? Bolland?'

'She lives next to the vicarage. Her family has lived here a long time. She was telling us how she'd come and stayed here when she was a child. She used to look forward to it. She said, because there were such wonderful gooseberries in the garden. And greengage trees too. Now that's a thing you practically never see nowadays, not real greengages. Something else called gage plums or something, but they're not a bit the same to taste.'

The ladies talked about things in the fruit line which did not taste like the things used to, which they remembered from their childhood.

'My great-uncle had greengage trees,' said Tuppence.

'Oh yes. Is that the one who was a canon at Anchester? Canon Henderson used to live there, with his sister, I believe. Very sad it was. She was eating seed cake one day, you know, and one of the seeds got the wrong way. Something like that and she choked and she choked and she choked and she died of it. Oh dear, that's very sad, isn't it?' said Mrs Barber. 'Very sad indeed. One of my cousins died choking,' she said. 'A piece of mutton. It's very easy to do, I believe, and there are people who die of hiccups because they can't stop, you know. They don't know the old rhyme,' she explained. 'Hic-up, hic-down, hic to the next town, three hics and one cup sure to cure the hiccups. You have to hold your breath while you say it.'

Chapter 7

More Problems

'Can I speak to you a moment, ma'am?'

'Oh dear,' said Tuppence. 'Not more problems?'

She was descending the stairs from the book-room, brushing dust off herself because she was dressed in her best coat and skirt, to which she was thinking of adding a feather hat and then proceeding out to a tea she had been asked to attend by a new friend she had met at the White Elephant Sale. It was no moment, she felt, to listen to the further difficulties of Beatrice.

'Well, no, no, it's not exactly a problem. It's just something I thought you might like to know about.'

'Oh,' said Tuppence, still feeling that this might be another problem in disguise. She came down carefully. 'I'm in rather a hurry because I have to go out to tea.'

'Well, it's just about someone as you asked about, it seems. Name of Mary Jordan, that was right? Only they thought perhaps it was Mary Johnson. You know, there was a Belinda Johnson as worked at the post office, but a good long time ago.'

'Yes,' said Tuppence, 'and there was a policeman called Johnson, too, so someone told me.'

'Yes, well, anyway, this friend of mine – Gwenda, her name is – you know the shop, the post office is one side and envelopes and dirty cards and things the other side, and some china things too, before Christmas, you see, and –'

'I know,' said Tuppence, 'it's called Mrs Garrison's or something like that.'

'Yes, but it isn't really Garrison nowadays as keep it. Quite a different name. But anyway, this friend of mine, Gwenda, she thought you might be interested to know because she says as she had heard of a Mary Jordan what lived here a long time ago. A very long time ago. Lived here, in this house I mean.'

'Oh, lived in The Laurels?'

'Well, it wasn't called that then. And she'd heard something about her, she said. And so she thought you might be interested. There was some rather sad story about her, she had an accident or something. Anyway she died.'

'You mean that she was living in this house when she died? Was she one of the family?'

'No. I think the family was called Parker, a name of that kind. A lot of Parkers there were, Parkers or

Parkinsons – something like that. I think she was just staying here. I believe Mrs Griffin knows about it. Do you know Mrs Griffin?'

'Oh, very slightly,' said Tuppence. 'Matter of fact, that's where I'm going to tea this afternoon. I talked to her the other day at the Sale. I hadn't met her before.'

'She's a very old lady. She's older than she looks, but I think she's got a very good memory. I believe one of the Parkinson boys was her godson.'

'What was his Christian name?'

'Oh, it was Alec, I think. Some name like that. Alec or Alex.'

'What happened to him? Did he grow up – go away – become a soldier or sailor or something like that?'

'Oh no. He died. Oh yes, I think he's buried right here. It's one of those things, I think, as people usedn't to know much about. It's one of those things with a name like a Christian name.'

'You mean somebody's disease?'

'Hodgkin's Disease, or something. No, it was a Christian name of some kind. I don't know, but they say as your blood grows the wrong colour or something. Nowadays I believe they take blood away from you and give you some good blood again, or something like that. But even then you usually die, they say. Mrs Billings –

the cake shop, you know – she had a little girl died of that and she was only seven. They say it takes them very young.'

'Leukaemia?'

'Oh now, fancy you knowing. Yes, it was that name, I'm sure. But they say now as one day there'll maybe be a cure for it, you know. Just like nowadays they give you inoculations and things to cure you from typhoid, or whatever it is.'

'Well,' said Tuppence, 'that's very interesting. Poor little boy.'

'Oh, he wasn't very young. He was at school somewhere, I think. Must have been about thirteen or fourteen.'

'Well,' said Tuppence, 'it's all very sad.' She paused, then said, 'Oh dear, I'm very late now. I must hurry off.'

'I dare say Mrs Griffin could tell you a few things. I don't mean things as she'd remember herself, but she was brought up here as a child and she heard a lot of things, and she tells people a lot sometimes about the families that were here before. Some of the things are real scandalous, too. You know, goings-on and all that. That was, of course, in what they call Edwardian times or Victorian times. I don't know which. You know. I should think it was Victorian because she was still alive, the old Queen. So that's Victorian, really.

They talk about it as Edwardian and something called "the Marlborough House set". Sort of high society, wasn't it?'

'Yes,' said Tuppence, 'yes. High society.'

'And goings-on,' said Beatrice, with some fervour.

'A good many goings-on,' said Tuppence.

'Young girls doing what they shouldn't do,' said Beatrice, loath to part with her mistress just when something interesting might be said.

'No,' said Tuppence, 'I believe the girls led very – well, pure and austere lives and they married young, though often into the peerage.'

'Oh dear,' said Beatrice, 'how nice for them. Lots of fine clothes, I suppose, race meetings and going to dances and ballrooms.'

'Yes,' said Tuppence, 'lots of ballrooms.'

'Well, I knew someone once, and her grandmother had been a housemaid in one of those smart houses, you know, as they all came to, and the Prince of Wales – the Prince of Wales as was then, you know, he was Edward VII afterwards, that one, the early one – well he was there and he was ever so nice. Ever so nice to all the servants and everything else. And when she left she took away the cake of soap that he'd used for his hands, and she kept it always. She used to show it to some of us children once.'

'Very thrilling for you,' said Tuppence. 'It must have

been very exciting times. Perhaps he stayed here in The Laurels.'

'No, I don't think as I ever heard that, and I would have heard it. No, it was only Parkinsons here. No countesses and marchionesses and lords and ladies. The Parkinsons, I think, were mostly in trade. Very rich, you know, and all that, but still there's nothing exciting in trade, is there?'

'It depends,' said Tuppence. She added, 'I think I ought –'

'Yes, you'd best be going along, ma'am.'

'Yes. Well, thank you very much, I don't think I'd better put on a hat. I've got my hair awfully mussed now.'

'Well, you put your head in that corner where the cobwebs is. I'll dust it off in case you do it again.'

Tuppence ran down the stairs.

'Alexander ran down there,' she said. 'Many times, I expect. And he knew it was "one of them". I wonder. I wonder more than ever now.'

Chapter 8
Mrs Griffin

'I am so very pleased that you and your husband have come here to live, Mrs Beresford,' said Mrs Griffin, as she poured out tea. 'Sugar? Milk?'

She pressed forward a dish of sandwiches, and Tuppence helped herself.

'It makes so much difference, you know, in the country where one has nice neighbours with whom one has something in common. Did you know this part of the world before?'

'No,' said Tuppence, 'not at all. We had, you know, a good many different houses to go and view – particulars of them were sent to us by the estate agents. Of course, most of them were very often quite frightful. One was called Full of Old World Charm.'

'I know,' said Mrs Griffin, 'I know exactly. Old world charm usually means that you have to put a new roof on and that the damp is very bad. And "thoroughly modernized" – well, one knows what that means. Lots of gadgets one doesn't want and usually a very bad view from the windows of really hideous houses. But The Laurels is a charming house. I expect, though, you have had a good deal to do to it. Everyone has in turn.'

'I suppose a lot of different people have lived there,' said Tuppence.

'Oh yes. Nobody seems to stay very long anywhere nowadays, do they? The Cuthbertsons were here and the Redlands, and before that the Seymours. And after them the Joneses.'

'We wondered a little why it was called The Laurels,' said Tuppence.

'Oh well, that was the kind of name people liked to give a house. Of course, if you go back far enough, probably to the time of the Parkinsons, I think there *were* laurels. Probably a drive, you know, curling round and a lot of laurels, including those speckled ones. I never liked speckled laurels.'

'No.' said Tuppence, 'I do agree with you. I don't like them either. There seem to have been a lot of Parkinsons here,' she added.

'Oh yes. I think they occupied it longer than anyone else.'

'Nobody seems able to tell one much about them.'

'Well, it was a long time ago, you see, dear. And after

the – well, I think after the – the trouble you know, and there was some feeling about it and of course one doesn't wonder they sold the place.'

'It had a bad reputation, did it?' said Tuppence, taking a chance. 'Do you mean the house was supposed to be insanitary, or something?'

'Oh no, not the house. No, really, the people you see. Well of course, there was the – the disgrace, in a way – it was during the first war. Nobody could believe it. My grandmother used to talk about it and say that it was something to do with naval secrets – about a new submarine. There was a girl living with the Parkinsons who was said to have been mixed up with it all.'

'Was that Mary Jordan?' said Tuppence.

'Yes. Yes, you're quite right. Afterwards they suspected that it wasn't her real name. I think somebody had suspected her for some time. The boy had, Alexander. Nice boy. Quite sharp too.'

Book II

Chapter 1

A Long Time Ago

Tuppence was selecting birthday cards. It was a wet afternoon and the post office was almost empty. People dropped letters into the post box outside or occasionally made a hurried purchase of stamps. Then they usually departed to get home as soon as possible. It was not one of those crowded shopping afternoons. In fact, Tuppence thought, she had chosen this particular day very well.

Gwenda, whom she had managed to recognize easily from Beatrice's description, had been only too pleased to come to her assistance. Gwenda represented the household shopping side of the post office. An elderly woman with grey hair presided over the government business of Her Majesty's mails. Gwenda, a chatty girl, interested always in new arrivals to the village, was happy among the Christmas cards, valentines, birthday cards, comic postcards, note paper and stationery, various types of chocolates and sundry china articles of domestic use. She and Tuppence were already on friendly terms.

'I'm so glad that the house has been opened again. Princes Lodge, I mean.'

'I thought it had always been The Laurels.'

'Oh no. I don't think it was ever called that. Houses change names a lot around here. People do like giving new names to houses, you know.'

'Yes, they certainly seem to,' said Tuppence thoughtfully. 'Even we have thought of a name or two. By the way, Beatrice told me that you knew someone once living here called Mary Jordan.'

'I didn't know her, but I have heard her mentioned. In the war it was, not the last war. The one long before that when there used to be zeppelins.'

'I remember hearing about zeppelins,' said Tuppence.

'In 1915 or 1916 – they came over London.'

'I remember I'd gone to the Army & Navy Stores one day with an old great-aunt and there was an alarm.'

'They used to come over at night sometimes, didn't they? Must have been rather frightening, I should think.'

'Well, I don't think it was really,' said Tuppence. 'People used to get quite excited. It wasn't nearly as frightening as the flying bombs – in this last war. One always felt rather as though *they* were following you to places. Following you down a street, or something like that?'

'Spend all your nights in the tube, did you? I had a friend in London. She used to spend all the nights in the tubes. Warren Street, I think it was. Everyone used to have their own particular tube station.'

'I wasn't in London in the last war,' said Tuppence. 'I don't think I'd have liked to spend all night in the tube.'

'Well, this friend of mine, Jenny her name was, oh she used to love the tube. She said it was ever so much fun. You know, you had your own particular stair in the tube. It was kept for you always, you slept there, and you took sandwiches in and things, and you had fun together and talked. Things went on all night and never stopped. Wonderful, you know. Trains going on right up to the morning. She told me she couldn't bear it when the war was over and she had to go home again, felt it was so dull, you know.'

'Anyway,' said Tuppence, 'there weren't any flying-bombs in 1914. Just the zeppelins.'

Zeppelins had clearly lost interest for Gwenda.

'It was someone called Mary Jordan I was asking about,' said Tuppence. 'Beatrice said you knew about her.'

'Not really – I just heard her name mentioned once or twice, but it was ages ago. Lovely golden hair she had, my grandmother said. German she was – one of those Frowlines as they were called. Looked after children – a kind of nurse. Had been with a naval family somewhere, that was up in Scotland, I think. And afterwards she came down here. Went to a family called Parks – or Perkins. She used to have one day off a week, you know, and go to London, and that's where she used to take the things, whatever they were.'

'What sort of things?' said Tuppence.

'I don't know – nobody ever said much. Things she'd stolen, I expect.'

'Was she discovered stealing?'

'Oh no, I don't think so. They were beginning to suspect, but she got ill and died before that.'

'What did she die of? Did she die down here? I suppose she went to hospital.'

'No – I don't think there were any hospitals to go to then. Wasn't any Welfare in those days. Somebody told me it was some silly mistake the cook made. Brought foxglove leaves into the house by mistake for spinach – or for lettuce, perhaps. No, I think that was someone else. Someone told me it was deadly nightshade but I don't believe *that* for a moment because, I mean, everyone knows about deadly nightshade, don't they, and anyway that's berries. Well, I think this was foxglove leaves brought in from the garden by mistake. Foxglove is Digoxo or some name like Digit – something that sounds like fingers. It's got something very deadly in it – the doctor came and he did what he could, but I think it was too late.'

'Were there many people in the house when it happened?'

'Oh, there was quite a lot I should think – yes, because there were always people staying, so I've heard, and children, you know, and weekenders and a nursery maid and a governess, I think, and parties. Mind you, I'm not knowing all about this myself. It's only what Granny used to tell me. And old Mr Bodlicott talks now and then. You know, the old gardener chap as works here now and then. He was gardener there, and they blamed him at first for sending the wrong leaves, but it wasn't *him* as did it. It was somebody who came out of the house, and wanted to help and picked the vegetables in the garden, and took them in to the cook. You know, spinach and lettuce and things like that and – er – I suppose they just made a mistake not knowing much about growing vegetables. I think they said at the inquest or whatever they had afterwards that it was a mistake that *anyone* could make because the spinach or the sorrel leaves were growing near the Digi – Digit-what-not, you see, so I suppose they just took a great handful of both leaves, possibly in a bunch together. Anyway, it was very sad because Granny said she was a very good-looking girl with golden hair and all that, you know.'

'And she used to go up to London every week? Naturally she'd have to have a day off.'

'Yes. Said she had friends there. Foreigner, she was – Granny says there was some as said she was actually a German spy.'

'And was she?'

'I shouldn't think so. The gentlemen liked her all right, apparently. You know, the naval officers and the ones up at Shelton Military Camp too. She had one or two friends there, you know. The military camp it was.'

'Was she really a spy?'

'Shouldn't think so. I mean, my grandmother said that was what people *said*. It wasn't in the last war. It was ages before that.'

'Funny,' said Tuppence, 'how easy it is to get mixed up over the wars. I knew an old man who had a friend in the Battle of Waterloo.'

'Oh, fancy that. Years before 1914. People did have foreign nurses – what were called Mamoselles as well as Frowlines, whatever a Frowline is. Very nice with children she was, Granny said. Everyone was very pleased with her and always liked her.'

'That was when she was living here, living at The Laurels?'

'Wasn't called that then – at least I don't think so. She was living with the Parkinsons or the Perkins, some name like that,' said Gwenda. 'What we call nowadays an *au pair* girl. She came from that place where the patty comes from, you know, Fortnum & Mason keep it – expensive patty for parties. Half German, half French, so someone told me.'

'Strasbourg?' suggested Tuppence.

'Yes, that was the name. She used to paint pictures. Did one of an old great-aunt of mine. It made her look too old, Aunt Fanny always said. Did one of one of the Parkinson boys. Old Mrs Griffin's got it still. The Parkinson boy found out something about her, I believe – the one she painted the picture of, I mean. Godson of Mrs Griffin, I believe he was.'

'Would that have been Alexander Parkinson?'

'Yes, that's the one. The one who's buried near the church.'

Chapter 2

Introduction to Mathilde, Truelove and KK

Tuppence, on the following morning, went in search of that well-known public character in the village known usually as Old Isaac, or, on formal occasions if one could remember, Mr Bodlicott. Isaac Bodlicott was one of the local 'characters'. He was a character because of his age – he claimed to be ninety (not generally believed) – and he was able to do repairs of many curious kinds. If your efforts to ring up the plumber met with no response, you went to old Isaac Bodlicott. Mr Bodlicott, whether or not he was in any way qualified for the repairs he did, had been well acquainted for many of the years of his long life with every type of sanitation problem, bath-water problems, difficulties with geysers, and sundry electrical problems on the side. His charges compared favourably with a real live qualified plumber, and his repairs were often surprisingly successful. He could do carpentering, he could attend to locks, he could hang pictures – rather crookedly sometimes – he understood about the springs of derelict armchairs. The main disadvantage of Mr Bodlicott's attentions was his garrulous habit of incessant conversation slightly hampered by a difficulty in adjusting his false teeth in such a way as to make what he said intelligible in his pronunciation. His memories of past inhabitants of the neighbourhood seemed to be unlimited. It was difficult, on the whole, to know how reliable they might be. Mr Bodlicott was not one to shirk giving himself the pleasure of retailing some really good story of past days. These flights of fancy, claimed usually as flights of memory, were usually ushered in with the same type of statement.

'You'd be surprised, you would, if I could tell you what I knew about that one. Yes indeed. Well, you know, everybody thought they knew all about it, but they were wrong. Absolutely wrong. It was the elder sister, you know. Yes, it was. Such a nice girl, she seemed. It was the butcher's dog that gave them all the clue. Followed her home, he did. Yes. Only it wasn't her own home, as you might say. Ah well, I could tell you a lot more about *that*. Then there was old Mrs Atkins. Nobody knew as she kept a revolver in the house, but I knew. I knew when I was sent for to mend her tallboy – that's what they call those high chests, isn't it? Yes. Tallboys. Well, that's right. Well, there she was, seventy-five, and in that drawer, the drawer of the tallboy as I went, you know, to mend – the hinges had gone, the lock too – that's where the revolver was. Wrapped up, it was, with a pair of women's shoes. No. 3 size. Or, I'm not sure as it wasn't No. 2. White satin. Tiny little foot. Her great-grandmother's wedding shoes, she said. Maybe. But somebody said she bought them at a curiosity shop once but I don't know about that. And there was the revolver wrapped up too. Yes. Well, they said as her son had brought it back. Brought it back from East Africa, he did. He'd been out there shooting elephants or something of that kind. And when he come home he brought this revolver. And do you know what that old lady used to do? Her son had taught her to shoot. She'd sit by her drawing-room window looking out and when people came up the drive she'd have her revolver with her and she'd shoot either side of them. Yes. Got them frightened to death and they ran away. She said she wouldn't have anyone coming in and disturbing the birds. Very keen on the birds, she was. Mind you, she never shot a bird. No, she didn't want to do that. Then there was all the stories about Mrs Letherby. Nearly had up, *she* was. Yes, shoplifting. Very clever at it, so they say. And yet as rich as they make them.'

Having persuaded Mr Bodlicott to replace the skylight in the bathroom, Tuppence wondered if she could direct his conversation to any memory of the past which would be useful to Tommy and herself in solving the mystery of the concealment in their house of some treasure or interesting secret of whose nature they had no knowledge whatever.

Old Isaac Bodlicott made no difficulties about coming to do repairs for the new tenants of the place. It was one of his pleasures in life to meet as many newcomers as possible. It was in his life one of the main events to be able to come across people who had not so far heard of his splendid memories and reminiscences. Those who were well acquainted with them did not often encourage him to repeat these tales. But a new audience! That was always a pleasant happening. That and displaying the wonderful amount of trades that he managed to combine among his various services to the community in which he lived. It was his pleasure to indulge in a running commentary.

'Luck it was, as old Joe didn't get cut. Might have ripped his face open.'

'Yes, it might indeed.'

'There's a bit more glass wants sweeping up on the floor still, missus.'

'I know,' said Tuppence, 'we haven't had time yet.'

'Ah, but you can't take risks with glass. You know

what glass is. A little splinter can do you all the harm in the world. Die of it, you can, if it gets into a blood vessel. I remember Miss Lavinia Shotacomb. You wouldn't believe . . .'

Tuppence was not tempted by Miss Lavinia Shotacomb. She had heard her mentioned by other local characters. She had apparently been between seventy and eighty, quite deaf and almost blind.

'I suppose,' said Tuppence, breaking in before Isaac's reminiscences of Lavinia Shotacomb could begin, 'that you must know a lot about all the various people and the extraordinary things that have happened in this place in the past.'

'Aw, well, I'm not as young as I was, you know. Over eighty-five, I am. Going on ninety. I've always had a good memory. There are things, you know, you don't forget. No. However long it is, something reminds you of it, you know, and brings it all back to you. The things I could tell you, you wouldn't believe.'

'Well, it's really wonderful, isn't it,' said Tuppence, 'to think how much you must know about what a lot of extraordinary people.'

'Ah no, there's no accounting for people, is there? Ones that aren't what you think they are, sometimes things as you wouldn't have believed in about them.'

'Spies, I suppose, sometimes,' said Tuppence, 'or criminals.'

She looked at him hopefully . . . Old Isaac bent and picked up a splinter of glass.

'Here you are,' he said. 'How'd you feel if *that* got in the sole of your foot?'

Tuppence began to feel that the replenishing of a glass skylight was not going to yield much in the way of Isaac's more exciting memories of the past. She noticed that the small so-called greenhouse attached to the wall of the house near the dining-room window was also in need of repair and replacement by an outlay of money upon glass. Would it be worth repairing or would it be better to have it pulled down? Isaac was quite pleased to transfer himself to this fresh problem. They went downstairs, and outside the house walked round its walls until they came to the erection in question.

'Ah, you mean that there, do you?'

Tuppence said yes, she did mean that there.

'Kay-kay,' said Isaac.

Tuppence looked at him. Two letters of the alphabet such as KK really meant nothing to her.

'What did you say?'

'I said KK. That's what it used to be called in old Mrs Lottie Jones's time.'

'Oh. Why did she call it KK?'

'I dunno. It was a sort of – sort of name I suppose they used to have for places like this. You know, it wasn't grand. Bigger houses have a real conservatory. You know, where they'd have maidenhair ferns in pots.'

'Yes,' said Tuppence, her own memories going back easily to such things.

'And a greenhouse you can call it, too. But this here, KK old Mrs Lottie Jones used to call it. I dunno why.'

'Did they have maidenhair ferns in it?'

'No, it wasn't used for that. No. The children had it for toys mostly. Well, when you say toys I expect they're here still if nobody has turned them out. You see, it's half falling down, isn't it? They just stuck up a bit then they put a bit of roofing over and I don't suppose that anyone will use it again. They used to bring the broken toys, or chairs out here and things like that. But then, you see, they already had the rocking-horse there and Truelove in the far corner.'

'Can we get inside it?' asked Tuppence, trying to apply her eye to a slightly clearer portion of a pane of window. 'There must be a lot of queer things inside.'

'Ah well, there's the key,' said Isaac. 'I expect it's hanging up in the same place.'

'Where's the same place?'

'Ah, there's a shed round here.'

They went round an adjacent path. The shed was

hardly worthy of being called a shed. Isaac kicked its door open, removed various bits of branches of trees, kicked away some rotting apples and, removing an old doormat hanging on the wall, showed three or four rusty keys hanging up on a nail.

'Lindop's keys, those,' he said. 'Last but one was as living here as gardener. Retired basket-maker, he was. Didn't do no good at anything. If you'd like to see inside KK –?'

'Oh yes,' said Tuppence hopefully. 'I'd like to see inside KK. How do you spell it?'

'How do you spell what?'

'I mean KK. Is it just two letters?'

'No. I think it was something different. I think it was two foreign words. I seem to remember now K-A-I and then another K-A-I. Kay-Kay, or Kye-Kye almost, they used to say it. I think it was a Japanese word.'

'Oh,' said Tuppence. 'Did any Japanese people ever live here?'

'Oh no, nothing like that. No. Not that kind of foreigner.'

The application of a little oil, which Isaac seemed to produce and apply quite quickly, had a wonderful effect on the rustiest of the keys which, inserted in the door and turned with a grinding noise, could be pushed open. Tuppence and her guide went in.

'There you are,' said Isaac, not displaying any particular pride in the objects within. 'Nothing but old rubbish, is it?'

'That's a rather wonderful-looking horse,' said Tuppence.

'That's Mackild, that is,' said Isaac.

'Mack-ild?' said Tuppence, rather doubtfully.

'Yes. It's a woman's name of some kind. Queen somebody, it was. Somebody said as it was William the Conqueror's wife but I think they were just boasting about that. Come from America, it did. American godfather brought it to one of the children.'

'To one of the –?'

'One of the Bassington children, that was. Before the other lot. I dunno. I suppose it's all rusted up now.'

Mathilde was a rather splendid-looking horse even in decay. Its length was quite the length of any horse or mare to be found nowadays. Only a few hairs were left of what must once have been a prolific mane. One ear was broken off. It had once been painted grey. Its front legs splayed out in front and its back legs at the back; it had a wispy tail.

'It doesn't work like any rocking-horse I've ever seen before,' said Tuppence, interested.

'No, it don't, do it?' said Isaac. 'You know, they go up and down, up and down, front to back. But this one here, you see – it sort of springs forwards. Once first, the front legs do it – whoop – and then the back legs do it. It's a very good action. Now if I was to get on it and show you –'

'Do be careful,' said Tuppence. 'It might – there might be nails or something which would stick into you, or you might fall off.'

'Ah. I've ridden on Mathilde, fifty or sixty years ago it must have been, but I remember. And it's still pretty solid, you know. It's not really falling to bits yet.'

With a sudden, unexpected, acrobatic action he sprang upon Mathilde. The horse raced forwards, then raced backwards.

'Got action, hasn't it?'

'Yes, it's got action,' said Tuppence.

'Ah, they loved that, you know. Miss Jenny, she used to ride it day after day.'

'Who was Miss Jenny?'

'Why, she was the eldest one, you know. She was the one that had the godfather as sent her this. Sent her Truelove, too,' he added.

Tuppence looked at him enquiringly. The remark did not seem to apply to any of the other contents of Kay-Kay.

'That's what they call it, you know. That little horse and cart what's there in the corner. Used to ride it down the hill, Miss Pamela did. Very serious, she was, Miss Pamela. She'd get in at the top of the hill and she'd put her feet on there – you see, it's meant to have pedals but they don't work, so she'd take it to the top of the hill and then she'd let it begin to go down the hill, and she'd put the brakes on, as it were, with her feet. Often she'd end up landing in the monkey puzzle, as a matter of fact.'

'That sounds very uncomfortable,' said Tuppence. 'I mean, to land in the monkey puzzle.'

'Ah well, she could stop herself a bit before that. Very serious, she was. She used to do that by the hour – three or four hours I've watched her. I was doing the Christmas rose bed very often, you know, and the pampas grass, and I'd see her going down. I didn't speak to her because she didn't like being spoken to. She wanted to go on with what she was doing or what she thought she was doing.'

'What did she think she was doing?' said Tuppence, beginning suddenly to get more interested in Miss Pamela than she had been in Miss Jenny.

'Well, I don't know. She used to say sometimes she was a princess, you know, escaping, or Mary, Queen of What-is-it – do I mean Ireland or Scotland?'

'Mary Queen of Scots,' suggested Tuppence.

'Yes, that's right. She went away or something, or escaped. Went into a castle. Lock something it was called. Not a real lock, you know, a piece of water, it was.'

'Ah yes, I see. And Pamela thought she was Mary Queen of Scots escaping from her enemies?'

'That's right. Going to throw herself into England on Queen Elizabeth's mercy, she said, but I don't think as Queen Elizabeth was very merciful.'

'Well,' said Tuppence, masking any disappointment she felt, 'it's all very interesting, I'm sure. Who were these people, did you say?'

'Oh, they were the Listers, they were.'

'Did you ever know a Mary Jordan?'

'Ah, I know who you mean. No, she was before my time a bit, I think. You mean the German spy girl, don't you?'

'Everyone seems to know about her here,' said Tuppence.

'Yes. They called her the Frow Line, or something. Sounds like a railway.'

'It does rather,' said Tuppence.

Isaac suddenly laughed. 'Ha, ha, ha,' he said. 'If it was a railway, a line, a railway line, oh, it didn't run straight, did it? No, indeed.' He laughed again.

'What a splendid joke,' said Tuppence kindly.

Isaac laughed again.

'It's about time,' he said, 'you thought of putting some vegetables in, isn't it? You know, if you want to get your broad beans on in good time you ought to put 'em in and prepare for the peas. And what about some early lettuce? Tom Thumbs now? Beautiful lettuce, those, small but crisp as anything.'

'I suppose you've done a lot of gardening work round here. I don't mean just this house, but a lot of places.'

'Ah yes, I've done odd jobbing, you know. I used to come along to most of the houses. Some of the gardeners they had weren't any good at all and I'd usually come in and help at certain times or other. Had a bit of an accident here once, you know. Mistake about vegetables. Before my time – but I heard about it.'

'Something about foxglove leaves, wasn't it?' said Tuppence.

'Ah, fancy you having heard of that already. That was a long time ago, too. Yes, several was taken ill with it. One of them died. At least so I heard. That was only hearsay. Old pal of mine told me that.'

'I think it was the Frow Line,' said Tuppence.

'What, the Frow Line as died? Well, I never heard that.'

'Well, perhaps I'm wrong,' said Tuppence. 'Supposing you take Truelove,' she said, 'or whatever this thing's called, and put it on the hill in the place where that child, Pamela, used to take it down the hill – if the hill is still there.'

'Well, of course the hill is still there. What do you think? It's all grass still, but be careful now. I don't know how much of Truelove is rusted away. I'll have a bit of a clean-up on it first, shall I?'

'That's right,' said Tuppence, 'and then you can think of a list of vegetables that we ought to be getting on with.'

'Ah well, I'll be careful you don't get foxglove and spinach planted together. Shouldn't like to hear that something happened to you when you've just got into a new house. Nice place here if you can just have a little money to spend on it.'

'Thank you very much,' said Tuppence.

'And I'll just see to that there Truelove so it won't break down under you. It's very old but you'd be surprised the way some old things work. Why, I knew a cousin of mine the other day and he got out an old bicycle. You wouldn't think it would go – nobody had ridden it for about forty years. But it went all right with a bit of oil. Ah, it's wonderful what a bit of oil can do.'

Chapter 3

Six Impossible Things Before Breakfast

'What on earth –' said Tommy.

He was used to finding Tuppence in unlikely spots when he returned to the house, but on this occasion he was more startled than usual.

Inside the house there was no trace of her, although outside there was a very slight patter of rain. It occurred to him that she might be engrossed in some portion of the garden, and he went out to see if this might be the case. And it was then that he remarked, 'What on earth –'

'Hullo, Tommy,' said Tuppence, 'you're back a bit earlier than I thought you would be.'

'What is that thing?'

'You mean Truelove?'

'What did you say?'

'I said Truelove,' said Tuppence, 'that's the name of it.'

'Are you trying to go for a ride on it – it's much too small for you.'

'Well, of course it is. It's a child's sort of thing – what you had, I suppose, before you had fairy-cycles, or whatever one had in my youth.'

'It doesn't really *go*, does it?' asked Tommy.

'Well, not exactly,' said Tuppence, 'but you see, you take it up to the top of the hill and then it – well, its wheels turn of their own accord, you see, and because of the hill you go down.'

'And crash at the bottom, I suppose. Is that what you've been doing?'

'Not at all,' said Tuppence. 'You brake it with your feet. Would you like me to give you a demonstration?'

'I don't think so,' said Tommy. 'It's beginning to rain rather harder. I just wanted to know why you – well, why you're doing it. I mean, it can't be very enjoyable, can it?'

'Actually,' said Tuppence, 'it's rather frightening. But you see I just wanted to find out and –'

'And are you asking this tree? What is this tree, anyway? A monkey puzzle, isn't it?'

'That's right,' said Tuppence. 'How clever of you to know.'

'Of course I know,' said Tommy. 'I know its other name, too.'

'So do I,' said Tuppence.

They looked at each other.

'Only at the moment I've forgotten it,' said Tommy. 'Is it an arti –'

'Well, it's something very like that,' said Tuppence. 'I think that's good enough, don't you?'

'What are you doing inside a prickly thing like that?'

'Well, because when you get to the end of the hill, I mean, if you didn't put your feet down to stop completely you could be in the arti – or whatever it is.'

'Do I mean arti –? What about urticaria? No, that's nettles, isn't it? Oh well,' said Tommy, 'everyone to their own kind of amusement.'

'I was just doing a little investigation, you know, of our latest problem.'

'Your problem? My problem? Whose problem?'

'I don't know,' said Tuppence. 'Both our problems, I hope.'

'But not one of Beatrice's problems, or anything like that?'

'Oh no. It's just that I wondered what other things there might be hidden in this house, so I went and looked at a lot of toys that seem to have been shoved away in a sort of queer old greenhouse probably years and years ago and there was this creature and there was Mathilde, which is a rocking-horse with a hole in its stomach.'

'A hole in its stomach?'

'Well, yes. People, I suppose, used to shove things in there. Children – for fun – and lots of old leaves and dirty papers and bits of sort of queer dusters and flannel, oily stuff that had been used to clean things with.'

'Come on, let's go into the house,' said Tommy.

II

'Well, Tommy,' said Tuppence, as she stretched out her feet to a pleasant wood fire which she had lit already for his return in the drawing-room, 'let's have your news. Did you go to the Ritz Hotel Gallery to see the show?'

'No. As a matter of fact, I hadn't time, really.'

'What do you mean, you hadn't time? I thought that's what you went for.'

'Well, one doesn't always do the things that one went for.'

'You must have gone somewhere and done *something*,' said Tuppence.

'I found a new possible place to park a car.'

'That's always useful,' said Tuppence. 'Where was that?'

'Near Hounslow.'

'What on earth did you want to go to Hounslow for?'

'Well, I didn't actually go to Hounslow. There's a

sort of car park there, then I took a tube, you know.'

'What, a tube to London?'

'Yes. Yes, it seemed the easiest way.'

'You have rather a guilty look about you,' said Tuppence. 'Don't tell me I have a rival who lives in Hounslow?'

'No,' said Tommy. 'You ought to be pleased with what I've been doing.'

'Oh. Have you been buying me a present?'

'No. No,' said Tommy, 'I'm afraid not. I never know what to give you, as a matter of fact.'

'Well, your guesses are very good sometimes,' said Tuppence hopefully. 'What have you been really doing, Tommy, and why should I be pleased?'

'Because I, too,' said Tommy, 'have been doing research.'

'Everyone's doing research nowadays,' said Tuppence. 'You know, all the teenagers and all one's nephews or cousins or other people's sons and daughters, they're all doing research. I don't know actually what they do research into nowadays, but they never seem to do it, whatever it is, afterwards. They just have the research and a good time doing the research and they're very pleased with themselves and – well, I don't quite know what does come next.'

'Betty, our adopted daughter, went to East Africa,' said Tommy. 'Have you heard from her?'

'Yes, she loves it there – loves poking into African families and writing articles about them.'

'Do you think the families appreciate her interest?' asked Tommy.

'I shouldn't think so,' said Tuppence. 'In my father's parish I remember, everyone disliked the District Visitors – Nosey Parkers they called them.'

'You may have something there,' said Tommy. 'You are certainly pointing out to me the difficulties of what I am undertaking, or trying to undertake.'

'Research into what? Not lawn-mowers, I hope.'

'I don't know why you mention lawn-mowers.'

'Because you're eternally looking at catalogues of them,' said Tuppence. 'You're mad about getting a lawn-mower.'

'In this house of ours it is historic research we are doing into things – crimes and others that seem to have happened at least sixty or seventy years ago.'

'Anyway, come on, tell me a little more about your research projects, Tommy.'

'I went to London,' said Tommy, 'and put certain things in motion.'

'Ah,' said Tuppence. 'Research? Research in motion. In a way I've been doing the same thing that you are, only our methods are different. And my period is very far back.'

'Do you mean that you're really beginning to take

an interest in the problem of Mary Jordan? So that's how you put it on the agenda nowadays,' said Tommy. 'It's definitely taken shape has it? The mystery, or the problem of Mary Jordan.'

'Such a very ordinary name, too. Couldn't have been her right name if she was German,' said Tuppence, 'and she was said to be a German spy or something like that, but she could have been English, I suppose.'

'I think the German story is just a kind of legend.'

'Do go on, Tommy. You're not telling me anything.'

'Well, I put certain – certain – certain –'

'Don't go on saying certain,' said Tuppence. 'I really can't understand.'

'Well, it's very difficult to explain things sometimes,' said Tommy, 'but I mean, there are certain ways of making enquiries.'

'You mean, things in the past?'

'Yes. In a sense. I mean, there are things that you can find out. Things that you could obtain information from. Not just by riding old toys and asking old ladies to remember things and cross-questioning an old gardener who probably will tell you everything quite wrong or going round to the post office and upsetting the staff by asking the girls there to tell their memories of what their great-great-aunts once said.'

'All of them have produced a little something,' said Tuppence.

'So will mine,' said Tommy.

'You've been making enquiries? Who do you go to to ask your questions?'

'Well, it's not quite like that, but you must remember, Tuppence, that occasionally in my life I have been in connection with people who do know how to go about these sort of things. You know, there are people you pay a certain sum to and they do the research for you from the proper quarters so that what you get is quite authentic.'

'What sort of things? What sort of places?'

'Well, there are lots of things. To begin with you can get someone to study deaths, births and marriages, that sort of thing.'

'Oh, I suppose you send them to Somerset House. Do you go there for deaths as well as marriages?'

'And births – one needn't go oneself, you get someone to go for you. And find out when someone dies or read somebody's will, look up marriages in churches or study birth certificates. All those things can be enquired into.'

'Have you been spending a lot of money?' asked Tuppence. 'I thought we were going to try and economize once we'd paid the expense of moving in here.'

'Well, considering the interest you're taking in problems, I consider that this can be regarded in the way of money well spent.'

'Well, did you find out anything?'

'Not as quickly as this. You have to wait until the research has been made. Then if they can get answers for you –'

'You mean somebody comes up and tells you that someone called Mary Jordan was born at Little Sheffield-on-the-Wold or something like that and then you go and make enquiries there later. Is that the sort of thing?'

'Not exactly. And then there are census returns and death certificates and causes of death and, oh, quite a lot of things that you can find out about.'

'Well,' said Tuppence, 'it sounds rather interesting anyway, which is always something.'

'And there are files in newspaper offices that you can read and study.'

'You mean accounts of something – like murders or court cases?'

'Not necessarily, but one has had contact with certain people from time to time. People who know things – one can look them up – ask a few questions – renew old friendships. Like the time we were being a private detective firm in London. There are a few people, I expect, who could give us information or tell us where to go. Things do depend a bit on who you know.'

'Yes,' said Tuppence, 'that's quite true. I know that myself from experience.'

'Our methods aren't the same,' said Tommy. 'I think yours are just as good as mine. I'll never forget the day I came suddenly into that boarding-house, or whatever it was, Sans Souci. The first thing I saw was you sitting there knitting and calling yourself Mrs Blenkinsop.'

'All because I *hadn't* applied research, or getting anyone to do research for me,' said Tuppence.

'No,' said Tommy, 'you got inside a wardrobe next door to the room where I was being interviewed in a very interesting manner, so you knew exactly where I was being sent and what I was meant to do, and you managed to get there first. Eavesdropping. Neither more nor less. Most dishonourable.'

'With very satisfactory results,' said Tuppence.

'Yes,' said Tommy. 'You have a kind of feeling for success. It seems to happen to you.'

'Well, some day we shall know all about everything here, only it's all such years and years ago. I can't help thinking that the idea of something really important being hidden round here or owned by someone here, or something to do with this house or people who once lived in it being important – I can't just believe it somehow. Oh well, I see what we shall have to do next.'

'What?' said Tommy.

'Believe six impossible things before breakfast, of

course,' said Tuppence. 'It's quarter to eleven now, and I want to go to bed. I'm tired. I'm sleepy and extremely dirty because of playing around with all those dusty, ancient toys and things. I expect there are even more things in that place that's called – by the way, why is it called Kay Kay?'

'I don't know. Do you spell it at all?'

'I don't know – I think it's spelt k-a-i. Not just KK.'

'Because it sounds more mysterious?'

'It sounds Japanese,' said Tuppence doubtfully.

'I can't see why it should sound to you like Japanese. It doesn't to me. It sounds like something you eat. A kind of rice, perhaps.'

'I'm going to bed and to wash thoroughly and to get all the cobwebs off me somehow,' said Tuppence.

'Remember,' said Tommy, 'six impossible things before breakfast.'

'I expect I shall be better at that than you would be,' said Tuppence.

'You're very unexpected sometimes,' said Tommy.

'*You're* more often right than *I* am,' said Tuppence. '*That's* very annoying sometimes. Well, these things are sent to try us. Who used to say that to us? Quite often, too.'

'Never mind,' said Tommy. 'Go and clean the dust of bygone years off you. Is Isaac any good at gardening?'

'He considers he is,' said Tuppence. 'We might experiment with him –'

'Unfortunately we don't know much about gardening ourselves. Yet another problem.'

Chapter 4

Expedition on Truelove; Oxford and Cambridge

'Six impossible things before breakfast indeed,' said Tuppence as she drained a cup of coffee and considered a fried egg remaining in the dish on the sideboard, flanked by two appetizing-looking kidneys. 'Breakfast is more worthwhile than thinking of impossible things. Tommy is the one who has gone after impossible things. Research, indeed. I wonder if he'll get anything out of it all.'

She applied herself to a fried egg and kidneys.

'How nice,' said Tuppence, 'to have a different kind of breakfast.'

For a long time she had managed to regale herself in the morning with a cup of coffee and either orange juice or grapefruit. Although satisfactory so long as any weight problems were thereby solved, the pleasures of this kind of breakfast were not much appreciated.

From the force of contrasts, hot dishes on the sideboard animated the digestive juices.

'I expect,' said Tuppence, 'it's what the Parkinsons used to have for breakfast here. Fried egg or poached eggs and bacon and perhaps –' she threw her mind a good long way back to remembrances of old novels – 'perhaps yes, perhaps cold grouse on the sideboard, delicious! Oh yes, I remember, delicious it sounded. Of course, I suppose children were so unimportant that they only let them have the legs. Legs of game are very good because you can nibble at them.' She paused with the last piece of kidney in her mouth.

Very strange noises seemed to be coming through the doorway.

'I wonder,' said Tuppence. 'It sounds like a concert gone wrong somewhere.'

She paused again, a piece of toast in her hand, and looked up as Albert entered the room.

'What is going on, Albert?' demanded Tuppence. 'Don't tell me that's our workmen playing something? A harmonium or something like that?'

'It's the gentleman what's come to do the piano,' said Albert.

'Come to do what to the piano?'

'To tune it. You said I'd have to get a piano tuner.'

'Good gracious,' said Tuppence, 'you've done it already? How wonderful you are, Albert.'

Albert looked pleased, though at the same time conscious of the fact that he *was* very wonderful in the speed with which he could usually supply the extraordinary demands made upon him sometimes by Tuppence and sometimes by Tommy.

'He says it needs it very bad,' he said.

'I expect it does,' said Tuppence.

She drank half a cup of coffee, went out of the room and into the drawing-room. A young man was at work at the grand piano, which was revealing to the world large quantities of its inside.

'Good morning, madam,' said the young man.

'Good morning,' said Tuppence. 'I'm so glad you've managed to come.'

'Ah, it needs tuning, it does.'

'Yes,' said Tuppence, 'I know. You see, we've only just moved in and it's not very good for pianos, being moved into houses and things. And it hasn't been tuned for a long time.'

'No, I can soon tell that,' said the young man.

He pressed three different chords in turn, two cheerful ones in a major key, two very melancholy ones in A Minor.

'A beautiful instrument, madam, if I may say so.'

'Yes,' said Tuppence. 'It's an Erard.'

'And a piano you wouldn't get so easily nowadays.'

'It's been through a few troubles,' said Tuppence.

'It's been through bombing in London. Our house there was hit. Luckily we were away, but it was mostly outside that was damaged.'

'Yes. Yes, the works are good. They don't need so very much doing to them.'

Conversation continued pleasantly. The young man played the opening bars of a Chopin Prelude and passed from that to a rendering of 'The Blue Danube'. Presently he announced that his ministrations had finished.

'I shouldn't leave it too long,' he warned her. 'I'd like the chance to come and try it again before too much time has gone by because you don't know quite when it might not – well, I don't know how I should put it – relapse a bit. You know, some little thing that you haven't noticed or haven't been able to get at.'

They parted with mutually appreciative remarks on music in general and on piano music in particular, and with the polite salutations of two people who agreed very largely in their ideas as to the joys that music generally played in life.

'Needs a lot doing to it, I expect, this house,' he said, looking round him.

'Well, I think it had been empty some time when we came into it.'

'Oh yes. It's changed hands a lot, you know.'

'Got quite a history, hasn't it,' said Tuppence. 'I mean, the people who lived in it in the past and the sort of queer things that happened.'

'Ah well, I expect you're talking of that time long ago. I don't know if it was the last war or the one before.'

'Something to do with naval secrets or something,' said Tuppence hopefully.

'Could be, I expect. There was a lot of talk, so they tell me, but of course I don't know anything about it myself.'

'Well before your time,' said Tuppence, looking appreciatively at his youthful countenance.

When he had gone, she sat down at the piano.

'I'll play "The Rain on the Roof",' said Tuppence, who had had this Chopin memory revived in her by the piano tuner's execution of one of the other preludes. Then she dropped into some chords and began playing the accompaniment to a song, humming it first and then murmuring the words as well.

Where has my true love gone a-roaming?
Where has my true love gone from me?
High in the woods the birds are calling.
When will my true love come back to me?

'I'm playing it in the wrong key, I believe,' said Tuppence, 'but at any rate, the piano's all right again now. Oh, it is great fun to be able to play the piano again. "Where has my true love gone a-roaming?"' she murmured. '"When will my true love" – Truelove,' said Tuppence thoughtfully. 'True love? Yes, I'm thinking of that perhaps as a sign. Perhaps I'd better go out and do something with Truelove.'

She put on her thick shoes and a pullover, and went out into the garden. Truelove had been pushed, not back into his former home in KK, but into the empty stable. Tuppence took him out, pulled him to the top of the grass slope, gave him a sharp flick with the duster she had brought out with her to remove the worst of the cobwebs which still adhered in many places, got into Truelove, placed her feet on the pedals and induced Truelove to display his paces as well as he could in his condition of general age and wear.

'Now, my true love,' she said, 'down the hill with you and not too fast.'

She removed her feet from the pedals and placed them in a position where she could brake with them when necessary.

Truelove was not inclined to go very fast in spite of the advantage to him of having only to go by weight down the hill. However, the slope increased in steepness suddenly. Truelove increased his pace, Tuppence applied her feet as brakes rather more sharply and she and Truelove arrived together at a rather more uncomfortable portion than usual of the monkey puzzle at the bottom of the hill.

'Most painful,' said Tuppence, excavating herself.

Having extricated herself from the pricking of various portions of the monkey puzzle, Tuppence brushed herself down and looked around her. She had come to a thick bit of shrubbery leading up the hill in the opposite direction. There were rhododendron bushes here and hydrangeas. It would look, Tuppence thought, very lovely later in the year. At the moment, there was no particular beauty about it, it was a mere thicket. However, she did seem to notice that there had once been a pathway leading up between the various flower bushes and shrubs. Everything was much grown together now but you could trace the direction of the path. Tuppence broke off a branch or two, pressed her way through the first bushes and managed to follow the hill. The path went winding up. It was clear that nobody had ever cleared it or walked down it for years.

'I wonder where it takes one,' said Tuppence. 'There must be a reason for it.'

Perhaps, she thought, as the path took a couple of sharp turns in opposite directions, making a zigzag and making Tuppence feel that she knew exactly what Alice in Wonderland had meant by saying that a path would suddenly shake itself and change direction. There were fewer bushes, there were laurels now, possibly fitting in with the name given to the property, and then a rather stony, difficult, narrow path wound up between them. It came very suddenly to four moss-covered steps leading up to a kind of niche made of what had once been metal and later seemed to have been replaced by bottles. A kind of shrine, and in it a pedestal and on this pedestal a stone figure, very much decayed. It was the figure of a boy with a basket on his head. A feeling of recognition came to Tuppence.

'This is the sort of thing you could date a place with,' she said. 'It's very like the one Aunt Sarah had in her garden. She had a lot of laurels too.'

Her mind went back to Aunt Sarah, whom she had occasionally visited as a child. She had played herself, she remembered, a game called River Horses. For River Horses you took your hoop out. Tuppence, it may be said, had been six years old at the time. Her hoop represented the horses. White horses with manes and flowing tails. In Tuppence's imagination, with that you had gone across a green, rather thick patch of grass and you had then gone round a bed planted with pampas grass waving feathery heads into the air, up the same kind of a path, and leaning there among some beech trees in the same sort of summer-house niche was a figure and a basket. Tuppence, when riding her winning horses here, had taken a gift always, a gift you put in the basket on top of the boy's head; at the same time you said it was an offering and you made a wish. The wish, Tuppence remembered, was nearly always to come true.

'But that,' said Tuppence, sitting down suddenly on the top step of the flight she had been climbing, 'that, of course, was because I cheated really. I mean, I wished for something that I knew was almost sure to happen, and then I could feel that my wish had come true and it really *was* a magic. It was a proper offering to a real god from the past. Though it wasn't a god really, it was just a podgy-looking little boy. Ah well – what fun it is, all the things one used to invent and believe in and play at.'

She sighed, went down the path again and found her way to the mysteriously named KK.

KK looked in just the same mess as ever. Mathilde was still looking forlorn and forsaken, but two more things attracted Tuppence's attention. They were in porcelain – porcelain stools with the figures of white swans curled round them. One stool was dark blue and the other stool was pale blue.

'Of course,' said Tuppence, 'I've seen things like that before when I was young. Yes, they used to be on verandas. One of my other aunts had them, I think. We used to call them Oxford and Cambridge. Very much the same. I think it was ducks – no, it *was* swans they had round them. And then there was the same sort of queer thing in the seat, a sort of hole that was like a letter S. The sort of thing you could put things into. Yes, I think I'll get Isaac to take these two stools out of here and give them a good wash, and then we'll have them on the loggia, or lodger as he will insist on calling it, though the veranda comes more natural to me. We'll put them on that and enjoy them when the good weather comes.'

She turned and started to run towards the door. Her foot caught in Mathilde's obtrusive rocker –

'Oh dear!' said Tuppence, 'now what have I done?'

What she had done was to catch her foot in the dark blue porcelain stool and it rolled down on to the floor and smashed in two pieces.

'Oh dear,' said Tuppence, 'now I've really killed Oxford, I suppose. We shall have to make do with Cambridge. I don't think you could stick Oxford together again. The pieces are too difficult.'

She sighed and wondered what Tommy was doing.

II

Tommy was sitting exchanging memories with some old friends.

'World's in a funny way nowadays,' said Colonel

Atkinson. 'I hear you and your what's-her-name, Prudence – no, you had a nickname for her, Tuppence, that's right – yes, I hear you've gone to live in the country. Somewhere down near Hollowquay. I wonder what took you there. Anything particular?'

'Well, we found this house fairly cheap,' said Tommy.

'Ah. Well, that's lucky always, isn't it? What's the name? You must give me your address.'

'Well, we think we may call it Cedar Lodge because there's a very nice cedar there. Its original name was The Laurels, but that's rather a Victorian hangover, isn't it?'

'The Laurels. The Laurels, Hollowquay. My word, what are *you* up to, eh? What are *you* up to?'

Tommy looked at the elderly face with the sprouting white moustache.

'On to something, are you?' said Colonel Atkinson. 'Are you employed in the service of your country again?'

'Oh, I'm too old for that,' said Tommy. 'I'm retired from all that sort of stuff.'

'Ah, I wonder now. Perhaps that's just the thing you say. Perhaps you've been told to say that. After all, you know, there's a good deal was never found out about all that business.'

'What business?' said Tommy.

'Well, I expect you've read about it or heard about it. The Cardington Scandal. You know, came after that other thing – the what-you-call-'em letters – and the Emlyn Johnson submarine business.'

'Oh,' said Tommy, 'I seem to remember something vaguely.'

'Well, it wasn't actually the submarine business, but that's what called attention to the whole thing. And there were those letters, you see. Gave the whole show away politically. Yes. Letters. If they'd been able to get hold of *them* it would have made a big difference. It would have drawn attention to several people who at the time were the most highly trusted people in the government. Astonishing how these things happen, isn't it? You know! The traitors in one's midst, always highly trusted, always splendid fellows, always the last people to be suspected – and all the time – well, a lot of all that never came to light.' He winked one eye. 'Perhaps you've been sent down there to have a look round, eh, my boy?'

'A look round at what?' said Tommy.

'Well, this house of yours, The Laurels, did you say? There used to be some silly jokes about The Laurels sometimes. Mind you, they'd had a good look round, the security people and the rest of them. They thought that somewhere in that house was valuable evidence of some kind. There was an idea it had been sent overseas

– Italy was mentioned – just before people got alerted. But other people thought it might be still hidden there in that part of the world somewhere. You know, it's the sort of place that has cellars and flagstones and various things. Come now, Tommy, my boy, I feel you're on the hunt again.'

'I assure you I don't do anything of that kind nowadays.'

'Well, that's what one thought before about you when you were at that other place. Beginning of the last war. You know, where you ran down that German chap. That and the woman with the nursery rhyme books. Yes. Sharp bit of work, all that. And now, perhaps, they've set you on another trail!'

'Nonsense,' said Tommy. 'You mustn't get all these ideas in your head. I'm an old gaffer now.'

'You're a cunning old dog. I bet you're better than some of these young ones. Yes. You sit there looking innocent, and really I expect, well, one mustn't ask you questions. Mustn't ask you to betray State secrets, must I? Anyway, be careful of your missus. You know she's always one to stick herself forward too much. She had a narrow escape last time in the N or M days.'

'Ah well,' said Tommy, 'I think Tuppence is just interested in the general antiquity of this place, you know. Who lived there and where. And pictures of the old people who used to live in the house, and all the rest of it. That and planning the garden. That's all we're really interested in nowadays. Gardens. Gardens and bulb catalogues and all the rest of it.'

'Well, maybe I'll believe that if a year passes and nothing exciting has happened. But I know you, Beresford, and I know our Mrs Beresford, too. The two of you together, you're a wonderful couple and I bet you'll come up with something. I tell you, if those papers ever come to light, it'll have a very, very great effect on the political front and there are several people who won't be pleased. No indeed. And those people who won't be pleased are looked on as – pillars of rectitude at the moment! But by some they are thought to be dangerous. Remember that. They're dangerous, and the ones that aren't dangerous are in contact with those who *are* dangerous. So you be careful and make your missus be careful too.'

'Really,' said Tommy, 'your ideas, you make me feel quite excited.'

'Well, go on feeling excited but look after Mrs Tuppence. I'm fond of Tuppence. She's a nice girl, always was and still is.'

'Hardly a girl,' said Tommy.

'Now don't say that of your wife. Don't get in that habit. One in a thousand, she is. But I'm sorry for someone who has her in the picture sleuthing him down. She's probably out on the hunt today.'

'I don't think she is. More likely gone to tea with an elderly lady.'

'Ah well. Elderly ladies can sometimes give you useful information. Elderly ladies and children of five years old. All the unlikely people come out sometimes with a truth nobody had ever dreamed of. I could tell you things –'

'I'm sure you could, Colonel.'

'Ah well, one mustn't give away secrets.'

Colonel Atkinson shook his head.

III

On his way home Tommy stared out of the railway carriage window and watched the rapidly retreating countryside. 'I wonder,' he said to himself, 'I really wonder. That old boy, he's usually in the know. Knows things. But what can there be that could matter *now*. It's all in the past – I mean there's nothing, *can't* be anything left from that war. Not nowadays.' Then he wondered. New ideas had taken over – Common Market ideas. Somewhere, as it were *behind* his mind rather than *in* it, because there were grandsons and nephews, new generations – younger members of families that had always meant something, that had pull, had got positions of influence, of power because they were born who they were, and if by any chance *they* were not loyal, they *could* be approached, could believe in new creeds or in old creeds revived, whichever way you liked to think of it. England was in a funny state, a different state from what it had been. Or was it really always in the same state? Always underneath the smooth surface there was some black mud. There wasn't clear water down to the pebbles, down to the shells, lying on the bottom of the sea. There was something moving, something sluggish somewhere, something that had to be found, suppressed. But surely not – surely not in a place like Hollowquay. Hollowquay was a has-been if there ever was. Developed first as a fishing village and then further developed as an English Riviera – and now a mere summer resort, crowded in August. Most people now preferred package trips abroad.

IV

'Well,' said Tuppence, as she left the dinner table that night and went into the other room to drink coffee, 'was it fun or not fun? How were all the old boys?'

'Oh, very much the old boys,' said Tommy. 'How was your old lady?'

'Oh the piano tuner came,' said Tuppence, 'and it rained in the afternoon so I didn't see her. Rather a pity, the old lady might have said some things that were interesting.'

'My old boy did,' said Tommy. 'I was quite surprised. What do you think of this place really, Tuppence?'

'Do you mean the house?'

'No, I didn't mean the house. I think I mean Hollowquay.'

'Well, I think it's a nice place.'

'What do you mean by nice?'

'Well, it's a good word really. It's a word one usually despises, but I don't know why one should. I suppose a place that's nice is a place where things don't happen and you don't want them to happen. You're glad they don't.'

'Ah. That's because of our age, I suppose.'

'No, I don't think it's because of that. It's because it's nice to know there *are* places where things don't happen. Though I must say something nearly happened today.'

'What do you mean by nearly happened? Have you been doing anything silly, Tuppence?'

'No, of course I haven't.'

'Then what do you mean?'

'I mean that pane of glass at the top of the greenhouse, you know, it was trembling the other day a bit, had the twitches. Well it practically came down on my head. Might have cut me to bits.'

'It doesn't seem to have cut you to bits,' said Tommy, looking at her.

'No. I was lucky. But still, it made me jump rather.'

'Oh, we'll have to get our old boy who comes and does things, what's-his-name? Isaac, isn't it? Have to get him to look at some of the other panes – I mean, we don't want you being done in, Tuppence.'

'Well, I suppose when you buy an old house there's always something wrong with it.'

'Do you think there's something wrong with this house, Tuppence?'

'What on earth do you mean by wrong with this house?'

'Well, because I heard something rather queer about it today.'

'What – queer about this house?'

'Yes.'

'Really, Tommy, that seems impossible,' said Tuppence.

'Why does it seem impossible? Because it looks so nice and innocent? Well painted and done up?'

'No. Well painted and done up and looking innocent, that's all due to us. It looked rather shabby and decayed when we bought it.'

'Well, of course, that's why it was cheap.'

'You look peculiar, Tommy,' said Tuppence. 'What is it?'

'Well, it was old Moustachio-Monty, you know.'

'Oh, dear old boy, yes. Did he send his love to me?'

'Yes, he certainly did. He told me to make you take care of yourself, and me to take care of you.'

'He always says that. Though why I should take care of myself here I don't know.'

'Well, it seems it's the sort of place you might have to take care of yourself.'

'Now what on earth do you mean by that, Tommy?'

'Tuppence, what would you think if I said that he suggested or hinted, whatever way you like, that we were here not as old retired has-beens but as people on active service? That we were once more, as in the N or M days, on duty here. Sent here by the forces of security and order to discover something. To find out what was wrong with this place.'

'Well, I don't know if you're dreaming, Tommy, or if it was old Moustachio-Monty who was, if it was he who suggested it.'

'Well, he did. He seemed to think that we were definitely here on some kind of mission, to find something.'

'To find something? What sort of thing?'

'Something that might be hidden in this house.'

'Something that might be hidden in this house! Tommy, are you mad, or was he mad?'

'Well, I rather thought he might be mad, but I'm not so sure.'

'What could there be to find in this house?'

'Something that I suppose was once hidden here.'

'Buried treasure, are you talking about? Russian crown jewels hidden in the basement, that sort of thing?'

'No. Not treasure. Something that would be dangerous to someone.'

'Well, that's very odd,' said Tuppence.

'Why, have you found something?'

'No, of course I haven't found anything. But it seems there was a scandal about this place donkey's years ago. I don't mean anyone actually remembers, but it's the sort of thing that your grandmother told you, or the servants gossiped about. Actually, Beatrice has a friend who seemed to know something about it. And Mary Jordan was mixed up in it. It was all very hush-hush.'

'Are you imagining things, Tuppence? Have you gone back to the glorious days of our youth, to the time when someone gave a girl on the *Lusitania* something secret, the days when we had adventure, when we tracked down the enigmatic Mr Brown?'

'Goodness, that was a long time ago, Tommy. The Young Adventurers we called ourselves. Doesn't seem real now, does it?'

'No, it doesn't. Not a bit. But it was real, yes, it was

real all right. Such a lot of things are real though you can't really bring yourself to believe it. Must be at least sixty or seventy years ago. More than that, even.'

'What did Monty actually say?'

'Letters or papers of some kind,' said Tommy. 'Something that would have created or did create some great political upheaval of some kind. Someone in a position of power and who oughtn't to have been in a position of power, and there were letters, or papers, or something that would definitely cook his goose if they ever came to light. All sorts of intrigues and all happening years ago.'

'In the time of Mary Jordan? It sounds very unlikely,' said Tuppence. 'Tommy, you must have gone to sleep in the train coming back, and dreamt all this.'

'Well, perhaps I did,' said Tommy. 'It certainly doesn't seem likely.'

'Well, I suppose we might as well have a look around,' said Tuppence, 'as we are living here.'

Her eyes passed round the room.

'I shouldn't think there would be anything hidden here, do you, Tommy?'

'It doesn't seem the sort of house where anything would have been likely to be hidden. Lots of other people have lived in the house since those days.'

'Yes. Family after family, as far as I can make out. Well, I suppose it might be hidden up in an attic or down in the cellar. Or perhaps buried under the summer-house floor. Anywhere.'

'Anyway, it'll be quite fun,' said Tuppence. 'Perhaps, you know, when we haven't got anything else to do and our backs are aching because of planting tulip bulbs, we might have a little sort of look round. You know, just to think. Starting from the point: "If I wanted to hide something, where would I choose to put it, and where would it be likely to remain undiscovered?"'

'I don't think anything could remain undiscovered here,' said Tommy. 'Not with gardeners and people, you know, tearing up the place, and different families living here, and house agents and everything else.'

'Well, you never know. It might be in a teapot somewhere.'

Tuppence rose to her feet, went towards the mantelpiece, stood up on a stool and took down a Chinese teapot. She took off the lid and peered inside.

'Nothing there,' she said.

'A most unlikely place,' said Tommy.

'Do you think,' said Tuppence, with a voice that was more hopeful than despondent, 'that somebody was trying to put an end to me and loosened the glass skylight in the conservatory so that it would fall on me?'

'Most unlikely,' said Tommy. 'It was probably meant to fall on old Isaac.'

'That's a disappointing thought,' said Tuppence. 'I would like to feel that I had had a great escape.'

'Well, you'd better be careful of yourself. I shall be careful of you too.'

'You always fuss over me,' said Tuppence.

'It's very nice of me to do so,' said Tommy. 'You should be very pleased to have a husband who fusses about you.'

'Nobody tried to shoot *you* in the train or derail it or anything, did they?' said Tuppence.

'No,' said Tommy. 'But we'd better look at the car brakes before we go out driving next time. Of course this is all completely ridiculous,' he added.

'Of course it is,' said Tuppence. 'Absolutely ridiculous. All the same –'

'All the same what?'

'Well, it's sort of fun just to *think* of things like that.'

'You mean Alexander was killed because he knew something?' asked Tommy.

'He knew something about who killed Mary Jordan. *It was one of us . . .*' Tuppence's face lit up. 'US,' she said with emphasis, 'we'll have to know just all about US. An "US" here in this house in the past. It's a crime we've got to solve. Go back to the past to solve it – to where it happened and why it happened. That's a thing we've never tried to do before.'

Chapter 5

Methods of Research

'Where on earth have you been, Tuppence?' demanded her husband when he returned to the family mansion the following day.

'Well, last of all I've been in the cellar,' said Tuppence.

'I can see that,' said Tommy. 'Yes, I do see. Do you know that your hair is absolutely full of cobwebs?'

'Well, it would be of course. The cellar is full of cobwebs. There wasn't anything there, anyway,' said Tuppence. 'At least there were some bottles of bay rum.'

'Bay rum?' said Tommy. 'That's interesting.'

'Is it?' said Tuppence. 'Does one drink it? It seems to me most unlikely.'

'No,' said Tommy, 'I think people used to put it on their hair. I mean men, not women.'

'I believe you're right,' said Tuppence. 'I remember my uncle – yes, I had an uncle who used bay rum. A friend of his used to bring it him from America.'

'Oh really? That seems very interesting,' said Tommy.

'I don't think it is particularly interesting,' said Tuppence. 'It's no help to us, anyway. I mean, you couldn't hide anything in a bottle of bay rum.'

'Oh, so that's what you've been doing.'

'Well, one has to start somewhere,' said Tuppence. 'It's just possible if what your pal said to you was true, something *could* be hidden in this house, though it's rather difficult to imagine where it could be or what it could be, because, you see, when you sell a house or die and go out of it, the house is then of course emptied, isn't it? I mean, anyone who inherits it takes the furniture out and sells it, or if it's left, the next person comes in and *they* sell it, and so anything that's left in now would have belonged to the last tenant but one and certainly not much further back than that.'

'Then why should somebody want to injure you or injure me or try to get us to leave this house – unless, I mean, there was something here that they didn't want us to find?'

'Well, that's all *your* idea,' said Tuppence. 'It mightn't be true at all. Anyway, it's not been an entirely wasted day. I have found *some* things.'

'Anything to do with Mary Jordan?'

'Not particularly. The cellar, as I say, is not much good. It had a few old things to do with photography,

I think. You know, a developing lamp or something like they used to use in old days, with red glass in it, and the bay rum. But there were no sort of flagstones that looked as though you could pull them up and find anything underneath. There were a few decayed trunks, some tin trunks and a couple of old suitcases, but things that just couldn't be used to put anything in any more. They'd fall to bits if you kicked them. No. It was a wash-out.'

'Well, I'm sorry,' said Tommy. 'So no satisfaction.'

'Well, there *were* some things that were interesting. I said to myself, one has to say something to oneself – I think I'd better go upstairs now and take the cobwebs off before I go on talking.'

'Well, I think perhaps you had,' said Tommy. 'I shall like looking at you better when you've done that.'

'If you want to get the proper Darby and Joan feeling,' said Tuppence, 'you must always look at me and consider that your wife, no matter what her age, still looks lovely to you.'

'Tuppence dearest,' said Tommy, 'you look excessively lovely to me. And there is a kind of roly-poly of a cobweb hanging down over your left ear which is most attractive. Rather like the curl that the Empress Eugenie is sometimes represented as having in pictures. You know, running along the corner of her neck. Yours seems to have got a spider in it, too.'

'Oh,' said Tuppence, 'I don't like that.'

She brushed the web away with her hand. She duly went upstairs and returned to Tommy later. A glass was awaiting her. She looked at it doubtfully.

'You aren't trying to make *me* drink bay rum, are you?'

'No. I don't think I particularly want to drink bay rum myself.'

'Well,' said Tuppence, 'if I may get on with what I was saying –'

'I should like you to,' said Tommy. 'You'll do it anyway, but I would like to feel it was because I urged you to do so.'

'Well, I said to myself, "Now if I was going to hide anything in this house that I didn't want anyone else to find, what sort of place would I choose?"'

'Yes,' said Tommy, 'very logical.'

'And so I thought, what places are there where one can hide things? Well, one of them of course is Mathilde's stomach.'

'I beg your pardon,' said Tommy.

'Mathilde's stomach. The rocking-horse. I told you about the rocking-horse. It's an American rocking-horse.'

'A lot of things seem to have come from America,' said Tommy. 'The bay rum too, you said.'

'Well, anyway, the rocking-horse did have a hole in

its stomach because old Isaac told me about it; it had a hole in its stomach and a lot of sort of queer old paper stuff came out of it. Nothing interesting. But anyway, that's the sort of place where anyone might have hidden anything, isn't it?'

'Quite possibly.'

'And Truelove, of course. I examined Truelove again. You know it's got a sort of rather old decayed mackintosh seat but there was nothing there. And of course there were no personal things belonging to anyone. So I thought again. Well, after all, there's still the bookcase and books. People hide things in books. And we haven't quite finished doing the book-room upstairs, have we?'

'I thought we had,' said Tommy hopefully.

'Not really. There was the bottom shelf still.'

'That doesn't really need doing. I mean, one hasn't got to get up a ladder and take things down.'

'No. So I went up there and sat down on the floor and looked through the bottom shelf. Most of it was sermons. Sermons of somebody in old times written by a Methodist minister, I think. Anyway, they weren't interesting, there was nothing in them. So I pulled all those books out on the floor. And then I did make a discovery. Underneath, some time or other, somebody had made a sort of gaping hole, and pushed all sorts of things in it, books all torn to pieces more or less. There was one rather big one. It had a brown paper cover on it and I just pulled it out to see. After all, one never knows, does one? And what do you think it was?'

'I've no idea. First edition of *Robinson Crusoe* or something valuable like that?'

'No. It was a birthday book.'

'A birthday book. What's that?'

'Well, they used to have them. Goes back a long time. Back to the Parkinsons, I think. Probably before that. Anyway, it was rather battered and torn. Not worth keeping, and I don't suppose anyone would have bothered about it. But it *does* date back and one *might* find something in it, I thought.'

'I see. You mean the sort of thing people might have slipped something into.'

'Yes. But nobody has done that, of course. Nothing so simple. But I'm still going through it quite carefully. I haven't gone through it properly yet. You see, it might have interesting names in it and one might find out something.'

'I suppose so,' said Tommy, sounding sceptical.

'Well, that's one thing. That's the only thing in the book line that I came across. There was nothing else on the bottom shelf. The other thing to look through, of course, is the cupboards.'

'What about furniture?' said Tommy. 'Lots of things like secret drawers in furniture, and all that.'

'No, Tommy, you're not looking at things straight. I mean, all the furniture in the house now is *ours*. We moved into an empty house and brought our furniture with us. The only thing we found here from really old times is all that mess out in the place called KK, old decayed toys and garden seats. I mean, there's no proper antique furniture left in the house. Whoever it was lived here last took it away or else sent it to be sold. There's been lots of people, I expect, since the Parkinsons, so there wouldn't be anything left of theirs here. But, I *did* find something. I don't know, it may mean something helpful.'

'What was that?'

'China menu cards.'

'China menu cards?'

'Yes. In that old cupboard we haven't been able to get into. The one off the larder. You know, they'd lost the key. Well, I found the key in an old box. Out in KK, as a matter of fact. I put some oil on it and I managed to get the cupboard door open. And, well, there was nothing in it. It was just a dirty cupboard with a few broken bits of china left in it. I should think from the last people who were here. But shoved up on the top shelf there was a little heap of the Victorian china menus people used to have at parties. Fascinating, the things they ate – really the most delicious meals. I'll read you some after we've had dinner. It was fascinating.

You know, two soups, clear and thick, and on top of that there were two kinds of fish and then there were two entrées, I think, and then you had a salad or something like that. And then after that you had the joint and after that – I'm not quite sure what came next. I think a sorbet – that's ice cream, isn't it? And actually after that – lobster salad! Can you believe it?'

'Hush, Tuppence,' said Tommy, 'I don't really think I can stand any more.'

'Well, anyway I thought it might be interesting. It dates back, you know. It dates back, I should think, quite a long time.'

'And what do you hope to get from all these discoveries?'

'Well, the only thing with possibilities is the birthday book. In it I see there is a mention of somebody called Winifred Morrison.'

'Well?'

'Well, Winifred Morrison, I gather, was the maiden name of old Mrs Griffin. That's the one I went to tea with the other day. She's one of the oldest inhabitants, you know, and she remembers or knows about a lot of things that happened before her time. Well, I think she might remember or have heard of some of the other names in the birthday book. We might get something from that.'

'We might,' said Tommy still sounding doubtful. 'I still think –'

'Well, what do you still think?' said Tuppence.

'I don't know what to think,' said Tommy. 'Let's go to bed and sleep. Don't you think we'd better give this business up altogether? Why should we want to know who killed Mary Jordan?'

'Don't you *want* to?'

'No, I don't,' said Tommy. 'At least – oh I give in. You've got me involved now, I admit.'

'Haven't *you* found out anything?' asked Tuppence.

'I hadn't time today. But I've got a few more sources of information. I put that woman I told you about – you know, the one who's quite clever about research – I put *her* on to a few things.'

'Oh well,' said Tuppence, 'we'll still hope for the best. It's all nonsense, but perhaps it *is* rather fun.'

'Only I'm not so sure it's going to be as much fun as you think,' said Tommy.

'Oh well. No matter,' said Tuppence, 'we'll have done our best.'

'Well, don't go on doing your best all by yourself,' said Tommy. 'That's exactly what worries me so much – when I'm away from you.'

Chapter 6

Mr Robinson

'I wonder what Tuppence is doing now,' said Tommy, sighing.

'Excuse me, I didn't quite hear what you said.'

Tommy turned his head to look at Miss Collodon more closely. Miss Collodon was thin, emaciated, had grey hair which was slowly passing through the stage of recovering from a peroxide rinse designated to make her look younger (which it had not done). She was now trying various shades of artistic grey, cloudy smoke, steel blue and other interesting shades suitable for a lady between sixty and sixty-five, devoted to the pursuit of research. Her face represented a kind of ascetic superiority and a supreme confidence in her own achievements.

'Oh, it was nothing really, Miss Collodon,' said Tommy. 'Just – just something I was considering, you know. Just thinking of.'

And what is it, I wonder, thought Thomas, being careful this time not to utter the words aloud, that she can be doing today. Something silly, I bet. Half killing herself in that extraordinary, obsolete child's toy that'll come to pieces carrying her down the hill, and she'll probably end up with a broken something or other. Hips, it seems to be nowadays, though I don't see why hips are more vulnerable than anything else. Tuppence, he thought, would at this moment be doing something silly or foolish or, if not that, she would be doing something which might not be silly or foolish but *would* be highly dangerous. Yes, dangerous. It was always difficult keeping Tuppence out of danger. His mind roved vaguely over various incidents in the past. Words of a quotation came into his mind, and he spoke them aloud:

'Postern of Fate . . .
Pass not beneath, O Caravan, or pass not singing.
Have you heard
That silence where the birds are dead, yet something
pipeth like a bird?'

Miss Collodon responded immediately, giving Tommy quite a shock of surprise.

'Flecker,' she said. 'Flecker. It goes on:

"Death's Caravan . . . Disaster's Cavern, Fort of Fear."'

Tommy stared at her, then realized that Miss Collodon had thought he was bringing her a poetic problem to be researched, full information on where a certain quotation came from and who the poet had been who had uttered it. The trouble with Miss Collodon was that her research covered such a broad field.

'I was just wondering about my wife,' said Tommy apologetically.

'Oh,' said Miss Collodon.

She looked at Tommy with a rather new expression in her eye. Marital trouble in the home, she was deducing. She would presently probably offer him the address of a marriage advice bureau wherein he might seek adjustment in his matrimonial affairs and troubles.

Tommy said hurriedly, 'Have you had any success with that enquiry I spoke to you about the day before yesterday?'

'Oh yes. Not very much trouble in *that*. Somerset House is very useful, you know, in all those things. I don't think, you know, that there is likely to be anything particular that you want there, but I've got the names and addresses of certain births, marriages and deaths.'

'What, are they all Mary Jordans?'

'Jordan, yes. A Mary. A Maria and a Polly Jordan. Also a Mollie Jordan. I don't know if any of them are likely to be what you want. Can I pass this to you?'

She handed him a small typewritten sheet.

'Oh, thank you. Thank you very much.'

'There are several addresses, too. The ones you asked me for. I have not been able to find out the address of Major Dalrymple. People change their addresses constantly nowadays. However, I think another two days ought to get that information all right. This is Dr Heseltine's address. He is at present living at Surbiton.'

'Thanks very much,' said Tommy. 'I might start on him, anyway.'

'Any more queries?'

'Yes. I've got a list here of about six. Some of them may not be in your line.'

'Oh well,' said Miss Collodon, with complete assurance, 'I have to make things my line, you know. You can easily find out first just where you can find out, if that isn't a rather foolish way of speech. But it does explain things, you know. I remember – oh, quite a long time ago, when I was first doing this work, I found how useful Selfridge's advice bureau was. You could ask them the most extraordinary questions about the most extraordinary things and they always seemed to be able to tell you something about it or where you could get the information quickly. But of course they don't do that sort of thing nowadays. Nowadays, you know, most enquiries that are made are – well, you know, if you want to commit suicide, things like that.

Samaritans. And legal questions about wills and a lot of extraordinary things for authors, of course. And jobs abroad and immigration problems. Oh yes, I cover a very wide field.'

'I'm sure you do,' said Tommy.

'And helping alcoholics. A lot of societies there are who specialize in that. Some of them are much better than others. I have quite a list – comprehensive – and some most reliable –'

'I'll remember it,' Tommy said, 'if I find myself shaping that way any time. It depends how far I get today.'

'Oh, I'm sure, Mr Beresford, I don't see any signs of alcoholic difficulties in you.'

'No red nose?' said Tommy.

'It's worse with women,' said Miss Collodon. 'More difficult, you know, to get them off it, as you might say. Men do relapse, but not so notably. But really, some women, they seem quite all right, quite happy drinking lemonade in large quantities and all that, and then some evening, in the middle of a party – well, it's all there again.'

In turn, she looked at her watch.

'Oh dear, I must go on to my next appointment. I have to get to Upper Grosvenor Street.'

'Thank you very much,' said Tommy, 'for all you've done.'

He opened the door politely, helped Miss Collodon on with her coat, went back into the room and said,

'I must remember to tell Tuppence this evening that our researches so far have led me to impress a research agent with the idea that my wife drinks and our marriage is breaking up because of it. Oh dear, what next!'

II

What next was an appointment in an inexpensive restaurant in the neighbourhood of Tottenham Court Road.

'Well I never!' said an elderly man, leaping up from his seat where he was sitting waiting. 'Carroty Tom, on my life. Shouldn't have known you.'

'Possibly not,' said Tommy. 'Not much carrots left about me. It's grey-haired Tom.'

'Ah well, we're all that. How's your health?'

'Much the same as I always was. Cracking. You know. Decomposing by degrees.'

'How long is it since I've seen you? Two years? Eight years? Eleven years?'

'Now you're going too far,' said Tommy. 'We met at the Maltese Cats dinner last autumn, don't you remember?'

'Ah, so we did. Pity that broke up, you know. I always thought it would. Nice premises, but the food was rotten. Well, what are you doing these days, old boy? Still in the espionage-up-to-date do?'

'No,' said Tommy, 'I'm nothing to do with espionage.'

'Dear me. What a waste of your activities.'

'And what about you, Mutton-Chop?'

'Oh, I'm much too old to serve my country in that way.'

'No espionage going on nowadays?'

'Lots of it, I expect. But probably they put the bright boys on to it. The ones who come bursting out of universities needing a job badly. Where are you now? I sent you a Christmas card this year. Well, I didn't actually post it till January but anyway it came back to me with "Not known at this address".'

'No. We've gone to the country to live now. Down near the sea. Hollowquay.'

'Hollowquay. Hollowquay? I seem to remember something. Something in your line going on there once, wasn't there?'

'Not in my time,' said Tommy. 'I've only just got to hear of it since going to live there. Legends of the past. At least sixty years ago.'

'Something to do with a submarine, wasn't it? Plans of a submarine sold to someone or other. I forget who we were selling to at that time. Might have been the

Japanese, might have been the Russians – oh, and lots of others. People always seemed to meet enemy agents in Regent's Park or somewhere like that. You know, they'd meet someone like a third Secretary from an Embassy. Not so many beautiful lady spies around as there used to be once in fiction.'

'I wanted to ask you a few things, Mutton-Chop.'

'Oh? Ask away. I've had a very uneventful life. Margery – do you remember Margery?'

'Yes, of course I remember Margery. I nearly got to your wedding.'

'I know. But you couldn't make it or something, or took the wrong train, as far as I remember. A train that was going to Scotland instead of Southall. Anyway, just as well you didn't. Nothing much came of it.'

'Didn't you get married?'

'Oh yes, I got married. But somehow or other it didn't take very well. No. A year and a half and it was done with. She's married again. I haven't, but I'm doing very nicely. I live at Little Pollon. Quite a decent golf-course there. My sister lives with me. She's a widow with a nice bit of money and we get on well together. She's a bit deaf so she doesn't hear what I say, but it only means shouting a bit.'

'You said you'd heard of Hollowquay. Was it really something to do with spying of some kind?'

'Well, to tell you the truth, old boy, it's so long ago that I can't remember much about it. It made a big stir at the time. You know, splendid young naval officer absolutely above suspicion in every way, ninety per cent British, rated about a hundred and five in reliability, but nothing of the kind really. In the pay of – well, I can't remember now who he was in the pay of. Germany, I suppose. Before the 1914 war. Yes, I think that was it.'

'And there was a woman too, I believe, associated with it all,' said Tommy.

'I seem to remember hearing something about a Mary Jordan, I think it was. Mind you, I am not clear about all this. Got into the papers and I think it was a wife of his – I mean of the above-suspicion naval officer. It was his wife who got in touch with the Russians and – no, no, that's something that happened since then. One mixes things up so – they all sound alike. Wife thought he wasn't getting enough money, which meant, I suppose, that *she* wasn't getting enough money. And so – well, why d'you want to dig up all this old history? What's it got to do with you after all this time? I know you had something to do once with someone who was on the *Lusitania* or went down with the *Lusitania* or something like that, didn't you? If we go back as far as that, I mean. That's what you were mixed up in once, or your wife was mixed up in.'

'We were both mixed up in it,' said Tommy, 'and it's such a very long time ago that I really can't remember anything about it now.'

'There was some woman associated with that, wasn't there? Name like Jane Fish, or something like that, or was it Jane Whale?'

'Jane Finn,' said Tommy.

'Where is she now?'

'She's married to an American.'

'Oh, I see. Well, all very nice. One always seems to get talking about one's old pals and what's happened to them all. When you talk about old friends, either they are dead, which surprises you enormously because you didn't think they would be, or else they're not dead and that surprises you even more. It's a very difficult world.'

Tommy said yes it was a very difficult world and here was the waiter coming. What could they have to eat . . . The conversation thereafter was gastronomic.

III

In the afternoon Tommy had another interview arranged. This time with a sad, grizzled man sitting in an office and obviously grudging the time he was giving Tommy.

'Well, I really couldn't say. Of course I know roughly what you're talking about – lot of talk about it at the time – caused a big political blow-up – but I really have no information about that sort of thing, you know. No. You see, these things, they don't last, do they? They soon pass out of one's mind once the Press gets hold of some other juicy scandal.'

He opened up slightly on a few of his own interesting moments in life when something he'd never suspected came suddenly to light or his suspicions had suddenly been aroused by some very peculiar event. He said:

'Well, I've just got one thing might help. Here's an address for you and I've made an appointment too. Nice chap. Knows everything. He's the tops, you know, absolutely the tops. One of my daughters was a godchild of his. That's why he's awfully nice to me and will always do me a good turn if possible. So I asked him if he would see you. I said there were some things you wanted the top news about, I said what a good chap you were and various things and he said yes, he'd heard of you already. Knew something about you, and he said, Of course come along. Three forty-five, I think. Here's the address. It's an office in the City, I think. Ever met him?'

'I don't think so,' said Tommy, looking at the card and the address. 'No.'

'Well you wouldn't think he knew anything, to look at him, I mean. Big, you know, and yellow.'

'Oh,' said Tommy, 'big and yellow.'

It didn't really convey much information to his mind.

'He's the tops,' said Tommy's grizzled friend, 'absolute tops. You go along there. He'll be able to tell you *something* anyway. Good luck, old chap.'

IV

Tommy, having successfully got himself to the City office in question, was received by a man of 35 to 40 years of age who looked at him with the eye of one determined to do the worst without delay. Tommy felt that he was suspected of many things, possibly carrying a bomb in some deceptive container, or prepared to hijack or kidnap anyone or to hold up with a revolver the entire staff. It made Tommy extremely nervous.

'You have an appointment with Mr Robinson? At what time, did you say? Ah, three forty-five.' He consulted a ledger. 'Mr Thomas Beresford, is that right?'

'Yes,' said Tommy.

'Ah. Just sign your name here, please.'

Tommy signed his name where he was told.

'Johnson.'

A nervous-looking young man of about twenty-three

seemed like an apparition rising out of a glass partitioned desk. 'Yes, sir?'

'Take Mr Beresford up to the fourth floor to Mr Robinson's office.'

'Yes, sir.'

He led Tommy to a lift, the kind of lift that always seemed to have its own idea of how it should deal with those who came into it. The doors rolled open. Tommy passed in, the doors very nearly pinched him in doing so and just managed to slam themselves shut about an inch from his spine.

'Cold afternoon,' said Johnson, showing a friendly attitude to someone who was clearly being allowed to approach the high one in the highest.

'Yes,' said Tommy, 'it always seems to be cold in the afternoons.'

'Some say it's pollution, some say it's all the natural gas they're taking out of the North Sea,' said Johnson.

'Oh, I haven't heard that,' said Tommy.

'Doesn't seem likely to me,' said Johnson.

They passed the second floor and the third floor and finally arrived at the fourth floor. Johnson led Tommy, again escaping the closing doors by a mere inch, along a passage to a door. He knocked, was told to enter, held the door open, insinuated Tommy across the threshold, and said:

'Mr Beresford, sir. By appointment.'

He went out and shut the door behind him. Tommy advanced. The room seemed to be mainly filled by an enormous desk. Behind the desk sat a rather enormous man, a man of great weight and many inches. He had, as Tommy had been prepared for by his friend, a very large and yellow face. What nationality he was Tommy had no idea. He might have been anything. Tommy had a feeling he was probably foreign. A German, perhaps? Or an Austrian? Possibly a Japanese. Or else he might be very decidedly English.

'Ah. Mr Beresford.'

Mr Robinson got up, shook hands.

'I'm sorry if I come taking a lot of your time,' said Tommy.

He had a feeling he had once seen Mr Robinson before or had had Mr Robinson pointed out to him. Anyway on the occasion, whatever it had been, he had been rather shy about it because obviously Mr Robinson was someone very important, and, he now gathered (or rather felt at once) he was still very important.

'There's something you want to know about, I gather. Your friend, What's-his-name, just gave me a brief résumé.'

'I don't suppose – I mean, it's something perhaps I oughtn't to bother you about. I don't suppose it's anything of any importance. It was just – just –'

'Just an idea?'

'Partly my wife's idea.'

'I've heard about your wife. I've heard about you, too. Let me see, the last time was M or N wasn't it? Or N or M. Mm. I remember. Remember all the facts and things. You got that Commander chap, didn't you? The one who was in the English Navy supposedly but was actually a very important Hun. I still call them Huns occasionally, you know. Of course I know we're all different now we're in the Common Market. All in the nursery school together, as you might say. I know. You did a good bit of work there. Very good bit indeed. And so did your missus. My word. All those children's books. I remember. Goosey, Goosey Gander wasn't it – the one that gave the show away? Where do you wander? Upstairs and downstairs and in my lady's chamber.'

'Fancy you remembering that,' said Tommy, with great respect.

'Yes, I know. One's always surprised when one remembers something. It just came back to me at that minute. So silly, you know, that really you'd never have suspected it of being anything else, would you?'

'Yes, it was a good show.'

'Now, what's the matter now? What are you up against?'

'Well, it's nothing, really,' said Tommy. 'It's just –'

'Come on, put it in your own words. You needn't make a thing of it. Just tell me the story. Sit down. Take the weight off your feet. Don't you know – or you will know, when you're some years older – resting your feet is important.'

'I'm old enough already, I should think,' said Tommy. 'There can't be much ahead of me now except a coffin, in due course.'

'Oh I wouldn't say that. I tell you, once you get above a certain age you can go on living practically for ever. Now then, what's all this about?'

'Well,' said Tommy, 'briefly, my wife and I went into a new house and there was all the fuss of getting into a new house –'

'I know,' said Mr Robinson, 'yes, I know the sort of thing. Electricians all over the floor. They pick holes and you fall into them and –'

'There were some books there the people moving out wanted to sell. A lot of children's books, all sorts of things. You know, Henty and things like that.'

'I remember. I remember Henty from my own youth.'

'And in one book my wife was reading we found a passage underlined. The letters were underlined and it made a sentence when you put it together. And – this sounds awfully silly, what I'm going to say next –'

'Well, that's hopeful,' said Mr Robinson. 'If a thing sounds silly, I always want to hear about it.'

'It said, *Mary Jordan did not die naturally. It must have been one of us.*'

'Very, very interesting,' said Mr Robinson. 'I've never come across anything like that before. It said that, did it? Mary Jordan did not die a natural death. And who was it who wrote it? Any clue of that?'

'Apparently a boy of school age. Parkinson was the family's name. They lived in this house and he was one of the Parkinsons, we gathered. Alexander Parkinson. At least, anyway, he's buried there in the churchyard.'

'Parkinson,' said Mr Robinson. 'Wait a bit. Let me think. Parkinson – yes, you know there was a name like that connected with things, but you don't always remember who or what and where.'

'And we've been very keen to learn who Mary Jordan was.'

'Because she didn't die a natural death. Yes, I suppose that would be rather your line of country. But it seems very odd. What did you find out about her?'

'Absolutely nothing,' said Tommy. 'Nobody seems to remember her there much, or say anything about her. At least somebody did say she was what we'd call an *au pair* girl nowadays or a governess or something like that. They couldn't remember. A Mamselle or a Frowline, they said. It's all very difficult, you see.'

'And she died – what did she die of?'

'Somebody brought a few foxglove leaves in with some spinach from the garden, by accident, and then they ate it. Mind you, that probably wouldn't kill you.'

'No,' said Mr Robinson. 'Not enough of it. But if you then put a strong dose of digitalin alkaloid in the coffee and just made sure that Mary Jordan got it in her coffee, or in a cocktail earlier, then – then, as you say, the foxglove leaves would be blamed and it would all be taken to be an accident. But Alexander Parker, or whatever the schoolboy's name was, was too sharp for that. He had other ideas, did he? Anything else, Beresford? When was this? First World War, Second World War, or before that?'

'Before. Rumours passed down through elderly ancestors say she was a German spy.'

'I remember that case – made a big sensation. Any German working in England before 1914 was always said to be a spy. The English officer involved was one always said to be "above suspicion". I always look very hard at anyone who is above suspicion. It's all a long time ago, I don't think it's ever been written up in recent years. I mean, not in the way that things are occasionally for public enjoyment when they release a bit of stuff from the records.'

'Yes, but it's all rather sketchy.'

'Yes, it would be by now. It's always been associated, of course, with the submarine secrets that were stolen around then. There was some aviation news as well. A lot of that side of it, and that's what caught the public interest, as you might say. But there are a lot of things, you know. There was the political side to it, too. A lot of our prominent politicians. You know, the sort of chaps people say, "Well, *he* has *real* integrity." Real integrity is just as dangerous as being above suspicion in the Services. Real integrity my foot,' said Mr Robinson. 'I remember it with this last war. Some people haven't got the integrity they are credited with. One chap lived down near here, you know. He had a cottage on the beach, I think. Made a lot of disciples, you know, praising Hitler. Saying our only chance was to get in with him. Really the fellow seemed such a noble man. Had some wonderful ideas. Was so terribly keen to abolish all poverty and difficulties and injustice – things of that kind. Oh yes. Blew the Fascist trumpet without calling it Fascism. And Spain too, you know. Was in with Franco and all that lot to begin with. And dear old Mussolini, naturally, spouting away. Yes, there are always a lot of side-lines to it just before wars. Things that never came out and nobody ever really knew about.'

'You seem to know everything,' said Tommy. 'I beg your pardon. Perhaps that's rather rude of me. But it really is very exciting to come across someone who does seem to know about everything.'

'Well, I've often had a finger in the pie, as you might say. You know, come into things on the side-lines, or in the background. One hears a good deal. One hears a good deal from one's old cronies too, who were in it up to the neck and who knew the lot. I expect you begin to find that, don't you?'

'Yes,' said Tommy, 'it's quite true. I meet old friends, you know, and they've seen other old friends and there're quite a lot of things that, well, one's friends knew and you knew. You didn't get together just then but now you *do* hear about them and they're very interesting sometimes.'

'Yes,' said Mr Robinson. 'I see where you're going – where you're tending, you might say. It's interesting that you should come across this.'

'The trouble is,' said Tommy, 'that I don't really know – I mean, perhaps we're being rather silly. I mean, we bought this house to live in, the sort of house we wanted. We've done it up the way we want and we're trying to get the garden in some kind of shape. But I mean, I don't want to get tied up in this sort of stuff again. It's just pure curiosity on our part. Something that happened long ago and you can't help thinking about it or wanting to know why. But there's no point in it. It's not going to do anybody any good.'

'I know. You just want to *know*. Well, that's the way the human being is made. That's what leads us to explore things, to go and fly to the moon, to bother about underwater discoveries, to find natural gas in the North Sea, to find oxygen supplied to us by the sea and not by the trees and forests. Quite a lot of things they're always finding out about. Just through curiosity. I suppose without curiosity a man would be a tortoise. Very comfortable life, a tortoise has. Goes to sleep all the winter and doesn't eat anything more than grass as far as I know, to live all the summer. Not an interesting life perhaps, but a very peaceful one. On the other hand –'

'On the other hand one might say man is more like a mongoose.'

'Good. You're a reader of Kipling. I'm so glad. Kipling's not appreciated as much as he should be nowadays. He was a wonderful chap. A wonderful person to read nowadays. His short stories, amazingly good, they are. I don't think it's ever been realized enough.'

'I don't want to make a fool of myself,' said Tommy. 'I don't want to mix myself up with a lot of things which have nothing to do with me. Not anything to do with anybody nowadays, I should say.'

'That you never know,' said Mr Robinson.

'I mean, really,' said Tommy, who was now completely swamped in a cloud of guilt for having disturbed a very important man, 'I mean, I'm not just trying to find out things.'

'Got to try and find out things just to satisfy your wife, I suppose. Yes, I've heard of her. I've never had the pleasure of meeting her, I don't think. Rather wonderful person, isn't she?'

'I think so,' said Tommy.

'That's good hearing. I like people who stick together and enjoy their marriage and go on enjoying it.'

'Really, I'm like the tortoise, I suppose. I mean, there we are. We're old and we're tired, and although we've got very good health for our age, we don't want to be mixed up in anything nowadays. We're not trying to butt into anything. We just –'

'I know. I know,' said Mr Robinson. 'Don't keep apologizing for it. You want to know. Like the mongoose, you want to know. And Mrs Beresford, she wants to know. Moreover, I should say from all I've heard of her and been told of her, I should say she will get to know somehow.'

'You think she's more likely to do it than I am?'

'Well, I don't think perhaps you're quite as keen on finding out things as she is, but I think you're just as likely to get on to it because I think you're rather good at finding sources. It's not easy to find sources for something as long ago as that.'

'That's why I feel awful about having come and disturbed you. But I wouldn't have done it on my own. It was only Mutton-Chop. I mean –'

'I know who you mean. Had mutton-chop whiskers and was rather pleased with them at one time. That's why he was called that. A nice chap. Done good work in his time. Yes. He sent you to me because he knew that I am interested in anything like that. I started quite early, you know. Poking about, I mean, and finding out things.'

'And now,' said Tommy, 'now you're the tops.'

'Now who told you that?' said Mr Robinson. 'All nonsense.'

'I don't think it is,' said Tommy.

'Well,' said Mr Robinson, 'some get to the tops and some have the tops forced upon them. I would say the latter applies to me, more or less. I've had a few things of surpassing interest forced upon me.'

'That business connected with – Frankfurt, wasn't it?'

'Ah, *you*'ve heard rumours, have you? Ah well, don't think about them any more. They're not supposed to be known much. Don't think I'm going to rebuff you for coming here asking me questions. I probably can answer some of the things you want to know. If I said there was something that happened years ago that might result in something being known that would be – possibly – interesting nowadays, sometimes that would give one a bit of information about things that might be going on nowadays, that might be true enough. I wouldn't put it past anyone or anything. I don't know what I can suggest to you, though. It's a question of worry about, listen to people, find out what you can about bygone years. If anything comes along that you think might be interesting to me, just give me a ring or something. We'll find some code words, you know. Just to make ourselves feel excited again, feel as though we really mattered. Crab-apple jelly, how would that be? You know, you say your wife's made some jars of crab-apple jelly and would I like a pot. I'll know what you mean.'

'You mean that – that I would have found out something about Mary Jordan. I don't see there's any point in going on with that. After all, she's dead.'

'Yes. She's dead. But – well, you see, sometimes one has the wrong ideas about people because of what you've been told. Or because of what's been written.'

'You mean we have wrong ideas about Mary Jordan. You mean, she wasn't important at all.'

'Oh yes, she could have been very important.' Mr Robinson looked at his watch. 'I have to push you off now. There's a chap coming in, in ten minutes. An awful bore, but he's high up in government circles, and you know what life is nowadays. Government, government, you've got to stand it everywhere. In the office, in the home, in the supermarkets, on the television. Private life. That's what we want more of nowadays.

Now this little fun and games that you and your wife are having, you're in private life and you can look at it from the background of private life. Who knows, you might find out something. Something that would be interesting. Yes. You may and you may not.

'I can't tell you anything more about it. I know some of the facts that probably nobody else can tell you and in due course I might be able to tell them to you. But as they're all dead and done with, that's not really practical.

'I'll tell you one thing that will help you perhaps in your investigations. You read about this case, the trial of Commander whatever-he-was – I've forgotten his name now – and he was tried for espionage, did a sentence for it and richly deserved it. He was a traitor to his country and that's that. But Mary Jordan –'

'Yes?'

'You want to know something about Mary Jordan. Well, I'll tell you one thing that might, as I say, help your point of view. Mary Jordan was – well, you can call it a spy but she wasn't a German spy. She wasn't an enemy spy. Listen to this, my boy. I can't keep calling you "my boy".'

Mr Robinson dropped his voice and leaned forward over his desk.

'*She was one of our lot.*'

Book III

Chapter 1

Mary Jordan

'But that alters everything,' said Tuppence.

'Yes,' said Tommy. 'Yes. It was – it was quite a shock.'

'Why did he tell you?'

'I don't know,' said Tommy. 'I thought – well, two or three different things.'

'Did he – what's he like, Tommy? You haven't really told me.'

'Well, he's yellow,' said Tommy. 'Yellow and big and fat and very, very ordinary, but at the same time, if you know what I mean, he isn't ordinary at all. He's – well, he's what my friend said he was. He's one of the tops.'

'You sound like someone talking about pop singers.'

'Well, one gets used to using these terms.'

'Yes, but why? Surely that was revealing something that he wouldn't have wanted to reveal, you'd think.'

'It was a long time ago,' said Tommy. 'It's all over, you see. I suppose none of it matters nowadays. I mean, look at all the things they're releasing now. Off the record. You know, not hushing up things any more. Letting it all come out, what really happened. What one person wrote and what another person said and what one row was about and how something else was all hushed up because of something you never heard about.'

'You make me feel horribly confused,' said Tuppence, 'when you say things like that. It makes everything wrong, too, doesn't it?'

'How do you mean, makes everything wrong?'

'Well, I mean, the way we've been looking at it. I mean – what do I mean?'

'Go on,' said Tommy. 'You must know what you mean.'

'Well, what I said. It's all wrong. I mean, we found this thing in *The Black Arrow*, and it was all clear enough. Somebody had written it in there, probably this boy Alexander, and it meant that somebody – one of them, he said, at least, one of us – I mean he put it that way but that's what he meant – one of the family or somebody in the house or something, had arranged to bring about the death of Mary Jordan, and we didn't know who Mary Jordan was, which was very baffling.'

'Goodness knows it's been baffling,' said Tommy.

'Well, it hasn't baffled you as much as me. It's baffled me a great deal. I haven't really found out anything about her. At least –'

'What you found out about her was that she had been apparently a German spy, isn't that what you mean? You found out that?'

'Yes, that is what was believed about her, and I supposed it was true. Only now –'

'Yes,' said Tommy, 'only now we know that it wasn't true. She was the opposite to a German spy.'

'She was a sort of English spy.'

'Well, she must have been in the English espionage or security whatever it was called. And she came here in some capacity to find out something. To find out something about – about – what's his name now? I wish I could remember names better. I mean the naval officer or the Army officer or whatever he was. The one who sold the secret of the submarine or something like that. Yes, I suppose there was a little cluster of German agents here, rather like in N or M all over again, all busy preparing things.'

'It would seem so, yes.'

'And she was sent here in that case, presumably, to find out all about it.'

'I see.'

'So "one of us" didn't mean what we thought it

meant. "One of us" meant – well, it had to be someone who was in this neighbourhood. And somebody who had something to do with this house, or was in this house for a special occasion. And so, when she died, her death wasn't a natural one, because somebody got wise to what she was doing. And Alexander found out about it.'

'She was pretending to spy, perhaps,' said Tuppence, 'for Germany. Making friends with Commander – whoever it was.'

'Call him Commander X,' said Tommy, 'if you can't remember.'

'All right, all right. Commander X. She was getting friendly with him.'

'There was also,' said Tommy, 'an enemy agent living down here. The head of a big organization. He lived in a cottage somewhere, down near the quay I think it was, and he wrote a lot of propaganda, and used to say that really our best plan would be to join in with Germany and get together with them – and things like that.'

'It is all so confusing,' said Tuppence. 'All these things – plans, and secret papers and plots and espionage – have been so confusing. Well, anyway, we've probably been looking in all the wrong places.'

'Not really,' said Tommy, 'I don't think so.'

'Why don't you think so?'

'Well, because if she, Mary Jordan, was here to find out something, and if she did find out something, then perhaps when *they* – I mean Commander X or other people – there must have been other people too in it – when *they* found out that she'd found out something –'

'Now don't get me muddled again,' said Tuppence. 'If you say things like that, it's very muddling. Yes. Go on.'

'All right. Well, when they found out that she'd found out a lot of things, well, then they had to –'

'To silence her,' said Tuppence.

'You make it sound like Phillips Oppenheim now,' said Tommy. 'And he was before 1914, surely.'

'Well, anyway, they had to silence Mary before she could report what she'd found out.'

'There must be a little more to it than that,' said Tommy. 'Perhaps she'd got hold of something important. Some kind of papers or written document. Letters that might have been sent or passed to someone.'

'Yes. I see what you mean. We've got to look among a different lot of people. But if she was one of the ones to die because of a mistake that had been made about the vegetables, then I don't see quite how it could be what Alexander called "one of us". It presumably wasn't one of *his* family.'

'It could have been like this,' said Tommy. 'It needn't

have been actually someone in the house. It's very easy to pick wrong leaves looking alike, bunch 'em all up together and take them into the kitchen; you wouldn't, I think, make them really – I mean, not *really* – too lethal. Just the people at one particular meal would get rather ill after it and they'd send for a doctor and the doctor would get the food analysed and he'd realize somebody'd made a mistake over vegetables. He wouldn't think anyone had done it on purpose.'

'But then everybody at that meal would have died,' said Tuppence. 'Or everybody would have been ill but *not* died.'

'Not necessarily,' said Tommy. 'Suppose they wanted a certain person – Mary J. – to die, and they were going to give a dose of poison to her, oh, in a cocktail *before* the lunch or dinner or whatever it was or in coffee or something after the meal – actual digitalin, or aconite or whatever it is in foxgloves –'

'Aconite's in monkshood, I think,' said Tuppence.

'Don't be so knowledgeable,' said Tommy. 'The point is everyone gets a mild dose by what is clearly a mistake, so everyone gets mildly ill – but one person dies. Don't you see, if most people were taken ill after whatever it was – dinner or lunch one day and it was looked into, and they found out about the mistake, well, things *do* happen like that. You know, people eat fungus instead of mushrooms, and deadly nightshade berries children eat by mistake because the berries look like fruit. Just a mistake and people are ill, but they don't usually all die. Just one of them does, and the one that did die would be assumed to have been particularly allergic to whatever it was and so *she* had died but the others *hadn't*. You see, it would pass off as really due to the mistake and they wouldn't have looked to see or even suspected there was some other way in which it happened –'

'She might have got a little ill like the others and then the real dose might have been put in her early tea the next morning,' said Tuppence.

'I'm sure, Tuppence, that you've lots of ideas.'

'About that part of it, yes,' said Tuppence. 'But what about the other things? I mean who and what and why? Who was the "one of us" – "one of them" as we'd better say now – who had the opportunity? Someone staying down here, friends of other people perhaps? People who brought a letter, forged perhaps, from a friend saying "Do be kind to my friend, Mr or Mrs Murray Wilson, or some name, who is down here. She is so anxious to see your pretty garden," or something. All that would be easy enough.'

'Yes, I think it would.'

'In that case,' said Tuppence, 'there's perhaps something still here in the house that would explain what happened to me today and yesterday, too.'

'What happened to you yesterday, Tuppence?'

'The wheels came off that beastly little cart and horse I was going down the hill in the other day, and so I came a terrible cropper right down behind the monkey puzzle and into it. And I very nearly – well, I might have had a serious accident. That silly old man Isaac ought to have seen that the thing was safe. He said he *did* look at it. He told me it was quite all right before I started.'

'And it wasn't?'

'No. He said afterwards that he thought someone had been playing about with it, tampering with the wheels or something, so that they came off.'

'Tuppence,' said Tommy, 'do you think that's the second or third thing that's happened here to us? You know that other thing that nearly came down on the top of me in the book-room?'

'You mean somebody wants to get rid of *us*? But that would mean –'

'That would mean,' said Tommy, 'that there must be *something*. Something that's *here* – in the house.'

Tommy looked at Tuppence and Tuppence looked at Tommy. It was the moment for consideration. Tuppence opened her mouth three times but checked herself each time, frowning, as she considered. It was Tommy who spoke at last.

'What did he think? What did he say about Truelove? Old Isaac, I mean.'

'That it was only to be expected, that the thing was pretty rotten anyway.'

'But he said somebody had been monkeying about with it?'

'Yes,' said Tuppence, 'very definitely. "Ah," he said, "these youngsters have been in tryin' it out, you know. Enjoy pulling wheels off things, they do, young monkeys." Not that I've seen anyone about. But then I suppose they'd be sure that I didn't catch them at it. They'd wait till I'm away from home, I expect.

'I asked him if he thought it was just – just something mischievous,' said Tuppence.

'What did he say to that?' said Tommy.

'He didn't really know what to say.'

'It could have been mischief, I suppose,' said Tommy. 'People do do those things.'

'Are you trying to say you think that it was meant in some way so that I should go on playing the fool with the cart and that the wheel would come off and the thing would fall to pieces – oh, but that is nonsense, Tommy.'

'Well, it sounds like nonsense,' said Tommy, 'but things aren't nonsense sometimes. It depends where and how they happen and why.'

'I don't see what "why" there could be.'

'One might make a guess – about the most likely thing,' said Tommy.

'Now what do you mean by the most likely?'

'I mean perhaps people want us to go away from here.'

'Why should they? If somebody wants the house for themselves, they could make us an offer for it.'

'Yes, they could.'

'Well, I wondered – Nobody else has wanted this house as far as we know. I mean, there was nobody else looking at it when we were. It seemed to be generally regarded as if it had come into the market rather cheap but not for any other reason, except that it was out of date and needed a lot doing to it.'

'I can't believe they wanted to do away with us, maybe it's because you've been nosing about, asking too many questions, copying things out of books.'

'You mean that I'm stirring up things that somebody doesn't want to be stirred up?'

'That sort of thing,' said Tommy. 'I mean, if we suddenly were meant to feel that we didn't like living here, and put the house up for sale and went away, that would be quite all right. They'd be satisfied with that. I don't think that they –'

'Who do you mean by "they"?'

'I've no idea,' said Tommy. 'We must get to "they" later. Just *they*. There's *We* and there's *They*. We must keep them apart in our minds.'

'What about Isaac?'

'What do you mean, what about Isaac?'

'I don't know. I just wondered if he was mixed up in this.'

'He's a very old man, he's been here a long time and he knows a few things. If somebody slipped him a five pound note or something, do you think he'd tamper with Truelove's wheels?'

'No, I don't,' said Tuppence. 'He hasn't got the brains to.'

'He wouldn't need brains for it,' said Tommy. 'He'd only need the brains to take the five pound note and to take out a few screws or break off a bit of wood here or there and just make it so that – well, it would come to grief next time you went down the hill in it.'

'I think what you are imagining is nonsense,' said Tuppence.

'Well, you've been imagining a few things that are nonsense already.'

'Yes, but they fitted in,' said Tuppence. 'They fitted in with the things we've heard.'

'Well,' said Tommy, 'as a result of my investigations or researches, whatever you like to call them, it seems that we haven't learnt quite the right things.'

'You mean what I said just now, that this turns things upside down. I mean now we know that Mary Jordan wasn't an enemy agent, instead she was a *British* agent. She was here for a purpose. Perhaps she had accomplished her purpose.'

'In that case,' said Tommy, 'now let's get it all clear, with this new bit of knowledge added. Her purpose here was to find out something.'

'Presumably to find out something about Commander X,' said Tuppence. 'You must find out his name, it seems so extraordinarily barren only to be able to say Commander X all the time.'

'All right, all right, but you know how difficult these things are.'

'And she did find them out, and she reported what she had found out. And perhaps someone opened the letter,' said Tuppence.

'What letter?' said Tommy.

'The letter she wrote to whoever was her "contact".'

'Yes.'

'Do you think he was her father or her grandfather or something like that.'

'I shouldn't think so,' said Tommy. 'I don't think that's the sort of way things would be done. She might just have chosen to take the name of Jordan, or they thought it was quite a good name because it was not associated in any way, which it wouldn't be if she was partly German, and had perhaps come from some other work that she had been doing for us but not for them.'

'For us and not for them,' agreed Tuppence, 'abroad. And so she came here as what?

'Oh, I don't know,' said Tuppence, 'we shall have to start all over again finding out *as what*, I suppose . . . Anyway, she came here and she found out something and she either passed it on to someone or didn't. I mean, she might not have written a letter. She might have gone to London and reported something. Met someone in Regent's Park, say.'

'That's rather the other way about, usually, isn't it?' said Tommy. 'I mean you meet somebody from whatever embassy it is you're in collusion with and you meet in Regent's Park and –'

'Hide things in a hollow tree sometimes. Do you think they really do that? It sounds so unlikely. It's so much more like people who are having a love-affair and putting love-letters in.'

'I dare say whatever they put in there was written as though they were love-letters and really had a code.'

'That's a splendid idea,' said Tuppence, 'only I suppose they – Oh dear, it's such years ago. How difficult it is to get anywhere. The more you know, I mean, the less use it is to you. But we're not going to stop, Tommy, are we?'

'I don't suppose we are for a moment,' said Tommy. He sighed.

'You wish we were?' said Tuppence.

'Almost. Yes. Far as I can see –'

'Well,' cut in Tuppence, 'I can't see you taking yourself off the trail. No, and it would be very difficult to get *me* off the trail. I mean, I'd go on thinking about it and it would worry me. I dare say I should go off my food and everything.'

'The point is,' said Tommy, 'do you think – we know in a way perhaps what this starts from. Espionage. Espionage by the enemy with certain objects in view, some of which were accomplished. Perhaps some which weren't quite accomplished. But we don't know – well – we don't know who was mixed up in it. From the enemy point of view. I mean, there were people here, I should think, people perhaps among security forces. People who were traitors but whose job it was to appear to be loyal servants of the State.'

'Yes,' said Tuppence. 'I'll go for that one. That seems to be very likely.'

'And Mary Jordan's job was to get in touch with them.'

'To get in touch with Commander X?'

'I should think so, yes. Or with friends of Commander X and to find out about things. But apparently it was necessary for her to come here to get it.'

'Do you mean that the Parkinsons – I suppose we're back at the Parkinsons again before we know where we are – were in it? That the Parkinsons were part of the enemy?'

'It seems very unlikely,' said Tommy.

'Well, then, I can't see what it all means.'

'I think the house might have something to do with it,' said Tommy.

'The house? Well, other people came and lived here afterwards, didn't they?'

'Yes, they did. But I don't suppose they were people quite like – well, quite like you, Tuppence.'

'What do you mean by quite like me?'

'Well, wanting old books and looking through them and finding out things. Being a regular mongoose, in fact. They just came and lived here and I expect the upstairs rooms and the books were probably servants' rooms and nobody went into them. There may be something that was hidden in this house. Hidden perhaps by Mary Jordan. Hidden in a place ready to deliver to someone who would come for them, or deliver them by going herself to London or somewhere on some excuse. Visit to a dentist. Seeing an old friend. Quite easy to do. She had something she had acquired, or got to know, hidden in this house. You're not saying it's still hidden in this house?'

'No,' said Tommy, 'I shouldn't have thought so. But one doesn't know. Somebody is afraid we may find it or have found it and they want to get us out of the house, or they want to get hold of whatever it is they think we've found but that they've never found, though perhaps they've looked for it in past years and then thought it had been hidden somewhere else outside.'

'Oh, Tommy,' said Tuppence, 'that makes it all much more exciting, really, doesn't it?'

'It's only what we *think*,' said Tommy.

'Now don't be such a wet blanket,' said Tuppence. 'I'm going to look outside as well as inside –'

'What are you going to do, dig up the kitchen garden?'

'No,' said Tuppence. 'Cupboards, the cellar, things like that. Who knows? Oh, Tommy!'

'Oh, Tuppence!' said Tommy. 'Just when we were looking forward to a delightful, peaceful old age.'

'No peace for the pensioners,' said Tuppence gaily. 'That's an idea too.'

'What?'

'I must go and talk to some old age pensioners at their club. I hadn't thought of them up to now.'

'For goodness' sake, look after yourself,' said Tommy. 'I think I'd better stay at home and keep an eye on you. But I've got to do some more research in London tomorrow.'

'I'm going to do some research here,' said Tuppence.

Chapter 2

Research by Tuppence

'I hope,' said Tuppence, 'that I'm not interrupting you, coming along like this? I thought I'd better ring up first in case you were out, you know, or busy. But, I mean, it's nothing particular so I could go away again at once if you liked. I mean, my feelings wouldn't be hurt or anything like that.'

'Oh, I'm delighted to see you, Mrs Beresford,' said Mrs Griffin.

She moved herself three inches along her chair so as to settle her back more comfortably and looked with what seemed to be distinct pleasure into Tuppence's somewhat anxious face.

'It's a great pleasure, you know, when somebody new comes and lives in this place. We're so used to all our neighbours that a new face, or if I may say so a couple of new faces, is a treat. An absolute *treat*! I hope indeed that you'll both come to dinner one day. I don't know what time your husband gets back. He goes to London, does he not, most days?'

'Yes,' said Tuppence. 'That's very nice of you. I hope you'll come and see our house when it's more or less finished. I'm always thinking it's going to be finished but it never is.'

'Houses are rather like that,' said Mrs Griffin.

Mrs Griffin, as Tuppence knew very well from her various sources of information which consisted of daily women, old Isaac, Gwenda in the post office and sundry others, was ninety-four. The upright position which she enjoyed arranging because it took the rheumatic pains out of her back, together with her erect carriage, gave her the air of someone much younger. In spite of the wrinkled face, the head of uprising white hair surmounted by a lace scarf tied round her head reminded Tuppence faintly of a couple of her great-aunts in past days. She wore bifocal spectacles and had a hearing aid which she sometimes, but very seldom as far as Tuppence could see, had to use. And she looked thoroughly alert and perfectly capable of reaching the age of a hundred or even a hundred and ten.

'What have you been doing with yourself lately?' enquired Mrs Griffin. 'I gather you've got the electricians out of the house now. So Dorothy told me. Mrs Rogers, you know. She used to be my housemaid once and she comes now and cleans twice a week.'

'Yes, thank goodness,' said Tuppence. 'I was always falling into the holes they made. I really came,' said Tuppence, 'and it may sound rather silly but it's something I just wondered about – I expect you'll think it's rather silly too. I've been turning out things, you know, a lot of old bookshelves and things like that. We bought some books with the house, mostly children's books years and years old but I found some old favourites among them.'

'Ah yes,' said Mrs Griffin, 'I quite understand that you must very much have enjoyed the prospect of being able to read certain old favourites again. *The Prisoner of Zenda*, perhaps. My grandmother used to read *The Prisoner of Zenda*, I believe. I read it once myself. Really very enjoyable. Romantic, you know. The first romantic book, I imagine, one is allowed to read. You know, novel reading was not encouraged. My mother and my grandmother never approved of reading anything like a novel in the mornings. A story book as it was called. You know, you could read history or something serious, but novels were only *pleasurable* and so to be read in the afternoon.'

'I know,' said Tuppence. 'Well, I found a good many books that I liked reading again. Mrs Molesworth.'

'*The Tapestry Room*?' said Mrs Griffin with immediate comprehension.

'Yes. *The Tapestry Room* was one of my favourites.'

'Well, I always liked *Four Winds Farm* best,' said Mrs Griffin.

'Yes, that was there too. And several others. Many different kinds of authors. Anyway, I got down to the last shelf and I think there must have been an accident there. You know, someone had banged it about a good deal. When they were moving furniture, I expect. There was a sort of hole and I scooped up a lot of old things out of that. Mostly torn books and among it there was this.'

She produced her parcel wrapped loosely in brown paper.

'It's a birthday book,' she said. 'An old-fashioned birthday book. And it had your name in it. Your name – I remember you told me – was Winifred Morrison, wasn't it?'

'Yes, my dear. Quite right.'

'And it was written in the birthday book. And so I wondered whether it would amuse you if I brought it along for you to see. It might have a lot of other old friends of yours in it and different things or names which would amuse you.'

'Well, that was very nice of you, my dear, and I should like to see it very much. You know, these things from the past, one does find very amusing to read in one's old age. A very kind thought of yours.'

'It's rather faded and torn and knocked about, said Tuppence, producing her offering.

'Well, well,' said Mrs Griffin, 'yes. You know, everyone had a birthday book. Not so much after my time as a girl. I expect this may be one of the last ones. All the girls at the school I went to had a birthday book. You know, you wrote your name in your friend's birthday book and they wrote their name in yours and so on.'

She took the book from Tuppence, opened it and began reading down the pages.

'Oh dear, oh dear,' she murmured, 'how it takes me back. Yes. Yes indeed. Helen Gilbert – yes, yes of course. And Daisy Sherfield. Sherfield, yes. Oh yes, I remember her. She had to have one of those tooth things in her mouth. A brace, I think they called it. And she was always taking it out. She said she couldn't stand it. And Edie Crone, Margaret Dickson. Ah yes. Good handwriting most of them had. Better than girls have nowadays. As for my nephew's letters, I really can't read them. Their handwriting is like hieroglyphics of some kind. One has to guess what most of the words are. Mollie Short. Ah yes, she had a stammer – it does bring things back.'

'I don't suppose there are many of them, I mean –' Tuppence paused, feeling that she might be about to say something tactless.

'You're thinking most of them are dead, I suppose, dear. Well, you're quite right. Most of them are. But not all of them. No. I've still got quite a lot of people living, with whom I was, as they say, girls together. Not living here, because most girls that one knew married and went somewhere else. Either they had husbands who were in the Services and they went abroad, or they went to some other different town altogether. Two of my oldest friends live up in Northumberland. Yes, yes, it's very interesting.'

'There weren't, I suppose, any Parkinsons left then?' said Tuppence. 'I don't see the name anywhere.'

'Oh no. It was after the Parkinsons' time. There's something you want to find out about the Parkinsons, isn't there?'

'Oh, yes, there is,' said Tuppence. 'It's pure curiosity, you know, nothing else. But – well, somehow in looking at things I got interested in the boy, Alexander Parkinson, and then, as I was walking through the churchyard the other day, I noticed that he'd died fairly young and his grave was there and that made me think about him more.'

'He died young,' said Mrs Griffin. 'Yes. Everyone seems to think it was sad that he should have done so. He was a very intelligent boy and they hoped for – well, quite a brilliant future for him. It wasn't really any illness, some food he had on a picnic, I believe. So

Mrs Henderson told me. She remembers a lot about the Parkinsons.'

'Mrs Henderson?' Tuppence looked up.

'Oh, you wouldn't know about her. She's in one of these old people's homes, you know. It's called Meadowside. It's about – oh, about twelve to fifteen miles from here. You ought to go and see her. She'd tell you a lot of things, I expect, about that house you're living in. Swallow's Nest, it was called then, it's called something else, isn't it now?'

'The Laurels.'

'Mrs Henderson is older than I am, although she was the youngest of quite a large family. She was a governess at one time. And then I think she was a kind of nurse-companion with Mrs Beddingfield who had Swallow's Nest, I mean The Laurels, then. And she likes talking about old times very much. You ought to go and see her, I think.'

'Oh, she wouldn't like –'

'Oh, my dear, I'm sure she *would* like. Go and see her. Just tell her that I suggested it. She remembers me and my sister Rosemary and I do go and see her occasionally, but not of late years because I haven't been able to get about. And you might go and see Mrs Hendley, who lives in – what is it now? – Apple Tree Lodge, I think it is. That's mainly old age pensioners. Not quite the same class, you know, but it's very well run and there's a lot of gossip going there! I'm sure they'd all be quite pleased with visits. You know, anything to break the monotony.'

Chapter 3

Tommy and Tuppence Compare Notes

'You look tired, Tuppence,' said Tommy as at the close of dinner they went into the sitting-room and Tuppence dropped into a chair, uttering several large sighs followed by a yawn.

'Tired? I'm dead beat,' said Tuppence.

'What have you been doing? Not things in the garden, I hope.'

'I have not been overworking myself physically,' said Tuppence, coldly. 'I've been doing like you. Mental research.'

'Also very exhausting, I agree,' said Tommy. 'Where, particularly? You didn't get an awful lot out of Mrs Griffin the day before yesterday, did you?'

'Well, I did get a good deal, I think. I didn't get much out of the first recommendation. At least, I suppose I did in a way.'

Opening her handbag, she tugged at a notebook of rather tiresome size, and finally got it out.

'I made various notes each time about things. I took some of the china menus along, for one thing.'

'Oh. And what did that produce?'

'Well, it's not names that I write down so much as the things they say to me and tell me. And they were very thrilled at that china menu because it seemed it was one particular dinner that everyone had enjoyed very much and they had had a wonderful meal – they hadn't had anything like it before, and apparently they had lobster salad for the first time. They'd heard of it being served after the joint in the richest and most fashionable houses, but it hadn't come their way.'

'Oh,' said Tommy, 'that wasn't very helpful.'

'Well, yes it was, in a way, because they said they'd always remember that evening. So I said why would they always remember that evening and they said it was because of the census.'

'What – a census?'

'Yes. You know what a census is, surely, Tommy? Why, we had one only last year, or was it the year before last? You know – having to say, or making everyone sign or enter particulars. Everyone who slept under your roof on a certain night. You know the sort of thing. On the night of November 15th who did you have sleeping under your roof? And you have to put it down, or they have to sign their names. I forget which. Anyway, they were having a census that day and so everyone had to say who was under their roof, and of course a lot of people were at the party and they talked about it. They said it was very unfair and a very stupid thing to have and that anyway they thought it was really a most disgraceful thing to go on having nowadays, because you had to say if you had children and if you were married, or if you were not married but did have children, and things like that. You had to put down a lot of very difficult particulars and you didn't think it was nice. Not nowadays. So they were very upset about it. I mean, they were upset, not about the old census because nobody minded then. It was just a thing that happened.'

'The census might come in useful if you've got the exact date of it,' said Tommy.

'Do you mean you could check up about the census?'

'Oh yes. If one knows the right people I think one could check up fairly easily.'

'And they remembered Mary Jordan being talked about. Everyone said what a nice girl she had *seemed* and how fond everyone was of her. And they would never have believed – you know how people say things. Then they said, Well, she was half German so perhaps people ought to have been more careful in engaging her.'

II

Tuppence put down her empty coffee cup and settled back in her chair.

'Anything hopeful?' said Tommy.

'No, not really,' said Tuppence, 'but it might be. Anyway, the old people talked about it and knew about it. Most of them had heard it from their elderly relations or something. Stories of where they had put things or found things. There was some story about a will that was hidden in a Chinese vase. Something about Oxford and Cambridge, though I don't see how anyone would know about things being hidden in Oxford or Cambridge. It seems very unlikely.'

'Perhaps someone had a nephew undergraduate,' said Tommy, 'who took something back with him to Oxford or Cambridge.'

'Possible, I suppose, but not likely.'

'Did anyone actually talk about Mary Jordan?'

'Only in the way of hearsay – not of actually knowing definitely about her being a German spy, only from their grandmothers or great-aunts or sisters or mothers' cousins or Uncle John's naval friend who knew all about it.'

'Did they talk about how Mary died?'

'They connected her death with the foxglove and

spinach episode. Everyone recovered, they said, except her.'

'Interesting,' said Tommy. 'Same story different setting.'

'Too many ideas perhaps,' said Tuppence. 'Someone called Bessie said, "Well. It was only my grandmother who talked about that and of course it had all been years before her time and I expect she got some of the details wrong. She usually did, I believe." You know, Tommy, with everyone talking at once it's all muddled up. There was all the talk about spies and poison on picnics and everything. I couldn't get any exact dates because of course nobody ever knows the exact date of anything your grandmother tells you. If she says, "I was only sixteen at the time and I was terribly thrilled," you probably don't know *now* how old your grandmother really was. She'd probably say she was ninety now because people like to say they're older than their age when they get to eighty, or if, of course, she's only about seventy, she says she's only fifty-two.'

'*Mary Jordan*,' said Tommy thoughtfully, as he quoted the words, '*did not die naturally. He* had his suspicions. Wonder if he ever talked to a policeman about them.'

'You mean Alexander?'

'Yes – And perhaps because of that he talked too much. He *had* to die.'

'A lot depends on Alexander, doesn't it?'

'We do know when Alexander died, because of his grave here. But Mary Jordan – we still don't know when or why.'

'We'll find out in the end,' said Tommy. 'You make a few lists of names you've got and dates and things. You'll be surprised. Surprised what one can check up through an odd word or two here and there.'

'You seem to have a lot of useful friends,' said Tuppence enviously.

'So do you,' said Tommy.

'Well, I don't really,' said Tuppence.

'Yes, you do, you set people in motion,' said Tommy. 'You go and see one old lady with a birthday book. The next thing I know you've been all through masses of people in an old pensioners' home or something, and you know all about things that happened at the time of their great-aunts, great-grandmothers and Uncle Johns and godfathers, and perhaps an old Admiral at sea who told tales about espionage and all that. Once we can figure a few dates down and get on with a few enquiries, we might – who knows? – get *something*.'

'I wonder who the undergraduates were who were mentioned – Oxford and Cambridge, the ones who were said to have hidden something.'

'They don't sound very like espionage,' said Tommy.

'No, they don't really,' said Tuppence.

'And doctors and old clergymen,' said Tommy. 'One could, I expect, check up on them, but I don't see it would lead one anywhere. It's all too far away. We're not near enough. We don't know – Has anybody tried anything more funny on you, Tuppence?'

'Do you mean has anyone attempted my life in the last two days? No, they haven't. Nobody's invited me to go on a picnic, the brakes of the car are all right, there's a jar of weedkiller in the potting shed but it doesn't even seem to be opened yet.'

'Isaac keeps it there to be handy in case you come out with some sandwiches one day.'

'Oh, poor Isaac,' said Tuppence. 'You are *not* to say things against Isaac. He is becoming one of my best friends. Now I wonder – that reminds me –'

'What does that remind you of?'

'I can't remember,' said Tuppence, blinking her eyes. 'It reminded me of something when you said that about Isaac.'

'Oh dear,' said Tommy and sighed.

'One old lady,' said Tuppence, 'was said to have always put her things in her mittens every night. Earrings, I think it was. That's the one who thought everyone was poisoning her. And somebody else remembered someone who put things in a missionary box or something. You know, the china thing for the waifs and strays, there was a label stuck on to it. But it wasn't for the waifs and strays at all, apparently. She used to put five pound notes in it so that she'd always have a nest egg, and when it got too full she used to take it away and buy another box and break the first one.'

'And spend the five pounds, I suppose,' said Tommy.

'I suppose that *was* the idea. My cousin Emlyn used to say,' said Tuppence, obviously quoting, 'nobody'd rob the waifs and strays or missionaries, would they? If anyone smashed a box like that somebody'd notice, wouldn't they?'

'You haven't found any books of rather dull-looking sermons, have you, in your book search in those rooms upstairs?'

'No. Why?' asked Tuppence.

'Well, I just thought that'd be a very good place to hide things in. You know, something really boring written about theology. An old crabbed book with the inside scooped out.'

'Hasn't been anything like that,' said Tuppence. 'I should have noticed it if there was.'

'Would you have read it?'

'Oh, of course I wouldn't,' said Tuppence.

'There you are then,' said Tommy. 'You wouldn't have read it, you'd have just thrown it away, I expect.'

'*The Crown of Success*. That's one book I remember,'

said Tuppence. 'There were two copies of that. Well, let's hope that success will crown our efforts.'

'It seems to me very unlikely. Who killed Mary Jordan? That's the book *we'll* have to write one day, I suppose?'

'If we ever find out,' said Tuppence gloomily.

Chapter 4

Possibility of Surgery on Mathilde

'What are you going to do this afternoon, Tuppence? Go on helping me with these lists of names and dates and things?'

'I don't think so,' said Tuppence. 'I've had all that. It really is most exhausting writing everything down. Every now and then I do get things a bit wrong, don't I?'

'Well, I wouldn't put it past you. You have made a few mistakes.'

'I wish you weren't more accurate than I am, Tommy. I find it so annoying sometimes.'

'What are you going to do instead?'

'I wouldn't mind having a good nap. Oh no, I'm not going to actually relax,' said Tuppence. 'I think I'm going to disembowel Mathilde.'

'I beg your pardon, Tuppence.'

'I said I was going to disembowel Mathilde.'

'What's the matter with you? You seem very set on violence.'

'Mathilde – she's in KK.'

'What do you mean, she's in KK?'

'Oh, the place where all the dumps are. You know, she's the rocking-horse, the one that's got a hole in her stomach.'

'Oh. And – you're going to examine her stomach, is that it?'

'That's the idea,' said Tuppence. 'Would you like to come and help me?'

'Not really,' said Tommy.

'Would you be *kind* enough to come and help me?' suggested Tuppence.

'Put like that,' said Tommy, with a deep sigh, 'I will force myself to consent. Anyway, it won't be as bad as making lists. Is Isaac anywhere about?'

'No. I think it's his afternoon off. Anyway, we don't want Isaac about. I think I've got all the information I can out of him.'

'He knows a good deal,' said Tommy thoughtfully. 'I found that out the other day, he was telling me a lot of things about the past. Things he can't remember himself.'

'Well, he must be nearly eighty,' said Tuppence. 'I'm quite sure of that.'

'Yes, I know, but things really far back.'

'People have always *heard* so many things,' said Tuppence. 'You never know if they're right or not in what they've heard. Anyway, let's go and disembowel Mathilde. I'd better change my clothes first because it's excessively dusty and cobwebby in KK and we have to burrow right inside her.

'You might get Isaac, if he's about, to turn her upside down, then we could get at her stomach more easily.'

'You really sound as though in your last reincarnation you must have been a surgeon.'

'Well, I suppose it is a little like that. We are now going to remove foreign matter which might be dangerous to the preservation of Mathilde's life, such as is left of it. We might have her painted up and Deborah's twins perhaps would like to ride on her when they next come to stay.'

'Oh, our grandchildren have so many toys and presents already.'

'That won't matter,' said Tuppence. 'Children don't particularly like expensive presents. They'll play with an old bit of string or a rag doll or something they call a pet bear which is only a bit of a hearthrug just made up into a bundle with a couple of black boot-button eyes put on it. Children have their own ideas about toys.'

'Well, come on,' said Tommy. 'Forward to Mathilde. To the operating theatre.'

The reversal of Mathilde to a position suitable for the necessary operation to take place was not an easy job. Mathilde was a very fair weight. In addition to that, she was very well studded with various nails which would on occasions reverse their position, and which had points sticking out. Tuppence wiped blood from her hand and Tommy swore as he caught his pullover which immediately tore itself in a somewhat disastrous fashion.

'Blow this damned rocking-horse,' said Tommy.

'Ought to have been put on a bonfire years ago,' said Tuppence.

It was at that moment that the aged Isaac suddenly appeared and joined them.

'Whatever now!' he said with some surprise. 'Whatever be you two doing here now? What do you want with this old bit of horse-flesh here? Can I help you at all? What do you want to do with it – do you want it taken out of here?'

'Not necessarily,' said Tuppence. 'We want to turn it upside down so that we can get at the hole there and pull things out.'

'You mean pull things out from inside her, as you might say? Who's been putting that idea into your head?'

'Yes,' said Tuppence, 'that's what we do mean to do.'

'What do you think you'll find there?'

'Nothing but rubbish, I expect,' said Tommy. 'But it would be nice,' he said in a rather doubtful voice, 'if things were cleared up a bit, you know. We might want to keep other things in here. You know – games, perhaps, a croquet set. Something like that.'

'There used to be a crookey lawn once. Long time ago. That was in Mrs Faulkner's time. Yes. Down where the rose garden is now. Mind you, it wasn't a full size one.'

'When was that?' asked Tommy.

'What, you mean the crookey lawn? Oh, well before my time, it was. There's always people as wants to tell you things about what used to happen – things as used to be hidden and why and who wanted to hide them. Lot of tall stories, some of them lies. Some maybe as was true.'

'You're very clever, Isaac,' said Tuppence, 'you always seem to know about everything. How do you know about the croquet lawn?'

'Oh, used to be a box of crookey things in here. Been there for ages. Shouldn't think there's much of it left now.'

Tuppence relinquished Mathilde and went over to a corner where there was a long wooden box. After releasing the lid with some difficulty as it had stuck under the ravages of time, it yielded a faded red ball, a blue ball and one mallet bent and warped. The rest of it was mainly cobwebs.

'Might have been in Mrs Faulkner's time, that might. They do say, you know, as she played in the tournaments in her time,' said Isaac.

'At Wimbledon?' said Tuppence, incredulous.

'Well, not exactly at Wimbledon, I don't think it was. No. The locals, you know. They used to have them down here. Pictures I've seen down at the photographer's –'

'The photographer's?'

'Ah. In the village, Durrance. You know Durrance, don't you?'

'Durrance?' said Tuppence vaguely. 'Oh, yes, he sells films and things like that, doesn't he?'

'That's right. Mind you, he's not the old Durrance, as manages it now. It's his grandson, or his great-grandson, I shouldn't wonder. He sells mostly postcards, you know, and Christmas cards and birthday cards and things like that. He used to take photographs of people. Got a whole lot tucked away. Somebody come in the other day, you know. Wanted a picture of her great-grandmother, she said. She said she'd had one but she'd broken it or burnt it or lost it or something, and she wondered if there was the negative left. But I don't think she found it. But there's a lot of old albums in there stuck away somewhere.'

'Albums,' said Tuppence thoughtfully.

'Anything more I can do?' said Isaac.

'Well, just give us a bit of a hand with Jane, or whatever her name is.'

'Not Jane, it's Mathilde, and it's not Matilda either, which it ought by rights to be, I should say. I believe it was always called Mathilde, for some reason. French, I expect.'

'French or American,' said Tommy, thoughtfully. 'Mathilde. Louise. That sort of thing.'

'Quite a good place to have hidden things, don't you think?' said Tuppence, placing her arm into the cavity in Mathilde's stomach. She drew out a dilapidated indiarubber ball, which had once been red and yellow but which now had gaping holes in it.

'I suppose that's children,' said Tuppence. 'They always put things in like this.'

'Whenever they see a hole,' said Isaac. 'But there was a young gentleman once as used to leave his letters in it, so I've heard. Same as though it was a post box.'

'Letters? Who were they for?'

'Some young lady, I'd think. But it was before my time,' said Isaac, as usual.

'The things that always happened long before Isaac's time,' said Tuppence, as Isaac, having adjusted Mathilde into a good position, left them on the pretext of having to shut up the frames.

Tommy removed his jacket.

'It's incredible,' said Tuppence, panting a little as she removed a scratched and dirty arm from the gaping wound in Mathilde's stomach, 'that anyone could put so many things or want to put them, in this thing, and that nobody should ever have cleaned it out.'

'Well, why should anyone clean it out? Why would anyone want to clean it out?'

'That's true,' said Tuppence. 'We do, though, don't we?'

'Only because we can't think of anything better to do. I don't think anything will come of it though. Ow!'

'What's the matter?' said Tuppence.

'Oh, I scratched myself on something.'

He drew his arm out slightly, readjusted it, and felt inside once more. A knitted scarf rewarded him. It had clearly been the sustenance of moths at one time and possibly after that had descended to an even lower level of social life.

'Disgusting,' said Tommy.

Tuppence pushed him aside slightly and fished in with her own arm, leaning over Mathilde while she felt about inside.

'Mind the nails,' said Tommy.

'What's this?' said Tuppence.

She brought her find out into the open air. It appeared to be the wheel off a bus or cart or some child's toy.

'I think,' she said, 'we're wasting our time.'

'I'm sure we are,' said Tommy.

'All the same, we might as well do it properly,' said Tuppence. 'Oh dear, I've got three spiders walking up my arm. It'll be a worm in a minute and I hate worms.'

'I don't think there'll be any worms inside Mathilde. I mean, worms like going underground in the earth. I don't think they'd care for Mathilde as a boarding-house, do you?'

'Oh well, it's getting empty at any rate, I think,' said Tuppence. 'Hullo, what's this? Dear me, it seems to be a needle book. What a funny thing to find. There's still some needles in it but they're all rusted.'

'Some child who didn't like to do her sewing, I expect,' said Tommy.

'Yes, that's a good idea.'

'I touched something that felt like a book just now,' said Tommy.

'Oh. Well, that might be helpful. What part of Mathilde?'

'I should thing the appendix or the liver,' said Tommy in a professional tone. 'On her right-hand side. I'm regarding this as an operation!' he added.

'All right, Surgeon. Better pull it out, whatever it is.'

The so-called book, barely recognizable as such, was

of ancient lineage. Its pages were loose and stained, and its binding was coming to pieces.

'It seems to be a manual of French,' said Tommy. '*Pour les enfants. Le Petit Précepteur.*'

'I see,' said Tuppence. 'I've got the same idea as you had. The child didn't want to learn her French lesson; so she came in here and deliberately lost it by putting it into Mathilde. Good old Mathilde.'

'If Mathilde was right side up, it must have been very difficult putting things through this hole in her stomach.'

'Not for a child,' said Tuppence. 'She'd be quite the right height and everything. I mean, she'd kneel and crawl underneath it. Hullo, here's something which feels slippery. Feels rather like an animal's skin.'

'How very unpleasant,' said Tommy. 'Do you think it's a dead rabbit or something?'

'Well, it's not furry or anything. I don't think it's very nice. Oh dear, there's a nail again. Well, it seems to be hung on a nail. There's a sort of bit of string or cord. Funny it hasn't rotted away, isn't it?'

She drew out her find cautiously.

'It's a pocket-book,' she said. 'Yes. Yes, it's been quite good leather once, I think. Quite good leather.'

'Let's see what's inside it, if there is anything inside it,' said Tommy.

'There's something inside it,' said Tuppence.

'Perhaps it's a lot of five pound notes,' she added hopefully.

'Well, I don't suppose they'd be usable still. Paper would rot, wouldn't it?'

'I don't know,' said Tuppence. 'A lot of queer things do survive, you know. I think five pound notes used to be made of wonderfully good paper once, you know. Sort of thin but very durable.'

'Oh well, perhaps it's a twenty pound note. It will help with the housekeeping.'

'What? The money'll be before Isaac's time too, I expect, or else *he'd* have found it. Ah well. Think! It might be a hundred pound note. I wish it were golden sovereigns. Sovereigns were always in purses. My Great-Aunt Maria had a great purse full of sovereigns. She used to show it to us as children. It was her nest egg, she said, in case the French came. I think it was the French. Anyway, it was for extremities or danger. Lovely fat golden sovereigns. I used to think it was wonderful and I'd think how lovely it would be, you know, once one was grown up and you'd have a purse full of sovereigns.'

'Who was going to give you a purse full of sovereigns?'

'I didn't think of anyone giving it to me,' said Tuppence. 'I thought of it as the sort of thing that belonged to you as a right, once you were a grown up person. You know, a real grown up wearing a mantle – that's what they called the things. A mantle with a sort of fur boa round it and a bonnet. You had this great fat purse jammed full of sovereigns, and if you had a favourite grandson who was going back to school, you always gave him a sovereign as a tip.'

'What about the girls, the grand-daughters?'

'I don't think they got any sovereigns,' said Tuppence. 'But sometimes she used to send me half a five pound note.'

'*Half* a five pound note? That wouldn't be much good.'

'Oh yes, it was. She used to tear the five pound note in half, send me one half first and then the other half in another letter later. You see, it was supposed in that way that nobody'd want to steal it.'

'Oh dear, what a lot of precautions everyone did take.'

'They did rather,' said Tuppence. 'Hullo, what's this?'

She was fumbling now in the leather case.

'Let's get out of KK for a minute,' said Tommy, 'and get some air.'

They got outside KK. In the air they saw better what their trophy was like. It was a thick leather wallet of good quality. It was stiff with age but not in any way destroyed.

'I expect it was kept from damp inside Mathilde,' said Tuppence. 'Oh, Tommy, do you know what I think this is?'

'No. What? It isn't money,' said Tuppence, 'but I think it's letters. I don't know whether we'll be able to read them now. They're very old and faded.'

Very carefully Tommy arranged the crinkled yellow paper of the letters, pushing them apart when he could. The writing was quite large and had once been written in a very deep blue-black ink.

'Meeting place changed,' said Tommy. 'Ken Gardens near Peter Pan. Wednesday 25th, 3.30 p.m. Joanna.'

'I really believe,' said Tuppence, 'we might have something at last.'

'You mean that someone who'd be going to London was told to go on a certain day and meet someone in Kensington Gardens bringing perhaps the papers or the plans or whatever it was. Who do you think got these things out of Mathilde or put them into Mathilde?'

'It couldn't have been a child,' said Tuppence. 'It must have been someone who lived in the house and so could move about without being noticed. Got things from the naval spy, I suppose, and took them to London.'

Tuppence wrapped up the old leather wallet in the

scarf she'd been wearing round her neck and she and Tommy returned to the house.

'There may be other papers in there,' said Tuppence, 'but most of them I think are perished and will more or less fall to pieces if you touch them. Hullo, what's this?'

On the hall table a rather bulky package was lying. Albert came out from the dining-room.

'It was left by hand, madam,' he said. 'Left by hand this morning for you.'

'Ah, I wonder what it is,' said Tuppence. She took it.

Tommy and she went into the sitting-room together. Tuppence undid the knot of the string and took off the brown paper wrapping.

'It's a kind of album,' she said, 'I think. Oh, there's a note with it. Ah, it's from Mrs Griffin.

'*Dear Mrs Beresford, It was so kind of you to bring me the birthday book the other day. I have had great pleasure looking over it and remembering various people from past days. One does forget so soon. Very often one only remembers somebody's Christian name and not their surname, sometimes it's the other way about. I came across, a little time ago, this old album. It doesn't really belong to me. I think it belonged to my grandmother, but it has a good many pictures in it and among them, I think, there are one or two of the Parkinsons, because my grandmother knew the Parkinsons. I thought perhaps you would like to see it as you seemed to be so interested in the history of your house and who has lived in it in the past. Please don't bother to send it back to me because it means nothing to me personally really, I can assure you. One has so many things in the house always belonging to aunts and grandmothers and the other day when I was looking in an old chest of drawers in the attic I came across six needle-books. Years and years old. And I believe that was not my grandmother but her grandmother again who used at one time always to give a needle-book to the maids for Christmas and I think these were some she had bought at a sale and would do for another year. Of course quite useless now. Sometimes it seems sad to think of how much waste there has always been.*

'A photo album,' said Tuppence. 'Well, that might be fun. Come along, let's have a look.'

They sat down on the sofa. The album was very typical of bygone days. Most of the prints were faded by now but every now and then Tuppence managed to recognize surroundings that fitted the gardens of their own house.

'Look, there's the monkey puzzle. Yes – and look, there's Truelove behind it. That must be a very old photograph, and a funny little boy hanging on to

Truelove. Yes, and there's the wistaria and there's the pampas grass. I suppose it must have been a tea-party or something. Yes, there are a lot of people sitting round a table in the garden. They've got names underneath them too. Mabel. Mabel's no beauty. And who's that?'

'Charles,' said Tommy. 'Charles and Edmund. Charles and Edmund seem to have been playing tennis. They've got rather queer tennis racquets. And there's William, whoever he was, and Major Coates.'

'And there's – oh Tommy, there's Mary.'

'Yes. Mary Jordan. Both names there, written under the photograph.'

'She was pretty. Very pretty, I think. It is very faded and old, but – oh Tommy, it really seems wonderful to see Mary Jordan.'

'I wonder who took the photograph?'

'Perhaps the photographer that Isaac mentioned. The one in the village here. Perhaps he'd have old photographs too. I think perhaps one day we'll go and ask.'

Tommy had pushed aside the album by now and was opening a letter which had come in the midday post.

'Anything interesting?' asked Tuppence. 'There are three letters here. Two are bills, I can see. This one – yes, this one is rather different. I asked you if it was interesting,' said Tuppence.

'It may be,' said Tommy. 'I'll have to go to London tomorrow again.'

'To deal with your usual committees?'

'Not exactly,' said Tommy. 'I'm going to call on someone. Actually it isn't London, it's out of London. Somewhere Harrow way, I gather.'

'What is?' said Tuppence. 'You haven't told me yet.'

'I'm going to call on someone called Colonel Pikeaway.'

'What a name,' said Tuppence.

'Yes, it is rather, isn't it?'

'Have I heard it before?' said Tuppence.

'I may have mentioned it to you once. He lives in a kind of permanent atmosphere of smoke. Have you got any cough lozenges, Tuppence?'

'Cough lozenges! Well, I don't know. Yes, I think I have. I've got an old box of them from last winter. But you haven't got a cough – not that I've noticed, at any rate.'

'No, but I shall have if I'm going to see Pikeaway. As far as I can remember, you take two choking breaths and then go on choking. You look hopefully at all the windows which are tightly shut, but Pikeaway would never take a hint of that kind.'

'Why do you think he wants to see you?'

'Can't imagine,' said Tommy. 'He mentions Robinson.'

'What – the yellow one? The one who's got a fat yellow face and is something very hush-hush?'

'That's the one, said Tommy.

'Oh well,' said Tuppence, 'perhaps what we're mixed up in here is hush-hush.'

'Hardly could be considering it all took place – whatever it was, if there is anything – years and years ago, before even Isaac can remember.'

'New sins have old shadows,' said Tuppence, 'if that's the saying I mean. I haven't got it quite right. New sins have old shadows. Or is it Old sins make long shadows?'

'I should forget it,' said Tommy. 'None of them sounds right.'

'I shall go and see that photographer man this afternoon, I think. Want to come?'

'No,' said Tommy. 'I think I shall go down and bathe.'

'Bathe? It'll be awfully cold.'

'Never mind. I feel I need something cold, bracing and refreshing to remove all the taste of cobwebs, the various remains of which seem to be clinging round my ears and round my neck and some even seem to have got between my toes.'

'This does seem a very dirty job,' said Tuppence. 'Well, I'll go and see Mr Durrell or Durrance, if that's his name. There was another letter, Tommy, which you haven't opened.'

'Oh, I didn't see it. Ah well, that might be something.'

'Who is it from?'

'My researcher,' said Tommy, in a rather grand voice. 'The one who has been running about England, in and out of Somerset House looking up deaths, marriages and births, consulting newspaper files and census returns. She's very good.'

'Good and beautiful?'

'Not beautiful so that you'd notice it,' said Tommy.

'I'm glad of that,' said Tuppence. 'You know, Tommy, now that you're getting on in years you might – you might get some rather dangerous ideas about a beautiful helper.'

'You don't appreciate a faithful husband when you've got one,' said Tommy.

'All my friends tell me you never know with husbands,' said Tuppence.

'You have the wrong kind of friends,' said Tommy.

Chapter 5

Interview with Colonel Pikeaway

Tommy drove through Regent's Park, then he passed through various roads he'd not been through for years. Once when he and Tuppence had had a flat near Belsize Park, he remembered walks on Hampstead Heath and a dog they had had who'd enjoyed the walks. A dog with a particularly self-willed nature. When coming out of the flat he had always wished to turn to the left on the road that would lead to Hampstead Heath. The efforts of Tuppence or Tommy to make him turn to the right and go into shopping quarters were usually defeated. James, a Sealyham of obstinate nature, had allowed his heavy sausage-like body to rest flat on the pavement, he would produce a tongue from his mouth and give every semblance of being a dog tired out by being given the wrong kind of exercise by those who owned him. People passing by usually could not refrain from comment.

'Oh, look at that dear little dog there. You know, the one with the white hair – looks rather like a sausage, doesn't he? And panting, poor fellow. Those people of his, they won't let him go the way he wants to, he looks tired out, just tired out.'

Tommy had taken the lead from Tuppence and had pulled James firmly in the opposite direction from the one he wanted to go.

'Oh dear,' said Tuppence, 'can't you pick him up, Tommy?'

'What, pick up James? He's too much of a weight.'

James, with a clever manoeuvre, turned his sausage body so that he was facing once more in the direction of his expectation.

'Look, poor little doggie, I expect he wants to go home, don't you?'

James tugged firmly on his lead.

'Oh, all right,' said Tuppence, 'we'll shop later. Come on, we'll have to let James go where he wants to go. He's such a heavy dog, you can't make him do anything else.'

James looked up and wagged his tail. 'I quite agree with you,' the wag seemed to say. 'You've got the point at last. Come on. Hampstead Heath it is.' And it usually had been.

Tommy wondered. He'd got the address of the place where he was going. The last time he had been to see

Colonel Pikeaway it had been in Bloomsbury. A small poky room full of smoke. Here, when he reached the address, it was a small, nondescript house fronting on the heath not far from the birthplace of Keats. It did not look particularly artistic or interesting.

Tommy rang a bell. An old woman with a close resemblance to what Tommy imagined a witch might look like, with a sharp nose and a sharp chin which almost met each other, stood there, looking hostile.

'Can I see Colonel Pikeaway?'

'Don't know I'm sure,' said the witch. 'Who would you be now?'

'My name is Beresford.'

'Oh, I see. Yes. He did say something about that.'

'Can I leave the car outside?'

'Yes, it'll be all right for a bit. Don't get many of the wardens poking around this street. No yellow lines just along here. Better lock it up, sir. You never know.'

Tommy attended to these rules as laid down, and followed the old woman into the house.

'One flight up,' she said, 'not more.'

Already on the stairs there was the strong smell of tobacco. The witch-woman tapped at a door, poked her head in, said, 'This must be the gentleman you wanted to see. Says you're expecting him.' She stood aside and Tommy passed into what he remembered before, an aroma of smoke which forced him almost immediately to choke and gulp. He doubted he would have remembered Colonel Pikeaway apart from the smoke and the cloud and smell of nicotine. A very old man lay back in an armchair – a somewhat ragged armchair with holes on the arms of it. He looked up thoughtfully as Tommy entered.

'Shut the door, Mrs Copes,' he said, 'don't want to let the cold air in, do we?'

Tommy rather thought that they did, but obviously it was his not to reason why, his but to inhale and in due course die, he presumed.

'Thomas Beresford,' said Colonel Pikeaway thoughtfully. 'Well, well, how many years is it since I saw you?'

Tommy had not made a proper computation.

'Long time ago,' said Colonel Pikeaway, 'came here with what's-his-name, didn't you? Ah well, never mind, one name's as good as another. A rose by any other name would smell as sweet. Juliet said that, didn't she? Silly things sometimes Shakespeare made them say. Of course, he couldn't help it, he was a poet. Never cared much for Romeo and Juliet, myself. All those suicides for love's sake. Plenty of 'em about, mind you. Always happening, even nowadays. Sit down, my boy, sit down.'

Tommy was slightly startled at being called 'my boy' again, but he availed himself of the invitation.

'You don't mind, sir,' he said, dispossessing the only possible-seeming chair of a large pile of books.

'No, no, shove 'em all on the floor. Just trying to look something up, I was. Well, well, I'm pleased to see you. You look a bit older than you did, but you look quite healthy. Ever had a coronary?'

'No,' said Tommy.

'Ah! Good. Too many people suffering from hearts, blood pressure – all those things. Doing too much. That's what it is. Running about all over the place, telling everyone how busy they are and the world can't get on without them, and how important they are and everything else. Do you feel the same? I expect you do.'

'No,' said Tommy, 'I don't feel very important. I feel – well, I feel that I really would enjoy relaxing nowadays.'

'Well, it's a splendid thought,' said Colonel Pikeaway. 'The trouble is there are so many people about who won't let you relax. What took you to this place of yours where you're living now? I've forgotten the name of it. Just tell me again, will you?'

Tommy obliged with his address.

'Ah, yes, ah yes, I put the right thing on the envelope then.'

'Yes, I got your letter.'

'I understand you've been to see Robinson. He's still

going. Just as fat as ever, just as yellow as ever, and just as rich or richer than ever, I expect. Knows all about it too. Knows about money, I mean. What took you there, boy?'

'Well, we had bought a new house, and a friend of mine advised me that Mr Robinson might be able to clear up a mystery that my wife and I found connected with it, relating to a long time back.'

'I remember now. I don't believe I ever met her but you've got a clever wife, haven't you? Did some sterling work in the – what is the thing? Sounded like the catechism. N or M, that was it, wasn't it?'

'Yes,' said Tommy.

'And now you're on to the same line again, are you? Looking into things. Had suspicions, had you?'

'No,' said Tommy, 'that's entirely wrong. We only went there because we were tired of the flat we were living in and they kept putting up the rent.'

'Nasty trick,' said Colonel Pikeaway. 'They do that to you nowadays, the landlords. Never satisfied. Talk about Daughters of the Horse Leech – sons of the horse leech are just as bad. All right, you went to live there. *Il faut cultiver son jardin*,' said Colonel Pikeaway, with a rather sudden onslaught on the French language. 'Trying to rub up my French again,' he explained. 'Got to keep in with the Common Market nowadays, haven't we? Funny stuff going on there, by the way.

You know, behind things. Not what you see on the surface. So you went to live at Swallow's Nest. What took you to Swallow's Nest, I'd like to know?'

'The house we bought – well, it's called The Laurels now,' said Tommy.

'Silly name,' said Colonel Pikeaway. 'Very popular at one time, though. I remember when I was a boy, all the neighbours, you know, they had those great Victorian drives up to the house. Always getting in loads of gravel for putting down on it and laurels on each side. Sometimes they were glossy green ones and sometimes the speckled ones. Supposed to be very showy. I suppose some of the people who've lived there called it that and the name stuck. Is that right?'

'Yes, I think so,' said Tommy. 'Not the last people. I believe the last people called it Katmandu, or some name abroad because they lived in a certain place they liked.'

'Yes, yes. Swallow's Nest goes back a long time. Yes, but one's got to go back sometimes. In fact, that's what I was going to talk to you about. Going back.'

'Did you ever know it, sir?'

'What – Swallow's Nest, alias The Laurels? No, I never went there. But it figured in certain things. It's tied up with certain periods in the past. People over a certain period. A period of great anxiety to this country.'

'I gather you've come in contact with some information pertaining to someone called Mary Jordan. Or known by that name. Anyway, that's what Mr Robinson told us.'

'Want to see what she looked like? Go over to the mantelpiece. There's a photograph on the left side.'

Tommy got up, went across to the mantelpiece and picked up the photograph. It represented an old-world type of a photograph. A girl wearing a picture hat and holding up a bunch of roses towards her head.

'Looks damn silly now, doesn't it?' said Colonel Pikeaway. 'But she was a good-looking girl, I believe. Unlucky though. She died young. Rather a tragedy, that was.'

'I don't know anything about her,' said Tommy.

'No, I don't suppose so,' said Colonel Pikeaway. 'Nobody does nowadays.'

'There was some idea locally that she was a German spy,' said Tommy. 'Mr Robinson told me that wasn't the case.'

'No, it wasn't the case. She belonged to us. And she did good work for us, too. But somebody got wise to her.'

'That was when there were some people called Parkinson living there,' said Tommy.

'Maybe. Maybe. I don't know all the details. Nobody does nowadays. I wasn't personally involved, you know.

All this has been raked up since. Because, you see, there's always trouble. There's trouble in every country. There's trouble all over the world now and not for the first time. No. You can go back a hundred years and you'll find trouble, and you can go back another hundred years and you'll find trouble. Go back to the Crusades and you'll find everyone dashing out of the country going to deliver Jerusalem, or you'll find risings all over the country. Wat Tyler and all the rest of them. This, that and the other, there's always trouble.'

'Do you mean there's some special trouble now?'

'Of course there is. I tell you, there's always trouble.'

'What sort of trouble?'

'Oh, we don't know,' said Colonel Pikeaway. 'They even come round to an old man like me and ask me what I can tell them, or what I can remember about certain people in the past. Well, I can't remember very much but I know about one or two people. You've got to look into the past sometimes. You've got to know what was happening then. What secrets people had, what knowledge they had that they kept to themselves, what they hid away, what they pretended was happening and what was really happening. You've done good jobs, you and your missus at different times. Do you want to go on with it now?'

'I don't know,' said Tommy. 'If – well, do you

think there is anything I could do? I'm rather an old man now.'

'Well, you look to me as though you've got better health than many people of your age. Look to me as though you've got better health than some of the younger ones too. And as for your wife, well, she was always good at nosing out things, wasn't she? Yes, good as a well-trained dog.'

Tommy could not repress a smile.

'But what is this all about?' said Tommy. 'I – of course I'm quite willing to do anything if – if you thought I could, but I don't know. Nobody's *told* me anything.'

'I don't suppose they will,' said Colonel Pikeaway. 'I don't think they want me to tell you anything. I don't suppose that Robinson told you much. He keeps his mouth shut, that large fat man. But I'll tell you, well, the bare facts. You know what the world's like – well, the same things always. Violence, swindles, materialism, rebellion by the young, love of violence and a good deal of sadism, almost as bad as the days of the Hitler Youth. All those things. Well, when you want to find out what's wrong not only with this country but world trouble as well, it's not easy. It's a good thing, the Common Market. It's what we always needed, always wanted. But it's got to be a real Common Market. That's got to be understood very clearly. It's got to be a united Europe. There's got to be a union of civilized countries with civilized ideas and with civilized beliefs and principles. The first thing is, when there's something wrong you've got to know where that something is and that's where that yellow whale of a fellow still knows his oats.'

'You mean Mr Robinson?'

'Yes, I mean Mr Robinson. They wanted to give him a peerage, you know, but he wouldn't have it. And you know what *he* means.'

'I suppose,' said Tommy, 'you mean – he stands for – *money*.'

'That's right. Not materialism, but he *knows* about money. He knows where it comes from, he knows where it goes, he knows why it goes, he knows who's behind things. Behind banks, behind big industrial undertakings, and he has to know who is responsible for certain things, big fortunes made out of drugs, drug pushers, drugs being sent all over the world, being marketed, a worship of money. Money not just for buying yourself a big house and two Rolls-Royces, but money for making more money and doing down, doing away with the old beliefs. Beliefs in honesty, in fair trading. You don't want equality in the world, you want the strong to help the weak. You want the rich to finance the poor. You want the honest and the good to be looked up to and admired. Finance! Things are coming back now to finance all the time. What finance is doing, where it's going, what it's supporting, how far hidden it is. There are people you knew, people in the past who had power and brains and their power and brains brought the money and means, and some of their activities were secret but we've got to find out about them. Find out who their secrets passed to, who they've been handed down to, who may be running things now. Swallow's Nest was a type of headquarters. A headquarters for what I should call evil. Later in Hollowquay there was something else. D'you remember Jonathan Kane at all?'

'It's a name,' said Tommy. 'I don't remember anything personally.'

'Well, he was said to be what was admired at one time – what came to be known later as a fascist. That was the time before we knew what Hitler was going to be like and all the rest of them. The time when we thought that something like fascism might be a splendid idea to reform the world with. This chap Jonathan Kane had followers. A lot of followers. Young followers, middle-aged followers, a lot of them. He had plans, he had sources of power, he knew the secrets of a lot of people. He had the kind of knowledge that gave him power. Plenty of blackmail about as always. We want to know what he knew, we want to know what he did, and I think it's possible that he left both plans and followers behind him. Young people who were enmeshed and perhaps still are in favour of his ideas. There have been secrets, you know, there are always secrets that are worth money. I'm not telling you anything exact because I don't know anything exact. The trouble with me is that nobody really knows. We think we know everything because of what we've been through. Wars, turmoil, peace, new forms of government. We think we know it all, but do we? Do we know anything about germ warfare? Do we know everything about gases, about means of inducing pollution? The chemists have their secrets, the Navy, the Air Force – all sorts of things. And they're not all in the present, some of them were in the past. Some of them were on the point of being developed but the development didn't take place. There wasn't time for it. But it was written down, it was committed to paper or committed to certain people, and those people had children and their children had children and maybe some of the things came down. Left in wills, left in documents, left with solicitors to be delivered at a certain time.

'Some people don't know what it is they've got hold of, some of them have just destroyed it as rubbish. But we've got to find out a little more than we do because things are happening all the time. In different countries, in different places, in wars, in Vietnam, in guerrilla wars, in Jordan, in Israel, even in the uninvolved countries. In Sweden and Switzerland – anywhere. There are these things and we want clues to them. And there's some idea that some of the clues could be found in the past. Well, you can't go back into the past, you can't go to a doctor and say, "Hypnotize me and let me see what happened in 1914," or in 1918 or earlier still perhaps. In 1890 perhaps. Something was being planned, something was never completely developed. Ideas. Just look far back. They were thinking of flying, you know, in the Middle Ages. They had some ideas about it. The ancient Egyptians, I believe, had certain ideas. They were never developed. But once the ideas passed on, once you come to the time when they get into the hands of someone who has the means and the kind of brain that can develop them, anything may happen – bad or good. We have a feeling lately that some of the things that have been invented – germ warfare, for example – are difficult to explain except through the process of some secret development, thought to be unimportant but it hasn't been unimportant. Somebody in whose hands it's got has made some adaptation of it which can produce very, very frightening results. Things that can change a character, can perhaps turn a good man into a fiend, and usually for the same reason. For money. Money and what money can buy, what money can get. The power that money can develop. Well, young Beresford, what do you say to all that?'

'I think it's a very frightening prospect,' said Tommy.

'That, yes. But do you think I'm talking nonsense? Do you think this is just an old man's fantasies?'

'No, sir,' said Tommy. 'I think you're a man who knows things. You always have been a man who knew things.'

'H'm. That's why they wanted me, wasn't it? They came here, complained about all the smoke, said it stifled them, but – well, you know there's a time – a time when there was that Frankfurt ring business – well, we managed to stop that. We managed to stop it by getting at who was behind it. There's a somebody, not just one somebody – several somebodies who are probably behind this. Perhaps we can know who they are, but even if not we can know perhaps what the things are.'

'I see,' said Tommy. 'I can almost understand.'

'Can you? Don't you think this is all rather nonsense? Rather fantastic?'

'I don't think anything's too fantastic to be true,' said Tommy. 'I've learnt that, at least, through a pretty long life. The most amazing things are true, things you couldn't believe could be true. But what I have to make you understand is that *I* have no qualifications. I have no scientific knowledge. I have been concerned always with security.'

'But,' said Colonel Pikeaway, 'you're a man who has always been able to find out things. You. You – and the other one. Your wife. I tell you, she's got a nose for things. She likes to find out things and you go about and take her about. These women are like that. They can get at secrets. If you're young and beautiful you do it like Delilah. When you're old – I can tell you, I had an old great-aunt once and there was no secret that she didn't nose into and find out the truth about. There's the money side. Robinson's on to that. He knows about money. He knows where the money goes, why it goes, where it goes to, and where it comes *from* and what it's *doing*. All the rest of it. He knows about money. It's like a doctor feeling your pulse. He can feel a financier's pulse. Where the headquarters of money are. Who's using it, what for and why. I'm putting you on to this because you're in the right place. You're in the right place by accident and you're not there for the reason anyone might suppose you were. For there you are, an ordinary couple, elderly, retired, seeking for a nice house to end your days in, poking about into the corners of it, interested in talking. Some sentence one day will tell you something. That's all I want you to do. Look about. Find out what legends or stories are told about the good old days or the bad old days.'

'A naval scandal, plans of a submarine or something, that's talked about still,' said Tommy. 'Several people keep mentioning it. But nobody seems to know anything really about it.'

'Yes, well, that's a good starting point. It was round about then Jonathan Kane lived in that part, you know. He had a cottage down near the sea and he ran his propaganda campaign round there. He had disciples who thought he was wonderful, Jonathan Kane. K-a-n-e. But I would rather spell it a different way. I'd spell it C-a-i-n. That would describe him better. He was set on destruction and methods of destruction. He left England. He went through Italy to countries rather far away, so it's said. How much is rumour I don't know. He went to Russia. He went to Iceland, he went to the American continent. Where he went and what he did and who went with him and listened to him, we don't know. But we think that he knew things, simple things; he was popular with his neighbours, he lunched with them and they with him. Now, one thing I've got to tell you. Look about you. Ferret out things, but for goodness' sake take care of yourselves, both of you. Take care of that – what's-her-name? Prudence?'

'Nobody ever called her Prudence. Tuppence,' said Tommy.

'That's right. Take care of Tuppence and tell Tuppence to take care of you. Take care of what you eat and what you drink and where you go and who is making up to you and being friendly and why should they? A little information comes along. Something odd or queer. Some story in the past that might mean something. Someone perhaps who's a descendant or a relative or someone who knew people in the past.'

'I'll do what I can,' said Tommy. 'We both will. But I don't feel that we'll be able to do it. We're too old. We don't know enough.'

'You can have ideas.'

'Yes. Tuppence has ideas. She thinks that something might be hidden in our house.'

'So it might. Others have had the same idea. Nobody's ever found anything so far, but then they haven't really looked with any assurance at all. Various houses and various families, they change. They get sold and somebody else comes and then somebody else and so they go on. Lestranges and Mortimers and Parkinsons. Nothing much in the Parkinsons except for one of the boys.'

'Alexander Parkinson?'

'So you know about him. How did you manage that?'

'He left a message for someone to find in one of Robert Louis Stevenson's books. *Mary Jordan did not die naturally*. We found it.'

'The fate of every man we have bound about his neck – some saying like that, isn't there? Carry on, you two. Pass through the Postern of Fate.'

Chapter 6

Postern of Fate

Mr Durrance's shop was half-way up the village. It was on a corner site, had a few photographs displayed in the window; a couple of marriage groups, a kicking baby in a nudist condition on a rug, one or two bearded young men taken with their girls. None of the photographs were very good, some of them already displayed signs of age. There were also postcards in large numbers; birthday cards and a few special shelves arranged in order of relationships. To my Husband. To my Wife. One or two bathing groups. There were a few pocket-books and wallets of rather poor quality and a certain amount of stationery and envelopes bearing floral designs. Boxes of small notepaper decorated with flowers and labelled For Notes.

Tuppence wandered about a little, picking up various specimens of the merchandise and waiting whilst a discussion about the results obtained from a certain camera were criticized, and advice was asked.

An elderly woman with grey hair and rather lack-lustre eyes attended to a good deal of the more ordinary requests. A rather tall young man with long flaxen hair and a budding beard seemed to be the principal attendant. He came along the counter towards Tuppence, looking at her questioningly.

'Can I help you in any way?'

'Really,' said Tuppence, 'I wanted to ask about albums. You know, photograph albums.'

'Ah, things to stick your photos in, you mean? Well, we've got one or two of those but you don't get so much of them nowadays, I mean, people go very largely for transparencies, of course.'

'Yes, I understand,' said Tuppence, 'but I collect them, you know. I collect old albums. Ones like this.'

She produced, with the air of a conjurer, the album she'd been sent.

'Ah, that goes back a long time, doesn't it?' said Mr Durrance. 'Ah, well now, over fifty years old, I should say. Of course, they did do a lot of those things around then, didn't they? Everyone had an album.'

'They had birthday books, too,' said Tuppence.

'Birthday books – yes, I remember something about them. My grandmother had a birthday book, I remember. Lots of people had to write their name in it. We've got birthday cards here still, but people don't buy them much nowadays. It's more Valentines, you know, and Happy Christmases, of course.'

'I don't know whether you had any old albums. You know, the sort of things people don't want any more, but they interest me as a collector. I like having different specimens.'

'Well, everyone collects something nowadays, that's true enough,' said Durrance. 'You'd hardly believe it, the things people collect. I don't think I've got anything as old as this one of yours, though. However, I could look around.'

He went behind the counter and pulled open a drawer against the wall.

'Lot of stuff in here,' he said. 'I meant to turn it out some time but I didn't know as there'd really be any market for it. A lot of weddings here, of course. But then, I mean, weddings date. People want them just at the time of the wedding but nobody comes back to look for weddings in the past.'

'You mean, nobody comes in and says "My grandmother was married here. I wonder if you've got any photographs of her wedding?"'

'Don't think anyone's ever asked me that,' said Durrance. 'Still, you never know. They do ask you for queer things sometimes. Sometimes, you know, someone comes in and wants to see whether you've kept a negative of a baby. You know what mothers are. They want pictures of their babies when they were young. Awful pictures, most of them are, anyway. Now and then we've even had the police round. You know, they want to identify someone. Someone who was here as a boy, and they want to see what he looks like – or rather what he looked like then, and whether he's likely to be the same one as one they're looking for now and whom they're after because he's wanted for murder or for swindles. I must say that cheers things up sometimes,' said Durrance with a happy smile.

'I see you're quite crime-minded,' said Tuppence.

'Oh well, you know, you're reading about things like that every day, why this man is supposed to have killed his wife about six months ago, and all that. Well, I mean, that's interesting, isn't it? Because, I mean, some people say that she's still alive. Other people say that he buried her somewhere and nobody's found her. Things like that. Well, a photograph of him might come in useful.'

'Yes,' said Tuppence.

'She felt that though she was getting on good terms with Mr Durrance nothing was coming of it.

'I don't suppose you'd have any photographs of someone called – I think her name was Mary Jordan. Some name like that. But it was a long time ago. About – oh, I suppose sixty years. I think she died here.'

'Well, it'd be well before my time,' said Mr Durrance.

'Father kept a good many things. You know, he was one of those – hoarders, they call them. Never wanted to throw anything away. Anyone he'd known he'd remember, especially if there was a history about it. Mary Jordan. I seem to remember something about her. Something to do with the Navy, wasn't it, and a submarine? And they said she was a spy, wasn't she? She was half foreign. Had a Russian mother or a German mother – might have been a Japanese mother or something like that.'

'Yes. I just wondered if you had any pictures of her.'

'Well, I don't think so. I'll have a look around some time when I've got a little time. I'll let you know if anything turns up. Perhaps you're a writer, are you?' he said hopefully.

'Well,' said Tuppence, 'I don't make a whole-time job of it, but I am thinking of bringing out a rather small book. You know, recalling the times of about anything from a hundred years ago down till today. You know, curious things that have happened including crimes and adventures. And, of course, old photographs are very interesting and would illustrate the book beautifully.'

'Well, I'll do everything I can to help you, I'm sure. Must be quite interesting, what you're doing. Quite interesting to do, I mean.'

'There were some people called Parkinson,' said

Tuppence. 'I think they lived in our house once.'

'Ah, you come from the house up on the hill, don't you? The Laurels or Katmandu – I can't remember what it was called last. Swallow's Nest it was called once, wasn't it? Can't think why.'

'I suppose there were a lot of swallows nesting in the roof,' suggested Tuppence. 'There still are.'

'Well, may have been, I suppose. But it seems a funny name for a house.'

Tuppence, having felt that she'd opened relations satisfactorily, though not hoping very much that any result would come of it, bought a few postcards and some flowered notes in the way of stationery, and wished Mr Durrance goodbye, got back to the gate, walked up the drive, then checked herself on the way to the house and went up the side path round it to have one more look at KK. She got near the door. She stopped suddenly, then walked on. It looked as though something like a bundle of clothes was lying near the door. Something they'd pulled out of Mathilde and not thought to look at, Tuppence wondered.

She quickened her pace, almost running. When she got near the door she stopped suddenly. It was not a bundle of old clothes. The clothes were old enough, and so was the body that wore them. Tuppence bent over and then stood up again, steadied herself with a hand on the door.

'Isaac!' she said. 'Isaac. Poor old Isaac. I believe – oh, I do believe that he's dead.'

Somebody was coming towards her on the path from the house as she called out, taking a step or two.

'Oh, Albert, Albert. Something awful's happened. Isaac, old Isaac. He's lying there and he's dead and I think – I think somebody has killed him.'

Chapter 7

The Inquest

The medical evidence had been given. Two passers-by not far from the gate had given their evidence. The family had spoken, giving evidence as to the state of his health, any possible people who had had reason for enmity towards him (one or two youngish adolescent boys who had before now been warned off by him) had been asked to assist the police and had protested their innocence. One or two of his employers had spoken including his latest employer, Mrs Prudence Beresford, and her husband, Mr Thomas Beresford. All had been said and done and a verdict had been brought in: Wilful Murder by a person or persons unknown.

Tuppence came out from the inquest and Tommy put an arm round her as they passed the little group of people waiting outside.

'You did very well, Tuppence,' he said, as they returned through the garden gate towards the house.

'Very well indeed. Much better than some of those people. You were very clear and you could be heard. The Coroner seemed to me to be very pleased with you.'

'I don't want anyone to be very pleased with me,' said Tuppence. 'I don't like old Isaac being coshed on the head and killed like that.'

'I suppose someone might have had it in for him,' said Tommy.

'Why should they?' said Tuppence.

'I don't know,' said Tommy.

'No,' said Tuppence, 'and I don't know either. But I just wondered if it's anything to do with us.'

'Do you mean – what do you mean, Tuppence?'

'You know what I mean really,' said Tuppence. 'It's this – this place. Our house. Our lovely new house. And garden and everything. It's as though – isn't it just the right place for us? We thought it was,' said Tuppence.

'Well, I still do,' said Tommy.

'Yes,' said Tuppence, 'I think you've got more hope than I have. I've got an uneasy feeling that there's something – something *wrong* with it all here. Something left over from the past.'

'Don't say it again,' said Tommy.

'Don't say what again?'

'Oh, just those two words.'

Tuppence dropped her voice. She got nearer to Tommy and spoke almost into his ear.

'Mary Jordan?'

'Well, yes. That *was* in my mind.'

'And in my mind, too, I expect. But I mean, what can anything then have to do with nowadays? What can the past matter?' said Tuppence. 'It oughtn't to have anything to do with – now.'

'The past oughtn't to have anything to do with the present – is that what you mean? But it does,' said Tommy. 'It does, in queer ways that one doesn't think of. I mean that one doesn't think would ever happen.'

'A lot of things, you mean, happen because of what there was in the past?'

'Yes. It's a sort of long chain. The sort of thing you have, with gaps and then with beads on it from time to time.'

'Jane Finn and all that. Like Jane Finn in our adventures when we were young because we wanted adventures.'

'And we had them,' said Tommy. 'Sometimes I look back on it and wonder how we got out of it alive.'

'And then – other things. You know, when we went into partnership, and we pretended to be detective agents.'

'Oh that was fun,' said Tommy. 'Do you remember –'

'No,' said Tuppence, 'I'm not going to remember.

I'm not anxious to go back to thinking of the past except – well, except as a stepping-stone, as you might say. No. Well, anyway that gave us practice, didn't it? And then we had the next bit.'

'Ah,' said Tommy. 'Mrs Blenkinsop, eh?'

Tuppence laughed.

'Yes. Mrs Blenkinsop. I'll never forget when I came into that room and saw you sitting there.'

'How you had the nerve, Tuppence, to do what you did, move that wardrobe or whatever it was, and listen in to me and Mr What's-his-name, talking. And then –'

'And then Mrs Blenkinsop,' said Tuppence. She laughed too. 'N or M and Goosey Goosey Gander.'

'But you don't –' Tommy hesitated – 'you don't believe that all those were what you call stepping-stones to this?'

'Well, they are in a way,' said Tuppence. 'I mean, I don't suppose that Mr Robinson would have said what he did to you if he hadn't had a lot of those things in his mind. Me for one of them.'

'Very much you for one of them.'

'But now,' said Tuppence, 'this makes it all different. This, I mean. Isaac. Dead. Coshed on the head. Just inside our garden gate.'

'You don't think *that's* connected with –'

'One can't help thinking it might be,' said Tuppence.

'That's what I mean. We're not just investigating a sort of detective mystery any more. Finding out, I mean, about the past and why somebody died in the past and things like that. It's become personal. Quite personal, I think. I mean, poor old Isaac being *dead*.'

'He was a very old man and possibly that had something to do with it.'

'Not after listening to the medical evidence this morning. Someone wanted to kill him. What for?'

'Why didn't they want to kill us if it was anything to do with us,' said Tommy.

'Well, perhaps they'll try that too. Perhaps, you know, he could have told us something. Perhaps he *was* going to tell us something. Perhaps he even threatened somebody else that he was going to talk to us, say something he knew about the girl or one of the Parkinsons. Or – or all this spying business in the 1914 war. The secrets that were sold. And then, you see, he had to be silenced. But if *we* hadn't come to live here and ask questions and wanted to find out, it wouldn't have happened.'

'Don't get so worked up.'

'I am worked up. And I'm not doing anything for fun any more. This isn't fun. We're doing something different now, Tommy. We're hunting down a killer. But who? Of course we don't know yet but we can find out. That's not the past, that's Now. That's something that happened – what – only days ago, six days ago. That's the present. It's here and it's connected with us and it's connected with this house. And we've got to find out and we're going to find out. I don't know how but we've got to go after all the clues and follow up things. I feel like a dog with my nose to the ground, following a trail. I'll have to follow it *here*, and you've got to be a hunting dog. Go round to different places. The way you're doing now. Finding out about things. Getting your – whatever you call it – research done. There must be people who know things, not of their own knowledge, but what people have told them. Stories they've heard. Rumours. Gossip.'

'But, Tuppence, you can't really believe there's any chance of our –'

'Oh yes I do,' said Tuppence. 'I don't know how or in what way, but I believe that when you've got a real, convincing idea, something that you know is black and bad and evil, and hitting old Isaac on the head *was* black and evil . . .' She stopped.

'We could change the name of the house again,' said Tommy.

'What do you mean? Call it Swallow's Nest and not The Laurels?'

A flight of birds passed over their heads. Tuppence turned her head and looked back towards the garden gate. 'Swallow's Nest was once its name. What's the rest of that quotation? The one your researcher quoted. Postern of Death, wasn't it?'

'No, Postern of Fate.'

'Fate. That's like a comment on what has happened to Isaac. Postern of Fate – *our* Garden Gate –'

'Don't worry so much, Tuppence.'

'I don't know why,' said Tuppence. 'It's just a sort of idea that came into my mind.'

Tommy gave her a puzzled look and shook his head.

'Swallow's nest is a nice name, really,' said Tuppence. 'Or it could be. Perhaps it will some day.'

'You have the most extraordinary ideas, Tuppence.'

'Yet something singeth like a bird. That was how it ended. Perhaps all this will end that way.'

Just before they reached the house, Tommy and Tuppence saw a woman standing on the doorstep.

'I wonder who that is,' said Tommy.

'Someone I've seen before,' said Tuppence. 'I don't remember who at the moment. Oh. I think it's one of old Isaac's family. You know they all lived together in one cottage. About three or four boys and this woman and another one, a girl. I may be wrong, of course.'

The woman on the doorstep had turned and came towards them.

'Mrs Beresford, isn't it?' she said, looking at Tuppence.

'Yes,' said Tuppence.

'And – I don't expect you know me. I'm Isaac's daughter-in-law, you know. Married to his son, Stephen, I was. Stephen – he got killed in an accident. One of them lorries. The big ones that go along. It was on one of the M roads, the M1 I think it was. M1 or the M5. No, the M5 was before that. The M4 it could be. Anyway, there it was. Five or six years ago it was. I wanted to – I wanted just to speak to you. You and – you and your husband –' She looked at Tommy. 'You sent flowers, didn't you, to the funeral? Isaac worked in the garden here for you, didn't he?'

'Yes,' said Tuppence. 'He did work for us here. It was such a terrible thing to have happened.'

'I came to thank you. Very lovely flowers they was, too. Good ones. Classy ones. A great bunch of them.'

'We thought we'd like to do it,' said Tuppence, 'because Isaac had been very helpful to us. He'd helped us a lot, you know, with getting into the house. Telling us about things, because we don't know much about the house. Where things were kept, and everything. And he gave me a lot of knowledge about planting things, too, and all that sort of thing.'

'Yes, he knew his stuff, as you might say. He wasn't much of a worker because he was old, you know, and he didn't like stooping. Got lumbago a lot, so he couldn't do as much as he'd have liked to do.'

'He was very nice and very helpful,' said Tuppence firmly. 'And he knew a lot about things here, and the people, and told us a lot.'

'Ah. He knew a lot, he did. A lot of his family, you know, worked before him. They lived round about and they'd known a good deal of what went on in years gone by. Not of their own knowledge, as you might say but – well, just hearing what went on. Well, ma'am, I won't keep you. I just came up to have a few words and say how much obliged I was.'

'That's very nice of you,' said Tuppence. 'Thank you very much.'

'You'll have to get someone else to do a bit of work in the garden, I expect.'

'I expect so,' said Tuppence. 'We're not very good at it ourselves. Do you – perhaps you –' she hesitated, feeling perhaps she was saying the wrong thing at the wrong moment – 'perhaps you know of someone who would like to come and work for us.'

'Well, I can't say I do offhand, but I'll keep it in mind. You never know. I'll send along Henry – that's my second boy, you know – I'll send him along and let you know if I hear of anyone. Well, good day for now.'

'What was Isaac's name? I can't remember,' said Tommy, as they went into the house. 'I mean, his surname.'

'Oh, Isaac Bodlicott, I think.'

'So that's a Mrs Bodlicott, is it?'

'Yes. Though I think she's got several sons, boys and a girl and they all live together. You know, in that cottage half-way up the Marshton Road. Do you think she knows who killed him?' said Tuppence.

'I shouldn't think so,' said Tommy. 'She didn't look as though she did.'

'I don't know how you'd look,' said Tuppence. 'It's rather difficult to say, isn't it?'

'I think she just came to thank you for the flowers. I don't think she had the look of someone who was – you know – revengeful. I think she'd have mentioned it if so.'

'Might. Might not,' said Tuppence.

She went into the house looking rather thoughtful.

Chapter 8

Reminiscences about an Uncle

The following morning Tuppence was interrupted in her remarks to an electrician who had come to adjust portions of his work which were not considered satisfactory.

'Boy at the door,' said Albert. 'Wants to speak to you, madam.'

'Oh. What's his name?'

'Didn't ask him, he's waiting there outside.'

Tuppence seized her garden hat, shoved it on her head and came down the stairs.

Outside the door a boy of about twelve or thirteen was standing. He was rather nervous, shuffling his feet.

'Hope it's all right to come along,' he said.

'Let me see,' said Tuppence, 'you're Henry Bodlicott, aren't you?'

'That's right. That was my – oh, I suppose he was by way of being an uncle, the one I mean whose inquest was on yesterday. Never been to an inquest before, I haven't.'

Tuppence stopped herself on the brink of saying 'Did you enjoy it?' Henry had the look of someone who was about to describe a treat.

'It was quite a tragedy, wasn't it?' said Tuppence. 'Very sad.'

'Oh well, he was an old one,' said Henry. 'Couldn't have expected to last much longer I don't think, you know. Used to cough something terrible in the autumn. Kept us all awake in the house. I just come along to ask if there's anything as you want done here. I understood – as a matter of fact Mom told me – as you had some lettuces ought to be thinned out now and I wonder if you'd like me to do it for you. I know just where they are because I used to come up sometimes and talk to old Izzy when he was at work. I could do it now if you liked.'

'Oh, that's very nice of you,' said Tuppence. 'Come out and show me.'

They moved into the garden together and went up to the spot designated.

'That's it, you see. They've been shoved in a bit tight and you've got to thin 'em out a bit and put 'em over there instead, you see, when you've made proper gaps.'

'I don't really know anything about lettuces,' Tuppence admitted. 'I know a little about flowers. Peas, Brussels sprouts and lettuces and other vegetables I'm not very good at. You don't want a job working in the garden, I suppose, do you?'

'Oh no, I'm still at school, I am. I takes the papers round and I do a bit of fruit picking in the summer, you know.'

'I see,' said Tuppence. 'Well, if you hear of anyone and you let me know, I'll be very glad.'

'Yes, I will do that. Well, so long, mum.'

'Just show me what you're doing to the lettuces. I'd like to know.'

She stood by, watching the manipulations of Henry Bodlicott.

'Now that's all right. Yes, nice ones, these, aren't they? Webb's Wonderful, aren't they? They keep a long time.'

'We finished the Tom Thumbs,' said Tuppence.

'That's right. Those are the little early ones, aren't they? Very crisp and good.'

'Well, thank you very much,' said Tuppence.

She turned away and started to walk towards the house. She noted she'd lost her scarf and turned back. Henry Bodlicott, just starting for home, stopped and came across to her.

'Just the scarf,' said Tuppence. 'Is it – oh, there it is on that bush.'

He handed it to her, then stood looking at her,

shuffling his feet. He looked so very worried and ill at ease that Tuppence wondered what was the matter with him.

'Is there anything?' she said.

Henry shuffled his feet, looked at her, shuffled his feet again, picked his nose and rubbed his left ear and then moved his feet in a kind of tattoo.

'Just something I – I wondered if you – I mean – if you wouldn't mind me asking you –'

'Well?' said Tuppence. She stopped and looked at him enquiringly.

Henry got very red in the face and continued to shuffle his feet.

'Well, I didn't like to – I don't like to ask, but I just wondered – I mean, people have been saying – they said things . . . I mean, I hear them say . . .'

'Yes?' said Tuppence, wondering what had upset Henry, what he could have heard concerning the lives of Mr and Mrs Beresford, the new tenants of The Laurels. 'Yes, you've heard what?'

'Oh, just as – as how it's you is the lady what caught spies or something in the last war. You did it, and the gentleman too. You were in it and you found someone who was a German spy pretending to be something else. And you found him out and you had a lot of adventures and in the end it was all cleared up. I mean, you were – I don't know what to call it – I suppose you were one of our Secret Service people and you did that and they said as you'd been wonderful. Of course, some time ago now but you was all mixed up with something – something about nursery rhymes too.'

'That's right,' said Tuppence. 'Goosey Goosey Gander was the one in question.'

'Goosey Goosey Gander! I remember that. Gosh, years ago, it was. Whither will you wander?'

'That's right,' said Tuppence. 'Upstairs, downstairs, in my lady's chamber. There he found an old man who wouldn't say his prayers and he took him by the left leg and threw him down the stairs. At least, I think that's right but it may be a different nursery rhyme I've tacked on to it.'

'Well, I never,' said Henry. 'Well, I mean, it's rather wonderful to have you living here just like anyone else, isn't it? But I don't know why the nursery rhymes were in it.'

'Oh there was a kind of code, a cypher,' said Tuppence.

'You mean it had to be sort of read and all that?' said Henry.

'Something of the kind,' said Tuppence. 'Anyway, it was all found out.'

'Well now, isn't that wonderful,' said Henry. 'You don't mind if I tell my friend, do you? My chum. Clarence, his name is. Silly name, I know. We all laugh at him for it. But he's a good chap, he is and he'll be ever so thrilled to know as we've got you really living amongst us.'

He looked at Tuppence with the admiration of an affectionate spaniel.

'Wonderful!' he said again.

'Oh, it was a long time ago,' said Tuppence. 'In the 1940s.'

'Was it fun, or were you ever so frightened?'

'Bits of both,' said Tuppence. 'Mostly, I think, I was frightened.'

'Oh well, I expect as you would be, too. Yes, but it's odd as you should come here and get mixed up in the same sort of thing. It was a naval gentleman, wasn't it? I mean as called himself an English commander in the Navy, but he wasn't really. He was a German. At least, that's what Clarence said.'

'Something like that,' said Tuppence.

'So perhaps that's why you come here. Because, you know, we had something here once – well it was a very, very long time ago – but it was the same thing, as you might say. He was a submarine officer. He sold plans of submarines. Mind you, it's only stories as I've heard people say.'

'I see,' said Tuppence. 'Yes. No, it's not the reason we came here. We just came here because it's a nice house to live in. I've heard these same rumours going about only I don't know exactly what happened.'

'Well, I'll try and tell you some time. Of course, one doesn't always know what's right or not but things aren't always known properly.'

'How did your friend Clarence manage to know so much about it?'

'Well, he heard from Mick, you know. He used to live a short time up by where the blacksmith used to be. He's been gone a long time, but he heard a lot from different people. And our uncle, old Isaac, he knew a good deal about it. He used to tell us things sometimes.'

'So he did know a good deal about it all?' said Tuppence.

'Oh yes. That's why I wondered, you know, when he was coshed the other day if that could be the reason. That he might have known a bit too much and – he told it all to you. So they did him in. That's what they do nowadays. They do people in, you know, if they know too much of anything that's going to involve them with the police or anything.'

'You think your Uncle Isaac – you think he knew a good deal about it?'

'Well, I think things got told him, you know. He heard a lot here and there. Didn't often talk of it but sometimes he would. Of an evening, you know, after smoking a pipe or hearing me and Clarrie talk and my other friend, Tom Gillingham. He used to want to know, too, and Uncle Izzy would tell us this, that and the other. Of course we didn't know if he was making it up or not. But I think he'd found things and knew where some things were. And he said if some people knew where they were there might be something interesting.'

'Did he?' said Tuppence. 'Well, I think that's very interesting to us also. You must try and remember some of the things he said or suggested some time because, well, it might lead to finding out who killed him. Because he was killed. It wasn't an accident, was it?'

'We thought at first it must have been an accident. You know, he had a bit of a heart or something and he used to fall down now and again or get giddy or have turns. But it seems – I went to the inquest, you know – as though he'd been done in deliberate.'

'Yes,' said Tuppence, 'I think he was done in deliberate.'

'And you don't know why?' said Henry.

Tuppence looked at Henry. It seemed to her as though she and Henry were for the moment two police dogs on the same scent.

'I think it was deliberate, and I think that you, because he was your relation, and I too, would like to know who it was who did such a cruel and wicked thing.

But perhaps you do know or have some idea already, Henry.'

'I don't have a proper idea, I don't,' said Henry. 'One just hears things and I know people that Uncle Izzy says – said – now and then had got it in for him for some reason and he said that was because he knew a bit too much about them and about what they knew and about something that happened. But it's always someone who's been dead so many years ago that one can't really remember it or get at it properly.'

'Well,' said Tuppence, 'I think you'll have to help us, Henry.'

'You mean you'll let me sort of be in it with you? I mean, doing a bit of finding out any time?'

'Yes,' said Tuppence, 'if you can hold your tongue about what you find out. I mean, tell me, but don't go talking to all your friends about it because that way things would get around.'

'I see. And then they might tell the coshers and go for you and Mr Beresford, mightn't they?'

'They might,' said Tuppence, 'and I'd rather they didn't.'

'Well, that's natural,' said Henry. 'Well, see here, if I come across anything or hear anything I'll come up and offer to do a bit of work here. How's that? Then I can tell you what I know and nobody'd hear us and –

but I don't know anything right at the moment. But I've got friends.' He drew himself up suddenly and put on an air clearly adopted from something he'd seen on television. 'I know things. People don't know as I know things. They don't think I've listened and they don't think I'd remember, but I know sometimes – you know, they'll say something and then they'll say who else knows about it and then they'll – well, you know, if you keep quiet you get to hear a lot. And I expect it's all very important, isn't it?'

'Yes,' said Tuppence, 'I think it's important. But we have to be very careful, Henry. You understand that?'

'Oh, I do. Of course I'll be careful. Careful as you know how. He knew a lot about this place, you know,' went on Henry. 'My Uncle Isaac did.'

'About this house, you mean, or this garden?'

'That's right. He knew some of the stories about it, you know. Where people were seen going and what they did with things maybe, and where they met people. Where there were hiding-places and things. He used to talk sometimes, he did. Of course Mom, she didn't listen much. She'd just think it was all silly. Johnny – that's my older brother – he thinks it's all nonsense and he didn't listen. But I listened and Clarence is interested in that sort of thing. You know, he liked those kind of films and all that. He said to me, "Chuck, it's just like a film." So we talked about it together.'

'Did you ever hear anyone talked about whose name was Mary Jordan?'

'Ah yes, of course. She was the German girl who was a spy, wasn't she? Got naval secrets out of naval officers, didn't she?'

'Something of that kind, I believe,' said Tuppence, feeling it safer to stick to that version, though in her mind apologizing to the ghost of Mary Jordan.

'I expect she was very lovely, wasn't she? Very beautiful?'

'Well, I don't know,' said Tuppence, 'because, I mean, she probably died when I was about three years old.'

'Yes, of course, it would be so, wouldn't it? Oh, one hears her talked about sometimes.'

II

'You seem very excited and out of breath, Tuppence,' said Tommy as his wife, dressed in her garden clothes, came in through the side door, panting a little as she came.

'Well,' said Tuppence, 'I am in a way.'

'Not been overdoing it in the garden?'

'No. Actually I haven't been doing anything at all. I've just been standing by the lettuces talking, or being talked to – whichever way you put it –'

'Who's been talking to you?'

'A boy,' said Tuppence. 'A boy.'

'Offering to help in the garden?'

'Not exactly,' said Tuppence. 'That would be very nice too, of course. No. Actually, he was expressing admiration.'

'Of the garden?'

'No,' said Tuppence, 'of me.'

'Of you?'

'Don't look surprised,' said Tuppence, 'and oh, don't sound surprised either. Still, I admit these *bonnes bouches* come in sometimes when you least expect them.'

'Oh. What is the admiration of – your beauty or your garden overall?'

'My past,' said Tuppence.

'Your past!'

'Yes. He was fairly thrilled to think I had been the lady, as he put it, who had unmasked a German spy in the last war. A false naval commander, retired, who was nothing of the kind.'

'Good gracious,' said Tommy. 'N or M again. Dear me, shan't we ever be able to live that down?'

'Well, I'm not very sure I want to live it down,' said

Tuppence. 'I mean, why should we? If we'd been a celebrated actress or actor we'd quite like to be reminded of it.'

'I see the point,' said Tommy.

'And I think it might be very useful with what we're trying to do here.'

'If he's a boy, how old did you say he was?'

'Oh, I should think about ten or twelve. Looks ten but he's twelve, I think. And he has a friend called Clarence.'

'What's that got to do with it?'

'Well, nothing at the moment,' said Tuppence, 'but he and Clarence are allies and would like, I think, to attach themselves to our service. To find out things or to tell us things.'

'If they're ten or twelve, how can they tell us things or remember things we want to know?' said Tommy. 'What sort of things did he say?'

'Most of his sentences were short,' said Tuppence, 'and consisted of mainly "well, you know", or "you see, it was like this", or "yes, and then you know". Anyway, "you know" was always a component part of everything he said.'

'And they were all things you didn't know.'

'Well, they were attempts at explaining things he'd heard about.'

'Heard about from whom?'

'Well, not first-hand knowledge, as you'd say, and I wouldn't say second-hand knowledge. I think it might go up to third-hand, fourth-hand, fifth-hand, sixth-hand knowledge. It consisted also of what Clarence had heard and what Clarence's friend, Algernon, had heard. What Algernon said Jimmy had heard –'

'Stop,' said Tommy, 'that's enough. And what had they heard?'

'That's more difficult,' said Tuppence, 'but I think one can get round to it. They'd heard certain places mentioned or stories told and they were very, very anxious to partake of the joys of what we had clearly come to do here.'

'Which is?'

'To discover something important. Something that's well known to be hidden here.'

'Ah,' said Tommy. 'Hidden. Hidden how, where and when?'

'Different stories about all those three,' said Tuppence, 'but it's exciting, you must admit, Tommy.'

Tommy said thoughtfully that perhaps it was.

'It ties in with old Isaac,' said Tuppence. 'I think Isaac must have known quite a lot of things which he could have told us.'

'And you think that Clarence and – what's this one's name again?'

'I'll remember it in a minute,' said Tuppence. 'I got

so confused with all the other people he'd heard things from. The ones with the grand names like Algernon and the ones with the ordinary names like Jimmy and Johnny and Mike.

'Chuck,' said Tuppence suddenly.

'Chuck what?' asked Tommy.

'No. I didn't mean it that way. I think that's his name. The boy, I mean. Chuck.'

'It seems a very odd name.'

'His real name is Henry but I expect his friends call him Chuck.'

'Like Chuck goes the weasel.'

'Pop goes the weasel, you mean.'

'Well, I know that's correct. But Chuck goes the weasel sounds much the same.'

'Oh Tommy, what I really want to say to you is that we've got to go on with this, specially now. Do you feel the same?'

'Yes,' said Tommy.

'Well, I thought perhaps you did. Not that you've said anything. But we've got to go on with it and I'll tell you why. Mainly because of Isaac. Isaac. Somebody killed him. They killed him because he knew something. He knew something that might have been dangerous to somebody. And we've got to find out who the person was it would be dangerous to.'

'You don't think,' said Tommy, 'that it's just –

oh, one of those things. You know, hooliganism or whatever they call it. You know, people go out and want to do people in and don't care who the people are, but they prefer them to be elderly and not to be able to put up any kind of a resistance.'

'Yes,' said Tuppence, 'in a way I do mean that. But – I don't think it was that. I think there *is* something, I don't know if hidden is the right word, there's something here. Something that throws light on something that happened in the past, something that someone left here or put here or gave to someone to keep here who has since died or put it somewhere. But something that someone doesn't want discovered. Isaac knew it and they must have been afraid he'd tell us because word's evidently going round now about us. You know, that we're famous anti-espionage people or whatever you call it. We've got a reputation for that sort of thing. And it's tied up in a way, you see, with Mary Jordan and all the rest of it.'

'Mary Jordan,' said Tommy, 'did not die a natural death.'

'Yes,' said Tuppence, 'and old Isaac was killed. We've got to find out who killed him and why. Otherwise –'

'You've got to be careful,' said Tommy, 'you've got to be careful of yourself, Tuppence. If anyone killed Isaac because he thought he was going to talk about things in the past that he'd heard about, someone may be only too pleased to wait in a dark corner for you one night and do the same thing. They wouldn't think there'd be any worry about it, they'd just think people would say: "Oh another of those things."'

'When old ladies are hit on the head and done in,' said Tuppence. 'Yes, quite so. That's the unfortunate result of having grey hair and walking with a slight arthritic limp. Of course I must be fair game for anyone. I shall look after myself. Do you think I ought to carry a small pistol about with me?'

'No,' said Tommy, 'certainly not.'

'Why? Do you think I'd make some mistake with it?'

'Well, I think you might trip over the root of a tree. You know you're always falling down. And then you might shoot yourself instead of just using the pistol for protection.'

'Oh, you don't really think I'd do anything stupid like that, do you?' said Tuppence.

'Yes, I do,' said Tommy. 'I'm sure you're quite capable of it.'

'I could carry a flick knife,' said Tuppence.

'I shouldn't carry anything at all,' said Tommy. 'I should just go about looking innocent and talking about gardening. Say, perhaps, we're not sure we like the house and we have plans for going to live elsewhere. That's what I suggest.'

'Who've I got to say that to?'

'Oh, almost anyone,' said Tommy. 'It'll get round.'

'Things always get round,' said Tuppence. 'Quite a place here for things getting round. Are you going to say the same things, Tommy?'

'Well, roughly. Say, perhaps, that we don't like the house as much as we thought we did.'

'But you want to go on, too, don't you?' said Tuppence.

'Yes,' said Tommy. 'I'm embroiled all right.'

'Have you thought how to set about it?'

'Go on doing what I'm doing at present. What about you, Tuppence? Have you got any plans?'

'Not quite yet,' said Tuppence. 'I've got a few ideas. I can get a bit more out of – what did I say his name was?'

'First Henry – then Clarence.'

Chapter 9

Junior Brigade

Having seen Tommy depart for London, Tuppence was wandering vaguely round the house trying to single out some particular activity which might yield successful results. However, her brain did not seem to be full of bright ideas this morning.

With the general feeling of one returning to the beginning, she climbed up to the book-room and walked round it vaguely, looking at the titles of various volumes. Children's books, lots of children's books, but really one couldn't go any farther than that, could one? She had gone as far as anyone could already. By now she was almost certain that she had looked at every single book in this particular room; Alexander Parkinson had not revealed any more of his secrets.

She was standing there running her fingers through her hair, frowning and kicking at a bottom shelf of theological works whose bindings were nearly all of them scaling away from the books, when Albert came up.

'Someone as wants to see you downstairs, madam.'

'What do you mean by someone?' said Tuppence. 'Anyone I know?'

'I dunno. Shouldn't think so. Boys they are, mainly. Boys and a girl or two all in a hump. Spect they want a subscription for something or other.'

'Oh. They didn't give any names or say anything?'

'Oh, one of them did. Said he was Clarence and you'd know all about him.'

'Oh,' said Tuppence. 'Clarence.' She considered for a moment.

Was this the fruit from yesterday? Anyway, it could do no harm to follow it up.

'Is the other boy here too? The one I was talking to yesterday in the garden?'

'Don't know. They all look much alike. Dirty, you know, and all the rest of it.'

'Oh well,' said Tuppence, 'I'll come down.'

When she had reached the ground floor she turned enquiringly to her guide.

Albert said, 'Oh, I didn't let them come into the house. Wouldn't be safe, I think. Never know what you might lose, these days. They're out in the garden. They said to tell you they was by the gold-mine.'

'They was by the what?' asked Tuppence.

'The gold-mine.'

'Oh,' said Tuppence.

'What way would that be?'

Tuppence pointed.

'Past the rose garden, and then right by the dahlia walk. I think I know. There's a sort of water thing there. I don't know if it's a brook or a canal or has once been a pond that has had goldfish in it. Anyway, give me my gumboots and I'd better take my mackintosh as well in case someone pushes me into it.'

'I should put it on if I was you, ma'am, it's going to rain presently.'

'Oh dear,' said Tuppence. 'Rain, rain. Always rain.'

She went out and came fairly quickly to what seemed to be a considerable deputation waiting for her. There were, she thought, about ten or twelve of assorted ages, mainly boys flanked by two long-haired girls, all looking rather excited. One of them said in a shrill voice as Tuppence approached:

'Here she comes! Here she is. Now then, who's going to speak? Go on, George, you'd better talk. You're the one as always talks.'

'Well, you're not going to now. I'm going to talk,' said Clarence.

'You shut up, Clarrie. You know your voice is weak. It makes you cough if you talk.'

'Now look here, this is my show. I –'

'Good morning, all,' said Tuppence, breaking in. 'You've come to see me about something, have you? What is it?'

'Got something for you, we have,' said Clarence. 'Information. That's what you're after, isn't it?'

'It depends,' said Tuppence. 'What kind of information?'

'Oh, not information about nowadays. All long ago.'

'Historical information,' said one of the girls, who appeared to be the intellectual chief of the group. 'Most interesting if you're doing research into the past.'

'I see,' said Tuppence, concealing the fact that she did not see. 'What's this place here?'

'It's a gold-mine.'

'Oh,' said Tuppence. 'Any gold in it?'

She looked about her.

'Well, really, it's a goldfish pool,' explained one of the boys. 'Used to be goldfish in it once, you know. Special ones with lots of tails, from Japan or somewhere. Oh, wonderful it used to be. That was in old Mrs Forrester's time. That's – oh, that's ten years ago.'

'Twenty-four years ago,' said one of the girls.

'Sixty years ago,' said a very small voice, 'every bit of sixty years ago. Lots of goldfish there were. Ever so many. Said to be valuable, they was. They used to die sometimes. Sometimes they ate each other, sometimes they were just lying on top, floating about, you know.'

'Well,' said Tuppence, 'what do you want to tell me about them? There are no goldfish to see here now.'

'No. It's information,' said the intellectual girl.

A large outbreak of voices occurred. Tuppence waved her hand.

'Not all at once,' she said. 'One or two speak at a time. What's all this about?'

'Something perhaps you ought to know about where things was hidden once. Hidden once and said to be very important.'

'And how do you know about them?' said Tuppence.

This provoked a chorus of replies. It was not very easy to hear everyone at once.

'It was Janie.'

'It was Janie's Uncle Ben,' said one voice.

'No, it wasn't. It was Harry, it was . . . Yes, it was Harry. Harry's cousin Tom . . . Much younger than that. It was his grandmother told him and his grandmother had been told by Josh. Yes. I don't know who Josh was. I think Josh was her husband . . . No, he wasn't her husband, he was her uncle.'

'Oh dear,' said Tuppence.

She looked over the gesticulating crowd and picked out a choice.

'Clarence,' she said. 'You're Clarence, aren't you? Your friend told me about you. You, well what do you know and what's it all about?'

'Well, if you want to find out you've got to go to the PPC.'

'Go to the what?' said Tuppence.

'The PPC.'

'What's the PPC?'

'Don't you know? Hasn't anyone told you? PPC is the Pensioners' Palace Club.'

'Oh dear,' said Tuppence, 'that sounds very grand.'

'It isn't grand at all,' said one boy of about nine. 'It isn't grand a bit. It's only old age pensioners saying things and getting together. Pack of lies, some people say they tell about things they knew. You know, knew in the last war and knew after it. Oh, all sorts of things they say.'

'Where is this PPC?' asked Tuppence.

'Oh, it's along at the end of the village. Half-way to Morton Cross, it is. If you're a pensioner you get a ticket for it and you go there and you have bingo and you have all sorts of things there. It's quite fun, it is. Oh, some of them are very old. Some of them are deaf and blind and everything else. But they all – well, they like getting together, you know.'

'Well, I should like to pay a visit to it,' said Tuppence. 'Certainly. Is there any particular time one goes there?'

'Well, any time you like, I suppose, but the afternoon would be a good time, you know. Yes. That's when they can say they've got a friend coming – if they've got a friend coming they get extra things for tea, you know. Biscuits sometimes, with sugar on. And crisps sometimes. Things like that. What did you say, Fred?'

Fred took a step forward. He gave a somewhat pompous bow to Tuppence.

'I shall be very happy,' he said, 'to escort you. Shall we say about half past three this afternoon?'

'Ah, be yourself,' said Clarence. 'Don't go talking like that.'

'I shall be very pleased to come,' said Tuppence. She looked at the water. 'I can't help being rather sorry that there aren't any goldfish any more.'

'You ought to have seen the ones with five tails. Wonderful, they was. Somebody's dog fell in here once. Mrs Faggett's, it was.'

He was contradicted. 'No it wasn't. It was somebody else, her name was Follyo, not Fagot –'

'It was Foliatt and it was spelt with a plain f. Not a capital letter.'

'Ah, don't be silly. It was someone quite different. It was that Miss French, that was. Two small ffs she spelt it with.'

'Did the dog drown?' asked Tuppence.

'No, he didn't drown. He was only a puppy, you see, and his mother was upset and she went along and she pulled at Miss French's dress. Miss Isabel was in the orchard picking apples and the mother dog pulled at her dress and Miss Isabel she come along and she saw the puppy drowning and she jumped right into this here and pulled it out. Wet through, she was, and the dress she was wearing was never fit for wearing again.'

'Oh dear,' said Tuppence, 'what a lot of things seem to have gone on here. All right,' she said, 'I'll be ready this afternoon. Perhaps two or three of you would come for me and take me to this Pensioners' Palace Club.'

'What three? Who's going to come?'

Uproar happened immediately.

'I'm coming . . . No, I'm not . . . No, Betty is . . . No, Betty shan't come. Betty went the other day. I mean, she went to the cinema party the other day. She can't go again.'

'Well, settle it between you,' said Tuppence, 'and come here at half past three.'

'I hope you'll find it interesting,' said Clarence.

'It will be of historical interest,' said the intellectual girl firmly.

'Oh, shut up, Janet!' said Clarence. He turned to Tuppence. 'She's always like that,' he said, 'Janet is. She goes to grammar school, that's why. She boasts about it, see? A comprehensive wasn't good enough for her and her parents made a fuss and now she's at grammar school. That's why she goes on like this all the time.'

II

Tuppence wondered, as she finished her lunch, whether the events of the morning would produce any sequel. Would anybody really come to escort her this afternoon and take her to the PPC? Was there any such thing really as the PPC or was it a nickname of some kind that the children had invented? Anyway, it might be fun, Tuppence thought, to sit waiting in case someone came.

However, the deputation was punctual to the minute. At half past three the bell rang, Tuppence rose from her seat by the fire, clapped a hat upon her head – an indiarubber hat because she thought it *would* probably rain – and Albert appeared to escort her to the front door.'

'Not going to let you go with just anyone,' he breathed into her ear.

'Look here, Albert,' whispered Tuppence, 'is there really such a place as the PPC here?'

'I thought that had something to do with visiting cards,' said Albert, who was always prone to show his complete knowledge of social customs. 'You know, what you leave on people when you're going away or when you're arriving, I'm not sure which.'

'I think it's something to do with pensioners.'

'Oh yes, they've got a sort of a place. Yes. Built just two or three years ago, I think it was. You know, it's just down after you pass the rectory and then you turn right and you see it. It's rather an ugly building, but it's nice for the old folk and any who like can go meeting there. They have games and things, and there's a lot of ladies goes and helps with things. Gets up concerts and – sort of – well, rather like, you know, Women's Institute. Only it's specially for the elderly people. They're all very, very old, and most of them deaf.'

'Yes,' said Tuppence, 'yes. It sounded rather like that.'

The front door opened. Janet, by reason of her intellectual superiority, stood there first. Behind her was Clarence, and behind him was a tall boy with a squint who appeared to answer to the name of Bert.

'Good afternoon, Mrs Beresford,' said Janet. 'Everybody is so pleased that you are coming. I think perhaps you'd better take an umbrella, the weather forecast was not very good today.'

'I've got to go that way anyway,' said Albert, 'so I'll come with you a short part of it.'

Certainly, Tuppence thought, Albert was always very protective. Perhaps just as well, but she did not think that either Janet, Bert or Clarence was likely to be a danger to her. The walk took about twenty minutes. When the red building was reached they went through the gate, up to the door and were received by a stout woman of about seventy.

'Ah, so we've got visitors. I'm so pleased you could come, my dear, so pleased.' She patted Tuppence upon the shoulder. 'Yes, Janet, thank you very much. Yes. This way. Yes. None of you need wait unless you like, you know.'

'Oh I think the boys will be very disappointed if they didn't wait to hear a little about what all this is about,' said Janet.

'Well, I think, you know, there are not so very many of us here. Perhaps it would be better for Mrs Beresford, not so worrying if there weren't too many of us. I wonder, Janet, if you would just go into the kitchen and tell Mollie that we are quite ready for tea to be brought in now.'

Tuppence had not really come for tea, but she could hardly say so. Tea appeared rather rapidly. It was excessively weak, it was served with some biscuits and some sandwiches with a rather nasty type of paste in between them with an extra fishy taste. Then they sat around and seemed slightly at a loss.

An old man with a beard who looked to Tuppence as though he was about a hundred came and sat firmly by her.

'I'd best have a word with you first, I think, my lady,' he said, elevating Tuppence to the peerage. 'Seeing as I'm about the oldest here and have heard more of the stories of the old days than anyone else. A lot of history about this place, you know. Oh, a lot of things has happened here, not that we can go into everything at once, can we? But we've all – oh, we've all heard something about the things that went on.'

'I gather,' said Tuppence, hastily rushing in before she could be introduced to some topic in which she had no interest whatever, 'I understand that quite a lot of interesting things went on here, not so much in the last war, but in the war before that, or even earlier. Not that any of your memories would go back as far as that. But one wonders perhaps if you could have heard things, you know, from your elderly relations.'

'Ah, that's right,' said the old man, 'that's right. Heard a lot, I did, from my Uncle Len. Yes, ah, he was a great chap, was Uncle Len. He knew about a lot of things. He knew what went on. It was like what went on down in the house on the quay before the last war. Yes, a bad show, that. What you call one of those fakists –'

'Fascists,' said one of the elderly ladies, a rather prim one with grey hair and a lace fichu rather the worse for wear round her neck.

'Well, fascist if you like to say it that way, what does it matter? Ah yes, one of those he was. Yes. Same sort of thing as that chap in Italy. Mussolini or something, wasn't it? Anyway, some sort of fishy name like that. Mussels or cockles. Oh yes, he did a lot of harm here. Had meetings, you know. All sorts of things like that. Someone called Mosley started it all.'

'But in the first war there was a girl called Mary Jordan, wasn't there?' said Tuppence, wondering if this was a wise thing to say or not.

'Ah yes. Said to be quite a good-looker, you know. Yes. Got hold of secrets out of the sailors and the soldiers.'

A very old lady piped up in a thin voice.

'He's not in the Navy and he's not in the Army,
But he's just the man for me.
Not in the Navy, not in the Army, he's in the
Royal Ar-till-er-rie!'

The old man took up his personal chant when she had got thus far:

'It's a long way to Tipperary,
It's a long way to go,
It's a long way to Tipperary
And the rest of it I don't know.'

'Now that's enough, Benny, that's quite enough,' said

a firm-looking woman who seemed to be either his wife or his daughter.

Another old lady sang in a quavering voice:

'All the nice girls love a sailor,
All the nice girls love a tar,
All the nice girls love a sailor,
And you know what sailors are.'

'Oh, shut up, Maudie, we're tired of that one. Now let the lady hear something,' said Uncle Ben. 'Let the lady hear something. She's come to hear something. She wants to hear where that thing there was all the fuss about was hidden, don't you? And all about it.'

'That sounds very interesting,' said Tuppence, cheering up. 'Something *was* hidden?'

'Ah yes, long before my time it was but I heard all about it. Yes. Before 1914. Word was handed down, you know, from one to another. Nobody knew exactly what it was and why there was all this excitement.'

'Something to do with the boat race it had,' said an old lady. 'You know, Oxford and Cambridge. I was taken once. I was taken to see the boat race in London under the bridges and everything. Oh, it was a wonderful day. Oxford won by a length.'

'A lot of nonsense you're all talking,' said a grim-looking woman with iron-grey hair. 'You don't know anything about it, you don't. I know more than most of you although it happened a long time before I was born. It was my Great-Aunt Mathilda who told *me* and she were told by her Aunty Lou. And that was a good forty years before them. Great talk about it, it was, and people went around looking for it. Some people thought as it was a gold-mine, you know. Yes, a gold ingot brought back from Australia. Somewhere like that.'

'Damn silly,' said an old man, who was smoking a pipe with an air of general dislike of his fellow members. 'Mixed it up with goldfish, they did. Was as ignorant as that.'

'It was worth a lot of money, whatever it was, or it wouldn't have been hidden,' said someone else. 'Yes, lots of people come down from the government, and yes, police too. They looked around but they couldn't find anything.'

'Ah well, they didn't have the right clues. There are clues, you know, if you know where to look for them.' Another old lady nodded her head wisely. 'There's always clues.'

'How interesting,' said Tuppence. 'Where? Where are these clues, I mean? In the village or somewhere outside it or –'

This was a rather unfortunate remark as it brought down at least six different replies, all uttered at once.

'On the moor, beyond Tower West,' one was saying.

'Oh no, it's past Little Kenny, it was. Yes, quite near Little Kenny.'

'No, it was the cave. The cave by the sea front. Over as far as Baldy's Head. You know, where the red rocks are. That's it. There's an old smugglers' tunnel. Wonderful, it must be. Some people say as it's there still.'

'I saw a story once of an old Spanish main or something. Right back to the time of the Armada, it was. A Spanish boat as went down there. Full of doubloons.'

Chapter 10

Attack on Tuppence

'Good gracious!' said Tommy, as he returned that evening. 'You look terribly tired, Tuppence. What have you been doing? You look worn out.'

'I am worn out,' said Tuppence. 'I don't know that I shall ever recover again. Oh dear.'

'What *have* you been doing? Not climbing up and finding more books or anything?'

'No, no,' said Tuppence, 'I don't want to look at books again. I'm off books.'

'Well, what is it? What have you been doing?'

'Do you know what a PPC is?'

'No,' said Tommy, 'at least, well, yes. It's something –' He paused.

'Yes, Albert knows,' said Tuppence, 'but it's not that kind of one. Now then, I'll just tell you in a minute, but you'd better have something first. A cocktail or a whisky or something. And I'll have something too.'

She more or less put Tommy wise to the events of the afternoon. Tommy said 'good gracious' again and added: 'The things you get yourself into, Tuppence. Was any of it interesting?'

'I don't know,' said Tuppence. 'When six people are talking at once, and most of them can't talk properly and they all say different things – you see, you don't really know what they're saying. But yes, I think I've got a few ideas for dealing with things.'

'What do you mean?'

'Well, there is a lot of legend, I think, going on about something that was once hidden here and was a secret connected with the 1914 war, or even before it.'

'Well, we know that already, don't we?' said Tommy. 'I mean, we've been briefed to know that.'

'Yes. Well, there are a few old tales still going around the village here. And everybody has got ideas about it put into their heads by their Aunt Marias or their Uncle Bens and it's been put into their Aunt Marias by their Uncle Stephens or Aunty Ruth or Grandmother Something else. It's been handed down for years and years. Well, one of the things might be the right one, of course.'

'What, lost among all the others?'

'Yes,' said Tuppence, 'like a needle in the haystack?

'I'm going to select a few what I call likely possibilities. People who might tell one something that they really *did* hear. I shall have to isolate them from everybody else, at any rate for a short period of time, and get them to tell me exactly what their Aunt Agatha or Aunt Betty or old Uncle James told them. Then I shall have to go on to the next one and possibly one of them might give me a further inkling. There must be something, you know, somewhere.'

'Yes,' said Tommy, 'I think there's something, but we don't know what it is.'

'Well, that's what we're trying to do, isn't it?'

'Yes, but I mean you've got to have some idea what a thing actually *is* before you go looking for it.'

'I don't think it's gold ingots on a Spanish Armada ship,' said Tuppence, 'and I don't think it's anything hidden in the smugglers' cave.'

'Might be some super brandy from France,' said Tommy hopefully.

'It might,' said Tuppence, 'but that wouldn't be really what we're looking for, would it?'

'I don't know,' said Tommy. 'I think it might be what I'm looking for sooner or later. Anyway, it's something I should enjoy finding. Of course it might be a sort of letter or something. A sexy letter that you could blackmail someone about, about sixty years ago. But I don't think it would cut much ice nowadays, do you?'

'No, I don't. But we've got to get some idea sooner or later. Do you think we'll *ever* get anywhere, Tommy?'

'I don't know,' said Tommy. '*I* got a little bit of help today.'

'Oh. What about?'

'Oh, about the census.'

'The what?'

'The census. There seems to have been a census in one particular year – I've got the year written down – and there were a good many people staying in this house with the Parkinsons.'

'How on earth did you find all that out?'

'Oh, by various methods of research by my Miss Collodon.'

'I'm getting jealous of Miss Collodon.'

'Well, you needn't be. She's very fierce and she ticks me off a good deal, and she is no ravishing beauty.'

'Well, that's just as well,' said Tuppence. 'But what has the census got to do with it?'

'Well, when Alexander said *it must be one of us* it could have meant, you see, someone who was in the house at that time and therefore you had to enter up their names on the census register. Anyone who spent the night under your roof, and I think probably there are records of these things in the census files. And if you know the right people – I don't mean I know them now, but I can get to know them through people I do know – then I think I could perhaps get a short list.'

'Well, I admit,' said Tuppence, 'you have ideas all

right. For goodness' sake let's have something to eat and perhaps I shall feel better and not so faint from trying to listen to sixteen very ugly voices all at once.'

II

Albert produced a very passable meal. His cooking was erratic. It had its moments of brilliance which tonight was exemplified by what he called cheese pudding, and Tuppence and Tommy preferred to call cheese soufflé. Albert reproved them slightly for the wrong nomenclature.

'Cheese soufflé is different,' he said, 'got more beaten up white of egg in it than this has.'

'Never mind,' said Tuppence, 'it's very good whether it's cheese pudding or cheese soufflé.'

Both Tommy and Tuppence were entirely absorbed with the eating of food and did not compare any more notes as to their procedure. When, however, they had both drunk two cups of strong coffee, Tuppence leaned back in her chair, uttered a deep sigh and said:

'Now I feel almost myself again. You didn't do much washing before dinner, did you, Tommy?'

'I couldn't be bothered to wait and wash,' said Tommy. 'Besides, I never know with you. You might have made me go upstairs to the book-room and stand on a dusty ladder and poke about on the shelves.'

'I wouldn't be so unkind,' said Tuppence. 'Now wait a minute. Let's see where we are.'

'Where we are or where you are?'

'Well, where I am, really,' said Tuppence. 'After all, that's the only thing I know about, isn't it? You know where you are and I know where I am. Perhaps, that is.'

'May be a bit of perhaps about it,' said Tommy.

'Pass me over my bag, will you, unless I've left it in the dining-room?'

'You usually do but you haven't this time. It's under the foot of your chair. No – the other side.'

Tuppence picked up her handbag.

'Very nice present, this was,' she said. 'Real crocodile, I think. Bit difficult to stuff things in sometimes.'

'And apparently to take them out again,' said Tommy.

Tuppence was wrestling.

'Expensive bags are always very difficult for getting things out of,' she said breathlessly. 'Those basket-work ones are the most comfortable. They bulge to any extent and you can stir them up like you stir up a pudding. Ah! I think I've got it.'

'What is it? It looks like a washing bill.'

'Oh, it's a little notebook. Yes, I used to write washing things in it, you know, what I had to complain about – torn pillowcase or something like that. But I thought it would come in useful, you see, because only three or four pages of it had been used. I put down here, you see, things we've heard. A great many of them don't seem to have any point but there it is. I added census, by the way, when you first mentioned it. I didn't know what it meant at that time or what you meant by it. But anyway I did add it.'

'Fine,' said Tommy.

'And I put down Mrs Henderson and someone called Dodo.'

'Who was Mrs Henderson?'

'Well, I don't suppose you'll remember and I needn't go back to it now but those were two of the names I put down that Mrs What's-her-name, you know, the old one, Mrs Griffin mentioned. And then there was a message or a notice. Something about Oxford and Cambridge. And I've come across another thing in one of the old books.'

'What about – Oxford and Cambridge? Do you mean an undergraduate?'

'I'm not sure whether there was an undergraduate or not, I think really it was a bet on the boat race.'

'Much more likely,' said Tommy. 'Not awfully apt to be useful to us.'

'Well, one never knows. So there's Mrs Henderson and there's somebody who lives in a house called Apple

Tree Lodge and there's something I found on a dirty bit of paper shoved into one of the books upstairs. I don't know if it was *Catriona* or whether it was in a book called *Shadow of the Throne*.'

'That's about the French Revolution. I read it when I was a boy,' said Tommy.

'Well, I don't see how that comes in. At any rate, I put it down.'

'Well, what is it?'

'It seems to be three pencil words. Grin, g-r-i-n, then hen, h-e-n and then Lo, capital L-o.'

'Let me guess,' said Tommy. 'Cheshire cat – that's a grin – Henny-Penny, that's another fairy story, isn't it, for the hen, and Lo –'

'Ah,' said Tuppence, 'Lo does you in, does it?'

'Lo and behold,' said Tommy, 'but it doesn't seem to make sense.'

Tuppence spoke rapidly. 'Mrs Henley, Apple Tree Lodge – I haven't done her yet, she's in Meadowside.' Tuppence recited quickly: 'Now, where are we? Mrs Griffin, Oxford and Cambridge, bet on a boat race, census, Cheshire cat, Henny-Penny, the story where the Hen went to the Dovrefell – Hans Andersen or something like that – and Lo. I suppose Lo means when they got there. Got to the Dovrefell, I mean.

'I don't think there's much else,' said Tuppence. 'There's the Oxford and Cambridge boat race or the bet.'

'I should think the odds are on our being rather silly. But I think if we go on being silly long enough, some gem of great price might come out of it, concealed among the rubbish, as you might say. Just as we found one significant book on the bookshelves upstairs.'

'Oxford and Cambridge,' said Tuppence thoughtfully. 'That makes me think of something. It makes me remember something. Now what could it be?'

'Mathilde?'

'No, it wasn't Mathilde, but –'

'Truelove,' suggested Tommy. He grinned from ear to ear. 'True love. Where can I my true love find?'

'Stop grinning, you ape,' said Tuppence. 'You've got that last thing on your brain. Grin-hen-lo. Doesn't make sense. And yet – I have a kind of feeling – Oh!'

'What's the Oh about?'

'Oh! Tommy, I've got an idea. Of course.'

'What's of course?'

'Lo,' said Tuppence. 'Lo. Grin is what made me think of it. You grinning like a Cheshire cat. Grin. Hen and then Lo. Of course. That must be it somehow.'

'What on earth are you talking about?'

'Oxford and Cambridge boat race.'

'Why does grin hen Lo make you think of Oxford and Cambridge boat race?'

'I'll give you three guesses,' said Tuppence.

'Well, I give up at once because I don't think it could possibly make sense.'

'It does really.'

'What, the boat race?'

'No, nothing to do with the boat race. The colour. Colours, I mean.'

'What *do* you mean, Tuppence?'

'Grin hen Lo. We've been reading it the wrong way round. It's meant to be read the other way round.'

'What do you mean? Ol, then n-e-h – it doesn't make sense. You couldn't go on n-i-r-g. Nirg or some word like that.'

'No. Just take the three words. A little bit, you know, like what Alexander did in the book – the first book that we looked at. Read those three words the other way round. Lo-hen-grin.'

Tommy scowled.

'Still haven't got it?' said Tuppence. 'Lohengrin, of course. The swan. The opera. You know, Lohengrin, Wagner.'

'Well, there's nothing to do with a swan.'

'Yes, there is. Those two pieces of china we found. Stools for the garden. You remember? One was a dark blue and one was a light blue, and old Isaac said to us, at least I think it was Isaac, he said, "That's Oxford, you see, and that's Cambridge."'

'Well, we smashed the Oxford one, didn't we?'

'Yes. But the Cambridge one is still there. The light blue one. Don't you see? Lohengrin. Something was hidden in one of those two swans. Tommy, the next thing we have to do is to go and look at the Cambridge one. The light blue one, it's still in KK. Shall we go now?'

'What – at eleven o'clock at night – no.'

'We'll go tomorrow. You haven't got to go to London tomorrow?'

'No.'

'Well, we'll go tomorrow and we'll see.'

III

'I don't know what you're doing about the garden,' said Albert. 'I did a spell once in a garden for a short time, but I'm not up in vegetables very much. There's a boy here that wants to see you, by the way, madam.'

'Oh, a boy,' said Tuppence. 'Do you mean the red-haired one?'

'No. I mean the other one, the one with a lot of messy yellow hair half down his back. Got rather a silly name.

Like a hotel. You know, the Royal Clarence. That's his name. Clarence.'

'Clarence, but not Royal Clarence.'

'Not likely,' said Albert. 'He's waiting in the front door. He says, madam, as he might be able to assist you in some way.'

'I see. I gather he used to assist old Isaac occasionally.'

She found Clarence sitting on a decayed basket chair on the veranda or loggia, whichever you liked to call it. He appeared to be making a late breakfast off potato crisps and held a bar of chocolate in his left hand.

'Morning, missus,' said Clarence. 'Come to see if I could be any help.'

'Well,' said Tuppence, 'of course we do want help in the garden. I believe you used to help Isaac at one time.'

'Ah well, now and again I did. Not that I know very much. Don't say that Isaac knew much neither. Lot of talk with him, lot of talking saying what a wonderful time he used to have. What a wonderful time it was for the people who employed him. Yes, he used to say he was the head gardener to Mr Bolingo. You know, as lives farther along the river. Great big house. Yes, it's turned into a school now. Head gardener there, he said he used to be. But my grandmother says there isn't a word of truth in that.'

'Well, never mind,' said Tuppence. 'Actually, I wanted to turn a few more things out of that little greenhouse place.'

'What d'you mean the shed, the glass shed? KK, isn't it?'

'Quite right,' said Tuppence. 'Fancy your knowing the proper name of it.'

'Oh well, it was always used to be called that. Everybody says so. They say it's Japanese. I don't know if that's true.'

'Come on,' said Tuppence. 'Let's go there.'

A procession formed consisting of Tommy, Tuppence, Hannibal, the dog, with Albert abandoning the washing up of breakfast for something more interesting bringing up the rear. Hannibal displayed a great deal of pleasure after attending to all the useful smells in the neighbourhood. He rejoined them at the door of KK and sniffed in an interested manner.

'Hullo, Hannibal,' said Tuppence, 'are you going to help us? You tell us something.'

'What kind of a dog is he?' asked Clarence. 'Somebody said as he is the kind of dog they used to keep for rats. Is that so?'

'Yes, that's quite true,' said Tommy. 'He's a Manchester Terrier, an old English Black and Tan.'

Hannibal, knowing he was being talked about, turned his head, waggled his body, beat his tail with a good deal of exuberance. He then sat down and looked proud of himself.

'He bites, doesn't he?' said Clarence. 'Everyone says so.'

'He's a very good guard dog,' said Tuppence. 'He looks after me.'

'That's quite right. When I'm away he looks after you,' said Tommy.

'The postman said he nearly got bitten four days age.'

'Dogs are rather like that with postmen,' said Tuppence. 'Do you know where the key of KK is?'

'I do,' said Clarence. 'Hanging up in the shed. You know, the shed where the flower-pots are.'

He went off and returned shortly with the once rusty but now more or less oiled key.

'Been oiling this key, Isaac must have,' he said.

'Yes, it wouldn't turn very easily before,' said Tuppence.

The door was opened.

The Cambridge china stool with the swan wreathed round it was looking rather handsome. Obviously Isaac had polished it up and washed it, with the idea of transferring it to the veranda when the weather was suitable for sitting out.

'Ought to be a dark blue one too,' said Clarence. 'Isaac used to say Oxford and Cambridge.'

'Is that true?'

'Yes. Dark blue Oxford and pale blue Cambridge. Oh, and Oxford was the one that smashed, was it?'

'Yes. Rather like the boat race, isn't it?'

'By the way, something's happened to that rocking-horse, hasn't it? There's a lot of mess about in KK.'

'Yes.'

'Funny name like Matilda, hasn't she?'

'Yes. She had to have an operation,' said Tuppence.

Clarence seemed to think this very amusing. He laughed heartily.

'My Great-Aunt Edith had to have an operation,' he said. 'Took out part of her inside but she got well.'

He sounded slightly disappointed.

'I suppose there's no real way of getting inside these things,' said Tuppence.

'Well, I suppose you can smash them like the dark blue one was smashed.'

'Yes. There's no other way, is there? Funny those sort of S-kind of slits around the top. Why, you could post things in there, couldn't you, like a post box.'

'Yes,' said Tommy, 'one could. It's an interesting idea. Very interesting, Clarence,' he said kindly.

Clarence looked pleased.

'You can unscrew 'em, you know,' he said.

'Unscrew them, can you?' said Tuppence. 'Who told you that?'

'Isaac. I've seen 'im do it often. You turn them upside down and then you begin to swing the top round. It's stiff sometimes. You pour a little oil round all the cracks and when it's soaked in a bit you can turn it round.'

'Oh.'

'The easiest way is to put it upside down.'

'Everything here always seems to have to be turned upside down,' said Tuppence. 'We had to do that to Mathilde before we could operate.'

For the moment Cambridge seemed to be entirely obstreperous, when quite suddenly the china began to revolve and very shortly afterwards they managed to unscrew it completely and lift it off.

'Lot of rubbish in here, I should think,' said Clarence.

Hannibal came to assist. He was a dog who liked helping in anything that was going on. Nothing, he thought, was complete unless he took a hand or a paw in it. But with him it was usually a nose in the investigation. He stuck his nose down, growled gently, retired an inch or two and sat down.

'Doesn't like it much, does he?' said Tuppence, and looked down into the somewhat unpleasant mass inside.

'Ow!' said Clarence.

'What's the matter?'

'Scratched myself. There's something hanging down

from a nail on the side here. I don't know if it's a nail or what it is. It's something. Ow!'

'Wuff, wuff!' said Hannibal, joining in.

'There's something hung on a nail just inside. Yes, I've got it. No, it's slipping. Yes, here I am. I've got it.'

Clarence lifted out a dark tarpaulin package.

Hannibal came and sat at Tuppence's feet. He growled.

'What's the matter, Hannibal?' said Tuppence.

Hannibal growled again. Tuppence bent down and smoothed the top of his head and ears.

'What's the matter, Hannibal?' said Tuppence. 'Did you want Oxford to win and now Cambridge have won, you see. Do you remember,' said Tuppence to Tommy, 'how we let him watch the boat race once on television?'

'Yes,' said Tommy, 'he got very angry towards the end and started barking so that we couldn't hear anything at all.'

'Well, we could still see things,' said Tuppence, 'that was something. But if you remember, he didn't like Cambridge winning.'

'Obviously,' said Tommy, 'he studied at the Oxford Dogs' University.'

Hannibal left Tuppence and came to Tommy and wagged his tail appreciatively.

'He likes your saying that,' said Tuppence, 'it must be true. I myself,' she added, 'think he has been educated at the Dogs' Open University.'

'What were his principal studies there?' asked Tommy, laughing.

'Bone disposal.'

'You know what he's like.'

'Yes, I know,' said Tuppence. 'Very unwisely, you know, Albert gave him the whole bone of a leg of mutton once. First of all I found him in the drawing-room putting it under a cushion, then I forced him out through the garden door and shut it. And I looked out of the window and he went into the flower-bed where I'd got gladioli, and buried it very carefully there. He's very tidy with his bones, you know. He never tries to eat them. He always puts them away for a rainy day.'

'Does he ever dig them up again?' asked Clarence, assisting on this point of dog lore.

'I think so,' said Tuppence. 'Sometimes when they're very, very old and would have been better if they had been left buried.'

'Our dog doesn't like dog biscuits,' said Clarence.

'He leaves them on the plate, I suppose,' said Tuppence, 'and eats the meat first.'

'He likes sponge cake, though, our dog does,' said Clarence.'

Hannibal sniffed at the trophy just disinterred from the inside of Cambridge. He wheeled round suddenly then and barked.

'See if there's anyone outside,' said Tuppence. 'It might be a gardener. Somebody told me the other day, Mrs Herring, I think it was, that she knew of an elderly man who'd been a very good gardener in his time and who did jobbing.'

Tommy opened the door and went outside. Hannibal accompanied him.

'Nobody here,' said Tommy.

Hannibal barked. First he growled again, then he barked and barked more loudly.

'He thinks there's someone or something in that great clump of pampas grass,' said Tommy. 'Perhaps someone is un-burying one of his bones there. Perhaps there's a rabbit there. Hannibal's very stupid about rabbits. He needs an awful lot of encouragement before he'll chase a rabbit. He seems to have a kindly feeling about them. He goes after pigeons and large birds. Fortunately he never catches them.'

Hannibal was now sniffing round the pampas grass, first growling, after which he began to bark loudly. At intervals he turned his head towards Tommy.

'I expect there's a cat in there,' said Tommy. 'You know what he's like when he thinks a cat is around. There's the big black cat that comes round here and the little one. The one that we call the Kitty-cat.'

'That's the one that's always getting into the house,' said Tuppence. 'It seems to get through the smallest chinks. Oh, do stop, Hannibal. Come back.'

Hannibal heard and turned his head. He was expressing a very high degree of fierceness. He gave Tuppence a look, went back a little way, then turned his attention once more to the clump of pampas grass and began barking furiously.

'There's something worries him,' said Tommy. 'Come on, Hannibal.'

Hannibal shook himself, shook his head, looked at Tommy, looked at Tuppence and made a prancing attack on the pampas grass, barking loudly.

There was a sudden sound. Two sharp explosions.

'Good Lord, somebody must be shooting rabbits,' exclaimed Tuppence.

'Get back. Get back inside KK, Tuppence,' said Tommy.

Something flew past his ear. Hannibal, now fully alerted, was racing round and round the pampas grass. Tommy ran after him.

'He's chasing someone now,' he said. 'He's chasing someone down the hill. He's running like mad.'

'Who was it – what was it?' said Tuppence.

'You all right, Tuppence?'

'No, I'm not quite all right,' said Tuppence.

'Something – something, I think, hit me here, just below the shoulder. Was it – what was it?'

'It was someone shooting at us. Someone who was hidden inside that pampas grass.'

'Someone who was watching what we were doing,' said Tuppence. 'Do you think that's it, perhaps?'

'I expect it's them Irish,' said Clarence hopefully. 'The IRA. You know. They've been trying to blow this place up.'

'I don't think it's of any political significance,' said Tuppence.

'Come into the house,' said Tommy. 'Come quickly. Come on, Clarence, you'd better come too.'

'You don't think your dog will bite me?' said Clarence uncertainly.

'No,' said Tommy. 'I think he is busy for the moment.'

They had just turned the corner into the garden door when Hannibal reappeared suddenly. He came racing up the hill very out of breath. He spoke to Tommy in the way a dog does speak. He came up to him, shook himself, put a paw on Tommy's trouser leg and tried to pull him in the direction from which he had just come.

'He wants me to go with him after whoever the man was,' said Tommy.

'Well, you're not to,' said Tuppence. 'If there's anyone there with a rifle or a pistol or something that shoots, I'm not going to have you shot. Not at your age. Who would look after me if anything happened to you? Come on, let's get indoors.'

They went into the house quickly. Tommy went out into the hall and spoke on the telephone.

'What are you doing?' said Tuppence.

'Telephoning the police,' said Tommy. 'Can't let anything like this pass. They may get on to someone if we're in time.'

'I think,' said Tuppence, 'that I want something put on my shoulder. This blood is ruining my best jumper.'

'Never mind your jumper,' said Tommy.

Albert appeared at that moment with a complete service of first aid.

'Well I never,' said Albert. 'You mean some dirty guy has shot at the missus? Whatever's happening next in this country?'

'You don't think you ought to go to the hospital, do you?'

'No, I don't,' said Tuppence. 'I'm quite all right but I want an outsize Band-Aid or something to stick on here. Put on something like friar's balsam first.'

'I've got some iodine.'

'I don't want iodine. It stings. Besides, they say now in hospitals that it isn't the right thing to put on.'

'I thought friar's balsam was something you breathed in out of an inhaler,' said Albert hopefully.

'That's one use,' said Tuppence, 'but it's very good to put on slight scratches or scars or if children cut themselves or anything like that. Have you got the thing all right?'

'What thing, what do you mean, Tuppence?'

'The thing we just got out of the Cambridge Lohengrin. That's what I mean. The thing that was hanging on a nail. Perhaps it's something important, you know. They saw us. And so if they tried to kill us – and tried to get whatever it was – that really would be something!'

Chapter 11

Hannibal Takes Action

Tommy sat with the police inspector in his office. The police officer, Inspector Norris, was nodding his head gently.

'I hope with any luck we may get results, Mr Beresford,' he said. 'Dr Crossfield, you say, is attending to your wife.'

'Yes,' said Tommy, 'it isn't serious, I gather. It was just grazing by a bullet and it bled a good deal, but she's going to be all right, I think. There's nothing really dangerous, Dr Crossfield said.'

'She's not very young, though, I suppose,' said Inspector Norris.

'She's over seventy,' said Tommy. 'We're both of us getting on, you know.'

'Yes, yes. Quite so,' said Inspector Norris. 'I've heard a good deal about her locally, you know, since you came here to live. People have taken to her in a big way. We've heard about her various activities. And about yours.'

'Oh, dear,' said Tommy.

'Can't live down your record, you know, whatever it is. Good or bad,' said Inspector Norris in a kindly voice. 'You can't live down a record if you're a criminal and you can't live down your record if you've been a hero either. Of one thing I can assure you. We'll do all we can to clear things up. You can't describe whoever it was, I suppose?'

'No,' said Tommy. 'When I saw him he was running with our dog after him. I should say he was not very old. He ran easily, I mean.'

'Difficult age round about fourteen, fifteen onwards.'

'It was someone older than that,' said Tommy.

'Not had any telephone calls or letters, demands for money or anything like that?' said the Inspector. 'Asking you to get out of your house, maybe?'

'No,' said Tommy, 'nothing like that.'

'And you've been here – how long?'

Tommy told him.

'Hmmm. Not very long. You go to London, I gather, most days of the week.'

'Yes,' said Tommy. 'If you want particulars –'

'No,' said Inspector Norris, 'no. No, I don't need any particulars. The only thing I should suggest is that – well, you don't go away too often. If you can manage to stay at home and look after Mrs Beresford yourself . . .'

'I thought of doing that anyway,' said Tommy. 'I think this is a good excuse for my not turning up always at the various appointments I've got in London.'

'Well, we'll do all we can to keep an eye on things, and if we could get hold of this whoever it is . . .'

'Do you feel – perhaps I oughtn't to ask this –' said Tommy – 'do you feel you know who it is? Do you know his name or his reasons?'

'Well, we know a good many things about some of the chaps around here. More than they think we know very often. Sometimes we don't make it apparent how much we do know because that's the best way to get at them in the end. You find out then who they're mixed up with, who's paying them for some of the things they do, or whether they thought of it themselves out of their own heads. But I think – well, I think somehow that this isn't one of our locals, as you might say.'

'Why do you think that?' asked Tommy.

'Ah. Well, one hears things, you know. One gets information from various headquarters elsewhere.'

Tommy and the Inspector looked at each other. For about five minutes neither of them spoke. They were just looking.

'Well,' said Tommy, 'I – I see. Yes. Perhaps I see.'

'If I may say one thing,' said Inspector Norris.

'Yes?' said Tommy, looking rather doubtful.

'This garden of yours. You want a bit of help in it, I understand.'

'Our gardener was killed, as you probably know.'

'Yes, I know all about that. Old Isaac Bodlicott, wasn't it? Fine old chap. Told tall stories now and then about the wonderful things he'd done in his time. But he was a well-known character and a fellow you could trust, too.'

'I can't imagine why he was killed or who killed him,' said Tommy. 'Nobody seems to have had any idea or to have found out.'

'You mean *we* haven't found out. Well, these things take a little time, you know. It doesn't come out at the time the inquest's on, and the Coroner sums up and says "Murder by some person unknown." That's only the beginning sometimes. Well, what I was going to say was it's likely someone may come and ask you whether you'd like a chap to come and do a bit of jobbing gardening for you. He'll come along and say that he could come two or three days a week. Perhaps more. He'll tell you, for reference, that he worked for some years for Mr Solomon. You'll remember that name, will you?'

'Mr Solomon,' said Tommy.

There seemed to be something like a twinkle for a moment in Inspector Norris's eye.

'Yes, he's dead, of course. Mr Solomon, I mean. But he *did* live here and he *did* employ several different jobbing gardeners. I'm not quite sure what name this chap will give you. We'll say I don't quite remember it. It might be one of several – it's likely to be Crispin, I think. Between thirty and fifty or so, and he worked for Mr Solomon. If anyone comes along and says he can do some jobbing gardening for you and *doesn't* mention Mr Solomon, in that case, I wouldn't accept him. That's just a word of warning.'

'I see,' said Tommy. 'Yes, I see. At least, I hope I see the point.'

'That's the point,' said Inspector Norris. 'You're quick on the uptake, Mr Beresford. Well, I suppose you've had to be quite often in your activities. Nothing more you want to know that we could tell you?'

'I don't think so,' said Tommy. 'I wouldn't know what to ask.'

'We shall be making enquiries, not necessarily round here, you know. I may be in London or other parts looking round. We all help to look round. Well, you'd know that, wouldn't you?'

'I want to try and keep Tuppence – keep my wife from getting herself too mixed up in things because – but it's difficult.'

'Women are always difficult,' said Inspector Norris.

Tommy repeated that remark later as he sat by

Tuppence's bedside and watched her eating grapes.

'Do you really eat all the pips of grapes?'

'Usually,' said Tuppence. 'It takes so much time getting them out, doesn't it? I don't think they hurt you.'

'Well, if they haven't hurt you by now, and you've been doing it all your life, I shouldn't think they would,' said Tommy.

'What did the police say?'

'Exactly what we thought they would say.'

'Do they know who it's likely to have been?'

'They say they don't think it's local.'

'Who did you see? Inspector Watson his name is, isn't it?'

'No. This was an Inspector Norris.'

'Oh, that's one I don't know. What else did he say?'

'He said women were always very difficult to restrain.'

'Really!' said Tuppence. 'Did he know you were coming back to tell me that?'

'Possibly not,' said Tommy. He got up. 'I must put in a telephone call or two to London. I'm not going up for a day or two.'

'You can go up all right. I'm quite safe here! There's Albert looking after me and all the rest of it. Dr Crossfield has been terribly kind and rather like a sort of broody hen watching over me.'

'I'll have to go out to get things for Albert. Anything you want?'

'Yes,' said Tuppence, 'you might bring me back a melon. I'm feeling very inclined to fruit. Nothing but fruit.'

'All right,' said Tommy.

II

Tommy rang up a London number.

'Colonel Pikeaway?'

'Yes. Hullo. Ah, it's you, Thomas Beresford, is it?'

'Ah, you recognized my voice. I wanted to tell you that –'

'Something about Tuppence. I've heard it all,' said Colonel Pikeaway. 'No need to talk. Stay where you are for the next day or two or a week. Don't come up to London. Report anything that happens.'

'There may be some things which we ought to bring to you.'

'Well, hang on to them for the moment. Tell Tuppence to invent a place to hide them until then.'

'She's good at that sort of thing. Like our dog. He hides bones in the garden.'

'I hear he chased the man who shot at you both, and saw him off the place –'

'You seem to know all about it.'

'We always know things here,' said Colonel Pikeaway.

'Our dog managed to get a snap at him and came back with a sample of his trousers in his mouth.'

Chapter 12

Oxford, Cambridge and Lohengrin

'Good man,' said Colonel Pikeaway, puffing out smoke. 'Sorry to send for you so urgently but I thought I'd better see you.'

'As I expect you know,' said Tommy, 'we've been having something a little unexpected lately.'

'Ah! Why should you think I know?'

'Because you always know everything here.'

Colonel Pikeaway laughed.

'Hah! Quoting me to myself, aren't you? Yes, that's what I say. We know everything. That's what we're here for. Did she have a very narrow escape? Your wife, I'm talking about, as you know.'

'She didn't have a narrow escape, but there might have been something serious. I expect you know most of the details, or do you want me to tell you?'

'You can run over it quickly if you like. There's a bit I didn't hear,' said Colonel Pikeaway, 'the bit about

Lohengrin. Grin-hen-lo. She's sharp, you know, your wife is. She saw the point of that. It seems idiotic, but there it was.'

'I've brought you the results today,' said Tommy. 'We hid them in the flour-bin until I could get up to see you. I didn't like to send them by post.'

'No. Quite right –'

'In a kind of tin – not tin but a better metal than that – box and hanging in Lohengrin. Pale blue Lohengrin. Cambridge, Victorian china outdoor garden stool.'

'Remember them myself in the old days. Had an aunt in the country who used to have a pair.'

'It was very well preserved, sewn up in tarpaulin. Inside it are letters. They are somewhat perished and that, but I expect with expert treatment –'

'Yes, we can manage that sort of thing all right.'

'Here they are then,' said Tommy, 'and I've got a list for you of things that we've noted down, Tuppence and I. Things that have been mentioned or told us.'

'Names?'

'Yes. Three or four. The Oxford and Cambridge clue and the mention of Oxford and Cambridge graduates staying there – I don't think there was anything in that, because really it referred simply to the Lohengrin porcelain stools, I suppose.'

'Yes – yes – yes, there are one or two other things here that are quite interesting.'

'After we were fired at,' said Tommy, 'I reported it at once to the police.'

'Quite right.'

'Then I was asked to go down to the police station the next day and I saw Inspector Norris there. I haven't come in contact with him before. I think he must be rather a new officer.'

'Yes. Probably on a special assignment,' said Colonel Pikeaway. He puffed out more smoke.

Tommy coughed.

'I expect you know all about him.'

'I know about him,' said Colonel Pikeaway. 'We know everything here. He's all right. He's in charge of this enquiry. Local people will perhaps be able to spot who it was who's been following you about, finding out things about you. You don't think, do you, Beresford, that it would be well if you left the place for a while and brought your wife along?'

'I don't think I could do that,' said Tommy.

'You mean she wouldn't come?' said Colonel Pikeaway.

'Again,' said Tommy, 'if I may mention it, you seem to know everything. I don't think you could draw Tuppence away. Mind you, she's not badly hurt, she's not ill and she's got a feeling now that – well, that we're on to something. We don't know what it is and we don't know what we shall find or do.'

'Nose around,' said Colonel Pikeaway, 'that's all you

can do in a case of this kind.' He tapped a nail on the metal box. 'This little box is going to tell us something, though, and it's going to tell us something we've always wanted to know. Who was involved a great many years ago in setting things going and doing a lot of dirty work behind the scenes.'

'But surely –'

'I know what you're going to say. You're going to say whoever it was is now dead. That's true. But it tells us nevertheless what was going on, how it was set in motion, who helped, who inspired it and who has inherited or carried on with something of the same business ever since. People who don't seem to amount to much but possibly they amount to more than we've ever thought. And people who've been in touch with the same group, as one calls it – one calls anything a group nowadays – the same group which may have different people in it now but who have the same ideas, the same love of violence and evil and the same people to communicate with elsewhere and other groups. Some groups are all right but some groups are worse because they are groups. It's a kind of technique, you know. We've taught it to ourselves in the last, oh, say fifty to a hundred years. Taught that if people cohere together and make a tight little mob of themselves, it's amazing what they are able to accomplish and what they are able to inspire other people to accomplish for them.'

'May I ask you something?'

'Anyone can always ask,' said Colonel Pikeaway. 'We know everything here but we don't always tell, I have to warn you of that.'

'Does the name of Solomon mean anything to you?'

'Ah,' said Colonel Pikeaway. 'Mr Solomon. And where did you get that name from?'

'It was mentioned by Inspector Norris.'

'I see. Well, if you're going by what Norris said, you're going right. I can tell you that. You won't see Solomon personally, I don't mind telling you. He's dead.'

'Oh,' said Tommy, 'I see.'

'At least you don't quite see,' said Colonel Pikeaway. 'We use his name sometimes. It's useful, you know, to have a name you can use. The name of a real person, a person who isn't there any longer but although dead is still highly regarded in the neighbourhood. It's sheer chance you ever came to live in The Laurels at all and we've got hopes that it may lead to a piece of luck for us. But I don't want it to be a cause of disaster to you or to your missus. Suspect everyone and everything. It's the best way.'

'I only trust two people there,' said Tommy. 'One's Albert, who's worked for us for years –'

'Yes, I remember Albert. Red-haired boy, wasn't he?'

'Not a boy any longer –'

'Who's the other one?'

'My dog Hannibal.'

'Hm. Yes – you may have something there. Who was it – Dr Watts who wrote a hymn beginning, "Dogs delight to bark and bite, It is their nature to." – What is he, an Alsatian?'

'No, he's a Manchester Terrier.'

'Ah, an old English Black and Tan, not as big as a Dobermann pinscher but the kind of dog that knows his stuff.'

Chapter 13

Visit from Miss Mullins

Tuppence, walking along the garden path, was accosted by Albert coming down at a quick pace from the house.

'Lady waiting to see you,' he said.

'Lady? Oh, who is it?'

'Miss Mullins, she says she is. Recommended by one of the ladies in the village to call on you.'

'Oh, of course,' said Tuppence. 'About the garden, isn't it?'

'Yes, she said something about the garden.'

'I think you'd better bring her out here,' said Tuppence.

'Yes, madam,' said Albert, falling into his role of experienced butler.

He went back to the house and returned a few moments later bringing with him a tall masculine-looking woman in tweed trousers and a Fair Isle pullover.

'Chilly wind this morning,' she said.

Her voice was deep and slightly hoarse.

'I'm Iris Mullins. Mrs Griffin suggested I should come along and see you. Wanting some help in the garden. Is that it?'

'Good morning,' said Tuppence, shaking hands. 'I'm very pleased to see you. Yes, we do want some help in the garden.'

'Only just moved in, haven't you?'

'Well, it feels almost like years,' said Tuppence, 'because we've only just got all the workmen out.'

'Ah yes,' said Miss Mullins, giving a deep hoarse chuckle. 'Know what it is to have workmen in the house. But you're quite right to come in yourself and not leave it to them. Nothing gets finished until the owner's moved in and even then you usually have to get them back again to finish something they've forgotten about. Nice garden you've got here but it's been let go a bit, hasn't it?'

'Yes, I'm afraid the last people who lived here didn't care much about how the garden looked.'

'People called Jones or something like that, weren't they? Don't think I actually know them. Most of my time here, you know, I've lived on the other side, the moor side, of the town. Two houses there I go to regularly. One, two days a week and the other one, one day. Actually, one day isn't enough, not to keep it right. You had old Isaac working here, didn't you? Nice old boy. Sad he had to get himself done in by some of this violent guerrilla material that's always going about bashing someone. The inquest was about a week ago, wasn't it? I hear they haven't found out who did it yet. Go about in little groups they do, and mug people. Nasty lot. Very often the younger they are, the nastier they are. That's a nice magnolia you've got there. *Soulangeana*, isn't it? Much the best to have. People always want the more exotic kinds but it's better to stick to old friends when it's magnolias in my opinion.'

'It's really been more the vegetables that we're thinking about.'

'Yes, you want to build up a good working kitchen garden, don't you? There doesn't seem to have been much attention paid before. People lose their spirit and think it's better really to buy their vegetables, and not try and grow them.'

'I'd always want to grow new potatoes and peas,' said Tuppence, 'and I think French beans too, because you then can have them all young.'

'That's right. You might as well add runner beans. Most gardeners are so proud of their runner beans that they like them a foot and a half in length. They think that's a fine bean. Always takes a prize at a local show. But you're quite right, you know. Young vegetables are the things that you really enjoy eating.'

Albert appeared suddenly.

'Mrs Redcliffe on the telephone, madam,' he said. 'Wanted to know if you could lunch tomorrow.'

'Tell her I'm very sorry,' said Tuppence. 'I'm afraid we may have to go to London tomorrow. Oh – wait a minute, Albert. Just wait while I write a word or two.'

She pulled out a small pad from her bag, wrote a few words on it and handed it to Albert.

'Tell Mr Beresford,' she said. 'Tell him Miss Mullins is here and we're in the garden. I forgot to do what he asked me to do, give him the name and address of the person he is writing to. I've written it here –'

'Certainly, madam,' said Albert, and disappeared.

Tuppence returned to the vegetable conversation.

'I expect you're very busy,' she said, 'as you are working three days already.'

'Yes, and as I said it's rather the other side of the town. I live the other side of town. I've got a small cottage there.'

At that moment Tommy arrived from the house. Hannibal was with him, running round in large circles. Hannibal reached Tuppence first. He stopped still for a moment, spread out his paws, and then rushed at Miss Mullins with a fierce array of barking. She took a step or two back in some alarm.

'This is our terrible dog,' said Tuppence. 'He doesn't really bite, you know. At least very seldom. It's usually only the postman he likes to bite.'

'All dogs bite postmen, or try to,' said Miss Mullins.

'He's a very good guard dog,' said Tuppence. 'He's a Manchester Terrier, you know, and they are good guard dogs. He protects the house in a wonderful way. He won't let anyone near it or come inside and he looks after me very carefully. He evidently regards me as his principal charge in life.'

'Oh well, of course I suppose it's a good thing nowadays.'

'I know. There are so many robberies about,' said Tuppence. 'Lots of our friends, you know, have had burglars. Some even who come in in broad daylight in the most extraordinary way. They set up ladders and take window-sashes out or pretend to be window-cleaners – oh, up to all kinds of tricks. So it's a good thing to let it be known that there's a fierce dog in the house, I think.'

'I think perhaps you're quite right.'

'Here is my husband,' said Tuppence. 'This is Miss Mullins, Tommy. Mrs Griffin very kindly told her that we wanted someone who could possibly do some gardening for us.'

'Would this be too heavy work for you perhaps, Miss Mullins?'

'Of course not,' said Miss Mullins in her deep voice. 'Oh, I can dig with anyone. You've got to dig the right way. It's not only trenching the sweet peas, it's everything needs digging, needs manuring. The ground's got to be prepared. Makes all the difference.'

Hannibal continued to bark.

'I think, Tommy,' said Tuppence, 'you'd really better take Hannibal back to the house. He seems to be in rather a protective mood this morning.'

'All right,' said Tommy.

'Won't you come back to the house,' said Tuppence to Miss Mullins, 'and have something to drink? It's rather a hot morning and I think it would be a good thing, don't you? And we can discuss plans together perhaps.'

Hannibal was shut into the kitchen and Miss Mullins accepted a glass of sherry. A few suggestions were made, then Miss Mullins looked at her watch and said she must hurry back.

'I have an appointment,' she explained. 'I mustn't be late.' She bade them a somewhat hurried farewell and departed.

'She *seems* all right,' said Tuppence.

'I know,' said Tommy – 'But one can't ever be sure –'

'One could ask questions?' said Tuppence doubtfully.

'You must be tired going all round the garden. We must leave our expedition this afternoon for another day – you have been ordered to rest.'

Chapter 14

Garden Campaign

'You understand, Albert,' said Tommy.

He and Albert were together in the pantry where Albert was washing up the tea tray he had just brought down from Tuppence's bedroom.

'Yes, sir,' said Albert. 'I understand.'

'You know, I think you will get a bit of a warning – from Hannibal.'

'He's a good dog in some ways,' said Albert. 'Doesn't take to everyone, of course.'

'No,' said Tommy, 'that's not his job in life. Not one of those dogs who welcome in the burglars and wag their tails at the wrong person. Hannibal knows a few things. But I have made it quite clear to you, haven't I?'

'Yes. I don't know what I am to do if the missus – well, am I to do what the missus says or tell her what you said or –'

'I think you'll have to use a certain amount of

diplomacy,' said Tommy. 'I'm making her stay in bed today. I'm leaving her in your charge more or less.'

Albert had just opened the front door to a youngish man in a tweed suit.

Albert looked up doubtfully at Tommy. The visitor stepped inside and advanced one step, a friendly smile on his face.

'Mr Beresford? I've heard you want a bit of help in your garden – just moved in here lately, haven't you? I noticed coming up the drive that it was getting rather overgrown. I did some work locally a couple of years ago – for a Mr Solomon – you may have heard of him.'

'Mr Solomon, yes, someone did mention him.'

'My name's Crispin, Angus Crispin. Perhaps we might take a look at what wants doing.'

II

'About time someone did something about the garden,' said Mr Crispin, as Tommy led him on a tour of the flower-beds and the vegetable garden.

'That's where they used to grow the spinach along this kitchen garden path here. Behind it were some frames. They used to grow melons too.'

'You seem to be very well aware of all this.'

'Well, one heard a lot you know of what had been

everywhere in the old days. Old ladies tell you about the flower-beds and Alexander Parkinson told a lot of his pals about the foxglove leaves.'

'He must have been a rather remarkable boy.'

'Well, he had ideas and he was very keen on crime. He made a kind of code message out in one of Stevenson's books: *The Black Arrow*.'

'Rather a good one, that, isn't it? I read it myself about five years ago. Before that I'd never got further than *Kidnapped*. When I was working for –' He hesitated.

'Mr Solomon?' suggested Tommy.

'Yes, yes, that's the name. I heard things. Heard things from old Isaac. I gather, unless I've heard the wrong rumours, I gather that old Isaac must have been, oh, getting on for a hundred and did some work for you here.'

'Yes,' said Tommy. 'For his age he was rather wonderful, really. He knew a lot of things he used to tell us, too. Things he couldn't have remembered himself.'

'No, but he liked the gossip of the old days. He's got relations here still, you know, who have listened to his tales and checked up on his stories. I expect you've heard a good many things yourself.'

'So far,' said Tommy, 'everything seems to work out in lists of names. Names from the past but names, naturally, that don't mean anything to me. They can't.'

'All hearsay?'

'Mostly. My wife has listened to a lot of it and made some lists. I don't know whether any of them mean anything. I've got one list myself. It only came into my hands yesterday, as a matter of fact.'

'Oh. What's your list?'

'Census,' said Tommy. 'You know, there was a census on – I've got the date written down so I'll give it to you – and the people who were entered up that day because they spent the night here. There was a big party. A dinner-party.'

'So you know on a certain date – and perhaps quite an interesting date – who was here?'

'Yes,' said Tommy.

'It might be valuable. It might be quite significant. You've only just moved in here, haven't you?'

'Yes,' said Tommy, 'but it's possible we might just want to move out of here.'

'Don't you like it? It's a nice house, and this garden – well, this garden could be made very beautiful indeed. You've got some fine shrubs – wants a bit of clearing out, superfluous trees and bushes, flowering shrubs that haven't flowered lately and may never flower again by the look of them. Yes, I don't know why you'd want to go and move.'

'The associations with the past aren't terribly pleasant here,' said Tommy.

'The past,' said Mr Crispin. 'How does the past tie up with the present?'

'One thinks it doesn't matter, it's all behind us. But there's always somebody left, you know. I don't mean walking about but somebody who comes alive when people tell you about her or him or it or them. You really would be prepared to do a bit of –'

'Bit of jobbing gardening for you? Yes, I would. It would interest me. It's rather a – well, it's rather a hobby of mine, gardening.'

'There was a Miss Mullins who came yesterday.'

'Mullins? Mullins? Is she a gardener?'

'I gather something in that line. It was a Mrs – a Mrs Griffin, I think it was – who mentioned her to my wife and who sent her along to see us.'

'Did you fix up with her or not?'

'Not definitely,' said Tommy. 'As a matter of fact we've got a rather enthusiastic guard dog here. A Manchester Terrier.'

'Yes, they can be very enthusiastic at guarding. I suppose he thinks your wife is his business and he practically never lets her go anywhere alone. He's always there.'

'Quite right,' said Tommy, 'and he's prepared to tear anyone limb from limb who lays a finger on her.'

'Nice dogs. Very affectionate, very loyal, very self-willed, very sharp teeth. I'd better look out for him, I suppose.'

'He's all right at the moment. He's up in the house.'

'Miss Mullins,' said Crispin thoughtfully. 'Yes. Yes, that's interesting.'

'Why is it interesting?'

'Oh, I think it's because – well, I wouldn't know her by that name, of course. Is she between fifty and sixty?'

'Yes. Very tweedy and countrified.'

'Yes. Got some country connections, too. Isaac could have told you something about her, I expect. I heard she'd come back to live here. Not so very long ago, either. Things tie up, you know.'

'I expect you know things about this place that I don't,' said Tommy.

'I shouldn't think so. Isaac could have told you a lot, though. He knew things. Old stories, as you say, but he had a memory. And they talked it over. Yes, in these clubs for old people, they talk things over. Tall stories – some of them not true, some of them based on fact. Yes, it's all very interesting. And – I suppose he knew too much.'

'It's a shame about Isaac,' said Tommy. 'I'd like to get even with whoever did him in. He was a nice old boy and he was good to us and did as much as he could to help us here. Come on, anyway, let's go on looking round.'

Chapter 15

Hannibal Sees Active Service with Mr Crispin

Albert tapped on the bedroom door and in answer to Tuppence's 'Come in' advanced his head round the side of it.

'The lady as came the other morning,' he said. 'Miss Mullins. She's here. Wants to speak to you for a minute or two. Suggestions about the garden, I understand. I said as you was in bed and I wasn't sure if you were receiving.'

'The words you use, Albert,' said Tuppence. 'All right. I am receiving.'

'I was just going to bring your morning coffee up.'

'Well, you can bring that up and another cup. That's all. There'll be enough for two, won't there?'

'Oh yes, madam.'

'Very well, then. Bring it up, put it on the table over there, and then bring Miss Mullins up.'

'What about Hannibal?' said Albert. 'Shall I take him down and shut him up in the kitchen?'

'He doesn't like being shut up in the kitchen. No. Just push him into the bathroom and shut the door of it when you've done so.'

Hannibal, resenting the insult which was being put upon him, allowed with a bad grace Albert's pushing him into the bathroom and adjustment to the door. He gave several loud fierce barks.

'Shut up!' Tuppence shouted to him. 'Shut up!'

Hannibal consented to shut up as far as barking went. He lay down with his paws in front of him and his nose pressed to the crack under the door and uttered long, non-cooperative growls.

'Oh, Mrs Beresford,' cried Miss Mullins, 'I'm afraid I am intruding, but I really thought you'd like to look at this book I have on gardening. Suggestions for planting at this time of year. Some very rare and interesting shrubs and they do quite well in this particular soil although some people say they won't . . . Oh dear – oh no, oh, it's very kind of you. Yes, I would like a cup of coffee. Please let me pour it out for you, it's so difficult when you're in bed. I wonder, perhaps –' Miss Mullins looked at Albert, who obligingly drew up a chair.

'That be all right for you, miss?' he demanded.

'Oh yes, very nice indeed. Dear me, is that another bell downstairs?'

'Milk, I expect,' said Albert. 'Or might be the grocer. It's his morning. Excuse me, won't you.'

He went out of the room, shutting the door behind him. Hannibal gave another growl.

'That's my dog,' said Tuppence, 'he's very annoyed at not being allowed to join the party but he makes so much noise.'

'Do you take sugar, Mrs Beresford?'

'One lump,' said Tuppence.

Miss Mullins poured out a cup of coffee. Tuppence said, 'Otherwise black.'

Miss Mullins put down the coffee beside Tuppence and went to pour out a cup for herself.

Suddenly she stumbled, clutched at an occasional table, and went down on her knees with an exclamation of dismay.

'Have you hurt yourself?' demanded Tuppence.

'No, oh no, but I've broken your vase. I caught my foot in something – so clumsy – and your beautiful vase is smashed. Dear Mrs Beresford, what will you think of me? I assure you it was an accident.'

'Of course it was,' said Tuppence kindly. 'Let me see. Well, it looks as if it could be worse. It's broken in two, which means we shall be able to glue it together. I dare say the join will hardly show.'

'I shall still feel awful about it,' declared Miss Mullins. 'I know you must perhaps be feeling ill and I oughtn't to have come today, but I did so want to tell you –'

Hannibal began to bark again.

'Oh, the poor wee doggie,' said Miss Mullins, 'shall I let him out?'

'Better not,' said Tuppence. 'He's not very reliable sometimes.'

'Oh dear, is that another bell downstairs?'

'No,' said Tuppence. 'Albert'll answer it. He can always bring up a message if necessary.'

It was, however, Tommy who answered the telephone.

'Hullo,' he said. 'Yes? Oh, I see. Who? I see – yes. Oh. An enemy, definite enemy. Yes, that's all right. We've taken the countermeasures all right. Yes. Thank you very much.'

He dropped the receiver back, and looked at Mr Crispin.

'Words of warning?' said Mr Crispin.

'Yes,' said Tommy.

He continued to look at Mr Crispin.

'Difficult to know, isn't it? I mean, who's your enemy and who's your friend.'

'Sometimes when you know it's too late. Postern of Fate, Disaster's Cavern,' said Tommy.

Mr Crispin looked at him in some surprise.

'Sorry,' said Tommy. 'For some reason or other we've got in the habit of reciting poetry in this house.'

'Flecker, isn't it? "Gates of Baghdad" or is it the "Gates of Damascus"?'

'Come up, will you?' said Tommy. 'Tuppence is only resting, she's not suffering from any peculiar disease or anything. Not even a sneezing cold in the head.'

'I've taken up coffee,' said Albert, reappearing suddenly, 'and an extra cup for Miss Mullins wot's up there now with a gardening book or something.'

'I see,' said Tommy. 'Yes. Yes, it's all going very well. Where's Hannibal?'

'Shut him in the bathroom.'

'Did you latch the door very tight, because he won't like that, you know?'

'No, sir, I've done just what you said.'

Tommy went upstairs. Mr Crispin came just behind him. Tommy gave a little tap on the bedroom door and then went in. From the bathroom door Hannibal gave one more outspoken bark of defiance, then he leapt at the door from the inside, the latch gave, he shot out into the room. He gave one quick glance at Mr Crispin, then came forward and lunged with all his might, growling furiously, at Miss Mullins.

'Oh dear,' said Tuppence, 'oh dear.'

'Good boy, Hannibal,' said Tommy, 'good boy. Don't you think so?'

He turned his head to Mr Crispin.

'Knows his enemies, doesn't he – and your enemies.'

'Oh dear,' said Tuppence. 'Has Hannibal bitten you?'

'A very nasty nip,' said Miss Mullins, rising to her feet and scowling at Hannibal.

'His second one, isn't it?' said Tommy. 'Chased you out of our pampas grass, didn't he?'

'He knows what's what,' said Mr Crispin. 'Doesn't he, Dodo, my dear? Long time since I've seen you, Dodo, isn't it?'

Miss Mullins got up, shot a glance at Tuppence, at Tommy and at Mr Crispin.

'Mullins,' said Mr Crispin. 'Sorry I'm not up to date. Is that a married name or are you now known as Miss Mullins?'

'I am Iris Mullins, as I always was.'

'Ah, I thought you were Dodo. You used to be Dodo to me. Well, dear, I think – nice to have seen you, but I think we'd better get out of here quickly. Drink your coffee. I expect that's all right. Mrs Beresford? I'm very pleased to meet you. If I might advise you, I shouldn't drink *your* coffee.'

'Oh dear, let me take the cup away.'

Miss Mullins pressed forward. In a moment Crispin stood between her and Tuppence.

'No, Dodo dear, I wouldn't do that,' he said. 'I'd rather have charge of it myself. The cup belongs to the house, you know, and of course it would be nice to have an analysis of exactly what's in it just now. Possibly you brought a little dose with you, did you? Quite easy to put a little dose into the cup as you're handing it to the invalid or the supposed invalid.'

'I assure you I did no such thing. Oh, do call your dog off.'

Hannibal showed every desire to pursue her down the staircase.

'He wants to see you off the premises,' said Tommy. 'He's rather particular about that. He likes biting people who are going out through the front door. Ah, Albert, there you are. I thought you'd be just outside the other door. Did you see what happened, by any chance?'

Albert put his head round the dressing-room door across the room.

'I saw all right. I watched her through the crack of the hinge. Yes. Put something in the missus's cup, she did. Very neat. Good as a conjuror, but she did it all right.'

'I don't know what you mean,' said Miss Mullins. 'I – oh dear, oh dear, I must go. I've got an appointment. It's very important.'

She shot out of the room and down the stairs. Hannibal gave one glance and went after her. Mr Crispin showed no sign of animosity, but he too left hurriedly in pursuit.

'I hope she's a good runner,' said Tuppence, 'because if she isn't Hannibal will catch up with her. My word, he's a good guard dog, isn't he?'

'Tuppence, that was Mr Crispin, sent us by Mr Solomon. Came at a very good moment, didn't he? I think he's been waiting his time to see what might be going to happen. Don't break that cup and don't pour any of that coffee away until we've got a bottle or something to put it in. It's going to be analysed and we're going to find out what's in it. Put your best dressing-gown on, Tuppence, and come down to the sitting-room and we'll have some drinks there before lunch.'

II

'And now, I suppose,' said Tuppence, 'we shall never know what any of it means or what it is all about.'

She shook her head in deep despondency. Rising from her chair, she went towards the fireplace.

'Are you trying to put a log on?' said Tommy. 'Let me. You've been told not to move about much.'

'My arm's quite all right now,' said Tuppence. 'Anyone would think I'd broken it or something. It was only a nasty scrape or graze.'

'You have more to boast about than that,' said

Tommy. 'It was definitely a bullet wound. You have been wounded in war.'

'War it seems to have been all right,' said Tuppence. 'Really!'

'Never mind,' said Tommy, 'we dealt with the Mullins very well, I think.'

'Hannibal,' said Tuppence, 'was a very good dog there, wasn't he?'

'Yes,' said Tommy, 'he told us. Told us very definitely. He just leapt for that pampas grass. His nose told him, I suppose. He's got a wonderful nose.'

'I can't say my nose warned me,' said Tuppence. 'I just thought she was rather an answer to prayer, turning up. And I quite forgot we were only supposed to take someone who had worked for Mr Solomon. Did Mr Crispin tell you anything more? I suppose his name isn't really Crispin.'

'Possibly not,' said Tommy.

'Did he come to do some sleuthing too? Too many of us here, I should say.'

'No,' said Tommy, 'not exactly a sleuth. I think he was sent for security purposes. To look after you.'

'To look after me,' said Tuppence, 'and you, I should say. Where is he now?'

'Dealing with Miss Mullins, I expect.'

'Yes, well, it's extraordinary how hungry these excitements make one. Quite peckish, as one might say. Do you know, there's nothing I can imagine I'd like to eat more than a nice hot crab with a sauce made of cream with just a touch of curry powder.'

'You're well again,' said Tommy. 'I'm delighted to hear you feeling like that about food.'

'I've never been ill,' said Tuppence. 'I've been wounded. That's quite different.'

'Well,' said Tommy, 'anyway you must have realized as I did that when Hannibal let go all out and told you an enemy was close at hand in the pampas grass, you must have realized that Miss Mullins was the person who, dressed as a man, hid there and shot at you –'

'But then,' said Tuppence, 'we thought that she'd have another go. I was immured with my wound in bed and we made our arrangements. Isn't that right, Tommy?'

'Quite right,' said Tommy, 'quite right. I thought probably she wouldn't leave it too long to come to the conclusion that one of her bullets had taken effect and that you'd be laid up in bed.'

'So she came along full of feminine solicitude,' said Tuppence.

'And our arrangement was very good, I thought,' said Tommy. 'There was Albert on permanent guard, watching every step she took, every single thing she did –'

'And also,' said Tuppence, 'bringing me up on a

tray a cup of coffee and adding another cup for the visitor.'

'Did you see Mullins – or Dodo, as Crispin called her – put anything in your cup of coffee?'

'No,' said Tuppence, 'I must admit that I didn't. You see, she seemed to catch her foot in something and she knocked over that little table with our nice vase on it, made a great deal of apology, and my eye of course was on the broken vase and whether it was too bad to mend. So I didn't see her.'

'Albert did,' said Tommy. 'Saw it through the hinge where he'd enlarged it a crack so that he could look through.'

'And then it was a very good idea to put Hannibal in confinement in the bathroom but leaving the door only half latched because, as we know, Hannibal is very good at opening doors. Not of course if they're completely latched, but if they only look latched or feel latched he takes one great spring and comes in like a – oh, like a Bengal tiger.'

'Yes,' said Tommy, 'that is quite a good description.'

'And now I suppose Mr Crispin or whatever his name is has finished making his enquiries, although how he thinks Miss Mullins can be connected with Mary Jordan, or with a dangerous figure like Jonathan Kane who only exists in the past –'

'I don't think he only exists in the past. I think there may be a new edition of him, a re-birth, as you might say. There are a lot of young members, lovers of violence, violence at any price, the merry muggers society if there's anything called that, and the super-fascists regretting the splendid days of Hitler and his merry group.'

'I've just been reading *Count Hannibal*,' said Tuppence. 'Stanley Weyman. One of his best. It was among the Alexander books upstairs.'

'What about it?'

'Well, I was thinking that nowadays it's really still like that. And probably always has been. All the poor children who went off to the Children's Crusade so full of joy and pleasure and vanity, poor little souls. Thinking they'd been appointed by the Lord to deliver Jerusalem, that the seas would part in front of them so that they could walk across, as Moses did in the Bible. And now all these pretty girls and young men who appear in courts the whole time, because they've smashed down some wretched old age pensioner or elderly person who had just got a little money or something in the bank. And there was St Bartholomew's Massacre. You see, all these things *do* happen again. Even the new fascists were mentioned the other day in connection with a perfectly respectable university. Ah well, I suppose nobody will ever really tell us anything.

Do you really think that Mr Crispin will find out something more about a hiding-place that nobody's yet discovered? Cisterns. You know, bank robberies. They often hid things in cisterns. Very damp place, I should have thought, to hide something. Do you think when he's finished making his enquiries or whatever it is, he'll come back here and continue looking after me – and you, Tommy?'

'I don't need him to look after me,' said Tommy.

'Oh, that's just arrogance,' said Tuppence.

'I think he'll come to say goodbye,' said Tommy.

'Oh yes, because he's got very nice manners, hasn't he?'

'He'll want to make sure that you're quite all right again.'

'I'm only wounded and the doctor's seen to that.'

'He's really very keen on gardening,' said Tommy. 'I realize that. He really did work for a friend of his who happened to be Mr Solomon, who has been dead for some years, but I suppose it makes a good cover, that, because he can say he worked for him and people will know he worked for him. So he'll appear to be quite *bona fide*.'

'Yes, I suppose one has to think of all those things,' said Tuppence.

The front door bell rang and Hannibal dashed from the room, tiger-style, to kill any intruder who might be wishing to enter the sacred precincts which he guarded. Tommy came back with an envelope.

'Addressed to us both,' he said. 'Shall I open it?'

'Go ahead,' said Tuppence.

He opened it.

'Well,' he said, 'this raises possibilities for the future.'

'What is it?'

'It's an invitation from Mr Robinson. To you and to me. To dine with him on a date the week after next when he hopes you'll be fully recovered and yourself again. In his country house. Somewhere in Sussex, I think.'

'Do you think he'll tell us anything then?' said Tuppence.

'I think he might,' said Tommy.

'Shall I take my list with me?' said Tuppence. 'I know it by heart now.'

She read rapidly.

'Black Arrow, Alexander Parkinson, Oxford and Cambridge porcelain Victorian seats, Grin-hen-lo, KK, Mathilde's stomach, Cain and Abel, Truelove . . .'

'Enough,' said Tommy. 'It sounds mad.'

'Well, it is mad, all of it. Think there'll be anyone else at Mr Robinson's?'

'Possibly Colonel Pikeaway.'

'In that case,' said Tuppence, 'I'd better take a cough lozenge with me, hadn't I? Anyway, I do want to see

Mr Robinson. I can't believe he's as fat and yellow as you say he is – Oh! – but, Tommy, isn't it the week after next that Deborah is bringing the children to stay with us?'

'No,' said Tommy, 'it's this *next* weekend as ever is.'

'Thank goodness, so that's all right,' said Tuppence.

Chapter 16

The Birds Fly South

'Was that the car?'

Tuppence came out of the front door peering curiously along the curve of the drive, eagerly awaiting the arrival of her daughter Deborah and the three children.

Albert emerged from the side door.

'They won't be here yet. No, that was the grocer, madam. You wouldn't believe it – eggs have gone up, *again.* Never vote for this Government again, *I* won't. I'll give the Liberals a go.'

'Shall I come and see to the rhubarb and strawberry fool for tonight?'

'I've seen to that, madam. I've watched you often and I know just how you do it.'

'You'll be a cordon bleu chef by the time you've finished, Albert,' said Tuppence. 'It's Janet's favourite sweet.'

'Yes, and I made a treacle tart – Master Andrew loves treacle tart.'

'The rooms are all ready?'

'Yes. Mrs Shacklebury came in good time this morning. I put the Guerlain Sandalwood Soap in Miss Deborah's bathroom. It's her favourite, I know.'

Tuppence breathed a sigh of relief at the knowledge that all was in order for the arrival of her family.

There was the sound of a motor horn and a few minutes later the car came up the drive with Tommy at the wheel and a moment later the guests were decanted on the doorstep – daughter Deborah still a very handsome woman, nearly forty, and Andrew, fifteen, Janet, eleven, and Rosalie, seven.

'Hullo, Grandma,' shouted Andrew.

'Where's Hannibal?' called Janet.

'I want my tea,' said Rosalie, showing a disposition to burst into tears.

Greetings were exchanged. Albert dealt with the disembarkation of all the family treasures including a budgerigar, a bowl of goldfish and a hamster in a hutch.

'So this is the new home,' said Deborah, embracing her mother. 'I like it – I like it very much.'

'Can we go round the garden?' asked Janet.

'After tea,' said Tommy.

'I want my tea,' reiterated Rosalie with an expression on her face of: First things first.

They went into the dining-room where tea was set out and met with general satisfaction.

'What's all this I've been hearing about you, Mum?' demanded Deborah, when they had finished tea and repaired to the open air – the children racing round to explore the possible pleasures of the garden in the joint company of Thomas and Hannibal who had rushed out to take part in the rejoicings.

Deborah, who always took a stern line with her mother, whom she considered in need of careful guardianship, demanded, 'What *have* you been doing?'

'Oh. We've settled in quite comfortably by now,' said Tuppence.

Deborah looked unconvinced.

'You've been doing things. She has, hasn't she, Dad?'

Tommy was returning with Rosalie riding him piggy-back, Janet surveying the new territory and Andrew looking around with an air of taking a full grown-up view.

'You have been *doing* things.' Deborah returned to the attack. 'You've been playing at being Mrs Blenkinsop all over again. The trouble with you is, there's no holding you – N or M – all over again. Derek heard something and wrote and told me.' She nodded as she mentioned her brother's name.

'Derek – what could *he* know?' demanded Tuppence.

'Derek always gets to know things.'

'You too, Dad.' Deborah turned on her father. '*You've* been mixing yourself up in things, too. I thought you'd come here, both of you, to retire, and take life quietly – and enjoy yourselves.'

'That *was* the idea,' said Tommy, 'but Fate thought otherwise.'

'Postern of Fate,' said Tuppence. 'Disaster's Cavern, Fort of Fear –'

'Flecker,' said Andrew, with conscious erudition. He was addicted to poetry and hoped one day to be a poet himself. He carried on with a full quotation:

'Four great gates has the City of Damascus . . .
Postern of Fate – the Desert Gate . . .
Pass not beneath, O Caravan – or pass not singing.
Have you heard that silence where the birds are dead,
yet something pipeth like a bird?'

With singularly apposite cooperation birds flew suddenly from the roof of the house over their heads.

'What are all those birds, Grannie?' asked Janet.

'Swallows flying south,' said Tuppence.

'Won't they ever come back again?'

'Yes, they'll come back next summer.'

'And pass through the Postern of Fate!' said Andrew with intense satisfaction.

'This house was called Swallow's Nest once,' said Tuppence.

'But you aren't going on living here, are you?' said Deborah. 'Dad wrote and said you're looking out for another house.'

'Why?' asked Janet – the Rosa Dartle of the family. 'I like this one.'

'I'll give you a few reasons,' said Tommy, plucking a sheet of paper from his pocket and reading aloud:

'Black Arrow
Alexander Parkinson
Oxford and Cambridge
Victorian china garden stools
Grin-hen-lo
KK
Mathilde's stomach
Cain and Abel
Gallant Truelove'

'Shut up, Tommy – that's *my* list. It's nothing to do with you,' said Tuppence.

'But what does it *mean*?' asked Janet, continuing her quiz.

'It sounds like a list of clues from a detective story,' said Andrew, who in his less poetical moments was addicted to that form of literature.

'It *is* a list of clues. It's the reason why we are looking for another house,' said Tommy.

'But I like it here,' said Janet, 'it's lovely.'

'It's a nice house,' said Rosalie. 'Chocolate biscuits,' she added, with memories of recently eaten tea.

'I like it,' said Andrew, speaking as an autocratic Czar of Russia might speak.

'Why don't *you* like it, Grandma?' asked Janet.

'I *do* like it,' said Tuppence with a sudden unexpected enthusiasm. 'I want to live here – to go on living here.'

'Postern of Fate,' said Andrew. 'It's an exciting name.'

'It used to be called Swallow's Nest,' said Tuppence. 'We could call it that again –'

'All those clues,' said Andrew. 'You could make a story out of them – even a book –'

'Too many names, too complicated,' said Deborah. 'Who'd read a book like that?'

'You'd be surprised,' said Tommy, 'what people *will* read – and enjoy!'

Tommy and Tuppence looked at each other.

'Couldn't I get some paint tomorrow?' asked Andrew. 'Or Albert could get some and he'd help me. We'd paint the new name on the gate.'

'And then the swallows would know they could come back next summer,' said Janet.

She looked at her mother.

'Not at all a bad idea,' said Deborah.

'*La Reine le veult*,' said Tommy and bowed to his daughter, who always considered that giving the Royal assent in the family was her perquisite.

Chapter 17

Last Words: Dinner with Mr Robinson

'What a lovely meal,' said Tuppence. She looked round at the assembled company.

They had passed from the dining table and were now assembled in the library round the coffee table.

Mr Robinson, as yellow and even larger than Tuppence had visualized him, was smiling behind a big and beautiful George II coffee-pot – next to him was Mr Crispin, now, it seemed, answering to the name of Horsham. Colonel Pikeaway sat next to Tommy, who had, rather doubtfully, offered him one of his own cigarettes.

Colonel Pikeaway, with an expression of surprise, said: 'I *never* smoke after *dinner*.'

Miss Collodon, whom Tuppence had found rather alarming, said, 'Indeed, Colonel Pikeaway? How *very*, *very* interesting.' She turned her head towards Tuppence.

'What a very well-behaved dog you have got, Mrs Beresford!'

Hannibal, who was lying under the table with his head resting on Tuppence's foot, looked out with his misleading best angelic expression and moved his tail gently.

'I understood he was a very *fierce* dog,' said Mr Robinson, casting an amused glance at Tuppence.

'You should see him in action,' said Mr Crispin – alias Horsham.

'He has party manners when he is asked out to dinner,' explained Tuppence. 'He loves it, feels he's really a prestige dog going into high society.' She turned to Mr Robinson. 'It was really very, *very* nice of you to send him an invitation and to have a plateful of liver ready for him. He loves liver.'

'All dogs love liver,' said Mr Robinson. 'I understand –' he looked at Crispin-Horsham – 'that if I were to pay a visit to Mr and Mrs Beresford at their *own* home I might be torn to pieces.'

'Hannibal takes his duties very seriously,' said Mr Crispin. 'He's a well-bred guard dog and never forgets it.'

'You understand his feelings, of course, as a security officer,' said Mr Robinson.

His eyes twinkled.

'You and your husband have done a very remarkable piece of work, Mrs Beresford,' said Mr Robinson. 'We are indebted to you. Colonel Pikeaway tells me that *you* were the initiator in the affair.'

'It just happened,' said Tuppence, embarrassed. 'I got – well – curious. I wanted to find out – about certain things –'

'Yes, I gathered that. And now, perhaps you feel an equally natural curiosity as to what all this has been about?'

Tuppence became even more embarrassed, and her remarks became slightly incoherent.

'Oh – oh of course – I mean – I do understand that all this is quite secret – I mean all very hush-hush – and that we can't ask questions – because you couldn't tell us things. I do understand that perfectly.'

'On the contrary, it is I who want to ask you a question. If you will answer it by giving me the information I shall be enormously pleased.'

Tuppence stared at him with wide-open eyes.

'I can't imagine –' She broke off.

'You have a list – or so your husband tells me. He didn't tell me what that list was. Quite rightly. That list is *your* secret property. But I, too, know what it is to suffer curiosity.'

Again his eyes twinkled. Tuppence was suddenly aware that she liked Mr Robinson very much.

She was silent for a moment or two, then she coughed and fumbled in her evening bag.

'It's terribly silly,' she said. 'In fact it's rather more than silly. It's mad.'

Mr Robinson responded unexpectedly: '"Mad, mad, all the whole world is *mad*." So Hans Sachs said, sitting under his elder tree in *Die Meistersinger* – my favourite opera. How right he was!'

He took the sheet of foolscap she handed to him.

'Read it aloud if you like,' said Tuppence. 'I don't really mind.'

Mr Robinson glanced at it, then handed it to Crispin. 'Angus, you have a clearer voice than I have.'

Mr Crispin took the sheet and read in an agreeable tenor with good enunciation:

> *'Black Arrow*
> *Alexander Parkinson*
> Mary Jordan did not die naturally
> *Oxford and Cambridge porcelain Victorian seats*
> *Grin-Hen-Lo*
> *KK*
> *Mathilde's stomach*
> *Cain and Abel*
> *Truelove'*

He stopped, looked at his host, who turned his head towards Tuppence.

'My dear,' said Mr Robinson. 'Let me congratulate

you – you must have a most unusual mind. To arrive from this list of clues at your final discoveries is really most remarkable.'

'Tommy was hard at it too,' said Tuppence.

'Nagged into it by you,' said Tommy.

'Very good research he did,' said Colonel Pikeaway appreciatively.

'The census date gave me a very good pointer.'

'You are a gifted pair,' said Mr Robinson. He looked at Tuppence again and smiled. 'I am still assuming that though you have displayed no indiscreet curiosity, you really want to know what all this has been about?'

'Oh,' exclaimed Tuppence. 'Are you really going to tell us something? How wonderful!'

'Some of it begins, as you surmised, with the Parkinsons,' said Mr Robinson. 'That is to say, in the distant past. My own great-grandmother was a Parkinson. Some things I learnt from her –

'The girl known as Mary Jordan was in our service. She had connections in the Navy – her mother was Austrian and so she herself spoke German fluently.

'As you may know, and as your husband certainly knows already, there are certain documents which will shortly be released for publication.

'The present trend of political thinking is that hush-hush, necessary as it is at certain times, should not be preserved indefinitely. There are things in the records that should be made known as a definite part of our country's past history.

'Three or four volumes are due to be published within the next couple of years authenticated by documentary evidence.

'What went on in the neighbourhood of Swallow's Nest (that was the name of your present house at that time) will certainly be included.

'There were leakages – as always there are leakages in times of war, or preceding a probable outbreak of war.

'There were politicians who had prestige and who were thought of very highly. There were one or two leading journalists who had enormous influence and used it unwisely. There were men even before the First World War who were intriguing against their own country. After that war there were young men who graduated from universities and who were fervent believers and often active members of the Communist Party without anyone knowing of that fact. And even more dangerous, Fascism was coming into favour with a full progressive programme of eventual union with Hitler, posing as a Lover of Peace and thereby bringing about a quick end to the war.

'And so on. A Continuous Behind the Scenes Picture. It has happened before in history. Doubtless it will always happen: a Fifth Column that is both active and dangerous, run by those who believed in it – as well as those who sought financial gain, those who aimed at eventual power being placed in their hands in the future. Some of this will make interesting reading. How often has the same phrase been uttered in all good faith: Old B.? A traitor? Nonsense. Last man in the world! Absolutely trustworthy!

'The complete confidence trick. The old, old story. Always on the same lines.

'In the commercial world, in the Services, in political life. Always a man with an honest face – a fellow you can't help liking and trusting. Beyond suspicion. "The last man in the world". Etc., etc., etc. Someone who's a natural for the job, like the man who can sell you a gold brick outside the Ritz.

'Your present village, Mrs Beresford, became the headquarters of a certain group just before the First World War. It was such a nice old-world village – nice people had always lived there – all patriotic, doing different kinds of war work. A good naval harbour – a good-looking young Naval commander – came of a good family, father had been an admiral. A good doctor practising there – much loved by all his patients – they enjoyed confiding their troubles to him. Just in general practice – hardly anyone knew that he had had a special training in chemical warfare – in poison-gases.

'And later, before the Second World War, Mr Kane

– spelt with a K – lived in a pretty thatched cottage by the harbour and had a particular political creed – not Fascist – oh no! Just Peace before Everything to save the world – a creed rapidly gaining a following on the Continent and in numerous other countries abroad.

'None of that is what you really want to know, Mrs Beresford – but you've got to realize the background first, a very carefully contrived one. That's where Mary Jordan was sent to find out, if she could, just what was going on.

'She was born before my time. I admired the work she had done for us when I heard the story of it – and I would have liked to have known her – she obviously had character and personality.

'Mary was her own Christian name though she was always known as Molly. She did good work. It was a tragedy she should die so young.'

Tuppence had been looking up to the wall at a picture which for some reason looked familiar. It was a mere sketch of a boy's head.

'Is that – surely –'

'Yes,' said Mr Robinson. 'That's the boy Alexander Parkinson. He was only eleven then. He was a grandson of a great-aunt of mine. That's how Molly went to the Parkinsons' in the role of a nursery governess. It seemed a good safe observation post. One wouldn't ever have thought –' he broke off, 'what would come of it.'

'It wasn't – one of the Parkinsons?' asked Tuppence.

'Oh no, my dear. I understand that the Parkinsons were not involved in any way. But there were others – guests and friends – staying in the house that night. It was your Thomas who found out that the evening in question was the date of a census return. The names of everyone sleeping under that roof had to be entered as well as the usual occupants. One of those names linked up in a significant manner. The daughter of the local doctor about whom I have just told you came down to visit her father as she often did and asked the Parkinsons to put her up that night as she had brought two friends with her. Those friends were all right – but later her father was found to be heavily involved in all that was going on in that part of the world. She herself, it seemed, had helped the Parkinsons in garden work some weeks earlier and was responsible for foxgloves and spinach being planted in close proximity. It was she who had taken the mixture of leaves to the kitchen on the fatal day. The illness of all the participants of the meal passed off as one of those unfortunate mistakes that happen sometimes. The doctor explained he had known such a thing happen before. His evidence at the inquest resulted in a verdict of Misadventure. The fact that a cocktail glass had been swept off a table and smashed by accident that same night attracted no attention.

'Perhaps, Mrs Beresford, you would be interested to know that history might have repeated itself. You were shot at from a clump of pampas grass, and later the lady calling herself Miss Mullins tried to add poison to your coffee cup. I understand she is actually a granddaughter or great-niece of the original criminal doctor, and before the Second World War she was a disciple of Jonathan Kane. That's how Crispin knew of her, of course. And your dog definitely disapproved of her and took prompt action. Indeed we now know that it was she who coshed old Isaac.

'We now have to consider an even more sinister character. The genial kindly doctor was idolized by everyone in the place, but it seems most probable on the evidence that it was the doctor who was responsible for Mary Jordan's death, though at the time no one would have believed it. He had wide scientific interests, and expert knowledge of poisons and did pioneering work in bacteriology. It has taken sixty years before the facts have become known. Only Alexander Parkinson, a schoolboy at the time, began having ideas.'

'*Mary Jordan did not die naturally*,' quoted Tuppence softly. '*It must have been one of us*.' She asked: 'Was it the doctor who found out what Mary was doing?'

'No. The doctor had not suspected. But somebody had. Up till then she had been completely successful. The Naval commander had worked with her as planned. The information she passed to him was genuine and he didn't realize that it was mainly stuff that didn't matter – though it had been made to sound important. So-called Naval plans and secrets which he passed to her, she duly delivered on her days off in London, obeying instructions as to when and where. Queen Mary's Garden in Regent's Park was one, I believe – and the Peter Pan statue in Kensington Gardens was another. We learned a good deal from these meetings and the minor officials in certain embassies concerned.

'But all that's in the past, Mrs Beresford, long, long in the past.'

Colonel Pikeaway coughed and suddenly took over. 'But history repeats itself, Mrs Beresford. Everyone learns that sooner or later. A nucleus recently reformed in Hollowquay. People who knew about it set things up again. Perhaps that's why Miss Mullins returned. Certain hiding-places were used again. Secret meetings took place. Once more money became significant – where it came from, where it went to. Mr Robinson here was called in. And then our old friend Beresford came along and started giving me some very interesting information. It fitted in with what we had already suspected. Background scenery, being set up in anticipation. A future being prepared to be controlled and run by one particular political figure in this country. A man with a certain reputation and making more converts and followers every day. The Confidence Trick in action once again. Man of Great Integrity – Lover of Peace. Not Fascism – oh no! Just something that looks like Fascism. Peace for all – and financial rewards to those who cooperate.'

'Do you mean it's still going on?' Tuppence's eyes opened wide.

'Well, we know more or less all we want and need to know now. And that's partly because of what you two have contributed – the operation of a surgical nature on a rocking-horse was particularly informative –'

'Mathilde!' exclaimed Tuppence. 'I *am* glad! I can hardly believe it. Mathilde's stomach!'

'Wonderful things, horses,' said Colonel Pikeaway. 'Never know what they will do, or won't do. Ever since the wooden horse of Troy.'

'Even Truelove helped, I hope,' said Tuppence. 'But, I mean, if it's all going on still. With children about –'

'It isn't,' said Mr Crispin. 'You don't need to worry. That area of England is purified – the wasps' nest cleared up. It's suitable for private living again. We've reason to believe they've shifted operations to the neighbourhood of Bury St Edmunds. And we'll be keeping an eye on you, so you needn't worry at all.'

Tuppence gave a sigh of relief. 'Thank you for telling me. You see, my daughter Deborah comes to stay from time to time and brings her three children –'

'You needn't worry,' said Mr Robinson. 'By the way, after the N and M business, didn't you adopt the child that figured in the case – the one that had the nursery rhyme books, Goosey Gander and all the rest of it?'

'Betty?' said Tuppence. 'Yes. She's done very well at university and she's gone off now to Africa to do research on how people live – that sort of thing. A lot of young people are very keen on that. She's a darling – and very happy.'

Mr Robinson cleared his throat and rose to his feet. 'I want to propose a toast. To Mr and Mrs Thomas Beresford in acknowledgement of the service they have rendered to their country.'

It was drunk enthusiastically.

'And if I may, I will propose a further toast,' said Mr Robinson. 'To Hannibal.'

'There, Hannibal,' said Tuppence, stroking his head. 'You've had your health drunk. Almost as good as being knighted or having a medal. I was reading Stanley Weyman's *Count Hannibal* only the other day.'

'Read it as a boy, I remember,' said Mr Robinson. '"Who touches my brother touches Tavanne," if I've got it right. Pikeaway, don't you think? Hannibal, may I be permitted to tap you on the shoulder?'

Hannibal took a step towards him, received a tap on the shoulder and gently wagged his tail.

'I hereby create you a Count of this Realm.'

'Count Hannibal. Isn't that lovely?' said Tuppence. 'What a proud dog you ought to be!'

N or M?

Agatha Christie is known throughout the world as the Queen of Crime. Her books have sold over a billion copies in English with another billion in 100 foreign languages. She is the most widely published author of all time and in any language, outsold only by the Bible and Shakespeare. She is the author of 80 crime novels and short story collections, 19 plays, and six novels written under the name of Mary Westmacott.

Agatha Christie's first novel, *The Mysterious Affair at Styles*, was written towards the end of the First World War, in which she served as a VAD. In it she created Hercule Poirot, the little Belgian detective who was destined to become the most popular detective in crime fiction since Sherlock Holmes. It was eventually published by The Bodley Head in 1920.

In 1926, after averaging a book a year, Agatha Christie wrote her masterpiece. *The Murder of Roger Ackroyd* was the first of her books to be published by Collins and marked the beginning of an author-publisher relationship which lasted for 50 years and well over 70 books. *The Murder of Roger Ackroyd* was also the first of Agatha Christie's books to be dramatized – under the name *Alibi* – and to have a successful run in London's West End. *The Mousetrap*, her most famous play of all, opened in 1952 and is the longest-running play in history.

Agatha Christie was made a Dame in 1971. She died in 1976, since when a number of books have been published posthumously: the bestselling novel *Sleeping Murder* appeared later that year, followed by her autobiography and the short story collections *Miss Marple's Final Cases*, *Problem at Pollensa Bay* and *While the Light Lasts*. In 1998 *Black Coffee* was the first of her plays to be novelized by another author, Charles Osborne.

By the same author

The ABC Murders
The Adventure of the Christmas Pudding
After the Funeral
And Then There Were None
Appointment with Death
At Bertram's Hotel
The Big Four
The Body in the Library
By the Pricking of My Thumbs
Cards on the Table
A Caribbean Mystery
Cat Among the Pigeons
The Clocks
Crooked House
Curtain: Poirot's Last Case
Dead Man's Folly
Death Comes as the End
Death in the Clouds
Death on the Nile
Destination Unknown
Dumb Witness
Elephants Can Remember
Endless Night
Evil Under the Sun
Five Little Pigs
4.50 from Paddington
Hallowe'en Party
Hercule Poirot's Christmas
Hickory Dickory Dock
The Hollow
The Hound of Death
The Labours of Hercules
The Listerdale Mystery
Lord Edgware Dies
The Man in the Brown Suit
The Mirror Crack'd from Side to Side
Miss Marple's Final Cases
The Moving Finger
Mrs McGinty's Dead
The Murder at the Vicarage
Murder in Mesopotamia
Murder in the Mews
A Murder is Announced
Murder is Easy
The Murder of Roger Ackroyd
Murder on the Links
Murder on the Orient Express
The Mysterious Affair at Styles
The Mysterious Mr Quin
The Mystery of the Blue Train
Nemesis
N or M?
One, Two, Buckle My Shoe
Ordeal by Innocence
The Pale Horse
Parker Pyne Investigates
Partners in Crime
Passenger to Frankfurt
Peril at End House
A Pocket Full of Rye
Poirot Investigates
Poirot's Early Cases
Postern of Fate
Problem at Pollensa Bay
Sad Cypress
The Secret Adversary
The Secret of Chimneys
The Seven Dials Mystery
The Sittaford Mystery
Sleeping Murder
Sparkling Cyanide
Taken at the Flood
They Came to Baghdad
They Do It With Mirrors
Third Girl
The Thirteen Problems
Three Act Tragedy
Towards Zero
While the Light Lasts
Why Didn't They Ask Evans?

Novels under the Nom de Plume of 'Mary Westmacott'

Absent in the Spring
The Burden
A Daughter's A Daughter
Giant's Bread
The Rose and the Yew Tree
Unfinished Portrait

Plays novelized by Charles Osborne

Black Coffee
Spider's Web
The Unexpected Guest

Memoirs

Agatha Christie: An Autobiography
Come, Tell Me How You Live

Agatha Christie

N or M?

HarperCollinsPublishers

HarperCollins*Publishers*
77–85 Fulham Palace Road
Hammersmith, London W6 8JB
www.**fireandwater**.com

This *Agatha Christie Signature Edition* published 2001
3 5 7 9 8 6 4 2

First published in Great Britain by Collins 1941

ISBN 0 00 711145 2

Typeset by Palimpsest Book Production Limited,
Polmont, Stirlingshire

Printed and bound in Great Britain by
Clays Ltd, St Ives plc

Chapter 1

Tommy Beresford removed his overcoat in the hall of the flat. He hung it up with some care, taking time over it. His hat went carefully on the next peg.

He squared his shoulders, affixed a resolute smile to his face and walked into the sitting-room, where his wife sat knitting a Balaclava helmet in khaki wool.

It was the spring of 1940.

Mrs Beresford gave him a quick glance and then busied herself by knitting at a furious rate. She said after a minute or two:

'Any news in the evening paper?'

Tommy said:

'The Blitzkrieg is coming, hurray, hurray! Things look bad in France.'

Tuppence said:

'It's a depressing world at the moment.'

There was a pause and then Tommy said:

'Well, why don't you ask? No need to be so damned tactful.'

'I know,' admitted Tuppence. 'There is something about conscious tact that is very irritating. But then it irritates you if I do ask. And anyway I don't *need* to ask. It's written all over you.'

'I wasn't conscious of looking a Dismal Desmond.'

'No, darling,' said Tuppence. 'You had a kind of nailed to the mast smile which was one of the most heartrending things I have ever seen.'

Tommy said with a grin:

'No, was it really as bad as all that?'

'And more! Well, come on, out with it. Nothing doing?'

'Nothing doing. They don't want me in any capacity. I tell you, Tuppence, it's pretty thick when a man of forty-six is made to feel like a doddering grandfather. Army, Navy, Air Force, Foreign Office, one and all say the same thing – I'm too old. I *may* be required later.'

Tuppence said:

'Well, it's the same for me. They don't want people of my age for nursing – no, thank you. Nor for anything else. They'd rather have a fluffy chit who's never seen a wound or sterilised a dressing than they would have me who worked for three years, 1915 to 1918, in various capacities, nurse in the surgical ward and operating theatre, driver of a trade delivery van and later of a General. This, that and the other – all, I assert firmly, with conspicuous success. And now I'm a poor, pushing, tiresome, middle-aged woman who won't sit at home quietly and knit as she ought to do.'

Tommy said gloomily:

'This war is hell.'

'It's bad enough having a war,' said Tuppence, 'but not being allowed to do anything in it just puts the lid on.'

Tommy said consolingly:

'Well, at any rate Deborah has got a job.'

Deborah's mother said:

'Oh, she's all right. I expect she's good at it, too. But I still think, Tommy, that I could hold my own with Deborah.'

Tommy grinned.

'She wouldn't think so.'

Tuppence said:

'Daughters can be very trying. Especially when they *will* be so kind to you.'

Tommy murmured:

'The way young Derek makes allowances for me is sometimes rather hard to bear. That "poor old Dad" look in his eye.'

'In fact,' said Tuppence, 'our children, although quite adorable, are also quite maddening.'

But at the mention of the twins, Derek and Deborah, her eyes were very tender.

'I suppose,' said Tommy thoughtfully, 'that it's always hard for people themselves to realise that they're getting middle-aged and past doing things.'

Tuppence gave a snort of rage, tossed her glossy dark head, and sent her ball of khaki wool spinning from her lap.

'Are we past doing things? *Are* we? Or is it only that everyone keeps insinuating that we are. Sometimes I feel that we never were any use.'

'Quite likely,' said Tommy.

'Perhaps so. But at any rate we did once feel important. And now I'm beginning to feel that all that never really happened. Did it happen, Tommy? Is it true that you were once crashed on the head and kidnapped by German agents? Is it true that we once tracked down a dangerous criminal – and got him! Is it true that we rescued a girl and got hold of important secret papers, and were practically thanked by a grateful country? Us! You and me! Despised, unwanted Mr and Mrs Beresford.'

'Now dry up, darling. All this does no good.'

'All the same,' said Tuppence, blinking back a tear, 'I'm disappointed in our Mr Carter.'

'He wrote us a very nice letter.'

'He didn't *do* anything – he didn't even hold out any hope.'

'Well, he's out of it all nowadays. Like us. He's quite old. Lives in Scotland and fishes.'

Tuppence said wistfully:

'They might have let us do *something* in the Intelligence.'

'Perhaps we couldn't,' said Tommy. 'Perhaps, nowadays, we wouldn't have the nerve.'

'I wonder,' said Tuppence. 'One feels just the same. But perhaps, as you say, when it came to the point –'

She sighed. She said:

'I wish we could find a job of some kind. It's so rotten when one has so much time to think.'

Her eyes rested just for a minute on the photograph of the very young man in the Air Force uniform, with the wide grinning smile so like Tommy's.

Tommy said:

'It's worse for a man. Women can knit, after all – and do up parcels and help at canteens.'

Tuppence said:

'I can do all that twenty years from now. I'm not old enough to be content with that. I'm neither one thing nor the other.'

The front door bell rang. Tuppence got up. The flat was a small service one.

She opened the door to find a broad-shouldered man with a big fair moustache and a cheerful red face, standing on the mat.

His glance, a quick one, took her in as he asked in a pleasant voice:

'Are you Mrs Beresford?'

'Yes.'

'My name's Grant. I'm a friend of Lord Easthampton's. He suggested I should look you and your husband up.'

'Oh, how nice, do come in.'

She preceded him into the sitting-room.

'My husband, er – Captain –'

'Mr'

'Mr Grant. He's a friend of Mr Car – of Lord Easthampton's.'

The old *nom de guerre* of the former Chief of the Intelligence, 'Mr Carter', always came more easily to her lips than their old friend's proper title.

For a few minutes the three talked happily together. Grant was an attractive person with an easy manner.

Presently Tuppence left the room. She returned a few minutes later with the sherry and some glasses.

After a few minutes, when a pause came, Mr Grant said to Tommy:

'I hear you're looking for a job, Beresford?'

An eager light came into Tommy's eye.

'Yes, indeed. You don't mean –'

Grant laughed, and shook his head.

'Oh, nothing of that kind. No, I'm afraid that has to

be left to the young active men – or to those who've been at it for years. The only things I can suggest are rather stodgy, I'm afraid. Office work. Filing papers. Tying them up in red tape and pigeon-holing them. That sort of thing.'

Tommy's face fell.

'Oh, I see!'

Grant said encouragingly:

'Oh well, it's better than nothing. Anyway, come and see me at my office one day. Ministry of Requirements. Room 22. We'll fix you up with something.'

The telephone rang. Tuppence picked up the receiver.

'Hallo – yes – *what*?' A squeaky voice spoke agitatedly from the other end. Tuppence's face changed. 'When? – Oh, my dear – of course – I'll come over right away . . .'

She put back the receiver.

She said to Tommy:

'That was Maureen.'

'I thought so – I recognised her voice from here.'

Tuppence explained breathlessly:

'I'm so sorry, Mr Grant. But I must go round to this friend of mine. She's fallen and twisted her ankle and there's no one with her but her little girl, so I must go round and fix up things for her and get hold of someone to come in and look after her. Do forgive me.'

'Of course, Mrs Beresford. I quite understand.'

Tuppence smiled at him, picked up a coat which had been lying over the sofa, slipped her arms into it and hurried out. The flat door banged.

Tommy poured out another glass of sherry for his guest.

'Don't go yet,' he said.

'Thank you.' The other accepted the glass. He sipped it for a moment in silence. Then he said, 'In a way, you know, your wife's being called away is a fortunate occurrence. It will save time.'

Tommy stared.

'I don't understand.'

Grant said deliberately:

'You see, Beresford, if you had come to see me at the Ministry, I was empowered to put a certain proposition before you.'

The colour came slowly up in Tommy's freckled face. He said:

'You don't mean –'

Grant nodded.

'Easthampton suggested you,' he said. 'He told us you were the man for the job.'

Tommy gave a deep sigh.

'Tell me,' he said.

'This is strictly confidential, of course.'

Tommy nodded.

'Not even your wife must know. You understand?'

'Very well – if you say so. But we worked together before.'

'Yes, I know. But this proposition is solely for you.'

'I see. All right.'

'Ostensibly you will be offered work – as I said just now – office work – in a branch of the Ministry functioning in Scotland – in a prohibited area where your wife cannot accompany you. Actually you will be somewhere very different.'

Tommy merely waited.

Grant said:

'You've read in the newspapers of the Fifth Column? You know, roughly at any rate, just what that term implies.'

Tommy murmured:

'The enemy within.'

'Exactly. This war, Beresford, started in an optimistic spirit. Oh, I don't mean the people who really knew – we've known all along what we were up against – the efficiency of the enemy, his aerial strength, his deadly determination, and the co-ordination of his well-planned war machine. I mean the people as a whole. The good-hearted, muddle-headed democratic fellow who believes what he wants to believe – that Germany will crack up, that she's on the verge of revolution, that her weapons of war are made of tin and that her men are so underfed that they'll fall down if they try to march – all that sort of stuff. Wishful thinking as the saying goes.

'Well, the war didn't go that way. It started badly and it went on worse. The men were all right – the men on the battleships and in the planes and in the dug-outs. But there was mismanagement and unpreparedness – the defects, perhaps, of our qualities. We don't want war, haven't considered it seriously, weren't good at preparing for it.

'The worst of that is over. We've corrected our mistakes, we're slowly getting the right men in the right place. We're beginning to run the war as it should be run – and we can win the war – make no mistake about that – but only if we don't lose it first. And the danger of losing it comes, not from outside – not from the might of Germany's bombers, not from her seizure of neutral countries and fresh vantage points from which to attack – but from within. Our danger is the danger of Troy – the wooden horse within our walls. Call it the Fifth Column if you like. It is here, among us. Men and women, some of them highly placed, some of them obscure, but all believing genuinely in the Nazi aims and the Nazi creed and desiring to substitute that sternly efficient creed for the muddled easy-going liberty of our democratic institutions.'

Grant leant forward. He said, still in that same pleasant unemotional voice:

'And we don't know who they are . . .'

Tommy said: 'But surely –'

Grant said with a touch of impatience:

'Oh, we can round up the small fry. That's easy enough. But it's the others. We know about them. We know that there are at least two highly placed in the Admiralty – that one must be a member of General G –'s staff – that there are three or more in the Air Force, and that two, at least, are members of the Intelligence, and have access to Cabinet secrets. We know that because it must be so from the way things have happened. The leakage – a leakage from the top – of information to the enemy, shows us that.'

Tommy said helplessly, his pleasant face perplexed:

'But what good should I be to you? I don't know any of these people.'

Grant nodded.

'Exactly. You don't know any of them – *and they don't know you.*'

He paused to let it sink in and then went on:

'These people, these high-up people, know most of our lot. Information can't be very well refused to them. I am at my wits' end. I went to Easthampton. He's out of it all now – a sick man – but his brain's the best I've ever known. He thought of you. Over twenty years since you worked for the department. Name quite unconnected with it. Your face not known. What do you say – will you take it on?'

Tommy's face was almost split in two by the magnitude of his ecstatic grin.

'Take it on? You bet I'll take it on. Though I can't see how I can be of any use. I'm just a blasted amateur.'

'My dear Beresford, amateur status is just what is needed. The professional is handicapped here. You'll take the place of the best man we had or are likely to have.'

Tommy looked a question. Grant nodded.

'Yes. Died in St Bridget's Hospital last Tuesday. Run down by a lorry – only lived a few hours. Accident case – but it wasn't an accident.'

Tommy said slowly: 'I see.'

Grant said quietly:

'And that's why we have reason to believe that Farquhar was on to something – that he was getting somewhere at last. By his death that wasn't an accident.'

Tommy looked a question.

Grant went on:

'Unfortunately we know next to nothing of what he had discovered. Farquhar had been methodically following up one line after another. Most of them led nowhere.'

Grant paused and then went on:

'Farquhar was unconscious until a few minutes before he died. Then he tried to say something. What he said was this: *N or M. Song Susie.*'

'That,' said Tommy, 'doesn't seem very illuminating.'

Grant smiled.

'A little more so than you might think. N or M, you see, is a term we have heard before. It refers to two of the most important and trusted German agents. We have come across their activities in other countries and we know just a little about them. It is their mission to organise a Fifth Column in foreign countries and to act as liaison officer between the country in question and Germany. N, we know, is a man. M is a woman. All we know about them is that these two are Hitler's most highly trusted agents and that in a code message we managed to decipher towards the beginning of the war there occurred this phrase – *Suggest N or M for England. Full powers* –'

'I see. And Farquhar –'

'As I see it, Farquhar must have got on the track of one or other of them. Unfortunately we don't know *which*. Song Susie sounds very cryptic – but Farquhar hadn't a high-class French accent! There was a return ticket to Leahampton in his pocket which is suggestive. Leahampton is on the south coast – a budding Bournemouth or Torquay. Lots of private hotels and guesthouses. Amongst them is one called *Sans Souci* –'

Tommy said again:

'Song Susie – Sans Souci – I see.'

Grant said: 'Do you?'

'The idea is,' Tommy said, 'that I should go there and – well – ferret round.'

'That *is* the idea.'

Tommy's smile broke out again.

'A bit vague, isn't it?' he asked. 'I don't even know what I'm looking for.'

'And I can't tell you. I don't know. It's up to you.'

Tommy sighed. He squared his shoulders.

'I can have a shot at it. But I'm not a very brainy sort of chap.'

'You did pretty well in the old days, so I've heard.'

'Oh, that was pure luck,' said Tommy hastily.

'Well, luck is rather what we need.'

Tommy considered a moment or two. Then he said:

'About this place, Sans Souci –'

Grant shrugged his shoulders.

'May be all a mare's nest. I can't tell. Farquhar may have been thinking of "Sister Susie sewing shirts for soldiers". It's all guesswork.'

'And Leahampton itself?'

'Just like any other of these places. There are rows of them. Old ladies, old Colonels, unimpeachable spinsters, dubious customers, fishy customers, a foreigner or two. In fact, a mixed bag.'

'And N or M amongst them?'

'Not necessarily. Somebody, perhaps, who's in touch with N or M. But it's quite likely to be N or M themselves. It's an inconspicuous sort of place, a boarding-house at a seaside resort.'

'You've no idea whether it's a man or a woman I've to look for?'

Grant shook his head.

Tommy said: 'Well, I can but try.'

'Good luck to your trying, Beresford. Now – to details –'

II

Half an hour later when Tuppence broke in, panting and eager with curiosity, Tommy was alone, whistling in an armchair with a doubtful expression on his face.

'Well?' demanded Tuppence, throwing an infinity of feeling into the monosyllable.

'Well,' said Tommy with a somewhat doubtful air, 'I've got a job – of kinds.'

'What kind?'

Tommy made a suitable grimace.

'Office work in the wilds of Scotland. Hush-hush and all that, but doesn't sound very thrilling.'

'Both of us, or only you?'

'Only me, I'm afraid.'

'Blast and curse you. How *could* our Mr Carter be so mean?'

'I imagine they segregate the sexes in these jobs. Otherwise too distracting for the mind.'

'Is it coding – or code breaking? Is it like Deborah's job? Do be careful, Tommy, people go queer doing that and can't sleep and walk about all night groaning and repeating 978345286 or something like that and finally have nervous breakdowns and go into homes.'

'Not me.'

Tuppence said gloomily:

'I expect you will sooner or later. Can I come too – not to work but just as a wife. Slippers in front of the fire and a hot meal at the end of the day?'

Tommy looked uncomfortable.

'Sorry, old thing. I *am* sorry. I hate leaving you –'

'But you feel you ought to go,' murmured Tuppence reminiscently.

'After all,' said Tommy feebly, 'you can knit, you know.'

'Knit?' said Tuppence. '*Knit?*'

Seizing her Balaclava helmet she flung it on the ground.

'I hate khaki wool,' said Tuppence, '*and* Navy wool *and* Air Force blue. I should like to knit something *magenta*!'

'It has a fine military sound,' said Tommy. 'Almost a suggestion of Blitzkrieg.'

He felt definitely very unhappy. Tuppence, however, was a Spartan and played up well, admitting freely that of course he had to take the job and that it didn't *really* matter about her. She added that she had heard they wanted someone to scrub down the First-Aid Post floors. She might possibly be found fit to do that.

Tommy departed for Aberdeen three days later. Tuppence saw him off at the station. Her eyes were bright and she blinked once or twice, but she kept resolutely cheerful.

Only as the train drew out of the station and Tommy saw the forlorn little figure walking away down the platform did he feel a lump in his own throat. War or no war he felt he was deserting Tuppence . . .

He pulled himself together with an effort. Orders were orders.

Having duly arrived in Scotland, he took a train the next day to Manchester. On the third day a train deposited him at Leahampton. Here he went to the principal hotel and on the following day made a tour of various private hotels and guesthouses, seeing rooms and inquiring terms for a long stay.

Sans Souci was a dark red Victorian villa, set on the side of a hill with a good view over the sea from its upper windows. There was a slight smell of dust and cooking in the hall and the carpet was worn, but it compared quite favourably with some of the other establishments Tommy had seen. He interviewed the proprietress, Mrs Perenna, in her office, a small untidy room with a large desk covered with loose papers.

Mrs Perenna herself was rather untidy looking, a woman of middle-age with a large mop of fiercely curling black hair, some vaguely applied make-up and a determined smile showing a lot of very white teeth.

Tommy murmured a mention of his elderly cousin, Miss Meadowes, who had stayed at Sans Souci two years ago. Mrs Perenna remembered Miss Meadowes quite well – such a dear old lady – at least perhaps not really old – very active and such a sensc of humour.

Tommy agreed cautiously. There was, he knew, a real Miss Meadowes – the department was careful about these points.

And how was dear Miss Meadowes?

Tommy explained sadly that Miss Meadowes was no more and Mrs Perenna clicked her teeth sympathetically and made the proper noises and put on a correct mourning face.

She was soon talking volubly again. She had, she was sure, just the room that would suit Mr Meadowes. A lovely sea view. She thought Mr Meadowes was so right to want to get out of London. Very depressing nowadays, so she understood, and, of course, after such a bad go of influenza –

Still talking, Mrs Perenna led Tommy upstairs and showed him various bedrooms. She mentioned a weekly sum. Tommy displayed dismay. Mrs Perenna explained that prices had risen so appallingly. Tommy explained that his income had unfortunately decreased and what with taxation and one thing and another –

Mrs Perenna groaned and said:

'This terrible war –'

Tommy agreed and said that in his opinion that fellow Hitler ought to be hanged. A madman, that's what he was, a madman.

Mrs Perenna agreed and said that what with rations and the difficulty the butchers had in getting the meat they wanted – and sometimes too much and sweetbreads and liver practically disappeared, it all made housekeeping very difficult, but as Mr Meadowes was a relation of Miss Meadowes, she would make it half a guinea less.

Tommy then beat a retreat with the promise to think it over and Mrs Perenna pursued him to the gate, talking more volubly than ever and displaying an archness that

Tommy found most alarming. She was, he admitted, quite a handsome woman in her way. He found himself wondering what her nationality was. Surely not quite English? The name was Spanish or Portuguese, but that would be her husband's nationality, not hers. She might, he thought, be Irish, though she had no brogue. But it would account for the vitality and the exuberance.

It was finally settled that Mr Meadowes should move in the following day.

Tommy timed his arrival for six o'clock. Mrs Perenna came out into the hall to greet him, threw a series of instructions about his luggage to an almost imbecile-looking maid, who goggled at Tommy with her mouth open, and then led him into what she called the lounge.

'I always introduce my guests,' said Mrs Perenna, beaming determinedly at the suspicious glares of five people. 'This is our new arrival, Mr Meadowes – Mrs O'Rourke.' A terrifying mountain of a woman with beady eyes and a moustache gave him a beaming smile.

'Major Bletchley.' Major Bletchley eyed Tommy appraisingly and made a stiff inclination of the head.

'Mr von Deinim.' A young man, very stiff, fair-haired and blue-eyed, got up and bowed.

'Miss Minton.' An elderly woman with a lot of beads, knitting with khaki wool, smiled and tittered.

'And Mrs Blenkensop.' More knitting – an untidy dark head which lifted from an absorbed contemplation of a Balaclava helmet.

Tommy held his breath, the room spun round.

Mrs Blenkensop! Tuppence! By all that was impossible and unbelievable – Tuppence, calmly knitting in the lounge of Sans Souci.

Her eyes met his – polite, uninterested stranger's eyes.

His admiration rose.

Tuppence!

Chapter 2

How Tommy got through that evening he never quite knew. He dared not let his eyes stray too often in the direction of Mrs Blenkensop. At dinner three more habitués of Sans Souci appeared – a middle-aged couple, Mr and Mrs Cayley, and a young mother, Mrs Sprot, who had come down with her baby girl from London and was clearly much bored by her enforced stay at Leahampton. She was placed next to Tommy and at intervals fixed him with a pair of pale gooseberry eyes and in a slightly adenoidal voice asked: 'Don't you think it's really quite safe now? Everyone's going back, aren't they?'

Before Tommy could reply to these artless queries, his neighbour on the other side, the beaded lady, struck in:

'What I say is one mustn't risk anything with children. Your sweet little Betty. You'd never forgive yourself and you know that Hitler has said the Blitzkrieg on England is coming quite soon now – and quite a new kind of gas, I believe.'

Major Bletchley cut in sharply:

'Lot of nonsense talked about gas. The fellows won't waste time fiddling round with gas. High explosive and incendiary bombs. That's what was done in Spain.'

The whole table plunged into the argument with gusto. Tuppence's voice, high-pitched and slightly fatuous, piped out: 'My son Douglas says –'

'Douglas, indeed,' thought Tommy. 'Why Douglas, I should like to know.'

After dinner, a pretentious meal of several meagre courses, all of which were equally tasteless, everyone drifted into the lounge. Knitting was resumed and Tommy was compelled to hear a long and extremely boring account of Major Bletchley's experiences on the North-West Frontier.

The fair young man with the bright blue eyes went out, executing a little bow on the threshold of the room.

Major Bletchley broke off his narrative and administered a kind of dig in the ribs to Tommy.

'That fellow who's just gone out. He's a refugee. Got out of Germany about a month before the war.'

'He's a German?'

'Yes. Not a Jew either. His father got into trouble

for criticising the Nazi régime. Two of his brothers are in concentration camps over there. This fellow got out just in time.'

At this moment Tommy was taken possession of by Mr Cayley, who told him at interminable length all about his health. So absorbing was the subject to the narrator that it was close upon bedtime before Tommy could escape.

On the following morning Tommy rose early and strolled down to the front. He walked briskly to the pier returning along the esplanade when he spied a familiar figure coming in the other direction. Tommy raised his hat.

'Good morning,' he said pleasantly. 'Er – Mrs Blenkensop, isn't it?'

There was no one within earshot. Tuppence replied:

'Dr Livingstone to you.'

'How on earth did you get here, Tuppence?' murmured Tommy. 'It's a miracle – an absolute miracle.'

'It's not a miracle at all – just brains.'

'Your brains, I suppose?'

'You suppose rightly. You and your uppish Mr Grant. I hope this will teach him a lesson.'

'It certainly ought to,' said Tommy. 'Come on, Tuppence, tell me how you managed it. I'm simply devoured with curiosity.'

'It was quite simple. The moment Grant talked of our

Mr Carter I guessed what was up. I knew it wouldn't be just some miserable office job. But his manner showed me that I wasn't going to be allowed in on this. So I resolved to go one better. I went to fetch some sherry and, when I did, I nipped down to the Browns' flat and rang up Maureen. Told her to ring me up and what to say. She played up loyally – nice high squeaky voice – you could hear what she was saying all over the room. I did my stuff, registered annoyance, compulsion, distressed friend, and rushed off with every sign of vexation. Banged the hall door, carefully remaining inside it, and slipped into the bedroom and eased open the communicating door that's hidden by the tallboy.'

'And you heard everything?'

'Everything,' said Tuppence complacently.

Tommy said reproachfully:

'And you never let on?'

'Certainly not. I wished to teach you a lesson. You and your Mr Grant.'

'He's not exactly my Mr Grant and I should say you have taught him a lesson.'

'Mr Carter wouldn't have treated me so shabbily,' said Tuppence. 'I don't think the Intelligence is anything like what it was in our day.'

Tommy said gravely: 'It will attain its former brilliance now we're back in it. But why Blenkensop?'

'Why not?'

'It seems such an odd name to choose.'

'It was the first one I thought of and it's handy for underclothes.'

'What do you mean, Tuppence?'

'B, you idiot. B for Beresford. B for Blenkensop. Embroidered on my camiknickers. Patricia Blenkensop. Prudence Beresford. Why did you choose Meadowes? It's a silly name.'

'To begin with,' said Tommy, 'I don't have large B's embroidered on my pants. And to continue, I didn't choose it. I was told to call myself Meadowes. Mr Meadowes is a gentleman with a respectable past – all of which I've learnt by heart.'

'Very nice,' said Tuppence. 'Are you married or single?'

'I'm a widower,' said Tommy with dignity. 'My wife died ten years ago at Singapore.'

'Why at Singapore?'

'We've all got to die somewhere. What's wrong with Singapore?'

'Oh, nothing. It's probably a most suitable place to die. I'm a widow.'

'Where did your husband die?'

'Does it matter? Probably in a nursing home. I rather fancy he died of cirrhosis of the liver.'

'I see. A painful subject. And what about your son Douglas?'

'Douglas is in the Navy.'

'So I heard last night.'

'And I've got two other sons. Raymond is in the Air Force and Cyril, my baby, is in the Territorials.'

'And suppose someone takes the trouble to check up on these imaginary Blenkensops?'

'They're not Blenkensops. Blenkensop was my second husband. My first husband's name was Hill. There are three pages of Hills in the telephone book. You couldn't check up on all the Hills if you tried.'

Tommy sighed.

'It's the old trouble with you, Tuppence. You will overdo things. Two husbands and three sons. It's too much. You'll contradict yourself over the details.'

'No, I shan't. And I rather fancy the sons may come in useful. I'm not under orders, remember. I'm a freelance. I'm in this to enjoy myself and I'm going to enjoy myself.'

'So it seems,' said Tommy. He added gloomily: 'If you ask me the whole thing's a farce.'

'Why do you say that?'

'Well, you've been at Sans Souci longer than I have. Can you honestly say you think any of these people who were there last night could be a dangerous enemy agent?'

Tuppence said thoughtfully:

'It does seem a little incredible. There's the young man, of course.'

'Carl von Deinim. The police check up on refugees, don't they?'

'I suppose so. Still, it might be managed. He's an attractive young man, you know.'

'Meaning, the girls will tell him things? But what girls? No Generals' or Admirals' daughters floating around here. Perhaps he walks out with a Company Commander in the ATS.'

'Be quiet, Tommy. We ought to be taking this seriously.'

'I am taking it seriously. It's just that I feel we're on a wild-goose chase.'

Tuppence said seriously:

'It's too early to say that. After all, nothing's going to be obvious about this business. What about Mrs Perenna?'

'Yes,' said Tommy thoughtfully. 'There's Mrs Perenna, I admit – she does want explaining.'

Tuppence said in a business-like tone:

'What about us? I mean, how are we going to co-operate?'

Tommy said thoughtfully:

'We mustn't be seen about too much together.'

'No, it would be fatal to suggest we know each other better than we appear to do. What we want to decide is the attitude. I think – yes, I think – pursuit is the best angle.'

'Pursuit?'

'Exactly. I pursue you. You do your best to escape, but being a mere chivalrous male don't always succeed. I've had two husbands and I'm on the look-out for a third. You act the part of the hunted widower. Every now and then I pin you down somewhere, pen you in a café, catch you walking on the front. Everyone sniggers and thinks it very funny.'

'Sounds feasible,' agreed Tommy.

Tuppence said: 'There's a kind of age-long humour about the chased male. That ought to stand us in good stead. If we are seen together, all anyone will do is to snigger and say, "Look at poor old Meadowes."'

Tommy gripped her arm suddenly.

'Look,' he said. 'Look ahead of you.'

By the corner of one of the shelters a young man stood talking to a girl. They were both very earnest, very wrapped up in what they were saying.

Tuppence said softly:

'Carl von Deinim. Who's the girl, I wonder?'

'She's remarkably good-looking, whoever she is.'

Tuppence nodded. Her eyes dwelt thoughtfully on the dark passionate face, and on the tight-fitting pull-over that revealed the lines of the girl's figure. She was talking earnestly, with emphasis. Carl von Deinim was listening to her.

Tuppence murmured:

'I think this is where you leave me.'

'Right,' agreed Tommy.

He turned and strolled in the opposite direction.

At the end of the promenade he encountered Major Bletchley. The latter peered at him suspiciously and then grunted out, 'Good morning.'

'Good morning.'

'See you're like me, an early riser,' remarked Bletchley.

Tommy said:

'One gets in the habit of it out East. Of course, that's many years ago now, but I still wake early.'

'Quite right, too,' said Major Bletchley with approval. 'God, these young fellows nowadays make me sick. Hot baths – coming down to breakfast at ten o'clock or later. No wonder the Germans have been putting it over on us. No stamina. Soft lot of young pups. Army's not what it was, anyway. Coddle 'em, that's what they do nowadays. Tuck 'em up at night with hot-water bottles. Faugh! Makes me sick!'

Tommy shook his head in melancholy fashion and Major Bletchley, thus encouraged, went on:

'Discipline, that's what we need. Discipline. How are we going to win the war without discipline? Do you know, sir, some of these fellows come on parade in slacks – so I've been told. Can't expect to win a war that way. Slacks! My God!'

Mr Meadowes hazarded the opinion that things were

very different from what they had been.

'It's all this democracy,' said Major Bletchley gloomily. 'You can overdo anything. In my opinion they're overdoing the democracy business. Mixing up the officers and the men, feeding together in restaurants – Faugh! – the men don't like it, Meadowes. The troops know. The troops always know.'

'Of course,' said Mr Meadowes, 'I have no real knowledge of Army matters myself –'

The Major interrupted him, shooting a quick sideways glance. 'In the show in the last war?'

'Oh yes.'

'Thought so. Saw you'd been drilled. Shoulders. What regiment?'

'Fifth Corfeshires.' Tommy remembered to produce Meadowes' military record.

'Ah yes, Salonica!'

'Yes.'

'I was in Mespot.'

Bletchley plunged into reminiscences. Tommy listened politely. Bletchley ended up wrathfully.

'And will they make use of me now? No, they will not. Too old. Too old be damned. I could teach one or two of these young cubs something about war.'

'Even if it's only what not to do?' suggested Tommy with a smile.

'Eh, what's that?'

A sense of humour was clearly not Major Bletchley's strong suit. He peered suspiciously at his companion. Tommy hastened to change the conversation.

'Know anything about that Mrs – Blenkensop, I think her name is?'

'That's right, Blenkensop. Not a bad-looking woman – bit long in the tooth – talks too much. Nice woman, but foolish. No, I don't know her. She's only been at Sans Souci a couple of days.' He added: 'Why do you ask?'

Tommy explained.

'Happened to meet her just now. Wondered if she was always out as early as this?'

'Don't know, I'm sure. Women aren't usually given to walking before breakfast – thank God,' he added.

'Amen,' said Tommy. He went on: 'I'm not much good at making polite conversation before breakfast. Hope I wasn't rude to the woman, but I wanted my exercise.'

Major Bletchley displayed instant sympathy.

'I'm with you, Meadowes. I'm with you. Women are all very well in their place, but not before breakfast.' He chuckled a little. 'Better be careful, old man. She's a widow, you know.'

'Is she?'

The Major dug him cheerfully in the ribs.

'*We* know what widows are. She's buried two husbands

and if you ask me she's on the look-out for number three. Keep a very wary eye open, Meadowes. A wary eye. That's my advice.'

And in high good humour Major Bletchley wheeled about at the end of the parade and set the pace for a smart walk back to breakfast at Sans Souci.

In the meantime, Tuppence had gently continued her walk along the esplanade, passing quite close to the shelter and the young couple talking there. As she passed she caught a few words. It was the girl speaking.

'But you must be careful, Carl. The very least suspicion –'

Tuppence was out of earshot. Suggestive words? Yes, but capable of any number of harmless interpretations. Unobtrusively she turned and again passed the two. Again words floated to her.

'Smug, detestable English . . .'

The eyebrows of Mrs Blenkensop rose ever so slightly. Carl von Deinim was a refugee from Nazi persecution, given asylum and shelter by England. Neither wise nor grateful to listen assentingly to such words.

Again Tuppence turned. But this time, before she reached the shelter, the couple had parted abruptly, the girl to cross the road leaving the sea front, Carl von Deinim to come along to Tuppence's direction.

He would not, perhaps, have recognised her but for

her own pause and hesitation. Then quickly he brought his heels together and bowed.

Tuppence twittered at him:

'Good morning, Mr von Deinim, isn't it? Such a lovely morning.'

'Ah, yes. The weather is fine.'

Tuppence ran on:

'It quite tempted me. I don't often come out before breakfast. But this morning, what with not sleeping very well – one often doesn't sleep well in a strange place, I find. It takes a day or two to accustom oneself, I always say.'

'Oh yes, no doubt that is so.'

'And really this little walk has quite given me an appetite for breakfast.'

'You go back to Sans Souci now? If you permit I will walk with you.' He walked gravely by her side.

Tuppence said:

'You also are out to get an appetite?'

Gravely, he shook his head.

'Oh no. My breakfast I have already had it. I am on my way to work.'

'Work?'

'I am a research chemist.'

'So that's what you are,' thought Tuppence, stealing a quick glance at him.

Carl von Deinim went on, his voice stiff:

'I came to this country to escape Nazi persecution. I had very little money – no friends. I do now what useful work I can.'

He stared straight ahead of him. Tuppence was conscious of some undercurrent of strong feeling moving him powerfully.

She murmured vaguely:

'Oh yes, I see. Very creditable, I am sure.'

Carl von Deinim said:

'My two brothers are in concentration camps. My father died in one. My mother died of sorrow and fear.'

Tuppence thought:

'The way he says that – as though he had learned it by heart.'

Again she stole a quick glance at him. He was still staring ahead of him, his face impassive.

They walked in silence for some moments. Two men passed them. One of them shot a quick glance at Carl. She heard him mutter to his companion:

'Bet you that fellow is a German.'

Tuppence saw the colour rise in Carl von Deinim's cheeks.

Suddenly he lost command of himself. That tide of hidden emotion came to the surface. He stammered:

'You heard – you heard – that is what they say – I –'

'My dear boy,' Tuppence reverted suddenly to her real self. Her voice was crisp and compelling. 'Don't be an idiot. You can't have it both ways.'

He turned his head and stared at her.

'What do you mean?'

'You're a refugee. You have to take the rough with the smooth. You're alive, that's the main thing. Alive and free. For the other – realise that it's inevitable. This country's at war. You're a German.' She smiled suddenly. 'You can't expect the mere man in the street – literally the man in the street – to distinguish between bad Germans and good Germans, if I may put it so crudely.'

He still stared at her. His eyes, so very blue, were poignant with suppressed feeling. Then suddenly he too smiled. He said:

'They said of Red Indians, did they not, that a good Indian was a dead Indian.' He laughed. 'To be a good German I must be on time at my work. Please. Good morning.'

Again that stiff bow. Tuppence stared after his retreating figure. She said to herself:

'Mrs Blenkensop, you had a lapse then. Strict attention to business in future. Now for breakfast at Sans Souci.'

The hall door of Sans Souci was open. Inside, Mrs Perenna was conducting a vigorous conversation with someone.

'And you'll tell him what I think of that last lot of margarine. Get the cooked ham at Quillers – it was twopence cheaper last time there, and be careful about the cabbages –' She broke off as Tuppence entered.

'Oh, good morning, Mrs Blenkensop, you are an early bird. You haven't had breakfast yet. It's all ready in the dining-room.' She added, indicating her companion: 'My daughter Sheila. You haven't met her. She's been away and only came home last night.'

Tuppence looked with interest at the vivid, handsome face. No longer full of tragic energy, bored now and resentful. 'My daughter Sheila.' Sheila Perenna.

Tuppence murmured a few pleasant words and went into the dining-room. There were three people breakfasting – Mrs Sprot and her baby girl, and big Mrs O'Rourke. Tuppence said 'Good morning' and Mrs O'Rourke replied with a hearty 'The top of the morning to you' that quite drowned Mrs Sprot's more anaemic salutation.

The old woman stared at Tuppence with a kind of devouring interest.

'Tis a fine thing to be out walking before breakfast,' she observed. 'A grand appetite it gives you.'

Mrs Sprot said to her offspring:

'*Nice* bread and milk, darling,' and endeavoured to insinuate a spoonful into Miss Betty Sprot's mouth.

The latter cleverly circumvented this endeavour by an adroit movement of her head, and continued to stare at Tuppence with large round eyes.

She pointed a milky finger at the newcomer, gave her a dazzling smile and observed in gurgling tones: 'Ga – ga bouch.'

'She likes you,' cried Mrs Sprot, beaming on Tuppence as on one marked out for favour. 'Sometimes she's so shy with strangers.'

'Bouch,' said Betty Sprot. 'Ah pooth ah bag,' she added with emphasis.

'And what would she be meaning by that?' demanded Mrs O'Rourke, with interest.

'She doesn't speak awfully clearly yet,' confessed Mrs Sprot. 'She's only just over two, you know. I'm afraid most of what she says is just bosh. She can say Mama, though, can't you, darling?'

Betty looked thoughtfully at her mother and remarked with an air of finality:

'Cuggle bick.'

''Tis a language of their own they have, the little angels,' boomed out Mrs O'Rourke. 'Betty, darling, say Mama now.'

Betty looked hard at Mrs O'Rourke, frowned and observed with terrific emphasis: 'Nazer –'

'There now, if she isn't doing her best! And a lovely sweet girl she is.'

Mrs O'Rourke rose, beamed in a ferocious manner at Betty, and waddled heavily out of the room.

'Ga, ga, ga,' said Betty with enormous satisfaction, and beat with a spoon on the table.

Tuppence said with a twinkle:

'What does Na-zer really mean?'

Mrs Sprot said with a flush: 'I'm afraid, you know, it's what Betty says when she doesn't like anyone or anything.'

'I rather thought so,' said Tuppence.

Both women laughed.

'After all,' said Mrs Sprot, 'Mrs O'Rourke means to be kind but she is rather alarming – with that deep voice and the beard and – and everything.'

With her head on one side Betty made a cooing noise at Tuppence.

'She has taken to you, Mrs Blenkensop,' said Mrs Sprot.

There was a slight jealous chill, Tuppence fancied, in her voice. Tuppence hastened to adjust matters.

'They always like a new face, don't they?' she said easily.

The door opened and Major Bletchley and Tommy appeared. Tuppence became arch.

'Ah, Mr Meadowes,' she called out. 'I've beaten you, you see. First past the post. But I've left you just a *little* breakfast!'

She indicated with the faintest of gestures the seat beside her.

Tommy, muttering vaguely: 'Oh – er – rather – thanks,' sat down at the other end of the table.

Betty Sprot said '*Putch!*' with a fine splutter of milk at Major Bletchley, whose face instantly assumed a sheepish but delighted expression.

'And how's little Miss Bo Peep this morning?' he asked fatuously. 'Bo Peep!' He enacted the play with a newspaper.

Betty crowed with delight.

Serious misgivings shook Tuppence. She thought:

'There must be some mistake. There *can't* be anything going on here. There simply can't!'

To believe in Sans Souci as a headquarters of the Fifth Column needed the mental equipment of the White Queen in *Alice*.

Chapter 3

On the sheltered terrace outside, Miss Minton was knitting.

Miss Minton was thin and angular, her neck was stringy. She wore pale sky-blue jumpers, and chains or bead necklaces. Her skirts were tweedy and had a depressed droop at the back. She greeted Tuppence with alacrity.

'Good morning, Mrs Blenkensop. I do hope you slept well.'

Mrs Blenkensop confessed that she never slept very well the first night or two in a strange bed. Miss Minton said, Now, wasn't that curious? It was exactly the same with *her*.

Mrs Blenkensop said, 'What a coincidence, and what a very pretty stitch that was.' Miss Minton, flushing with pleasure, displayed it. Yes, it was rather uncommon, and really quite simple. She could easily show it to Mrs Blenkensop if Mrs Blenkensop liked. Oh, that was very kind of Miss Minton, but Mrs Blenkensop was so stupid, she wasn't really very good at knitting, not at following patterns, that was to say. She could only do simple things like Balaclava helmets, and even now she was afraid she had gone wrong somewhere. It didn't look *right,* somehow, did it?

Miss Minton cast an expert eye over the knaki mass. Gently she pointed out just what had gone wrong. Thankfully, Tuppence handed the faulty helmet over. Miss Minton exuded kindness and patronage. Oh, no, it wasn't a trouble at all. She had knitted for so many years.

'I'm afraid I've never done any before this dreadful war,' confessed Tuppence. 'But one feels so terribly, doesn't one, that one must do *something.*'

'Oh yes, indeed. And you actually have a boy in the Navy, I think I heard you say last night?'

'Yes, my eldest boy. Such a splendid boy he is – though I suppose a mother shouldn't say so. Then I have a boy in the Air Force and Cyril, my baby, is out in France.'

'Oh dear, dear, how terribly anxious you must be.'

Tuppence thought:

'Oh Derek, my darling Derek . . . Out in the hell and mess – and here I am playing the fool – acting the thing I'm really feeling . . .'

She said in her most righteous voice:

'We must all be brave, mustn't we? Let's hope it will all be over soon. I was told the other day on very high authority indeed that the Germans can't possibly last out more than another two months.'

Miss Minton nodded with so much vigour that all her bead chains rattled and shook.

'Yes, indeed, and I believe' – (her voice lowered mysteriously) – 'that Hitler is suffering from a *disease* – absolutely fatal – he'll be raving mad by August.'

Tuppence replied briskly:

'All this Blitzkrieg is just the Germans' last effort. I believe the shortage is something frightful in Germany. The men in the factories are very dissatisfied. The whole thing will crack up.'

'What's this? What's all this?'

Mr and Mrs Cayley came out on the terrace, Mr Cayley putting his questions fretfully. He settled himself in a chair and his wife put a rug over his knees. He repeated fretfully:

'What's that you are saying?'

'We're saying,' said Miss Minton, 'that it will all be over by the autumn.'

'Nonsense,' said Mr Cayley. 'This war is going to last at least six years.'

'Oh, Mr Cayley,' protested Tuppence. 'You don't really think so?'

Mr Cayley was peering about him suspiciously.

'Now I wonder,' he murmured. 'Is there a draught? Perhaps it would be better if I moved my chair back into the corner.'

The resettlement of Mr Cayley took place. His wife, an anxious-faced woman who seemed to have no other aim in life than to minister to Mr Cayley's wants, manipulating cushions and rugs, asking from time to time: 'Now how is that, Alfred? Do you think that will be all right? Ought you, perhaps, to have your sun-glasses? There is rather a glare this morning.'

Mr Cayley said irritably:

'No, no. Don't fuss, Elizabeth. Have you got my muffler? No, no, my silk muffler. Oh well, it doesn't matter. I dare say this will do – for once. But I don't want to get my throat overheated, and wool – in this sunlight – well, perhaps you *had* better fetch the other.' He turned his attention back to matters of public interest. 'Yes,' he said. 'I give it six years.'

He listened with pleasure to the protests of the two women.

'You dear ladies are just indulging in what we call wishful thinking. Now I know Germany. I may say I know Germany extremely well. In the course of my business before I retired I used to be constantly to and fro. Berlin, Hamburg, Munich, I know them all. I can assure you that Germany can hold out practically indefinitely. With Russia behind her –'

Mr Cayley plunged triumphantly on, his voice rising and falling in pleasurably melancholy cadences, only interrupted when he paused to receive the silk muffler his wife brought him and wind it round his throat.

Mrs Sprot brought out Betty and plumped her down with a small woollen dog that lacked an ear and a woolly doll's jacket.

'There, Betty,' she said. 'You dress up Bonzo ready for his walk while Mummy gets ready to go out.'

Mr Cayley's voice droned on, reciting statistics and figures, all of a depressing character. The monologue was punctuated by a cheerful twittering from Betty talking busily to Bonzo in her own language.

'Truckle – truckly – pah bat,' said Betty. Then, as a bird alighted near her, she stretched out loving hands to it and gurgled. The bird flew away and Betty glanced round the assembled company and remarked clearly:

'Dicky,' and nodded her head with great satisfaction.

'That child is learning to talk in the most wonderful way,' said Miss Minton. 'Say "Ta ta", Betty. "Ta ta."'

Betty looked at her coldly and remarked:

'Gluck!'

Then she forced Bonzo's one arm into his woolly coat and, toddling over to a chair, picked up the cushion and pushed Bonzo behind it. Chuckling gleefully, she said with terrific pains:

'Hide! Bow wow. Hide!'

Miss Minton, acting as a kind of interpreter, said with vicarious pride:

'She loves hide-and-seek. She's always hiding things.' She cried out with exaggerated surprise:

'*Where* is Bonzo? Where *is* Bonzo? Where *can* Bonzo have gone?'

Betty flung herself down and went into ecstasies of mirth.

Mr Cayley, finding attention diverted from his explanation of Germany's methods of substitution of raw materials, looked put out and coughed aggressively.

Mrs Sprot came out with her hat on and picked up Betty.

Attention returned to Mr Cayley.

'You were saying, Mr Cayley?' said Tuppence.

But Mr Cayley was affronted. He said coldly:

'That woman is always plumping that child down and expecting people to look after it. I think I'll have the woollen muffler after all, dear. The sun is going in.'

'Oh, but, Mr Cayley, do go on with what you were telling us. It was so interesting,' said Miss Minton.

Mollified, Mr Cayley weightily resumed his discourse, drawing the folds of the woolly muffler closer round his stringy neck.

'As I was saying, Germany has so perfected her system of –'

Tuppence turned to Mrs Cayley, and asked:

'What do you think about the war, Mrs Cayley?'

Mrs Cayley jumped.

'Oh, what do I think? What – what do you mean?'

'Do you think it will last as long as six years?'

Mrs Cayley said doubtfully:

'Oh, I hope not. It's a very long time, isn't it?'

'Yes. A long time. What do you really think?'

Mrs Cayley seemed quite alarmed by the question. She said:

'Oh, I – I don't know. I don't know at all. Alfred says it will.'

'But you don't think so?'

'Oh, I don't know. It's difficult to say, isn't it?'

Tuppence felt a wave of exasperation. The chirruping Miss Minton, the dictatorial Mr Cayley, the nit-witted Mrs Cayley – were these people really typical of her fellow-countrymen? Was Mrs Sprot any better with her slightly vacant face and boiled gooseberry eyes? What could she, Tuppence, ever find out here? Not one of these people, surely –

Her thought was checked. She was aware of a shadow. Someone behind her who stood between her and the sun. She turned her head.

Mrs Perenna, standing on the terrace, her eyes on

the group. And something in those eyes – scorn, was it? A kind of withering contempt. Tuppence thought:

'I must find out more about Mrs Perenna.'

II

Tommy was establishing the happiest of relationships with Major Bletchley.

'Brought down some golf clubs with you, didn't you, Meadowes?'

Tommy pleaded guilty.

'Ha! I can tell you, *my* eyes don't miss much. Splendid. We must have a game together. Ever played on the links here?'

Tommy replied in the negative.

'They're not bad – not bad at all. Bit on the short side, perhaps, but lovely view over the sea and all that. And never very crowded. Look here, what about coming along with me this morning? We might have a game.'

'Thanks very much. I'd like it.'

'Must say I'm glad you've arrived,' remarked Bletchley as they were trudging up the hill. 'Too many women in that place. Gets on one's nerves. Glad I've got another fellow to keep me in countenance. You can't count Cayley – the man's a kind of walking chemist's shop.

Talks of nothing but his health and the treatment he's tried and the drugs he's taking. If he threw away all his little pill-boxes and went out for a good ten-mile walk every day he'd be a different man. The only other male in the place is von Deinim, and to tell you the truth, Meadowes, I'm not too easy in my mind about him.'

'No?' said Tommy.

'No. You take my word for it, this refugee business is dangerous. If I had my way I'd intern the lot of them. Safety first.'

'A bit drastic, perhaps.'

'Not at all. War's war. And I've got my suspicions of Master Carl. For one thing he's clearly not a Jew. Then he came over here just a month – only a month, mind you – before war broke out. That's a bit suspicious.'

Tommy said invitingly:

'Then you think –?'

'*Spying* – that's his little game!'

'But surely there's nothing of great military or naval importance hereabouts?'

'Ah, old man, that's where the artfulness comes in! If he were anywhere near Plymouth or Portsmouth he'd be under supervision. In a sleepy place like this, nobody bothers. But it's on the coast, isn't it? The truth of it is the Government is a great deal too easy with these enemy aliens. Anyone who cared could come over here and pull a long face and talk about their brothers in concentration camps. Look at that young man – arrogance in every line of him. He's a Nazi – that's what he is – a Nazi.'

'What we really need in this country is a witch doctor or two,' said Tommy pleasantly.

'Eh, what's that?'

'To smell out the spies,' Tommy explained gravely.

'Ha, very good that – very good. Smell 'em out – yes, of course.'

Further conversation was brought to an end, for they had arrived at the clubhouse.

Tommy's name was put down as a temporary member, he was introduced to the secretary, a vacant-looking elderly man, and the subscription duly paid. Tommy and the Major started on their round.

Tommy was a mediocre golfer. He was glad to find that his standard of play was just about right for his new friend. The Major won by two up and one to play, a very happy state of events.

'Good match, Meadowes, very good match – you had bad luck with that mashie shot, just turned off at the last minute. We must have a game fairly often. Come along and I'll introduce you to some of the fellows. Nice lot on the whole, some of them inclined to be rather old women, if you know what I mean? Ah, here's Haydock – you'll like Haydock. Retired naval wallah. Has that house on the cliff next door to us. He's our local ARP warden.'

Commander Haydock was a big hearty man with a weather-beaten face, intensely blue eyes, and a habit of shouting most of his remarks.

He greeted Tommy with friendliness.

'So you're going to keep Bletchley countenance at Sans Souci? He'll be glad of another man. Rather swamped by female society, eh, Bletchley?'

'I'm not much of a ladies' man,' said Major Bletchley.

'Nonsense,' said Haydock. 'Not your type of lady, my boy, that's it. Old boarding-house pussies. Nothing to do but gossip and knit.'

'You're forgetting Miss Perenna,' said Bletchley.

'Ah, Sheila – she's an attractive girl all right. Regular beauty if you ask me.'

'I'm a bit worried about her,' said Bletchley.

'What do you mean? Have a drink, Meadowes? What's yours, Major?'

The drinks ordered and the men settled on the veranda of the clubhouse, Haydock repeated his question.

Major Bletchley said with some violence:

'That German chap. She's seeing too much of him.'

'Getting sweet on him, you mean? H'm, that's bad. Of course he's a good-looking young chap in his way. But it won't do. It won't do, Bletchley. We can't have that sort of thing. Trading with the enemy, that's what it amounts to. These girls – where's their proper spirit? Plenty of decent young English fellows about.'

Bletchley said:

'Sheila's a queer girl – she gets odd sullen fits when she will hardly speak to anyone.'

'Spanish blood,' said the Commander. 'Her father was half Spanish, wasn't he?'

'Don't know. It's a Spanish name, I should think.'

The Commander glanced at his watch.

'About time for the news. We'd better go in and listen to it.'

The news was meagre that day, little more in it than had been already in the morning papers. After commenting with approval on the latest exploits of the Air Force – first-rate chaps, brave as lions – the Commander went on to develop his own pet theory – that sooner or later the Germans would attempt a landing at Leahampton itself – his argument being that it was such an unimportant spot.

'Not even an anti-aircraft gun in the place! Disgraceful!'

The argument was not developed, for Tommy and the Major had to hurry back to lunch at Sans Souci. Haydock extended a cordial invitation to Tommy to come and see his little place, 'Smugglers' Rest'. 'Marvellous view – my own beach – every kind of handy gadget in the house. Bring him along, Bletchley.'

It was settled that Tommy and Major Bletchley should come in for drinks on the evening of the following day.

III

After lunch was a peaceful time at Sans Souci. Mr Cayley went to have his 'rest' with the devoted Mrs Cayley in attendance. Mrs Blenkensop was conducted by Miss Minton to a depot to pack and address parcels for the Front.

Mr Meadowes strolled gently out into Leahampton and along the front. He bought a few cigarettes, stopped at Smith's to purchase the latest number of *Punch*, then after a few minutes of apparent irresolution, he entered a bus bearing the legend, 'OLD PIER'.

The old pier was at the extreme end of the promenade. That part of Leahampton was known to house agents as the least desirable end. It was West Leahampton and poorly thought of. Tommy paid 2d, and strolled up the pier. It was a flimsy and weather-worn affair, with a few moribund penny-in-the-slot machines placed at far distant intervals. There was no one on it but some children running up and down and screaming in voices that matched quite accurately the screaming of the gulls, and one solitary man sitting on the end fishing.

Mr Meadowes strolled up to the end and gazed down into the water. Then he asked gently:

'Caught anything?'

The fisherman shook his head.

'Don't often get a bite.' Mr Grant reeled in his line a bit. He said without turning his head:

'What about you, Meadowes?'

Tommy said:

'Nothing much to report as yet, sir. I'm digging myself in.'

'Good. Tell me.'

Tommy sat on an adjacent bollard, so placed that he commanded the length of the pier. Then he began:

'I've gone down quite all right, I think. I gather you've already got a list of the people there?' Grant nodded. 'There's nothing to report as yet. I've struck up a friendship with Major Bletchley. We played golf this morning. He seems the ordinary type of retired officer. If anything, a shade too typical. Cayley seems a genuine hypochondriacal invalid. That, again, would be an easy part to act. He has, by his own admission, been a good deal in Germany during the last few years.'

'A point,' said Grant laconically.

'Then there's von Deinim.'

'Yes, I don't need to tell you, Meadowes, that von Deinim's the one I'm most interested in.'

'You think he's N?'

Grant shook his head.

'No, I don't. As I see it, N couldn't afford to be a German.'

'Not a refugee from Nazi persecution, even?'

'Not even that. We watch, and they know we watch all the enemy aliens in this country. Moreover – this is in confidence, Beresford – very nearly all enemy aliens between 16 and 60 will be interned. Whether our adversaries are aware of that fact or not, they can at any rate anticipate that such a thing might happen. They would never risk the head of their organisation being interned. N therefore must be either a neutral – or else he is (apparently) an Englishman. The same, of course, applies to M. No, my meaning about von Deinim is this. He may be a link in the chain. N or M may not be at Sans Souci, it may be Carl von Deinim who is there and through him we may be led to our objective. That does seem to me highly possible. The more so as I cannot very well see that any of the other inmates of Sans Souci are likely to be the person we are seeking.'

'You've had them more or less vetted, I suppose, sir?'

Grant sighed – a sharp, quick sigh of vexation.

'No, that's just what it's impossible for me to do. I could have them looked up by the department easily enough – *but I can't risk it, Beresford.* For, you see, the rot is in the department itself. One hint that I've got my eye on Sans Souci for any reason – and the organisation may be put wise. That's where *you* come in, the outsider. That's why you've got to work in the dark, without help from us. It's our only chance – and I daren't risk alarming them. There's only one person I've been able to check up on.'

'Who's that, sir?'

'Carl von Deinim himself. That's easy enough. Routine. I can have him looked up – not from the Sans Souci angle, but from the enemy alien angle.'

Tommy asked curiously:

'And the result?'

A curious smile came over the other's face.

'Master Carl is exactly what he says he is. His father was indiscreet, was arrested and died in a concentration camp. Carl's elder brothers are in camps. His mother died in great distress of mind a year ago. He escaped to England a month before war broke out. Von Deinim has professed himself anxious to help this country. His work in a chemical research laboratory has been excellent and most helpful on the problem of immunising certain gases and in general decontamination experiments.'

Tommy said:

'Then he's all right?'

'Not necessarily. Our German friends are notorious for their thoroughness. If von Deinim was sent as an agent to England, special care would be taken that his record should be consistent with his own account of himself. There are two possibilities. The whole von Deinim family may be parties to the arrangement – not improbable under the painstaking Nazi régime. Or else this is not really Carl von Deinim but *a man playing the part of Carl von Deinim*.'

Tommy said slowly: 'I see.' He added inconsequently:

'He seems an awfully nice young fellow.'

Sighing, Grant said: 'They are – they nearly always are. It's an odd life this service of ours. We respect our adversaries and they respect us. You usually like your opposite number, you know – even when you're doing your best to down him.'

There was silence as Tommy thought over the strange anomaly of war. Grant's voice broke into his musings.

'But there are those for whom we've neither respect nor liking – and those are the traitors within our own ranks – the men who are willing to betray their country and accept office and promotion from the foreigner who has conquered it.'

Tommy said with feeling:

'My God, I'm with you, sir. That's a skunk's trick.'

'And deserves a skunk's end.'

Tommy said incredulously:

'And there really are these – these swine?'

'Everywhere. As I told you. In our service. In the fighting forces. On Parliamentary benches. High up in the Ministries. We've got to comb them out – we've *got* to! And we must do it quickly. It can't be done from the bottom – the small fry, the people who speak in the parks, who sell their wretched little news-sheets, they don't know who the big bugs are. It's the big bugs we want, they're the people who can do untold damage – and will do it unless we're in time.'

Tommy said confidently:

'We shall be in time, sir.'

Grant asked:

'What makes you say that?'

Tommy said:

'You've just said it – we've *got* to be!'

The man with the fishing line turned and looked full at his subordinate for a minute or two, taking in anew the quiet resolute line of the jaw. He had a new liking and appreciation of what he saw. He said quietly:

'Good man.'

He went on:

'What about the women in this place? Anything strike you as suspicious there?'

'I think there's something odd about the woman who runs it.'

'Mrs Perenna?'

'Yes. You don't – know anything about her?'

Grant said slowly:

'I might see what I could do about checking her antecedents, but as I told you, it's risky.'

'Yes, better not take any chances. She's the only one who strikes me as suspicious in any way. There's a young mother, a fussy spinster, the hypochondriac's brainless wife, and a rather fearsome-looking old Irishwoman. All seem harmless enough on the face of it.'

'That's the lot, is it?'

'No. There's a Mrs Blenkensop – arrived three days ago.'

'Well?'

Tommy said: 'Mrs Blenkensop is my wife.'

'What?'

In the surprise of the announcement Grant's voice was raised. He spun round, sharp anger in his gaze. 'I thought I told you, Beresford, not to breathe a word to your wife!'

'Quite right, sir, and I didn't. If you'll just listen –'

Succinctly, Tommy narrated what had occurred. He did not dare look at the other. He carefully kept out of his voice the pride that he secretly felt.

There was a silence when he brought the story to an end. Then a queer noise escaped from the other. Grant was laughing. He laughed for some minutes.

He said: 'I take my hat off to the woman! She's one in a thousand!'

'I agree,' said Tommy.

'Easthampton will laugh when I tell him this. He warned me not to leave her out. Said she'd get the better of me if I did. I wouldn't listen to him. It shows you, though, how damned careful you've got to be. I thought I'd taken every precaution against being overheard. I'd satisfied myself beforehand that you and your wife were alone in the flat. I actually heard the voice in the telephone asking your wife to come round at once, and so – and so I was tricked by the old simple device of the banged door. Yes, she's a smart woman, your wife.'

He was silent for a minute, then he said:

'Tell her from me, will you, that I eat dirt?'

'And I suppose, now, she's in on this?'

Mr Grant made an expressive grimace.

'She's in on it whether we like it or not. Tell her the department will esteem it an honour if she will condescend to work with us over the matter.'

'I'll tell her,' said Tommy with a faint grin.

Grant said seriously:

'You couldn't persuade her, I suppose, to go home and stay home?'

Tommy shook his head.

'You don't know Tuppence.'

'I think I am beginning to. I said that because – well, it's a dangerous business. If they get wise to you or to her –'

He left the sentence unfinished.

Tommy said gravely: 'I do understand that, sir.'

'But I suppose even you couldn't persuade your wife to keep out of danger.'

Tommy said slowly:

'I don't know that I really would want to do that . . . Tuppence and I, you see, aren't on those terms. We go into things – together!'

In his mind was that phrase, uttered years ago, at the close of an earlier war. A *joint venture* . . .

That was what his life with Tuppence had been and would always be – a Joint Venture . . .

Chapter 4

When Tuppence entered the lounge at Sans Souci just before dinner, the only occupant of the room was the monumental Mrs O'Rourke, who was sitting by the window looking like some gigantic Buddha.

She greeted Tuppence with a lot of geniality and verve.

'Ah now, if it isn't Mrs Blenkensop! You're like myself; it pleases you to be down to time and get a quiet minute or two before going into the dining-room, and a pleasant room this is in good weather with the windows open in the way that you'll not be noticing the smell of cooking. Terrible that is, in all of these places, and more especially if it's onion or cabbage that's on the fire. Sit here now, Mrs Blenkensop, and tell me what you've been doing with yourself this fine day and how you like Leahampton.'

There was something about Mrs O'Rourke that had

an unholy fascination for Tuppence. She was rather like an ogress dimly remembered from early fairy tales. With her bulk, her deep voice, her unabashed beard and moustache, her deep twinkling eyes and the impression she gave of being more than life-size, she was indeed not unlike some childhood's fantasy.

Tuppence replied that she thought she was going to like Leahampton very much, and be happy there.

'That is,' she added in a melancholy voice, 'as happy as I can be anywhere with this terrible anxiety weighing on me all the time.'

'Ah now, don't you be worrying yourself,' Mrs O'Rourke advised comfortably. 'Those boys of yours will come back to you safe and sound. Not a doubt of it. One of them's in the Air Force, so I think you said?'

'Yes, Raymond.'

'And is he in France now, or in England?'

'He's in Egypt at the moment, but from what he said in his last letter – not exactly *said* – but we have a little private code if you know what I mean? – certain sentences mean certain things. I think that's quite justified, don't you?'

Mrs O'Rourke replied promptly:

'Indeed I do. 'Tis a mother's privilege.'

'Yes, you see I feel I must know just where he is.'

Mrs O'Rourke nodded the Buddha-like head.

'I feel for you entirely, so I do. If I had a boy out there

I'd be deceiving the censor in the very same way, so I would. And your other boy, the one in the Navy?'

Tuppence entered obligingly upon a saga of Douglas.

'You see,' she cried, 'I feel so lost without my three boys. They've never been all away together from me before. They're all so sweet to me. I really do think they treat me more as a *friend* than a mother.' She laughed self-consciously. 'I have to scold them sometimes and *make* them go out without me.'

('What a pestilential woman I sound,' thought Tuppence to herself.)

She went on aloud:

'And really I didn't know quite *what* to do or *where* to go. The lease of my house in London was up and it seemed so foolish to renew it, and I thought if I came somewhere quiet, and yet with a good train service –' She broke off.

Again the Buddha nodded.

'I agree with you entirely. London is no place at the present. Ah! the gloom of it! I've lived there myself for many a year now. I'm by way of being an antique dealer, you know. You may know my shop in Cornaby Street, Chelsea? Kate Kelly's the name over the door. Lovely stuff I had there too – oh, lovely stuff – mostly glass – Waterford, Cork – beautiful. Chandeliers and lustres and punchbowls and all the rest of it. Foreign glass, too. And small furniture – nothing large – just small period pieces – mostly walnut and oak. Oh, lovely stuff – and I had some good customers. But there, when there's a war on, all that goes west. I'm lucky to be out of it with as little loss as I've had.'

A faint memory flickered through Tuppence's mind. A shop filled with glass, through which it was difficult to move, a rich persuasive voice, a compelling massive woman. Yes, surely, she had been into that shop.

Mrs O'Rourke went on:

'I'm not one of those that like to be always complaining – not like some that's in this house. Mr Cayley for one, with his muffler and his shawls and his moans about his business going to pieces. Of course it's to pieces, there's a war on – and his wife with never boo to say to a goose. Then there's that little Mrs Sprot, always fussing about her husband.'

'Is he out at the Front?'

'Not he. He's a tuppenny-halfpenny clerk in an insurance office, that's all, and so terrified of air raids he's had his wife down here since the beginning of the war. Mind you, I think that's right where the child's concerned – and a nice wee mite she is – but Mrs Sprot she frets, for all that her husband comes down when he can . . . Keeps saying Arthur must miss her so. But if you ask me Arthur's not missing her overmuch – maybe he's got other fish to fry.'

Tuppence murmured:

'I'm terribly sorry for all these mothers. If you let your children go away without you, you never stop worrying. And if you go with them it's hard on the husbands being left.'

'Ah! yes, and it comes expensive running two establishments.'

'This place seems quite reasonable,' said Tuppence.

'Yes, I'd say you get your money's worth. Mrs Perenna's a good manager. There's a queer woman for you now.'

'In what way?' asked Tuppence.

Mrs O'Rourke said with a twinkle:

'You'll be thinking I'm a terrible talker. It's true. I'm interested in all my fellow creatures, that's why I sit in this chair as often as I can. You see who goes in and who goes out and who's on the veranda and what goes on in the garden. What were we talking of now – ah yes, Mrs Perenna, and the queerness of her. There's been a grand drama in that woman's life, or I'm much mistaken.'

'Do you really think so?'

'I do now. And the mystery she makes of herself! "And where might you come from in Ireland?" I asked her. And would you believe it, she held out on me, declaring she was not from Ireland at all.'

'You think she is Irish?'

'Of course she's Irish. I know my own countrywomen. I could name you the county she comes from. But there! "I'm English," she says. "And my husband was a Spaniard" –'

Mrs O'Rourke broke off abruptly as Mrs Sprot came in, closely followed by Tommy.

Tuppence immediately assumed a sprightly manner.

'Good evening, Mr Meadowes. You look very brisk this evening.'

Tommy said:

'Plenty of exercise, that's the secret. A round of golf this morning and a walk along the front this afternoon.'

Millicent Sprot said:

'I took baby down to the beach this afternoon. She wanted to paddle but I really thought it was rather cold. I was helping her build a castle and a dog ran off with my knitting and pulled out yards of it. So annoying, and so difficult picking up all the stitches again. I'm such a bad knitter.'

'You're getting along fine with that helmet, Mrs Blenkensop,' said Mrs O'Rourke, suddenly turning her attention to Tuppence. 'You've been just racing along. I thought Miss Minton said that you were an inexperienced knitter.'

Tuppence flushed faintly. Mrs O'Rourke's eyes were

sharp. With a slightly vexed air, Tuppence said:

'I have really done quite a lot of knitting. I told Miss Minton so. But I think she likes teaching people.'

Everybody laughed in agreement, and a few minutes later the rest of the party came in and the gong was sounded.

The conversation during the meal turned on the absorbing subject of spies. Well-known hoary chestnuts were retold. The nun with the muscular arm, the clergyman descending from his parachute and using unclergymanlike language as he landed with a bump, the Austrian cook who secreted a wireless in her bedroom chimney, and all the things that had happened or nearly happened to aunts and second cousins of those present. That led easily to Fifth Column activities. To denunciations of the British Fascists, of the Communists, of the Peace Party, of conscientious objectors. It was a very normal conversation of the kind that may be heard almost every day, nevertheless Tuppence watched keenly the faces and demeanour of the people as they talked, striving to catch some tell-tale expression or word. But there was nothing. Sheila Perenna alone took no part in the conversation, but that might be put down to her habitual taciturnity. She sat there, her dark rebellious face sullen and brooding.

Carl von Deinim was out tonight, so tongues could be quite unrestrained.

Sheila only spoke once toward the end of dinner.

Mrs Sprot had just said in her thin fluting voice:

'Where I do think the Germans made such a mistake in the last war was to shoot Nurse Cavell. It turned everybody against them.'

It was then that Sheila, flinging back her head, demanded in her fierce young voice: 'Why shouldn't they shoot her? She was a spy, wasn't she?'

'Oh, no, not a spy.'

'She helped English people to escape – in an enemy country. That's the same thing. Why shouldn't she be shot?'

'Oh, but shooting a woman – and a nurse.'

Sheila got up.

'I think the Germans were quite right,' she said.

She went out of the window into the garden.

Dessert, consisting of some under-ripe bananas, and some tired oranges, had been on the table some time. Everyone rose and adjourned to the lounge for coffee.

Only Tommy unobtrusively betook himself to the garden. He found Sheila Perenna leaning over the terrace wall staring out at the sea. He came and stood beside her.

By her hurried, quick breathing he knew that something had upset her badly. He offered her a cigarette, which she accepted.

He said: 'Lovely night.'

In a low intense voice the girl answered:

'It could be . . .'

Tommy looked at her doubtfully. He felt, suddenly, the attraction and the vitality of this girl. There was a tumultuous life in her, a kind of compelling power. She was the kind of girl, he thought, that a man might easily lose his head over.

'If it weren't for the war, you mean?' he said.

'I don't mean that at all. I hate the war.'

'So do we all.'

'Not in the way I mean. I hate the cant about it, the smugness – the horrible, horrible patriotism.'

'Patriotism?' Tommy was startled.

'Yes, I hate patriotism, do you understand? All this *country, country, country*! Betraying your country – dying for your country – serving your country. Why should one's country mean anything at all?'

Tommy said simply: 'I don't know. It just does.'

'Not to me! Oh, it would to you – you go abroad and buy and sell in the British Empire and come back bronzed and full of clichés, talking about the natives and calling for Chota Pegs and all that sort of thing.'

Tommy said gently:

'I'm not quite as bad as that, I hope, my dear.'

'I'm exaggerating a little – but you know what I mean. You believe in the British Empire – and – and – the stupidity of dying for one's country.'

'My country,' said Tommy dryly, 'doesn't seem particularly anxious to allow me to die for it.'

'Yes, but you *want* to. And it's so *stupid*! *Nothing's* worth dying for. It's all an *idea* – talk, talk – froth – high-flown idiocy. My country doesn't mean anything to me at all.'

'Some day,' said Tommy, 'you'll be surprised to find that it does.'

'No. Never. I've suffered – I've seen –'

She broke off – then turned suddenly and impetuously upon him.

'Do you know who my father was?'

'No!' Tommy's interest quickened.

'His name was Patrick Maguire. He – he was a follower of Casement in the last war. He was shot as a traitor! All for nothing! For an idea – he worked himself up with those other Irishmen. Why couldn't he just stay at home quietly and mind his own business? He's a martyr to some people and a traitor to others. I think he was just – *stupid*!'

Tommy could hear the note of pent-up rebellion, coming out into the open. He said:

'So that's the shadow you've grown up with?'

'Shadow's right. Mother changed her name. We lived in Spain for some years. She always says that my father was half a Spaniard. We always tell lies wherever we go. We've been all over the Continent.

Finally we came here and started this place. I think this is quite the most hateful thing we've done yet.'

Tommy asked:

'How does your mother feel about – things?'

'You mean – about my father's death?' Sheila was silent a moment, frowning, puzzled. She said slowly: 'I've never really known . . . she never talks about it. It's not easy to know what Mother feels or thinks.'

Tommy nodded his head thoughtfully.

Sheila said abruptly:

'I – I don't know why I've been telling you this. I got worked up. Where did it all start?'

'A discussion on Edith Cavell.'

'Oh yes – patriotism. I said I hated it.'

'Aren't you forgetting Nurse Cavell's own words?'

'What words?'

'Before she died. Don't you know what she said?'

He repeated the words:

'*Patriotism is not enough . . . I must have no hatred in my heart.*'

'Oh.' She stood there stricken for a moment.

Then, turning quickly, she wheeled away into the shadow of the garden.

II

'So you see, Tuppence, it would all fit in.'

Tuppence nodded thoughtfully. The beach around them was empty. She herself leaned against a breakwater, Tommy sat above her and the breakwater itself, from which post he could see anyone who approached along the esplanade. Not that he expected to see anyone, having ascertained with a fair amount of accuracy where people would be this morning. In any case his rendezvous with Tuppence had borne all the signs of a casual meeting, pleasurable to the lady and slightly alarming to himself.

Tuppence said:

'Mrs Perenna?'

'Yes. M not N. She satisfies the requirements.'

Tuppence nodded thoughtfully again.

'Yes. She's Irish – as spotted by Mrs O'Rourke – won't admit the fact. Has done a good deal of coming and going on the Continent. Changed her name to Perenna, came here and started this boarding-house. A splendid bit of camouflage, full of innocuous bores. Her husband was shot as a traitor – she's got every incentive for running a Fifth Column show in this country. Yes, it fits. Is the girl in it too, do you think?'

Tommy said finally:

'Definitely not. She'd never have told me all this otherwise. I – I feel a bit of a cad, you know.'

Tuppence nodded with complete understanding.

'Yes, one does. In a way it's a foul job, this.'

'But very necessary.'

'Oh, of course.'

Tommy said, flushing slightly:

'I don't like lying any better than you do –'

Tuppence interrupted him.

'I don't mind lying in the least. To be quite honest I get a lot of artistic pleasure out of my lies. What gets me down is those moments when one forgets to lie – the times when one is just oneself – and gets results that way that you couldn't have got any other.' She paused and went on: 'That's what happened to you last night – with the girl. She responded to the *real* you – that's why you feel badly about it.'

'I believe you're right, Tuppence.'

'I know. Because I did the same thing myself – with the German boy.'

Tommy said:

'What do you think about him?'

Tuppence said quickly:

'If you ask me, I don't think he's got anything to do with it.'

'Grant thinks he has.'

'Your Mr Grant!' Tuppence's mood changed. She chuckled. 'How I'd like to have seen his face when you told him about me.'

'At any rate, he's made the *amende honorable*. You're definitely on the job.'

Tuppence nodded, but she looked a trifle abstracted. She said:

'Do you remember after the last war – when we were hunting down Mr Brown? Do you remember what fun it was? How excited we were?'

Tommy agreed, his face lighting up.

'Rather!'

'Tommy – why isn't it the same now?'

He considered the question, his quiet ugly face grave. Then he said:

'I suppose it's really – a question of age.'

Tuppence said sharply:

'You don't think – we're too old?'

'No, I'm sure we're not. It's only that – this time – it won't be *fun*. It's the same in other ways. This is the second war we've been in – and we feel quite different about this one.'

'I know – we see the pity of it and the waste – and the horror. All the things we were too young to think about before.'

'That's it. In the last war I was scared every now and then – and had some pretty close shaves, and went through hell once or twice, but there were good times too.'

Tuppence said:

'I suppose Derek feels like that?'

'Better not think about him, old thing,' Tommy advised.

'You're right.' Tuppence set her teeth. 'We've got a job. We're going to *do* that job. Let's get on with it. Have we found what we're looking for in Mrs Perenna?'

'We can at least say that she's strongly indicated. There's no one else, is there, Tuppence, that you've got your eye on?'

Tuppence considered.

'No, there isn't. The first thing I did when I arrived, of course, was to size them all up and assess, as it were, possibilities. Some of them seem quite impossible.'

'Such as?'

'Well, Miss Minton for instance, the "compleat" British spinster, and Mrs Sprot and her Betty, and the vacuous Mrs Cayley.'

'Yes, but nitwittishness can be assumed.'

'Oh, quite, but the fussy spinster and the absorbed young mother are parts that would be fatally easy to overdo – and these people are quite natural. Then, where Mrs Sprot is concerned, there's the child.'

'I suppose,' said Tommy, 'that even a secret agent might have a child.'

'Not with her on the job,' said Tuppence. 'It's not the kind of thing you'd bring a child into. I'm quite sure about that, Tommy. I *know*. You'd keep a child out of it.'

'I withdraw,' said Tommy. 'I'll give you Mrs Sprot and Miss Minton, but I'm not so sure about Mrs Cayley.'

'No, she might be a possibility. Because she really does overdo it. I mean there can't be many women *quite* as idiotic as she seems.'

'I have often noticed that being a devoted wife saps the intellect,' murmured Tommy.

'And where have you noticed that?' demanded Tuppence.

'Not from you, Tuppence. Your devotion has never reached those lengths.'

'For a man,' said Tuppence kindly, 'you don't really make an undue fuss when you are ill.'

Tommy reverted to a survey of possibilities.

'Cayley,' said Tommy thoughtfully. 'There might be something fishy about Cayley.'

'Yes, there might. Then there's Mrs O'Rourke?'

'What do you feel about her?'

'I don't quite know. She's disturbing. Rather *fee fo fum* if you know what I mean.'

'Yes, I think I know. But I rather fancy that's just the predatory note. She's that kind of woman.'

Tuppence said slowly:

'She – notices things.'

She was remembering the remark about knitting.

'Then there's Bletchley,' said Tommy.

'I've hardly spoken to him. He's definitely your chicken.'

'I *think* he's just the ordinary pukka old school tie. I *think* so.'

'That's just it,' said Tuppence, answering a stress rather than actual words. 'The worst of this sort of show is that you look at quite ordinary everyday people and twist them to suit your morbid requirements.'

'I've tried a few experiments on Bletchley,' said Tommy.

'What sort of thing? I've got some experiments in mind myself.'

'Well – just gentle ordinary little traps – about dates and places – all that sort of thing.'

'Could you condescend from the general to the particular?'

'Well, say we're talking of duck-shooting. He mentions the Fayum – good sport there such and such a year, such and such a month. Some other time I mention Egypt in quite a different connection. Mummies, Tutankhamen, something like that – has he seen that stuff? When was he there? Check up on the answers. Or P & O boats – I mention the names of one or two, say so and so was a comfortable boat. He mentions some trip or other, later I check that. Nothing important, or anything that puts him on his guard – just a check up on accuracy.'

'And so far he hasn't slipped up in any way?'

'Not once. And that's a pretty good test, let me tell you, Tuppence.'

'Yes, but I suppose *if* he was N he would have his story quite pat.'

'Oh yes – the main outlines of it. But it's not so easy not to trip up on unimportant details. And then occasionally you remember too much – more, that is, than a bona fide person would do. An ordinary person doesn't usually remember offhand whether they took a certain shooting trip in 1926 or 1927. They have to think a bit and search their memory.'

'But so far you haven't caught Bletchley out?'

'So far he's responded in a perfectly normal manner.'

'Result – negative.'

'Exactly.'

'Now,' said Tuppence. 'I'll tell you some of my ideas.'

And she proceeded to do so.

III

On her way home, Mrs Blenkensop stopped at the post office. She bought stamps and on her way out went into one of the public call boxes. There she rang up a certain number, and asked for 'Mr Faraday'. This was the accepted method of communication with Mr Grant. She came out smiling and walked slowly homewards, stopping on the way to purchase some knitting wool.

It was a pleasant afternoon with a light breeze. Tuppence curbed the natural energy of her own brisk trot to that leisurely pace that accorded with her conception of the part of Mrs Blenkensop. Mrs Blenkensop had nothing on earth to do with herself except knit (not too well) and write letters to her boys. She was always writing letters to her boys – sometimes she left them about half finished.

Tuppence came slowly up the hill towards Sans Souci. Since it was not a through road (it ended at Smugglers' Rest, Commander Haydock's house) there was never much traffic – a few tradesmen's vans in the morning. Tuppence passed house after house, amusing herself by noting their names. Bella Vista (inaccurately named, since the merest glimpse of the sea was to be obtained, and the main view was the vast Victorian bulk of Edenholme on the other side of the road). Karachi was the next house. After that came Shirley Tower. Then Sea View (appropriate this time), Castle Clare (somewhat grandiloquent, since it was a small house), Trelawny, a rival establishment to that of Mrs Perenna, and finally the vast maroon bulk of Sans Souci.

It was just as she came near to it that Tuppence became aware of a woman standing by the gate peering inside. There was something tense and vigilant about the figure.

Almost unconsciously, Tuppence softened the sound of her own footsteps, stepping cautiously upon her toes.

It was not until she was close behind her, that the woman heard her and turned. Turned with a start.

She was a tall woman, poorly, even meanly dressed, but her face was unusual. She was not young – probably just under forty – but there was a contrast between her face and the way she was dressed. She was fair-haired, with wide cheekbones, and had been – indeed still was – beautiful. Just for a minute Tuppence had a feeling that the woman's face was somehow familiar to her, but the feeling faded. It was not, she thought, a face easily forgotten.

The woman was obviously startled, and the flash of alarm that flitted across her face was not lost on Tuppence. (Something odd here?)

Tuppence said:

'Excuse me, are you looking for someone?'

The woman spoke in a slow, foreign voice, pronouncing the words carefully as though she had learnt them by heart.

'This 'ouse is Sans Souci?'

'Yes. I live there. Did you want someone?'

There was an infinitesimal pause, then the woman said:

'You can tell me please. There is a Mr Rosenstein there, no?'

'Mr Rosenstein?' Tuppence shook her head. 'No. I'm afraid not. Perhaps he has been there and left. Shall I ask for you?'

But the strange woman made a quick gesture of refusal. She said:

'No – no. I make mistake. Excuse, please.'

Then, quickly, she turned and walked rapidly down the hill again.

Tuppence stood staring after her. For some reason, her suspicions were aroused. There was a contrast between the woman's manner and her words. Tuppence had an idea that 'Mr Rosenstein' was a fiction, that the woman had seized at the first name that came into her head.

Tuppence hesitated a minute, then she started down the hill after the other. What she could only describe as a 'hunch' made her want to follow the woman.

Presently, however, she stopped. To follow would be to draw attention to herself in a rather marked manner. She had clearly been on the point of entering Sans Souci when she spoke to the woman; to reappear on her trail would be to arouse suspicion that Mrs Blenkensop was something other than appeared on the surface – that is to say if this strange woman was indeed a member of the enemy plot.

No, at all costs Mrs Blenkensop must remain what she seemed.

Tuppence turned and retraced her steps up the hill. She entered Sans Souci and paused in the hall. The house seemed deserted, as was usual early in the afternoon. Betty was having her nap, the elder members were either resting or had gone out.

Then, as Tuppence stood in the dim hall thinking over her recent encounter, a faint sound came to her ears. It was a sound she knew quite well – the faint echo of a ting.

The telephone at Sans Souci was in the hall. The sound that Tuppence had just heard was the sound made when the receiver of an extension is taken off or replaced. There was one extension in the house – in Mrs Perenna's bedroom.

Tommy might have hesitated. Tuppence did not hesitate for a minute. Very gently and carefully she lifted off the receiver and put it to her ear.

Someone was using the extension. It was a man's voice. Tuppence heard:

'– Everything going well. On the fourth, then, as arranged.'

A woman's voice said: 'Yes, carry on.'

There was a click as the receiver was replaced.

Tuppence stood there, frowning. Was that Mrs Perenna's voice? Difficult to say with only those three words to go upon. If there had been only a little more to the conversation. It might, of course, be quite an ordinary conversation – certainly there was nothing in the words she had overheard to indicate otherwise.

A shadow obscured the light from the door. Tuppence jumped and replaced the receiver as Mrs Perenna spoke.

'Such a pleasant afternoon. Are you going out, Mrs Blenkensop, or have you just come in?'

So it was not Mrs Perenna who had been speaking from Mrs Perenna's room. Tuppence murmured something about having had a pleasant walk and moved to the staircase.

Mrs Perenna moved along the hall after her. She seemed bigger than usual. Tuppence was conscious of her as a strong athletic woman.

She said:

'I must get my things off,' and hurried up the stairs.

As she turned the corner of the landing she collided with Mrs O'Rourke, whose vast bulk barred the top of the stairs.

'Dear, dear, now, Mrs Blenkensop, it's a great hurry you seem to be in.'

She did not move aside, just stood there smiling down at Tuppence just below her. There was, as always, a frightening quality about Mrs O'Rourke's smile.

And suddenly, for no reason, Tuppence felt afraid.

The big smiling Irishwoman, with her deep voice, barring her way, and below Mrs Perenna closing in at the foot of the stairs.

Tuppence glanced over her shoulder. Was it her fancy that there was something definitely menacing in Mrs Perenna's upturned face? Absurd, she told herself, absurd. In broad daylight – in a commonplace seaside boarding-house. But the house was so very quiet. Not a sound. And she herself here on the stairs between the two of them. Surely there *was* something a little queer in Mrs O'Rourke's smile – some fixed ferocious quality about it, Tuppence thought wildly, 'like a cat with a mouse'.

And then suddenly the tension broke. A little figure darted along the top-landing uttering shrill squeals of mirth. Little Betty Sprot in vest and knickers. Darting past Mrs O'Rourke, shouting happily, 'Peek bo,' as she flung herself on Tuppence.

The atmosphere had changed. Mrs O'Rourke, a big genial figure, was crying out:

'Ah, the darlin'. It's a great girl she's getting.'

Below, Mrs Perenna had turned away to the door that led into the kitchen. Tuppence, Betty's hand clasped in hers, passed Mrs O'Rourke and ran along the passage to where Mrs Sprot was waiting to scold the truant.

Tuppence went in with the child.

She felt a queer sense of relief at the domestic atmosphere – the child's clothes lying about, the woolly toys, the painted crib, the sheeplike and somewhat unattractive face of Mr Sprot in its frame on the dressing-table, the burble of Mrs Sprot's denunciation of laundry prices and really she thought Mrs Perenna was a little unfair in refusing to sanction guests having their own electric irons –

All so normal, so reassuring, so everyday.

And yet – just now – on the stairs.

'Nerves,' said Tuppence to herself. 'Just nerves!'

But had it been nerves? Someone *had* been telephoning from Mrs Perenna's room. Mrs O'Rourke? Surely a very odd thing to do. It ensured, of course, that you would not be overheard by the household.

It must have been, Tuppence thought, a very short conversation. The merest brief exchange of words.

'Everything going well. On the fourth as arranged.'

It might mean nothing – or a good deal.

The fourth. Was that a date? The fourth, say of a month?

Or it might mean the fourth seat, or the fourth lamp-post, or the fourth breakwater – impossible to know.

It might just conceivably mean the Forth Bridge. There had been an attempt to blow that up in the last war.

Did it mean anything at all?

It might quite easily have been the confirmation of some perfectly ordinary appointment. Mrs Perenna might have told Mrs O'Rourke she could use the telephone in her bedroom any time she wanted to do so.

And the atmosphere on the stairs, that tense moment, might have been just her own overwrought nerves . . .

The quiet house – the feeling that there was something sinister – something evil . . .

'Stick to facts, Mrs Blenkensop,' said Tuppence sternly. 'And get on with your job.'

Chapter 5

Commander Haydock turned out to be a most genial host. He welcomed Mr Meadowes and Major Bletchley with enthusiasm, and insisted on showing the former 'all over my little place'.

Smugglers' Rest had been originally a couple of coastguards' cottages standing on the cliff overlooking the sea. There was a small cove below, but the access to it was perilous, only to be attempted by adventurous boys.

Then the cottages had been bought by a London business man who had thrown them into one and attempted half-heartedly to make a garden. He had come down occasionally for short periods in summer.

After that, the cottages had remained empty for some years, being let with a modicum of furniture to summer visitors.

'Then, some years ago,' explained Haydock, 'it was

sold to a man called Hahn. He was a German, and if you ask me, he was neither more or less than a spy.'

Tommy's ears quickened.

'That's interesting,' he said, putting down the glass from which he had been sipping sherry.

'Damned thorough fellows they are,' said Haydock. 'Getting ready even then for this show – at least that is my opinion. Look at the situation of this place. Perfect for signalling out to sea. Cove below where you could land a motor-boat. Completely isolated owing to the contour of the cliff. Oh yes, don't tell me that fellow Hahn wasn't a German agent.'

Major Bletchley said:

'Of course he was.'

'What happened to him?' asked Tommy.

'Ah!' said Haydock. 'Thereby hangs a tale. Hahn spent a lot of money on this place. He had a way cut down to the beach for one thing – concrete steps – expensive business. Then he had the whole of the house done over – bathrooms, every expensive gadget you can imagine. And who did he set to do all this? Not a local man. No, a firm from London, so it was said – but a lot of the men who came down were foreigners. Some of them *didn't speak a word of English*. Don't you agree with me that that sounds extremely fishy?'

'A little odd, certainly,' agreed Tommy.

'I was in the neighbourhood myself at the time, living in a bungalow, and I got interested in what this fellow was up to. I used to hang about to watch the workmen. Now I'll tell you this – they didn't like it – they didn't like it at all. Once or twice they were quite threatening about it. Why should they be if everything was all square and above board?'

Bletchley nodded agreement.

'You ought to have gone to the authorities,' he said.

'Just what I did do, my dear fellow. Made a positive nuisance of myself pestering the police.'

He poured himself out another drink.

'And what did I get for my pains? Polite inattention. Blind and deaf, that's what we were in this country. Another war with Germany was out of the question – there was peace in Europe – our relations with Germany were excellent. Natural sympathy between us nowadays. I was regarded as an old fossil, a war maniac, a diehard old sailor. What was the good of pointing out to people that the Germans were building the finest Air Force in Europe and not just to fly round and have picnics!'

Major Bletchley said explosively:

'Nobody believed it! Damned fools! "Peace in our time." "Appeasement." All a lot of blah!'

Haydock said, his face redder than usual with

suppressed anger: 'A warmonger, that's what they called me. The sort of chap, they said, who was an obstacle to peace. Peace! I knew what our Hun friends were at! And mind this, they prepare things a long time beforehand. I was convinced that Mr Hahn was up to no good. I didn't like his foreign workmen. I didn't like the way he was spending money on this place. I kept on badgering away at people.'

'Stout fellow,' said Bletchley appreciatively.

'And finally,' said the Commander, 'I began to make an impression. We had a new Chief Constable down here – retired soldier. And he had the sense to listen to me. His fellows began to nose around. Sure enough, Hahn decamped. Just slipped out and disappeared one fine night. The police went over this place with a search-warrant. In a safe which had been built-in in the dining-room they found a wireless transmitter and some pretty damaging documents. Also a big store place under the garage for petrol – great tanks. I can tell you I was cock-a-hoop over that. Fellows at the club used to rag me about my German spy complex. They dried up after that. Trouble with us in this country is that we're so absurdly unsuspicious.'

'It's a crime. Fools – that's what we are – fools. Why don't we intern all these refugees?' Major Bletchley was well away.

'End of the story was I bought the place when it came

into the market,' continued the Commander, not to be side-tracked from his pet story. 'Come and have a look round, Meadowes?'

'Thanks, I'd like to.'

Commander Haydock was as full of zest as a boy as he did the honours of the establishment. He threw open the big safe in the dining-room to show where the secret wireless had been found. Tommy was taken out to the garage and was shown where the big petrol tanks had lain concealed, and finally, after a superficial glance at the two excellent bathrooms, the special lighting, and the various kitchen 'gadgets', he was taken down the steep concreted path to the little cove beneath, whilst Commander Haydock told him all over again how extremely useful the whole lay-out would be to an enemy in wartime.

He was taken into the cave which gave the place its name, and Haydock pointed out enthusiastically how it could have been used.

Major Bletchley did not accompany the two men on their tour, but remained peacefully sipping his drink on the terrace. Tommy gathered that the Commander's spy hunt with its successful issue was that good gentleman's principal topic of conversation, and that his friends had heard it many times.

In fact, Major Bletchley said as much when they were walking down to Sans Souci a little later.

'Good fellow, Haydock,' he said. 'But he's not content to let a good thing alone. We've heard all about that business again and again until we're sick of it. He's as proud of the whole bag of tricks up there as a cat of its kittens.'

The simile was not too far-fetched, and Tommy assented with a smile.

The conversation then turning to Major Bletchley's own successful unmasking of a dishonest bearer in 1923, Tommy's attention was free to pursue its own inward line of thought punctuated by sympathetic 'Not reallys?' – 'You don't say so?' and 'What an extraordinary business' which was all Major Bletchley needed in the way of encouragement.

More than ever now Tommy felt that when the dying Farquhar had mentioned Sans Souci he had been on the right track. Here, in this out of the world spot, preparations had been made a long time beforehand. The arrival of the German Hahn and his extensive installation showed clearly enough that this particular part of the coast had been selected for a rallying point, a focus of enemy activity.

That particular game had been defeated by the unexpected activity of the suspicious Commander Haydock. Round one had gone to Britain. But supposing that Smugglers' Rest had been only the first outpost of a complicated scheme of attack? Smugglers'

Rest, that is to say, had represented sea communications. Its beach, inaccessible save for the path down from above, would lend itself admirably to the plan. But it was only a part of the whole.

Defeated on that part of the plan by Haydock, what had been the enemy's response? Might not he have fallen back upon the next best thing – that is to say, Sans Souci. The exposure of Hahn had come about four years ago. Tommy had an idea, from what Sheila Perenna had said, that it was very soon after that that Mrs Perenna had returned to England and bought Sans Souci. The next move in the game?

It would seem therefore that Leahampton was definitely an enemy centre – that there were already installations and affiliations in the neighbourhood.

His spirits rose. The depression engendered by the harmless and futile atmosphere of Sans Souci disappeared. Innocent as it seemed, that innocence was no more than skin deep. Behind that innocuous mask things were going on.

And the focus of it all, so far as Tommy could judge, was Mrs Perenna. The first thing to do was to know more about Mrs Perenna, to penetrate behind her apparently simple routine of running her boarding establishment. Her correspondence, her acquaintances, her social or war-working activities – somewhere in all these must lie the essence of her real activities. If

Mrs Perenna was the renowned woman agent – M – then it was she who controlled the whole of the Fifth Column activities in this country. Her identity would be known to few – only to those at the top. But communications she must have with her chiefs of staff, and it was those communications that he and Tuppence had got to tap.

At the right moment, as Tommy saw well enough, Smugglers' Rest could be seized and held – by a few stalwarts operating from Sans Souci. That moment was not yet, but it might be very near.

Once the German army was established in control of the channel ports in France and Belgium, they could concentrate on the invasion and subjugation of Britain, and things were certainly going very badly in France at the moment.

Britain's Navy was all-powerful on the sea, so the attack must come by air and by internal treachery – and if the threads of internal treachery were in Mrs Perenna's keeping there was no time to lose.

Major Bletchley's words chimed in with his thoughts:

'I saw, you know, that there was no time to lose. I got hold of Abdul, my syce – good fellow, Abdul –'

The story droned on.

Tommy was thinking:

'Why Leahampton? Any reason? It's out of the mainstream – bit of a backwater. Conservative, old-fashioned.

All those points make it desirable. Is there anything else?'

There was a stretch of flat agricultural country behind it running inland. A lot of pasture. Suitable, therefore, for the landing of troop-carrying airplanes or of parachute troops. But that was true of many other places. There was also a big chemical works where, it might be noted, Carl von Deinim was employed.

Carl von Deinim. How did he fit in? Only too well. He was not, as Grant had pointed out, the real head. A cog, only, in the machine. Liable to suspicion and internment at any moment. But in the meantime he might have accomplished what had been his task. He had mentioned to Tuppence that he was working on decontamination problems and on the immunising of certain gases. There were probabilities there – probabilities unpleasant to contemplate.

Carl, Tommy decided (a little reluctantly), was in it. A pity, because he rather liked the fellow. Well, he was working for his country – taking his life in his hands. Tommy had respect for such an adversary – down him by all means – a firing-party was the end, but you knew that when you took on your job.

It was the people who betrayed their own land – from within – that really roused a slow vindictive passion in him. By God, he'd get them!

'– And that's how I got them!' The Major wound up his story triumphantly. 'Pretty smart bit of work, eh?'

Unblushingly Tommy said:

'Most ingenious thing I've heard in my life, Major.'

II

Mrs Blenkensop was reading a letter on thin foreign paper stamped outside with the censor's mark.

Incidentally the direct result of her conversation with 'Mr Faraday'.

'Dear Raymond,' she murmured. 'I was so happy about him out in Egypt, and now, it seems, there is a big change round. All *very* secret, of course, and he can't *say* anything – just that there really is a marvellous plan and that I'm to be ready for some *big surprise* soon. I'm glad to know where he's being sent, but I really don't see why –'

Bletchley grunted.

'Surely he's not allowed to tell you that?'

Tuppence gave a deprecating laugh and looked round the breakfast table as she folded up her precious letter.

'Oh! we have our methods,' she said archly. 'Dear Raymond knows that if only I know where he is or where he's going I don't worry quite so much. It's quite a simple way, too. Just a certain word, you know, and after it the initial letters of the next words spell out the place. Of course it makes rather a funny sentence sometimes – but Raymond is really most ingenious. I'm sure *nobody* would notice.'

Little murmurs arose round the table. The moment was well chosen; everybody happened to be at the breakfast table together for once.

Bletchley, his face rather red, said:

'You'll excuse me, Mrs Blenkensop, but that's a damned foolish thing to do. Movements of troops and air squadrons are just what the Germans want to know.'

'Oh, but I never tell anyone,' cried Tuppence. 'I'm very, very careful.'

'All the same it's an unwise thing to do – and your boy will get into trouble over it some day.'

'Oh, I do hope not. I'm his *mother*, you see. A mother *ought* to know.'

'Indeed and I think you're right,' boomed out Mrs O'Rourke. 'Wild horses wouldn't drag the information from you – we know that.'

'Letters can be read,' said Bletchley.

'I'm very careful never to leave letters lying about,' said Tuppence with an air of outraged dignity. 'I always keep them locked up.'

Bletchley shook his head doubtfully.

III

It was a grey morning with the wind blowing coldly from the sea. Tuppence was alone at the far end of the beach.

She took from her bag two letters that she had just called for at a small newsagent's in the town.

They had taken some time in coming since they had been readdressed there, the second time to a Mrs Spender. Tuppence liked crossing her tracks. Her children believed her to be in Cornwall with an old aunt.

She opened the first letter.

'Dearest Mother,

'Lots of funny things I could tell you only I mustn't. We're putting up a good show, I think. Five German planes before breakfast is today's market quotation. Bit of a mess at the moment and all that, but we'll get there all right in the end.

'It's the way they machine-gun the poor civilian devils on the roads that gets me. It makes us all see red. Gus and Trundles want to be remembered to you. They're still going strong.

'Don't worry about me. I'm all right. Wouldn't have missed this show for the world. Love to old Carrot Top –

have the W.O. given him a job yet?

'Yours ever,

'Derek.'

Tuppence's eyes were very bright and shining as she read and re-read this.

Then she opened the other letter.

'Dearest Mum,

'How's old Aunt Gracie? Going strong? I think you're wonderful to stick it. I couldn't.

'No news. My job is very interesting, but so hush-hush I can't tell you about it. But I really do feel I'm doing something worthwhile. Don't fret about not getting any war work to do – it's so silly all these elderly women rushing about wanting to do *things. They only really want people who are young and efficient. I wonder how Carrots is getting on at his job up in Scotland? Just filling up forms, I suppose. Still he'll be happy to feel he is doing something.*

'Lots of love,

'Deborah.'

Tuppence smiled.

She folded the letters, smoothed them lovingly, and then under the shelter of a breakwater she struck a match and set them on fire. She waited until they were reduced to ashes.

Taking out her fountain-pen and a small writing-pad, she wrote rapidly.

'Langherne,
Cornwall.

'Dearest Deb,

'It seems so remote from the war here that I can hardly believe there is a war going on. Very glad to get your letter and know that your work is interesting.

'Aunt Gracie has grown much more feeble and very hazy in her mind. I think she is glad to have me here. She talks a good deal about the old days and sometimes, I think, confuses me with my own mother. They are growing more vegetables than usual – have turned the rose-garden into potatoes. I help old Sikes a bit. It makes me feel I am doing something in the war. Your father seems a bit disgruntled, but I think, as you say, he too is glad to be doing something.

'Love from your
'TUPPENNY MOTHER.'

She took a fresh sheet.

'Darling Derek,

'A great comfort to get your letter. Send field postcards often if you haven't time to write.

'I've come down to be with Aunt Gracie a bit. She is very feeble. She will talk of you as though you were seven and gave me ten shillings yesterday to send you as a tip.

'I'm still on the shelf and nobody wants my invaluable services! Extraordinary! Your father, as I told you, has got a job in the Ministry of Requirements. He is up north somewhere. Better than nothing, but not what he wanted, poor old Carrot Top. Still I suppose we've got to be humble and take a back seat and leave the war to you young idiots.

'I won't say "Take care of yourself", because I gather that the whole point is that you should do just the opposite. But don't go and be stupid.

'Lots of love,

'TUPPENCE.'

She put the letters into envelopes, addressed and stamped them, and posted them on her way back to Sans Souci.

As she reached the bottom of the cliff her attention was caught by two figures standing talking a little way up.

Tuppence stopped dead. It was the same woman

she had seen yesterday and talking to her was Carl von Deinim.

Regretfully Tuppence noted the fact that there was no cover. She could not get near them unseen and overhear what was being said.

Moreover, at that moment, the young German turned his head and saw her. Rather abruptly, the two figures parted. The woman came rapidly down the hill, crossing the road and passing Tuppence on the other side.

Carl von Deinim waited until Tuppence came up to him.

Then, gravely and politely, he wished her good morning.

Tuppence said immediately:

'What a very odd-looking woman that was to whom you were talking, Mr Deinim.'

'Yes. It is a Central European type. She is a Pole.'

'Really? A – a friend of yours?'

Tuppence's tone was a very good copy of the inquisitive voice of Aunt Gracie in her younger days.

'Not at all,' said Carl stiffly. 'I never saw the woman before.'

'Oh really. I thought –' Tuppence paused artistically.

'She asked me only for a direction. I speak German to her because she does not understand much English.'

'I see. And she was asking the way somewhere?'

'She asked me if I knew a Mrs Gottlieb near here. I do not, and she says she has, perhaps, got the name of the house wrong.'

'I see,' said Tuppence thoughtfully.

Mr Rosenstein. Mrs Gottlieb.

She stole a swift glance at Carl von Deinim. He was walking beside her with a set stiff face.

Tuppence felt a definite suspicion of this strange woman. And she felt almost convinced that when she had first caught sight of them, the woman and Carl had been already talking some time together.

Carl von Deinim?

Carl and Sheila that morning. '*You must be careful.*'

Tuppence thought:

'I hope – I hope these young things *aren't* in it!'

Soft, she told herself, middle-aged and soft! That's what she was! The Nazi creed was a youth creed. Nazi agents would in all probability be young. Carl and Sheila. Tommy said Sheila wasn't in it. Yes, but Tommy was a man, and Sheila was beautiful with a queer breath-taking beauty.

Carl and Sheila, and behind them that enigmatic figure: Mrs Perenna. Mrs Perenna, sometimes the voluble commonplace guesthouse hostess, sometimes, for fleeting minutes, a tragic, violent personality.

Tuppence went slowly upstairs to her bedroom.

That evening, when she went to bed, she pulled out

the long drawer of her bureau. At one side of it was a small japanned box with a flimsy cheap lock. Tuppence slipped on gloves, unlocked the box, and opened it. A pile of letters lay inside. On the top was the one received that morning from 'Raymond'. Tuppence unfolded it with due precautions.

Then her lips set grimly. There had been an eyelash in the fold of the paper this morning. The eyelash was not there now.

She went to the washstand. There was a little bottle labelled innocently: 'Grey powder' with a dose.

Adroitly Tuppence dusted a little of the powder on to the letter and on to the surface of the glossy japanned enamel of the box.

There were no fingerprints on either of them.

Again Tuppence nodded her head with a certain grim satisfaction.

For there should have been fingerprints – her own.

A servant might have read the letters out of curiosity, though it seemed unlikely – certainly unlikely that she should have gone to the trouble of finding a key to fit the box.

But a servant would not think of wiping off fingerprints.

Mrs Perenna? Sheila? Somebody else? Somebody, at least, who was interested in the movements of British armed forces.

IV

Tuppence's plan of campaign had been simple in its outlines. First, a general sizing up of probabilities and possibilities. Second, an experiment to determine whether there was or was not an inmate of Sans Souci who was interested in troop movements and anxious to conceal the fact. Third – who that person was?

It was concerning that third operation that Tuppence pondered as she lay in bed the following morning. Her train of thought was slightly hampered by Betty Sprot, who had pranced in at an early hour, preceding indeed the cup of somewhat tepid inky liquid known as Morning Tea.

Betty was both active and voluble. She had taken a great fancy to Tuppence. She climbed up on the bed and thrust an extremely tattered picture-book under Tuppence's nose, commanding with brevity:

'Wead.'

Tuppence read obediently.

'Goosey goosey gander, whither will you wander?

'Upstairs, downstairs, in my lady's chamber.'

Betty rolled with mirth – repeating in an ecstasy:

'Upstares – upstares – upstares –' and then with a sudden climax, '*Down* –' and proceeded to roll off the bed with a thump.

This proceeding was repeated several times until it palled. Then Betty crawled about the floor, playing with Tuppence's shoes and muttering busily to herself in her own particular idiom:

'Ag do – bah pit – soo – soodah – putch –'

Released to fly back to its own perplexities, Tuppence's mind forgot the child. The words of the nursery rhyme seemed to mock at her.

'Goosey – goosey, gander, whither shall ye wander?'

Whither indeed? Goosey, that was her, Gander was Tommy. It was, at any rate, what they appeared to be! Tuppence had the heartiest contempt for Mrs Blenkensop. Mr Meadowes, the thought, was a little better – stolid, British, unimaginative – quite incredibly stupid. Both of them, she hoped, fitting nicely into the background of Sans Souci. Both such possible people to be there.

All the same, one must not relax – a slip was so easy. She had made one the other day – nothing that mattered, but just a sufficient indication to warn her to be careful. Such an easy approach to intimacy and good relations – an indifferent knitter asking for guidance. But she had forgotten that one evening, her fingers had slipped into their own practised efficiency, the needles clicking busily with the even note of the experienced knitter. Mrs O'Rourke had noticed it. Since then, she had carefully struck a medium course – not so clumsy as she had been at first – but not so rapid as she could be.

'Ag boo bate?' demanded Betty. She reiterated the question: 'Ag boo bate?'

'Lovely, darling,' said Tuppence absently. 'Beautiful.'

Satisfied, Betty relapsed into murmurs again.

Her next step, Tuppence thought, could be managed easily enough. That is to say with the connivance of Tommy. She saw exactly how to do it –

Lying there planning, time slipped by. Mrs Sprot came in, breathless, to seek for Betty.

'Oh, here she is. I couldn't think where she had got to. Oh, Betty, you naughty girl – oh, dear, Mrs Blenkensop, I am so sorry.'

Tuppence sat up in bed. Betty, with an angelic face, was contemplating her handiwork.

She had removed all the laces from Tuppence's shoes and had immersed them in a toothglass of water. She was prodding them now with a gleeful finger.

Tuppence laughed and cut short Mrs Sprot's apologies.

'How frightfully funny. Don't worry, Mrs Sprot, they'll recover all right. It's my fault. I should have noticed what she was doing. She was rather quiet.'

'I know,' Mrs Sprot sighed. 'Whenever they're quiet,

it's a bad sign. I'll get you some more laces this morning, Mrs Blenkensop.'

'Don't bother,' said Tuppence. 'They'll dry none the worse.'

Mrs Sprot bore Betty away and Tuppence got up to put her plan into execution.

Chapter 6

Tommy looked rather gingerly at the packet that Tuppence thrust upon him.

'Is this it?'

'Yes. Be careful. Don't get it over you.'

Tommy took a delicate sniff at the packet and replied with energy.

'No, indeed. What is this frightful stuff?'

'Asafoetida,' replied Tuppence. 'A pinch of that and you will wonder why your boy-friend is no longer attentive, as the advertisements say.'

'Shades of BO,' murmured Tommy.

Shortly after that, various incidents occurred.

The first was the smell in Mr Meadowes' room.

Mr Meadowes, not a complaining man by nature, spoke about it mildly at first, then with increasing firmness.

Mrs Perenna was summoned into conclave. With all

the will to resist in the world, she had to admit that there was a smell. A pronounced unpleasant smell. Perhaps, she suggested, the gas tap of the fire was leaking.

Bending down and sniffing dubiously, Tommy remarked that he did not think the smell came from there. Nor from under the floor. He himself thought, definitely – a dead rat.

Mrs Perenna admitted that she had heard of such things – but she was sure there were no rats at Sans Souci. Perhaps a mouse – though she herself had never seen a mouse.

Mr Meadowes said with firmness that he thought the smell indicated at least a rat – and he added, still more firmly, that he was not going to sleep another night in the room until the matter had been seen to. He would ask Mrs Perenna to change his room.

Mrs Perenna said, 'Of course, she had just been about to suggest the same thing. She was afraid that the only room vacant was rather a small one and unfortunately it had no sea view, but if Mr Meadowes did not mind that –'

Mr Meadowes did not. His only wish was to get away from the smell. Mrs Perenna thereupon accompanied him to a small bedroom, the door of which happened to be just opposite the door of Mrs Blenkensop's room, and summoned the adenoidal semi-idiotic Beatrice to 'move

Mr Meadowes' things'. She would, she explained, send for 'a man' to take up the floor and search for the origin of the smell.

Matters were settled satisfactorily on this basis.

II

The second incident was Mr Meadowes' hay fever. That was what he called it at first. Later he admitted doubtfully that he might just possibly have caught cold. He sneezed a good deal, and his eyes ran. If there was a faint elusive suggestion of raw onion floating in the breeze in the vicinity of Mr Meadowes' large silk handkerchief nobody noticed the fact, and indeed a pungent amount of eau de cologne masked the more penetrating odour.

Finally, defeated by incessant sneezing and nose-blowing, Mr Meadowes retired to bed for the day.

It was on the morning of that day that Mrs Blenkensop received a letter from her son Douglas. So excited and thrilled was Mrs Blenkensop that everybody at Sans Souci heard about it. The letter had not been censored at all, she explained, because fortunately one of Douglas's friends coming on leave had brought it, so for once Douglas had been able to write quite fully.

'And it just shows,' declared Mrs Blenkensop, wagging her head sagely, 'how little we know really of what is going on.'

After breakfast she went upstairs to her room, opened the japanned box and put the letter away. Between the folded pages were some unnoticeable grains of rice powder. She closed the box again, pressing her fingers firmly on its surface.

As she left her room she coughed, and from opposite came the sound of a highly histrionic sneeze.

Tuppence smiled and proceeded downstairs.

She had already made known her intention of going up to London for the day – to see her lawyer on some business and to do a little shopping.

Now she was given a good send-off by the assembled boarders and entrusted with various commissions – 'only if you have time, of course'.

Major Bletchley held himself aloof from this female chatter. He was reading his paper and uttering appropriate comments aloud. 'Damned swines of Germans. Machine-gunning civilian refugees on the roads. Damned brutes. If I were our people –'

Tuppence left him still outlining what *he* would do if he were in charge of operations.

She made a detour through the garden to ask Betty Sprot what she would like as a present from London.

Betty ecstatically clasping a snail in two hot hands

gurgled appreciatively. In response to Tuppence's suggestions – 'A pussy. A picture-book? Some coloured chalks to draw with?' – Betty decided, 'Betty dwar.' So the coloured chalks were noted down on Tuppence's list.

As she passed on meaning to rejoin the drive by the path at the end of the garden she came unexpectedly upon Carl von Deinim. He was standing leaning on the wall. His hands were clenched, and as Tuppence approached he turned on her, his usually impassive face convulsed with emotion.

Tuppence paused involuntarily and asked:

'Is anything the matter?'

'Ach, yes, everything is the matter.' His voice was hoarse and unnatural. 'You have a saying here that a thing is neither fish, flesh, fowl, nor good red herring, have you not?'

Tuppence nodded.

Carl went on bitterly:

'That is what I am. It cannot go on, that is what I say. It cannot go on. It would be best, I think, to end everything.'

'What do you mean?'

The young man said:

'You have spoken kindly to me. You would, I think, understand. I fled from my own country because of injustice and cruelty. I came here to find freedom. I hated Nazi Germany. But, alas, I am still a German. Nothing can alter that.'

Tuppence murmured:

'You may have difficulties, I know –'

'It is not that. I am a German, I tell you. In my heart – in my feeling. Germany is still my country. When I read of German cities bombed, of German soldiers dying, of German aeroplanes brought down – they are my people who die. When that old fire-eating Major reads out from his paper, when he say "those swine" – I am moved to fury – I cannot bear it.'

He added quietly:

'And so I think it would be best, perhaps, to end it all. Yes, to end it.'

Tuppence took hold of him firmly by the arm.

'Nonsense,' she said robustly. 'Of course you feel as you do. Anyone would. But you've got to stick it.'

'I wish they would intern me. It would be easier so.'

'Yes, probably it would. But in the meantime you're doing useful work – or so I've heard. Useful not only to England but to humanity. You're working on decontamination problems, aren't you?'

His face lit up slightly.

'Ah yes, and I begin to have much success. A process very simple, easily made and not complicated to apply.'

'Well,' said Tuppence, 'that's worth doing. Anything that mitigates suffering is worthwhile – and anything that's constructive and not destructive. Naturally we've got to call the other side names. They're doing just the same in Germany. Hundreds of Major Bletchleys – foaming at the mouth. I hate the Germans myself. "The Germans," I say, and feel waves of loathing. But when I think of individual Germans, mothers sitting anxiously waiting for news of their sons, and boys leaving home to fight, and peasants getting in the harvests, and little shopkeepers and some of the nice kindly German people I know, I feel quite different. I know then that they are just human beings and that we're all feeling alike. That's the real thing. The other is just the war mask that you put on. It's a part of war – probably a necessary part – but it's ephemeral.'

As she spoke she thought, as Tommy had done not long before, of Nurse Cavell's words: 'Patriotism is not enough. I must have no hatred in my heart.'

That saying of a most truly patriotic woman had always seemed to them both the high-water mark of sacrifice.

Carl von Deinim took her hand and kissed it. He said:

'I thank you. What you say is good and true. I will have more fortitude.'

'Oh, dear,' thought Tuppence as she walked down

the road into the town. 'How very unfortunate that the person I like best in this place should be a German. It makes everything cock-eyed!'

III

Tuppence was nothing if not thorough. Although she had no wish to go to London, she judged it wise to do exactly as she had said she was going to do. If she merely made an excursion somewhere for the day, somebody might see her and the fact would get round to Sans Souci.

No, Mrs Blenkensop had said she was going to London, and to London she must go.

She purchased a third return, and was just leaving the booking-office window when she ran into Sheila Perenna.

'Hallo,' said Sheila. 'Where are you off to? I just came to see about a parcel which seems to have gone astray.'

Tuppence explained her plans.

'Oh, yes, of course,' said Sheila carelessly. 'I do remember you saying something about it, but I hadn't realised it was today you were going. I'll come and see you into the train.'

Sheila was more animated than usual. She looked

neither bad-tempered nor sulky. She chatted quite amiably about small details of daily life at Sans Souci. She remained talking to Tuppence until the train left the station.

After waving from the window and watching the girl's figure recede, Tuppence sat down in her corner seat again and gave herself up to serious meditation.

Was it, she wondered, an accident that Sheila had happened to be at the station just at that time? Or was it a proof of enemy thoroughness? Did Mrs Perenna want to make quite sure that the garrulous Mrs Blenkensop really *had* gone to London?

It looked very much like it.

IV

It was not until the next day that Tuppence was able to have a conference with Tommy. They had agreed never to attempt to communicate with each other under the roof of Sans Souci.

Mrs Blenkensop met Mr Meadowes as the latter, his hay fever somewhat abated, was taking a gentle stroll on the front. They sat down on one of the promenade seats.

'Well?' said Tuppence.

Slowly, Tommy nodded his head. He looked rather unhappy.

'Yes,' he said. 'I got something. But Lord, what a day. Perpetually with an eye to the crack of the door. I've got quite a stiff neck.'

'Never mind your neck,' said Tuppence unfeelingly. 'Tell me.'

'Well, the maids went in to do the bed and the room, of course. And Mrs Perenna went in – but that was when the maids were there and she was just blowing them up about something. And the kid ran in once and came out with a woolly dog.'

'Yes, yes. Anyone else?'

'One person,' said Tommy slowly.

'Who?'

'Carl von Deinim.'

'Oh!' Tuppence felt a swift pang. So, after all –

'When?' she asked.

'Lunch time. He came out from the dining-room early, came up to his room, then sneaked across the passage and into yours. He was there about a quarter of an hour.'

He paused.

'That settles it, I think?'

Tuppence nodded.

Yes, it settled it all right. Carl von Deinim could have had no reason for going into Mrs Blenkensop's bedroom and remaining there for a quarter of an hour save one. His complicity was proved. He must be, Tuppence thought, a marvellous actor . . .

His words to her that morning had rung so very true. Well, perhaps they had been true in a way. To know when to use the truth was the essence of successful deception. Carl von Deinim was a patriot all right; he was an enemy agent working for his country. One could respect him for that. Yes – but destroy him too.

'I'm sorry,' she said slowly.

'So am I,' said Tommy. 'He's a good chap.'

Tuppence said:

'You and I might be doing the same thing in Germany.'

Tommy nodded. Tuppence went on.

'Well, we know more or less where we are. Carl von Deinim working in with Sheila and her mother. Probably Mrs Perenna is the big noise. Then there is that foreign woman who was talking to Carl yesterday. She's in it somehow.'

'What do we do now?'

'We must go through Mrs Perenna's room sometime. There might be something there that would give us a hint. And we must tail her – see where she goes and whom she meets. Tommy, let's get Albert down here.'

Tommy considered the point.

Many years ago Albert, a pageboy in a hotel, had joined forces with the young Beresfords and shared their adventures. Afterwards he had entered their service and been the sole domestic prop of the establishment. Some six years ago he had married and was now the proud proprietor of The Duck and Dog pub in South London.

Tuppence continued rapidly:

'Albert will be thrilled. We'll get him down here. He can stay at the pub near the station and he can shadow the Perennas for us – or anyone else.'

'What about Mrs Albert?'

'She was going to her mother in Wales with the children last Monday. Because of air raids. It all fits in perfectly.'

'Yes, that's a good idea, Tuppence. Either of us following the woman about would be rather conspicuous. Albert will be perfect. Now another thing – I think we ought to watch out for that so-called Polish woman who was talking to Carl and hanging about here. It seems to me that she probably represents the other end of the business – and that's what we're anxious to find.'

'Oh yes, I do agree. She comes here for orders, or to take messages. Next time we see her, one of us must follow her and find out more about her.'

'What about looking through Mrs Perenna's room – and Carl's too, I suppose?'

'I don't suppose you'll find anything in his. After all, as a German, the police are liable to search it and so he'd be careful not to have anything suspicious. The Perenna is going to be difficult. When she's out of the house, Sheila is often there, and there's Betty and Mrs Sprot running about all over the landings, and Mrs O'Rourke spends a lot of time in her bedroom.'

She paused. 'Lunch time is the best.'

'Master Carl's time?'

'Exactly. I could have a headache and go to my room – no, someone might come up and want to minister to me. I know, I'll just come in quietly before lunch and go up to my room without telling anyone. Then, after lunch, I can say I had a headache.'

'Hadn't I better do it? My hay fever could recrudesce tomorrow.'

'I think it had better be me. If I'm caught I could always say I was looking for aspirin or something. One of the gentlemen boarders in Mrs Perenna's room would cause far more speculation.'

Tommy grinned.

'Of a scandalous character.'

Then the smile died. He looked grave and anxious.

'As soon as we can, old thing. The news is bad today. We must get on to something soon.'

V

Tommy continued his walk and presently entered the post office, where he put through a call to Mr Grant, and reported 'the recent operation was successful and our friend C is definitely involved'.

Then he wrote a letter and posted it. It was addressed to Mr Albert Batt, The Duck and Dog, Glamorgan St, Kennington.

Then he bought himself a weekly paper which professed to inform the English world of what was really going to happen and strolled innocently back in the direction of Sans Souci.

Presently he was hailed by the hearty voice of Commander Haydock leaning from his two-seater car and shouting, 'Hallo, Meadowes, want a lift?'

Tommy accepted a lift gratefully and got in.

'So you read that rag, do you?' demanded Haydock, glancing at the scarlet cover of the *Inside Weekly News*.

Mr Meadowes displayed the slight confusion of all readers of the periodical in question when challenged.

'Awful rag,' he agreed. 'But sometimes, you know, they really do seem to know what's going on behind the scenes.'

'And sometimes they're wrong.'

'Oh, quite so.'

'Truth of it is,' said Commander Haydock, steering rather erratically round a one-way island and narrowly missing collision with a large van, 'when the beggars are right, one remembers it, and when they're wrong you forget it.'

'Do you think there's any truth in this rumour about Stalin having approached us?'

'Wishful thinking, my boy, wishful thinking,' said Commander Haydock. 'The Russkys are as crooked as hell and always have been. Don't trust 'em, that's what I say. Hear you've been under the weather?'

'Just a touch of hay fever. I get it about this time of year.'

'Yes, of course. Never suffered from it myself, but I had a pal who did. Used to lay him out regularly every June. Feeling fit enough for a game of golf?'

Tommy said he'd like it very much.

'Right. What about tomorrow? Tell you what, I've got to go to a meeting about this Parashot business, raising a corps of local volunteers – jolly good idea if you ask me. Time we were all made to pull our weight. So shall we have a round about six?'

'Thanks very much. I'd like to.'

'Good. Then that's settled.'

The Commander drew up abruptly at the gate of Sans Souci.

'How's the fair Sheila?' he asked.

'Quite well, I think. I haven't seen much of her.'

Haydock gave his loud barking laugh.

'Not as much as you'd like to, I bet! Good-looking girl that, but damned rude. She sees too much of that German fellow. Damned unpatriotic, I call it. Dare say she's got no use for old fogies like you and me, but there are plenty of nice lads going about in our own Services. Why take up with a bloody German? That sort of thing riles me.'

Mr Meadowes said:

'Be careful, he's just coming up the hill behind us.'

'Don't care if he does hear! Rather hope he does. I'd like to kick Master Carl's behind for him. Any decent German's fighting for his country – not slinking over here to get out of it!'

'Well,' said Tommy, 'it's one less German to invade England at all events.'

'You mean he's here already? Ha ha! Rather good, Meadowes! Not that I believe this tommy rot about invasion. We never have been invaded and never will be. We've got a Navy, thank God!'

With which patriotic announcement the Commander let in his clutch with a jerk and the car leaped forward up the hill to Smugglers' Rest.

VI

Tuppence arrived at the gates of Sans Souci at twenty minutes to two. She turned off from the drive and went through the garden and into the house through the open drawing-room window. A smell of Irish stew and the clatter of plates and murmur of voices came from afar. Sans Souci was hard at work on its mid-day meal.

Tuppence waited by the drawing-room door until Martha, the maid, had passed across the hall and into the dining-room, then she ran quickly up the stairs, shoeless.

She went into her room, put on her soft felt bedroom slippers, and then went along the landing and into Mrs Perenna's room.

Once inside she looked round her and felt a certain distaste sweep over her. Not a nice job, this. Quite unpardonable if Mrs Perenna was simply Mrs Perenna. Prying into people's private affairs –

Tuppence shook herself, an impatient terrier shake that was a reminiscence of her girlhood. *There was a war on!*

She went over to the dressing-table.

Quick and deft in her movements, she had soon gone through the contents of the drawers there. In the tall bureau, one of the drawers was locked. That seemed more promising.

Tommy had been entrusted with certain tools and had received some brief instruction on the manipulation of them. These indications he had passed on to Tuppence.

A deft twist or two of the wrist and the drawer yielded.

There was a cash box containing twenty pounds in notes and some piles of silver – also a jewel case. And there were a heap of papers. These last were what interested Tuppence most. Rapidly she went through them; necessarily it was a cursory glance. She could not afford time for more.

Papers relating to a mortgage on Sans Souci, a bank account, letters. Time flew past; Tuppence skimmed through the documents, concentrating furiously on anything that might bear a double meaning. Two letters from a friend in Italy, rambling, discursive letters, seemingly quite harmless. But possibly not so harmless as they sounded. A letter from one Simon Mortimer, of London – a dry business-like letter containing so little of moment that Tuppence wondered why it had been kept. Was Mr Mortimer not so harmless as he seemed? At the bottom of the pile a letter in faded ink signed Pat and beginning '*This will be the last letter I'll be writing you, Eileen my darling –*'

No, not that! Tuppence could not bring herself to read that! She refolded it, tidied the letters on top of it and then, suddenly alert, pushed the drawer to – no time to relock it – and when the door opened and Mrs Perenna came in, she was searching vaguely amongst the bottles on the washstand.

Mrs Blenkensop turned a flustered, but foolish face towards her hostess.

'Oh, Mrs Perenna, do forgive me. I came in with such a blinding headache, and I thought I would lie down on my bed with a little aspirin, and I couldn't find mine, so I thought you wouldn't mind – I know you must have some because you offered it to Miss Minton the other day.'

Mrs Perenna swept into the room. There was a sharpness in her voice as she said:

'Why, of course, Mrs Blenkensop, why ever didn't you come and ask me?'

'Well, of course, yes, I should have done really. But I knew you were all at lunch, and I do so hate, you know, making a *fuss* –'

Passing Tuppence, Mrs Perenna caught up the bottle of aspirin from the washstand.

'How many would you like?' she demanded crisply.

Mrs Blenkensop accepted three. Escorted by Mrs Perenna she crossed to her own room and hastily demurred to the suggestion of a hot-water bottle.

Mrs Perenna used her parting shot as she left the room.

'But you have some aspirin of your own, Mrs Blenkensop. I've seen it.'

Tuppence cried quickly:

'Oh, I know. I know I've got some somewhere, but, so stupid of me, I simply couldn't lay my hands on it.'

Mrs Perenna said with a flash of her big white teeth:

'Well, have a good rest until tea time.'

She went out, closing the door behind her. Tuppence drew a deep breath, lying on her bed rigidly lest Mrs Perenna should return.

Had the other suspected anything? Those teeth, so big and so white – the better to eat you with, my dear. Tuppence always thought of that when she noticed those teeth. Mrs Perenna's hands too, big cruel-looking hands.

She had appeared to accept Tuppence's presence in her bedroom quite naturally. But later she would find the bureau drawer unlocked. Would she suspect then? Or would she think she had left it unlocked herself by accident? One did do such things. Had Tuppence been able to replace the papers in such a way that they looked much the same as before?

Surely, even if Mrs Perenna did notice anything amiss she would be more likely to suspect one of the servants than she would 'Mrs Blenkensop'. And if she did suspect the latter, wouldn't it be a mere case of suspecting her of undue curiosity? There were people, Tuppence knew, who did poke and pry.

But then, if Mrs Perenna were the renowned German agent M., she would be suspicious of counter-espionage.

Had anything in her bearing revealed undue alertness?

She had seemed natural enough – only that one sharply pointed remark about the aspirin.

Suddenly, Tuppence sat up on her bed. She remembered that her aspirin, together with some iodine and a bottle of soda mints, were at the back of the writing-table drawer where she had shoved them when unpacking.

It would seem, therefore, that she was not the only person to snoop in other people's rooms. Mrs Perenna had got there first.

Chapter 7

On the following day Mrs Sprot went up to London.

A few tentative remarks on her part had led immediately to various offers on the part of the inhabitants of Sans Souci to look after Betty.

When Mrs Sprot, with many final adjurations to Betty to be a very good girl, had departed, Betty attached herself to Tuppence, who had elected to take morning duty.

'Play,' said Betty. 'Play hide seek.'

She was talking more easily every day and had adopted a most fetching habit of laying her head on one side, fixing her interlocutor with a bewitching smile and murmuring *'Peese'*.

Tuppence had intended taking her for a walk, but it was raining hard, so the two of them adjourned to the bedroom where Betty led the way to the bottom drawer of the bureau where her playthings were kept.

'Hide Bonzo, shall we?' asked Tuppence.

But Betty had changed her mind and demanded instead:

'Wead me story.'

Tuppence pulled out a rather tattered book from one end of the cupboard – to be interrupted by a squeal from Betty.

'No, no. Nasty . . . Bad . . .'

Tuppence stared at her in surprise and then down at the book, which was a coloured version of *Little Jack Horner*.

'Was Jack a bad boy?' she asked. 'Because he pulled out a plum?'

Betty reiterated with emphasis:

'B-a-ad!' and with a terrific effort, 'Dirrrty!'

She seized the book from Tuppence and replaced it in the line, then tugged out an identical book from the other end of the shelf, announcing with a beaming smile:

'K-k-klean ni'tice Jackorner!'

Tuppence realised that the dirty and worn books had been replaced by new and cleaner editions and was rather amused. Mrs Sprot was very much what Tuppence thought of as 'the hygienic mother'. Always terrified of germs, of impure food, or of the child sucking a soiled toy.

Tuppence, brought up in a free and easy rectory

life, was always rather contemptuous of exaggerated hygiene and had brought up her own two children to absorb what she called a 'reasonable amount' of dirt. However, she obediently took out the clean copy of *Jack Horner* and read it to the child with the comments proper to the occasion. Betty murmuring '*That's* Jack! – Plum! – In a *Pie*!' pointing out these interesting objects with a sticky finger that bade fair to soon consign this second copy to the scrap heap. They proceeded to *Goosey Goosey Gander* and *The Old Woman Who Lived in a Shoe*, and then Betty hid the books and Tuppence took an amazingly long time to find each of them, to Betty's great glee, and so the morning passed rapidly away.

After lunch Betty had her rest and it was then that Mrs O'Rourke invited Tuppence into her room.

Mrs O'Rourke's room was very untidy and smelt strongly of peppermint, and stale cake with a faint odour of moth balls added. There were photographs on every table of Mrs O'Rourke's children and grandchildren and nieces and nephews and great-nieces and great-nephews. There were so many of them that Tuppence felt as though she were looking at a realistically produced play of the late Victorian period.

''Tis a grand way you have with children, Mrs Blenkensop,' observed Mrs O'Rourke genially.

'Oh well,' said Tuppence, 'with my own two –'

Mrs O'Rourke cut in quickly:

'Two? It was three boys I understood you had?'

'Oh yes, three. But two of them are very near in age and I was thinking of the days spent with them.'

'Ah! I see. Sit down now, Mrs Blenkensop. Make yourself at home.'

Tuppence sat down obediently and wished that Mrs O'Rourke did not always make her feel so uncomfortable. She felt now exactly like Hansel or Gretel accepting the witch's invitation.

'Tell me now,' said Mrs O'Rourke. 'What do you think of Sans Souci?'

Tuppence began a somewhat gushing speech of eulogy, but Mrs O'Rourke cut her short without ceremony.

'What I'd be asking you is if you don't feel there's something odd about the place?'

'Odd? No, I don't think so.'

'Not about Mrs Perenna? You're interested in her, you must allow. I've seen you watching her and watching her.'

Tuppence flushed.

'She – she's an interesting woman.'

'She is not then,' said Mrs O'Rourke. 'She's a commonplace woman enough – that is if she's what she seems. But perhaps she isn't. Is that your idea?'

'Really, Mrs O'Rourke, I don't know *what* you mean.'

'Have you ever stopped to think that many of us are that way – different to what we seem on the surface. Mr Meadowes, now. He's a puzzling kind of man. Sometimes I'd say he was a typical Englishman, stupid to the core, and there's other times I'll catch a look or a word that's not stupid at all. It's odd that, don't you think so?'

Tuppence said firmly:

'Oh, I really think Mr Meadowes is *very* typical.'

'There are others. Perhaps you'll know who I'll be meaning?'

Tuppence shook her head.

'The name,' said Mrs O'Rourke encouragingly, 'begins with an S.'

She nodded her head several times.

With a sudden spark of anger and an obscure impulse to spring to the defence of something young and vulnerable, Tuppence said sharply:

'Sheila's just a rebel. One usually is, at that age.'

Mrs O'Rourke nodded her head several times, looking just like an obese china mandarin that Tuppence remembered on her Aunt Gracie's mantelpiece. A vast smile tilted up the corners of her mouth. She said softly:

'You mayn't know it, but Miss Minton's Christian name is Sophia.'

'Oh,' Tuppence was taken aback. 'Was it Miss Minton you meant?'

'It was not,' said Mrs O'Rourke.

Tuppence turned away to the window. Queer how this old woman could affect her, spreading about her an atmosphere of unrest and fear. 'Like a mouse between a cat's paws,' thought Tuppence. 'That's what I feel like . . .'

This vast smiling monumental old woman, sitting there, almost purring – and yet there was the pat pat of paws playing with something that wasn't, in spite of the purring, to be allowed to get away . . .

'Nonsense – all nonsense! I imagine these things,' thought Tuppence, staring out of the window into the garden. The rain had stopped. There was a gentle patter of raindrops off the trees.

Tuppence thought: 'It isn't all my fancy. I'm not a fanciful person. There is something, some focus of evil there. If I could see –'

Her thoughts broke off abruptly.

At the bottom of the garden the bushes parted slightly. In the gap a face appeared, staring stealthily up at the house. It was the face of the foreign woman who had stood talking to Carl von Deinim in the road.

It was so still, so unblinking in its regard, that it seemed to Tuppence as though it was not human. Staring, staring up at the windows of Sans Souci. It was devoid of expression, and yet there was – yes, undoubtedly there was – menace about it. Immobile, implacable. It represented some spirit, some force, alien to Sans Souci and the commonplace banality of English guesthouse life. 'So,' Tuppence thought, 'might Jael have looked, awaiting to drive the nail through the forehead of sleeping Sisera.'

These thoughts took only a second or two to flash through Tuppence's mind. Turning abruptly from the window, she murmured something to Mrs O'Rourke, hurried out of the room and ran downstairs and out of the front door.

Turning to the right she ran down the side garden path to where she had seen the face. There was no one there now. Tuppence went through the shrubbery and out on to the road and looked up and down the hill. She could see no one. Where had the woman gone?

Vexed, she turned and went back into the grounds of Sans Souci. Could she have imagined the whole thing? No, the woman had been there.

Obstinately she wandered round the garden, peering behind bushes. She got very wet and found no trace of the strange woman. She retraced her steps to the house with a vague feeling of foreboding – a queer formless dread of something about to happen.

She did not guess, would never have guessed, what that something was going to be.

II

Now that the weather had cleared, Miss Minton was dressing Betty preparatory to taking her out for a walk. They were going down to the town to buy a celluloid duck to sail in Betty's bath.

Betty was very excited and capered so violently that it was extremely difficult to insert her arms into her woolly pullover. The two set off together, Betty chattering violently: 'Byaduck. Byaduck. For Bettibarf. For Bettibarf,' and deriving great pleasure from a ceaseless reiteration of these important facts.

Two matches, left carelessly crossed on the marble table in the hall, informed Tuppence that Mr Meadowes was spending the afternoon on the trail of Mrs Perenna. Tuppence betook herself to the drawing-room and the company of Mr and Mrs Cayley.

Mr Cayley was in a fretful mood. He had come to Leahampton, he explained, for absolute rest and quiet, and what quiet could there be with a child in the house? All day long it went on, screaming and running about, jumping up and down on the floors –

His wife murmured pacifically that Betty was really a dear little mite, but the remark met with no favour.

'No doubt, no doubt,' said Mr Cayley, wriggling his long neck. 'But her mother should keep her quiet.

There are other people to consider. Invalids, people whose nerves need repose.'

Tuppence said: 'It's not easy to keep a child of that age quiet. It's not natural – there would be something wrong with the child if she was quiet.'

Mr Cayley gobbled angrily.

'Nonsense – nonsense – this foolish modern spirit. Letting children do exactly as they please. A child should be made to sit down quietly and – and nurse a doll – or read, or something.'

'She's not three yet,' said Tuppence, smiling. 'You can hardly expect her to be able to read.'

'Well, something must be done about it. I shall speak to Mrs Perenna. The child was singing, singing in her bed before seven o'clock this morning. I had had a bad night and just dropped off towards morning – and it woke me right up.'

'It's very important that Mr Cayley should get as much sleep as possible,' said Mrs Cayley anxiously. 'The doctor said so.'

'You should go to a nursing home,' said Tuppence.

'My dear lady, such places are ruinously expensive and besides it's not the right atmosphere. There is a suggestion of illness that reacts unfavourably on my subconscious.'

'Bright society, the doctor said,' Mrs Cayley explained helpfully. 'A normal life. He thought a guesthouse would be better than just taking a furnished house. Mr Cayley would not be so likely to brood, and would be stimulated by exchanging ideas with other people.'

Mr Cayley's method of exchanging ideas was, so far as Tuppence could judge, a mere recital of his own ailments and symptoms and the exchange consisted in the sympathetic or unsympathetic reception of them.

Adroitly, Tuppence changed the subject.

'I wish you would tell me,' she said, 'of your own views on life in Germany. You told me you had travelled there a good deal in recent years. It would be interesting to have the point of view of an experienced man of the world like yourself. I can see you are the kind of man, quite unswayed by prejudice, who could really give a clear account of conditions there.'

Flattery, in Tuppence's opinion, should always be laid on with a trowel where a man was concerned. Mr Cayley rose at once to the bait.

'As you say, dear lady, I am capable of taking a clear unprejudiced view. Now, in my opinion –'

What followed constituted a monologue. Tuppence, throwing in an occasional 'Now that's very interesting' or 'What a shrewd observer you are', listened with an attention that was not assumed for the occasion. For Mr Cayley, carried away by the sympathy of his listener, was displaying himself as a decided admirer of the Nazi system. How much better it would have been, he hinted, if did not say, for England and Germany to have allied themselves against the rest of Europe.

The return of Miss Minton and Betty, the celluloid duck duly obtained, broke in upon the monologue, which had extended unbroken for nearly two hours. Looking up, Tuppence caught rather a curious expression on Mrs Cayley's face. She found it hard to define. It might be merely pardonable wifely jealousy at the monopoly of her husband's attention by another woman. It might be alarm at the fact that Mr Cayley was being too outspoken in his political views. It certainly expressed dissatisfaction.

Tea was the next move and hard on that came the return of Mrs Sprot from London exclaiming:

'I do hope Betty's been good and not troublesome? Have you been a good girl, Betty?' To which Betty replied laconically by the single word:

'Dam!'

This, however, was not to be regarded as an expression of disapproval at her mother's return, but merely as a request for blackberry preserve.

It elicited a deep chuckle from Mrs O'Rourke and a reproachful:

'Please, Betty, dear,' from the young lady's parent.

Mrs Sprot then sat down, drank several cups of

tea, and plunged into a spirited narrative of her purchases in London, the crowd on the train, what a soldier recently returned from France had told the occupants of her carriage, and what a girl behind the stocking counter had told her of a stocking shortage to come.

The conversation was, in fact, completely normal. It was prolonged afterwards on the terrace outside, for the sun was now shining and the wet day a thing of the past.

Betty rushed happily about, making mysterious expeditions into the bushes and returning with a laurel leaf, or a heap of pebbles which she placed in the lap of one of the grown-ups with a confused and unintelligible explanation of what it represented. Fortunately she required little co-operation in her game, being satisfied with an occasional 'How nice, darling. Is it really?'

Never had there been an evening more typical of Sans Souci at its most harmless. Chatter, gossip, speculations as to the course of the war – Can France rally? Will Weygand pull things together? What is Russia likely to do? Could Hitler invade England if he tried? Will Paris fall if the 'bulge' is not straightened out? Was it true that . . . ? It had been said that . . . And it was rumoured that . . .

Political and military scandal was happily bandied about.

Tuppence thought to herself: 'Chatterbugs a danger? Nonsense, they're a safety valve. People *enjoy* these rumours. It gives them the stimulation to carry on with their own private worries and anxieties.' She contributed a nice tit-bit prefixed by 'My son told me – of course this is *quite* private, you understand –'

Suddenly, with a start, Mrs Sprot glanced at her watch.

'Goodness, it's nearly seven. I ought to have put that child to bed hours ago. Betty – Betty!'

It was some time since Betty had returned to the terrace, though no one had noticed her defection.

Mrs Sprot called her with rising impatience.

'Bett – eeee! Where can the child be?'

Mrs O'Rourke said with her deep laugh:

'Up to mischief, I've no doubt of it. 'Tis always the way when there's peace.'

'Betty! I want you.'

There was no answer and Mrs Sprot rose impatiently.

'I suppose I must go and look for her. I wonder where she can be?'

Miss Minton suggested that she was hiding somewhere and Tuppence, with memories of her own childhood, suggested the kitchen. But Betty could not be found, either inside or outside the house. They went round the garden calling, looking all over the bedrooms. There was no Betty anywhere.

Mrs Sprot began to get annoyed.

'It's very naughty of her – very naughty indeed! Do you think she can have gone out on the road?'

Together she and Tuppence went out to the gate and looked up and down the hill. There was no one in sight except a tradesman's boy with a bicycle standing talking to a maid at the door of St Lucian's opposite.

On Tuppence's suggestion, she and Mrs Sprot crossed the road and the latter asked if either of them had noticed a little girl. They both shook their heads and then the servant asked, with sudden recollection:

'A little girl in a green checked gingham dress?'

Mrs Sprot said eagerly:

'That's right.'

'I saw her about half an hour ago – going down the road with a woman.'

Mrs Sprot said with astonishment:

'With a woman? What sort of a woman?'

The girl seemed slightly embarrassed.

'Well, what I'd call an odd-looking kind of woman. A foreigner she was. Queer clothes. A kind of shawl thing and no hat, and a strange sort of face – queer like, if you know what I mean. I've seen her about once or twice lately, and to tell the truth I thought she was a bit wanting – if you know what I mean,' she added helpfully.

In a flash Tuppence remembered the face she had seen that afternoon peering through the bushes and the foreboding that had swept over her.

But she had never thought of the woman in connection with the child, could not understand it now.

She had little time for meditation, however, for Mrs Sprot almost collapsed against her.

'Oh Betty, my little girl. She's been kidnapped. She – what did the woman look like – a gipsy?'

Tuppence shook her head energetically.

'No, she was fair, very fair, a broad face with high cheekbones and blue eyes set very far apart.'

She saw Mrs Sprot staring at her and hastened to explain.

'I saw the woman this afternoon – peering through the bushes at the bottom of the garden. And I've noticed her hanging about. Carl von Deinim was speaking to her one day. It must be the same woman.'

The servant girl chimed in to say:

'That's right. Fair-haired she was. And wanting, if you ask me. Didn't understand nothing that was said to her.'

'Oh God,' moaned Mrs Sprot. 'What shall I do?'

Tuppence passed an arm round her.

'Come back to the house, have a little brandy and then we'll ring up the police. It's all right. We'll get her back.'

Mrs Sprot went with her meekly, murmuring in a dazed fashion:

'I can't imagine how Betty would go like that with a stranger.'

'She's very young,' said Tuppence. 'Not old enough to be shy.'

Mrs Sprot cried out weakly:

'Some dreadful German woman, I expect. She'll kill my Betty.'

'Nonsense,' said Tuppence robustly. 'It will be all right. I expect she's just some woman who's not quite right in her head.' But she did not believe her own words – did not believe for one moment that the calm blonde woman was an irresponsible lunatic.

Carl! Would Carl know? Had Carl something to do with this?

A few minutes later she was inclined to doubt this. Carl von Deinim, like the rest, seemed amazed, unbelieving, completely surprised.

As soon as the facts were made plain, Major Bletchley assumed control.

'Now then, dear lady,' he said to Mrs Sprot. 'Sit down here – just drink a little drop of this – brandy – it won't hurt you – and I'll get straight on to the police station.'

Mrs Sprot murmured:

'Wait a minute – there might be something –'

She hurried up the stairs and along the passage to hers and Betty's room.

A minute or two later they heard her footsteps running wildly along the landing. She rushed down the stairs like a demented woman and clutched Major Bletchley's hand from the telephone receiver, which he was just about to lift.

'No, no,' she panted. 'You mustn't – you mustn't . . .'

And sobbing wildly, she collapsed into a chair.

They crowded round her. In a minute or two, she recovered her composure. Sitting up, with Mrs Cayley's arm round her, she held something out for them to see.

'I found this on the floor of my room. It had been wrapped round a stone and thrown through the window. Look – look what it says.'

Tommy took it from her and unfolded it.

It was a note, written in a queer stiff foreign handwriting, big and bold.

> WE HAVE GOT YOUR CHILD IN SAFE KEEPING. YOU WILL BE TOLD WHAT TO DO IN DUE COURSE. IF YOU GO TO THE POLICE YOUR CHILD WILL BE KILLED. SAY NOTHING. WAIT FOR INSTRUCTIONS. IF NOT –

It was signed with a skull and crossbones.

Mrs Sprot was moaning faintly:

'Betty – Betty –'

Everyone was talking at once. 'The dirty murdering scoundrels' from Mrs O'Rourke. 'Brutes!' from Sheila Perenna. 'Fantastic, fantastic – I don't believe a word of it. Silly practical joke' from Mr Cayley. 'Oh, the dear wee mite' from Miss Minton. 'I do not understand. It is incredible' from Carl von Deinim. And above everyone else the stentorian voice of Major Bletchley.

'Damned nonsense. Intimidation. We must inform the police at once. They'll soon get to the bottom of it.'

Once more he moved towards the telephone. This time a scream of outraged motherhood from Mrs Sprot stopped him.

He shouted:

'But my dear madam, it's *got* to be done. This is only a crude device to prevent you getting on the track of these scoundrels.'

'They'll kill her.'

'Nonsense. They wouldn't dare.'

'I won't have it, I tell you. I'm her mother. It's for me to say.'

'I know. I know. That's what they're counting on – your feeling like that. Very natural. But you must take it from me, a soldier and an experienced man of the world, the police are what we need.'

'*No!*'

Bletchley's eyes went round seeking allies.

'Meadowes, you agree with me?'

Slowly Tommy nodded.

'Cayley? Look, Mrs Sprot, both Meadowes and Cayley agree.'

Mrs Sprot said with sudden energy:

'Men! All of you! Ask the women!'

Tommy's eyes sought Tuppence. Tuppence said, her voice low and shaken:

'I – I agree with Mrs Sprot.'

She was thinking: 'Deborah! Derek! If it were them, I'd feel like her. Tommy and the others are right, I've no doubt, but all the same I couldn't do it. I couldn't risk it.'

Mrs O'Rourke was saying:

'No mother alive could risk it and that's a fact.'

Mrs Cayley murmured:

'I do think, you know, that – well –' and tailed off into incoherence.

Miss Minton said tremulously:

'Such awful things happen. We'd never forgive ourselves if anything happened to dear little Betty.'

Tuppence said sharply:

'You haven't said anything, Mr von Deinim?'

Carl's blue eyes were very bright. His face was a mask. He said slowly and stiffly:

'I am a foreigner. I do not know your English police. How competent they are – how quick.'

Someone had come into the hall. It was Mrs Perenna, her cheeks were flushed. Evidently she had been hurrying up the hill. She said:

'What's all this?' And her voice was commanding, imperious, not the complaisant guesthouse hostess, but a woman of force.

They told her – a confused tale told by too many people, but she grasped it quickly.

And with her grasping of it, the whole thing seemed, in a way, to be passed up to her for judgement. She was the Supreme Court.

She held the hastily scrawled note a minute, then she handed it back. Her words came sharp and authoritative.

'The police? They'll be no good. You can't risk their blundering. Take the law into your own hands. Go after the child yourselves.'

Bletchley said, shrugging his shoulders:

'Very well. If you won't call the police, it's the best thing to be done.'

Tommy said:

'They can't have got much of a start.'

'Half an hour, the maid said,' Tuppence put in.

'Haydock,' said Bletchley. 'Haydock's the man to help us. He's got a car. The woman's unusual looking, you say? And a foreigner? Ought to leave a trail that we can follow. Come on, there's no time to be lost. You'll come along, Meadowes?'

Mrs Sprot got up.

'I'm coming too.'

'Now, my dear lady, leave it to us –'

'I'm coming too.'

'Oh, well –'

He gave in – murmuring something about the female of the species being deadlier than the male.

III

In the end Commander Haydock, taking in the situation with commendable Naval rapidity, drove the car, Tommy sat beside him, and behind were Bletchley, Mrs Sprot and Tuppence. Not only did Mrs Sprot cling to her, but Tuppence was the only one (with the exception of Carl von Deinim) who knew the mysterious kidnapper by sight.

The Commander was a good organiser and a quick worker. In next to no time he had filled up the car with petrol, tossed a map of the district and a larger scale map of Leahampton itself to Bletchley and was ready to start off.

Mrs Sprot had run upstairs again, presumably to

her room to get a coat. But when she got into the car and they had started down the hill she disclosed to Tuppence something in her handbag. It was a small pistol.

She said quietly:

'I got it from Major Bletchley's room. I remembered his mentioning one day that he had one.'

Tuppence looked a little dubious.

'You don't think that –?'

Mrs Sprot said, her mouth a thin line:

'It may come in useful.'

Tuppence sat marvelling at the strange forces maternity will set loose in an ordinary commonplace young woman. She could visualise Mrs Sprot, the kind of woman who would normally declare herself frightened to death of fire-arms, coolly shooting down any person who had harmed her child.

They drove first, on the Commander's suggestion, to the railway station. A train had left Leahampton about twenty minutes earlier and it was possible that the fugitives had gone by it.

At the station they separated, the Commander taking the ticket collector, Tommy the booking office, and Bletchley the porters outside. Tuppence and Mrs Sprot went into the ladies' room on the chance that the woman had gone in there to change her appearance before taking the train.

One and all drew a blank. It was now more difficult to shape a course. In all probability, as Haydock pointed out, the kidnappers had had a car waiting, and once Betty had been persuaded to come away with the woman, they had made their get-away in that. It was here, as Bletchley pointed out once more, that the co-operation of the police was so vital. It needed an organisation of that kind who could send out messages all over the country, covering the different roads.

Mrs Sprot merely shook her head, her lips pressed tightly together.

Tuppence said:

'We must put ourselves in their places. Where would they have waited in the car? Somewhere as near Sans Souci as possible, but where a car wouldn't be noticed. Now let's *think.* The woman and Betty walk down the hill together. At the bottom is the esplanade. The car might have been drawn up there. So long as you don't leave it unattended you can stop there for quite a while. The only other places are the car park in James's Square, also quite near, or else one of the small streets that lead off from the esplanade.'

It was at that moment that a small man, with a diffident manner and pince nez, stepped up to them and said, stammering a little:

'Excuse me . . . No offence, I hope . . . but I c-c-couldn't help overhearing what you were asking the porter just now' (he now directed his remarks to Major Bletchley). 'I was not listening, of course, just come down to see about a parcel – extraordinary how long things are delayed just now – movements of troops, they say – but really most difficult when it's perishable – the parcel, I mean – and so, you see, I happened to overhear – and really it did seem the most wonderful coincidence . . .'

Mrs Sprot sprang forward. She seized him by the arm.

'You've seen her? You've seen my little girl?'

'Oh really, your little girl, you say? Now fancy that –'

Mrs Sprot cried: 'Tell me.' And her fingers bit into the little man's arm so that he winced.

Tuppence said quickly:

'Please tell us anything you have seen as quickly as you can. We shall be most grateful if you would.'

'Oh, well, really, of course, it may be nothing at all. But the description fitted so well –'

Tuppence felt the woman beside her trembling, but she herself strove to keep her manner calm and unhurried. She knew the type with which they were dealing – fussy, muddle-headed, diffident, incapable of going straight to the point and worse if hurried. She said:

'Please tell us.'

'It was only – my name is Robbins, by the way, Edward Robbins –'

'Yes, Mr Robbins?'

'I live at Whiteways in Ernes Cliff Road, one of those new houses on the new road – most labour-saving, and really every convenience, and a beautiful view and the downs only a stone's throw away.'

Tuppence quelled Major Bletchley, who she saw was about to break out, with a glance, and said:

'And you saw the little girl we are looking for?'

'Yes, I really think it *must* be. A little girl with a foreign-looking woman, you said? It was really the woman I noticed. Because, of course, we are all on the look-out nowadays for Fifth Columnists, aren't we? A sharp look-out, that is what they say, and I always try to do so, and so, as I say, I noticed this woman. A nurse, I thought, or a maid – a lot of spies came over here in that capacity, and this woman was most unusual looking and walking up the road and on to the downs – with a little girl – and the little girl seemed tired and rather lagging, and half-past seven, well, most children go to bed then, so I looked at the woman pretty sharply. I think it flustered her. She hurried up the road, pulling the child after her, and finally picked her up and went on up the path out on to the cliff, which I thought *strange*, you know, because there are no houses there at all – nothing – not until you get to Whitehaven – about five miles over the downs – a favourite walk for hikers. But in this case I thought it odd. I wondered if the woman was going to signal, perhaps. One hears of so much enemy activity, and she certainly looked uneasy when she saw me staring at her.'

Commander Haydock was back in the car and had started the engine. He said:

'Ernes Cliff Road, you say. That's right the other side of the town, isn't it?'

'Yes, you go along the esplanade and past the old town and then up –'

The others had jumped in, not listening further to Mr Robbins.

Tuppence called out:

'Thank you, Mr Robbins,' and they drove off, leaving him staring after them with his mouth open.

They drove rapidly through the town, avoiding accidents more by good luck than by skill. But the luck held. They came out at last at a mass of straggling building development, somewhat marred by proximity to the gas works. A series of little roads led up towards the downs, stopping abruptly a short way up the hill. Ernes Cliff Road was the third of these.

Commander Haydock turned smartly into it and drove up. At the end the road petered out on to bare hillside, up which a footpath meandered upwards.

'Better get out and walk here,' said Bletchley.

Haydock said dubiously:

'Could almost take the car up. Ground's firm enough. Bit bumpy but I think she could do it.'

Mrs Sprot cried:

'Oh yes, please, please . . . We must be quick.'

The Commander murmured to himself:

'Hope to goodness we're after the right lot. That little pipsqueak may have seen any woman with a kid.'

The car groaned uneasily as it ploughed its way up over the rough ground. The gradient was severe, but the turf was short and springy. They came out without mishap on the top of the rise. Here the view was uninterrupted till it rested in the distance on the curve of Whitehaven Bay.

Bletchley said:

'Not a bad idea. The woman could spend the night up here if need be, drop down into Whitehaven tomorrow morning and take a train there.'

Haydock said:

'No sign of them as far as I can see.'

He was standing up holding some field glasses that he had thoughtfully brought with him to his eyes. Suddenly his figure became tense as he focused the glasses on two small moving dots.

'Got 'em, by Jove . . .'

He dropped into the driver's seat again and the car bucketed forward. The chase was a short one now. Shot up in the air, tossed from side to side, the occupants of the car gained rapidly on those two small dots. They could be distinguished now – a tall figure and a short one – nearer still, a woman holding a child by the hand – still nearer, yes, a child in a green gingham frock. Betty.

Mrs Sprot gave a strangled cry.

'All right now, my dear,' said Major Bletchley, patting her kindly. 'We've got 'em.'

They went on. Suddenly the woman turned and saw the car advancing towards her.

With a cry she caught up the child in her arms and began running.

She ran, not forwards, but sideways towards the edge of the cliff.

The car, after a few yards, could not follow; the ground was too uneven and blocked with big boulders. It stopped and the occupants tumbled out.

Mrs Sprot was out first and running wildly after the two fugitives.

The others followed her.

When they were within twenty yards, the other woman turned at bay. She was standing now at the very edge of the cliff. With a hoarse cry she clutched the child closer.

Haydock cried out:

'My God, she's going to throw the kid over the cliff . . .'

The woman stood there, clutching Betty tightly. Her face was disfigured with a frenzy of hate. She uttered a long hoarse sentence that none of them understood. And still she held the child and looked from time to time at the drop below – not a yard from where she stood.

It seemed clear that she was threatening to throw the child over the cliff.

All of them stood there, dazed, terrified, unable to move for fear of precipitating a catastrophe.

Haydock was tugging at his pocket. He pulled out a service revolver.

He shouted: 'Put that child down – or I fire.'

The foreign woman laughed. She held the child closer to her breast. The two figures were moulded into one.

Haydock muttered:

'I daren't shoot. I'd hit the child.'

Tommy said:

'The woman's crazy. She'll jump over with the child in another moment.'

Haydock said again, helplessly:

'I daren't shoot –'

But at that moment a shot rang out. The woman swayed and fell, the child still clasped in her arms.

The men ran forward, Mrs Sprot stood swaying, the smoking pistol in her hands, her eyes dilated.

She took a few stiff steps forward.

Tommy was kneeling by the bodies. He turned them gently. He saw the woman's face – noted appreciatively its strange wild beauty. The eyes opened, looked at him, then went blank. With a sigh, the woman died, shot through the head.

Unhurt, little Betty Sprot wriggled out and ran towards the woman standing like a statue.

Then, at last, Mrs Sprot crumpled. She flung away the pistol and dropped down, clutching the child to her.

She cried:

'She's safe – she's safe – oh, Betty – *Betty.*' And then, in a low, awed whisper:

'Did I – did I – kill her?'

Tuppence said firmly:

'Don't think about it – don't think about it. Think about Betty. Just think about Betty.'

Mrs Sprot held the child close against her, sobbing.

Tuppence went forward to join the men.

Haydock murmured:

'Bloody miracle. I couldn't have brought off a shot like that. Don't believe the woman's ever handled a pistol before either – sheer instinct. A miracle, that's what it is.'

Tuppence said:

'Thank God! It was a near thing!' And she looked down at the sheer drop to the sea below and shuddered.

Chapter 8

The inquest on the dead woman was held some days later. There had been an adjournment whilst the police identified her as a certain Vanda Polonska, a Polish refugee.

After the dramatic scene on the cliffs, Mrs Sprot and Betty, the former in a state of collapse, had been driven back to Sans Souci, where hot bottles, nice cups of tea, ample curiosity, and finally a stiff dollop of brandy had been administered to the half-fainting heroine of the night.

Commander Haydock had immediately got in touch with the police, and under his guidance they had gone out to the scene of the tragedy on the cliff.

But for the disturbing war news, the tragedy would probably have been given much greater space in the papers than it was. Actually it occupied only one small paragraph.

Both Tuppence and Tommy had to give evidence at the inquest, and in case any reporters should think fit to take pictures of the more unimportant witnesses, Mr Meadowes was unfortunate enough to get something in his eye which necessitated a highly disfiguring eyeshade. Mrs Blenkensop was practically obliterated by her hat.

However, such interest as there was focused itself entirely on Mrs Sprot and Commander Haydock. Mr Sprot, hysterically summoned by telegraph, rushed down to see his wife, but had to go back again the same day. He seemed an amiable but not very interesting young man.

The inquest opened with the formal identification of the body by a certain Mrs Calfont, a thin-lipped, gimlet-eyed woman who had been dealing for some months with refugee relief.

Polonska, she said, had come to England in company with a cousin and his wife who were her only relatives, so far as she knew. The woman, in her opinion, was slightly mental. She understood from her that she had been through scenes of great horror in Poland and that her family, including several children, had all been killed. The woman seemed not at all grateful for anything done for her, and was suspicious and taciturn. She muttered to herself a lot, and did not seem normal. A domestic post was found for her, but she had left it without notice some weeks ago and without reporting to the police.

The coroner asked why the woman's relatives had not come forward, and at this point Inspector Brassey made an explanation.

The couple in question were being detained under the Defence of the Realm Act for an offence in connection with a Naval dockyard. He stated that these two aliens had posed as refugees to enter the country, but had immediately tried to obtain employment near a Naval base. The whole family was looked upon with suspicion. They had had a larger sum of money in their possession than could be accounted for. Nothing was actually known against the deceased woman Polonska – except that her sentiments were believed to have been anti-British. It was possible that she also had been an enemy agent, and that her pretended stupidity was assumed.

Mrs Sprot, when called, dissolved at once into tears. The coroner was gentle with her, leading her tactfully along the path of what had occurred.

'It's so awful,' gasped Mrs Sprot. 'So awful to have killed someone. I didn't mean to do that – I mean I never thought – but it was Betty – and I thought that woman was going to throw her over the cliff and I had to stop her – and oh, dear – I don't know how I did it.'

'You are accustomed to the use of firearms?'

'Oh, no! Only those rifles at regattas – at fairs – when you shoot at booths, and even then I never used to hit anything. Oh, dear – I feel as though I'd *murdered* someone.'

The coroner soothed her and asked if she had ever come in contact with the dead woman.

'Oh, *no*. I'd never seen her in my life. I think she must have been quite mad – because she didn't even *know* me or Betty.'

In reply to further questions, Mrs Sprot said that she had attended a sewing party for comforts for Polish refugees, but that that was the extent of her connection with Poles in this country.

Haydock was the next witness, and he described the steps he had taken to track down the kidnapper and what had eventually happened.

'You are clear in your mind that the woman was definitely preparing to jump over the cliff?'

'Either that or to throw the child over. She seemed to be quite demented with hate. It would have been impossible to reason with her. It was a moment for immediate action. I myself conceived the idea of firing and crippling her, but she was holding up the child as a shield. I was afraid of killing the child if I fired. Mrs Sprot took the risk and was successful in saving her little girl's life.'

Mrs Sprot began to cry again.

Mrs Blenkensop's evidence was short – a mere confirming of the Commander's evidence.

Mr Meadowes followed.

'You agree with Commander Haydock and Mrs Blenkensop as to what occurred?'

'I do. The woman was definitely so distraught that it was impossible to get near her. She was about to throw herself and the child over the cliff.'

There was little more evidence. The coroner directed the jury that Vanda Polonska came to her death by the hand of Mrs Sprot and formally exonerated the latter from blame. There was no evidence to show what was the state of the dead woman's mind. She might have been actuated by hate of England. Some of the Polish 'comforts' distributed to refugees bore the names of the ladies sending them, and it was possible that the woman got Mrs Sprot's name and address this way, but it was not easy to get at her reason for kidnapping the child – possibly some crazy motive quite incomprehensible to the normal mind. Polonska, according to her own story, had suffered great bereavement in her own country, and that might have turned her brain. On the other hand, she might be an enemy agent.

The verdict was in accordance with the coroner's summing up.

II

On the day following the inquest Mrs Blenkensop and Mr Meadowes met to compare notes.

'Exit Vanda Polonska and a blank wall as usual,' said Tommy gloomily.

Tuppence nodded.

'Yes, they seal up both ends, don't they? No papers, no hints of any kind as to where the money came from that she and her cousins had, no record of whom they had dealings with.'

'Too damned efficient,' said Tommy.

He added: 'You know, Tuppence, I don't like the look of things.'

Tuppence assented. The news was indeed far from reassuring.

The French Army was in retreat and it seemed doubtful if the tide could be turned. Evacuation from Dunkirk was in progress. It was clearly a matter of a few days only before Paris fell. There was a general dismay at the revelation of lack of equipment and of material for resisting the Germans' great mechanised units.

Tommy said:

'Is it only our usual muddling and slowness? Or has there been deliberate engineering behind this?'

'The latter, I think, but they'll never be able to prove it.'

'No. Our adversaries are too damned clever for that.'

'We are combing out a lot of the rot now.'

'Oh, yes, we're rounding up the obvious people, but I don't believe we've got at the brains that are behind it all. Brains, organisation, a whole carefully thought-out plan – a plan which uses our habits of dilatoriness, and our petty feuds, and our slowness for its own ends.'

Tuppence said:

'That's what we're here for – and we haven't got results.'

'We've done something,' Tommy reminded her.

'Carl von Deinim and Vanda Polonska, yes. The small fry.'

'You think they were working together?'

'I think they must have been,' said Tuppence thoughtfully. 'Remember I saw them talking.'

'Then Carl von Deinim must have engineered the kidnapping?'

'I suppose so.'

'But why?'

'I know,' said Tuppence. 'That's what I keep thinking and thinking about. It doesn't make *sense*.'

'Why kidnap that particular child? Who are the

Sprots? They've no money – so it isn't ransom. They're neither of them employed by Government in any capacity.'

'I know, Tommy. It just doesn't make any sense at all.'

'Hasn't Mrs Sprot any idea herself?'

'That woman,' said Tuppence scornfully, 'hasn't got the brains of a hen. She doesn't think at all. Just says it's the sort of thing the wicked Germans would do.'

'Silly ass,' said Tommy. 'The Germans are efficient. If they send one of their agents to kidnap a brat, it's for some reason.'

'I've a feeling, you know,' said Tuppence, 'that Mrs Sprot *could* get at the reason if only she'd *think* about it. There must be *something* – some piece of information that she herself has inadvertently got hold of, perhaps without knowing what it is exactly.'

'*Say nothing. Wait for instructions*,' Tommy quoted from the note found on Mrs Sprot's bedroom floor. 'Damn it all, that means *something*.'

'Of course it does – it must. The only thing I can think of is that Mrs Sprot, or her husband, has been given something to keep by someone else – given it, perhaps, just because they are such humdrum ordinary people that no one would ever suspect they had it – whatever "it" may be.'

'It's an idea, that.'

'I know – but it's awfully like a spy story. It doesn't seem real somehow.'

'Have you asked Mrs Sprot to rack her brains a bit?'

'Yes, but the trouble is that she isn't really interested. All she cares about is getting Betty back – that, and having hysterics because she's shot someone.'

'Funny creatures, women,' mused Tommy. 'There was that woman, went out that day like an avenging fury, she'd have shot down a regiment in cold blood without turning a hair just to get her child back, and then, having shot the kidnapper by a perfectly incredible fluke, she breaks down and comes all over squeamish about it.'

'The coroner exonerated her all right,' said Tuppence.

'Naturally. By Jove, I wouldn't have risked firing when she did.'

Tuppence said:

'No more would she, probably, if she'd known more about it. It was sheer ignorance of the difficulty of the shot that made her bring it off.'

Tommy nodded.

'Quite Biblical,' he said. 'David and Goliath.'

'Oh!' said Tuppence.

'What is it, old thing?'

'I don't quite know. When you said that something twanged somewhere in my brain, and now it's gone again!'

'Very useful,' said Tommy.

'Don't be scathing. That sort of thing does happen sometimes.'

'Gentlemen who draw a bow at a venture, was that it?'

'No, it was – wait a minute – I think it was something to do with Solomon.'

'Cedars, temples, a lot of wives and concubines?'

'Stop,' said Tuppence, putting her hands to her ears. 'You're making it worse.'

'Jews?' said Tommy hopefully. 'Tribes of Israel?'

But Tuppence shook her head. After a minute or two she said:

'I wish I could remember who it was that woman reminded me of.'

'The late Vanda Polonska?'

'Yes. The first time I saw her, her face seemed vaguely familiar.'

'Do you think you had come across her somewhere else?'

'No, I'm sure I hadn't.'

'Mrs Perenna and Sheila are a totally different type.'

'Oh, yes, it wasn't them. You know, Tommy, about those two. I've been thinking.'

'To any good purpose?'

'I'm not sure. It's about that note – the one Mrs Sprot found on the floor in her room when Betty was kidnapped.'

'Well?'

'All that about its being wrapped round a stone and thrown through the window is rubbish. It was put there by someone – ready for Mrs Sprot to find – and I think it was Mrs Perenna who put it there.'

'Mrs Perenna, Carl, Vanda Polonska – all working together.'

'Yes. Did you notice how Mrs Perenna came in just at the critical moment and clinched things – not to ring up the police? She took command of the whole situation.'

'So she's still your selection for M.'

'Yes, isn't she yours?'

'I suppose so,' said Tommy slowly.

'Why, Tommy, have you got another idea?'

'It's probably an awfully dud one.'

'Tell me.'

'No, I'd rather not. I've nothing to go on. Nothing whatever. But if I'm right, it's not M we're up against, but N.'

He thought to himself.

'Bletchley. I suppose he's all right. Why shouldn't he be? He's a true enough type – almost too true, and after all, it was he who wanted to ring up the police. Yes, but he could have been pretty sure that the child's mother couldn't stand for the idea. The threatening note made sure of that. He could afford to urge the opposite point of view –'

And that brought him back again to the vexing, teasing problem to which as yet he could find no answer.

Why kidnap Betty Sprot?

III

There was a car standing outside Sans Souci bearing the word Police on it.

Absorbed in her own thoughts Tuppence took little notice of that. She turned in at the drive, and entering the front door went straight upstairs to her own room.

She stopped, taken aback, on the threshold, as a tall figure turned away from the window.

'Dear me,' said Tuppence. 'Sheila?'

The girl came straight towards her. Now Tuppence saw her more clearly, saw the blazing eyes deep set in the white tragic face.

Sheila said:

'I'm glad you've come. I've been waiting for you.'

'What's the matter?'

The girl's voice was quiet and devoid of emotion. She said:

'They have arrested Carl!'

'The police?'

'Yes.'

'Oh, dear,' said Tuppence. She felt inadequate to the situation. Quiet as Sheila's voice had been, Tuppence was under no apprehension as to what lay behind it.

Whether they were fellow-conspirators or not, this girl loved Carl von Deinim, and Tuppence felt her heart aching in sympathy with this tragic young creature.

Sheila asked:

'What shall I do?'

The simple forlorn question made Tuppence wince. She said helplessly:

'Oh, my dear.'

Sheila said, and her voice was like a mourning harp:

'They've taken him away. I shall never see him again.'

She cried out:

'What shall I do? What shall I do?' And flinging herself down on her knees by the bed she wept her heart out.

Tuppence stroked the dark head. She said presently, in a weak voice:

'It – it may not be true. Perhaps they are only

going to intern him. After all, he is an enemy alien, you know.'

'That's not what they said. They're searching his room now.'

Tuppence said slowly, 'Well, if they find nothing –'

'They will find nothing, of course! What should they find?'

'I don't know. I thought perhaps you might?'

'I?'

Her scorn, her amazement were too real to be feigned. Any suspicions Tuppence had had that Sheila Perenna was involved died at this moment. The girl knew nothing, had never known anything.

Tuppence said:

'If he is innocent –'

Sheila interrupted her.

'What does it matter? The police will make a case against him.'

Tuppence said sharply:

'Nonsense, my dear child, that really isn't true.'

'The English police will do anything. My mother says so.'

'Your mother may say so, but she's wrong. I assure you that it isn't so.'

Sheila looked at her doubtfully for a minute or two. Then she said:

'Very well. If you say so. I trust you.'

Tuppence felt very uncomfortable. She said sharply:

'You trust too much, Sheila. You may have been unwise to trust Carl.'

'Are you against him too? I thought you liked him. He thinks so too.'

Touching young things – with their faith in one's liking for them. And it was true – she had liked Carl – she did like him.

Rather wearily she said:

'Listen, Sheila, liking or not liking has nothing to do with facts. This country and Germany are at war. There are many ways of serving one's country. One of them is to get information – and to work behind the lines. It is a brave thing to do, for when you are caught, it is' – her voice broke a little – 'the end.'

Sheila said:

'You think Carl –'

'Might be working for his country that way? It is a possibility, isn't it?'

'No,' said Sheila.

'It would be his job, you see, to come over here as a refugee, to appear to be violently anti-Nazi and then to gather information.'

Sheila said quietly:

'It's not true. I know Carl. I know his heart and his mind. He cares most for science – for his work – for the truth and the knowledge in it. He is grateful to

England for letting him work here. Sometimes, when people say cruel things, he feels German and bitter. But he hates the Nazis always, and what they stand for – their denial of freedom.'

Tuppence said: 'He would say so, of course.'

Sheila turned reproachful eyes upon her.

'So you believe he is a spy?'

'I think it is' – Tuppence hesitated – 'a possibility.'

Sheila walked to the door.

'I see. I'm sorry I came to ask you to help us.'

'But what did you think I could do, dear child?'

'You know people. Your sons are in the Army and Navy, and I've heard you say more than once that they knew influential people. I thought perhaps you could get them to – to do – something?'

Tuppence thought of those mythical creatures, Douglas and Raymond and Cyril.

'I'm afraid,' she said, 'that they couldn't do anything.'

Sheila flung her head up. She said passionately:

'Then there's no hope for us. They'll take him away and shut him up, and one day, early in the morning, they'll stand him against a wall and shoot him – and that will be the end.'

She went out, shutting the door behind her.

'Oh, damn, damn, damn the Irish!' thought Tuppence in a fury of mixed feelings. 'Why have they got that terrible power of twisting things until you don't know where you are? If Carl von Deinim's a spy, he deserves to be shot. I must hang on to that, not let this girl with her Irish voice bewitch me into thinking it's the tragedy of a hero and a martyr!'

She recalled the voice of a famous actress speaking a line from *Riders to the Sea*:

'It's the fine quiet time they'll be having . . .'

Poignant . . . carrying you away on a tide of feeling . . .

She thought: 'If it weren't true. Oh, if only it weren't true . . .'

Yet, knowing what she did, how could she doubt?

IV

The fisherman on the end of the Old Pier cast in his line and reeled it cautiously in.

'No doubt whatever, I'm afraid,' he said.

'You know,' said Tommy, 'I'm sorry about it. He's – well, he's a nice chap.'

'They are, my dear fellow, they usually are. It isn't the skunks and the rats of a land who volunteer to go to the enemy's country. It's the brave men. We know that well enough. But there it is, the case is proved.'

'No doubt whatever, you say?'

'No doubt at all. Among his chemical formulae was a list of people in the factory to be approached, as possible Fascist sympathisers. There was also a very clever scheme of sabotage and a chemical process that, applied to fertilisers, would have devastated large areas of food stocks. All well up Master Carl's street.'

Rather unwillingly, Tommy said, secretly anathematising Tuppence, who had made him promise to say it:

'I suppose it's not possible that these things could have been planted on him?'

Mr Grant smiled, rather a diabolical smile.

'Oh,' he said. 'Your wife's idea, no doubt.'

'Well – er – yes, as a matter of fact it is.'

'He's an attractive lad,' said Mr Grant tolerantly.

Then he went on:

'No, seriously, I don't think we can take that suggestion into account. He'd got a supply of secret ink, you know. That's a pretty good clinching test. And it wasn't obvious as it would have been if planted. It wasn't "The mixture to be taken when required" on the wash hand-stand, or anything like that. In fact, it was damned ingenious. Only came across the method once before, and then it was waistcoat buttons. Steeped in the stuff, you know. When the fellow wants to use it, he soaks a button in water. Carl von Deinim's wasn't buttons. It was a shoelace. Pretty neat.'

'Oh!' Something stirred in Tommy's mind – vague – wholly nebulous . . .

Tuppence was quicker. As soon as he retailed the

conversation to her, she seized on the salient point.

'A shoelace? Tommy, that explains it!'

'What?'

'Betty, you idiot! Don't you remember that funny thing she did in my room, taking out my laces and soaking them in water. I thought at the time it was a funny thing to think of doing. But, of course, she'd seen Carl do it and was imitating him. He couldn't risk her talking about it, and arranged with that woman for her to be kidnapped.'

Tommy said, 'Then that's cleared up.'

'Yes. It's nice when things begin to fall into shape. One can put them behind you and get on a bit.'

'We need to get on.'

Tuppence nodded.

The times were gloomy indeed. France had astonishingly and suddenly capitulated – to the bewilderment and dismay of her own people.

The destination of the French Navy was in doubt.

Now the coasts of France were entirely in the hands of Germany, and the talk of invasion was no longer a remote contingency.

Tommy said:

'Carl von Deinim was only a link in the chain. Mrs Perenna's the fountain head.'

'Yes, we've got to get the goods on her. But it won't be easy.'

'No. After all, if she's the brains of the whole thing one can't expect it to be.'

'So M is Mrs Perenna?'

Tommy supposed she must be. He said slowly:

'You really think the girl isn't in this at all?'

'I'm quite sure of it.'

Tommy sighed.

'Well, you should know. But if so, it's tough luck on her. First the man she loves – and then her mother. She's not going to have much left, is she?'

'We can't help that.'

'Yes, but supposing we're wrong – that M or N is someone else?'

Tuppence said rather coldly:

'So you're still harping on that? Are you sure it isn't a case of wishful thinking?'

'What do you mean?'

'Sheila Perenna – that's what I mean.'

'Aren't you being rather absurd, Tuppence?'

'No, I'm not. She's got round you, Tommy, just like any other man –'

Tommy replied angrily:

'Not at all. It's simply that I've got my own ideas.'

'Which are?'

'I think I'll keep them to myself for a bit. We'll see which of us is right.'

'Well, I think we've got to go all out after Mrs

Perenna. Find out where she goes, whom she meets – everything. There must be a link somewhere. You'd better put Albert on to her this afternoon.'

'You can do that. I'm busy.'

'Why, what are you doing?'

Tommy said:

'I'm playing golf.'

Chapter 9

'Seems quite like old times, doesn't it, madam?' said Albert. He beamed happily. Though now, in his middle years, running somewhat to fat, Albert had still the romantic boy's heart which had first led him into associations with Tommy and Tuppence in their young and adventurous days.

'Remember how you first came across me?' demanded Albert. 'Cleanin' of the brasses, I was, in those top-notch flats. Coo, wasn't that hallporter a nasty bit of goods? Always on to me, he was. And the day you come along and strung me a tale! Pack of lies it was too, all about a crook called Ready Rita. Not but what some of it didn't turn out to be true. And since then, as you might say, I've never looked back. Many's the adventures we had afore we all settled down, so to speak.'

Albert sighed, and, by a natural association of ideas,

Tuppence inquired after the health of Mrs Albert.

'Oh, the missus is all right – but she doesn't take to the Welsh much, she says. Thinks they ought to learn proper English, and as for raids – why, they've had two there already, and holes in the field what you could put a motor-car in, so she says. So – how's that for safety? Might as well be in Kennington, she says, where she wouldn't have to see all the melancholy trees and could get good clean milk in a bottle.'

'I don't know,' said Tuppence, suddenly stricken, 'that we ought to get you into this, Albert.'

'Nonsense, madam,' said Albert. 'Didn't I try and join up and they were so haughty they wouldn't look at me. Wait for my age-group to be called up, they said. And me in the pink of health and only too eager to get at them perishing Germans – if you'll excuse the language. You just tell me how I can put a spoke in their wheel and spoil their goings on – and I'm there. Fifth Column, that's what we're up against, so the papers say – though what's happened to the other four they don't mention. But the long and short of it is, I'm ready to assist you and Captain Beresford in any way you like to indicate.'

'Good. Now I'll tell you what we want you to do.'

II

'How long have you known Bletchley?' asked Tommy as he stepped off the tee and watched with approval his ball leaping down the centre of the fairway.

Commander Haydock, who had also done a good drive, had a pleased expression on his face as he shouldered his clubs and replied:

'Bletchley? Let me see. Oh! About nine months or so. He came here last autumn.'

'Friend of friends of yours, I think you said?' Tommy suggested mendaciously.

'Did I?' The Commander looked a little surprised. 'No, I don't think so. Rather fancy I met him here at the club.'

'Bit of a mystery man, I gather?'

The Commander was clearly surprised this time.

'Mystery man? Old Bletchley?' He sounded frankly incredulous.

Tommy sighed inwardly. He supposed he was imagining things.

He played his next shot and topped it. Haydock had a good iron shot that stopped just short of the green. As he rejoined the other, he said:

'What on earth makes you call Bletchley a mystery man? I should have said he was a painfully prosaic chap

– typical Army. Bit set in his ideas and all that – narrow life, an Army life – but mystery!'

Tommy said vaguely:

'Oh well, I just got the idea from something somebody said –'

They got down to the business of putting. The Commander won the hole.

'Three up and two to play,' he remarked with satisfaction.

Then, as Tommy had hoped, his mind, free of the preoccupation of the match, harked back to what Tommy had said.

'What sort of mystery do you mean?' he asked.

Tommy shrugged his shoulders.

'Oh, it was just that nobody seemed to know much about him.'

'He was in the Rugbyshires.'

'Oh, you know that definitely?'

'Well, I – well, no, I don't know myself. I say, Meadowes, what's the idea? Nothing wrong about Bletchley, is there?'

'No, no, of course not.' Tommy's disclaimer came hastily. He had started his hare. He could now sit back and watch the Commander's mind chasing after it.

'Always struck me as an almost absurdly typical sort of chap,' said Haydock.

'Just so, just so.'

'Ah, yes – see what you mean. Bit too much of a type, perhaps?'

'I'm leading the witness,' thought Tommy. 'Still perhaps something may crop up out of the old boy's mind.'

'Yes, I do see what you mean,' the Commander went on thoughtfully. 'And now I come to think of it I've never actually come across anyone who knew Bletchley before he came down here. He doesn't have any old pals to stay – nothing of that kind.'

'Ah!' said Tommy, and added, 'Shall we play the bye? Might as well get a bit more exercise. It's a lovely evening.'

They drove off, then separated to play their next shots. When they met again on the green, Haydock said abruptly:

'Tell me what you heard about him.'

'Nothing – nothing at all.'

'No need to be so cautious with me, Meadowes. I hear all sorts of rumours. You understand? Everyone comes to me. I'm known to be pretty keen on the subject. What's the idea – that Bletchley isn't what he seems to be?'

'It was only the merest suggestion.'

'What do they think he is? A Hun? Nonsense, the man's as English as you and I.'

'Oh, yes, I'm sure he's quite all right.'

'Why, he's always yelling for more foreigners to be interned. Look how violent he was against that young German chap – and quite right, too, it seems. I heard unofficially from the Chief Constable that they found enough to hang von Deinim a dozen times over. He'd got a scheme to poison the water supply of the whole country and he was actually working out a new gas – working on it in one of our factories. My God, the short-sightedness of our people! Fancy letting the fellow inside the place to begin with. Believe anything, our Government would! A young fellow has only to come to this country just before war starts and whine a bit about persecution, and they shut both eyes and let him into all our secrets. They were just as dense about that fellow Hahn –'

Tommy had no intention of letting the Commander run ahead on the well-grooved track. He deliberately missed a putt.

'Hard lines,' cried Haydock. He played a careful shot. The ball rolled into the hole.

'My hole. A bit off your game today. What were we talking about?'

Tommy said firmly:

'About Bletchley being perfectly all right.'

'Of course. Of course. I wonder now – I did hear a rather funny story about him – didn't think anything of it at the time –'

Here, to Tommy's annoyance, they were hailed by two other men. The four returned to the clubhouse together and had drinks. After that, the Commander looked at his watch and remarked that he and Meadowes must be getting along. Tommy had accepted an invitation to supper with the Commander.

Smugglers' Rest was in its usual condition of apple-pie order. A tall middle-aged manservant waited on them with the professional deftness of a waiter. Such perfect service was somewhat unusual to find outside of a London restaurant.

When the man had left the room, Tommy commented on the fact.

'Yes, I was lucky to get Appledore.'

'How did you get hold of him?'

'He answered an advertisement as a matter of fact. He had excellent references, was clearly far superior to any of the others who applied and asked remarkably low wages. I engaged him on the spot.'

Tommy said with a laugh:

'The war has certainly robbed us of most of our good restaurant service. Practically all good waiters were foreigners. It doesn't seem to come naturally to the Englishman.'

'Bit too servile, that's why. Bowing and scraping doesn't come kindly to the English bulldog.'

Sitting outside, sipping coffee, Tommy gently asked:

'What was it you were going to say on the links? Something about a funny story – apropos of Bletchley.'

'What was it now? Hallo, did you see that? Light being shown out at sea. Where's my telescope?'

Tommy sighed. The stars in their courses seemed to be fighting against him. The Commander fussed into the house and out again, swept the horizon with his glass, outlined a whole system of signalling by the enemy to likely spots on shore, most of the evidence for which seemed to be non-existent, and proceeded to give a gloomy picture of a successful invasion in the near future.

'No organisation, no proper co-ordination. You're an LDV yourself, Meadowes – you know what it's like. With a man like old Andrews in charge –'

This was well-worn ground. It was Commander Haydock's pet grievance. He ought to be the man in command and he was quite determined to oust Col Andrews if it could possibly be done.

The manservant brought out whisky and liqueurs while the Commander was still holding forth.

'– and we're still honeycombed with spies – riddled with 'em. It was the same in the last war – hairdressers, waiters –'

Tommy, leaning back, catching the profile of Appledore as the latter hovered deft-footed, thought

– 'Waiters? You could call that fellow Fritz easier than Appledore . . .'

Well, why not? The fellow spoke perfect English, true, but then many Germans did. They had perfected their English by years in English restaurants. And the racial type was not unlike. Fair-haired, blue-eyed – often betrayed by the shape of the head – yes, the head – where had he seen a head lately . . .

He spoke on an impulse. The words fitted in appositely enough with what the Commander was just saying.

'All these damned forms to fill in. No good at all, Meadowes. Series of idiotic questions –'

Tommy said:

'I know. Such as "What is your name?" Answer N or M.'

There was a swerve – a crash. Appledore, the perfect servant, had blundered. A stream of crême de menthe soaked over Tommy's cuff and hand.

The man stammered, 'Sorry, sir.'

Haydock blazed out in fury:

'You damned clumsy fool! What the hell do you think you're doing?'

His usually red face was quite purple with anger. Tommy thought, 'Talk of an Army temper – Navy beats it hollow!' Haydock continued with a stream of abuse. Appledore was abject in apologies.

Tommy felt uncomfortable for the man, but suddenly, as though by magic, the Commander's wrath passed and he was his hearty self again.

'Come along and have a wash. Beastly stuff. It would be the crême de menthe.'

Tommy followed him indoors and was soon in the sumptuous bathroom with the innumerable gadgets. He carefully washed off the sticky sweet stuff. The Commander talked from the bedroom next door. He sounded a little shamefaced.

'Afraid I let myself go a bit. Poor old Appledore – he knows I let go a bit more than I mean always.'

Tommy turned from the wash-basin drying his hands. He did not notice that a cake of soap had slipped on to the floor. His foot stepped on it. The linoleum was highly polished.

A moment later Tommy was doing a wild ballet dancer step. He shot across the bathroom, arms outstretched. One came up against the right-hand tap of the bath, the other pushed heavily against the side of a small bathroom cabinet. It was an extravagant gesture never likely to be achieved except by some catastrophe such as had just occurred.

His foot skidded heavily against the end panel of the bath.

The thing happened like a conjuring trick. The bath slid out from the wall, turning on a concealed pivot.

Tommy found himself looking into a dim recess. He had no doubt whatever as to what occupied that recess. It contained a transmitting wireless apparatus.

The Commander's voice had ceased. He appeared suddenly in the doorway. And with a click, several things fell into place in Tommy's brain.

Had he been blind up to now? That jovial florid face – the face of a 'hearty Englishman' – was only a mask. Why had he not seen it all along for what it was – the face of a bad-tempered overbearing Prussian officer. Tommy was helped, no doubt, by the incident that had just happened. For it recalled to him another incident, a Prussian bully turning on a subordinate and rating him with the Junker's true insolence. So had Commander Haydock turned on his subordinate that evening when the latter had been taken unawares.

And it all fitted in – it fitted in like magic. The double bluff. The enemy agent Hahn, sent first, preparing the place, employing foreign workmen, drawing attention to himself and proceeding finally to the next stage in the plan, his own unmasking by the gallant British sailor Commander Haydock. And then how natural that the Englishman should buy the place and tell the story to everyone, boring them by constant repetition. And so N, securely settled in his appointed place, with sea communications and his secret wireless and his staff officers at Sans Souci close at hand, is ready to carry out Germany's plan.

Tommy was unable to resist a flash of genuine admiration. The whole thing had been so perfectly planned. He himself had never suspected Haydock – he had accepted Haydock as the genuine article – only a completely unforeseen accident had given the show away.

All this passed through Tommy's mind in a few seconds. He knew, only too well, that he was, that he must necessarily be, in deadly peril. If only he could act the part of the credulous thick-headed Englishman well enough.

He turned to Haydock with what he hoped was a natural-sounding laugh.

'By Jove, one never stops getting surprises at your place. Was this another of Hahn's little gadgets? You didn't show me this the other day.'

Haydock was standing still. There was a tensity about his big body as it stood there blocking the door.

'More than a match for me,' Tommy thought. 'And there's that confounded servant, too.'

For an instant Haydock stood as though moulded in stone, then he relaxed. He said with a laugh:

'Damned funny, Meadowes. You went skating over the floor like a ballet dancer! Don't suppose a thing like that would happen once in a thousand times. Dry your hands and come into the other room.'

Tommy followed him out of the bathroom. He was alert and tense in every muscle. Somehow or other he must get safely away from this house with his knowledge. Could he succeed in fooling Haydock? The latter's tone sounded natural enough.

With an arm round Tommy's shoulders, a casual arm, perhaps (or perhaps not), Haydock shepherded him into the sitting-room. Turning, he shut the door behind them.

'Look here, old boy, I've got something to say to you.'

His voice was friendly, natural – just a shade embarrassed. He motioned to Tommy to sit down.

'It's a bit awkward,' he said. 'Upon my word, it's a bit awkward! Nothing for it, though, but to take you into my confidence. Only you'll have to keep dark about it, Meadowes. You understand that?'

Tommy endeavoured to throw an expression of eager interest upon his face.

Haydock sat down and drew his chair confidentially close.

'You see, Meadowes, it's like this. Nobody's supposed to know it but I'm working on Intelligence MI42 BX – that's my department. Ever heard of it?'

Tommy shook his head and intensified the eager expression.

'Well, it's pretty secret. Kind of inner ring, if you know what I mean. We transmit certain information from here – but it would be absolutely fatal if that fact got out, you understand?'

'Of course, of course,' said Mr Meadowes. 'Most interesting! Naturally you can count on me not to say a word.'

'Yes, that's absolutely vital. The whole thing is extremely confidential.'

'I quite understand. Your work must be most thrilling. Really most thrilling. I should like so much to know more about it – but I suppose I mustn't ask that?'

'No, I'm afraid not. It's very secret, you see.'

'Oh yes, I see. I really do apologise – a most extraordinary accident –'

He thought to himself, 'Surely he can't be taken in? He can't imagine I'd fall for this stuff?'

It seemed incredible to him. Then he reflected that vanity had been the undoing of many men. Commander Haydock was a clever man, a big fellow – this miserable chap Meadowes was a stupid Britisher – the sort of man who would believe anything! If only Haydock continued to think that.

Tommy went on talking. He displayed keen interest and curiosity. He knew he mustn't ask questions but – He supposed Commander Haydock's work must be very dangerous? Had he ever been in Germany, working there?

Haydock replied genially enough. He was intensely

the British sailor now – the Prussian officer had disappeared. But Tommy, watching him with a new vision, wondered how he could ever have been deceived. The shape of the head – the line of the jaw – nothing British about them.

Presently Mr Meadowes rose. It was the supreme test. Would it go off all right?

'I really must be going now – getting quite late – feel terribly apologetic, but can assure you will not say a word to anybody.'

('It's now or never. Will he let me go or not? I must be ready – a straight to his jaw would be best –')

Talking amiably and with pleasurable excitement, Mr Meadowes edged towards the door.

He was in the hall . . . he had opened the front door . . .

Through the door on the right he caught a glimpse of Appledore setting the breakfast things ready on a tray for the morning. (The damned fools were going to let him get away with it!)

The two men stood in the porch, chatting – fixing up another match for next Saturday.

Tommy thought grimly: 'There'll be no next Saturday for you, my boy.'

Voices came from the road outside. Two men returning from a tramp on the headland. They were men that both Tommy and the Commander knew slightly.

Tommy hailed them. They stopped. Haydock and he exchanged a few words with them, all standing at the gate, then Tommy waved a genial farewell to his host and stepped off with the two men.

He had got away with it.

Haydock, damned fool, had been taken in!

He heard Haydock go back to his house, go in and shut the door. Tommy tramped carefully down the hill with his two new-found friends.

Weather looked likely to change.

Old Monroe was off his game again.

That fellow Ashby refused to join the LDV. Said it was no damned good. Pretty thick, that. Young Marsh, the assistant caddy master, was a conscientious objector. Didn't Meadowes think that matter ought to be put up to the committee. There had been a pretty bad raid on Southampton the night before last – quite a lot of damage done. What did Meadowes think about Spain? Were they turning nasty? Of course, ever since the French collapse –

Tommy could have shouted aloud. Such good casual normal talk. A stroke of providence that these two men had turned up just at that moment.

He said goodbye to them at the gate of Sans Souci and turned in.

He walked up the drive whistling softly to himself.

He had just turned the dark corner by the rhododendrons when something heavy descended on his head. He crashed forward, pitching into blackness and oblivion.

Chapter 10

'Did you say Three Spades, Mrs Blenkensop?'

Yes, Mrs Blenkensop had said Three Spades. Mrs Sprot, returning breathless from the telephone: 'And they've changed the time of the ARP exam, again, it's *too* bad,' demanded to have the bidding again.

Miss Minton, as usual, delayed things by ceaseless reiterations.

'Was it Two Clubs I said? Are you sure? I rather thought, you know, that it might have been one No Trump – Oh yes, of course, I remember now. Mrs Cayley said One Heart, didn't she? I was going to say one No Trump although I hadn't quite got the count, but I do think one should play a plucky game – and then Mrs Cayley said One Heart and so I had to go Two Clubs. I always think it's so difficult when one has two short suits –'

'Sometimes,' Tuppence thought to herself, 'it would

save time if Miss Minton just put her hand down on the table to show them all. She was quite incapable of not telling exactly what was in it.'

'So now we've got it right,' said Miss Minton triumphantly. 'One Heart, Two Clubs.'

'Two Spades,' said Tuppence.

'I passed, didn't I?' said Mrs Sprot.

They looked at Mrs Cayley, who was leaning forward listening. Miss Minton took up the tale.

'Then Mrs Cayley said Two Hearts and I said Three Diamonds.'

'And I said Three Spades,' said Tuppence.

'Pass,' said Mrs Sprot.

Mrs Cayley sat in silence. At last she seemed to become aware that everyone was looking at her.

'Oh dear,' she flushed. 'I'm so sorry. I thought perhaps Mr Cayley needed me. I hope he's all right out there on the terrace.'

She looked from one to the other of them.

'Perhaps, if you don't mind, I'd better just go and *see*. I heard rather an odd noise. Perhaps he's dropped his book.'

She fluttered out of the window. Tuppence gave an exasperated sigh.

'She ought to have a string tied to her wrist,' she said. 'Then he could pull it when he wanted her.'

'Such a devoted wife,' said Miss Minton. 'It's very

nice to see, isn't it?'

'Is it?' said Tuppence, who was feeling far from good-tempered.

The three women sat in silence for a minute or two.

'Where's Sheila tonight?' asked Miss Minton.

'She went to the pictures,' said Mrs Sprot.

'Where's Mrs Perenna?' asked Tuppence.

'She said she was going to do accounts in her room,' said Miss Minton. 'Poor dear. So tiring, doing accounts.'

'She's not been doing accounts all evening,' said Mrs Sprot, 'because she came in just now when I was telephoning in the hall.'

'I wonder where she'd been,' said Miss Minton, whose life was taken up with such small wonderments. 'Not to the pictures, they wouldn't be out yet.'

'She hadn't got a hat on,' said Mrs Sprot. 'Nor a coat. Her hair was all anyhow and I think she'd been running or something. Quite out of breath. She ran upstairs without a word and she glared – positively glared at me – and I'm sure *I* hadn't done anything.'

Mrs Cayley reappeared at the window.

'Fancy,' she said. 'Mr Cayley has walked all round the garden by himself. He quite enjoyed it, he said. Such a mild night.'

She sat down again.

'Let me see – oh, do you think we could have the bidding over again?'

Tuppence suppressed a rebellious sigh. They had the bidding all over again and she was left to play Three Spades.

Mrs Perenna came in just as they were cutting for the next deal.

'Did you enjoy your walk?' asked Miss Minton.

Mrs Perenna stared at her. It was a fierce and unpleasant stare. She said:

'I've not been out.'

'Oh – oh – I thought Mrs Sprot said you'd come in just now.'

Mrs Perenna said:

'I just went outside to look at the weather.'

Her tone was disagreeable. She threw a hostile glance at the meek Mrs Sprot, who flushed and looked frightened.

'Just fancy,' said Mrs Cayley, contributing her item of news. 'Mr Cayley walked all round the garden.'

Mrs Perenna said sharply:

'Why did he do that?'

Mrs Cayley said:

'It is such a mild night. He hasn't even put on his second muffler and he *still* doesn't want to come in. I do *hope* he won't get a chill.'

Mrs Perenna said:

'There are worse things than chills. A bomb might come any minute and blow us all to bits!'

'Oh, dear, I hope it won't.'

'Do you? *I* rather wish it would.'

Mrs Perenna went out of the window. The four bridge players stared after her.

'She seems very *odd* tonight,' said Mrs Sprot.

Miss Minton leaned forward.

'You don't think, do you –' She looked from side to side. They all leaned nearer together. Miss Minton said in a sibilant whisper:

'You don't suspect, do you, that she drinks?'

'Oh, dear,' said Mrs Cayley. 'I wonder now? That would explain it. She really is so – so unaccountable sometimes. What do you think, Mrs Blenkensop?'

'Oh, I don't *really* think so. I think she's worried about something. Er – it's your call, Mrs Sprot.'

'Dear me, what shall I say?' asked Mrs Sprot, surveying her hand.

Nobody volunteered to tell her, though Miss Minton, who had been gazing with unabashed interest into her hand, might have been in a position to advise.

'That isn't Betty, is it?' demanded Mrs Sprot, her head upraised.

'No, it isn't,' said Tuppence firmly.

'She felt that she might scream unless they could get on with the game.

Mrs Sprot looked at her hand vaguely, her mind still apparently maternal. Then she said:

'Oh, One Diamond, I *think.*'

The call went round. Mrs Cayley led.

'When in doubt lead a Trump, they say,' she twittered, and laid down the Nine of Diamonds.

A deep genial voice said:

''Tis the curse of Scotland that you've played there!'

Mrs O'Rourke stood in the window. She was breathing deeply – her eyes were sparkling. She looked sly and malicious. She advanced into the room.

'Just a nice quiet game of bridge, is it?'

'What's that in your hand?' asked Mrs Sprot, with interest.

''Tis a hammer,' said Mrs O'Rourke amiably. 'I found it lying in the drive. No doubt someone left it there.'

'It's a funny place to leave a hammer,' said Mrs Sprot doubtfully.

'It is that,' agreed Mrs O'Rourke.

She seemed in a particularly good humour. Swinging the hammer by its handle she went out into the hall.

'Let me see,' said Miss Minton. 'What's trumps?'

The game proceeded for five minutes without further interruption, and then Major Bletchley came in. He had been to the pictures and proceeded to tell them in detail the plot of *Wandering Minstrel*, laid in the reign of Richard the First. The Major, as a military man, criticised at some length the crusading battle scenes.

The rubber was not finished, for Mrs Cayley, looking at her watch, discovered the lateness of the hour with shrill little cries of horror and rushed out to Mr Cayley. The latter, as a neglected invalid, enjoyed himself a great deal, coughing in a sepulchral manner, shivering dramatically and saying several times:

'*Quite* all right, my dear. I hope you enjoyed your game. It doesn't matter about *me* at all. Even if I *have* caught a severe chill, what does it really matter? There's a war on!'

II

At breakfast the next morning, Tuppence was aware at once of a certain tension in the atmosphere.

Mrs Perenna, her lips pursed very tightly together, was distinctly acrid in the few remarks she made. She left the room with what could only be described as a flounce.

Major Bletchley, spreading marmalade thickly on his toast, gave vent to a deep chuckle.

'Touch of frost in the air,' he remarked. 'Well, well! Only to be expected, I suppose.'

'Why, what has happened?' demanded Miss Minton, leaning forward eagerly, her thin neck twitching with pleasurable anticipation.

'Don't know that I ought to tell tales out of school,' replied the Major irritatingly.

'Oh! Major Bletchley!'

'*Do* tell us,' said Tuppence.

Major Bletchley looked thoughtfully at his audience: Miss Minton, Mrs Blenkensop, Mrs Cayley and Mrs O'Rourke. Mrs Sprot and Betty had just left. He decided to talk.

'It's Meadowes,' he said. 'Been out on the tiles all night. Hasn't come home yet.'

'*What?*' exclaimed Tuppence.

Major Bletchley threw her a pleased and malicious glance. He enjoyed the discomfiture of the designing widow.

'Bit of a gay dog, Meadowes,' he chortled. 'The Perenna's annoyed. Naturally.'

'Oh dear,' said Miss Minton, flushing painfully. Mrs Cayley looked shocked. Mrs O'Rourke merely chuckled.

'Mrs Perenna told me already,' she said. 'Ah, well, the boys will be the boys.'

Miss Minton said eagerly:

'Oh, but surely – perhaps Mr Meadowes has met with an accident. In the black-out, you know.'

'Good old black-out,' said Major Bletchley. 'Responsible for a lot. I can tell you, it's been an eye-opener being on patrol in the LDV. Stopping cars and all that. The amount of wives "just seeing their husbands home". And different names on their identity cards! And the wife or the husband coming back the other way alone a few hours later. Ha ha!' He chuckled, then quickly composed his face as he received the full blast of Mrs Blenkensop's disapproving stare.

'Human nature – a bit humorous, eh?' he said appeasingly.

'Oh, but Mr Meadowes,' bleated Miss Minton. 'He may really have met with an accident. Been knocked down by a car.'

'That'll be his story, I expect,' said the Major. 'Car hit him and knocked him out and he came to in the morning.'

'He may have been taken to hospital.'

'They'd have let us know. After all, he's carrying his identity card, isn't he?'

'Oh dear,' said Mrs Cayley, 'I wonder what Mr Cayley will say?'

This rhetorical question remained unanswered. Tuppence, rising with an assumption of affronted dignity, got up and left the room.

Major Bletchley chuckled when the door closed behind her.

'Poor old Meadowes,' he said. 'The fair widow's annoyed about it. Thought she'd got her hooks into him.'

'Oh, Major *Bletchley*,' bleated Miss Minton.

Major Bletchley winked.

'Remember your Dickens? *Beware of widders, Sammy.*'

III

Tuppence was a little upset by Tommy's unannounced absence, but she tried to reassure herself. He might possibly have struck some hot trail and gone off upon it. The difficulties of communication with each other under such circumstances had been foreseen by them both, and they had agreed that the other one was not to be unduly perturbed by unexplained absences. They had arranged certain contrivances between them for such emergencies.

Mrs Perenna had, according to Mrs Sprot, been out last night. The vehemence of her own denial of the fact only made that absence of hers more interesting to speculate upon.

It was possible that Tommy had trailed her on her secret errand and had found something worth following up.

Doubtless he would communicate with Tuppence in his special way, or else turn up, very shortly.

Nevertheless, Tuppence was unable to avoid a certain feeling of uneasiness. She decided that in her role of Mrs Blenkensop it would be perfectly natural to display some curiosity and even anxiety. She went without more ado in search of Mrs Perenna.

Mrs Perenna was inclined to be short with her upon the subject. She made it clear that such conduct on the part of one of her lodgers was not to be condoned or glossed over. Tuppence exclaimed breathlessly:

'Oh, but he may have met with an *accident*. I'm sure he *must* have done. He's not at all that sort of man – not at all loose in his ideas, or *anything* of that kind. He must have been run down by a car or something.'

'We shall probably soon hear one way or another,' said Mrs Perenna.

But the day wore on and there was no sign of Mr Meadowes.

In the evening, Mrs Perenna, urged on by the pleas of her boarders, agreed extremely reluctantly to ring up the police.

A sergeant called at the house with a notebook and took particulars. Certain facts were then elicited. Mr Meadowes had left Commander Haydock's house at half-past ten. From there he had walked with a Mr Walters and a Dr Curtis as far as the gate of Sans

Souci, where he had said goodbye to them and turned into the drive.

From that moment, Mr Meadowes seemed to have disappeared into space.

In Tuppence's mind, two possibilities emerged from this.

When walking up the drive, Tommy may have seen Mrs Perenna coming towards him, have slipped into the bushes and then have followed her. Having observed her rendezvous with some unknown person, he might then have followed the latter, whilst Mrs Perenna returned to Sans Souci. In that case, he was probably very much alive, and busy on a trail. In which case the well-meant endeavours of the police to find him might prove most embarrassing.

The other possibility was not so pleasant. It resolved itself into two pictures – one that of Mrs Perenna returning 'out of breath and dishevelled' – the other, one that would not be laid aside, a picture of Mrs O'Rourke standing smiling in the window, holding a heavy hammer.

That hammer had horrible possibilities.

For what should a hammer be doing lying outside?

As to who had wielded it, that was more difficult. A good deal depended on the exact time when Mrs Perenna had re-entered the house. It was certainly somewhere in the neighbourhood of half-past ten, but none of the bridge party happened to have noted the time exactly. Mrs Perenna had declared vehemently that she had not been out except just to look at the weather. But one does not get out of breath just looking at the weather. It was clearly extremely vexing to her to have been seen by Mrs Sprot. With ordinary luck the four ladies might have been safely accounted for as busy playing bridge.

What had the time been exactly?

Tuppence found everybody extremely vague on the subject.

If the time agreed, Mrs Perenna was clearly the most likely suspect. But there were other possibilities. Of the inhabitants of Sans Souci, three had been out at the time of Tommy's return. Major Bletchley had been out at the cinema – but he had been to it alone, and the way that he had insisted on retailing the whole picture so meticulously might suggest to a suspicious mind that he was deliberately establishing an alibi.

Then there was the valetudinarian Mr Cayley who had gone for a walk all round the garden. But for the accident of Mrs Cayley's anxiety over her spouse, no one might have ever heard of that walk and might have imagined Mr Cayley to have remained securely encased in rugs like a mummy in his chair on the terrace. (Rather unlike him, really, to risk the contamination of the night air so long.)

And there was Mrs O'Rourke herself, swinging the hammer, and smiling . . .

IV

'What's the matter, Deb? You're looking worried, my sweet.'

Deborah Beresford started, and then laughed, looking frankly into Tony Marsdon's sympathetic brown eyes. She liked Tony. He had brains – was one of the most brilliant beginners in the coding department – and was thought likely to go far.

Deborah enjoyed her job, though she found it made somewhat strenuous demands on her powers of concentration. It was tiring, but it was worthwhile and it gave her a pleasant feeling of importance. This was real work – not just hanging about a hospital waiting for a chance to nurse.

She said:

'Oh, nothing. Just *family*! *You* know.'

'Families *are* a bit trying. What's yours been up to?'

'It's my mother. To tell the truth, I'm just a bit worried about her.'

'Why? What's happened?'

'Well, you see, she went down to Cornwall to a

frightfully trying old aunt of mine. Seventy-eight and completely ga ga.'

'Sounds grim,' commented the young man sympathetically.

'Yes, it was really very noble of Mother. But she was rather hipped anyway because nobody seemed to want her in this war. Of course, she nursed and did things in the last one – but it's all quite different now, and they don't want these middle-aged people. They want people who are young and on the spot. Well, as I say, Mother got a bit hipped over it all, and so she went off down to Cornwall to stay with Aunt Gracie, and she's been doing a bit in the garden, extra vegetable growing and all that.'

'Quite sound,' commented Tony.

'Yes, much the best thing she could do. She's quite active still, you know,' said Deborah kindly.

'Well, that sounds all right.'

'Oh yes, it isn't *that*. I was quite happy about her – had a letter only two days ago sounding quite cheerful.'

'What's the trouble, then?'

'The trouble is that I told Charles, who was going down to see his people in that part of the world, to go and look her up. And he did. And she wasn't there.'

'Wasn't *there*?'

'No. And she hadn't been there! Not at all apparently!'

Tony looked a little embarrassed.

'Rather odd,' he murmured. 'Where's – I mean – your father?'

'Carrot Top? Oh, he's in Scotland somewhere. In one of those dreadful Ministries where they file papers in triplicate all day long.'

'Your mother hasn't gone to join him, perhaps?'

'She can't. He's in one of those area things where wives can't go.'

'Oh – er – well, I suppose she's just slopped off somewhere.'

Tony was decidedly embarrassed now – especially with Deborah's large worried eyes fixed plaintively upon him.

'Yes, but why? It's so *queer*. All her letters – talking about Aunt Gracie and the garden and everything.'

'I know, I know,' said Tony hastily. 'Of course, she'd want you to think – I mean – nowadays – well, people *do* slope off now and again if you know what I mean –'

Deborah's gaze, from being plaintive, became suddenly wrathful.

'If you think Mother's just gone off weekending with someone you're absolutely wrong. Absolutely. Mother and Father are devoted to each other – really devoted. It's quite a joke in the family. She'd never –'

Tony said hastily:

'Of course not. Sorry. I really didn't mean –'

Deborah, her wrath appeased, creased her forehead.

'The odd thing is that someone the other day said they'd seen Mother in Leahampton, of all places, and of course I said it couldn't be her because she was in Cornwall, but now I wonder –'

Tony, his match held to a cigarette, paused suddenly and the match went out.

'Leahampton?' he said sharply.

'Yes. Just the last place you could imagine Mother going off to. Nothing to do and all old Colonels and maiden ladies.'

'Doesn't sound a likely spot, certainly,' said Tony.

He lit his cigarette and asked casually:

'What did your mother do in the last war?'

Deborah answered mechanically:

'Oh, nursed a bit and drove a General – Army, I mean, not a bus. All the usual sort of things.'

'Oh, I thought perhaps she'd been like you – in the Intelligence.'

'Oh, Mother would never have had the head for this sort of work. I believe, though, that she and Father did do something in the sleuthing line. Secret papers and master spies – that sort of thing. Of course, the darlings exaggerate it all a good deal and make it all sound as though it had been frightfully important. We don't really encourage them to talk about it much because you know what one's family is – the same old story over and over again.'

'Oh, rather,' said Tony Marsdon heartily. 'I quite agree.'

It was on the following day that Deborah, returning to her digs, was puzzled by something unfamiliar in the appearance of her room.

It took her a few minutes to fathom what it was. Then she rang the bell and demanded angrily of her landlady what had happened to the big photograph that always stood on the top of the chest of drawers.

Mrs Rowley was aggrieved and resentful.

She couldn't say, she was sure. She hadn't touched it herself. Maybe Gladys –

But Gladys also denied having removed it. The man had been about the gas, she said hopefully.

But Deborah declined to believe that an employee of the Gas Co. would have taken a fancy to and removed the portrait of a middle-aged lady.

Far more likely, in Deborah's opinion, that Gladys had smashed the photograph frame and had hastily removed all traces of the crime to the dustbin.

Deborah didn't make a fuss about it. Sometime or other she'd get her mother to send her another photo.

She thought to herself with rising vexation:

'What's the old darling up to? She might tell me. Of course, it's absolute nonsense to suggest, as Tony did, that she's gone off with someone, but all the same it's very queer . . .'

Chapter 11

It was Tuppence's turn to talk to the fisherman on the end of the pier.

She had hoped against hope that Mr Grant might have had some comfort for her. But her hopes were soon dashed. He stated definitely that no news of any kind had come from Tommy.

Tuppence said, trying her best to make her voice assured and business-like:

'There's no reason to suppose that anything has – happened to him?'

'None whatever. But let's suppose it has.'

'What?'

'I'm saying – supposing it has. What about you?'

'Oh, I see – I – carry on, of course.'

'That's the stuff. *There is time to weep after the battle.* We're in the thick of the battle now. And time is short. One piece of information you brought us has been proved correct. You overheard a reference to the *fourth*. The fourth referred to is the fourth of next month. It's the date fixed for the big attack on this country.'

'You're sure?'

'Fairly sure. They're methodical people, our enemies. All their plans neatly made and worked out. Wish we could say the same of ourselves. Planning isn't our strong point. Yes, the fourth is The Day. All these raids aren't the real thing – they're mostly reconnaissance – testing our defences and our reflexes to air attack. On the fourth comes the real thing.'

'But if you know that –'

'We know The Day is fixed. We know, or think we know, roughly, *where* . . . (But we may be wrong there.) We're as ready as we can be. But it's the old story of the siege of Troy. They knew, as we know, all about the forces without. It's the forces within we want to know about. The men in the Wooden Horse! For they are the men who can deliver up the keys of the fortress. A dozen men in high places, in command, in vital spots, by issuing conflicting orders, can throw the country into just that state of confusion necessary for the German plan to succeed. We've *got* to have inside information in time.'

Tuppence said despairingly:

'I feel so futile – so inexperienced.'

'Oh, you needn't worry about that. We've got experienced people working, all the experience and talent we've got – but when there's treachery within we can't tell who to trust. You and Beresford are the irregular forces. Nobody knows about you. That's why you've got a chance to succeed – that's why you *have* succeeded up to a certain point.'

'Can't you put some of your people on to Mrs Perenna? There *must* be some of them you can trust absolutely?'

'Oh, we've done that. Working from "information received that Mrs Perenna is a member of the IRA with anti-British sympathies". That's true enough, by the way – but we can't get proof of anything further. Not of the vital facts we want. So stick to it, Mrs Beresford. Go on, and do your darndest.'

'The fourth,' said Tuppence. 'That's barely a week ahead?'

'It's a week exactly.'

Tuppence clenched her hands.

'We *must* get *something*! I say *we* because I believe Tommy is on to something, and that that's why he hasn't come back. He's following up a lead. If I could only get something too. I wonder how. If I –'

She frowned, planning a new form of attack.

II

'You see, Albert, it's a possibility.'

'I see what you mean, madam, of course. But I don't like the idea very much, I must say.'

'I think it might work.'

'Yes, madam, but it's exposing yourself to attack – that's what I don't like – and I'm sure the master wouldn't like it.'

'We've tried all the usual ways. That is to say, we've done what we could keeping under cover. It seems to me that now the only chance is to come out into the open.'

'You are aware, madam, that thereby you may be sacrificing an advantage?'

'You're frightfully BBC in your language this afternoon, Albert,' said Tuppence, with some exasperation.

Albert looked slightly taken aback and reverted to a more natural form of speech.

'I was listening to a very interesting talk on pond life last night,' he explained.

'We've no time to think about pond life now,' said Tuppence.

'Where's Captain Beresford, that's what I'd like to know?'

'So should I,' said Tuppence, with a pang.

'Don't seem natural, his disappearing without a word. He ought to have tipped you the wink by now. That's why –'

'Yes, Albert?'

'What I mean is, if *he's* come out in the open, perhaps *you'd* better not.'

He paused to arrange his ideas and then went on.

'I mean, they've blown the gaff on *him*, but *they mayn't know about you* – and so it's up to you to keep under cover still.'

'I wish I could make up my mind,' sighed Tuppence.

'Which way were you thinking of managing it, madam?'

Tuppence murmured thoughtfully:

'I thought I might lose a letter I'd written – make a lot of fuss about it, seem very upset. Then it would be found in the hall and Beatrice would probably put it on the hall table. Then the right person would get a look at it.'

'What would be in the letter?'

'Oh, roughly – that I'd been successful in discovering the *identity of the person in question* and that I was to make a full report personally tomorrow. Then, you see, Albert, N or M would have to come out in the open and have a shot at eliminating me.'

'Yes, and maybe they'd manage it, too.'

'Not if I was on my guard. They'd have, I think, to decoy me away somewhere – some lonely spot. That's where *you'd* come in – because they don't know about you.'

'I'd follow them up and catch them red-handed, so to speak?'

Tuppence nodded.

'That's the idea. I must think it out carefully – I'll meet you tomorrow.'

III

Tuppence was just emerging from the local lending library with what had been recommended to her as a 'nice book' clasped under her arm when she was startled by a voice saying:

'Mrs Beresford.'

She turned abruptly to see a tall dark young man with an agreeable but slightly embarrassed smile.

He said:

'Er – I'm afraid you don't remember me?'

Tuppence was thoroughly used to the formula. She could have predicted with accuracy the words that were coming next.

'I – er – came to the flat with Deborah one day.'

Deborah's friends! So many of them, and all, to

Tuppence, looking singularly alike! Some dark like this young man, some fair, an occasional red-haired one – but all cast in the same mould – pleasant, well-mannered, their hair, in Tuppence's view, just slightly too long. (But when this was hinted, Deborah would say, 'Oh, *Mother*, don't be so terribly 1916. I can't *stand* short hair.')

Annoying to have run across and been recognised by one of Deborah's young men just now. However, she could probably soon shake him off.

'I'm Anthony Marsdon,' explained the young man.

Tuppence murmured mendaciously, 'Oh, of course,' and shook hands.

Tony Marsdon went on:

'I'm awfully glad to have found you, Mrs Beresford. You see, I'm working at the same job as Deborah, and as a matter of fact something rather awkward has happened.'

'Yes?' said Tuppence. 'What is it?'

'Well, you see, Deborah's found out that you're not down in Cornwall as she thought, and that makes it a bit awkward, doesn't it, for you?'

'Oh, bother,' said Tuppence, concerned. 'How did she find out?'

Tony Marsdon explained. He went on rather diffidently:

'Deborah, of course, has no idea of what you're really doing.'

He paused discreetly, and then went on:

'It's important, I imagine, that she shouldn't know. My job, actually, is rather the same line. I'm supposed to be just a beginner in the coding department. Really my instructions are to express views that are mildly Fascist – admiration of the German system, insinuations that a working alliance with Hitler wouldn't be a bad thing – all that sort of thing – just to see what response I get. There's a good deal of rot going on, you see, and we want to find out who's at the bottom of it.'

'Rot everywhere,' thought Tuppence.

'But as soon as Deb told me about you,' continued the young man, 'I thought I'd better come straight down and warn you so that you can cook up a likely story. You see, I happen to know what you are doing and that it's of vital importance. It would be fatal if any hint of who you are got about. I thought perhaps you could make it seem as though you'd joined Captain Beresford in Scotland or wherever he is. You might say that you'd been allowed to work with him there.'

'I might do that, certainly,' said Tuppence thoughtfully.

Tony Marsdon said anxiously:

'You don't think I'm butting in?'

'No, no, I'm very grateful to you.'

Tony said rather inconsequentially:

'I'm – well – you see – I'm rather fond of Deborah.'

Tuppence flashed him an amused quick glance.

How far away it seemed, that world of attentive young men and Deb with her rudeness to them that never seemed to put them off. This young man was, she thought, quite an attractive specimen.

She put aside what she called to herself 'peace-time thoughts' and concentrated on the present situation.

After a moment or two she said slowly:

'My husband isn't in Scotland.'

'Isn't he?'

'No, he's down here with me. At least he was! Now – he's disappeared.'

'I say, that's bad – or isn't it? Was he on to something?'

Tuppence nodded.

'I think so. That's why I don't think that his disappearing like this is really a bad sign. I think, sooner or later, he'll communicate with me – in his own way.' She smiled a little.

Tony said, with some slight embarrassment:

'Of course, you know the game well, I expect. But you ought to be careful.'

Tuppence nodded.

'I know what you mean. Beautiful heroines in books are always easily decoyed away. But Tommy and I have our methods. We've got a slogan,' she smiled. '*Penny plain and tuppence coloured.*'

'What?' The young man stared at her as though she had gone mad.

'I ought to explain that my family nickname is Tuppence.'

'Oh, I see.' The young man's brow cleared. 'Ingenious – what?'

'I hope so.'

'I don't want to butt in – but couldn't I help in any way?'

'Yes,' said Tuppence thoughtfully. 'I think perhaps you might.'

Chapter 12

After long aeons of unconsciousness, Tommy began to be aware of a fiery ball swimming in space. In the centre of the fiery ball was a core of pain, the universe shrank, the fiery ball swung more slowly – he discovered suddenly that the nucleus of it was his own aching head.

Slowly he became aware of other things – of cold cramped limbs, of hunger, of an inability to move his lips.

Slower and slower swung the fiery ball . . . It was now Thomas Beresford's head and it was resting on solid ground. Very solid ground. In fact something suspiciously like stone.

Yes, he was lying on hard stones, and he was in pain, unable to move, extremely hungry, cold and uncomfortable.

Surely, although Mrs Perenna's beds had never been unduly soft, this could not be –

Of course – Haydock! The wireless! The German waiter! Turning in at the gates of Sans Souci . . .

Someone, creeping up behind him, had struck him down. That was the reason of his aching head.

And he'd thought he'd got away with it all right! So Haydock, after all, hadn't been quite such a fool?

Haydock? Haydock had gone back into Smugglers' Rest, and closed the door. How had he managed to get down the hill and be waiting for Tommy in the grounds of Sans Souci?

It couldn't be done. Not without Tommy seeing him.

The manservant, then? Had he been sent ahead to lie in wait? But surely, as Tommy had crossed the hall, he had seen Appledore in the kitchen of which the door was slightly ajar? Or did he only fancy he had seen him? Perhaps that was the explanation.

Anyway it didn't matter. The thing to do was to find out where he was now.

His eyes, accustomed to the darkness, picked out a small rectangle of dim light. A window or small grating. The air smelt chilly and musty. He was, he fancied, lying in a cellar. His hands and feet were tied and a gag in his mouth was secured by a bandage.

'Seems rather as though I'm for it,' thought Tommy.

He tried gingerly to move his limbs or body, but he could not succeed.

At that moment, there was a faint creaking sound and a door somewhere behind him was pushed open. A man with a candle came in. He set down the candle on the ground. Tommy recognised Appledore. The latter disappeared again and then returned carrying a tray on which was a jug of water, a glass, and some bread and cheese.

Stooping down he first tested the cords binding the other limbs. He then touched the gag.

He said in a quiet level voice:

'I am about to take this off. You will then be able to eat and drink. If, however, you make the slightest sound, I shall replace it immediately.'

Tommy tried to nod his head which proved impossible, so he opened and shut his eyes several times instead.

Appledore, taking this for consent, carefully unknotted the bandage.

His mouth freed, Tommy spent some minutes easing his jaw. Appledore held the glass of water to his lips. He swallowed at first with difficulty, then more easily. The water did him the world of good.

He murmured stiffly:

'That's better. I'm not quite so young as I was. Now for the eats, Fritz – or is it Franz?'

The man said quietly:

'My name here is Appledore.'

He held the slice of bread and cheese up and Tommy bit at it hungrily.

The meal washed down with water, he then asked:

'And what's the next part of the programme?'

For answer, Appledore picked up the gag again.

Tommy said quickly:

'I want to see Commander Haydock.'

Appledore shook his head. Deftly he replaced the gag and went out.

Tommy was left to meditate in darkness. He was awakened from a confused sleep by the sound of the door reopening. This time Haydock and Appledore came in together. The gag was removed and the cords that held his arms were loosened so that he could sit up and stretch his arms.

Haydock had an automatic pistol with him.

Tommy, without much inward confidence, began to play his part.

He said indignantly:

'Look here, Haydock, what's the meaning of all this? I've been set upon – kidnapped –'

The Commander was gently shaking his head.

He said:

'Don't waste your breath. It's not worth it.'

'Just because you're a member of our Secret Service, you think you can –'

Again the other shook his head.

'No, no, Meadowes. You weren't taken in by that story. No need to keep up the pretence.'

But Tommy showed no signs of discomfiture. He argued to himself that the other could not really be sure. If he continued to play his part –

'Who the devil do you think you are?' he demanded. 'However great your powers you've no right to behave like this. I'm perfectly capable of holding my tongue about any of our vital secrets!'

The other said coldly:

'You do your stuff very well, but I may tell you that it's immaterial to me whether you're a member of the British Intelligence, or merely a muddling amateur –'

'Of all the damned cheek –'

'Cut it out, Meadowes.'

'I tell you –'

Haydock thrust a ferocious face forwards.

'Be quiet, damn you. Earlier on it would have mattered to find out who you were and who sent you. Now it doesn't matter. The time's short, you see. And you didn't have the chance to report to anyone what you'd found out.'

'The police will be looking for me as soon as I'm reported missing.'

Haydock showed his teeth in a sudden gleam.

'I've had the police here this evening. Good fellows – both friends of mine. They asked me all about Mr

Meadowes. Very concerned about his disappearance. How he seemed that evening – what he said. They never dreamt, how should they, that the man they were talking about was practically underneath their feet where they were sitting. It's quite clear, you see, that you left this house well and alive. They'd never dream of looking for you here.'

'You can't keep me here for ever,' Tommy said vehemently.

Haydock said with a resumption of his most British manner:

'It won't be necessary, my dear fellow. Only until tomorrow night. There's a boat due in at my little cove – and we're thinking of sending you on a voyage for your health – though actually I don't think you'll be alive, or even on board, when they arrive at their destination.'

'I wonder you didn't knock me on the head straight away.'

'It's such hot weather, my dear fellow. Just occasionally our sea communications are interrupted, and if that were to be so – well, a dead body on the premises has a way of announcing its presence.'

'I see,' said Tommy.

He did see. The issue was perfectly clear. He was to be kept alive until the boat arrived. Then he would be killed, or drugged, and his dead body taken out to sea.

Nothing would ever connect this body, when found, with Smugglers' Rest.

'I just came along,' continued Haydock, speaking in the most natural manner, 'to ask whether there is anything we could – er – do for you – afterwards?'

Tommy reflected. Then he said:

'Thanks – but I won't ask you to take a lock of my hair to the little woman in St John's Wood, or anything of that kind. She'll miss me when pay day comes along – but I dare say she'll soon find a friend elsewhere.'

At all costs, he felt, he must create the impression that he was playing a lone hand. So long as no suspicion attached itself to Tuppence, then the game might still be won through, though he was not there to play it.

'As you please,' said Haydock. 'If you did care to send a message to – your friend – we would see that it was delivered.'

So he was, after all, anxious to get a little information about this unknown Mr Meadowes? Very well, then, Tommy would keep him guessing.

He shook his head. 'Nothing doing,' he said.

'Very well.' With an appearance of the utmost indifference Haydock nodded to Appledore. The latter replaced the bonds and the gag. The two men went out, locking the door behind them.

Left to his reflections, Tommy felt anything but cheerful. Not only was he faced with the prospect of rapidly approaching death, but he had no means of leaving any clue behind him as to the information he had discovered.

His body was completely helpless. His brain felt singularly inactive. Could he, he wondered, have utilised Haydock's suggestion of a message? Perhaps if his brain had been working better . . . But he could think of nothing helpful.

There was, of course, still Tuppence. But what could Tuppence do? As Haydock had just pointed out, Tommy's disappearance would not be connected with him. Tommy had left Smugglers' Rest alive and well. The evidence of two independent witnesses would confirm that. Whoever Tuppence might suspect, it would not be Haydock. And she might not suspect at all. She might think that he was merely following up a trail.

Damn it all, if only he had been more on his guard –

There was a little light in the cellar. It came through the grating which was high up in one corner. If only he could get his mouth free, he could shout for help. Somebody might hear, though it was very unlikely.

For the next half-hour he busied himself straining at the cords that bound him, and trying to bite through the gag. It was all in vain, however. The people who had adjusted those things knew their business.

It was, he judged, late afternoon. Haydock, he fancied, had gone out; he had heard no sounds from overhead.

Confound it all, he was probably playing golf, speculating at the clubhouse over what could have happened to Meadowes!

'Dined with me night before last – seemed quite normal, then. Just vanished into the blue.'

Tommy writhed with fury. That hearty English manner! Was everyone blind not to see that bullet-headed Prussian skull? He himself hadn't seen it. Wonderful what a first-class actor could get away with.

So here he was – a failure – an ignominious failure – trussed up like a chicken, with no one to guess where he was.

If only Tuppence could have second sight! She might suspect. She had, sometimes, an uncanny insight . . .

What was that?

He strained his ears listening to a far-off sound.

Only some man humming a tune.

And here he was, unable to make a sound to attract anyone's attention.

The humming came nearer. A most untuneful noise.

But the tune, though mangled, was recognisable. It dated from the last war – had been revived for this one.

'If you were the only girl in the world and I was the only boy.'

How often he had hummed that in 1917.

Dash this fellow. Why couldn't he sing in tune?

Suddenly Tommy's body grew taut and rigid. Those particular lapses were strangely familiar. Surely there was only one person who always went wrong in that one particular place and in that one particular way!

'Albert, by gosh!' thought Tommy.

Albert prowling round Smugglers' Rest. Albert quite close at hand, and here he was, trussed up, unable to move hand or foot, unable to make a sound . . .

Wait a minute. Was he?

There was just one sound – not so easy with the mouth shut as with the mouth open, but it could be done.

Desperately Tommy began to snore. He kept his eyes closed, ready to feign a deep sleep if Appledore should come down, and he snored, he snored . . .

Short snore, short snore, short snore – pause – long snore, long snore, long snore – pause – short snore, short snore, short snore . . .

II

Albert, when Tuppence had left him, was deeply perturbed.

With the advance of years he had become a person

of slow mental processes, but those processes were tenacious.

The state of affairs in general seemed to him quite wrong.

The war was all wrong to begin with.

'Those Germans,' thought Albert gloomily and almost without rancour. Heiling Hitler, and goose-stepping and over-running the world and bombing and machine-gunning, and generally making pestilential nuisances of themselves. They'd got to be stopped, no two ways about it – and so far it seemed as though nobody had been able to stop them.

And now here was Mrs Beresford, a nice lady if there ever was one, getting herself mixed up in trouble and looking out for more trouble, and how was he going to stop her? Didn't look as though he could. Up against this Fifth Column and a nasty lot they must be. Some of 'em English-born, too! A disgrace, that was!

And the master, who was always the one to hold the missus back from her impetuous ways – the master was missing.

Albert didn't like that at all. It looked to him as though 'those Germans' might be at the bottom of that.

Yes, it looked bad, it did. Looked as though he might have copped one.

Albert was not given to the exercise of deep reasoning. Like most Englishmen, he felt something strongly, and proceeded to muddle around until he had, somehow or other, cleared up the mess. Deciding that the master had got to be found, Albert, rather after the manner of a faithful dog, set out to find him.

He acted upon no settled plan, but proceeded in exactly the same way as he was wont to embark upon the search for his wife's missing handbag or his own spectacles when either of those essential articles were mislaid. That is to say, he went to the place where he had last seen the missing objects and started from there.

In this case, the last thing known about Tommy was that he had dined with Commander Haydock at Smuglers' Rest, and had then returned to Sans Souci and been last seen turning in at the gate.

Albert accordingly climbed the hill as far as the gate of Sans Souci, and spent some five minutes staring hopefully at the gate. Nothing of a scintillating character having occurred to him, he sighed and wandered slowly up the hill to Smugglers' Rest.

Albert, too, had visited the Ornate Cinema that week, and had been powerfully impressed by the theme of *Wandering Minstrel.* Romantic, it was! He could not but be struck by the similarity of his own predicament. He, like that hero of the screen, Larry Cooper, was a faithful Blondel seeking his imprisoned master. Like Blondel, he had fought at that master's side in bygone days.

Now his master was betrayed by treachery, and there was none but his faithful Blondel to seek for him and restore him to the loving arms of Queen Berengaria.

Albert heaved a sigh as he remembered the melting strains of 'Richard, O mon roi', which the faithful troubadour had crooned so feelingly beneath tower after tower.

Pity he himself wasn't better at picking up a tune.

Took him a long time to get hold of a tune, it did.

His lips shaped themselves into a tentative whistle.

Begun playing the old tunes again lately, they had.

'If you were the only girl in the world and I was the only boy –'

Albert paused to survey the neat white-painted gate of Smugglers' Rest. That was it, that was where the master had gone to dinner.

He went up the hill a little farther and came out on the downs.

Nothing here. Nothing but grass and a few sheep.

The gate of Smugglers' Rest swung open and a car passed out. A big man in plus fours with golf clubs drove out and down the hill.

'That would be Commander Haydock, that would,' Albert deduced.

He wandered down again and stared at Smugglers' Rest. A tidy little place. Nice bit of garden. Nice view.

He eyed it benignly. 'I would say such wonderful things to you,' he hummed.

Through a side door of the house a man came out with a hoe and passed out of sight through a little gate.

Albert, who grew nasturtiums and a bit of lettuce in his back garden, was instantly interested.

He edged nearer to Smugglers' Rest and passed through the open gate. Yes, tidy little place.

He circled slowly round it. Some way below him, reached by steps, was a flat plateau planted as a vegetable garden. The man who had come out of the house was busy down there.

Albert watched him with interest for some minutes. Then he turned to contemplate the house.

Tidy little place, he thought for the third time. Just the sort of place a retired Naval gentleman would like to have. This was where the master had dined that night.

Slowly Albert circled round and round the house. He looked at it much as he had looked at the gate of Sans Souci – hopefully, as though asking it to tell him something.

And as he went he hummed softly to himself, a twentieth-century Blondel in search of his master.

'There would be such wonderful things to do,' hummed Albert. 'I would say such wonderful things to you.

There would be such wonderful things to do –' Gone wrong somewhere, hadn't he? He'd hummed that bit before.

Hallo, funny, so the Commander kept pigs, did he? A long-drawn grunt came to him. Funny – seemed almost as though it were underground. Funny place to keep pigs.

Couldn't be pigs. No, it was someone having a bit of shut-eye. Bit of shut-eye in the cellar, so it seemed . . .

Right kind of day for a snooze, but funny place to go for it. Humming like a bumble bee Albert approached nearer.

That's where it was coming from – through that little grating. Grunt, grunt, grunt, snoooooore. Snoooooore, snoooooooore – grunt, grunt, grunt. Funny sort of snore – reminded him of something . . .

'Coo!' said Albert. 'That's what it is – SOS. Dot, dot, dot, dash, dash, dash, dot, dot, dot.'

He looked round him with a quick glance.

Then kneeling down, he tapped a soft message on the iron grille of the little window of the cellar.

Chapter 13

Although Tuppence went to bed in an optimistic frame of mind, she suffered a severe reaction in those waking hours of early dawn when human morale sinks to its lowest.

On descending to breakfast, however, her spirits were raised by the sight of a letter sitting on her plate addressed in a painfully backhanded script.

This was no communication from Douglas, Raymond or Cyril, or any other of the camouflaged correspondence that arrived punctually for her, and which included this morning a brightly coloured Bonzo postcard with a scrawled, 'Sorry I haven't written before. All well, Maudie,' on it.

Tuppence thrust this aside and opened the letter.

'*Dear Patricia* (it ran),

'*Auntie Grace is, I am afraid, much worse today. The*

doctors do not actually say she is sinking, but I am afraid that there cannot be much hope. If you want to see her before the end I think it would be well to come today. If you will take the 10.20 train to Yarrow, a friend will meet you with his car.

'Shall look forward to seeing you again, dear, in spite of the melancholy reason.

'Yours ever,

'Penelope Playne.'

It was all Tuppence could do to restrain her jubilation.

Good old Penny Plain!

With some difficulty she assumed a mourning expression – and sighed heavily as she laid the letter down.

To the two sympathetic listeners present, Mrs O'Rourke and Miss Minton, she imparted the contents of the letter, and enlarged freely on the personality of Aunt Gracie, her indomitable spirit, her indifference to air raids and danger, and her vanquishment by illness. Miss Minton tended to be curious as to the exact nature of Aunt Gracie's sufferings, and compared them interestedly with the diseases of her own cousin Selina. Tuppence, hovering slightly between dropsy and diabetes, found herself slightly confused, but compromised on complications with the kidneys.

Mrs O'Rourke displayed an avid interest as to whether Tuppence would benefit pecuniarily by the old lady's death and learned that dear Cyril had always been the old lady's favourite grand-nephew as well as being her godson.

After breakfast, Tuppence rang up the tailor's and cancelled a fitting of a coat and skirt for that afternoon, and then sought out Mrs Perenna and explained that she might be away from home for a night or two.

Mrs Perenna expressed the usual conventional sentiments. She looked tired this morning, and had an anxious harassed expression.

'Still no news of Mr Meadowes,' she said. 'It really is *most* odd, is it not?'

'I'm sure he must have met with an accident,' sighed Mrs Blenkensop. 'I always said so.'

'Oh, but surely, Mrs Blenkensop, the accident would have been reported by this time.'

'Well, what do you think?' asked Tuppence.

Mrs Perenna shook her head.

'I really don't know *what* to say. I quite agree that he can't have gone away of his own free will. He would have sent word by now.'

'It was always a most unjustified suggestion,' said Mrs Blenkensop warmly. 'That horrid Major Bletchley started it. No, if it isn't an accident, it must be loss of memory. I believe that is far more common than is generally known, especially at times of stress like those we are living through now.'

Mrs Perenna nodded her head. She pursed up her lips with rather a doubtful expression. She shot a quick look at Tuppence.

'You know, Mrs Blenkensop,' she said, 'we don't know very much *about* Mr Meadowes, do we?'

Tuppence said sharply: 'What do you mean?'

'Oh, please, don't take me up so sharply. *I* don't believe it – not for a minute.'

'Don't believe what?'

'This story that's going round.'

'What story? I haven't heard anything.'

'No – well – perhaps people wouldn't tell you. I don't really know how it started. I've an idea that Mr Cayley mentioned it first. Of course he's rather a suspicious man, if you know what I mean?'

Tuppence contained herself with as much patience as possible.

'Please tell me,' she said.

'Well, it was just a suggestion, you know, that Mr Meadowes might be an enemy agent – one of these dreadful Fifth Column people.'

Tuppence put all she could of an outraged Mrs Blenkensop into her indignant:

'I never *heard* of such an absurd idea!'

'No. I don't think there's anything in it. But of course

Mr Meadowes was seen about a good deal with that German boy – and I believe he asked a lot of questions about the chemical processes at the factory – and so people think that perhaps the two of them might have been working together.'

Tuppence said:

'*You* don't think there's any doubt about Carl, do you, Mrs Perenna?'

She saw a quick spasm distort the other woman's face.

'I wish I *could* think it was not true.'

Tuppence said gently: 'Poor Sheila . . .'

Mrs Perenna's eyes flashed.

'Her heart's broken, the poor child. Why should it be that way? Why couldn't it be someone else she set her heart upon?'

Tuppence shook her head.

'Things don't happen that way.'

'You're right.' The other spoke in a deep, bitter voice. 'It's got to be sorrow and bitterness and dust and ashes. It's got to be the way things tear you to pieces. . . . I'm sick of the cruelty – the unfairness of this world. I'd like to smash it and break it – and let us all start again near to the earth and without these rules and laws and the tyranny of nation over nation. I'd like –'

A cough interrupted her. A deep, throaty cough. Mrs

O'Rourke was standing in the doorway, her vast bulk filling the aperture completely.

'Am I interrupting now?' she demanded.

Like a sponge across a slate, all evidence of Mrs Perenna's outburst vanished from her face – leaving in their wake only the mild worried face of the proprietress of a guesthouse whose guests were causing trouble.

'No, indeed, Mrs O'Rourke,' she said. 'We were just talking about what had become of Mr Meadowes. It's amazing the police can find no trace of him.'

'Ah, the police!' said Mrs O'Rourke in tones of easy contempt. 'What good would they be? No good at all, at all! Only fit for fining motor-cars, and dropping on poor wretches who haven't taken out their dog licences.'

'What's your theory, Mrs O'Rourke?' asked Tuppence.

'You'll have been hearing the story that's going about?'

'About his being a Fascist and an enemy agent – yes,' said Tuppence coldly.

'It might be true now,' said Mrs O'Rourke thoughtfully. 'For there's been something about the man that's intrigued me from the beginning. I've watched him, you know,' she smiled directly at Tuppence – and like all Mrs O'Rourke's smiles it had a vaguely terrifying quality – the smile of an ogress. 'He'd not the look of a man who'd retired from business and had nothing to do with himself. If I was backing my judgement, I'd say he came here with a purpose.'

'And when the police got on his track he disappeared, is that it?' demanded Tuppence.

'It might be so,' said Mrs O'Rourke. 'What's your opinion, Mrs Perenna?'

'I don't know,' sighed Mrs Perenna. 'It's a most vexing thing to happen. It makes so much *talk*.'

'Ah! Talk won't hurt you. They're happy now out there on the terrace wondering and surmising. They'll have it in the end that the quiet, inoffensive man was going to blow us all up in our beds with bombs.'

'You haven't told us what you think?' said Tuppence.

Mrs O'Rourke smiled, that same slow ferocious smile.

'I'm thinking that the man is safe somewhere – quite safe . . .'

Tuppence thought:

'She might say that if she knew . . . but he isn't where she thinks he is!'

She went up to her room to get ready. Betty Sprot came running out of the Cayleys' bedroom with a smile of mischievous and impish glee on her face.

'What have you been up to, minx?' demanded Tuppence.

Betty gurgled:

'Goosey, goosey gander . . .'

Tuppence chanted:

'Whither will you wander? *Up*stairs!' She snatched up Betty high over her head. '*Down*stairs!' She rolled her on the floor –

At this minute Mrs Sprot appeared and Betty was led off to be attired for her walk.

'Hide?' said Betty hopefully. 'Hide?'

'You can't play hide-and-seek now,' said Mrs Sprot.

Tuppence went into her room, donned her hat (a nuisance having to wear a hat – Tuppence Beresford never did – but Patricia Blenkensop would certainly wear one, Tuppence felt).

Somebody, she noted, had altered the position of the hats in her hat-cupboard. Had someone been searching her room? Well, let them. They wouldn't find anything to cast doubt on blameless Mrs Blenkensop.

She left Penelope Playne's letter artistically on the dressing-table and went downstairs and out of the house.

It was ten o'clock as she turned out of the gate. Plenty of time. She looked up at the sky, and in doing so stepped into a dark puddle by the gatepost, but without apparently noticing it she went on.

Her heart was dancing wildly. Success – success – they were going to succeed.

II

Yarrow was a small country station where the village was some distance from the railway.

Outside the station a car was waiting. A good-looking young man was driving it. He touched his peaked cap to Tuppence, but the gesture seemed hardly natural.

Tuppence kicked the off-side tyre dubiously.

'Isn't this rather flat?'

'We haven't got far to go, madam.'

She nodded and got in.

They drove, not towards the village, but towards the downs. After winding up over a hill, they took a side-track that dropped sharply into a deep cleft. From the shadow of a small copse of trees a figure stepped out to meet them.

The car stopped and Tuppence, getting out, went to meet Anthony Marsdon.

'Beresford's all right,' he said quickly. 'We located him yesterday. He's a prisoner – the other side got him – and for good reasons he's remaining put for another twelve hours. You see, there's a small boat due in at a certain spot – and we want to catch her badly. That's why Beresford's lying low – we don't want to give the show away until the last minute.'

He looked at her anxiously.

'You do understand, don't you?'

'Oh, yes!' Tuppence was staring at a curious tangled mass of canvas material half-hidden by the trees.

'He'll be absolutely all right,' continued the young man earnestly.

'Of course Tommy will be all right,' said Tuppence impatiently. 'You needn't talk to me as though I were a child of two. We're both ready to run a few risks. What's that thing over there?'

'Well –' The young man hesitated. 'That's just it. I've been ordered to put a certain proposition before you. But – but well, frankly, I don't like doing it. You see –'

Tuppence treated him to a cold stare.

'Why don't you like doing it?'

'Well – dash it – you're Deborah's mother. And I mean – what would Deb say to me if – if –'

'If I got it in the neck?' inquired Tuppence. 'Personally, if I were you, I shouldn't mention it to her. The man who said explanations were a mistake was quite right.'

Then she smiled kindly at him.

'My dear boy, I know exactly how you feel. That it's all very well for you and Deborah and the young generally to run risks, but that the mere middle-aged must be shielded. All complete nonsense, because if anyone is going to be liquidated it is much better it should be the middle-aged, who have had the best part of their lives. Anyway, stop looking upon me as that sacred object, Deborah's mother, and just tell me what dangerous and unpleasant job there is for me to do.'

'You know,' said the young man with enthusiasm, 'I think you're splendid, simply splendid.'

'Cut out the compliments,' said Tuppence. 'I'm admiring myself a good deal, so there's no need for you to chime in. What exactly *is* the big idea?'

Tony indicated the mass of crumpled material with a gesture.

'That,' he said, 'is the remains of a parachute.'

'Aha,' said Tuppence. Her eyes sparkled.

'There was just an isolated parachutist,' went on Marsdon. 'Fortunately the LDVs around here are quite a bright lot. The descent was spotted, and they got her.'

'Her?'

'Yes, *her*! Woman dressed as a hospital nurse.'

'I'm sorry she wasn't a nun,' said Tuppence. 'There have been so many good stories going around about nuns paying their fares in buses with hairy muscular arms.'

'Well, she wasn't a nun and she wasn't a man in disguise. She was a woman of medium height, middle-aged, with dark hair and of slight build.'

'In fact,' said Tuppence, 'a woman not unlike me?'

'You've hit it exactly,' said Tony.

'Well?' said Tuppence.

Marsdon said slowly:

'The next part of it is up to you.'

Tuppence smiled. She said:

'I'm *on* all right. Where do I go and what do I do?'

'I say, Mrs Beresford, you really *are* a sport. Magnificent nerve you've got.'

'Where do I go and what do I do?' repeated Tuppence, impatiently.

'The instructions are very meagre, unfortunately. In the woman's pocket there was a piece of paper with these words on it in German. "Walk to Leatherbarrow – due east from the stone cross. 14 St Asalph's Rd. Dr Binion."'

Tuppence looked up. On the hilltop nearby was a stone cross.

'That's it,' said Tony. 'Signposts have been removed, of course. But Leatherbarrow's a biggish place, and walking due east from the cross you're bound to strike it.'

'How far?'

'Five miles at least.'

Tuppence made a slight grimace.

'Healthy walking exercise before lunch,' she commented. 'I hope Dr Binion offers me lunch when I get there.'

'Do you know German, Mrs Beresford?'

'Hotel variety only. I shall have to be firm about speaking English – say my instructions were to do so.'

'It's an awful risk,' said Marsdon.

'Nonsense. Who's to imagine there's been a substitution? Or does everyone know for miles round that there's been a parachutist brought down?'

'The two LDV men who reported it are being kept by the Chief Constable. Don't want to risk their telling their friends how clever they have been!'

'Somebody else may have seen it – or heard about it?'

Tony smiled.

'My dear Mrs Beresford, every single day word goes round that one, two, three, four, up to a hundred parachutists have been seen!'

'That's probably quite true,' agreed Tuppence. 'Well, lead me to it.'

Tony said:

'We've got the kit here – and a policewoman who's an expert in the art of make-up. Come with me.'

Just inside the copse there was a tumble-down shed. At the door of it was a competent-looking middle-aged woman.

She looked at Tuppence and nodded approvingly.

Inside the shed, seated on an upturned packing case, Tuppence submitted herself to expert ministrations.

Finally the operator stood back, nodded approvingly and remarked:

'There, now, I think we've made a very nice job of it. What do you think, sir?'

'Very good indeed,' said Tony.

Tuppence stretched out her hand and took the mirror the other woman held. She surveyed her own face earnestly and could hardly repress a cry of surprise.

The eyebrows had been trimmed to an entirely different shape, altering the whole expression. Small pieces of adhesive plaster hidden by curls pulled forward over the ears that tightened the skin of the face and altered its contours. A small amount of nose putty had altered the shape of the nose, giving Tuppence an unexpectedly beak-like profile. Skilful make-up had added several years to her age, with heavy lines running down each side of the mouth. The whole face had a complacent, rather foolish look.

'It's frightfully clever,' said Tuppence admiringly. She touched her nose gingerly.

'You must be careful,' the other woman warned her. She produced two slices of thin india-rubber. 'Do you think you could bear to wear these in your cheeks?'

'I suppose I shall have to,' said Tuppence gloomily.

She slipped them in and worked her jaws carefully.

'It's not really too uncomfortable,' she had to admit.

Tony then discreetly left the shed and Tuppence shed her own clothing and got into the nurse's kit. It was not too bad a fit, though inclined to strain a little over the shoulders. The dark blue bonnet put the final touch to her new personality. She rejected, however, the stout square-toed shoes.

'If I've got to walk five miles,' she said decidedly, 'I do it in my own shoes.'

They both agreed that this was reasonable – particularly as Tuppence's own shoes were dark blue brogues that went well with the uniform.

She looked with interest into the dark blue handbag – powder; no lipstick; two pounds fourteen and sixpence in English money; a handkerchief and an identity card in the name of Freda Elton, 4 Manchester Road, Sheffield.

Tuppence transferred her own powder and lipstick and stood up, prepared to set out.

Tony Marsdon turned his head away. He said gruffly:

'I feel a swine letting you do this.'

'I know just how you feel.'

'But, you see, it's absolutely vital – that we should get some idea of just where and how the attack will come.'

Tuppence patted him on the arm. 'Don't you worry, my child. Believe it or not, I'm enjoying myself.'

Tony Marsdon said again:

'I think you're simply wonderful!'

III

Somewhat weary, Tuppence stood outside 14 St Asalph's Road and noted that Dr Binion was a dental surgeon and not a doctor.

From the corner of her eye she noted Tony Marsdon. He was sitting in a racy-looking car outside a house farther down the street.

It had been judged necessary for Tuppence to walk to Leatherbarrow exactly as instructed, since if she had been driven there in a car the fact might have been noted.

It was certainly true that two enemy aircraft had passed over the downs, circling low before making off, and they could have noted the nurse's lonely figure walking across country.

Tony, with the expert policewoman, had driven off in the opposite direction and had made a big detour before approaching Leatherbarrow and taking up his position in St Asalph's Road. Everything was now set.

'The arena doors open,' murmured Tuppence. 'Enter one Christian *en route* for the lions. Oh, well, nobody can say I'm not seeing life.'

She crossed the road and rang the bell, wondering as she did so exactly how much Deborah liked that young man. The door was opened by an elderly woman with a stolid peasant face – not an English face.

'Dr Binion?' said Tuppence.

The woman looked her slowly up and down.

'You will be Nurse Elton, I suppose.'

'Yes.'

'Then you will come up to the doctor's surgery.'

She stood back, the door closed behind Tuppence, who found herself standing in a narrow linoleum-lined hall.

The maid preceded her upstairs and opened a door on the first floor.

'Please to wait. The doctor will come to you.'

She went out, shutting the door behind her.

A very ordinary dentist's surgery – the appointments somewhat old and shabby.

Tuppence looked at the dentist's chair and smiled to think that for once it held none of the usual terrors. She had the 'dentist feeling' all right – but from quite different causes.

Presently the door would open and 'Dr Binion' would come in. Who would Dr Binion be? A stranger? Or someone she had seen before? If it was the person she was half expecting to see –

The door opened.

The man who entered was not at all the person Tuppence had half fancied she might see! It was someone she had never considered as a likely starter.

It was Commander Haydock.

Chapter 14

A flood of wild surmises as to the part Commander Haydock had played in Tommy's disappearance surged through Tuppence's brain, but she thrust them resolutely aside. This was a moment for keeping all her wits about her.

Would or would not the Commander recognise her? It was an interesting question.

She had so steeled herself beforehand to display no recognition or surprise herself, no matter whom she might see, that she felt reasonably sure that she herself had displayed no signs untoward to the situation.

She rose now to her feet and stood there, standing in a respectable attitude, as befitted a mere German woman in the presence of a Lord of creation.

'So you have arrived,' said the Commander.

He spoke in English and his manner was precisely the same as usual.

'Yes,' said Tuppence, and added, as though presenting her credentials: 'Nurse Elton.'

Haydock smiled as though at a joke.

'Nurse Elton! Excellent.'

He looked at her approvingly.

'You look absolutely right,' he said kindly.

Tuppence inclined her head, but said nothing. She was leaving the initiative to him.

'You know, I suppose, what you have to do?' went on Haydock. 'Sit down, please.'

Tuppence sat down obediently. She replied:

'I was to take detailed instructions from you.'

'Very proper,' said Haydock. There was a faint suggestion of mockery in his voice.

He said:

'You know the day?'

'The fourth.'

Haydock looked startled. A heavy frown creased his forehead.

'So you know that, do you?' he muttered.

There was a pause, then Tuppence said:

'You will tell me, please, what I have to do?'

Haydock said:

'All in good time, my dear.'

He paused a minute, and then asked:

'You have heard, no doubt, of Sans Souci?'

'No,' said Tuppence.

'You haven't?'

'No,' said Tuppence firmly.

'Let's see how you deal with this one!' she thought.

There was a queer smile on the Commander's face. He said:

'So you haven't heard of Sans Souci? That surprises me very much – since I was under the impression, you know, *that you'd been living there for the last month* . . .'

There was a dead silence. The Commander said:

'What about that, Mrs Blenkensop?'

'I don't know what you mean, Dr Binion. I landed by parachute this morning.'

Again Haydock smiled – definitely an unpleasant smile.

He said:

'A few yards of canvas thrust into a bush create a wonderful illusion. And I am not Dr Binion, dear lady. Dr Binion is, officially, my dentist – he is good enough to lend me his surgery now and again.'

'Indeed?' said Tuppence.

'Indeed, Mrs Blenkensop! Or perhaps you would prefer me to address you by your real name of Beresford?'

Again there was a poignant silence. Tuppence drew a deep breath.

Haydock nodded.

'The game's up, you see. "*You've walked into my parlour,*" *said the spider to the fly.*'

There was a faint click and a gleam of blue steel showed in his hand. His voice took on a grim note as he said:

'And I shouldn't advise you to make any noise or try to arouse the neighbourhood! You'd be dead before you got so much as a yelp out, and even if you did manage to scream it wouldn't arouse attention. Patients under gas, you know, often cry out.'

Tuppence said composedly:

'You seem to have thought of everything. Has it occurred to you that I have friends who know where I am?'

'Ah! Still harping on the blue-eyed boy – actually brown-eyed! Young Anthony Marsdon. I'm sorry, Mrs Beresford, but young Anthony happens to be one of our most stalwart supporters in this country. As I said just now, a few yards of canvas creates a wonderful effect. You swallowed the parachute idea quite easily.'

'I don't see the point of all this rigmarole!'

'Don't you? We don't want your friends to trace you too easily, you see. *If* they pick up your trail it will lead to Yarrow and to a man in a car. The fact that a hospital nurse, of quite different facial appearance, walked into Leatherbarrow between one and two will hardly be connected with your disappearance.'

'Very elaborate,' said Tuppence.

Haydock said:

'I admire your nerve, you know. I admire it very much. I'm sorry to have to coerce you – but it's vital that we should know just exactly how much you *did* discover at Sans Souci.'

Tuppence did not answer.

Haydock said quietly:

'I'd advise you, you know, to come clean. There are certain – possibilities – in a dentist's chair and instruments.'

Tuppence merely threw him a scornful look.

Haydock leant back in his chair. He said slowly:

'Yes – I dare say you've got a lot of fortitude – your type often has. But what about the other half of the picture?'

'What do you mean?'

'I'm talking about Thomas Beresford, your husband, who has lately been living at Sans Souci under the name of Mr Meadowes, and who is now very conveniently trussed up in the cellar of my house.'

Tuppence said sharply:

'I don't believe it.'

'Because of the Penny Plain letter? Don't you realise that that was just a smart bit of work on the part of young Anthony. You played into his hands nicely when you gave him the code.'

Tuppence's voice trembled.

'Then Tommy – then Tommy –'

'Tommy,' said Commander Haydock, 'is where he has been all along – completely in my power! It's up to you now. If you answer my questions satisfactorily, there's a chance for him. If you don't – well, the original plan holds. He'll be knocked on the head, taken out to sea and put overboard.'

Tuppence was silent for a minute or two – then she said:

'What do you want to know?'

'I want to know who employed you, what your means of communication with that person or persons are, what you have reported so far, and exactly what you know?'

Tuppence shrugged her shoulders.

'I could tell you what lies I choose,' she pointed out.

'No, because I shall proceed to test what you say.' He drew his chair a little nearer. His manner was now definitely appealing. 'My dear woman – I know just what you feel about it all, but believe me when I say I really do admire both you and your husband immensely. You've got grit and pluck. It's people like you that will be needed in the new State – the State that will arise in this country when your present imbecile Government is vanquished. We want to turn some of our enemies into friends – those that are worthwhile. If I have to give the order that ends your husband's life, I shall do it – it's my duty – but I shall feel really badly about having to do it! He's a fine fellow – quiet, unassuming and clever. Let me impress upon you what so few people in this country seem to understand. Our Leader does not intend to conquer this country in the sense that you all think. He aims at creating a new Britain – a Britain strong in its own power – ruled over, *not* by Germans, but by Englishmen. And the best *type* of Englishmen – Englishmen with brains and breeding and courage. *A brave new world*, as Shakespeare puts it.'

He leaned forward.

'We want to do away with muddle and inefficiency. With bribery and corruption. With self-seeking and money-grabbing – *and in this new state we want people like you and your husband* – brave and resourceful – enemies that have been, friends to be. You would be surprised if you knew how many there are in this country, as in others, who have sympathy with and belief in our aims. Between us all we will create a new Europe – a Europe of peace and progress. Try and see it that way – because, I assure you – it *is* that way . . .'

His voice was compelling, magnetic. Leaning forward, he looked the embodiment of a straightforward British sailor.

Tuppence looked at him and searched her mind for

a telling phrase. She was only able to find one that was both childish and rude.

'Goosey, goosey gander!' said Tuppence . . .

II

The effect was so magical that she was quite taken aback.

Haydock jumped to his feet, his face went dark purple with rage, and in a second all likeness to a hearty British sailor had vanished. She saw what Tommy had once seen – an infuriated Prussian.

He swore at her fluently in German. Then, changing to English, he shouted:

'You infernal little fool! Don't you realise you give yourself away completely answering like that? You've done for yourself now – you and your precious husband.'

Raising his voice he called:

'Anna!'

The woman who had admitted Tuppence came into the room. Haydock thrust the pistol into her hand.

'Watch her. Shoot if necessary.'

He stormed out of the room.

Tuppence looked appealingly at Anna, who stood in front of her with an impassive face.

'Would you really shoot me?' said Tuppence.

Anna answered quietly:

'You need not try to get round me. In the last war my son was killed, my Otto. I was thirty-eight, then – I am sixty-two now – but I have not forgotten.'

Tuppence looked at the broad, impassive face. It reminded her of the Polish woman, Vanda Polonska. That same frightening ferocity and singleness of purpose. Motherhood – unrelenting! So, no doubt, felt many quiet Mrs Joneses and Mrs Smiths all over England. There was no arguing with the female of the species – the mother deprived of her young.

Something stirred in the recesses of Tuppence's brain – some nagging recollection – something that she had always known but had never succeeded in getting into the forefront of her mind. Solomon – Solomon came into it somewhere . . .

The door opened. Commander Haydock came back into the room.

He howled out, beside himself with rage:

'Where is it? Where have you hidden it?'

Tuppence stared at him. She was completely taken aback. What he was saying did not make sense to her.

She had taken nothing and hidden nothing.

Haydock said to Anna:

'Get out.'

The woman handed the pistol to him and left the room promptly.

Haydock dropped into a chair and seemed to be striving to pull himself together. He said:

'You can't get away with it, you know. I've got you – and I've got ways of making people speak – not pretty ways. You'll have to tell the truth in the end. Now then, *what have you done with it?*'

Tuppence was quick to see that here, at least, was something that gave her the possibility of bargaining. If only she could find out what it was she was supposed to have in her possession.

She said cautiously:

'How do you know I've got it?'

'From what you said, you damned little fool. You haven't got it on you – that we know, since you changed completely into this kit.'

'Suppose I posted it to someone?' said Tuppence.

'Don't be a fool. Everything you posted since yesterday has been examined. You didn't post it. No, there's only one thing you *could* have done. Hidden it in Sans Souci before you left this morning. I give you just three minutes to tell me where that hiding-place is.'

He put his watch down on the table.

'Three minutes, Mrs Thomas Beresford.'

The clock on the mantelpiece ticked.

Tuppence sat quite still with a blank impassive face.

It revealed nothing of the racing thoughts behind it.

In a flash of bewildering light she saw everything – saw the whole business revealed in terms of blinding clarity and realised at last who was the centre and pivot of the whole organisation.

It came quite as a shock to her when Haydock said: *'Ten seconds more . . .'*

Like one in a dream she watched him, saw the pistol arm rise, heard him count:

'One, two, three, four, five –'

He had reached *eight* when the shot rang out and he collapsed forward on his chair, an expression of bewilderment on his broad red face. So intent had he been on watching his victim that he had been unaware of the door behind him slowly opening.

In a flash Tuppence was on her feet. She pushed her way past the uniformed men in the doorway, and seized on a tweed-clad arm.

'Mr Grant.'

'Yes, yes, my dear, it's all right now – you've been wonderful –'

Tuppence brushed aside these reassurances.

'*Quick!* There's no time to lose. You've got a car here?'

'Yes.' He stared.

'A fast one? We must get to Sans Souci *at once*. If

only we're in time. Before they telephone here, and get no answer.'

Two minutes later they were in the car, and it was threading its way through the streets of Leatherbarrow. Then they were out in the open country and the needle of the speedometer was rising.

Mr Grant asked no questions. He was content to sit quietly whilst Tuppence watched the speedometer in an agony of apprehension. The chauffeur had been given his orders and he drove with all the speed of which the car was capable.

Tuppence only spoke once.

'Tommy?'

'Quite all right. Released half an hour ago.'

She nodded.

Now, at last, they were nearing Leahampton. They darted and twisted through the town, up the hill.

Tuppence jumped out and she and Mr Grant ran up the drive. The hall door, as usual, was open. There was no one in sight. Tuppence ran lightly up the stairs.

She just glanced inside her own room in passing, and noted the confusion of open drawers and disordered bed. She nodded and passed on, along the corridor and into the room occupied by Mr and Mrs Cayley.

The room was empty. It looked peaceful and smelt slightly of medicines.

Tuppence ran across to the bed and pulled at the coverings.

They fell to the ground and Tuppence ran her hand under the mattress. She turned triumphantly to Mr Grant with a tattered child's picture-book in her hand.

'Here you are. It's all in here –'

'What on –?'

They turned. Mrs Sprot was standing in the doorway staring.

'And now,' said Tuppence, '*let me introduce you to M*! Yes. *Mrs Sprot!* I ought to have known it all along.'

It was left to Mrs Cayley arriving in the doorway a moment later to introduce the appropriate anticlimax.

'Oh *dear*,' said Mrs Cayley, looking with dismay at her spouse's dismantled bed. 'Whatever *will* Mr Cayley say?'

Chapter 15

'I ought to have known it all along,' said Tuppence.

She was reviving her shattered nerves by a generous tot of old brandy, and was beaming alternately at Tommy and at Mr Grant – and at Albert, who was sitting in front of a pint of beer and grinning from ear to ear.

'Tell us all about it, Tuppence,' urged Tommy.

'You first,' said Tuppence.

'There's not much for me to tell,' said Tommy. 'Sheer accident let me into the secret of the wireless transmitter. I thought I'd get away with it, but Haydock was too smart for me.'

Tuppence nodded and said:

'He telephoned to Mrs Sprot at once. And she ran out into the drive and laid in wait for you with the hammer. She was only away from the bridge table for about three minutes. I *did* notice she was a little out of breath – but I never suspected her.'

'After that,' said Tommy, 'the credit belongs entirely to Albert. He came sniffing round like a faithful dog. I did some impassioned morse snoring and he cottoned on to it. He went off to Mr Grant with the news and the two of them came back late that night. More snoring! Result was, I agreed to remain put so as to catch the sea forces when they arrived.'

Mr Grant added his quota.

'When Haydock went off this morning, our people took charge at Smugglers' Rest. We nabbed the boat this evening.'

'And now, Tuppence,' said Tommy. 'Your story.'

'Well, to begin with, I've been the most frightful fool all along! I suspected everybody here except Mrs Sprot! I *did* once have a terrible feeling of menace, as though I was in danger – that was after I overheard the telephone message about the fourth of the month. There were three people there at the time – I put down my feeling of apprehension to either Mrs Perenna or Mrs O'Rourke. Quite wrong – it was the colourless Mrs Sprot who was the really dangerous personality.

'I went muddling on, as Tommy knows, until after he disappeared. Then I was just cooking up a plan with Albert when suddenly, out of the blue, Anthony Marsdon turned up. It seemed all right to begin with – the usual sort of young man that Deb often has in tow. But two things made me think a bit. First I became more and more sure as I talked to him that I *hadn't* seen him before and that he never had been to the flat. The second was that, though he seemed to know all about my working at Leahampton, he assumed that *Tommy* was in Scotland. Now, that seemed all wrong. If he knew about anyone, it would be *Tommy* he knew about, since I was more or less unofficial. That struck me as very odd.

'Mr Grant had told me that Fifth Columnists were everywhere – in the most unlikely places. So why shouldn't one of them be working in Deborah's show? I wasn't convinced, but I was suspicious enough to lay a trap for him. I told him that Tommy and I had fixed up a code for communicating with each other. Our real one, of course, was a Bonzo postcard, but I told Anthony a fairy tale about the Penny plain, tuppence coloured saying.

'As I hoped, he rose to it beautifully! I got a letter this morning which gave him away completely.

'The arrangements had been all worked out beforehand. All I had to do was to ring up a tailor and cancel a fitting. That was an intimation that the fish had risen.'

'Coo-er!' said Albert. 'It didn't half give me a turn. I drove up with a baker's van and we dumped a pool of stuff just outside the gate. Aniseed, it was – or smelt like it.'

'And then –' Tuppence took up the tale. 'I came out and walked in it. Of course it was easy for the baker's van to follow me to the station and someone came up behind me and heard me book to Yarrow. It was after that that it might have been difficult.'

'The dogs followed the scent well,' said Mr Grant. 'They picked it up at Yarrow station and again on the track the tyre had made after you rubbed your shoe on it. It led us down to the copse and up again to the stone cross and after you where you had walked over the downs. The enemy had no idea we could follow you easily after they themselves had seen you start and driven off themselves.'

'All the same,' said Albert, 'it gave me a turn. Knowing you were in that house and not knowing what might come to you. Got in a back window, we did, and nabbed the foreign woman as she came down the stairs. Come in just in the nick of time, we did.'

'I knew you'd come,' said Tuppence. 'The thing was for me to spin things out as long as I could. I'd have pretended to tell if I hadn't seen the door opening. What was really exciting was the way I suddenly saw the whole thing and what a fool I'd been.'

'How did you see it?' asked Tommy.

'*Goosey, goosey, gander,*' said Tuppence promptly. 'When I said that to Commander Haydock he went absolutely livid. And not just because it was silly and rude. No, I saw at once that it *meant* something to him. And then there was the expression on that woman's face – Anna – it was like the Polish woman's, and then, of course, I thought of Solomon and I saw the whole thing.'

Tommy gave a sigh of exasperation.

'Tuppence, if you say that once again, I'll shoot you myself. Saw all *what*? And what on earth has Solomon got to do with it?'

'Do you remember that two women came to Solomon with a baby and both said it was hers, but Solomon said, "Very well, cut it in two." And the false mother said, "All right." But the real mother said, "No, let the other woman have it." You see, she couldn't face her child being killed. Well, that night that Mrs Sprot shot the other woman, you all said what a miracle it was and how easily she might have shot the child. Of course, it ought to have been quite plain then! If it had been her child, she *couldn't* have risked that shot for a minute. It meant that Betty *wasn't* her child. And that's why she absolutely had to shoot the other woman.'

'Why?'

'Because, of course, the other woman was *the child's real mother*.' Tuppence's voice shook a little.

'Poor thing – poor hunted thing. She came over a penniless refugee and gratefully agreed to let Mrs Sprot adopt her baby.'

'Why did Mrs Sprot want to adopt the child?'

'*Camouflage*! Supreme psychological camouflage. You just can't conceive of a master spy dragging her kid into the business. That's the main reason why I never considered Mrs Sprot seriously. Simply because of the child. But Betty's real mother had a terrible hankering for her baby and she found out Mrs Sprot's address and came down here. She hung about waiting for her chance, and at last she got it and went off with the child.

'Mrs Sprot, of course, was frantic. At all costs she didn't want the police. So she wrote that message and pretended she found it in her bedroom, and roped in Commander Haydock to help. Then, when we'd tracked down the wretched woman, she was taking no chances, and shot her . . . Far from not knowing anything about firearms, she was a very fine shot! Yes, she killed that wretched woman – and because of that I've no pity for her. She was bad through and through.'

Tuppence paused, then she went on:

'Another thing that ought to have given me a hint was the likeness between Vanda Polonska and Betty. It was *Betty* the woman reminded me of all along. And then the child's absurd play with my shoelaces. How much more likely that she'd seen her so-called mother do that – not Carl von Deinim! But as soon as Mrs

Sprot saw what the child was doing, she planted a lot of evidence in Carl's room for us to find and added the master touch of a shoelace dipped in secret ink.'

'I'm glad that Carl wasn't in it,' said Tommy. 'I liked him.'

'He's not been shot, has he?' asked Tuppence anxiously, noting the past tense.

Mr Grant shook his head.

'He's all right,' he said. 'As a matter of fact I've got a little surprise for you there.'

Tuppence's face lit up as she said:

'I'm terribly glad – for Sheila's sake! Of course we were idiots to go on barking up the wrong tree after Mrs Perenna.'

'She was mixed up in some IRA activities, nothing more,' said Mr Grant.

'I suspected Mrs O'Rourke a little – and sometimes the Cayleys –'

'And I suspected Bletchley,' put in Tommy.

'And all the time,' said Tuppence, 'it was that milk and water creature we just thought of as – Betty's mother.'

'Hardly milk and water,' said Mr Grant. 'A very dangerous woman and a very clever actress. And, I'm sorry to say, English by birth.'

Tuppence said:

'Then I've no pity or admiration for her – it wasn't

even her country she was working for.' She looked with fresh curiosity at Mr Grant. 'You found what you wanted?'

Mr Grant nodded.

'It was all in that battered set of duplicate children's books.'

'The ones that Betty said were "nasty",' Tuppence exclaimed.

'They *were* nasty,' said Mr Grant dryly. '*Little Jack Horner* contained very full details of our naval dispositions. *Johnny Head in Air* did the same for the Air Force. Military matters were appropriately embodied in: *There Was a Little Man and He Had a Little Gun.*'

'And *Goosey, Goosey, Gander*?' asked Tuppence.

Mr Grant said:

'Treated with the appropriate reagent, that book contains written in invisible ink a full list of all prominent personages who are pledged to assist an invasion of this country. Amongst them were two Chief Constables, an Air Vice-Marshal, two Generals, the Head of an Armaments Works, a Cabinet Minister, many Police Superintendents, Commanders of Local Volunteer Defence Organisations, and various military and naval lesser fry, as well as members of our own Intelligence Force.'

Tommy and Tuppence stared.

'*Incredible!*' said the former.

Grant shook his head.

'You do not know the force of the German propaganda. It appeals to something in man, some desire or lust for power. These people were ready to betray their country not for money, but in a kind of megalomaniacal pride in what they, *they themselves*, were going to achieve for that country. In every land it has been the same. It is the Cult of Lucifer – Lucifer, Son of the Morning. Pride and a desire for *personal glory*!'

He added:

'You can realise that, with such persons to issue contradictory orders and confuse operations, how the threatened invasion would have had every chance to succeed.'

'And now?' said Tuppence.

Mr Grant smiled.

'And now,' he said, '*let them come! We'll be ready* for them!'

Chapter 16

'Darling,' said Deborah. 'Do you know I almost thought the most terrible things about you?'

'Did you?' said Tuppence. 'When?'

Her eyes rested affectionately on her daughter's dark head.

'That time when you sloped off to Scotland to join Father and I thought you were with Aunt Gracie. I almost thought you were having an affair with someone.'

'Oh, Deb, did you?'

'Not really, of course. Not at your age. And of course I knew you and Carrot Top are devoted to each other. It was really an idiot called Tony Marsdon who put it into my head. Do you know, Mother – I think I might tell you – he was found afterwards to be a Fifth Columnist. He always did talk rather oddly – how things would be just the same, perhaps better if Hitler did win.'

'Did you – er – like him at all?'

'Tony? Oh no – he was always rather a bore. I must dance this.'

She floated away in the arms of a fair-haired young man, smiling up at him sweetly. Tuppence followed their revolutions for a few minutes, then her eyes shifted to where a tall young man in Air Force uniform was dancing with a fair-haired slender girl.

'I do think, Tommy,' said Tuppence, 'that our children are rather nice.'

'Here's Sheila,' said Tommy.

He got up as Sheila Perenna came towards their table. She was dressed in an emerald evening dress which showed up her dark beauty. It was a sullen beauty tonight and she greeted her host and hostess somewhat ungraciously.

'I've come, you see,' she said, 'as I promised. But I can't think why you wanted to ask me.'

'Because we like you,' said Tommy smiling.

'Do you really?' said Sheila. 'I can't think why. I've been perfectly foul to you both.'

She paused and murmured:

'But I am grateful.'

Tuppence said:

'We must find a nice partner to dance with you.'

'I don't want to dance. I loathe dancing. I came just to see you two.'

'You will like the partner we've asked to meet you,' said Tuppence smiling.

'I –' Sheila began. Then stopped – for Carl von Deinim was walking across the floor.

Sheila looked at him like one dazed. She muttered:

'You –'

'I, myself,' said Carl.

There was something a little different about Carl von Deinim this evening. Sheila stared at him, a trifle perplexed. The colour had come up on her cheeks, turning them a deep glowing red.

She said a little breathlessly:

'I knew that you would be all right now – but I thought they would still keep you interned?'

Carl shook his head.

'There is no reason to intern me.'

He went on:

'You have got to forgive me, Sheila, for deceiving you. I am not, you see, Carl von Deinim at all. I took his name for reasons of my own.'

He looked questioningly at Tuppence, who said:

'Go ahead. Tell her.'

'Carl von Deinim was my friend. I knew him in England some years ago. I renewed acquaintanceship with him in Germany just before the war. I was there then on special business for this country.'

'You were in the Intelligence?' asked Sheila.

'Yes. When I was there, queer things began to happen. Once or twice I had some very near escapes. My plans were known when they should not have been known. I realised that there was something wrong and that "the rot", to express it in their terms, had penetrated actually into the service in which I was. I had been let down by my own people. Carl and I had a certain superficial likeness (my grandmother was a German), hence my suitability for work in Germany. Carl was not a Nazi. He was interested solely in his job – a job I myself had also practised – research chemistry. He decided, shortly before war broke out, to escape to England. His brothers had been sent to concentration camps. There would, he thought, be great difficulties in the way of his own escape, but in an almost miraculous fashion all these difficulties smoothed themselves out. The fact, when he mentioned it to me, made me somewhat suspicious. Why were the authorities making it so easy for von Deinim to leave Germany when his brothers and other relations were in concentration camps and he himself was suspected because of his anti-Nazi sympathies? It seemed as though they wanted him in England for some reason. My own position was becoming increasingly precarious. Carl's lodgings were in the same house as mine and one day I found him, to my sorrow, lying dead on his bed. He had succumbed to depression and taken his own life, leaving a letter behind which I read and pocketed.

'I decided then to effect a substitution. I wanted to get out of Germany – and I wanted to know why Carl was being encouraged to do so. I dressed his body in my clothes and laid it on my bed. It was disfigured by the shot he had fired into his head. My landlady, I knew, was semi-blind.

'With Carl von Deinim's papers I travelled to England and went to the address to which he had been recommended to go. The address was Sans Souci.

'Whilst I was there I played the part of Carl von Deinim and never relaxed. I found arrangements had been made for me to work in the chemical factory there. At first I thought that the idea was I should be compelled to do work for the Nazis. I realised later that the part for which my poor friend had been cast was that of scapegoat.

'When I was arrested on faked evidence, I said nothing. I wanted to leave the revelation of my own identity as late as possible. I wanted to see what would happen.

'It was only a few days ago that I was recognised by one of our people and the truth came out.'

Sheila said reproachfully:

'You should have told me.'

He said gently:

'If you feel like that – I am sorry.'

His eyes looked into hers. She looked at him angrily

and proudly – then the anger melted. She said:

'I suppose you had to do what you did . . .'

'Darling –'

He caught himself up.

'Come and dance . . .'

They moved off together.

Tuppence sighed.

'What's the matter?' said Tommy.

'I do hope Sheila will go on caring for him now that he isn't a German outcast with everyone against him.'

'She looks as though she cares all right.'

'Yes, but the Irish are terribly perverse. And Sheila is a born rebel.'

'Why did he search your room that day? That's what led us up the garden path so terribly.'

Tommy gave a laugh.

'I gather he thought Mrs Blenkensop wasn't a very convincing person. In fact – while we were suspecting him he was suspecting us.'

'Hallo, you two,' said Derek Beresford as he and his partner danced past his parents' table. 'Why don't you come and dance?'

He smiled encouragingly at them.

'They are so kind to us, bless 'em,' said Tuppence.

Presently the twins and their partners returned and sat down.

Derek said to his father:

'Glad you got a job all right. Not very interesting, I suppose?'

'Mainly routine,' said Tommy.

'Never mind, you're doing something. That's the great thing.'

'And I'm glad Mother was allowed to go and work too,' said Deborah. 'She looks ever so much happier. It wasn't too dull, was it, Mother?'

'I didn't find it at all dull,' said Tuppence.

'Good,' said Deborah. She added: 'When the war's over, I'll be able to tell you something about my job. It's really frightfully interesting, but very confidential.'

'How thrilling,' said Tuppence.

'Oh, it is! Of course, it's not so thrilling as flying –'

She looked enviously at Derek.

She said, 'He's going to be recommended for –'

Derek said quickly:

'Shut up, Deb.'

Tommy said:

'Hallo, Derek, what have you been up to?'

'Oh, nothing much – sort of show all of us are doing. Don't know why they pitched on me,' murmured the young airman, his face scarlet. He looked as embarrassed as though he had been accused of the most deadly of sins.

He got up and the fair-haired girl got up too.

Derek said:

'Mustn't miss any of this – last night of my leave.'

'Come on, Charles,' said Deborah.

The two of them floated away with their partners.

Tuppence prayed inwardly:

'Oh let them be safe – don't let anything happen to them . . .'

She looked up to meet Tommy's eyes. He said, 'About that child – shall we?'

'Betty? Oh, Tommy, I'm glad you've thought of it, too! I thought it was just me being maternal. You really mean it?'

'That we should adopt her? Why not? She's had a raw deal, and it will be fun for us to have something young growing up.'

'Oh Tommy!'

She stretched out her hand and squeezed his. They looked at each other.

'We always do want the same things,' said Tuppence happily.

Deborah, passing Derek on the floor, murmured to him:

'Just look at those two – actually holding hands! They're rather sweet, aren't they? We must do all we can to make up to them for having such a dull time in this war . . .'

By the Pricking of My Thumbs

Agatha Christie is known throughout the world as the Queen of Crime. Her books have sold over a billion copies in English with another billion in 100 foreign languages. She is the most widely published author of all time and in any language, outsold only by the Bible and Shakespeare. She is the author of 80 crime novels and short story collections, 19 plays, and six novels written under the name of Mary Westmacott.

Agatha Christie's first novel, *The Mysterious Affair at Styles*, was written towards the end of the First World War, in which she served as a VAD. In it she created Hercule Poirot, the little Belgian detective who was destined to become the most popular detective in crime fiction since Sherlock Holmes. It was eventually published by The Bodley Head in 1920.

In 1926, after averaging a book a year, Agatha Christie wrote her masterpiece. *The Murder of Roger Ackroyd* was the first of her books to be published by Collins and marked the beginning of an author-publisher relationship which lasted for 50 years and well over 70 books. *The Murder of Roger Ackroyd* was also the first of Agatha Christie's books to be dramatized – under the name *Alibi* – and to have a successful run in London's West End. *The Mousetrap*, her most famous play of all, opened in 1952 and is the longest-running play in history.

Agatha Christie was made a Dame in 1971. She died in 1976, since when a number of books have been published posthumously: the bestselling novel *Sleeping Murder* appeared later that year, followed by her autobiography and the short story collections *Miss Marple's Final Cases*, *Problem at Pollensa Bay* and *While the Light Lasts*. In 1998 *Black Coffee* was the first of her plays to be novelized by another author, Charles Osborne.

By the same author

The ABC Murders
The Adventure of the Christmas Pudding
After the Funeral
And Then There Were None
Appointment with Death
At Bertram's Hotel
The Big Four
The Body in the Library
By the Pricking of My Thumbs
Cards on the Table
A Caribbean Mystery
Cat Among the Pigeons
The Clocks
Crooked House
Curtain: Poirot's Last Case
Dead Man's Folly
Death Comes as the End
Death in the Clouds
Death on the Nile
Destination Unknown
Dumb Witness
Elephants Can Remember
Endless Night
Evil Under the Sun
Five Little Pigs
4.50 from Paddington
Hallowe'en Party
Hercule Poirot's Christmas
Hickory Dickory Dock
The Hollow
The Hound of Death
The Labours of Hercules
The Listerdale Mystery
Lord Edgware Dies
The Man in the Brown Suit
The Mirror Crack'd from Side to Side
Miss Marple's Final Cases
The Moving Finger
Mrs McGinty's Dead
The Murder at the Vicarage
Murder in Mesopotamia
Murder in the Mews
A Murder is Announced
Murder is Easy
The Murder of Roger Ackroyd
Murder on the Links
Murder on the Orient Express
The Mysterious Affair at Styles
The Mysterious Mr Quin
The Mystery of the Blue Train
Nemesis
N or M?
One, Two, Buckle My Shoe
Ordeal by Innocence
The Pale Horse
Parker Pyne Investigates
Partners in Crime
Passenger to Frankfurt
Peril at End House
A Pocket Full of Rye
Poirot Investigates
Poirot's Early Cases
Postern of Fate
Problem at Pollensa Bay
Sad Cypress
The Secret Adversary
The Secret of Chimneys
The Seven Dials Mystery
The Sittaford Mystery
Sleeping Murder
Sparkling Cyanide
Taken at the Flood
They Came to Baghdad
They Do It With Mirrors
Third Girl
The Thirteen Problems
Three Act Tragedy
Towards Zero
While the Light Lasts
Why Didn't They Ask Evans?

Novels under the Nom de Plume of 'Mary Westmacott'

Absent in the Spring
The Burden
A Daughter's A Daughter
Giant's Bread
The Rose and the Yew Tree
Unfinished Portrait

Plays novelized by Charles Osborne

Black Coffee
Spider's Web
The Unexpected Guest

Memoirs

Agatha Christie: An Autobiography
Come, Tell Me How You Live

Agatha Christie

By the Pricking of My Thumbs

HarperCollins*Publishers*

HarperCollins*Publishers*
77–85 Fulham Palace Road
Hammersmith, London W6 8JB
www.**fire**and**water**.com

This *Agatha Christie Signature Edition* published 2001
1 3 5 7 9 8 6 4 2

First published in Great Britain by
Collins 1968

ISBN 0 00 711149 5

Typeset by Palimpsest Book Production Limited,
Polmont, Stirlingshire

Printed and bound in Great Britain by
Omnia Books Limited, Glasgow

This book is dedicated to the many readers in this and other countries who write to me asking: 'What has happened to Tommy and Tuppence? What are they doing now?' My best wishes to you all, and I hope you will enjoy meeting Tommy and Tuppence again, years older, but with spirit unquenched!

Agatha Christie

Contents

Book 3

Missing – A Wife

Book 4

Here is a Church and here is the Steeple
Open the Doors and there are the People

By the pricking of my thumbs
Something wicked this way comes.

Macbeth

'What's the matter, Tommy?'

'Matter?' said Tommy vaguely. 'Matter?'

'That's what I said,' said Mrs Beresford.

'Nothing is the matter,' said Mr Beresford. 'What should it be?'

'You've thought of something,' said Tuppence accusingly.

'I don't think I was thinking of anything at all.'

'Oh yes, you were. Has anything happened?'

'No, of course not. What should happen?' He added, 'I got the plumber's bill.'

'Oh,' said Tuppence with the air of one enlightened. 'More than you expected, I suppose.'

'Naturally,' said Tommy, 'it always is.'

'I can't think why we didn't train as plumbers,' said Tuppence. 'If you'd only trained as a plumber, I could have been a plumber's mate and we'd be raking in money day by day.'

'Very short-sighted of us not to see these opportunities.'

'Was that the plumber's bill you were looking at just now?'

'Oh no, that was just an Appeal.'

'Delinquent boys – Racial integration?'

'No. Just another Home they're opening for old people.'

'Well, that's more sensible anyway,' said Tuppence,

'but I don't see why you have to have that worried look about it.'

'Oh, I wasn't thinking of that.'

'Well, what *were* you thinking of?'

'I suppose it put it into my mind,' said Mr Beresford.

'What?' said Tuppence. 'You know you'll tell me in the end.'

'It really wasn't anything important. I just thought that perhaps – well, it was Aunt Ada.'

'Oh, I see,' said Tuppence, with instant comprehension. 'Yes,' she added, softly, meditatively. 'Aunt Ada.'

Their eyes met. It is regrettably true that in these days there is in nearly every family, the problem of what might be called an 'Aunt Ada'. The names are different – Aunt Amelia, Aunt Susan, Aunt Cathy, Aunt Joan. They are varied by grandmothers, aged cousins and even great-aunts. But they exist and present a problem in life which has to be dealt with. Arrangements have to be made. Suitable establishments for looking after the elderly have to be inspected and full questions asked about them. Recommendations are sought from doctors, from friends, who have Aunt Adas of their own who had been 'perfectly happy until she had died' at 'The Laurels, Bexhill', or 'Happy Meadows at Scarborough'.

The days are past when Aunt Elisabeth, Aunt Ada

and the rest of them lived on happily in the homes where they had lived for many years previously, looked after by devoted if sometimes somewhat tyrannical old servants. Both sides were thoroughly satisfied with the arrangement. Or there were the innumerable poor relations, indigent nieces, semi-idiotic spinster cousins, all yearning for a good home with three good meals a day and a nice bedroom. Supply and demand complemented each other and all was well. Nowadays, things are different.

For the Aunt Adas of today arrangements have to be made suitable, not merely to an elderly lady who, owing to arthritis or other rheumatic difficulties, is liable to fall downstairs if she is left alone in a house, or who suffers from chronic bronchitis, or who quarrels with her neighbours and insults the tradespeople.

Unfortunately, the Aunt Adas are far more trouble than the opposite end of the age scale. Children can be provided with foster homes, foisted off on relations, or sent to suitable schools where they stay for the holidays, or arrangements can be made for pony treks or camps and on the whole very little objection is made by the children to the arrangements so made for them. The Aunt Adas are very different. Tuppence Beresford's own aunt – Great-aunt Primrose – had been a notable troublemaker. Impossible to satisfy her. No sooner did she enter an establishment guaranteed to provide a good home and all comforts for elderly ladies than after writing a few highly complimentary letters to her niece praising this particular establishment, the next news would be that she had indignantly walked out of it without notice.

'Impossible. I couldn't stay there another minute!'

Within the space of a year Aunt Primrose had been in and out of eleven such establishments, finally writing to say that she had now met a very charming young man. 'Really a very devoted boy. He lost his mother at a young age and he badly needs looking after. I have rented a flat and he is coming to live with me. This arrangement will suit us both perfectly. We are natural affinities. You need have no more anxieties, dear Prudence. My future is settled. I am seeing my lawyer tomorrow as it is necessary that I should make some provision for Mervyn if I should pre-decease him which is, of course, the natural course of events, though I assure you at the moment I feel in the pink of health.'

Tuppence had hurried north (the incident had taken place in Aberdeen). But as it happened, the police had arrived there first and had removed the glamorous Mervyn, for whom they had been seeking for some time, on a charge of obtaining money under false pretences. Aunt Primrose had been highly indignant, and had called it persecution – but after attending the

Court proceedings (where twenty-five other cases were taken into account) – had been forced to change her views of her *protégé*.

'I think I ought to go and see Aunt Ada, you know, Tuppence,' said Tommy. 'It's been some time.'

'I suppose so,' said Tuppence, without enthusiasm. 'How long has it been?'

Tommy considered. 'It must be nearly a year,' he said.

'It's more than that,' said Tuppence. 'I think it's over a year.'

'Oh dear,' said Tommy, 'the time does go so fast, doesn't it? I can't believe it's been as long as that. Still, I believe you're right, Tuppence.' He calculated. 'It's awful the way one forgets, isn't it? I really feel very badly about it.'

'I don't think you need,' said Tuppence. 'After all, we send her things and we write letters.'

'Oh yes, I know. You're awfully good about those sort of things, Tuppence. But all the same, one does read things sometimes that are very upsetting.'

'You're thinking of that dreadful book we got from the library,' said Tuppence, 'and how awful it was for the poor old dears. How they suffered.'

'I suppose it was true – taken from life.'

'Oh yes,' said Tuppence, 'there must be places like that. And there are people who are terribly unhappy, who can't help being unhappy. But what else is one to do, Tommy?'

'What can anyone do except be as careful as possible. Be very careful what you choose, find out all about it and make sure she's got a nice doctor looking after her.'

'Nobody could be nicer than Dr Murray, you must admit that.'

'Yes,' said Tommy, the worried look receding from his face. 'Murray's a first-class chap. Kind, patient. If anything was going wrong he'd let us know.'

'So I don't think you need worry about it,' said Tuppence. 'How old is she by now?'

'Eighty-two,' said Tommy. 'No – no. I think it's eighty-three,' he added. 'It must be rather awful when you've outlived everybody.'

'That's only what *we* feel,' said Tuppence. '*They* don't feel it.'

'You can't really tell.'

'Well, your Aunt Ada doesn't. Don't you remember the glee with which she told us the number of her old friends that she'd already outlived? She finished up by saying "and as for Amy Morgan, I've heard she won't last more than another six months. She always used to say I was so delicate and now it's practically a certainty that I shall outlive her. Outlive her by a good many years too." Triumphant, that's what she was at the prospect.'

'All the same –' said Tommy.

'I know,' said Tuppence, 'I know. All the same you feel it's your duty and so you've got to go.'

'Don't you think I'm right?'

'Unfortunately,' said Tuppence, 'I do think you're right. Absolutely right. And I'll come too,' she added, with a slight note of heroism in her voice.

'No,' said Tommy. 'Why should you? She's not your aunt. No, I'll go.'

'Not at all,' said Mrs Beresford. 'I like to suffer too. We'll suffer together. You won't enjoy it and I shan't enjoy it and I don't think for one moment that Aunt Ada will enjoy it. But I quite see it is one of those things that has got to be done.'

'No, I don't want you to go. After all, the last time, remember how frightfully rude she was to you?'

'Oh, I didn't mind that,' said Tuppence. 'It's probably the only bit of the visit that the poor old girl enjoyed. I don't grudge it to her, not for a moment.'

'You've always been nice to her,' said Tommy, 'even though you don't like her very much.'

'Nobody could like Aunt Ada,' said Tuppence. 'If you ask me I don't think anyone ever has.'

'One can't help feeling sorry for people when they get old,' said Tommy.

'I can,' said Tuppence. 'I haven't got as nice a nature as you have.'

'Being a woman you're more ruthless,' said Tommy.

'I suppose that might be it. After all, women haven't really got time to be anything but realistic over things. I mean I'm very sorry for people if they're old or sick or anything, if they're nice people. But if they're not nice people, well, it's different, you must admit. If you're pretty nasty when you're twenty and just as nasty when you're forty and nastier still when you're sixty, and a perfect devil by the time you're eighty – well, really, I don't see why one should be particularly sorry for people, just because they're old. You can't change yourself really. I know some absolute ducks who are seventy and eighty. Old Mrs Beauchamp, and Mary Carr and the baker's grandmother, dear old Mrs Poplett, who used to come in and clean for us. They were all dears and sweet and I'd do anything I could for them.'

'All right, all right,' said Tommy, 'be realistic. But if you really want to be noble and come with me –'

'I want to come with you,' said Tuppence. 'After all, I married you for better or for worse and Aunt Ada is decidedly the worse. So I shall go with you hand in hand. And we'll take her a bunch of flowers and a box of chocolates with soft centres and perhaps a magazine or two. You might write to Miss What's-her-name and say we're coming.'

'One day next week? I could manage Tuesday,' said Tommy, 'if that's all right for you.'

'Tuesday it is,' said Tuppence. 'What's the name of the woman? I can't remember – the matron or the superintendent or whoever she is. Begins with a P.'

'Miss Packard.'

'That's right.'

'Perhaps it'll be different this time,' said Tommy.

'Different? In what way?'

'Oh, I don't know. Something interesting might happen.'

'We might be in a railway accident on the way there,' said Tuppence, brightening up a little.

'Why on earth do you want to be in a railway accident?'

'Well I don't really, of course. It was just –'

'Just what?'

'Well, it would be an adventure of some kind, wouldn't it? Perhaps we could save lives or do something useful. Useful and at the same time exciting.'

'What a hope!' said Mr Beresford.

'I know,' agreed Tuppence. 'It's just that these sort of ideas come to one sometimes.'

Chapter 2

Was it your Poor Child?

How Sunny Ridge had come by its name would be difficult to say. There was nothing prominently ridge-like about it. The grounds were flat, which was eminently more suitable for the elderly occupants. It had an ample, though rather undistinguished garden. It was a fairly large Victorian mansion kept in a good state of repair. There were some pleasant shady trees, a Virginia creeper running up the side of the house, and two monkey puzzles gave an exotic air to the scene. There were several benches in advantageous places to catch the sun, one or two garden chairs and a sheltered veranda on which the old ladies could sit sheltered from the east winds.

Tommy rang the front door bell and he and Tuppence were duly admitted by a rather harassed-looking young woman in a nylon overall. She showed them into a small sitting-room saying rather breathlessly, 'I'll tell

Miss Packard. She's expecting you and she'll be down in a minute. You won't mind waiting just a little, will you, but it's old Mrs Carraway. She's been and swallowed her thimble again, you see.'

'How on earth did she do a thing like that?' asked Tuppence, surprised.

'Does it for fun,' explained the household help briefly. 'Always doing it.'

She departed and Tuppence sat down and said thoughtfully, 'I don't think I should like to swallow a thimble. It'd be awfully bobbly as it went down. Don't you think so?'

They had not very long to wait however before the door opened and Miss Packard came in, apologizing as she did so. She was a big, sandy-haired woman of about fifty with the air of calm competence about her which Tommy had always admired.

'I'm sorry if I have kept you waiting, Mr Beresford,' she said. 'How do you do, Mrs Beresford, I'm so glad you've come too.'

'Somebody swallowed something, I hear,' said Tommy.

'Oh, so Marlene told you that? Yes, it was old Mrs Carraway. She's always swallowing things. Very difficult, you know, because one can't watch them all the time. Of course one knows children do it, but it seems a funny thing to be a hobby of an elderly woman, doesn't it? It's grown upon her, you know. She gets worse every year. It doesn't seem to do her any harm, that's the cheeriest thing about it.'

'Perhaps her father was a sword swallower,' suggested Tuppence.

'Now that's a very interesting idea, Mrs Beresford. Perhaps it *would* explain things.' She went on, 'I've told Miss Fanshawe that you were coming, Mr Beresford. I don't know really whether she quite took it in. She doesn't always, you know.'

'How has she been lately?'

'Well, she's failing rather rapidly now, I'm afraid,' said Miss Packard in a comfortable voice. 'One never really knows how much she takes in and how much she doesn't. I told her last night and she said she was sure I must be mistaken because it was term time. She seemed to think that you were still at school. Poor old things, they get very muddled up sometimes, especially over time. However, this morning when I reminded her about your visit, she just said it was quite impossible because you were dead. Oh well,' Miss Packard went on cheerfully, 'I expect she'll recognize you when she sees you.'

'How is she in health? Much the same?'

'Well, perhaps as well as can be expected. Frankly, you know, I don't think she'll be with us very much longer. She doesn't suffer in any way but her heart condition's no better than it was. In fact, it's rather worse. So I think I'd like you to know that it's just as well to be prepared, so that if she did go suddenly it wouldn't be any shock to you.'

'We brought her some flowers,' said Tuppence.

'And a box of chocolates,' said Tommy.

'Oh, that's very kind of you I'm sure. She'll be very pleased. Would you like to come up now?'

Tommy and Tuppence rose and followed Miss Packard from the room. She led them up the broad staircase. As they passed one of the rooms in the passage upstairs, it opened suddenly and a little woman about five foot high trotted out, calling in a loud shrill voice, 'I want my cocoa. I want my cocoa. Where's Nurse Jane? I want my cocoa.'

A woman in a nurse's uniform popped out of the next door and said, 'There, there, dear, it's all right. You've had your cocoa. You had it twenty minutes ago.'

'No I didn't, Nurse. It's not true. I haven't had my cocoa. I'm thirsty.'

'Well, you shall have another cup if you like.'

'I can't have another when I haven't had one.'

They passed on and Miss Packard, after giving a brief rap on a door at the end of the passage, opened it and passed in.

'Here you are, Miss Fanshawe,' she said brightly.

'Here's your nephew come to see you. Isn't that nice?'

In a bed near the window an elderly lady sat up abruptly on her raised pillows. She had iron-grey hair, a thin wrinkled face with a large, high-bridged nose and a general air of disapprobation. Tommy advanced.

'Hullo, Aunt Ada,' he said. 'How are you?'

Aunt Ada paid no attention to him, but addressed Miss Packard angrily.

'I don't know what you mean by showing gentlemen into a lady's bedroom,' she said. 'Wouldn't have been thought proper at all in my young days! Telling me he's my nephew indeed! Who is he? A plumber or the electrician?'

'Now, now, that's not very nice,' said Miss Packard mildly.

'I'm your nephew, Thomas Beresford,' said Tommy. He advanced the box of chocolates. 'I've brought you a box of chocolates.'

'You can't get round me that way,' said Aunt Ada. 'I know your kind. Say anything, you will. Who's this woman?' She eyed Mrs Beresford with an air of distaste.

'I'm Prudence,' said Mrs Beresford. 'Your niece, Prudence.'

'What a ridiculous name,' said Aunt Ada. 'Sounds like a parlourmaid. My Great-uncle Mathew had a parlourmaid called Comfort and the housemaid was called Rejoice-in-the-Lord. Methodist she was. But my Great-aunt Fanny soon put a stop to that. Told her she was going to be called Rebecca as long as she was in *her* house.'

'I brought you a few roses,' said Tuppence.

'I don't care for flowers in a sick-room. Use up all the oxygen.'

'I'll put them in a vase for you,' said Miss Packard.

'You won't do anything of the kind. You ought to have learnt by now that I know my own mind.'

'You seem in fine form, Aunt Ada,' said Mr Beresford. 'Fighting fit, I should say.'

'I can take your measure all right. What d'you mean by saying that you're my nephew? What did you say your name was? Thomas?'

'Yes. Thomas or Tommy.'

'Never heard of you,' said Aunt Ada. 'I only had one nephew and he was called William. Killed in the last war. Good thing, too. He'd have gone to the bad if he'd lived. I'm tired,' said Aunt Ada, leaning back on her pillows and turning her head towards Miss Packard. 'Take 'em away. You shouldn't let strangers in to see me.'

'I thought a nice little visit might cheer you up,' said Miss Packard unperturbed.

Aunt Ada uttered a deep bass sound of ribald mirth.

'All right,' said Tuppence cheerfully. 'We'll go away

again. I'll leave the roses. You might change your mind about them. Come on, Tommy,' said Tuppence. She turned towards the door.

'Well, goodbye, Aunt Ada. I'm sorry you don't remember me.'

Aunt Ada was silent until Tuppence had gone out of the door with Miss Packard and Tommy followed her.

'Come back, *you*, said Aunt Ada, raising her voice. 'I know you perfectly. You're Thomas. Red-haired you used to be. Carrots, that's the colour your hair was. Come back. I'll talk to you. I don't want the woman. No good her pretending she's your wife. I know better. Shouldn't bring that type of woman in here. Come and sit down here in this chair and tell me about your dear mother. You go away,' added Aunt Ada as a kind of postscript, waving her hand towards Tuppence who was hesitating in the doorway.

Tuppence retired immediately.

'Quite in one of her moods today,' said Miss Packard, unruffled, as they went down the stairs. 'Sometimes, you know,' she added, 'she can be quite pleasant. You would hardly believe it.'

Tommy sat down in the chair indicated to him by Aunt Ada and remarked mildly that he couldn't tell her much about his mother as she had been dead now for nearly forty years. Aunt Ada was unperturbed by this statement.

'Fancy,' she said, 'is it as long as that? Well, time does pass quickly.' She looked him over in a considering manner. 'Why don't you get married?' she said. 'Get some nice capable woman to look after you. You're getting on, you know. Save you taking up with all these loose women and bringing them round and speaking as though they were your wife.'

'I can see,' said Tommy, 'that I shall have to get Tuppence to bring her marriage lines along next time we come to see you.'

'Made an honest woman of her, have you?' said Aunt Ada.

'We've been married over thirty years,' said Tommy, 'and we've got a son and a daughter, and they're both married too.'

'The trouble is,' said Aunt Ada, shifting her ground with dexterity, 'that nobody tells me anything. If you'd kept me properly up to date –'

Tommy did not argue the point. Tuppence had once laid upon him a serious injunction. 'If anybody over the age of sixty-five finds fault with you,' she said, 'never argue. Never try to say you're right. Apologize at once and say it was all your fault and you're very sorry and you'll never do it again.'

It occurred to Tommy at this moment with some force that that would certainly be the line to take with Aunt Ada, and indeed always had been.

'I'm very sorry, Aunt Ada,' he said. 'I'm afraid, you know, one does tend to get forgetful as time goes on. It's not everyone,' he continued unblushingly, 'who has your wonderful memory for the past.'

Aunt Ada smirked. There was no other word for it. 'You have something there,' she said. 'I'm sorry if I received you rather roughly, but I don't care for being imposed upon. You never know in this place. They let in anyone to see you. Anyone at all. If I accepted everyone for what they said they were, they might be intending to rob and murder me in my bed.'

'Oh, I don't think that's very likely,' said Tommy.

'You never know,' said Aunt Ada. 'The things you read in the paper. And the things people come and tell you. Not that I believe everything I'm told. But I keep a sharp look-out. Would you believe it, they brought a strange man in the other day – never seen him before. Called himself Dr Williams. Said Dr Murray was away on his holiday and this was his new partner. New partner! How was I to know he was his new partner? He just said he was, that's all.'

'Was he his new partner?'

'Well, as a matter of fact,' said Aunt Ada, slightly annoyed at losing ground, 'he actually was. But nobody could have known it for sure. There he was, drove up in a car, had that little kind of black box with him, which doctors carry to do blood pressure – and all that sort of thing. It's like the magic box they all used to talk about so much. Who was it, Joanna Southcott's?'

'No,' said Tommy. 'I think that was rather different. A prophecy of some kind.'

'Oh, I see. Well, my point is anyone could come into a place like this and say he was a doctor, and immediately all the nurses would smirk and giggle and say yes, Doctor, of course, Doctor, and more or less stand to attention, silly girls! And if the patient swore she didn't know the man, they'd only say she was forgetful and forgot people. I never forget a face,' said Aunt Ada firmly. 'I never have. How is your Aunt Caroline? I haven't heard from her for some time. Have you seen anything of her?'

Tommy said, rather apologetically, that his Aunt Caroline had been dead for fifteen years. Aunt Ada did not take this demise with any signs of sorrow. Aunt Caroline had after all not been her sister, but merely her first cousin.

'Everyone seems to be dying,' she said, with a certain relish. 'No stamina. That's what's the matter with them. Weak heart, coronary thrombosis, high blood pressure, chronic bronchitis, rheumatoid arthritis – all the rest of it. Feeble folk, all of them. That's how the doctors make their living. Giving them boxes and boxes and bottles and bottles of tablets. Yellow tablets, pink tablets, green tablets, even black tablets, I shouldn't be surprised. Ugh! Brimstone and treacle they used to use in my grandmother's day. I bet that was as good as anything. With the choice of getting well or having brimstone and treacle to drink, you chose getting well every time.' She nodded her head in a satisfied manner. 'Can't really trust doctors, can you? Not when it's a professional matter – some new fad – I'm told there's a lot of poisoning going on here. To get hearts for the surgeons, so I'm told. Don't think it's true, myself. Miss Packard's not the sort of woman who would stand for that.'

Downstairs Miss Packard, her manner slightly apologetic, indicated a room leading off the hall.

'I'm so sorry about this, Mrs Beresford, but I expect you know how it is with elderly people. They take fancies or dislikes and persist in them.'

'It must be very difficult running a place of this kind,' said Tuppence.

'Oh, not really,' said Miss Packard. 'I quite enjoy it, you know. And really, I'm quite fond of them all. One gets fond of people one has to look after, you know. I mean, they have their little ways and their fidgets, but they're quite easy to manage, if you know how.'

Tuppence thought to herself that Miss Packard was one of those people who would know how.

'They're like children, really,' said Miss Packard indulgently. 'Only children are far more logical which makes it difficult sometimes with them. But these people are illogical, they want to be reassured by your telling them what they want to believe. Then they're quite happy again for a bit. I've got a very nice staff here. People with patience, you know, and good temper, and not too brainy, because if you have people who are brainy they are bound to be very impatient. Yes, Miss Donovan, what is it?' She turned her head as a young woman with *pince-nez* came running down the stairs.

'It's Mrs Lockett again, Miss Packard. She says she's dying and she wants the doctor called at once.'

'Oh,' said Miss Packard, unimpressed, 'what's she dying from this time?'

'She says there was mushroom in the stew yesterday and that there must have been fungi in it and that she's poisoned.'

'That's a new one,' said Miss Packard. 'I'd better come up and talk to her. So sorry to leave you, Mrs Beresford. You'll find magazines and papers in that room.'

'Oh, I'll be quite all right,' said Tuppence.

She went into the room that had been indicated to her. It was a pleasant room overlooking the garden with french windows that opened on it. There were easy chairs, bowls of flowers on the tables. One wall had a bookshelf containing a mixture of modern novels and travel books, and also what might be described as old favourites, which possibly many of the inmates might be glad to meet again. There were magazines on a table.

At the moment there was only one occupant in the room. An old lady with white hair combed back off her face who was sitting in a chair, holding a glass of milk in her hand, and looking at it. She had a pretty pink and white face, and she smiled at Tuppence in a friendly manner.

'Good morning,' she said. 'Are you coming to live here or are you visiting?'

'I'm visiting,' said Tuppence. 'I have an aunt here. My husband's with her now. We thought perhaps two people at once was rather too much.'

'That was very thoughtful of you,' said the old lady. She took a sip of milk appreciatively. 'I wonder – no, I think it's quite all right. Wouldn't you like something? Some tea or some coffee perhaps? Let me ring the bell. They're very obliging here.'

'No thank you,' said Tuppence, 'really.'

'Or a glass of milk perhaps. It's not poisoned today.'

'No, no, not even that. We shan't be stopping very much longer.'

'Well, if you're quite sure – but it wouldn't be any trouble, you know. Nobody ever thinks anything is any trouble here. Unless, I mean, you ask for something quite impossible.'

'I daresay the aunt we're visiting sometimes asks for quite impossible things,' said Tuppence. 'She's a Miss Fanshawe,' she added.

'Oh, Miss Fanshawe,' said the old lady. 'Oh yes.'

Something seemed to be restraining her but Tuppence said cheerfully,

'She's rather a tartar, I should imagine. She always has been.'

'Oh, yes indeed she is. I used to have an aunt myself, you know, who was very like that, especially as she grew older. But we're all quite fond of Miss Fanshawe. She can be very, very amusing if she likes. About people, you know.'

'Yes, I daresay she could be,' said Tuppence. She reflected a moment or two, considering Aunt Ada in this new light.

'Very acid,' said the old lady. 'My name is Lancaster, by the way, Mrs Lancaster.'

'My name's Beresford,' said Tuppence.

'I'm afraid, you know, one does enjoy a bit of malice now and then. Her descriptions of some of the other guests here, and the things she says about them. Well, you know, one oughtn't, of course, to find it funny but one does.'

'Have you been living here long?'

'A good while now. Yes, let me see, seven years – eight years. Yes, yes it must be more than eight years.'

She sighed. 'One loses touch with things. And people too. Any relations I have left live abroad.'

'That must be rather sad.'

'No, not really. I didn't care for them very much. Indeed, I didn't even known them well. I had a bad illness – a very bad illness – and I was alone in the world, so they thought it was better for me to live in a place like this. I think I'm very lucky to have come here. They are so kind and thoughtful. And the gardens are really beautiful. I know myself that I shouldn't like to be living on my own because I do get very confused sometimes, you know. Very confused.' She tapped her forehead. 'I get confused here. I mix things up. I don't always remember properly the things that have happened.'

'I'm sorry,' said Tuppence. 'I suppose one always has to have something, doesn't one?'

'Some illnesses are very painful. We have two poor women living here with very bad rheumatoid arthritis. They suffer terribly. So I think perhaps it doesn't matter so much if one gets, well, just a little confused about what happened and where, and who it was, and all that sort of thing, you know. At any rate it's not painful physically.'

'No. I think perhaps you're quite right,' said Tuppence.

The door opened and a girl in a white overall came in with a little tray with a coffee pot on it and a plate with two biscuits, which she set down at Tuppence's side.

'Miss Packard thought you might care for a cup of coffee,' she said.

'Oh. Thank you,' said Tuppence.

The girl went out again and Mrs Lancaster said,

'There, you see. Very thoughtful, aren't they?'

'Yes indeed.'

Tuppence poured out her coffee and began to drink it. The two women sat in silence for some time. Tuppence offered the plate of biscuits but the old lady shook her head.

'No thank you, dear. I just like my milk plain.'

She put down the empty glass and leaned back in her chair, her eyes half closed. Tuppence thought that perhaps this was the moment in the morning when she took a little nap, so she remained silent. Suddenly however, Mrs Lancaster seemed to jerk herself awake again. Her eyes opened, she looked at Tuppence and said,

'I see you're looking at the fireplace.'

'Oh. Was I?' said Tuppence, slightly startled.

'Yes. I wondered –' she leant forward and lowered her voice. '– Excuse me, was it your poor child?'

Tuppence slightly taken aback, hesitated.

'I – no, I don't think so,' she said.

'I wondered. I thought perhaps you'd come for that reason. Someone ought to come some time. Perhaps they will. And looking at the fireplace, the way you did. That's where it is, you know. Behind the fireplace.'

'Oh,' said Tuppence. 'Oh. Is it?'

'Always the same time,' said Mrs Lancaster, in a low voice. 'Always the same time of day.' She looked up at the clock on the mantelpiece. Tuppence looked up also. 'Ten past eleven,' said the old lady. 'Ten past eleven. Yes, it's always the same time every morning.'

She sighed. 'People didn't understand – I told them what I knew – but they wouldn't believe me!'

Tuppence was relieved that at that moment the door opened and Tommy came in. Tuppence rose to her feet.

'Here I am. I'm ready.' She went towards the door turning her head to say, 'Goodbye, Mrs Lancaster.'

'How did you get on?' she asked Tommy, as they emerged into the hall.

'After *you* left,' said Tommy, 'like a house on fire.'

'I seem to have had a bad effect on her, don't I?' said Tuppence. 'Rather cheering, in a way.'

'Why cheering?'

'Well, at my age,' said Tuppence, 'and what with my neat and respectable and slightly boring appearance, it's nice to think that you might be taken for a depraved woman of fatal sexual charm.'

'Idiot,' said Tommy, pinching her arm affectionately. 'Who were you hobnobbing with? She looked a very nice fluffy old lady.'

'She was very nice,' said Tuppence. 'A dear old thing, I think. But unfortunately bats.'

'Bats?'

'Yes. Seemed to think there was a dead child behind the fireplace or something of the kind. She asked me if it was my poor child.'

'Rather unnerving,' said Tommy. 'I suppose there must be some people who are slightly batty here, as well as normal elderly relatives with nothing but age to trouble them. Still, she looked nice.'

'Oh, she was nice,' said Tuppence. 'Nice and very sweet, I think. I wonder what exactly her fancies are and why.'

Miss Packard appeared again suddenly.

'Goodbye, Mrs Beresford. I hope they brought you some coffee?'

'Oh yes, they did, thank you.'

'Well, it's been very kind of you to come, I'm sure,' said Miss Packard. Turning to Tommy, she said, 'And I know Miss Fanshawe has enjoyed your visit very much. I'm sorry she was rude to your wife.'

'I think that gave her a lot of pleasure too,' said Tuppence.

'Yes, you're quite right. She does like being rude to people. She's unfortunately rather good at it.'

'And so she practises the art as often as she can,' said Tommy.

'You're very understanding, both of you,' said Miss Packard.

'The old lady I was talking to,' said Tuppence. 'Mrs Lancaster, I think she said her name was?'

'Oh yes, Mrs Lancaster. We're all very fond of her.'

'She's – is she a little peculiar?'

'Well, she has fancies,' said Miss Packard indulgently. 'We have several people here who have fancies. Quite harmless ones. But – well, there they are. Things that they believe have happened to them. Or to other people. We try not to take any notice, not to encourage them. Just play it down. I think really it's just an exercise in imagination, a sort of phantasy they like to live in. Something exciting or something sad and tragic. It doesn't matter which. But no persecution mania, thank goodness. That would never do.'

'Well, that's over,' said Tommy with a sigh, as he got into the car. 'We shan't need to come again for at least six months.'

But they didn't need to go and see her in six months, for three weeks later Aunt Ada died in her sleep.

Chapter 3

A Funeral

'Funerals are rather sad, aren't they?' said Tuppence.

They had just returned from attending Aunt Ada's funeral, which had entailed a long and troublesome railway journey since the burial had taken place at the country village in Lincolnshire where most of Aunt Ada's family and forebears had been buried.

'What do you expect a funeral to be?' said Tommy reasonably. 'A scene of mad gaiety?'

'Well, it could be in some places,' said Tuppence. 'I mean the Irish enjoy a wake, don't they? They have a lot of keening and wailing first and then plenty of drink and a sort of mad whoopee. *Drink*?' she added, with a look towards the sideboard.

Tommy went over to it and duly brought back what he considered appropriate. In this case a White Lady.

'Ah, that's more like it,' said Tuppence.

She took off her black hat and threw it across the room and slipped off her long black coat.

'I hate mourning,' she said. 'It always smells of moth balls because it's been laid up somewhere.'

'You don't need to go on wearing mourning. It's only to go to the funeral in,' said Tommy.

'Oh no, I know that. In a minute or two I'm going to go up and put on a scarlet jersey just to cheer things up. You can make me another White Lady.'

'Really, Tuppence, I had no idea that funerals would bring out this party feeling.'

'I said funerals were sad,' said Tuppence when she reappeared a moment or two later, wearing a brilliant cherry-red dress with a ruby and diamond lizard pinned to the shoulder of it, 'because it's funerals like Aunt Ada's that are sad. I mean elderly people and not many flowers. Not a lot of people sobbing and sniffing round. Someone old and lonely who won't be missed much.'

'I should have thought it would be much easier for you to stand that than it would if it were my funeral, for instance.'

'That's where you're entirely wrong,' said Tuppence. 'I don't particularly want to think of your funeral because I'd much prefer to die before you do. But I mean, if I were going to your funeral, at any rate it would be an orgy of grief. I should take a lot of handkerchiefs.'

'With black borders?'

'Well, I hadn't thought of black borders but it's a nice idea. And besides, the Burial service is rather lovely. Makes you feel uplifted. Real grief is real. It makes you feel awful but it *does* something to you. I mean, it works it out like perspiration.'

'Really, Tuppence, I find your remarks about my decease and the effect it will have upon you in exceedingly bad taste. I don't like it. Let's forget about funerals.'

'I agree. Let's forget.'

'The poor old bean's gone,' said Tommy, 'and she went peacefully and without suffering. So, let's leave it at that. I'd better clear up all these, I suppose.'

He went over to the writing table and ruffled through some papers.

'Now where did I put Mr Rockbury's letter?'

'Who's Mr Rockbury? Oh, you mean the lawyer who wrote to you.'

'Yes. About winding up her affairs. I seem to be the only one of the family left by now.'

'Pity she hadn't got a fortune to leave you,' said Tuppence.

'If she had had a fortune she'd have left it to that Cats' Home,' said Tommy. 'The legacy that she's left to them in her will will pretty well eat up all the spare cash. There won't be much left to come to me. Not that I need it or want it anyway.'

'Was she so fond of cats?'

'I don't know. I suppose so. I never heard her mention them. I believe,' said Tommy thoughtfully, 'she used to get rather a lot of fun out of saying to old friends of hers when they came to see her "I've left you a little something in my will, dear" or "This brooch that you're so fond of I've left you in my will." She didn't actually leave anything to anyone except the Cats' Home.'

'I bet she got rather a kick out of that,' said Tuppence. 'I can just see her saying all the things you told me to a lot of her old friends – or so-called old friends because I don't suppose they were people she really liked at all. She just enjoyed leading them up the garden path. I must say she was an old devil, wasn't she, Tommy? Only, in a funny sort of way one likes her for being an old devil. It's something to be able to get some fun out of life when you're old and stuck away in a Home. Shall we have to go to Sunny Ridge?'

'Where's the other letter, the one from Miss Packard? Oh yes, here it is. I put it with Rockbury's. Yes, she says there are certain things there, I gather, which apparently are now my property. She took some furniture with her, you know, when she went to live there. And of course there are her personal effects. Clothes and things like that. I suppose somebody will have to go through them. And letters and things. I'm her executor, so I suppose it's up to me. I don't suppose there's anything we want really, is there? Except there's a small desk there that I always liked. Belonged to old Uncle William, I believe.'

'Well, you might take that as a memento,' said Tuppence. 'Otherwise, I suppose, we just send the things to be auctioned.'

'So you don't really need to go there at all,' said Tommy.

'Oh, I think I'd like to go there,' said Tuppence.

'You'd like to? Why? Won't it be rather a bore to you?'

'What, looking through her things? No, I don't think so. I think I've got a certain amount of curiosity. Old letters and antique jewellery are always interesting and I think one ought to look at them oneself, not just send them to auction or let strangers go through them. No, we'll go and look through the things and see if there's anything we would like to keep and otherwise settle up.'

'Why do you really want to go? You've got some other reason, haven't you?'

'Oh dear,' said Tuppence, 'it is awful being married to someone who knows too much about one.'

'So you *have* got another reason?'

'Not a real one.'

'Come on, Tuppence. You're not really so fond of turning over people's belongings.'

'That, I think, is my duty,' said Tuppence firmly. 'No, the only other reason is –'

'Come on. Cough it up.'

'I'd rather like to see that – that other old pussy again.'

'What, the one who thought there was a dead child behind the fireplace?'

'Yes,' said Tuppence. 'I'd like to talk to her again. I'd like to know what was in her mind when she said all those things. Was it something she remembered or was it something that she'd just imagined? The more I think about it the more extraordinary it seems. Is it a sort of story that she wrote to herself in her mind or is there – was there once something real that happened about a fireplace or about a dead child. What made her think that the dead child might have been *my* dead child? Do I look as though I had a dead child?'

'I don't know how you expect anyone to look who has a dead child,' said Tommy. 'I shouldn't have thought so. Anyway, Tuppence, it is our duty to go and you can enjoy yourself in your *macabre* way on the side. So that's settled. We'll write to Miss Packard and fix a day.'

Chapter 4

Picture of a House

Tuppence drew a deep breath.

'It's just the same,' she said.

She and Tommy were standing on the front doorstep of Sunny Ridge.

'Why shouldn't it be?' asked Tommy.

'I don't know. It's just a feeling I have – something to do with time. Time goes at a different pace in different places. Some places you come back to, and you feel that time has been bustling along at a terrific rate and that all sorts of things will have happened – and changed. But here – Tommy – do you remember Ostend?'

'Ostend? We went there on our honeymoon. Of course I remember.'

'And do you remember the sign written up? TRAMSTILLSTAND – It made us laugh. It seemed so ridiculous.'

'I think it was Knock – not Ostend.'

'Never mind – you remember it. Well, this is like that word – *Tramstillstand* – a portmanteau word. Timestillstand – nothing's happened here. Time has just stood still. Everything's going on here just the same. It's like ghosts, only the other way round.'

'I don't know what you are talking about. Are you going to stand here all day talking about time and not even ring the bell? – Aunt Ada isn't here, for one thing. That's different.' He pressed the bell.

'That's the only thing that will be different. My old lady will be drinking milk and talking about fire-places, and Mrs Somebody-or-other will have swallowed a thimble or a teaspoon and a funny little woman will come squeaking out of a room demanding her cocoa, and Miss Packard will come down the stairs, and –'

The door opened. A young woman in a nylon overall said: 'Mr and Mrs Beresford? Miss Packard's expecting you.'

The young woman was just about to show them into the same sitting-room as before when Miss Packard came down the stairs and greeted them. Her manner was suitably not quite as brisk as usual. It was grave, and had a kind of semi-mourning about it – not too much – that might have been embarrassing. She was an expert in the exact amount of condolence which would be acceptable.

Three score years and ten was the Biblical accepted span of life, and the deaths in her establishment seldom occurred below that figure. They were to be expected and they happened.

'So good of you to come. I've got everything laid out tidily for you to look through. I'm glad you could come so soon because as a matter of fact I have already three or four people waiting for a vacancy to come here. You will understand, I'm sure, and not think that I was trying to hurry you in any way.'

'Oh no, of course, we quite understand,' said Tommy.

'It's all still in the room Miss Fanshawe occupied,' Miss Packard explained.

Miss Packard opened the door of the room in which they had last seen Aunt Ada. It had that deserted look a room has when the bed is covered with a dust sheet, with the shapes showing beneath it of folded-up blankets and neatly arranged pillows.

The wardrobe doors stood open and the clothes it had held had been laid on the top of the bed neatly folded.

'What do you usually do – I mean, what do people do mostly with clothes and things like that?' said Tuppence.

Miss Packard, as invariably, was competent and helpful.

'I can give you the name of two or three societies who are only too pleased to have things of that kind. She had quite a good fur stole and a good quality coat but I don't suppose you would have any personal use for them? But perhaps you have charities of your own where you would like to dispose of things.'

Tuppence shook her head.

'She had some jewellery,' said Miss Packard. 'I removed that for safe keeping. You will find it in the right-hand drawer of the dressing-table. I put it there just before you were due to arrive.'

'Thank you very much,' said Tommy, 'for the trouble you have taken.'

Tuppence was staring at a picture over the mantelpiece. It was a small oil painting representing a pale pink house standing adjacent to a canal spanned by a small hump-backed bridge. There was an empty boat drawn up under the bridge against the bank of the canal. In the distance were two poplar trees. It was a very pleasant little scene but nevertheless Tommy wondered why Tuppence was staring at it with such earnestness.

'How funny,' murmured Tuppence.

Tommy looked at her inquiringly. The things that Tuppence thought funny were, he knew by long experience, not really to be described by such an adjective at all.

'What do you mean, Tuppence?'

'It is funny. I never noticed that picture when I was here before. But the odd thing is that I have seen that house somewhere. Or perhaps it's a house just like that that I have seen. I remember it quite well . . . Funny that I can't remember when and where.'

'I expect you noticed it without really noticing you were noticing,' said Tommy, feeling his choice of words was rather clumsy and nearly as painfully repetitive as Tuppence's reiteration of the word 'funny'.

'Did *you* notice it, Tommy, when we were here last time?'

'No, but then I didn't look particularly.'

'Oh, that picture,' said Miss Packard. 'No, I don't think you would have seen it when you were here the last time because I'm almost sure it wasn't hanging over the mantelpiece then. Actually it was a picture belonging to one of our other guests, and she gave it to your aunt. Miss Fanshawe expressed admiration of it once or twice and this other old lady made her a present of it and insisted she should have it.'

'Oh I see,' said Tuppence, 'so of course I couldn't have seen it here before. But I still feel I know the house quite well. Don't you, Tommy?'

'No,' said Tommy.

'Well, I'll leave you now,' said Miss Packard briskly. 'I shall be available at any time that you want me.'

She nodded with a smile, and left the room, closing the door behind her.

'I don't think I really like that woman's teeth,' said Tuppence.

'What's wrong with them?'

'Too many of them. Or too big – "*The better to eat you with, my child*" – Like Red Riding Hood's grandmother.'

'You seem in a very odd sort of mood today, Tuppence.'

'I am rather. I've always thought of Miss Packard as very nice – but today, somehow, she seems to me rather sinister. Have you ever felt that?'

'No, I haven't. Come on, let's get on with what we came here to do – look over poor old Aunt Ada's "effects", as the lawyers call them. That's the desk I told you about – Uncle William's desk. Do you like it?'

'It's lovely. Regency, I should think. It's nice for the old people who come here to be able to bring some of their own things with them. I don't care for the horsehair chairs, but I'd like that little work-table. It's just what we need for that corner by the window where we've got that perfectly hideous whatnot.'

'All right,' said Tommy. 'I'll make a note of those two.'

'And we'll have the picture over the mantelpiece.

It's an awfully attractive picture and I'm quite sure that I've seen that house somewhere. Now, let's look at the jewellery.'

They opened the dressing-table drawer. There was a set of cameos and a Florentine bracelet and ear-rings and a ring with different-coloured stones in it.

'I've seen one of these before,' said Tuppence. 'They spell a name usually. Dearest sometimes. Diamond, emerald, amethyst, no, it's not dearest. I don't think it would be really. I can't imagine anyone giving your Aunt Ada a ring that spelt dearest. Ruby, emerald – the difficulty is one never knows where to begin. I'll try again. Ruby, emerald, another ruby, no, I think it's a garnet and an amethyst and another pinky stone, it must be a ruby this time and a small diamond in the middle. Oh, of course, it's *regard*. Rather nice really. So old-fashioned and sentimental.'

She slipped it on to her finger.

'I think Deborah might like to have this,' she said, 'and the Florentine set. She's frightfully keen on Victorian things. A lot of people are nowadays. Now, I suppose we'd better do the clothes. That's always rather *macabre*, I think. Oh, this is the fur stole. Quite valuable, I should think. I wouldn't want it myself. I wonder if there's anyone here – anyone who was especially nice to Aunt Ada – or perhaps some special friend among the other inmates – visitors, I mean. They call them visitors or guests, I notice. It would be nice to offer her the stole if so. It's real sable. We'll ask Miss Packard. The rest of the things can go to the charities. So that's all settled, isn't it? We'll go and find Miss Packard now. Goodbye, Aunt Ada,' she remarked aloud, her eyes turning to the bed. 'I'm glad we came to see you that last time. I'm sorry you didn't like me, but if it was fun to you *not* to like me and say those rude things, I don't begrudge it to you. You had to have *some* fun. And we won't forget you. We'll think of you when we look at Uncle William's desk.'

They went in search of Miss Packard. Tommy explained that they would arrange for the desk and the small work-table to be called for and despatched to their own address and that he would arrange with the local auctioneers to dispose of the rest of the furniture. He would leave the choice of any societies willing to receive clothing to Miss Packard if she wouldn't mind the trouble.

'I don't know if there's anyone here who would like her sable stole,' said Tuppence. 'It's a very nice one. One of her special friends, perhaps? Or perhaps one of the nurses who had done some special waiting on Aunt Ada?'

'That is a very kind thought of yours, Mrs Beresford. I'm afraid Miss Fanshawe hadn't any special friends among our visitors, but Miss O'Keefe, one of the nurses, did do a lot for her and was especially good and tactful, and I think she'd be pleased and honoured to have it.'

'And there's the picture over the mantelpiece,' said Tuppence. 'I'd like to have that – but perhaps the person whom it belonged to, and who gave it to her, would want to have it back. I think we ought to ask her –?'

Miss Packard interrupted. 'Oh, I'm sorry, Mrs Beresford, I'm afraid we can't do that. It was a Mrs Lancaster who gave it to Miss Fanshawe and she isn't with us any longer.'

'Isn't with you?' said Tuppence, surprised. 'A Mrs Lancaster? The one I saw last time I was here – with white hair brushed back from her face. She was drinking milk in the sitting-room downstairs. She's gone away, you say?'

'Yes. It was all rather sudden. One of her relations, a Mrs Johnson, took her away about a week ago. Mrs Johnson had returned from Africa where she's been living for the last four or five years – quite unexpectedly. She is now able to take care of Mrs Lancaster in her own home, since she and her husband are taking a house in England. I don't think,' said Miss Packard, 'that Mrs Lancaster really wanted to leave us. She had become so – set in her ways here, and she got on very well with everyone and was happy. She was very disturbed, quite tearful about it – but what can one do? She hadn't really very much say in the matter, because of course the Johnsons were paying for her stay here. I did suggest that as she had been here so long and settled down so well, it might be advisable to let her remain –'

'How long had Mrs Lancaster been with you? asked Tuppence.

'Oh, nearly six years, I think. Yes, that's about it. That's why, of course, she'd really come to feel that this was her home.'

'Yes,' said Tuppence. 'Yes, I can understand that.' She frowned and gave a nervous glance at Tommy and then stuck a resolute chin into the air.

'I'm sorry she's left. I had a feeling when I was talking to her that I'd met her before – her face seemed familiar to me. And then afterwards it came back to me that I'd met her with an old friend of mine, a Mrs Blenkinsop. I thought when I came back here again to visit Aunt Ada, that I'd find out from her if that was so. But of course if she's gone back to her own people, that's different.'

'I quite understand, Mrs Beresford. If any of our visitors can get in touch with some of their old friends or someone who knew their relations at one time, it makes a great difference to them. I can't remember a Mrs Blenkinsop ever having been mentioned by her, but then I don't suppose that would be likely to happen in any case.'

'Can you tell me a little more about her, who her relations were, and how she came to come here?'

'There's really very little to tell. As I said, it was about six years ago that we had letters from Mrs Johnson inquiring about the Home, and then Mrs Johnson herself came here and inspected it. She said she'd had mentions of Sunny Ridge from a friend and she inquired the terms and all that and – then she went away. And about a week or a fortnight later we had a letter from a firm of solicitors in London making further inquiries, and finally they wrote saying that they would like us to accept Mrs Lancaster and that Mrs Johnson would bring her here in about a week's time if we had a vacancy. As it happened, we had, and Mrs Johnson brought Mrs Lancaster here and Mrs Lancaster seemed to like the place and liked the room that we proposed to allot her. Mrs Johnson said that Mrs Lancaster would like to bring some of her own things. I quite agreed, because people usually do that and find they're much happier. So it was all arranged very satisfactorily. Mrs Johnson explained that Mrs Lancaster was a relation of her husband's, not a very near one, but that they felt worried about her because they themselves were going out to Africa – to Nigeria I think it was, her husband was taking up an appointment there and it was likely they'd be there for some years before they returned to England, so as they had no home to offer Mrs Lancaster, they wanted to make sure that she was accepted in a place where she would be really happy. They were quite sure from what they'd heard about this place that that was so. So it was all arranged very happily indeed and Mrs Lancaster settled down here very well.'

'I see.'

'Everyone here liked Mrs Lancaster very much. She was a little bit – well, you know what I mean – woolly in the head. I mean, she forgot things, confused things and couldn't remember names and addresses sometimes.'

'Did she get many letters?' said Tuppence. 'I mean letters from abroad and things?'

'Well, I think Mrs Johnson – or Mr Johnson – wrote once or twice from Africa but not after the first year. People, I'm afraid, do forget, you know. Especially when they go to a new country and a different life, and I don't think they'd been very closely in touch with her at any time. I think it was just a distant relation, and a family responsibility, and that was all it meant to them. All the financial arrangements were done through the lawyer, Mr Eccles, a very nice, reputable firm. Actually we'd had one or two dealings with that firm before so that we new about them, as they knew about us. But I think most of Mrs Lancaster's friends and relations had passed over and so she didn't hear much from anyone, and I think hardly anyone ever came to visit her. One very nice-looking man came about a year later, I think. I don't think he knew her personally at all well but he was a friend of Mr Johnson's and had also been in the Colonial service overseas. I think he just came to make sure she was well and happy.'

'And after that,' said Tuppence, 'everyone forgot about her.'

'I'm afraid so,' said Miss Packard. 'It's sad, isn't it? But it's the usual rather than the unusual thing to happen. Fortunately, most visitors to us make their own friends here. They get friendly with someone who has their own tastes or certain memories in common, and so things settle down quite happily. I think most of them forget most of their past life.'

'Some of them, I suppose,' said Tommy, 'are a little –' he hesitated for a word '– a little –' his hand went slowly to his forehead, but he drew it away. 'I don't mean –' he said.

'Oh, I know perfectly what you mean,' said Miss Packard. 'We don't take mental patients, you know, but we do take what you might call borderline cases. I mean, people who are rather senile – can't look after themselves properly, or who have certain fancies and imaginations. Sometimes they imagine themselves to be historical personages. Quite in a harmless way. We've had two Marie Antoinettes here, one of them was always talking about something called the *Petit Trianon* and drinking a lot of milk which she seemed to associate with the place. And we had one dear old soul who insisted that she was Madame Curie and that she had discovered radium. She used to read the papers with great interest, especially any news of atomic bombs or scientific discoveries. Then she always explained it was she and her husband who had first started experiments on these lines. Harmless delusions are things that manage to keep you very happy when you're elderly. They don't usually last all the time, you know. You're not Marie Antoinette every day or even Madame Curie. Usually it comes on about once a fortnight. Then I suppose presumably one gets tired of keeping the play-acting up. And of course more often it's just forgetfulness that people suffer from. They can't quite remember who they are. Or they keep saying there's something very important they've forgotten and if they could only remember it. That sort of thing.'

'I see,' said Tuppence. She hesitated, and then said, 'Mrs Lancaster – Was it always things about that particular fireplace in the sitting-room she remembered, or was it any fireplace?'

Miss Packard stared – 'A fireplace? I don't understand what you mean.'

'It was something she said that I didn't understand –

Perhaps she'd had some unpleasant association with a fireplace, or read some story that had frightened her.'

'Possibly.'

Tuppence said: 'I'm still rather worried about the picture she gave to Aunt Ada.'

'I really don't think you need worry, Mrs Beresford. I expect she's forgotten all about it by now. I don't think she prized it particularly. She was just pleased that Miss Fanshawe admired it and was glad for her to have it, and I'm sure she'd be glad for you to have it because you admire it. It's a nice picture, I thought so myself. Not that I know much about pictures.'

'I tell you what I'll do. I'll write to Mrs Johnson if you'll give me her address, and just ask if it's all right to keep it.'

'The only address I've got is the hotel in London they were going to – the Cleveland, I think it was called. Yes, the Cleveland Hotel, George Street, W1. She was taking Mrs Lancaster there for about four or five days and after that I think they were going to stay with some relations in Scotland. I expect the Cleveland Hotel will have a forwarding address.'

'Well, thank you – And now, about this fur stole of Aunt Ada's.'

'I'll go and bring Miss O'Keefe to you.'

She went out of the room.

'You and your Mrs Blenkinsops,' said Tommy.

Tuppence looked complacent.

'One of my best creations,' she said. 'I'm glad I was able to make use of her – I was just trying to think of a name and suddenly Mrs Blenkinsop came into my mind. What fun it was, wasn't it?'

'It's a long time ago – No more spies in wartime and counter-espionage for us.'

'More's the pity. It *was* fun – living in that guest house – inventing a new personality for myself – I really began to believe I *was* Mrs Blenkinsop.'

'You were lucky you got away safely with it,' said Tommy, 'and in my opinion, as I once told you, you overdid it.'

'I did not. I was perfectly in character. A nice woman, rather silly, and far too much taken up with her three sons.'

'That's what I mean,' said Tommy. 'One son would have been quite enough. Three sons were too much to burden yourself with.'

'They became quite real to me,' said Tuppence. 'Douglas, Andrew and – goodness, I've forgotten the name of the third one now. I know exactly what they looked like and their characters and just where they were stationed, and I talked most indiscreetly about the letters I got from them.'

'Well, that's over,' said Tommy. 'There's nothing to find out in this place – so forget about Mrs Blenkinsop. When I'm dead and buried and you've suitably mourned me and taken up your residence in a home for the aged, I expect you'll be thinking you are Mrs Blenkinsop half of the time.'

'It'll be rather boring to have only one role to play,' said Tuppence.

'Why do you think old people *want* to be Marie Antoinette, and Madame Curie and all the rest of it?' asked Tommy.

'I expect because they get so bored. One does get bored. I'm sure *you* would if you couldn't use your legs and walk about, or perhaps your fingers get too stiff and you can't knit. Desperately you want something to do to amuse yourself so you try on some public character and see what it feels like when you are it. I can understand that perfectly.'

'I'm sure you can,' said Tommy. 'God help the home for the aged that you go to. You'll be Cleopatra most of the time, I expect.'

'I won't be a famous person,' said Tuppence. 'I'll be someone like a kitchenmaid at Anne of Cleves' castle retailing a lot of spicy gossip that I'd heard.'

The door opened, and Miss Packard appeared in company with a tall, freckle-faced young woman in nurse's dress and a mop of red hair.

'This is Miss O'Keefe – Mr and Mrs Beresford. They have something to tell you. Excuse me, will you? One of the patients is asking for me.'

Tuppence duly made the presentation of Aunt Ada's fur stole and Nurse O'Keefe was enraptured.

'Oh! It's lovely. It's too good for me, though. You'll be wanting it yourself –'

'No, I don't really. It's on the big side for me. I'm too small. It's just right for a tall girl like you. Aunt Ada was tall.'

'Ah! she was the grand old lady – she must have been very handsome as a girl.'

'I suppose so,' said Tommy doubtfully. 'She must have been a tartar to look after, though.'

'Oh, she was that, indeed. But she had a grand spirit. Nothing got her down. And she was no fool either. You'd be surprised the way she got to know things. Sharp as a needle, she was.'

'She had a temper, though.'

'Yes, indeed. But it's the whining kind that gets you down – all complaints and moans. Miss Fanshawe was never dull. Grand stories she'd tell you of the old days – Rode a horse once up the staircase of a country house when she was a girl – or so she said – Would that be true now?'

'Well, I wouldn't put it past her,' said Tommy.

'You never know what you can believe here. The

tales the old dears come and tell you. Criminals that they've recognized – We must notify the police at once – if not, we're all in danger.'

'Somebody was being poisoned last time we were here, I remember,' said Tuppence.

'Ah! that was only Mrs Lockett. It happens to her every day. But it's not the police she wants, it's a doctor to be called – she's that crazy about doctors.'

'And somebody – a little woman – calling out for cocoa –'

'That would be Mrs Moody. Poor soul, she's gone.'

'You mean left here – gone away?'

'No – it was a thrombosis took her – very sudden. She was one who was very devoted to your Aunt – not that Miss Fanshawe always had time for her – always talking nineteen to the dozen, as she did –'

'Mrs Lancaster has left, I hear.'

'Yes, her folk came for her. She didn't want to go, poor thing.'

'What was the story she told me – about the fireplace in the sitting-room?'

'Ah! she'd lots of stories, that one – about the things that happened to her – and the secrets she knew –'

'There was something about a child – a kidnapped child or a murdered child –'

'It's strange it is, the things they think up. It's the TV as often as not that gives them the ideas –'

'Do you find it a strain, working here with all these old people? It must be tiring.'

'Oh no – I like old people – That's why I took up Geriatric work –'

'You've been here long?'

'A year and a half –' She paused. '– But I'm leaving next month.'

'Oh! why?'

For the first time a certain constraint came into Nurse O'Keefe's manner.

'Well, you see, Mrs Beresford, one needs a change –'

'But you'll be doing the same kind of work?'

'Oh yes –' She picked up the fur stole. 'I'm thanking you again very much – and I'm glad, too, to have something to remember Miss Fanshawe by – She was a grand old lady – You don't find many like her nowadays.'

Chapter 5

Disappearance of an Old Lady

Aunt Ada's things arrived in due course. The desk was installed and admired. The little work-table dispossessed the whatnot – which was relegated to a dark corner of the hall. And the picture of the pale pink house by the canal bridge Tuppence hung over the mantelpiece in her bedroom where she could see it every morning when drinking her early morning tea.

Since her conscience still troubled her a little, Tuppence wrote a letter explaining how the picture had come into their possession but that if Mrs Lancaster would like it returned, she had only got to let them know. This she dispatched to Mrs Lancaster, c/o Mrs Johnson, at the Cleveland Hotel, George Street, London, W1.

To this there was no reply, but a week later the letter was returned with 'Not known at this address' scrawled on it.

'How tiresome,' said Tuppence.

'Perhaps they only stayed for a night or two,' suggested Tommy.

'You'd think they'd have left a forwarding address –'

'Did you put "Please forward" on it?'

'Yes, I did. I know, I'll ring them up and ask – They must have put an address in the hotel register –'

'I'd let it go if I were you,' said Tommy. 'Why make all this fuss? I expect the old pussy has forgotten all about the picture.'

'I might as well try.'

Tuppence sat down at the telephone and was presently connected to the Cleveland Hotel.

She rejoined Tommy in his study a few minutes later.

'It's rather curious, Tommy – they haven't even *been* there. No Mrs Johnson – no Mrs Lancaster – no rooms booked for them – or any trace of their having stayed there before.'

'I expect Miss Packard got the name of the hotel wrong. Wrote it down in a hurry – and then perhaps lost it – or remembered it wrong. Things like that often happen, you know.'

'I shouldn't have thought it would at Sunny Ridge. Miss Packard is so efficient always.'

'Perhaps they didn't book beforehand at the hotel and it was full, so they had to go somewhere else. You know what accommodation in London is like – *Must* you go on fussing?'

Tuppence retired.

Presently she came back.

'I know what I'm going to do. I'll ring up Miss Packard and I'll get the address of the lawyers –'

'What lawyers?'

'Don't you remember she said something about a firm of solicitors who made all the arrangements because the Johnsons were abroad?'

Tommy, who was busy over a speech he was drafting for a Conference he was shortly to attend, and murmuring under his breath – '*the proper policy if such a contingency should arise*' – said: 'How do you spell contingency, Tuppence?'

'Did you hear what I was saying?'

'Yes, very good idea – splendid – excellent – you do that –'

Tuppence went out – stuck her head in again and said:

'C-o-n-s-i-s-t-e-n-c-y.'

'Can't be – you've got the wrong word.'

'What are you writing about?'

'The Paper I'm reading next at the I.U.A.S. and I do wish you'd let me do it in peace.'

'Sorry.'

Tuppence removed herself. Tommy continued to

write sentences and then scratch them out. His face was just brightening, as the pace of his writing increased – when once more the door opened.

'Here it is,' said Tuppence. 'Partingdale, Harris, Lockeridge and Partingdale, 32 Lincoln Terrace, W.C.2. Tel. Holborn 051386. The operative member of the firm is Mr Eccles.' She placed a sheet of paper by Tommy's elbow. 'Now *you* take on.'

'No!' said Tommy firmly.

'Yes! She's *your* Aunt Ada.'

'Where does Aunt Ada come in? Mrs Lancaster is no aunt of mine.'

'But it's *lawyers*,' Tuppence insisted. 'It's a man's job always to deal with lawyers. They just think women are silly and don't pay attention –'

'A very sensible point of view,' said Tommy.

'Oh! Tommy – *do* help. You go and telephone and I'll find the dictionary and look how to spell contingency.'

Tommy gave her a look, but departed.

He returned at last and spoke firmly – 'This matter is now *closed*, Tuppence.'

'You got Mr Eccles?'

'Strictly speaking I got a Mr Wills who is doubtless the dogsbody of the firm of Partingford, Lockjaw and Harrison. But he was fully informed and glib. All letters and communications go via the Southern Counties

Bank, Hammersmith branch, who will forward all communications. And there, Tuppence, let me tell you, the trail *stops*. Banks will forward things – but they won't yield any addresses to you or anyone else who asks. They have their code of rules and they'll stick to them – Their lips are sealed like our more pompous Prime Ministers.'

'All right, I'll send a letter care of the Bank.'

'Do that – and for goodness' sake, *leave me alone* – or I shall never get my speech done.'

'Thank you, darling,' said Tuppence. 'I don't know what I'd do without you.' She kissed the top of his head.

'It's the best butter,' said Tommy.

II

It was not until the following Thursday evening that Tommy asked suddenly, 'By the way, did you ever get any answer to the letter you sent care of the Bank to Mrs Johnson –'

'It's nice of you to ask,' said Tuppence sarcastically. 'No, I didn't.' She added meditatively, 'I don't think I shall, either.'

'Why not?'

'You're not really interested,' said Tuppence coldly.

'Look here, Tuppence – I know I've been rather preoccupied – It's all this I.U.A.S. – It's only once a year, thank goodness.'

'It starts on Monday, doesn't it? For five days –'

'Four days.'

'And you all go down to a Hush Hush, top secret house in the country somewhere, and make speeches and read Papers and vet young men for Super Secret assignments in Europe and beyond. I've forgotten what I.U.A.S. stands for. All these initials they have nowadays –'

'International Union of Associated Security.'

'What a mouthful! Quite ridiculous. And I expect the whole place is bugged, and everybody knows everybody else's most secret conversations.'

'Highly likely,' said Tommy with a grin.

'And I suppose you enjoy it?'

'Well, I do in a way. One sees a lot of old friends.'

'All quite ga-ga by now, I expect. Does any of it do any good?'

'Heavens, what a question! Can one ever let oneself believe that you can answer that by a plain Yes or No –'

'And are any of the people any good?'

'I'd answer Yes to that. Some of them are very good indeed.'

'Will old Josh be there?'

'Yes, he'll be there.'

'What is he like nowadays?'

'Extremely deaf, half blind, crippled with rheumatism – and you'd be surprised at the things that *don't* get past him.'

'I see,' said Tuppence. She meditated. 'I wish I were in it, too.'

Tommy looked apologetic.

'I expect you'll find something to do while I'm away.'

'I might at that,' said Tuppence meditatively.

Her husband looked at her with the vague apprehension that Tuppence could always arouse in him.

'Tuppence – what are you up to?'

'Nothing, yet – So far I'm only thinking.'

'What about?'

'Sunny Ridge. And a nice old lady sipping milk and talking in a scatty kind of way about dead children and fireplaces. It intrigued me. I thought then that I'd try and find out more from her next time we came to see Aunt Ada – But there wasn't a next time because Aunt Ada died – And when we were next in Sunny Ridge – Mrs Lancaster had – disappeared!'

'You mean her people had taken her away? That's not a disappearance – it's quite natural.'

'It's a disappearance – no traceable address – no answer to letters – it's a planned disappearance. I'm more and more sure of it.'

'But –'

Tuppence broke in upon his 'But'.

'Listen, Tommy – supposing that sometime or other a crime happened – It seemed all safe and covered up – But then suppose that someone in the family had seen something, or known something – someone elderly and garrulous – someone who chattered to people – someone whom you suddenly realized might be a danger to you – What would you do about it?'

'Arsenic in the soup?' suggested Tommy cheerfully. 'Cosh them on the head – Push them down the staircase –?'

'That's rather extreme – Sudden deaths attract attention. You'd look about for some simpler way – and you'd find one. A nice respectable Home for Elderly Ladies. You'd pay a visit to it, calling yourself Mrs Johnson or Mrs Robinson – or you would get some unsuspecting third party to make arrangements – You'd fix the financial arrangements through a firm of reliable solicitors. You've already hinted, perhaps, that your elderly relative has fancies and mild delusions sometimes – so do a good many of the other old ladies – Nobody will think it odd – if she cackles on about poisoned milk, or dead children behind a fireplace, or a sinister kidnapping; nobody will really listen. They'll just think it's old Mrs So-and-So having her fancies again – nobody will take any *notice at all.*'

'Except Mrs Thomas Beresford,' said Tommy.

'All right, *yes*,' said Tuppence. '*I've* taken notice –'

'But why did you?'

'I don't quite know,' said Tuppence slowly. 'It's like the fairy stories. *By the pricking of my thumbs – Something evil this way comes* – I felt suddenly scared. I'd always thought of Sunny Ridge as such a normal happy place – and suddenly I began to wonder – That's the only way I can put it. I wanted to find out more. And now poor old Mrs Lancaster has disappeared. Somebody's spirited her away.'

'But why should they?'

'I can only think because she was getting worse – worse from their point of view – remembering more, perhaps, talking to people more, or perhaps she recognized someone – or someone recognized her – or told her something that gave her new ideas about something that had once happened. Anyway, for some reason or other she became dangerous to someone.'

'Look here, Tuppence, this whole thing is all somethings and someones. It's just an idea you've thought up. You don't want to go mixing yourself up in things that are no business of yours –'

'There's nothing to be mixed up in according to you,' said Tuppence. 'So you needn't worry at all.'

'You leave Sunny Ridge alone.'

'I don't mean to go back to Sunny Ridge. I think

they've told me all they know there. I think that that old lady was quite safe whilst she was there. I want to find out where she is *now* – I want to get to her wherever she is *in time* – before something happens to her.'

'What on earth do you think might happen to her?'

'I don't like to think. But I'm on the trail – I'm going to be Prudence Beresford, Private Investigator. Do you remember when we were Blunts Brilliant Detectives?'

'*I* was,' said Tommy. '*You* were Miss Robinson, my private secretary.'

'Not all the time. Anyway, that's what I'm going to do while you're playing at International Espionage at Hush Hush Manor. It's the "Save Mrs Lancaster" that I'm going to be busy with.'

'You'll probably find her perfectly all right.'

'I hope I shall. Nobody would be better pleased than I should.'

'How do you propose to set about it?'

'As I told you, I've got to think first. Perhaps an advertisement of some kind? No, that would be a mistake.'

'Well, be careful,' said Tommy, rather inadequately.

Tuppence did not deign to reply.

III

On Monday morning, Albert, the domestic mainstay of the Beresfords' life for many long years, ever since he had been roped into anti-criminal activities by them as a carroty-haired lift-boy, deposited the tray of early morning tea on the table between the two beds, pulled back the curtains, announced that it was a fine day, and removed his now portly form from the room.

Tuppence yawned, sat up, rubbed her eyes, poured out a cup of tea, dropped a slice of lemon in it, and remarked that it seemed a nice day, but you never knew.

Tommy turned over and groaned.

'Wake up,' said Tuppence. 'Remember you're going places today.'

'Oh Lord,' said Tommy. 'So I am.'

He, too, sat up and helped himself to tea. He looked with appreciation at the picture over the mantelpiece.

'I must say, Tuppence, your picture looks very nice.'

'It's the way the sun comes in from the window sideways and lights it up.'

'Peaceful,' said Tommy.

'If only I could remember where it was I'd seen it before.'

'I can't see that it matters. You'll remember sometime or other.'

'That's no good. I want to remember *now*.'

'But why?'

'Don't you see? It's the only clue I've got. It was Mrs Lancaster's picture –'

'But the two things don't tie up together anyway,' said Tommy. 'I mean, it's true that the picture once belonged to Mrs Lancaster. But it may have been just a picture she bought at an exhibition or that somebody in her family did. It may have been a picture that somebody gave her as a present. She took it to Sunny Ridge with her because she thought it looked nice. There's no reason it should have anything to do with her *personally*. If it had, she wouldn't have given it to Aunt Ada.'

'It's the only clue I've got,' said Tuppence.

'It's a nice peaceful house,' said Tommy.

'All the same, I think it's an empty house.'

'What do you mean, empty?'

'I don't think,' said Tuppence, 'there's anybody living in it. I don't think anybody's ever going to come out of that house. Nobody's going to walk across that bridge, nobody's going to untie that boat and row away in it.'

'For goodness' sake, Tuppence.' Tommy stared at her. 'What's the matter with you?'

'I thought so the first time I saw it,' said Tuppence. 'I thought "What a nice house that would be to live in." And then I thought "But nobody does live here, I'm sure they don't." That shows you that I have seen it before. Wait a minute. Wait a minute . . . it's coming. It's coming.'

Tommy stared at her.

'Out of a *window*,' said Tuppence breathlessly. 'Out of a car window? No, no, that would be the wrong angle. Running alongside the canal . . . and a little hump-backed bridge and the pink walls of the house, the two poplar trees, more than two. There were *lots* more poplar trees. Oh dear, oh dear, if I could –'

'Oh, come off it, Tuppence.'

'It will come back to me.'

'Good Lord,' Tommy looked at his watch. 'I've got to hurry. You and your *déjà vu* picture.'

He jumped out of bed and hastened to the bathroom. Tuppence lay back on her pillows and closed her eyes, trying to force a recollection that just remained elusively out of reach.

Tommy was pouring out a second cup of coffee in the dining-room when Tuppence appeared flushed with triumph.

'I've got it – I know where I saw that house. It was out of the window of a railway train.'

'Where? When?'

'I don't know. I'll have to think. I remember saying to myself: "Someday I'll go and look at that house" – and I tried to see what the name of the next station was. But you know what railways are nowadays. They've pulled down half the stations – and the next one we went through was all torn down, and grass growing over the platforms, and no name board or anything.'

'Where the hell's my brief-case? Albert!'

A frenzied search took place.

Tommy came back to say a breathless goodbye. Tuppence was sitting looking meditatively at a fried egg.

'Goodbye,' said Tommy. 'And for God's sake, Tuppence, don't go poking into something that's none of your business.'

'I think,' said Tuppence, meditatively, 'that what I shall really do, is to take a few railway journeys.'

Tommy looked slightly relieved.

'Yes,' he said encouragingly, 'you try that. Buy yourself a season ticket. There's some scheme where you can travel a thousand miles all over the British Isles for a very reasonable fixed sum. That ought to suit you down to the ground, Tuppence. You travel by all the trains you can think of in all the likely parts. That ought to keep you happy until I come home again.'

'Give my love to Josh.'

'I will.' He added, looking at his wife in a worried manner, 'I wish you were coming with me. Don't – don't do anything stupid, will you?'

'Of course not,' said Tuppence.

Chapter 6

Tuppence on the Trail

'Oh dear,' sighed Tuppence, 'oh dear.' She looked round her with gloomy eyes. Never, she said to herself, had she felt more miserable. Naturally she had known she would miss Tommy, but she had no idea how much she was going to miss him.

During the long course of their married life they had hardly ever been separated for any length of time. Starting before their marriage, they had called themselves a pair of 'young adventurers'. They had been through various difficulties and dangers together, they had married, they had had two children and just as the world was seeming rather dull and middle-aged to them, the second war had come about and in what seemed an almost miraculous way they had been tangled up yet again on the outskirts of the British Intelligence. A somewhat unorthodox pair, they had been recruited by a quiet nondescript man who called himself 'Mr

Carter', but to whose word everybody seemed to bow. They had had adventures, and once again they had had them together. This, by the way, had not been planned by Mr Carter. Tommy alone had been recruited. But Tuppence displaying all her natural ingenuity, had managed to eavesdrop in such a fashion that when Tommy had arrived at a guest house on the sea coast in the role of a certain Mr Meadows, the first person he had seen there had been a middle-aged lady plying knitting needles, who had looked up at him with innocent eyes and whom he had been forced to greet as Mrs Blenkinsop. Thereafter they had worked as a pair.

'However,' thought Tuppence to herself, 'I can't do it this time.' No amount of eavesdropping, of ingenuity, or anything else would take her to the recesses of Hush Hush Manor or to participation in the intricacies of I.U.A.S. Just an Old Boys Club, she thought resentfully. Without Tommy the flat was empty, the world was lonely, and 'What on earth,' thought Tuppence, 'am I to do with myself?'

The question was really purely rhetorical for Tuppence had already started on the first steps of what she planned to do with herself. There was no question this time of intelligence work, of counter-espionage or anything of that kind. Nothing of an official nature. 'Prudence Beresford, Private Investigator, that's what I am,' said Tuppence to herself.

After a scrappy lunch had been hastily cleared away, the dining-room table was strewn with railway time-tables, guide-books, maps, and a few old diaries which Tuppence had managed to disinter.

Some time in the last three years (not longer, she was sure) she had taken a railway journey, and looking out of the carriage window, had noticed a house. But, what railway journey?

Like most people at the present time, the Beresfords travelled mainly by car. The railway journeys they took were few and far between.

Scotland, of course, when they went to stay with their married daughter Deborah – but that was a night journey.

Penzance – summer holidays – but Tuppence knew that line by heart.

No, this had been a much more casual journey.

With diligence and perseverance, Tuppence had made a meticulous list of all the possible journeys she had taken which might correspond to what she was looking for. One or two race meetings, a visit to Northumberland, two possible places in Wales, a christening, two weddings, a sale they had attended, some puppies she had once delivered for a friend who bred them and who had gone down with influenza. The meeting place had been an arid-looking country junction whose name she couldn't remember.

Tuppence sighed. It seemed as though Tommy's solution was the one she might have to adopt – Buy a kind of circular ticket and actually travel over the most likely stretches of railway line.

In a small notebook she had jotted down any snatches of extra memories – vague flashes – in case they might help.

A hat, for instance – Yes, a hat that she had thrown up on the rack. She had been wearing a hat – so – a wedding or the christening – certainly not puppies.

And – another flash – kicking off her shoes – because her feet hurt. Yes – that was definite – she had been actually looking at the House – and she had kicked off her shoes because her feet hurt.

So, then, it had definitely been a social function she had either been going to, or returning from – Returning from, of course – because of the painfulness of her feet from long standing about in her best shoes. And what kind of a hat? Because that would help – a flowery hat – a summer wedding – or a velvet winter one?

Tuppence was busy jotting down details from the Railway timetables of different lines when Albert came in to ask what she wanted for supper – and what she wanted ordered in from the butcher and the grocer.

'I think I'm going to be away for the next few days,'

said Tuppence. 'So you needn't order in anything. I'm going to take some railway journeys.'

'Will you be wanting some sandwiches?'

'I might. Get some ham or something.'

'Egg and cheese do you? Or there's a tin of *pâté* in the larder – it's been there a long while, time it was eaten.' It was a somewhat sinister recommendation, but Tuppence said,

'All right. That'll do.'

'Want letters forwarded?'

'I don't even know where I'm going yet,' said Tuppence.

'I see,' said Albert.

The comfortable thing about Albert was that he always accepted everything. Nothing ever had to be explained to him.

He went away and Tuppence settled down to her planning – what she wanted was: a social engagement involving a hat and party shoes. Unfortunately the ones she had listed involved different railway lines – One wedding on the Southern Railway, the other in East Anglia. The christening north of Bedford.

If she could remember a little more about the scenery . . . She had been sitting on the right-hand side of the train. What had she been looking at *before* the canal – Woods? Trees? Farmland? A distant village?

Straining her brain, she looked up with a frown –

Albert had come back. How far she was at that moment from knowing that Albert standing there waiting for attention was neither more nor less than an answer to prayer –

'Well, what is it *now*, Albert?'

'If it's that you're going to be away all day tomorrow –'

'And the day after as well, probably –'

'Would it be all right for me to have the day off?'

'Yes, of course.'

'It's Elizabeth – come out in spots she has. Milly thinks it's measles –'

'Oh dear.' Milly was Albert's wife and Elizabeth was the youngest of his children. 'So Milly wants you at home, of course.'

Albert lived in a small neat house a street or two away.

'It's not that so much – She likes me out of the way when she's got her hands full – she doesn't want me messing things up – But it's the other kids – I could take 'em somewhere out of her way.'

'Of course. You're all in quarantine, I suppose.'

'Oh! well, best for 'em all to get it, and get it over. Charlie's had it, and so has Jean. Anyway, that'll be all right?'

Tuppence assured him that it would be all right.

Something was stirring in the depths of her subconscious – A happy anticipation – a recognition – Measles

– Yes, measles. Something to do with measles.

But why should the house by the canal have anything to do with measles . . . ?

Of course! Anthea. Anthea was Tuppence's god-daughter – and Anthea's daughter Jane was at school – her first term – and it was Prize Giving and Anthea had rung up – her two younger children had come out in a measle rash and she had nobody in the house to help and Jane would be terribly disappointed if nobody came – Could Tuppence possibly? –

And Tuppence had said of course – She wasn't doing anything particular – she'd go down to the school and take Jane out and give her lunch and then go back to the sports and all the rest of it. There was a special school train.

Everything came back into her mind with astonishing clarity – even the dress she'd worn – a summer print of cornflowers!

She had seen the house on the return journey.

Going down there she had been absorbed in a magazine she had bought, but coming back she had had nothing to read, and she had looked out of the window until, exhausted by the activities of the day, and the pressure of her shoes, she had dropped off to sleep.

When she had woken up the train had been running beside a canal. It was partially wooded country, an occasional bridge, sometimes a twisting lane or minor road – a distant farm – no villages.

The train began to slow down, for no reason it would seem, except that a signal must be against it. It drew jerkily to a halt by a bridge, a little hump-backed bridge which spanned the canal, a disused canal presumably. On the other side of the canal, close to the water, was the house – a house that Tuppence thought at once was one of the most attractive houses she had ever seen – a quiet, peaceful house, irradiated by the golden light of the late afternoon sun.

There was no human being to be seen – no dogs, or livestock. Yet the green shutters were not fastened. The house must be lived in, but now, at this moment, it was empty.

'I must find out about that house,' Tuppence had thought. 'Someday I must come back here and look at it. It's the kind of house I'd like to live in.'

With a jerk the train lurched slowly forwards.

'I'll look out for the name of the next station – so that I'll know where it is.'

But there had been no appropriate station. It was the time when things were beginning to happen to railways – small stations were closed, even pulled down, grass sprouted on the decayed platforms. For twenty minutes – half an hour – the train ran on, but nothing identifiable was to be seen. Over fields, in the far distance, Tuppence once saw the spire of a church.

Then had come some factory complex – tall chimneys – a line of pre-fab houses, then open country again.

Tuppence had thought to herself – That house was rather like a dream! Perhaps it was a dream – I don't suppose I'll ever go and look for it – too difficult. Besides, rather a pity, perhaps –

Someday, maybe, I'll come across it by accident!

And so – she had forgotten all about it – until a picture hanging on a wall had reawakened a veiled memory.

And now, thanks to one word uttered unwittingly by Albert, the quest was ended.

Or, to speak correctly, a quest was beginning.

Tuppence sorted out three maps, a guide-book, and various other accessories.

Roughly now she knew the area she would have to search. Jane's school she marked with a large cross – the branch railway line, which ran into the main line to London – the time lapse whilst she had slept.

The final area as planned covered a considerable mileage – north of Medchester, south-east of Market Basing which was a small town, but was quite an important railway junction, west probably of Shaleborough.

She'd take the car, and start early tomorrow morning.

She got up and went into the bedroom and studied the picture over the mantelpiece.

Yes, there was no mistake. That was the house she had seen from the train three years ago. The house she had promised to look for someday –

Someday had come – Someday was tomorrow.

was nothing to suggest that anyone lived in it. She went back to the car and drove a little farther. The wall, a moderately high one, ran along to her right. The left-hand side of the road was merely a hedge giving on green fields.

Presently she came to a wrought-iron gate in the wall. She parked the car by the side of the road, got out and went over to look through the ironwork of the gate. By standing on tiptoe she could look over it. What she looked into was a garden. The place was certainly not a farm now, though it might have been once. Presumably it gave on fields beyond it. The garden was tended and cultivated. It was not particularly tidy but it looked as though someone was trying rather unsuccessfully to keep it tidy.

From the iron gate a circular path curved through the garden and round to the house. This must be presumably the front door, though it didn't look like a front door. It was inconspicuous though sturdy – a back door. The house looked quite different from this side. To begin with, it was not empty. People lived there. Windows were open, curtains fluttered at them, a garbage pail stood by the door. At the far end of the garden Tuppence could see a large man digging, a big elderly man who dug slowly and with persistence. Certainly looked at from here the house held no enchantment, no artist would have wanted particularly to paint it. It was just a house and somebody lived in it. Tuppence wondered. She hesitated. Should she go on and forget the house altogether? No, she could hardly do that, not after all the trouble she had taken. What time was it? She looked at her watch but her watch had stopped. The sound of a door opening came from inside. She peered through the gate again.

The door of the house had opened and a woman came out. She put down a milk bottle and then, straightening up, glanced towards the gate. She saw Tuppence and hesitated for a moment, and then seeming to make up her mind, she came down the path towards the gate. 'Why,' said Tuppence to herself, 'why, it's a friendly witch!'

It was a woman of about fifty. She had long straggly hair which when caught by the wind, flew out behind her. It reminded Tuppence vaguely of a picture (by Nevinson?) of a young witch on a broomstick. That is perhaps why the term witch had come into her mind. But there was nothing young or beautiful about this woman. She was middle-aged, with a lined face, dressed in a rather slipshod way. She had a kind of steeple hat perched on her head and her nose and her chin came up towards each other. As a description she could have been sinister but she did not look sinister. She seemed to have a beaming and boundless good will. 'Yes,' thought Tuppence, 'you're exactly *like* a witch, but you're a *friendly* witch. I expect you're what they used to call a "white witch".'

The woman came down in a hesitating manner to the gate and spoke. Her voice was pleasant with a faint country burr in it of some kind.

'Were you looking for anything?' she said.

'I'm sorry,' said Tuppence, 'you must think it very rude of me looking into your garden in this way, but – but I wondered about this house.'

'Would you like to come in and look round the garden?' said the friendly witch.

'Well – well – thank you but I don't want to bother you.'

'Oh, it's no bother. I've nothing to do. Lovely afternoon, isn't it?'

'Yes, it is,' said Tuppence.

'I thought perhaps you'd lost your way,' said the friendly witch. 'People do sometimes.'

'I just thought,' said Tuppence, 'that this was a very attractive-looking house when I came down the hill on the other side of the bridge.'

'That's the prettiest side,' said the woman. 'Artists come and sketch it sometimes – or they used to – once.'

'Yes,' said Tuppence, 'I expect they would. I believe I – I saw a picture – at some exhibition,' she added hurriedly. 'Some house very like this. Perhaps it *was* this.'

'Oh, it may have been. Funny, you know, artists

come and do a picture. And then other artists seem to come too. It's just the same when they have the local picture show every year. Artists all seem to choose the same spot. I don't know why. You know, it's either a bit of meadow and brook, or a particular oak tree, or a clump of willows, or it's the same view of the Norman church. Five or six different pictures of the same thing, most of them pretty bad, I should think. But then I don't know anything about art. Come in, do.'

'You're very kind,' said Tuppence. 'You've got a very nice garden,' she added.

'Oh, it's not too bad. We've got a few flowers and vegetables and things. But my husband can't do much work nowadays and I've got no time with one thing and another.'

'I saw this house once from the train,' said Tuppence. 'The train slowed up and I saw this house and I wondered whether I'd ever see it again. Quite some time ago.'

'And now suddenly you come down the hill in your car and there it is,' said the woman. 'Funny, things happen like that, don't they?'

'Thank goodness,' Tuppence thought, 'this woman is extraordinarily easy to talk to. One hardly has to imagine anything to explain oneself. One can almost say just what comes into one's head.'

'Like to come inside the house?' said the friendly

witch. 'I can see you're interested. It's quite an old house, you know. I mean, late Georgian or something like that, they say, only it's been added on to. Of course, we've only got half the house, you know.'

'Oh I see,' said Tuppence. 'It's divided in two, is that it?'

'This is really the back of it,' said the woman. 'The front's the other side, the side you saw from the bridge. It was a funny way to partition it, I should have thought. I'd have thought it would have been easier to do it the other way. You know, right and left, so to speak. Not back and front. This is all really the back.'

'Have you lived here long?' asked Tuppence.

'Three years. After my husband retired we wanted a little place somewhere in the country where we'd be quiet. Somewhere cheap. This was going cheap because of course it's very lonely. You're not near a village or anything.'

'I saw a church steeple in the distance.'

'Ah, that's Sutton Chancellor. Two and a half miles from here. We're in the parish, of course, but there aren't any houses until you get to the village. It's a very small village too. You'll have a cup of tea?' said the friendly witch. 'I just put the kettle on not two minutes ago when I looked out and saw you.' She raised both hands to her mouth and shouted. 'Amos,' she shouted, 'Amos.'

The big man in the distance turned his head.

'Tea in ten minutes,' she called.

He acknowledged the signal by raising his hand. She turned, opened the door and motioned Tuppence to go in.

'Perry, my name is,' she said in a friendly voice. 'Alice Perry.'

'Mine's Beresford,' said Tuppence. 'Mrs Beresford.'

'Come in, Mrs Beresford, and have a look round.'

Tuppence paused for a second. She thought 'Just for a moment I feel like Hansel and Gretel. The witch asks you into her house. Perhaps it's a gingerbread house . . . It ought to be.'

Then she looked at Alice Perry again and thought that it wasn't the gingerbread house of Hansel and Gretel's witch. This was just a perfectly ordinary woman. No, not quite ordinary. She had a rather strange wild friendliness about her. 'She might be able to do spells,' thought Tuppence, 'but I'm sure they'd be good spells.' She stooped her head a little and stepped over the threshold into the witch's house.

It was rather dark inside. The passages were small. Mrs Perry led her through a kitchen and into a sitting-room beyond it which was evidently the family living-room. There was nothing exciting about the house. It was, Tuppence thought, probably a late Victorian addition to the main part. Horizontally it was narrow.

It seemed to consist of a horizontal passage, rather dark, which served a string of rooms. She thought to herself that it certainly was rather an odd way of dividing a house.

'Sit down and I'll bring the tea in,' said Mrs Perry.

'Let me help you.'

'Oh, don't worry, I shan't be a minute. It's all ready on the tray.'

A whistle rose from the kitchen. The kettle had evidently reached the end of its span of tranquillity. Mrs Perry went out and returned in a minute or two with the tea tray, a plate of scones, a jar of jam and three cups and saucers.

'I expect you're disappointed, now you've got inside,' said Mrs Perry.

It was a shrewd remark and very near to the truth.

'Oh no,' said Tuppence.

'Well, I should be if I was you. Because they don't match a bit, do they? I mean the front and the back side of the house don't match. But it is a comfortable house to live in. Not many rooms, not too much light but it makes a great difference in price.'

'Who divided the house and why?'

'Oh, a good many years ago, I believe. I suppose whoever had it thought it was too big or too inconvenient. Only wanted a weekend place or something of that kind. So they kept the good rooms, the dining-room and the drawing-room and made a kitchen out of a small study there was, and a couple of bedrooms and bathroom upstairs, and then walled it up and let the part that was kitchens and old-fashioned sculleries and things, and did it up a bit.'

'Who lives in the other part? Someone who just comes down for weekends?'

'Nobody lives there now,' said Mrs Perry. 'Have another scone, dear.'

'Thank you,' said Tuppence.

'At least nobody's come down here in the last two years. I don't know even who it belongs to now.'

'But when you first came here?'

'There was a young lady used to come down here – an actress they said she was. At least that's what we heard. But we never saw her really. Just caught a glimpse sometimes. She used to come down late on a Saturday night after the show, I suppose. She used to go away on the Sunday evenings.'

'Quite a mystery woman,' said Tuppence, encouragingly.

'You know that's just the way I used to think of her. I used to make up stories about her in my head. Sometimes I'd think she was like Greta Garbo. You know, the way *she* went about always in dark glasses and pulled-down hats. Goodness now, *I've* got *my* peak hat on.'

She removed the witch's headgear from her head and laughed.

'It's for a play we're having at the parish rooms in Sutton Chancellor,' she said. 'You know – a sort of fairy story play for the children mostly. I'm playing the witch,' she added.

'Oh,' said Tuppence, slightly taken aback, then added quickly, 'What fun.'

'Yes, it is fun, isn't it?' said Mrs Perry. 'Just right for the witch, aren't I?' She laughed and tapped her chin. 'You know. I've got the face for it. Hope it won't put ideas into people's heads. They'll think I've got the evil eye.'

'I don't think they'd think that of you,' said Tuppence. 'I'm sure you'd be a beneficent witch.'

'Well, I'm glad you think so,' said Mrs Perry. 'As I was saying, this actress – I can't remember her name now – Miss Marchment I think it was, but it might have been something else – you wouldn't believe the things I used to make up about her. Really, I suppose, I hardly ever saw or spoke to her. Sometimes I think she was just terribly shy and neurotic. Reporters'd come down after her and things like that, but she never would see them. At other times I used to think – well, you'll say I'm foolish – I used to think quite sinister things about her. You know, that she was afraid of being *recognized.* Perhaps she wasn't an actress at all. Perhaps the police were looking for her. Perhaps she was a criminal of some kind. It's exciting sometimes, making things up in your head. Especially when you don't – well – see many people.'

'Did nobody ever come down here with her?'

'Well, I'm not so sure about that. Of course these partition walls, you know, that they put in when they turned the house into two, well, they're pretty thin and sometimes you'd hear voices and things like that. I think she did bring down someone for weekends occasionally.' She nodded her head. 'A man of some kind. That may have been why they wanted somewhere quiet like this.'

'A married man,' said Tuppence, entering into the spirit of make-believe.

'Yes, it would be a married man, wouldn't it?' said Mrs Perry.

'Perhaps it was her husband who came down with her. He'd taken this place in the country because he wanted to murder her and perhaps he buried her in the garden.'

'My!' said Mrs Perry. 'You do have an imagination, don't you? I never thought of that one.'

'I suppose *someone* must have known all about her,' said Tuppence. 'I mean house agents. People like that.'

'Oh, I suppose so,' said Mrs Perry. 'But I rather liked *not* knowing, if you understand what I mean.'

'Oh yes,' said Tuppence, 'I do understand.'

'It's got an atmosphere, you know, this house. I mean there's a feeling in it, a feeling that anything might have happened.'

'Didn't she have any people come in to clean for her or anything like that?'

'Difficult to get anyone here. There's nobody near at hand.'

The outside door opened. The big man who had been digging in the garden came in. He went to the scullery tap and turned it, obviously washing his hands. Then he came through into the sitting-room.

'This is my husband,' said Mrs Perry. 'Amos. We've got a visitor, Amos. This is Mrs Beresford.'

'How do you do?' said Tuppence.

Amos Perry was a tall, shambling-looking man. He was bigger and more powerful than Tuppence had realized. Although he had a shambling gait and walked slowly, he was a big man of muscular build. He said,

'Pleased to meet you, Mrs Beresford.'

His voice was pleasant and he smiled, but Tuppence wondered for a brief moment whether he was really what she would have called 'all there'. There was a kind of wondering simplicity about the look in his eyes and she wondered, too, whether Mrs Perry had wanted a quiet place to live in because of some mental disability on the part of her husband.

'Ever so fond of the garden, he is,' said Mrs Perry.

At his entrance the conversation dimmed down. Mrs Perry did most of the talking but her personality seemed to have changed. She talked with rather more nervousness and with particular attention to her husband. Encouraging him, Tuppence thought, rather in a way that a mother might prompt a shy boy to talk, to display the best of himself before a visitor, and to be a little nervous that he might be inadequate. When she'd finished her tea, Tuppence got up. She said,

'I must be going. Thank you, Mrs Perry, very much for your hospitality.'

'You'll see the garden before you go.' Mr Perry rose. 'Come on, *I'll* show you.'

She went with him outdoors and he took her down to the corner beyond where he had been digging.

'Nice, them flowers, aren't they?' he said. 'Got some old-fashioned roses here – See this one, striped red and white.'

'"Commandant Beaurepaire",' said Tuppence.

'Us calls it "York and Lancaster" here,' said Perry. 'Wars of the Roses. Smells sweet, don't it?'

'Smells lovely.'

'Better than them new-fashioned Hybrid Teas.'

In a way the garden was rather pathetic. The weeds were imperfectly controlled, but the flowers themselves were carefully tied up in an amateurish fashion.

'Bright colours,' said Mr Perry. 'I like bright colours. We often get folk to see our garden,' he said. 'Glad you came.'

'Thank you very much,' said Tuppence. 'I think your garden and your house are very nice indeed.'

'You ought to see t'other side of it.'

'Is it to let or to be sold? Your wife says there's nobody living there now.'

'We don't know. We've not seen anyone and there's no board up and nobody's ever come to see over it.'

'It would be a nice house, I think, to live in.'

'You wanting a house?'

'Yes,' said Tuppence, making up her mind quickly. 'Yes, as a matter of fact, we are looking round for some small place in the country, for when my husband retires. That'll be next year probably, but we like to look about in plenty of time.'

'It's quiet here if you like quiet.'

'I suppose,' said Tuppence, 'I could ask the local house agents. Is that how you got your house?'

'Saw an advertisement first we did in the paper. Then we went to the house agents, yes.'

'Where was that – in Sutton Chancellor? That's your village, isn't it?'

'Sutton Chancellor? No. Agents' place is in Market Basing. Russell & Thompson, that's the name. You could go to them and ask.'

'Yes,' said Tuppence, 'so I could. How far is Market Basing from here?'

'It's two miles to Sutton Chancellor and it's seven miles to Market Basing from there. There's a proper road from Sutton Chancellor, but it's all lanes hereabouts.'

'I see,' said Tuppence. 'Well, goodbye, Mr Perry, and thank you very much for showing me your garden.'

'Wait a bit.' He stooped, cut off an enormous paeony and taking Tuppence by the lapel of her coat, he inserted this through the buttonhole in it. 'There,' he said, 'there you are. Looks pretty, it does.'

For a moment Tuppence felt a sudden feeling of panic. This large, shambling, good-natured man suddenly frightened her. He was looking down at her, smiling. Smiling rather wildly, almost leering. 'Pretty it looks on you,' he said again. 'Pretty.'

Tuppence thought 'I'm glad I'm not a young girl . . . I don't think I'd like him putting a flower on me then.' She said goodbye again and hurried away.

The house door was open and Tuppence went in to say goodbye to Mrs Perry. Mrs Perry was in the kitchen, washing up the tea things and Tuppence almost automatically pulled a teacloth off the rack and started drying.

'Thank you so much,' she said, 'both you and your

husband. You've been so kind and hospitable to me – *What's that*?'

From the wall of the kitchen, or rather behind the wall where an old-fashioned range had once stood, there came a loud screaming and squawking and a scratching noise too.

'That'll be a jackdaw,' said Mrs Perry, 'dropped down the chimney in the other house. They do this time of the year. One came down our chimney last week. They make nests in the chimneys, you know.'

'What – in the other house?'

'Yes, there it is again.'

Again the squawking and crying of a distressed bird came to their ears. Mrs Perry said, 'There's no one to bother, you see, in the empty house. The chimneys ought to be swept and all that.'

The squawking scratching noises went on.

'Poor bird,' said Tuppence.

'I know. It won't be able to get up again.'

'You mean it'll just die there?'

'Oh yes. One came down our chimney as I say. Two of them, actually. One was a young bird. It was all right, we put it out and it flew away. The other one was dead.'

The frenzied scuffling and squeaking went on.

'Oh,' said Tuppence, 'I wish we could get at it.'

Mr Perry came in through the door. 'Anything the matter?' he said, looking from one to the other.

'There's a bird, Amos. It must be in the drawing-room chimney next door. Hear it?'

'Eh, it's come down from the jackdaws' nest.'

'I wish we could get in there,' said Mrs Perry.

'Ah, you can't do anything. They'll die from the fright, if nothing else.'

'Then it'll smell,' said Mrs Perry.

'You won't smell anything in here. You're soft-hearted,' he went on, looking from one to the other, 'like all females. We'll get it if you like.'

'Why, is one of the windows open?'

'We can get in through the door.'

'What door?'

'Outside here in the yard. The key's hanging up among those.'

He went outside and along to the end, opening a small door there. It was a kind of potting shed really, but a door from it led into the other house and near the door of the potting shed were six or seven rusty keys hanging on a nail.

'This one fits,' said Mr Perry.

He took down the key and put it in the door, and after exerting a good deal of cajolery and force, the key turned rustily in the lock.

'I went in once before,' he said, 'when I heard water running. Somebody'd forgotten to turn the water off properly.'

He went in and the two women followed him. The door led into a small room which still contained various flower vases on a shelf and a sink with a tap.

'A flower room, I shouldn't wonder,' he said. 'Where people used to do the flowers. See? A lot of the vases left here.'

There was a door out of the flower room. This was not even locked. He opened it and they went through. It was like, Tuppence thought, going through into another world. The passageway outside was covered with a pile carpet. A little way along there was a door half-open and from there the sounds of a bird in distress were coming. Perry pushed the door open and his wife and Tuppence went in.

The windows were shuttered but one side of a shutter was hanging loose and light came in. Although it was dim, there was a faded but beautiful carpet on the floor, a deep sage-green in colour. There was a bookshelf against the wall but no chairs or tables. The furniture had been removed no doubt, the curtains and carpets had been left as fittings to be passed on to the next tenant.

Mrs Perry went towards the fireplace. A bird lay in the grate scuffling and uttering loud squawking sounds of distress. She stooped, picked it up, and said,

'Open the window if you can, Amos.'

Amos went over, pulled the shutter aside, unfastened

the other side of it and then pushed at the latch of the window. He raised the lower sash which came gratingly. As soon as it was open Mrs Perry leaned out and released the jackdaw. It flopped on to the lawn, hopped a few paces.

'Better kill it,' said Perry. 'It's damaged.'

'Leave it a bit,' said his wife. 'You never know. They recover very quickly, birds. It's fright that makes them so paralysed looking.'

Sure enough, a few moments later the jackdaw, with a final struggle, a squawk, a flapping of wings flew off.

'I only hope,' said Alice Perry, 'that it doesn't come down that chimney again. Contrary things, birds. Don't know what's good for them. Get into a room, they can never get out of it by themselves. Oh,' she added, 'what a mess.'

She, Tuppence and Mr Perry all stared at the grate. From the chimney had come down a mass of soot, of odd rubble and of broken bricks. Evidently it had been in a bad state of repair for some time.

'Somebody ought to come and live here,' said Mrs Perry, looking round her.

'Somebody ought to look after it,' Tuppence agreed with her. 'Some builder ought to look at it or do something about it or the whole house will come down soon.'

'Probably water has been coming through the roof

in the top rooms. Yes, look at the ceiling up there, it's come through there.'

'Oh, what a shame,' said Tuppence, 'to ruin a beautiful house – it really is a beautiful room, isn't it.'

She and Mrs Perry looked together round it appreciatively. Built in 1790 it had all the graciousness of a house of that period. It had had originally a pattern of willow leaves on the discoloured paper.

'It's a ruin now,' said Mr Perry.

Tuppence poked the debris in the grate.

'One ought to sweep it up,' said Mrs Perry.

'Now what do you want to bother yourself with a house that doesn't belong to you?' said her husband. 'Leave it alone, woman. It'll be in just as bad a state tomorrow morning.'

Tuppence stirred the bricks aside with a toe.

'Ooh,' she said with an exclamation of disgust.

There were two dead birds lying in the fireplace. By the look of them they had been dead for some time.

'That's the nest that came down a good few weeks ago. It's a wonder it doesn't smell more than it does,' said Perry.

'What's this thing?' said Tuppence.

She poked with her toe at something lying half hidden in the rubble. Then she bent and picked it up.

'Don't you touch a dead bird,' said Mrs Perry.

'It's not a bird,' said Tuppence. 'Something else

must have come down the chimney. Well I never,' she added, staring at it. 'It's a doll. It's a child's doll.'

They looked down at it. Ragged, torn, its clothes in rags, its head lolling from the shoulders, it had originally been a child's doll. One glass eye dropped out. Tuppence stood holding it.

'I wonder,' she said, 'I wonder how a child's doll ever got up a chimney. Extraordinary.'

Chapter 8

Sutton Chancellor

After leaving the canal house, Tuppence drove slowly on along the narrow winding road which she had been assured would lead her to the village of Sutton Chancellor. It was an isolated road. There were no houses to be seen from it – only field gates from which muddy tracks led inwards. There was little traffic – one tractor came along, and one lorry proudly announcing that it carried Mother's Delight and the picture of an enormous and unnatural-looking loaf. The church steeple she had noticed in the distance seemed to have disappeared entirely – but it finally reappeared quite near at hand after the lane had bent suddenly and sharply round a belt of trees. Tuppence glanced at the speedometer and saw she had come two miles since the canal house.

It was an attractive old church standing in a sizeable churchyard with a lone yew tree standing by the church door.

Tuppence left the car outside the lych-gate, passed through it, and stood for a few moments surveying the church and the churchyard round it. Then she went to the church door with its rounded Norman arch and lifted the heavy handle. It was unlocked and she went inside.

The inside was unattractive. The church was an old one, undoubtedly, but it had had a zealous wash and brush up in Victorian times. Its pitch pine pews and its flaring red and blue glass windows had ruined any antique charm it had once possessed. A middle-aged woman in a tweed coat and skirt was arranging flowers in brass vases round the pulpit – she had already finished the altar. She looked round at Tuppence with a sharply inquiring glance. Tuppence wandered up an aisle looking at memorial tablets on the walls. A family called Warrender seemed to be most fully represented in early years. All of The Priory, Sutton Chancellor. Captain Warrender, Major Warrender, Sarah Elisabeth Warrender, dearly beloved wife of George Warrender. A newer tablet recorded the death of Julia Starke (another beloved wife) of Philip Starke, also of The Priory, Sutton Chancellor – so it would seem the Warrenders had died out. None of them were particularly suggestive or interesting. Tuppence passed out of the church again and walked round it on the outside. The outside, Tuppence thought, was much more attractive than the inside. 'Early Perp. and Dec.,' said Tuppence to herself, having been brought up on familiar terms with ecclesiastical architecture. She was not particularly fond of early Perp. herself.

It was a fair-sized church and she thought that the village of Sutton Chancellor must once have been a rather more important centre of rural life than it was now. She left the car where it was and walked on to the village. It had a village shop and a post office and about a dozen small houses or cottages. One or two of them were thatched but the others were rather plain and unattractive. There were six council houses at the end of the village street looking slightly self-conscious. A brass plate on a door announced 'Arthur Thomas, Chimney Sweep'.

Tuppence wondered if any responsible house agents were likely to engage his services for the house by the canal which certainly needed them. How silly she had been, she thought, not to have asked the name of the house.

She walked back slowly towards the church, and her car, pausing to examine the churchyard more closely. She liked the churchyard. There were very few new burials in it. Most of the stones commemorated Victorian burials, and earlier ones – half defaced by lichen and time. The old stones were attractive. Some of them were upright slabs with cherubs on the tops, with wreaths round them. She wandered about, looking at the inscriptions. Warrenders again. Mary Warrender, aged 47, Alice Warrender, aged 33, Colonel John Warrender killed in Afghanistan. Various infant Warrenders – deeply regretted – and eloquent verses of pious hopes. She wondered if any Warrenders lived here still. They'd left off being buried here apparently. She couldn't find any tombstones later than 1843. Rounding the big yew tree she came upon an elderly clergyman who was stooping over a row of old tombstones near a wall behind the church. He straightened up and turned round as Tuppence approached.

'Good afternoon,' he said pleasantly.

'Good afternoon,' said Tuppence, and added, 'I've been looking at the church.'

'Ruined by Victorian renovation,' said the clergyman.

He had a pleasant voice and a nice smile. He looked about seventy, but Tuppence presumed he was not quite as far advanced in age as that, though he was certainly rheumatic and rather unsteady on his legs.

'Too much money about in Victorian times,' he said sadly. 'Too many ironmasters. They were pious, but had, unfortunately, no sense of the artistic. No taste. Did you see the east window?' he shuddered.

'Yes,' said Tuppence. 'Dreadful,' she said.

'I couldn't agree with you more. I'm the vicar,' he added, rather unnecessarily.

'I thought you must be,' said Tuppence politely. 'Have you been here long?' she added.

'Ten years, my dear,' he said. 'It's a nice parish. Nice people, what there are of them. I've been very happy here. They don't like my sermons very much,' he added sadly. 'I do the best I can, but of course I can't pretend to be really modern. Sit down,' he added hospitably, waving to a nearby tombstone.

Tuppence sat down gratefully and the vicar took a seat on another one nearby.

'I can't stand very long,' he said, apologetically. He added, 'Can I do anything for you or are you just passing by?'

'Well, I'm really just passing by,' said Tuppence. 'I thought I'd just look at the church. I'd rather lost myself in a car wandering around the lanes.'

'Yes, yes. Very difficult to find one's way about round here. A lot of signposts are broken, you know, and the council don't repair them as they should.' He added, 'I don't know that it matters very much. People who drive down these lanes aren't usually trying to get anywhere in particular. People who *are* keep to the main roads. Dreadful,' he added again. 'Especially the new Motorway. At least, *I* think so. The noise and the speed and the reckless driving. Oh well! pay no attention to me. I'm a crusty old fellow. You'd never guess what I'm doing here,' he went on.

'I saw you were examining some of the gravestones,' said Tuppence. 'Has there been any vandalism? Have teenagers been breaking bits off them?'

'No. One's mind *does* turn that way nowadays what with so many telephone boxes wrecked and all those other things that these young vandals do. Poor children, they don't know any better, I suppose. Can't think of anything more amusing to do than to smash things. Sad, isn't it? Very sad. No,' he said, 'there's been no damage of that kind here. The boys round here are a nice lot on the whole. No, I'm just looking for a child's grave.'

Tuppence stirred on her tombstone. 'A child's grave?' she said.

'Yes. Somebody wrote to me. A Major Waters, he asked if by any possibility a child had been buried here. I looked it up in the parish register, of course, but there was no record of any such name. All the same, I came out here and looked round the stones. I thought, you know, that perhaps whoever wrote might have got hold of some wrong name, or that there had been a mistake.'

'What was the Christian name?' asked Tuppence.

'He didn't know. Perhaps Julia after the mother.'

'How old was the child?'

'Again he wasn't sure – Rather vague, the whole thing. I think myself that the man must have got hold of the wrong village altogether. I never remember a Waters living here or having heard of one.'

'What about the Warrenders?' asked Tuppence, her mind going back to the names in the church. 'The church seems full of tablets to them and their names are on lots of gravestones out here.'

'Ah, that family's died out by now. They had a fine property, an old fourteenth-century Priory. It was burnt down – oh, nearly a hundred years ago now, so I suppose any Warrenders there were left, went away and didn't come back. A new house was built on the site, by a rich Victorian called Starke. A very ugly house but comfortable, they say. Very comfortable. Bathrooms, you know, and all that. I suppose that sort of thing *is* important.'

'It seems a very odd thing,' said Tuppence, 'that someone should write and ask you about a child's grave. Somebody – a relation?'

'The father of the child,' said the vicar. 'One of these war tragedies, I imagine. A marriage that broke up when the husband was on service abroad. The young wife ran away with another man while the husband was serving abroad. There was a child, a child he'd never seen. She'd be grown up by now, I suppose, if she were alive. It must be twenty years ago or more.'

'Isn't it a long time after to be looking for her?'

'Apparently he only heard there *was* a child quite recently. The information came to him by pure chance. Curious story, the whole thing.'

'What made him think that the child had been buried here?'

'I gather somebody who had come across his wife in wartime had told him that his wife had said she was living at Sutton Chancellor. It happens, you know. You meet someone, a friend or acquaintance you haven't seen for years, and they sometimes can give you news from the past that you wouldn't get in any other way. But she's certainly not living here now. Nobody of that name has lived here – not since I've been here. Or in the neighbourhood as far as I know. Of course, the mother *might* have been going by another name. However, I gather the father is employing solicitors and inquiry agents and all that sort of thing, and they will probably be able to get results in the end. It will take time –'

'*Was it your poor child?*' murmured Tuppence.

'I beg your pardon, my dear?'

'Nothing,' said Tuppence. 'Something somebody said to me the other day. "*Was it your poor child?*" It's rather a startling thing to hear suddenly. But I don't really think the old lady who said it knew what she was talking about.'

'I know. I know. I'm often the same. I say things and

I don't really know what I mean by them. Most vexing.'

'I expect you know everything about the people who live here *now*?' said Tuppence.

'Well, there certainly aren't very many to know. Yes. Why? Is there someone you wanted to know about?'

'I wondered if there had ever been a Mrs Lancaster living here.'

'Lancaster? No, I don't think I recollect that name.'

'And there's a house – I was driving today rather aimlessly – not minding particularly where I went, just following lanes –'

'I know. Very nice, the lanes round here. And you can find quite rare specimens. Botanical, I mean. In the hedges here. Nobody ever picks flowers in these hedges. We never get any tourists round here or that sort of thing. Yes, I've found some very rare specimens sometimes. Dusty Cranesbell, for instance –'

'There was a house by a canal,' said Tuppence, refusing to be side-tracked into botany. 'Near a little hump-backed bridge. It was about two miles from here. I wondered what its name was.'

'Let me see. Canal – hump-backed bridge. Well . . . there are several houses like that. There's Merricot Farm.'

'It wasn't a farm.'

'Ah, now, I expect it was the Perrys' house – Amos and Alice Perry.'

'That's right,' said Tuppence. 'A Mr and Mrs Perry.'

'She's a striking-looking woman, isn't she? Interesting, I always think. Very interesting. Medieval face, didn't you think so? She's going to play the witch in our play we're getting up. The school children, you know. She looks rather like a witch, doesn't she?'

'Yes,' said Tuppence. 'A friendly witch.'

'As you say, my dear, absolutely rightly. Yes, a friendly witch.'

'But he –'

'Yes, poor fellow,' said the vicar. 'Not completely *compos mentis* – but no harm in him.'

'They were very nice. They asked me in for a cup of tea,' said Tuppence. 'But what I wanted to know was the *name* of the house. I forgot to ask them. They're only living in half of it, aren't they?'

'Yes, yes. In what used to be the old kitchen quarters. *They* call it "Waterside", I think, though I believe the ancient name for it was "Watermead". A pleasanter name, I think.'

'Who does the other part of the house belong to?'

'Well, the whole house used to belong originally to the Bradleys. That was a good many years ago. Yes, thirty or forty at least, I should think. And then it was sold, and then sold again and then it remained empty for a long time. When I came here it was just being used as a kind of weekend place. By some actress – Miss Margrave, I believe. She was not here very much. Just used to come down from time to time. I never knew her. She never came to church. I saw her in the distance sometimes. A beautiful creature. A very beautiful creature.'

'Who does it actually belong to *now*?' Tuppence persisted.

'I've no idea. Possibly it still belongs to her. The part the Perrys live in is only rented to them.'

'I recognized it, you know,' said Tuppence, 'as soon as I saw it, because I've got a picture of it.'

'Oh really? That must have been one of Boscombe's, or was his name Boscobel – I can't remember now. Some name like that. He was a Cornishman, fairly well-known artist, I believe. I rather imagine he's dead now. Yes, he used to come down here fairly often. He used to sketch all round this part of the world. He did some oils here, too. Very attractive landscapes, some of them.'

'This particular picture,' said Tuppence, 'was given to an old aunt of mine who died about a month ago. It was given to her by a Mrs Lancaster. That's why I asked if you knew the name.'

But the vicar shook his head once more.

'Lancaster? Lancaster. No, I don't seem to remember the name. Ah! but here's the person you must ask.

Our dear Miss Bligh. Very active, Miss Bligh is. She knows all about the parish. She runs everything. The Women's Institute, the Boy Scouts and the Guides – everything. You ask *her*. She's very active, very active indeed.'

The vicar sighed. The activity of Miss Bligh seemed to worry him. 'Nellie Bligh, they call her in the village. The boys sing it after her sometimes. *Nellie Bligh, Nellie Bligh.* It's not her proper name. That's something more like Gertrude or Geraldine.'

Miss Bligh, who was the tweed-clad woman Tuppence had seen in the church, was approaching them at a rapid trot, still holding a small watering can. She eyed Tuppence with deep curiosity as she approached, increasing her pace and starting a conversation before she reached them.

'Finished my job,' she exclaimed merrily. 'Had a bit of a rush today. Oh yes, had a bit of a rush. Of course, as you know, Vicar, I usually do the church in the morning. But today we had the emergency meeting in the parish rooms and really you wouldn't believe the time it took! So much *argument*, you know. I really think sometimes people object to things just for the fun of doing so. Mrs Partington was particularly irritating. Wanting everything fully discussed, you know, and wondering whether we'd got enough different prices from different firms. I mean, the whole thing is such a small cost anyway, that really a few shillings here or there can't make much difference. And Burkenheads have always been most reliable. I don't think really, Vicar, you know, that you ought to sit on that tombstone.'

'Irreverent, perhaps?' suggested the vicar.

'Oh no, no, of course I didn't mean that *at all*, Vicar. I meant the *stone*, you know, the damp does come through and with your rheumatism –' Her eyes slid sideways to Tuppence questioningly.

'Let me introduce you to Miss Bligh,' said the vicar. 'This is – this is –' he hesitated.

'Mrs Beresford,' said Tuppence.

'Ah yes,' said Miss Bligh. 'I saw you in the church, didn't I, just now, looking round it. I would have come and spoken to you, called your attention to one or two interesting points, but I was in such a hurry to finish my job.'

'I ought to have come and helped you,' said Tuppence, in her sweetest voice. 'But it wouldn't have been much use, would it, because I could see you knew so exactly where every flower ought to go.'

'Well now, it's very nice of you to say so, but it's quite true. I've done the flowers in the church for – oh, I don't know *how* many years it is. We let the school children arrange their own particular pots of wild flowers for festivals, though of course they haven't the least idea, poor little things. I do think a *little* instruction, but Mrs Peake will never have any instruction. She's so particular. She says it spoils their initiative. Are you staying down here?' she asked Tuppence.

'I was going on to Market Basing,' said Tuppence. 'Perhaps you can tell me a nice quiet hotel to stay there?'

'Well, I expect you'll find it a little disappointing. It's just a market town, you know. It doesn't cater at all for the motoring trade. The Blue Dragon is a two-star but really I don't think these stars mean anything *at all* sometimes. I think you'd find The Lamb better. Quieter, you know. Are you staying there for long?'

'Oh no,' said Tuppence, 'just a day or two while I'm looking round the neighbourhood.'

'Not very much to see, I'm afraid. No interesting antiquities or anything like that. We're purely a rural and agricultural district,' said the vicar. 'But peaceful, you know, very peaceful. As I told you, some interesting wild flowers.'

'Ah yes,' said Tuppence, 'I've heard that and I'm anxious to collect a few specimens in the intervals of doing a little mild house hunting,' she added.

'Oh dear, how interesting,' said Miss Bligh. 'Are you thinking of settling in this neighbourhood?'

'Well, my husband and I haven't decided very definitely on any one neighbourhood in particular,' said

Tuppence. 'And we're in no hurry. He won't be retiring for another eighteen months. But it's always as well, I think, to look about. Personally, what *I* prefer to do is to stay in one neighbourhood for four or five days, get a list of likely small properties and drive about to see them. Coming down for one day from London to see one particular house is very tiring, I find.'

'Oh yes, you've got your car here, have you?'

'Yes,' said Tuppence. 'I shall have to go to a house agent in Market Basing tomorrow morning. There's nowhere, I suppose, to stay in the village here, is there?'

'Of course, there's Mrs Copleigh,' said Miss Bligh. 'She takes people in the summer, you know. Summer visitors. She's beautifully clean. All her rooms are. Of course, she only does bed and breakfast and perhaps a light meal in the evening. But I don't think she takes anyone in much before August or July at the earliest.'

'Perhaps I could go and see her and find out,' said Tuppence.

'She's a very worthy woman,' said the vicar. 'Her tongue wags a good deal,' he added. 'She never stops talking, not for one single minute.'

'A lot of gossip and chattering is always going on in these small villages,' said Miss Bligh. 'I think it would be a very good idea if I helped Mrs Beresford.

I could take her along to Mrs Copleigh and just see what chances there are.'

'That would be very kind of you,' said Tuppence.

'Then we'll be off,' said Miss Bligh briskly. 'Goodbye, Vicar. Still on your quest? A sad task and so unlikely to meet with success. I really think it was a *most* unreasonable request to make.'

Tuppence said goodbye to the vicar and said she would be glad to help him if she could.

'I could easily spend an hour or two looking at the various gravestones. I've got very good eyesight for my age. It's just the name Waters you are looking for?'

'Not really,' said the vicar. 'It's the age that matters, I think. A child of perhaps seven, it would be. A girl. Major Waters thinks that his wife might have changed her name and that probably the child might be known by the name she had taken. And as he doesn't know what that name is, it makes it all very difficult.'

'The whole thing's impossible, so far as I can see,' said Miss Bligh. 'You ought never to have said you would do such a thing, Vicar. It's monstrous, suggesting anything of the kind.'

'The poor fellow seems very upset,' said the vicar. 'A sad history altogether, so far as I can make out. But I mustn't keep you.'

Tuppence thought to herself as she was shepherded by Miss Bligh that no matter what the reputation of

Mrs Copleigh for talking, she could hardly talk more than Miss Bligh did. A stream of pronouncements both rapid and dictatorial poured from her lips.

Mrs Copleigh's cottage proved to be a pleasant and roomy one set back from the village street with a neat garden of flowers in front, a whitened doorstep and a brass handle well polished. Mrs Copleigh herself seemed to Tuppence like a character straight out of the pages of Dickens. She was very small and very round, so that she came rolling towards you rather like a rubber ball. She had bright twinkling eyes, blonde hair rolled up in sausage curls on her head and an air of tremendous vigour. After displaying a little doubt to begin with – 'Well, I don't usually, you know. No. My husband and I say "summer visitors, that's different". Everyone does that if they can nowadays. And have to, I'm sure. But not this time of year so much, we don't. Not until July. However, if it's just for a few days and the lady wouldn't mind things being a bit rough, perhaps –'

Tuppence said she didn't mind things being rough and Mrs Copleigh, having surveyed her with close attention, whilst not stopping her flow of conversation, said perhaps the lady would like to come up and see the room, and then things might be arranged.

At that point Miss Bligh tore herself away with some regret because she had not so far been able to extract all the information she wanted from Tuppence, as to where she came from, what her husband did, how old she was, if she had any children and other matters of interest. But it appeared that she had a meeting at her house over which she was going to preside and was terrified at the risk that someone else might seize that coveted post.

'You'll be quite all right with Mrs Copleigh,' she assured Tuppence, 'she'll look after you, I'm sure. Now what about your car?'

'Oh, I'll fetch it presently,' said Tuppence. 'Mrs Copleigh will tell me where I had better put it. I can leave it outside here really because it isn't a very narrow street, is it?'

'Oh, my husband can do better than that for you,' said Mrs Copleigh. 'He'll put it in the field for you. Just round the side lane here, and it'll be quite all right, there. There's a shed he can drive it into.'

Things were arranged amicably on that basis and Miss Bligh hurried away to her appointment. The question of an evening meal was next raised. Tuppence asked if there was a pub in the village.

'Oh, we have nothing as a lady could go to,' said Mrs Copleigh, 'but if you'd be satisfied with a couple of eggs and a slice of ham and maybe some bread and homemade jam –'

Tuppence said that would be splendid. Her room

was small but cheerful and pleasant with a rosebud wallpaper and a comfortable-looking bed and a general air of spotless cleanliness.

'Yes, it's a nice wallpaper, miss,' said Mrs Copleigh, who seemed determined to accord Tuppence single status. 'Chose it we did so that any newly married couple should come here on honeymoon. Romantic, if you know what I mean.'

Tuppence agreed that romance was a very desirable thing.

'They haven't got so much to spend nowadays, newly marrieds. Not what they used to. Most of them you see are saving for a house or are making down payments already. Or they've got to buy some furniture on the hire purchase and it doesn't leave anything over for having a posh honeymoon or anything of that kind. They're careful, you know, most of the young folk. They don't go bashing all their money.'

She clattered downstairs again talking briskly as she went. Tuppence lay down on the bed to have half an hour's sleep after a somewhat tiring day. She had, however, great hopes of Mrs Copleigh, and felt that once thoroughly rested herself, she would be able to lead the conversation to the most fruitful subjects possible. She would hear, she was sure, all about the house by the bridge, who had lived there, who had been of evil or good repute in the neighbourhood, what scandals there were and other such likely topics. She was more convinced of this than ever when she had been introduced to Mr Copleigh, a man who barely opened his mouth. His conversation was mostly made up of amiable grunts, usually signifying an affirmative. Sometimes, in more muted tones, a disagreement.

He was content so far as Tuppence could see, to let his wife talk. He himself more or less abstracted his attention, part of the time busy with his plans for the next day which appeared to be market day.

As far as Tuppence was concerned nothing could have turned out better. It could have been distinguished by a slogan – 'You want information, we have it'. Mrs Copleigh was as good as a wireless set or a television. You had only to turn the button and words poured out accompanied by gestures and lots of facial expression. Not only was her figure like a child's rubber ball, her face might also have been made of indiarubber. The various people she was talking about almost came alive in caricature before Tuppence's eyes.

Tuppence ate bacon and eggs and had slices of thick bread and butter and praised the blackberry jelly, home-made, her favourite kind, she truthfully announced, and did her best to absorb the flood of information so that she could write notes down in her notebook later. A whole panorama of the past in this country district seemed to be spread out before her.

There was no chronological sequence which occasionally made things difficult. Mrs Copleigh jumped from fifteen years ago to two years ago to last month, and then back to somewhere in the twenties. All this would want a lot of sorting out. And Tuppence wondered whether in the end she would get anything.

The first button she had pressed had not given her any result. That was a mention of Mrs Lancaster.

'I think she came from hereabouts,' said Tuppence, allowing a good deal of vagueness to appear in her voice. 'She had a picture – a very nice picture done by an artist who I believe was known down here.'

'Who did you say now?'

'A Mrs Lancaster.'

'No, I don't remember any Lancasters in these parts. Lancaster. Lancaster. A gentleman had a car accident, I remember. No, it's the car I'm thinking of. A Lancaster that was. No Mrs Lancaster. It wouldn't be Miss Bolton, would it? She'd be about seventy now I think. She might have married a Mr Lancaster. She went away and travelled abroad and I do hear she married someone.'

'The picture she gave my aunt was by a Mr Boscobel – I think the name was,' said Tuppence. 'What a lovely jelly.'

'I don't put no apple in it either, like most people

do. Makes it jell better, they say, but it takes all the flavour out.'

'Yes,' said Tuppence. 'I quite agree with you. It does.'

'Who did you say now? It began with a B but I didn't quite catch it.'

'Boscobel, I think.'

'Oh, I remember Mr Boscowan well. Let's see now. That must have been – fifteen years ago it was at least that he came down here. He came several years running, he did. He liked the place. Actually rented a cottage. One of Farmer Hart's cottages it was, that he kept for his labourer. But they built a new one, they did, the Council. Four new cottages specially for labourers.

'Regular artist, Mr B was,' said Mrs Copleigh. 'Funny kind of coat he used to wear. Sort of velvet or corduroy. It used to have holes in the elbows and he wore green and yellow shirts, he did. Oh, very colourful, he was. I liked his pictures, I did. He had a showing of them one year. Round about Christmas time it was, I think. No, of course not, it must have been in the summer. He wasn't here in the winter. Yes, very nice. Nothing exciting, if you know what I mean. Just a house with a couple of trees or two cows looking over a fence. But all nice and quiet and pretty colours. Not like some of these young chaps nowadays.'

'Do you have a lot of artists down here?'

'Not really. Oh no, not to speak of. One or two ladies comes down in the summer and does sketching sometimes, but I don't think much of them. We had a young fellow a year ago, called himself an artist. Didn't shave properly. I can't say I liked any of his pictures much. Funny colours all swirled round anyhow. Nothing you could recognize a bit. Sold a lot of his pictures, he did at that. And they weren't cheap, mind you.'

'Ought to have been five pounds,' said Mr Copleigh entering the conversation for the first time so suddenly that Tuppence jumped.

'What my husband thinks is,' said Mrs Copleigh, resuming her place as interpreter to him. 'He thinks no picture ought to cost more than five pounds. Paints wouldn't cost as much as that. That's what he says, don't you, George?'

'Ah,' said George.

'Mr Boscowan painted a picture of that house by the bridge and the canal – Waterside or Watermead, isn't it called? I came that way today.'

'Oh, you came along that road, did you? It's not much of a road, is it? Very narrow. Lonely that house is, I always think. *I* wouldn't like to live in that house. Too lonely. Don't you agree, George?'

George made the noise that expressed faint disagreement and possibly contempt at the cowardice of women.

'That's where Alice Perry lives, that is,' said Mrs Copleigh.

Tuppence abandoned her researches on Mr Boscowan to go along with an opinion on the Perrys. It was, she perceived, always better to go along with Mrs Copleigh who was a jumper from subject to subject.

'Queer couple *they* are,' said Mrs Copleigh.

George made his agreeing sound.

'Keep themselves to themselves, they do. Don't mingle much, as you'd say. And she goes about looking like nothing on earth, Alice Perry does.'

'Mad,' said Mr Copleigh.

'Well, I don't know as I'd say *that*. She *looks* mad all right. All that scatty hair flying about. And she wears men's coats and great rubber boots most of the time. And she says odd things and doesn't sometimes answer you right when you ask her a question. But I wouldn't say she was *mad*. Peculiar, that's all.'

'Do people like her?'

'Nobody knows her hardly, although they've been there several years. There's all sorts of *tales* about her but then, there's always tales.'

'What sort of tales?'

Direct questions were never resented by Mrs Copleigh, who welcomed them as one who was only too eager to answer.

'Calls up spirits, they say, at night. Sitting round a

table. And there's stories of lights moving about the house at night. And she reads a lot of clever books, they say. With things drawn in them – circles and stars. If you ask me, it's Amos Perry as is the one that's not quite all right.'

'He's just simple,' said Mr Copleigh indulgently.

'Well, you may be right about that. But there were tales said of him once. Fond of his garden, but doesn't know much.'

'It's only half a house though, isn't it?' said Tuppence. 'Mrs Perry asked me in very kindly.'

'Did she now? Did she really? I don't know as I'd have liked to go into that house,' said Mrs Copleigh.

'Their part of it's all right,' said Mr Copleigh.

'Isn't the other part all right?' said Tuppence. 'The front part that gives on the canal.'

'Well, there used to be a lot of stories about it. Of course, nobody's lived in it for years. They say there's something queer about it. Lot of stories told. But when you come down to it, it's not stories in anybody's memory here. It's all long ago. It was built over a hundred years ago, you know. They say as there was a pretty lady kept there first, built for her, it was, by one of the gentlemen at Court.'

'Queen Victoria's Court?' asked Tuppence with interest.

'I don't think it would be her. *She* was particular, the

old Queen was. No, I'd say it was before that. Time of one of them Georges. This gentlemen, he used to come down and see her and the story goes that they had a quarrel and he cut her throat one night.'

'How terrible!' said Tuppence. 'Did they hang him for it?'

'No. Oh no, there was nothing of that sort. The story is, you see, that he had to get rid of the body and he walled her up in the fireplace.'

'Walled her up in the fireplace!'

'Some ways they tell it, they say she was a nun, and she had run away from a convent and that's why she had to be walled up. That's what they do at convents.'

'But it wasn't nuns who walled her up.'

'No, no. He did it. Her lover, what had done her in. And he bricked up all the fireplace, they say, and nailed a big sheet of iron over it. Anyway, she was never seen again, poor soul, walking about in her fine dresses. Some said, of course, she'd gone away with him. Gone away to live in town or back to some other place. People used to hear noises and see lights in the house, and a lot of people don't go near it after dark.'

'But what happened later?' said Tuppence, feeling that to go back beyond the reign of Queen Victoria seemed a little too far into the past for what she was looking for.

'Well, I don't rightly know as there was very much.

A farmer called Blodgick took it over when it came up for sale, I believe. He weren't there long either. What they called a gentleman farmer. That's why he liked the house, I suppose, but the farming land wasn't much use to him, and he didn't know how to deal with it. So he sold it again. Changed hands ever so many times it has – Always builders coming along and making alterations – new bathrooms – that sort of thing – A couple had it who were doing chicken farming, I believe, at one time. But it got a name, you know, for being unlucky. But all that's a bit before my time. I believe Mr Boscowan himself thought of buying it at one time. That was when he painted the picture of it.'

'What sort of age was Mr Boscowan when he was down here?'

'Forty, I would say, or maybe a bit more than that. He was a good-looking man in his way. Run into fat a bit, though. Great one for the girls, he was.'

'Ah,' said Mr Copleigh. It was a warning grunt this time.

'Ah well, we all know what artists are like,' said Mrs Copleigh, including Tuppence in this knowledge. 'Go over to France a lot, you know, and get French ways, they do.'

'He wasn't married?'

'Not then he wasn't. Not when he was first down

here. Bit keen he was on Mrs Charrington's daughter, but nothing came of it. She was a lovely girl, though, but too young for him. She wasn't more than twenty-five.'

'Who was Mrs Charrington?' Tuppence felt bewildered at this introduction of new characters.

'What the hell am I doing here, anyway?' she thought suddenly as waves of fatigue swept over her – 'I'm just listening to a lot of gossip about people, and imagining things like murder which aren't true at all. *I can see now* – It started when a nice but addle-headed old pussy got a bit mixed up in her head and began reminiscing about stories this Mr Boscowan, or someone like him who may have given the picture to her, told about the house and the legends about it, of someone being walled up alive in a fireplace and she thought it was a child for some reason. And here I am going round investigating mares' nests. Tommy told me I was a fool, and he was quite right – I *am* a fool.'

She waited for a break to occur in Mrs Copleigh's even flow of conversation, so that she could rise, say good night politely and go upstairs to bed.

Mrs Copleigh was still in full and happy spate.

'Mrs Charrington? Oh, she lived in Watermead for a bit,' said Mrs Copleigh. 'Mrs Charrington, and her daughter. She was a nice lady, she was, Mrs Charrington. Widow of an army officer, I believe.

Badly off, but the house was being rented cheap. Did a lot of gardening. She was very fond of gardening. Not much good at keeping the house clean, she wasn't. I went and obliged for her, once or twice, but I couldn't keep it up. I had to go on my bicycle, you see, and it's over two miles. Weren't any buses along that road.'

'Did she live there long?'

'Not more than two or three years, I think. Got scared, I expect, after the troubles came. And then she had her own troubles about her daughter, too. Lilian, I think her name was.'

Tuppence took a draught of the strong tea with which the meal was fortified, and resolved to get finished with Mrs Charrington before seeking repose.

'What was the trouble about the daughter? Mr Boscowan?'

'No, it wasn't Mr Boscowan as got her into trouble. I'll never believe that. It was the other one.'

'Who was the other one?' asked Tuppence. 'Someone else who lived down here?'

'I don't think he lived down in these parts. Someone she'd met up in London. She went up there to study ballet dancing, would it be? Or art? Mr Boscowan arranged for her to join some school there. Slate I think its name was.'

'Slade?' suggested Tuppence.

'May have been. That sort of name. Anyway, she used to go up there and that's how she got to know this fellow, whoever he was. Her mother didn't like it. She forbade her to meet him. Fat lot of good that was likely to do. She was a silly woman in some ways. Like a lot of those army officers' wives were, you know. She thought girls would do as they were told. Behind the times, she was. Been out in India and those parts, but when it's a question of a good-looking young fellow and you take your eye off a girl, you won't find she's doing what you told her. Not her. He used to come down here now and then and they used to meet outside.'

'And then she got into trouble, did she?' Tuppence said, using the well-known euphemism, hoping that under that form it would not offend Mr Copleigh's sense of propriety.

'Must have been him, I suppose. Anyway, there it was plain as plain. I saw how it was long before her own mother did. Beautiful creature, she was. Big and tall and handsome. But I don't think, you know, that she was one that could stand up to things. She'd break up, you know. She used to walk about rather wild-like, muttering to herself. If you ask me he treated her bad, that fellow did. Went away and left her when he found out what was happening. Of course, a mother as was a mother would have gone and talked to him and made him see where his duty lay, but Mrs Charrington, she wouldn't have had the spirit to do that. Anyway, her mother got wise, and she took the girl away. Shut up the house, she did and afterwards it was put up for sale. They came back to pack up, I believe, but they never came to the village or said anything to anyone. They never come back here, neither of them. There was some story got around. I never knew if there was any truth in it.'

'Some folk'll make up anything,' said Mr Copleigh unexpectedly.

'Well, you're right there, George. Still they may have been true. Such things happen. And as you say, that girl didn't look quite right in the head to me.'

'What was the story?' demanded Tuppence.

'Well, really, I don't like to say. It's a long time since and I wouldn't like to say anything as I wasn't sure of it. It was Mrs Badcock's Louise who put it about. Awful liar that girl was. The things she'd say. Anything to make up a good story.'

'But what was it?' said Tuppence.

'Said this Charrington girl had killed the baby and after that killed herself. Said her mother went half mad with grief and her relations had to put her in a nursing home.'

Again Tuppence felt confusion mounting in her head. She felt almost as though she was swaying in her chair. Could Mrs Charrington be Mrs Lancaster? Changed her name, gone slightly batty, obsessed about her daughter's fate. Mrs Copleigh's voice was going on remorselessly.

'I never believed a word of that myself. That Badcock girl would say anything. We weren't listening much to hearsay and stories just then – we'd had other things to worry about. Scared stiff we'd been, all over the countryside on account of the things that had been going on – REAL things –'

'Why? What had been happening?' asked Tuppence, marvelling at the things that seemed to happen, and to centre round the peaceful-looking village of Sutton Chancellor.

'I daresay as you'll have read about it all in the papers at the time. Let's see, near as possible it would have been twenty years ago. You'll have read about it for sure. Child murders. Little girl of nine years old first. Didn't come home from school one day. Whole neighbourhood was out searching for her. Dingley Copse she was found in. Strangled, she'd been. It makes me shiver still to think of it. Well, that was the first, then about three weeks later another. The other side of Market Basing, that was. But within the district, as you might say. A man with a car could have done it easy enough.

'And then there were others. Not for a month or two

sometimes. And then there'd be another one. Not more than a couple of miles from here, one was; almost in the village, though.'

'Didn't the police – didn't anyone know who'd done it?'

'They tried hard enough,' said Mrs Copleigh. 'Detained a man quite soon, they did. Someone from t'other side of Market Basing. Said he was helping them in their inquiries. You know what that always means. They think they've got him. They pulled in first one and then another but always after twenty-four hours or so they had to let him go again. Found out he couldn't have done it or wasn't in these parts or somebody gave him an alibi.'

'You don't know, Liz,' said Mr Copleigh. 'They may have known quite well who done it. I'd say they *did*. That's often the way of it, or so I've heard. The police know who it is but they can't get the evidence.'

'That's wives, that is,' said Mrs Copleigh, 'wives or mothers or fathers even. Even the police can't do much no matter what they may think. A mother says "my boy was here that night at dinner" or his young lady says she went to the pictures with him that night, and he was with her the whole time, or a father says that he and his son were out in the far field together doing something – well, you can't do anything against it. They may think the father or the mother or his sweetheart's lying, but unless someone else come along and say they saw the boy or the man or whatever it is in some other place, there's not much they can do. It was a terrible time. Right het up we all were round here. When we heard another child was missing we'd make parties up.'

'Aye, that's right,' said Mr Copleigh.

'When they'd got together they'd go out and they'd search. Sometimes they found her at once and sometimes they wouldn't find her for weeks. Sometimes she was quite near her home in a place you'd have thought we must have looked at already. Maniac, I suppose it must have been. It's awful,' said Mrs Copleigh in a righteous tone, 'it's awful, that there should be men like that. They ought to be shot. They ought to be strangled themselves. And I'd do it to them for one, if anyone would let me. Any man who kills children and assaults them. What's the good putting them in loony bins and treating them with all the home comforts and living soft. And then sooner or later they let 'em out again, say they're cured and send them home. That happened somewhere in Norfolk. My sister lives there and she told me about it. He went back home and two days later he'd done in someone else. Crazy they are, these doctors, some of them, saying these men are cured when they are not.'

'And you've no idea down here who it might have

been?' said Tuppence. 'Do you think really it was a stranger?'

'Might have been a stranger to us. But it must have been someone living within – oh! I'd say a range of twenty miles around. It mightn't have been here in this village.'

'You always thought it was, Liz.'

'You get het up,' said Mrs Copleigh. 'You think it's sure to be here in your own neighbourhood because you're afraid, I suppose. I used to look at people. So did you, George. You'd say to yourself I wonder if it could be *that* chap, he's seemed a bit queer lately. That sort of thing.'

'I don't suppose really he looked queer at all,' said Tuppence. 'He probably looked just like everyone else.'

'Yes, it could be you've got something there. I've heard it said that you wouldn't know, and whoever it was had never seemed mad at all, but other people say there's always a terrible glare in their eyes.'

'Jeffreys, he was the sergeant of police here then,' said Mr Copleigh, 'he always used to say he had a good idea but there was nothing doing.'

'They never caught the man?'

'No. Over six months it was, nearly a year. Then the whole thing stopped. And there's never been anything of that kind round here since. No, I think he must have gone away. Gone away altogether. That's what makes people think they might know who it was.'

'You mean because of people who *did* leave the district?'

'Well, of course it made people talk, you know. They'd say it might be so-and-so.'

Tuppence hesitated to ask the next question, but she felt that with Mrs Copleigh's passion for talking it wouldn't matter if she did.

'Who did *you* think it was?' she asked.

'Well, it's that long ago I'd hardly like to say. But there *was* names mentioned. Talked of, you know, and looked at. Some as thought it might be Mr Boscowan.'

'Did they?'

'Yes, being an artist and all, artists are queer. They say that. But I didn't think it was him!'

'There was more as said it was Amos Perry,' said Mr Copleigh.

'Mrs Perry's husband?'

'Yes. He's a bit queer, you know, simple-minded. He's the sort of chap that might have done it.'

'Were the Perrys living here then?'

'Yes. Not at Watermead. They had a cottage about four or five miles away. Police had an eye on him, I'm sure of that.'

'Couldn't get anything on him, though,' said Mrs

Copleigh. 'His wife spoke for him always. Stayed at home with her in the evenings, he did. Always, she said. Just went along sometimes to the pub on a Saturday night, but none of these murders took place on a Saturday night, so there wasn't anything in that. Besides, Alice Perry was the kind you'd believe when she gave evidence. She'd never let up or back down. You couldn't frighten her out of it. Anyway, *he's* not the one. I never thought so. I know I've nothing to go on but I've a sort of feeling if I'd had to put my finger on anyone I'd have put it on Sir Philip.'

'Sir Philip?' Again Tuppence's head reeled. Yet another character was being introduced. Sir Philip. 'Who's Sir Philip?' she asked.

'Sir Philip Starke – Lives up in the Warrender House. Used to be called the Old Priory when the Warrenders lived in it – before it burnt down. You can see the Warrender graves in the churchyard and tablets in the church, too. Always been Warrenders here practically since the time of King James.'

'Was Sir Philip a relation of the Warrenders?'

'No. Made his money in a big way, I believe, or his father did. Steelworks or something of that kind. Odd sort of man was Sir Philip. The works were somewhere up north, but he lived here. Kept to himself he did. What they call a rec – rec – rec-something.'

'Recluse,' suggested Tuppence.

'That's the word I'm looking for. Pale he was, you know, and thin and bony and fond of flowers. He was a botanist. Used to collect all sorts of silly little wild flowers, the kind you wouldn't look at twice. He even wrote a book on them, I believe. Oh yes, he was clever, very clever. His wife was a nice lady, and very handsome, but sad looking, I always thought.'

Mr Copleigh uttered one of his grunts. 'You're daft,' he said. 'Thinking it might have been Sir Philip. He was fond of children, Sir Philip was. He was always giving parties for them.'

'Yes I know. Always giving fêtes, having lovely prizes for the children. Egg and spoon races – all those strawberry and cream teas he'd give. He'd no children of his own, you see. Often he'd stop children in a lane and give them a sweet or give them a sixpence to buy sweets. But I don't know. *I* think he overdid it. He was an odd man. I thought there was something wrong when his wife suddenly up and left him.'

'When did his wife leave him?'

'It'd be about six months after all this trouble began. Three children had been killed by then. Lady Starke went away suddenly to the south of France and she never came back. She wasn't the kind, you'd say, to do that. She was a quiet lady, respectable. It's not as though she left him for any other man. No, she wasn't the kind to do that. So *why* did she go and leave him?

I always say it's because she knew something – found out about something –'

'Is he still living here?'

'Not regular, he isn't. He comes down once or twice a year but the house is kept shut up most of the time with a caretaker there. Miss Bligh in the village – she used to be his secretary – she sees to things for him.'

'And his wife?'

'She's dead, poor lady. Died soon after she went abroad. There's a tablet put up to her in the church. Awful for her it would be. Perhaps she wasn't sure at first, then perhaps she began to suspect her husband, and then perhaps she got to be quite sure. She couldn't bear it and she went away.'

'The things you women imagine,' said Mr Copleigh.

'All I say is there was *something* that wasn't right about Sir Philip. He was too fond of children, I think, and it wasn't in a natural kind of way.'

'Women's fancies,' said Mr Copleigh.

Mrs Copleigh got up and started to move things off the table.

'About time,' said her husband. 'You'll give this lady here bad dreams if you go on about things as were over years ago and have nothing to do with anyone here any more.'

'It's been very interesting hearing,' said Tuppence. 'But I am very sleepy. I think I'd better go to bed now.'

'Well, we usually goes early to bed,' said Mrs Copleigh, 'and you'll be tired after the long day you've had.'

'I am. I'm frightfully sleepy.' Tuppence gave a large yawn. 'Well, good night and thank you very much.'

'Would you like a call and a cup of tea in the morning? Eight o'clock too early for you?'

'No, that would be fine,' said Tuppence. 'But don't bother if it's a lot of trouble.'

'No trouble at all,' said Mrs Copleigh.

Tuppence pulled herself wearily up to bed. She opened her suitcase, took out the few things she needed, undressed, washed and dropped into bed. It was true what she had told Mrs Copleigh. She was dead tired. The things she had heard passed through her head in a kind of kaleidoscope of moving figures and of all sorts of horrific imaginings. Dead children – too many dead children. Tuppence wanted just one dead child behind a fireplace. The fireplace had to do perhaps with Waterside. The child's doll. A child that had been killed by a demented young girl driven off her rather weak brains by the fact that her lover had deserted her. Oh dear me, what melodramatic language I'm using, thought Tuppence. All such a muddle – the chronology all mixed up – one can't be sure what happened when.

She went to sleep and dreamt. There was a kind of Lady of Shalott looking out of the window of the house. There was a scratching noise coming from the chimney. Blows were coming from behind a great iron plate nailed up there. The clanging sounds of the hammer. Clang, clang, clang. Tuppence woke up. It was Mrs Copleigh knocking on the door. She came in brightly, put the tea down by Tuppence's bed, pulled the curtains, hoped Tuppence had slept well. No one had ever, Tuppence thought, looked more cheerful than Mrs Copleigh did. *She* had had no bad dreams!

Chapter 9

A Morning in Market Basing

'Ah well,' said Mrs Copleigh, as she bustled out of the room. 'Another day. That's what I always say when I wake up.'

'Another day?' thought Tuppence, sipping strong black tea. 'I wonder if I'm making an idiot of myself . . . ? Could be . . . Wish I had Tommy here to talk to. Last night muddled me.'

Before she left her room, Tuppence made entries in her notebook on the various facts and names that she had heard the night before, which she had been far too tired to do when she went up to bed. Melodramatic stories, of the past, containing perhaps grains of truth here and there but mostly hearsay, malice, gossip, romantic imagination.

'Really,' thought Tuppence. 'I'm beginning to know the love lives of a quantity of people right back to the eighteenth century, I think. But what does it all amount to? And what am I looking for? I don't even *know* any longer. The awful thing is that I've got involved and I can't leave off.'

Having a shrewd suspicion that the first thing she might be getting involved with was Miss Bligh, whom Tuppence recognized as the overall menace of Sutton Chancellor, she circumvented all kind offers of help by driving off to Market Basing post haste, only pausing, when the car was accosted by Miss Bligh with shrill cries, to explain to that lady that she had an urgent appointment . . . When would she be back? Tuppence was vague – Would she care to lunch? – Very kind of Miss Bligh, but Tuppence was afraid –

'Tea, then. Four-thirty I'll expect you.' It was almost a Royal Command. Tuppence smiled, nodded, let in the clutch and drove on.

Possibly, Tuppence thought – if she got anything interesting out of the house agents in Market Basing – Nellie Bligh might provide additional useful information. She was the kind of woman who prided herself on knowing all about everyone. The snag was that she would be determined to know all about Tuppence. Possibly by this afternoon Tuppence would have recovered sufficiently to be once more her own inventive self!

'Remember, Mrs Blenkinsop,' said Tuppence, edging round a sharp corner and squeezing into a hedge to avoid being annihilated by a frolicsome tractor of immense bulk.

Arrived in Market Basing she put the car in a parking lot in the main square, and went into the post office and entered a vacant telephone box.

The voice of Albert answered – using his usual response – a single 'Hallo' uttered in a suspicious voice.

'Listen, Albert – I'll be home tomorrow. In time for dinner, anyway – perhaps earlier. Mr Beresford will be back, too, unless he rings up. Get us something – chicken, I think.'

'Right, Madam. Where are you –'

But Tuppence had rung off.

The life of Market Basing seemed centred in its important main square – Tuppence had consulted a classified directory before leaving the post office and three out of the four house and estate agents were situated in the square – the fourth in something called George Street.

Tuppence scribbled down the names and went out to look for them.

She started with Messrs Lovebody & Slicker which appeared to be the most imposing.

A girl with spots received her.

'I want to make some inquiries about a house.'

The girl received this news without interest. Tuppence

might have been inquiring about some rare animal.

'I don't know, I'm sure,' said the girl, looking round to ascertain if there was one of her colleagues to whom she could pass Tuppence on –

'A *house*,' said Tuppence. 'You *are* house agents, aren't you?'

'House agents and auctioneers. The Cranberry Court auction's on Wednesday if it's that you're interested in, catalogues two shillings.'

'I'm not interested in auctions. I want to ask about a house.'

'Furnished?'

'Unfurnished – To buy – or rent.'

Spots brightened a little.

'I think you'd better see Mr Slicker.'

Tuppence was all for seeing Mr Slicker and was presently seated in a small office opposite a tweed-suited young man in horsy checks, who began turning over a large number of particulars of desirable residences – murmuring comments to himself . . . '8 Mandeville Road – architect built, three bed, American kitchen – Oh, no, that's gone – Amabel Lodge – picturesque residence, four acres – reduced price for quick sale –'

Tuppence interrupted him forcefully: 'I have seen a house I like the look of – In Sutton Chancellor – or rather, near Sutton Chancellor – by a canal –'

'Sutton Chancellor,' Mr Slicker looked doubtful –

'I don't think we have any property there on our books at present. What name?'

'It doesn't seem to have any written up – Possibly Waterside. Rivermead – once called Bridge House. I gather,' said Tuppence, 'the house is in two parts. One half is let but the tenant there could not tell me anything about the other half, which fronts on the canal and which is the one in which I am interested. It appears to be unoccupied.'

Mr Slicker said distantly that he was afraid he couldn't help her, but condescended to supply the information that perhaps Messrs Blodget & Burgess might do so. By the tone in his voice the clerk seemed to imply this Messrs Blodget & Burgess were a very inferior firm.

Tuppence transferred herself to Messrs Blodget & Burgess who were on the opposite side of the square – and whose premises closely resembled those of Messrs Lovebody & Slicker – the same kind of sale bills and forthcoming auctions in their rather grimy windows. Their front door had recently been repainted a rather bilious shade of green, if that was accounted to be a merit.

The reception arrangements were equally discouraging, and Tuppence was given over to a Mr Sprig, an elderly man of apparently despondent disposition. Once more Tuppence retailed her wants and requirements.

Mr Sprig admitted to being aware of the existence of the residence in question, but was not helpful, or as far as it seemed, much interested.

'It's not in the market, I'm afraid. The owner doesn't want to sell.'

'Who is the owner?'

'Really I doubt if I know. It has changed hands rather frequently – there was a rumour at one moment of a compulsory purchase order.'

'What did any local government want it for?'

'Really, Mrs – er – (he glanced down at Tuppence's name jotted down on his blotter) – Mrs Beresford, if you could tell me the answer to that question you would be wiser than most victims are these days. The ways of local councils and planning societies are always shrouded in mystery. The rear portion of the house had a few necessary repairs done to it and was let at an exceedingly low rent to a – er – ah yes, a Mr and Mrs Perry. As to the actual owners of the property, the gentleman in question lives abroad and seems to have lost interest in the place. I imagine there was some question of a minor inheriting, and it was administered by executors. Some small legal difficulties arose – the law tends to be expensive, Mrs Beresford – I fancy the owner is quite content for the house to fall down – no repairs are done except to the portion the Perrys inhabit. The actual land, of course, might always prove valuable in the future – the repair of derelict houses is seldom profitable. If you are interested in a property of that kind, I am sure we could offer you something far more worth your while. What, if I may ask, is there which especially appealed to you in this property?'

'I liked the look of it,' said Tuppence. 'It's a very *pretty* house – I saw it first from the train –'

'Oh, I see –' Mr Sprig masked as best he could an expression of 'the foolishness of women is incredible' – and said soothingly, 'I should really forget all about it if I were you.'

'I suppose you could write and ask the owners if they would be prepared to sell – or if you would give me their – or his address –'

'We will get into communication with the owners' solicitors if you insist – but I can't hold out much hope.'

'I suppose one always has to go through solicitors for everything nowadays.' Tuppence sounded both foolish and fretful . . . 'And lawyers are always so *slow* over everything.'

'Ah yes – the law is prolific of delays –'

'And so are *banks* – just as bad!'

'Banks –' Mr Sprig sounded a little startled.

'So many people give you a *bank* as an address. That's tiresome too.'

'Yes – yes – as you say – But people are so restless

these days and move about so much – living abroad and all that.' He opened a desk drawer. 'Now I have a property here, Crossgates – two miles from Market Basing – very good condition – nice garden –'

Tuppence rose to her feet.

'No thank you.'

She bade Mr Sprig a firm goodbye and went out into the square.

She paid a brief visit to the third establishment which seemed to be mainly preoccupied with sales of cattle, chicken farms and general farms in a derelict condition.

She paid a final visit to Messrs Roberts & Wiley in George Street – which seemed to be a small but pushing business, anxious to oblige – but generally uninterested and ignorant of Sutton Chancellor and anxious to sell residences as yet only half built at what seemed ridiculously exorbitant sums – an illustration of one made Tuppence shudder. The eager young man seeing his possible client firm in departure, admitted unwillingly that such a place as Sutton Chancellor did exist.

'Sutton Chancellor you mentioned. Better try Blodget & Burgess in the square. They handle some property thereabouts – but it's all in very poor condition – run down –'

'There's a pretty house near there, by a canal bridge

– I saw it from the train. Why does nobody want to live there?'

'Oh! I know the place, this – Riverbank – You wouldn't get anyone to live in it – Got a reputation as haunted.'

'You mean – ghosts?'

'So they say – Lots of tales about it. Noises at nights. And groans. If you ask me, it's death-watch beetle.'

'Oh dear,' said Tuppence. 'It looked to me so nice and isolated.'

'Much too isolated most people would say. Floods in winter – think of that.'

'I see that there's a lot to think about,' said Tuppence bitterly.

She murmured to herself as she sent her steps towards The Lamb and Flag at which she proposed to fortify herself with lunch.

'A lot to think about – floods, death-watch beetle, ghosts, clanking chains, absentee owners and landlords, solicitors, banks – a house that nobody wants or loves – except perhaps *me* . . . Oh well, what I want now is FOOD.'

The food at The Lamb and Flag was good and plentiful – hearty food for farmers rather than phony French menus for tourists passing through – Thick savoury soup, leg of pork and apple sauce, Stilton cheese – or plums and custard if you preferred it – which Tuppence didn't –

After a desultory stroll round, Tuppence retrieved her car and started back to Sutton Chancellor – unable to feel that her morning had been fruitful.

As she turned the last corner and Sutton Chancellor church came into view, Tuppence saw the vicar emerging from the churchyard. He walked rather wearily. Tuppence drew up by him.

'Are you still looking for that grave?' she asked.

The vicar had one hand at the small of his back.

'Oh dear,' he said, 'my eyesight is not very good. So many of the inscriptions are nearly erased. My back troubles me, too. So many of these stones lie flat on the ground. Really, when I bend over sometimes I fear that I shall never get up again.'

'I shouldn't do it any more,' said Tuppence. 'If you've looked in the parish register and all that, you've done all you can.'

'I know, but the poor fellow seemed so keen, so earnest. I'm quite sure that it's all wasted labour. However, I really felt it was my duty. I have still got a short stretch I haven't done, over there from beyond the yew tree to the far wall – although most of the stones are eighteenth century. But I should like to feel I had finished my task properly. Then I could not reproach myself. However, I shall leave it till tomorrow.'

'Quite right,' said Tuppence. 'You mustn't do too much in one day. I tell you what,' she added. 'After I've had a cup of tea with Miss Bligh, I'll go and have a look myself. From the yew tree to the wall, do you say?'

'Oh, but I couldn't possibly ask you –'

'That's all right. I shall quite like to do it. I think it's very interesting prowling round in a churchyard. You know, the older inscriptions give you a sort of picture of the people who lived here and all that sort of thing. I shall quite enjoy it, I shall really. Do go back home and rest.'

'Well, of course, I really have to do something about my sermon this evening, it's quite true. You are a very kind friend, I'm sure. A *very* kind friend.'

He beamed at her and departed into the vicarage. Tuppence glanced at her watch. She stopped at Miss Bligh's house. 'Might as well get it over,' thought Tuppence. The front door was open and Miss Bligh was just carrying a plate of fresh-baked scones across the hall into the sitting-room.

'Oh! so there you are, dear Mrs Beresford. I'm *so* pleased to see you. Tea's quite ready. The kettle is on. I've only got to fill up the teapot. I hope you did all the shopping you wanted,' she added, looking in a rather marked manner at the painfully evident empty shopping bag hanging on Tuppence's arm.

'Well, I didn't have much luck really,' said Tuppence, putting as good a face on it as she could. 'You know how it is sometimes – just one of those days when people just haven't got the particular colour or the particular kind of thing you want. But I always enjoy looking round a new place even if it isn't a very interesting one.'

A whistling kettle let forth a strident shriek for attention and Miss Bligh shot back into the kitchen to attend to it, scattering a batch of letters waiting for the post on the hall table.

Tuppence stooped and retrieved them, noticing as she put them back on the table that the topmost one was addressed to a Mrs Yorke, Rosetrellis Court for Elderly Ladies – at an address in Cumberland.

'Really,' thought Tuppence. 'I am beginning to feel as if the whole of the country is full of nothing but Homes for the Elderly! I suppose in next to no time Tommy and I will be living in one!'

Only the other day, some would-be kind and helpful friend had written to recommend a very nice address in Devon – married couples – mostly retired Service people. Quite good cooking – You brought your own furniture and personal belongings.

Miss Bligh reappeared with the teapot and the two ladies sat down to tea.

Miss Bligh's conversation was of a less melodramatic and juicy nature than that of Mrs Copleigh, and was concerned more with the procuring of information, than of giving it.

Tuppence murmured vaguely of past years of Service abroad – the domestic difficulties of life in England, gave details of a married son and a married daughter both with children and gently steered the conversation to the activities of Miss Bligh in Sutton Chancellor which were numerous – The Women's Institute, Guides, Scouts, the Conservative Ladies Union, Lectures, Greek Art, Jam Making, Flower Arrangement, the Sketching Club, the Friends of Archaeology – The vicar's health, the necessity of making him take care of himself, his absentmindedness – Unfortunate differences of opinion between churchwardens –

Tuppence praised the scones, thanked her hostess for her hospitality and rose to go.

'You are so wonderfully energetic, Miss Bligh,' she said. 'How you manage to do all you do, I cannot imagine. I must confess that after a day's excursion and shopping, I like just a nice little rest on my bed – just half an hour or so of shut-eye – A very comfortable bed, too. I must thank you very much for recommending me to Mrs Copleigh –'

'A most reliable woman, though of course she talks too much –'

'Oh! I found all her local tales most entertaining.'

'Half the time she doesn't know what she's talking about! Are you staying here for long?'

'Oh no – I'm going home tomorrow. I'm disappointed at not having heard of any suitable little property – I had hopes of that very picturesque house by the canal –'

'You're well out of that. It's in a very poor state of repair – Absentee landlords – it's a disgrace –'

'I couldn't even find out who it belongs to. I expect *you* know. You seem to know everything here –'

'I've never taken much interest in that house. It's always changing hands – One can't keep pace. The Perrys live in half of it – and the other half just goes to rack and ruin.'

Tuppence said goodbye again and drove back to Mrs Copleigh's. The house was quiet and apparently empty. Tuppence went up to her bedroom, deposited her empty shopping bag, washed her face and powdered her nose, tiptoed out of the house again, looking up and down the street, then leaving her car where it was, she walked swiftly round the corner, and took a footpath through the field behind the village which eventually led to a stile into the churchyard.

Tuppence went over the stile into the churchyard, peaceful in the evening sun, and began to examine the tombstones as she had promised. She had not really had any ulterior motive in doing so. There was nothing here she hoped to discover. It was really just kindliness on her part. The elderly vicar was rather a dear, and she would like him to feel that his conscience was entirely satisfied. She had brought a notebook and pencil with her in case there was anything of interest to note down for him. She presumed she was merely to look for a gravestone that might have been put up commemorating the death of some child of the required age. Most of the graves here were of an older date. They were not very interesting, not old enough to be quaint or to have touching or tender inscriptions. They were mostly of fairly elderly people. Yet she lingered a little as she went along, making mental pictures in her mind. Jane Elwood, departed this life January the 6th, aged 45. William Marl, departed this life January the 5th, deeply regretted. Mary Treves, five years old. March 14th 1835. That was too far back. 'In thy presence is the fulness of joy.' Lucky little Mary Treves.

She had almost reached the far wall now. The graves here were neglected and overgrown, nobody seemed to care about this bit of the cemetery. Many of the stones were no longer upright but lay about on the ground. The wall here was damaged and crumbling. In places it had been broken down.

Being right behind the church, it could not be seen from the road – and no doubt children came here to do what damage they could. Tuppence bent over one of the stone slabs – The original lettering was worn away and unreadable – But heaving it up sideways, Tuppence saw some coarsely scrawled letters and words, also by now partly overgrown.

She stopped to trace them with a forefinger, and got a word here and there –

Whoever . . . offend . . . one of these little ones . . .

Millstone . . . Millstone . . . Millstone . . . and below – in uneven cutting by an amateur hand:

Here lies Lily Waters.

Tuppence drew a deep breath – She was conscious of a shadow behind her, but before she could turn her head – something hit her on the back of her head and she fell forwards on to the tombstone into pain and darkness.

Book 3

Missing – A Wife

Chapter 10

A Conference – and After

'Well, Beresford,' said Major-General Sir Josiah Penn, K.M.G., C.B., D.S.O., speaking with the weight appropriate to the impressive stream of letters after his name. 'Well, what do you think of all that yackety-yack?'

Tommy gathered by that remark that Old Josh, as he was irreverently spoken of behind his back, was not impressed with the result of the course of the conferences in which they had been taking part.

'Softly, softly catchee monkey,' said Sir Josiah, going on with his remarks. 'A lot of talk and nothing said. If anybody does say anything sensible now and then, about four beanstalks immediately get up and howl it down. *I* don't know why we come to these things. At least, I *do* know. I know why I do. Nothing else to do. If I didn't come to these shows, I'd have to stay at home. Do you know what happens to me there? I get bullied, Beresford. Bullied by my housekeeper, bullied by my gardener. He's an elderly Scot and he won't so much as let me touch my own peaches. So I come along here, throw my weight about and pretend to myself that I'm performing a useful function, ensuring the security of this country! Stuff and nonsense.

'What about you? You're a relatively young man. What do you come and waste your time for? Nobody'll listen to you, even if you do say something worth hearing.'

Tommy, faintly amused that despite his own, as he considered, advanced age, he could be regarded as a youngster by Major-General Sir Josiah Penn, shook his head. The General must be, Tommy thought, considerably past eighty, he was rather deaf, heavily bronchial, but he was nobody's fool.

'Nothing would ever get done at all if you weren't here, sir,' said Tommy.

'I like to think so,' said the General. 'I'm a toothless bulldog – but I can still bark. How's Mrs Tommy? Haven't seen her for a long time.'

Tommy replied that Tuppence was well and active.

'She was always active. Used to make me think of a dragonfly sometimes. Always darting off after some apparently absurd idea of her own and then we'd find it wasn't absurd. Good fun!' said the General, with approval. 'Don't like these earnest middle-aged women you meet nowadays, all got a Cause with a capital C. And as for the girls nowadays –' he shook his head. 'Not what they used to be when I was a young man. Pretty as a picture, they used to be then. Their muslin frocks! *Cloche* hats, they used to wear at one time. Do you remember? No, I suppose you'd have been at school. Had to look right down underneath the brim before you could see the girl's face. Tantalizing it was, *and* they knew it! I remember now – let me see – she was a relative of yours – an aunt wasn't she? – Ada. Ada Fanshawe –'

'Aunt Ada?'

'Prettiest girl I ever knew.'

Tommy managed to contain the surprise he felt. That his Aunt Ada could ever have been considered pretty seemed beyond belief. Old Josh was dithering on.

'Yes, pretty as a picture. Sprightly, too! Gay! Regular tease. Ah, I remember last time I saw her. I was a subaltern just off to India. We were at a moonlight picnic on the beach . . . She and I wandered away together and sat on a rock looking at the sea.'

Tommy looked at him with great interest. At his double chins, his bald head, his bushy eyebrows and his enormous paunch. He thought of Aunt Ada, of her incipient moustache, her grim smile, her iron-grey hair, her malicious glance. Time, he thought. What Time does to one! He tried to visualize a handsome young subaltern and a pretty girl in the moonlight. He failed.

'Romantic,' said Sir Josiah Penn with a deep sigh. 'Ah yes, romantic. I would have liked to propose to her that night, but you couldn't propose if you were a subaltern. Not on your pay. We'd have had to wait five years before we could be married. That was too long an engagement to ask any girl to agree to. Ah well! you know how things happen. I went out to India and it was a long time before I came home on leave. We wrote to one another for a bit, then things slacked off. As it usually happens. I never saw her again. And yet, you know, I never quite forgot her. Often thought of her. I remember I nearly wrote to her once, years later. I'd heard she was in the neighbourhood where I was staying with some people. I thought I'd go and see her, ask if I could call. Then I thought to myself "Don't be a damn' fool. She probably looks quite different by now."

'I heard a chap mention her some years later. Said she was one of the ugliest women he'd ever seen. I could hardly believe it when I heard him say that, but I think now perhaps I was lucky I never *did* see her again. What's she doing now? Alive still?'

'No. She died about two or three weeks ago, as a matter of fact,' said Tommy.

'Did she really, did she really? Yes, I suppose she'd

be – what now, she'd be seventy-five or seventy-six? Bit older than that perhaps.'

'She was eighty,' said Tommy.

'Fancy now. Dark-haired lively Ada. Where did she die? Was she in a nursing home or did she live with a companion or – she never married, did she?'

'No,' said Tommy, 'she never married. She was in an old ladies' home. Rather a nice one, as a matter of fact. Sunny Ridge, it's called.'

'Yes, I've heard of that. Sunny Ridge. Someone my sister knew was there, I believe. A Mrs – now what was the name – a Mrs Carstairs? D'you ever come across her?'

'No. I didn't come across anyone much there. One just used to go and visit one's own particular relative.'

'Difficult business, too, I think. I mean, one never knows what to say to them.'

'Aunt Ada was particularly difficult,' said Tommy. 'She was a tartar, you know.'

'She would be.' The General chuckled. 'She could be a regular little devil when she liked when she was a girl.'

He sighed.

'Devilish business, getting old. One of my sister's friends used to get fancies, poor old thing. Used to say she'd killed somebody.'

'Good Lord,' said Tommy. 'Had she?'

'Oh, I don't suppose so. Nobody seems to think she had. I suppose,' said the General, considering the idea thoughtfully, 'I suppose she *might* have, you know. If you go about saying things like that quite cheerfully, nobody *would* believe you, would they? Entertaining thought that, isn't it?'

'Who did she think she'd killed?'

'Blessed if I know. Husband perhaps? Don't know who he was or what he was like. She was a widow when we first came to know her. Well,' he added with a sigh, 'sorry to hear about Ada. Didn't see it in the paper. If I had I'd have sent flowers or something. Bunch of rosebuds or something of that kind. That's what girls used to wear on their evening dresses. A bunch of rosebuds on the shoulder of an evening dress. Very pretty it was. I remember Ada had an evening dress – sort of hydrangea colour, mauvy. Mauvy-blue and she had pink rosebuds on it. She gave me one once. They weren't real, of course. Artificial. I kept it for a long time – years. I know,' he added, catching Tommy's eye, 'makes you laugh to think of it, doesn't it. I tell you, my boy, when you get really old and *gaga* like I am, you get sentimental again. Well, I suppose I'd better toddle off and go back to the last act of this ridiculous show. Best regards to Mrs T. when you get home.'

In the train the next day, Tommy thought back over this conversation, smiling to himself and trying again to picture his redoubtable aunt and the fierce Major-General in their young days.

'I must tell Tuppence this. It'll make her laugh,' said Tommy. 'I wonder what Tuppence has been doing while I've been away?'

He smiled to himself.

II

The faithful Albert opened the front door with a beaming smile of welcome.

'Glad to see you back, sir.'

'I'm glad to be back –' Tommy surrendered his suitcase – 'Where's Mrs Beresford?'

'Not back yet, sir.'

'Do you mean she's away?'

'Been away three or four days. But she'll be back for dinner. She rang up yesterday and said so.'

'What's she up to, Albert?'

'I couldn't say, sir. She took the car, but she took a lot of railway guides as well. She might be anywhere, as you might say.'

'You might indeed,' said Tommy with feeling. 'John o' Groat's – or Land's End – and probably missed the connection at Little Dither on the Marsh on the way back. God bless British Railways. She rang up yesterday, you say. Did she say where she was ringing from?'

'She didn't say.'

'What time yesterday was this?'

'Yesterday morning. Before lunch. Just said everything was all right. She wasn't quite sure of what time she'd get home, but she thought she'd be back well before dinner and suggested a chicken. That do you all right, sir?'

'Yes,' said Tommy, regarding his watch, 'but she'll have to make it pretty quickly now.'

'I'll hold the chicken back,' said Albert.

Tommy grinned. 'That's right,' he said. 'Catch it by the tail. How've you been, Albert? All well at home?'

'Had a scare of measles – But it's all right. Doctor says it's only strawberry rash.'

'Good,' said Tommy. He went upstairs, whistling a tune to himself. He went into the bathroom, shaved and washed, strode from there into the bedroom and looked around him. It had that curious look of disoccupancy some bedrooms put on when their owner is away. Its atmosphere was cold and unfriendly. Everything was scrupulously tidy and scrupulously clean. Tommy had the depressed feeling that a faithful dog might have had. Looking round him, he thought it was as though

Tuppence had never been. No spilled powder, no book cast down open with its back splayed out.

'Sir.'

It was Albert, standing in the doorway.

'Well?'

'I'm getting worried about the chicken.'

'Oh damn the chicken,' said Tommy. 'You seem to have that chicken on your nerves.'

'Well, I took it as you and she wouldn't be later than eight. Not later than eight, sitting down, I mean.'

'I should have thought so, too,' said Tommy, glancing at his wrist watch. 'Good Lord, is it nearly five and twenty to nine?'

'Yes it is, sir. And the chicken –'

'Oh, come on,' said Tommy, 'you get that chicken out of the oven and you and I'll eat it between us. Serve Tuppence right. Getting back well before dinner indeed!'

'Of course some people do eat dinner late,' said Albert. 'I went to Spain once and believe me, you couldn't get a meal before ten o'clock. Ten p.m. I ask you! Heathens!'

'All right,' said Tommy, absentmindedly. 'By the way, have you no idea where she has been all this time?'

'You mean the missus? I dunno, sir. Rushing around, I'd say. Her first idea was going to places by train, as far as I can make out. She was always looking in A.B.C.s and timetables and things.'

'Well,' said Tommy, 'we all have our ways of amusing ourselves, I suppose. Hers seems to have been railway travel. I wonder where she is all the same. Sitting in the Ladies' Waiting Room at Little Dither on the Marsh, as likely as not.'

'She knew as you was coming home today though, didn't she, sir?' said Albert. 'She'll get here somehow. Sure to.'

Tommy perceived that he was being offered loyal allegiance. He and Albert were linked together in expressing disapprobation of a Tuppence who in the course of her flirtations with British Railways was neglecting to come home in time to give a returning husband his proper welcome.

Albert went away to release the chicken from its possible fate of cremation in the oven.

Tommy, who had been about to follow him, stopped and looked towards the mantelpiece. He walked slowly to it and looked at the picture that hung there. Funny, her being so sure that she had seen that particular house before. Tommy felt quite certain that *he* hadn't seen it. Anyway, it was quite an ordinary house. There must be plenty of houses like that.

He stretched up as far as he could towards it and then, still not able to get a good view, unhooked it and took it close to the electric lamp. A quiet, gentle house. There was the artist's signature. The name began with a B though he couldn't make out exactly what the name was. Bosworth – Bouchier – He'd get a magnifying glass and look at it more closely. A merry chime of cowbells came from the hall. Albert had highly approved of the Swiss cowbells that Tommy and Tuppence had brought back some time or other from Grindelwald. He was something of a virtuoso on them. Dinner was served. Tommy went to the dining-room. It was odd, he thought, that Tuppence hadn't turned up by now. Even if she had had a puncture, which seemed probable, he rather wondered that she hadn't rung up to explain or excuse her delay.

'She might know that I'd worry,' said Tommy to himself. Not, of course, that he ever *did* worry – not about Tuppence. Tuppence was always all right. Albert contradicted this mood.

'Hope she hasn't had an accident,' he remarked, presenting Tommy with a dish of cabbage, and shaking his head gloomily.

'Take that away. You know I hate cabbage,' said Tommy. 'Why should she have had an accident? It's only half past nine now.'

'Being on the road is plain murder nowadays,' said Albert. 'Anyone might have an accident.'

The telephone bell rang. 'That's her,' said Albert.

Hastily reposing the dish of cabbage on the sideboard, he hurried out of the room. Tommy rose, abandoning his plate of chicken, and followed Albert. He was just saying 'Here, I'll take it,' when Albert spoke.

'Yes, sir? Yes, Mr Beresford is at home. Here he is now.' He turned his head to Tommy. 'It's a Dr Murray for you, sir.'

'Dr Murray?' Tommy thought for a moment. The name seemed familiar but for the moment he couldn't remember who Dr Murray was. If Tuppence had had an accident – and then with a sigh of relief he remembered that Dr Murray had been the doctor who attended the old ladies at Sunny Ridge. Something, perhaps, to do with Aunt Ada's funeral forms. True child of his time, Tommy immediately assumed that it must be a question of some form or other – something he ought to have signed, or Dr Murray ought to have signed.

'Hullo,' he said, 'Beresford here.'

'Oh, I'm glad to catch you. You remember me, I hope. I attended your aunt, Miss Fanshawe.'

'Yes, of course I remember. What can I do?'

'I really wanted to have a word or two with you sometime. I don't know if we can arrange a meeting, perhaps in town one day?'

'Oh I expect so, yes. Quite easily. But – er – is it something you can't say over the phone?'

'I'd rather not say it over the telephone. There's no immediate hurry. I won't pretend there is but – but I should like to have a chat with you.'

'Nothing wrong?' said Tommy, and wondered why he put it that way. Why should there be anything wrong?

'Not really. I may be making a mountain out of a molehill. Probably am. But there have been some rather curious developments at Sunny Ridge.'

'Nothing to do with Mrs Lancaster, is it?' asked Tommy.

'Mrs Lancaster?' The doctor seemed surprised. 'Oh no. She left some time ago. In fact – before your aunt died. This is something quite different.'

'I've been away – only just got back. May I ring you up tomorrow morning – we could fix something then.'

'Right. I'll give you my telephone number. I shall be at my surgery until ten a.m.'

'Bad news?' asked Albert as Tommy returned to the dining-room.

'For God's sake, don't croak, Albert,' said Tommy irritably. 'No – of course it isn't bad news.'

'I thought perhaps the missus –'

'She's all right,' said Tommy. 'She always is. Probably gone haring off after some wild-cat clue or other – You know what she's like. I'm not going to worry any more. Take away this plate of chicken – You've been keeping it hot in the oven and it's inedible. Bring me some coffee. And then I'm going to bed.

'There will probably be a letter tomorrow. Delayed in the post – you know what our posts are like – or there will be a wire from her – or she'll ring up.'

But there was no letter next day – no telephone call – no wire.

Albert eyed Tommy, opened his mouth and shut it again several times, judging quite rightly that gloomy predictions on his part would not be welcomed.

At last Tommy had pity on him. He swallowed a last mouthful of toast and marmalade, washed it down with coffee, and spoke –

'All right, Albert, I'll say it first – *Where is she?* What's happened to her? And what are we going to do about it?'

'Get on to the police, sir?'

'I'm not sure. You see –' Tommy paused.

'If she's had an accident –'

'She's got her driving licence on her – and plenty of identifying papers – Hospitals are very prompt at reporting these things – and getting in touch with relatives – all that. I don't want to be precipitate – she – she mightn't want it. You've no idea – no idea at all, Albert, where she was going – Nothing she said? No particular place – or county. Not a mention of some name?'

Albert shook his head.

'What was she feeling like? Pleased? – Excited? Unhappy? Worried?'

Albert's response was immediate.

'Pleased as Punch – Bursting with it.'

'Like a terrier off on the trail,' said Tommy.

'That's right, sir – you know how she gets –'

'On to something – Now I wonder –' Tommy paused in consideration.

Something had turned up, and, as he had just said to Albert, Tuppence had rushed off like a terrier on the scent. The day before yesterday she had rung up to announce her return. Why, then, hadn't she returned? Perhaps, at this moment, thought Tommy, she's sitting somewhere telling lies to people so hard that she can't think of anything else!

If she were engrossed in pursuit, she would be extremely annoyed if he, Tommy, were to rush off to the police bleating like a sheep that his wife had disappeared – He could hear Tuppence saying 'How you could be so fatuous as to do such a thing! I can look after myself *perfectly*. You ought to know that by this time!' (But could she look after herself?)

One was never quite sure where Tuppence's imagination could take her.

Into *danger*? There hadn't, so far, been any evidence

of danger in this business – Except, as aforesaid, in Tuppence's imagination.

If he were to go to the police, saying his wife had not returned home as she announced she was going to do – The police would sit there, looking tactful though possibly grinning inwardly, and would then presumably, still in a tactful way, ask what men friends his wife had got!

'I'll find her myself,' declared Tommy. 'She's *somewhere.* Whether it's north, south, east or west I've no idea – and she was a silly cuckoo not to leave word when she rang up, where she was.'

'A gang's got her, perhaps –' said Albert.

'Oh! be your age, Albert, you've outgrown that sort of stuff years ago!'

'What are you going to do, sir?'

'I'm going to London,' said Tommy, glancing at the clock. 'First I'm going to have lunch at my club with Dr Murray who rang me up last night, and who's got something to say to me about my late deceased aunt's affairs – I might possibly get a useful hint from him – After all, this business started at Sunny Ridge. I am also taking that picture that's hanging over our bedroom mantelpiece up with me –'

'You mean you're taking it to Scotland Yard?'

'No,' said Tommy. 'I'm taking it to Bond Street.'

Chapter 11

Bond Street and Dr Murray

Tommy jumped out of a taxi, paid the driver and leaned back into the cab to take out a rather clumsily done up parcel which was clearly a picture. Tucking as much of it as he could under his arm, he entered the New Athenian Galleries, one of the longest established and most important picture galleries in London.

Tommy was not a great patron of the arts but he had come to the New Athenian because he had a friend who officiated there.

'Officiated' was the only word to use because the air of sympathetic interest, the hushed voice, the pleasurable smile, all seemed highly ecclesiastical.

A fair-haired young man detached himself and came forward, his face lighting up with a smile of recognition.

'Hullo, Tommy,' he said. 'Haven't seen you for a long time. What's that you've got under your arm?

Don't tell me you've been taking to painting pictures in your old age? A lot of people do – results usually deplorable.'

'I doubt if creative art was ever my long suit,' said Tommy. 'Though I must admit I found myself strongly attracted the other day by a small book telling in the simplest terms how a child of five can learn to paint in water colours.'

'God help us if you're going to take to that. Grandma Moses in reverse.'

'To tell you the truth, Robert, I merely want to appeal to your expert knowledge of pictures. I want your opinion on this.'

Deftly Robert took the picture from Tommy and skilfully removed its clumsy wrappings with the expertise of a man accustomed to handle the parcelling up and deparcelling of all different-sized works of art. He took the picture and set it on a chair, peered into it to look at it, and then withdrew five or six steps away. He turned his gaze towards Tommy.

'Well,' he said, 'what about it? What do you want to know? Do you want to sell it, is that it?'

'No,' said Tommy, 'I don't want to sell it, Robert. I want to know about it. To begin with, I want to know who painted it.'

'Actually,' said Robert, 'if you *had* wanted to sell it, it would be quite saleable nowadays. It wouldn't have been, ten years ago. But Boscowan's just coming into fashion again.'

'Boscowan?' Tommy looked at him inquiringly. 'Is that the name of the artist? I saw it was signed with something beginning with B but I couldn't read the name.'

'Oh, it's Boscowan all right. Very popular painter about twenty-five years ago. Sold well, had plenty of shows. People bought him all right. Technically a very good painter. Then, in the usual cycle of events, he went out of fashion. Finally, hardly any demand at all for his works but lately he's had a revival. He, Stitchwort, and Fondella. They're all coming up.'

'Boscowan,' repeated Tommy.

'B-o-s-c-o-w-a-n,' said Robert obligingly.

'Is he still painting?'

'No. He's dead. Died some years ago. Quite an old chap by then. Sixty-five, I think, when he died. Quite a prolific painter, you know. A lot of his canvases about. Actually we're thinking of having a show of him here in about four or five months' time. We ought to do well over it, I think. Why are you so interested in him?'

'It'd be too long a story to tell you,' said Tommy. 'One of these days I'll ask you out to lunch and give you the doings from the beginning. It's a long, complicated and really rather an idiotic story. All I wanted to know is all about this Boscowan and if you happen to know by any chance where this house is that's represented here.'

'I couldn't tell you the last for a moment. It's the sort of thing he did paint, you know. Small country houses in rather isolated spots usually, sometimes a farmhouse, sometimes just a cow or two around. Sometimes a farm cart, but if so, in the far distance. Quiet rural scenes. Nothing sketchy or messy. Sometimes the surface looks almost like enamel. It was a peculiar technique and people liked it. A good many of the things he painted were in France, Normandy mostly. Churches. I've got one picture of his here now. Wait a minute and I'll get it for you.'

He went to the head of the staircase and shouted down to someone below. Presently he came back holding a small canvas which he propped on another chair.

'There you are,' he said. 'Church in Normandy.'

'Yes,' said Tommy, 'I see. The same sort of thing. My wife says nobody ever lived in that house – the one I brought in. I see now what she meant. I don't see that anybody was attending service in that church or ever will.'

'Well, perhaps your wife's got something. Quiet, peaceful dwellings with no human occupancy. He didn't often paint people, you know. Sometimes there's a figure or two in the landscape, but more often not. In a way I think that gives them their special charm. A sort of isolationist feeling. It was as though he removed all the human beings, and the peace of the countryside was all the better without them. Come to think of it, that's maybe why the general taste has swung round to him. Too many people nowadays, too many cars, too many noises on the road, too much noise and bustle. Peace, perfect peace. Leave it all to Nature.'

'Yes, I shouldn't wonder. What sort of a man was he?'

'I didn't know him personally. Before my time. Pleased with himself by all accounts. Thought he was a better painter than he was, probably. Put on a bit of side. Kindly, quite likeable. Eye for the girls.'

'And you've no idea where this particular piece of countryside exists? It *is* England, I suppose.'

'I should think so, yes. Do you want me to find out for you?'

'Could you?'

'Probably the best thing to do would be to ask his wife, his widow rather. He married Emma Wing, the sculptor. Well known. Not very productive. Does quite powerful work. You could go and ask her. She lives in Hampstead. I can give you the address. We've been corresponding with her a good deal lately over the question of this show of her husband's work we're doing. We're having a few of her smaller pieces of sculpture as well. I'll get the address for you.'

He went to the desk, turned over a ledger, scrawled something on a card and brought it back.

'There you are, Tommy,' he said. 'I don't know what the deep dark mystery is. Always been a man of mystery, haven't you? It's a nice representation of Boscowan's work you've got there. We might like to use it for the show. I'll send you a line to remind you nearer the time.'

'You don't know a Mrs Lancaster, do you?'

'Well, I can't think of one off-hand. Is she an artist or something of the kind?'

'No, I don't think so. She's just an old lady living for the last few years in an old ladies' home. She comes into it because this picture belonged to her until she gave it away to an aunt of mine.'

'Well I can't say the name means anything to me. Better go and talk to Mrs Boscowan.'

'What's she like?'

'She was a good bit younger than he was, I should say. Quite a personality.' He nodded his head once or twice. 'Yes, quite a personality. You'll find that out I expect.'

He took the picture, handed it down the staircase with instructions to someone below to do it up again.

'Nice for you having so many myrmidons at your beck and call,' said Tommy.

He looked round him, noticing his surroundings for the first time.

'What's this you've got here now?' he said with distaste.

'Paul Jaggerowski – Interesting young Slav. Said to produce all his works under the influence of drugs – Don't you like him?'

Tommy concentrated his gaze on a big string bag which seemed to have enmeshed itself in a metallic green field full of distorted cows.

'Frankly, no.'

'Philistine,' said Robert. 'Come out and have a bite of lunch.'

'Can't. I've got a meeting with a doctor at my club.'

'Not ill, are you?'

'I'm in the best of health. My blood pressure is so good that it disappoints every doctor to whom I submit it.'

'Then what do you want to see a doctor for?'

'Oh,' said Tommy cheerfully – 'I've just got to see a doctor about a body. Thanks for your help. Good-bye.'

II

Tommy greeted Dr Murray with some curiosity – He presumed it was some formal matter to do with Aunt Ada's decease, but why on earth Dr Murray would not at least mention the subject of his visit over the telephone, Tommy couldn't imagine.

'I'm afraid I'm a little late,' said Dr Murray, shaking hands, 'but the traffic was pretty bad and I wasn't exactly sure of the locality. I don't know this part of London very well.'

'Well, too bad you had to come all the way here,' said Tommy. 'I could have met you somewhere more convenient, you know.'

'You've time on your hands then just now?'

'Just at the moment, yes. I've been away for the last week.'

'Yes, I believe someone told me so when I rang up.'

Tommy indicated a chair, suggested refreshment, placed cigarettes and matches by Dr Murray's side. When the two men had established themselves comfortably Dr Murray opened the conversation.

'I'm sure I've aroused your curiosity,' he said, 'but as a matter of fact we're in a spot of trouble at Sunny Ridge. It's a difficult and perplexing matter and in one way it's nothing to do with you. I've no earthly right to trouble you with it but there's just an off chance that you might know something which would help me.'

'Well, of course, I'll do anything I can. Something to do with my aunt, Miss Fanshawe?'

'Not directly, no. But in a way she does come into it. I can speak to you in confidence, can't I, Mr Beresford?'

'Yes, certainly.'

'As a matter of fact I was talking the other day to a mutual friend of ours. He was telling me a few things about you. I gather that in the last war you had rather a delicate assignment.'

'Oh, I wouldn't put it quite as seriously as that,' said Tommy, in his most non-committal manner.

'Oh no, I quite realize that it's not a thing to be talked about.'

'I don't really think that matters nowadays. It's a good long time since the war. My wife and I were younger then.'

'Anyway, it's nothing to do with that, that I want to talk to you about, but at least I feel that I can speak frankly to you, that I can trust you not to repeat what I am now saying, though it's possible that it all may have to come out later.'

'A spot of trouble at Sunny Ridge, you say?'

'Yes. Not very long ago one of our patients died. A Mrs Moody. I don't know if you ever met her or if your aunt ever talked about her.'

'Mrs Moody?' Tommy reflected. 'No, I don't think so. Anyway, not so far as I remember.'

'She was not one of our older patients. She was still on the right side of seventy and she was not seriously ill in any way. It was just a case of a woman with no near relatives and no one to look after her in the domestic line. She fell into the category of what I often call to myself a flutterer. Women who more and more resemble hens as they grow older. They cluck. They forget things. They run themselves into difficulties and they worry. They get themselves wrought up about nothing at all. There is very little the matter with them. They are not strictly speaking mentally disturbed.'

'But they just cluck,' Tommy suggested.

'As you say. Mrs Moody clucked. She caused the nurses a fair amount of trouble although they were quite fond of her. She had a habit of forgetting when she'd had her meals, making a fuss because no dinner had been served to her when as a matter of fact she had actually just eaten a very good dinner.'

'Oh,' said Tommy, enlightened, 'Mrs Cocoa.'

'I beg your pardon?'

'I'm sorry,' said Tommy, 'it's a name my wife and I had for her. She was yelling for Nurse Jane one day when we passed along the passage and saying she hadn't had her cocoa. Rather a nice-looking scatty little woman. But it made us both laugh, and we fell into the habit of calling her Mrs Cocoa. And so she's died.'

'I wasn't particularly surprised when the death happened,' said Dr Murray. 'To be able to prophesy with any exactitude when elderly women will die is practically impossible. Women whose health is seriously affected, who, one feels as a result of physical examination, will hardly last the year out, sometimes are good for another ten years. They have a tenacious hold on life which mere physical disability will not quench. There are other people whose health is reasonably good and who may, one thinks, make old bones. They on the other hand, catch bronchitis, or 'flu, seem unable to have the stamina to recuperate from it, and die with surprising ease. So, as I say, as a medical attendant to an elderly ladies' home, I am not surprised when what might be called a fairly unexpected death occurs. This case of Mrs Moody, however, was somewhat different. She died in her sleep without having exhibited any sign of illness and I could not help feeling that in my opinion her death was unexpected. I will use the phrase that has always intrigued me in Shakespeare's play, *Macbeth.* I have always wondered what Macbeth meant when he said of his wife, "She should have died hereafter."'

'Yes, I remember wondering once myself what Shakespeare was getting at,' said Tommy. 'I forget whose production it was and who was playing Macbeth, but there was a strong suggestion in that particular production, and Macbeth certainly played it in a way to suggest that he was hinting to the medical attendant that Lady Macbeth would be better out of the way. Presumably the medical attendant took the hint. It was then that Macbeth, feeling safe after his wife's death, feeling that she could no longer damage him by her indiscretions or her rapidly failing mind, expresses his genuine affection and grief for her. "She should have died hereafter."'

'Exactly,' said Dr Murray. 'It is what I felt about Mrs Moody. I felt that she should have died hereafter. Not just three weeks ago of no apparent cause –'

Tommy did not reply. He merely looked at the doctor inquiringly.

'Medical men have certain problems. If you are puzzled over the cause of a patient's death there is only one sure way to tell. By a post mortem. Post mortems are not appreciated by relatives of the deceased, but if a doctor demands a post mortem and the result is, as it perfectly well may be, a case of natural causes, or some disease or malady which does not always give outward signs or symptoms, then the doctor's career can be quite seriously affected by his having made a questionable diagnosis –'

'I can see that it must have been difficult.'

'The relatives in question are distant cousins. So I took it upon myself to get their consent as it was a matter of medical interest to know the cause of death. When a patient dies in her sleep it is advisable to add to one's medical knowledge. I wrapped it up a good bit, mind you, didn't make it too formal. Luckily they couldn't care less. I felt very relieved in mind. Once the autopsy had been performed and if all was well, I could give a death certificate without a qualm. Anyone can die of what is amateurishly called heart failure, from one of several different causes. Actually Mrs Moody's heart was in really very good shape for her age. She suffered from arthritis and rheumatism and occasional trouble with her liver, but none of these things seemed to accord with her passing away in her sleep.'

Dr Murray came to a stop. Tommy opened his lips and then shut them again. The doctor nodded.

'Yes, Mr Beresford. You can see where I am tending. Death has resulted from an overdose of morphine.'

'Good Lord!' Tommy stared and the ejaculation escaped him.

'Yes. It seemed quite incredible, but there was no getting away from the analysis. The question was: How was that morphia administered? She was not on morphia. She was not a patient who suffered pain. There were three possibilities, of course. She might have taken it by accident. Unlikely. She might have got hold of some other patient's medicine by mistake but that again is not particularly likely. Patients are not entrusted with supplies of morphia, and we do not accept drug addicts who might have a supply of such things in their possession. It could have been deliberate suicide but I should be very slow to accept that. Mrs Moody, though a worrier, was of a perfectly cheerful disposition and I am quite sure had never thought of ending her life. The third possibility is that a fatal overdose was deliberately administered to her. But by whom, and why? Naturally, there are supplies of morphia and other drugs which Miss Packard as a registered hospital nurse and matron, is perfectly entitled to have in her possession and which she keeps in a locked cupboard. In such cases as sciatica or rheumatoid arthritis there can be such severe and desperate pain that morphia is occasionally administered. We have hoped that we may come across some circumstance in which Mrs Moody had a dangerous amount of morphia administered to her by mistake or which she herself took under the delusion that it was a cure for indigestion or insomnia. We have not been able to find any such circumstances possible. The next thing we have done, at Miss Packard's suggestion and I agreed with her, is to look carefully into the records of such deaths as have taken place at Sunny Ridge in the last two years. There have not been many of them, I am glad to say. I think seven in all, which is a pretty fair average for people of that age group. Two deaths of bronchitis, perfectly straightforward, two of 'flu, always a possible killer during the winter months owing to the slight resistance offered by frail, elderly women. And three others.'

He paused and said, 'Mr Beresford, I am not satisfied about those three others, certainly not about two of them. They were perfectly probable, they were not unexpected, but I will go as far as saying that they were *unlikely*. They are not cases that on reflection and research I am entirely satisfied about. One has to accept the possibility that, unlikely as it seems, there is someone at Sunny Ridge who is, possibly for mental reasons, a killer. An entirely unsuspected killer.'

There was silence for some moments. Tommy gave a sigh.

'I don't doubt what you've told me,' he said, 'but all the same, frankly, it seems unbelievable. These things – surely, they can't happen.'

'Oh yes,' said Dr Murray grimly, 'they happen all right. You go over some of the pathological cases. A woman who took on domestic service. She worked as a cook in various households. She was a nice, kind, pleasant-seeming woman, gave her employers faithful service, cooked well, enjoyed being with them. Yet, sooner or later, things happened. Usually a plate of sandwiches. Sometimes picnic food. For no apparent motive arsenic was added. Two or three poisoned sandwiches among the rest. Apparently sheer chance dictated who took and ate them. There seemed no personal venom. Sometimes no tragedy happened. The same woman was three or four months in a situation and there was no trace of illness. Nothing. Then she left to go to another job, and in that next job, within three weeks, two of the family died after eating bacon for breakfast. The fact that all these things happened in different parts of England and at irregular intervals made it some time before the police got on her track. She used a different name, of course, each time. But there are so many pleasant, capable, middle-aged women who can cook, it was hard to find out which particular woman it was.'

'Why did she do it?'

'I don't think anybody has ever really known. There have been several different theories, especially of course by psychologists. She was a somewhat religious woman and it seems possible that some form of religious insanity made her feel that she had a divine command to rid the world of certain people, but it does not seem that she herself had borne them any personal animus.

'Then there was the French woman, Jeanne Gebron, who was called The Angel of Mercy. She was so upset when her neighbours had ill children, she hurried to nurse those children. Sat devotedly at their bedside. There again it was some time before people discovered that the children she nursed *never recovered. Instead they all died.* And *why*? It is true that when she was young her own child died. She appeared to be prostrated with grief. Perhaps that was the cause of her career of crime. If *her* child died so should the children of other women. Or it may be, as some thought, that her own child was also one of the victims.'

'You're giving me chills down my spine,' said Tommy.

'I'm taking the most melodramatic examples,' said the doctor. 'It may be something much simpler than that. You remember in the case of Armstrong, anyone who had in any way offended him or insulted him, or indeed, if he even thought anyone had insulted him, that person was quickly asked to tea and given arsenic sandwiches. A sort of intensified touchiness. His first crimes were obviously mere crimes for personal advantage. Inheriting of money. The removal of a wife so that he could marry another woman.

'Then there was Nurse Warriner who kept a Home for elderly people. They made over what means they had to her, and were guaranteed a comfortable old age until death came – But death did not delay very long. There, too, it was morphia that was administered – a very kindly woman, but with no scruples – she regarded herself, I believe, as a benefactor.'

'You've no idea, if your surmise about these deaths is true, who it could be?'

'No. There seems no pointer of any kind. Taking the view that the killer is probably insane, insanity is a very difficult thing to recognize in some of its manifestations. Is it somebody, shall we say, who dislikes elderly people, who had been injured or has had her life ruined or so she thinks, by somebody elderly? Or is it possibly someone who has her own ideas of mercy killing and thinks that everyone over sixty years of age should be kindly exterminated. It could be anyone, of course. A patient? Or a member of the staff – a nurse or a domestic worker?

'I have discussed this at great length with Millicent Packard who runs the place. She is a highly competent woman, shrewd, businesslike, with keen supervision both of the guests there and of her own staff. She insists that she has no suspicion and no clue whatever and I am sure that is perfectly true.'

'But why come to me? What can I do?'

'Your aunt, Miss Fanshawe, was a resident there for some years – she was a woman of very considerable mental capacity, though she often pretended otherwise. She had unconventional ways of amusing herself by putting on an appearance of senility. But she was actually very much all there – What I want you to try and do, Mr Beresford, is to think hard – you and your wife, too – Is there anything you can remember that Miss Fanshawe ever said or hinted, that might give us a clue – Something she had seen or noticed, something that someone had told her, something that she herself had thought peculiar. Old ladies see and notice a lot, and a really shrewd one like Miss Fanshawe would know a surprising amount of what went on in a place like Sunny Ridge. These old ladies are not busy, you see, they have all the time in the world to look around them and make deductions – and even jump to conclusions – that may seem fantastic, but are sometimes, surprisingly, entirely correct.'

Tommy shook his head.

'I know what you mean – But I can't remember anything of that kind.'

'Your wife's away from home, I gather. You don't think she might remember something that hadn't struck you?'

'I'll ask her – but I doubt it.' He hesitated, then made up his mind. 'Look here, there was something that worried my wife – about one of the old ladies, a Mrs Lancaster.'

'Mrs Lancaster? Yes?'

'My wife's got it into her head that Mrs Lancaster has been taken away by some so-called relations very suddenly. As a matter of fact, Mrs Lancaster gave a picture to my aunt as a present, and my wife felt that she ought to offer to return the picture to Mrs Lancaster, so she tried to get in touch with her to know if Mrs Lancaster would like the picture returned to her.'

'Well, that was very thoughtful of Mrs Beresford, I'm sure.'

'Only she found it very hard to get in touch with her. She got the address of the hotel where they were supposed to be staying – Mrs Lancaster and her relations – but nobody of that name had been staying there or had booked rooms there.'

'Oh? That was rather odd.'

'Yes. Tuppence thought it was rather odd, too. They had left no other forwarding address at Sunny Ridge. In fact, we have made several attempts to get in touch with Mrs Lancaster, or with this Mrs – Johnson I think the name was – but have been quite unable to get in touch with them. There was a solicitor who I believe paid all the bills – and made all the arrangements with Miss Packard and we got into communication with him. But he could only give me the address of a bank. Banks,' said Tommy drily, 'don't give you any information.'

'Not if they've been told not to by their clients, I agree.'

'My wife wrote to Mrs Lancaster care of the bank, and also to Mrs Johnson, but she's never had any reply.'

'That seems a little unusual. Still, people don't always answer letters. They may have gone abroad.'

'Quite so – it didn't worry me. But it has worried my wife. She seems convinced that something has happened to Mrs Lancaster. In fact, during the time I was away from home, she said she was going to investigate further – I don't know what exactly she meant to do, perhaps see the hotel personally, or the bank, or try the solicitor. Anyway, she was going to try and get a little more information.'

Dr Murray looked at him politely, but with a trace of patient boredom in his manner.

'What did she think exactly –?'

'She thinks that Mrs Lancaster is in danger of some kind – even that something may have happened to her.'

The doctor raised his eyebrows.

'Oh! really, I should hardly think –'

'This may seem quite idiotic to you,' said Tommy, 'but you see, my wife rang up saying she would be back yesterday evening – and – *she didn't arrive*.'

'She said definitely that she *was* coming back?'

'Yes. She knew I was coming home, you see, from this conference business. So she rang up to let our man, Albert, know that she'd be back to dinner.'

'And that seems to you an unlikely thing for her to do?' said Murray. He was now looking at Tommy with some interest.

'Yes,' said Tommy. 'It's *very* unlike Tuppence. If she'd been delayed or changed her plans she would have rung up again or sent a telegram.'

'And you're worried about her?'

'Yes, I am,' said Tommy.

'H'm! Have you consulted the police?'

'No,' said Tommy. 'What'd the police think? It's not as though I had any reason to believe that she is in trouble or danger or anything of that kind. I mean, if she'd had an accident or was in a hospital, anything like that, somebody would communicate with me soon enough, wouldn't they?'

'I should say so – yes – if she had some means of identification on her.'

'She'd have her driving licence on her. Probably letters and various other things.'

Dr Murray frowned.

Tommy went on in a rush:

'And now you come along – And bring up all this business of Sunny Ridge – People who've died when they oughtn't to have died. Supposing this old bean got on to something – saw something, or suspected something – and began chattering about it – She'd have to be silenced in some way, so she was whisked out of it quickly, and taken off to some place or other where she wouldn't be traced. I can't help feeling that the whole thing ties up somehow –'

'It's odd – it's certainly odd – What do you propose to do next?'

'I'm going to do a bit of searching myself – Try these solicitors first – They may be quite all right, but I'd like to have a look at them, and draw my own conclusions.'

Chapter 12

Tommy Meets an Old Friend

From the opposite side of the road, Tommy surveyed the premises of Messrs. Partingdale, Harris, Lockeridge and Partingdale.

They looked eminently respectable and old-fashioned. The brass plate was well worn but nicely polished. He crossed the street and passed through swing doors to be greeted by the muted note of typewriters at full speed.

He addressed himself to an open mahogany window on his right which bore the legend INQUIRIES –

Inside was a small room where three women were typing and two male clerks were bending over desks copying documents.

There was a faint, musty atmosphere with a decidedly legal flavour.

A woman of thirty-five odd, with a severe air, faded blonde hair, and *pince-nez* rose from her typewriter and came to the window.

'Can I help you?'

'I would like to see Mr Eccles.'

The woman's air of severity redoubled.

'Have you an appointment?'

'I'm afraid not. I'm just passing through London today.'

'I'm afraid Mr Eccles is rather busy this morning. Perhaps another member of the firm –'

'It was Mr Eccles I particularly wanted to see. I have already had some correspondence with him.'

'Oh I see. Perhaps you'll give me your name.'

Tommy gave his name and address and the blonde woman retired to confer with the telephone on her desk. After a murmured conversation she returned.

'The clerk will show you into the waiting-room. Mr Eccles will be able to see you in about ten minutes' time.'

Tommy was ushered into a waiting-room which had a bookcase of rather ancient and ponderous-looking law tomes and a round table covered with various financial papers. Tommy sat there and went over in his own mind his planned methods of approach. He wondered what Mr Eccles would be like. When he was shown in at last and Mr Eccles rose from a desk to receive him, he decided for no particular reason that he could name to himself that he did not like Mr Eccles. He also wondered why he did not like Mr Eccles. There seemed no valid reason for dislike. Mr

Eccles was a man of between forty and fifty with greyish hair thinning a little at the temples. He had a long rather sad-looking face with a particularly wooden expression, shrewd eyes, and quite a pleasant smile which from time to time rather unexpectedly broke up the natural melancholy of his countenance.

'Mr Beresford?'

'Yes. It is really rather a trifling matter, but my wife has been worried about it. She wrote to you, I believe, or possibly she may have rung you up, to know if you could give her the address of a Mrs Lancaster.'

'Mrs Lancaster,' said Mr Eccles, retaining a perfect poker face. It was not even a question. He just left the name hanging in the air.

'A cautious man,' thought Tommy, 'but then it's second nature for lawyers to be cautious. In fact, if they were one's own lawyers one would prefer them to be cautious.'

He went on:

'Until lately living at a place called Sunny Ridge, an establishment – and a very good one – for elderly ladies. In fact, an aunt of my own was there and was extremely happy and comfortable.'

'Oh yes, of course, of course. I remember now. Mrs Lancaster. She is, I think, no longer living there? That is right, is it not?'

'Yes,' said Tommy.

'At the moment I do not exactly recall –' he stretched out a hand towards the telephone – 'I will just refresh my memory –'

'I can tell you quite simply,' said Tommy. 'My wife wanted Mrs Lancaster's address because she happens to be in possession of a piece of property which originally belonged to Mrs Lancaster. A picture, in fact. It was given by Mrs Lancaster as a present to my aunt, Miss Fanshawe. My aunt died recently, and her few possessions have come into our keeping. This included the picture which was given her by Mrs Lancaster. My wife likes it very much but she feels rather guilty about it. She thinks that it may be a picture Mrs Lancaster values and in that case she feels she ought to offer to return it to Mrs Lancaster.'

'Ah, I see,' said Mr Eccles. 'It is very conscientious of your wife, I am sure.'

'One never knows,' said Tommy, smiling pleasantly, 'what elderly people may feel about their possessions. She may have been glad for my aunt to have it since my aunt admired it, but as my aunt died very soon after having received this gift, it seems, perhaps, a little unfair that it should pass into the possession of strangers. There is no particular title on the picture. It represents a house somewhere in the country. For all I know it may be some family house associated with Mrs Lancaster.'

'Quite, quite,' said Mr Eccles, 'but I don't think –'

There was a knock and the door opened and a clerk entered and produced a sheet of paper which he placed before Mr Eccles. Mr Eccles looked down.

'Ah yes, ah yes, I remember now. Yes, I believe Mrs –' he glanced down at Tommy's card lying on his desk – 'Beresford rang up and had a few words with me. I advised her to get into touch with the Southern Counties Bank, Hammersmith branch. This is the only address I myself know. Letters addressed to the bank's address, care of Mrs Richard Johnson would be forwarded. Mrs Johnson is, I believe, a niece or distant cousin of Mrs Lancaster's and it was Mrs Johnson who made all the arrangements with me for Mrs Lancaster's reception at Sunny Ridge. She asked me to make full inquiries about the establishment, since she had only heard about it casually from a friend. We did so, I can assure you, most carefully. It was said to be an excellent establishment and I believe Mrs Johnson's relative, Mrs Lancaster, spent several years there quite happily.'

'She left there, though, rather suddenly,' Tommy suggested.

'Yes. Yes, I believe she did. Mrs Johnson, it seems, returned rather unexpectedly recently from East Africa – so many people have done so! She and her husband had, I believe, resided in Kenya for many years. They were making various new arrangements and felt able to assume personal care of their elderly relative. I am afraid I have no knowledge of Mrs Johnson's present whereabouts. I had a letter from her thanking me and settling accounts she owed, and directing that if there was any necessity for communicating with her I should address my letters care of the bank as she was undecided as yet where she and her husband would actually be residing. I am afraid, Mr Beresford, that that is all I know.'

His manner was gentle but firm. It displayed no embarrassment of any kind nor disturbance. But the finality of his voice was very definite. Then he unbent and his manner softened a little.

'I shouldn't really worry, you know, Mr Beresford,' he said reassuringly. 'Or rather, I shouldn't let your wife worry. Mrs Lancaster, I believe, is quite an old lady and inclined to be forgetful. She's probably forgotten all about this picture that she gave away. She is, I believe, seventy-five or seventy-six years of age. One forgets very easily at that age, you know.'

'Did you know her personally?'

'No, I never actually met her.'

'But you knew Mrs Johnson?'

'I met her when she came here occasionally to consult me as to arrangements. She seemed a pleasant, business-like woman. Quite competent in the arrangements she was making.' He rose and said, 'I am so sorry I can't help you, Mr Beresford.'

It was a gentle but firm dismissal.

Tommy came out on to the Bloomsbury street and looked about him for a taxi. The parcel he was carrying, though not heavy, was of a fairly awkward size. He looked up for a moment at the building he had just left. Eminently respectable, long established. Nothing you could fault there, nothing apparently wrong with Messrs Partingdale, Harris, Lockeridge and Partingdale, nothing wrong with Mr Eccles, no signs of alarm or despondency, no shiftiness or uneasiness. In books, Tommy thought gloomily, a mention of Mrs Lancaster or Mrs Johnson should have brought a guilty start or a shifty glance. Something to show that the names registered, that all was not well. Things didn't seem to happen like that in real life. All Mr Eccles had looked like was a man who was too polite to resent having his time wasted by such an inquiry as Tommy had just made.

But all the same, thought Tommy to himself, *I don't like Mr Eccles*. He recalled to himself vague memories of the past, of other people that he had for some reason not liked. Very often those hunches – for hunches is all they were – had been right. But perhaps it was simpler than that. If you had had a good many dealings in your time with personalities, you had a sort of feeling about them, just as an expert antique dealer knows instinctively the taste and look and feel of a forgery before getting down to expert tests and examinations. The thing just is *wrong*. The same with pictures. The same presumably with a cashier in a bank who is offered a first-class spurious banknote.

'He sounds all right,' thought Tommy. 'He looks all right, he speaks all right, but all the same –' He waved frantically at a taxi which gave him a direct and cold look, increased its speed and drove on. 'Swine,' thought Tommy.

His eyes roved up and down the street, seeking for a more obliging vehicle. A fair amount of people were walking on the pavement. A few hurrying, some strolling, one man gazing at a brass plate just across the road from him. After a close scrutiny, he turned round and Tommy's eyes opened a little wider. He knew that face. He watched the man walk to the end of the street, pause, turn and walk back again. Somebody came out of the building behind Tommy and at that moment the man opposite increased his pace a little, still walking on the other side of the road but keeping pace with the man who had come out of the door. The man who had come out of Messrs Partingdale, Harris, Lockeridge and Partingdale's doorway was, Tommy thought, looking after his retreating figure, almost certainly Mr Eccles. At the same moment a taxi lingering in a pleasant tempting manner, came along.

Tommy raised his hand, the taxi drew up, he opened the door and got in.

'Where to?'

Tommy hesitated for a moment, looking at his parcel. About to give an address he changed his mind and said, '14 Lyon Street.'

A quarter of an hour later he had reached his destination. He rang the bell after paying off the taxi and asked for Mr Ivor Smith. When he entered a second-floor room, a man sitting at a table facing the window, swung round and said with faint surprise,

'Hullo, Tommy, fancy seeing you. It's a long time. What are you doing here? Just tooling round looking up your old friends?'

'Not quite as good as that, Ivor.'

'I suppose you're on your way home after the Conference?'

'Yes.'

'All a lot of the usual talky-talky, I suppose? No conclusions drawn and nothing helpful said.'

'Quite right. All a sheer waste of time.'

'Mostly listening to old Bogie Waddock shooting his mouth off, I expect. Crashing bore. Gets worse every year.'

'Oh! well –'

Tommy sat down in the chair that was pushed towards him, accepted a cigarette, and said,

'I just wondered – it's a very long shot – whether you know anything of a derogatory nature about one Eccles, solicitor, of the firm of Messrs Partingdale, Harris, Lockeridge and Partingdale.'

'Well, well, well,' said the man called Ivor Smith. He raised his eyebrows. They were very convenient eyebrows for raising. The end of them near the nose went up and the opposite end of the cheek went down for an almost astonishing extent. They made him on very little provocation look like a man who had had a severe shock, but actually it was quite a common gesture with him. 'Run up against Eccles somewhere have you?'

'The trouble is,' said Tommy, 'that I know nothing about him.'

'And you want to know something about him?'

'Yes.'

'Hm. What made you come to see me?'

'I saw Anderson outside. It was a long time since I'd seen him but I recognized him. He was keeping someone or other under observation. Whoever it was, it was someone in the building from which I had just emerged. Two firms of lawyers practise there and one firm of chartered accountants. Of course it may be any one of them or any member of any one of them. But a man walking away down the street looked to me like Eccles. And I just wondered if by a lucky chance it could have been my Mr Eccles that Anderson was giving his attention to?'

'Hm,' said Ivor Smith. 'Well, Tommy, you always were a pretty good guesser.'

'Who *is* Eccles?'

'Don't you know? Haven't you any idea?'

'I've no idea whatever,' said Tommy. 'Without going into a long history, I went to him for some information about an old lady who has recently left an old ladies' home. The solicitor employed to make arrangements for her was Mr Eccles. He appears to have done it with perfect decorum and efficiency. I wanted her present address. He says he hasn't got it. Quite possibly he hasn't . . . but I wondered. He's the only clue to her whereabouts I've got.'

'And you want to find her?'

'Yes.'

'I don't think it sounds as though I'm going to be much good to you. Eccles is a very respectable, sound solicitor who makes a large income, has a good many highly respectable clients, works for the landed gentry, professional classes and retired soldiers and sailors, generals and admirals and all that sort of thing. He's the acme of respectability. I should imagine from what you're talking about, that he was strictly within his lawful activities.'

'But you're – interested in him,' suggested Tommy.

'Yes, we're very interested in Mr James Eccles.' He sighed. 'We've been interested in him for at least six years. We haven't progressed very far.'

'Very interesting,' said Tommy. 'I'll ask you again. Who exactly *is* Mr Eccles?'

'You mean what do we suspect Eccles of? Well, to put it in a sentence, we suspect him of being one of the best organizing brains in criminal activity in this country.'

'Criminal activity?' Tommy looked surprised.

'Oh yes, yes. No cloak and dagger. No espionage, no counter-espionage. No, plain criminal activity. He is a man who has so far as we can discover never performed a criminal act in his life. He has never stolen anything, he's never forged anything, he's never converted funds, we can't get any kind of evidence against him. But all the same whenever there's a big planned organized robbery, there we find, somewhere in the background, Mr Eccles leading a blameless life.'

'Six years,' said Tommy thoughtfully.

'Possibly even longer than that. It took a little time, to get on to the pattern of things. Bank holdups, robberies of private jewels, all sorts of things where the big money was. They're all jobs that followed a certain pattern. You couldn't help feeling that the same mind had planned them. The people who directed them and who carried them out never had to do any planning at all. They went where they were told, they did what they were ordered, they never had to think. Somebody else was doing the thinking.'

'And what made you hit on Eccles?'

Ivor Smith shook his head thoughtfully. 'It would take too long to tell you. He's a man who has a lot of acquaintances, a lot of friends. There are people he plays golf with, there are people who service his car, there are firms of stockbrokers who act for him. There are companies doing a blameless business in which he is interested. The plan is getting clearer but his part in it hasn't got much clearer, except that he is very conspicuously absent on certain occasions. A big bank robbery cleverly planned (and no expense spared, mind you), consolidating the get-away and all the rest of it, and where's Mr Eccles when it happens? Monte Carlo or Zurich or possibly even fishing for salmon in Norway. You can be quite sure Mr Eccles is never within a hundred miles of where criminal activities are happening.'

'Yet you suspect him?'

'Oh yes. I'm quite sure in my own mind. But whether we'll ever catch him I don't know. The man who tunnelled through the floor of a bank, the man who knocked out the night watchman, the cashier who was in it from the beginning, the bank manager who supplied the information, none of them know Eccles, probably they've never even seen him. There's a long chain leading away – and no one seems to know more than just one link beyond themselves.'

'The good old plan of the cell?'

'More or less, yes, but there's some original thinking. Some day we'll get a chance. Somebody who oughtn't to know *anything*, will know *something*. Something silly and trivial, perhaps, but something that strangely enough may be evidence at last.'

'Is he married – got a family?'

'No, he has never taken risks like that. He lives alone with a housekeeper and a gardener and a butler-valet. He entertains in a mild and pleasant way, and I dare swear that every single person who's entered his house as his guest is beyond suspicion.'

'And nobody's getting rich?'

'That's a good point you've put your finger on, Thomas. Somebody *ought* to be getting rich. Somebody ought to be *seen* to be getting rich. But that part of it's very cleverly arranged. Big wins on race courses, investments in stocks and shares, all things which are natural, just chancy enough to make big money at, and all apparently genuine transactions. There's a lot of money stacked up abroad in different countries and different places. It's a great big, vast, money-making concern – and the money's always on the move – going from place to place.'

'Well,' said Tommy, 'good luck to you. I hope you get your man.'

'I think I shall, you know, some day. There might be a hope if one could jolt him out of his routine.'

'Jolt him with what?'

'Danger,' said Ivor. 'Make him feel he's in danger. Make him feel someone's on to him. Get him uneasy. If you once get a man uneasy, he may do something foolish. He may make a mistake. That's the way you get chaps, you know. Take the cleverest man there is, who can plan brilliantly and never put a foot wrong. Let some little thing rattle him and he'll make a mistake. So I'm hoping. Now let's hear your story. You might know something that would be useful.'

'Nothing to do with crime, I'm afraid – very small beer.'

'Well, let's hear about it.'

Tommy told his story without undue apologies for the triviality of it. Ivor, he knew, was not a man to despise triviality. Ivor, indeed, went straight to the point which had brought Tommy on his errand.

'And your wife's disappeared, you say?'

'It's not like her.'

'That's serious.'

'Serious to me all right.'

'So I can imagine. I only met your missus once. She's sharp.'

'If she goes after things she's like a terrier on a trail,' said Thomas.

'You've not been to the police?'

'No.'

'Why not?'

'Well, first because I can't believe that she's anything but all right. Tuppence is always all right. She just goes all out after any hare that shows itself. She mayn't have had time to communicate.'

'Mmm. I don't like it very much. She's looking for a house, you say? That just *might* be interesting because among various odds and ends that we followed, which incidentally have not led to much, are a kind of trail of house agents.'

'House agents?' Tommy looked surprised.

'Yes. Nice, ordinary, rather mediocre house agents in small provincial towns in different parts of England, but none of them so very far from London. Mr Eccles's firm does a lot of business with and for house agents. Sometimes he's the solicitor for the buyers and sometimes for the sellers, and he employs various house agencies, on behalf of clients. Sometimes we rather wondered why. None of it seems very profitable, you see –'

'But you think it might mean something or lead to something?'

'Well, if you remember the big London Southern

Bank robbery some years ago, there was a house in the country – a lonely house. That was the thieves' rendezvous. They weren't very noticeable there, but that's where the stuff was brought and cached away. People in the neighbourhood began to have a few stories about them, and wonder who these people were who came and went at rather unusual hours. Different kinds of cars arriving in the middle of the night and going away again. People are curious about their neighbours in the country. Sure enough, the police raided the place, they got some of the loot, and they got three men, including one who was recognized and identified.'

'Well, didn't that lead you somewhere?'

'Not really. The men wouldn't talk, they were well defended and represented, they got long sentences in gaol and within a year and a half they were all out of the jug again. Very clever rescues.'

'I seem to remember reading about it. One man disappeared from a criminal court where he was brought up by two warders.'

'That's right. All very cleverly arranged and an enormous amount of money spent on the escape.

'But we think that whoever was responsible for the staff work realized he made a mistake in having one house for too long a time, so that the local people got interested. Somebody, perhaps, thought it would be a better idea to get subsidiaries living in, say, as many as *thirty* houses in *different places*. People come and take a house, mother and daughter, say, a widow, or a retired army man and his wife. Nice quiet people. They have a few repairs done to the house, get a local builder in and improve the plumbing, and perhaps some other firm down from London to decorate, and then after a year or a year and a half circumstances arise, and the occupiers sell the house and go off abroad to live. Something like that. All very natural and pleasant. During their tenancy that house has been used perhaps for rather unusual purposes! But no one suspects such a thing. Friends come to see them, not very often. Just occasionally. One night, perhaps, a kind of anniversary party for a middle-aged, or elderly couple; or a coming of age party. A lot of cars coming and going. Say there are five major robberies done within six months but each time the loot passes through, or is cached in, not just one of these houses, but five different houses in five different parts of the countryside. It's only a supposition as yet, my dear Tommy, but we're working on it. Let's say your old lady lets a picture of a certain house go out of her possession and supposing that's a *significant* house. And supposing that that's the house that your missus has recognized somewhere, and has gone dashing off to investigate. And supposing someone doesn't want that particular house investigated – It might tie up, you know.'

'It's very far-fetched.'

'Oh yes – I agree. But these times we live in are far-fetched times – In our particular world incredible things happen.'

II

Somewhat wearily Tommy alighted from his fourth taxi of the day and looked appraisingly at his surroundings. The taxi had deposited him in a small *cul-de-sac* which tucked itself coyly under one of the protuberances of Hampstead Heath. The *cul-de-sac* seemed to have been some artistic 'development'. Each house was wildly different from the house next to it. This particular one seemed to consist of a large studio with skylights in it, and attached to it (rather like a gumboil), on one side was what seemed to be a little cluster of three rooms. A ladder staircase painted bright green ran up the outside of the house. Tommy opened the small gate, went up a path and not seeing a bell applied himself to the knocker. Getting no response, he paused for a few moments and then started again with the knocker, a little louder this time.

The door opened so suddenly that he nearly fell backwards. A woman stood on the doorstep. At first sight Tommy's first impression was that this was one of the plainest women he had ever seen. She had a large expanse of flat, pancake-like face, two enormous eyes which seemed of impossibly different colours, one green and one brown, a noble forehead with a quantity of wild hair rising up from it in a kind of thicket. She wore a purple overall with blotches of clay on it, and Tommy noticed that the hand that held the door open was one of exceeding beauty of structure.

'Oh,' she said. Her voice was deep and rather attractive. 'What is it? I'm busy.'

'Mrs Boscowan?'

'Yes. What do you want?'

'My name's Beresford. I wondered if I might speak to you for a few moments.'

'I don't know. Really, must you? What is it – something about a picture?' Her eye had gone to what he held under his arm.

'Yes. It's something to do with one of your husband's pictures.'

'Do you want to sell it? I've got plenty of his pictures. I don't want to buy any more of them. Take it to one of these galleries or something. They're beginning to buy him now. You don't look as though you needed to sell pictures.'

'Oh no, I don't want to sell anything.'

Tommy felt extraordinary difficulty in talking to this particular woman. Her eyes, unmatching though they were, were very fine eyes and they were looking now over his shoulder down the street with an air of some peculiar interest at something in the far distance.

'Please,' said Tommy. 'I wish you would let me come in. It's so difficult to explain.'

'If you're a painter I don't want to talk to you,' said Mrs Boscowan. 'I find painters very boring always.'

'I'm not a painter.'

'Well, you don't look like one, certainly.' Her eyes raked him up and down. 'You look more like a civil servant,' she said disapprovingly.

'Can I come in, Mrs Boscowan?'

'I'm not sure. Wait.'

She shut the door rather abruptly. Tommy waited. After about four minutes had passed the door opened again.

'All right,' she said. 'You can come in.'

She led him through the doorway, up a narrow staircase and into the large studio. In a corner of it there was a figure and various implements standing by it. Hammers and chisels. There was also a clay head. The whole place looked as though it had recently been savaged by a gang of hooligans.

'There's never any room to sit up here,' said Mrs Boscowan.

She threw various things off a wooden stool and pushed it towards him.

'There. Sit down here and speak to me.'

'It's very kind of you to let me come in.'

'It is rather, but you looked so worried. You are worried, aren't you, about something?'

'Yes I am.'

'I thought so. What are you worried about?'

'My wife,' said Tommy, surprising himself by his answer.

'Oh, worried about your wife? Well, there's nothing unusual in that. Men are always worrying about their wives. What's the matter – has she gone off with someone or playing up?'

'No. Nothing like that.'

'Dying? Cancer?'

'No,' said Tommy. 'It's just that I don't know where she is.'

'And you think I might? Well, you'd better tell me her name and something about her if you think I can find her for you. I'm not sure, mind you,' said Mrs Boscowan, 'that I shall want to. I'm warning you.'

'Thank God,' said Tommy, 'you're more easy to talk to than I thought you were going to be.'

'What's the picture got to do with it? It is a picture, isn't it – must be, that shape.'

Tommy undid the wrappings.

'It's a picture signed by your husband,' said Tommy. 'I want you to tell me what you can about it.'

'I see. What exactly do you want to know?'

'When it was painted and where it is.'

Mrs Boscowan looked at him and for the first time there was a slight look of interest in her eyes.

'Well, that's not difficult,' she said. 'Yes, I can tell you all about it. It was painted about fifteen years ago – no, a good deal longer than that I should think. It's one of his fairly early ones. Twenty years ago, I should say.'

'You know where it is – the place I mean?'

'Oh yes, I can remember quite well. Nice picture. I always liked it. That's the little hump-backed bridge and the house and the name of the place is Sutton Chancellor. About seven or eight miles from Market Basing. The house itself is about a couple of miles from Sutton Chancellor. Pretty place. Secluded.'

She came up to the picture, bent down and peered at it closely.

'That's funny,' she said. 'Yes, that's very odd. I wonder now.'

Tommy did not pay much attention.

'What's the name of the house?' he asked.

'I can't really remember. It got renamed, you know. Several times. I don't know what there was about it. A couple of rather tragic things happened there, I think, then the next people who came along renamed it. Called the Canal House once, or Canal Side. Once it was called Bridge House then Meadowside – or Riverside was another name.'

'Who lived there – or who lives there now? Do you know?'

'Nobody I know. Man and a girl lived there when first I saw it. Used to come down for weekends. Not married, I think. The girl was a dancer. May have been an actress – no, I think she was a dancer. Ballet dancer. Rather beautiful but dumb. Simple, almost wanting. William was quite soft about her, I remember.'

'Did he paint her?'

'No. He didn't often paint people. He used to say sometimes he wanted to do a sketch of them, but he never did much about it. He was always silly over girls.'

'They were the people who were there when your husband was painting the house?'

'Yes, I think so. Part of the time anyway. They only came down weekends. Then there was some kind of a bust up. They had a row, I think, or he went away and left her or she went away and left him. I wasn't down there myself. I was working in Coventry then doing a group. After that I think there was just a governess in the house and the child. I don't know who the child was or where she came from but I suppose the governess was looking after her. Then I think something happened to the child. Either the governess took her away somewhere or perhaps she died. What do you want to know about the people who lived in the house twenty years ago? Seems to me idiotic.'

'I want to hear anything I can about that house,' said Tommy. 'You see, my wife went away to look for that house. She said she'd seen it out of a train somewhere.'

'Quite right,' said Mrs Boscowan, 'the railway line runs just the other side of the bridge. You can see the house very well from it, I expect.' Then she said, 'Why did she want to find that house?'

Tommy gave a much abridged explanation – she looked at him doubtfully.

'You haven't come out of a mental home or anything, have you?' said Mrs Boscowan. 'On parole or something, whatever they call it.'

'I suppose I must sound a little like that,' said Tommy, 'but it's quite simple really. My wife wanted to find out about this house and so she tried to take various train journeys to find out where it was she'd seen it. Well, I think she did find out. I think she went there to this place – something Chancellor?'

'Sutton Chancellor, yes. Very one-horse place it used to be. Of course it may be a big development or even one of these new dormitory towns by now.'

'It might be anything, I expect,' said Tommy. 'She telephoned she was coming back but she didn't come back. And I want to know what's happened to her. I think she went and started investigating that house and perhaps – perhaps she ran into danger.'

'What's dangerous about it?'

'I don't know,' said Tommy. 'Neither of us knew. I didn't even think there could be any danger about it, but my wife did.'

'E.S.P.?'

'Possibly. She's a little like that. She has hunches. You never heard of or knew a Mrs Lancaster twenty years ago or any time up to a month ago?'

'Mrs Lancaster? No, I don't think so. Sort of name one might remember, mightn't it be. No. What about Mrs Lancaster?'

'She was the woman who owned this picture. She gave it as a friendly gesture to an aunt of mine. Then she left an old people's home rather suddenly. Her relatives took her away. I've tried to trace her but it isn't easy.'

'Who's the one who's got the imagination, you or your wife? You seem to have thought up a lot of things and to be rather in a state, if I may say so.'

'Oh yes, you can say so,' said Tommy. 'Rather in a state and all about nothing at all. That's what you mean, isn't it? I suppose you're right too.'

'No,' said Mrs Boscowan. Her voice had altered slightly. 'I wouldn't say about nothing at all.'

Tommy looked at her inquiringly.

'There's one thing that's odd about that picture,' said Mrs Boscowan. 'Very odd. I remember it quite well, you know. I remember most of William's pictures although he painted such a lot of them.'

'Do you remember who it was sold to, if it was sold?'

'No, I don't remember that. Yes, I think it was sold. There was a whole batch of his paintings sold from one of his exhibitions. They ran back for about three or four years before this and a couple of years later than this. Quite a lot of them were sold. Nearly all of them. But I can't remember by now who it was sold to. That's asking too much.'

'I'm very grateful to you for all you have remembered.'

'You haven't asked me yet why I said there was something odd about the picture. This picture that you brought here.'

'You mean it isn't your husband's – somebody else painted it?'

'Oh no. That's the picture that William painted. "House by a Canal", I think he called it in the catalogue. But it isn't as it was. You see, there's something wrong with it.'

'What's wrong with it?'

Mrs Boscowan stretched out a clay-smeared finger

and jabbed at a spot just below the bridge spanning the canal.

'There,' she said. 'You see? There's a boat tied up under the bridge, isn't there?'

'Yes,' said Tommy puzzled.

'Well, that boat wasn't there, not when I saw it last. William never painted that boat. When it was exhibited *there was no boat of any kind.*'

'You mean that somebody not your husband painted the boat in here afterwards?'

'Yes. Odd, isn't it? I wonder why. First of all I was surprised to see the boat there, a place where there wasn't any boat, then I can see quite well that it wasn't painted by William. *He* didn't put it in at any time. Somebody else did. I wonder who?'

She looked at Tommy.

'And I wonder why?'

Tommy had no solution to offer. He looked at Mrs Boscowan. His Aunt Ada would have called her a scatty woman but Tommy did not think of her in that light. She was vague, with an abrupt way of jumping from one subject to another. The things she said seemed to have very little relation to the last thing she had said a minute before. She was the sort of person, Tommy thought, who might know a great deal more than she chose to reveal. Had she loved her husband or been jealous of her husband or despised her husband?

There was really no clue whatever in her manner, or indeed her words. But he had the feeling that that small painted boat tied up under the bridge had caused her uneasiness. She hadn't liked the boat being there. Suddenly he wondered if the statement she had made was true. Could she really remember from long years back whether Boscowan had painted a boat at the bridge or had not? It seemed really a very small and insignificant item. If it had been only a year ago when she had seen the picture last – but apparently it was a much longer time than that. And it had made Mrs Boscowan uneasy. He looked at her again and saw that she was looking at him. Her curious eyes resting on him not defiantly, but only thoughtfully. Very, very thoughtfully.

'What are you going to do now?' she said.

That at least was easy. Tommy had no difficulty in knowing what he was going to do now.

'I shall go home tonight – see if there is any news of my wife – any word from her. If not, tomorrow I shall go to this place,' he said. 'Sutton Chancellor. I hope that I may find my wife there.'

'It would depend,' said Mrs Boscowan.

'Depend on what?' said Tommy sharply.

Mrs Boscowan frowned. Then she murmured, seemingly to herself, 'I wonder where she is?'

'You wonder where who is?'

Mrs Boscowan had turned her glance away from him. Now her eyes swept back.

'Oh,' she said. 'I meant your wife.' Then she said, 'I hope she is all right.'

'Why shouldn't she be all right? Tell me, Mrs Boscowan, is there something wrong with that place – with Sutton Chancellor?'

'With Sutton Chancellor? With the place?' She reflected. 'No, I don't think so. Not with the *place*.'

'I suppose I meant the house,' said Tommy. 'This house by the canal. Not Sutton Chancellor village.'

'Oh, the house,' said Mrs Boscowan. 'It was a good house really. Meant for lovers, you know.'

'Did lovers live there?'

'Sometimes. Not often enough really. If a house is built for lovers, it ought to be lived in by lovers.'

'Not put to some other use by someone.'

'You're pretty quick,' said Mrs Boscowan. 'You saw what I meant, didn't you? You mustn't put a house that was meant for one thing to the wrong use. It won't like it if you do.'

'Do you know anything about the people who have lived there of late years?'

She shook her head. 'No. No. I don't know anything about the house at all. It was never important to me, you see.'

'But you're thinking of something – no, someone?'

'Yes,' said Mrs Boscowan. 'I suppose you're right about that. I was thinking of – someone.'

'Can't you tell me about the person you were thinking of?'

'There's really nothing to say,' said Mrs Boscowan. 'Sometimes, you know, one just wonders where a person is. What's happened to them or how they might have – developed. There's a sort of feeling –' She waved her hands – 'Would you like a kipper?' she said unexpectedly.

'A kipper?' Tommy was startled.

'Well, I happen to have two or three kippers here. I thought perhaps you ought to have something to eat before you catch a train. Waterloo is the station,' she said. 'For Sutton Chancellor, I mean. You used to have to change at Market Basing. I expect you still do.'

It was a dismissal. He accepted it.

Chapter 13

Albert on Clues

Tuppence blinked her eyes. Vision seemed rather dim. She tried to lift her head from the pillow but winced as a sharp pain ran through it, and let it drop again on to the pillow. She closed her eyes. Presently she opened them again and blinked once more.

With a feeling of achievement she recognized her surroundings. 'I'm in a hospital ward,' thought Tuppence. Satisfied with her mental progress so far, she attempted no more brainy deduction. She was in a hospital ward and her head ached. Why it ached, why she was in a hospital ward, she was not quite sure. 'Accident?' thought Tuppence.

There were nurses moving around beds. That seemed natural enough. She closed her eyes and tried a little cautious thought. A faint vision of an elderly figure in clerical dress, passed across a mental screen. 'Father?' said Tuppence doubtfully. 'Is it Father?' She couldn't really remember. She supposed so.

'But what am I doing being ill in a hospital?' thought Tuppence. 'I mean, I nurse in a hospital, so I ought to be in uniform. V.A.D. uniform. Oh dear,' said Tuppence.

Presently a nurse materialized near her bed.

'Feeling better now, dear?' said the nurse with a kind of false cheerfulness. 'That's nice, isn't it?'

Tuppence wasn't quite sure whether it *was* nice. The nurse said something about a nice cup of tea.

'I seem to be a patient,' said Tuppence rather disapprovingly to herself. She lay still, resurrecting in her own mind various detached thoughts and words.

'Soldiers,' said Tuppence. 'V.A.D.s. That's it, of course. I'm a V.A.D.'

The nurse brought her some tea in a kind of feeding cup and supported her whilst she sipped it. The pain went through her head again. 'A V.A.D., that's what I am,' said Tuppence aloud.

The nurse looked at her in an uncomprehending fashion.

'My head hurts,' said Tuppence, adding a statement of fact.

'It'll be better soon,' said the nurse.

She removed the feeding cup, reporting to a sister as she passed along. 'Number 14's awake. She's a bit wonky, though, I think.'

'Did she say anything?'

'Said she was a V.I.P.,' said the nurse.

The ward sister gave a small snort indicating that that was how she felt towards unimportant patients who reported themselves to be V.I.P.s.

'We shall see about that,' said the sister. 'Hurry up, Nurse, don't be all day with that feeding cup.'

Tuppence remained half drowsy on her pillows. She had not yet got beyond the stage of allowing thoughts to flit through her mind in a rather disorganized procession.

There was somebody who ought to be here, she felt, somebody she knew quite well. There was something very strange about this hospital. It wasn't the hospital she remembered. It wasn't the one she had nursed in. 'All soldiers, that was,' said Tuppence to herself. 'The surgical ward, I was on A and B rows.' She opened her eyelids and took another look round. She decided it was a hospital she had never seen before and that it had nothing to do with the nursing of surgical cases, military or otherwise.

'I wonder where this is,' said Tuppence. 'What place?' She tried to think of the name of some place. The only places she could think of were London and Southampton.

The ward sister now made her appearance at the bedside.

'Feeling a little better, I hope,' she said.

'I'm all right,' said Tuppence. 'What's the matter with me?'

'You hurt your head. I expect you find it rather painful, don't you?'

'It aches,' said Tuppence. 'Where am I?'

'Market Basing Royal Hospital.'

Tuppence considered this information. It meant nothing to her at all.

'An old clergyman,' she said.

'I beg your pardon?'

'Nothing particular. I –'

'We haven't been able to write your name on your diet sheet yet,' said the ward sister.

She held her Biro pen at the ready and looked inquiringly at Tuppence.

'My name?'

'Yes,' said the sister. 'For the records,' she added helpfully.

Tuppence was silent, considering. Her name. What was her name? 'How silly,' said Tuppence to herself, 'I seem to have forgotten it. And yet I must have a name.' Suddenly a faint feeling of relief came to her. The elderly clergyman's face flashed suddenly across her mind and she said with decision,

'Of course. Prudence.'

'P-r-u-d-e-n-c-e?'

'That's right,' said Tuppence.

'That's your Christian name. The surname?'

'Cowley. C-o-w-l-e-y.'

'Glad to get that straight,' said the sister, and moved away again with the air of one whose records were no longer worrying her.

Tuppence felt faintly pleased with herself. Prudence Cowley. Prudence Cowley in the V.A.D. and her father was a clergyman at – at something vicarage and it was wartime and . . . 'Funny,' said Tuppence to herself, 'I seem to be getting this all wrong. It seems to me it all happened a long time ago.' She murmured to herself, 'Was it your poor child?' She wondered. Was it she who had just said that or was it somebody else said it to her?

The sister was back again.

'Your address,' she said, 'Miss – Miss Cowley, or is it Mrs Cowley? Did you ask about a child?'

'Was it your poor child? Did somebody say that to me or am I saying it to them?'

'I think I should sleep a little if I were you now, dear,' said the sister.

She went away and took the information she had obtained to the proper place.

'She seems to have come to herself, Doctor,' she remarked, 'and she says her name is Prudence Cowley. But she doesn't seem to remember her address. She said something about a child.'

'Oh well,' said the doctor, with his usual casual air, 'we'll give her another twenty-four hours or so. She's coming round from the concussion quite nicely.'

II

Tommy fumbled with his latchkey. Before he could use it the door came open and Albert stood in the open aperture.

'Well,' said Tommy, 'is she back?'

Albert slowly shook his head.

'No word from her, no telephone message, no letters waiting – no telegrams?'

'Nothing I tell you, sir. Nothing whatever. And nothing from anyone else either. They're lying low – but they've got her. That's what I think. They've got her.'

'What the devil do you mean – they've got her?' said Tommy. 'The things you read. Who've got her?'

'Well, you know what I mean. The gang.'

'What gang?'

'One of those gangs with flick knives maybe. Or an international one.'

'Stop talking rubbish,' said Tommy. 'D'you know what I think?'

Albert looked inquiringly at him.

'I think it's extremely inconsiderate of her not to send us word of some kind,' said Tommy.

'Oh,' said Albert, 'well, I see what you mean. I suppose you *could* put it that way. If it makes you happier,' he added rather unfortunately. He removed the parcel from Tommy's arms. 'I see you brought that picture back,' he said.

'Yes, I've brought the bloody picture back,' said Tommy. 'A fat lot of use it's been.'

'You haven't learnt anything from it?'

'That's not quite true,' said Tommy. 'I *have* learnt something from it but whether what I've learnt is going to be any use to me I don't know.' He added, 'Dr Murray didn't ring up, I suppose, or Miss Packard from Sunny Ridge Nursing Home? Nothing like that?'

'Nobody's rung up except the greengrocer to say he's got some nice aubergines. He knows the missus is fond of aubergines. He always lets her know. But I told him she wasn't available just now.' He added, 'I've got a chicken for your dinner.'

'It's extraordinary that you can never think of anything but chickens,' said Tommy, unkindly.

'It's what they call a *poussin* this time,' said Albert. 'Skinny,' he added.

'It'll do,' said Tommy.

The telephone rang. Tommy was out of his seat and had rushed to it in a moment.

'Hallo . . . hallo?'

A faint and far-away voice spoke. 'Mr Thomas Beresford? Can you accept a personal call from Invergashly?'

'Yes.'

'Hold the line, please.'

Tommy waited. His excitement was calming down. He had to wait some time. Then a voice he knew, crisp and capable, sounded. The voice of his daughter.

'Hallo, is that you, Pop?'

'Deborah!'

'Yes. Why are you sounding so breathless, have you been running?'

Daughters, Tommy thought, were always critical.

'I wheeze a bit in my old age,' he said. 'How are you, Deborah?'

'Oh, I'm all right. Look here, Dad, I saw something in the paper. Perhaps you've seen it too. I wondered about it. Something about someone who had had an accident and was in hospital.'

'Well? I don't think I saw anything of that kind. I mean, not to notice it in any way. Why?'

'Well it – it didn't sound too bad. I supposed it was a car accident or something like that. It mentioned that the woman, whoever it was – an elderly woman – gave her name as Prudence Cowley but they were unable to find her address.'

'Prudence Cowley? You mean –'

'Well yes. I only – well – I only wondered. That *is* Mother's name, isn't it? I mean it was her name.'

'Of course.'

'I always forget about the Prudence. I mean we've never thought of her as Prudence, you and I, or Derek either.'

'No,' said Tommy. 'No. It's not the kind of Christian name one would associate much with your mother.'

'No, I know it isn't. I just thought it was – rather odd. You don't think it might be some relation of hers?'

'I suppose it might be. Where was this?'

'Hospital at Market Basing, I think it said. They wanted to know more about her, I gather. I just wondered – well, I know it's awfully silly, there must be quantities of people called Cowley and quantities of people called Prudence. But I thought I'd just ring up and find out. Make sure, I mean, that Mother was at home and all right and all that.'

'I see,' said Tommy. 'Yes, I see.'

'Well, go on, Pop, is she at home?'

'No,' said Tommy, 'she isn't at home and I don't know either whether she is all right or not.'

'What do you mean?' said Deborah. 'What's Mother been doing? I suppose you've been up in London with that hush-hush utterly secret idiotic survival from past days, jawing with all the old boys.'

'You're quite right,' said Tommy. 'I got back from that yesterday evening.'

'And you found Mother away – or did you know she was away? Come on, Pop, tell me about it. You're worried. I know when you're worried well enough. What's Mother been doing? She's been up to something, hasn't she? I wish at her age she'd learn to sit quiet and not do things.'

'She's been worried,' said Tommy. 'Worried about something that happened in connection with your Great-aunt Ada's death.'

'What sort of thing?'

'Well, something that one of the patients at the nursing home said to her. She got worried about this old lady. She started talking a good deal and your mother was worried about some of the things she said. And so, when we went to look through Aunt Ada's things we suggested talking to this old lady and it seems she'd left rather suddenly.'

'Well, that seems quite natural, doesn't it?'

'Some of her relatives came and fetched her away.'

'It still seems quite natural,' said Deborah. 'Why did Mother get the wind up?'

'She got it into her head,' said Tommy, 'that something might have happened to this old lady.'

'I see.'

'Not to put too fine a point on it, as the saying goes,

she seems to have disappeared. All in quite a natural way. I mean, vouched for by lawyers and banks and all that. Only – we haven't been able to find out where she is.'

'You mean Mother's gone off to look for her somewhere?'

'Yes. And she didn't come back when she said she was coming back, two days ago.'

'And haven't you heard from her?'

'No.'

'I wish to goodness you could look after Mother properly,' said Deborah, severely.

'None of us have ever been able to look after her properly,' said Tommy. 'Not you either, Deborah, if it comes to that. It's the same way she went off in the war and did a lot of things that she'd no business to be doing.'

'But it's different now. I mean, she's quite *old*. She ought to sit at home and take care of herself. I suppose she's been getting bored. That's at the bottom of it all.'

'Market Basing Hospital, did you say?' said Tommy.

'Melfordshire. It's about an hour or an hour and a half from London, I think, by train.'

'That's it,' said Tommy. 'And there's a village near Market Basing called Sutton Chancellor.'

'What's that got to do with it?' said Deborah.

'It's too long to go into now,' said Tommy. 'It has to do with a picture painted of a house near a bridge by a canal.'

'I don't think I can hear you very well,' said Deborah. 'What are you talking about?'

'Never mind,' said Tommy. 'I'm going to ring up Market Basing Hospital and find out a few things. I've a feeling that it's your mother, all right. People, if they've had concussion, you know, often remember things first that happened when they were a child, and only get slowly to the present. She's gone back to her maiden name. She may have been in a car accident, but I shouldn't be surprised if somebody hadn't given her a conk on the head. It's the sort of thing that happens to your mother. She gets into things. I'll let you know what I find out.'

Forty minutes later, Tommy Beresford glanced at his wrist watch and breathed a sigh of utter weariness, as he replaced the receiver with a final clang on the telephone rest. Albert made an appearance.

'What about your dinner, sir?' he demanded. 'You haven't eaten a thing, and I'm sorry to say I forgot about that chicken – Burnt to a cinder.'

'I don't want anything to eat,' said Tommy. 'What I want is a drink. Bring me a double whisky.'

'Coming, sir,' said Albert.

A few moments later he brought the required refreshment to where Tommy had slumped down in the worn but comfortable chair reserved for his special use.

'And now, I suppose,' said Tommy, 'you want to hear everything.'

'Matter of fact, sir,' said Albert in a slightly apologetic tone, 'I know most of it. You see, seeing as it was a question of the missus and all that, I took the liberty of lifting up the extension in the bedroom. I didn't think you'd mind, sir, not as it was the missus.'

'I don't blame you,' said Tommy. 'Actually, I'm grateful to you. If I had to start explaining –'

'Got on to everyone, didn't you? The hospital and the doctor and the matron.'

'No need to go over it all again,' said Tommy.

'Market Basing Hospital,' said Albert. 'Never breathed a word of that, she didn't. Never left it behind as an address or anything like that.'

'She didn't intend it to be her address,' said Tommy. 'As far as I can make out she was probably coshed on the head in an out of the way spot somewhere. Someone took her along in a car and dumped her at the side of the road somewhere, to be picked up as an ordinary hit and run.' He added, 'Call me at six-thirty tomorrow morning. I want to get an early start.'

'I'm sorry about your chicken getting burnt up again

in the oven. I only put it in to keep warm and forgot about it.'

'Never mind chickens,' said Tommy. 'I've always thought they were very silly birds, running under cars and clucking about. Bury the corpse tomorrow morning and give it a good funeral.'

'She's not at death's door or anything, is she, sir?' asked Albert.

'Subdue your melodramatic fancies,' said Tommy. 'If you'd done any proper listening you'd have heard that she's come nicely to herself again, knows who she is or was and where she is and they've sworn to keep her there waiting for me until I arrive to take charge of her again. On no account is she to be allowed to slip out by herself and go off again doing some more tomfool detective work.'

'Talking of detective work,' said Albert, and hesitated with a slight cough.

'I don't particularly want to talk about it,' said Tommy. 'Forget it, Albert. Teach yourself book-keeping or window-box gardening or something.'

'Well, I was just thinking – I mean, as a matter of clues –'

'Well, what about clues?'

'I've been thinking.'

'That's where all the trouble in life comes from. Thinking.'

'Clues,' said Albert again. 'That picture, for instance. That's a clue, isn't it?'

Tommy observed that Albert had hung the picture of the house by the canal up on the wall.

'If that picture's a clue to something, what do you think it's a clue to?' He blushed slightly at the inelegancy of the phrase he had just coined. 'I mean – what's it all about? It ought to mean something. What I was thinking of,' said Albert, 'if you'll excuse me mentioning it –'

'Go ahead, Albert.'

'What I was thinking of was that desk.'

'Desk?'

'Yes. The one that came by the furniture removers with the little table and the two chairs and the other things. Family property, it was, you said?'

'It belonged to my Aunt Ada,' said Tommy.

'Well, that's what I meant, sir. That's the sort of place where you find clues. In old desks. Antiques.'

'Possibly,' said Tommy.

'It wasn't my business, I know, and I suppose I really oughtn't to have gone messing about with it, but while you were away, sir, I couldn't help it. I had to go and have a look.'

'What – a look into the desk?'

'Yes, just to see if there might be a clue there. You see, desks like that, they have secret drawers.'

'Possibly,' said Tommy.

'Well, there you are. There might be a clue there, hidden. Shut up in the secret drawer.'

'It's an agreeable idea,' said Tommy. 'But there's no reason as far as I know for my Aunt Ada to hide things away in secret drawers.'

'You never know with old ladies. They like tucking things away. Like jackdaws, they are, or magpies. I forget which it is. There might be a secret will in it or something written in invisible ink or a treasure. Where you'd find some hidden treasure.'

'I'm sorry, Albert, but I think I'm going to have to disappoint you. I'm pretty sure there's nothing of that kind in that nice old family desk which once belonged to my Uncle William. Another man who turned crusty in his old age besides being stone deaf and having a very bad temper.'

'What I thought is,' said Albert, 'it wouldn't do any harm to look, would it?' He added virtuously, 'It needed cleaning out anyway. You know how old things are with old ladies. They don't turn them out much – not when they're rheumatic and find it hard to get about.'

Tommy paused for a moment or two. He remembered that Tuppence and he had looked quickly through the drawers of the desk, had put their contents such as they were in two large envelopes and removed a few skeins of wool, two cardigans, a black velvet stole and three fine pillow-cases from the lower drawers which they had placed with other clothing and odds and ends for disposal. They had also looked through such papers as there had been in the envelopes after their return home with them. There had been nothing there of particular interest.

'We looked through the contents, Albert,' he said. 'Spent a couple of evenings really. One or two quite interesting old letters, some recipes for boiling ham, some other recipes for preserving fruit, some ration books and coupons and things dating back to the war. There was nothing of any interest.'

'Oh, that,' said Albert, 'but that's just papers and things, as you might say. Just ordinary go and come what everybody gets holed up in desks and drawers and things. I mean real secret stuff. When I was a boy, you know, I did six months with an antique dealer – helping him fake up things as often as not. But I got to know about secret drawers that way. They usually run to the same pattern. Three or four well-known kinds and they very it now and then. Don't you think, sir, you ought to have a look? I mean, I didn't like to go it meself with you not here. I would have been presuming.' He looked at Tommy with the air of a pleading dog.

'Come on, Albert,' said Tommy, giving in. 'Let's go and presume.'

'A very nice piece of furniture,' thought Tommy, as

he stood by Albert's side, surveying this specimen of his inheritance from Aunt Ada. 'Nicely kept, beautiful old polish on it, showing the good workmanship and craftsmanship of days gone by.'

'Well, Albert,' he said, 'go ahead. This is your bit of fun. But don't go and strain it.'

'Oh, I was ever so careful. I didn't crack it, or slip knives into it or anything like that. First of all we let down the front and put it on these two slab things that pull out. That's right, you see, the flap comes down this way and that's where the old lady used to sit. Nice little mother-of-pearl blotting case your Aunt Ada had. It was in the left-hand drawer.'

'There are these two things,' said Tommy.

He drew out two delicate pilastered shallow vertical drawers.

'Oh, them, sir. You can push papers in them, but there's nothing really secret about them. The most usual place is to open the little middle cupboard – and then at the bottom of it usually there's a little depression and you slide the bottom out and there's a space. But there's other ways and places. This desk is the kind that has a kind of well underneath.'

'That's not very secret either, is it? You just slide back a panel –'

'The point is, it looks as though you'd found all there was to find. You push back the panel, there's the cavity and you can put a good many things in there that you want to keep a bit from being pawed over and all that. But that's not all, as you might say. Because you see, here there's a little piece of wood in front, like a little ledge. And you can pull that up, you see.'

'Yes,' said Tommy, 'yes, I can see that. You pull that up.'

'And you've got a secret cavity here, just behind the middle lock.'

'But there's nothing in it.'

'No,' said Albert, 'it looks disappointing. But if you slip your hand into that cavity and you wiggle it along either to the left or the right, there are two little thin drawers, one each side. There's a little semi-circle cut out of the top, and you can hook your finger over that – and pull gently towards you –' During these remarks Albert seemed to be getting his wrist in what was almost a contortionist position. 'Sometimes they stick a little. Wait – wait – here she comes.'

'Albert's hooked forefinger drew something towards him from inside. He clawed it gently forward until the narrow small drawer showed in the opening. He hooked it out and laid it before Tommy, with the air of a dog bringing his bone to his master.

'Now wait a minute, sir. There's something in here, something wrapped up in a long thin envelope. Now we'll do the other side.'

He changed hands and resumed his contortionist clawings. Presently a second drawer was brought to light and was laid beside the first one.

'There's something in here, too,' said Albert. 'Another sealed-up envelope that someone's hidden here one time or another. I've not tried to open either of them – I wouldn't do such a thing.' His voice was virtuous in the extreme. 'I left that to you – But what I say is – they may be *clues* –'

Together he and Tommy extracted the contents of the dusty drawers. Tommy took out first a sealed envelope rolled up lengthways with an elastic band round it. The elastic band parted as soon as it was touched.

'Looks valuable,' said Albert.

Tommy glanced at the envelope. It bore the superscription 'Confidential'.

'There you are,' said Albert. '"Confidential". It's a clue.'

Tommy extracted the contents of the envelope. In a faded handwriting, and very scratchy handwriting at that, there was a half-sheet of notepaper. Tommy turned it this way and that and Albert leaned over his shoulder, breathing heavily.

'Mrs MacDonald's recipe for Salmon Cream,' Tommy read. 'Given to me as a special favour. Take 2 pounds of middle cut of salmon, 1 pint of Jersey cream, a wineglass of brandy and a fresh cucumber.' He broke off. 'I'm sorry, Albert, it's a clue which will lead us to good cookery, no doubt.'

Albert uttered sounds indicative of disgust and disappointment.

'Never mind,' said Tommy. 'Here's another one to try.'

The next sealed envelope did not appear to be one of quite such antiquity. It had two pale grey wax seals affixed to it, each bearing a representation of a wild rose.

'Pretty,' said Tommy, 'rather fanciful for Aunt Ada. How to cook a beef steak pie, I expect.'

Tommy ripped open the envelope. He raised his eyebrows. Ten carefully folded five-pound notes fell out.

'Nice thin ones,' said Tommy. 'They're the old ones. You know, the kind we used to have in the war. Decent paper. Probably aren't legal tender nowadays.'

'Money!' said Albert. 'What she want all that money for?'

'Oh, that's an old lady's nest egg,' said Tommy. 'Aunt Ada always had a nest egg. Years ago she told me that every woman should always have fifty pounds in five-pound notes with her in case of what she called emergencies.'

'Well, I suppose it'll still come in handy,' said Albert.

'I don't suppose they're absolutely obsolete. I think

you can make some arrangement to change them at a bank.'

'There's another one still,' said Albert. 'The one from the other drawer –'

The next was bulkier. There seemed to be more inside it and it had three large important-looking red seals. On the outside was written in the same spiky hand 'In the event of my death, this envelope should be sent unopened to my solicitor, Mr Rockbury of Rockbury & Tomkins, or to my nephew Thomas Beresford. Not to be opened by any unauthorized person.'

There were several sheets of closely written paper. The handwriting was bad, very spiky and here and there somewhat illegible. Tommy read it aloud with some difficulty.

'I, Ada Maria Fanshawe, am writing down here certain matters which have come to my knowledge and which have been told me by people who are residing in this nursing home called Sunny Ridge. I cannot vouch for any of this information being correct but there seems to be some reason to believe that suspicious – possibly criminal – activities are taking place here or have taken place here. Elizabeth Moody, a foolish woman, but not I think untruthful, declares that she has recognized here a well-known criminal. There may be a poisoner at work among us. I myself prefer to keep an open mind, but I shall remain watchful.

I propose to write down here any facts that come to my knowledge. The whole thing may be a mare's nest. Either my solicitor or my nephew Thomas Beresford, is asked to make full investigation.'

'There,' said Albert triumphantly – 'Told you so! It's a CLUE!'

Book 4

Here is a Church and here is the Steeple Open the Doors and there are the People

Chapter 14

Exercise in Thinking

'I suppose what we ought to do is think,' said Tuppence.

After a glad reunion in the hospital, Tuppence had eventually been honourably discharged. The faithful pair were now comparing notes together in the sitting-room of the best suite in The Lamb and Flag at Market Basing.

'You leave thinking alone,' said Tommy. 'You know what that doctor told you before he let you go. No worries, no mental exertion, very little physical activity – take everything easy.'

'What else am I doing now?' demanded Tuppence. 'I've got my feet up, haven't I, and my head on two cushions? And as for thinking, thinking isn't necessarily mental exertion. I'm not doing mathematics, or studying economics, or adding up the household accounts. Thinking is just resting comfortably, and leaving one's mind open in case something interesting or important should just come floating in. Anyway, wouldn't you rather I did a little thinking with my feet up and my head on cushions, rather than go in for action again?'

'I certainly don't want you going in for action again,' said Tommy. 'That's *out.* You understand? Physically, Tuppence, you will remain quiescent. If possible, I shan't let you out of my sight because I don't trust you.'

'All right,' said Tuppence. 'Lecture ends. Now let's think. Think together. Pay no attention to what doctors have said to you. If you knew as much as I do about doctors –'

'Never mind about the doctors,' said Tommy, 'you do as *I* tell you.'

'All right. I've no wish at present for physical activity, I assure you. The point is that we've got to compare notes. We've got hold of a lot of things. It's as bad as a village jumble sale.'

'What do you mean by things?'

'Well, facts. All sorts of facts. Far too many facts. And not only facts – Hearsay, suggestions, legends, gossip. The whole thing is like a bran tub with different kinds of parcels wrapped up and shoved down in the sawdust.'

'Sawdust is right,' said Tommy.

'I don't quite know whether you're being insulting or modest,' said Tuppence. 'Anyway, you do agree with me, don't you? We've got far too *much* of everything. There are wrong things and right things, and important things and unimportant things and they're all mixed up together. We don't know where to start.'

'I do,' said Tommy.

'All right,' said Tuppence. 'Where are you starting?'

'I'm starting with your being coshed on the head,' said Tommy.

Tuppence considered a moment. 'I don't see really that that's a starting point. I mean, it's the last thing that happened, not the first.'

'It's the first in my mind,' said Tommy. 'I won't have people coshing my wife. And it's a *real* point to start from. It's not imagination. It's a *real* thing that *really* happened.'

'I couldn't agree with you more,' said Tuppence. 'It really happened and it happened to me, and I'm not forgetting it. I've been thinking about it – Since I regained the power of thought, that is.'

'Have you any idea as to who did it?'

'Unfortunately, no. I was bending down over a gravestone and whoosh!'

'Who could it have been?'

'I suppose it must have been somebody in Sutton Chancellor. And yet that seems so unlikely. I've hardly spoken to anyone.'

'The vicar?'

'It couldn't have been the vicar,' said Tuppence. 'First because he's a nice old boy. And secondly because he wouldn't have been nearly strong enough. And thirdly because he's got very asthmatic breathing. He couldn't possibly have crept up behind me without my hearing him.'

'Then if you count the vicar out –'

'Don't you?'

'Well,' said Tommy, 'yes, I do. As you know, I've been to see him and talked to him. He's been a vicar here for years and everyone knows him. I suppose a fiend incarnate *could* put on a show of being a kindly vicar, but not for more than about a week or so at the outside, I'd say. Not for about ten or twelve years.'

'Well, then,' said Tuppence, 'the next suspect would be Miss Bligh. Nellie Bligh. Though heaven knows why. She can't have thought I was trying to steal a tombstone.'

'Do you feel it might have been her?'

'Well, I don't really. Of course, she's *competent.* If she wanted to follow me and see what I was doing, and conk me, she'd make a success of it. And like the vicar, she was there – on the spot – She was in Sutton Chancellor, popping in and out of her house to do this and that, and she could have caught sight of me in the churchyard, come up behind me on tiptoe out of curiosity, seen me examining a grave, objected to my doing so for some particular reason, and hit me with one of the church metal flower vases or anything else handy. But don't ask me *why*. There seems no possible reason.'

'Who next, Tuppence? Mrs Cockerell, if that's her name?'

'Mrs Copleigh,' said Tuppence. 'No, it wouldn't be Mrs Copleigh.'

'Now why are you so sure of that? She lives in Sutton Chancellor, she could have seen you go out of the house and she could have followed you.'

'Oh yes, yes, but she talks too much,' said Tuppence.

'I don't see where talking too much comes into it.'

'If you'd listened to her a whole evening as I did,' said Tuppence, 'you'd realize that anyone who talks as much as she does, non-stop in a constant flow, could not possibly be a woman of action as well! She couldn't have come up anywhere near me without talking at the top of her voice as she came.'

Tommy considered this.

'All right,' he said. 'You have good judgement in that kind of thing, Tuppence. Wash out Mrs Copleigh. Who else is there?'

'Amos Perry,' said Tuppence. 'That's the man who lives at the Canal House. (I have to call it the Canal House because it's got so many other odd names. And it was called that originally.) The husband of the friendly witch. There's something a bit queer about him. He's a bit simple minded and he's a big powerful man, and he could cosh anyone on the head if he wanted to, and I even think it's possible in certain circumstances he might want to – though I don't exactly know why he should want to cosh *me*. He's a better possibility really than Miss Bligh who seems to me just one of those tiresome, efficient women who go about running parishes and poking their noses into things. Not at all the type who would get up to the point of physical attack, except for some wildly emotional reason.' She added, with a slight shiver, 'You know, I felt frightened of Amos Perry the first time I saw him. He was showing me his garden. I felt suddenly that I – well, that I wouldn't like to get on the wrong side of him – or meet him in a dark road at night. I felt he was a man that wouldn't often want to be violent but who could be violent if something took him that way.'

'All right,' said Tommy. 'Amos Perry. Number one.'

'And there's his wife,' said Tuppence slowly. 'The friendly witch. She was nice and I liked her – I don't want it to be her – I don't think it *was* her, but she's mixed up in things, I think . . . Things that have to do with that house. That's another point, you see, Tommy – We don't know what the important thing is in all this – I've begun to wonder whether everything doesn't circulate round that *house* – whether the *house* isn't the central point. The picture – That picture does mean something, doesn't it, Tommy? It must, I think.'

'Yes,' said Tommy, 'I think it must.'

'I came here trying to find Mrs Lancaster – but nobody here seems to have heard of her. I've been wondering whether I got things the wrong way round – that Mrs Lancaster was in danger (because I'm still sure of that) *because she owned that picture.* I don't think *she* was ever in Sutton Chancellor – but she was either given, or she bought, a picture of a house here. And that picture *means* something – is in some way a menace to someone.'

'Mrs Cocoa – Mrs Moody – told Aunt Ada that she recognized someone at Sunny Ridge – someone connected with 'criminal activities'. I think the criminal activities are connected with the picture and with the house by the canal, and a child who perhaps was killed there.'

'Aunt Ada admired Mrs Lancaster's picture – and Mrs Lancaster gave it to her – and perhaps she talked about it – where she got it, or who had given it to her, and where the house was –'

'Mrs Moody was bumped off because she definitely recognized someone who had been "connected with criminal activities".'

'Tell me again about your conversation with Dr Murray,' said Tuppence. 'After telling you about Mrs Cocoa, he went on to talk about certain types of killers, giving examples of real life cases. One was a woman who ran a nursing home for elderly patients – I remember reading about it vaguely, though I can't remember the woman's name. But the idea was that they made over what money they had to her, and then they lived there until they died, well fed and looked after, and without any money worries. And they *were* very happy – only they usually died well within a year – quite peacefully in their sleep. And at last people began to notice. She was tried and convicted of murder – But had no conscience pangs and protested that what she had done was really a kindness to the old dears.'

'Yes. That's right,' said Tommy. 'I can't remember the name of the woman now.'

'Well, never mind about that,' said Tuppence. 'And then he cited another case. A case of a woman, a domestic worker or a cook or a housekeeper. She used to go into service into different families. Sometimes nothing happened, I believe, and sometimes it was a kind of mass poisoning. Food poisoning, it was supposed to be. All with quite reasonable symptoms. Some people recovering.'

'She used to prepare sandwiches,' said Tommy, 'and make them up into packets and send them out for picnics with them. She was very nice and very devoted and she used to get, if it was a mass poisoning, some of the symptoms and signs herself. Probably exaggerating their effect. Then she'd go away after that and she'd take another place, in quite a different part of England. It went on for some years.'

'That's right, yes. Nobody, I believe, has ever been able to understand *why* she did it. Did she get a sort of addiction for it – a sort of habit of it? Was it fun for her? Nobody really ever knew. She never seems to have had any personal malice for any of the people whose deaths she seems to have caused. Bit wrong in the top storey?'

'Yes. I think she must have been, though I suppose one of the trick cyclists would probably do a great deal of analysis and find out it had all something to do with a canary of a family she'd known years and years ago as a child who had given her a shock or upset her or something. But anyway, that's the sort of thing it was.'

'The third one was queerer still,' said Tommy. 'A French woman. A woman who'd suffered terribly from the loss of her husband and her child. She was broken-hearted and she was an angel of mercy.'

'That's right,' said Tuppence, 'I remember. They called her the angel of whatever the village was. *Givon* or something like that. She went to all the neighbours and nursed them when they were ill. Particularly she used to go to children when they were ill. She nursed them devotedly. But sooner or later, after apparently a slight recovery, they grew much worse and died. She spent hours crying and went to the funeral crying and everybody said they wouldn't know what they'd have done without the angel who'd nursed their darlings and done everything she could.'

'Why do you want to go over all this again, Tuppence?'

'Because I wondered if Dr Murray had a reason for mentioning them.'

'You mean he connected –'

'I think he connected up three classical cases that are well known, and tried them on, as it were, like a glove, to see if they fitted anyone at Sunny Ridge. I think in a way any of them might have fitted. Miss Packard would fit in with the first one. The efficient matron of a Home.'

'You really have got your knife into that woman. I always liked her.'

'I daresay people *have* liked murderers,' said Tuppence very reasonably. 'It's like swindlers and confidence tricksmen who always look so honest and seem so honest. I daresay murderers all seem very nice and particularly soft-hearted. That sort of thing. Anyway, Miss Packard *is* very efficient and she has all the means to hand whereby she could produce a nice natural death without suspicion. And only someone like Mrs Cocoa would be likely to suspect her. Mrs Cocoa might suspect her because she's a bit batty herself and can understand batty people, or she might have come across her somewhere before.'

'I don't think Miss Packard would profit financially by any of her elderly inmates' deaths.'

'You don't know,' said Tuppence. 'It would be a cleverer way to do it, *not* to benefit from all of them. Just get one or two of them, perhaps, rich ones, to leave you a lot of money, but to always have some deaths that were quite natural as well, and where you didn't get anything. So you see I think that Dr Murray might, just *might*, have cast a glance at Miss Packard and said to himself, "Nonsense, I'm imagining things." But all the same the thought stuck in his mind. The second case he mentioned would fit with a domestic worker, or cook, or even some kind of hospital nurse. Somebody employed in the place, a middle-aged reliable woman, but who was batty in that particular way. Perhaps used to have little grudges, dislikes for some of the patients there. We can't go guessing at that because I don't think we know anyone well enough –'

'And the third one?'

'The third one's more difficult,' Tuppence admitted. 'Someone devoted. Dedicated.'

'Perhaps he just added that for good measure,' said Tommy. He added, 'I wonder about that Irish nurse.'

'The nice one we gave the fur stole to?'

'Yes, the nice one Aunt Ada liked. The very sympathetic one. She seemed so fond of everyone, so sorry if they died. She was very worried when she spoke to us, wasn't she? You said so – she was leaving, and she didn't really tell us why.'

'I suppose she might have been a rather neurotic type. Nurses aren't supposed to be too sympathetic. It's bad for patients. They are told to be cool and efficient and inspire confidence.'

'Nurse Beresford speaking,' said Tommy, and grinned.

'But to come back to the picture,' said Tuppence. 'If we just concentrate on the picture. Because I think it's very interesting what you told me about Mrs Boscowan, when you went to see her. She sounds – she sounds *interesting*.'

'She was interesting,' said Tommy. 'Quite the most interesting person I think we've come across in this unusual business. The sort of person who seems to *know* things, but not by thinking about them. It was as though she knew something about this place that I didn't, and that perhaps you don't. But she knows *something*.'

'It was odd what she said about the boat,' said Tuppence. 'That the picture hadn't had a boat originally. Why do you think it's got a boat now?'

'Oh,' said Tommy, 'I don't know.'

'Was there any name painted on the boat? I don't

remember seeing one – but then I never looked at it very closely.'

'It's got *Waterlily* on it.'

'A very appropriate name for a boat – what does that remind me of?'

'I've no idea.'

'And she was quite positive that her husband didn't paint that boat – He could have put it in afterwards.'

'She says *not* – she was very definite.'

'Of course,' said Tuppence, 'there's another possibility we haven't gone into. About my coshing, I mean – the outsider – somebody perhaps who followed me here from Market Basing that day to see what I was up to. Because I'd been there asking all those questions. Going into all those house agents. Blodget & Burgess and all the rest of them. They put me off about the house. They were evasive. More evasive than would be natural. It was the same sort of evasion as we had when we were trying to find out where Mrs Lancaster had gone. Lawyers and banks, an owner who can't be communicated with because he's abroad. The same sort of *pattern*. They send someone to follow my car, they want to see what I am doing, and in due course I am coshed. Which brings us,' said Tuppence, 'to the gravestone in the churchyard. Why didn't anyone want me to look at old gravestones? They were all pulled about anyway – a group of boys, I should say, who'd got bored with wrecking telephone boxes, and went into the churchyard to have some fun and sacrilege behind the church.'

'You say there were painted words – or roughly carved words?'

'Yes – done with a chisel, I should think. Someone who gave it up as a bad job.

'The name – Lily Waters – and the age – seven years old. That was done properly – and then the other bits of words – It looked like "Whosoever . . ." and then "offend least of these" – and – "Millstone" –'

'Sounds familiar.'

'It should do. It's definitely biblical – but done by someone who wasn't quite sure what the words he wanted to remember were –'

'Very odd – the whole thing.'

'And why anyone should object – I was only trying to help the vicar – and the poor man who was trying to find his lost child – There we are – back to the lost child motif again – Mrs Lancaster talked about a poor child walled up behind a fireplace, and Mrs Copleigh chattered about walled-up nuns and murdered children, and a mother who killed a baby, and a lover, and an illegitimate baby, and a suicide – It's all old tales and gossip and hearsay and legends, mixed up in the most glorious kind of hasty pudding! All the same, Tommy, there was one actual *fact* – not just hearsay or legend –'

'You mean?'

'I mean that in the chimney of this Canal House, this old rag doll fell out – A child's doll. It had been there a very, very long time, all covered with soot and rubble –'

'Pity we haven't got it,' said Tommy.

'I *have*,' said Tuppence. She spoke triumphantly.

'You brought it away with you?'

'Yes. It startled me, you know. I thought I'd like to take it and examine it. Nobody wanted it or anything. I should imagine the Perrys would just have thrown it into the ashcan straight away. I've got it here.'

She rose from her sofa, went to her suitcase, rummaged a little and then brought out something wrapped in newspaper.

'Here you are, Tommy, have a look.'

With some curiosity Tommy unwrapped the newspaper. He took out carefully the wreck of a child's doll. It's limp arms and legs hung down, faint festoons of clothing dropped off as he touched them. The body seemed made of a very thin suède leather sewn up over a body that had once been plump with sawdust and now was sagging because here and there the sawdust had escaped. As Tommy handled it, and he was quite gentle in his touch, the body suddenly disintegrated, flapping over in a great wound from which there poured out a cupful of sawdust and with it small pebbles that ran to and fro about the floor. Tommy went round picking them up carefully.

'Good Lord,' he said to himself, 'Good Lord!'

'How odd,' Tuppence said, 'it's full of pebbles. Is that a bit of the chimney disintegrating, do you think? The plaster or something crumbling away?'

'No,' said Tommy. 'These pebbles were *inside* the body.'

He had gathered them up now carefully, he poked his finger into the carcase of the doll and a few more pebbles fell out. He took them over to the window and turned them over in his hand. Tuppence watched him with uncomprehending eyes.

'It's a funny idea, stuffing a doll with pebbles,' she said.

'Well, they're not exactly the usual kind of pebbles,' said Tommy. 'There was a very good reason for it, I should imagine.'

'What do you mean?'

'Have a look at them. Handle a few.'

She took some wonderingly from his hand.

'They're nothing but pebbles,' she said. 'Some are rather large and some small. Why are you so excited?'

'Because, Tuppence, I'm beginning to understand things. Those aren't pebbles, my dear girl, they're *diamonds*.'

Chapter 15

Evening at the Vicarage

'Diamonds!' Tuppence gasped.

Looking from him to the pebbles she still held in her hand, she said:

'These dusty-looking things, *diamonds*?'

Tommy nodded.

'It's beginning to make sense now, you see, Tuppence. It ties up. The Canal House. The picture. You wait until Ivor Smith hears about that doll. He's got a bouquet waiting for you already, Tuppence –'

'What for?'

'For helping to round up a big criminal gang!'

'You and your Ivor Smith! I suppose that's where you've been all this last week, abandoning me in my last days of convalescence in that dreary hospital – just when I wanted brilliant conversation and a lot of cheering up.'

'I came in visiting hours practically every evening.'

'You didn't tell me much.'

'I was warned by that dragon of a sister not to excite you. But Ivor himself is coming here the day after tomorrow, and we've got a little social evening laid on at the vicarage.'

'Who's coming?'

'Mrs Boscowan, one of the big local landowners, your friend Miss Nellie Bligh, the vicar, of course, you and I –'

'And Mr Ivor Smith – what's his real name?'

'As far as I know, it's Ivor Smith.'

'You are always so cautious –' Tuppence laughed suddenly.

'What's amusing you?'

'I was just thinking that I'd like to have seen you and Albert discovering secret drawers in Aunt Ada's desk.'

'All the credit goes to Albert. He positively delivered a lecture on the subject. He learnt all about it in his youth from an antique dealer.'

'Fancy your Aunt Ada really leaving a secret document like that, all done up with seals all over. She didn't actually know anything, but she was ready to believe there was somebody in Sunny Ridge who was dangerous. I wonder if she knew it was Miss Packard.'

'That's only your idea.'

'It's a very good idea if its a criminal gang we're looking for. They'd need a place like Sunny Ridge, respectable and well run, with a competent criminal to run it. Someone properly qualified to have access to drugs whenever she needed them. And by accepting any deaths that occurred as quite natural, it would influence a doctor to think they were quite all right.'

'You've got it all taped out, but actually the real reason you started to suspect Miss Packard was because you didn't like her teeth –'

'The better to eat you with,' said Tuppence meditatively. 'I'll tell you something else, Tommy – Supposing this picture – the picture of the Canal House – *never belonged to Mrs Lancaster at all* –'

'But we know it did.' Tommy stared at her.

'No, we don't. We only know that Miss Packard said so – It was Miss Packard who said that Mrs Lancaster gave it to Aunt Ada.'

'But why should –' Tommy stopped –

'Perhaps that's why Mrs Lancaster was taken away – so that she shouldn't tell us that the picture didn't belong to her, and that she didn't give it to Aunt Ada.'

'I think that's a very far-fetched idea.'

'Perhaps – But the picture was painted in Sutton Chancellor – The house in the picture is a house in Sutton Chancellor – We've reason to believe that that house is – or was – used as one of their hidey-holes by a criminal association – Mr Eccles is believed to be the man behind this gang. Mr Eccles was the man responsible for sending Mrs Johnson to remove Mrs Lancaster. I don't believe Mrs Lancaster was ever in Sutton Chancellor, or was ever in the Canal House, or had a picture of it – though I think she heard someone at Sunny Ridge talk about it – Mrs Cocoa perhaps? So she started chattering, and that was dangerous, so she had to be removed. And one day I shall find her! Mark my words, Tommy.'

'The Quest of Mrs Thomas Beresford.'

II

'You look remarkably well, if I may say so, Mrs Tommy,' said Mr Ivor Smith.

'I'm feeling perfectly well again,' said Tuppence. 'Silly of me to let myself get knocked out, I suppose.'

'You deserve a medal – Especially for this doll business. How you get on to these things, I don't know!'

'She's the perfect terrier,' said Tommy. 'Puts her nose down on the trail and off she goes.'

'You're not keeping me out of this party tonight,' said Tuppence suspiciously.

'Certainly not. A certain amount of things, you know, have been cleared up. I can't tell you how grateful I am to you two. We were getting *somewhere*, mind you, with this remarkably clever association of criminals who have been responsible for a stupendous amount of robberies over the last five or six years. As I told Tommy when he came to ask me if I knew anything about our clever legal gentleman, Mr Eccles, we've had our suspicions of him for a long time but he's not the man you'll easily get evidence against. Too careful by far. He practises as a solicitor – an ordinary genuine business with perfectly genuine clients.

'As I told Tommy, one of the important points has been this chain of houses. Genuine respectable houses with quite genuine respectable people living in them, living there for a short time – then leaving.

'Now, thanks to you, Mrs Tommy, and your investigation of chimneys and dead birds, we've found quite certainly one of those houses. The house where a particular amount of the spoil was concealed. It's been quite a clever system, you know, getting jewels or various things of that kind changed into packets of rough diamonds, hiding them, and then when the time comes they are flown abroad, or taken abroad in fishing boats, when all the hue and cry about one particular robbery has died down.'

'What about the Perrys? Are they – I hope they're not – mixed up in it?'

'One can't be sure,' said Mr Smith. 'No, one can't be sure. It seems likely to me that Mrs Perry, at least, knows something, or certainly knew something once.'

'Do you mean she really is one of the criminals?'

'It mightn't be that. It might be, you know, that they had a hold on her.'

'What sort of hold?'

'Well, you'll keep this confidential, I know you can hold your tongue in these things, but the local police have always had the idea that the husband, Amos Perry, might just possibly have been the man who was responsible for a wave of child murders a good many years ago. He is not fully competent mentally. The medical opinion was that he *might* quite easily have had a compulsion to do away with children. There was never any direct evidence, but his wife was perhaps overanxious to provide him always with adequate alibis. If so, you see, that might give a gang of unscrupulous people a hold on her and they may have put her in as tenant of part of a house where they knew she'd keep her mouth shut. They may really have had some form of damaging evidence against her husband. You met them – what do you feel about them both, Mrs Tommy?'

'I liked *her*,' said Tuppence. 'I think she was – well, as I say I summed her up as a friendly witch, given to white magic but not black.'

'What about him?'

'I was frightened of him,' said Tuppence. 'Not all the time. Just once or twice. He seemed suddenly to go big and terrifying. Just for a minute or two. I couldn't think what I was frightened of, but I was frightened. I suppose, as you say, I felt that he wasn't quite right in his head.'

'A lot of people are like that,' said Mr Smith. 'And very often they're not dangerous at all. But you can't tell, and you can't be sure.'

'What are we going to do at the vicarage tonight?'

'Ask some questions. See a few people. Find out things that may give us a little more of the information we need.'

'Will Major Waters be there? The man who wrote to the vicar about his child?'

'There doesn't seem to be any such person! There was a coffin buried where the old gravestone had been removed – a child's coffin, lead lined – And it was full of loot. Jewels and gold objects from a burglary near St Albans. The letter to the vicar was with the object of finding out what had happened to the grave. The local lads' sabotage had messed things up.'

III

'I am so deeply sorry, my dear,' said the vicar, coming to meet Tuppence with both hands outstretched. 'Yes, indeed, my dear, I have been so terribly upset that this should happen to you when you have been so kind. When you were doing this to help me. I really felt – yes, indeed I have, that it was all my fault. I shouldn't have let you go poking among gravestones, though really we had no reason to believe – no reason at all – that some band of young hooligans –'

'Now don't disturb yourself, Vicar,' said Miss Bligh, suddenly appearing at his elbow. 'Mrs Beresford knows, I'm sure, that it was nothing to do with *you*. It was indeed extremely kind of her to offer to help, but it's all over now, and she's quite well again. Aren't you, Mrs Beresford?'

'Certainly,' said Tuppence, faintly annoyed, however, that Miss Bligh should answer for her health so confidently.

'Come and sit down here and have a cushion behind your back,' said Miss Bligh.

'I don't need a cushion,' said Tuppence, refusing to accept the chair that Miss Bligh was officiously pulling forward. Instead, she sat down in an upright and exceedingly uncomfortable chair on the other side of the fireplace.

There was a sharp rap on the front door and everyone in the room jumped. Miss Bligh hurried out.

'Don't worry, Vicar,' she said. 'I'll go.'

'Please, if you will be so kind.'

There were low voices outside in the hall, then Miss

Bligh came back shepherding a big woman in a brocade shift, and behind her a very tall thin man, a man of cadaverous appearance. Tuppence stared at him. A black cloak was round his shoulders, and his thin gaunt face was like the face from another century. He might have come, Tuppence thought, straight out of an El Greco canvas.

'I'm very pleased to see you,' said the vicar, and turned. 'May I introduce Sir Philip Starke, Mr and Mrs Beresford. Mr Ivor Smith. Ah! Mrs Boscowan. I've not seen you for many, many years – Mr and Mrs Beresford.'

'I've met Mr Beresford,' said Mrs Boscowan. She looked at Tuppence. 'How do you do,' she said. 'I'm glad to meet you. I heard you'd had an accident.'

'Yes. I'm all right again now.'

The introductions completed, Tuppence sat back in her chair. Tiredness swept over her as it seemed to do rather more frequently than formerly, which she said to herself was possibly a result of concussion. Sitting quietly, her eyes half closed, she was nevertheless scrutinizing everyone in the room with close attention. She was not listening to the conversation, she was only looking. She had a feeling that a few of the characters in the drama – the drama in which she had unwittingly involved herself – were assembled here as they might be in a dramatic scene. Things were drawing together, forming themselves into a compact nucleus. With the coming of Sir Philip Starke and Mrs Boscowan it was as though two hitherto unrevealed characters were suddenly presenting themselves. They had been there all along, as it were, outside the circle, but now they had come inside. They were somehow concerned, implicated. They had come here this evening – why, she wondered? Had someone summoned them? Ivor Smith? Had he commanded their presence, or only gently demanded it? Or were they perhaps as strange to him as they were to her? She thought to herself: 'It all began in Sunny Ridge, but Sunny Ridge isn't the real heart of the matter. That was, had always been, here, in Sutton Chancellor. Things had happened here. Not very lately, almost certainly not lately. Long ago. Things which had nothing to do with Mrs Lancaster – but Mrs Lancaster had become unknowingly involved. So where was Mrs Lancaster now?'

A little cold shiver passed over Tuppence.

'I think,' thought Tuppence, 'I think perhaps she's *dead . . .*'

If so, Tuppence felt, she herself had failed. She had set out on her quest worried about Mrs Lancaster, feeling that Mrs Lancaster was threatened with some danger and she had resolved to find Mrs Lancaster, protect her.

'And if she isn't dead,' thought Tuppence, 'I'll still do it!'

Sutton Chancellor . . . That was where the beginning of something meaningful and dangerous had happened. The house with the canal was part of it. Perhaps it was the centre of it all, or was it Sutton Chancellor itself? A place where people had lived, had come to, had left, had run away, had vanished, had disappeared and reappeared. Like Sir Philip Starke.

Without turning her head Tuppence's eyes went to Sir Philip Starke. She knew nothing about him except what Mrs Copleigh had poured out in the course of her monologue on the general inhabitants. A quiet man, a learned man, a botanist, an industrialist, or at least one who owned a big stake in industry. Therefore a rich man – and a man who loved children. There she was, back at it. Children again. The house by the canal and the bird in the chimney, and out of the chimney had fallen a child's doll, shoved up there by someone. A child's doll that held within its skin a handful of diamonds – the proceeds of crime. This was one of the headquarters of a big criminal undertaking. But there had been crimes more sinister than robberies. Mrs Copleigh had said 'I always fancied myself as *he* might have done it.'

Sir Philip Starke. A murderer? Behind her half-closed eyelids, Tuppence studied him with the knowledge clearly in her mind that she was studying him to find out if he fitted in any way with her conception of a murderer – and a child murderer at that.

How old was he, she wondered. Seventy at least, perhaps older. A worn ascetic face. Yes, definitely ascetic. Very definitely a tortured face. Those large dark eyes. El Greco eyes. The emaciated body.

He had come here this evening, why, she wondered? Her eyes went on to Miss Bligh. Sitting a little restlessly in her chair, occasionally moving to push a table nearer someone, to offer a cushion, to move the position of the cigarette box or matches. Restless, ill at ease. She was looking at Philip Starke. Every time she relaxed, her eyes went to him.

'Doglike devotion,' thought Tuppence. 'I think she must have been in love with him once. I think in a way perhaps she still is. You don't stop being in love with anyone because you get old. People like Derek and Deborah think you do. They can't imagine anyone who isn't young being in love. But I think she – I think she is still in love with him, hopelessly, devotedly in love. Didn't someone say – was it Mrs Copleigh or the vicar who had said, that Miss Bligh had been his secretary as a young woman, that she still looked after his affairs here?

'Well,' thought Tuppence, 'it's natural enough. Secretaries often fall in love with their bosses. So say Gertrude Bligh had loved Philip Starke. Was that a useful fact at all? Had Miss Bligh known or suspected that behind Philip Starke's calm ascetic personality there ran a horrifying thread of madness? *So fond of children always*.'

'Too fond of children, I thought,' Mrs Copleigh had said.

Things did take you like that. Perhaps that was a reason for his looking so tortured.

'Unless one is a pathologist or a psychiatrist or something, one doesn't know anything about mad murderers,' thought Tuppence. '*Why* do they want to kill children? What gives them that urge? Are they sorry about it afterwards? Are they disgusted, are they desperately unhappy, are they terrified?'

At that moment she noticed that his gaze had fallen on her. His eyes met hers and seemed to leave some message.

'You are thinking about me,' those eyes said. 'Yes, it's true what you are thinking. I am a haunted man.'

Yes, that described him exactly – He was a haunted man.

She wrenched her eyes away. Her gaze went to the vicar. She liked the vicar. He was a dear. Did he know anything? He might, Tuppence thought, or he might be living in the middle of some evil tangle that he never even suspected. Things happened all round him, perhaps, but he wouldn't know about them, because he had that rather disturbing quality of innocence.

Mrs Boscowan? But Mrs Boscowan was difficult to know anything about. A middle-aged woman, a personality, as Tommy had said, but that didn't express enough. As though Tuppence had summoned her, Mrs Boscowan rose suddenly to her feet.

'Do you mind if I go upstairs and have a wash?' she said.

'Oh! of course.' Miss Bligh jumped to her feet. 'I'll take you up, shall I, Vicar?'

'I know my way perfectly,' said Mrs Boscowan. 'Don't bother – Mrs Beresford?'

Tuppence jumped slightly.

'I'll show you,' said Mrs Boscowan, 'where things are. Come with me.'

Tuppence got up as obediently as a child. She did not describe it so to herself. But she knew that she had been summoned and when Mrs Boscowan summoned, you obeyed.

By then Mrs Boscowan was through the door to the hall and Tuppence had followed her. Mrs Boscowan started up the stairs – Tuppence came up behind her.

'The spare room is at the top of the stairs,' said Mrs Boscowan. 'It's always kept ready. It has a bathroom leading out of it.'

She opened the door at the top of the stairs, went through, switched on the light and Tuppence followed her in.

'I'm very glad to have found you here,' said Mrs Boscowan. 'I hoped I should. I was worried about you. Did your husband tell you?'

'I gathered you'd said something,' said Tuppence.

'Yes, I was worried.' She closed the door behind them, shutting them, as it were, into a private place of private consultation. 'Have you felt at all,' said Emma Boscowan, 'that Sutton Chancellor is a dangerous place?'

'It's been dangerous for me,' said Tuppence.

'Yes, I know. It's lucky it wasn't worse, but then – yes, I think I can understand that.'

'You know something,' said Tuppence. 'You know something about all this, don't you?'

'In a way,' said Emma Boscowan, 'in a way I do, and in a way I don't. One has instincts, feelings, you know. When they turn out to be right, it's worrying. This whole criminal gang business, it seems so extraordinary. It doesn't seem to have anything to do with –' She stopped abruptly.

'I mean, it's just one of those things that are going on – that have always gone on really. But they're very well organized now, like businesses. There's nothing really dangerous, you know, not about the criminal part of it. It's the *other*. It's knowing just where the danger is and how to guard against it. You must be careful, Mrs Beresford, you really must. You're one of those people who rush into things and it wouldn't be safe to do that. Not here.'

Tuppence said slowly, 'My old aunt – or rather Tommy's old aunt, she wasn't mine – someone told her in the nursing home where she died – that there was a killer.'

Emma nodded her head slowly.

'There were two deaths in that nursing home,' said Tuppence, 'and the doctor isn't satisfied about them.'

'Is that what started you off?'

'No,' said Tuppence, 'it was before that.'

'If you have time,' said Emma Boscowan, 'will you tell me very quickly – as quickly as you can because someone may interrupt us – just what happened at that nursing home or old ladies' home or whatever it was, to start you off?'

'Yes, I can tell you very quickly,' said Tuppence. She proceeded to do so.

'I see,' said Emma Boscowan. 'And you don't know where this old lady, this Mrs Lancaster, is now?'

'No, I don't.'

'Do you think she's dead?'

'I think she – might be.'

'Because she knew something?'

'Yes. She knew about something. Some murder. Some child perhaps who was killed.'

'I think you've gone wrong there,' said Mrs Boscowan.

'I think the child got mixed up in it and perhaps she got it mixed up. Your old lady, I mean. She got the child mixed up with something else, some other kind of killing.'

'I suppose it's possible. Old people do get mixed up. But there *was* a child murderer loose here, wasn't there? Or so the woman I lodged with here said.'

'There were several child murders in this part of the country, yes. But that was a good long time ago, you know. I'm not sure. The vicar wouldn't know. He wasn't there then. But Miss Bligh was. Yes, yes, she must have been here. She must have been a fairly young girl then.'

'I suppose so.'

Tuppence said, 'Has she always been in love with Sir Philip Starke?'

'You saw that, did you? Yes, I think so. Completely devoted beyond idolatry. We noticed it when we first came here, William and I.'

'What made you come here? Did you live in the Canal House?'

'No, we never lived there. He liked to paint it. He painted it several times. What's happened to the picture your husband showed me?'

'He brought it home again,' said Tuppence. 'He told me what you said about the boat – that your husband didn't paint it – the boat called *Waterlily* –'

'Yes. It wasn't painted by my husband. When I last saw the picture there was no boat there. Somebody painted it in.'

'And called it *Waterlily* – And a man who didn't exist, Major *Waters* – wrote about a child's grave – a child called Lilian – but there was no child buried in that grave, only a child's coffin, full of the proceeds of a big robbery. The painting of the boat must have been a message – a message to say where the loot was hidden – It all seems to tie up with crime . . .'

'It seems to, yes – But one can't be sure what –'

Emma Boscowan broke off abruptly. She said quickly, 'She's coming up to find us. Go into the bathroom –'

'Who?'

'Nellie Bligh. Pop into the bathroom – bolt the door.'

'She's just a busybody,' said Tuppence, disappearing into the bathroom.

'Something a little more than that,' said Mrs Boscowan.

Miss Bligh opened the door and came in, brisk and helpful.

'Oh, I hope you found everything you wanted?' she said. 'There were fresh towels and soap, I hope? Mrs Copleigh comes in to look after the vicar, but I really have to see she does things properly.'

Mrs Boscowan and Miss Bligh went downstairs together. Tuppence joined them just as they reached the drawing-room door. Sir Philip Starke rose as she came into the room, rearranged her chair and sat down beside her.

'Is that the way you like it, Mrs Beresford?'

'Yes, thank you,' said Tuppence. 'It's very comfortable.'

'I'm sorry to hear –' his voice had a vague charm to it, though it had some elements of a ghostlike voice, far-away, lacking in resonance, yet with a curious depth – 'about your accident,' he said. 'It's so sad nowadays – all the accidents there are.'

His eyes were wandering over her face and she thought to herself, 'He's making just as much a study of me as I made of him.' She gave a sharp half-glance at Tommy, but Tommy was talking to Emma Boscowan.

'What made you come to Sutton Chancellor in the first place, Mrs Beresford?'

'Oh, we're looking for a house in the country in a vague sort of way,' said Tuppence. 'My husband was away from home attending some congress or other and I thought I'd have a tour round a likely part of the countryside – just to see what there was going, and the kind of price one would have to pay, you know.'

'I hear you went and looked at the house by the canal bridge?'

'Yes, I did. I believe I'd once noticed it from the train. It's a very attractive-looking house – from the outside.'

'Yes. I should imagine, though, that even the outside

needs a great deal doing to it, to the roof and things like that. Not so attractive on the wrong side, is it?'

'No, it seems to me a curious way to divide up a house.'

'Oh well,' said Philip Starke, 'people have different ideas, don't they?'

'You never lived in it, did you?' asked Tuppence.

'No, no, indeed. My house was burnt down many years ago. There's part of it left still. I expect you've seen it or had it pointed out to you. It's above this vicarage, you know, a bit up the hill. At least what they call a hill in this part of the world. It was never much to boast of. My father built it way back in 1890 or so. A proud mansion. Gothic overlays, a touch of Balmoral. Our architects nowadays rather admire that kind of thing again, though actually forty years ago it was shuddered at. It had everything a so-called gentleman's house ought to have.' His voice was gently ironic. 'A billiard room, a morning room, ladies' parlour, colossal dining-room, a ballroom, about fourteen bedrooms, and once had – or so I should imagine – a staff of fourteen servants to look after it.'

'You sound as though you never liked it much yourself.'

'I never did. I was a disappointment to my father. He was a very successful industrialist. He hoped I would follow in his footsteps. I didn't. He treated me very well. He gave me a large income, or allowance – as it used to be called – and let me go my own way.'

'I heard you were a botanist.'

'Well, that was one of my great relaxations. I used to go looking for wild flowers, especially in the Balkans. Have you ever been to the Balkans looking for wild flowers? It's a wonderful place for them.'

'It sounds very attractive. Then you used to come back and live here?'

'I haven't lived here for a great many years now. In fact, I've never been back to live here since my wife died.'

'Oh,' said Tuppence, slightly embarrassed. 'Oh, I'm – I'm sorry.'

'It's quite a long time ago now. She died before the war. In 1938. She was a very beautiful woman,' he said.

'Do you have pictures of her in your house here still?'

'Oh no, the house is empty. All the furniture, pictures and things were sent away to be stored. There's just a bedroom and an office and a sitting-room where my agent comes, or I come if I have to come down here and see to any estate business.'

'It's never been sold?'

'No. There's some talk of having a development of the land there. I don't know. Not that I have any feeling for it. My father hoped that he was starting a kind of feudal domain. I was to succeed him and my children were to succeed me and so on and so on and so on.' He paused a minute and said then, 'But Julia and I never had any children.'

'Oh,' said Tuppence softly, 'I see.'

'So there's nothing to come hère for. In fact I hardly ever do. Anything that needs to be done here Nellie Bligh does for me.' He smiled over at her. 'She's been the most wonderful secretary. She still attends to my business affairs or anything of that kind.'

'You never come here and yet you don't want to sell it?' said Tuppence.

'There's a very good reason why not,' said Philip Starke.

A faint smile passed over the austere features.

'Perhaps after all I do inherit some of my father's business sense. The land, you know, is improving enormously in value. It's a better investment than money would be, if I sold it. Appreciates every day. Some day, who knows, we'll have a grand new dormitory town built on that land.'

'Then you'll be rich?'

'Then I'll be an even richer man than I am at present,' said Sir Philip. 'And I'm quite rich enough.'

'What do you do most of the time?'

'I travel, and I have interests in London. I have a

picture gallery there. I'm by way of being an art dealer. All those things are interesting. They occupy one's time – till the moment when the hand is laid on your shoulder which says "Depart".'

'Don't,' said Tuppence. 'That sounds – it gives me the shivers.'

'It needn't give you the shivers. I think you're going to have a long life, Mrs Beresford, and a very happy one.'

'Well, I'm very happy at present,' said Tuppence. 'I suppose I shall get all the aches and pains and troubles that old people do get. Deaf and blind and arthritis and a few other things.'

'You probably won't mind them as much as you think you will. If I may say so, without being rude, you and your husband seem to have a very happy life together.'

'Oh, we have,' said Tuppence. 'I suppose really,' she said, 'there's nothing in life like being happily married, is there?'

A moment later she wished she had not uttered these words. When she looked at the man opposite her, who she felt had grieved for so many years and indeed might still be grieving for the loss of a very much loved wife, she felt even more angry with herself.

Chapter 16

The Morning After

It was the morning after the party.

Ivor Smith and Tommy paused in their conversation and looked at each other, then they looked at Tuppence. Tuppence was staring into the grate. Her mind looked far away.

'Where have we got to?' said Tommy.

With a sigh Tuppence came back from where her thoughts had been wandering, and looked at the two men.

'It seems all tied up still to me,' she said. 'The party last night? What was it for? What did it all mean?' She looked at Ivor Smith. 'I suppose it meant something to you two. You know where we are?'

'I wouldn't go as far as that,' said Ivor. 'We're not all after the same thing, are we?'

'Not quite,' said Tuppence.

The men both looked at her inquiringly.

'All right,' said Tuppence. 'I'm a woman with an

obsession. *I want to find Mrs Lancaster.* I want to be sure that she's all right.'

'You want to find Mrs Johnson first,' said Tommy. 'You'll never find Mrs Lancaster till you find Mrs Johnson.'

'Mrs Johnson,' said Tuppence. 'Yes, I wonder – But I suppose none of that part of it interests you,' she said to Ivor Smith.

'Oh it does, Mrs Tommy, it does very much.'

'What about Mr Eccles?'

Ivor smiled. 'I think,' he said, 'that retribution might be overtaking Mr Eccles shortly. Still, I wouldn't bank on it. He's a man who covers his tracks with incredible ingenuity. So much so, that one imagines that there aren't really any tracks at all.' He added thoughtfully under his breath, 'A great administrator. A great planner.'

'Last night –' began Tuppence, and hesitated – 'Can I ask questions?'

'You can ask them,' Tommy told her. 'But don't bank on getting any satisfactory answers from old Ivor here.'

'Sir Philip Starke,' said Tuppence – 'Where does he come in? He doesn't seem to fit as a likely criminal – unless he was the kind that –'

She stopped, hastily biting off a reference to Mrs Copleigh's wilder suppositions as to child murderers –

'Sir Philip Starke comes in as a very valuable source

of information,' said Ivor Smith. 'He's the biggest landowner in these parts – and in other parts of England as well.'

'In Cumberland?'

Ivor Smith looked at Tuppence sharply. 'Cumberland? Why do you mention Cumberland? What do you know about Cumberland, Mrs Tommy?'

'Nothing,' said Tuppence. 'For some reason or other it just came into my head.' She frowned and looked perplexed. 'And a red and white striped rose on the side of a house – one of those old-fashioned roses.'

She shook her head.

'Does Sir Philip Starke own the Canal House?'

'He owns the land – He owns most of the land hereabouts.'

'Yes, he said so last night.'

'Through him, we've learned a good deal about leases and tenancies that have been cleverly obscured through legal complexities –'

'Those house agents I went to see in the Market Square – Is there something phony about them, or did I imagine it?'

'You didn't imagine it. We're going to pay them a visit this morning. We are going to ask some rather awkward questions.'

'Good,' said Tuppence.

'We're doing quite nicely. We've cleared up the big

post office robbery of 1965, and the Albury Cross robberies, and the Irish Mail train business. We've found some of the loot. Clever places they manufactured in these houses. A new bath installed in one, a service flat made in another – a couple of its rooms a little smaller than they ought to have been thereby providing for an interesting recess. Oh yes, we've found out a great deal.'

'But what about the *people*?' said Tuppence. 'I mean the people who thought of it, or ran it – apart from Mr Eccles, I mean. There must have been others who knew something.'

'Oh yes. There were a couple of men – one who ran a night club, conveniently just off the M1. Happy Hamish they used to call him. Slippery as an eel. And a woman they called Killer Kate – but that was a long time ago – one of our more interesting criminals. A beautiful girl, but her mental balance was doubtful. They eased her out – she might have become a danger to them. They were a strictly business concern – in it for loot – not for murder.'

'And was the Canal House one of their hideaway places?'

'At one time, Ladymead, they called it then. It's had a lot of different names in its time.'

'Just to make things more difficult, I suppose,' said Tuppence. 'Ladymead. I wonder if that ties up with some particular thing.'

'What should it tie up with?'

'Well, it doesn't really,' said Tuppence. 'It just started off another hare in my mind, if you know what I mean. The trouble is,' she added, 'I don't really know what I mean myself now. The picture, too. Boscowan painted the picture and then somebody else painted a boat into it, with a name on the boat –'

'Tiger Lily.'

'No, *Waterlily*. And his wife says that he didn't paint the boat.'

'Would she know?'

'I expect she would. If you were married to a painter, and especially if you were an artist yourself, I think you'd know if it was a different style of painting. She's rather frightening, I think,' said Tuppence.

'Who – Mrs Boscowan?'

'Yes. If you know what I mean, powerful. Rather overwhelming.'

'Possibly. Yes.'

'She knows things,' said Tuppence, 'but I'm not sure that she knows them because she knows them, if you know what I mean.'

'I don't,' said Tommy firmly.

'Well, I mean, there's one way of knowing things. The other way is that you sort of feel them.'

'That's rather the way you go in for, Tuppence.'

'You can say what you like,' said Tuppence, apparently

following her own track of thought, 'the whole thing ties up round Sutton Chancellor. Round Ladymead, or Canal House or whatever you like to call it. And all the people who lived there, now and in past times. Some things I think might go back a long way.'

'You're thinking of Mrs Copleigh.'

'On the whole,' said Tuppence, 'I think Mrs Copleigh just put in a lot of things which have made everything more difficult. I think she's got all her times and dates mixed up too.'

'People do,' said Tommy, 'in the country.'

'I know that,' said Tuppence, 'I was brought up in a country vicarage, after all. They date things by events, they don't date them by years. They don't say "that happened in 1930" or "that happened in 1925" or things like that. They say "that happened the year after the old mill burned down" or "that happened after the lightning struck the big oak and killed Farmer James" or "that was the year we had the polio epidemic". So naturally, of course, the things they do remember don't go in any particular sequence. Everything's very difficult,' she added. 'There are just bits poking up here and there, if you know what I mean. Of course the point is,' said Tuppence with the air of someone who suddenly makes an important discovery, 'the trouble is that I'm old myself.'

'You are eternally young,' said Ivor gallantly.

'Don't be daft,' said Tuppence, scathingly. I'm old because I remember things that same way. I've gone back to being primitive in my aids to memory.'

She got up and walked round the room.

'This is an annoying kind of hotel,' she said.

She went through the door into her bedroom and came back again shaking her head.

'No Bible,' she said.

'Bible?'

'Yes. You know, in old-fashioned hotels, they've always got a Gideon Bible by your bed. I suppose so that you can get saved any moment of the day or night. Well, they don't have that here.'

'Do you want a Bible?'

'Well, I do rather. I was brought up properly and I used to know my Bible quite well, as any good clergyman's daughter should. But now, you see, one rather forgets. Especially as they don't read the lessons properly any more in churches. They give you some new version where all the wording, I suppose, is technically right and a proper translation, but sounds nothing like it used to. While you two go to the house agents, I shall drive into Sutton Chancellor,' she added.

'What for? I forbid you,' said Tommy.

'Nonsense – I'm not going to sleuth. I shall just go into the church and look at the Bible. If it's some modern version, I shall go and ask the vicar, he'll have a Bible, won't he? The proper kind, I mean. Authorized Version.'

'What do you want the Authorized Version for?'

'I just want to refresh my memory over those words that were scratched on the child's tombstone . . . They interested me.'

'It's all very well – but I don't trust you, Tuppence – don't trust you not to get into trouble once you're out of my sight.'

'I give you my word I'm not going to prowl about in graveyards any more. The church on a sunny morning and the vicar's study – that's all – what could be more harmless?'

Tommy looked at his wife doubtfully and gave in.

II

Having left her car by the lych-gate at Sutton Chancellor, Tuppence looked round her carefully before entering the church precincts. She had the natural distrust of one who has suffered grievous bodily harm in a certain geographical spot. There did not on this occasion seem to be any possible assailants lurking behind the tombstones.

She went into the church, where an elderly woman was on her knees polishing some brasses. Tuppence tiptoed up to the lectern and made a tentative examination of the volume that rested there. The woman cleaning the brasses looked up with a disapproving glance.

'I'm not going to steal it,' said Tuppence reassuringly, and carefully closing it again, she tiptoed out of the church.

She would have liked to examine the spot where the recent excavations had taken place, but that she had undertaken on no account to do.

'*Whosoever shall offend*,' she murmured to herself. 'It might mean that, but if so it would have to be someone –'

She drove the car the short distance to the vicarage, got out and went up the path to the front door. She rang but could hear no tinkle from inside. 'Bell's broken, I expect,' said Tuppence, knowing the habits of vicarage bells. She pushed the door and it responded to her touch.

She stood inside in the hall. On the hall table a large envelope with a foreign stamp took up a good deal of space. It bore the printed legend of a Missionary Society in Africa.

'I'm glad I'm not a missionary,' thought Tuppence.

Behind that vague thought, there lay something else, something connected with some hall table somewhere, something that she ought to remember . . . Flowers? Leaves? Some letter or parcel?

At that moment the vicar came out from the door on the left.

'Oh,' he said. 'Do you want me? I – oh, it's Mrs Beresford, isn't it?'

'Quite right,' said Tuppence. 'What I really came to ask you was whether by any chance you had a Bible.'

'Bible,' said the vicar, looking rather unexpectedly doubtful. 'A Bible.'

'I thought it likely that you might have,' said Tuppence.

'Of course, of course,' said the vicar. 'As a matter of fact, I suppose I've got several. I've got a Greek Testament,' he said hopefully. 'That's not what you want, I suppose?'

'No,' said Tuppence. 'I want,' she said firmly, 'the Authorized Version.'

'Oh dear,' said the vicar. 'Of course, there must be several in the house. Yes, several. We don't use that version in the church now, I'm sorry to say. One has to fall in with the bishop's ideas, you know, and the bishop is very keen on modernization, for young people and all that. A pity, I think. I have so many books in my library here that some of them, you know, get pushed behind the others. But I *think* I can find you what you want. I *think* so. If not, we'll ask Miss Bligh. She's here somewhere looking out the vases for the children who arrange their wild flowers for the Children's Corner in the church.' He left Tuppence in the hall and went back into the room where he had come from.

Tuppence did not follow him. She remained in the

hall, frowning and thinking. She looked up suddenly as the door at the end of the hall opened and Miss Bligh came through it. She was holding up a very heavy metal vase.

Several things clicked together in Tuppence's head.

'Of course,' said Tuppence, '*of course*.'

'Oh, can I help – I – oh, it's Mrs Beresford.'

'Yes,' said Tuppence, and added, 'And *it's Mrs Johnson, isn't it*?'

The heavy vase fell to the floor. Tuppence stooped and picked it up. She stood weighing it in her hand. 'Quite a handy weapon,' she said. She put it down. 'Just the thing to cosh anyone with from behind,' she said – 'That's what you did to me, didn't you, *Mrs Johnson*.'

'I – I – what did you say? I – I – I never –'

But Tuppence had no need to stay longer. She had seen the effect of her words. At the second mention of Mrs Johnson, Miss Bligh had given herself away in an unmistakable fashion. She was shaking and panic-stricken.

'There was a letter on your hall table the other day,' said Tuppence, 'addressed to a Mrs Yorke at an address in Cumberland. That's where you took her, isn't it, Mrs Johnson, when you took her away from Sunny Ridge? That's where she is now. Mrs Yorke or Mrs Lancaster – you used either name – York and Lancaster like the striped red and white rose in the Perrys' garden –'

She turned swiftly and went out of the house leaving Miss Bligh in the hall, still supporting herself on the stair rail, her mouth open, staring after her. Tuppence ran down the path to the gate, jumped into her car and drove away. She looked back towards the front door, but no one emerged. Tuppence drove past the church and back towards Market Basing, but suddenly changed her mind. She turned the car, drove back the way she had come, and took the left-hand road leading to the Canal House bridge. She abandoned the car, looked over the gate to see if either of the Perrys were in the garden, but there was no sign of them. She went through the gate and up the path to the back door. That was closed too and the windows were shut.

Tuppence felt annoyed. Perhaps Alice Perry had gone to Market Basing to shop. She particularly wanted to see Alice Perry. Tuppence knocked at the door, rapping first gently then loudly. Nobody answered. She turned the handle but the door did not give. It was locked. She stood there, undecided.

There were some questions she wanted badly to ask Alice Perry. Possibly Mrs Perry might be in Sutton Chancellor. She might go back there. The difficulty of Canal House was that there never seemed to be anyone in sight and hardly any traffic came over the bridge. There was no one to ask where the Perrys might be this morning.

Chapter 17

Mrs Lancaster

Tuppence stood there frowning, and then, suddenly, quite unexpectedly, the door opened. Tuppence drew back a step and gasped. The person confronting her was the last person in the world she expected to see. In the doorway, dressed exactly the same as she had been at Sunny Ridge, and smiling the same way with that air of vague amiability, was Mrs Lancaster in person.

'Oh,' said Tuppence.

'Good morning. Were you wanting Mrs Perry?' said Mrs Lancaster. 'It's market day, you know. So lucky I was able to let you in. I couldn't find the key for some time. I think it must be a duplicate anyway, don't you? But do come in. Perhaps you'd like a cup of tea or something.'

Like one in a dream, Tuppence crossed the threshold. Mrs Lancaster, still retaining the gracious air of a hostess, led Tuppence along into the sitting-room.

'Do sit down,' she said. 'I'm afraid I don't know where all the cups and things are. I've only been here a day or two. Now – let me see . . . But – surely – I've met you before, haven't I?'

'Yes,' said Tuppence, 'when you were at Sunny Ridge.'

'Sunny Ridge, now, Sunny Ridge. That seems to remind me of something. Oh, of course, dear Miss Packard. Yes, a very nice place.'

'You left it in rather a hurry, didn't you?' said Tuppence.

'People are so very bossy,' said Mrs Lancaster. 'They hurry you so. They don't give you time to *arrange* things or *pack* properly or *anything*. Kindly meant, I'm sure. Of course, I'm very fond of dear Nellie Bligh, but she's a very masterful kind of woman. I sometimes think,' Mrs Lancaster added, bending forward to Tuppence, 'I sometimes think, you know, that she is not quite –' she tapped her forehead significantly. 'Of course it *does* happen. Especially to spinsters. Unmarried women, you know. Very given to good works and all that but they take very odd fancies sometimes. Curates suffer a great deal. They seem to think sometimes, these women, that the curate has made them an offer of marriage but really he never thought of doing anything of the kind. Oh yes, poor Nellie. So sensible in some ways. She's been wonderful in the parish here. And she was always a first-class secretary, I believe. But all the same she has some very curious ideas at times. Like taking me away at a moment's notice from dear Sunny Ridge, and then up to Cumberland – a very bleak house, and, again quite suddenly, bringing me here –'

'Are you living here?' said Tuppence.

'Well, if you can *call* it that. It's a very peculiar arrangement altogether. I've only been here two days.'

'Before that, you were at Rosetrellis Court, in Cumberland –'

'Yes, I believe that was the name of it. Not such a pretty name as Sunny Ridge, do you think? In fact I never really settled down, if you know what I mean. And it wasn't nearly as well run. The service wasn't as good and they had a very inferior brand of coffee. Still, I was getting used to things and I had found one or two interesting acquaintances there. One of them who knew an aunt of mine quite well years ago in India. It's so nice, you know, when you find *connections*.'

'It must be,' said Tuppence.

Mrs Lancaster continued cheerfully.

'Now let me see, you came to Sunny Ridge, but not to stay, I think. I think you came to see one of the guests there.'

'My husband's aunt,' said Tuppence, 'Miss Fanshawe.'

'Oh yes. Yes of course. I remember now. And wasn't

there something about a child of yours behind the chimney piece?'

'No,' said Tuppence, 'no, it wasn't my child.'

'But that's why you've come here, isn't it? They've had trouble with a chimney here. A bird got into it, I understand. This place wants repairing. I don't like being here at *all*. No, not at all and I shall tell Nellie so as soon as I see her.'

'You're lodging with Mrs Perry?'

'Well, in a way I am, and in a way I'm not. I think I could trust you with a secret, couldn't I?'

'Oh yes,' said Tuppence, 'you can trust me.'

'Well, I'm not really here at all. I mean not in this part of the house. This is the Perrys' part of the house.' She leaned forward. 'There's another one, you know, if you go upstairs. Come with me. I'll take you.'

Tuppence rose. She felt that she was in rather a crazy kind of dream.

'I'll just lock the door first, it's safer,' said Mrs Lancaster.

She led Tuppence up a rather narrow staircase to the first floor. She took her through a double bedroom with signs of occupation – presumably the Perrys' room – and through a door leading out of that into another room next door. It contained a washstand and a tall wardrobe of maple wood. Nothing else. Mrs Lancaster went to the maple wardrobe, fumbled at the back of it, then with sudden ease pushed it aside. There seemed to be castors on the wardrobe and it rolled out from the wall easily enough. Behind the wardrobe there was, rather strangely, Tuppence thought, a grate. Over the mantelpiece there was a mirror with a small shelf under the mirror on which were china figures of birds.

To Tuppence's astonishment Mrs Lancaster seized the bird in the middle of the mantelshelf and gave it a sharp pull. Apparently the bird was stuck to the mantelpiece. In fact, by a swift touch Tuppence perceived that all the birds were firmly fastened down. But as a result of Mrs Lancaster's action there was a click and the whole mantelpiece came away from the wall and swung forward.

'Clever, isn't it?' said Mrs Lancaster. 'It was done a long time ago, you know, when they altered the house. The priest's hole, you know, they used to call this room but I don't think it was really a priest's hole. No, nothing to do with priests. I've never thought so. Come through. This is where I live now.'

She gave another push. The wall in front of her also swung back and a minute or two later they were in a large attractive-looking room with windows that gave out on the canal and the hill opposite.

'A lovely room, isn't it?' said Mrs Lancaster. 'Such a lovely view. I always liked it. I lived here for a time as a girl, you know.'

'Oh, I see.'

'Not a lucky house,' said Mrs Lancaster. 'No, they always said it wasn't a lucky house. I think, you know,' she added, 'I think I'll shut up this again. One can't be too careful, can one?'

She stretched out a hand and pushed the door they had come through back again. There was a sharp click as the mechanism swung into place.

'I suppose,' said Tuppence, 'that this was one of the alterations they made to the house when they wanted to use it as a hiding place.'

'They did a lot of alterations,' said Mrs Lancaster. 'Sit down, do. Do you like a high chair or a low one? I like a high one myself. I'm rather rheumatic, you know. I suppose you thought there might have been a child's body there,' added Mrs Lancaster. 'An absurd idea really, don't you think so?'

'Yes, perhaps.'

'Cops and robbers,' said Mrs Lancaster, with an indulgent air. 'One is so foolish when one is young, you know. All that sort of thing. Gangs – big robberies – it has such an appeal for one when one is young. One thinks being a gunman's moll would be the most wonderful thing in the world. I thought so once. Believe me –' she leaned forward and tapped Tuppence on the knee '– believe me, *it's not true.* It isn't really. I thought so once, but one wants more than that, you know.

There's no thrill really in just stealing things and getting away with it. It needs good organization, of course.'

'You mean Mrs Johnson or Miss Bligh – whichever you call her –'

'Well, of course, she's always Nellie Bligh to me. But for some reason or other – to facilitate things, she says – she calls herself Mrs Johnson now and then. But she's never been married, you know. Oh no. She's a regular spinster.'

A sound of knocking came to them from below.

'Dear me,' said Mrs Lancaster, 'that must be the Perrys back again. I'd no idea they were going to be back so soon.'

The knocking went on.

'Perhaps we ought to let them in,' suggested Tuppence.

'No, dear, we won't do that,' said Mrs Lancaster. 'I can't stand people always interfering. We're having such a nice little talk up here, aren't we? I think we'll just stay up here – oh dear, now they're calling under the window. Just look out and see who it is.'

Tuppence went to the window.

'It's Mr Perry,' she said.

From below, Mr Perry shouted,

'Julia! Julia!'

'Impertinence,' said Mrs Lancaster. 'I don't allow people like Amos Perry to call me by my Christian name. No, indeed. Don't worry, dear,' she added, 'we're quite safe here. And we can have a nice little talk. I'll tell you all about myself – I've really had a very interesting life – Eventful – Sometimes I think I ought to write it down. I was mixed up, you see. I was a wild girl, and I was mixed up with – well, really just a common gang of criminals. No other word for it. Some of them *very* undesirable people. Mind you, there *were* nice people among them. Quite good class.'

'Miss Bligh?'

'No, no, Miss Bligh never had anything to do with crime. Not Nellie Bligh. Oh no, she's very churchy, you know. Religious. All that. But there are different ways of religion. Perhaps you know that, do you?'

'I suppose there are a lot of different sects,' Tuppence suggested.

'Yes, there have to be, for ordinary people. But there are others besides ordinary people. There are some special ones, under special commands. There are special legions. Do you understand what I mean, my dear?'

'I don't think I do,' said Tuppence. 'Don't you think we ought to let the Perrys into their own house? They're getting rather upset –'

'No, we're not going to let the Perrys in. Not till – well, not till I've told you all about it. You mustn't be frightened, my dear. It's all quite – quite natural, quite harmless. There's no pain of any kind. It'll be just like going to sleep. Nothing worse.'

Tuppence stared at her, then she jumped up and went towards the door in the wall.

'You can't get out that way,' said Mrs Lancaster. 'You don't know where the catch is. It's not where you think it is at all. Only I know that. I know all the secrets of this place. I lived here with the criminals when I was a girl until I went away from them all and got salvation. Special salvation. That's what was given to me – to expiate my sin – The child, you know – I killed it. I was a dancer – I didn't want a child – Over there, on the wall – that's my picture – as a dancer –'

Tuppence followed the pointing finger. On the wall hung an oil painting, full length, of a girl in a costume of white satin leaves with the legend 'Waterlily'.

'Waterlily was one of my best roles. Everyone said so.'

Tuppence came back slowly and sat down. She stared at Mrs Lancaster. As she did so words repeated in her head. Words heard at Sunny Ridge. '*Was it your poor child*?' She had been frightened then, frightened. She was frightened now. She was as yet not quite sure what she was frightened of, but the same fear was there. Looking at that benignant face, that kindly smile.

'I had to obey the commands given me – There have to be agents of destruction. I was appointed to that. I accepted my appointment. They go free of sin, you see. I mean, the children went free of sin. They were not old enough to sin. So I sent them to Glory as I was appointed to do. Still innocent. Still not knowing evil. You can see what a great honour it was to be chosen. To be one of the specially chosen. I always loved children. I had none of my own. That was very cruel, wasn't it, or it seemed cruel. But it was retribution really for what I'd done. You know perhaps what I'd done.'

'No,' said Tuppence.

'Oh, you seem to know so much. I thought perhaps you'd know that too. There was a doctor. I went to him. I was only seventeen then and I was frightened. He said it would be all right to have the child taken away so that nobody would ever know. But it wasn't all right, you see. I began to have dreams. I had dreams that the child was always there, asking me why it had never had life. The child told me it wanted companions. It was a girl, you know. Yes, I'm sure it was a girl. She came and she wanted other children. Then I got the command. *I* couldn't have any children. I'd married and I thought I'd have children, then my husband wanted children passionately but the children never came, because I was cursed, you see. You understand that, don't you? But there was a way, a way to atone. To atone for what I'd done. What I'd done was murder, wasn't it, and you could only atone for murder with other murders, because the other murders wouldn't be really murders, they would be *sacrifices.* They would be offered up. You do see the difference, don't you? The children went to keep my child company. Children of different ages but young. The command would come and then –' she leaned forward and touched Tuppence '– it was such a happy thing to do. You understand that, don't you? It was so happy to release them so that they'd never know sin like I knew sin. I couldn't tell anyone, of course, nobody was ever to know. That was the thing I had to be sure about. But there were people sometimes who got to know or to suspect. Then of course – well, I mean it had to be death for them too, so that *I* should be safe. So I've always been quite safe. You understand, don't you?'

'Not – not quite.'

'But you do *know.* That's why you came here, isn't it? You knew. You knew the day I asked you at Sunny Ridge. I saw by your face. I said "Was it your poor child?" I thought you'd come, perhaps because you were a mother. One of those whose children I'd killed. I hoped you'd come back another time and then we'd have a glass of milk together. It was usually milk. Sometimes cocoa. Anyone who knew about me.'

She moved slowly across the room and opened a cupboard in a corner of the room.

'Mrs Moody –' said Tuppence, 'was she one?'

'Oh, you know about her – she wasn't a mother – she'd been a dresser at the theatre. She recognized me so she had to go.' Turning suddenly she came towards Tuppence holding a glass of milk and smiling persuasively.

'Drink it up,' she said. 'Just drink it up.'

Tuppence sat silent for a moment, then she leapt to her feet and rushed to the window. Catching up a chair, she crashed the glass. She leaned her head out and screamed:

'Help! Help!'

Mrs Lancaster laughed. She put the glass of milk down on a table and leant back in her chair and laughed.

'How stupid you are. Who do you think will come? Who do you think *can* come? They'd have to break down doors, they'd have to get through that wall and by that time – there are other things, you know. It needn't be milk. Milk is the easy way. Milk and cocoa and even tea. For little Mrs Moody I put it in cocoa – she loved cocoa.'

'The morphia? How did you get it?'

'Oh, that was easy. A man I lived with years ago – he had cancer – the doctor gave me supplies for him – to keep in my charge – other drugs too – I said later that they'd all been thrown away – but I kept them, and other drugs and sedatives too – I thought they might come in useful some day – and they did – I've still got a supply – I never take anything of the kind myself – I don't believe in it.' She pushed the glass of milk towards Tuppence – 'Drink it up, it's much the easiest way. The other way – the trouble is, I can't be sure just where I put it.'

She got up from her chair and began walking round the room.

'Where *did* I put it? Where did I? I forget everything now I'm getting old.'

Tuppence yelled again. 'Help!' but the canal bank was empty still. Mrs Lancaster was still wandering round the room.

'I thought – I certainly thought – oh, of course, in my knitting bag.'

Tuppence turned from the window. Mrs Lancaster was coming towards her.

'What a silly woman you are,' said Mrs Lancaster, 'to want it this way.'

Her left arm shot out and she caught Tuppence's shoulder. Her right hand came from behind her back. In it was a long thin stiletto blade. Tuppence struggled. She thought, 'I can stop her easily. Easily. She's an old woman. Feeble. She can't –'

Suddenly in a cold tide of fear she thought, 'But *I'm* an old woman too. I'm not as strong as I think myself. I'm not as strong as she is. Her hands, her grasp, her fingers. I suppose because she's mad and mad people, I've always heard, are strong.'

The gleaming blade was approaching near her. Tuppence screamed. Down below she heard shouts and blows. Blows now on the doors as though someone were trying to force the doors or windows. 'But they'll never get through,' thought Tuppence. 'They'll never get through this trick doorway here. Not unless they know the mechanism.'

She struggled fiercely. She was still managing to hold Mrs Lancaster away from her. But the other was the bigger woman. A big strong woman. Her face was still smiling but it no longer had the benignant look. It had the look now of someone enjoying herself.

'Killer Kate,' said Tuppence.

'You know my nickname? Yes, but I've sublimated that. I've become a killer of the Lord. It's the Lord's will that I should kill you. So that makes it all right. You do see that, don't you? You see, it makes it all right.'

Tuppence was pressed now against the side of a big chair. With one arm Mrs Lancaster held her against the chair, and the pressure increased – no further recoil was possible. In Mrs Lancaster's right hand the sharp steel of the stiletto approached.

Tuppence thought, 'I mustn't panic – I mustn't panic –' But following that came with sharp insistence, '*But what can I do*?' To struggle was unavailing.

Fear came then – the same sharp fear of which she had the first indication in Sunny Ridge –

'*Is it your poor child*?'

That had been the first warning – but she had misunderstood it – she had not known it was a warning.

Her eyes watched the approaching steel but strangely enough it was not the gleaming metal and its menace that frightened her into a state of paralysis; it was the face above it – it was the smiling benignant face of Mrs Lancaster – smiling happily, contentedly – a woman pursuing her appointed task, with gentle reasonableness.

'She doesn't *look* mad,' thought Tuppence – 'That's what's so awful – Of course she doesn't because in her own mind she's sane. She's a perfectly normal, reasonable human being – that's what she *thinks* – Oh Tommy, Tommy, what have I got myself into this time?'

Dizziness and limpness submerged her. Her muscles relaxed – somewhere there was a great crash of broken glass. It swept her away, into darkness and unconsciousness.

II

'That's better – you're coming round – drink this, Mrs Beresford.'

A glass pressed against her lips – she resisted fiercely – Poisoned milk – who had said that once – something about 'poisoned milk'? She wouldn't drink poisoned milk . . . No, not milk – quite a different smell –

She relaxed, her lips opened – she sipped –

'Brandy,' said Tuppence with recognition.

'Quite right! Go on – drink some more –'

Tuppence sipped again. She leaned back against cushions, surveyed her surroundings. The top of a ladder showed through the window. In front of the window there was a mass of broken glass on the floor.

'I heard the glass break.'

She pushed away the brandy glass and her eyes followed up the hand and arm to the face of the man who had been holding it.

'El Greco,' said Tuppence.

'I beg your pardon.'

'It doesn't matter.'

She looked round the room.

'Where is she – Mrs Lancaster, I mean?'

'She's – resting – in the next room –'

'I see.' But she wasn't sure that she did see. She would see better presently. Just now only one idea would come at a time –

'Sir Philip Starke.' She said it slowly and doubtfully. 'That's right?'

'Yes – Why did you say El Greco?'

'Suffering.'

'I beg your pardon.'

'The picture – In Toledo – Or in the Prado – I thought so a long time ago – no, not very long ago –' She thought about it – made a discovery – 'Last night. A party – At the vicarage –'

'You're doing fine,' he said encouragingly.

It seemed very natural, somehow, to be sitting here, in this room with broken glass on the floor, talking to this man – with the dark agonized face –

'I made a mistake – at Sunny Ridge. I was all wrong about her – I was afraid, then – a – wave of fear – But I got it wrong – I wasn't afraid of *her* – I was afraid *for* her – I thought something was going to happen to her – I wanted to protect her – to save her – I –' She looked doubtfully at him. 'Do you understand? Or does it sound silly?'

'Nobody understands better than I do – nobody in this world.'

Tuppence stared at him – frowning.

'Who – who was she? I mean Mrs Lancaster – Mrs Yorke – that's not real – that's just taken from a rose tree – who was she – herself?'

Philip Starke said harshly:

'*Who was she? Herself? The real one, the true one*

Who was she – with God's Sign upon her brow?'

'Did you ever read Peer Gynt, Mrs Beresford?'

He went to the window. He stood there a moment, looking out – Then he turned abruptly.

'She was my wife, God help me.'

'Your wife – But she died – the tablet in the church –'

'She died abroad – that was the story I circulated – And I put up a tablet to her memory in the church. People don't like to ask too many questions of a bereaved widower. I didn't go on living here.'

'Some people said she had left you.'

'That made an acceptable story, too.'

'You took her away when you found out – about the children –'

'So you know about the children?'

'She told me – It seemed – unbelievable.'

'Most of the time she was quite normal – no one would have guessed. But the police were beginning to suspect – I had to act – I had to save her – to protect her – You understand – can you understand – in the very least?'

'Yes,' said Tuppence, 'I can understand quite well.'

'She was – so lovely once –' His voice broke a little. 'You see her – there,' he pointed to the painting on the wall. 'Waterlily – She was a wild girl – always. Her mother was the last of the Warrenders – an old family – inbred – Helen Warrender – ran away from home. She took up with a bad lot – a gaolbird – her daughter went on the stage – she trained as a dancer – Waterlily was her most popular role – then she took up with a criminal gang – for excitement – purely to get a kick out of it – She was always being disappointed –

'When she married me, she had finished with all that – she wanted to settle down – to live quietly – a family life – with children. I was rich – I could give her all the things she wanted. But we had no children. It was a sorrow to both of us. She began to have obsessions of guilt – Perhaps she had always been slightly unbalanced – I don't know – What do causes matter? – She was –'

He made a despairing gesture.

'I loved her – I always loved her – no matter what she was – what she did – I wanted her safe – to keep her safe – not shut up – a prisoner for life, eating her heart out. And we did keep her safe – for many many years.'

'We?'

'Nellie – my dear faithful Nellie Bligh. My dear Nellie Bligh. She was wonderful – planned and arranged it all. The Homes for the Elderly – every comfort and luxury. And no temptations – *no children* – keep children out of her way – It seemed to work – these homes were in faraway places – Cumberland – North Wales – no one was likely to recognize her – or so we thought. It was on Mr Eccles's advice – a very shrewd lawyer – his charges were high – but I relied on him.'

'Blackmail?' suggested Tuppence.

'I never thought of it like that. He was a friend, and an adviser –'

'Who painted the boat in the picture – the boat called *Waterlily*?'

'I did. It pleased her. She remembered her triumph on the stage. It was one of Boscowan's pictures. She liked his pictures. Then, one day, she wrote a name in black pigment on the bridge – the name of a dead child – So I painted a boat to hide it and labelled the boat *Waterlily* –'

The door in the wall swung open – The friendly witch came through it.

She looked at Tuppence and from Tuppence to Philip Starke.

'All right again?' she said in a matter-of-fact way.

'Yes,' said Tuppence. The nice thing about the

friendly witch, she saw, was that there wasn't going to be any fuss.

'Your husband's down below, waiting in the car. I said I'd bring you down to him – if that's the way you want it?'

'That's the way I want it,' said Tuppence.

'I thought you would.' She looked towards the door into the bedroom. 'Is she – in there?'

'Yes,' said Philip Starke.

Mrs Perry went to the bedroom. She came out again –

'I see –' She looked at him inquiringly.

'She offered Mrs Beresford a glass of milk – Mrs Beresford didn't want it.'

'And so, I suppose, she drank it herself?'

He hesitated.

'Yes.'

'Dr Mortimer will be along later,' said Mrs Perry.

She came to help Tuppence to her feet, but Tuppence rose unaided.

'I'm not hurt,' she said. 'It was just shock – I'm quite all right now.'

She stood facing Philip Starke – neither of them seemed to have anything to say. Mrs Perry stood by the door in the wall.

Tuppence spoke at last.

'There is nothing I can do, is there?' she said, but it was hardly a question.

'Only one thing – It was Nellie Bligh who struck you down in the churchyard that day.'

Tuppence nodded.

'I've realized it must have been.'

'She lost her head. She thought you were on the track of her, of our, secret. She – I'm bitterly remorseful for the terrible strain I've subjected her to all these long years. It's been more than any woman ought to be asked to bear –'

'She loved you very much, I suppose,' said Tuppence. 'But I don't think we'll go on looking for any Mrs Johnson, if that is what you want to ask *us* not to do.'

'Thank you – I'm very grateful.'

There was another silence. Mrs Perry waited patiently. Tuppence looked round her. She went to the broken window and looked at the peaceful canal down below.

'I don't suppose I shall ever see this house again. I'm looking at it very hard, so that I shall be able to remember it.'

'Do you want to remember it?'

'Yes, I do. Someone said to me that it was a house that had been put to the wrong use. I know what they meant now.'

He looked at her questioningly, but did not speak.

'Who sent you here to find me?' asked Tuppence.

'Emma Boscowan.'

'I thought so.'

She joined the friendly witch and they went through the secret door and on down.

A house for lovers, Emma Boscowan had said to Tuppence. Well, that was how she was leaving it – in the possession of two lovers – one dead and one who suffered and lived –

She went out through the door to where Tommy and the car were waiting.

She said goodbye to the friendly witch. She got into the car.

'Tuppence,' said Tommy.

'I know,' said Tuppence.

'Don't do it again,' said Tommy. 'Don't ever do it again.'

'I won't.'

'That's what you say now, but you will.'

'No, I shan't. I'm too old.'

Tommy pressed the starter. They drove off.

'Poor Nellie Bligh,' said Tuppence.

'Why do you say that?'

'So terribly in love with Philip Starke. Doing all those things for him all those years – such a lot of wasted doglike devotion.'

'Nonsense!' said Tommy. 'I expect she's enjoyed every minute of it. Some women do.'

'Heartless brute,' said Tuppence.

'Where do you want to go – The Lamb and Flag at Market Basing?'

'No,' said Tuppence. 'I want to go home. HOME, Thomas. And stay there.'

'Amen to that,' said Mr Beresford. '*And if Albert welcomes us with a charred chicken, I'll kill him*!'

Partners in Crime

Agatha Christie is known throughout the world as the Queen of Crime. Her books have sold over a billion copies in English with another billion in 100 foreign languages. She is the most widely published author of all time and in any language, outsold only by the Bible and Shakespeare. She is the author of 80 crime novels and short story collections, 19 plays, and six novels written under the name of Mary Westmacott.

Agatha Christie's first novel, *The Mysterious Affair at Styles*, was written towards the end of the First World War, in which she served as a VAD. In it she created Hercule Poirot, the little Belgian detective who was destined to become the most popular detective in crime fiction since Sherlock Holmes. It was eventually published by The Bodley Head in 1920.

In 1926, after averaging a book a year, Agatha Christie wrote her masterpiece. *The Murder of Roger Ackroyd* was the first of her books to be published by Collins and marked the beginning of an author-publisher relationship which lasted for 50 years and well over 70 books. *The Murder of Roger Ackroyd* was also the first of Agatha Christie's books to be dramatized – under the name *Alibi* – and to have a successful run in London's West End. *The Mousetrap*, her most famous play of all, opened in 1952 and is the longest-running play in history.

Agatha Christie was made a Dame in 1971. She died in 1976, since when a number of books have been published posthumously: the bestselling novel *Sleeping Murder* appeared later that year, followed by her autobiography and the short story collections *Miss Marple's Final Cases*, *Problem at Pollensa Bay* and *While the Light Lasts*. In 1998 *Black Coffee* was the first of her plays to be novelized by another author, Charles Osborne.

The Agatha Christie Collection

The Man In The Brown Suit
The Secret of Chimneys
The Seven Dials Mystery
The Mysterious Mr Quin
The Sittaford Mystery
The Hound of Death
The Listerdale Mystery
Why Didn't They Ask Evans?
Parker Pyne Investigates
Murder Is Easy
And Then There Were None
Towards Zero
Death Comes as the End
Sparkling Cyanide
Crooked House
They Came to Baghdad
Destination Unknown
Spider's Web *
The Unexpected Guest *
Ordeal by Innocence
The Pale Horse
Endless Night
Passenger To Frankfurt
Problem at Pollensa Bay
While the Light Lasts

Poirot

The Mysterious Affair at Styles
The Murder on the Links
Poirot Investigates
The Murder of Roger Ackroyd
The Big Four
The Mystery of the Blue Train
Black Coffee *
Peril at End House
Lord Edgware Dies
Murder on the Orient Express
Three-Act Tragedy
Death in the Clouds
The ABC Murders
Murder in Mesopotamia
Cards on the Table
Murder in the Mews
Dumb Witness
Death on the Nile
Appointment With Death
Hercule Poirot's Christmas
Sad Cypress
One, Two, Buckle My Shoe
Evil Under the Sun
Five Little Pigs

* novelised by Charles Osborne

The Hollow
The Labours of Hercules
Taken at the Flood
Mrs McGinty's Dead
After the Funeral
Hickory Dickory Dock
Dead Man's Folly
Cat Among the Pigeons
The Adventure of the Christmas Pudding
The Clocks
Third Girl
Hallowe'en Party
Elephants Can Remember
Poirot's Early Cases
Curtain: Poirot's Last Case

Marple

The Murder at the Vicarage
The Thirteen Problems
The Body in the Library
The Moving Finger
A Murder is Announced
They Do It With Mirrors
A Pocket Full of Rye
The 4.50 from Paddington
The Mirror Crack'd from Side to Side
A Caribbean Mystery
At Bertram's Hotel
Nemesis
Sleeping Murder
Miss Marple's Final Cases

Tommy & Tuppence

The Secret Adversary
Partners in Crime
N or M?
By the Pricking of My Thumbs
Postern of Fate

Published as Mary Westmacott

Giant's Bread
Unfinished Portrait
Absent in the Spring
The Rose and the Yew Tree
A Daughter's a Daughter
The Burden

Memoirs

An Autobiography
Come, Tell Me How You Live

Play Collections

The Mousetrap and Selected Plays
Witness for the Prosecution and
Selected Plays

Agatha Christie

Partners in Crime

HarperCollinsPublishers

HarperCollins*Publishers*
77–85 Fulham Palace Road
Hammersmith, London W6 8JB
www.**fire**and**water**.com

This *Agatha Christie Signature Edition* published 2001
3 5 7 9 8 6 4 2

First published in Great Britain by
Collins 1929

ISBN 0 00 711150 9

Typeset by Palimpsest Book Production Limited,
Polmont, Stirlingshire

Printed in Great Britain by
Clays Ltd, St Ives plc

Contents

Chapter 1

A Fairy in the Flat

Mrs Thomas Beresford shifted her position on the divan and looked gloomily out of the window of the flat. The prospect was not an extended one, consisting solely of a small block of flats on the other side of the road. Mrs Beresford sighed and then yawned.

'I wish,' she said, 'something would happen.'

Her husband looked up reprovingly.

'Be careful, Tuppence, this craving for vulgar sensation alarms me.'

Tuppence sighed and closed her eyes dreamily.

'So Tommy and Tuppence were married,' she chanted, 'and lived happily ever afterwards. And six years later they were still living together happily ever afterwards. It is extraordinary,' she said, 'how different everything always is from what you think it is going to be.'

'A very profound statement, Tuppence. But not

original. Eminent poets and still more eminent divines have said it before – and if you will excuse me saying so, have said it better.'

'Six years ago,' continued Tuppence, 'I would have sworn that with sufficient money to buy things with, and with you for a husband, all life would have been one grand sweet song, as one of the poets you seem to know so much about puts it.'

'Is it me or the money that palls upon you?' inquired Tommy coldly.

'Palls isn't exactly the word,' said Tuppence kindly. 'I'm used to my blessings, that's all. Just as one never thinks what a boon it is to be able to breathe through one's nose until one has a cold in the head.'

'Shall I neglect you a little?' suggested Tommy. 'Take other women about to night clubs. That sort of thing.'

'Useless,' said Tuppence. 'You would only meet me there with other men. And I should know perfectly well that you didn't care for the other women, whereas you would never be quite sure that I didn't care for the other men. Women are so much more thorough.'

'It's only in modesty that men score top marks,' murmured her husband. 'But what is the matter with you, Tuppence? Why this yearning discontent?'

'I don't know. I want things to happen. Exciting things. Wouldn't you like to go chasing German spies again, Tommy? Think of the wild days of peril we went through once. Of course I know you're more or less in the Secret Service now, but it's pure office work.'

'You mean you'd like them to send me into darkest Russia disguised as a Bolshevik bootlegger, or something of that sort?'

'That wouldn't be any good,' said Tuppence. 'They wouldn't let me go with you and I'm the person who wants something to do so badly. Something to do. That is what I keep saying all day long.'

'Women's sphere,' suggested Tommy, waving his hand.

'Twenty minutes' work after breakfast every morning keeps the flag going to perfection. You have nothing to complain of, have you?'

'Your housekeeping is so perfect, Tuppence, as to be almost monotonous.'

'I do like gratitude,' said Tuppence.

'You, of course, have got your work,' she continued, 'but tell me, Tommy, don't you ever have a secret yearning for excitement, for things to *happen*?'

'No,' said Tommy, 'at least I don't think so. It is all very well to want things to happen – they might not be pleasant things.'

'How prudent men are,' sighed Tuppence. 'Don't you ever have a wild secret yearning for romance – adventure – life?'

'What *have* you been reading, Tuppence?' asked Tommy.

'Think how exciting it would be,' went on Tuppence, 'if we heard a wild rapping at the door and went to open it and in staggered a dead man.'

'If he was dead he couldn't stagger,' said Tommy critically.

'You know what I mean,' said Tuppence. 'They always stagger in just before they die and fall at your feet, just gasping out a few enigmatic words. "The Spotted Leopard", or something like that.'

'I advise a course of Schopenhauer or Emmanuel Kant,' said Tommy.

'That sort of thing would be good for you,' said Tuppence. 'You are getting fat and comfortable.'

'I am not,' said Tommy indignantly. 'Anyway you do slimming exercises yourself.'

'Everybody does,' said Tuppence. 'When I said you were getting fat I was really speaking metaphorically, you are getting prosperous and sleek and comfortable.'

'I don't know what has come over you,' said her husband.

'The spirit of adventure,' murmured Tuppence. 'It is better than a longing for romance anyway. I have that sometimes too. I think of meeting a man, a really handsome man –'

'You have met me,' said Tommy. 'Isn't that enough for you?'

'A brown, lean man, terrifically strong, the kind of man who can ride anything and lassoes wild horses –'

'Complete with sheepskin trousers and a cowboy hat,' interpolated Tommy sarcastically.

'– and has lived in the Wilds,' continued Tuppence. 'I should like him to fall simply madly in love with me. I should, of course, rebuff him virtuously and be true to my marriage vows, but my heart would secretly go out to him.'

'Well,' said Tommy, 'I often wish that I may meet a really beautiful girl. A girl with corn coloured hair who will fall desperately in love with me. Only I don't think I rebuff her – in fact I am quite sure I don't.'

'That,' said Tuppence, 'is naughty temper.'

'What,' said Tommy, 'is really the matter with you, Tuppence? You have never talked like this before.'

'No, but I have been boiling up inside for a long time,' said Tuppence. 'You see it is very dangerous to have everything you want – including enough money to buy things. Of course there are always hats.'

'You have got about forty hats already,' said Tommy, 'and they all look alike.'

'Hats are like that,' said Tuppence. 'They are not really alike. There are *nuances* in them. I saw rather a nice one in Violette's this morning.'

'If you haven't anything better to do than going on buying hats you don't need –'

'That's it,' said Tuppence, 'that's exactly it. If I had something better to do. I suppose I ought to take up good works. Oh, Tommy, I do wish something exciting would happen. I feel – I really do feel it would be good for us. If we could find a fairy –'

'Ah!' said Tommy. 'It is curious your saying that.'

He got up and crossed the room. Opening a drawer of the writing table he took out a small snapshot print and brought it to Tuppence.

'Oh!' said Tuppence, 'so you have got them developed. Which is this, the one you took of this room or the one I took?'

'The one I took. Yours didn't come out. You under exposed it. You always do.'

'It is nice for you,' said Tuppence, 'to think that there is one thing you can do better than me.'

'A foolish remark,' said Tommy, 'but I will let it pass for the moment. What I wanted to show you was this.'

He pointed to a small white speck on the photograph.

'That is a scratch on the film,' said Tuppence.

'Not at all,' said Tommy. 'That, Tuppence, is a fairy.'

'Tommy, you idiot.'

'Look for yourself.'

He handed her a magnifying glass. Tuppence studied the print attentively through it. Seen thus by a slight stretch of fancy the scratch on the film could be imagined to represent a small winged creature on the fender.

'It has got wings,' cried Tuppence. 'What fun, a real live fairy in our flat. Shall we write to Conan Doyle about it? Oh, Tommy. Do you think she'll give us wishes?'

'You will soon know,' said Tommy. 'You have been wishing hard enough for something to happen all the afternoon.'

At that minute the door opened, and a tall lad of fifteen who seemed undecided as to whether he was a butler or a page boy inquired in a truly magnificent manner.

'Are you at home, madam? The front-door bell has just rung.'

'I wish Albert wouldn't go to the Pictures,' sighed Tuppence, after she had signified her assent, and Albert had withdrawn. 'He's copying a Long Island butler now. Thank goodness I've cured him of asking for people's cards and bringing them to me on a salver.'

The door opened again, and Albert announced: 'Mr Carter,' much as though it were a Royal title.

'The Chief,' muttered Tommy, in great surprise.

Tuppence jumped up with a glad exclamation, and greeted a tall grey-haired man with piercing eyes and a tired smile.

'Mr Carter, I *am* glad to see you.'

'That's good, Mrs Tommy. Now answer me a question. How's life generally?'

'Satisfactory, but dull,' replied Tuppence with a twinkle.

'Better and better,' said Mr Carter. 'I'm evidently going to find you in the right mood.'

'This,' said Tuppence, 'sounds exciting.'

Albert, still copying the Long Island butler, brought in tea. When this operation was completed without mishap and the door had closed behind him Tuppence burst out once more.

'You did mean something, didn't you, Mr Carter? Are you going to send us on a mission into darkest Russia?'

'Not exactly that,' said Mr Carter.

'But there is something.'

'Yes – there is something. I don't think you are the kind who shrinks from risks, are you, Mrs Tommy?'

Tuppence's eyes sparkled with excitement.

'There is certain work to be done for the Department – and I fancied – I just fancied – that it might suit you two.'

'Go on,' said Tuppence.

'I see that you take the *Daily Leader*,' continued Mr Carter, picking up that journal from the table.

He turned to the advertisement column and indicating a certain advertisement with his finger pushed the paper across to Tommy.

'Read that out,' he said.

Tommy complied.

'The International Detective Agency, Theodore Blunt, Manager. Private Inquiries. Large staff of confidential and highly skilled Inquiry Agents. Utmost discretion. Consultations free. 118 Haleham St, W.C.'

He looked inquiringly at Mr Carter. The latter nodded. 'That detective agency has been on its last legs for some time,' he murmured. 'Friend of mine acquired it for a mere song. We're thinking of setting it going again – say, for a six months' trial. And during that time, of course, it will have to have a manager.'

'What about Mr Theodore Blunt?' asked Tommy.

'Mr Blunt has been rather indiscreet, I'm afraid. In fact, Scotland Yard have had to interfere. Mr Blunt is being detained at Her Majesty's expense, and he won't tell us half of what we'd like to know.'

'I see, sir,' said Tommy. 'At least, I think I see.'

'I suggest that you have six months leave from the office. Ill health. And, of course, if you like to run a

Detective Agency under the name of Theodore Blunt, it's nothing to do with me.'

Tommy eyed his Chief steadily.

'Any instructions, sir?'

'Mr Blunt did some foreign business, I believe. Look out for blue letters with a Russian stamp on them. From a ham merchant anxious to find his wife who came as a refugee to this country some years ago. Moisten the stamp and you'll find the number 16 written underneath. Make a copy of these letters and send the originals on to me. Also if any one comes to the office and makes a reference to the number 16, inform me immediately.'

'I understand, sir,' said Tommy. 'And apart from these instructions?'

Mr Carter picked up his gloves from the table and prepared to depart.

'You can run the Agency as you please. I fancied' – his eyes twinkled a little – 'that it might amuse Mrs Tommy to try her hand at a little detective work.'

Chapter 2

A Pot of Tea

Mr and Mrs Beresford took possession of the offices of the International Detective Agency a few days later. They were on the second floor of a somewhat dilapidated building in Bloomsbury. In the small outer office, Albert relinquished the role of a Long Island butler, and took up that of office boy, a part which he played to perfection. A paper bag of sweets, inky hands, and a tousled head was his conception of the character.

From the outer office, two doors led into inner offices. On one door was painted the legend 'Clerks'. On the other 'Private'. Behind the latter was a small comfortable room furnished with an immense business-like desk, a lot of artistically labelled files, all empty, and some solid leather-seated chairs. Behind the desk sat the pseudo Mr Blunt trying to look as though he had run a Detective Agency all his life. A telephone, of course, stood at his elbow. Tuppence and he had rehearsed several good telephone effects, and Albert also had his instructions.

In the adjoining room was Tuppence, a typewriter, the necessary tables and chairs of an inferior type to those in the room of the great Chief, and a gas ring for making tea.

Nothing was wanting, in fact, save clients.

Tuppence, in the first ecstasies of initiation, had a few bright hopes.

'It will be too marvellous,' she declared. 'We will hunt down murderers, and discover the missing family jewels, and find people who've disappeared and detect embezzlers.'

At this point Tommy felt it his duty to strike a more discouraging note.

'Calm yourself, Tuppence, and try to forget the cheap fiction you are in the habit of reading. Our clientèle, if we have any clientèle at all – will consist solely of husbands who want their wives shadowed, and wives who want their husbands shadowed. Evidence for divorce is the sole prop of private inquiry agents.'

'Ugh!' said Tuppence, wrinkling a fastidious nose. 'We shan't touch divorce cases. We must raise the tone of our new profession.'

'Ye-es,' said Tommy doubtfully.

And now a week after installation they compared notes rather ruefully.

'Three idiotic women whose husbands go away for weekends,' sighed Tommy. 'Anyone come whilst I was out at lunch?'

'A fat old man with a flighty wife,' sighed Tuppence sadly. 'I've read in the papers for years that the divorce evil was growing, but somehow I never seemed to realise it until this last week. I'm sick and tired of saying, "We don't undertake divorce cases."'

'We've put it in the advertisements now,' Tommy reminded her. 'So it won't be so bad.'

'I'm sure we advertise in the most tempting way too,' said Tuppence in a melancholy voice. 'All the same, I'm not going to be beaten. If necessary, I shall commit a crime myself, and you will detect it.'

'And what good would that do? Think of my feelings when I bid you a tender farewell at Bow Street – or is it Vine Street?'

'You are thinking of your bachelor days,' said Tuppence pointedly.

'The Old Bailey, that is what I mean,' said Tommy.

'Well,' said Tuppence, 'something has got to be done about it. Here we are bursting with talent and no chance of exercising it.'

'I always like your cheery optimism, Tuppence. You seem to have no doubt whatever that you have talent to exercise.'

'Of course,' said Tuppence, opening her eyes very wide.

'And yet you have no expert knowledge whatever.'

'Well, I have read every detective novel that has been published in the last ten years.'

'So have I,' said Tommy, 'but I have a sort of feeling that that wouldn't really help us much.'

'You always were a pessimist, Tommy. Belief in oneself – that is the great thing.'

'Well, you have got it all right,' said her husband.

'Of course it is easy in detective stories,' said Tuppence thoughtfully, 'because one works backwards. I mean if one knows the solution one can arrange the clues. I wonder now –'

She paused wrinkling her brows.

'Yes?' said Tommy inquiringly.

'I have got a sort of idea,' said Tuppence. 'It hasn't quite come yet, but it's coming.' She rose resolutely. 'I think I shall go and buy that hat I told you about.'

'Oh, God!' said Tommy, 'another hat!'

'It's a very nice one,' said Tuppence with dignity.

She went out with a resolute look on her face.

Once or twice in the following days Tommy inquired curiously about the idea. Tuppence merely shook her head and told him to give her time.

And then, one glorious morning, the first client arrived, and all else was forgotten.

There was a knock on the outer door of the office and Albert, who had just placed an acid drop between his lips, roared out an indistinct 'Come in.' He then swallowed the acid drop whole in his surprise and delight. For this looked like the Real Thing.

A tall young man, exquisitely and beautifully dressed, stood hesitating in the doorway.

'A toff, if ever there was one,' said Albert to himself. His judgement in such matters was good.

The young man was about twenty-four years of age, had beautifully slicked back hair, a tendency to pink rims round the eyes, and practically no chin to speak of.

In an ecstasy, Albert pressed a button under his desk and almost immediately a perfect fusilade of typing broke out from the direction of 'Clerks'. Tuppence had rushed to the post of duty. The effect of this hum of industry was to overawe the young man still further.

'I say,' he remarked. 'Is this the whatnot – detective agency – Blunt's Brilliant Detectives? All that sort of stuff, you know? Eh?'

'Did you want, sir, to speak to Mr Blunt himself?' inquired Albert, with an air of doubts as to whether such a thing could be managed.

'Well – yes, laddie, that was the jolly old idea. Can it be done?'

'You haven't an appointment, I suppose?'

The visitor became more and more apologetic.

'Afraid I haven't.'

'It's always wise, sir, to ring up on the phone first. Mr Blunt is so terribly busy. He's engaged on the telephone at the moment. Called into consultation by Scotland Yard.'

The young man seemed suitably impressed.

Albert lowered his voice, and imparted information in a friendly fashion.

'Important theft of documents from a Government Office. They want Mr Blunt to take up the case.'

'Oh! really. I say. He must be no end of a fellow.'

'The Boss, sir,' said Albert, 'is It.'

The young man sat down on a hard chair, completely unconscious of the fact that he was being subjected to keen scrutiny by two pairs of eyes looking through cunningly contrived peep-holes – those of Tuppence, in the intervals of frenzied typing, and those of Tommy awaiting the suitable moment.

Presently a bell rang with violence on Albert's desk.

'The Boss is free now. I will find out whether he can see you,' said Albert, and disappeared through the door marked 'Private'.

He reappeared immediately.

'Will you come this way, sir?'

The visitor was ushered into the private office, and a pleasant faced young man with red hair and an air of brisk capability rose to greet him.

'Sit down. You wish to consult me? I am Mr Blunt.'

'Oh! Really. I say, you're awfully young, aren't you?'

'The day of the Old Men is over,' said Tommy, waving his hand. 'Who caused the war? The Old Men. Who is responsible for the present state of unemployment? The Old Men. Who is responsible for every single rotten thing that has happened? Again I say, the Old Men!'

'I expect you are right,' said the client, 'I know a fellow who is a poet – at least he says he is a poet – and he always talks like that.'

'Let me tell you this, sir, not a person on my highly trained staff is a day over twenty-five. That is the truth.'

Since the highly trained staff consisted of Tuppence and Albert, the statement was truth itself.

'And now – the facts,' said Mr Blunt.

'I want you to find someone that's missing,' blurted out the young man.

'Quite so. Will you give me the details?'

'Well, you see, it's rather difficult. I mean, it's a frightfully delicate business and all that. She might be frightfully waxy about it. I mean – well, it's so dashed difficult to explain.'

He looked helplessly at Tommy. Tommy felt annoyed. He had been on the point of going out to lunch, but he foresaw that getting the facts out of this client would be a long and tedious business.

'Did she disappear of her own free will, or do you suspect abduction?' he demanded crisply.

'I don't know,' said the young man. 'I don't know anything.'

Tommy reached for a pad and pencil.

'First of all,' he said, 'will you give me your name? My office boy is trained never to ask names. In that way consultations can remain completely confidential.'

'Oh! rather,' said the young man. 'Jolly good idea. My name – er – my name's Smith.'

'Oh! no,' said Tommy. 'The real one, please.'

His visitor looked at him in awe.

'Er – St Vincent,' he said. 'Lawrence St Vincent.'

'It's a curious thing,' said Tommy, 'how very few people there are whose real name is Smith. Personally, I don't know anyone called Smith. But nine men out of ten who wish to conceal their real name give that of Smith. I am writing a monograph upon the subject.'

At that moment a buzzer purred discreetly on his desk. That meant that Tuppence was requesting to take hold. Tommy, who wanted his lunch, and who felt profoundly unsympathetic towards Mr St Vincent, was only too pleased to relinquish the helm.

'Excuse me,' he said, and picked up the telephone.

Across his face there shot rapid changes – surprise, consternation, slight elation.

'You don't say so,' he said into the phone. 'The

Prime Minister himself? Of course, in that case, I will come round at once.'

He replaced the receiver on the hook, and turned to his client.

'My dear sir, I must ask you to excuse me. A most urgent summons. If you will give the facts of the case to my confidential secretary, she will deal with them.'

He strode to the adjoining door.

'Miss Robinson.'

Tuppence, very neat and demure with smooth black head and dainty collars and cuffs, tripped in. Tommy made the necessary introductions and departed.

'A lady you take an interest in has disappeared, I understand, Mr St Vincent,' said Tuppence, in her soft voice, as she sat down and took up Mr Blunt's pad and pencil. 'A young lady?'

'Oh! rather,' said St Vincent. 'Young – and – and – awfully good-looking and all that sort of thing.'

Tuppence's face grew grave.

'Dear me,' she murmured. 'I hope that –'

'You don't think anything's really happened to her?' demanded Mr St Vincent, in lively concern.

'Oh! we must hope for the best,' said Tuppence, with a kind of false cheerfulness which depressed Mr St Vincent horribly.

'Oh! look here, Miss Robinson. I say, you must do something. Spare no expense. I wouldn't have anything happen to her for the world. You seem awfully sympathetic, and I don't mind telling you in confidence that I simply worship the ground that girl walks on. She's a topper, an absolute topper.'

'Please tell me her name and all about her.'

'Her name's Jeanette – I don't know her second name. She works in a hat shop – Madame Violette's in Brook Street – but she's as straight as they make them. Has ticked me off no end of times – I went round there yesterday – waiting for her to come out – all the others came, but not her. Then I found that she'd never turned up that morning to work at all – sent no message either – old Madame was furious about it. I got the address of her lodgings, and I went round there. She hadn't come home the night before, and they didn't know where she was. I was simply frantic. I thought of going to the police. But I knew that Jeanette would be absolutely furious with me for doing that if she were really all right and had gone off on her own. Then I remembered that she herself had pointed out your advertisement to me one day in the paper and told me that one of the women who'd been in buying hats had simply raved about your ability and discretion and all that sort of thing. So I toddled along here right away.'

'I see,' said Tuppence. 'What is the address of her lodgings?'

The young man gave it to her.

'That's all, I think,' said Tuppence reflectively. 'That is to say – am I to understand that you are engaged to this young lady?'

Mr St Vincent turned a brick red.

'Well, no – not exactly. I never said anything. But I can tell you this, I mean to ask her to marry me as soon as ever I see her – if I ever do see her again.'

Tuppence laid aside her pad.

'Do you wish for our special twenty-four hour service?' she asked in business-like tones.

'What's that?'

'The fees are doubled, but we put all our available staff on to the case. Mr St Vincent, if the lady is alive, I shall be able to tell you where she is by this time tomorrow.'

'What? I say, that's wonderful.'

'We only employ experts – and we guarantee results,' said Tuppence crisply.

'But I say, you know. You must have the most topping staff.'

'Oh! we have,' said Tuppence. 'By the way, you haven't given me a description of the young lady.'

'She's got the most marvellous hair – sort of golden but very deep, like a jolly old sunset – that's it, a jolly old sunset. You know, I never noticed things like sunsets until lately. Poetry too, there's a lot more in poetry than I ever thought.'

'Red hair,' said Tuppence unemotionally, writing it down. 'What height should you say the lady was?'

'Oh! tallish, and she's got ripping eyes, dark blue, I think. And a sort of decided manner with her – takes a fellow up short sometimes.'

Tuppence wrote down a few words more, then closed her notebook and rose.

'If you will call here tomorrow at two o'clock, I think we shall have news of some kind for you,' she said. 'Good-morning, Mr St Vincent.'

When Tommy returned Tuppence was just consulting a page of Debrett.

'I've got all the details,' she said succinctly. 'Lawrence St Vincent is the nephew and heir of the Earl of Cheriton. If we pull this through we shall get publicity in the highest places.'

Tommy read through the notes on the pad.

'What do you really think has happened to the girl?' he asked.

'I think,' said Tuppence, 'that she has fled at the dictates of her heart, feeling that she loves this young man too well for her peace of mind.'

Tommy looked at her doubtfully.

'I know they do it in books,' he said, 'but I've never known any girl who did it in real life.'

'No?' said Tuppence. 'Well, perhaps you're right. But I dare say Lawrence St Vincent will swallow that sort of slush. He's full of romantic notions just now. By the way, I guaranteed results in twenty-four hours – our special service.'

'Tuppence – you congenital idiot, what made you do that?'

'The idea just came into my head. I thought it sounded rather well. Don't you worry. Leave it to mother. Mother knows best.'

She went out leaving Tommy profoundly dissatisfied.

Presently he rose, sighed, and went out to do what could be done, cursing Tuppence's over-fervent imagination.

When he returned weary and jaded at half-past four, he found Tuppence extracting a bag of biscuits from their place of concealment in one of the files.

'You look hot and bothered,' she remarked. 'What have you been doing?'

Tommy groaned.

'Making a round of the hospitals with that girl's description.'

'Didn't I tell you to leave it to me?' demanded Tuppence.

'You can't find that girl single-handed before two o'clock tomorrow.'

'I can – and what's more, I have!'

'You have? What do you mean?'

'A simple problem, Watson, very simple indeed.'

'Where is she now?'

Tuppence pointed a hand over her shoulder.

'She's in my office next door.'

'What is she doing there?'

Tuppence began to laugh.

'Well,' she said, 'early training will tell, and with a kettle, a gas ring, and half a pound of tea staring her in the face, the result is a foregone conclusion.

'You see,' continued Tuppence gently. 'Madame Violette's is where I go for my hats, and the other day I ran across an old pal of hospital days amongst the girls there. She gave up nursing after the war and started a hat shop, failed, and took this job at Madame Violette's. We fixed up the whole thing between us. She was to rub the advertisement well into young St Vincent, and then disappear. Wonderful efficiency of Blunt's Brilliant Detectives. Publicity for us, and the necessary fillip to young St Vincent to bring him to the point of proposing. Janet was in despair about it.'

'Tuppence,' said Tommy. 'You take my breath away! The whole thing is the most immoral business I ever heard of. You aid and abet this young man to marry out of his class –'

'Stuff,' said Tuppence. 'Janet is a splendid girl – and the queer thing is that she really adores that week-kneed young man. You can see with half a glance what *his* family needs. Some good red blood in it. Janet will be the making of him. She'll look after him like a mother, ease down the cocktails and the night clubs and make him lead a good healthy country gentleman's life. Come and meet her.'

Tuppence opened the door of the adjoining office and Tommy followed her.

A tall girl with lovely auburn hair, and a pleasant face, put down the steaming kettle in her hand, and turned with a smile that disclosed an even row of white teeth.

'I hope you'll forgive me, Nurse Cowley – Mrs Beresford, I mean. I thought that very likely you'd be quite ready for a cup of tea yourself. Many's the pot of tea you've made for me in the hospital at three o'clock in the morning.'

'Tommy,' said Tuppence. 'Let me introduce you to my old friend, Nurse Smith.'

'Smith, did you say? How curious!' said Tommy shaking hands. 'Eh? Oh! nothing – a little monograph that I was thinking of writing.'

'Pull yourself together, Tommy,' said Tuppence.

She poured him out a cup of tea.

'Now, then, let's drink together. Here's to the success of the International Detective Agency. Blunt's Brilliant Detectives! May they never know failure!'

Chapter 3

The Affair of the Pink Pearl

'What on earth are you doing?' demanded Tuppence, as she entered the inner sanctum of the International Detective Agency – (Slogan – Blunt's Brilliant Detectives) and discovered her lord and master prone on the floor in a sea of books.

Tommy struggled to his feet.

'I was trying to arrange these books on the top shelf of that cupboard,' he complained. 'And the damned chair gave way.'

'What are they, anyway?' asked Tuppence, picking up a volume. '*The Hound of the Baskervilles*. I wouldn't mind reading that again some time.'

'You see the idea?' said Tommy, dusting himself with care. 'Half-hours with the Great Masters – that sort of thing. You see, Tuppence, I can't help feeling that we are more or less amateurs at this business – of course amateurs in one sense we cannot help being, but it would do no harm to acquire the technique, so to speak. These books are detective stories by the leading masters of the art. I intend to try different styles, and compare results.'

'H'm,' said Tuppence. 'I often wonder how these detectives would have got on in real life.' She picked up another volume. 'You'll find a difficulty in being a Thorndyke. You've no medical experience, and less legal, and I never heard that science was your strong point.'

'Perhaps not,' said Tommy. 'But at any rate I've bought a very good camera, and I shall photograph footprints and enlarge the negatives and all that sort of thing. Now, *mon ami*, use your little grey cells – what does this convey to you?'

He pointed to the bottom shelf of the cupboard. On it lay a somewhat futuristic dressing-gown, a turkish slipper, and a violin.

'Obvious, my dear Watson,' said Tuppence.

'Exactly,' said Tommy. 'The Sherlock Holmes touch.'

He took up the violin and drew the bow idly across the strings, causing Tuppence to give a wail of agony.

At that moment the buzzer rang on the desk, a sign that a client had arrived in the outer office and was being held in parley by Albert, the office boy.

Tommy hastily replaced the violin in the cupboard and kicked the books behind the desk.

'Not that there's any great hurry,' he remarked. 'Albert will be handing them out the stuff about my being engaged with Scotland Yard on the phone. Get into your office and start typing, Tuppence. It makes the office sound busy and active. No, on second thoughts you shall be taking notes in shorthand from my dictation. Let's have a look before we get Albert to send the victim in.'

They approached the peephole which had been artistically contrived so as to command a view of the outer office.

The client was a girl of about Tuppence's age, tall and dark with a rather haggard face and scornful eyes.

'Clothes cheap and striking,' remarked Tuppence. 'Have her in, Tommy.'

In another minute the girl was shaking hands with the celebrated Mr Blunt, whilst Tuppence sat by with eyes demurely downcast, and pad and pencil in hand.

'My confidential secretary, Miss Robinson,' said Mr Blunt with a wave of his hand. 'You may speak freely before her.' Then he lay back for a minute, half closed his eyes and remarked in a tired tone: 'You must find travelling in a bus very crowded at this time of day.'

'I came in a taxi,' said the girl.

'Oh!' said Tommy aggrieved. His eyes rested reproachfully on a blue bus ticket protruding from her glove.

The girl's eyes followed his glance, and she smiled and drew it out.

'You mean this? I picked it up on the pavement. A little neighbour of ours collects them.'

Tuppence coughed, and Tommy threw a baleful glare at her.

'We must get to business,' he said briskly. 'You are in need of our services, Miss –?'

'Kingston Bruce is my name,' said the girl. 'We live at Wimbledon. Last night a lady who is staying with us lost a valuable pink pearl. Mr St Vincent was also dining with us, and during dinner he happened to mention your firm. My mother sent me off to you this morning to ask you if you would look into the matter for us.'

The girl spoke sullenly, almost disagreeably. It was clear as daylight that she and her mother had not agreed over the matter. She was here under protest.

'I see,' said Tommy, a little puzzled. 'You have not called in the police?'

'No,' said Miss Kingston Bruce, 'we haven't. It would be idiotic to call in the police and then find the silly thing had rolled under the fireplace, or something like that.'

'Oh!' said Tommy. 'Then the jewel may only be lost after all?'

Miss Kingston Bruce shrugged her shoulders.

'People make such a fuss about things,' she murmured. Tommy cleared his throat.

'Of course,' he said doubtfully. 'I am extremely busy just now –'

'I quite understand,' said the girl, rising to her feet. There was a quick gleam of satisfaction in her eyes which Tuppence, for one, did not miss.

'Nevertheless,' continued Tommy. 'I think I can manage to run down to Wimbledon. Will you give me the address, please?'

'The Laurels, Edgeworth Road.'

'Make a note of it, please, Miss Robinson.'

Miss Kingston Bruce hesitated, then said rather ungraciously.

'We'll expect you then. Good-morning.'

'Funny girl,' said Tommy when she had left. 'I couldn't quite make her out.'

'I wonder if she stole the thing herself,' remarked Tuppence meditatively. 'Come on, Tommy, let's put away these books and take the car and go down there. By the way, who are you going to be, Sherlock Holmes still?'

'I think I need practice for that,' said Tommy. 'I came rather a cropper over that bus ticket, didn't I?'

'You did,' said Tuppence. 'If I were you I shouldn't try too much on that girl – she's as sharp as a needle. She's unhappy too, poor devil.'

'I suppose you know all about her already,' said Tommy with sarcasm, 'simply from looking at the shape of her nose!'

'I'll tell you my idea of what we shall find at The Laurels,' said Tuppence, quite unmoved. 'A household of snobs, very keen to move in the best society; the father, if there is a father, is sure to have a military title. The girl falls in with their way of life and despises herself for doing so.'

Tommy took a last look at the books now neatly arranged upon the shelf.

'I think,' he said thoughtfully, 'that I shall be Thorndyke today.'

'I shouldn't have thought there was anything medico-legal about this case,' remarked Tuppence.

'Perhaps not,' said Tommy. 'But I'm simply dying to use that new camera of mine! It's supposed to have the most marvellous lens that ever was or could be.'

'I know those kind of lenses,' said Tuppence. 'By the time you've adjusted the shutter and stopped down and calculated the exposure and kept your eye on the spirit level, your brain gives out, and you yearn for the simple Brownie.'

'Only an unambitious soul is content with the simple Brownie.'

'Well, I bet I shall get better results with it than you will.'

Tommy ignored the challenge.

'I ought to have a "Smoker's Companion",' he said regretfully. 'I wonder where one buys them?'

'There's always the patent corkscrew Aunt Araminta gave you last Christmas,' said Tuppence helpfully.

'That's true,' said Tommy. 'A curious-looking engine of destruction I thought it at the time, and rather a humorous present to get from a strictly tee-total aunt.'

'I,' said Tuppence, 'shall be Polton.'

Tommy looked at her scornfully.

'Polton indeed. You couldn't begin to do one of the things that he does.'

'Yes, I can,' said Tuppence. 'I can rub my hands together when I'm pleased. That's quite enough to get on with. I hope you're going to take plaster casts of footprints?'

Tommy was reduced to silence. Having collected the corkscrew they went round to the garage, got out the car and started for Wimbledon.

The Laurels was a big house. It ran somewhat to gables and turrets, had an air of being very newly painted and was surrounded with neat flower beds filled with scarlet geraniums.

A tall man with a close-cropped white moustache, and an exaggeratedly martial bearing opened the door before Tommy had time to ring.

'I've been looking out for you,' he explained fussily. 'Mr Blunt, is it not? I am Colonel Kingston Bruce. Will you come into my study?'

He let them into a small room at the back of the house.

'Young St Vincent was telling me wonderful things about your firm. I've noticed your advertisements myself. This guaranteed twenty-four hours' service of yours – a marvellous notion. That's exactly what I need.'

Inwardly anathematising Tuppence for her irresponsibility in inventing this brilliant detail, Tommy replied: 'Just so, Colonel.'

'The whole thing is most distressing, sir, most distressing.'

'Perhaps you would kindly give me the facts,' said Tommy, with a hint of impatience.

'Certainly I will – at once. We have at the present moment staying with us a very old and dear friend of ours, Lady Laura Barton. Daughter of the late Earl of Carrowway. The present earl, her brother, made a striking speech in the House of Lords the other day. As I say, she is an old and dear friend of ours. Some American friends of mine who have just come over, the Hamilton Betts, were most anxious to meet her. "Nothing easier," I said. "She is staying with me now. Come down for the weekend." You know what Americans are about titles, Mr Blunt.'

'And others beside Americans sometimes, Colonel Kingston Bruce.'

'Alas! only too true, my dear sir. Nothing I hate more

than a snob. Well, as I was saying, the Betts came down for the weekend. Last night – we were playing bridge at the time – the clasp of a pendant Mrs Hamilton Betts was wearing broke, so she took it off and laid it down on a small table, meaning to take it upstairs with her when she went. This, however, she forgot to do. I must explain, Mr Blunt, that the pendant consisted of two small diamond wings, and a big pink pearl depending from them. The pendant was found this morning lying where Mrs Betts had left it, but the pearl, a pearl of enormous value, had been wrenched off.'

'Who found the pendant?'

'The parlourmaid – Gladys Hill.'

'Any reason to suspect her?'

'She has been with us some years, and we have always found her perfectly honest. But, of course, one never knows –'

'Exactly. Will you describe your staff, and also tell me who was present at dinner last night?'

'There is the cook – she has been with us only two months, but then she would have no occasion to go near the drawing-room – the same applies to the kitchenmaid. Then there is the housemaid, Alice Cummings. She also has been with us for some years. And Lady Laura's maid, of course. She is French.'

Colonel Kingston Bruce looked very impressive as he said this. Tommy, unaffected by the revelation of the maid's nationality, said: 'Exactly. And the party at dinner?'

'Mr and Mrs Betts, ourselves – my wife and daughter – and Lady Laura. Young St Vincent was dining with us, and Mr Rennie looked in after dinner for a while.'

'Who is Mr Rennie?'

'A most pestilential fellow – an arrant socialist. Good looking, of course, and with a certain specious power of argument. But a man, I don't mind telling you, whom I wouldn't trust a yard. A dangerous sort of fellow.'

'In fact,' said Tommy drily, 'it is Mr Rennie whom you suspect?'

'I do, Mr Blunt. I'm sure, holding the views he does, that he can have no principles whatsoever. What could have been easier for him than to have quietly wrenched off the pearl at a moment when we were all absorbed in our game? There were several absorbing moments – a redoubled no trump hand, I remember, and also a painful argument when my wife had the misfortune to revoke.'

'Quite so,' said Tommy. 'I should just like to know one thing – what is Mrs Betts's attitude in all this?'

'She wanted me to call in the police,' said Colonel Kingston Bruce reluctantly. 'That is, when we had searched everywhere in case the pearl had only dropped off.'

'But you dissuaded her?'

'I was very averse to the idea of publicity and my wife and daughter backed me up. Then my wife remembered young St Vincent speaking about your firm at dinner last night – and the twenty-four hours' special service.'

'Yes,' said Tommy, with a heavy heart.

'You see, in any case, no harm will be done. If we call in the police tomorrow, it can be supposed that we thought the jewel merely lost and were hunting for it. By the way, nobody has been allowed to leave the house this morning.'

'Except your daughter, of course,' said Tuppence, speaking for the first time.

'Except my daughter,' agreed the Colonel. 'She volunteered at once to go and put the case before you.'

Tommy rose.

'We will do our best to give you satisfaction, Colonel,' he said. 'I should like to see the drawing-room, and the table on which the pendant was laid down. I should also like to ask Mrs Betts a few questions. After that, I will interview the servants – or rather my assistant, Miss Robinson, will do so.'

He felt his nerve quailing before the terrors of questioning the servants.

Colonel Kingston Bruce threw open the door and led them across the hall. As he did so, a remark came to them clearly through the open door of the room they were approaching and the voice that uttered it was that of the girl who had come to see them that morning.

'You know perfectly well, Mother,' she was saying, 'that she *did* bring home a teaspoon in her muff.'

In another minute they were being introduced to Mrs Kingston Bruce, a plaintive lady with a languid manner. Miss Kingston Bruce acknowledged their presence with a short inclination of the head. Her face was more sullen than ever.

Mrs Kingston Bruce was voluble.

'– but I know who *I* think took it,' she ended. 'That dreadful socialist young man. He loves the Russians and the Germans and hates the English – what else can you expect?'

'He never touched it,' said Miss Kingston Bruce fiercely. 'I was watching him – all the time. I couldn't have failed to see if he had.'

She looked at them defiantly with her chin up.

Tommy created a diversion by asking for an interview with Mrs Betts. When Mrs Kingston Bruce had departed accompanied by her husband and daughter to find Mrs Betts, he whistled thoughtfully.

'I wonder,' he said gently, 'who it was who had a teaspoon in her muff?'

'Just what I was thinking,' replied Tuppence.

Mrs Betts, followed by her husband, burst into the room. She was a big woman with a determined voice. Mr Hamilton Betts looked dyspeptic and subdued.

'I understand, Mr Blunt, that you are a private inquiry agent, and one who hustles things through at a great rate?'

'Hustle,' said Tommy, 'is my middle name, Mrs Betts. Let me ask you a few questions.'

Thereafter things proceeded rapidly. Tommy was shown the damaged pendant, the table on which it had lain, and Mr Betts emerged from his taciturnity to mention the value, in dollars, of the stolen pearl.

And withal, Tommy felt an irritating certainty that he was not getting on.

'I think that will do,' he said, at length. 'Miss Robinson, will you kindly fetch the special photographic apparatus from the hall?'

Miss Robinson complied.

'A little invention of my own,' said Tommy. 'In appearance, you see, it is just like an ordinary camera.'

He had some slight satisfaction in seeing that the Betts were impressed.

He photographed the pendant, the table on which it had lain, and took several general views of the apartment. Then 'Miss Robinson' was delegated to interview the servants, and in view of the eager expectancy on the faces of Colonel Kingston Bruce and Mrs Betts,

Tommy felt called upon to say a few authoritative words.

'The position amounts to this,' he said. 'Either the pearl is still in the house, or it is not still in the house.'

'Quite so,' said the Colonel with more respect than was, perhaps, quite justified by the nature of the remark.

'If it is not in the house, it may be anywhere – but if it is in the house, it must necessarily be concealed somewhere –'

'And a search must be made,' broke in Colonel Kingston Bruce. 'Quite so. I give you carte blanche, Mr Blunt. Search the house from attic to cellar.'

'Oh! Charles,' murmured Mrs Kingston Bruce tearfully, 'do you think that is wise? The servants won't *like* it. I'm sure they'll leave.'

'We will search their quarters last,' said Tommy soothingly. 'The thief is sure to have hidden the gem in the most unlikely place.'

'I seem to have read something of the kind,' agreed the Colonel.

'Quite so,' said Tommy. 'You probably remember the case of Rex v Bailey, which created a precedent.'

'Oh – er – yes,' said the Colonel, looking puzzled.

'Now, the most unlikely place is in the apartment of Mrs Betts,' continued Tommy.

'My! Wouldn't that be too cute?' said Mrs Betts admiringly.

Without more ado she took him up to her room, where Tommy once more made use of the special photographic apparatus.

Presently Tuppence joined him there.

'You have no objection, I hope, Mrs Betts, to my assistant's looking through your wardrobe?'

'Why, not at all. Do you need me here any longer?'

Tommy assured her that there was no need to detain her, and Mrs Betts departed.

'We might as well go on bluffing it out,' said Tommy. 'But personally I don't believe we've a dog's chance of finding the thing. Curse you and your twenty-four hours' stunt, Tuppence.'

'Listen,' said Tuppence. 'The servants are all right, I'm sure, but I managed to get something out of the French maid. It seems that when Lady Laura was staying here a year ago, she went out to tea with some friends of the Kingston Bruces, and when she got home a teaspoon fell out of her muff. Everyone thought it must have fallen in by accident. But, talking about similar robberies, I got hold of a lot more. Lady Laura is always staying about with people. She hasn't got a bean, I gather, and she's out for comfortable quarters with people to whom a title still means something. It may be a coincidence – or it may be something more, but five distinct thefts have taken place whilst she has been staying in various houses, sometimes trivial things, sometimes valuable jewels.'

'Whew!' said Tommy, and gave vent to a prolonged whistle. 'Where's the old bird's room, do you know?'

'Just across the passage.'

'Then I think, I rather think, that we'll just slip across and investigate.'

The room opposite stood with its door ajar. It was a spacious apartment, with white enamelled fitments and rose pink curtains. An inner door led to a bathroom. At the door of this appeared a slim, dark girl, very neatly dressed.

Tuppence checked the exclamation of astonishment on the girl's lips.

'This is Elise, Mr Blunt,' she said primly. 'Lady Laura's maid.'

Tommy stepped across the threshold of the bathroom, and approved inwardly its sumptuous and up-to-date fittings. He set to work to dispel the wide stare of suspicion on the French girl's face.

'You are busy with your duties, eh, Mademoiselle Elise?'

'Yes, Monsieur, I clean Milady's bath.'

'Well, perhaps you'll help me with some photography instead. I have a special kind of camera here, and I am photographing the interiors of all the rooms in this house.'

He was interrupted by the communicating door to the bedroom banging suddenly behind him. Elise jumped at the sound.

'What did that?'

'It must have been the wind,' said Tuppence.

'We will come into the other room,' said Tommy.

Elise went to open the door for them, but the door knob rattled aimlessly.

'What's the matter?' said Tommy sharply.

'Ah, Monsieur, but somebody must have locked it on the other side.' She caught up a towel and tried again. But this time the door handle turned easily enough, and the door swung open.

'*Voilà ce qui est curieux.* It must have been stuck,' said Elise.

There was no one in the bedroom.

Tommy fetched his apparatus. Tuppence and Elise worked under his orders. But again and again his glance went back to the communicating door.

'I wonder,' he said between his teeth – 'I wonder why that door stuck?'

He examined it minutely, shutting and opening it. It fitted perfectly.

'One picture more,' he said with a sigh. 'Will you loop back that rose curtain, Mademoiselle Elise? Thank you. Just hold it so.'

The familiar click occurred. He handed a glass slide to Elise to hold, relinquished the tripod to Tuppence, and carefully readjusted and closed the camera.

He made some easy excuse to get rid of Elise, and as soon as she was out of the room, he caught hold of Tuppence and spoke rapidly.

'Look here, I've got an idea. Can you hang on here? Search all the rooms – that will take some time. Try and get an interview with the old bird – Lady Laura – but don't alarm her. Tell her you suspect the parlourmaid. But whatever you do don't let her leave the house. I'm going off in the car. I'll be back as soon as I can.'

'All right,' said Tuppence. 'But don't be too cocksure. You've forgotten one thing.

'The girl. There's something funny about that girl. Listen, I've found out the time she started from the house this morning. It took her two hours to get to our office. That's nonsense. Where did she go before she came to us?'

'There's something in that,' admitted her husband. 'Well, follow up any old clue you like, but don't let Lady Laura leave the house. What's that?'

His quick ear had caught a faint rustle outside on the landing. He strode across to the door, but there was no one to be seen.

'Well, so long,' he said, 'I'll be back as soon as I can.'

II

Tuppence watched him drive off in the car with a faint misgiving. Tommy was very sure – she herself was not so sure. There were one or two things she did not quite understand.

She was still standing by the window, watching the road, when she saw a man leave the shelter of a gateway opposite, cross the road and ring the bell.

In a flash Tuppence was out of the room and down the stairs. Gladys Hill, the parlourmaid, was emerging from the back part of the house, but Tuppence motioned her back authoritatively. Then she went to the front door and opened it.

A lanky young man with ill-fitting clothes and eager dark eyes was standing on the step.

He hesitated a moment, and then said:

'Is Miss Kingston Bruce in?'

'Will you come inside?' said Tuppence.

She stood aside to let him enter, closing the door.

'Mr Rennie, I think?' she said sweetly.

He shot a quick glance at her.

'Er – yes.'

'Will you come in here, please?'

She opened the study door. The room was empty, and Tuppence entered it after him, closing the door behind her. He turned on her with a frown.

'I want to see Miss Kingston Bruce.'

'I am not quite sure that you can,' said Tuppence composedly.

'Look here, who the devil are you?' said Mr Rennie rudely.

'International Detective Agency,' said Tuppence succinctly – and noticed Mr Rennie's uncontrollable start.

'Please sit down, Mr Rennie,' she went on. 'To begin with, we know all about Miss Kingston Bruce's visit to you this morning.'

It was a bold guess, but it succeeded. Perceiving his consternation, Tuppence went on quickly.

'The recovery of the pearl is the great thing, Mr Rennie. No one in this house is anxious for – publicity. Can't we come to some arrangement?'

The young man looked at her keenly.

'I wonder how much you know,' he said thoughtfully. 'Let me think for a moment.'

He buried his head in his hands – then asked a most unexpected question.

'I say, is it really true that young St Vincent is engaged to be married?'

'Quite true,' said Tuppence. 'I know the girl.'

Mr Rennie suddenly became confidential.

'It's been hell,' he confided. 'They've been asking

her morning, noon and night – chucking Beatrice at his head. All because he'll come into a title some day. If I had my way –'

'Don't let's talk politics,' said Tuppence hastily. 'Do you mind telling me, Mr Rennie, why you think Miss Kingston Bruce took the pearl?'

'I – I don't.'

'You do,' said Tuppence calmly. 'You wait to see the detective, as you think, drive off and the coast clear, and then you come and ask for her. It's obvious. If you'd taken the pearl yourself, you wouldn't be half so upset.'

'Her manner was so odd,' said the young man. 'She came this morning and told me about the robbery, explaining that she was on her way to a firm of private detectives. She seemed anxious to say something, and yet not able to get it out.'

'Well,' said Tuppence. 'All I want is the pearl. You'd better go and talk to her.'

But at that moment Colonel Kingston Bruce opened the door.

'Lunch is ready, Miss Robinson. You will lunch with us, I hope. The –'

Then he stopped and glared at the guest.

'Clearly,' said Mr Rennie, 'you don't want to ask me to lunch. All right, I'll go.'

'Come back later,' whispered Tuppence, as he passed her.

Tuppence followed Colonel Kingston Bruce, still growling into his moustache about the pestilential impudence of some people, into a massive dining-room where the family was already assembled. Only one person present was unknown to Tuppence.

'This, Lady Laura, is Miss Robinson, who is kindly assisting us.'

Lady Laura bent her head, and then proceeded to stare at Tuppence through her pince-nez. She was a tall, thin woman, with a sad smile, a gentle voice, and very hard shrewd eyes. Tuppence returned her stare, and Lady Laura's eyes dropped.

After lunch Lady Laura entered into conversation with an air of gentle curiosity. How was the inquiry proceeding? Tuppence laid suitable stress on the suspicion attaching to the parlourmaid, but her mind was not really on Lady Laura. Lady Laura might conceal teaspoons and other articles in her clothing, but Tuppence felt fairly sure that she had not taken the pink pearl.

Presently Tuppence proceeded with her search of the house. Time was going on. There was no sign of Tommy, and, what mattered far more to Tuppence, there was no sign of Mr Rennie. Suddenly Tuppence came out of a bedroom and collided with Beatrice Kingston Bruce, who was going downstairs. She was fully dressed for the street.

'I'm afraid,' said Tuppence, 'that you mustn't go out just now.'

The other girl looked at her haughtily.

'Whether I go out or not is no business of yours,' she said coldly.

'It is my business whether I communicate with the police or not, though,' said Tuppence.

In a minute the girl had turned ashy pale.

'You mustn't – you mustn't – I won't go out – but don't do that.' She clung to Tuppence beseechingly.

'My dear Miss Kingston Bruce,' said Tuppence, smiling, 'the case has been perfectly clear to me from the start – I –'

But she was interrupted. In the stress of her encounter with the girl, Tuppence had not heard the front-door bell. Now, to her astonishment, Tommy came bounding up the stairs, and in the hall below she caught sight of a big burly man in the act of removing a bowler hat.

'Detective Inspector Marriot of Scotland Yard,' he said with a grin.

With a cry, Beatrice Kingston Bruce tore herself from Tuppence's grasp and dashed down the stairs, just as the front door was opened once more to admit Mr Rennie.

'Now you *have* torn it,' said Tuppence bitterly.

'Eh?' said Tommy, hurrying into Lady Laura's room. He passed on into the bathroom and picked up a large cake of soap which he brought out in his hands. The Inspector was just mounting the stairs.

'She went quite quietly,' he announced. 'She's an old hand and knows when the game is up. What about the pearl?'

'I rather fancy,' said Tommy, handing him the soap, 'that you'll find it in here.'

The Inspector's eyes lit up appreciatively.

'An old trick, and a good one. Cut a cake of soap in half, scoop out a place for the jewel, clap it together again, and smooth the join well over with hot water. A very smart piece of work on your part, sir.'

Tommy accepted the compliment gracefully. He and Tuppence descended the stairs. Colonel Kingston Bruce rushed at him and shook him warmly by the hand.

'My dear sir, I can't thank you enough. Lady Laura wants to thank you also –'

'I am glad we have given you satisfaction,' said Tommy. 'But I'm afraid I can't stop. I have a most urgent appointment. Member of the Cabinet.'

He hurried out to the car and jumped in. Tuppence jumped in beside him.

'But Tommy,' she cried. 'Haven't they arrested Lady Laura after all?'

'Oh!' said Tommy. 'Didn't I tell you? They've not arrested Lady Laura. They've arrested Elise.'

'You see,' he went on, as Tuppence sat dumbfounded, 'I've often tried to open a door with soap on my hands myself. It can't be done – your hands slip. So I wondered what Elise could have been doing with the soap to get her hands as soapy as all that. She caught up a towel, you remember, so there were no traces of soap on the handle afterwards. But it occurred to me that if you were a professional thief, it wouldn't be a bad plan to be maid to a lady suspected of kleptomania who stayed about a good deal in different houses. So I managed to get a photo of her as well as of the room, induced her to handle a glass slide and toddled off to dear old Scotland Yard. Lightning development of negative, successful identification of finger-prints – and photo. Elise was a long lost friend. Useful place, Scotland Yard.'

'And to think,' said Tuppence, finding her voice, 'that those two young idiots were only suspecting each other in that weak way they do it in books. But why didn't you tell me what you were up to when you went off?'

'In the first place, I suspected that Elise was listening on the landing, and in the second place –'

'Yes?'

'My learned friend forgets,' said Tommy. 'Thorndyke

never tells until the last moment. Besides, Tuppence, you and your pal Janet Smith put one over on me last time. This makes us all square.'

Chapter 4

The Adventure of the Sinister Stranger

'It's been a darned dull day,' said Tommy, and yawned widely.

'Nearly tea time,' said Tuppence and also yawned.

Business was not brisk in the International Detective Agency. The eagerly expected letter from the ham merchant had not arrived and *bona fide* cases were not forthcoming.

Albert, the office boy, entered with a sealed package which he laid on the table.

'The Mystery of the Sealed Packet,' murmured Tommy. 'Did it contain the fabulous pearls of the Russian Grand Duchess? Or was it an infernal machine destined to blow Blunt's Brilliant Detectives to pieces?'

'As a matter of fact,' said Tuppence, tearing open the package. 'It's my wedding present to Francis Haviland. Rather nice, isn't it?'

Tommy took a slender silver cigarette case from her outstretched hand, noted the inscription engraved in her own handwriting, '*Francis from Tuppence*,' opened and shut the case, and nodded approvingly.

'You do throw your money about, Tuppence,' he remarked. 'I'll have one like it, only in gold, for my birthday next month. Fancy wasting a thing like that on Francis Haviland, who always was and always will be one of the most perfect asses God ever made!'

'You forget I used to drive him about during the war, when he was a General. Ah! those were the good old days.'

'They were,' agreed Tommy. 'Beautiful women used to come and squeeze my hand in hospital, I remember. But I don't send them all wedding presents. I don't believe the bride will care much for this gift of yours, Tuppence.'

'It's nice and slim for the pocket, isn't it?' said Tuppence, disregarding his remarks.

Tommy slipped it into his own pocket.

'Just right,' he said approvingly. 'Hullo, here is Albert with the afternoon post. Very possibly the Duchess of Perthshire is commissioning us to find her prize Peke.'

They sorted through the letters together. Suddenly Tommy gave vent to a prolonged whistle and held up one of them in his hand.

'A blue letter with a Russian stamp on it. Do you remember what the Chief said? We were to look out for letters like that.'

'How exciting,' said Tuppence. 'Something has happened at last. Open it and see if the contents are up to schedule. A ham merchant, wasn't it? Half a minute. We shall want some milk for tea. They forgot to leave it this morning. I'll send Albert out for it.'

She returned from the outer office, after despatching Albert on his errand, to find Tommy holding the blue sheet of paper in his hand.

'As we thought, Tuppence,' he remarked. 'Almost word for word what the Chief said.'

Tuppence took the letter from him and read it.

It was couched in careful stilted English, and purported to be from one Gregor Feodorsky, who was anxious for news of his wife. The International Detective Agency was urged to spare no expense in doing their utmost to trace her. Feodorsky himself was unable to leave Russia at the moment owing to a crisis in the pork trade.

'I wonder what it really means,' said Tuppence thoughtfully, smoothing out the sheet on the table in front of her.

'Code of some kind, I suppose,' said Tommy. 'That's not our business. Our business is to hand it over to the Chief as soon as possible. Better just verify it by soaking off the stamp and seeing if the number 16 is underneath.'

'All right,' said Tuppence. 'But I should think –'

She stopped dead, and Tommy, surprised by her sudden pause, looked up to see a man's burly figure blocking the doorway.

The intruder was a man of commanding presence, squarely built, with a very round head and a powerful jaw. He might have been about forty-five years of age.

'I must beg your pardon,' said the stranger, advancing into the room, hat in hand. 'I found your outer office empty and this door open, so I ventured to intrude. This is Blunt's International Detective Agency, is it not?'

'Certainly it is.'

'And you are, perhaps, Mr Blunt? Mr Theodore Blunt?'

'I am Mr Blunt. You wish to consult me? This is my secretary, Miss Robinson.'

Tuppence inclined her head gracefully, but continued to scrutinise the stranger narrowly through her downcast eyelashes. She was wondering how long he had been standing in the doorway, and how much he had seen and heard. It did not escape her observation that even while he was talking to Tommy, his eyes kept coming back to the blue paper in her hand.

Tommy's voice, sharp with a warning note, recalled her to the needs of the moment.

'Miss Robinson, please, take notes. Now, sir, will you kindly state the matter on which you wish to have my advice?'

Tuppence reached for her pad and pencil.

The big man began in rather a harsh voice.

'My name is Bower. Dr Charles Bower. I live in Hampstead, where I have a practice. I have come to you, Mr Blunt, because several rather strange occurrences have happened lately.'

'Yes, Dr Bower?'

'Twice in the course of the last week I have been summoned by telephone to an urgent case – in each case to find that the summons has been a fake. The first time I thought a practical joke had been played upon me, but on my return the second time I found that some of my private papers had been displaced and disarranged, and now I believe that the same thing had happened the first time. I made an exhaustive search and came to the conclusion that my whole desk had been thoroughly ransacked, and the various papers replaced hurriedly.'

Dr Bower paused and gazed at Tommy.

'Well, Mr Blunt?'

'Well, Dr Bower,' replied the young man, smiling.

'What do you think of it, eh?'

'Well, first I should like the facts. What do you keep in your desk?'

'My private papers.'

'Exactly. Now, what do those private papers consist of? What value are they to the common thief – or any particular person?'

'To the common thief I cannot see that they would have any value at all, but my notes on certain obscure alkaloids would be of interest to anyone possessed of technical knowledge of the subject. I have been making a study of such matters for the last few years. These alkaloids are deadly and virulent poisons, and are in addition, almost untraceable. They yield no known reactions.'

'The secret of them would be worth money, then?'

'To unscrupulous persons, yes.'

'And you suspect – whom?'

The doctor shrugged his massive shoulders.

'As far as I can tell, the house was not entered forcibly from the outside. That seems to point to some member of my household, and yet I cannot believe –' He broke off abruptly, then began again, his voice very grave.

'Mr Blunt, I must place myself in your hands unreservedly. I dare not go to the police in the matter. Of my three servants I am almost entirely sure. They have served me long and faithfully. Still, one never knows. Then I have living with me my two nephews, Bertram and Henry. Henry is a good boy – a very good boy – he has never caused me any anxiety, an excellent hard-working young fellow. Bertram, I regret to say, is of quite a different character – wild, extravagant, and persistently idle.'

'I see,' said Tommy thoughtfully. 'You suspect your nephew Bertram of being mixed up in this business. Now I don't agree with you. I suspect the good boy – Henry.'

'But why?'

'Tradition. Precedent.' Tommy waved his hand airily. 'In my experience, the suspicious characters are always innocent – and vice versa, my dear sir. Yes, decidedly, I suspect Henry.'

'Excuse me, Mr Blunt,' said Tuppence, interrupting in a deferential tone. 'Did I understand Dr Bower to say that these notes on – er – obscure alkaloids – are kept in the desk with the other papers?'

'They are kept in the desk, my dear young lady, but in a secret drawer, the position of which is known only to myself. Hence they have so far defied the search.'

'And what exactly do you want me to do, Dr Bower?' asked Tommy. 'Do you anticipate that a further search will be made?'

'I do, Mr Blunt. I have every reason to believe so. This afternoon I received a telegram from a patient of mine whom I ordered to Bournemouth a few weeks ago. The telegram states that my patient is in a critical condition, and begs me to come down at once. Rendered suspicious by the events I have told you of, I myself despatched a telegram, prepaid, to the patient in question, and elicited the fact that he was in good health and had sent no summons to me of any kind. It occurred to me that if I pretended to have been taken in, and duly departed to Bournemouth, we should have a very good chance of finding the miscreants at work. They – or he – will doubtless wait until the household has retired to bed before commencing operations. I suggest that you should meet me outside my house at eleven o'clock this evening, and we will investigate the matter together.'

'Hoping, in fact, to catch them in the act.' Tommy drummed thoughtfully on the table with a paper-knife. 'Your plan seems to me an excellent one, Dr Bower. I cannot see any hitch in it. Let me see, your address is –?'

'The Larches, Hangman's Lane – rather a lonely part, I am afraid. But we command magnificent views over the Heath.'

'Quite so,' said Tommy.

The visitor rose.

'Then I shall expect you tonight, Mr Blunt. Outside The Larches at – shall we say, five minutes to eleven – to be on the safe side?'

'Certainly. Five minutes to eleven. Good-afternoon, Dr Bower.'

Tommy rose, pressed a buzzer on his desk, and Albert appeared to show the client out. The doctor walked with a decided limp, but his powerful physique was evident in spite of it.

'An ugly customer to tackle,' murmured Tommy to himself. 'Well, Tuppence, old girl, what do you think of it?'

'I'll tell you in one word,' said Tuppence. '*Clubfoot!*'

'What?'

'I said Clubfoot! My study of the classics has not been in vain. Tommy, this thing's a plant. Obscure alkaloids indeed – I never heard a weaker story.'

'Even I did not find it very convincing,' admitted her husband.

'Did you see his eyes on the letter? Tommy, he's one of the gang. They've got wise to the fact that you're not the real Mr Blunt, and they're out for our blood.'

'In that case,' said Tommy, opening the side cupboard and surveying his rows of books with an affectionate eye, 'our role is easy to select. We are the brothers Okewood! And I am Desmond,' he added firmly.

Tuppence shrugged her shoulders.

'All right. Have it your own way. I'd as soon be Francis. Francis was much the more intelligent of the two. Desmond always gets into a mess, and Francis turns up as the gardener or something in the nick of time and saves the situation.'

'Ah!' said Tommy, 'but I shall be a super Desmond. When I arrive at the Larches –'

Tuppence interrupted him unceremoniously.

'You're not going to Hampstead tonight?'

'Why not?'

'Walk into a trap with your eyes shut!'

'No, my dear girl, walk into a trap with my eyes open. There's a lot of difference. I think our friend, Dr Bower, will get a little surprise.'

'I don't like it,' said Tuppence. 'You know what happens when Desmond disobeys the Chief's orders and acts on his own. Our orders were quite clear. To send on the letters at once and to report immediately on anything that happened.'

'You've not got it quite right,' said Tommy. 'We were to report immediately if any one came in and mentioned the number 16. Nobody has.'

'That's a quibble,' said Tuppence.

'It's no good. I've got a fancy for playing a lone hand. My dear old Tuppence, I shall be all right. I shall go armed to the teeth. The essence of the whole thing is that I shall be on my guard and they won't know it. The Chief will be patting me on the back for a good night's work.'

'Well,' said Tuppence. 'I don't like it. That man's as strong as a gorilla.'

'Ah!' said Tommy, 'but think of my blue-nosed automatic.'

The door of the outer office opened and Albert appeared. Closing the door behind him, he approached them with an envelope in his hand.

'A gentleman to see you,' said Albert. 'When I began the usual stunt of saying you were engaged with Scotland Yard, he told me he knew all about that. Said he came from Scotland Yard himself! And he wrote something on a card and stuck it up in this envelope.'

Tommy took the envelope and opened it. As he read the card, a grin passed across his face.

'The gentleman was amusing himself at your expense by speaking the truth, Albert,' he remarked. 'Show him in.'

He tossed the card to Tuppence. It bore the name Detective Inspector Dymchurch, and across it was scrawled in pencil – 'A friend of Marriot's.'

In another minute the Scotland Yard detective was entering the inner office. In appearance, Inspector Dymchurch was of the same type as Inspector Marriot, short and thick set, with shrewd eyes.

'Good-afternoon,' said the detective breezily. 'Marriot's away in South Wales, but before he went he asked me to keep an eye on you two, and on this place in general. Oh, bless you, sir,' he went on, as Tommy seemed about to interrupt him, '*we* know all about it. It's not our department, and we don't interfere. But somebody's got wise lately to the fact that all is not what it seems. You've had a gentleman here this afternoon. I don't know what he called himself, and I don't know what his real name is, but I know just a little about him. Enough to want to know more. Am I right in assuming that he made a date with you for some particular spot this evening?'

'Quite right.'

'I thought as much. 16 Westerham Road, Finsbury Park – was that it?'

'You're wrong there,' said Tommy with a smile. 'Dead wrong. The Larches, Hampstead.'

Dymchurch seemed honestly taken aback. Clearly he had not expected this.

'I don't understand it,' he muttered. 'It must be a new layout. The Larches, Hampstead, you said?'

'Yes. I'm to meet him there at eleven o'clock tonight.'

'Don't you do it, sir.'

'There!' burst from Tuppence.

Tommy flushed.

'If you think, Inspector –' he began heatedly.

But the Inspector raised a soothing hand.

'I'll tell you what I think, Mr Blunt. The place

you want to be at eleven o'clock tonight is here in this office.'

'What?' cried Tuppence, astonished.

'Here in this office. Never mind how I know – departments overlap sometimes – but you got one of those famous "Blue" letters today. Old what's-his-name is after that. He lures you up to Hampstead, makes quite sure of your being out of the way, and steps in here at night when all the building is empty and quiet to have a good search round at his leisure.'

'But why should he think the letter would be here? He'd know I should have it on me or else have passed it on.'

'Begging your pardon, sir, that's just what he wouldn't know. He may have tumbled to the fact that you're not the original Mr Blunt, but he probably thinks that you're a *bona fide* gentleman who's bought the business. In that case, the letter would be all in the way of regular business and would be filed as such.'

'I see,' said Tuppence.

'And that's just what we've got to let him think. We'll catch him red-handed here tonight.'

'So that's the plan, is it?'

'Yes. It's the chance of a lifetime. Now, let me see, what's the time? Six o'clock. What time do you usually leave here, sir?'

'About six.'

'You must seem to leave the place as usual. Actually we'll sneak back to it as soon as possible. I don't believe they'll come here till about eleven, but of course they might. If you'll excuse me, I'll just go and take a look round outside and see if I can make out anyone watching the place.'

Dymchurch departed, and Tommy began an argument with Tuppence.

It lasted some time and was heated and acrimonious. In the end Tuppence suddenly capitulated.

'All right,' she said. 'I give in. I'll go home and sit there like a good little girl whilst you tackle crooks and hobnob with detectives – but you wait, young man. I'll be even with you yet for keeping me out of the fun.'

Dymchurch returned at that moment.

'Coast seems clear enough,' he said. 'But you can't tell. Better seem to leave in the usual manner. They won't go on watching the place once you've gone.'

Tommy called Albert and gave him instructions to lock up.

Then the four of them made their way to the garage near by where the car was usually left. Tuppence drove and Albert sat beside her. Tommy and the detective sat behind.

Presently they were held up by a block in the traffic. Tuppence looked over her shoulder and nodded. Tommy and the detective opened the right hand door and stepped out into the middle of Oxford Street. In a minute or two Tuppence drove on.

II

'Better not go in just yet,' said Dymchurch as he and Tommy hurried into Haleham Street. 'You've got the key all right?'

Tommy nodded.

'Then what about a bite of dinner? It's early, but there's a little place here right opposite. We'll get a table by the window, so that we can watch the place all the time.'

They had a very welcome little meal, in the manner the detective had suggested. Tommy found Inspector Dymchurch quite an entertaining companion. Most of his official work had lain amongst international spies, and he had tales to tell which astonished his simple listener.

They remained in the little restaurant until eight o'clock, when Dymchurch suggested a move.

'It's quite dark now, sir,' he explained. 'We shall be able to slip in without any one being the wiser.'

It was, as he said, quite dark. They crossed the road, looked quickly up and down the deserted street, and slipped inside the entrance. Then they mounted the stairs, and Tommy inserted his key in the lock of the outer office.

Just as he did so, he heard, as he thought, Dymchurch whistle beside him.

'What are you whistling for?' he asked sharply.

'*I* didn't whistle,' said Dymchurch, very much astonished. 'I thought *you* did.'

'Well, some one –' began Tommy.

He got no further. Strong arms seized him from behind, and before he could cry out, a pad of something sweet and sickly was pressed over his mouth and nose.

He struggled valiantly, but in vain. The chloroform did its work. His head began to whirl and the floor heaved up and down in front of him. Choking, he lost consciousness . . .

He came to himself painfully, but in full possession of his faculties. The chloroform had been only a whiff. They had kept him under long enough to force a gag into his mouth and ensure that he did not cry out.

When he came to himself, he was half-lying, half-sitting, propped against the wall in a corner of his own inner office. Two men were busily turning out the contents of the desk and ransacking the cupboards, and as they worked they cursed freely.

'Swelp me, guv'nor,' said the taller of the two hoarsely,

'we've turned the whole b—y place upside down and inside out. It's not there.'

'It must be here,' snarled the other. 'It isn't on him. And there's no other place it can be.'

As he spoke he turned, and to Tommy's utter amazement he saw that the last speaker was none other than Inspector Dymchurch. The latter grinned when he saw Tommy's astonished face.

'So our young friend is awake again,' he said. 'And a little surprised – yes, a little surprised. But it was so simple. We suspect that all is not as it should be with the International Detective Agency. I volunteer to find out if that is so, or not. If the new Mr Blunt is indeed a spy, he will be suspicious, so I send first my dear old friend, Carl Bauer. Carl is told to act suspiciously and pitch an improbable tale. He does so, and then I appear on the scene. I used the name of Inspector Marriot to gain confidence. The rest is easy.'

He laughed.

Tommy was dying to say several things, but the gag in his mouth prevented him. Also, he was dying to *do* several things – mostly with his hands and feet – but alas, that too had been attended to. He was securely bound.

The thing that amazed him most was the astounding change in the man standing over him. As Inspector Dymchurch the fellow had been a typical Englishman.

Now, no one could have mistaken him for a moment for anything but a well-educated foreigner who talked English perfectly without a trace of accent.

'Coggins, my good friend,' said the erstwhile Inspector, addressing his ruffianly-looking associate, 'take your life-preserver and stand by the prisoner. I am going to remove the gag. You understand, my dear Mr Blunt, do you not, that it would be criminally foolish on your part to cry out? But I am sure you do. For your age, you are quite an intelligent lad.'

Very deftly he removed the gag and stepped back.

Tommy eased his stiff jaws, rolled his tongue round his mouth, swallowed twice – and said nothing at all.

'I congratulate you on your restraint,' said the other. 'You appreciate the position, I see. Have you nothing at all to say?'

'What I have to say will keep,' said Tommy. 'And it won't spoil by waiting.'

'Ah! What I have to say will not keep. In plain English, Mr Blunt, where is that letter?'

'My dear fellow, I don't know,' said Tommy cheerfully. 'I haven't got it. But you know that as well as I do. I should go on looking about if I were you. I like to see you and friend Coggins playing hide-and-seek together.'

The other's face darkened.

'You are pleased to be flippant, Mr Blunt. You see

that square box over there. That is Coggins's little outfit. In it there is vitriol . . . yes, vitriol . . . and irons that can be heated in the fire, so that they are red hot and burn . . .'

Tommy shook his head sadly.

'An error in diagnosis,' he murmured. 'Tuppence and I labelled this adventure wrong. It's not a Clubfoot story. It's a Bull-dog Drummond, and you are the inimitable Carl Peterson.'

'What is this nonsense you are talking,' snarled the other.

'Ah!' said Tommy. 'I see you are unacquainted with the classics. A pity.'

'Ignorant fool! Will you do what we want or will you not? Shall I tell Coggins to get out his tools and begin?'

'Don't be so impatient,' said Tommy. 'Of course I'll do what you want, as soon as you tell me what it is. You don't suppose I want to be carved up like a filleted sole and fried on a gridiron? I loathe being hurt.'

Dymchurch looked at him in contempt.

'Gott! What cowards are these English.'

'Common sense, my dear fellow, merely common sense. Leave the vitriol alone and let us come down to brass tacks.'

'I want the letter.'

'I've already told you I haven't got it.'

'We know that – we also know who must have it. The girl.'

'Very possibly you're right,' said Tommy. 'She may have slipped it into her handbag when your pal Carl startled us.'

'Oh, you do not deny. That is wise. Very good, you will write to this Tuppence, as you call her, bidding her bring the letter here immediately.'

'I can't do that,' began Tommy.

The other cut in before he had finished the sentence.

'Ah! You can't? Well, we shall soon see. Coggins!'

'Don't be in such a hurry,' said Tommy. 'And do wait for the end of the sentence. I was going to say that I can't do that unless you untie my arms. Hang it all, I'm not one of those freaks who can write with their noses or their elbows.'

'You are willing to write, then?'

'Of course. Haven't I been telling you so all along? I'm all out to be pleasant and obliging. You won't do anything unkind to Tuppence, of course. I'm sure you won't. She's such a nice girl.'

'We only want the letter,' said Dymchurch, but there was a singularly unpleasant smile on his face.

At a nod from him the brutal Coggins knelt down and unfastened Tommy's arms. The latter swung them to and fro.

'That's better,' he said cheerfully. 'Will kind Coggins

hand me my fountain pen? It's on the table, I think, with my other miscellaneous property.'

Scowling, the man brought it to him, and provided a sheet of paper.

'Be careful what you say,' Dymchurch said menacingly. 'We leave it to you, but failure means – death – and slow death at that.'

'In that case,' said Tommy, 'I will certainly do my best.'

He reflected a minute or two, then began to scribble rapidly.

'How will this do?' he asked, handing over the completed epistle.

Dear Tuppence,

Can you come along at once and bring that blue letter with you? We want to decode it here and now.

In haste,

Francis.

'Francis?' queried the bogus Inspector, with lifted eyebrows. 'Was that the name she called you?'

'As you weren't at my christening,' said Tommy, 'I don't suppose you can know whether it's my name or not. But I think the cigarette case you took from my pocket is a pretty good proof that I'm speaking the truth.'

The other stepped over to the table and took up the case, read 'Francis from Tuppence' with a faint grin and laid it down again.

'I am glad to find you are behaving so sensibly,' he said. 'Coggins, give that note to Vassilly. He is on guard outside. Tell him to take it at once.'

The next twenty minutes passed slowly, the ten minutes after that more slowly still. Dymchurch was striding up and down with a face that grew darker and darker. Once he turned menacingly on Tommy.

'If you have dared to double-cross us,' he growled.

'If we'd had a pack of cards here, we might have had a game of picquet to pass the time,' drawled Tommy. 'Women always keep one waiting. I hope you're not going to be unkind to little Tuppence when she comes?'

'Oh, no,' said Dymchurch. 'We shall arrange for you to go to the same place – together.'

'Will you, you swine,' said Tommy under his breath.

Suddenly there was a stir in the outer office. A man whom Tommy had not yet seen poked his head in and growled something in Russian.

'Good,' said Dymchurch. 'She is coming – and coming alone.'

For a moment a faint anxiety caught at Tommy's heart.

The next minute he heard Tuppence's voice.

'Oh! there you are, Inspector Dymchurch. I've brought the letter. Where is Francis?'

With the last words she came through the door, and Vassilly sprang on her from behind, clapping his hand over her mouth. Dymchurch tore the handbag from her grasp and turned over its contents in a frenzied search.

Suddenly he uttered an ejaculation of delight and held up a blue envelope with a Russian stamp on it. Coggins gave a hoarse shout.

And just in that minute of triumph the other door, the door into Tuppence's own office, opened noiselessly and Inspector Marriot and two men armed with revolvers stepped into the room, with the sharp command: 'Hands up.'

There was no fight. The others were taken at a hopeless disadvantage. Dymchurch's automatic lay on the table, and the two others were not armed.

'A very nice little haul,' said Inspector Marriot with approval, as he snapped the last pair of handcuffs. 'And we'll have more as time goes on, I hope.'

White with rage, Dymchurch glared at Tuppence.

'You little devil,' he snarled. 'It was you put them on to us.'

Tuppence laughed.

'It wasn't all my doing. I ought to have guessed, I admit, when you brought in the number sixteen this afternoon. But it was Tommy's note clinched matters. I rang up Inspector Marriot, got Albert to meet him with the duplicate key of the office, and came along myself with the empty blue envelope in my bag. The letter I forwarded according to my instructions as soon as I had parted with you two this afternoon.'

But one word had caught the other's attention.

'*Tommy*?' he queried.

Tommy, who had just been released from his bonds, came towards them.

'Well done, brother Francis,' he said to Tuppence, taking both her hands in his. And to Dymchurch: 'As I told you, my dear fellow, you really ought to read the classics.'

Chapter 5

Finessing the King

It was a wet Wednesday in the offices of the International Detective Agency. Tuppence let the *Daily Leader* fall idly from her hand.

'Do you know what I've been thinking, Tommy?'

'It's impossible to say,' replied her husband. 'You think of so many things, and you think of them all at once.'

'I think it's time we went dancing again.'

Tommy picked up the *Daily Leader* hastily.

'Our advertisement looks well,' he remarked, his head on one side. 'Blunt's Brilliant Detectives. Do you realise, Tuppence, that you and you alone are Blunt's Brilliant Detectives? There's glory for you, as Humpty Dumpty would say.'

'I was talking about dancing.'

'There's a curious point that I have observed about newspapers. I wonder if you have ever noticed it. Take these three copies of the *Daily Leader*. Can you tell me how they differ one from the other?'

Tuppence took them with some curiosity.

'It seems fairly easy,' she remarked witheringly. 'One is today's, one is yesterday's, and one is the day before's.'

'Positively scintillating, my dear Watson. But that was not my meaning. Observe the headline, "Daily Leader." Compare the three – do you see any difference between them?'

'No, I don't,' said Tuppence, 'and what's more, I don't believe there is any.'

Tommy sighed and brought the tips of his fingers together in the most approved Sherlock Holmes fashion.

'Exactly. Yet you read the papers as much – in fact, more than I do. But I have observed and you have not. If you will look at today's *Daily Leader*, you will see that in the middle of the downstroke of the D is a small white dot, and there is another in the L of the same word. But in yesterday's paper the white dot is not in DAILY at all. There are two white dots in the L of LEADER. That of the day before again has two dots in the D of DAILY. In fact, the dot, or dots, are in a different position every day.'

'Why?' asked Tuppence.

'That's a journalistic secret.'

'Meaning you don't know, and can't guess.'

'I will merely say this – the practice is common to all newspapers.'

'Aren't you clever?' said Tuppence. 'Especially at drawing red herrings across the track. Let's go back to what we were talking about before.'

'What were we talking about?'

'The Three Arts Ball.'

Tommy groaned.

'No, no, Tuppence. Not the Three Arts Ball. I'm not young enough. I assure you I'm not young enough.'

'When I was a nice young girl,' said Tuppence, 'I was brought up to believe that men – especially husbands – were dissipated beings, fond of drinking and dancing and staying up late at night. It took an exceptionally beautiful and clever wife to keep them at home. Another illusion gone! All the wives I know are hankering to go out and dance, and weeping because their husbands will wear bedroom slippers and go to bed at half-past nine. And you do dance so nicely, Tommy dear.'

'Gently with the butter, Tuppence.'

'As a matter of fact,' said Tuppence, 'it's not purely for pleasure that I want to go. I'm intrigued by this advertisement.'

She picked up the *Daily Leader* again and read it out.

'I should go three hearts. 12 tricks. Ace of Spades. Necessary to finesse the King.'

'Rather an expensive way of learning bridge,' was Tommy's comment.

'Don't be an ass. That's nothing to do with bridge. You see, I was lunching with a girl yesterday at the Ace of Spades. It's a queer little underground den in Chelsea, and she told me that it's quite the fashion at these big shows to trundle round there in the course of the evening for bacon and eggs and Welsh rarebits – Bohemian sort of stuff. It's got screened-off booths all around it. Pretty hot place, I should say.'

'And your idea is –?'

'Three hearts stands for the Three Arts Ball, tomorrow night, 12 tricks is twelve o'clock, and the Ace of Spades is the Ace of Spades.'

'And what about its being necessary to finesse the King?'

'Well, that's what I thought we'd find out.'

'I shouldn't wonder if you weren't right, Tuppence,' said Tommy magnanimously. 'But I don't quite see why you want to butt in upon other people's love affairs.'

'I shan't butt in. What I'm proposing is an interesting experiment in detective work. We *need* practice.'

'Business is certainly not too brisk,' agreed Tommy. 'All the same, Tuppence, what you want is to go to the Three Arts Ball and dance! Talk of red herrings.'

Tuppence laughed shamelessly.

'Be a sport, Tommy. Try and forget you're thirty-two and have got one grey hair in your left eyebrow.'

'I was always weak where women were concerned,' murmured her husband. 'Have I got to make an ass of myself in fancy dress?'

'Of course, but you can leave that to me. I've got a splendid idea.'

Tommy looked at her with some misgiving. He was always profoundly mistrustful of Tuppence's brilliant ideas.

When he returned to the flat on the following evening, Tuppence came flying out of her bedroom to meet him.

'It's come,' she announced.

'What's come?'

'The costume. Come and look at it.'

Tommy followed her. Spread out on the bed was a complete fireman's kit with shining helmet.

'Good God!' groaned Tommy. 'Have I joined the Wembley fire brigade?'

'Guess again,' said Tuppence. 'You haven't caught the idea yet. Use your little grey cells, *mon ami.* Scintillate, Watson. Be a bull that has been more than ten minutes in the arena.'

'Wait a minute,' said Tommy. 'I begin to see. There is a dark purpose in this. What are you going to wear, Tuppence?'

'An old suit of your clothes, an American hat and some horn spectacles.'

'Crude,' said Tommy. 'But I catch the idea. McCarty incog. And I am Riordan.'

'That's it. I thought we ought to practise American detective methods as well as English ones. Just for once I am going to be the star, and you will be the humble assistant.'

'Don't forget,' said Tommy warningly, 'that it's always an innocent remark by the simple Denny that puts McCarty on the right track.'

But Tuppence only laughed. She was in high spirits.

It was a most successful evening. The crowds, the music, the fantastic dresses – everything conspired to make the young couple enjoy themselves. Tommy forgot his role of the bored husband dragged out against his will.

At ten minutes to twelve they drove off in the car to the famous – or infamous – Ace of Spades. As Tuppence had said, it was an underground den, mean and tawdry in appearance, but it was nevertheless crowded with couples in fancy dress. There were closed-in booths round the walls, and Tommy and Tuppence secured one of these. They left the doors purposely a little ajar so that they could see what was going on outside.

'I wonder which they are – our people, I mean,' said

Tuppence. 'What about that Columbine over there with the red Mephistopheles?'

'I fancy the wicked Mandarin and the lady who calls herself a Battleship – more of a fast Cruiser, I should say.'

'Isn't he witty?' said Tuppence. 'All done on a little drop of drink! Who's this coming in dressed as the Queen of Hearts – rather a good get-up, that.'

The girl in question passed into the booth next to them, accompanied by her escort, who was 'the gentleman dressed in newspaper' from *Alice in Wonderland*. They were both wearing masks – it seemed to be rather a common custom at the Ace of Spades.

'I'm sure we're in a real den of iniquity,' said Tuppence with a pleased face. 'Scandals all round us. What a row everyone makes.'

A cry, as of protest, rang out from the booth next door and was covered by a man's loud laugh. Everybody was laughing and singing. The shrill voices of the girls rose above the booming of their male escorts.

'What about that shepherdess?' demanded Tommy. 'The one with the comic Frenchman. They might be our little lot.'

'Any one might be,' confessed Tuppence. 'I'm not going to bother. The great thing is that we are enjoying ourselves.'

'I could have enjoyed myself better in another costume,' grumbled Tommy. 'You've no idea of the heat of this one.'

'Cheer up,' said Tuppence. 'You look lovely.'

'I'm glad of that,' said Tommy. 'It's more than you do. You're the funniest little guy I've ever seen.'

'Will you keep a civil tongue in your head, Denny, my boy. Hullo, the gentleman in newspaper is leaving his lady alone. Where's he going, do you think?'

'Going to hurry up the drinks, I expect,' said Tommy. 'I wouldn't mind doing the same thing.'

'He's a long time doing it,' said Tuppence, when four or five minutes had passed. 'Tommy, would you think me an awful ass –' She paused.

Suddenly she jumped up.

'Call me an ass if you like. I'm going in next door.'

'Look here, Tuppence – you can't –'

'I've a feeling there's something wrong. I *know* there is. Don't try and stop me.'

She passed quickly out of their own booth, and Tommy followed her. The doors of the one next door were closed. Tuppence pushed them apart and went in, Tommy on her heels.

The girl dressed as the Queen of Hearts sat in the corner leaning up against the wall in a queer huddled position. Her eyes regarded them steadily through her mask, but she did not move. Her dress was carried out in a bold design of red and white, but on the left hand side the pattern seemed to have got mixed. There was more red than there should have been . . .

With a cry Tuppence hurried forward. At the same time, Tommy saw what she had seen, the hilt of a jewelled dagger just below the heart. Tuppence dropped on her knees by the girl's side.

'Quick, Tommy, she's still alive. Get hold of the manager and make him get a doctor at once.'

'Right. Mind you don't touch the handle of that dagger, Tuppence.'

'I'll be careful. Go quickly.'

Tommy hurried out, pulling the doors to behind him. Tuppence passed her arm round the girl. The latter made a faint gesture, and Tuppence realised that she wanted to get rid of the mask. Tuppence unfastened it gently. She saw a fresh, flower-like face, and wide starry eyes that were full of horror, suffering, and a kind of dazed bewilderment.

'My dear,' said Tuppence, very gently. 'Can you speak at all? Will you tell me, if you can, who did this?'

She felt the eyes fix themselves on her face. The girl was sighing, the deep palpitating sighs of a failing heart. And still she looked steadily at Tuppence. Then her lips parted.

'Bingo did it –' she said in a strained whisper.

Then her hands relaxed, and she seemed to nestle down on Tuppence's shoulder.

Tommy came in, two men with him. The bigger of the two came forward with an air of authority, the word doctor written all over him.

Tuppence relinquished her burden.

'She's dead, I'm afraid,' she said with a catch in her voice.

The doctor made a swift examination.

'Yes,' he said. 'Nothing to be done. We had better leave things as they are till the police come. How did the thing happen?'

Tuppence explained rather haltingly, slurring over her reasons for entering the booth.

'It's a curious business,' said the doctor. 'You heard nothing?'

'I heard her give a kind of cry, but then the man laughed. Naturally I didn't think –'

'Naturally not,' agreed the doctor. 'And the man wore a mask you say. You wouldn't recognise him?'

'I'm afraid not. Would you, Tommy?'

'No. Still there is his costume.'

'The first thing will be to identify this poor lady,' said the doctor. 'After that, well, I suppose the police will get down to things pretty quickly. It ought not to be a difficult case. Ah, here they come.'

Chapter 6

The Gentleman Dressed in Newspaper

It was after three o'clock when, weary and sick at heart, the husband and wife reached home. Several hours passed before Tuppence could sleep. She lay tossing from side to side, seeing always that flower-like face with the horror-stricken eyes.

The dawn was coming in through the shutters when Tuppence finally dropped off to sleep. After the excitement, she slept heavily and dreamlessly. It was broad daylight when she awoke to find Tommy, up and dressed, standing by the bedside, shaking her gently by the arm.

'Wake up, old thing. Inspector Marriot and another man are here and want to see you.'

'What time is it?'

'Just on eleven. I'll get Alice to bring you your tea right away.'

'Yes, do. Tell Inspector Marriot I'll be there in ten minutes.'

A quarter of an hour later, Tuppence came hurrying into the sitting-room. Inspector Marriot, who was sitting looking very straight and solemn, rose to greet her.

'Good-morning, Mrs Beresford. This is Sir Arthur Merivale.'

Tuppence shook hands with a tall thin man with haggard eyes and greying hair.

'It's about this sad business last night,' said Inspector Marriot. 'I want Sir Arthur to hear from your own lips what you told me – the words the poor lady said before she died. Sir Arthur has been very hard to convince.'

'I can't believe,' said the other, 'and I won't believe, that Bingo Hale ever hurt a hair of Vere's head.'

Inspector Marriot went on.

'We've made some progress since last night, Mrs Beresford,' he said. 'First of all we managed to identify the lady as Lady Merivale. We communicated with Sir Arthur here. He recognised the body at once, and was horrified beyond words, of course. Then I asked him if he knew anyone called Bingo.'

'You must understand, Mrs Beresford,' said Sir Arthur, 'that Captain Hale, who is known to all his friends as Bingo, is the dearest pal I have. He practically lives with us. He was staying at my house when they arrested him this morning. I cannot but believe that you have made a mistake – it was not his name that my wife uttered.'

'There is no possibility of mistake,' said Tuppence gently. 'She said, "Bingo did it –"'

'You see, Sir Arthur,' said Marriot.

The unhappy man sank into a chair and covered his face with his hands.

'It's incredible. What earthly motive could there be? Oh, I know your idea, Inspector Marriot. You think Hale was my wife's lover, but even if that were so – which I don't admit for a moment – what motive was there for killing her?'

Inspector Marriot coughed.

'It's not a very pleasant thing to say, sir. But Captain Hale has been paying a lot of attention to a certain young American lady of late – a young lady with a considerable amount of money. If Lady Merivale liked to turn nasty, she could probably stop his marriage.'

'This is outrageous, Inspector.'

Sir Arthur sprang angrily to his feet. The other calmed him with a soothing gesture.

'I beg your pardon, I'm sure, Sir Arthur. You say that you and Captain Hale both decided to attend this show. Your wife was away on a visit at the time, and you had no idea that she was to be there?'

'Not the least idea.'

'Just show him that advertisement you told me about, Mrs Beresford.'

Tuppence complied.

'That seems to me clear enough. It was inserted by Captain Hale to catch your wife's eye. They had already arranged to meet there. But you only made up your mind to go the day before, hence it was necessary to warn her. That is the explanation of the phrase, "Necessary to finesse the King." You ordered your costume from a theatrical firm at the last minute, but Captain Hale's was a home-made affair. He went as the Gentleman dressed in Newspaper. Do you know, Sir Arthur, what we found clasped in the dead lady's hand? A fragment torn from a newspaper. My men have orders to take Captain Hale's costume away with them from your house. I shall find it at the Yard when I get back. If there's a tear in it corresponding to the missing piece – well, it'll be the end of the case.'

'You won't find it,' said Sir Arthur. 'I know Bingo Hale.'

Apologising to Tuppence for disturbing her, they took their leave.

Late that evening there was a ring at the bell, and somewhat to the astonishment of the young pair Inspector Marriot once more walked in.

'I thought Blunt's Brilliant Detectives would like to

hear the latest developments,' he said, with a hint of a smile.

'They would,' said Tommy. 'Have a drink?'

He placed materials hospitably at Inspector Marriot's elbow.

'It's a clear case,' said the latter, after a minute or two. 'Dagger was the lady's own – the idea was to have made it look like suicide evidently, but thanks to you two being on the spot, that didn't come off. We've found plenty of letters – they'd been carrying on together for some time, that's clear – without Sir Arthur tumbling to it. Then we found the last link –'

'The last what?' said Tuppence sharply.

'The last link in the chain – that fragment of the *Daily Leader*. It was torn from the dress he wore – fits exactly. Oh, yes, it's a perfectly clear case. By the way, I brought round a photograph of those two exhibits – I thought they might interest you. It's very seldom that you get such a perfectly clear case.'

'Tommy,' said Tuppence, when her husband returned from showing the Scotland Yard man out, 'why do you think Inspector Marriot keeps repeating that it's a perfectly clear case?'

'I don't know. Smug satisfaction, I suppose.'

'Not a bit of it. He's trying to get us irritated. You know, Tommy, butchers, for instance, know something about meat, don't they?'

'I should say so, but what on earth –'

'And in the same way, greengrocers know all about vegetables, and fishermen about fish. Detectives, professional detectives, must know all about criminals. They know the real thing when they see it – and they know when it isn't the real thing. Marriot's expert knowledge tells him that Captain Hale isn't a criminal – but all the facts are dead against him. As a last resource Marriot is egging us on, hoping against hope that some little detail or other will come back to us – something that happened last night – which will throw a different light on things. Tommy, why shouldn't it be suicide, after all?'

'Remember what she said to you.'

'I know – but take that a different way. It was Bingo's doing – his conduct that drove her to kill herself. It's just possible.'

'Just. But it doesn't explain that fragment of newspaper.'

'Let's have a look at Marriot's photographs. I forgot to ask him what Hale's account of the matter was.'

'I asked him that in the hall just now. Hale declared he had never spoken to Lady Merivale at the show. Says somebody shoved a note into his hand which said, 'Don't try and speak to me tonight. Arthur suspects.' He couldn't produce the piece of paper, though, and it doesn't sound a very likely story. Anyway, you and

I *know* he was with her at the Ace of Spades, because we saw him.'

Tuppence nodded and pored over the two photographs.

One was a tiny fragment with the legend DAILY LE – and the rest torn off. The other was the front sheet of the *Daily Leader* with the small round tear at the top of it. There was no doubt about it. Those two fitted together perfectly.

'What are all those marks down the side?' asked Tommy.

'Stitches,' said Tuppence. 'Where it was sewn to the others, you know.'

'I thought it might be a new scheme of dots,' said Tommy. Then he gave a slight shiver. 'My word, Tuppence, how creepy it makes one feel. To think that you and I were discussing dots and puzzling over that advertisement – all as lighthearted as anything.'

Tuppence did not answer. Tommy looked at her and was startled to observe that she was staring ahead of her, her mouth slightly open, and a bewildered expression on her face.

'Tuppence,' said Tommy gently, shaking her by the arm, 'what's the matter with you? Are you just going to have a stroke or something?'

But Tuppence remained motionless. Presently she said in a faraway voice:

'Denis Riordan.'

'Eh?' said Tommy, staring.

'It's just as you said. One simple innocent remark! Find me all this week's *Daily Leaders*.'

'What are you up to?'

'I'm being McCarty. I've been worrying round, and thanks to you, I've got a notion at last. This is the front sheet of Tuesday's paper. I seem to remember that Tuesday's paper was the one with two dots in the L of LEADER. This has a dot in the D of DAILY – and one in the L too. Get me the papers and let's make sure.'

They compared them anxiously. Tuppence had been quite right in her remembrance.

'You see? This fragment wasn't torn from Tuesday's paper.'

'But Tuppence, we can't be sure. It may merely be different editions.'

'It may – but at any rate it's given me an idea. It can't be coincidence – that's certain. There's only one thing it can be if I'm right in my idea. Ring up Sir Arthur, Tommy. Ask him to come round here at once. Say I've got important news for him. Then get hold of Marriot. Scotland Yard will know his address if he's gone home.'

Sir Arthur Merivale, very much intrigued by the summons, arrived at the flat in about half an hour's time. Tuppence came forward to greet him.

'I must apologise for sending for you in such a peremptory fashion,' she said. 'But my husband and I have discovered something that we think you ought to know at once. Do sit down.'

Sir Arthur sat down, and Tuppence went on.

'You are, I know, very anxious to clear your friend.'

Sir Arthur shook his head sadly.

'I was, but even I have had to give in to the overwhelming evidence.'

'What would you say if I told you that chance has placed in my hands a piece of evidence that will certainly clear him of all complicity?'

'I should be overjoyed to hear it, Mrs Beresford.'

'Supposing,' continued Tuppence, 'that I had come across a girl who was actually dancing with Captain Hale last night at twelve o'clock – the hour when he was supposed to be at the Ace of Spades.'

'Marvellous!' cried Sir Arthur. 'I knew there was some mistake. Poor Vere must have killed herself after all.'

'Hardly that,' said Tuppence. 'You forget the other man.'

'What other man?'

'The one my husband and I saw leave the booth. You see, Sir Arthur, there must have been a second man dressed in newspaper at the ball. By the way, what was your own costume?'

'Mine? I went as a seventeenth century executioner.'

'How very appropriate,' said Tuppence softly.

'Appropriate, Mrs Beresford. What do you mean by appropriate?'

'For the part you played. Shall I tell you my ideas on the subject, Sir Arthur? The newspaper dress is easily put on over that of an executioner. Previously a little note has been slipped into Captain Hale's hand, asking him not to speak to a certain lady. But the lady herself knows nothing of that note. She goes to the Ace of Spades at the appointed time and sees the figure she expects to see. They go into the booth. He takes her in his arms, I think, and kisses her – the kiss of a Judas, and as he kisses he strikes with the dagger. She only utters one faint cry and he covers that with a laugh. Presently he goes away – and to the last, horrified and bewildered, she believes her lover is the man who killed her.

'But she has torn a small fragment from the costume. The murderer notices that – he is a man who pays great attention to detail. To make the case absolutely clear against his victim the fragment must seem to have been torn from Captain Hale's costume. That would present great difficulties unless the two men happened to be living in the same house. Then, of course, the thing would be simplicity itself. He makes an exact duplicate of the tear in Captain Hale's costume – then he burns his own and prepares to play the part of the loyal friend.'

Tuppence paused.

'Well, Sir Arthur?'

Sir Arthur rose and made her a bow.

'The rather vivid imagination of a charming lady who reads too much fiction.'

'You think so?' said Tommy.

'And a husband who is guided by his wife,' said Sir Arthur. 'I do not fancy you will find anybody to take the matter seriously.'

He laughed out loud, and Tuppence stiffened in her chair.

'I would swear to that laugh anywhere,' she said. 'I heard it last in the Ace of Spades. And you are under a little misapprehension about us both. Beresford is our real name, but we have another.'

She picked up a card from the table and handed it to him. Sir Arthur read it aloud.

'International Detective Agency . . .' He drew his breath sharply. 'So that is what you really are! That was why Marriot brought me here this morning. It was a trap –'

He strolled to the window.

'A fine view you have from here,' he said. 'Right over London.'

'Inspector Marriot,' cried Tommy sharply.

In a flash the Inspector appeared from the communicating door in the opposite wall.

A little smile of amusement came to Sir Arthur's lips.

'I thought as much,' he said. 'But you won't get me this time, I'm afraid, Inspector. I prefer to take my own way out.'

And putting his hands on the sill, he vaulted clean through the window.

Tuppence shrieked and clapped her hands to her ears to shut out the sound she had already imagined – the sickening thud far beneath. Inspector Marriot uttered an oath.

'We should have thought of the window,' he said. 'Though, mind you, it would have been a difficult thing to prove. I'll go down and – and – see to things.'

'Poor devil,' said Tommy slowly. 'If he was fond of his wife –'

But the Inspector interrupted him with a snort.

'Fond of her? That's as may be. He was at his wits' end where to turn for money. Lady Merivale had a large fortune of her own, and it all went to him. If she'd bolted with young Hale, he'd never have seen a penny of it.'

'That was it, was it?'

'Of course, from the very start, I sensed that Sir Arthur was a bad lot, and that Captain Hale was all right. We know pretty well what's what at the Yard – but it's awkward when you're up against facts. I'll be going down now – I should give your wife a glass of brandy if I were you, Mr Beresford – it's been upsetting like for her.'

'Greengrocers,' said Tuppence in a low voice as the door closed behind the imperturbable Inspector, 'butchers, fishermen, detectives. I was right, wasn't I? He knew.'

Tommy, who had been busy at the sideboard, approached her with a large glass.

'Drink this.'

'What is it? Brandy?'

'No, it's a large cocktail – suitable for a triumphant McCarty. Yes, Marriot's right all round – that was the way of it. A bold finesse for game and rubber.'

Tuppence nodded.

'But he finessed the wrong way round.'

'And so,' said Tommy, 'exit the King.'

Chapter 7

The Case of the Missing Lady

The buzzer on Mr Blunt's desk – International Detective Agency, Manager, Theodore Blunt – uttered its warning call. Tommy and Tuppence both flew to their respective peepholes which commanded a view of the outer office. There it was Albert's business to delay the prospective client with various artistic devices.

'I will see, sir,' he was saying. 'But I'm afraid Mr Blunt is very busy just at present. He is engaged with Scotland Yard on the phone just now.'

'I'll wait,' said the visitor. 'I haven't got a card with me, but my name is Gabriel Stavansson.'

The client was a magnificent specimen of manhood, standing over six foot high. His face was bronzed and weatherbeaten, and the extraordinary blue of his eyes made an almost startling contrast to the brown skin.

Tommy swiftly made up his mind. He put on his

hat, picked up some gloves and opened the door. He paused on the threshold.

'This gentleman is waiting to see you, Mr Blunt,' said Albert.

A quick frown passed over Tommy's face. He took out his watch.

'I am due at the Duke's at a quarter to eleven,' he said. Then he looked keenly at the visitor. 'I can give you a few minutes if you will come this way.'

The latter followed him obediently into the inner office, where Tuppence was sitting demurely with pad and pencil.

'My confidential secretary, Miss Robinson,' said Tommy. 'Now, sir, perhaps you will state your business? Beyond the fact that it is urgent, that you came here in a taxi, and that you have lately been in the Arctic – or possibly the Antarctic, I know nothing.'

The visitor stared at him in amazement.

'But this is marvellous,' he cried. 'I thought detectives only did such things in books! Your office boy did not even give you my name!'

Tommy sighed deprecatingly.

'Tut, tut, all that was very easy,' he said. 'The rays of the midnight sun within the Arctic circle have a peculiar action upon the skin – the actinic rays have certain properties. I am writing a little monograph on the subject shortly. But all this is wide of the point.

What is it that has brought you to me in such distress of mind?'

'To begin with, Mr Blunt, my name is Gabriel Stavansson –'

'Ah! of course,' said Tommy. 'The well-known explorer. You have recently returned from the region of the North Pole, I believe?'

'I landed in England three days ago. A friend who was cruising in northern waters brought me back on his yacht. Otherwise I should not have got back for another fortnight. Now I must tell you, Mr Blunt, that before I started on this last expedition two years ago, I had the great good fortune to become engaged to Mrs Maurice Leigh Gordon –'

Tommy interrupted.

'Mrs Leigh Gordon was, before her marriage –?'

'The Honourable Hermione Crane, second daughter of Lord Lanchester,' reeled off Tuppence glibly.

Tommy threw her a glance of admiration.

'Her first husband was killed in the war,' added Tuppence.

Gabriel Stavansson nodded.

'That is quite correct. As I was saying, Hermione and I became engaged. I offered, of course, to give up this expedition, but she wouldn't hear of such a thing – bless her! She's the right kind of woman for an explorer's wife. Well, my first thought on landing was to see Hermione. I sent a telegram from Southampton, and rushed up to town by the first train. I knew that she was living for the time being with an aunt of hers, Lady Susan Clonray, in Pont Street, and I went straight there. To my great disappointment, I found that Hermy was away visiting some friends in Northumberland. Lady Susan was quite nice about it, after getting over her first surprise at seeing me. As I told you, I wasn't expected for another fortnight. She said Hermy would be returning in a few days' time. Then I asked for her address, but the old woman hummed and hawed – said Hermy was staying at one or two different places and that she wasn't quite sure what order she was taking them in. I may as well tell you, Mr Blunt, that Lady Susan and I have never got on very well. She's one of those fat women with double chins. I loathe fat women – always have – fat women and fat dogs are an abomination unto the Lord – and unfortunately they so often go together! It's an idiosyncrasy of mine, I know – but there it is – I never can get on with a fat woman.'

'Fashion agrees with you, Mr Stavansson,' said Tommy dryly. 'And every one has their own pet aversion – that of the late Lord Roberts was cats.'

'Mind you, I'm not saying that Lady Susan isn't a perfectly charming woman – she may be, but I've never taken to her. I've always felt, deep down, that she disapproved of our engagement, and I feel sure that she would influence Hermy against me if that were possible. I'm telling you this for what it's worth. Count it out as prejudice if you like. Well, to go on with my story, I'm the kind of obstinate brute who likes his own way. I didn't leave Pont Street until I'd got out of her the names and addresses of the people Hermy was likely to be staying with. Then I took the mail train north.'

'You are, I perceive, a man of action, Mr Stavansson,' said Tommy, smiling.

'The thing came upon me like a bombshell. Mr Blunt, none of these people had seen a sign of Hermy. Of the three houses, only one had been expecting her – Lady Susan must have made a bloomer over the other two – and she had put off her visit there at the last moment by telegram. I returned post haste to London, of course, and went straight to Lady Susan. I will do her the justice to say that she seemed upset. She admitted that she had no idea where Hermy could be. All the same, she strongly negatived any idea of going to the police. She pointed out that Hermy was not a silly young girl, but an independent woman who had always been in the habit of making her own plans. She was probably carrying out some idea of her own.

'I thought it quite likely that Hermy didn't want to report all her movements to Lady Susan. But I was still worried. I had that queer feeling one gets when something is wrong. I was just leaving when a telegram was brought to Lady Susan. She read it with an expression of relief and handed it to me. It ran as follows: '*Changed my plans. Just off to Monte Carlo for a week. – Hermy.*'

Tommy held out his hand.

'You have got the telegram with you?'

'No, I haven't. But it was handed in at Maldon, Surrey. I noticed that at the time, because it struck me as odd. What should Hermy be doing at Maldon. She'd no friends there that I had ever heard of.'

'You didn't think of rushing off to Monte Carlo in the same way that you had rushed north?'

'I thought of it, of course. But I decided against it. You see, Mr Blunt, whilst Lady Susan seemed quite satisfied by that telegram, I wasn't. It struck me as odd that she should always telegraph, not write. A line or two in her own handwriting would have set all my fears at rest. But anyone can sign a telegram "Hermy." The more I thought it over, the more uneasy I got. In the end I went down to Maldon. That was yesterday afternoon. It's a fair-sized place – good links there and all that – two hotels. I inquired everywhere I could think of, but there wasn't a sign that Hermy had ever been there. Coming back in the train I read your advertisement and I thought I'd put it up to you. If Hermy has really gone off to Monte Carlo, I don't want to set the police on her track and make a scandal, but I'm not going to be sent off on a wild goose chase myself. I stay here in London, in case – in case there's been foul play of any kind.'

Tommy nodded thoughtfully.

'What do you suspect exactly?'

'I don't know. But I feel there's something wrong.'

With a quick movement, Stavansson took a case from his pocket and laid it open before them.

'That is Hermione,' he said. 'I will leave it with you.'

The photograph represented a tall, willowy woman, no longer in her first youth, but with a charming frank smile and lovely eyes.

'Now, Mr Stavansson,' said Tommy, 'there is nothing you have omitted to tell me?'

'Nothing whatever.'

'No detail, however small?'

'I don't think so.'

Tommy sighed.

'That makes the task harder,' he observed. 'You must often have noticed, Mr Stavansson, in reading of crime, how one small detail is all the great detective needs to set him on the track. I may say that this case presents some unusual features. I have, I think, partially solved it already, but time will show.'

He picked up a violin which lay on the table and drew

the bow once or twice across the strings. Tuppence ground her teeth, and even the explorer blenched. The performer laid the instrument down again.

'A few chords from Mosgovskensky,' he murmured. 'Leave me your address, Mr Stavansson, and I will report progress to you.'

As the visitor left the office, Tuppence grabbed the violin, and putting it in the cupboard turned the key in the lock.

'If you must be Sherlock Holmes,' she observed, 'I'll get you a nice little syringe and a bottle labelled cocaine, but for God's sake leave that violin alone. If that nice explorer man hadn't been as simple as a child, he'd have seen through you. Are you going on with the Sherlock Holmes touch?'

'I flatter myself that I have carried it through very well so far,' said Tommy with some complacence. 'The deductions were good, weren't they? I had to risk the taxi. After all, it's the only sensible way of getting to this place.'

'It's lucky I had just read the bit about his engagement in this morning's *Daily Mirror*,' remarked Tuppence.

'Yes, that looked well for the efficiency of Blunt's Brilliant Detectives. This is decidedly a Sherlock Holmes case. Even you cannot have failed to notice the similarity between it and the disappearance of Lady Frances Carfax.'

'Do you expect to find Mrs Leigh Gordon's body in a coffin?'

'Logically, history should repeat itself. Actually – well, what do you think?'

'Well,' said Tuppence. 'The most obvious explanation seems to be that for some reason or other, Hermy, as he calls her, is afraid to meet her fiancé, and that Lady Susan is backing her up. In fact, to put it bluntly, she's come a cropper of some kind, and has got the wind up about it.'

'That occurred to me also,' said Tommy. 'But I thought we'd better make pretty certain before suggesting that explanation to a man like Stavansson. What about a run down to Maldon, old thing? And it would do no harm to take some golf clubs with us.'

Tuppence agreeing, the International Detective Agency was left in the charge of Albert.

Maldon, though a well-known residential place, did not cover a large area. Tommy and Tuppence, making every possible inquiry that ingenuity could suggest, nevertheless drew a complete blank. It was as they were returning to London that a brilliant idea occurred to Tuppence.

'Tommy, why did they put Maldon, Surrey, on the telegram?'

'Because Maldon is in Surrey, idiot.'

'Idiot yourself – I don't mean that. If you get a

telegram from – Hastings, say, or Torquay, they don't put the county after it. But from Richmond, they do put Richmond, Surrey. That's because there are two Richmonds.'

Tommy, who was driving, slowed up.

'Tuppence,' he said affectionately, 'your idea is not so dusty. Let us make inquiries at yonder post office.'

They drew up before a small building in the middle of a village street. A very few minutes sufficed to elicit the information that there were two Maldons. Maldon, Surrey, and Maldon, Sussex, the latter, a tiny hamlet but possessed of a telegraph office.

'That's it,' said Tuppence excitedly. 'Stavansson knew Maldon was in Surrey, so he hardly looked at the word beginning with S after Maldon.'

'Tomorrow,' said Tommy, 'we'll have a look at Maldon, Sussex.'

Maldon, Sussex, was a very different proposition to its Surrey namesake. It was four miles from a railway station, possessed two public houses, two small shops, a post and telegraph office combined with a sweet and picture postcard business, and about seven small cottages. Tuppence took on the shops whilst Tommy betook himself to the Cock and Sparrow. They met half an hour later.

'Well?' said Tuppence.

'Quite good beer,' said Tommy, 'but no information.'

'You'd better try the King's Head,' said Tuppence. 'I'm going back to the post office. There's a sour old woman there, but I heard them yell to her that dinner was ready.'

She returned to the place and began examining postcards. A fresh-faced girl, still munching, came out of the back room.

'I'd like these, please,' said Tuppence. 'And do you mind waiting whilst I just look over these comic ones?'

She sorted through a packet, talking as she did so.

'I'm ever so disappointed you couldn't tell me my sister's address. She's staying near here and I've lost her letter. Leigh Gordon, her name is.'

The girl shook her head.

'I don't remember it. And we don't get many letters through here either – so I probably should if I'd seen it on a letter. Apart from the Grange, there isn't many big houses round about.'

'What is the Grange?' asked Tuppence. 'Who does it belong to?'

'Dr Horriston has it. It's turned into a nursing home now. Nerve cases mostly, I believe. Ladies that come down for rest cures, and all that sort of thing. Well, it's quiet enough down here, heaven knows.' She giggled.

Tuppence hastily selected a few cards and paid for them.

'That's Doctor Horriston's car coming along now,' exclaimed the girl.

Tuppence hurried to the shop door. A small two-seater was passing. At the wheel was a tall dark man with a neat black beard and a powerful unpleasant face. The car went straight on down the street. Tuppence saw Tommy crossing the road towards her.

'Tommy, I believe I've got it. Doctor Horriston's nursing home.'

'I heard about it at the King's Head, and I thought there might be something in it. But if she's had a nervous breakdown or anything of that sort, her aunt and her friends would know about it surely.'

'Ye-es. I didn't mean that. Tommy, did you see that man in the two-seater?'

'Unpleasant-looking brute, yes.'

'That was Doctor Horriston.'

Tommy whistled.

'Shifty looking beggar. What do you say about it, Tuppence? Shall we go and have a look at the Grange?'

They found the place at last, a big rambling house, surrounded by deserted grounds, with a swift mill stream running behind the house.

'Dismal sort of abode,' said Tommy. 'It gives me the creeps, Tuppence. You know, I've a feeling this is going to turn out a far more serious matter than we thought at first.'

'Oh, don't. If only we are in time. That woman's in some awful danger; I feel it in my bones.'

'Don't let your imagination run away with you.'

'I can't help it. I mistrust that man. What shall we do? I think it would be a good plan if I went and rang the bell alone first and asked boldly for Mrs Leigh Gordon just to see what answer I get. Because, after all, it may be perfectly fair and above board.'

Tuppence carried out her plan. The door was opened almost immediately by a manservant with an impassive face.

'I want to see Mrs Leigh Gordon, if she is well enough to see me.'

She fancied that there was a momentary flicker of the man's eyelashes, but he answered readily enough.

'There is no one of that name here, madam.'

'Oh, surely. This is Doctor Horriston's place, The Grange, is it not?'

'Yes, madam, but there is nobody of the name of Mrs Leigh Gordon here.'

Baffled, Tuppence was forced to withdraw and hold a further consultation with Tommy outside the gate.

'Perhaps he was speaking the truth. After all, we don't *know*.'

'He wasn't. He was lying. I'm sure of it.'

'Wait until the doctor comes back,' said Tommy. 'Then I'll pass myself off as a journalist anxious to discuss his new system of rest cure with him. That will give me a chance of getting inside and studying the geography of the place.'

The doctor returned about half an hour later. Tommy gave him about five minutes, then he in turn marched up to the front door. But he too returned baffled.

'The doctor was engaged and couldn't be disturbed. And he never sees journalists. Tuppence, you're right. There's something fishy about this place. It's ideally situated – miles from anywhere. Any mortal thing could go on here, and no one would ever know.'

'Come on,' said Tuppence, with determination.

'What are you going to do?'

'I'm going to climb over the wall and see if I can't get up to the house quietly without being seen.'

'Right. I'm with you.'

The garden was somewhat overgrown and afforded a multitude of cover. Tommy and Tuppence managed to reach the back of the house unobserved.

Here there was a wide terrace with some crumbling steps leading down from it. In the middle some french windows opened on to the terrace, but they dared not step out into the open, and the windows where they were crouching were too high for them to be able to look in. It did not seem as though their reconnaissance would be much use, when suddenly Tuppence tightened her grasp of Tommy's arm.

Someone was speaking in the room close to them. The window was open and the fragment of conversation came clearly to their ears.

'Come in, come in, and shut the door,' said a man's voice irritably. 'A lady came about an hour ago, you said, and asked for Mrs Leigh Gordon?'

Tuppence recognised the answering voice as that of the impassive manservant.

'Yes, sir.'

'You said she wasn't here, of course?'

'Of course, sir.'

'And now this journalist fellow,' fumed the other.

He came suddenly to the window, throwing up the sash, and the two outside, peering through a screen of bushes, recognised Dr Horriston.

'It's the woman I mind most about,' continued the doctor. 'What did she look like?'

'Young, good-looking, and very smartly dressed, sir.'

Tommy nudged Tuppence in the ribs.

'Exactly,' said the doctor between his teeth, 'as I feared. Some friend of the Leigh Gordon woman's. It's getting very difficult. I shall have to take steps –'

He left the sentence unfinished. Tommy and Tuppence heard the door close. There was silence.

Gingerly Tommy led the retreat. When they had reached a little clearing not far away, but out of earshot from the house, he spoke.

'Tuppence, old thing, this is getting serious. They mean mischief. I think we ought to get back to town at once and see Stavansson.'

To his surprise Tuppence shook her head.

'We must stay down here. Didn't you hear him say he was going to take steps – That might mean anything.'

'The worst of it is we've hardly got a case to go to the police on.'

'Listen, Tommy. Why not ring up Stavansson from the village? I'll stay around here.'

'Perhaps that is the best plan,' agreed her husband. 'But I say – Tuppence –'

'Well?'

'Take care of yourself – won't you?'

'Of course I shall, you silly old thing. Cut along.'

It was some two hours later that Tommy returned. He found Tuppence awaiting him near the gate.

'Well?'

'I couldn't get on to Stavansson. Then I tried Lady Susan. She was out too. Then I thought of ringing up old Brady. I asked him to look up Horriston in the Medical Directory or whatever the thing calls itself.'

'Well, what did Dr Brady say?'

'Oh, he knew the name at once. Horriston was once a *bona fide* doctor, but he came a cropper of some kind. Brady called him a most unscrupulous quack, and said he, personally, wouldn't be surprised at anything. The question is, what are we to do now?'

'We must stay here,' said Tuppence instantly. 'I've a feeling they mean something to happen tonight. By the way, a gardener has been clipping ivy round the house. Tommy, *I saw where he put the ladder*.'

'Good for you, Tuppence,' said her husband appreciatively. 'Then tonight –'

'As soon as it's dark –'

'We shall see –'

'What we shall see.'

Tommy took his turn at watching the house whilst Tuppence went to the village and had some food.

Then she returned and they took up the vigil together. At nine o'clock they decided that it was dark enough to commence operations. They were now able to circle round the house in perfect freedom. Suddenly Tuppence clutched Tommy by the arm.

'Listen.'

The sound she had heard came again, borne faintly on the night air. It was the moan of a woman in pain. Tuppence pointed upward to a window on the first floor.

'It came from that room,' she whispered.

Again that low moan rent the stillness of the night.

The two listeners decided to put their original plan into action. Tuppence led the way to where she had seen the gardener put the ladder. Between them they carried it to the side of the house from which they had heard the moaning. All the blinds of the ground floor rooms were drawn, but this particular window upstairs was unshuttered.

Tommy put the ladder as noiselessly as possible against the side of the house.

'I'll go up,' whispered Tuppence. 'You stay below. I don't mind climbing ladders and you can steady it better than I could. And in case the doctor should come round the corner you'd be able to deal with him and I shouldn't.'

Nimbly Tuppence swarmed up the ladder and raised her head cautiously to look in at the window. Then she ducked it swiftly, but after a minute or two brought it very slowly up again. She stayed there for about five minutes. Then she descended again.

'It's her,' she said breathlessly and ungrammatically. 'But, oh, Tommy, it's horrible. She's lying there in bed, moaning, and turning to and fro – and just as I got there a woman dressed as a nurse came in. She bent over her and injected something in her arm and then went away again. What shall we do?'

'Is she conscious?'

'I think so. I'm almost sure she is. I fancy she may be strapped to the bed. I'm going up again, and if I can I'm going to get into that room.'

'I say, Tuppence –'

'If I'm in any sort of danger, I'll yell for you. So long.'

Avoiding further argument Tuppence hurried up the ladder again. Tommy saw her try the window, then noiselessly push up the sash. Another second and she had disappeared inside.

And now an agonising time came for Tommy. He could hear nothing at first. Tuppence and Mrs Leigh Gordon must be talking in whispers if they were talking at all. Presently he did hear a low murmur of voices and drew a breath of relief. But suddenly the voices stopped. Dead silence.

Tommy strained his ears. Nothing. What could they be doing?

Suddenly a hand fell on his shoulder.

'Come on,' said Tuppence's voice out of the darkness.

'Tuppence! How did you get here?'

'Through the front door. Let's get out of this.'

'Get out of this?'

'That's what I said.'

'But – Mrs Leigh Gordon?'

In a tone of indescribable bitterness Tuppence replied:

'Getting thin!'

Tommy looked at her, suspecting irony.

'What do you mean?'

'What I say. Getting thin. Slinkiness. Reduction of weight. Didn't you hear Stavansson say he hated fat women? In the two years he's been away, his Hermy has put on weight. Got a panic when she knew he was coming back and rushed off to do this new treatment of Dr Horriston's. It's injections of some sort, and he makes a deadly secret of it, and charges through the nose. I dare say he *is* a quack – but he's a damned successful one! Stavansson comes home a fortnight too soon, when she's only beginning the treatment. Lady Susan has been sworn to secrecy and plays up. And we come down here and make blithering idiots of ourselves!'

Tommy drew a deep breath.

'I believe, Watson,' he said with dignity, 'that there is a very good concert at the Queen's Hall tomorrow. We shall be in plenty of time for it. And you will oblige me by not placing this case upon your records. It has absolutely *no* distinctive features.'

Chapter 8

Blindman's Buff

'Right,' said Tommy, and replaced the receiver on its hook.

Then he turned to Tuppence.

'That was the Chief. Seems to have got the wind up about us. It appears that the parties we're after have got wise to the fact that I'm not the genuine Mr Theodore Blunt. We're to expect excitements at any minute. The Chief begs you as a favour to go home and stay at home, and not mix yourself up in it any more. Apparently the hornet's nest we've stirred up is bigger than anyone imagined.'

'All that about my going home is nonsense,' said Tuppence decidedly. 'Who is going to look after you if I go home? Besides, I like excitement. Business hasn't been very brisk just lately.'

'Well, one can't have murders and robberies every day,' said Tommy. 'Be reasonable. Now, my idea is this. When business is slack, we ought to do a certain amount of home exercises every day.'

'Lie on our backs and wave our feet in the air? That sort of thing?'

'Don't be so literal in your interpretation. When I say exercises, I mean exercises in the detective art. Reproductions of the great masters. For instance –'

From the drawer beside him Tommy took out a formidable dark green eyeshade, covering both eyes. This he adjusted with some care. Then he drew a watch from his pocket.

'I broke the glass this morning,' he remarked. 'That paved the way for its being the crystalless watch which my sensitive fingers touch so lightly.'

'Be careful,' said Tuppence. 'You nearly had the short hand off then.'

'Give me your hand,' said Tommy. He held it, one finger feeling for the pulse. 'Ah! the keyboard of silence. This woman has *not* got heart disease.'

'I suppose,' said Tuppence, 'that you are Thornley Colton?'

'Just so,' said Tommy. 'The blind Problemist. And you're thingummybob, the black haired, apple-cheeked secretary –'

'The bundle of baby clothes picked up on the banks of the river,' finished Tuppence.

'And Albert is the Fee, alias Shrimp.'

'We must teach him to say, "Gee,"' said Tuppence. 'And his voice isn't shrill. It's dreadfully hoarse.'

'Against the wall by the door,' said Tommy, 'you perceive the slim hollow cane which held in my sensitive hand tells me so much.'

He rose and cannoned into a chair.

'Damn!' said Tommy. 'I forgot that chair was there.'

'It must be beastly to be blind,' said Tuppence with feeling.

'Rather,' agreed Tommy heartily. 'I'm sorrier for all those poor devils who lost their eyesight in the war than for anyone else. But they say that when you live in the dark you really do develop special senses. That's what I want to try and see if one couldn't do. It would be jolly handy to train oneself to be some good in the dark. Now, Tuppence, be a good Sydney Thames. How many steps to that cane?'

Tuppence made a desperate guess.

'Three straight, five left,' she hazarded.

Tommy paced it uncertainly, Tuppence interrupting with a cry of warning as she realised that the fourth step left would take him slap against the wall.

'There's a lot in this,' said Tuppence. 'You've no idea how difficult it is to judge how many steps are needed.'

'It's jolly interesting,' said Tommy. 'Call Albert in. I'm going to shake hands with you both, and see if I know which is which.'

'All right,' said Tuppence, 'but Albert must wash his hands first. They're sure to be sticky from those beastly acid drops he's always eating.'

Albert, introduced to the game, was full of interest.

Tommy, the handshakes completed, smiled complacently.

'The keyboard of silence cannot lie,' he murmured. 'The first was Albert, the second, you, Tuppence.'

'Wrong!' shrieked Tuppence. 'Keyboard of silence indeed! You went by my dress ring. And I put that on Albert's finger.'

Various other experiments were carried out, with indifferent success.

'But it's coming,' declared Tommy. 'One can't expect to be infallible straight away. I tell you what. It's just lunch time. You and I will go to the Blitz, Tuppence. Blind man and his keeper. Some jolly useful tips to be picked up there.'

'I say, Tommy, we shall get into trouble.'

'No, we shan't. I shall behave quite like the little gentleman. But I bet you that by the end of luncheon I shall be startling you.'

All protests being thus overborne, a quarter of an hour later saw Tommy and Tuppence comfortably ensconced at a corner table in the Gold Room of the Blitz.

Tommy ran his fingers lightly over the Menu.

'Pilaff de homar and grilled chicken for me,' he murmured.

Tuppence also made her selection, and the waiter moved away.

'So far, so good,' said Tommy. 'Now for a more ambitious venture. What beautiful legs that girl in the short skirt has – the one who has just come in.'

'How was that done, Thorn?'

'Beautiful legs impart a particular vibration to the floor, which is received by my hollow cane. Or, to be honest, in a big restaurant there is nearly always a girl with beautiful legs standing in the doorway looking for her friends, and with short skirts going about, she'd be sure to take advantage of them.'

The meal proceeded.

'The man two tables from us is a very wealthy profiteer, I fancy,' said Tommy carelessly. 'Jew, isn't he?'

'Pretty good,' said Tuppence appreciatively. 'I don't follow that one.'

'I shan't tell you how it's done every time. It spoils my show. The head waiter is serving champagne three tables off to the right. A stout woman in black is about to pass our table.'

'Tommy, how can you –'

'Aha! You're beginning to see what I can do. That's a nice girl in brown just getting up at the table behind you.'

'Snoo!' said Tuppence. 'It's a young man in grey.'

'Oh!' said Tommy, momentarily disconcerted.

And at that moment two men who had been sitting at a table not far away, and who had been watching the young pair with keen interest, got up and came across to the corner table.

'Excuse me,' said the elder of the two, a tall, well-dressed man with an eyeglass, and a small grey moustache. 'But you have been pointed out to me as Mr Theodore Blunt. May I ask if that is so?'

Tommy hesitated a minute, feeling somewhat at a disadvantage. Then he bowed his head.

'That is so. I am Mr Blunt!'

'What an unexpected piece of good fortune! Mr Blunt, I was going to call at your offices after lunch. I am in trouble – very grave trouble. But – excuse me – you have had some accident to your eyes?'

'My dear sir,' said Tommy in a melancholy voice, 'I'm blind – completely blind.'

'What?'

'You are astonished. But surely you have heard of blind detectives?'

'In fiction. Never in real life. And I have certainly never heard that you were blind.'

'Many people are not aware of the fact,' murmured Tommy. 'I am wearing an eyeshade today to save my eyeballs from glare. But without it, quite a host of people have never suspected my infirmity – if you call it that. You see, my eyes cannot mislead me. But, enough of all this. Shall we go at once to my office, or will you give me the facts of the case here? The latter would be best, I think.'

A waiter brought up two extra chairs, and the two men sat down. The second man who had not yet spoken, was shorter, sturdy in build, and very dark.

'It is a matter of great delicacy,' said the older man dropping his voice confidentially. He looked uncertainly at Tuppence. Mr Blunt seemed to feel the glance.

'Let me introduce my confidential secretary,' he said. 'Miss Ganges. Found on the banks of the Indian river – a mere bundle of baby clothes. Very sad history. Miss Ganges is my eyes. She accompanies me everywhere.'

The stranger acknowledged the introduction with a bow.

'Then I can speak out. Mr Blunt, my daughter, a girl of sixteen, has been abducted under somewhat peculiar circumstances. I discovered this half an hour ago. The circumstances of the case were such that I dared not call in the police. Instead, I rang up your office. They told me you were out to lunch, but would be back by half-past two. I came in here with my friend, Captain Harker –'

The short man jerked his head and muttered something.

'By the greatest good fortune you happened to be lunching here also. We must lose no time. You must return with me to my house immediately.'

Tommy demurred cautiously.

'I can be with you in half an hour. I must return to my office first.'

Captain Harker, turning to glance at Tuppence, may have been surprised to see a half smile lurking for a moment at the corners of her mouth.

'No, no, that will not do. You must return with me.' The grey-haired man took a card from his pocket and handed it across the table. 'That is my name.'

Tommy fingered it.

'My fingers are hardly sensitive enough for that,' he said with a smile, and handed it to Tuppence, who read out in a low voice: 'The Duke of Blairgowrie.'

She looked with great interest at their client. The Duke of Blairgowrie was well known to be a most haughty and inaccessible nobleman who had married as a wife, the daughter of a Chicago pork butcher, many years younger than himself, and of a lively temperament that augured ill for their future together. There had been rumours of disaccord lately.

'You will come at once, Mr Blunt?' said the Duke, with a tinge of acerbity in his manner.

Tommy yielded to the inevitable.

'Miss Ganges and I will come with you,' he said

quietly. 'You will excuse my just stopping to drink a large cup of black coffee? They will serve it immediately. I am subject to very distressing headaches, the result of my eye trouble, and the coffee steadies my nerves.'

He called a waiter and gave the order. Then he spoke to Tuppence.

'Miss Ganges – I am lunching here tomorrow with the French Prefect of Police. Just note down the luncheon, and give it to the head waiter with instructions to reserve me my usual table. I am assisting the French police in an important case. *The fee*' – he paused – 'is considerable. Are you ready, Miss Ganges.'

'Quite ready,' said Tuppence, her stylo poised.

'We will start with that special salad of shrimps that they have here. Then to follow – let me see, *to follow* – Yes, Omelette Blitz, and perhaps a couple of *Tournedos à l'Etranger*.'

He paused and murmured apologetically:

'You will forgive me, I hope. Ah! yes, *Souffle en surprise*. That will conclude the repast. A most interesting man, the French Prefect. You know him, perhaps?'

The other replied in the negative, as Tuppence rose and went to speak to the head waiter. Presently she returned, just as the coffee was brought.

Tommy drank a large cup of it, sipping it slowly, then rose.

'My cane, Miss Ganges? Thank you. Directions, please?'

It was a moment of agony for Tuppence.

'One right, eighteen straight. About the fifth step, there is a waiter serving the table on your left.'

Swinging his cane jauntily, Tommy set out. Tuppence kept close beside him, and endeavoured unobtrusively to steer him. All went well until they were just passing out through the doorway. A man entered rather hurriedly, and before Tuppence could warn the blind Mr Blunt, he had barged right into the newcomer. Explanations and apologies ensued.

At the door of the Blitz, a smart landaulette was waiting. The Duke himself aided Mr Blunt to get in.

'Your car here, Harker?' he asked over his shoulder.

'Yes. Just round the corner.'

'Take Miss Ganges in it, will you.'

Before another word could be said, he had jumped in beside Tommy, and the car rolled smoothly away.

'A very delicate matter,' murmured the Duke. 'I can soon acquaint you with all the details.'

Tommy raised his hand to his head.

'I can remove my eyeshade now,' he observed pleasantly. 'It was only the glare of artificial light in the restaurant necessitated its use.'

But his arm was jerked down sharply. At the same

time he felt something hard and round being poked between his ribs.

'No, my dear Mr Blunt,' said the Duke's voice – but a voice that seemed suddenly different. 'You will not remove that eyeshade. You will sit perfectly still and not move in any way. You understand? I don't want this pistol of mine to go off. You see, I happen not to be the Duke of Blairgowrie at all. I borrowed his name for the occasion, knowing that you would not refuse to accompany such a celebrated client. I am something much more prosaic – a ham merchant who has lost his wife.'

He felt the start the other gave.

'That tells you something,' he laughed. 'My dear young man, you have been incredibly foolish. I'm afraid – I'm very much afraid that your activities will be curtailed in future.'

He spoke the last words with a sinister relish.

Tommy sat motionless. He did not reply to the other's taunts.

Presently the car slackened its pace and drew up.

'Just a minute,' said the pseudo Duke. He twisted a handkerchief deftly into Tommy's mouth, and drew up his scarf over it.

'In case you should be foolish enough to think of calling for help,' he explained suavely.

The door of the car opened and the chauffeur stood

ready. He and his master took Tommy between them and propelled him rapidly up some steps and in at the door of a house.

The door closed behind them. There was a rich oriental smell in the air. Tommy's feet sank deep into velvet pile. He was propelled in the same fashion up a flight of stairs and into a room which he judged to be at the back of the house. Here the two men bound his hands together. The chauffeur went out again, and the other removed the gag.

'You may speak freely now,' he announced pleasantly. 'What have you to say for yourself, young man?'

Tommy cleared his throat and eased the aching corners of his mouth.

'I hope you haven't lost my hollow cane,' he said mildly. 'It cost me a lot to have that made.'

'You have nerve,' said the other, after a minute's pause. 'Or else you are just a fool. Don't you understand that I have got you – got you in the hollow of my hand? That you're absolutely in my power? That no one who knows you is ever likely to see you again.'

'Can't you cut out the melodrama?' asked Tommy plaintively. 'Have I got to say, "You villain, I'll foil you yet"? That sort of thing is so very much out of date.'

'What about the girl?' said the other, watching him. 'Doesn't that move you?'

'Putting two and two together during my enforced

silence just now,' said Tommy. 'I have come to the inevitable conclusion that that chatty lad Harker is another of the doers of desperate deeds, and that therefore my unfortunate secretary will shortly join this little tea party.'

'Right as to one point, but wrong on the other. Mrs Beresford – you see, I know all about you – Mrs Beresford will not be brought here. That is a little precaution I took. It occurred to me that just probably your friends in high places might be keeping you shadowed. In that case, by dividing the pursuit, you could not both be trailed. I should still keep one in my hands. I am waiting now –'

He broke off as the door opened. The chauffeur spoke.

'We've not been followed, sir. It's all clear.'

'Good. You can go, Gregory.'

The door closed again.

'So far, so good,' said the 'Duke.' 'And now what are we to do with you, Mr Beresford Blunt?'

'I wish you'd take this confounded eyeshade off me,' said Tommy.

'I think not. With it on, you are truly blind – without it you would see as well as I do – and that would not suit my little plan. For I have a plan. You are fond of sensational fiction, Mr Blunt. This little game that you and your wife were playing today proves that. Now I, too, have arranged a little game – something rather ingenious, as I am sure you will admit when I explain it to you.

'You see, this floor on which you are standing is made of metal, and here and there on its surface are little projections. I touch a switch – so.' A sharp click sounded. 'Now the electric current is switched on. To tread on one of those little knobs now means – death! You understand? If you could see . . . but you cannot see. You are in the dark. That is the game – Blindman's Buff with death. If you can reach the door in safety – freedom! But I think that long before you reach it you will have trodden on one of the danger spots. And that will be very amusing – for me!'

He came forward and unbound Tommy's hands. Then he handed him his cane with a little ironical bow.

'The blind Problemist. Let us see if he will solve this problem. I shall stand here with my pistol ready. If you raise your hands to your head to remove that eyeshade, I shoot. Is that clear?'

'Perfectly clear,' said Tommy. He was rather pale, but determined. 'I haven't a dog's chance, I suppose?'

'Oh! that –' the other shrugged his shoulders.

'Damned ingenious devil, aren't you?' said Tommy. 'But you've forgotten one thing. May I light a cigarette by the way? My poor little heart's going pit-a-pat.'

'You may light a cigarette – but no tricks. I am watching you, remember, with the pistol ready.'

'I'm not a performing dog,' said Tommy. 'I don't do tricks.' He extracted a cigarette from his case, then felt for a match box. 'It's all right. I'm not feeling for a revolver. But you know well enough that I'm not armed. All the same, as I said before, you've forgotten one thing.'

'What is that?'

Tommy took a match from the box, and held it ready to strike.

'I'm blind and you can see. That's admitted. The advantage is with you. But supposing we were both in the dark – eh? Where's your advantage then?'

He struck the match.

'Thinking of shooting at the switch of the lights? Plunging the room into darkness? It can't be done.'

'Just so,' said Tommy. 'I can't give you darkness. But extremes meet, you know. What about *light*?'

As he spoke, he touched the match to something he held in his hand, and threw it down upon the table.

A blinding glare filled the room.

Just for a minute, blinded by the intense white light, the 'Duke' blinked and fell back, his pistol hand lowered.

He opened his eyes again to feel something sharp pricking his breast.

'Drop that pistol,' ordered Tommy. 'Drop it quick. I agree with you that a hollow cane is a pretty rotten affair. So I didn't get one. A good *sword stick* is a very useful weapon, though. Don't you think so? Almost as useful as magnesium wire. *Drop that pistol.*'

Obedient to the necessity of that sharp point, the man dropped it. Then, with a laugh, he sprang back.

'But I still have the advantage,' he mocked. 'For I can see, and you cannot.'

'That's where you're wrong,' said Tommy. 'I can see perfectly. The eyeshade's a fake. I was going to put one over on Tuppence. Make one or two bloomers to begin with, and then put in some perfectly marvellous stuff towards the end of lunch. Why, bless you, I could have walked to the door and avoided all the knobs with perfect ease. But I didn't trust you to play a sporting game. You'd never have let me get out of this alive. Careful now –'

For, with his face distorted with rage, the 'Duke' sprang forward, forgetting in his fury to look where he put his feet.

There was a sudden blue crackle of flame, and he swayed for a minute, then fell like a log. A faint odour of singed flesh filled the room, mingling with a stronger smell of ozone.'

'Whew,' said Tommy.

He wiped his face.

Then, moving gingerly, and with every precaution, he reached the wall, and touched the switch he had seen the other manipulate.

He crossed the room to the door, opened it carefully, and looked out. There was no one about. He went down the stairs and out through the front door.

Safe in the street, he looked up at the house with a shudder, noting the number. Then he hurried to the nearest telephone box.

There was a moment of agonising anxiety, and then a well-known voice spoke.

'Tuppence, thank goodness!'

'Yes, I'm all right. I got all your points. The Fee, Shrimp, Come to the Blitz and follow the two strangers. Albert got there in time, and when we went off in separate cars, followed me in a taxi, saw where they took me, and rang up the police.'

'Albert's a good lad,' said Tommy. 'Chivalrous. I was pretty sure he'd choose to follow you. But I've been worried, all the same. I've got lots to tell you. I'm coming straight back now. And the first thing I shall do when I get back is to write a thumping big cheque for St Dunstan's. Lord, it must be awful not to be able to see.'

Chapter 9

The Man in the Mist

Tommy was not pleased with life. Blunt's Brilliant Detectives had met with a reverse, distressing to their pride if not to their pockets. Called in professionally to elucidate the mystery of a stolen pearl necklace at Adlington Hall, Adlington, Blunt's Brilliant Detectives had failed to make good. Whilst Tommy, hard on the track of a gambling Countess, was tracking her in the disguise of a Roman Catholic priest, and Tuppence was 'getting off' with the nephew of the house on the golf links, the local Inspector of Police had unemotionally arrested the second footman who proved to be a thief well known at headquarters, and who admitted his guilt without making any bones about it.

Tommy and Tuppence, therefore, had withdrawn with what dignity they could muster, and were at the present moment solacing themselves with cocktails at the Grand Adlington Hotel. Tommy still wore his clerical disguise.

'Hardly a Father Brown touch, that,' he remarked gloomily. 'And yet I've got just the right kind of umbrella.'

'It wasn't a Father Brown problem,' said Tuppence. 'One needs a certain atmosphere from the start. One must be doing something quite ordinary, and then bizarre things begin to happen. That's the idea.'

'Unfortunately,' said Tommy, 'we have to return to town. Perhaps something bizarre will happen on the way to the station.'

He raised the glass he was holding to his lips, but the liquid in it was suddenly spilled, as a heavy hand smacked him on the shoulder, and a voice to match the hand boomed out words of greeting.

'Upon my soul, it is! Old Tommy! And Mrs Tommy too. Where did you blow in from? Haven't seen or heard anything of you for years.'

'Why, it's Bulger!' said Tommy, setting down what was left of the cocktail, and turning to look at the intruder, a big square-shouldered man of thirty years of age, with a round red beaming face, and dressed in golfing kit. 'Good old Bulger!'

'But I say, old chap,' said Bulger (whose real name, by the way, was Marvyn Estcourt), 'I never knew you'd taken orders. Fancy you a blinking parson.'

Tuppence burst out laughing, and Tommy looked embarrassed. And then they suddenly became conscious of a fourth person.

A tall, slender creature, with very golden hair and very round blue eyes, almost impossibly beautiful, with an effect of really expensive black topped by wonderful ermines, and very large pearl earrings. She was smiling. And her smile said many things. It asserted, for instance, that she knew perfectly well that she herself was the thing best worth looking at, certainly in England, and possibly in the whole world. She was not vain about it in any way, but she just knew, with certainty and confidence, that it was so.

Both Tommy and Tuppence recognised her immediately. They had seen her three times in *The Secret of the Heart*, and an equal number of times in that other great success, *Pillars of Fire*, and in innumerable other plays. There was, perhaps, no other actress in England who had so firm a hold on the British public, as Miss Gilda Glen. She was reported to be the most beautiful woman in England. It was also rumoured that she was the stupidest.

'Old friends of mine, Miss Glen,' said Estcourt, with a tinge of apology in his voice for having presumed, even for a moment, to forget such a radiant creature. 'Tommy and Mrs Tommy, let me introduce you to Miss Gilda Glen.'

The ring of pride in his voice was unmistakable. By merely being seen in his company, Miss Glen had conferred great glory upon him.

The actress was staring with frank interest at Tommy.

'Are you really a priest?' she asked. 'A Roman Catholic priest, I mean? Because I thought they didn't have wives.'

Estcourt went off in a boom of laughter again.

'That's good,' he exploded. 'You sly dog, Tommy. Glad he hasn't renounced you, Mrs Tommy, with all the rest of the pomps and vanities.'

Gilda Glen took not the faintest notice of him. She continued to stare at Tommy with puzzled eyes.

'Are you a priest?' she demanded.

'Very few of us are what we seem to be,' said Tommy gently. 'My profession is not unlike that of a priest. I don't give absolution – but I listen to confessions – I –'

'Don't you listen to him,' interrupted Estcourt. 'He's pulling your leg.'

'If you're not a clergyman, I don't see why you're dressed up like one,' she puzzled. 'That is, unless –'

'Not a criminal flying from justice,' said Tommy. 'The other thing.'

'Oh!' she frowned, and looked at him with beautiful bewildered eyes.

'I wonder if she'll ever get that,' thought Tommy to himself. 'Not unless I put it in words of one syllable for her, I should say.'

Aloud he said:

'Know anything about the trains back to town, Bulger? We've got to be pushing for home. How far is it to the station?'

'Ten minutes' walk. But no hurry. Next train up is the 6.35 and it's only about twenty to six now. You've just missed one.'

'Which way is it to the station from here?'

'Sharp to the left when you turn out of the hotel. Then – let me see – down Morgan's Avenue would be the best way, wouldn't it?'

'Morgan's Avenue?' Miss Glen started violently, and stared at him with startled eyes.

'I know what you're thinking of,' said Estcourt, laughing. 'The Ghost. Morgan's Avenue is bounded by the cemetery on one side, and tradition has it that a policeman who met his death by violence gets up and walks on his old beat, up and down Morgan's Avenue. A spook policeman! Can you beat it? But lots of people swear to having seen him.'

'A policeman?' said Miss Glen. She shivered a little. 'But there aren't really any ghosts, are there? I mean – there aren't such things?'

She got up, folding her wrap tighter round her.

'Goodbye,' she said vaguely.

She had ignored Tuppence completely throughout, and now she did not even glance in her direction. But, over her shoulder, she threw one puzzled questioning glance at Tommy.

Just as she got to the door, she encountered a tall man with grey hair and a puffy face, who uttered an exclamation of surprise. His hand on her arm, he led her through the doorway, talking in an animated fashion.

'Beautiful creature, isn't she?' said Estcourt. 'Brains of a rabbit. Rumour has it that she's going to marry Lord Leconbury. That was Leconbury in the doorway.'

'He doesn't look a very nice sort of man to marry,' remarked Tuppence.

Estcourt shrugged his shoulders.

'A title has a kind of glamour still, I suppose,' he said. 'And Leconbury is not an impoverished peer by any means. She'll be in clover. Nobody knows where she sprang from. Pretty near the gutter, I dare say. There's something deuced mysterious about her being down here anyway. She's not staying at the hotel. And when I tried to find out where she was staying, she snubbed me – snubbed me quite crudely, in the only way she knows. Blessed if I know what it's all about.'

He glanced at his watch and uttered an exclamation.

'I must be off. Jolly glad to have seen you two again. We must have a bust in town together some night. So long.'

He hurried away, and as he did so, a page approached with a note on a salver. The note was unaddressed.

'But it's for you, sir,' he said to Tommy. 'From Miss Gilda Glen.'

Tommy tore it open and read it with some curiosity. Inside were a few lines written in a straggling untidy hand.

I'm not sure, but I think you might be able to help me. And you'll be going that way to the station. Could you be at The White House, Morgan's Avenue, at ten minutes past six?

Yours sincerely,

Gilda Glen.

Tommy nodded to the page, who departed, and then handed the note to Tuppence.

'Extraordinary!' said Tuppence. 'Is it because she still thinks you're a priest?'

'No,' said Tommy thoughtfully. 'I should say it's because she's at last taken in that I'm not one. Hullo! what's this?'

'This,' was a young man with flaming red hair, a pugnacious jaw, and appallingly shabby clothes. He had walked into the room and was now striding up and down muttering to himself.

'Hell!' said the red-haired man, loudly and forcibly. 'That's what I say – Hell!'

He dropped into a chair near the young couple and stared at them moodily.

'Damn all women, that's what I say,' said the young man, eyeing Tuppence ferociously. 'Oh! all right, kick up a row if you like. Have me turned out of the hotel. It won't be for the first time. Why shouldn't we say what we think? Why should we go about bottling up our feelings, and smirking, and saying things exactly like everyone else. I don't feel pleasant and polite. I feel like getting hold of someone round the throat and gradually choking them to death.'

He paused.

'Any particular person?' asked Tuppence. 'Or just anybody?'

'One particular person,' said the young man grimly.

'This is very interesting,' said Tuppence. 'Won't you tell us some more?'

'My name's Reilly,' said the red-haired man. 'James Reilly. You may have heard it. I wrote a little volume of Pacifist poems – good stuff, although I say so.'

'*Pacifist poems*?' said Tuppence.

'Yes – why not?' demanded Mr Reilly belligerently.

'Oh! nothing,' said Tuppence hastily.

'I'm for peace all the time,' said Mr Reilly fiercely. 'To Hell with war. And women! Women! Did you see that creature who was trailing around here just now? Gilda Glen, she calls herself. Gilda Glen! God! how I've worshipped that woman. And I'll tell you this – if she's got a heart at all, it's on my side. She cared once for me, and I could make her care again. And if she sells herself to that muck heap, Leconbury – well, God help her. I'd as soon kill her with my own hands.'

And on this, suddenly, he rose and rushed from the room.

Tommy raised his eyebrows.

'A somewhat excitable gentleman,' he murmured. 'Well, Tuppence, shall we start?'

A fine mist was coming up as they emerged from the hotel into the cool outer air. Obeying Estcourt's directions, they turned sharp to the left, and in a few minutes they came to a turning labelled Morgan's Avenue.

The mist had increased. It was soft and white, and hurried past them in little eddying drifts. To their left was the high wall of the cemetery, on their right a row of small houses. Presently these ceased, and a high hedge took their place.

'Tommy,' said Tuppence. 'I'm beginning to feel jumpy. The mist – and the silence. As though we were miles from anywhere.'

'One does feel like that,' agreed Tommy. 'All alone in the world. It's the effect of the mist, and not being able to see ahead of one.'

Tuppence nodded.

'Just our footsteps echoing on the pavement. What's that?'

'What's what?'

'I thought I heard other footsteps behind us.'

'You'll be seeing the ghost in a minute if you work yourself up like this,' said Tommy kindly. 'Don't be so nervy. Are you afraid the spook policeman will lay his hands on your shoulder?'

Tuppence emitted a shrill squeal.

'Don't, Tommy. Now you've put it into my head.'

She craned her head back over her shoulder, trying to peer into the white veil that was wrapped all round them.

'There they are again,' she whispered. 'No, they're in front now. Oh! Tommy, don't say you can't hear them?'

'I do hear something. Yes, it's footsteps behind us. Somebody else walking this way to catch the train. I wonder –'

He stopped suddenly, and stood still, and Tuppence gave a gasp.

For the curtain of mist in front of them suddenly parted in the most artificial manner, and there, not twenty feet away, a gigantic policeman suddenly appeared, as though materialised out of the fog. One minute he was not there, the next minute he was – so at least it seemed to the rather superheated imaginations of the two watchers. Then as the mist rolled back still more, a little scene appeared, as though set on a stage.

The big blue policeman, a scarlet pillar box, and on the right of the road the outlines of a white house.

'Red, white, and blue,' said Tommy. 'It's damned pictorial. Come on, Tuppence, there's nothing to be afraid of.'

For, as he had already seen, the policeman was a real policeman. And, moreover, he was not nearly so gigantic as he had at first seemed looming up out of the mist.

But as they started forward, footsteps came from behind them. A man passed them, hurrying along. He turned in at the gate of the white house, ascended the steps, and beat a deafening tattoo upon the knocker. He was admitted just as they reached the spot where the policeman was standing staring after him.

'There's a gentleman seems to be in a hurry,' commented the policeman.

He spoke in a slow reflective voice, as one whose thoughts took some time to mature.

'He's the sort of gentleman always would be in a hurry,' remarked Tommy.

The policeman's stare, slow and rather suspicious, came round to rest on his face.

'Friend of yours?' he demanded, and there was distinct suspicion now in his voice.

'No,' said Tommy. 'He's not a friend of mine, but I happen to know who he is. Name of Reilly.'

'Ah!' said the policeman. 'Well, I'd better be getting along.'

'Can you tell me where the White House is?' asked Tommy.

The constable jerked his head sideways.

'This is it. Mrs Honeycott's.' He paused, and added, evidently with the idea of giving them valuable information, 'Nervous party. Always suspecting burglars is around. Always asking me to have a look around the place. Middle-aged women get like that.'

'Middle-aged, eh?' said Tommy. 'Do you happen to know if there's a young lady staying there?'

'A young lady,' said the policeman, ruminating. 'A young lady. No, I can't say I know anything about that.'

'She mayn't be staying here, Tommy,' said Tuppence. 'And anyway, she mayn't be here yet. She could only have started just before we did.'

'Ah!' said the policeman suddenly. 'Now that I call it to mind, a young lady did go in at this gate. I saw her as I was coming up the road. About three or four minutes ago it might be.'

'With ermine furs on?' asked Tuppence eagerly.

'She had some kind of white rabbit round her throat,' admitted the policeman.

Tuppence smiled. The policeman went on in the direction from which they had just come, and they prepared to enter the gate of the White House.

Suddenly, a faint, muffled cry sounded from inside the house, and almost immediately afterwards the front door opened and James Reilly came rushing down the steps. His face was white and twisted, and his eyes glared in front of him unseeingly. He staggered like a drunken man.

He passed Tommy and Tuppence as though he did not see them, muttering to himself with a kind of dreadful repetition.

'My God! My God! Oh, my God!'

He clutched at the gatepost, as though to steady himself, and then, as though animated by sudden panic, he raced off down the road as hard as he could go in the opposite direction from that taken by the policeman.

II

Tommy and Tuppence stared at each other in bewilderment.

'Well,' said Tommy, 'something's happened in that

house to scare our friend Reilly pretty badly.'

Tuppence drew her finger absently across the gate-post.

'He must have put his hand on some wet red paint somewhere,' she said idly.

'H'm,' said Tommy. 'I think we'd better go inside rather quickly. I don't understand this business.'

In the doorway of the house a white-capped maid-servant was standing, almost speechless with indignation.

'Did you ever see the likes of that now, Father,' she burst out, as Tommy ascended the steps. 'That fellow comes here, asks for the young lady, rushes upstairs without how or by your leave. She lets out a screech like a wild cat – and what wonder, poor pretty dear, and straightaway he comes rushing down again, with the white face on him, like one who's seen a ghost. What will be the meaning of it all?'

'Who are you talking with at the front door, Ellen?' demanded a sharp voice from the interior of the hall.

'Here's Missus,' said Ellen, somewhat unnecessarily.

She drew back, and Tommy found himself confronting a grey-haired, middle-aged woman, with frosty blue eyes imperfectly concealed by pince-nez, and a spare figure clad in black with bugle trimming.

'Mrs Honeycott?' said Tommy. 'I came here to see Miss Glen.'

'Mrs Honeycott gave him a sharp glance, then went on to Tuppence and took in every detail of her appearance.

'Oh, you did, did you?' she said. 'Well, you'd better come inside.'

She led the way into the hall and along it into a room at the back of the house, facing on the garden. It was a fair-sized room, but looked smaller than it was, owing to the large amount of chairs and tables crowded into it. A big fire burned in the grate, and a chintz-covered sofa stood at one side of it. The wallpaper was a small grey stripe with a festoon of roses round the top. Quantities of engravings and oil paintings covered the walls.

It was a room almost impossible to associate with the expensive personality of Miss Gilda Glen.

'Sit down,' said Mrs Honeycott. 'To begin with, you'll excuse me if I say I don't hold with the Roman Catholic religion. Never did I think to see a Roman Catholic priest in my house. But if Gilda's gone over to the Scarlet Woman, it's only what's to be expected in a life like hers – and I dare say it might be worse. She mightn't have any religion at all. I should think more of Roman Catholics if their priests were married – I always speak my mind. And to think of those convents – quantities of beautiful young girls shut up there, and no one knowing what becomes of them – well, it won't bear thinking about.'

Mrs Honeycott came to a full stop, and drew a deep breath.

Without entering upon a defence of the celibacy of the priesthood or the other controversial points touched upon, Tommy went straight to the point.

'I understand, Mrs Honeycott, that Miss Glen is in this house.'

'She is. Mind you, I don't approve. Marriage is marriage and your husband's your husband. As you make your bed, so you must lie on it.'

'I don't quite understand –' began Tommy, bewildered.

'I thought as much. That's the reason I brought you in here. You can go up to Gilda after I've spoken my mind. She came to me – after all these years, think of it! – and asked me to help her. Wanted me to see this man and persuade him to agree to a divorce. I told her straight out I'd have nothing whatever to do with it. Divorce is sinful. But I couldn't refuse my own sister shelter in my house, could I now?'

'Your sister?' exclaimed Tommy.

'Yes, Gilda's my sister. Didn't she tell you?'

Tommy stared at her openmouthed. The thing seemed fantastically impossible. Then he remembered that the angelic beauty of Gilda Glen had been in evidence for many years. He had been taken to see her act as quite a small boy. Yes, it was possible after all. But what a piquant contrast. So it was from this lower middle-class respectability that Gilda Glen had sprung. How well she had guarded her secret!

'I am not yet quite clear,' he said. 'Your sister is married?'

'Ran away to be married as a girl of seventeen,' said Mrs Honeycott succinctly. 'Some common fellow far below her in station. And our father a reverend. It was a disgrace. Then she left her husband and went on the stage. Play-acting! I've never been inside a theatre in my life. I hold no truck with wickedness. Now, after all these years, she wants to divorce the man. Means to marry some big wig, I suppose. But her husband's standing firm – not to be bullied and not to be bribed – I admire him for it.'

'What is his name?' asked Tommy suddenly.

'That's an extraordinary thing now, but I can't remember! It's nearly twenty years ago, you know, since I heard it. My father forbade it to be mentioned. And I've refused to discuss the matter with Gilda. She knows what I think, and that's enough for her.'

'It wasn't Reilly, was it?'

'Might have been. I really can't say. It's gone clean out of my head.'

'The man I mean was here just now.'

'That man! I thought he was an escaped lunatic. I'd been in the kitchen giving orders to Ellen. I'd just got back into this room, and was wondering whether Gilda had come in yet (she has a latchkey), when I heard her. She hesitated a minute or two in the hall and then went straight upstairs. About three minutes later all this tremendous rat-tatting began. I went out into the hall, and just saw a man rushing upstairs. Then there was a sort of cry upstairs, and presently down he came again and rushed out like a madman. Pretty goings on.'

Tommy rose.

'Mrs Honeycott, let us go upstairs at once. I am afraid –'

'What of?'

'Afraid that you have no red wet paint in the house.'

Mrs Honeycott stared at him.

'Of course I haven't.'

'That is what I feared,' said Tommy gravely. 'Please let us go to your sister's room at once.'

Momentarily silenced, Mrs Honeycott led the way. They caught a glimpse of Ellen in the hall, backing hastily into one of the rooms.

Mrs Honeycott opened the first door at the top of the stairs. Tommy and Tuppence entered close behind her.

Suddenly she gave a gasp and fell back.

A motionless figure in black and ermine lay stretched

on the sofa. The face was untouched, a beautiful soulless face like a mature child asleep. The wound was on the side of the head, a heavy blow with some blunt instrument had crushed in the skull. Blood was dripping slowly on to the floor, but the wound itself had long ceased to bleed . . .

Tommy examined the prostrate figure, his face very white.

'So,' he said at last, 'he didn't strangle her after all.'

'What do you mean? Who?' cried Mrs Honeycott. 'Is she dead?'

'Oh, yes, Mrs Honeycott, she's dead. Murdered. The question is – by whom? Not that it is much of a question. Funny – for all his ranting words, I didn't think the fellow had got it in him.'

He paused a minute, then turned to Tuppence with decision.

'Will you go out and get a policeman, or ring up the police station from somewhere?'

Tuppence nodded. She too, was very white. Tommy led Mrs Honeycott downstairs again.

'I don't want there to be any mistake about this,' he said. 'Do you know exactly what time it was when your sister came in?'

'Yes, I do,' said Mrs Honeycott. 'Because I was just setting the clock on five minutes as I have to do every evening. It loses just five minutes a day. It was exactly eight minutes past six by my watch, and that never loses or gains a second.'

Tommy nodded. That agreed perfectly with the policeman's story. He had seen the woman with the white furs go in at the gate, probably three minutes had elapsed before he and Tuppence had reached the same spot. He had glanced at his own watch then and had noted that it was just one minute after the time of their appointment.

There was just the faint chance that some one might have been waiting for Gilda Glen in the room upstairs. But if so, he must still be hiding in the house. No one but James Reilly had left it.

He ran upstairs and made a quick but efficient search of the premises. But there was no one concealed anywhere.

Then he spoke to Ellen. After breaking the news to her, and waiting for her first lamentations and invocations to the saints to have exhausted themselves, he asked a few questions.

Had any one else come to the house that afternoon asking for Miss Glen? No one whatsoever. Had she herself been upstairs at all that evening? Yes she'd gone up at six o'clock as usual to draw the curtains – or it might have been a few minutes after six. Anyway it was just before that wild fellow came breaking the knocker down. She'd run downstairs to answer the door. And him a black-hearted murderer all the time.

Tommy let it go at that. But he still felt a curious pity for Reilly, and unwillingness to believe the worst of him. And yet there was no one else who could have murdered Gilda Glen. Mrs Honeycott and Ellen had been the only two people in the house.

He heard voices in the hall, and went out to find Tuppence and the policeman from the beat outside. The latter had produced a notebook, and a rather blunt pencil, which he licked surreptitiously. He went upstairs and surveyed the victim stolidly, merely remarking that if he was to touch anything the Inspector would give him beans. He listened to all Mrs Honeycott's hysterical outbursts and confused explanations, and occasionally he wrote something down. His presence was calming and soothing.

Tommy finally got him alone for a minute or two on the steps outside ere he departed to telephone headquarters.

'Look here,' said Tommy, 'you saw the deceased turning in at the gate, you say. Are you sure she was alone?'

'Oh! she was alone all right. Nobody with her.'

'And between that time and when you met us, nobody came out of the gate?'

'Not a soul.'

'You'd have seen them if they had?'

'Of course I should. Nobody come out till that wild chap did.'

The majesty of the law moved portentously down the steps and paused by the white gatepost, which bore the imprint of a hand in red.

'Kind of amateur he must have been,' he said pityingly. 'To leave a thing like that.'

Then he swung out into the road.

III

It was the day after the crime. Tommy and Tuppence were still at the Grand Hotel, but Tommy had thought it prudent to discard his clerical disguise.

James Reilly had been apprehended, and was in custody. His solicitor, Mr Marvell, had just finished a lengthy conversation with Tommy on the subject of the crime.

'I never would have believed it of James Reilly,' he said simply. 'He's always been a man of violent speech, but that's all.'

Tommy nodded.

'If you disperse energy in speech, it doesn't leave you too much over for action. What I realise is that I shall be one of the principal witnesses against him.

That conversation he had with me just before the crime was particularly damning. And, in spite of everything, I like the man, and if there was anyone else to suspect, I should believe him to be innocent. What's his own story?'

The solicitor pursed up his lips.

'He declares that he found her lying there dead. But that's impossible, of course. He's using the first lie that comes into his head.'

'Because, if he happened to be speaking the truth, it would mean that the garrulous Mrs Honeycott committed the crime – and that is fantastic. Yes, he must have done it.'

'The maid heard her cry out, remember.'

'The maid – yes –'

Tommy was silent a moment. Then he said thoughtfully.

'What credulous creatures we are, really. We believe evidence as though it were gospel truth. And what is it really? Only the impression conveyed to the mind by the senses – and suppose they're the wrong impressions?'

The lawyer shrugged his shoulders.

'Oh! we all know that there are unreliable witnesses, witnesses who remember more and more as time goes on, with no real intention to deceive.'

'I don't mean only that. I mean all of us – we say

things that aren't really so, and never know that we've done so. For instance, both you and I, without doubt, have said some time or other, "There's the post," when what we really meant was that we'd heard a double knock and the rattle of the letter-box. Nine times out of ten we'd be right, and it would be the post, but just possibly the tenth time it might be only a little urchin playing a joke on us. See what I mean?'

'Ye-es,' said Mr Marvell slowly. 'But I don't see what you're driving at?'

'Don't you? I'm not so sure that I do myself. But I'm beginning to see. It's like the stick, Tuppence. You remember? One end of it pointed one way – but the other end always points the opposite way. It depends whether you get hold of it by the right end. Doors open – but they also shut. People go upstairs, but they also go downstairs. Boxes shut, but they also open.'

'What *do* you mean?' demanded Tuppence.

'It's so ridiculously easy, really,' said Tommy. 'And yet it's only just come to me. How do you know when a person's come into the house. You hear the door open and bang to, and if you're expecting any one to come in, you will be quite sure it is them. But it might just as easily be someone going *out*.'

'But Miss Glen didn't go out?'

'No, I know *she* didn't. But some one else did – the murderer.'

'But how did she get in, then?'

'She came in whilst Mrs Honeycott was in the kitchen talking to Ellen. They didn't hear her. Mrs Honeycott went back to the drawing-room, wondered if her sister had come in and began to put the clock right, and then, as she thought, she heard her come in and go upstairs.'

'Well, what about that? The footsteps going upstairs?'

'That was Ellen, going up to draw the curtains. You remember, Mrs Honeycott said her sister paused before going up. That pause was just the time needed for Ellen to come out from the kitchen into the hall. She just missed seeing the murderer.'

'But, Tommy,' cried Tuppence. 'The cry she gave?'

'That was James Reilly. Didn't you notice what a high-pitched voice he has? In moments of great emotion, men often squeal just like a woman.'

'But the murderer? We'd have seen him?'

'We *did* see him. We even stood talking to him. Do you remember the sudden way that policeman appeared? That was because he stepped out of the gate, just after the mist cleared from the road. It made us jump, don't you remember? After all, though we never think of them as that, policemen are men just like any other men. They love and they hate. They marry . . .

'I think Gilda Glen met her husband suddenly just

outside that gate, and took him in with her to thrash the matter out. He hadn't Reilly's relief of violent words, remember. He just saw red – and he had his truncheon handy . . .'

Chapter 10

The Crackler

'Tuppence,' said Tommy. 'We shall have to move into a much larger office.'

'Nonsense,' said Tuppence. 'You mustn't get swollen-headed and think you are a millionaire just because you solved two or three twopenny halfpenny cases with the aid of the most amazing luck.'

'What some call luck, others call skill.'

'Of course, if you really think you are Sherlock Holmes, Thorndyke, McCarty and the Brothers Okewood all rolled into one, there is no more to be said. Personally I would much rather have luck on my side than all the skill in the world.'

'Perhaps there is something in that,' conceded Tommy. 'All the same, Tuppence, we do need a larger office.'

'Why?'

'The classics,' said Tommy. 'We need several hundreds

of yards of extra bookshelf if Edgar Wallace is to be properly represented.'

'We haven't had an Edgar Wallace case yet.'

'I'm afraid we never shall,' said Tommy. 'If you notice he never does give the amateur sleuth much of a chance. It is all stern Scotland Yard kind of stuff – the real thing and no base counterfeit.'

Albert, the office boy, appeared at the door.

'Inspector Marriot to see you,' he announced.

'The mystery man of Scotland Yard,' murmured Tommy.

'The busiest of the Busies,' said Tuppence. 'Or is it "Noses"? I always get mixed between Busies and Noses.'

The Inspector advanced upon them with a beaming smile of welcome.

'Well, and how are things?' he asked breezily. 'None the worse for our little adventure the other day?'

'Oh, rather not,' said Tuppence. 'Too, too marvellous, wasn't it?'

'Well, I don't know that I would describe it exactly that way myself,' said Marriot cautiously.

'What has brought you here today, Marriot?' asked Tommy. 'Not just solicitude for our nervous systems, is it?'

'No,' said the Inspector. 'It is work for the brilliant Mr Blunt.'

'Ha!' said Tommy. 'Let me put my brilliant expression on.'

'I have come to make you a proposition, Mr Beresford. What would you say to rounding up a really big gang?'

'Is there such a thing?' asked Tommy.

'What do you mean, is there such a thing?'

'I always thought that gangs were confined to fiction – like master crooks and super criminals.'

'The master crook isn't very common,' agreed the Inspector. 'But Lord bless you, sir, there's any amount of gangs knocking about.'

'I don't know that I should be at my best dealing with a gang,' said Tommy. 'The amateur crime, the crime of quiet family life – that is where I flatter myself that I shine. Drama of strong domestic interest. That's the thing – with Tuppence at hand to supply all those little feminine details which are so important, and so apt to be ignored by the denser male.'

His eloquence was arrested abruptly as Tuppence threw a cushion at him and requested him not to talk nonsense.

'Will have your little bit of fun, won't you, sir?' said Inspector Marriot, smiling paternally at them both. 'If you'll not take offence at my saying so, it's a pleasure to see two young people enjoying life as much as you two do.'

'Do we enjoy life?' said Tuppence, opening her eyes

very wide. 'I suppose we do. I've never thought about it before.'

'To return to that gang you were talking about,' said Tommy. 'In spite of my extensive private practice – duchesses, millionaires, and all the best charwomen – I might, perhaps, condescend to look into the matter for you. I don't like to see Scotland Yard at fault. You'll have the *Daily Mail* after you before you know where you are.'

'As I said before, you must have your bit of fun. Well, it's like this.' Again he hitched his chair forward. 'There's any amount of forged notes going about just now – hundreds of 'em! The amount of counterfeit Treasury notes in circulation would surprise you. Most artistic bit of work it is. Here's one of 'em.'

He took a one pound note from his pocket and handed it to Tommy.

'Looks all right, doesn't it?'

Tommy examined the note with great interest.

'By Jove, I'd never spot there was anything wrong with that.'

'No more would most people. Now here's a genuine one. I'll show you the differences – very slight they are, but you'll soon learn to tell them apart. Take this magnifying glass.'

At the end of five minutes' coaching both Tommy and Tuppence were fairly expert.

'What do you want us to do, Inspector Marriot?' asked Tuppence. 'Just keep our eyes open for these things?'

'A great deal more than that, Mrs Beresford. I'm pinning my faith on you to get to the bottom of the matter. You see, we've discovered that the notes are being circulated from the West End. Somebody pretty high up in the social scale is doing the distributing. They're passing them the other side of the Channel as well. Now there's a certain person who is interesting us very much. A Major Laidlaw – perhaps you've heard the name?'

'I think I have,' said Tommy. 'Connected with racing, isn't that it?'

'Yes. Major Laidlaw is pretty well known in connection with the Turf. There's nothing actually against him, but there's a general impression that he's been a bit too smart over one or two rather shady transactions. Men in the know look queer when he's mentioned. Nobody knows much of his past or where he came from. He's got a very attractive French wife who's seen about everywhere with a train of admirers. They must spend a lot of money, the Laidlaws, and I'd like to know where it comes from.'

'Possibly from the train of admirers,' suggested Tommy.

'That's the general idea. But I'm not so sure. It

may be coincidence, but a lot of notes have been forthcoming from a certain very smart little gambling club which is much frequented by the Laidlaws and their set. This racing, gambling set get rid of a lot of loose money in notes. There couldn't be a better way of getting it into circulation.'

'And where do we come in?'

'This way. Young St Vincent and his wife are friends of yours, I understand? They're pretty thick with the Laidlaw set – though not as thick as they were. Through them it will be easy for you to get a footing in the same set in a way that none of our people could attempt. There's no likelihood of their spotting you. You'll have an ideal opportunity.'

'What have we got to find out exactly?'

'Where they get the stuff from, if they *are* passing it.'

'Quite so,' said Tommy. 'Major Laidlaw goes out with an empty suit-case. When he returns it is crammed to the bursting point with Treasury notes. How is it done? I sleuth him and find out. Is that the idea?'

'More or less. But don't neglect the lady, and her father, M. Heroulade. Remember the notes are being passed on both sides of the Channel.'

'My dear Marriot,' exclaimed Tommy reproachfully, 'Blunt's Brilliant Detectives do not know the meaning of the word neglect.'

The Inspector rose.

'Well, good luck to you,' he said, and departed.

'Slush,' said Tuppence enthusiastically.

'Eh?' said Tommy, perplexed.

'Counterfeit money,' explained Tuppence. 'It is always called slush. I know I'm right. Oh, Tommy, we have got an Edgar Wallace case. At last we are Busies.'

'We are,' said Tommy. 'And we are out to get the Crackler, and we will get him good.'

'Did you say the Cackler or the Crackler?'

'The Crackler.'

'Oh, what is a Crackler?'

'A new word that I have coined,' said Tommy. 'Descriptive of one who passes false notes into circulation. Banknotes crackle, therefore he is called a crackler. Nothing could be more simple.'

'That is rather a good idea,' said Tuppence. 'It makes it seem more real. I like the Rustler myself. Much more descriptive and sinister.'

'No,' said Tommy, 'I said the Crackler first, and I stick to it.'

'I shall enjoy this case,' said Tuppence. 'Lots of night clubs and cocktails in it. I shall buy some eyelash-black tomorrow.'

'Your eyelashes are black already,' objected her husband.

'I could make them blacker,' said Tuppence. 'And

cherry lipstick would be useful too. That ultra-bright kind.'

'Tuppence,' said Tommy, 'you're a real rake at heart. What a good thing it is that you are married to a sober steady middle-aged man like myself.'

'You wait,' said Tuppence. 'When you have been to the Python Club a bit, you won't be so sober yourself.'

Tommy produced from a cupboard various bottles, two glasses, and a cocktail shaker.

'Let's start now,' he said. 'We are after you, Crackler, and we mean to get you.'

II

Making the acquaintance of the Laidlaws proved an easy affair. Tommy and Tuppence, young, well-dressed, eager for life, and with apparently money to burn, were soon made free of that particular coterie in which the Laidlaws had their being.

Major Laidlaw was a tall, fair man, typically English in appearance, with a hearty sportsmanlike manner, slightly belied by the hard lines round his eyes and the occasional quick sideways glance that assorted oddly with his supposed character.

He was a very dexterous card player, and Tommy

noticed that when the stakes were high he seldom rose from the table a loser.

Marguerite Laidlaw was quite a different proposition. She was a charming creature, with the slenderness of a wood nymph and the face of a Greuze picture. Her dainty broken English was fascinating, and Tommy felt that it was no wonder most men were her slaves. She seemed to take a great fancy to Tommy from the first, and playing his part, he allowed himself to be swept into her train.

'My Tommee,' she would say; 'but positively I cannot go without my Tommee. His 'air, eet ees the colour of the sunset, ees eet not?'

Her father was a more sinister figure. Very correct, very upright, with his little black beard and his watchful eyes.

Tuppence was the first to report progress. She came to Tommy with ten one pound notes.

'Have a look at these. They're wrong 'uns, aren't they?'

Tommy examined them and confirmed Tuppence's diagnosis.

'Where did you get them from?'

'That boy, Jimmy Faulkener. Marguerite Laidlaw gave them to him to put on a horse for her. I said I wanted small notes and gave him a tenner in exchange.'

'All new and crisp,' said Tommy thoughtfully. 'They

can't have passed through many hands. I suppose young Faulkener is all right?'

'Jimmy? Oh, he's a dear. He and I are becoming great friends.'

'So I have noticed,' said Tommy coldly. 'Do you really think it is necessary?'

'Oh, it isn't business,' said Tuppence cheerfully. 'It's pleasure. He's such a nice boy. I'm glad to get him out of that woman's clutches. You've no idea of the amount of money she's cost him.'

'It looks to me as though he were getting rather a pash for you, Tuppence.'

'I've thought the same myself sometimes. It's nice to know one's still young and attractive, isn't it?'

'Your moral tone, Tuppence, is deplorably low. You look at these things from the wrong point of view.'

'I haven't enjoyed myself so much for years,' declared Tuppence shamelessly. 'And anyway, what about you? Do I ever see you nowadays? Aren't you always living in Marguerite Laidlaw's pocket?'

'Business,' said Tommy crisply.

'But she is attractive, isn't she?'

'Not my type,' said Tommy. 'I don't admire her.'

'Liar,' laughed Tuppence. 'But I always did think I'd rather marry a liar than a fool.'

'I suppose,' said Tommy, 'that there's no absolute necessity for a husband to be either?'

But Tuppence merely threw him a pitying glance and withdrew.

Amongst Mrs Laidlaw's train of admirers was a simple but extremely wealthy gentleman of the name of Hank Ryder.

Mr Ryder came from Alabama, and from the first he was disposed to make a friend and confidant of Tommy.

'That's a wonderful woman, sir,' said Mr Ryder following the lovely Marguerite with reverential eyes. 'Plumb full of civilisation. Can't beat *la gaie France*, can you? When I'm near her, I feel as though I was one of the Almighty's earliest experiments. I guess he'd got to get his hand in before he attempted anything so lovely as that perfectly lovely woman.'

Tommy agreeing politely with these sentiments, Mr Ryder unburdened himself still further.

'Seems kind of a shame a lovely creature like that should have money worries.'

'Has she?' asked Tommy.

'You betcha life she has. Queer fish, Laidlaw. She's skeered of him. Told me so. Daren't tell him about her little bills.'

'Are they *little* bills?' asked Tommy.

'Well – when I say little! After all, a woman's got to wear clothes, and the less there are of them the more they cost, the way I figure it out. And a pretty woman like that doesn't want to go about in last season's goods. Cards too, the poor little thing's been mighty unlucky at cards. Why, she lost fifty to me last night.'

'She won two hundred from Jimmy Faulkener the night before,' said Tommy drily.

'Did she indeed? That relieves my mind some. By the way, there seems to be a lot of dud notes floating around in your country just now. I paid in a bunch at my bank this morning, and twenty-five of them were down-and-outers, so the polite gentleman behind the counter informed me.'

'That's rather a large proportion. Were they new looking?'

'New and crisp as they make 'em. Why, they were the ones Mrs Laidlaw paid over to me, I reckon. Wonder where she got 'em from. One of these toughs on the racecourse as likely as not.'

'Yes,' said Tommy. 'Very likely.'

'You know, Mr Beresford, I'm new to this sort of high life. All these swell dames and the rest of the outfit. Only made my pile a short while back. Came right over to Yurrop to see life.'

Tommy nodded. He made a mental note to the effect that with the aid of Marguerite Laidlaw Mr Ryder would probably see a good deal of life and that the price charged would be heavy.

Meantime, for the second time, he had evidence that

the forged notes were being distributed pretty near at hand, and that in all probability Marguerite Laidlaw had a hand in their distribution.

On the following night he himself was given a proof.

It was at that small select meeting place mentioned by Inspector Marriot. There was dancing there, but the real attraction of the place lay behind a pair of imposing folding doors. There were two rooms there with green baize-covered tables, where vast sums changed hands nightly.

Marguerite Laidlaw, rising at last to go, thrust a quantity of small notes into Tommy's hands.

'They are so bulkee, Tommee – you will change them, yes? A beeg note. See my so sweet leetle bag, it bulges him to distraction.'

Tommy brought her the hundred pound note she asked for. Then in a quiet corner he examined the notes she had given him. At least a quarter of them were counterfeit.

But where did she get her supplies from? To that he had as yet no answer. By means of Albert's co-operation, he was almost sure that Laidlaw was not the man. His movements had been watched closely and had yielded no result.

Tommy suspected her father, the saturnine M. Heroulade. He went to and fro to France fairly often. What could be simpler than to bring the notes across with him? A false bottom to the trunk – something of that kind.

Tommy strolled slowly out of the Club, absorbed in these thoughts, but was suddenly recalled to immediate necessities. Outside in the street was Mr Hank P. Ryder, and it was clear at once that Mr Ryder was not strictly sober. At the moment he was trying to hang his hat on the radiator of a car, and missing it by some inches every time.

'This goddarned hatshtand, this goddarned hatshtand,' said Mr Ryder tearfully. 'Not like that in the Shtates. Man can hang up his hat every night – every night, sir. You're wearing two hatshs. Never sheen a man wearing two hatshs before. Must be effect – climate.'

'Perhaps I've got two heads,' said Tommy gravely.

'Sho you have,' said Mr Ryder. 'Thatsh odd. Thatsh remarkable fac'. Letsh have a cocktail. Prohibition – probishun thatsh whatsh done me in. I guess I'm drunk – constootionally drunk. Cocktailsh – mixed 'em – Angel's Kiss – that's Marguerite – lovely creature, fon o' me too. Horshes Neck, two Martinis – three Road to Ruinsh – no, roadsh to roon – mixed 'em all – in a beer tankard. Bet me I wouldn't – I shaid – to hell, I shaid –'

Tommy interrupted.

'That's all right,' he said soothingly. 'Now what about getting home?'

'No home to go to,' said Mr Ryder sadly, and wept.

'What hotel are you staying at?' asked Tommy.

'Can't go home,' said Mr Ryder. 'Treasure hunt. Swell thing to do. She did it. Whitechapel – white heartsh, white headsn shorrow to the grave –'

But Mr Ryder became suddenly dignified. He drew himself erect and attained a sudden miraculous command over his speech.

'Young man, I'm telling you. Margee took me. In her car. Treasure hunting. English aristocrashy all do it. Under the cobblestones. Five hundred poundsh. Solemn thought, '*tis* solemn thought. I'm *telling* you, young man. You've been kind to me. I've got your welfare at heart, sir, at heart. We Americans –'

Tommy interrupted him this time with even less ceremony.

'What's that you say? Mrs Laidlaw took you in a car?'

The American nodded with a kind of owlish solemnity.

'To Whitechapel?' Again that owlish nod.

'And you found five hundred pounds there?'

Mr Ryder struggled for words.

'S-she did,' he corrected his questioner. 'Left me outside. Outside the door. Always left outside. It's kinder sad. Outside – always outside.'

'Would you know your way there?'

'I guess so. Hank Ryder doesn't lose his bearings –'

Tommy hauled him along unceremoniously. He found his own car where it was waiting, and presently they were bowling eastward. The cool air revived Mr Ryder. After slumping against Tommy's shoulder in a kind of stupor, he awoke clear-headed and refreshed.

'Say, boy, where are we?' he demanded.

'Whitechapel,' said Tommy crisply. 'Is this where you came with Mrs Laidlaw tonight?'

'It looks kinder familiar,' admitted Mr Ryder, looking round. 'Seems to me we turned off to the left somewhere down here. That's it – that street there.'

Tommy turned off obediently. Mr Ryder issued directions.

'That's it. Sure. And round to the right. Say, aren't the smells awful. Yes, past that pub at the corner – sharp round, and stop at the mouth of that little alley. But what's the big idea? Hand it to me. Some of the oof left behind? Are we going to put one over on them?'

'That's exactly it,' said Tommy. 'We're going to put one over on them. Rather a joke, isn't it?'

'I'll tell the world,' assented Mr Ryder. 'Though I'm just a mite hazed about it all,' he ended wistfully.

Tommy got out and assisted Mr Ryder to alight also. They advanced into the alley way. On the left were the backs of a row of dilapidated houses, most of which had doors opening into the alley. Mr Ryder came to a stop before one of these doors.

'In here she went,' he declared. 'It was this door – I'm plumb certain of it.'

'They all look very alike,' said Tommy. 'Reminds me of the story of the soldier and the Princess. You remember, they made a cross on the door to show which one it was. Shall we do the same?'

Laughing, he drew a piece of white chalk from his pocket and made a rough cross low down on the door. Then he looked up at various dim shapes that prowled high on the walls of the alley, one of which was uttering a blood-curdling yawl.

'Lots of cats about,' he remarked cheerfully.

'What is the procedure?' asked Mr Ryder. 'Do we step inside?'

'Adopting due precautions, we do,' said Tommy.

He glanced up and down the alley way, then softly tried the door. It yielded. He pushed it open and peered into a dim yard.

Noiselessly he passed through, Mr Ryder on his heels.

'Gee,' said the latter, 'there's someone coming down the alley.'

He slipped outside again. Tommy stood still for a minute, then hearing nothing went on. He took a torch from his pocket and switched on the light for a brief second. That momentary flash enabled him to see his way ahead. He pushed forward and tried the closed door ahead of him. That too gave, and very softly he pushed it open and went in.

After standing still a second and listening, he again switched on the torch, and at that flash, as though at a given signal, the place seemed to rise round him. Two men were in front of him, two men were behind him. They closed in on him and bore him down.

'Lights,' growled a voice.

An incandescent gas burner was lit. By its light Tommy saw a circle of unpleasing faces. His eyes wandered gently round the room and noted some of the objects in it.

'Ah!' he said pleasantly. 'The headquarters of the counterfeiting industry, if I am not mistaken.'

'Shut your jaw,' growled one of the men.

The door opened and shut behind Tommy, and a genial and well-known voice spoke.

'Got him, boys. That's right. Now, Mr Busy, let me tell you you're up against it.'

'That dear old word,' said Tommy. 'How it thrills me. Yes. I am the Mystery Man of Scotland Yard. Why, it's Mr Hank Ryder. This *is* a surprise.'

'I guess you mean that too. I've been laughing fit to bust all this evening – leading you here like a little child. And you so pleased with your cleverness. Why, sonny, I was on to you from the start. You weren't in with that crowd for your health. I let you play about for a while, and when you got real suspicious of the lovely Marguerite, I said to myself: "Now's the time to lead him to it." I guess your friends won't be hearing of you for some time.'

'Going to do me in? That's the correct expression, I believe. You have got it in for me.'

'You've got a nerve all right. No, we shan't attempt violence. Just keep you under restraint, so to speak.'

'I'm afraid you're backing the wrong horse,' said Tommy. 'I've no intention of being "kept under restraint," as you call it.'

Mr Ryder smiled genially. From outside a cat uttered a melancholy cry to the moon.

'Banking on that cross you put on the door, eh, sonny?' said Mr Ryder. 'I shouldn't if I were you. Because I know that story you mentioned. Heard it when I was a little boy. I stepped back into the alley-way to enact the part of the dog with eyes as big as cart-wheels. If you were in that alley now, you would observe that every door in the alley is marked with an identical cross.'

Tommy dropped his head despondently.

'Thought you were mighty clever, didn't you?' said Ryder.

As the words left his lips a sharp rapping sounded on the door.

'What's that?' he cried, starting.

At the same time an assault began on the front of the house. The door at the back was a flimsy affair. The lock gave almost immediately and Inspector Marriot showed in the doorway.

'Well done, Marriot,' said Tommy. 'You were quite right as to the district. I'd like you to make the acquaintance of Mr Hank Ryder who knows all the best fairy tales.

'You see, Mr Ryder,' he added gently, 'I've had my suspicions of you. Albert (that important-looking boy with the big ears is Albert) had orders to follow on his motorcycle if you and I went off joy-riding at any time. And whilst I was ostentatiously marking a chalk cross on the door to engage your attention, I also emptied a little bottle of valerian on the ground. Nasty smell, but cats love it. All the cats in the neighbourhood were assembled outside to mark the right house when Albert and the police arrived.'

He looked at the dumbfounded Mr Ryder with a smile, then rose to his feet.

'I said I would get you Crackler, and I have got you,' he observed.

'What the hell are you talking about?' asked Mr Ryder. 'What do you mean – Crackler?'

'You will find it in the glossary of the next criminal dictionary,' said Tommy. 'Etymology doubtful.'

He looked round him with a happy smile.

'And all done without a nose,' he murmured brightly. 'Good-night, Marriot. I must go now to where the happy ending of the story awaits me. No reward like the love of a good woman – and the love of a good woman awaits me at home – that is, I hope it does, but one never knows nowadays. This has been a very dangerous job, Marriot. Do you know Captain Jimmy Faulkener? His dancing is simply too marvellous, and as for his taste in cocktails –! Yes, Marriot, it has been a very dangerous job.'

Chapter 11

The Sunningdale Mystery

'Do you know where we are going to lunch today, Tuppence?'

Mrs Beresford considered the question.

'The Ritz?' she suggested hopefully.

'Think again.'

'That nice little place in Soho?'

'No.' Tommy's tone was full of importance. 'An ABC shop. This one, in fact.'

He drew her deftly inside an establishment of the kind indicated, and steered her to a corner marble-topped table.

'Excellent,' said Tommy with satisfaction, as he seated himself. 'Couldn't be better.'

'Why has this craze for the simple life come upon you?' demanded Tuppence.

'*You see, Watson, but you do not observe.* I wonder now whether one of these haughty damsels would condescend to notice us? Splendid, she drifts this way. It is true that she appears to be thinking of something else, but doubtless her sub-conscious mind is functioning busily with such matters as ham and eggs and pots of tea. Chop and fried potatoes, please, miss, and a large coffee, a roll and butter, and a plate of tongue for the lady.'

The waitress repeated the order in a scornful tone, but Tuppence leant forward suddenly and interrupted her.

'No, not a chop and fried potatoes. This gentleman will have a cheesecake and a glass of milk.'

'A cheesecake and a milk,' said the waitress with even deeper scorn, if that were possible. Still thinking of something else, she drifted away again.

'That was uncalled for,' said Tommy coldly.

'But I'm right, aren't I? You are the Old Man in the Corner? Where's your piece of string?'

Tommy drew a long twisted mesh of string from his pocket and proceeded to tie a couple of knots in it.

'Complete to the smallest detail,' he murmured.

'You made a small mistake in ordering your meal, though.'

'Women are so literal-minded,' said Tommy. 'If there's one thing I hate it's milk to drink, and cheesecakes are always so yellow and bilious-looking.'

'Be an artist,' said Tuppence. 'Watch me attack my cold tongue. Jolly good stuff, cold tongue. Now then, I'm all ready to be Miss Polly Burton. Tie a large knot and begin.'

'First of all,' said Tommy, 'speaking in a strictly unofficial capacity, let me point out this. Business is not too brisk lately. If business does not come to us, we must go to business. Apply our minds to one of the great public mysteries of the moment. Which brings me to the point – the Sunningdale Mystery.'

'Ah!' said Tuppence, with deep interest. 'The Sunningdale Mystery!'

Tommy drew a crumpled piece of newspaper from his pocket and laid it on the table.

'That is the latest portrait of Captain Sessle as it appeared in the *Daily Leader*.'

'Just so,' said Tuppence. 'I wonder someone doesn't sue these newspapers sometimes. You can see it's a man and that's all.'

'When I said the Sunningdale Mystery, I should have said the so-called Sunningdale Mystery,' went on Tommy rapidly.

'A mystery to the police perhaps, but not to an intelligent mind.'

'Tie another knot,' said Tuppence.

'I don't know how much of the case you remember,' continued Tommy quietly.

'All of it,' said Tuppence, 'but don't let me cramp your style.'

'It was just over three weeks ago,' said Tommy, 'that the gruesome discovery was made on the famous golf links. Two members of the club, who were enjoying an early round, were horrified to find the body of a man lying face downwards on the seventh tee. Even before they turned him over they had guessed him to be Captain Sessle, a well-known figure on the links, and who always wore a golf coat of a peculiarly bright blue colour.

'Captain Sessle was often seen out on the links early in the morning, practising, and it was thought at first that he had been suddenly overcome by some form of heart disease. But examination by a doctor revealed the sinister fact that he had been murdered, stabbed to the heart with a significant object, *a woman's hatpin*. He was also found to have been dead at least twelve hours.

'That put an entirely different complexion on the matter, and very soon some interesting facts came to light. Practically the last person to see Captain Sessle alive was his friend and partner, Mr Hollaby of the Porcupine Assurance Co, and he told his story as follows:

'Sessle and he had played a round earlier in the day. After tea the other suggested that they should play a few more holes before it got too dark to see. Hollaby assented. Sessle seemed in good spirits, and was in excellent form. There is a public footpath that crosses the links, and just as they were playing up to the sixth green, Hollaby noticed a woman coming along it. She was very tall, and dressed in brown, but he did not observe her particularly, and Sessle, he thought, did not notice her at all.

'The footpath in question crossed in front of the seventh tee,' continued Tommy. 'The woman had passed along this and was standing at the farther side, as though waiting. Captain Sessle was the first to reach the tee, as Mr Hollaby was replacing the pin in the hole. As the latter came towards the tee, he was astonished to see Sessle and the woman talking together. As he came nearer, they both turned abruptly, Sessle calling over his shoulder: "Shan't be a minute."

'The two of them walked off side by side, still deep in earnest conversation. The footpath there leaves the course, and, passing between the two narrow hedges of neighbouring gardens, comes out on the road to Windlesham.

'Captain Sessle was as good as his word. He reappeared within a minute or two, much to Hollaby's satisfaction, as two other players were coming up behind them, and the light was failing rapidly. They drove off, and at once Hollaby noticed that something had occurred to upset his companion. Not only did he foozle his drive badly, but his face was worried and his forehead creased in a big frown. He hardly answered his companion's remarks, and his golf was atrocious. Evidently something had occurred to put him completely off his game.

'They played that hole and the eighth, and then Captain Sessle declared abruptly that the light was too bad and that he was off home. Just at that point there is another of those narrow "slips" leading to the Windlesham road, and Captain Sessle departed that way, which was a short cut to his home, a small bungalow on the road in question. The other two players came up, a Major Barnard and Mr Lecky, and to them Hollaby mentioned Captain Sessle's sudden change of manner. They also had seen him speaking to the woman in brown, but had not been near enough to see her face. All three men wondered what she could have said to upset their friend to that extent.

'They returned to the clubhouse together, and as far as was known at the time, were the last people to see Captain Sessle alive. The day was a Wednesday, and on Wednesday cheap tickets to London are issued. The man and wife who ran Captain Sessle's small bungalow were up in town, according to custom, and did not return until the late train. They entered the bungalow as usual, and supposed their master to be in his room asleep. Mrs Sessle, his wife, was away on a visit.

'The murder of the Captain was a nine days' wonder. Nobody could suggest a motive for it. The identity of the tall woman in brown was eagerly discussed, but without result. The police were, as usual, blamed for their supineness – most unjustly, as time was to show. For a week later, a girl called Doris Evans was arrested and charged with the murder of Captain Anthony Sessle.

'The police had had little to work upon. A strand of fair hair caught in the dead man's fingers and a few threads of flame-coloured wool caught on one of the buttons of his blue coat. Diligent inquiries at the railway station and elsewhere had elicited the following facts.

'A young girl dressed in a flame-coloured coat and skirt had arrived by train that evening about seven o'clock and had asked the way to Captain Sessle's house. The same girl had reappeared again at the station, two hours later. Her hat was awry and her hair tousled, and she seemed in a state of great agitation. She inquired about the trains back to town, and was continually looking over her shoulder as though afraid of something.

'Our police force is in many ways very wonderful. With this slender evidence to go upon, they managed to track down the girl and identify her as one Doris Evans. She was charged with murder and cautioned that anything she might say would be used against her, but she nevertheless persisted in making a statement, and this statement she repeated again in detail, without any subsequent variation, at the subsequent proceedings.

'Her story was this. She was a typist by profession, and had made friends one evening, in a cinema, with a well-dressed man, who declared he had taken a fancy to her. His name, he told her, was Anthony, and he suggested that she should come down to his bungalow at Sunningdale. She had no idea then, or at any other time, that he had a wife. It was arranged between them that she should come down on the following Wednesday – the day, you will remember, when the servants would be absent and his wife away from home. In the end he told her his full name was Anthony Sessle, and gave her the name of his house.

'She duly arrived at the bungalow on the evening in question, and was greeted by Sessle, who had just come in from the links. Though he professed himself delighted to see her, the girl declared that from the first his manner was strange and different. A half-acknowledged fear sprang up in her, and she wished fervently that she had not come.

'After a simple meal, which was all ready and prepared, Sessle suggested going out for a stroll. The girl consenting, he took her out of the house, down the road, and along the "slip" on to the golf course. And then suddenly, just as they were crossing the seventh tee, he seemed to go completely mad. Drawing a revolver from his pocket, he brandished it in the air, declaring that he had come to the end of his tether.

'"Everything must go! I'm ruined – done for. And you shall go with me. I shall shoot you first – then myself. They will find our bodies here in the morning side by side – together in death."

'And so on – a lot more. He had hold of Doris Evans by the arm, and she, realising she had to do with a madman, made frantic efforts to free herself, or failing that to get the revolver away from him. They struggled together, and in that struggle he must have torn out a piece of her hair and got the wool of her coat entangled on a button.

'Finally, with a desperate effort, she freed herself, and ran for her life across the golf links, expecting every minute to be shot down with a revolver bullet. She fell twice, tripping over the heather, but eventually regained the road to the station and realised that she was not being pursued.

'That is the story that Doris Evans tells – and from which she has never varied. She strenuously denies that she ever struck at him with a hatpin in self-defence – a natural enough thing to do under the circumstances, though – and one which may well be the truth. In support of her story, a revolver has been found in the furze bushes near where the body was lying. It had not been fired.

'Doris Evans has been sent for trial, but the mystery still remains a mystery. If her story is to be believed, who was it who stabbed Captain Sessle? The other woman, the tall woman in brown, whose appearance so upset him? So far no one has explained her connection with the case. She appears out of space suddenly on the footpath across the links, she disappears along the slip, and no one ever hears of her again. Who was she? A local resident? A visitor from London? If so, did she come by car or by train? There is nothing remarkable about her except her height; no one seems to be able to describe her appearance. She could not have been Doris Evans, for Doris Evans is small and fair, and moreover was only just then arriving at the station.'

'The wife?' suggested Tuppence. 'What about the wife?'

'A very natural suggestion. But Mrs Sessle is also a small woman, and besides, Mr Hollaby knows her well by sight, and there seems no doubt that she was really away from home. One further development has come to light. The Porcupine Assurance Co is in liquidation. The accounts reveal the most daring misappropriation of funds. The reasons for Captain Sessle's wild words to Doris Evans are now quite apparent. For some years past he must have been systematically embezzling money. Neither Mr Hollaby nor his son had any idea of what was going on. They are practically ruined.

'The case stands like this. Captain Sessle was on the verge of discovery and ruin. Suicide would be a natural solution, but the nature of the wound rules that theory out. Who killed him? Was it Doris Evans? Was it the mysterious woman in brown?'

Tommy paused, took a sip of milk, made a wry face, and bit cautiously at the cheesecake.

II

'Of course,' murmured Tommy, 'I saw at once where the hitch in this particular case lay, and just where the police were going astray.'

'Yes?' said Tuppence eagerly.

Tommy shook his head sadly.

'I wish I did. Tuppence, it's dead easy being the Old Man in the Corner up to a certain point. But the solution beats me. Who did murder the beggar? I don't know.'

He took some more newspaper cuttings out of his pocket.

'Further exhibits – Mr Hollaby, his son, Mrs Sessle, Doris Evans.'

Tuppence pounced on the last and looked at it for some time.

'She didn't murder him anyway,' she remarked at last. 'Not with a hatpin.'

'Why this certainty?'

'A lady Molly touch. She's got bobbed hair. Only one woman in twenty uses hatpins nowadays, anyway – long hair or short. Hats fit tight and pull on – there's no need for such a thing.'

'Still, she might have had one by her.'

'My dear boy, we don't keep them as heirlooms! What on earth should she have brought a hatpin down to Sunningdale for?'

'Then it must have been the other woman, the woman in brown.'

'I wish she hadn't been tall. Then she could have been the wife. I always suspect wives who are away at the time and so couldn't have had anything to do with it. If she found her husband carrying on with that girl, it would be quite natural for her to go for him with a hatpin.'

'I shall have to be careful, I see,' remarked Tommy.

But Tuppence was deep in thought and refused to be drawn.

'What were the Sessles like?' she asked suddenly. 'What sort of things did people say about them?'

'As far as I can make out, they were very popular.

He and his wife were supposed to be devoted to one another. That's what makes the business of the girl so odd. It's the last thing you'd have expected of a man like Sessle. He was an ex-soldier, you know. Came into a good bit of money, retired, and went into this Insurance business. The last man in the world, apparently, whom you would have suspected of being a crook.'

'It is absolutely certain that he was the crook? Couldn't it have been the other two who took the money?'

'The Hollabys? They say they're ruined.'

'Oh, they say! Perhaps they've got it all in a bank under another name. I put it foolishly, I dare say, but you know what I mean. Suppose they'd been speculating with the money for some time, unbeknownst to Sessle, and lost it all. It might be jolly convenient for them that Sessle died just when he did.'

Tommy tapped the photograph of Mr Hollaby senior with his finger-nail.

'So you're accusing this respectable gentleman of murdering his friend and partner? You forget that he parted from Sessle on the links in full view of Barnard and Lecky, and spent the evening in the Dormy House. Besides, there's the hatpin.'

'Bother the hatpin,' said Tuppence impatiently. 'That hatpin, you think, points to the crime having been committed by a woman?'

'Naturally. Don't you agree?'

'No. Men are notoriously old-fashioned. It takes them ages to rid themselves of preconceived ideas. They associate hatpins and hairpins with the female sex, and call them "women's weapons." They may have been in the past, but they're both rather out of date now. Why, I haven't had a hatpin or a hairpin for the last four years.'

'Then you think –?'

'That it was a *man* killed Sessle. The hatpin was used to make it seem a woman's crime.'

'There's something in what you say, Tuppence,' said Tommy slowly. 'It's extraordinary how things seem to straighten themselves out when you talk a thing over.'

Tuppence nodded.

'Everything must be logical – if you look at it the right way. And remember what Marriot once said about the amateur point of view – that it had the *intimacy*. We know something about people like Captain Sessle and his wife. We know what they're likely to do – and what they're not likely to do. And we've each got our special knowledge.'

Tommy smiled.

'You mean,' he said, 'that you are an authority on what people with bobbed and shingled heads are likely to have in their possession, and that you have an intimate acquaintance with what wives are likely to feel and do?'

'Something of the sort.'

'And what about me? What is my special knowledge? Do husbands pick up girls, etc?'

'No,' said Tuppence gravely. 'You know the course – you've been on it – not as a detective searching for clues, but as a golfer. You know about golf, and what's likely to put a man off his game.'

'It must have been something pretty serious to put Sessle off his game. His handicap's two, and from the seventh tee on he played like a child, so they say.'

'Who say?'

'Barnard and Lecky. They were playing just behind him, you remember.'

'That was after he met the woman – the tall woman in brown. They saw him speaking to her, didn't they?'

'Yes – at least –'

Tommy broke off. Tuppence looked up at him and was puzzled. He was staring at the piece of string in his fingers, but staring with the eyes of one who sees something very different.

'Tommy – what is it?'

'Be quiet, Tuppence. I'm playing the sixth hole at Sunningdale. Sessle and old Hollaby are holing out on the sixth green ahead of me. It's getting dusk, but I can see that bright blue coat of Sessle's clearly enough. And on the footpath to the left of me there's a woman coming along. She hasn't crossed from the ladies' course – that's on the right – I should have seen her if she had done so. And it's odd I didn't see her on the footpath before – from the fifth tee, for instance.'

He paused.

'You said just now I knew the course, Tuppence. Just behind the sixth tee there's a little hut or shelter made of turf. Any one could wait in there until – the right moment came. They could change their appearance there. I mean – tell me, Tuppence, this is where your special knowledge comes in again – would it be very difficult for a man to look like a woman, and then change back to being a man again? Could he wear a skirt over plus-fours, for instance?'

'Certainly he could. The woman would look a bit bulky, that would be all. A longish brown skirt, say a brown sweater of the kind both men and women wear, and a woman's felt hat with a bunch of side curls attached each side. That would be all that was needed – I'm speaking, of course, of what would pass at a distance, which I take to be what you are driving at. Switch off the skirt, take off the hat and curls, and put on a man's cap which you can carry rolled up in your hand, and there you'd be – back as a man again.'

'And the time required for the transformation?'

'From woman to man, a minute and a half at the outside, probably a good deal less. The other way about would take longer, you'd have to arrange the hat and curls a bit, and the skirt would stick getting it on over the plus fours.'

'That doesn't worry me. It's the time for the first that matters. As I tell you, I'm playing the sixth hole. The woman in brown has reached the seventh tee now. She crosses it and waits. Sessle in his blue coat goes towards her. They stand together a minute, and then they follow the path round the trees out of sight. Hollaby is on the tee alone. Two or three minutes pass. I'm on the green now. The man in the blue coat comes back and drives off, foozling badly. The light's getting worse. I and my partner go on. Ahead of us are those two, Sessle slicing and topping and doing everything he shouldn't do. At the eighth green, I see him stride off and vanish down the slip. What happened to him to make him play like a different man?'

'The woman in brown – or the man, if you think it was a man.'

'Exactly, and where they were standing – out of sight, remember, of those coming after them – there's a deep tangle of furze bushes. You could thrust a body in there, and it would be pretty certain to lie hidden until the morning.'

'Tommy! You think it was *then*. – But someone would have heard –'

'Heard what? The doctors agreed death must have

been instantaneous. I've seen men killed instantaneously in the war. They don't cry out as a rule – just a gurgle, or a moan – perhaps just a sigh, or a funny little cough. Sessle comes towards the seventh tee, and the woman comes forward and speaks to him. He recognises her, perhaps, as a man he knows masquerading. Curious to learn the why and wherefore, he allows himself to be drawn along the footpath out of sight. One stab with the deadly hatpin as they walk along. Sessle falls – dead. The other man drags his body into the furze bushes, strips off the blue coat, then sheds his own skirt and the hat and curls. He puts on Sessle's well-known blue coat and cap and strides back to the tee. Three minutes would do it. The others behind can't see his face, only the peculiar blue coat they know so well. They never doubt that it's Sessle – *but he doesn't play Sessle's brand of golf.* They all say he played like a different man. Of course he did. He *was* a different man.'

'But –'

'Point No. 2. His action in bringing the girl down there was the action of *a different man.* It wasn't Sessle who met Doris Evans at a cinema and induced her to come down to Sunningdale. It was a man *calling* himself Sessle. Remember, Doris Evans wasn't arrested until a fortnight after the time. *She never saw the body.* If she had, she might have bewildered everyone by declaring that that wasn't the man who took her out on the golf links that night and spoke so wildly of suicide. It was a carefully laid plot. The girl invited down for Wednesday when Sessle's house would be empty, then the hatpin which pointed to its being a woman's doing. The murderer meets the girl, takes her into the bungalow and gives her supper, then takes her out on the links, and when he gets to the scene of the crime, brandishes his revolver and scares the life out of her. Once she has taken to her heels, all he has to do is to pull out the body and leave it lying on the tee. The revolver he chucks into the bushes. Then he makes a neat parcel of the skirt and – now I admit I'm guessing – in all probability walks to Woking, which is only about six or seven miles away, and goes back to town from there.'

'Wait a minute,' said Tuppence. 'There's one thing you haven't explained. What about Hollaby?'

'Hollaby?'

'Yes. I admit that the people behind couldn't have seen whether it was really Sessle or not. But you can't tell me that the man who was playing with him was so hypnotised by the blue coat that he never looked at his face.'

'My dear old thing,' said Tommy. 'That's just the point. Hollaby knew all right. You see, I'm adopting your theory – that Hollaby and his son were the real embezzlers. The murderer's got to be a man who knew Sessle pretty well – knew, for instance, about the servants being always out on a Wednesday, and that his wife was away. And also someone who was able to get an impression of Sessle's latch key. I think Hollaby junior would fulfil all these requirements. He's about the same age and height as Sessle, and they were both clean-shaven men. Doris Evans probably saw several photographs of the murdered man reproduced in the papers, but as you yourself observed – one can just see that it's a man and that's about all.'

'Didn't she ever see Hollaby in Court?'

'The son never appeared in the case at all. Why should he? He had no evidence to give. It was old Hollaby, with his irreproachable alibi, who stood in the limelight throughout. Nobody has ever bothered to inquire what his son was doing that particular evening.'

'It all fits in,' admitted Tuppence. She paused a minute and then asked: 'Are you going to tell all this to the police?'

'I don't know if they'd listen.'

'They'd listen all right,' said an unexpected voice behind him.

Tommy swung round to confront Inspector Marriot. The Inspector was sitting at the next table. In front of him was a poached egg.

'Often drop in here to lunch,' said Inspector Marriot.

'As I was saying, we'll listen all right – in fact I've been listening. I don't mind telling you that we've not been quite satisfied all along over those Porcupine figures. You see, we've had our suspicions of those Hollabys, but nothing to go upon. Too sharp for us. Then this murder came, and that seemed to upset all our ideas. But thanks to you and the lady, sir, we'll confront young Hollaby with Doris Evans and see if she recognises him. I rather fancy she will. That's a very ingenious idea of yours about the blue coat. I'll see that Blunt's Brilliant Detectives get the credit for it.'

'You *are* a nice man, Inspector Marriot,' said Tuppence gratefully.

'We think a lot of you two at the Yard,' replied that stolid gentleman. 'You'd be surprised. If I may ask you, sir, what's the meaning of that piece of string?'

'Nothing,' said Tommy, stuffing it into his pocket. 'A bad habit of mine. As to the cheesecake and the milk – I'm on a diet. Nervous dyspepsia. Busy men are always martyrs to it.'

'Ah!' said the detective. 'I thought perhaps you'd been reading – well, it's of no consequence.'

But the Inspector's eyes twinkled.

Chapter 12

The House of Lurking Death

'What –' began Tuppence, and then stopped.

She had just entered the private office of Mr Blunt from the adjoining one marked 'Clerks,' and was surprised to behold her lord and master with his eye riveted to the private peep-hole into the outer office.

'Ssh,' said Tommy warningly. 'Didn't you hear the buzzer? It's a girl – rather a nice girl – in fact she looks to me a frightfully nice girl. Albert is telling her all that tosh about my being engaged with Scotland Yard.'

'Let *me* see,' demanded Tuppence.

Somewhat unwillingly, Tommy moved aside. Tuppence in her turn glued her eye to the peep-hole.

'She's not bad,' admitted Tuppence. 'And her clothes are simply the latest shout.'

'She's perfectly lovely,' said Tommy. 'She's like those girls Mason writes about – you know, frightfully sympathetic, and beautiful, and distinctly intelligent without being too saucy. I think, yes – I certainly think – I shall be the great Hanaud this morning.'

'H'm,' said Tuppence. 'If there is one detective out of all the others whom you are most unlike – I should say it was Hanaud. Can you do the lightning changes of personality? Can you be the great comedian, the little gutter boy, the serious and sympathetic friend – all in five minutes?'

'I know this,' said Tommy, rapping sharply on the desk, 'I am the Captain of the Ship – and don't you forget it, Tuppence. I'm going to have her in.'

He pressed the buzzer on his desk. Albert appeared ushering in the client.

The girl stopped in the doorway as though undecided. Tommy came forward.

'Come in, mademoiselle,' he said kindly, 'and seat yourself here.'

Tuppence choked audibly and Tommy turned upon her with a swift change of manner. His tone was menacing.

'You spoke, Miss Robinson? Ah, no, I thought not.'

He turned back to the girl.

'We will not be serious or formal,' he said. 'You will just tell me about it, and then we will discuss the best way to help you.'

'You are very kind,' said the girl. 'Excuse me, but are you a foreigner?'

A fresh choke from Tuppence. Tommy glared in her direction out of the corner of his eye.

'Not exactly,' he said with difficulty. 'But of late years I have worked a good deal abroad. My methods are the methods of the Sûreté.'

'Oh!' The girl seemed impressed.

She was, as Tommy had indicated, a very charming girl. Young and slim, with a trace of golden hair peeping out from under her little brown felt hat, and big serious eyes.

That she was nervous could be plainly seen. Her little hands were twisting themselves together, and she kept clasping and unclasping the catch of her lacquered handbag.

'First of all, Mr Blunt, I must tell you that my name is Lois Hargreaves. I live in a great rambling old-fashioned house called Thurnly Grange. It is in the heart of the country. There is the village of Thurnly nearby, but it is very small and insignificant. There is plenty of hunting in winter, and we get tennis in summer, and I have never felt lonely there. Indeed I much prefer country to town life.

'I tell you this so that you may realise that in a country village like ours, everything that happens is of supreme importance. About a week ago, I got a box of chocolates sent through the post. There was nothing inside to indicate who they came from. Now I myself am not particularly fond of chocolates, but the others in the house are, and the box was passed round. As a result, everyone who had eaten any chocolates was taken ill. We sent for the doctor, and after various inquiries as to what other things had been eaten, he took the remains of the chocolates away with him, and had them analysed. Mr Blunt, those chocolates contained arsenic! Not enough to kill anyone, but enough to make anyone quite ill.'

'Extraordinary,' commented Tommy.

'Dr Burton was very excited over the matter. It seems that this was the third occurrence of the kind in the neighbourhood. In each case a big house was selected, and the inmates were taken ill after eating the mysterious chocolates. It looked as though some local person of weak intellect was playing a particularly fiendish practical joke.'

'Quite so, Miss Hargreaves.'

'Dr Burton put it down to Socialist agitation – rather absurdly, I thought. But there are one or two malcontents in Thurnly village, and it seemed possible that they might have had something to do with it. Dr Burton was very keen that I should put the whole thing in the hands of the police.'

'A very natural suggestion,' said Tommy. 'But you have not done so, I gather, Miss Hargreaves?'

'No,' admitted the girl. 'I hate the fuss and the

publicity that would ensue – and you see, I know our local Inspector. I can never imagine him finding out anything! I have often seen your advertisements, and I told Dr Burton that it would be much better to call in a private detective.'

'I see.'

'You say a great deal about discretion in your advertisement. I take that to mean – that – that – well, that you would not make anything public without my consent?'

Tommy looked at her curiously, but it was Tuppence who spoke.

'I think,' she said quietly, 'that it would be as well if Miss Hargreaves told us *everything*.'

She laid especial stress upon the last word, and Lois Hargreaves flushed nervously.

'Yes,' said Tommy quickly, 'Miss Robinson is right. You must tell us everything.'

'You will not –' she hesitated.

'Everything you say is understood to be strictly in confidence.'

'Thank you. I know that I ought to have been quite frank with you. I have a reason for not going to the police. Mr Blunt, that box of chocolates was sent by someone in our house!'

'How do you know that, mademoiselle?'

'It's very simple. I've got a habit of drawing a little

silly thing – three fish intertwined – whenever I have a pencil in my hand. A parcel of silk stockings arrived from a certain shop in London not long ago. We were at the breakfast table. I'd just been marking something in the newspaper, and without thinking, I began to draw my silly little fish on the label of the parcel before cutting the string and opening it. I thought no more about the matter, but when I was examining the piece of brown paper in which the chocolates had been sent, I caught sight of the corner of the original label – most of which had been torn off. My silly little drawing was on it.'

Tommy drew his chair forward.

'That is very serious. It creates, as you say, a very strong presumption that the sender of the chocolates is a member of your household. But you will forgive me if I say that I still do not see why that fact should render you indisposed to call in the police?'

Lois Hargreaves looked him squarely in the face.

'I will tell you, Mr Blunt. I may want the whole thing hushed up.'

Tommy retired gracefully from the position.

'In that case,' he murmured, 'we know where we are. I see, Miss Hargreaves, that you are not disposed to tell me who it is you suspect?'

'I suspect no one – but there are possibilities.'

'Quite so. Now will you describe the household to me in detail?'

'The servants, with the exception of the parlourmaid, are all old ones who have been with us many years. I must explain to you, Mr Blunt, that I was brought up by my aunt, Lady Radclyffe, who was extremely wealthy. Her husband made a big fortune, and was knighted. It was he who bought Thurnly Grange, but he died two years after going there, and it was then that Lady Radclyffe sent for me to come and make my home with her. I was her only living relation. The other inmate of the house was Dennis Radclyffe, her husband's nephew. I have always called him cousin, but of course he is really nothing of the kind. Aunt Lucy always said openly that she intended to leave her money, with the exception of a small provision for me, to Dennis. It was Radclyffe money, she said, and it ought to go to a Radclyffe. However, when Dennis was twenty-two, she quarrelled violently with him – over some debts that he had run up, I think. When she died, a year later, I was astonished to find that she had made a will leaving all her money to me. It was, I know, a great blow to Dennis, and I felt very badly about it. I would have given him the money if he would have taken it, but it seems that kind of thing can't be done. However, as soon as I was twenty-one, I made a will leaving it all to him. That's the least I can do. So if I'm run over by a motor, Dennis will come into his own.'

'Exactly,' said Tommy. 'And when were you twenty-one, if I may ask the question?'

'Just three weeks ago.'

'Ah!' said Tommy. 'Now will you give me fuller particulars of the members of your household at this minute?'

'Servants – or – others?'

'Both.'

'The servants, as I say, have been with us some time. There is old Mrs Holloway, the cook, and her niece Rose, the kitchenmaid. Then there are two elderly housemaids, and Hannah who was my aunt's maid and who has always been devoted to me. The parlourmaid is called Esther Quant, and seems a very nice quiet girl. As for ourselves, there is Miss Logan, who was Aunt Lucy's companion, and who runs the house for me, and Captain Radclyffe – Dennis, you know, whom I told you about, and there is a girl called Mary Chilcott, an old school friend of mine who is staying with us.'

Tommy thought for a moment.

'That all seems fairly clear and straightforward, Miss Hargreaves,' he said after a minute or two. 'I take it that you have no special reason for attaching suspicion more to one person than another? You are only afraid it might prove to be – well – not a servant, shall we say?'

'That's it exactly, Mr Blunt. I have honestly no idea

who used that piece of brown paper. The handwriting was printed.'

'There seems only one thing to be done,' said Tommy. 'I must be on the spot.'

The girl looked at him inquiringly.

Tommy went on after a moment's thought.

'I suggest that you prepare the way for the arrival of – say, Mr and Miss Van Dusen – American friends of yours. Will you be able to do that quite naturally?'

'Oh, yes. There will be no difficulty at all. When will you come down – tomorrow – or the day after?'

'Tomorrow, if you please. There is no time to waste.'

'That is settled then.'

The girl rose and held out her hand.

'One thing, Miss Hargreaves, not a word, mind, to anyone – anyone at all, that we are not what we seem.'

'What do you think of it, Tuppence?' he asked, when he returned from showing the visitor out.

'I don't like it,' said Tuppence decidedly. 'Especially I don't like the chocolates having so little arsenic in them.'

'What *do* you mean?'

'Don't you see? All those chocolates being sent round the neighbourhood were a blind. To establish the idea of a local maniac. Then, when the girl was really poisoned, it would be thought to be the same thing.

You see, but for a stroke of luck, no one would ever have guessed that the chocolates were actually sent by someone in the house itself.'

'That was a stroke of luck. You're right. You think it's a deliberate plot against the girl herself?'

'I'm afraid so. I remember reading about old Lady Radclyffe's will. That girl has come into a terrific lot of money.'

'Yes, and she came of age and made a will three weeks ago. It looks bad – for Dennis Radclyffe. He gains by her death.'

Tuppence nodded.

'The worst of it is – that she thinks so too! That's why she won't have the police called in. Already she suspects him. And she must be more than half in love with him to act as she has done.'

'In that case,' said Tommy thoughtfully, 'why the devil doesn't he marry her? Much simpler and safer.'

Tuppence stared at him.

'You've said a mouthful,' she observed. 'Oh, boy! I'm getting ready to be Miss Van Dusen, you observe.'

'Why rush to crime, when there is a lawful means near at hand?'

Tuppence reflected for a minute or two.

'I've got it,' she announced. 'Clearly he must have married a barmaid whilst at Oxford. Origin of the quarrel with his aunt. That explains everything.'

'Then why not send the poisoned sweets to the barmaid?' suggested Tommy. 'Much more practical. I wish you wouldn't jump to these wild conclusions, Tuppence.'

'They're deductions,' said Tuppence, with a good deal of dignity. 'This is your first *corrida*, my friend, but when you have been twenty minutes in the arena –'

Tommy flung the office cushion at her.

II

'Tuppence, I say, Tuppence, come here.'

It was breakfast time the next morning. Tuppence hurried out of her bedroom and into the dining-room. Tommy was striding up and down, the open newspaper in his hand.

'What's the matter?'

Tommy wheeled round, and shoved the paper into her hand, pointing to the headlines.

MYSTERIOUS POISONING CASE
DEATHS FROM FIG SANDWICHES

Tuppence read on. This mysterious outbreak of ptomaine poisoning had occurred at Thurnly Grange. The deaths so far reported were those of Miss Lois Hargreaves, the owner of the house, and the parlourmaid, Esther

Quant. A Captain Radclyffe and a Miss Logan were reported to be seriously ill. The cause of the outbreak was supposed to be some fig paste used in sandwiches, since another lady, a Miss Chilcott, who had not partaken of these was reported to be quite well.

'We must get down there at once,' said Tommy. 'That girl! That perfectly ripping girl! Why the devil didn't I go straight down there with her yesterday?'

'If you had,' said Tuppence, 'you'd probably have eaten fig sandwiches too for tea, and then you'd have been dead. Come on, let's start at once. I see it says that Dennis Radclyffe is seriously ill also.'

'Probably shamming, the dirty blackguard.'

They arrived at the small village of Thurnly about midday. An elderly woman with red eyes opened the door to them when they arrived at Thurnly Grange.

'Look here,' said Tommy quickly before she could speak. 'I'm not a reporter or anything like that. Miss Hargreaves came to see me yesterday, and asked me to come down here. Is there anyone I can see?'

'Dr Burton is here now, if you'd like to speak to him,' said the woman doubtfully. 'Or Miss Chilcott. She's making all the arrangements.'

But Tommy had caught at the first suggestion.

'Dr Burton,' he said authoritatively. 'I should like to see him at once if he is here.'

The woman showed them into a small morning-room. Five minutes later the door opened, and a tall, elderly man with bent shoulders and a kind, but worried face, came in.

'Dr Burton,' said Tommy. He produced his professional card. 'Miss Hargreaves called on me yesterday with reference to those poisoned chocolates. I came down to investigate the matter at her request – alas! too late.'

The doctor looked at him keenly.

'You are Mr Blunt himself?'

'Yes. This is my assistant, Miss Robinson.'

The doctor bowed to Tuppence.

'Under the circumstances, there is no need for reticence. But for the episode of the chocolates, I might have believed these deaths to be the result of severe ptomaine poisoning – but ptomaine poisoning of an unusually virulent kind. There is gastro-intestinal inflammation and haemorrhage. As it is, I am taking the fig paste to be analysed.'

'You suspect arsenic poisoning?'

'No. The poison, if a poison has been employed, is something far more potent and swift in its action. It looks more like some powerful vegetable toxin.'

'I see. I should like to ask you, Dr Burton, whether you are thoroughly convinced that Captain Radclyffe is suffering from the same form of poisoning?'

The doctor looked at him.

'Captain Radclyffe is not suffering from any sort of poisoning now.'

'Aha,' said Tommy. 'I –'

'Captain Radclyffe died at five o'clock this morning.'

Tommy was utterly taken aback. The doctor prepared to depart.

'And the other victim, Miss Logan?' asked Tuppence.

'I have every reason to hope that she will recover since she has survived so far. Being an older woman, the poison seems to have had less effect on her. I will let you know the result of the analysis, Mr Blunt. In the meantime, Miss Chilcott, will, I am sure, tell you anything you want to know.'

As he spoke, the door opened, and a girl appeared. She was tall, with a tanned face, and steady blue eyes.

Dr Burton performed the necessary introductions.

'I am glad you have come, Mr Blunt,' said Mary Chilcott. 'This affair seems too terrible. Is there anything you want to know that I can tell you?'

'Where did the fig paste come from?'

'It is a special kind that comes from London. We often have it. No one suspected that this particular pot differed from any of the others. Personally I dislike the flavour of figs. That explains my immunity. I cannot understand how Dennis was affected, since he was out for tea. He must have picked up a sandwich when he came home, I suppose.'

Tommy felt Tuppence's hand press his arm ever so slightly.

'What time did he come in?' he asked.

'I don't really know. I could find out.'

'Thank you, Miss Chilcott. It doesn't matter. You have no objection, I hope, to my questioning the servants?'

'Please do anything you like, Mr Blunt. I am nearly distraught. Tell me – you don't think there has been – foul play?'

Her eyes were very anxious, as she put the question.

'I don't know what to think. We shall soon know.'

'Yes, I suppose Dr Burton will have the paste analysed.'

Quickly excusing herself, she went out by the window to speak to one of the gardeners.

'You take the housemaids, Tuppence,' said Tommy, 'and I'll find my way to the kitchen. I say, Miss Chilcott may feel very distraught, but she doesn't look it.'

Tuppence nodded assent without replying.

Husband and wife met half an hour later.

'Now to pool results,' said Tommy. 'The sandwiches came out for tea, and the parlourmaid ate one – that's how she got it in the neck. Cook is positive Dennis Radclyffe hadn't returned when tea was cleared away. Query – how did *he* get poisoned?'

'He came in at a quarter to seven,' said Tuppence. 'Housemaid saw him from one of the windows. He had a cocktail before dinner – in the library. She was just clearing away the glass now, and luckily I got it from her before she washed it. It was after that that he complained of feeling ill.'

'Good,' said Tommy. 'I'll take that glass along to Burton, presently. Anything else?'

'I'd like you to see Hannah, the maid. She's – she's queer.'

'How do you mean – queer?'

'She looks to me as though she were going off her head.'

'Let me see her.'

Tuppence led the way upstairs. Hannah had a small sitting-room of her own. The maid sat upright on a high chair. On her knees was an open Bible. She did not look towards the two strangers as they entered. Instead she continued to read aloud to herself.

'*Let hot burning coals fall upon them, let them be cast into the fire and into the pit, that they never rise up again.*'

'May I speak to you a minute?' asked Tommy.

Hannah made an impatient gesture with her hand.

'This is no time. The time is running short, I say. *I*

will follow upon mine enemies and overtake them, neither will I turn again till I have destroyed them. So it is written. The word of the Lord has come to me. I am the scourge of the Lord.'

'Mad as a hatter,' murmured Tommy.

'She's been going on like that all the time,' whispered Tuppence.

Tommy picked up a book that was lying open, face downwards on the table. He glanced at the title and slipped it into his pocket.

Suddenly the old woman rose and turned towards them menacingly.

'Go out from here. The time is at hand! I am the flail of the Lord. The wind bloweth where it listeth – so do I destroy. The ungodly shall perish. This is a house of evil – of evil, I tell you! Beware of the wrath of the Lord whose handmaiden I am.'

She advanced upon them fiercely. Tommy thought it best to humour her and withdrew. As he closed the door, he saw her pick up the Bible again.

'I wonder if she's always been like that,' he muttered.

He drew from his pocket the book he had picked up off the table.

'Look at that. Funny reading for an ignorant maid.'

Tuppence took the book.

'Materia Medica,' she murmured. She looked at the

flyleaf, 'Edward Logan. It's an old book. Tommy, I wonder if we could see Miss Logan? Dr Burton said she was better.'

'Shall we ask Miss Chilcott?'

'No. Let's get hold of a housemaid, and send her in to ask.'

After a brief delay, they were informed that Miss Logan would see them. They were taken into a big bedroom facing over the lawn. In the bed was an old lady with white hair, her delicate face drawn by suffering.

'I have been very ill,' she said faintly. 'And I can't talk much, but Ellen tells me you are detectives. Lois went to consult you then? She spoke of doing so.'

'Yes, Miss Logan,' said Tommy. 'We don't want to tire you, but perhaps you can answer a few questions. The maid, Hannah, is she quite right in her head?'

Miss Logan looked at them with obvious surprise.

'Oh, yes. She is very religious – but there is nothing wrong with her.'

Tommy held out the book he had taken from the table.

'Is this yours, Miss Logan?'

'Yes. It was one of my father's books. He was a great doctor, one of the pioneers of serum therapeutics.'

The old lady's voice rang with pride.

'Quite so,' said Tommy. 'I thought I knew his name.'

he added mendaciously. 'This book now, did you lend it to Hannah?'

'To Hannah?' Miss Logan raised herself in bed with indignation. 'No, indeed. She wouldn't understand the first word of it. It is a highly technical book.'

'Yes. I see that. Yet I found it in Hannah's room.'

'Disgraceful,' said Miss Logan. 'I will not have the servants touching my things.'

'Where ought it to be?'

'In the bookshelf in my sitting-room – or – stay, I lent it to Mary. The dear girl is very interested in herbs. She has made one or two experiments in my little kitchen. I have a little place of my own, you know, where I brew liqueurs and make preserves in the old-fashioned way. Dear Lucy, Lady Radclyffe, you know, used to swear by my tansy tea – a wonderful thing for a cold in the head. Poor Lucy, she was subject to colds. So is Dennis. Dear boy, his father was my first cousin.'

Tommy interrupted these reminiscences.

'This kitchen of yours? Does anyone else use it except you and Miss Chilcott?'

'Hannah clears up there. And she boils the kettle there for our early morning tea.'

'Thank you, Miss Logan,' said Tommy. 'There is nothing more I want to ask you at present. I hope we haven't tired you too much.'

He left the room and went down the stairs, frowning to himself.

'There is something here, my dear Mr Ricardo, that I do not understand.'

'I hate this house,' said Tuppence with a shiver. 'Let's go for a good long walk and try to think things out.'

Tommy complied and they set out. First they left the cocktail glass at the doctor's house, and then set off for a good tramp across the country, discussing the case as they did so.

'It makes it easier somehow if one plays the fool,' said Tommy. 'All this Hanaud business. I suppose some people would think I didn't care. But I do, most awfully. I feel that somehow or other we ought to have prevented this.'

'I think that's foolish of you,' said Tuppence. 'It is not as though we advised Lois Hargreaves not to go to Scotland Yard or anything like that. Nothing would have induced her to bring the police into the matter. If she hadn't come to us, she would have done nothing at all.'

'And the result would have been the same. Yes, you are right, Tuppence. It's morbid to reproach oneself over something one couldn't help. What I would like to do is to make good now.'

'And that's not going to be easy.'

'No, it isn't. There are so many possibilities, and

yet all of them seem wild and improbable. Supposing Dennis Radclyffe put the poison in the sandwiches. He knew he would be out to tea. That seems fairly plain sailing.'

'Yes,' said Tuppence, 'that's all right so far. Then we can put against that the fact that he was poisoned himself – so that seems to rule him out. There is one person we mustn't forget – and that is Hannah.'

'Hannah?'

'People do all sorts of queer things when they have religious mania.'

'She is pretty far gone with it too,' said Tommy. 'You ought to drop a word to Dr Burton about it.'

'It must have come on very rapidly,' said Tuppence. 'That is if we go by what Miss Logan said.'

'I believe religious mania does,' said Tommy. 'I mean, you go on singing hymns in your bedroom with the door open for years, and then you go suddenly right over the line and become violent.'

'There is certainly more evidence against Hannah than against anybody else,' said Tuppence thoughtfully. 'And yet I have an idea –' She stopped.

'Yes?' said Tommy encouragingly.

'It is not really an idea. I suppose it is just a prejudice.'

'A prejudice against someone?'

Tuppence nodded.

'Tommy – did *you* like Mary Chilcott?'

Tommy considered.

'Yes, I think I did. She struck me as extremely capable and business-like – perhaps a shade too much so – but very reliable.'

'You didn't think it was odd that she didn't seem more upset?'

'Well, in a way that is a point in her favour. I mean, if she had done anything, she would make a point of being upset – lay it on rather thick.'

'I suppose so,' said Tuppence. 'And anyway there doesn't seem to be any motive in her case. One doesn't see what good this wholesale slaughter can do her.'

'I suppose none of the servants are concerned?'

'It doesn't seem likely. They seem a quiet, reliable lot. I wonder what Esther Quant, the parlourmaid, was like.'

'You mean, that if she was young and good-looking there was a chance that she was mixed up in it some way.'

'That is what I mean,' Tuppence sighed. 'It is all very discouraging.'

'Well, I suppose the police will get down to it all right,' said Tommy.

'Probably. I should like it to be us. By the way, did you notice a lot of small red dots on Miss Logan's arm?'

'I don't think I did. What about them?'

'They looked as though they were made by a hypodermic syringe,' said Tuppence.

'Probably Dr Burton gave her a hypodermic injection of some kind.'

'Oh, very likely. But he wouldn't give her about forty.'

'The cocaine habit,' suggested Tommy helpfully.

'I thought of that,' said Tuppence, 'but her eyes were all right. You could see at once if it was cocaine or morphia. Besides, she doesn't look that sort of old lady.'

'Most respectable and God-fearing,' agreed Tommy.

'It is all very difficult,' said Tuppence. 'We have talked and talked and we don't seem any nearer now than we were. Don't let's forget to call at the doctor's on our way home.'

The doctor's door was opened by a lanky boy of about fifteen.

'Mr Blunt?' he inquired. 'Yes, the doctor is out, but he left a note for you in case you should call.'

He handed them the note in question and Tommy tore it open.

Dear Mr Blunt,

There is reason to believe that the poison employed was

Ricin, a vegetable toxalbumose of tremendous potency.
Please keep this to yourself for the present.

Tommy let the note drop, but picked it up quickly.

'Ricin,' he murmured. 'Know anything about it, Tuppence? You used to be rather well up in these things.'

'Ricin,' said Tuppence, thoughtfully. 'You get it out of castor oil, I believe.'

'I never did take kindly to castor oil,' said Tommy. 'I am more set against it than ever now.'

'The oil's all right. You get Ricin from the seeds of the castor oil plant. I believe I saw some castor oil plants in the garden this morning – big things with glossy leaves.'

'You mean that someone extracted the stuff on the premises. Could Hannah do such a thing?'

Tuppence shook her head.

'Doesn't seem likely. She wouldn't know enough.'

Suddenly Tommy gave an exclamation.

'That book. Have I got it in my pocket still? Yes.' He took it out, and turned over the leaves vehemently. 'I thought so. Here's the page it was open at this morning. Do you see, Tuppence? Ricin!'

Tuppence seized the book from him.

'Can you make head or tail of it? I can't.'

'It's clear enough to me,' said Tuppence. She walked

along, reading busily, with one hand on Tommy's arm to steer herself. Presently she shut the book with a bang. They were just approaching the house again.

'Tommy, will you leave this to me? Just for once, you see, I am the bull that has been more than twenty minutes in the arena.'

Tommy nodded.

'You shall be the Captain of the Ship, Tuppence,' he said gravely. 'We've got to get to the bottom of this.'

'First of all,' said Tuppence as they entered the house, 'I must ask Miss Logan one more question.'

She ran upstairs. Tommy followed her. She rapped sharply on the old lady's door and went in.

'Is that you, my dear?' said Miss Logan. 'You know you are much too young and pretty to be a detective. Have you found out anything?'

'Yes,' said Tuppence. 'I have.'

Miss Logan looked at her questioningly.

'I don't know about being pretty,' went on Tuppence, 'but being young, I happened to work in a hospital during the War. I know something about serum therapeutics. I happen to know that when Ricin is injected in small doses hypodermically, immunity is produced, antiricin is formed. That fact paved the way for the foundation of serum therapeutics. You knew that, Miss Logan. You injected Ricin for some time hypodermically into yourself. Then you let yourself be poisoned with the rest. You helped your father in his work, and you knew all about Ricin and how to obtain it and extract it from the seeds. You chose a day when Dennis Radclyffe was out for tea. It wouldn't do for him to be poisoned at the same time – he might die before Lois Hargreaves. So long as she died first, he inherited her money, and at his death it passes to you, his next-of-kin. You remember, you told us this morning that his father was your first cousin.'

The old lady stared at Tuppence with baleful eyes.

Suddenly a wild figure burst in from the adjoining room. It was Hannah. In her hand she held a lighted torch which she waved frantically.

'Truth has been spoken. That is the wicked one. I saw her reading the book and smiling to herself and I knew. I found the book and the page – but it said nothing to me. But the voice of the Lord spoke to me. She hated my mistress, her ladyship. She was always jealous and envious. She hated my own sweet Miss Lois. But the wicked shall perish, the fire of the Lord shall consume them.'

Waving her torch she sprang forward to the bed.

A cry arose from the old lady.

'Take her away – take her away. It's true – but take her away.'

Tuppence flung herself upon Hannah, but the woman managed to set fire to the curtains of the bed before

Tuppence could get the torch from her and stamp on it. Tommy, however, had rushed in from the landing outside. He tore down the bed hangings and managed to stifle the flames with a rug. Then he rushed to Tuppence's assistance, and between them they subdued Hannah just as Dr Burton came hurrying in.

A very few words sufficed to put him *au courant* of the situation.

He hurried to the bedside, lifted Miss Logan's hand, then uttered a sharp exclamation.

'The shock of fire has been too much for her. She's dead. Perhaps it is as well under the circumstances.'

He paused, and then added, 'There was Ricin in the cocktail glass as well.'

'It's the best thing that could have happened,' said Tommy, when they had relinquished Hannah to the doctor's care, and were alone together. 'Tuppence, you were simply marvellous.'

'There wasn't much Hanaud about it,' said Tuppence.

'It was too serious for play-acting. I still can't bear to think of that girl. I won't think of her. But, as I said before, you were marvellous. The honours are with you. To use a familiar quotation, "It is a great advantage to be intelligent and not to look it."'

'Tommy,' said Tuppence, 'you're a beast.'

Chapter 13

The Unbreakable Alibi

Tommy and Tuppence were busy sorting correspondence. Tuppence gave an exclamation and handed a letter across to Tommy.

'A new client,' she said importantly.

'Ha!' said Tommy. 'What do we deduce from this letter, Watson? Nothing much, except the somewhat obvious fact that Mr – er – Montgomery Jones is not one of the world's best spellers, thereby proving that he has been expensively educated.'

'Montgomery Jones?' said Tuppence. 'Now what do I know about a Montgomery Jones? Oh, yes, I have got it now. I think Janet St Vincent mentioned him. His mother was Lady Aileen Montgomery, very crusty and high church, with gold crosses and things, and she married a man called Jones who is immensely rich.'

'In fact the same old story,' said Tommy. 'Let me

see, what time does this Mr M. J. wish to see us? Ah, eleven-thirty.'

At eleven-thirty precisely, a very tall young man with an amiable and ingenuous countenance entered the outer office and addressed himself to Albert, the office boy.

'Look here – I say. Can I see Mr – er – Blunt?'

'Have you an appointment, sir?' said Albert.

'I don't quite know. Yes, I suppose I have. What I mean is, I wrote a letter –'

'What name, sir?'

'Mr Montgomery Jones.'

'I will take your name in to Mr Blunt.'

He returned after a brief interval.

'Will you wait a few minutes please, sir. Mr Blunt is engaged on a very important conference at present.'

'Oh – er – yes – certainly,' said Mr Montgomery Jones.

Having, he hoped, impressed his client sufficiently Tommy rang the buzzer on his desk, and Mr Montgomery Jones was ushered into the inner office by Albert.

Tommy rose to greet him, and shaking him warmly by the hand motioned towards the vacant chair.

'Now, Mr Montgomery Jones,' he said briskly. 'What can we have the pleasure of doing for you?'

Mr Montgomery Jones looked uncertainly at the third occupant of the office.

'My confidential secretary, Miss Robinson,' said Tommy. 'You can speak quite freely before her. I take it that this is some family matter of a delicate kind?'

'Well – not exactly,' said Mr Montgomery Jones.

'You surprise me,' said Tommy. 'You are not in trouble of any kind yourself, I hope?'

'Oh, rather not,' said Mr Montgomery Jones.

'Well,' said Tommy, 'perhaps you will – er – state the facts plainly.'

That, however, seemed to be the one thing that Mr Montgomery Jones could not do.

'It's a dashed odd sort of thing I have got to ask you,' he said hesitatingly. 'I – er – I really don't know how to set about it.'

'We never touch divorce cases,' said Tommy.

'Oh Lord, no,' said Mr Montgomery Jones. 'I don't mean that. It is just, well – it's a deuced silly sort of a joke. That's all.'

'Someone has played a practical joke on you of a mysterious nature?' suggested Tommy.

But Mr Montgomery Jones once more shook his head.

'Well,' said Tommy, retiring gracefully from the position, 'take your own time and let us have it in your own words.'

There was a pause.

'You see,' said Mr Jones at last, 'it was at dinner. I sat next to a girl.'

'Yes?' said Tommy encouragingly.

'She was a – oh well, I really can't describe her, but she was simply one of the most sporting girls I ever met. She's an Australian, over here with another girl, sharing a flat with her in Clarges Street. She's simply game for anything. I absolutely can't tell you the effect that girl had on me.'

'We can quite imagine it, Mr Jones,' said Tuppence.

She saw clearly that if Mr Montgomery Jones's troubles were ever to be extracted a sympathetic feminine touch was needed, as distinct from the businesslike methods of Mr Blunt.

'We can understand,' said Tuppence encouragingly.

'Well, the whole thing came as an absolute shock to me,' said Mr Montgomery Jones, 'that a girl could well – knock you over like that. There had been another girl – in fact two other girls. One was awfully jolly and all that, but I didn't much like her chin. She danced marvellously though, and I have known her all my life, which makes a fellow feel kind of safe, you know. And then there was one of the girls at the "Frivolity." Frightfully amusing, but of course there would be a lot of ructions with the matter over that, and anyway I didn't really want to marry either of them, but I was thinking about things, you know, and then – slap out of the blue – I sat next to this girl and –'

'The whole world was changed,' said Tuppence in a feeling voice.

Tommy moved impatiently in his chair. He was by now somewhat bored by the recital of Mr Montgomery Jones's love affairs.

'You put it awfully well,' said Mr Montgomery Jones. 'That is absolutely what it was like. Only, you know, I fancy she didn't think much of me. You mayn't think it, but I am not terribly clever.'

'Oh, you mustn't be too modest,' said Tuppence.

'Oh, I do realise that I am not much of a chap,' said Mr Jones with an engaging smile. 'Not for a perfectly marvellous girl like that. That is why I just feel I have got to put this thing through. It's my only chance. She's such a sporting girl that she would never go back on her word.'

'Well, I am sure we wish you luck and all that,' said Tuppence kindly. 'But I don't exactly see what you want us to do.'

'Oh Lord,' said Mr Montgomery Jones. 'Haven't I explained?'

'No,' said Tommy, 'you haven't.'

'Well, it was like this. We were talking about detective stories. Una – that's her name – is just as keen about them as I am. We got talking about one in particular. It all hinges on an alibi. Then we got talking about alibis and faking them. Then I said – no, she said – now which of us was it that said it?'

'Never mind which of you it was,' said Tuppence.

'I said it would be a jolly difficult thing to do. She disagreed – said it only wanted a bit of brain work. We got all hot and excited about it and in the end she said, "I will make you a sporting offer. What do you bet that I can produce an alibi that nobody can shake?"'

'"Anything you like," I said, and we settled it then and there. She was frightfully cocksure about the whole thing. "It's an odds on chance for me," she said. "Don't be so sure of that," I said. "Supposing you lose and I ask you for anything I like?" She laughed and said she came of a gambling family and I could.'

'Well?' said Tuppence as Mr Jones came to a pause and looked at her appealingly.

'Well, don't you see? It is up to me. It is the only chance I have got of getting a girl like that to look at me. You have no idea how sporting she is. Last summer she was out in a boat and someone bet her she wouldn't jump overboard and swim ashore in her clothes, and she did it.'

'It is a very curious proposition,' said Tommy. 'I am not quite sure I yet understand it.'

'It is perfectly simple,' said Mr Montgomery Jones. 'You must be doing this sort of thing all the time. Investigating fake alibis and seeing where they fall down.'

'Oh – er – yes, of course,' said Tommy. 'We do a lot of that sort of work.'

'Someone has got to do it for me,' said Montgomery Jones. 'I shouldn't be any good at that sort of thing myself. You have only got to catch her out and everything is all right. I dare say it seems rather a futile business to you, but it means a lot to me and I am prepared to pay – er – all necessary whatnots, you know.'

'That will be all right,' said Tuppence. 'I am sure Mr Blunt will take this case on for you.'

'Certainly, certainly,' said Tommy. 'A most refreshing case, most refreshing indeed.'

Mr Montgomery Jones heaved a sigh of relief, pulled a mass of papers from his pocket and selected one of them. 'Here it is,' he said. 'She says, "I am sending you proof I was in two distinct places at one and the same time. According to one story I dined at the Bon Temps Restaurant in Soho by myself, went to the Duke's Theatre and had supper with a friend, Mr le Marchant, at the Savoy – *but* I was also staying at the Castle Hotel, Torquay, and only returned to London on the following morning. You have got to find out which of the two stories is the true one and how I managed the other."'

'There,' said Mr Montgomery Jones. 'Now you see what it is that I want you to do.'

'A most refreshing little problem,' said Tommy. 'Very naive.'

'Here is Una's photograph,' said Mr Montgomery Jones. 'You will want that.'

'What is the lady's full name?' inquired Tommy.

'Miss Una Drake. And her address is 180 Clarges Street.'

'Thank you,' said Tommy. 'Well, we will look into the matter for you, Mr Montgomery Jones. I hope we shall have good news for you very shortly.'

'I say, you know, I am no end grateful,' said Mr Jones, rising to his feet and shaking Tommy by the hand. 'It has taken an awful load off my mind.'

Having seen his client out, Tommy returned to the inner office. Tuppence was at the cupboard that contained the classic library.

'Inspector French,' said Tuppence.

'Eh?' said Tommy.

'Inspector French, of course,' said Tuppence. 'He always does alibis. I know the exact procedure. We have to go over everything and check it. At first it will seem all right and then when we examine it more closely we shall find the flaw.'

'There ought not to be much difficulty about that,' agreed Tommy. 'I mean, knowing that one of them is a fake to start with makes the thing almost a certainty, I should say. That is what worries me.'

'I don't see anything to worry about in that.'

'I am worrying about the girl,' said Tommy. 'She will

probably be let in to marry that young man whether she wants to or not.'

'Darling,' said Tuppence, 'don't be foolish. Women are never the wild gamblers they appear. Unless that girl was already perfectly prepared to marry that pleasant, but rather empty-headed young man, she would never have let herself in for a wager of this kind. But, Tommy, believe me, she will marry him with more enthusiasm and respect if he wins the wager than if she has to make it easy for him some other way.'

'You do think you know about everything,' said her husband.

'I do,' said Tuppence.

'And now to examine our data,' said Tommy, drawing the papers towards him. 'First the photograph – h'm – quite a nice looking girl – and quite a good photograph, I should say. Clear and easily recognisable.'

'We must get some other girls' photographs,' said Tuppence.

'Why?'

'They always do,' said Tuppence. 'You show four or five to waiters and they pick out the right one.'

'Do you think they do?' said Tommy – 'pick out the right one, I mean.'

'Well, they do in books,' said Tuppence.

'It is a pity that real life is so different from fiction,' said Tommy. 'Now then, what have we here? Yes, this is the London lot. Dined at the Bon Temps seven-thirty. Went to Duke's Theatre and saw *Delphiniums Blue.* Counterfoil of theatre ticket enclosed. Supper at the Savoy with Mr le Marchant. We can, I suppose, interview Mr le Marchant.'

'That tells us nothing at all,' said Tuppence, 'because if he is helping her to do it he naturally won't give the show away. We can wash out anything he says now.'

'Well, here is the Torquay end,' went on Tommy. 'Twelve o'clock from Paddington, had lunch in the Restaurant Car, receipted bill enclosed. Stayed at Castle Hotel for one night. Again receipted bill.'

'I think this is all rather weak,' said Tuppence. 'Anyone can buy a theatre ticket, you need never go near the theatre. The girl just went to Torquay and the London thing is a fake.'

'If so, it is rather a sitter for us,' said Tommy. 'Well, I suppose we might as well go and interview Mr le Marchant.'

Mr le Marchant proved to be a breezy youth who betrayed no great surprise on seeing them.

'Una has got some little game on, hasn't she?' he asked. 'You never know what that kid is up to.'

'I understand, Mr le Marchant,' said Tommy, 'that Miss Drake had supper with you at the Savoy last Tuesday evening.'

'That's right,' said Mr le Marchant, 'I know it was

Tuesday because Una impressed it on me at the time and what's more she made me write it down in a little book.'

With some pride he showed an entry faintly pencilled. 'Having supper with Una. Savoy. Tuesday 19th.'

'Where had Miss Drake been earlier in the evening? Do you know?'

'She had been to some rotten show called *Pink Peonies* or something like that. Absolute slosh, so she told me.'

'You are quite sure Miss Drake was with you that evening?'

Mr le Marchant stared at him.

'Why, of course. Haven't I been telling you.'

'Perhaps she asked you to tell us,' said Tuppence.

'Well, for a matter of fact she did say something that was rather dashed odd. She said – what was it now? "You think you are sitting here having supper with me, Jimmy, but really I am having supper two hundred miles away in Devonshire." Now that was a dashed odd thing to say, don't you think so? Sort of astral body stuff. The funny thing is that a pal of mine, Dicky Rice, thought he saw her there.'

'Who is this Mr Rice?'

'Oh, just a friend of mine. He had been down in Torquay staying with an aunt. Sort of old bean who is always going to die and never does. Dicky had been down doing the dutiful nephew. He said, "I saw that Australian girl one day – Una something or other. Wanted to go and talk to her, but my aunt carried me off to chat with an old pussy in a bath chair." I said: "When was this?" and he said, "Oh, Tuesday about tea time." I told him, of course, that he had made a mistake, but it was odd, wasn't it? With Una saying that about Devonshire that evening?'

'Very odd,' said Tommy. 'Tell me, Mr le Marchant, did anyone you know have supper near you at the Savoy?'

'Some people called Oglander were at the next table.'

'Do they know Miss Drake?'

'Oh yes, they know her. They are not frightful friends or anything of that kind.'

'Well, if there's nothing more you can tell us, Mr le Marchant, I think we will wish you good-morning.'

'Either that chap is an extraordinarily good liar,' said Tommy as they reached the street, 'or else he is speaking the truth.'

'Yes,' said Tuppence, 'I have changed my opinion. I have a sort of feeling now that Una Drake was at the Savoy for supper that night.'

'We will now go to the Bon Temps,' said Tommy. 'A little food for starving sleuths is clearly indicated. Let's just get a few girls' photographs first.'

This proved rather more difficult than was expected.

Turning into a photographers and demanding a few assorted photographs, they were met with a cold rebuff.

'Why are all the things that are so easy and simple in books so difficult in real life,' wailed Tuppence. 'How horribly suspicious they looked. What do you think they thought we wanted to do with the photographs? We had better go and raid Jane's flat.'

Tuppence's friend Jane proved of an accommodating disposition and permitted Tuppence to rummage in a drawer and select four specimens of former friends of Jane's who had been shoved hastily in to be out of sight and mind.

Armed with this galaxy of feminine beauty they proceeded to the Bon Temps where fresh difficulties and much expense awaited them. Tommy had to get hold of each waiter in turn, tip him and then produce the assorted photographs. The result was unsatisfactory. At least three of the photographs were promising starters as having dined there last Tuesday. They then returned to the office where Tuppence immersed herself in an A.B.C.

'Paddington twelve o'clock. Torquay three thirty-five. That's the train and le Marchant's friend, Mr Sago or Tapioca or something saw her there about tea time.'

'We haven't checked his statement, remember,' said Tommy. 'If, as you said to begin with, le Marchant is a friend of Una Drake's he may have invented this story.'

'Oh, we'll hunt up Mr Rice,' said Tuppence. 'I have a kind of hunch that Mr le Marchant was speaking the truth. No, what I am trying to get at now is this. Una Drake leaves London by the twelve o'clock train, possibly takes a room at a hotel and unpacks. Then she takes a train back to town arriving in time to get to the Savoy. There is one at four-forty gets up to Paddington at nine-ten.'

'And then?' said Tommy.

'And then,' said Tuppence frowning, 'it is rather more difficult. There is a midnight train from Paddington down again, but she could hardly take that, that would be too early.'

'A fast car,' suggested Tommy.

'H'm,' said Tuppence. 'It is just on two hundred miles.'

'Australians, I have always been told, drive very recklessly.'

'Oh, I suppose it could be done,' said Tuppence. 'She would arrive there about seven.'

'Are you supposing her to have nipped into her bed at the Castle Hotel without being seen? Or arriving there explaining that she had been out all night and could she have her bill, please?'

'Tommy,' said Tuppence, 'we are idiots. She needn't

have gone back to Torquay at all. She has only got to get a friend to go to the hotel there and collect her luggage and pay her bill. Then you get the receipted bill with the proper date on it.'

'I think on the whole we have worked out a very sound hypothesis,' said Tommy. 'The next thing to do is to catch the twelve o'clock train to Torquay tomorrow and verify our brilliant conclusions.'

Armed with a portfolio of photographs, Tommy and Tuppence duly established themselves in a first-class carriage the following morning, and booked seats for the second lunch.

'It probably won't be the same dining car attendants,' said Tommy. 'That would be too much luck to expect. I expect we shall have to travel up and down to Torquay for days before we strike the right ones.'

'This alibi business is very trying,' said Tuppence. 'In books it is all passed over in two or three paragraphs. Inspector Something then boarded the train to Torquay and questioned the dining car attendants and so ended the story.'

For once, however, the young couple's luck was in. In answer to their question the attendant who brought their bill for lunch proved to be the same one who had been on duty the preceding Tuesday. What Tommy called the ten-shilling touch then came into action and Tuppence produced the portfolio.

'I want to know,' said Tommy, 'if any of these ladies had lunch on this train on Tuesday last?'

In a gratifying manner worthy of the best detective fiction the man at once indicated the photograph of Una Drake.

'Yes, sir, I remember that lady, and I remember that it was Tuesday, because the lady herself drew attention to the fact, saying it was always the luckiest day in the week for her.'

'So far, so good,' said Tuppence as they returned to their compartment. 'And we will probably find that she booked at the hotel all right. It is going to be more difficult to prove that she travelled back to London, but perhaps one of the porters at the station may remember.'

Here, however, they drew a blank, and crossing to the up platform Tommy made inquiries of the ticket collector and of various porters. After the distribution of half-crowns as a preliminary to inquiring, two of the porters picked out one of the other photographs with a vague remembrance that someone like that travelled to town by the four-forty that afternoon, but there was no identification of Una Drake.

'But that doesn't prove anything,' said Tuppence as they left the station. 'She may have travelled by that train and no one noticed her.'

'She may have gone from the other station, from Torre.'

'That's quite likely,' said Tuppence, 'however, we can see to that after we have been to the hotel.'

The Castle Hotel was a big one overlooking the sea. After booking a room for the night and signing the register, Tommy observed pleasantly.

'I believe you had a friend of ours staying here last Tuesday. Miss Una Drake.'

The young lady in the bureau beamed at him.

'Oh, yes, I remember quite well. An Australian young lady, I believe.'

At a sign from Tommy, Tuppence produced the photograph.

'That is rather a charming photograph of her, isn't it?' said Tuppence.

'Oh, very nice, very nice indeed, quite stylish.'

'Did she stay here long?' inquired Tommy.

'Only the one night. She went away by the express the next morning back to London. It seemed a long way to come for one night, but of course I suppose Australian ladies don't think anything of travelling.'

'She is a very sporting girl,' said Tommy, 'always having adventures. It wasn't here, was it, that she went out to dine with some friends, went for a drive in their car afterwards, ran the car into a ditch and wasn't able to get home till morning?'

'Oh, no,' said the young lady. 'Miss Drake had dinner here in the hotel.'

'Really,' said Tommy, 'are you sure of that? I mean – how do you know?'

'Oh, I saw her.'

'I asked because I understood she was dining with some friends in Torquay,' explained Tommy.

'Oh, no, sir, she dined here.' The young lady laughed and blushed a little. 'I remember she had on a most sweetly pretty frock. One of those new flowered chiffons all over pansies.'

'Tuppence, this tears it,' said Tommy when they had been shown upstairs to their room.

'It does rather,' said Tuppence. 'Of course that woman may be mistaken. We will ask the waiter at dinner. There can't be very many people here just at this time of year.'

This time it was Tuppence who opened the attack.

'Can you tell me if a friend of mine was here last Tuesday?' she asked the waiter with an engaging smile. 'A Miss Drake, wearing a frock all over pansies, I believe.' She produced a photograph. 'This lady.'

The waiter broke into immediate smiles of recognition.

'Yes, yes, Miss Drake, I remember her very well. She told me she came from Australia.'

'She dined here?'

'Yes. It was last Tuesday. She asked me if there was anything to do afterwards in the town.'

'Yes?'

'I told her the theatre, the Pavilion, but in the end she decided not to go and she stayed here listening to our orchestra.'

'Oh, damn!' said Tommy, under his breath.

'You don't remember what time she had dinner, do you?' asked Tuppence.

'She came down a little late. It must have been about eight o'clock.'

'Damn, Blast, and Curse,' said Tuppence as she and Tommy left the dining-room. 'Tommy, this is all going wrong. It seemed so clear and lovely.'

'Well, I suppose we ought to have known it wouldn't all be plain sailing.'

'Is there any train she could have taken after that, I wonder?'

'Not one that would have landed her in London in time to go to the Savoy.'

'Well,' said Tuppence, 'as a last hope I am going to talk to the chambermaid. Una Drake had a room on the same floor as ours.'

The chambermaid was a voluble and informative woman. Yes, she remembered the young lady quite well. That was her picture right enough. A very nice young lady, very merry and talkative. Had told her a lot about Australia and the kangaroos.

The young lady rang the bell about half-past nine and

asked for her bottle to be filled and put in her bed, and also to be called the next morning at half-past seven – with coffee instead of tea.

'You did call her and she was in her bed?' asked Tuppence.

'Why, yes, Ma'am, of course.'

'Oh, I only wondered if she was doing exercises or anything,' said Tuppence wildly. 'So many people do in the early morning.'

'Well, that seems cast-iron enough,' said Tommy when the chambermaid had departed. 'There is only one conclusion to be drawn from it. It is the London side of the thing that *must* be faked.'

'Mr le Marchant must be a more accomplished liar than we thought,' said Tuppence.

'We have a way of checking his statements,' said Tommy. 'He said there were people sitting at the next table whom Una knew slightly. What was their name – Oglander, that was it. We must hunt up these Oglanders, and we ought also to make inquiries at Miss Drake's flat in Clarges Street.'

The following morning they paid their bill and departed somewhat crestfallen.

Hunting out the Oglanders was fairly easy with the aid of the telephone book. Tuppence this time took the offensive and assumed the character of a representative of a new illustrated paper. She called on Mrs Oglander, asking for a few details of their 'smart' supper party at the Savoy on Tuesday evening. These details Mrs Oglander was only too willing to supply. Just as she was leaving Tuppence added carelessly. 'Let me see, wasn't Miss Drake sitting at the table next to you? Is it really true that she is engaged to the Duke of Perth? You know her, of course.'

'I know her slightly,' said Mrs Oglander. 'A very charming girl, I believe. Yes, she was sitting at the next table to ours with Mr le Marchant. My girls know her better than I do.'

Tuppence's next port of call was the flat in Clarges Street. Here she was greeted by Miss Marjory Leicester, the friend with whom Miss Drake shared a flat.

'Do tell me what all this is about?' asked Miss Leicester plaintively. 'Una has some deep game on and I don't know what it is. Of course she slept here on Tuesday night.'

'Did you see her when she came in?'

'No, I had gone to bed. She has got her own latch key, of course. She came in about one o'clock, I believe.'

'When did you see her?'

'Oh, the next morning about nine – or perhaps it was nearer ten.'

As Tuppence left the flat she almost collided with a tall gaunt female who was entering.

'Excuse me, Miss, I'm sure,' said the gaunt female.

'Do you work here?' asked Tuppence.

'Yes, Miss, I come daily.'

'What time do you get here in the morning?'

'Nine o'clock is my time, Miss.'

Tuppence slipped a hurried half-crown into the gaunt female's hand.

'Was Miss Drake here last Tuesday morning when you arrived?'

'Why, yes, Miss, indeed she was. Fast asleep in her bed and hardly woke up when I brought her in her tea.'

'Oh, thank you,' said Tuppence and went disconsolately down the stairs.

She had arranged to meet Tommy for lunch in a small restaurant in Soho and there they compared notes.

'I have seen that fellow Rice. It is quite true he did see Una Drake in the distance at Torquay.'

'Well,' said Tuppence, 'we have checked these alibis all right. Here, give me a bit of paper and a pencil, Tommy. Let us put it down neatly like all detectives do.'

1.30	Una Drake seen in Luncheon Car of train.
4 o'clock	Arrives at Castle Hotel.
5 o'clock	Seen by Mr Rice.
8 o'clock	Seen dining at hotel.

9.30	Asks for hot water bottle.
11.30	Seen at Savoy with Mr le Marchant.
7.30 a.m.	Called by chambermaid at Castle Hotel.
9 o'clock.	Called by charwoman at flat at Clarges Street.

They looked at each other.

'Well, it looks to me as if Blunt's Brilliant Detectives are beat,' said Tommy.

'Oh, we mustn't give up,' said Tuppence. 'Somebody *must* be lying!'

'The queer thing is that it strikes me nobody was lying. They all seemed perfectly truthful and straightforward.'

'Yet there must be a flaw. We know there is. I think of all sorts of things like private aeroplanes, but that doesn't really get us any forwarder.'

'I am inclined to the theory of an astral body.'

'Well,' said Tuppence, 'the only thing to do is to sleep on it. Your sub-conscious works in your sleep.'

'H'm,' said Tommy. 'If your sub-conscious provides you with a perfectly good answer to this riddle by tomorrow morning, I take off my hat to it.'

They were very silent all that evening. Again and again Tuppence reverted to the paper of times. She wrote things on bits of paper. She murmured to herself, she sought perplexedly through Rail Guides. But in the end they both rose to go to bed with no faint glimmer of light on the problem.

'This is very disheartening,' said Tommy.

'One of the most miserable evenings I have ever spent,' said Tuppence.

'We ought to have gone to a Music Hall,' said Tommy. 'A few good jokes about mothers-in-law and twins and bottles of beer would have done us no end of good.'

'No, you will see this concentration will work in the end,' said Tuppence. 'How busy our sub-conscious will have to be in the next eight hours!' And on this hopeful note they went to bed.

'Well,' said Tommy next morning. 'Has the subconscious worked?'

'I have got an idea,' said Tuppence.

'You have. What sort of an idea?'

'Well, rather a funny idea. Not at all like anything I have ever read in detective stories. As a matter of fact it is an idea that *you* put into my head.'

'Then it must be a good idea,' said Tommy firmly. 'Come on, Tuppence, out with it.'

'I shall have to send a cable to verify it,' said Tuppence. 'No, I am not going to tell you. It's a perfectly wild idea, but it's the only thing that fits the facts.'

'Well,' said Tommy, 'I must away to the office.

A roomful of disappointed clients must not wait in vain. I leave this case in the hands of my promising subordinate.'

Tuppence nodded cheerfully.

She did not put in an appearance at the office all day. When Tommy returned that evening about half-past five it was to find a wildly exultant Tuppence awaiting him.

'I have done it, Tommy. I have solved the mystery of the alibi. We can charge up all these half-crowns and ten-shilling notes and demand a substantial fee of our own from Mr Montgomery Jones and he can go right off and collect his girl.'

'What is the solution?' cried Tommy.

'A perfectly simple one,' said Tuppence. '*Twins*.'

'What do you mean? – Twins?'

'Why, just that. Of course it is the only solution. I will say you put it into my head last night talking about mothers-in-law, twins, and bottles of beer. I cabled to Australia and got back the information I wanted. Una has a twin sister, Vera, who arrived in England last Monday. That is why she was able to make this bet so spontaneously. She thought it would be a frightful rag on poor Montgomery Jones. The sister went to Torquay and she stayed in London.'

'Do you think she'll be terribly despondent that she's lost?' asked Tommy.

'No,' said Tuppence, 'I don't. I gave you my views about that before. She will put all the kudos down to Montgomery Jones. I always think respect for your husband's abilities should be the foundation of married life.'

'I am glad to have inspired these sentiments in you, Tuppence.'

'It is not a really satisfactory solution,' said Tuppence. 'Not the ingenious sort of flaw that Inspector French would have detected.'

'Nonsense,' said Tommy. 'I think the way I showed these photographs to the waiter in the restaurant was exactly like Inspector French.'

'He didn't have to use nearly so many half-crowns and ten-shilling notes as we seem to have done,' said Tuppence.

'Never mind,' said Tommy. 'We can charge them all up with additions to Mr Montgomery Jones. He will be in such a state of idiotic bliss that he would probably pay the most enormous bill without jibbing at it.'

'So he should,' said Tuppence. 'Haven't Blunt's Brilliant Detectives been brilliantly successful? Oh, Tommy, I do think we are extraordinarily clever. It quite frightens me sometimes.'

'The next case we have shall be a Roger Sheringham case, and you, Tuppence, shall be Roger Sheringham.'

'I shall have to talk a lot,' said Tuppence.

'You do that naturally,' said Tommy. 'And now I suggest that we carry out my programme of last night and seek out a Music Hall where they have plenty of jokes about mothers-in-law, bottles of beer, *and Twins*.'

Chapter 14

The Clergyman's Daughter

'I wish,' said Tuppence, roaming moodily round the office, 'that we could befriend a clergyman's daughter.'

'Why?' asked Tommy.

'You may have forgotten the fact, but I was once a clergyman's daughter myself. I remember what it was like. Hence this altruistic urge – this spirit of thoughtful consideration for others – this –'

'You are getting ready to be Roger Sheringham, I see,' said Tommy. 'If you will allow me to make a criticism, you talk quite as much as he does, but not nearly so well.'

'On the contrary,' said Tuppence. 'There is a feminine subtlety about my conversation, a *je ne sais quoi* that no gross male could ever attain to. I have, moreover, powers unknown to my prototype – do I mean prototype? Words are such uncertain things, they so often sound well, but mean the opposite of what one thinks they do.'

'Go on,' said Tommy kindly.

'I was. I was only pausing to take breath. Touching these powers, it is my wish today to assist a clergyman's daughter. You will see, Tommy, the first person to enlist the aid of Blunt's Brilliant Detectives will be a clergyman's daughter.'

'I'll bet you it isn't,' said Tommy.

'Done,' said Tuppence. 'Hist! To your typewriters, Oh! Israel. One comes.'

Mr Blunt's office was humming with industry as Albert opened the door and announced:

'Miss Monica Deane.'

A slender, brown-haired girl, rather shabbily dressed, entered and stood hesitating. Tommy came forward.

'Good-morning, Miss Deane. Won't you sit down and tell us what we can do for you? By the way, let me introduce my confidential secretary, Miss Sheringham.'

'I am delighted to make your acquaintance, Miss Deane,' said Tuppence. 'Your father was in the Church, I think.'

'Yes, he was. But how *did* you know that?'

'Oh! we have our methods,' said Tuppence. 'You mustn't mind me rattling on. Mr Blunt likes to hear me talk. He always says it gives him ideas.'

The girl stared at her. She was a slender creature,

not beautiful, but possessing a wistful prettiness. She had a quantity of soft mouse-coloured hair, and her eyes were dark blue and very lovely, though the dark shadows round them spoke of trouble and anxiety.

'Will you tell me your story, Miss Deane?' said Tommy.

The girl turned to him gratefully.

'It's such a long rambling story,' said the girl. 'My name is Monica Deane. My father was the rector of Little Hampsley in Suffolk. He died three years ago, and my mother and I were left very badly off. I went out as a governess, but my mother became a confirmed invalid, and I had to come home to look after her. We were desperately poor, but one day we received a lawyer's letter telling us that an aunt of my father's had died and had left everything to me. I had often heard of this aunt, who had quarrelled with my father many years ago, and I knew that she was very well off, so it really seemed that our troubles were at an end. But matters did not turn out quite as well as we had hoped. I inherited the house she had lived in, but after paying one or two small legacies, there was no money left. I suppose she must have lost it during the war, or perhaps she had been living on her capital. Still, we had the house, and almost at once we had a chance of selling it at quite an advantageous price. But, foolishly perhaps, I refused the offer. We were in tiny, but expensive lodgings, and I thought it would be much nicer to live in the Red House, where my mother could have comfortable rooms and take in paying guests to cover our expenses.

'I adhered to this plan, notwithstanding a further tempting offer from the gentleman who wanted to buy. We moved in, and I advertised for paying guests. For a time, all went well, we had several answers to our advertisement; my aunt's old servant remained on with us, and she and I between us did the work of the house. And then these unaccountable things began to happen.'

'What things?'

'The queerest things. The whole place seemed bewitched. Pictures fell down, crockery flew across the room and broke; one morning we came down to find all the furniture moved round. At first we thought someone was playing a pracitcal joke, but we had to give up that explanation. Sometimes when we were all sitting down to dinner, a terrific crash would be heard overhead. We would go up and find no one there, but a piece of furniture thrown violently to the ground.'

'A *poltergeist*,' cried Tuppence, much interested.

'Yes, that's what Dr O'Neill said – though I don't know what it means.'

'It's a sort of evil spirit that plays tricks,' explained Tuppence, who in reality knew very little about the subject, and was not even sure that she had got the word *poltergeist* right.

'Well, at any rate, the effect was disastrous. Our visitors were frightened to death, and left as soon as possible. We got new ones, and they too left hurriedly. I was in despair, and, to crown all, our own tiny income ceased suddenly – the Company in which it was invested failed.'

'You poor dear,' said Tuppence sympathetically. 'What a time you have had. Did you want Mr Blunt to investigate this "haunting" business?'

'Not exactly. You see, three days ago, a gentleman called upon us. His name was Dr O'Neill. He told us that he was a member of the Society for Physical Research, and that he had heard about the curious manifestations that had taken place in our house and was much interested. So much so, that he was prepared to buy it from us, and conduct a series of experiments there.'

'Well?'

'Of course, at first, I was overcome with joy. It seemed the way out of all our difficulties. But –'

'Yes?'

'Perhaps you will think me fanciful. Perhaps I am. But – oh! I'm sure I haven't made a mistake. It was the same man!'

'What same man?'

'The same man who wanted to buy it before. Oh! I'm sure I'm right.'

'But why shouldn't it be?'

'You don't understand. The two men were quite different, different name and everything. The first man was quite young, a spruce, dark young man of thirty odd. Dr O'Neill is about fifty, he has a grey beard and wears glasses and stoops. But when he talked I saw a gold tooth one side of his mouth. It only shows when he laughs. The other man had a tooth in just the same position, and then I looked at his ears. I had noticed the other man's ears, because they were a peculiar shape with hardly any lobe. Dr O'Neill's were just the same. Both things couldn't be a coincidence, could they? I thought and thought and finally I wrote and said I would let him know in a week. I had noticed Mr Blunt's advertisement some time ago – as a matter of fact in an old paper that lined one of the kitchen drawers. I cut it out and came up to town.'

'You were quite right,' said Tuppence, nodding her head with vigour. 'This needs looking into.'

'A very interesting case, Miss Deane,' observed Tommy.

'We shall be pleased to look into this for you – eh, Miss Sheringham?'

'Rather,' said Tuppence, 'and we'll get to the bottom of it too.'

'I understand, Miss Deane,' went on Tommy, 'that the household consists of you and your mother and a servant. Can you give me any particulars about the servant?'

'Her name is Crockett. She was with my aunt about eight or ten years. She is an elderly woman, not very pleasant in manner, but a good servant. She is inclined to give herself airs because her sister married out of her station. Crockett has a nephew whom she is always telling us is "quite the gentleman".'

'H'm,' said Tommy, rather at a loss how to proceed.

Tuppence had been eyeing Monica keenly, now she spoke with sudden decision.

'I think the best plan would be for Miss Deane to come out and lunch with me. It's just one o'clock. I can get full details from her.'

'Certainly, Miss Sheringham,' said Tommy. 'An excellent plan.'

'Look here,' said Tuppence, when they were comfortably ensconced at a little table in a neighbouring restaurant, 'I want to know: Is there any special reason why you want to find out about all this?'

Monica blushed.

'Well, you see –'

'Out with it,' said Tuppence encouragingly.

'Well – there are two men who – who – want to marry me.'

'The usual story, I suppose? One rich, one poor, and the poor one is the one you like!'

'I don't know how you know all these things,' murmured the girl.

'That's a sort of law of Nature,' explained Tuppence. 'It happens to everybody. It happened to me.'

'You see, even if I sell the house, it won't bring us in enough to live on. Gerald is a dear, but he's desperately poor – though he's a very clever engineer; and if only he had a little capital, his firm would take him into partnership. The other, Mr Partridge, is a very good man, I am sure – and well off, and if I married him, it would be an end to all our troubles. But – but –'

'I know,' said Tuppence sympathetically. 'It isn't the same thing at all. You can go on telling yourself how good and worthy he is, and adding up his qualities as though they were an addition sum – and it all has a simply refrigerating effect.'

Monica nodded.

'Well,' said Tuppence, 'I think it would be as well if we went down to the neighbourhood and studied matters upon the spot. What is the address?'

'The Red House, Stourton-in-the-Marsh.'

Tuppence wrote down the address in her notebook.

'I didn't ask you,' Monica began – 'about terms –' she ended, blushing a little.

'Our payments are strictly by results,' said Tuppence

gravely. 'If the secret of the Red House is a profitable one, as seems possible from the anxiety displayed to acquire the property, we should expect a small percentage, otherwise – nothing!'

'Thank you very much,' said the girl gratefully.

'And now,' said Tuppence, 'don't worry. Everything's going to be all right. Let's enjoy lunch and talk of interesting things.'

Chapter 15

The Red House

'Well,' said Tommy, looking out of the window of the Crown and Anchor, 'here we are at Toad in the Hole – or whatever this blasted village is called.'

'Let us review the case,' said Tuppence.

'By all means,' said Tommy. 'To begin with, getting my say in first, *I* suspect the invalid mother!'

'Why?'

'My dear Tuppence, grant that this *poltergeist* business is all a put-up job, got up in order to persuade the girl to sell the house, someone must have thrown the things about. Now the girl said everyone was at dinner – but if the mother is a thoroughgoing invalid, she'd be upstairs in her room.'

'If she was an invalid she could hardly throw furniture about.'

'Ah! but she wouldn't be a real invalid. She'd be shamming.'

'Why?'

'There you have me,' confessed her husband. 'I was really going on the well-known principle of suspecting the most unlikely person.'

'You always make fun of everything,' said Tuppence severely. 'There must be *something* that makes these people so anxious to get hold of the house. And if you don't care about getting to the bottom of this matter, I do. I like that girl. She's a dear.'

Tommy nodded seriously enough.

'I quite agree. But I never can resist ragging you, Tuppence. Of course, there's something queer about the house, and whatever it is, it's something that's difficult to get at. Otherwise a mere burglary would do the trick. But to be willing to buy the house means either that you've got to take up floors or pull down walls, or else that there's a coal mine under the back garden.'

'I don't want it to be a coal mine. Buried treasure is much more romantic.'

'H'm,' said Tommy. 'In that case I think that I shall pay a visit to the local Bank Manager, explain that I am staying here over Christmas and probably buying the Red House, and discuss the question of opening an account.'

'But why –?'

'Wait and see.'

Tommy returned at the end of half an hour. His eyes were twinkling.

'We advance, Tuppence. Our interview proceeded on the lines indicated. I then asked casually whether he had had much gold paid in, as is often the case nowadays in these small country banks – small farmers who hoarded it during the war, you understand. From that we proceeded quite naturally to the extraordinary vagaries of old ladies. I invented an aunt who on the outbreak of war drove to the Army and Navy Stores in a four-wheeler, and returned with sixteen hams. He immediately mentioned a client of his own, who had insisted on drawing out every penny of money she had – in gold as far as possible, and who also insisted on having her securities, bearer bonds and such things, given into her own custody. I exclaimed on such an act of folly, and he mentioned casually that she was the former owner of the Red House. You see, Tuppence? She drew out all this money, and she hid it somewhere. You remember that Monica Deane mentioned that they were astonished at the small amount of her estate? Yes, she hid it in the Red House, and someone knows about it. I can make a pretty good guess who that someone is too.'

'Who?'

'What about the faithful Crockett? She would know all about her mistress's peculiarities.'

'And that gold-toothed Dr O'Neill?'

'The gentlemanly nephew, of course! That's it. But whereabouts did she hide it. You know more about old ladies than I do, Tuppence. Where do they hide things?'

'Wrapped up in stockings and petticoats, under mattresses.'

Tommy nodded.

'I expect you're right. All the same, she can't have done that because it would have been found when her things were turned over. It worries me – you see, an old lady like that can't have taken up floors or dug holes in the garden. All the same it's there in the Red House somewhere. Crockett hasn't found it, but she knows it's there, and once they get the house to themselves, she and her precious nephew, they can turn it upside down until they find what they're after. We've got to get ahead of them. Come on, Tuppence. We'll go to the Red House.'

Monica Deane received them. To her mother and Crockett they were represented as would-be purchasers of the Red House, which would account for their being taken all over the house and grounds. Tommy did not tell Monica of the conclusions he had come to, but he asked her various searching questions. Of the garments and personal belongings of the dead woman, some had been given to Crockett and the others sent to various poor families. Everything had been gone through and turned out.

'Did your aunt leave any papers?'

'The desk was full, and there were some in a drawer in her bedroom, but there was nothing of importance amongst them.'

'Have they been thrown away?'

'No, my mother is always very loath to throw away old papers. There were some old-fashioned recipes among them which she intends to go through one day.'

'Good,' said Tommy approvingly. Then, indicating an old man who was at work upon one of the flower beds in the garden, he asked: 'Was that old man the gardener here in your aunt's time?'

'Yes, he used to come three days a week. He lives in the village. Poor old fellow, he is past doing any really useful work. We have him just once a week to keep things tidied up. We can't afford more.'

Tommy winked at Tuppence to indicate that she was to keep Monica with her, and he himself stepped across to where the gardener was working. He spoke a few pleasant words to the old man, asked him if he had been there in the old lady's time, and then said casually.

'You buried a box for her once, didn't you?'

'No, sir, I never buried naught for her. What should she want to bury a box for?'

Tommy shook his head. He strolled back to the house frowning. It was to be hoped that a study of the old lady's papers would yield some clue – otherwise the problem was a hard one to solve. The house itself was old fashioned, but not old enough to contain a secret room or passage.

Before leaving, Monica brought them down a big cardboard box tied with string.

'I've collected all the papers,' she whispered. 'And they're in here. I thought you could take it away with you, and then you'll have plenty of time to go over them – but I'm sure you won't find anything to throw light on the mysterious happenings in this house –'

Her words were interrupted by a terrific crash overhead. Tommy ran quickly up the stairs. A jug and a basin in one of the front rooms was lying on the ground broken to pieces. There was no one in the room.

'The ghost up to its tricks again,' he murmured with a grin.

He went downstairs again thoughtfully.

'I wonder, Miss Deane, if I might speak to the maid, Crockett, for a minute.'

'Certainly. I will ask her to come to you.'

Monica went off to the kitchen. She returned with the elderly maid who had opened the door to them earlier.

'We are thinking of buying this house,' said Tommy

pleasantly, 'and my wife was wondering whether, in that case, you would care to remain on with us?'

Crockett's respectable face displayed no emotion of any kind.

'Thank you, sir,' she said. 'I should like to think it over if I may.'

Tommy turned to Monica.

'I am delighted with the house, Miss Deane. I understand that there is another buyer in the market. I know what he has offered for the house, and I will willingly give a hundred more. And mind you, that is a good price I am offering.'

Monica murmured something noncommittal, and the Beresfords took their leave.

'I was right,' said Tommy, as they went down the drive, 'Crockett's in it. Did you notice that she was out of breath? That was from running down the backstairs after smashing the jug and basin. Sometimes, very likely, she has admitted her nephew secretly, and he has done a little poltergeisting, or whatever you call it, whilst she has been innocently with the family. You'll see Dr O'Neill will make a further offer before the day is out.'

True enough, after dinner, a note was brought. It was from Monica.

'I have just heard from Dr O'Neill. He raises his previous offer by £150.'

'The nephew must be a man of means,' said Tommy thoughtfully. 'And I tell you what, Tuppence, the prize he's after must be well worth while.'

'Oh! Oh! Oh! if only we could find it!'

'Well, let's get on with the spade work.'

They were sorting through the big box of papers, a wearisome affair, as they were all jumbled up pell mell without any kind of order or method. Every few minutes they compared notes.

'What's the latest, Tuppence?'

'Two old receipted bills, three unimportant letters, a recipe for preserving new potatoes and one for making lemon cheesecake. What's yours?'

'One bill, a poem on Spring, two newspaper cuttings: "Why Women buy Pearls – a sound investment", and "Man with Four Wives – Extraordinary Story", and a recipe for Jugged Hare.'

'It's heart-breaking,' said Tuppence, and they fell to once more. At last the box was empty. They looked at each other.

'I put this aside,' said Tommy, picking up a half sheet of notepaper, 'because it struck me as peculiar. But I don't suppose it's got anything to do with what we're looking for.'

'Let's see it. Oh! it's one of these funny things, what do they call them? Anagrams, charades or something.' She read it:

'My first *you put on glowing coal*
And into it you put my whole*;*
My second *really is the first;*
My third mislikes the winter blast.'

'H'm,' said Tommy critically. 'I don't think much of the poet's rhymes.'

'I don't see what you find peculiar about it, though,' said Tuppence. 'Everybody used to have a collection of these sort of things about fifty years ago. You saved them up for winter evenings round the fire.'

'I wasn't referring to the verse. It's the words written below it that strike me as peculiar.'

'St Luke, xi, 9,' she read. 'It's a text.'

'Yes. Doesn't that strike you as odd? Would an old lady of a religious persuasion write a text just under a charade?'

'It is rather odd,' agreed Tuppence thoughtfully.

'I presume that you, being a clergyman's daughter, have got your Bible with you?'

'As a matter of fact, I have. Aha! you didn't expect that. Wait a sec.'

Tuppence ran to her suitcase, extracted a small red volume and returned to the table. She turned the leaves rapidly. 'Here we are. Luke, chapter xi, verse 9. Oh! Tommy, look.'

Tommy bent over and looked where Tuppence's

small finger pointed to a portion of the verse in question.

'*Seek and ye shall find.*'

'That's it,' cried Tuppence. 'We've got it! Solve the cryptogram and the treasure is ours – or rather Monica's.'

'Well, let's get to work on the cryptogram, as you call it. "My *first* you put on glowing coal." What does that mean, I wonder? Then – "My *second* really is the first." That's pure gibberish.'

'It's quite simple, really,' said Tuppence kindly. 'It's just a sort of knack. Let *me* have it.'

Tommy surrendered it willingly. Tuppence ensconced herself in an armchair, and began muttering to herself with bent brows.

'It's quite simple, really,' murmured Tommy when half an hour had elapsed.

'Don't crow! We're the wrong generation for this. I've a good mind to go back to town tomorrow and call on some old pussy who would probably read it as easy as winking. It's a knack, that's all.'

'Well, let's have one more try.'

'There aren't many things you can put on glowing coal,' said Tuppence thoughtfully. 'There's water, to put it out, or wood, or a kettle.'

'It must be one syllable, I suppose? What about *wood*, then?'

'You couldn't put anything *into* wood, though.'

'There's no one syllable word instead of *water*, but there must be one syllable things you can put on a fire in the kettle line.'

'Saucepans,' mused Tuppence. 'Frying pans. How about *pan?* or *pot?* What's a word beginning pan or pot that is something you cook?'

'Pottery,' suggested Tommy. 'You bake that in the fire. Wouldn't that be near enough?'

'The rest of it doesn't fit. Pancakes? No. Oh! bother.'

They were interrupted by the little serving-maid, who told them that dinner would be ready in a few minutes.

'Only Mrs Lumley, she wanted to know if you like your potatoes fried, or boiled in their jackets? She's got some of each.'

'Boiled in their jackets,' said Tuppence promptly. 'I love potatoes –' She stopped dead with her mouth open.

'What's the matter, Tuppence? Have you seen a ghost?'

'Tommy,' cried Tuppence. 'Don't you see? That's it! The word, I mean. *Potatoes*! "My first you put on glowing coal" – that's pot. "And into it you put my *whole*." "My *second* really is the first." That's A, the first letter of the alphabet. "My *third* mislikes the wintry blast" – cold *toes* of course!'

'You're right, Tuppence. Very clever of you. But I'm afraid we've wasted an awful lot of time over nothing. Potatoes don't fit in at all with missing treasure. Half a sec, though. What did you read out just now, when we were going through the box? Something about a recipe for New Potatoes. I wonder if there's anything in that.'

He rummaged hastily through the pile of recipes.

'Here it is. "To KEEP NEW POTATOES. Put the new potatoes into tins and bury them in the garden. Even in the middle of winter, they will taste as though freshly dug."'

'We've got it,' screamed Tuppence. 'That's it. The treasure is in the garden, buried in a tin.'

'But I asked the gardener. He said he'd never buried anything.'

'Yes, I know, but that's because people never really answer what you say, they answer what they think you mean. He knew he'd never buried anything out of the common. We'll go tomorrow and ask him where he buried the potatoes.'

The following morning was Christmas Eve. By dint of inquiry they found the old gardener's cottage. Tuppence broached the subject after some minutes' conversation.

'I wish one could have new potatoes at Christmas time,' she remarked. 'Wouldn't they be good with turkey? Do people round here ever bury them in tins? I've heard that keeps them fresh.'

'Ay, that they do,' declared the old man. 'Old Miss Deane, up to the Red House, she allus had three tins buried every summer, and as often as not forgot to have 'em dug up again!'

'In the bed by the house, as a rule, didn't she?'

'No, over against the wall by the fir tree.'

Having got the information they wanted, they soon took their leave of the old man, presenting him with five shillings as a Christmas box.

'And now for Monica,' said Tommy.

'Tommy! You have no sense of the dramatic. Leave it to me. I've got a beautiful plan. Do you think you could manage to beg, borrow or steal a spade?'

Somehow or other, a spade was duly produced, and that night, late, two figures might have been seen stealing into the grounds of the Red House. The place indicated by the gardener was easily found, and Tommy set to work. Presently his spade rang on metal, and a few seconds later he had unearthed a big biscuit tin. It was sealed round with adhesive plaster and firmly fastened down, but Tuppence, by the aid of Tommy's knife, soon managed to open it. Then she gave a groan. The tin was full of potatoes. She poured them out, so that the tin was completely empty, but there were no other contents.

'Go on digging, Tommy.'

It was some time before a second tin rewarded their search. As before, Tuppence unsealed it.

'Well?' demanded Tommy anxiously.

'Potatoes again!'

'Damn!' said Tommy, and set to once more.

'The third time is lucky,' said Tuppence consolingly.

'I believe the whole thing's a mare's nest,' said Tommy gloomily, but he continued to dig.

At last a third tin was brought to light.

'Potatoes aga –' began Tuppence, then stopped. 'Oh, Tommy, we've got it. It's only potatoes on top. Look!'

She held up a big old-fashioned velvet bag.

'Cut along home,' cried Tommy. 'It's icy cold. Take the bag with you. I must shovel back the earth. And may a thousand curses light upon your head, Tuppence, if you open that bag before I come!'

'I'll play fair. Ouch! I'm frozen.' She beat a speedy retreat.

On arrival at the inn she had not long to wait. Tommy was hard upon her heels, perspiring freely after his digging and the final brisk run.

'Now then,' said Tommy, 'the private inquiry agents make good! Open the loot, Mrs Beresford.'

Inside the bag was a package done up in oil silk

and a heavy chamois leather bag. They opened the latter first. It was full of gold sovereigns. Tommy counted them.

'Two hundred pounds. That was all they would let her have, I suppose. Cut open the package.'

Tuppence did so. It was full of closely folded banknotes. Tommy and Tuppence counted them carefully. They amounted to exactly twenty thousand pounds.

'Whew!' said Tommy. 'Isn't it lucky for Monica that we're both rich and honest? What's that done up in tissue paper?'

Tuppence unrolled the little parcel and drew out a magnificent string of pearls, exquisitely matched.

'I don't know much about these things,' said Tommy slowly. 'But I'm pretty sure that those pearls are worth another five thousand pounds at least. Look at the size of them. Now I see why the old lady kept that cutting about pearls being a good investment. She must have realised all her securities and turned them into notes and jewels.'

'Oh, Tommy, isn't it wonderful? Darling Monica. Now she can marry her nice young man and live happily ever afterwards, like me.'

'That's rather sweet of you, Tuppence. So you *are* happy with me?'

'As a matter of fact,' said Tuppence, 'I am. But I didn't mean to say so. It slipped out. What with being excited, and Christmas Eve, and one thing and another –'

'If you really love me,' said Tommy, 'will you answer me one question?'

'I hate these catches,' said Tuppence, 'but – well – all right.'

'Then how did you know that Monica was a clergyman's daughter?'

'Oh, that was just cheating,' said Tuppence happily. 'I opened her letter making an appointment, and a Mr Deane was father's curate once, and he had a little girl called Monica, about four or five years younger than me. So I put two and two together.'

'You are a shameless creature,' said Tommy. 'Hullo, there's twelve o'clock striking. Happy Christmas, Tuppence.'

'Happy Christmas, Tommy. It'll be a Happy Christmas for Monica too – and all owing to US. I am glad. Poor thing, she has been so miserable. Do you know, Tommy, I feel all queer and choky about the throat when I think of it.'

'Darling Tuppence,' said Tommy.

'Darling Tommy,' said Tuppence. 'How awfully sentimental we are getting.'

'Christmas comes but once a year,' said Tommy sententiously. 'That's what our great-grandmothers said, and I expect there's a lot of truth in it still.'

Chapter 16

The Ambassador's Boots

'My dear fellow, my dear fellow,' said Tuppence, and waved a heavily buttered muffin.

Tommy looked at her for a minute or two, then a broad grin spread over his face and he murmured.

'We do have to be so very careful.'

'That's right,' said Tuppence, delighted. 'You guessed. I am the famous Dr Fortune and you are Superintendent Bell.'

'Why are you being Reginald Fortune?'

'Well, really because I feel like a lot of hot butter.'

'That is the pleasant side of it,' said Tommy. 'But there is another. You will have to examine horribly smashed faces and very extra dead bodies a good deal.'

In answer Tuppence threw across a letter. Tommy's eyebrows rose in astonishment.

'Randolph Wilmott, the American Ambassador. I wonder what he wants.'

'We shall know tomorrow at eleven o'clock.'

Punctually to the time named, Mr Randolph Wilmott, United States Ambassador to the Court of St James, was ushered into Mr Blunt's office. He cleared his throat and commenced speaking in a deliberate and characteristic manner.

'I have come to you, Mr Blunt – By the way, it is Mr Blunt himself to whom I am speaking, is it not?'

'Certainly,' said Tommy. 'I am Theodore Blunt, the head of the firm.'

'I always prefer to deal with heads of departments,' said Mr Wilmott. 'It is more satisfactory in every way. As I was about to say, Mr Blunt, this business gets my goat. There's nothing in it to trouble Scotland Yard about – I'm not a penny the worse in any way, and it's probably all due to a simple mistake. But all the same, I don't see just how that mistake arose. There's nothing criminal in it, I dare say, but I'd like just to get the thing straightened out. It makes me mad not to see the why and wherefore of a thing.'

'Absolutely,' said Tommy.

Mr Wilmott went on. He was slow and given to much detail. At last Tommy managed to get a word in.

'Quite so,' he said, 'the position is this. You arrived by the liner *Nomadic* a week ago. In some way your kitbag and the kitbag of another gentleman, Mr Ralph Westerham, whose initials are the same as yours, got mixed up. You took Mr Westerham's kitbag, and he took yours. Mr Westerham discovered the mistake immediately, sent round your kitbag to the Embassy, and took away his own. Am I right so far?'

'That is precisely what occurred. The two bags must have been practically identical, and with the initials R. W. being the same in both cases, it is not difficult to understand that an error might have been made. I myself was not aware of what had happened until my valet informed me of the mistake, and that Mr Westerham – he is a Senator, and a man for whom I have a great admiration – had sent round for his bag and returned mine.'

'Then I don't see –'

'But you will see. That's only the beginning of the story. Yesterday, as it chanced, I ran up against Senator Westerham, and I happened to mention the matter to him jestingly. To my great surprise, he did not seem to know what I was talking about, and when I explained, he denied the story absolutely. He had not taken my bag off the ship in mistake for his own – in fact, he had not travelled with such an article amongst his luggage.'

'What an extraordinary thing!'

'Mr Blunt, it *is* an extraordinary thing. There seems no rhyme or reason in it. Why, if any one wanted to steal my kitbag, he could do so easily enough without resorting to all this roundabout business. And anyway, it was *not* stolen, but returned to me. On the other hand, if it were taken by mistake, why use Senator Westerham's name? It's a crazy business – but just for curiosity I mean to get to the bottom of it. I hope the case is not too trivial for you to undertake?'

'Not at all. It is a very intriguing little problem, capable as you say, of many simple explanations, but nevertheless baffling on the face of it. The first thing, of course, is the *reason* of the substitution, if substitution it was. You say nothing was missing from your bag when it came back into your possession?'

'My man says not. He would know.'

'What was in it, if I may ask?'

'Mostly boots.'

'Boots,' said Tommy, discouraged.

'Yes,' said Mr Wilmott. 'Boots. Odd, isn't it?'

'You'll forgive my asking you,' said Tommy, 'but you didn't carry any secret papers, or anything of that sort sewn in the lining of a boot or screwed into a false heel?'

The Ambassador seemed amused by the question.

'Secret diplomacy hasn't got to that pitch, I hope.'

'Only in fiction,' said Tommy with an answering smile, and a slightly apologetic manner. 'But you see, we've got to account for the thing somehow. Who came for the bag – the other bag, I mean?'

'Supposed to be one of Westerham's servants. Quite

a quiet, ordinary man, so I understand. My valet saw nothing wrong with him.'

'Had it been unpacked, do you know?'

'That I can't say. I presume not. But perhaps you'd like to ask the valet a few questions? He can tell you more than I can about the business.'

'I think that would be the best plan, Mr Wilmott.'

The Ambassador scribbled a few words on a card and handed it to Tommy.

'I opine that you would prefer to go round to the Embassy and make your inquiries there? If not, I will have the man, his name is Richards, by the way – sent round here.'

'No, thank you, Mr Wilmott. I should prefer to go to the Embassy.'

The Ambassador rose, glancing at his watch.

'Dear me, I shall be late for an appointment. Well, goodbye, Mr Blunt. I leave the matter in your hands.'

He hurried away. Tommy looked at Tuppence, who had been scribbling demurely on her pad in the character of the efficient Miss Robinson.

'What about it, old thing?' he asked. 'Do you see, as the old bird put it, any rhyme or reason in the proceedings?'

'None whatever,' replied Tuppence cheerily.

'Well, that's a start, anyway! It shows that there is really something very deep at the back of it.'

'You think so?'

'It's a generally accepted hypothesis. Remember Sherlock Holmes and the depth the butter had sunk into the parsley – I mean the other way round. I've always had a devouring wish to know all about that case. Perhaps Watson will disinter it from his notebook one of these days. Then I shall die happy. But we must get busy.'

'Quite so,' said Tuppence. 'Not a quick man, the esteemed Wilmott, but sure.'

'She knows men,' said Tommy. 'Or do I say *he* knows men. It is so confusing when you assume the character of a male detective.'

'Oh, my dear fellow, my dear fellow!'

'A little more action, Tuppence, and a little less repetition.'

'A classic phrase cannot be repeated too often,' said Tuppence with dignity.

'Have a muffin,' said Tommy kindly.

'Not at eleven o'clock in the morning, thank you. Silly case, this. Boots – you know. Why boots?'

'Well,' said Tommy. 'Why not?'

'It doesn't fit. Boots.' She shook her head. 'All wrong. Who wants other people's boots? The whole thing's mad.'

'Possibly they got hold of the wrong bag,' suggested Tommy.

'That's possible. But if they were after papers, a despatch case would be more likely. Papers are the only things one thinks of in connection with ambassadors.'

'Boots suggest footprints,' said Tommy thoughtfully. 'Do you think they wanted to lay a trail of Wilmott's footsteps somewhere?'

Tuppence considered the suggestion, abandoning her role, then shook her head.

'It seems wildly impossible,' she said. 'No, I believe we shall have to resign ourselves to the fact that the boots have nothing to do with it.'

'Well,' said Tommy with a sigh, 'the next step is to interview friend Richards. He may be able to throw some light on the mystery.'

On production of the Ambassador's card, Tommy was admitted to the Embassy, and presently a pale young man, with a respectful manner and a subdued voice, presented himself to undergo examination.

'I am Richards, sir. Mr Wilmott's valet. I understood you wished to see me?'

'Yes, Richards. Mr Wilmott called on me this morning, and suggested that I should come round and ask you a few questions. It is this matter of the kitbag.'

'Mr Wilmott was rather upset over the affair, I know, sir. I can hardly see why, since no harm was done. I certainly understood from the man who called for the other bag that it belonged to Senator Westerham, but of course, I may have been mistaken.'

'What kind of man was he?'

'Middle-aged. Grey hair. Very good class, I should say – most respectable. I understood he was Senator Westerham's valet. He left Mr Wilmott's bag and took away the other.'

'Had it been unpacked at all?'

'Which one, sir?'

'Well, I meant the one you brought from the boat. But I should like to know about the other as well – Mr Wilmott's own. Had that been unpacked, do you fancy?'

'I should say not, sir. It was just as I strapped it up on the boat. I should say the gentleman – whoever he was – just opened it – realised it wasn't his, and shut it up again.'

'Nothing missing? No small article?'

'I don't think so, sir. In fact, I'm quite sure.'

'And now the other one. Had you started to unpack that?'

'As a matter of fact, sir, I was just opening it at the very moment Senator Westerham's man arrived. I'd just undone the straps.'

'Did you open it at all?'

'We just unfastened it together, sir, to be sure no mistake had been made this time. The man said it was all right, and he strapped it up again and took it away.'

'What was inside? Boots also?'

'No, sir, mostly toilet things, I fancy. I know I saw a tin of bath salts.'

Tommy abandoned that line of research.

'You never saw anyone tampering with anything in your master's cabin on board ship, I suppose?'

'Oh, no, sir.'

'Never anything suspicious of any kind?'

'And what do I mean by that, I wonder,' he thought to himself with a trace of amusement. 'Anything suspicious – just words!'

But the man in front of him hesitated.

'Now that I remember it –'

'Yes,' said Tommy eagerly. 'What?'

'I don't think it could have anything to do with it. But there was a young lady.'

'Yes? A young lady, you say, what was she doing?'

'She was taken faint, sir. A very pleasant young lady. Miss Eileen O'Hara, her name was. A dainty looking lady, not tall, with black hair. Just a little foreign looking.'

'Yes?' said Tommy, with even greater eagerness.

'As I was saying, she was taken queer. Just outside Mr Wilmott's cabin. She asked me to fetch the doctor. I helped her to the sofa, and then went off for the doctor.

I was some time finding him, and when I found him and brought him back, the young lady was nearly all right again.'

'Oh!' said Tommy.

'You don't think, sir –'

'It's difficult to know what to think,' said Tommy noncommittally. 'Was this Miss O'Hara travelling alone?'

'Yes, I think so, sir.'

'You haven't seen her since you landed?'

'No, sir.'

'Well,' said Tommy, after a minute or two spent in reflection. 'I think that's all. Thank you, Richards.'

'Thank *you*, sir.'

Back at the office of the Detective Agency, Tommy retailed his conversation with Richards to Tuppence, who listened attentively.

'What do you think of it, Tuppence?'

'Oh, my dear fellow, we doctors are always sceptical of a sudden faintness! So very convenient. And Eileen as well as O'Hara. Almost too impossibly Irish, don't you think?'

'It's something to go upon at last. Do you know what I am going to do, Tuppence? Advertise for the lady.'

'What?'

'Yes, any information respecting Miss Eileen O'Hara known to have travelled such and such a ship and such and such a date. Either she'll answer it herself if she's genuine, or someone may come forward to give us information about her. So far, it's the only hope of a clue.'

'You'll also put her on her guard, remember.'

'Well,' said Tommy, 'one's got to risk something.'

'I still can't see any sense in the thing,' said Tuppence, frowning. 'If a gang of crooks get hold of the Ambassador's bag for an hour or two, and then send it back, what possible good can it do them. Unless there are papers in it they want to copy, and Mr Wilmott swears there was nothing of the kind.'

Tommy stared at her thoughtfully.

'You put these things rather well, Tuppence,' he said at last. 'You've given me an idea.'

II

It was two days later. Tuppence was out to lunch. Tommy, alone in the austere office of Mr Theodore Blunt, was improving his mind by reading the latest sensational thriller.

The door of the office opened and Albert appeared.

'A young lady to see you, sir. Miss Cicely March. She says she has called in answer to an advertisement.'

'Show her in at once,' cried Tommy, thrusting his novel into a convenient drawer.

In another minute, Albert had ushered in the young

lady. Tommy had just time to see that she was fair haired and extremely pretty, when the amazing occurrence happened.

The door through which Albert had just passed out was rudely burst open. In the doorway stood a picturesque figure – a big dark man, Spanish in appearance, with a flaming red tie. His features were distorted with rage, and in his hand was a gleaming pistol.

'So this is the office of Mr Busybody Blunt,' he said in perfect English. His voice was low and venomous. 'Hands up at once – or I shoot.'

It sounded no idle threat. Tommy's hands went up obediently. The girl, crouched against the wall, gave a gasp of terror.

'This young lady will come with me,' said the man. 'Yes, you will, my dear. You have never seen me before, but that doesn't matter. I can't have my plans ruined by a silly little chit like you. I seem to remember that you were one of the passengers on the *Nomadic*. You must have been peering into things that didn't concern you – but I've no intention of letting you blab any secrets to Mr Blunt here. A very clever gentleman, Mr Blunt, with his fancy advertisements. But as it happens, I keep an eye on the advertisement columns. That's how I got wise to his little game.'

'You interest me exceedingly,' said Tommy. 'Won't you go on?'

'Cheek won't help you, Mr Blunt. From now on, you're a marked man. Give up this investigation, and we'll leave you alone. Otherwise – God help you! Death comes swiftly to those who thwart our plans.'

Tommy did not reply. He was staring over the intruder's shoulder as though he saw a ghost.

As a matter of fact he was seeing something that caused him far more apprehension than any ghost could have done. Up to now, he had not given a thought to Albert as a factor in the game. He had taken for granted that Albert had already been dealt with by the mysterious stranger. If he had thought of him at all, it was as one lying stunned on the carpet in the outer office.

He now saw that Albert had miraculously escaped the stranger's attention. But instead of rushing out to fetch a policeman in good sound British fashion, Albert had elected to play a lone hand. The door behind the stranger had opened noiselessly, and Albert stood in the aperture enveloped in a coil of rope.

An agonised yelp of protest burst from Tommy, but too late. Fired with enthusiasm, Albert flung a loop of rope over the intruder's head, and jerked him backwards off his feet.

The inevitable happened. The pistol went off with a roar and Tommy felt the bullet scorch his ear in passing, ere it buried itself in the plaster behind him.

'I've got him, sir,' cried Albert, flushed with triumph. 'I've lassoed him. I've been practising with a lasso in my spare time, sir. Can you give me a hand? He's very violent.'

Tommy hastened to his faithful henchman's assistance, mentally determining that Albert should have no further spare time.

'You damned idiot,' he said. 'Why didn't you go for a policeman? Owing to this fool's play of yours, he as near as anything plugged me through the head. Whew! I've never had such a near escape.'

'Lassoed him in the nick of time, I did,' said Albert, his ardour quite undamped. 'It's wonderful what those chaps can do on the prairies, sir.'

'Quite so,' said Tommy, 'but we're not on the prairies. We happen to be in a highly civilised city. And now, my dear sir,' he added to his prostrate foe. 'What are we going to do with you?'

A stream of oaths in a foreign language was his only reply.

'Hush,' said Tommy. 'I don't understand a word of what you're saying, but I've got a shrewd idea it's not the kind of language to use before a lady. You'll excuse him, won't you, Miss – do you know, in the excitement of this little upset, I've quite forgotten your name?'

'March,' said the girl. She was still white and shaken. But she came forward now and stood by Tommy looking down on the recumbent figure of the discomfited stranger. 'What are you going to do with him?'

'I could fetch a bobby now,' said Albert helpfully.

But Tommy, looking up, caught a very faint negative movement of the girl's head, and took his cue accordingly.

'We'll let him off this time,' he remarked. 'Nevertheless I shall give myself the pleasure of kicking him downstairs – if it's only to teach him manners to a lady.'

He removed the rope, hauled the victim to his feet, and propelled him briskly through the outer office.

A series of shrill yelps was heard and then a thud. Tommy came back, flushed but smiling.

The girl was staring at him with round eyes.

'Did you – hurt him?'

'I hope so,' said Tommy. 'But these dagoes make a practice of crying out before they're hurt – so I can't be quite sure about it. Shall we come back into my office, Miss March, and resume our interrupted conversation? I don't think we shall be interrupted again.'

'I'll have my lasso ready, sir, in case,' said the helpful Albert.

'Put it away,' ordered Tommy sternly.

He followed the girl into the inner office and sat down at his desk, whilst she took a chair facing him.

'I don't quite know where to begin,' said the girl. 'As you heard that man say, I was a passenger on the *Nomadic*. The lady you advertised about, Miss O'Hara, was also on board.'

'Exactly,' said Tommy. 'That we know already but I suspect you must know something about her doings on board that boat, or else that picturesque gentleman would not have been in such a hurry to intervene.'

'I will tell you everything. The American Ambassador was on board. One day, as I was passing his cabin, I saw this woman inside, and she was doing something so extraordinary that I stopped to watch. She had a man's boot in her hand –'

'A boot?' cried Tommy excitedly. 'I'm sorry, Miss March, go on.'

'With a little pair of scissors, she was slitting up the lining. Then she seemed to push something inside. Just at that minute the doctor and another man came down the passage, and immediately she dropped back on the couch and groaned. I waited, and I gathered from what was being said that she had pretended to feel faint. I say *pretended* – because when I first caught sight of her, she was obviously feeling nothing of the kind.'

Tommy nodded.

'Well?'

'I rather hate to tell you the next part. I was – curious. And also, I'd been reading silly books, and I wondered if she'd put a bomb or a poisoned needle or something like that in Mr Wilmott's boot. I know it's absurd – but I did think so. Anyway, next time I passed the empty cabin, I slipped in and examined the boot. I drew out from the lining a slip of paper. Just as I had it in my hand, I heard the steward coming, and I hurried out so as not to be caught. The folded paper was still in my hand. When I got into my own cabin I examined it. Mr Blunt, it was nothing but some verses from the Bible.'

'Verses from the Bible?' said Tommy, very much intrigued.

'At least I thought so at the time. I couldn't understand it, but I thought perhaps it was the work of a religious maniac. Anyway, I didn't feel it was worth while replacing it. I kept it without thinking much about it until yesterday when I used it to make into a boat for my little nephew to sail in his bath. As the paper got wet, I saw a queer kind of design coming out all over it. I hastily took it out of the bath, and smoothed it out flat again. The water had brought out the hidden message. It was a kind of tracing – and looked like the mouth of a harbour. Immediately after that I read your advertisement.'

Tommy sprang from his chair.

'But this is most important. I see it all now. That tracing is probably the plan of some important harbour defences. It had been stolen by this woman. She feared someone was on her track, and not daring to conceal it amongst her own belongings, she contrived this hiding-place. Later, she obtained possession of the bag in which the boot was packed – only to discover that the paper had vanished. Tell me, Miss March, you have brought this paper with you?'

The girl shook her head.

'It's at my place of business. I run a beauty parlour in Bond Street. I am really an agent for the "Cyclamen" preparations in New York. That is why I had been over there. I thought the paper might be important, so I locked it up in the safe before coming out. Ought not Scotland Yard to know about it?'

'Yes, indeed.'

'Then shall we go there now, get it out, and take it straight to Scotland Yard?'

'I am very busy this afternoon,' said Tommy, adopting his professional manner and consulting his watch. 'The Bishop of London wants me to take up a case for him. A very curious problem, concerning some vestments and two curates.'

'Then in that case,' said Miss March, rising, 'I will go alone.'

Tommy raised a hand in protest.

'As I was about to say,' he said, 'the Bishop must wait. I will leave a few words with Albert. I am convinced, Miss March, that until that paper has been safely deposited with Scotland Yard you are in active danger.'

'Do you think so?' said the girl doubtfully.

'I don't think so, I'm sure. Excuse me.' He scribbled some words on the pad in front of him, then tore off the leaf and folded it.

Taking his hat and stick, he intimated to the girl that he was ready to accompany her. In the outer office he handed the folded paper to Albert with an air of importance.

'I am called out on an urgent case. Explain that to his lordship if he comes. Here are my notes on the case for Miss Robinson.'

'Very good, sir,' said Albert, playing up. 'And what about the Duchess's pearls?'

Tommy waved his hand irritably.

'That must wait also.'

He and Miss March hurried out. Half-way down the stairs they encountered Tuppence coming up. Tommy passed her with a brusque: 'Late again, Miss Robinson. I am called out on an important case.'

Tuppence stood still on the stairs and stared after them. Then, with raised eyebrows, she went on up to the office.

As they reached the street, a taxi came sailing up to them. Tommy, on the point of hailing it, changed his mind.

'Are you a good walker, Miss March?' he asked seriously.

'Yes, why? Hadn't we better take that taxi? It will be quicker.'

'Perhaps you did not notice. That taxi driver has just refused a fare a little lower down the street. He was waiting for us. Your enemies are on the look-out. If you feel equal to it, it would be better for us to walk to Bond Street. In the crowded streets they will not be able to attempt much against us.'

'Very well,' said the girl, rather doubtfully.

They walked westwards. The streets, as Tommy had said, were crowded, and progress was slow. Tommy kept a sharp look out. Occasionally he drew the girl to one side with a quick gesture, though she herself had seen nothing suspicious.

Suddenly glancing at her, he was seized with compunction.

'I say, you look awfully done up. The shock of that man. Come into this place and have a good cup of strong coffee. I suppose you wouldn't hear of a nip of brandy.'

The girl shook her head, with a faint smile.

'Coffee be it then,' said Tommy. 'I think we can safely risk its being poisoned.'

They lingered some time over their coffee, and finally set off at a brisker pace.

'We've thrown them off, I think,' said Tommy, looking over his shoulder.

Cyclamen Ltd was a small establishment in Bond Street, with pale pink taffeta curtains, and one or two jars of face cream and a cake of soap decorating the window.

Cicely March entered, and Tommy followed. The place inside was tiny. On the left was a glass counter with toilet preparations. Behind this counter was a middle-aged woman with grey hair and an exquisite complexion, who acknowledged Cicely March's entrance with a faint inclination of the head before continuing to talk to the customer she was serving.

This customer was a small dark woman. Her back was to them and they could not see her face. She was speaking in slow difficult English. On the right was a sofa and a couple of chairs with some magazines on a table. Here sat two men – apparently bored husbands waiting for their wives.

Cicely March passed straight on through a door at the end which she held ajar for Tommy to follow her. As he did so, the woman customer exclaimed, 'Ah, but I think that is an *amico* of mine,' and rushed after them, inserting her foot in the door just in time to prevent its closing. At the same time the two men rose to their feet. One followed her through the door, the other advanced to the shop attendant and clapped his hand over her mouth to drown the scream rising to her lips.

In the meantime, things were happening rather quickly beyond the swing door. As Tommy passed through a cloth was flung over his head, and a sickly odour assailed his nostrils. Almost as soon however, it was jerked off again, and a woman's scream rang out.

Tommy blinked a little and coughed as he took in the scene in front of him. On his right was the mysterious stranger of a few hours ago, and busily fitting handcuffs upon him was one of the bored men from the shop parlour. Just in front of him was Cicely March wrestling vainly to free herself, whilst the woman customer from the shop held her firmly pinioned. As the latter turned her head, and the veil she wore unfastened itself and fell off, the well-known features of Tuppence were revealed.

'Well done, Tuppence,' said Tommy, moving forward. 'Let me give you a hand. I shouldn't struggle if I were you, Miss O'Hara – or do you prefer to be called Miss March?'

'This is Inspector Grace, Tommy,' said Tuppence. 'As soon as I read the note you left I rang up Scotland Yard, and Inspector Grace and another man met me outside here.'

'Very glad to get hold of this gentleman,' said the Inspector, indicating his prisoner. 'He's wanted badly.

But we've never had cause to suspect this place – thought it was a genuine beauty shop.'

'You see,' explained Tommy gently, 'we do have to be so very careful! Why should anyone want the Ambassador's bag for an hour or so? I put the question the other way round. Supposing it was the other bag that was the important one. Someone wanted that bag to be in the Ambassador's possession for an hour or so. Much more illuminating! Diplomatic luggage is not subjected to the indignities of a Customs examination. Clearly smuggling. But smuggling of what? Nothing too bulky. At once I thought of drugs. Then that picturesque comedy was enacted in my office. They'd seen my advertisement and wanted to put me off the scent – or failing that, out of the way altogether. But I happened to notice an expression of blank dismay in the charming lady's eyes when Albert did his lasso act. That didn't fit in very well with her supposed part. The stranger's attack was meant to assure my confidence in her. I played the part of the credulous sleuth with all my might – swallowed her rather impossible story and permitted her to lure me here, carefully leaving behind full instructions for dealing with the situation. Under various pretexts I delayed our arrival, so as to give you all plenty of time.'

Cicely March was looking at him with a stony expression.

'You are mad. What do you expect to find here?'

'Remembering that Richards saw a tin of bath salts, what do you say about beginning with the bath salts, eh, Inspector?'

'A very sound idea, sir.'

He picked up one of the dainty pink tins, and emptied it on the table. The girl laughed.

'Genuine crystals, eh?' said Tommy. 'Nothing more deadly than carbonate of soda?'

'Try the safe,' suggested Tuppence.

There was a small wall safe in the corner. The key was in the lock. Tommy swung it open and gave a shout of satisfaction. The back of the safe opened out into a big recess in the wall, and that recess was stacked with the same elegant tins of bath salts. Rows and rows of them. He took one out and prised up the lid. The top showed the same pink crystals, but underneath was a fine white powder.

The Inspector uttered an ejaculation.

'You've got it, sir. Ten to one, that tin's full of pure cocaine. We knew there was a distributing area somewhere round here, handy to the West End, but we haven't been able to get a clue to it. This is a fine coup of yours, sir.'

'Rather a triumph for Blunt's Brilliant Detectives,' said Tommy to Tuppence, as they emerged into the street together. 'It's a great thing to be a married man. Your persistent schooling has at last taught me to recognise peroxide when I see it. Golden hair has got to be the genuine article to take me in. We will concoct a business-like letter to the Ambassador, informing him that the matter has been dealt with satisfactorily. And now, my dear fellow, what about tea, and lots of hot buttered muffins?'

Chapter 17

The Man Who Was No. 16

Tommy and Tuppence were closeted with the Chief in his private room. His commendation had been warm and sincere.

'You have succeeded admirably. Thanks to you we have laid our hands on no less than five very interesting personages, and from them we have received much valuable information. Meanwhile I learn from a creditable source that headquarters in Moscow have taken alarm at the failure of their agents to report. I think that in spite of all our precautions they have begun to suspect that all is not well at what I may call the distributing centre – the office of Mr Theodore Blunt – the International Detective Bureau.'

'Well,' said Tommy, 'I suppose they were bound to tumble to it some time or other, sir.'

'As you say, it was only to be expected. But I am a little worried – about Mrs Tommy.'

'I can look after her all right, sir,' said Tommy, at exactly the same minute as Tuppence said, 'I can take care of myself.'

'H'm,' said Mr Carter. 'Excessive self-confidence was always a characteristic of you two. Whether your immunity is entirely due to your own superhuman cleverness, or whether a small percentage of luck creeps in, I'm not prepared to say. But luck changes, you know. However, I won't argue the point. From my extensive knowledge of Mrs Tommy, I suppose it's quite useless to ask her to keep out of the limelight for the next week or two?'

Tuppence shook her head very energetically.

'Then all I can do is to give you all the information that I can. We have reason to believe that a special agent has been despatched from Moscow to this country. We don't know what name he is travelling under, we don't know when he will arrive. But we do know something about him. He is a man who gave us great trouble in the war, an ubiquitous kind of fellow who turned up all over the place where we least wanted him. He is a Russian by birth, and an accomplished linguist – so much so that he can pass as half a dozen other nationalities, including our own. He is also a past-master in the art of disguise. And he has brains. It was he who devised the No. 16 code.

'When and how he will turn up, I do not know. But

I am fairly certain that he *will* turn up. We do know this – he was not personally acquainted with the real Mr Theodore Blunt. I think that he will turn up at your office, on the pretext of a case which he will wish you to take up, and will try you with the pass words. The first, as you know, is the mention of the number sixteen – which is replied to by a sentence containing the same number. The second, which we have only just learnt, is an inquiry as to whether you have ever crossed the Channel. The answer to that is: "I was in Berlin on the 13th of last month." As far as we know that is all. I would suggest that you reply correctly, and so endeavour to gain his confidence. Sustain the fiction if you possibly can. But even if he appears to be completely deceived, remain on your guard. Our friend is particularly astute, and can play a double game as well, or better, than you can. But in either case I hope to get him through you. From this day forward I am adopting special precautions. A dictaphone was installed last night in your office, so that one of my men in the room below will be able to hear everything that passes in your office. In this way I shall be immediately informed if anything arises, and can take the necessary steps to safeguard you and your wife whilst securing the man I am after.'

After a few more instructions, and a general discussion of tactics, the two young people departed and made their way as rapidly as possible to the offices of Blunt's Brilliant Detectives.

'It's late,' said Tommy, looking at his watch. 'Just on twelve o'clock. We've been a long time with the Chief. I hope we haven't missed a particularly spicy case.'

'On the whole,' said Tuppence, 'we've not done badly. I was tabulating results the other day. We've solved four baffling murder mysteries, rounded up a gang of counterfeiters, ditto gang of smugglers –'

'Actually two gangs,' interpolated Tommy. 'So we have! I'm glad of that. "Gangs" sounds so professional.'

Tuppence continued, ticking off the items on her fingers.

'One jewel robbery, two escapes from violent death, one case of missing lady reducing her figure, one young girl befriended, an alibi successfully exploded, and alas! one case where we made utter fools of ourselves. On the whole, jolly good! We're *very* clever, I think.'

'You would think so,' said Tommy. 'You always do. Now I have a secret feeling that once or twice we've been rather lucky.'

'Nonsense,' said Tuppence. 'All done by the little grey cells.'

'Well, I was damned lucky once,' said Tommy. 'The day that Albert did his lasso act! But you speak, Tuppence, as though it was all over?'

'So it is,' said Tuppence. She lowered her voice impressively. 'This is our last case. When they have laid the super spy by the heels, the great detectives intend to retire and take to bee keeping or vegetable marrow growing. It's always done.'

'Tired of it, eh?'

'Ye-es, I think I am. Besides, we're so successful now – the luck might change.'

'Who's talking about luck now?' asked Tommy triumphantly.

At that moment they turned in at the doorway of the block of buildings in which the International Detective Bureau had its offices, and Tuppence did not reply.

Albert was on duty in the outer office, employing his leisure in balancing, or endeavouring to balance, the office ruler upon his nose.

With a stern frown of reproof, the great Mr Blunt passed into his own private office. Divesting himself of his overcoat and hat, he opened the cupboard, on the shelves of which reposed his classic library of the great detectives of fiction.

'The choice narrows,' murmured Tommy. 'On whom shall I model myself today?'

Tuppence's voice, with an unusual note in it, made him turn sharply.

'Tommy,' she said, 'what day of the month is it?'

'Let me see – the eleventh – why?'

'Look at the calendar.'

Hanging on the wall was one of those calendars from which you tear a leaf every day. It bore the legend of Sunday the 16th. Today was Monday.

'By Jove, that's odd. Albert must have torn off too many. Careless little devil.'

'I don't believe he did,' said Tuppence. 'But we'll ask him.'

Albert, summoned and questioned, seemed very astonished. He swore he had only torn off two leaves, those of Saturday and Sunday. His statement was presently supported, for whereas the two leaves torn off by Albert were found in the grate, the succeeding ones were lying neatly in the wastepaper basket.

'A neat and methodical criminal,' said Tommy. 'Who's been here this morning, Albert? A client of any kind?'

'Just one, sir.'

'What was he like?'

'It was a she. A hospital nurse. Very upset and anxious to see you. Said she'd wait until you came. I put her in "Clerks" because it was warmer.'

'And from there she could walk in here, of course, without your seeing her. How long has she been gone?'

'About half an hour, sir. Said she'd call again this afternoon. A nice motherly-looking body.'

'A nice motherly – oh, get out, Albert.'

Albert withdrew, injured.

'Queer start, that,' said Tommy. 'It seems a little purposeless. Puts us on our guard. I suppose there isn't a bomb concealed in the fireplace or anything of that kind?'

He reassured himself on that point, then he seated himself at the desk and addressed Tuppence.

'*Mon ami*,' he said, 'we are here faced with a matter of the utmost gravity. You recall, do you not, the man who was No. 4. Him whom I crushed like an egg shell in the Dolomites – with the aid of high explosives, *bien entendu*. But he was not really dead – ah, no, they are never really dead, these super-criminals. This is the man – but even more so, if I may put it. He is the 4 squared – in other words, he is now the No. 16. You comprehend, my friend?'

'Perfectly,' said Tuppence. 'You are the great Hercule Poirot.'

'Exactly. No moustaches, but lots of grey cells.'

'I've a feeling,' said Tuppence, 'that this particular adventure will be called the "Triumph of Hastings".'

'Never,' said Tommy. 'It isn't done. Once the idiot friend, always the idiot friend. There's an etiquette in these matters. By the way, *mon ami*, can you not part your hair in the middle instead of one side? The present effect is unsymmetrical and deplorable.'

The buzzer rang sharply on Tommy's desk. He

returned the signal, and Albert appeared bearing a card.

'Prince Vladiroffsky,' read Tommy, in a low voice. He looked at Tuppence. 'I wonder – Show him in, Albert.'

The man who entered was of middle height, graceful in bearing, with a fair beard, and apparently about thirty-five years of age.

'Mr Blunt?' he inquired. His English was perfect. 'You have been most highly recommended to me. Will you take up a case for me?'

'If you will give me the details –?'

'Certainly. It concerns the daughter of a friend of mine – a girl of sixteen. We are anxious for no scandal – you understand.'

'My dear sir,' said Tommy, 'this business has been running successfully for sixteen years owing to our strict attention to that particular principle.'

He fancied he saw a sudden gleam in the other's eye. If so, it passed as quickly as it came.

'You have branches, I believe, on the other side of the Channel?'

'Oh, yes. As a matter of fact,' he brought out the word with great deliberation. 'I myself was in Berlin on the 13th of last month.'

'In that case,' said the stranger, 'it is hardly necessary to keep up the little fiction. The daughter of my friend can be conveniently dismissed. You know who I am – at any rate I see you have had warning of my coming.'

He nodded towards the calendar on the wall.

'Quite so,' said Tommy.

'My friends – I have come over here to investigate matters. What has been happening?'

'Treachery,' said Tuppence, no longer able to remain quiescent.

The Russian shifted his attention to her, and raised his eyebrows.

'Ah ha, that is so, is it? I thought as much. Was it Sergius?'

'We think so,' said Tuppence unblushingly.

'It would not surprise me. But you yourselves, you are under no suspicion?'

'I do not think so. We handle a good deal of *bona fide* business, you see,' explained Tommy.

The Russian nodded.

'That is wise. All the same, I think it would be better if I did not come here again. For the moment I am staying at the Blitz. I will take Marise – this is Marise, I suppose?'

Tuppence nodded.

'What is she known as here?'

'Oh, Miss Robinson.'

'Very well, Miss Robinson, you will return with me to the Blitz and lunch with me there. We will all meet at headquarters at three o'clock. Is that clear?' He looked at Tommy.

'Perfectly clear,' replied Tommy, wondering where on earth headquarters might be.

But he guessed that it was just those headquarters that Mr Carter was so anxious to discover.

Tuppence rose and slipped on her long black coat with its leopardskin collar. Then, demurely, she declared herself ready to accompany the Prince.

They went out together, and Tommy was left behind, a prey to conflicting emotions.

Supposing something had gone wrong with the dictaphone? Supposing the mysterious hospital nurse had somehow or other learnt of its installation, and had rendered it useless.

He seized the telephone and called a certain number. There was a moment's delay, and then a well-known voice spoke.

'Quite O.K. Come round to the Blitz at once.'

Five minutes later Tommy and Mr Carter met in the Palm Court of the Blitz. The latter was crisp and reassuring.

'You've done excellently. The Prince and the little lady are at lunch in the restaurant. I've got two of my men in there as waiters. Whether he suspects, or whether he doesn't – and I'm fairly sure he doesn't – we've got him on toast. There are two men posted upstairs to watch his suite, and more outside ready to follow wherever they go. Don't be worried about your wife. She'll be kept in sight the whole time. I'm not going to run any risks.'

Occasionally one of the Secret Service men came to report progress. The first time it was a waiter, who took their orders for cocktails, the second time it was a fashionable vacant-faced young man.

'They're coming out,' said Mr Carter. 'We'll retire behind this pillar in case they sit down here, but I fancy he'll take her up to his suite. Ah, yes, I thought so.'

From their post of vantage, Tommy saw the Russian and Tuppence cross the hall and enter the lift.

The minutes passed, and Tommy began to fidget.

'Do you think, sir. I mean, alone in that suite –'

'One of my men's inside – behind the sofa. Don't worry, man.'

A waiter crossed the hall and came up to Mr Carter.

'Got the signal they were coming up, sir – but they haven't come. Is it all right?'

'What?' Mr Carter spun round. 'I saw them go into the lift myself. Just,' he glanced up at the clock – 'four and a half minutes ago. And they haven't shown up . . .'

He hurried across to the lift which had just at that minute come down again, and spoke to the uniformed attendant.

'You took up a gentleman with a fair beard and a young lady a few minutes ago to the second floor.'

'Not the second floor, sir. Third floor the gentleman asked for.'

'Oh!' The Chief jumped in, motioning Tommy to accompany him. 'Take us up to the third floor, please.'

'I don't understand this,' he murmured in a low voice. 'But keep calm. Every exit from the hotel is watched, and I've got a man on the third floor as well – on every floor, in fact. I was taking no chances.'

The lift door opened on the third floor and they sprang out, hurrying down the corridor. Half-way along it, a man dressed as a waiter came to meet them.

'It's all right, Chief. They're in No. 318.'

Carter breathed a sigh of relief.

'That's all right. No other exit?'

'It's a suite, but there are only these two doors into the corridor, and to get out from any of these rooms, they'd have to pass us to get to the staircase or the lifts.'

'That's all right then. Just telephone down and find out who is supposed to occupy this suite.'

The waiter returned in a minute or two.

'Mrs Cortlandt Van Snyder of Detroit.'

Mr Carter became very thoughtful.

'I wonder now. Is this Mrs Van Snyder an accomplice, or is she –'

He left the sentence unfinished.

'Hear any noise from inside?' he asked abruptly.

'Not a thing. But the doors fit well. One couldn't hope to hear much.'

Mr Carter made up his mind suddenly.

'I don't like this business. We're going in. Got the master key?'

'Of course, sir.'

'Call up Evans and Clydesly.'

Reinforced by the other two men, they advanced towards the door of the suite. It opened noiselessly when the first man inserted his key.

They found themselves in a small hall. To the right was the open door of a bathroom, and in front of them was the sitting-room. On the left was a closed door and from behind it a faint sound – rather like an asthmatic pug – could be heard. Mr Carter pushed the door open and entered.

The room was a bedroom, with a big double bed, ornately covered with a bedspread of rose and gold. On it, bound hand and foot, with her mouth secured by a gag and her eyes almost starting out of her head with pain and rage, was a middle-aged fashionably-dressed woman.

On a brief order from Mr Carter, the other men had covered the whole suite. Only Tommy and his Chief had entered the bedroom. As he leant over the bed and strove to unfasten the knots, Carter's eyes went roving round the room in perplexity. Save for an immense quantity of truly American luggage, the room was empty. There was no sign of the Russian or Tuppence.

In another minute the waiter came hurrying in, and reported that the other rooms were also empty. Tommy went to the window, only to draw back and shake his head. There was no balcony – nothing but a sheer drop to the street below.

'Certain it was this room they entered?' asked Carter peremptorily.

'Sure. Besides –' The man indicated the woman on the bed.

With the aid of a pen-knife, Carter parted the scarf that was half choking her and it was at once clear that whatever her sufferings they had not deprived Mrs Cortlandt Van Snyder of the use of her tongue.

When she had exhausted her first indignation, Mr Carter spoke mildly.

'Would you mind telling me exactly what happened – from the beginning?'

'I guess I'll sue the hotel for this. It's a perfect outrage. I was just looking for my bottle of "Killagrippe", when a man sprung on me from behind and broke a little glass bottle right under my nose, and before I could get my breath I was all in. When I came to I was lying here, all trussed up, and goodness knows what's happened to my jewels. He's gotten the lot, I guess.'

'Your jewels are quite safe, I fancy,' said Mr Carter drily. He wheeled round and picked up something from the floor. 'You were standing just where I am when he sprang upon you?'

'That's so,' assented Mrs Van Snyder.

It was a fragment of thin glass that Mr Carter had picked up. He sniffed it and handed it to Tommy.

'Ethyl chloride,' he murmured. 'Instant anaesthetic. But it only keeps one under for a moment or two. Surely he must still have been in the room when you came to, Mrs Van Snyder?'

'Isn't that just what I'm telling you? Oh! it drove me half crazy to see him getting away and me not able to move or do anything at all.'

'Getting away?' said Mr Carter sharply. 'Which way?'

'Through that door.' She pointed to one in the opposite wall. 'He had a girl with him, but she seemed kind of limp as though she'd had a dose of the same dope.'

Carter looked a question at his henchman.

'Leads into the next suite, sir. But double doors – supposed to be bolted on each side.'

Mr Carter examined the door carefully. Then he straightened himself up and turned towards the bed.

'Mrs Van Snyder,' he said quietly, 'do you still persist in your assertion that the man went out this way?'

'Why, certainly he did. Why shouldn't he?'

'Because the door happens to be bolted on this side,' said Mr Carter dryly. He rattled the handle as he spoke.

A look of the utmost astonishment spread over Mrs Van Snyder's face.

'Unless someone bolted the door behind him,' said Mr Carter, 'he cannot have gone out that way.'

He turned to Evans, who had just entered the room.

'Sure they're not anywhere in this suite? Any other communicating doors?'

'No, sir, and I'm quite sure.'

Carter turned his gaze this way and that about the room. He opened the big hanging-wardrobe, looked under the bed, up the chimney and behind all the curtains. Finally, struck by a sudden idea, and disregarding Mrs Van Snyder's shrill protests, he opened the large wardrobe trunk and rummaged swiftly in the interior.

Suddenly Tommy, who had been examining the communicating door, gave an exclamation.

'Come here, sir, look at this. They did go this way.'

The bolt had been very cleverly filed through, so close to the socket that the join was hardly perceptible.

'The door won't open because it's locked on the other side,' explained Tommy.

In another minute they were out in the corridor again and the waiter was opening the door of the adjoining suite with his pass key. This suite was untenanted. When they came to the communicating door, they saw that the same plan had been adopted. The bolt had been filed through, and the door was locked, the key having been removed. But nowhere in the suite was there any sign of Tuppence or the fair-bearded Russian and there was no other communicating door, only the one on the corridor.

'But I'd have seen them come out,' protested the waiter. 'I couldn't have helped seeing them. I can take my oath they never did.'

'Damn it all,' cried Tommy. 'They can't have vanished into thin air!'

Carter was calm again now, his keen brain working.

'Telephone down and find out who had this suite last and when.'

Evans who had come with them, leaving Clydesly on guard in the other suite, obeyed. Presently he raised his head from the telephone.

'An invalid French lad, M. Paul de Vareze. He had a hospital nurse with him. They left this morning.'

An exclamation burst from the other Secret Service man, the waiter. He had gone deathly pale.

'The invalid boy – the hospital nurse,' he stammered. 'I – they passed me in the passage. I never dreamed – I had seen them so often before.'

'Are you sure they were the same?' cried Mr Carter. 'Are you sure, man? You looked at them well?'

The man shook his head.

'I hardly glanced at them. I was waiting, you understand, on the alert for the others, the man with the fair beard and the girl.'

'Of course,' said Mr Carter, with a groan. 'They counted on that.'

With a sudden exclamation, Tommy stooped down and pulled something from under the sofa. It was a small rolled-up bundle of black. Tommy unrolled it and several articles fell out. The outside wrapper was the long black coat Tuppence had worn that day. Inside was her walking dress, her hat and a long fair beard.'

'It's clear enough now,' he said bitterly. 'They've got her – got Tuppence. That Russian devil has given us the slip. The hospital nurse and the boy were accomplices. They stayed here for a day or two to get the hotel people accustomed to their presence. The man must have realised at lunch that he was trapped and proceeded to carry out his plan. Probably he counted on the room next door being empty since it was when he fixed the bolts. Anyway he managed to silence both the woman next door and Tuppence, brought her in here, dressed her in boy's clothes, altered his own appearance, and walked out bold as brass. The clothes must have been hidden ready. But I don't quite see how he managed Tuppence's acquiescence.'

'I can see,' said Mr Carter. He picked up a little shining piece of steel from the carpet. 'That's a fragment of a hypodermic needle. She was doped.'

'My God!' groaned Tommy. 'And he's got clear away.'

'We don't know that,' said Carter quickly. 'Remember every exit is watched.'

'For a man and a girl. Not for a hospital nurse and an invalid boy. They'll have left the hotel by now.'

Such, on inquiry, proved to be the case. The nurse and her patient had driven away in a taxi some five minutes earlier.

'Look here, Beresford,' said Mr Carter, 'for God's sake pull yourself together. You know that I won't leave a stone unturned to find that girl. I'm going back to my office at once and in less than five minutes every resource of the department will be at work. We'll get them yet.'

'Will you, sir? He's a clever devil, that Russian. Look at the cunning of this coup of his. But I know you'll do your best. Only – pray God it's not too late. They've got it in for us badly.'

He left the Blitz Hotel and walked blindly along the street, hardly knowing where he was going. He felt completely paralysed. Where to search? What to do?

He went into the Green Park, and dropped down upon a seat. He hardly noticed when someone else sat down at the opposite end, and was quite startled to hear a well-known voice.

'If you please, sir, if I might make so bold –'

Tommy looked up.

'Hullo, Albert,' he said dully.

'I know all about it, sir – but don't take on so.'

'Don't take on –' He gave a short laugh. 'Easily said, isn't it?'

'Ah, but think, sir. Blunt's Brilliant Detectives! Never beaten. And if you'll excuse my saying so I happened to overhear what you and the Missus was ragging about this morning. Mr Poirot, and his little grey cells. Well, sir, why not use your little grey cells, and see what you can do.'

'It's easier to use your little grey cells in fiction than it is in fact, my boy.'

'Well,' said Albert stoutly, 'I don't believe anybody could put the Missus out, for good and all. You know what she is, sir, just like one of those rubber bones you buy for little dorgs – guaranteed indestructible.'

'Albert,' said Tommy, 'you cheer me.'

'Then what about using your little grey cells, sir?'

'You're a persistent lad, Albert. Playing the fool has

served us pretty well up to now. We'll try it again. Let us arrange our facts neatly, and with method. At ten minutes past two exactly, our quarry enters the lift. Five minutes later we speak to the lift man, and having heard what he says we also go up to the third floor. At say, nineteen minutes past two we enter the suite of Mrs Van Snyder. And now, what significant fact strikes us?'

There was a pause, no significant fact striking either of them.

'There wasn't such a thing as a trunk in the room, was there?' asked Albert, his eyes lighting suddenly.

'*Mon ami*,' said Tommy, 'you do not understand the psychology of an American woman who has just returned from Paris. There were, I should say, about nineteen trunks in the room.'

'What I meantersay is, a trunk's a handy thing if you've got a dead body about you want to get rid of – not that she *is* dead, for a minute.'

'We searched the only two there were big enough to contain a body. What is the next fact in chronological order?'

'You've missed one out – when the Missus and the bloke dressed up as a hospital nurse passed the waiter in the passage.'

'It must have been just before we came up in the lift,' said Tommy. 'They must have had a narrow escape of meeting us face to face. Pretty quick work, that. I –'

He stopped.

'What is it, sir?'

'Be silent, *mon ami*. I have the kind of little idea – colossal, stupendous – that always comes sooner or later to Hercule Poirot. But if so – if that's it – Oh, Lord, I hope I'm in time.'

He raced out of the Park, Albert hard on his heels, inquiring breathlessly as he ran, 'What's up, sir? I don't understand.'

'That's all right,' said Tommy. 'You're not supposed to. Hastings never did. If your grey cells weren't of a very inferior order to mine, what fun do you think I should get out of this game? I'm talking damned rot – but I can't help it. You're a good lad, Albert. You know what Tuppence is worth – she's worth a dozen of you and me.'

Thus talking breathlessly as he ran, Tommy re-entered the portals of the Blitz. He caught sight of Evans, and drew him aside with a few hurried words. The two men entered the lift, Albert with them.

'Third floor,' said Tommy.

At the door of No. 318 they paused. Evans had a pass key, and used it forthwith. Without a word of warning, they walked straight into Mrs Van Snyder's bedroom. The lady was still lying on the bed, but was now arrayed in a becoming negligee. She stared at them in surprise.

'Pardon my failure to knock,' said Tommy pleasantly. 'But I want my wife. Do you mind getting off that bed?'

'I guess you've gone plumb crazy,' cried Mrs Van Snyder.

Tommy surveyed her thoughtfully, his head on one side.

'Very artistic,' he pronounced, 'but it won't do. We looked *under* the bed – but not *in* it. I remember using that hiding-place myself when young. Horizontally across the bed, underneath the bolster. And that nice wardrobe trunk all ready to take away the body in later. But we were a bit too quick for you just now. You'd had time to dope Tuppence, put her under the bolster, and be gagged and bound by your accomplices next door, and I'll admit we swallowed your story all right for the moment. But when one came to think it out – with order and method – impossible to drug a girl, dress her in boys' clothes, gag and bind another woman, and change one's own appearance – all in five minutes. Simply a physical impossibility. The hospital nurse and the boy were to be a decoy. We were to follow that trail, and Mrs Van Snyder was to be pitied as a victim. Just help the lady off the bed, will you, Evans? You have your automatic? Good.'

Protesting shrilly, Mrs Van Snyder was hauled from

her place of repose. Tommy tore off the coverings and the bolster.

There, lying horizontally across the top of the bed was Tuppence, her eyes closed, and her face waxen. For a moment Tommy felt a sudden dread, then he saw the slight rise and fall of her breast. She was drugged – not dead.

He turned to Albert and Evans.

'And now, Messieurs,' he said dramatically, 'the final *coup*!'

With a swift, unexpected gesture he seized Mrs Van Snyder by her elaborately dressed hair. It came off in his hand.

'As I thought,' said Tommy. '*No.* 16!'

II

It was about half an hour later when Tuppence opened her eyes and found a doctor and Tommy bending over her.

Over the events of the next quarter of an hour a decent veil had better be drawn, but after that period the doctor departed with the assurance that all was now well.

'*Mon ami*, Hastings,' said Tommy fondly. 'How I rejoice that you are still alive.'

'Have we got No. 16?'

'Once more I have crushed him like an egg-shell – in other words, Carter's got him. The little grey cells! By the way, I'm raising Albert's wages.'

'Tell me all about it.'

Tommy gave her a spirited narrative, with certain omissions.

'Weren't you half frantic about me?' asked Tuppence faintly.

'Not particularly. One must keep calm, you know.'

'Liar!' said Tuppence. 'You look quite haggard still.'

'Well, perhaps, I was just a little worried, darling. I say – we're going to give it up now, aren't we?'

'Certainly we are.'

Tommy gave a sigh of relief.

'I hoped you'd be sensible. After a shock like this –'

'It's not the shock. You know I never mind shocks.'

'A rubber bone – indestructible,' murmured Tommy.

'I've got something better to do,' continued Tuppence. 'Something ever so much more exciting. Something I've never done before.'

Tommy looked at her with lively apprehension.

'I forbid it, Tuppence.'

'You can't,' said Tuppence. 'It's a law of nature.'

'What are you talking about, Tuppence?'

'I'm talking,' said Tuppence, 'of Our Baby. Wives don't whisper nowadays. They shout. OUR BABY! Tommy, isn't everything marvellous?'

The Secret Adversary

Agatha Christie is known throughout the world as the Queen of Crime. Her books have sold over a billion copies in English with another billion in 100 foreign languages. She is the most widely published author of all time and in any language, outsold only by the Bible and Shakespeare. She is the author of 80 crime novels and short story collections, 19 plays, and six novels written under the name of Mary Westmacott.

Agatha Christie's first novel, *The Mysterious Affair at Styles*, was written towards the end of the First World War, in which she served as a VAD. In it she created Hercule Poirot, the little Belgian detective who was destined to become the most popular detective in crime fiction since Sherlock Holmes. It was eventually published by The Bodley Head in 1920.

In 1926, after averaging a book a year, Agatha Christie wrote her masterpiece. *The Murder of Roger Ackroyd* was the first of her books to be published by Collins and marked the beginning of an author-publisher relationship which lasted for 50 years and well over 70 books. *The Murder of Roger Ackroyd* was also the first of Agatha Christie's books to be dramatized – under the name *Alibi* – and to have a successful run in London's West End. *The Mousetrap*, her most famous play of all, opened in 1952 and is the longest-running play in history.

Agatha Christie was made a Dame in 1971. She died in 1976, since when a number of books have been published posthumously: the bestselling novel *Sleeping Murder* appeared later that year, followed by her autobiography and the short story collections *Miss Marple's Final Cases*, *Problem at Pollensa Bay* and *While the Light Lasts*. In 1998 *Black Coffee* was the first of her plays to be novelized by another author, Charles Osborne.

The Agatha Christie Collection

The Man In The Brown Suit
The Secret of Chimneys
The Seven Dials Mystery
The Mysterious Mr Quin
The Sittaford Mystery
The Hound of Death
The Listerdale Mystery
Why Didn't They Ask Evans?
Parker Pyne Investigates
Murder Is Easy
And Then There Were None
Towards Zero
Death Comes as the End
Sparkling Cyanide
Crooked House
They Came to Baghdad
Destination Unknown
Spider's Web *
The Unexpected Guest *
Ordeal by Innocence
The Pale Horse
Endless Night
Passenger To Frankfurt
Problem at Pollensa Bay
While the Light Lasts

Poirot

The Mysterious Affair at Styles
The Murder on the Links
Poirot Investigates
The Murder of Roger Ackroyd
The Big Four
The Mystery of the Blue Train
Black Coffee *
Peril at End House
Lord Edgware Dies
Murder on the Orient Express
Three-Act Tragedy
Death in the Clouds
The ABC Murders
Murder in Mesopotamia
Cards on the Table
Murder in the Mews
Dumb Witness
Death on the Nile
Appointment With Death
Hercule Poirot's Christmas
Sad Cypress
One, Two, Buckle My Shoe
Evil Under the Sun
Five Little Pigs
The Hollow
The Labours of Hercules
Taken at the Flood
Mrs McGinty's Dead
After the Funeral
Hickory Dickory Dock
Dead Man's Folly
Cat Among the Pigeons
The Adventure of the Christmas Pudding
The Clocks
Third Girl
Hallowe'en Party
Elephants Can Remember
Poirot's Early Cases
Curtain: Poirot's Last Case

Marple

The Murder at the Vicarage
The Thirteen Problems
The Body in the Library
The Moving Finger
A Murder is Announced
They Do It With Mirrors
A Pocket Full of Rye
The 4.50 from Paddington
The Mirror Crack'd from Side to Side
A Caribbean Mystery
At Bertram's Hotel
Nemesis
Sleeping Murder
Miss Marple's Final Cases

Tommy & Tuppence

The Secret Adversary
Partners in Crime
N or M?
By the Pricking of My Thumbs
Postern of Fate

Published as Mary Westmacott

Giant's Bread
Unfinished Portrait
Absent in the Spring
The Rose and the Yew Tree
A Daughter's a Daughter
The Burden

Memoirs

An Autobiography
Come, Tell Me How You Live

Play Collections

The Mousetrap and Selected Plays
Witness for the Prosecution and Selected Plays

* novelised by Charles Osborne

Agatha Christie

The Secret Adversary

HarperCollinsPublishers

HarperCollins*Publishers*
77–85 Fulham Palace Road
Hammersmith, London W6 8JB
www.**fire**and**water**.com

This *Agatha Christie Signature Edition* published 2001
9 8 7 6 5 4 3 2

First published in Great Britain by
Bodley Head Limited 1922

ISBN 0 00 711146 0

Typeset by Palimpsest Book Production Limited,
Polmont, Stirlingshire

Printed and bound in Great Britain by
Clays Ltd, St Ives plc

To all those who lead monotonous lives in the hope that they may experience at second-hand the delights and dangers of adventure.

Agatha Christie

Contents

Prologue

It was 2 p.m. on the afternoon of May 7th, 1915. The *Lusitania* had been struck by two torpedoes in succession and was sinking rapidly, while the boats were being launched with all possible speed. The women and children were being lined up awaiting their turn. Some still clung desperately to husbands and fathers; others clutched their children closely to their breasts. One girl stood alone, slightly apart from the rest. She was quite young, not more than eighteen. She did not seem afraid, and her grave steadfast eyes looked straight ahead.

'I beg your pardon.'

A man's voice beside her made her start and turn. She had noticed the speaker more than once amongst the first-class passengers. There had been a hint of mystery about him which had appealed to her imagination. He spoke to no one. If anyone spoke to him he was quick to rebuff the overture. Also he had a nervous way of looking over his shoulder with a swift, suspicious glance.

She noticed now that he was greatly agitated. There were beads of perspiration on his brow. He was evidently in a state of overmastering fear. And yet he did not strike her as the kind of man who would be afraid to meet death!

'Yes?' Her grave eyes met his inquiringly.

He stood looking at her with a kind of desperate irresolution.

'It must be!' he muttered to himself. 'Yes – it is the only way.' Then aloud he said abruptly: 'You are an American?'

'Yes.'

'A patriotic one?'

The girl flushed.

'I guess you've no right to ask such a thing! Of course I am!'

'Don't be offended. You wouldn't be if you knew how much there was at stake. But I've got to trust someone – and it must be a woman.'

'Why?'

'Because of "women and children first."' He looked round and lowered his voice. 'I'm carrying papers – vitally important papers. They may make all the difference to the Allies in the war. You understand? These papers have *got* to be saved! They've more chance with you than with me. Will you take them?'

The girl held out her hand.

'Wait – I must warn you. There may be a risk – if I've been followed. I don't think I have, but one never knows. If so, there will be danger. Have you the nerve to go through with it?'

The girl smiled.

'I'll go through with it all right. And I'm real proud to be chosen! What am I to do with them afterwards?'

'Watch the newspapers! I'll advertise in the personal column of *The Times*, beginning "Shipmate." At the end of three days if there's nothing – well, you'll know I'm down and out. Then take the packet to the American Embassy, and deliver it into the Ambassador's own hands. Is that clear?'

'Quite clear.'

'Then be ready – I'm going to say goodbye.' He took her hand in his. 'Goodbye. Good luck to you,' he said in a louder tone.

Her hand closed on the oilskin packet that had lain in his palm.

The *Lusitania* settled with a more decided list to starboard. In answer to a quick command, the girl went forward to take her place in the boat.

Chapter 1

The Young Adventurers, Ltd.

'Tommy, old thing!'

'Tuppence, old bean!'

The two young people greeted each other affectionately, and momentarily blocked the Dover Street Tube exit in doing so. The adjective 'old' was misleading. Their united ages would certainly not have totalled forty-five.

'Not seen you for simply centuries,' continued the young man. 'Where are you off to? Come and chew a bun with me. We're getting a bit unpopular here – blocking the gangway as it were. Let's get out of it.'

The girl assenting, they started walking down Dover Street towards Piccadilly.

'Now then,' said Tommy, 'where shall we go?'

The very faint anxiety which underlay his tone did not escape the astute ears of Miss Prudence Cowley, known to her intimate friends for some mysterious reason as 'Tuppence.' She pounced at once.

'Tommy, you're stony!'

'Not a bit of it,' declared Tommy unconvincingly. 'Rolling in cash.'

'You always were a shocking liar,' said Tuppence severely, 'though you did once persuade Sister Greenbank that the doctor had ordered you beer as a tonic, but forgotten to write it on the chart. Do you remember?'

Tommy chuckled.

'I should think I did! Wasn't the old cat in a rage when she found out? Not that she was a bad sort really, old Mother Greenbank! Good old hospital – demobbed like everything else, I suppose?'

Tuppence sighed.

'Yes. You too?'

Tommy nodded.

'Two months ago.'

'Gratuity?' hinted Tuppence.

'Spent.'

'Oh, Tommy!'

'No, old thing, not in riotous dissipation. No such luck! The cost of living – ordinary plain, or garden living nowadays is, I assure you, if you do not know –'

'My dear child,' interrupted Tuppence, 'there is nothing I do *not* know about the cost of living. Here we are at Lyons', and we will each of us pay for our own. That's that!' And Tuppence led the way upstairs.

The place was full, and they wandered about looking for a table, catching odds and ends of conversation as they did so.

'And – do you know, she sat down and *cried* when I told her she couldn't have the flat after all.' 'It was simply a *bargain*, my dear! Just like the one Mabel Lewis brought from Paris –'

'Funny scraps one does overhear,' murmured Tommy. 'I passed two Johnnies in the street today talking about someone called Jane Finn. Did you ever hear such a name?'

But at that moment two elderly ladies rose and collected parcels, and Tuppence deftly ensconced herself in one of the vacant seats.

Tommy ordered tea and buns. Tuppence ordered tea and buttered toast.

'And mind the tea comes in separate teapots,' she added severely.

Tommy sat down opposite her. His bared head revealed a shock of exquisitely slicked-back red hair. His face was pleasantly ugly – nondescript, yet unmistakably the face of a gentleman and a sportsman. His brown suit was well cut, but perilously near the end of its tether.

They were an essentially modern-looking couple as they sat there. Tuppence had no claim to beauty, but there was character and charm in the elfin lines of her little face, with its determined chin and large, wide-apart grey eyes that looked mistily out from under straight, black brows. She wore a small bright green toque over her black bobbed hair, and her extremely short and rather shabby skirt revealed a pair of uncommonly dainty ankles. Her appearance presented a valiant attempt at smartness.

The tea came at last, and Tuppence, rousing herself from a fit of meditation, poured it out.

'Now then,' said Tommy, taking a large bite of bun, 'lets's get up-to-date. Remember, I haven't seen you since that time in hospital in 1916.'

'Very well.' Tuppence helped herself liberally to buttered toast. 'Abridged biography of Miss Prudence Cowley, fifth daughter of Archdeacon Cowley of Little Missendell, Suffolk. Miss Cowley left the delights (and drudgeries) of her home life early in the war and came up to London, where she entered an officers' hospital. First month: Washed up six hundred and forty-eight plates every day. Second month: Promoted to drying aforesaid plates. Third month: Promoted to peeling potatoes. Fourth month: Promoted to cutting bread and butter. Fifth month: Promoted one floor up to duties of wardmaid with mop and pail. Sixth month: Promoted to waiting at table. Seventh month: Pleasing appearance and nice manners so striking that am promoted to waiting on the Sisters! Eighth month: Slight check in career. Sister Bond ate Sister Westhaven's egg!

Grand row! Wardmaid clearly to blame! Inattention in such important matters cannot be too highly censured. Mop and pail again! How are the mighty fallen! Ninth month: Promoted to sweeping out wards, where I found a friend of my childhood in Lieutenant Thomas Beresford (bow, Tommy!), whom I had not seen for five long years. The meeting was affecting! Tenth month: Reproved by matron for visiting the pictures in company with one of the patients, namely: the aforementioned Lieutenant Thomas Beresford. Eleventh and twelfth months: Parlourmaid duties resumed with entire success. At the end of the year left hospital in a blaze of glory. After that, the talented Miss Cowley drove successively a trade delivery van, a motor-lorry and a general. The last was the pleasantest. He was quite a young general!'

'What blighter was that?' inquired Tommy. 'Perfectly sickening the way those brass hats drove from the War Office to the Savoy, and from the Savoy to the War Office!'

'I've forgotten his name now,' confessed Tuppence. 'To resume, that was in a way the apex of my career. I next entered a Government office. We had several very enjoyable tea parties. I had intended to become a land girl, a post-woman, and a bus conductress by way of rounding off my career – but the Armistice intervened! I clung to the office with the true limpet touch for many long months, but, alas, I was combed out at last. Since then I've been looking for a job. Now then – your turn.'

'There's not so much promotion in mine,' said Tommy regretfully, 'and a great deal less variety. I went out to France again, as you know. Then they sent me to Mesopotamia, and I got wounded for the second time, and went into hospital out there. Then I got stuck in Egypt till the Armistice happened, kicked my heels there some time longer, and, as I told you, finally got demobbed. And, for ten long, weary months I've been job hunting! There aren't any jobs! And, if there were, they wouldn't give 'em to me. What good am I? What do I know about business? Nothing.'

Tuppence nodded gloomily.

'What about the colonies?' she suggested.

Tommy shook his head.

'I shouldn't like the colonies – and I'm perfectly certain they wouldn't like me!'

'Rich relations?'

Again Tommy shook his head.

'Oh, Tommy, not even a great-aunt?'

'I've got an old uncle who's more or less rolling, but he's no good.'

'Why not?'

'Wanted to adopt me once. I refused.'

'I think I remember hearing about it,' said Tuppence

slowly. 'You refused because of your mother –'

Tommy flushed.

'Yes, it would have been a bit rough on the mater. As you know, I was all she had. Old boy hated her – wanted to get me away from her. Just a bit of spite.'

'Your mother's dead, isn't she?' said Tuppence gently.

Tommy nodded.

Tuppence's large grey eyes looked misty.

'You're a good sort, Tommy. I always knew it.'

'Rot!' said Tommy hastily. 'Well, that's my position. I'm just about desperate.'

'So am I! I've hung out as long as I could. I've touted round. I've answered advertisements. I've tried every mortal blessed thing. I've screwed and saved and pinched! But it's no good. I shall have to go home!'

'Don't you want to?'

'Of course I don't want to! What's the good of being sentimental? Father's a dear – I'm awfully fond of him – but you've no idea how I worry him! He has that delightful early Victorian view that short skirts and smoking are immoral. You can imagine what a thorn in the flesh I am to him! He just heaved a sigh of relief when the war took me off. You see, there are seven of us at home. It's awful! All housework and mothers' meetings! I have always been the changeling. I don't want to go back, but – oh, Tommy, what else is there to do?'

Tommy shook his head sadly. There was a silence, and then Tuppence burst out:

'Money, money, money! I think about money morning, noon and night! I dare say it's mercenary of me, but there it is!'

'Same here,' agreed Tommy with feeling.

'I've thought over every imaginable way of getting it too,' continued Tuppence. 'There are only three! To be left it, to marry it, or to make it. First is ruled out. I haven't got any rich elderly relatives. Any relatives I have are in homes for decayed gentlewomen! I always help old ladies over crossings, and pick up parcels for old gentlemen, in case they should turn out to be eccentric millionaires. But not one of them has ever asked me my name – and quite a lot never said "Thank you."'

There was a pause.

'Of course,' resumed Tuppence, 'marriage is my best chance. I made up my mind to marry money when I was quite young. Any thinking girl would! I'm not sentimental, you know.' She paused. 'Come now, you can't say I'm sentimental,' she added sharply.

'Certainly not,' agreed Tommy hastily. 'No one would ever think of sentiment in connexion with you.'

'That's not very polite,' replied Tuppence. 'But I

dare say you mean it all right. Well, there it is! I'm ready and willing – but I never meet any rich men! All the boys I know are about as hard up as I am.'

'What about the general?' inquired Tommy.

'I fancy he keeps a bicycle shop in time of peace,' explained Tuppence. 'No, there it is! Now *you* could marry a rich girl.'

'I'm like you. I don't know any.'

'That doesn't matter. You can always get to know one. Now, if I see a man in a fur coat come out of the Ritz I can't rush up to him and say: "Look here, you're rich. I'd like to know you."'

'Do you suggest that I should do that to a similarly garbed female?'

'Don't be silly. You tread on her foot, or pick up her handkerchief, or something like that. If she thinks you want to know her she's flattered, and will manage it for you somehow.'

'You overrate my manly charms,' murmured Tommy.

'On the other hand,' proceeded Tuppence, 'my millionaire would probably run for his life! No – marriage is fraught with difficulties. Remains – to *make* money!'

'We've tried that, and failed,' Tommy reminded her.

'We've tried all the orthodox ways, yes. But suppose we try the unorthodox. Tommy, let's be adventurers!'

'Certainly,' replied Tommy cheerfully. 'How do we begin?'

'That's the difficulty. If we could make ourselves known, people might hire us to commit crimes for them.'

'Delightful,' commented Tommy. 'Especially coming from a clergyman's daughter!'

'The moral guilt,' Tuppence pointed out, 'would be theirs – not mine. You must admit that there's a difference between stealing a diamond necklace for yourself and being hired to steal it?'

'There wouldn't be the least difference if you were caught!'

'Perhaps not. But I shouldn't be caught. I'm so clever.'

'Modesty always was your besetting sin,' remarked Tommy.

'Don't rag. Look here, Tommy, shall we really? Shall we form a business partnership?'

'Form a company for the stealing of diamond necklaces?'

'That was only an illustration. Let's have a – what do you call it in book-keeping?'

'Don't know. Never did any.'

'I have – but I always got mixed up, and used to put credit entries on the debit side, and vice versa – so they fired me out. Oh, I know – a joint venture! It struck me as such a romantic phrase to come across in the middle of musty old figures. It's got an Elizabethan flavour about it – makes one think of galleons and doubloons. A joint venture!'

'Trading under the name of the Young Adventurers, Ltd.? Is that your idea, Tuppence?'

'It's all very well to laugh, but I feel there might be something in it.'

'How do you propose to get in touch with your would-be employers?'

'Advertisement,' replied Tuppence promptly. 'Have you got a bit of paper and a pencil? Men usually seem to have. Just like we have hairpins and powder-puffs.'

Tommy handed over a rather shabby green note-book, and Tuppence began writing busily.

'Shall we begin: "Young officer, twice wounded in the war –"'

'Certainly not.'

'Oh, very well, my dear boy. But I can assure you that that sort of thing might touch the heart of an elderly spinster, and she might adopt you, and then there would be no need for you to be a young adventurer at all.'

'I don't want to be adopted.'

'I forgot you had a prejudice against it. I was only ragging you! The papers are full up to the brim with that type of thing. Now listen – how's this? "Two young adventurers for hire. Willing to do anything, go anywhere. Pay must be good." (We might as well make that clear from the start.) Then we might add: "No reasonable offer refused" – like flats and furniture.'

'I should think any offer we get in answer to that would be a pretty *un*reasonable one!'

'Tommy! You're a genius! That's ever so much more chic. "No unreasonable offer refused – if pay is good." How's that?'

'I shouldn't mention pay again. It looks rather eager.'

'It couldn't look as eager as I feel! But perhaps you are right. Now I'll read it straight through. "Two young adventures for hire. Willing to do anything, go anywhere. Pay must be good. No unreasonable offer refused." How would that strike you if you read it?'

'It would strike me as either being a hoax, or else written by a lunatic.'

'It's not half so insane as a thing I read this morning beginning "Petunia" and signed "Best Boy."' She tore out the leaf and handed it to Tommy. 'There you are. *The Times*, I think. Reply to Box so-and-so. I expect it will be about five shillings. Here's half a crown for my share.'

Tommy was holding the paper thoughtfully. His face burned a deeper red.

'Shall we really try it?' he said at last. 'Shall we, Tuppence? Just for the fun of the thing?'

'Tommy, you're a sport! I knew you would be! Let's

drink to success.' She poured some cold dregs of tea into the two cups.

'Here's to our joint venture, and may it prosper!'

'The Young Adventurers, Ltd.!' responded Tommy.

They put down the cups and laughed rather uncertainly. Tuppence rose.

'I must return to my palatial suite at the hostel.'

'Perhaps it is time I strolled round to the Ritz,' agreed Tommy with a grin. 'Where shall we meet? And when?'

'Twelve o'clock tomorrow. Piccadilly Tube station. Will that suit you?'

'My time is my own,' replied Mr Beresford magnificently.

'So long, then.'

'Goodbye, old thing.'

The two young people went off in opposite directions. Tuppence's hostel was situated in what was charitably called Southern Belgravia. For reasons of economy she did not take a bus.

She was half-way across St James's Park, when a man's voice behind her made her start.

'Excuse me,' it said. 'But may I speak to you for a moment?'

Chapter 2
Mr Whittington's Offer

Tuppence turned sharply, but the words hovering on the tip of her tongue remained unspoken for the man's appearance and manner did not bear out her first and most natural assumption. She hesitated. As if he read her thoughts, the man said quickly:

'I can assure you I mean no disrespect.'

Tuppence believed him. Although she disliked and distrusted him instinctively, she was inclined to acquit him of the particular motive which she had at first attributed to him. She looked him up and down. He was a big man, clean shaven, with a heavy jowl. His eyes were small and cunning, and shifted their glance under her direct gaze.

'Well, what is it?' she asked.

The man smiled.

'I happened to overhear part of your conversation with the young gentleman in Lyons'.'

'Well – what of it?'

'Nothing – except that I think I may be of some use to you.'

Another inference forced itself into Tuppence's mind.

'You followed me here?'

'I took that liberty.'

'And in what way do you think you could be of use to me?'

The man took a card from his pocket and handed it to her with a bow.

Tuppence took it and scrutinized it carefully. It bore the inscription 'Mr Edward Whittington.' Below the name were the words 'Esthonia Glassware Co.,' and the address of a city office. Mr Whittington spoke again:

'If you will call upon me tomorrow morning at eleven o'clock, I will lay the details of my proposition before you.'

'At eleven o'clock?' said Tuppence doubtfully.

'At eleven o'clock.'

Tuppence made up her mind.

'Very well. I'll be there.'

'Thank you. Good evening.'

He raised his hat with a flourish, and walked away. Tuppence remained for some minutes gazing after him. Then she gave a curious movement of her shoulders, rather as a terrier shakes himself.

'The adventures have begun,' she murmured to herself. 'What does he want me to do, I wonder? There's something about you, Mr Whittington, that I don't like at all. But, on the other hand, I'm not the least bit afraid of you. And as I've said before, and shall doubtless say again, little Tuppence can look after herself, thank you!'

And with a short, sharp nod of her head she walked briskly onward. As a result of further meditations, however, she turned aside from the direct route and entered a post office. There she pondered for some moments, a telegraph form in her hand. The thought of a possible five shillings spent unnecessarily spurred her to action, and she decided to risk the waste of ninepence.

Disdaining the spiky pen and thick, black treacle which a beneficent Government had provided, Tuppence drew out Tommy's pencil which she had retained and wrote rapidly: 'Don't put in advertisement. Will explain tomorrow.' She addressed it to Tommy at his club, from which in one short month he would have to resign, unless a kindly fortune permitted him to renew his subscription.

'It may catch him,' she murmured. 'Anyway it's worth trying.'

After handing it over the counter she set out briskly for home, stopping at a baker's to buy three-pennyworth of new buns.

Later, in her tiny cubicle at the top of the house she munched buns and reflected on the future. What was the Esthonia Glassware Co., and what earthly need could it have for her services? A pleasurable thrill of excitement made Tuppence tingle. At any rate, the country vicarage had retreated into the background again. The morrow held possibilities.

It was a long time before Tuppence went to sleep that night, and, when at length she did, she dreamed that Mr Whittington had set her to washing up a pile of Esthonia Glassware, which bore an unaccountable resemblance to hospital plates!

It wanted some five minutes to eleven when Tuppence reached the block of buildings in which the offices of the Esthonia Glassware Co. were situated. To arrive before the time would look over-eager. So Tuppence decided to walk to the end of the street and back again. She did so. On the stroke of eleven she plunged into the recesses of the building. The Esthonia Glassware Co. was on the top floor. There was a lift, but Tuppence chose to walk up.

Slightly out of breath, she came to a halt outside the ground glass door with the legend painted across it: 'Esthonia Glassware Co.'

Tuppence knocked. In response to a voice from within, she turned the handle and walked into a small, rather dirty office.

A middle-aged clerk got down from a high stool at a desk near the window and came towards her inquiringly.

'I have an appointment with Mr Whittington,' said Tuppence.

'Will you come this way, please.' He crossed to a partition door with 'Private' on it, knocked, then opened the door and stood aside to let her pass in.

Mr Whittington was seated behind a large desk covered with papers. Tuppence felt her previous judgment confirmed. There was something wrong about Mr Whittington. The combination of his sleek prosperity and his shifty eye was not attractive.

He looked up and nodded.

'So you've turned up all right? That's good. Sit down, will you?'

Tuppence sat down on the chair facing him. She looked particularly small and demure this morning. She sat there meekly with downcast eyes whilst Mr Whittington sorted and rustled amongst his papers. Finally he pushed them away, and leaned over the desk.

'Now, my dear young lady, let us come to business.' His large face broadened into a smile. 'You want work? Well, I have work to offer you. What should you say now to £100 down, and all expenses paid?' Mr Whittington leaned back in his chair, and thrust his thumbs into the arm-holes of his waistcoat.

Tuppence eyed him warily.

'And the nature of the work?' she demanded.

'Nominal – purely nominal. A pleasant trip, that is all.'

'Where to?'

Mr Whittington smiled again.

'Paris.'

'Oh!' said Tuppence thoughtfully. To herself she said: 'Of course, if father heard that he would have a fit! But somehow I don't see Mr Whittington in the rôle of the gay deceiver.'

'Yes,' continued Whittington. 'What could be more delightful? To put the clock back a few years – a very few, I am sure – and re-enter one of those charming *pensionnats de jeunes filles* with which Paris abounds –'

Tuppence interrupted him.

'A *pensionnat*?'

'Exactly. Madame Colombier's in the Avenue de Neuilly.'

Tuppence knew the name well. Nothing could have been more select. She had had several American friends there. She was more than ever puzzled.

'You want me to go to Madame Colombier's? For how long?'

'That depends. Possibly three months.'

'And that is all? There are no other conditions?'

'None whatever. You would, of course, go in the character of my ward, and you would hold no communication with your friends. I should have to request absolute secrecy for the time being. By the way, you are English, are you not?'

'Yes.'

'Yet you speak with a slight American accent?'

'My great pal in hospital was a little American girl. I dare say I picked it up from her. I can soon get out of it again.'

'On the contrary, it might be simpler for you to pass as an American. Details about your past life in England might be more difficult to sustain. Yes, I think that would be decidedly better. Then –'

'One moment, Mr Whittington! You seem to be taking my consent for granted.'

Whittington looked surprised.

'Surely you are not thinking of refusing? I can assure you that Madame Colombier's is a most high-class and orthodox establishment. And the terms are most liberal.'

'Exactly,' said Tuppence. 'That's just it. The terms are almost too liberal, Mr Whittington. I cannot see any way in which I can be worth that amount of money to you.'

'No?' said Whittington softly. 'Well, I will tell you.

I could doubtless obtain someone else for very much less. What I am willing to pay for is a young lady with sufficient intelligence and presence of mind to sustain her part well, and also one who will have sufficient discretion not to ask too many questions.'

Tuppence smiled a little. She felt that Whittington had scored.

'There's another thing. So far there has been no mention of Mr Beresford. Where does he come in?'

'Mr Beresford?'

'My partner,' said Tuppence with dignity. 'You saw us together yesterday.'

'Ah, yes. But I'm afraid we shan't require his services.'

'Then it's off!' Tuppence rose. 'It's both or neither. Sorry – but that's how it is. Good morning, Mr Whittington.'

'Wait a minute. Let us see if something can't be managed. Sit down again, Miss –' He paused interrogatively.

Tuppence's conscience gave her a passing twinge as she remembered the archdeacon. She seized hurriedly on the first name that came into her head.

'Jane Finn,' she said hastily; and then paused open-mouthed at the effect of those two simple words.

All the geniality had faded out of Whittington's face. It was purple with rage, and the veins stood out on the forehead. And behind it all there lurked a sort of incredulous dismay. He leaned forward and hissed savagely:

'So that's your little game, is it?'

Tuppence, though utterly taken aback, nevertheless kept her head. She had not the faintest comprehension of his meaning, but she was naturally quick-witted, and felt it imperative to 'keep her end up' as she phrased it.

Whittington went on:

'Been playing with me, have you, all the time, like a cat and mouse? Knew all the time what I wanted you for, but kept up the comedy. Is that it, eh?' He was cooling down. The red colour was ebbing out of his face. He eyed her keenly. 'Who's been blabbing? Rita?'

Tuppence shook her head. She was doubtful as to how long she could sustain this illusion, but she realized the importance of not dragging an unknown Rita into it.

'No,' she replied with perfect truth. 'Rita knows nothing about me.'

His eyes still bored into her like gimlets.

'How much do you know?' he shot out.

'Very little indeed,' answered Tuppence, and was pleased to note that Whittington's uneasiness was augmented instead of allayed. To have boasted that she knew a lot might have raised doubts in his mind.

'Anyway,' snarled Whittington, 'you knew enough to come in here and plump out that name.'

'It might be my own name,' Tuppence pointed out.

'It's likely, isn't it, that there would be two girls with a name like that?'

'Or I might just have hit upon it by chance,' continued Tuppence, intoxicated with the success of truthfulness.

Mr Whittington brought his fist down upon the desk with a bang.

'Quit fooling! How much do you know? And how much do you want?'

The last five words took Tuppence's fancy mightily, especially after a meagre breakfast and a supper of buns the night before. Her present part was of the adventuress rather than the adventurous order, but she did not deny its possibilities. She sat up and smiled with the air of one who has the situation thoroughly well in hand.

'My dear Mr Whittington,' she said, 'let us by all means lay our cards upon the table. And pray do not be so angry. You heard me say yesterday that I proposed to live by my wits. It seems to me that I have now proved I have some wits to live by! I admit I have knowledge of a certain name, but perhaps my knowledge ends there.'

'Yes – and perhaps it doesn't,' snarled Whittington.

'You insist on misjudging me,' said Tuppence, and sighed gently.

'As I said once before,' said Whittington angrily, 'quit fooling, and come to the point. You can't play the innocent with me. You know a great deal more than you're willing to admit.'

Tuppence paused a moment to admire her own ingenuity, and then said softly:

'I shouldn't like to contradict you, Mr Whittington.'

'So we come to the usual question – how much?'

Tuppence was in a dilemma. So far she had fooled Whittington with complete success, but to mention a palpably impossible sum might awaken his suspicions. An idea flashed across her brain.

'Suppose we say a little something down, and a fuller discussion of the matter later?'

Whittington gave her an ugly glance.

'Blackmail, eh?'

Tuppence smiled sweetly.

'Oh no! Shall we say payment of services in advance?'

Whittington grunted.

'You see,' explained Tuppence sweetly, 'I'm not so very fond of money!'

'You're about the limit, that's what you are,' growled Whittington, with a sort of unwilling admiration. 'You took me in all right. Thought you were quite a meek little kid with just enough brains for my purpose.'

'Life,' moralized Tuppence, 'is full of surprises.'

'All the same,' continued Whittington, 'someone's been talking. You say it isn't Rita. Was it –? Oh, come in?'

The clerk followed his discreet knock into the room, and laid a paper at his master's elbow.

'Telephone message just come for you, sir.'

Whittington snatched it up and read it. A frown gathered on his brow.

'That'll do, Brown. You can go.'

The clerk withdrew, closing the door behind him. Whittington turned to Tuppence.

'Come tomorrow at the same time. I'm busy now. Here's fifty to go on with.'

He rapidly sorted out some notes, and pushed them across the table to Tuppence, then stood up, obviously impatient for her to go.

The girl counted the notes in a business-like manner, secured them in her handbag, and rose.

'Good morning, Mr Whittington,' she said politely. 'At least *au revoir*, I should say.'

'Exactly. *Au revoir*!' Whittington looked almost genial again, a reversion that aroused in Tuppence a faint misgiving. '*Au revoir*, my clever and charming young lady.'

Tuppence sped lightly down the stairs. A wild elation possessed her. A neighbouring clock showed the time to be five minutes to twelve.

'Let's give Tommy a surprise!' murmured Tuppence, and hailed a taxi.

The cab drew up outside the Tube station. Tommy

was just within the entrance. His eyes opened to their fullest extent as he hurried forward to assist Tuppence to alight. She smiled at him affectionately, and remarked in a slightly affected voice:

'Pay the thing, will you, old bean? I've got nothing smaller than a five-pound note!'

Chapter 3
A Setback

The moment was not quite so triumphant as it ought to have been. To begin with, the resources of Tommy's pockets were somewhat limited. In the end the fare was managed, the lady recollecting a plebeian twopence, and the driver, still holding the varied assortment of coins in his hand, was prevailed upon to move on, which he did after one last hoarse demand as to what the gentleman thought he was giving him?

'I think you've given him too much, Tommy,' said Tuppence innocently. 'I fancy he wants to give some of it back.'

It was possibly this remark which induced the driver to move away.

'Well,' said Mr Beresford, at length able to relieve his feelings, 'what the – dickens, did you want to take a taxi for?'

'I was afraid I might be late and keep you waiting,'

said Tuppence gently.

'Afraid – you – might – be – late! Oh, Lord, I give it up!' said Mr Beresford.

'And really and truly,' continued Tuppence, opening her eyes very wide, 'I haven't got anything smaller than a five-pound note.'

'You did that part of it very well, old bean, but all the same the fellow wasn't taken in – not for a moment!'

'No,' said Tuppence thoughtfully, 'he didn't believe it. That's the curious part about speaking the truth. No one does believe it. I found that out this morning. Now let's go to lunch. How about the Savoy?'

Tommy grinned.

'How about the Ritz?'

'On second thoughts, I prefer the Piccadilly. It's nearer. We shan't have to take another taxi. Come along.'

'Is this a new brand of humour? Or is your brain really unhinged?' inquired Tommy.

'Your last supposition is the correct one. I have come into money, and the shock has been too much for me! For that particular form of mental trouble an eminent physician recommends unlimited *hors d'oeuvre*, lobster *à l'américaine*, chicken Newberg, and *pêche Melba*! Let's go and get them!'

'Tuppence, old girl, what has really come over you?'

'Oh, unbelieving one!' Tuppence wrenched open her bag. 'Look here, and here, and here!'

'My dear girl, don't wave pound notes aloft like that!'

'They're not pound notes. They're five times better, and this one's ten times better!'

Tommy groaned.

'I must have been drinking unawares! Am I dreaming, Tuppence, or do I really behold a large quantity of five-pound notes being waved about in a dangerous fashion?'

'Even so, O King! *Now*, will you come and have lunch?'

'I'll come anywhere. But what have you been doing? Holding up a bank?'

'All in good time. What an awful place Piccadilly Circus is. There's a huge bus bearing down on us. It would be too terrible if they killed the five-pound notes!'

'Grill room?' inquired Tommy, as they reached the opposite pavement in safety.

'The other's more expensive,' demurred Tuppence.

'That's mere wicked wanton extravagance. Come on below.'

'Are you sure I can get all the things I want there?'

'That extremely unwholesome menu you were outlining just now? Of course you can – or as much as is good for you, anyway.'

'And now tell me,' said Tommy, unable to restrain his pent-up curiosity any longer, as they sat in state surrounded by the many *hors d'oeuvre* of Tuppence's dreams.

Miss Cowley told him.

'And the curious part of it is,' she ended, 'that I really did invent the name of Jane Finn! I didn't want to give my own because of poor father – in case I should get mixed up in anything shady.'

'Perhaps that's so,' said Tommy slowly. 'But you didn't invent it.'

'What?'

'No. *I* told it to you. Don't you remember, I said yesterday I'd overheard two people talking about a female called Jane Finn? That's what brought the name into your mind so pat.'

'So you did. I remember now. How extraordinary –' Tuppence tailed off into silence. Suddenly she roused herself. 'Tommy!'

'Yes?'

'What were they like, the two men you passed?'

Tommy frowned in an effort at remembrance.

'One was a big fat sort of chap. Clean shaven. I think – and dark.'

'That's him,' cried Tuppence, in an ungrammatical squeal. 'That's Whittington! What was the other man like?'

'I can't remember. I didn't notice him particularly. It was really the outlandish name that caught my attention.'

'And people say that coincidences don't happen!' Tuppence tackled her *pêche Melba* happily.

But Tommy had become serious.

'Look here, Tuppence, old girl, what is this going to lead to?'

'More money,' replied his companion.

'I know that. You've only got one idea in your head. What I mean is, what about the next step? How are you going to keep the game up?'

'Oh!' Tuppence laid down her spoon. 'You're right, Tommy, it is a bit of a poser.'

'After all, you know, you can't bluff him for ever. You're sure to slip up sooner or later. And, anyway, I'm not at all sure that it isn't actionable – blackmail, you know.'

'Nonsense. Blackmail is saying you'll tell unless you are given money. Now, there's nothing I could tell, because I don't really know anything.'

'H'm,' said Tommy doubtfully. 'Well, anyway, what *are* we going to do? Whittington was in a hurry to get rid of you this morning, but next time he'll want to know something more before he parts with his money. He'll want to know how much you know, and where you got your information from, and a lot of other things that you can't cope with. What are you going to do about it?'

Tuppence frowned severely.

'We must think. Order some Turkish coffee, Tommy. Stimulating to the brain. Oh, dear, what a lot I have eaten!'

'You have made rather a hog of yourself! So have I for that matter, but I flatter myself that my choice of dishes was more judicious than yours. Two coffees.' (This was to the waiter.) 'One Turkish, one French.'

Tuppence sipped her coffee with a deeply reflective air, and snubbed Tommy when he spoke to her.

'Be quiet. I'm thinking.'

'Shades of Pelmanism!' said Tommy, and relapsed into silence.

'There!' said Tuppence at last. 'I've got a plan. Obviously what we've got to do is find out more about it all.'

Tommy applauded.

'Don't jeer. We can only find out through Whittington. We must discover where he lives, what he does – sleuth him, in fact! Now I can't do it, because he knows me, but he only saw you for a minute or two in Lyons'. He's not likely to recognize you. After all, one young man is much like another.'

'I repudiate that remark utterly. I'm sure my pleasing features and distinguished appearance would single me out from any crowd.'

'My plan is this,' Tuppence went on calmly. 'I'll go alone tomorrow. I'll put him off again like I did today. It doesn't matter if I don't get any more money at once. Fifty pounds ought to last us a few days.'

'Or even longer!'

'You'll hang about outside. When I come out I shan't speak to you in case he's watching. But I'll take up my stand somewhere near, and when he comes out of the building I'll drop a handkerchief or something, and off you go!'

'Off I go where?'

'Follow him, of course, silly! What do you think of the idea?'

'Sort of thing one reads about in books. I somehow feel that in real life one will feel a bit of an ass standing in the street for hours with nothing to do. People will wonder what I'm up to.'

'Not in the city. Everyone's in such a hurry. Probably no one will even notice you at all.'

'That's the second time you've made that sort of remark. Never mind, I forgive you. Anyway, it will be rather a lark. What are you doing this afternoon?'

'Well,' said Tuppence meditatively. 'I *had* thought of hats! Or perhaps silk stockings! Or perhaps –'

'Hold hard,' admonished Tommy. 'There's a limit to fifty pounds! But let's do dinner and a show tonight at all events.'

'Rather.'

The day passed pleasantly. The evening even more so. Two of the five-pound notes were now irretrievably dead.

They met by arrangement the following morning, and proceeded citywards. Tommy remained on the opposite side of the road while Tuppence plunged into the building.

Tommy strolled slowly down to the end of the street, then back again. Just as he came abreast of the buildings, Tuppence darted across the road.

'Tommy!'

'Yes. What's up?'

'The place is shut. I can't make anyone hear.'

'That's odd.'

'Isn't it? Come up with me, and let's try again.'

Tommy followed her. As they passed the third floor landing a young clerk came out of an office. He hesitated a moment, then addressed himself to Tuppence.

'Were you wanting the Esthonia Glassware?'

'Yes, please.'

'It's closed down. Since yesterday afternoon. Company being wound up, they say. Not that I've ever heard of it myself. But anyway the office is to let.'

'Th – thank you,' faltered Tuppence. 'I suppose you don't know Mr Whittington's address?'

'Afraid I don't. They left rather suddenly.'

'Thank you very much,' said Tommy. 'Come on, Tuppence.'

They descended to the street again where they gazed at one another blankly.

'That's torn it,' said Tommy at length.

'And I never suspected it,' wailed Tuppence.

'Cheer up, old thing, it can't be helped.'

'Can't it, though!' Tuppence's little chin shot out defiantly. 'Do you think this is the end? If so, you're wrong. It's just the beginning!'

'The beginning of what?'

'Of our adventure! Tommy, don't you see, if they are scared enough to run away like this, it shows that there must be a lot in this Jane Finn business! Well, we'll get to the bottom of it. We'll run them down! We'll be sleuths in earnest!'

'Yes, but there's no one left to sleuth.'

'No, that's why we'll have to start all over again. Lend me that bit of pencil. Thanks. Wait a minute – don't interrupt. There!' Tuppence handed back the pencil, and surveyed the piece of paper on which she had written with a satisfied eye.

'What's that?'

'Advertisement.'

'You're not going to put that thing in after all?'

'No, it's a different one.' She handed him the slip of paper.

Tommy read the words on it aloud:

'WANTED, any information respecting Jane Finn. Apply Y. A.'

Chapter 4

Who is Jane Finn?

The next day passed slowly. It was necessary to curtail expenditure. Carefully husbanded, forty pounds will last a long time. Luckily the weather was fine, and 'walking is cheap,' dictated Tuppence. An outlying picture house provided them with recreation for the evening.

The day of disillusionment had been a Wednesday. On Thursday the advertisement had duly appeared. On Friday letters might be expected to arrive at Tommy's rooms.

He had been bound by an honourable promise not to open any such letters if they did arrive, but to repair to the National Gallery, where his colleague would meet him at ten o'clock.

Tuppence was first at the rendezvous. She ensconced herself on a red velvet seat, and gazed at the Turners with unseeing eyes until she saw the familiar figure enter the room.

'Well?'

'Well,' returned Mr Beresford provokingly. 'Which is your favourite picture?'

'Don't be a wretch. Aren't there *any* answers?'

Tommy shook his head with a deep and somewhat overacted melancholy.

'I didn't want to disappoint you, old thing, by telling you right off. It's too bad. Good money wasted.' He sighed. 'Still, there it is. The advertisement has appeared, and – there are only two answers!'

'Tommy, you devil!' almost screamed Tuppence. 'Give them to me. How could you be so mean!'

'Your luggage, Tuppence, your luggage! They're very particular at the National Gallery. Government show, you know. And do remember, as I have pointed out to you before, that as a clergyman's daughter –'

'I ought to be on the stage!' finished Tuppence with a snap.

'That is not what I intended to say. But if you are sure that you have enjoyed to the full the reaction of joy after despair with which I have kindly provided you free of charge, let us get down to our mail, as the saying goes.'

Tuppence snatched the two precious envelopes from him unceremoniously, and scrutinized them carefully.

'Thick paper, this one. It looks rich. We'll keep it to the last and open the other first.'

'Right you are. One, two, three, go!'

Tuppence's little thumb ripped open the envelope, and she extracted the contents.

Dear Sir,

Referring to your advertisement in this morning's paper, I may be able to be of some use to you. Perhaps you could call and see me at the above address at eleven o'clock tomorrow morning.

Yours truly,

A. Carter

'27 Carshalton Terrace,' said Tuppence, referring to the address. 'That's Gloucester Road way. Plenty of time to get there if we Tube.'

'The following,' said Tommy, 'is the plan of campaign. It is my turn to assume the offensive. Ushered into the presence of Mr Carter, he and I wish each other good morning as is customary. He then says: "Please take a seat, Mr – er?" To which I reply promptly and significantly: "Edward Whittington!" whereupon Mr Carter turns purple in the face and gasps out: "How much?" Pocketing the usual fee of fifty pounds, I rejoin you in the road outside, and we proceed to the next address and repeat the performance.'

'Don't be absurd, Tommy. Now for the other letter. Oh, this is from the Ritz!'

'A hundred pounds instead of fifty!'

'I'll read it:

'Dear Sir,

'Re your advertisement, I should be glad if you would call round somewhere about lunch-time.

'Yours truly,

'Julius P. Hersheimmer.'

'Ha!' said Tommy. 'Do I smell a Boche? Or only an American millionaire of unfortunate ancestry? At all events we'll call at lunch-time. It's a good time – frequently leads to free food for two.'

Tuppence nodded assent.

'Now for Carter. We'll have to hurry.'

Carshalton Terrace proved to be an unimpeachable row of what Tuppence called 'ladylike looking houses.' They rang the bell at No. 27, and a neat maid answered the door. She looked so respectable that Tuppence's heart sank. Upon Tommy's request for Mr Carter, she showed them into a small study on the ground floor, where she left them. Hardly a minute elapsed, however, before the door opened, and a tall man with a lean hawklike face and a tired manner entered the room.

'Mr Y.A.?' he said, and smiled. His smile was distinctly attractive. 'Do sit down, both of you.'

They obeyed. He himself took a chair opposite to

Tuppence and smiled at her encouragingly. There was something in the quality of his smile that made the girl's usual readiness desert her.

As he did not seem inclined to open the conversation, Tuppence was forced to begin.

'We wanted to know – that is, would you be so kind as to tell us anything you know about Jane Finn?'

'Jane Finn? Ah!' Mr Carter appeared to reflect. 'Well, the question is, what do you know about her?'

Tuppence drew herself up.

'I don't see that that's got anything to do with it.'

'No? But it has, you know, really it has.' He smiled again in his tired way, and continued reflectively. 'So that brings us down to it again. What do *you* know about Jane Finn?'

'Come now,' he continued, as Tuppence remained silent. 'You must know *something* to have advertised as you did?' He leaned forward a little, his weary voice held a hint of persuasiveness. 'Suppose you tell me . . .'

There was something very magnetic about Mr Carter's personality. Tuppence seemed to shake herself free of it with an effort, as she said:

'We couldn't do that, could we, Tommy?'

But to her surprise, her companion did not back her up. His eyes were fixed on Mr Carter, and his tone when he spoke held an unusual note of deference.

'I dare say the little we know won't be any good to

you, sir. But such as it is, you're welcome to it.'

'Tommy!' cried out Tuppence in surprise.

Mr Carter slewed round in his chair. His eyes asked a question.

Tommy nodded.

'Yes, sir, I recognized you at once. Saw you in France when I was with the Intelligence. As soon as you came into the room, I knew –'

Mr Carter held up his hand.

'No names, please. I'm known as Mr Carter here. It's my cousin's house, by the way. She's willing to lend it to me sometimes when it's a case of working on strictly unofficial lines. Well, now,' – he looked from one to the other – 'who's going to tell me the story?'

'Fire ahead, Tuppence,' directed Tommy. 'It's your yarn.'

'Yes, little lady, out with it.'

And obediently Tuppence did out with it, telling the whole story from the forming of the Young Adventurers, Ltd., downwards.

Mr Carter listened in silence with a resumption of his tired manner. Now and then he passed his hand across his lips as though to hide a smile. When she had finished he nodded gravely.

'Not much. But suggestive. Quite suggestive. If you'll excuse me saying so, you're a curious young couple. I don't know – you might succeed where others have failed . . . I believe in luck, you know – always have . . .'

He paused a moment and then went on.

'Well, how about it? You're out for adventure. How would you like to work for me? All quite unofficial, you know. Expenses paid, and a moderate screw?'

Tuppence gazed at him, her lips parted, her eyes growing wider and wider. 'What should we have to do?' she breathed.

Mr Carter smiled.

'Just go on with what you're doing now. *Find Jane Finn.*'

'Yes, but – who is Jane Finn?'

Mr Carter nodded gravely.

'Yes, you're entitled to know that, I think.'

He leaned back in his chair, crossed his legs, brought the tips of his fingers together, and began in a low monotone:

'Secret diplomacy (which, by the way, is nearly always bad policy!) does not concern you. It will be sufficient to say that in the early days of 1915 a certain document came into being. It was the draft of a secret agreement – treaty – call it what you like. It was drawn up ready for signature by the various representatives, and drawn up in America – at that time a neutral country. It was dispatched to England by a special messenger selected for that purpose, a young fellow called Danvers. It was hoped that the whole affair had been kept so secret that nothing would have leaked out. That kind of hope is usually disappointed. Somebody always talks!

'Danvers sailed for England on the *Lusitania*. He carried the precious papers in an oilskin packet which he wore next his skin. It was on that particular voyage that the *Lusitania* was torpedoed and sunk. Danvers was among the list of those missing. Eventually his body was washed ashore, and identified beyond any possible doubt. But the oilskin packet was missing!

'The question was, had it been taken from him, or had he himself passed it on into another's keeping? There were a few incidents that strengthened the possibility of the latter theory. After the torpedo struck the ship, in the few moments during the launching of the boats, Danvers was seen speaking to a young American girl. No one actually saw him pass anything to her, but he might have done so. It seems to me quite likely that he entrusted the papers to this girl, believing that she, as a woman, had a greater chance of bringing them safely to shore.

'But if so, where was the girl, and what had she done with the papers? By later advice from America it seemed likely that Danvers had been closely shadowed on the way over. Was this girl in league with his enemies? Or had she, in her turn, been shadowed and either tricked or forced into handing over the precious packet?

'We set to work to trace her out. It proved unexpectedly difficult. Her name was Jane Finn, and it duly appeared among the list of the survivors, but the girl herself seemed to have vanished completely. Inquiries into her antecedents did little to help us. She was an orphan, and had been what we should call over here a pupil teacher in a small school out West. Her passport had been made out for Paris, where she was going to join the staff of a hospital. She had offered her services voluntarily, and after some correspondence they had been accepted. Having seen her name in the list of the saved from the *Lusitania*, the staff of the hospital were naturally very surprised at her not arriving to take up her billet, and at not hearing from her in any way.

'Well, every effort was made to trace the young lady – but all in vain. We tracked her across Ireland, but nothing could be heard of her after she set foot in England. No use was made of the draft treaty – as might very easily have been done – and we therefore came to the conclusion that Danvers had, after all, destroyed it. The war entered on another phase, the diplomatic aspect changed accordingly, and the treaty was never redrafted. Rumours as to its existence were emphatically denied. The disappearance of Jane Finn was forgotten and the whole affair was lost in oblivion.'

Mr Carter paused, and Tuppence broke in impatiently:

'But why has it all cropped up again? The war's over.'

A hint of alertness came into Mr Carter's manner.

'Because it seemed that the papers were not destroyed after all, and that they might be resurrected today with a new and deadly significance.'

Tuppence stared. Mr Carter nodded.

'Yes, five years ago, that draft treaty was a weapon in our hands; today it is a weapon against us. It was a gigantic blunder. If its terms were made public, it would mean disaster . . . It might possibly bring about another war – not with Germany this time! That is an extreme possibility, and I do not believe in its likelihood myself, but that document undoubtedly implicates a number of our statesmen whom we cannot afford to have discredited in any way at the present moment. As a party cry for Labour it would be irresistible, and a Labour Government at this juncture would, in my opinion, be a grave disability for British trade, but that is a mere nothing to the *real* danger.'

He paused, and then said quietly:

'You may perhaps have heard or read that there is Bolshevist influence at work behind the present labour unrest?'

Tuppence nodded.

'That is the truth, Bolshevist gold is pouring into this country for the specific purpose of procuring a Revolution. And there is a certain man, a man whose real name is unknown to us, who is working in the dark for his own ends. The Bolshevists are behind the labour unrest – but this man is *behind the Bolshevists*. Who is he? We do not know. He is always spoken of by the unassuming title of "Mr Brown." But one thing is certain, he is the master criminal of this age. He controls a marvellous organization. Most of the peace propaganda during the war was originated and financed by him. His spies are everywhere.'

'A naturalized German?' asked Tommy.

'On the contrary, I have every reason to believe he is an Englishman. He was pro-German, as he would have been pro-Boer. What he seeks to attain we do not know – probably supreme power for himself, of a kind unique in history. We have no clue as to his real personality. It is reported that even his own followers are ignorant of it. Where we have come across his tracks, he has always played a secondary part. Somebody else assumes the chief rôle. But afterwards we always find that there had been some nonentity, a servant or a clerk, who had remained in the background unnoticed, and that the elusive Mr Brown has escaped us once more.'

'Oh!' Tuppence jumped. 'I wonder –'

'Yes?'

'I remember in Mr Whittington's office. The clerk – he called him Brown. You don't think –'

Carter nodded thoughtfully.

'Very likely. A curious point is that the name is usually mentioned. An idiosyncracy of genius. Can you describe him at all?'

'I really didn't notice. He was quite ordinary – just like anyone else.'

Mr Carter sighed in his tired manner.

'That is the invariable description of Mr Brown! Brought a telephone message to the man Whittington, did he? Notice a telephone in the outer office?'

Tuppence thought.

'No, I don't think I did.'

'Exactly. That "message" was Mr Brown's way of giving an order to his subordinate. He overheard the whole conversation of course. Was it after that that Whittington handed you over the money, and told you to come the following day?'

Tuppence nodded.

'Yes, undoubtedly the hand of Mr Brown!' Mr Carter paused. 'Well, there it is, you see what you are pitting yourself against? Possibly the finest criminal brain of the age. I don't quite like it, you know. You're such young things, both of you. I shouldn't like anything to happen to you.'

'It won't,' Tuppence assured him positively.

'I'll look after her, sir,' said Tommy.

'And *I'll* look after you,' retorted Tuppence, resenting the manly assertion.

'Well, then, look after each other,' said Mr Carter, smiling. 'Now let's get back to business. There's something mysterious about this draft treaty that we haven't fathomed yet. We've been threatened with it – in plain and unmistakable terms. The Revolutionary elements as good as declared that it's in their hands, and that they intend to produce it at a given moment. On the other hand, they are clearly at fault about many of its provisions. The Government consider it as mere bluff on their part, and, rightly or wrongly, have stuck to the policy of absolute denial. I'm not so sure. There have been hints, indiscreet allusions, that seem to indicate that the menace is a real one. The position is much as though they had got hold of an incriminating document, but couldn't read it because it was in cipher – but we know that the draft treaty wasn't in cipher – couldn't be in the nature of things – so that won't wash. But there's *something*. Of course, Jane Finn may be dead for all we know – but I don't think so. The curious thing is that *they're trying to get information about the girl from us*.'

'What?'

'Yes. One or two little things have cropped up. And your story, little lady, confirms my idea. They know we're looking for Jane Finn. Well, they'll produce a Jane Finn of their own – say at a *pensionnat* in Paris.' Tuppence gasped, and Mr Carter smiled. 'No one knows in the least what she looks like, so that's all right. She's primed with a trumped-up tale, and her real business is to get as much information as possible out of us. See the idea?'

'Then you think' – Tuppence paused to grasp the supposition fully – 'that it *was* as Jane Finn that they wanted me to go to Paris?'

Mr Carter smiled more wearily than ever.

'I believe in coincidences, you know,' he said.

Chapter 5

Mr Julius P. Hersheimmer

'Well,' said Tuppence, recovering herself, 'it really seems as though it were meant to be.'

Carter nodded.

'I know what you mean. I'm superstitious myself. Luck, and all that sort of thing. Fate seems to have chosen you out to be mixed up in this.'

Tommy indulged in a chuckle.

'My word! I don't wonder Whittington got the wind up when Tuppence plumped out that name! I should have myself. But look here, sir, we're taking up an awful lot of your time. Have you any tips to give us before we clear out?'

'I think not. My experts, working in stereotyped ways, have failed. You will bring imagination and an open mind to the task. Don't be discouraged if that too does not succeed. For one thing there is a likelihood of the pace being forced.'

Tuppence frowned uncomprehendingly.

'When you had that interview with Whittington, they had time before them. I have information that the big *coup* was planned for early in the new year. But the Government is contemplating legislative action which will deal effectually with the strike menace. They'll get wind of it soon, if they haven't already, and it's possible that they may bring things to a head. I hope it will myself. The less time they have to mature their plans the better. I'm just warning you that you haven't much time before you, and that you needn't be cast down if you fail. It's not an easy proposition anyway. That's all.'

Tuppence rose.

'I think we ought to be business-like. What exactly can we count upon you for, Mr Carter?'

Mr Carter's lips twitched slightly, but he replied succinctly:

'Funds within reason, detailed information on any point, and no *official recognition.* I mean that if you get yourselves into trouble with the police, I can't officially help you out of it. You're on your own.'

Tuppence nodded sagely.

'I quite understand that. I'll write out a list of the things I want to know when I've had time to think. Now – about money –'

'Yes, Miss Tuppence. Do you want to say how much?'

'Not exactly. We've got plenty to go on with for the present, but when we want more –'

'It will be waiting for you.'

'Yes, but – I'm sure I don't want to be rude about the Government if you've got anything to do with it, but you know one really has the devil of a time getting anything out of it! And if we have to fill up a blue form and send it in, and then, after three months, they send us a green one, and so on – well, that won't be much use, will it?'

Mr Carter laughed outright.

'Don't worry, Miss Tuppence. You will send a personal demand to me here, and the money, in notes, shall be sent by return of post. As to salary, shall we say at the rate of three hundred a year? And an equal sum for Mr Beresford, of course.'

Tuppence beamed upon him.

'How lovely. You are kind. I do love money! I'll keep beautiful accounts of our expenses – all debit and credit, and the balance on the right side, and a red line drawn sideways with the totals the same at the bottom. I really know how to do it when I think.'

'I'm sure you do. Well, goodbye, and good luck to you both.'

He shook hands with them and in another minute they were descending the steps of 27 Carshalton Terrace with their heads in a whirl.

'Tommy! Tell me at once, who is "Mr Carter"?'

Tommy murmured a name in her ear.

'Oh!' said Tuppence, impressed.

'And I can tell you, old bean, he's rr!'

'Oh!' said Tuppence again. Then she added reflectively: 'I like him, don't you? He looks so awfully tired and bored, and yet you feel that underneath he's just like steel, all keen and flashing. Oh!' She gave a skip. 'Pinch me, Tommy, do pinch me. I can't believe it's real!'

Mr Beresford obliged.

'Ow! That's enough! Yes, we're not dreaming. We've got a job!'

'And what a job! The joint venture has really begun.'

'It's more respectable than I thought it would be,' said Tuppence thoughtfully.

'Luckily I haven't got your craving for crime! What time is it? Let's have lunch – oh!'

The same thought sprang to the minds of each. Tommy voiced it first.

'Julius P. Hersheimmer!'

'We never told Mr Carter about hearing from him.'

'Well, there wasn't much to tell – not till we've seen him. Come on, we'd better take a taxi.'

'Now who's being extravagant?'

'All expenses paid, remember. Hop in.'

'At any rate, we shall make a better effect arriving

this way,' said Tuppence, leaning back luxuriously. 'I'm sure blackmailers never arrive in buses!'

'We've ceased being blackmailers,' Tommy pointed out.

'I'm not sure I have,' said Tuppence darkly.

On inquiring for Mr Hersheimmer, they were at once taken up to his suite. An impatient voice cried 'Come in' in answer to the page-boy's knock, and the lad stood aside to let then pass in.

Mr Julius P. Hersheimmer was a great deal younger than either Tommy or Tuppence had pictured him. The girl put him down as thirty-five. He was of middle height, and squarely built to match his jaw. His face was pugnacious but pleasant. No one could have mistaken him for anything but an American, though he spoke with very little accent.

'Get my note?' Sit down and tell me right away all you know about my cousin.'

'Your cousin?'

'Sure thing. Jane Finn.'

'Is she your cousin?'

'My father and her mother were brother and sister,' explained Mr Hersheimmer meticulously.

'Oh!' cried Tuppence. 'Then you know where she is?'

'No!' Mr Hersheimmer brought down his fist with a bang on the table. 'I'm darned if I do! Don't you?'

'We advertised to receive information, not to give it,' said Tuppence severely.

'I guess I know that. I can read. But I thought maybe it was her back history you were after, and that you'd know where she was now?'

'Well, we wouldn't mind hearing her back history,' said Tuppence guardedly.

But Mr Hersheimmer seemed to grow suddenly suspicious.

'See here,' he declared. 'This isn't Sicily! No demanding ransom or threatening to crop her ears if I refuse. These are the British Isles, so quit the funny business, or I'll just sing out for that beautiful big British policeman I see out there in Piccadilly.'

Tommy hastened to explain.

'We haven't kidnapped your cousin. On the contrary, we're trying to find her. We're employed to do so.'

Mr Hersheimmer leant back in his chair.

'Put me wise,' he said succinctly.

Tommy fell in with this demand in so far as he gave him a guarded version of the disappearance of Jane Finn, and of the possibility of her having been mixed up unawares in 'some political show.' He alluded to Tuppence and himself as 'private inquiry agents' commissioned to find her, and added that they would therefore be glad of any details Mr Hersheimmer could give them.

That gentleman nodded approval.

'I guess that's my right. I was just a mite hasty. But London gets my goat! I only know little old New York. Just trot your questions and I'll answer.'

For the moment this paralysed the Young Adventurers, but Tuppence, recovering herself, plunged boldly into the breach with a reminiscence culled from detective fiction.

'When did you last see the dece – your cousin, I mean?'

'Never seen her,' responded Mr Hersheimmer.

'What?' demanded Tommy astonished.

Hersheimmer turned to him.

'No, sir. As I said before, my father and her mother were brother and sister, just as you might be' – Tommy did not correct this view of their relationship – 'but they didn't always get on together. And when my aunt made up her mind to marry Amos Finn, who was a poor school teacher out West, my father was just mad! Said if he made his pile, as he seemed in a fair way to do, she'd never see a cent of it. Well, the upshot was that Aunt Jane went out West and we never heard from her again.

'The old man *did* pile it up. He went into oil, and he went into steel, and he played a bit with railroads, and I can tell you he made Wall Street sit up!' He paused. 'Then he died – last fall – and I got the dollars. Well, would you believe it, my conscience got busy! Kept knocking me up and saying: What about your Aunt Jane, way out West? It worried me some. You see, I figured it out that Amos Finn would never make good. He wasn't the sort. End of it was, I hired a man to hunt her down. Result, she was dead, and Amos Finn was dead, but they'd left a daughter – Jane – who'd been torpedoed in the *Lusitania* on her way to Paris. She was saved all right, but they didn't seem able to hear of her over this side. I guessed they weren't hustling any, so I thought I'd come along over, and speed things up. I phoned Scotland Yard and the Admiralty first thing. The Admiralty rather choked me off, but Scotland Yard were very civil – said they would make inquiries, even sent a man round this morning to get her photograph. I'm off to Paris tomorrow, just to see what the Prefecture is doing. I guess if I go to and fro hustling them, they ought to get busy!'

The energy of Mr Hersheimmer was tremendous. They bowed before it.

'But say now,' he ended, 'you're not after her for anything? Contempt of court, or something British? A proud-spirited young American girl might find your rules and regulations in wartime rather irksome, and get up against it. If that's the case, and there's such a thing as graft in this country, I'll buy her off.'

Tuppence reassured him.

'That's good. Then we can work together. What about some lunch? Shall we have it up here, or go down to the restaurant?'

Tuppence expressed a preference for the latter, and Julius bowed to her decision.

Oysters had just given place to Sole Colbert when a card was brought to Hersheimmer.

'Inspector Japp, C.I.D. Scotland Yard again. Another man this time. What does he expect I can tell him that I didn't tell the first chap? I hope they haven't lost that photograph. That Western photographer's place was burned down and all his negatives destroyed – this is the only copy in existence. I got it from the principal of the college there.'

An unformulated dread swept over Tuppence.

'You – you don't know the name of the man who came this morning?'

'Yes, I do. No, I don't. Half a second. It was on his card. Oh, I know! Inspector Brown. Quiet unassuming sort of chap.'

Chapter 6

A Plan of Campaign

A veil might with profit be drawn over the events of the next half-hour. Suffice it to say that no such person as 'Inspector Brown' was known to Scotland Yard. The photograph of Jane Finn, which would have been of the utmost value to the police in tracing her, was lost beyond recovery. Once again 'Mr Brown' had triumphed.

The immediate result of this set-back was to effect a *rapprochement* between Julius Hersheimmer and the Young Adventurers. All barriers went down with a crash, and Tommy and Tuppence felt they had known the young American all their lives. They abandoned the discreet reticence of 'private inquiry agents,' and revealed to him the whole history of the joint venture, whereat the young man declared himself 'tickled to death.'

He turned to Tuppence at the close of the narration.

'I've always had a kind of idea that English girls were just a mite moss-grown. Old-fashioned and sweet, you know, but scared to move round without a foot-man or a maiden aunt. I guess I'm a bit behind the times!'

The upshot of these confidential relations was that Tommy and Tuppence took up their abode forthwith at the Ritz, in order, as Tuppence put it, to keep in touch with Jane Finn's only living relation. 'And put like that,' she added confidentially to Tommy, 'nobody could boggle at the expense!'

Nobody did, which was the great thing.

'And now,' said the young lady on the morning after their installation, 'to work!'

Mr Beresford put down the *Daily Mail*, which he was reading, and applauded with somewhat unnecessary vigour. He was politely requested by his colleague not to be an ass.

'Dash it all, Tommy, we've got to *do* something for our money.'

Tommy sighed.

'Yes, I fear even the dear old Government will not support us at the Ritz in idleness for ever.'

'Therefore, as I said before, we must *do* something.'

'Well,' said Tommy, picking up the *Daily Mail* again, '*do* it. I shan't stop you.'

'You see,' continued Tuppence. 'I've been thinking –'

She was interrupted by a fresh bout of applause.

'It's all very well for you to sit there being funny, Tommy. It would do you no harm to do a little brain work too.'

'My union, Tuppence, my union! It does not permit me to work before 11 a.m.'

'Tommy, do you want something thrown at you? It is absolutely essential that we should without delay map out a plan of campaign.'

'Hear, hear!'

'Well, let's do it.'

Tommy laid his paper finally aside. 'There's something of the simplicity of the truly great mind about you, Tuppence. Fire ahead. I'm listening.'

'To begin with,' said Tuppence, 'what have we to go upon?'

'Absolutely nothing,' said Tommy cheerily.

'Wrong!' Tuppence wagged an energetic finger. 'We have two distinct clues.'

'What are they?'

'First clue, we know one of the gang.'

'Whittington?'

'Yes. I'd recognize him anywhere.'

'Hum,' said Tommy doubtfully. 'I don't call that much of a clue. You don't know where to look for him, and it's about a thousand to one against your running against him by accident.'

'I'm not so sure about that,' replied Tuppence thoughtfully. 'I've often noticed that once coincidences start happening they go on happening in the most extraordinary way. I dare say it's some natural law that we haven't found out. Still, as you say, we can't rely on that. But there *are* places in London where simply everyone is bound to turn up sooner or later. Piccadilly Circus, for instance. One of my ideas was to take up my stand there every day with a tray of flags.'

'What about meals?' inquired the practical Tommy.

'How like a man! What does mere food matter?'

'That's all very well. You've just had a thundering good breakfast. No one's got a better appetite than you have, Tuppence, and by tea-time you'd be eating the flags, pins and all. But, honestly, I don't think much of the idea. Whittington mayn't be in London at all.'

'That's true. Anyway, I think clue No. 2 is more promising.'

'Let's hear it.'

'It's nothing much. Only a Christian name – Rita. Whittington mentioned it that day.'

'Are you proposing a third advertisement: Wanted, female crook, answering to the name of Rita?'

'I am not. I propose to reason in a logical manner. That man, Danvers, was shadowed on the way over, wasn't he? And it's more likely to have been a woman than a man –'

'I don't see that at all.'

'I am absolutely certain that it would be a woman, and a good-looking one,' replied Tuppence calmly.

'On these technical points I bow to your decision,' murmured Mr Beresford.

'Now, obviously, this woman, whoever she was, was saved.'

'How do you make that out?'

'If she wasn't, how would they have known Jane Finn had got the papers?'

'Correct. Proceed, O Sherlock!'

'Now there's just a chance, I admit it's only a chance, that this woman may have been "Rita".'

'And if so?'

'If so, we've got to hunt through the survivors of the *Lusitania* till we find her.'

'Then the first thing is to get a list of the survivors.'

'I've got it. I wrote a long list of things I wanted to know, and sent it to Mr Carter. I got his reply this morning, and among other things it encloses the official statement of those saved from the *Lusitania*. How's that for clever little Tuppence?'

'Full marks for industry, zero for modesty. But the great point is, is there a "Rita" on the list?'

'That's just what I don't know,' confessed Tuppence.

'Don't know?'

'Yes, look here.' Together they bent over the list. 'You see, very few Christian names are given. They're nearly all Mrs or Miss.'

Tommy nodded.

'That complicates matters,' he murmured thoughtfully.

Tuppence gave her characteristic 'terrier' shake.

'Well, we've just got to get down to it, that's all. We'll start with the London area. Just note down the addresses of any of the females who live in London or roundabout, while I put on my hat.'

Five minutes later the young couple emerged into Piccadilly, and a few seconds later a taxi was bearing them to The Laurels, Glendower Road, N.7., the residence of Mrs Edgar Keith, whose name figured first in a list of seven reposing in Tommy's pocket-book.

The Laurels was a dilapidated house, standing back from the road with a few grimy bushes to support the fiction of a front garden. Tommy paid off the taxi, and accompanied Tuppence to the front door bell. As she was about to ring it, he arrested her hand.

'What are you going to say?'

'What am I going to say? Why, I shall say – Oh dear, I don't know. It's very awkward.'

'I thought as much,' said Tommy with satisfaction. 'How like a woman! No foresight! Now just stand aside, and see how easily the mere male deals with the situation.' He pressed the bell. Tuppence withdrew to a suitable spot.

A slatternly-looking servant, with an extremely dirty face and a pair of eyes that did not match, answered the door.

Tommy had produced a notebook and pencil.

'Good morning,' he said briskly and cheerfully. 'From the Hampstead Borough Council. The New Voting Register. Mrs Edgar Keith lives here, does she not?'

'Yaas,' said the servant.

'Christian name?' asked Tommy, his pencil poised.

'Missus's? Eleanor Jane.'

'Eleanor,' spelt Tommy. 'Any sons or daughters over twenty-one?'

'Naow.'

'Thank you.' Tommy closed the notebook with a brisk snap. 'Good morning.'

The servant volunteered her first remark:

'I thought perhaps as you'd come about the gas,' she observed cryptically, and shut the door.

Tommy rejoined his accomplice.

'You see, Tuppence,' he observed. 'Child's play to the masculine mind.'

'I don't mind admitting that for once you've scored handsomely. I should never have thought of that.'

'Good wheeze, wasn't it? And we can repeat it *ad lib.*'

Lunch-time found the young couple attacking steak and chips in an obscure hostelry with avidity. They had collected a Gladys Mary and a Marjorie, been baffled by one change of address, and had been forced to listen to a long lecture on universal suffrage from a vivacious American lady whose Christian name had proved to be Sadie.

'Ah!' said Tommy, imbibing a long draught of beer. 'I feel better. Where's the next draw?'

The notebook lay on the table between them. Tuppence picked it up.

'Mrs Vandemeyer,' she read, '20 South Audley Mansions. Miss Wheeler, 43 Clapington Road, Battersea. She's a lady's maid, as far as I remember, so probably won't be there, and, anyway, she's not likely.'

'Then the Mayfair lady is clearly indicated as the first port of call.'

'Tommy, I'm getting discouraged.'

'Buck up, old bean. We always knew it was an outside chance. And, anyway, we're only starting. If we draw a blank in London, there's a fine tour of England, Ireland and Scotland before us.'

'True,' said Tuppence, her flagging spirits reviving. 'And all expenses paid! But, oh, Tommy, I do like things to happen quickly. So far, adventure has succeeded adventure, but this morning has been dull as dull.'

'You must stifle this longing for vulgar sensation, Tuppence. Remember that if Mr Brown is all he is reported to be, it's a wonder that he has not ere now done us to death. That's a good sentence, quite a literary flavour about it.'

'You're really more conceited than I am – with less excuse! Ahem! But it certainly is queer that Mr Brown has not yet wreaked vengeance upon us. (You see, I can do it too.) We pass on our way unscathed.'

'Perhaps he doesn't think us worth bothering about,' suggested the young man simply.

Tuppence received the remark with great disfavour.

'How horrid you are, Tommy. Just as though we didn't count.'

'Sorry, Tuppence. What I meant was that we work like moles in the dark, and that he has no suspicion of our nefarious schemes. Ha ha!'

'Ha ha!' echoed Tuppence approvingly, as she rose.

South Audley Mansions was an imposing looking block of flats just off Park Lane. No. 20 was on the second floor.

Tommy had by this time the glibness born of practice. He rattled off the formula to the elderly woman, looking more like a housekeeper than a servant, who opened the door to him.

'Christian name?'

'Margaret.'

Tommy spelt it, but the other interrupted him.

'No, *g u e*.'

'Oh, Marguerite; French way, I see.' He paused then plunged boldly. 'We had her down as Rita Vandermeyer, but I suppose that's correct?'

'She's mostly called that, sir, but Marguerite's her name.'

'Thank you. That's all. Good morning.'

Hardly able to contain his excitement, Tommy hurried down the stairs. Tuppence was waiting at the angle of the turn.

'You heard?'

'Yes. Oh, *Tommy*!'

Tommy squeezed her arm sympathetically.

'I know, old thing. I feel the same.'

'It's – it's so lovely to think of things – and then for them really to happen!' cried Tuppence enthusiastically.

Her hand was still in Tommy's. They had reached the entrance hall. There were footsteps on the stairs above them, and voices.

Suddenly, to Tommy's complete surprise, Tuppence dragged him into the little space by the side of the lift where the shadow was deepest.

'What the –'

'Hush!'

Two men came down the stairs and passed out

through the entrance. Tuppence's hand closed tighter on Tommy's arm.

'Quick – follow them. I daren't. He might recognize me. I don't know who the other man is, but the bigger of the two was Whittington.'

Chapter 7

The House in Soho

Whittington and his companion were walking at a good pace. Tommy started in pursuit at once, and was in time to see them turn the corner of the street. His vigorous strides soon enabled him to gain upon them, and by the time he, in his turn, reached the corner the distance between them was sensibly lessened. The small Mayfair streets were comparatively deserted, and he judged it wise to content himself with keeping them in sight.

The sport was a new one to him. Though familiar with the technicalities from a course of novel reading, he had never before attempted to 'follow' anyone, and it appeared to him at once that, in actual practice, the proceeding was fraught with difficulties. Supposing, for instance, that they should suddenly hail a taxi? In books, you simply leapt into another, promised the driver a sovereign – or its modern equivalent – and there you were. In actual fact, Tommy foresaw that it was extremely likely there would be no second taxi. Therefore he would have to run. What happened in actual fact to a young man who ran incessantly and persistently through the London streets? In a main road he might hope to create the illusion that he was merely running for a bus. But in these obscure aristocratic byways he could not but feel that an officious policeman might stop him to explain matters.

At this juncture in his thoughts a taxi with flag erect turned the corner of the street ahead. Tommy held his breath. Would they hail it?

He drew a sigh of relief as they allowed it to pass unchallenged. Their course was a zigzag one designed to bring them as quickly as possible to Oxford Street. When at length they turned into it, proceeding in an easterly direction, Tommy slightly increased his pace. Little by little he gained upon them. On the crowded pavement there was little chance of his attracting their notice, and he was anxious if possible to catch a word or two of their conversation. In this he was completely foiled: they spoke low and the din of the traffic drowned their voices effectually.

Just before the Bond Street Tube station they crossed the road, Tommy, unperceived, faithfully at their heels, and entered the big Lyons'. There they went up to the first floor, and sat at a small table in the window. It was late, and the place was thinning out. Tommy took a seat at the table next to them sitting directly behind Whittington in case of recognition. On the other hand, he had a full view of the second man and studied him attentively. He was fair, with a weak, unpleasant face, and Tommy put him down as being either a Russian or a Pole. He was probably about fifty years of age, his shoulders cringed a little as he talked, and his eyes, small and crafty, shifted unceasingly.

Having already lunched heartily, Tommy contented himself with ordering a Welsh rarebit and a cup of coffee. Whittington ordered a substantial lunch for himself and his companion; then, as the waitress withdrew, he moved his chair a little closer to the table and began to talk earnestly in a low voice. The other man joined in. Listen as he would, Tommy could only catch a word here and there; but the gist of it seemed to be some directions or orders which the big man was impressing on his companion, and with which the latter seemed from time to time to disagree. Whittington addressed the other as Boris.

Tommy caught the word 'Ireland' several times, also 'propaganda,' but of Jane Finn there was no mention. Suddenly, in a lull in the clatter of the room, he got one phrase entire. Whittington was speaking. 'Ah, but you don't know Flossie. She's a marvel. An archbishop would swear she was his own mother. She gets the voice right every time, and that's really the principal thing.'

Tommy did not hear Boris's reply, but in response to it Whittington said something that sounded like: 'of course – only in an emergency . . .'

Then he lost the thread again. But presently the phrases became distinct again, whether because the other two had insensibly raised their voices, or because Tommy's ears were getting more attuned, he could not tell. But two words certainly had a most stimulating effect upon the listener. They were uttered by Boris and they were: 'Mr Brown.'

Whittington seemed to remonstrate with him, but he merely laughed.

'Why not, my friend? It is a name most respectable – most common. Did he not choose it for that reason? Ah, I should like to meet him – Mr Brown.'

There was a steely ring in Whittington's voice as he replied:

'Who knows? You may have met him already.'

'Bah!' retorted the other. 'That is children's talk – a fable for the police. Do you know what I say to myself sometimes? That he is a fable invented by the Inner Ring, a bogy to frighten us with. It might be so.'

'And it might not.'

'I wonder . . . or is it indeed true that he is with us and amongst us, unknown to all but a chosen few? If so, he keeps his secret well. And the idea is a good one, yes. We never know. We look at each other –

one of us is Mr Brown – which? He commands – but also he serves. Among us – in the midst of us. And no one knows which he is . . .'

With an effort the Russian shook off the vagary of his fancy. He looked at his watch.

'Yes,' said Whittington. 'We might as well go.'

He called the waitress and asked for his bill. Tommy did likewise, and a few moments later was following the two men down the stairs.

Outside, Whittington hailed a taxi, and directed the driver to Waterloo.

Taxis were plentiful here, and before Whittington's had driven off another was drawing up to the curb in obedience to Tommy's peremptory hand.

'Follow that other taxi,' directed the young man. 'Don't lose it.'

The elderly chauffeur showed no interest. He merely grunted and jerked down his flag. The drive was uneventful. Tommy's taxi came to rest at the departure platform just after Whittington's. Tommy was behind him at the booking-office. He took a first-class single to Bournemouth, Tommy did the same. As he emerged, Boris remarked, glancing up at the clock: 'You are early. You have nearly half an hour.'

Boris's words had aroused a new train of thought in Tommy's mind. Clearly Whittington was making the journey alone, while the other remained in London.

Therefore he was left with a choice as to which he would follow. Obviously, he could not follow both of them unless – Like Boris, he glanced up at the clock, and then to the announcement board of the trains. The Bournemouth train left at 3.30. It was now ten past. Whittington and Boris were walking up and down by the bookstall. He gave one doubtful look at them, then hurried into an adjacent telephone box. He dared not waste time in trying to get hold of Tuppence. In all probability she was still in the neighbourhood of South Audley Mansions. But there remained another ally. He rang up the Ritz and asked for Julius Hersheimmer. There was a click and a buzz. Oh, if only the young American was in his room! There was another click, and then 'Hello' in unmistakable accents came over the wire.

'That you, Hersheimmer? Beresford speaking. I'm at Waterloo. I've followed Whittington and another man here. No time to explain. Whittington's off to Bournemouth by the 3.30. Can you get here by then?'

The reply was reassuring.

'Sure. I'll hustle.'

The telephone rang off. Tommy put back the receiver with a sigh of relief. His opinion of Julius's power of hustling was high. He felt instinctively that the American would arrive in time.

Whittington and Boris were still where he had left

them. If Boris remained to see his friend off, all was well. Then Tommy fingered his pocket thoughtfully. In spite of the carte blanche assured to him, he had not yet acquired the habit of going about with any considerable sum of money on him. The taking of the first-class ticket to Bournemouth had left him with only a few shillings in his pocket. It was to be hoped that Julius would arrive better provided.

In the meantime, the minutes were creeping by: 3.15, 3.20, 3.25, 3.27. Supposing Julius did not get there in time. 3.29. . . . Doors were banging. Tommy felt cold waves of despair pass over him. Then a hand fell on his shoulder.

'Here I am, son. Your British traffic beats description! Put me wise to the crooks right away.'

'That's Whittington – there, getting in now, that big dark man. The other is the foreign chap he's talking to.'

'I'm on to them. Which of the two is my bird?'

Tommy had thought out this question.

'Got any money with you?'

Julius shook his head, and Tommy's face fell.

'I guess I haven't more than three or four hundred dollars with me at the moment,' explained the American.

Tommy gave a faint whoop of relief.

'Oh, Lord, you millionaires! You don't talk the same

language! Climb aboard the lugger. Here's your ticket. Whittington's your man.'

'Me for Whittington!' said Julius darkly. The train was just starting as he swung himself aboard. 'So long, Tommy.' The train slid out of the station.

Tommy drew a deep breath. The man Boris was coming along the platform towards him. Tommy allowed him to pass and then took up the chase once more.

From Waterloo Boris took the Tube as far as Piccadilly Circus. Then he walked up Shaftesbury Avenue, finally turning off into the maze of mean streets round Soho. Tommy followed him at a judicious distance.

They reached at length a small dilapidated square. The houses there had a sinister air in the midst of their dirt and decay. Boris looked round, and Tommy drew back into the shelter of a friendly porch. The place was almost deserted. It was a cul-de-sac, and consequently no traffic passed that way. The stealthy way the other had looked round stimulated Tommy's imagination. From the shelter of the doorway he watched him go up the steps of a particularly evil-looking house and rap sharply, with a peculiar rhythm, on the door. It was opened promptly, he said a word or two to the doorkeeper, then passed inside. The door was shut to again.

It was at this juncture that Tommy lost his head. What he ought to have done, what any sane man would have done, was to remain patiently where he was and wait for his man to come out again. What he did do was entirely foreign to the sober common sense which was, as a rule, his leading characteristic. Something, as he expressed it, seemed to snap in his brain. Without a moment's pause for reflection he, too, went up the steps, and reproduced as far as he was able the peculiar knock.

The door swung open with the same promptness as before. A villainous-faced man with close-cropped hair stood in the doorway.

'Well?' he grunted.

It was at that moment that the full realization of his folly began to come home to Tommy. But he dared not hesitate. He seized at the first words that came into his mind.

'Mr Brown?' he said.

To his surprise the man stood aside.

'Upstairs,' he said, jerking his thumb over his shoulder, 'second door on your left.'

Chapter 8

The Adventures of Tommy

Taken aback though he was by the man's words, Tommy did not hesitate. If audacity had successfully carried him so far, it was to be hoped it would carry him yet farther. He quietly passed into the house and mounted the ramshackle staircase. Everything in the house was filthy beyond words. The grimy paper, of a pattern now indistinguishable, hung in loose festoons from the wall. In every angle was a grey mass of cobweb.

Tommy proceeded leisurely. By the time he reached the bend of the staircase, he had heard the man below disappear into a back room. Clearly no suspicion attached to him as yet. To come to the house and ask for 'Mr Brown' appeared indeed to be a reasonable and natural proceeding.

At the top of the stairs Tommy halted to consider his next move. In front of him ran a narrow passage, with doors opening on either side of it. From the one nearest him on the left came a low murmur of voices. It was this room which he had been directed to enter. But what held his glance fascinated was a small recess immediately on his right, half concealed by a torn velvet curtain. It was directly opposite the left-hand door and, owing to its angle, it also commanded a good view of the upper part of the staircase. As a hiding-place for one or, at a pinch, two men, it was ideal, being about two feet deep and three feet wide. It attracted Tommy mightily. He thought things over in his usual slow and steady way, deciding that the mention of 'Mr Brown' was not a request for an individual, but in all probability a password used by the gang. His lucky use of it had gained him admission. So far he had aroused no suspicion. But he must decide quickly on his next step.

Suppose he were boldly to enter the room on the left of the passage. Would the mere fact of his having been admitted to the house be sufficient? Perhaps a further password would be required, or, at any rate, some proof of identity. The doorkeeper clearly did not know all the members of the gang by sight, but it might be different upstairs. On the whole it seemed to him that luck had served him very well so far, but that there was such a thing as trusting it too far. To enter that room was a colossal risk. He could not hope to sustain his part indefinitely; sooner or later he was almost bound to betray himself, and then he would have thrown away a vital chance in mere foolhardiness.

A repetition of the signal sounded on the door below, and Tommy, his mind made up, slipped quickly into the recess, and cautiously drew the curtain farther across so that it shielded him completely from sight. There were several rents and slits in the ancient material which afforded him a good view. He would watch events, and any time he chose could, after all, join the assembly, modelling his behaviour on that of the new arrival.

The man who came up the staircase with a furtive, soft-footed tread was quite unknown to Tommy. He was obviously of the very dregs of society. The low beetling brows, and the criminal jaw, the bestiality of the whole countenance were new to the young man, though he was of a type that Scotland Yard would have recognized at a glance.

The man passed the recess, breathing heavily as he went. He stopped at the door opposite, and gave a repetition of the signal knock. A voice inside called out something, and the man opened the door and passed in, affording Tommy a momentary glimpse of the room inside. He thought there must be about four or five people seated round a long table that took up most of the space, but his attention was caught and held by a tall man with close-cropped hair and a short, pointed, naval-looking beard, who sat at the head of the table with papers in front of him. As the new-comer entered he glanced up, and with a correct, but curiously precise enunciation, which attracted Tommy's notice, he asked: 'Your number, comrade?'

'Fourteen, guv'nor,' replied the other hoarsely.

'Correct.'

The door shut again.

'If that isn't a Hun, I'm a Dutchman!' said Tommy to himself. 'And running the show darned systematically, too – as they always do. Lucky I didn't roll in. I'd have given the wrong number, and there would have been the deuce to pay. No, this is the place for me. Hullo, here's another knock.'

This visitor proved to be of an entirely different type to the last. Tommy recognized in him an Irish Sinn Feiner. Certainly Mr Brown's organization was a far-reaching concern. The common criminal, the well-bred Irish gentleman, the pale Russian, and the efficient German master of the ceremonies! Truly a strange and sinister gathering! Who was this man who held in his fingers these curiously variegated links of an unknown chain?

In this case, the procedure was exactly the same. The signal knock, the demand for a number, and the reply 'Correct.'

Two knocks followed in quick succession on the door below. The first man was quite unknown to Tommy, who put him down as a city clerk. A quiet, intelligent-looking man, rather shabbily dressed. The second was of the working classes, and his face was vaguely familiar to the young man.

Three minutes later came another, a man of commanding appearance, exquisitely dressed, and evidently well born. His face, again, was not unknown to the watcher, though he could not for the moment put a name to it.

After his arrival there was a long wait. In fact, Tommy concluded that the gathering was now complete, and was just cautiously creeping out from his hiding-place, when another knock sent him scuttling back to cover.

This last-comer came up the stairs so quietly that he was almost abreast of Tommy before the young man had realized his presence.

He was a small man, very pale, with a gentle almost womanish air. The angle of the cheek-bones hinted at his Slavonic ancestry, otherwise there was nothing to indicate his nationality. As he passed the recess, he turned his head slowly. The strange light eyes seemed to burn through the curtain; Tommy could hardly believe that the man did not know he was there and in spite of himself he shivered. He was no more fanciful than the majority of young Englishmen, but he could not rid himself of the impression that some unusually potent force emanated from the man. The creature reminded him of a venomous snake.

A moment later his impression was proved correct. The new-comer knocked on the door as all had done, but his reception was very different. The bearded man rose to his feet, and all the others followed suit. The German came forward and shook hands. His heels clicked together.

'We are honoured,' he said. 'We are greatly honoured. I much feared that it would be impossible.'

The other answered in a low voice that had a kind of hiss in it:

'There were difficulties. It will not be possible again, I fear. But one meeting is essential – to define my policy. I can do nothing without – Mr Brown. He is here?'

The change in the German's air was audible as he replied with slight hesitation:

'We have received a message. It is impossible for him to be present in person.' He stopped, giving a curious impression of having left the sentence unfinished.

A very slow smile overspread the face of the other. He looked round at a circle of uneasy faces.

'Ah! I understand. I have read of his methods. He works in the dark and trusts no one. But, all the same, it is possible that he is among us now . . .' He looked round him again, and again that expression of fear swept over the group. Each man seemed eyeing his neighbour doubtfully.

The Russian tapped his cheek.

'So be it. Let us proceed.'

The German seemed to pull himself together. He indicated the place he had been occupying at the head of the table. The Russian demurred, but the other insisted.

'It is the only possible place,' he said, 'for – Number One. Perhaps Number Fourteen will shut the door!'

In another moment Tommy was once more confronting bare wooden panels, and the voices within had sunk once more to a mere undistinguishable murmur. Tommy became restive. The conversation he had overheard had stimulated his curiosity. He felt that, by hook or by crook, he must hear more.

There was no sound from below, and it did not seem likely that the door-keeper would come upstairs. After listening intently for a minute or two, he put his head round the curtain. The passage was deserted. Tommy bent down and removed his shoes, then, leaving them behind the curtain, he walked gingerly out on his stockinged feet, and kneeling down by the closed door he laid his ear cautiously to the crack. To his intense annoyance he could distinguish little more; just a chance word here and there if a voice was raised, which merely served to whet his curiosity still further.

He eyed the handle of the door tentatively. Could he turn it by degrees so gently and imperceptibly that those in the room would notice nothing? He decided that with great care it could be done. Very slowly, a fraction of an inch at a time, he moved it round, holding his breath in his excessive care. A little more – a little more still – would it never be finished? Ah! at last it would turn no farther.

He stayed so for a minute or two, then drew a deep breath, and pressed it ever so slightly inward. The door did not budge. Tommy was annoyed. If he had to use too much force, it would almost certainly creak. He waited until the voices rose a little, then he tried again. Still nothing happened. He increased the pressure. Had the beastly thing stuck? Finally, in desperation, he pushed with all his might. But the door remained firm, and at last the truth dawned upon him. It was locked or bolted on the inside.

For a moment or two Tommy's indignation got the better of him.

'Well, I'm damned!' he said. 'What a dirty trick!'

As his indignation cooled, he prepared to face the situation. Clearly the first thing to be done was to restore the handle to its original position. If he let it go suddenly, the men inside would be almost certain to notice it, so with the same infinite pains he reversed his former tactics. All went well, and with a sigh of relief the young man rose to his feet. There was a certain bulldog tenacity about Tommy that made him slow to admit defeat. Checkmated for the moment, he was far from abandoning the conflict. He still intended to hear what was going on in the locked room. As one plan had failed, he must hunt about for another.

He looked round him. A little farther along the passage on the left was a second door. He slipped silently along to it. He listened for a moment or two, then tried the handle. It yielded, and he slipped inside.

The room, which was untenanted, was furnished as a bedroom. Like everything else in the house, the furniture was falling to pieces, and the dirt was, if anything, more abundant.

But what interested Tommy was the thing he had hoped to find, a communicating door between the two rooms, up on the left by the window. Carefully closing the door into the passage behind him, he stepped across to the other and examined it closely. The bolt was shot across it. It was very rusty, and had clearly not been used for some time. By gently wriggling it to and fro, Tommy managed to draw it back without making too much noise. Then he repeated his former manœuvres with the handle – this time with complete success. The door swung open – a crack, a mere fraction, but enough for Tommy to hear what went on. There was a velvet *portière* on the inside of this door which prevented him from seeing, but he was able to recognize the voices with a reasonable amount of accuracy.

The Sinn Feiner was speaking. His rich Irish voice was unmistakable:

'That's all very well. But more money is essential. No money – no results!'

Another voice which Tommy rather thought was that of Boris replied:

'Will you guarantee that there *are* results?'

'In a month from now – sooner or later as you wish – I will guarantee you such a reign of terror in Ireland as shall shake the British Empire to its foundations.'

There was a pause, and then came the soft, sibilant accents of Number One:

'Good! You shall have the money. Boris, you will see to that.'

Boris asked a question:

'Via the Irish Americans, and Mr Potter as usual?'

'I guess that'll be all right!' said a new voice, with a transatlantic intonation, 'though I'd like to point out, here and now, that things are getting a mite difficult. There's not the sympathy there was, and a growing disposition to let the Irish settle their own affairs without interference from America.'

Tommy felt that Boris had shrugged his shoulders as he answered:

'Does that matter, since the money only nominally comes from the States?'

'The chief difficulty is the landing of the ammunition,' said the Sinn Feiner. 'The money is conveyed in easily enough – thanks to our colleague here.'

Another voice, which Tommy fancied was that of the tall, commanding-looking man whose face had seemed familiar to him, said:

'Think of the feelings of Belfast if they could hear you!'

'That is settled, then,' said the sibilant tones. 'Now, in the matter of the loan to an English newspaper, you have arranged the details satisfactorily, Boris?'

'I think so.'

'That is good. An official denial from Moscow will be forthcoming if necessary.'

There was a pause, and then the clear voice of the German broke the silence:

'I am directed by – Mr Brown, to place the summaries of the reports from the different unions before you. That of the miners is most satisfactory. We must hold back the railways. There may be trouble with the A.S.E.'

For a long time there was a silence, broken only by the rustle of papers and an occasional word of explanation from the German. Then Tommy heard the light tap-tap of fingers drumming on the table.

'And – the date, my friend?' said Number One.

'The 29th.'

The Russian seemed to consider.

'That is rather soon.'

'I know. But it was settled by the principal Labour leaders, and we cannot seem to interfere too much. They must believe it to be entirely their own show.'

The Russian laughed softly, as though amused.

'Yes, yes,' he said. 'That is true. They must have no inkling that we are using them for our own ends. They are honest men – and that is their value to us. It is curious – but you cannot make a revolution without honest men. The instinct of the populace is infallible.' He paused, and then repeated, as though the phrase pleased him: 'Every revolution has had its honest men. They are soon disposed of afterwards.'

There was a sinister note in his voice.

The German resumed:

'Clymes must go. He is too far-seeing. Number Fourteen will see to that.'

There was a hoarse murmur.

'That's all right, guv'nor.' And then after a moment or two: 'Suppose I'm nabbed.'

'You will have the best legal talent to defend you,' replied the German quietly. 'But in any case you will wear gloves fitted with the finger-prints of a notorious housebreaker. You have little to fear.'

'Oh, I ain't afraid, guv'nor. All for the good of the cause. The streets is going to run with blood, so they say.' He spoke with a grim relish. 'Dreams of it, sometimes, I does. And diamonds and pearls rolling about in the gutter for anyone to pick up!'

Tommy heard a chair shifted. Then Number One spoke:

'Then all is arranged. We are assured of success?'

'I – I think so.' But the German spoke with less than his usual confidence.

Number One's voice held suddenly a dangerous quality:

'What has gone wrong?'

'Nothing; but –'

'But what?'

'The labour leaders. Without them, as you say, we can do nothing. If they do not declare a general strike on the 29th –'

'Why should they not?'

'As you've said, they're honest. And, in spite of everything we've done to discredit the Government in their eyes, I'm not sure that they haven't got a sneaking faith and belief in it.'

'But –'

'I know. They abuse it unceasingly. But, on the whole, public opinion swings to the side of the Government. They will not go against it.'

Again the Russian's fingers drummed on the table.

'To the point, my friend. I was given to understand that there was a certain document in existence which assured success.'

'That is so. If that document were placed before the leaders, the result would be immediate. They would publish it broadcast throughout England, and declare for the revolution without a moment's hesitation. The Government would be broken finally and completely.'

'Then what more do you want?'

'The document itself,' said the German bluntly.

'Ah! It is not in your possession? But you know where it is?'

'No.'

'Does anyone know where it is?'

'One person – perhaps. And we are not sure of that even.'

'Who is this person?'

'A girl.'

Tommy held his breath.

'A girl?' The Russian's voice rose contemptuously. 'And you have not made her speak? In Russia we have ways of making a girl talk.'

'This case is different,' said the German sullenly.

'How – different?' He paused a moment, then went on: 'Where is the girl now?'

'The girl?'

'Yes.'

'She is –'

But Tommy heard no more. A crashing blow descended on his head, and all was darkness.

Chapter 9

Tuppence Enters Domestic Service

When Tommy set forth on the trail of the two men, it took all Tuppence's self-command to refrain from accompanying him. However, she contained herself as best she might, consoled by the reflection that her reasoning had been justified by events. The two men had undoubtedly come from the second floor flat, and that one slender thread of the name 'Rita' had set the Young Adventurers once more upon the track of the abductors of Jane Finn.

The question was what to do next? Tuppence hated letting the grass grow under her feet. Tommy was amply employed, and debarred from joining him in the chase, the girl felt at a loose end. She retraced her steps to the entrance hall of the mansions. It was now tenanted by a small lift-boy, who was polishing brass fittings, and whistling the latest air with a good deal of vigour and a reasonable amount of accuracy.

He glanced round at Tuppence's entry. There was a certain amount of the gamin element in the girl, at all events she invariably got on well with small boys. A sympathetic bond seemed instantly to be formed. She reflected that an ally in the enemy's camp, so to speak, was not to be despised.

'Well, William,' she remarked cheerfully, in the best approved hospital-early-morning style, 'getting a good shine up?'

The boy grinned responsively.

'Albert, miss,' he corrected.

'Albert be it,' said Tuppence. She glanced mysteriously round the hall. The effect was purposely a broad one in case Albert should miss it. She leaned towards the boy and dropped her voice: 'I want a word with you, Albert.'

Albert ceased operations on the fittings and opened his mouth slightly.

'Look! Do you know what this is?' With dramatic gesture she flung back the left side of her coat and exposed a small enamelled badge. It was extremely unlikely that Albert would have any knowledge of it – indeed, it would have been fatal for Tuppence's plans, since the badge in question was the device of a local training corps originated by the archdeacon in the early days of the war. Its presence in Tuppence's coat was due to the fact that she had used it for pinning in some flowers a day or two before. But Tuppence had sharp eyes, and had noted the corner of a threepenny detective novel protruding from Albert's pocket, and the immediate enlargement of his eyes told her that her tactics were good, and that the fish would rise to the bait.

'American Detective Force!' she hissed.

Albert fell for it.

'Lord!' he murmured ecstatically.

Tuppence nodded at him with the air of one who has established a thorough understanding.

'Know who I'm after?' she inquired genially.

Albert, still round-eyed, demanded breathlessly:

'One of the flats?'

Tuppence nodded and jerked a thumb up the stairs.

'No. 20. Calls herself Vandemeyer. Vandemeyer! Ha! ha!'

Albert's hand stole to his pocket.

'A crook?' he queried eagerly.

'A crook? I should say so. Ready Rita they call her in the States.'

'Ready Rita,' repeated Albert deliriously. 'Oh, ain't it just like the pictures!'

It was. Tuppence was a great frequenter of the cinema.

'Annie always said as how she was a bad lot,' continued the boy.

'Who's Annie?' inquired Tuppence idly.

''Ouse-parlourmaid. She's leaving today. Many's the time Annie's said to me: "Mark my words, Albert, I wouldn't wonder if the police was to come after her one of these days." Just like that. But she's a stunner to look at, ain't she?'

'She's some peach,' allowed Tuppence carefully. 'Finds it useful in her lay-out, you bet. Has she been wearing any of the emeralds, by the way?'

'Emeralds? Them's the green stones, isn't they?'

Tuppence nodded.

'That's what we're after her for. You know old man Rysdale?'

Albert shook his head.

'Peter B. Rysdale, the oil king?'

'It seems sort of familiar to me.'

'The sparklers belonged to him. Finest collection of emeralds in the world. Worth a million dollars!'

'Lumme!' came ecstatically from Albert. 'It sounds more like the pictures every minute.'

Tuppence smiled, gratified at the success of her efforts.

'We haven't exactly proved it yet. But we're after her. And' – she produced a long drawn-out wink – 'I guess she won't get away with the goods this time.'

Albert uttered another ejaculation indicative of delight.

'Mind you, sonny, not a word of this,' said Tuppence

suddenly. 'I guess I oughtn't to have put you wise, but in the States we know a real smart lad when we see one.'

'I'll not breathe a word,' protested Albert eagerly. 'Ain't there anything I could do? A bit of shadowing, maybe, or suchlike?'

Tuppence affected to consider, then shook her head.

'Not at the moment, but I'll bear you in mind, son. What's this about the girl you say is leaving?'

'Annie? Regular turn up, they 'ad. As Annie said, servants is someone nowadays, and to be treated accordingly, and, what with her passing the word round, she won't find it so easy to get another.'

'Won't she?' said Tuppence thoughtfully. 'I wonder –'

An idea was dawning in her brain. She thought a minute or two, then tapped Albert on the shoulder.

'See here, son, my brain's got busy. How would it be if you mentioned that you'd got a young cousin, or a friend of yours had, that might suit the place. You get me?'

'I'm there,' said Albert instantly. 'You leave it to me, miss, and I'll fix the whole thing up in two ticks.'

'Some lad!' commented Tuppence, with a nod of approval. 'You might say that the young woman could come right away. You let me know, and if it's O.K. I'll be round tomorrow at eleven o'clock.'

'Where am I to let you know to?'

'Ritz,' replied Tuppence laconically. 'Name of Cowley.'

Albert eyed her enviously.

'It must be a good job, this tec business.'

'It sure is,' drawled Tuppence, 'especially when old man Rysdale backs the bill. But don't fret, son. If this goes well, you shall come in on the ground floor.'

With which promise she took leave of her new ally, and walked briskly away from South Audley Mansions, well pleased with her morning's work.

But there was no time to be lost. She went straight back to the Ritz and wrote a few brief words to Mr Carter. Having dispatched this, and Tommy not having yet returned – which did not surprise her – she started off on a shopping expedition which, with an interval for tea and assorted creamy cakes, occupied her until well after six o'clock, and she returned to the hotel jaded, but satisfied with her purchases. Starting with a cheap clothing store, and passing through one or two second-hand establishments, she had finished the day at a well-known hairdresser's. Now, in the seclusion of her bedroom, she unwrapped that final purchase. Five minutes later she smiled contentedly at her reflection in the glass. With an actress's pencil she had slightly altered the line of her eyebrows, and that, taken in conjunction with the new luxuriant growth of fair hair above, so changed her appearance that she felt confident that even if she came face to face with Whittington he would not recognize her. She would wear elevators in her shoes, and the cap and apron would be an even more valuable disguise. From hospital experience she knew only too well that a nurse out of uniform is frequently unrecognized by her patients.

'Yes,' said Tuppence aloud, nodding at the pert reflection in the glass, 'you'll do.' She then resumed her normal appearance.

Dinner was a solitary meal. Tuppence was rather surprised at Tommy's non-return. Julius, too, was absent – but that to the girl's mind was more easily explained. His 'hustling' activities were not confined to London, and his abrupt appearances and disappearances were fully accepted by the Young Adventurers as part of the day's work. It was quite on the cards that Julius P. Hersheimmer had left for Constantinople at a moment's notice if he fancied that a clue to his cousin's disappearance was to be found there. The energetic young man had succeeded in making the lives of several Scotland Yard men unbearable to them, and the telephone girls at the Admiralty had learned to know and dread the familiar 'Hullo!' He had spent three hours in Paris hustling the Prefecture, and had returned from there imbued with the idea, possibly inspired by a weary French official, that the true clue to the mystery was to be found in Ireland.

'I dare say he's dashed off there now,' thought Tuppence. 'All very well, but this is very dull for *me*! Here I am bursting with news, and absolutely no one to tell it to! Tommy might have wired, or something. I wonder where he is. Anyway, he can't have "lost the trail" as they say. That reminds me –' And Miss Cowley broke off in her meditations, and summoned a small boy.

Ten minutes later the lady was ensconced comfortably on her bed, smoking cigarettes and deep in the perusal of *Barnaby Williams, the Boy Detective*, which, with other threepenny works of lurid fiction, she had sent out to purchase. She felt, and rightly, that before the strain of attempting further intercourse with Albert, it would be as well to fortify herself with a good supply of local colour.

The morning brought a note from Mr Carter:

Dear Miss Tuppence

You have made a splendid start, and I congratulate you. I feel, though, that I should like to point out to you once more the risks you are running, especially if you pursue the course you indicate. Those people are absolutely desperate and incapable of either mercy or pity. I feel that you probably underestimate the danger, and therefore warn you again that I can promise you no protection. You have given us valuable information, and if you choose to withdraw now no one could blame you. At any rate, think the matter over well before you decide.

If, in spite of my warnings, you make up your mind to go through with it, you will find everything arranged. You have lived for two years with Miss Dufferin, the Parsonage, Llanelly, and Mrs Vendemeyer can apply to her for a reference.

May I be permitted a word or two of advice? Stick as near to the truth as possible – it minimizes the danger of 'slips'. I suggest that you should represent yourself to be what you are, a former V.A.D., who has chosen domestic service as a profession. There are many such at the present time. That explains away any incongruities of voice or manner which otherwise might awaken suspicion.

Whichever way you decide, good luck to you.

Your sincere friend,

Mr Carter

Tuppence's spirits rose mercurially. Mr Carter's warnings passed unheeded. The young lady had far too much confidence in herself to pay any heed to them.

With some reluctance she abandoned the interesting part she had sketched out for herself. Although she had no doubts of her own powers to sustain a rôle indefinitely, she had too much common sense not to recognize the force of Mr Carter's arguments.

There was still no word or message from Tommy, but the morning post brought a somewhat dirty post-card with the words: 'It's O.K.' scrawled upon it.

At 10.30 Tuppence surveyed with pride a slightly battered tin trunk containing her new possessions. It was artistically corded. It was with a slight blush that she rang the bell and ordered it to be placed in a taxi. She drove to Paddington, and left the box in the cloak room. She then repaired with a handbag to the fastnesses of the ladies' waiting-room. Ten minutes later a metamorphosed Tuppence walked demurely out of the station and entered a bus.

It was a few minutes past eleven when Tuppence again entered the hall of South Audley Mansions. Albert was on the look-out, attending to his duties in a somewhat desultory fashion. He did not immediately recognize Tuppence. When he did, his admiration was unbounded.

'Blest if I'd have known you! That rig-out's top-hole.'

'Glad you like it, Albert,' replied Tuppence modestly. 'By the way, am I your cousin, or am I not?'

'Your voice too,' cried the delighted boy. 'It's as English as anything! No, I said as a friend of mine knew a young gal. Annie wasn't best pleased. She stopped on till today – to oblige, *she* said, but really it's so as to put you against the place.'

'Nice girl,' said Tuppence.

Albert suspected no irony.

'She's style about her, and keeps her silver a treat – but, my word, ain't she got a temper. Are you going up now, miss? Step inside the lift. No. 20 did you say?' And he winked.

Tuppence quelled him with a stern glance, and stepped inside.

As she rang the bell of No. 20 she was conscious of Albert's eyes descending beneath the level of the floor.

A smart young woman opened the door.

'I've come about the place,' said Tuppence.

'It's a rotten place,' said the young woman without hesitation. 'Regular old cat – always interfering. Accused me of tampering with her letters. Me! The flap was half undone anyway. There's never anything in the waste-paper basket – she burns everything. She's a wrong 'un, that's what she is. Swell clothes but no class. Cook knows something about her – but she won't tell – scared to death of her. And suspicious! She's on to you in a minute if you as much as speak to a fellow. I can tell you –'

'But what more Annie could tell, Tuppence was never destined to learn, for at that moment a clear voice with a peculiarly steely ring to it called:

'Annie!'

The smart young woman jumped as if she had been shot.

'Yes, ma'am?'

'Who are you talking to?'

'It's a young woman about the situation, ma'am.'

'Show her in then. At once.'

'Yes, ma'am.'

Tuppence was ushered into a room on the right of the long passage. A woman was standing by the fire-place. She was no longer in her first youth, and the beauty she undeniably possessed was hardened and coarsened. In her youth she must have been dazzling. Her pale gold hair, owing a slight assistance to art, was coiled low on her neck, her eyes, of a piercing electric blue, seemed to possess a faculty of boring into the very soul of the person she was looking at. Her exquisite figure was enhanced by a wonderful gown of indigo charmeuse. And yet, despite her swaying grace, and the almost ethereal beauty of her face, you felt instinctively the presence of something hard and menacing, a kind of metallic strength that found expression in the tones of her voice and in that gimlet-like quality of her eyes.

For the first time Tuppence felt afraid. She had not feared Whittington, but this woman was different. As if fascinated, she watched the long cruel line of the red curving mouth, and again she felt that sensation of panic pass over her. Her usual self-confidence deserted her. Vaguely she felt that deceiving this woman would be very different to deceiving Whittington. Mr Carter's warning recurred to her mind. Here, indeed, she might expect no mercy.

Fighting down that instinct of panic which urged her to turn tail and run without further delay, Tuppence returned the lady's gaze firmly and respectfully.

As though that first scrutiny had been satisfactory, Mrs Vandemeyer motioned to a chair.

'You can sit down. How did you hear I wanted a house-parlourmaid?'

'Through a friend who knows the lift boy here. He thought the place might suit me.'

Again that basilisk glance seemed to pierce her through.

'You speak like an educated girl?'

Glibly enough, Tuppence ran through her imaginary career on the lines suggested by Mr Carter. It seemed to her, as she did so, that the tension of Mrs Vandemeyer's attitude relaxed.

'I see,' she remarked at length. 'Is there anyone I can write to for a reference?'

'I lived last with a Miss Dufferin, The Parsonage, Llanelly. I was with her two years.'

'And then you thought you would get more money by coming to London, I suppose? Well, it doesn't matter to me. I will give you £50-£60 – whatever you want. You can come at once?'

'Yes, ma'am. Today, if you like. My box is at Paddington.'

'Go and fetch it by taxi, then. It's an easy place. I am out a good deal. By the way, what's your name?'

'Prudence Cooper, ma'am.'

'Very well, Prudence. Go away and fetch your box. I shall be out to lunch. The cook will show you where everything is.'

'Thank you, ma'am.'

Tuppence withdrew. The smart Annie was not in evidence. In the hall below a magnificent hall porter had relegated Albert to the background. Tuppence did not even glance at him as she passed meekly out.

The adventure had begun, but she felt less elated than she had done earlier in the morning. It crossed her mind that if the unknown Jane Finn had fallen into the hands of Mrs Vandemeyer, it was likely to have gone hard with her.

Chapter 10

Enter Sir James Peel Edgerton

Tuppence betrayed no awkwardness in her new duties. The daughters of the archdeacon were well grounded in household tasks. They were also experts in training a 'raw girl,' the inevitable result being that the raw girl, once trained, departed somewhere where her newly-acquired knowledge commanded a more substantial remuneration than the archdeacon's meagre purse allowed.

Tuppence had therefore very little fear of proving inefficient. Mrs Vandemeyer's cook puzzled her. She evidently went in deadly terror of her mistress. The girl thought it probable that the other woman had some hold over her. For the rest, she cooked like a *chef*, as Tuppence had an opportunity of judging that evening. Mrs Vandemeyer was expecting a guest to dinner, and Tuppence accordingly laid the beautifully polished table for two. She was a little exercised in her own mind as to this visitor. It was highly possible that it might prove to be Whittington. Although she felt fairly confident that he would not recognize her, yet she would have been better pleased had the guest proved to be a total stranger. However, there was nothing for it but to hope for the best.

At a few minutes past eight the front door bell rang, and Tuppence went to answer it with some inward trepidation. She was relieved to see that the visitor was the second of the two men whom Tommy had taken upon himself to follow.

He gave his name as Count Stepanov. Tuppence announced him, and Mrs Vandemeyer rose from her seat on a low divan with a quick murmur of pleasure.

'It is delightful to see you, Boris Ivanovitch,' she said.

'And you, madame!' He bowed low over her hand.

Tuppence returned to the kitchen.

'Count Stepanov, or some such,' she remarked, and affecting a frank and unvarnished curiosity: 'Who's he?'

'A Russian gentleman, I believe.'

'Come here much?'

'Once in a while. What d'you want to know for?'

'Fancied he might be sweet on the missus, that's all,' explained the girl, adding with an appearance of sulkiness: 'How you do take one up!'

'I'm not quite easy in my mind about the *soufflé*,' explained the other.

'You know something,' thought Tuppence to herself, but aloud she only said: 'Going to dish up now? Right-o.'

Whilst waiting at table, Tuppence listened closely to all that was said. She remembered that this was one of the men Tommy was shadowing when she had last seen him. Already, although she would hardly admit it, she was becoming uneasy about her partner. Where was he? Why had no word of any kind come from him? She had arranged before leaving the Ritz to have all letters or messages sent on at once by special messenger to a small stationer's shop near at hand where Albert was to call in frequently. True, it was only yesterday morning that she had parted from Tommy, and she told herself that any anxiety on his behalf would be absurd. Still, it was strange he had sent no word of any kind.

But, listen as she might, the conversation presented no clue. Boris and Mrs Vandemeyer talked on purely indifferent subjects: plays they had seen, new dances, and the latest society gossip. After dinner they repaired to the small boudoir where Mrs Vandemeyer, stretched on the divan, looked more wickedly beautiful than ever. Tuppence brought in the coffee and liqueurs and unwillingly retired. As she did so, she heard Boris say:

'New, isn't she?'

'She came in today. The other was a fiend. This girl seems all right. She waits well.'

Tuppence lingered a moment longer by the door which she had carefully neglected to close, and heard him say:

'Quite safe, I suppose?'

'Really, Boris, you are absurdly suspicious. I believe she's the cousin of the hall porter, or something of the kind. And nobody even dreams that I have any connexion with our – mutual friend, Mr Brown.'

'For Heaven's sake, be careful, Rita. That door isn't shut.'

'Well, shut it then,' laughed the woman.

Tuppence removed herself speedily.

She dared not absent herself longer from the back premises, but she cleared away and washed up with a breathless speed acquired in hospital. Then she slipped quietly back to the boudoir door. The cook, more leisurely, was still busy in the kitchen and, if she missed the other, would only suppose her to be turning down the beds.

Alas! The conversation inside was being carried on in too low a tone to permit of her hearing anything of it. She dared not reopen the door, however gently. Mrs Vandemeyer was sitting almost facing it, and Tuppence respected her mistress's lynx-eyed powers of observation.

Nevertheless, she felt she would give a good deal to overhear what was going on. Possibly, if anything unforeseen had happened, she might get news of Tommy. For some moments she reflected desperately, then her face brightened. She went quickly along the passage to Mrs Vandemeyer's bedroom, which had long French windows leading on to a balcony that ran the length of the flat. Slipping quickly through the window, Tuppence crept noiselessly along till she reached the boudoir window. As she had thought it stood a little ajar, and the voices within were plainly audible.

Tuppence listened attentively, but there was no mention of anything that could be twisted to apply to Tommy. Mrs Vandemeyer and the Russian seemed to be at variance over some matter, and finally the latter exclaimed bitterly:

'With your persistent recklessness, you will end by ruining us!'

'Bah!' laughed the woman. 'Notoriety of the right kind is the best way of disarming suspicion. You will realize that one of these days – perhaps sooner than you think!'

'In the meantime, you are going about everywhere with Peel Edgerton. Not only is he, perhaps, the most celebrated K. C. in England, but his special hobby is criminology! It is madness!'

'I know that his eloquence has saved untold men

from the gallows,' said Mrs Vandemeyer calmly. 'What of it? I may need his assistance in that line myself some day. If so, how fortunate to have such a friend at court – or perhaps it would be more to the point to say *in* court.'

Boris got up and began striding up and down. He was very excited.

'You are a clever woman, Rita; but you are also a fool! Be guided by me, and give up Peel Edgerton.'

Mrs Vandemeyer shook her head gently.

'I think not.'

'You refuse?' There was an ugly ring in the Russian's voice.

'I do.'

'Then, by Heaven,' snarled the Russian, 'we will see –'

But Mrs Vandemeyer also rose to her feet, her eyes flashing.

'You forget, Boris,' she said. 'I am accountable to no one. I take my orders only from – Mr Brown.'

The other threw up his hands in despair.

'You are impossible,' he muttered. 'Impossible! Already it may be too late. They say Peel Edgerton can *smell* a criminal! How do we know what is at the bottom of his sudden interest in you? Perhaps even now his suspicions are aroused. He guesses –'

Mrs Vandemeyer eyed him scornfully.

'Reassure yourself, my dear Boris. He suspects nothing. With less than your usual chivalry, you seem to forget that I am commonly accounted a beautiful woman. I assure you that is all that interests Peel Edgerton.'

Boris shook his head doubtfully.

'He has studied crime as no other man in this kingdom has studied it. Do you fancy that you can deceive him?'

Mrs Vandemeyer's eyes narrowed.

'If he is all that you say – it would amuse me to try!'

'Good heavens, Rita –'

'Besides,' added Mrs Vandemeyer, 'he is extremely rich. I am not one who despises money. The "sinews of war" you know, Boris!'

'Money – money! That is always the danger with you, Rita. I believe you would sell your soul for money. I believe –' He paused, then in a low, sinister voice he said slowly: 'Sometimes I believe that you would sell – *us*!'

Mrs Vandemeyer smiled and shrugged her shoulders.

'The price, at any rate, would have to be enormous,' she said lightly. 'It would be beyond the power of anyone but a millionaire to pay.'

'Ah!' snarled the Russian. 'You see, I was right.'

'My dear Boris, can you not take a joke?'

'Was it a joke?'

'Of course.'

'Then all I can say is that your ideas of humour are peculiar, my dear Rita.'

Mrs Vandemeyer smiled.

'Let us not quarrel, Boris. Touch the bell. We will have some drinks.'

Tuppence beat a hasty retreat. She paused a moment to survey herself in Mrs Vandemeyer's long glass, and be sure that nothing was amiss with her appearance. Then she answered the bell demurely.

The conversation that she had overheard, although interesting in that it proved beyond doubt the complicity of both Rita and Boris, threw very little light on the present preoccupations. The name of Jane Finn had not even been mentioned.

The following morning a few brief words with Albert informed her that nothing was waiting for her at the stationer's. It seemed incredible that Tommy, if all was well with him, should not send any word to her. A cold hand seemed to close round her heart . . . Supposing . . . She choked her fears down bravely. It was no good worrying. But she leapt at a chance offered her by Mrs Vandemeyer.

'What day do you usually go out, Prudence?'

'Friday's my usual day, ma'am.'

Mrs Vandemeyer lifted her eyebrows.

'And today is Friday! But I suppose you hardly wish

to go out today, as you only came yesterday.'

'I was thinking of asking you if I might, ma'am.'

Mrs Vandemeyer looked at her a minute longer, and then smiled.

'I wish Count Stepanov could hear you. He made a suggestion about you last night.' Her smile broadened, cat-like. 'Your request is very – typical. I am satisfied. You do not understand all this – but you can go out today. It makes no difference to me, as I shall not be dining at home.'

'Thank you, ma'am.'

Tuppence felt a sensation of relief once she was out of the other's presence. Once again she admitted to herself that she was afraid, horribly afraid, of the beautiful woman with the cruel eyes.

In the midst of a final desultory polishing of her silver, Tuppence was disturbed by the ringing of the front door bell, and went to answer it. This time the visitor was neither Whittington nor Boris, but a man of striking appearance.

Just a shade over average height, he nevertheless conveyed the impression of a big man. His face, clean-shaven and exquisitely mobile, was stamped with an expression of power and force far beyond the ordinary. Magnetism seemed to radiate from him.

Tuppence was undecided for the moment whether to put him down as an actor or a lawyer, but her doubts were soon solved as he gave her his name: Sir James Peel Edgerton.

She looked at him with renewed interest. This, then, was the famous K. C. whose name was familiar all over England. She had heard it said that he might one day be Prime Minister. He was known to have refused office in the interests of his profession, preferring to remain a simple Member for a Scotch constituency.

Tuppence went back to her pantry thoughtfully. The great man had impressed her. She understood Boris's agitation. Peel Edgerton would not be an easy man to deceive.

In about a quarter of an hour the bell rang, and Tuppence repaired to the hall to show the visitor out. He had given her a piercing glance before. Now, as she handed him his hat and stick, she was conscious of his eyes raking her through. As she opened the door and stood aside to let him pass out, he stopped in the doorway.

'Not been doing this long, eh?'

Tuppence raised her eyes, astonished. She read in his glance kindliness, and something else more difficult to fathom.

He nodded as though she had answered.

'V.A.D. and hard up, I suppose?'

'Did Mrs Vandemeyer tell you that?' asked Tuppence suspiciously.

'No, child. The look of you told me. Good place here?'

'Very good, thank you, sir.'

'Ah, but there are plenty of good places nowadays. And a change does no harm sometimes.'

'Do you mean –?' began Tuppence.

But Sir James was already on the topmost stair. He looked back with his kindly, shrewd glance.

'Just a hint,' he said. 'That's all.'

Tuppence went back to the pantry more thoughtful than ever.

Chapter 11

Julius Tells a Story

Dressed appropriately, Tuppence duly sallied forth for her 'afternoon out'. Albert was in temporary abeyance, but Tuppence went herself to the stationer's to make quite sure that nothing had come for her. Satisfied on this point, she made her way to the Ritz. On inquiry she learnt that Tommy had not yet returned. It was the answer she had expected, but it was another nail in the coffin of her hopes. She resolved to appeal to Mr Carter, telling him when and where Tommy had started on his quest, and asking him to do something to trace him. The prospect of his aid revived her mercurial spirits, and she next inquired for Julius Hersheimmer. The reply she got was to the effect that he had returned about half an hour ago, but had gone out immediately.

Tuppence's spirits revived still more. It would be something to see Julius. Perhaps he could devise some plan for finding out what had become of Tommy. She wrote her note to Mr Carter in Julius's sitting-room, and was just addressing the envelope when the door burst open.

'What the hell –' began Julius, but checked himself abruptly. 'I beg your pardon, Miss Tuppence. Those fools down at the office would have it that Beresford wasn't here any longer – hadn't been here since Wednesday. Is that so?'

Tuppence nodded.

'You don't know where he is?' she asked faintly.

'I? How should I know? I haven't had one darned word from him, though I wired him yesterday morning.'

'I expect your wire's at the office unopened.'

'But where is he?'

'I don't know. I hoped you might.'

'I tell you I haven't had one darned word from him since we parted at the depot on Wednesday.'

'What depot?'

'Waterloo. Your London and South Western road.'

'Waterloo?' frowned Tuppence.

'Why, yes. Didn't he tell you?'

'I haven't seen him either,' replied Tuppence impatiently. 'Go on about Waterloo. What were you doing there?'

'He gave me a call. Over the phone. Told me to get a move on, and hustle. Said he was trailing two crooks.'

'Oh!' said Tuppence, her eyes opening. 'I see. Go on.'

'I hurried along right away. Beresford was there. He pointed out the crooks. The big one was mine, the guy you bluffed. Tommy shoved a ticket into my hand and told me to get aboard the cars. He was going to sleuth the other crook.' Julius paused. 'I thought for sure you'd know all this.'

'Julius,' said Tuppence firmly, 'stop walking up and down. It makes me giddy. Sit down in that arm-chair, and tell me the whole story with as few fancy turns of speech as possible.'

Mr Hersheimmer obeyed.

'Sure,' he said. 'Where shall I begin?'

'Where you left off. At Waterloo.'

'Well,' began Julius, 'I got into one of your dear old-fashioned first-class British compartments. The train was just off. First thing I knew a guard came along and informed me mightily politely that I wasn't in a smoking-carriage. I handed him out half a dollar, and that settled that. I did a bit of prospecting along the corridor to the next coach. Whittington was there right enough. When I saw the skunk, with his big sleek fat face, and thought of poor little Jane in his clutches, I felt real mad that I hadn't got a gun with me. I'd have tickled him up some.

'We got to Bournemouth all right. Whittington took

a cab and gave the name of an hotel. I did likewise, and we drove up within three minutes of each other. He hired a room, and I hired one too. So far it was all plain sailing. He hadn't the remotest notion that anyone was on to him. Well, he just sat around in the hotel lounge, reading the papers and so on, till it was time for dinner. He didn't hurry any over that either.

'I began to think that there was nothing doing, that he'd just come on the trip for his health, but I remembered that he hadn't changed for dinner, though it was by way of being a slap-up hotel, so it seemed likely enough that he'd be going out on his real business afterwards.

'Sure enough, about nine o'clock, so he did. Took a car across the town – mighty pretty place by the way, I guess I'll take Jane there for a spell when I find her – and then paid it off and struck out along those pine-woods on the top of the cliff. I was there too, you understand. We walked, maybe, for half an hour. There's a lot of villas all the way along, but by degrees they seemed to get more and more thinned out, and in the end we got to one that seemed the last of the bunch. Big house it was, with a lot of piny grounds around it.

'It was a pretty black night, and the carriage drive up to the house was dark as pitch. I could hear him ahead, though I couldn't see him. I had to walk carefully in case he might get on to it that he was being followed. I turned a curve and I was just in time to see him ring the bell and get admitted to the house. I just stopped where I was. It was beginning to rain, and I was soon pretty near soaked through. Also, it was almighty cold.

'Whittington didn't come out again, and by and by I got kind of restive, and began to mooch around. All the ground floor windows were shuttered tight, but upstairs, on the first floor (it was a two-storied house) I noticed a window with a light burning and the curtains not drawn.

'Now, just opposite to that window, there was a tree growing. It was about thirty foot away from the house, maybe, and I sort of got it into my head that, if I climbed up that tree, I'd very likely be able to see into that room. Of course, I knew there was no reason why Whittington should be in that room rather than in any other – less reason, in fact, for the betting would be on his being in one of the reception-rooms downstairs. But I guess I'd got the hump from standing so long in the rain, and anything seemed better than going on doing nothing. So I started up.

'It wasn't so easy, by a long chalk! The rain had made the boughs mighty slippery, and it was all I could do to keep a foothold, but bit by bit I managed it, until at last there I was level with the window.

'But then I was disappointed. I was too far to the

left. I could only see sideways into the room. A bit of curtain, and a yard of wall-paper was all I could command. Well, that wasn't any manner of good to me, but just as I was going to give it up, and climb down ignominiously, someone inside moved and threw his shadow on my little bit of wall – and, by gum, it was Whittington!

'After that, my blood was up. I'd just *got* to get a look into that room. It was up to me to figure out how. I noticed that there was a long branch running out from the tree in the right direction. If I could only swarm about half-way along it, the proposition would be solved. But it was mighty uncertain whether it would bear my weight. I decided I'd just got to risk that, and I started. Very cautiously, inch by inch, I crawled along. The bough creaked and swayed in a nasty fashion, and it didn't do to think of the drop below, but at last I got safely to where I wanted to be.

'The room was medium-sized, furnished in a kind of bare hygienic way. There was a table with a lamp on it in the middle of the room, and sitting at that table, facing towards me, was Whittington right enough. He was talking to a woman dressed as a hospital nurse. She was sitting with her back to me, so I couldn't see her face. Although the blinds were up, the window itself was shut, so I couldn't catch a word of what they said. Whittington seemed to be doing all the talking, and the nurse just listened. Now and then she nodded, and sometimes she'd shake her head, as though she were answering questions. He seemed very emphatic – once or twice he beat with his fist on the table. The rain had stopped now, and the sky was clearing in that sudden way it does.

'Presently, he seemed to get to the end of what he was saying. He got up, and so did she. He looked towards the window and asked something – I guess it was whether it was raining. Anyway, she came right across and looked out. Just then the moon came out from behind the clouds. I was scared the woman would catch sight of me, for I was full in the moonlight. I tried to move back a bit. The jerk I gave was too much for that rotten old branch. With an almighty crash, down it came, and Julius P. Hersheimmer with it!'

'Oh, Julius,' breathed Tuppence, 'how exciting! Go on.'

'Well, luckily for me, I pitched down into a good soft bed of earth – but it put me out of action for the time, sure enough. The next thing I knew, I was lying in bed with a hospital nurse (not Whittington's one) on one side of me, and a little black-bearded man with gold glasses, and medical man written all over him, on the other. He rubbed his hands together, and raised his eyebrows as I stared at him. "Ah!" he said. "So our young friend is coming round again. Capital. Capital."

'I did the usual stunt. Said: "What's happened?" And "Where am I?" But I knew the answer to the last well enough. There's no moss growing on my brain. "I think that'll do for the present, sister," said the little man, and the nurse left the room in a sort of brisk well-trained way. But I caught her handing me out a look of deep curiosity as she passed through the door.

'That look of hers gave me an idea. "Now then, doc," I said, and tried to sit up in bed, but my right foot gave me a nasty twinge as I did so. "A slight sprain," explained the doctor. "Nothing serious. You'll be about again in a couple of days."

'I noticed you walked lame,' interpolated Tuppence.

Julius nodded, and continued:

'"How did it happen?" I asked again. He replied dryly. "You fell, with a considerable portion of one of my trees, into one of my newly-planted flower-beds."

'I liked the man. He seemed to have a sense of humour. I felt sure that he, at least, was plumb straight. "Sure, doc," I said, "I'm sorry about the tree, and I guess the new bulbs will be on me. But perhaps you'd like to know what I was doing in your garden?" "I think the facts do call for an explanation," he replied. "Well, to begin with, I wasn't after the spoons."

'He smiled. "My first theory. But I soon altered my mind. By the way, you are an American, are you not?" I told him my name. "And you?" "I am Dr Hall, and this, as you doubtless know, is my private nursing home."

'I didn't know, but wasn't going to put him wise. I was just thankful for the information. I liked the man, and I felt he was straight, but I wasn't going to give him the whole story. For one thing he probably wouldn't have believed it.

'I made up my mind in a flash. "Why, doctor," I said, "I guess I feel an almighty fool, but I owe it to you to let you know that it wasn't the Bill Sikes business I was up to." Then I went on and mumbled out something about a girl. I trotted out the stern guardian business, and a nervous breakdown, and finally explained that I had fancied I recognized her among the patients at the home, hence my nocturnal adventures.

'I guess it was just the kind of story he was expecting. "Quite a romance," he said genially, when I'd finished. "Now, doc," I went on, "will you be frank with me? Have you here now, or have you had here at any time, a young girl called Jane Finn?" He repeated the name thoughtfully. "Jane Finn?" he said. "No."

'I was chagrined, and I guess I showed it. "You are sure?" "Quite sure, Mr Hersheimmer. It is an uncommon name, and I should not have been likely to forget it."

'Well, that was flat. It laid me out for a space. I'd kind of hoped my search was at an end. "That's that," I said at last. "Now, there's another matter. When I was hugging that darned branch I thought I recognized an old friend of mine talking to one of your nurses." I purposely didn't mention any name because, of course, Whittington might be calling himself something quite different down here, but the doctor answered at once. "Mr Whittington, perhaps?" "That's the fellow," I replied. "What's he doing down here? Don't tell me *his* nerves are out of order?"

'Dr Hall laughed. "No. He came down to see one of my nurses, Nurse Edith, who is a niece of his." "Why, fancy that!" I exclaimed, "Is he still here?" "No, he went back to town almost immediately." "What a pity!" I ejaculated. "But perhaps I could speak to his niece – Nurse Edith, did you say her name was?"

'But the doctor shook his head. "I'm afraid that, too, is impossible. Nurse Edith left with a patient tonight also." "I seem to be real unlucky," I remarked. "Have you Mr Whittington's address in town? I guess I'd like to look him up when I get back." "I don't know his address. I can write to Nurse Edith for it if you like." I thanked him. "Don't say who it is wants it. I'd like to give him a little surprise."

'That was about all I could do for the moment. Of course, if the girl was really Whittington's niece, she might be too cute to fall into the trap, but it was worth trying. Next thing I did was to write out a wire to Beresford saying where I was, and that I was laid up with a sprained foot, and telling him to come down if he wasn't busy. I had to be guarded in what I said. However, I didn't hear from him, and my foot soon got all right. It was only ricked, not really sprained, so today I said goodbye to the little doctor chap, asked him to send me word if he heard from Nurse Edith, and came right away back to town. Say, Miss Tuppence, you're looking mighty pale?'

'It's Tommy,' said Tuppence. 'What can have happened to him?'

'Buck up, I guess he's all right really. Why shouldn't he be? See here, it was a foreign-looking guy he went off after. Maybe they've gone abroad – to Poland, or something like that?'

Tuppence shook her head.

'He couldn't without passports and things. Besides I've seen that man, Boris Something, since. He dined with Mrs Vandemeyer last night.'

'Mrs Who?'

'I forgot. Of course you don't know all that.'

'I'm listening,' said Julius, and gave vent to his favourite expression. 'Put me wise.'

Tuppence thereupon related the events of the last two days. Julius's astonishment and admiration were unbounded.

'Bully for you! Fancy you a menial. It just tickles me to death!' Then he added seriously: 'But say now, I don't like it, Miss Tuppence, I sure don't. You're just as plucky as they make 'em, but I wish you'd keep right out of this. These crooks we're up against would as soon croak a girl as a man any day.'

'Do you think I'm afraid?' said Tuppence indignantly, valiantly repressing memories of the steely glitter in Mrs Vandemeyer's eyes.

'I said before you were darned plucky. But that doesn't alter facts.'

'Oh, bother *me*!' said Tuppence impatiently. 'Let's think about what can have happened to Tommy. I've written to Mr Carter about it,' she added, and told him the gist of her letter.

Julius nodded gravely.

'I guess that's good as far as it goes. But it's for us to get busy and do something.'

'What can we do?' asked Tuppence, her spirits rising.

'I guess we'd better get on the track of Boris. You say he's been to your place. Is he likely to come again?'

'He might. I really don't know.'

'I see. Well, I guess I'd better buy a car, a slap-up one, dress as a chauffeur and hang about outside. Then if Boris comes, you could make some kind of signal, and I'd trail him. How's that?'

'Splendid, but he mightn't come for weeks.'

'We'll have to chance that. I'm glad you like the plan.' He rose.

'Where are you going?'

'To buy the car, of course,' replied Julius, surprised. 'What make do you like? I guess you'll do some riding in it before we've finished.'

'Oh,' said Tuppence faintly. 'I *like* Rolls-Royces, but –'

'Sure,' agreed Julius. 'What you say goes. I'll get one.'

'But you can't at once,' cried Tuppence. 'People wait ages sometimes.'

'Little Julius doesn't,' affirmed Mr Hersheimmer. 'Don't you worry any. I'll be round in the car in half an hour.'

Tuppence got up.

'You're awfully good, Julius. But I can't help feeling that it's rather a forlorn hope. I'm really pinning my faith to Mr Carter.'

'Then I shouldn't.'

'Why?'

'Just an idea of mine.'

'Oh, but he must do something. There's no one else. By the way, I forgot to tell you of a queer thing that happened this morning.'

And she narrated her encounter with Sir James Peel Edgerton. Julius was interested.

'What did the guy mean, do you think?' he asked.

'I don't quite know,' said Tuppence meditatively.

'But I think that, in an ambiguous, legal, without prejudicish lawyer's way, he was trying to warn me.'

'Why should he?'

'I don't know,' confessed Tuppence. 'But he looked kind, and simply awfully clever. I wouldn't mind going to him and telling him everything.'

Somewhat to her surprise, Julius negatived the idea sharply.

'See here,' he said, 'we don't want any lawyers mixed up in this. That guy couldn't help us any.'

'Well, I believe he could,' reiterated Tuppence obstinately.

'Don't you think it. So long. I'll be back in half an hour.'

Thirty-five minutes had elapsed when Julius returned. He took Tuppence by the arm, and walked her to the window.

'There she is.'

'Oh!' said Tuppence with a note of reverence in her voice, as she gazed down at the enormous car.

'She's some pace-maker, I can tell you,' said Julius complacently.

'How did you get it?' gasped Tuppence.

'She was just being sent home to some bigwig.'

'Well?'

'I went round to his house,' said Julius. 'I said that I reckoned a car like that was worth every penny of twenty thousand dollars. Then I told him that it was worth just about fifty thousand dollars to me if he'd get out.'

'Well?' said Tuppence, intoxicated.

'Well,' returned Julius, 'he got out, that's all.'

Chapter 12

A Friend in Need

Friday and Saturday passed uneventfully. Tuppence had received a brief answer to her appeal from Mr Carter. In it he pointed out that the Young Adventurers had undertaken the work at their own risk, and had been fully warned of the dangers. If anything had happened to Tommy he regretted it deeply, but he could do nothing.

This was cold comfort. Somehow, without Tommy, all the savour went out of the adventure, and, for the first time, Tuppence felt doubtful of success. While they had been together she had never questioned it for a minute. Although she was accustomed to take the lead, and to pride herself on her quick-wittedness, in reality she had relied upon Tommy more than she realized at the time. There was something so eminently sober and clear-headed about him, his common sense and soundness of vision were so unvarying, that without him Tuppence felt much like a rudderless ship. It was curious that Julius, who was undoubtedly much cleverer than Tommy, did not give her the same feeling of support. She had accused Tommy of being a pessimist, and it is certain that he always saw the disadvantages and difficulties which she herself was optimistically given to overlooking, but nevertheless she had really relied a good deal on his judgment. He might be slow, but he was very sure.

It seemed to the girl that, for the first time, she realized the sinister character of the mission they had undertaken so light-heartedly. It had begun like a page of romance. Now, shorn of its glamour, it seemed to be turning to grim reality. Tommy – that was all that mattered. Many times in the day Tuppence blinked the tears out of her eyes resolutely. 'Little fool,' she would apostrophize herself, 'don't snivel. Of course you're fond of him. You've known him all your life. But there's no need to be sentimental about it.'

In the meantime, nothing more was seen of Boris. He did not come to the flat, and Julius and the car waited in vain. Tuppence gave herself over to new meditations. Whilst admitting the truth of Julius's objections, she had nevertheless not entirely relinquished the idea of appealing to Sir James Peel Edgerton. Indeed, she had gone so far as to look up his address in the *Red Book*. Had he meant to warn her that day? If so, why? Surely she was at least entitled to demand an explanation. He had looked at her so kindly. Perhaps he might tell them something concerning Mrs Vandemeyer which might lead to a clue to Tommy's whereabouts.

Anyway, Tuppence decided, with her usual shake of the shoulders, it was worth trying, and try it she would. Sunday was her afternoon out. She would meet Julius, persuade him to her point of view, and they would beard the lion in his den.

When the day arrived Julius needed a considerable amount of persuading, but Tuppence held firm. 'It can do no harm,' was what she always came back to. In the end Julius gave in, and they proceeded in the car to Carlton House Terrace.

The door was opened by an irreproachable butler. Tuppence felt a little nervous. After all, perhaps it *was* colossal cheek on her part. She had decided not to ask if Sir James was 'at home,' but to adopt a more personal attitude.

'Will you ask Sir James if I can see him for a few minutes? I have an important message for him.'

The butler retired, returning a moment or two later.

'Sir James will see you. Will you step this way?'

He ushered them into a room at the back of the house, furnished as a library. The collection of books was a magnificent one, and Tuppence noticed that all one wall was devoted to works on crime and criminology.

There were several deep-padded leather armchairs, and an old-fashioned open hearth. In the window was a big roll-top desk strewn with papers at which the master of the house was sitting.

He rose as they entered.

'You have a message for me? Ah' – he recognized Tuppence with a smile – 'it's you, is it? Brought a message from Mrs Vandemeyer, I suppose?'

'Not exactly,' said Tuppence. 'In fact, I'm afraid I only said that to be quite sure of getting in. Oh, by the way, this is Mr Hersheimmer, Sir James Peel Edgerton.'

'Pleased to meet you,' said the American, shooting out a hand.

'Won't you both sit down?' asked Sir James. He drew forward two chairs.

'Sir James,' said Tuppence, plunging boldly, 'I dare say you will think it is most awful cheek of me coming here like this. Because, of course, it's nothing whatever to do with you, and then you're a very important person, and of course Tommy and I are very unimportant.' She paused for breath.

'Tommy?' queried Sir James, looking across at the American.

'No, that's Julius,' explained Tuppence. 'I'm rather nervous, and that makes me tell it badly. What I really want to know is what you meant by what you said to me the other day? Did you mean to warn me against Mrs Vandemeyer? You did, didn't you?'

'My dear young lady, as far as I recollect I only mentioned that there were equally good situations to be obtained elsewhere.'

'Yes, I know. But it was a hint, wasn't it?'

'Well, perhaps it was,' admitted Sir James gravely.

'Well, I want to know more. I want to know just *why* you gave me a hint.'

Sir James smiled at her earnestness.

'Suppose the lady brings a libel action against me for defamation of character?'

'Of course,' said Tuppence. 'I know lawyers are always dreadfully careful. But can't we say "without prejudice" first, and then say just what we want to.'

'Well,' said Sir James, still smiling, 'without prejudice, then, if I had a young sister forced to earn her living, I should not like to see her in Mrs Vandemeyer's service. I felt it incumbent on me just to give you a hint. It is no place for a young and inexperienced girl. That is all I can tell you.'

'I see,' said Tuppence thoughtfully. 'Thank you very much. But I'm not *really* inexperienced, you know. I knew perfectly that she was a bad lot when I went there – as a matter of fact that's *why* I went –' She broke off, seeing some bewilderment on the lawyer's face, and went on: 'I think perhaps I'd better tell you the whole story, Sir James. I've a sort of feeling that you'd know in a minute if I didn't tell the truth, and so you might as well know all about it from the beginning. What do you think, Julius?'

'As you're bent on it, I'd go right ahead with the facts,' replied the American, who had so far sat in silence.

'Yes, tell me all about it,' said Sir James. 'I want to know who Tommy is.'

Thus encouraged Tuppence plunged into her tale, and the lawyer listened with close attention.

'Very interesting,' he said, when she finished. 'A great deal of what you tell me, child, is already known to me. I've had certain theories of my own about this Jane Finn. You've done extraordinarily well so far, but it's rather too bad of – what do you know him as? – Mr Carter to pitchfork you two young things into an affair of this kind. By the way, where did Mr Hersheimmer come in originally? You didn't make that clear?'

Julius answered for himself.

'I'm Jane's first cousin,' he explained, returning the lawyer's keen gaze.

'Ah!'

'Oh, Sir James,' broke out Tuppence, 'what do you think has become of Tommy?'

'H'm.' The lawyer rose, and paced slowly up and

down. 'When you arrived, young lady, I was just packing up my traps. Going to Scotland by the night train for a few days' fishing. But there are different kinds of fishing. I've a good mind to stay, and see if we can't get on the track of that young chap.'

'Oh!' Tuppence clasped her hands ecstatically.

'All the same, as I said before, it's too bad of – of Carter to set you two babies on a job like this. Now, don't get offended, Miss – er –'

'Cowley. Prudence Cowley. But my friends call me Tuppence.'

'Well, Miss Tuppence, then, as I'm certainly going to be a friend. Don't be offended because I think you're young. Youth is a failing only too easily outgrown. Now, about this young Tommy of yours –'

'Yes.' Tuppence clasped her hands.

'Frankly, things look bad for him. He's been butting in somewhere where he wasn't wanted. Not a doubt of it. But don't give up hope.'

'And you really will help us? There, Julius! He didn't want me to come,' she added by way of explanation.

'H'm,' said the lawyer, favouring Julius with another keen glance. 'And why was that?'

'I reckoned it would be no good worrying you with a petty little business like this.'

'I see.' He paused a moment. 'This petty little business, as you call it, bears directly on a very big business, bigger perhaps than either of you or Miss Tuppence know. If this boy is alive, he may have very valuable information to give us. Therefore, we must find him.'

'Yes, but how?' cried Tuppence. 'I've tried to think of everything.'

Sir James smiled.

'And yet there's one person quite near at hand who in all probability knows where he is, or at all events where he is likely to be.'

'Who is that?' asked Tuppence, puzzled.

'Mrs Vandemeyer.'

'Yes, but she'd never tell us.'

'Ah, that is where I come in. I think it quite likely that I shall be able to make Mrs Vandemeyer tell me what I want to know.'

'How?' demanded Tuppence, opening her eyes very wide.

'Oh, just by asking her questions,' replied Sir James easily. 'That's the way we do it, you know.'

He tapped with his fingers on the table, and Tuppence felt again the intense power that radiated from the man.

'And if she won't tell?' asked Julius suddenly.

'I think she will. I have one or two powerful levers. Still, in that unlikely event, there is always the possibility of bribery.'

'Sure. And that's where I come in!' cried Julius, bringing his fist down on the table with a bang. 'You can count on me, if necessary, for one million dollars. Yes, sir, one million dollars!'

Sir James sat down and subjected Julius to a long scrutiny.

'Mr Hersheimmer,' he said at last, 'that is a very large sum.'

'I guess it'll have to be. These aren't the kind of folk to offer sixpence to.'

'At the present rate of exchange it amounts to considerably over two hundred and fifty thousand pounds.'

'That's so. Maybe you think I'm talking through my hat, but I can deliver the goods all right, with enough over to spare for your fee.'

Sir James flushed slightly.

'There is no question of a fee, Mr Hersheimmer. I am not a private detective.'

'Sorry. I guess I was just a mite hasty, but I've been feeling bad about this money question. I wanted to offer a big reward for news of Jane some days ago, but your crusted institution of Scotland Yard advised me against it. Said it was undesirable.'

'They were probably right,' said Sir James dryly.

'But it's all O.K. about Julius,' put in Tuppence. 'He's not pulling your leg. He's got simply pots of money.'

'The old man piled it up in style,' explained Julius. 'Now, let's get down to it. What's your idea?'

Sir James considered for a moment or two.

'There is no time to be lost. The sooner we strike the better.' He turned to Tuppence. 'Is Mrs Vandemeyer dining out tonight, do you know?'

'Yes, I think so, but she will not be out late. Otherwise, she would have taken the latchkey.'

'Good. I will call upon her about ten o'clock. What time are you supposed to return?'

'About nine-thirty or ten, but I could go back earlier.'

'You must not do that on any account. It might arouse suspicion if you did not stay out till the usual time. Be back by nine-thirty. I will arrive at ten. Mr Hersheimmer will wait below in a taxi perhaps.'

'He's got a new Rolls-Royce car,' said Tuppence with vicarious pride.

'Even better. If I succeed in obtaining the address from her, we can go there at once, taking Mrs Vandemeyer with us if necessary. You understand?'

'Yes.' Tuppence rose to her feet with a skip of delight. 'Oh, I feel so much better!'

'Don't build on it too much, Miss Tuppence. Go easy.'

Julius turned to the lawyer.

'Say, then, I'll call for you in the car round about nine-thirty. Is that right?'

'Perhaps that will be the best plan. It would be unnecessary to have two cars waiting about. Now, Miss Tuppence, my advice to you is to go and have a good dinner, a *really* good one, mind. And don't think ahead more than you can help.'

He shook hands with them both, and a moment later they were outside.

'Isn't he a duck?' inquired Tuppence ecstatically, as she skipped down the steps. 'Oh, Julius, isn't he just a duck?'

'Well, I allow he seems to be the goods all right. And I was wrong about its being useless to go to him. Say, shall we go right away back to the Ritz?'

'I must walk a bit, I think. I feel so excited. Drop me in the Park, will you? Unless you'd like to come too?'

Julius shook his head.

'I want to get some petrol,' he explained. 'And send off a cable or two.'

'All right. I'll meet you at the Ritz at seven. We'll have to dine upstairs. I can't show myself in these glad rags.'

'Sure. I'll get Felix to help me choose the menu. He's some head waiter, that. So long.'

Tuppence walked briskly along towards the Serpentine, first glancing at her watch. It was nearly six o'clock. She remembered that she had had no tea, but felt too excited to be conscious of hunger. She walked as far as Kensington Gardens and then slowly retraced her steps, feeling infinitely better for the fresh air and exercise. It was not so easy to follow Sir James's advice and put the possible events of the evening out of her head. As she drew nearer and nearer to Hyde Park corner, the temptation to return to South Audley Mansions was almost irresistible.

At any rate, she decided, it would do no harm just to go and *look* at the building. Perhaps, then, she could resign herself to waiting patiently for ten o'clock.

South Audley Mansions looked exactly the same as usual. What Tuppence had expected she hardly knew, but the sight of its red brick solidity slightly assuaged the growing and entirely unreasonable uneasiness that possessed her. She was just turning away when she heard a piercing whistle, and the faithful Albert came running from the building to join her.

Tuppence frowned. It was no part of the programme to have attention called to her presence in the neighbourhood, but Albert was purple with suppressed excitement.

'I say, miss, she's a-going!'

'Who's going?' demanded Tuppence sharply.

'The crook. Ready Rita. Mrs Vandemeyer. She's a-packing up, and she's just sent down word for me to get her a taxi.'

'What?' Tuppence clutched his arm.

'It's the truth, miss. I thought maybe as you didn't know about it.'

'Albert,' cried Tuppence, 'you're a brick. If it hadn't been for you we'd have lost her.'

Albert flushed with pleasure at this tribute.

'There's no time to lose,' said Tuppence, crossing the road. 'I've got to stop her. At all costs I must keep her here until –' She broke off. 'Albert, there's a telephone here, isn't there?'

The boy shook his head.

'The flats mostly have their own, miss. But there's a box just round the corner.'

'Go to it then, at once, and ring up the Ritz Hotel. Ask for Mr Hersheimmer, and when you get him tell him to get Sir James and come at once, as Mrs Vandemeyer is trying to hook it. If you can't get him, ring up Sir James Peel Edgerton, you'll find his number in the book, and tell him what's happening. You won't forget the names, will you?'

Albert repeated them glibly. 'You trust to me, miss, it'll be all right. But what about you? Aren't you afraid to trust yourself with her?'

'No, no, that's all right. *But go and telephone.* Be quick.'

Drawing a long breath, Tuppence entered the Mansions and ran up to the door of No. 20. How she was to detain Mrs Vandemeyer until the two men arrived, she did not know, but somehow or other it had to be done, and she must accomplish the task single-handed. What had occasioned this precipitate departure? Did Mrs Vandemeyer suspect her?

Speculations were idle. Tuppence pressed the bell firmly. She might learn something from the cook.

Nothing happened and, after waiting some minutes, Tuppence pressed the bell again, keeping her finger on the button for some little while. At last she heard footsteps inside, and a moment later Mrs Vandemeyer herself opened the door. She lifted her eyebrows at the sight of the girl.

'You?'

'I had a touch of toothache, ma'am,' said Tuppence glibly. 'So thought it better to come home and have a quiet evening.'

Mrs Vandemeyer said nothing, but she drew back and let Tuppence pass into the hall.

'How unfortunate for you,' she said coldly. 'You had better go to bed.'

'Oh, I shall be all right in the kitchen, ma'am. Cook will –'

'Cook is out,' said Mrs Vandemeyer, in a rather disagreeable tone. 'I sent her out. So you see you had better go to bed.'

Suddenly Tuppence felt afraid. There was a ring in

Mrs Vandemeyer's voice that she did not like at all. Also, the other woman was slowly edging her up the passage. Tuppence turned at bay.

'I don't want –'

Then, in a flash, a rim of cold steel touched her temple, and Mrs Vandemeyer's voice rose cold and menacing:

'You damned little fool! Do you think I don't know? No, don't answer. If you struggle or cry out, I'll shoot you like a dog.'

The rim of steel pressed a little harder against the girl's temple.

'Now then, march,' went on Mrs Vandemeyer. 'This way – into my room. In a minute, when I've done with you, you'll go to bed as I told you to. And you'll sleep – oh yes, my little spy, you'll sleep all right!'

There was a sort of hideous geniality in the last words which Tuppence did not at all like. For the moment there was nothing to be done, and she walked obediently into Mrs Vandemeyer's bedroom. The pistol never left her forehead. The room was in a state of wild disorder, clothes were flung about right and left, a suit-case and a hat box, half-packed, stood in the middle of the floor.

Tuppence pulled herself together with an effort. Her voice shook a little, but she spoke out bravely.

'Come now,' she said, 'this is nonsense. You can't

shoot me. Why, everyone in the building would hear the report.'

'I'd risk that,' said Mrs Vandemeyer cheerfully. 'But, as long as you don't sing out for help, you're all right – and I don't think you will. You're a clever girl. You deceived *me* all right. I hadn't a suspicion of you! So I've no doubt that you understand perfectly well that this is where I'm on top and you're underneath. Now then – sit on the bed. Put your hands above your head, and if you value your life don't move them.'

Tuppence obeyed passively. Her good sense told her that there was nothing else to do but accept the situation. If she shrieked for help there was very little chance of anyone hearing her, whereas there was probably quite a good chance of Mrs Vandemeyer's shooting her. In the meantime, every minute of delay gained was valuable.

Mrs Vandemeyer laid down the revolver on the edge of the wash-stand within reach of her hand, and, still eyeing Tuppence like a lynx in case the girl should attempt to move, she took a little stoppered bottle from its place on the marble and poured some of its contents into a glass which she filled up with water.

'What's that?' asked Tuppence sharply.

'Something to make you sleep soundly.'

Tuppence paled a little.

'Are you going to poison me?' she asked in a whisper.

'Perhaps,' said Mrs Vandemeyer, smiling agreeably.

'Then I shan't drink it,' said Tuppence firmly. 'I'd much rather be shot. At any rate that would make a row, and someone might hear it. But I won't be killed off quietly like a lamb.'

Mrs Vandemeyer stamped her foot.

'Don't be a little fool! Do you really think I want a hue and cry for murder out after me? If you've any sense at all, you'll realize that poisoning you wouldn't suit my book at all. It's a sleeping-draught, that's all. You'll wake up tomorrow morning none the worse. I simply don't want the bother of tying you up and gagging you. That's the alternative – and you won't like it, I can tell you! I can be very rough if I choose. So drink this down like a good girl, and you'll be none the worse for it.'

In her heart of hearts Tuppence believed her. The arguments she had adduced rang true. It was a simple and effective method of getting her out of the way for the time being. Nevertheless, the girl did not take kindly to the idea of being tamely put to sleep without as much as one bid for freedom. She felt that once Mrs Vandemeyer gave them the slip, the last hope of finding Tommy would be gone.

Tuppence was quick in her mental processes. All

these reflections passed through her mind in a flash, and she saw where a chance, a very problematic chance, lay, and she determined to risk all in one supreme effort.

Accordingly, she lurched suddenly off the bed and fell on her knees before Mrs Vandemeyer, clutching her skirts frantically.

'I don't believe it,' she moaned. 'It's poison – I know it's poison. Oh, don't make me drink it' – her voice rose to a shriek – 'don't make me drink it!'

Mrs Vandemeyer, glass in hand, looked down with a curling lip at this sudden collapse.

'Get up, you little idiot! Don't go on drivelling there. How you ever had the nerve to play your part as you did I can't think.' She stamped her foot. 'Get up, I say.'

But Tuppence continued to cling and sob, interjecting her sobs with incoherent appeals for mercy. Every minute gained was to the good. Moreover, as she grovelled, she moved imperceptibly nearer to her objective.

Mrs Vandemeyer gave a sharp impatient exclamation, and jerked the girl to her knees.

'Drink it at once!' Imperiously she pressed the glass to the girl's lips.

Tuppence gave one last despairing moan.

'You swear it won't hurt me?' she temporized.

'Of course it won't hurt you. Don't be a fool.'

'Will you swear it?'

'Yes, yes,' said the other impatiently. 'I swear it.'

Tuppence raised a trembling left hand to the glass.

'Very well.' Her mouth opened meekly.

Mrs Vandemeyer gave a sigh of relief, off her guard for the moment. Then, quick as a flash, Tuppence jerked the glass upward as hard as she could. The fluid in it splashed into Mrs Vandemeyer's face, and during her momentary gasp, Tuppence's right hand shot out and grasped the revolver where it lay on the edge of the wash-stand. The next moment she had sprung back a pace, and the revolver pointed straight at Mrs Vandemeyer's heart, with no unsteadiness in the hand that held it.

In the moment of victory, Tuppence betrayed a somewhat unsportsman-like triumph.

'Now who's on top and who's underneath?' she crowed.

The other's face was convulsed with rage. For a minute Tuppence thought she was going to spring upon her, which would have placed the girl in an unpleasant dilemma, since she meant to draw the line at actually letting off the revolver. However, with an effort, Mrs Vandemeyer controlled herself, and at last a slow evil smile crept over her face.

'Not a fool then, after all! You did that well, girl. But you shall pay for it – oh, yes, you shall pay for it! I have a long memory!'

'I'm surprised you should have been gulled so easily,' said Tuppence scornfully. 'Did you really think I was the kind of girl to roll about on the floor and whine for mercy?'

'You may do – some day!' said the other significantly.

The cold malignity of her manner sent an unpleasant chill down Tuppence's spine, but she was not going to give in to it.

'Supposing we sit down,' she said pleasantly. 'Our present attitude is a little melodramatic. No – not on the bed. Draw a chair up to the table, that's right. Now I'll sit opposite you with the revolver in front of me – just in case of accidents. Splendid. Now, let's talk.'

'What about?' said Mrs Vandemeyer sullenly.

Tuppence eyed her thoughtfully for a minute. She was remembering several things. Boris's words, 'I believe you would sell – *us*!' and her answer, 'The price would have to be enormous,' given lightly, it was true, yet might not there be a substratum of truth in it? Long ago, had not Whittington asked: 'Who's been blabbing? Rita?' Would Rita Vandemeyer prove to be the weak spot in the armour of Mr Brown?

Keeping her eyes fixed steadily on the other's face, Tuppence replied quietly:

'Money –'

Mrs Vandemeyer started. Clearly, the reply was unexpected.

'What do you mean?'

'I'll tell you. You said just now that you had a long memory. A long memory isn't half as useful as a long purse! I dare say it relieves your feelings a good deal to plan out all sorts of dreadful things to do to me, but is that *practical*? Revenge is very unsatisfactory. Everyone always says so. But money' – Tuppence warmed to her pet creed – 'well, there's nothing unsatisfactory about money, is there?'

'Do you think,' said Mrs Vandemeyer scornfully, 'that I am the kind of woman to sell my friends?'

'Yes,' said Tuppence promptly, 'if the price was big enough.'

'A paltry hundred pounds or so!'

'No,' said Tuppence. 'I should suggest – a hundred thousand!'

Her economical spirit did not permit her to mention the whole million dollars suggested by Julius.

A flush crept over Mrs Vandemeyer's face.

'What did you say?' she asked, her fingers playing nervously with a brooch on her breast. In that moment Tuppence knew that the fish was hooked, and for the first time she felt a horror of her own money-loving spirit. It gave her a dreadful sense of kinship to the woman fronting her.

'A hundred thousand pounds,' repeated Tuppence.

The light died out of Mrs Vandemeyer's eyes. She leaned back in her chair.

'Bah!' she said. 'You haven't got it.'

'No,' admitted Tuppence, 'I haven't – but I know someone who has.'

'Who?'

'A friend of mine.'

'Must be a millionaire,' remarked Mrs Vandemeyer unbelievingly.

'As a matter of fact he is. He's an American. He'll pay you that without a murmur. You can take it from me that it's a perfectly genuine proposition.'

Mrs Vandemeyer sat up again.

'I'm inclined to believe you,' she said slowly.

There was silence between them for some time, then Mrs Vandemeyer looked up.

'What does he want to know, this friend of yours?'

Tuppence want through a momentary struggle, but it was Julius's money, and his interests must come first.

'He wants to know where Jane Finn is,' she said boldly.

Mrs Vandemeyer showed no surprise.

'I'm not sure where she is at the present moment,' she replied.

'But you could find out?'

'Oh, yes,' returned Mrs Vandemeyer carelessly. 'There would be no difficulty about that.'

'Then' – Tuppence's voice shook a little – 'there's a boy, a friend of mine. I'm afraid something's happened to him, through your pal, Boris.'

'What's his name?'

'Tommy Beresford.'

'Never heard of him. But I'll ask Boris. He'll tell me anything he knows.'

'Thank you.' Tuppence felt a terrific rise in her spirits. It impelled her to more audacious efforts. 'There's one thing more.'

'Well?'

Tuppence leaned forward and lowered her voice.

'*Who is Mr Brown?*'

Her quick eyes saw the sudden paling of the beautiful face. With an effort Mrs Vandemeyer pulled herself together and tried to resume her former manner. But the attempt was a mere parody.

She shrugged her shoulders.

'You can't have learnt much about us if you don't know that *nobody knows who Mr Brown is . . .*'

'You do,' said Tuppence quietly.

Again the colour deserted the other's face.

'What makes you think that?'

'I don't know,' said the girl truthfully. 'But I'm sure.'

Mrs Vandemeyer stared in front of her for a long time.

'Yes,' she said hoarsely, at last, '*I* know. I was beautiful, you see – very beautiful –'

'You are still,' said Tuppence with admiration.

Mrs Vandemeyer shook her head. There was a strange gleam in her electric-blue eyes.

'Not beautiful enough,' she said in a soft dangerous voice. 'Not – beautiful – enough! And sometimes, lately, I've been afraid . . . It's dangerous to know too much!' She leaned forward across the table. 'Swear that my name shan't be brought into it – that no one shall ever know.'

'I swear it. And, once he's caught, you'll be out of danger.'

A terrified look swept across Mrs Vandemeyer's face.

'Shall I? Shall I ever be?' She clutched Tuppence's arm. 'You're sure about the money?'

'Quite sure.'

'When shall I have it? There must be no delay.'

'This friend of mine will be here presently. He may have to send cables, or something like that. But there won't be any delay – he's a terrific hustler.'

A resolute look settled on Mrs Vandemeyer's face.

'I'll do it. It's a great sum of money, and besides' – she gave a curious smile – 'it is not – wise to throw over a woman like me!'

For a moment or two, she remained smiling, and lightly tapping her fingers on the table. Suddenly she started, and her face blanched.

'What was that?'

'I heard nothing.'

Mrs Vandemeyer gazed round her fearfully.

'If there should be someone listening –'

'Nonsense. Who could there be?'

'Even the walls might have ears,' whispered the other. 'I tell you I'm frightened. You don't know him!'

'Think of the hundred thousand pounds,' said Tuppence soothingly.

Mrs Vandemeyer passed her tongue over her dried lips.

'You don't know him,' she reiterated hoarsely. 'He's – ah!'

With a shriek of terror she sprang to her feet. Her outstretched hand pointed over Tuppence's head. Then she swayed to the ground in a dead faint.

Tuppence looked round to see what had startled her.

In the doorway were Sir James Peel Edgerton and Julius Hersheimmer.

Chapter 13

The Vigil

Sir James brushed past Julius and hurriedly bent over the fallen woman.

'Heart,' he said sharply. 'Seeing us so suddenly must have given her a shock. Brandy – and quickly, or she'll slip through our fingers.'

Julius hurried to the wash-stand.

'Not here,' said Tuppence over her shoulder. 'In the tantalus in the dining-room. Second door down the passage.'

Between them Sir James and Tuppence lifted Mrs Vandemeyer and carried her to the bed. There they dashed water on her face, but with no result. The lawyer fingered her pulse.

'Touch and go,' he muttered. 'I wish that young fellow would hurry up with the brandy.'

At that moment Julius re-entered the room, carrying a glass half full of the spirit which he handed to Sir

James. While Tuppence lifted her head the lawyer tried to force a little of the spirit between her closed lips. Finally the woman opened her eyes feebly. Tuppence held the glass to her lips.

'Drink this.'

Mrs Vandemeyer complied. The brandy brought the colour back to her white cheeks, and revived her in a marvellous fashion. She tried to sit up – then fell back with a groan, her hand to her side.

'It's my heart,' she whispered. 'I mustn't talk.'

She lay back with closed eyes.

Sir James kept his finger on her wrist a minute longer, then withdrew it with a nod.

'She'll do now.'

All three moved away, and stood together talking in low voices. One and all were conscious of a certain feeling of anticlimax. Clearly any scheme for cross-questioning the lady was out of the question for the moment. For the time being they were baffled, and could do nothing.

Tuppence related how Mrs Vandemeyer had declared herself willing to disclose the identity of Mr Brown, and how she had consented to discover and reveal to them the whereabouts of Jane Finn. Julius was congratulatory.

'That's all right, Miss Tuppence. Splendid! I guess that hundred thousand pounds will look just as good in the morning to the lady as it did over night. There's nothing to worry over. She won't speak without the cash anyway, you bet!'

There was certainly a good deal of common sense in this, and Tuppence felt a little comforted.

'What you say is true,' said Sir James meditatively. 'I must confess, however, that I cannot help wishing we had not interrupted at the minute we did. Still, it cannot be helped, it is only a matter of waiting until the morning.'

He looked across at the inert figure on the bed. Mrs Vandemeyer lay perfectly passive with closed eyes. He shook his head.

'Well,' said Tuppence, with an attempt at cheerfulness, 'we must wait until the morning, that's all. But I don't think we ought to leave the flat.'

'What about leaving that bright boy of yours on guard?'

'Albert? And suppose she came round again and hooked it. Albert couldn't stop her.'

'I guess she won't want to make tracks away from the dollars.'

'She might. She seemed very frightened of "Mr Brown."'

'What? Real plumb scared of him?'

'Yes. She looked round and said even walls had ears.'

'Maybe she meant a dictaphone,' said Julius with interest.

'Miss Tuppence is right,' said Sir James quietly. 'We must not leave the flat – if only for Mrs Vandemeyer's sake.'

Julius stared at him.

'You think he'd get after her? Between now and tomorrow morning. How could he know, even?'

'You forget your own suggestion of a dictaphone,' said Sir James dryly. 'We have a very formidable adversary. I believe, if we exercise all due care, that there is a very good chance of his being delivered into our hands. But we must neglect no precaution. We have an important witness, but she must be safeguarded. I would suggest that Miss Tuppence should go to bed, and that you and I, Mr Hersheimmer, should share the vigil.'

Tuppence was about to protest, but happening to glance at the bed she saw Mrs Vandemeyer, her eyes half-open, with such an expression of mingled fear and malevolence on her face that it quite froze the words on her lips.

For a moment she wondered whether the faint and the heart attack had been a gigantic sham, but remembering the deadly pallor she could hardly credit the supposition. As she looked the expression disappeared as by magic, and Mrs Vandemeyer lay inert and motionless as before. For a moment the girl fancied she must have dreamt it. But she determined nevertheless to be on the alert.

'Well,' said Julius, 'I guess we'd better make a move out of here anyway.'

The others fell in with his suggestion. Sir James again felt Mrs Vandemeyer's pulse.

'Perfectly satisfactory,' he said in a low voice to Tuppence. 'She'll be absolutely all right after a night's rest.'

The girl hesitated a moment by the bed. The intensity of the expression she had surprised had impressed her powerfully. Mrs Vandemeyer lifted her eyelids. She seemed to be struggling to speak. Tuppence bent over her.

'Don't – leave –' she seemed unable to proceed, murmuring something that sounded like 'sleepy'. Then she tried again.

Tuppence bent lower still. It was only a breath.

'Mr – Brown –' The voice stopped.

But the half-closed eyes seemed still to send an agonized message.

Moved by a sudden impulse, the girl said quickly:

'I shan't leave the flat. I shall sit up all night.'

A flash of relief showed before the lids descended once more. Apparently Mrs Vandemeyer slept. But her words had awakened a new uneasiness in Tuppence. What had she meant by that low murmur. 'Mr Brown?'

Tuppence caught herself nervously looking over her shoulder. The big wardrobe loomed up in a sinister fashion before her eyes. Plenty of room for a man to hide in that . . . Half-ashamed of herself Tuppence pulled it open and looked inside. No one – of course! She stooped down and looked under the bed. There was no other possible hiding-place.

Tuppence gave her familiar shake of the shoulders. It was absurd, this giving way to nerves! Slowly she went out of the room. Julius and Sir James were talking in a low voice. Sir James turned to her.

'Lock the door on the outside, please, Miss Tuppence, and take out the key. There must be no chance of anyone entering that room.'

The gravity of his manner impressed them, and Tuppence felt less ashamed of her attack of 'nerves.'

'Say,' remarked Julius suddenly, 'there's Tuppence's bright boy. I guess I'd better go down and ease his young mind. That's some lad, Tuppence.'

'How did you get in, by the way?' asked Tuppence suddenly. 'I forgot to ask.'

'Well, Albert got me on the phone all right. I ran round for Sir James here, and we came right on. The boy was on the look out for us, and was just a mite worried about what might have happened to you. He'd been listening outside the door of the flat, but couldn't hear anything. Anyhow he suggested sending us up in the coal lift instead of ringing the bell. And sure enough we landed in the scullery and came right along to find you. Albert's still below, and must be hopping mad by this time.' With which Julius departed abruptly.

'Now then, Miss Tuppence,' said Sir James, 'you know this place better than I do. Where do you suggest we should take up our quarters?'

Tuppence considered for a moment or two.

'I think Mrs Vandemeyer's boudoir would be the most comfortable,' she said at last, and led the way there.

Sir James looked round approvingly.

'This will do very well, and now, my dear young lady, do go to bed and get some sleep.'

Tuppence shook her head resolutely.

'I couldn't, thank you, Sir James. I should dream of Mr Brown all night!'

'But you'll be so tired, child.'

'No, I shan't. I'd rather stay up – really.'

The lawyer gave in.

Julius reappeared some minutes later, having reassured Albert and rewarded him lavishly for his services. Having in his turn failed to persuade Tuppence to go to bed, he said decisively:

'At any rate, you've got to have something to eat right away. Where's the larder?'

Tuppence directed him, and he returned in a few minutes with a cold pie and three plates.

After a hearty meal, the girl felt inclined to pooh-pooh her fancies of half an hour before. The power of the money bribe could not fail.

'And now, Miss Tuppence,' said Sir James, 'we want to hear your adventures.'

'That's so,' agreed Julius.

Tuppence narrated her adventures with some complacence. Julius occasionally interjected an admiring 'Bully.' Sir James said nothing until she had finished, when his quiet 'Well done, Miss Tuppence,' made her flush with pleasure.

'There's one thing I don't get clearly,' said Julius. 'What put her up to clearing out?'

'I don't know,' confessed Tuppence.

Sir James stroked his chin thoughtfully.

'The room was in great disorder. That looks as though her flight was unpremeditated. Almost as though she got a sudden warning to go from someone.'

'Mr Brown, I suppose,' said Julius scoffingly.

The lawyer looked at him deliberately for a minute or two.

'Why not?' he said. 'Remember, you yourself have once been worsted by him.'

Julius flushed with vexation.

'I feel just mad when I think of how I handed out Jane's photograph to him like a lamb. Gee, if I ever lay hands on it again, I'll freeze on to it – like hell!'

'That contingency is likely to be a remote one,' said the other dryly.

'I guess you're right,' said Julius frankly. 'And, in any case, it's the original I'm out after. Where do you think she can be, Sir James?'

The lawyer shook his head.

'Impossible to say. But I've a very good idea where she *has* been.'

'You have? Where?'

Sir James smiled.

'At the scene of your nocturnal adventures, the Bournemouth nursing home.'

'There? Impossible. I asked.'

'No, my dear sir, you asked if anyone of the name of Jane Finn had been there. Now, if the girl had been placed there it would almost certainly be under an assumed name.'

'Bully for you,' cried Julius. 'I never thought of that!'

'It was fairly obvious,' said the other.

'Perhaps the doctor's in it too,' suggested Tuppence.

Julius shook his head.

'I don't think so. I took to him at once. No, I'm pretty sure Dr Hall's all right.'

'Hall, did you say?' asked Sir James. 'That is curious – really very curious.'

'Why?' demanded Tuppence.

'Because I happened to meet him this morning. I've known him slightly on and off for some years, and this morning I ran across him in the street. Staying at the Metropole, he told me.' He turned to Julius. 'Didn't he tell you he was coming up to town?'

Julius shook his head.

'Curious,' mused Sir James. 'You did not mention his name this afternoon, or I would have suggested your going to him for further information with my card as introduction.'

'I guess I'm a mutt,' said Julius with unusual humility. 'I ought to have thought of the false name stunt.'

'How could you think of anything after falling out of that tree?' cried Tuppence. 'I'm sure anyone else would have been killed right off.'

'Well, I guess it doesn't matter now, anyway,' said Julius. 'We've got Mrs Vandemeyer on a string, and that's all we need.'

'Yes,' said Tuppence, but there was a lack of assurance in her voice.

A silence settled down over the party. Little by little the magic of the night began to gain hold on them. There were sudden creaks in the furniture, imperceptible rustlings in the curtains. Suddenly Tuppence sprang up with a cry.

'I can't help it. I know Mr Brown's somewhere in the flat! I can *feel* him.'

'Sure, Tuppence, how could he be? This door's open into the hall. No one could have come in by the front door without our seeing and hearing him.'

'I can't help it. I *feel* he's here!'

She looked appealingly at Sir James, who replied gravely:

'With due deference to your feelings, Miss Tuppence (and mine as well for that matter), I do not see how it is humanly possible for anyone to be in the flat without our knowledge.'

The girl was a little comforted by his words.

'Sitting up at night is always rather jumpy,' she confessed.

'Yes,' said Sir James. 'We are in the condition of people holding a séance. Perhaps if a medium were present we might get some marvellous results.'

'Do you believe in spiritualism?' asked Tuppence, opening her eyes wide.

The lawyer shrugged his shoulders.

'There is some truth in it, without a doubt. But most of the testimony would not pass muster in the witness-box.'

The hours drew on. With the first faint glimmerings of dawn, Sir James drew aside the curtains. They beheld, what few Londoners see, the slow rising of the sun over the sleeping city. Somehow, with the coming of the light, the dreads and fancies of the past night seemed absurd. Tuppence's spirits revived to the normal.

'Hooray!' she said. 'It's going to be a gorgeous day. And we shall find Tommy. And Jane Finn. And everything will be lovely. I shall ask Mr Carter if I can't be made a Dame!'

At seven o'clock Tuppence volunteered to go and make some tea. She returned with a tray, containing the teapot and four cups.

'Who's the other cup for?' inquired Julius.

'The prisoner, of course. I suppose we might call her that?'

'Taking her tea seems a kind of anti-climax to last night,' said Julius thoughtfully.

'Yes, it does,' admitted Tuppence. 'But, anyway, here goes. Perhaps you'd both come, too, in case she springs on me, or anything. You see, we don't know what mood she'll wake up in.'

Sir James and Julius accompanied her to the door.

'Where's the key? Oh, of course, I've got it myself.'

She put it in the lock, and turned it, then paused.

'Supposing, after all, she's escaped?' she murmured in a whisper.

'Plumb impossible,' replied Julius reassuringly.

But Sir James said nothing.

Tuppence drew a long breath and entered. She heaved a sigh of relief as she saw that Mrs Vandemeyer was lying on the bed.

'Good morning,' she remarked cheerfully. 'I've brought you some tea.'

Mrs Vandemeyer did not reply. Tuppence put down the cup on the table by the bed and went across to draw up the blinds. When she turned, Mrs Vandemeyer still lay without a movement. With a sudden fear clutching at her heart, Tuppence ran to the bed. The hand she lifted was cold as ice . . . Mrs Vandemeyer would never speak now . . .

Her cry brought the others. A very few minutes sufficed. Mrs Vandemeyer was dead – must have been dead some hours. She had evidently died in her sleep.

'If that isn't the cruellest luck,' cried Julius in despair.

The lawyer was calmer, but there was a curious gleam in his eyes.

'If it is luck,' he replied.

'You don't think – but, say, that's plumb impossible – no one could have got in.'

'No,' admitted the lawyer. 'I don't see how they could. And yet – she is on the point of betraying Mr Brown, and – she dies. Is it only chance?'

'But how –'

'Yes, *how*! That is what we must find out.' He stood there silently, gently stroking his chin. 'We must find out,' he said quietly, and Tuppence felt that if she was Mr Brown she would not like the tone of those simple words.

Julius's glance went to the window.

'The window's open,' he remarked. 'Do you think –'

Tuppence shook her head.

'The balcony only goes along as far as the boudoir. We were there.'

'He might have slipped out –' suggested Julius.

But Sir James interrupted him.

'Mr Brown's methods are not so crude. In the meantime we must send for a doctor, but before we do so is there anything in this room that might be of value to us?'

Hastily, the three searched. A charred mass in the grate indicated that Mrs Vandemeyer had been burning papers on the eve of her flight. Nothing of importance remained, though they searched the other rooms as well.

'There's that,' said Tuppence suddenly, pointing to a small, old-fashioned safe let into the wall. 'It's for jewellery, I believe, but there might be something else in it.'

The key was in the lock, and Julius swung open the door, and searched inside. He was some time over the task.

'Well,' said Tuppence impatiently.

There was a pause before Julius answered, then he withdrew his head and shut the door.

'Nothing,' he said.

In five minutes a brisk young doctor arrived, hastily summoned. He was deferential to Sir James, whom he recognized.

'Heart failure, or possibly an overdose of some sleeping-draught. He sniffed. 'Rather an odour of chloral in the air.'

Tuppence remembered the glass she had upset. A new thought drove her to the wash-stand. She found the little bottle from which Mrs Vandemeyer had poured a few drops.

It had been three parts full. Now – *it was empty.*

Chapter 14

A Consultation

Nothing was more surprising and bewildering to Tuppence than the ease and simplicity with which everything was arranged, owing to Sir James's skilful handling. The doctor accepted quite readily the theory that Mrs Vandemeyer had accidentally taken an overdose of chloral. He doubted whether an inquest would be necessary. If so, he would let Sir James know. He understood that Mrs Vandemeyer was on the eve of departure for abroad, and that the servants had already left? Sir James and his young friends had been paying a call upon her, when she was suddenly stricken down and they had spent the night in the flat, not liking to leave her alone. Did they know of any relatives? They did not, but Sir James referred him to Mrs Vandemeyer's solicitor.

Shortly afterwards a nurse arrived to take charge, and the others left the ill-omened building.

'And what now?' asked Julius, with a gesture of despair. 'I guess we're down and out for good.'

Sir James stroked his chin thoughtfully.

'No,' he said quietly. 'There is still the chance that Dr Hall may be able to tell us something.'

'Gee! I'd forgotten him.'

'The chance is slight, but it must not be neglected. I think I told you that he is staying at the Metropole. I should suggest that we call upon him there as soon as possible. Shall we say after a bath and breakfast?'

It was arranged that Tuppence and Julius should return to the Ritz, and call for Sir James in the car. The programme was faithfully carried out, and a little after eleven they drew up before the Metropole. They asked for Dr Hall, and a page-boy went in search of him. In a few minutes the little doctor came hurrying towards them.

'Can you spare us a few minutes, Dr Hall?' said Sir James pleasantly. 'Let me introduce you to Miss Cowley. Mr Hersheimmer, I think, you already know.'

A quizzical gleam came into the doctor's eye as he shook hands with Julius.

'Ah, yes, my young friend of the tree episode! Ankle all right, eh?'

'I guess it's cured owing to your skilful treatment, doc.'

'And the heart trouble? Ha! ha!'

'Still searching,' said Julius briefly.

'To come to the point, can we have a word with you in private?' asked Sir James.

'Certainly. I think there is a room here where we shall be quite undisturbed.'

He led the way, and the others followed him. They sat down, and the doctor looked inquiringly at Sir James.

'Dr Hall, I am very anxious to find a certain young lady for the purpose of obtaining a statement from her. I have reason to believe that she has been at one time or another in your establishment at Bournemouth. I hope I am transgressing no professional etiquette in questioning you on the subject?'

'I suppose it is a matter of testimony?'

Sir James hesitated a moment, then he replied:

'Yes.'

'I shall be pleased to give you any information in my power. What is the young lady's name? Mr Hersheimmer asked me, I remember –' He half turned to Julius.

'The name,' said Sir James bluntly, 'is really immaterial. She would be almost certainly sent to you under an assumed one. But I should like to know if you are acquainted with a Mrs Vandemeyer?'

'Mrs Vandemeyer, of 20 South Audley Mansions? I know her slightly.'

'You are not aware of what has happened?'

'What do you mean?'

'You do not know that Mrs Vandemeyer is dead?'

'Dear, dear, I had no idea of it! When did it happen?'

'She took an overdose of chloral last night.'

'Purposely?'

'Accidentally, it is believed. I should not like to say myself. Anyway, she was found dead this morning.'

'Very sad. A singularly handsome woman. I presume she was a friend of yours, since you are acquainted with all these details.'

'I am acquainted with the details because – well, it was I who found her dead.'

'Indeed,' said the doctor, starting.

'Yes,' said Sir James, and stroked his chin reflectively.

'This is very sad news, but you will excuse me if I say that I do not see how it bears on the subject of your inquiry?'

'It bears on it in this way, is it not a fact that Mrs Vandemeyer committed a young relative of hers to your charge?'

Julius leaned forward eagerly.

'That is the case,' said the doctor quietly.

'Under the name of –?'

'Janet Vandemeyer. I understood her to be a niece of Mrs Vandemeyer's.'

'And she came to you?'

'As far as I can remember in June or July of 1915.'

'Was she a mental case?'

'She is perfectly sane, if that is what you mean. I understood from Mrs Vandemeyer that the girl had been with her on the *Lusitania* when that ill-fated ship was sunk, and had suffered a severe shock in consequence.'

'We're on the right track, I think?' Sir James looked round.

'As I said before, I'm a mutt!' returned Julius.

The doctor looked at them all curiously.

'You spoke of wanting a statement from her,' he said. 'Supposing she is not able to give one?'

'What? You have just said that she is perfectly sane.'

'So she is. Nevertheless, if you want a statement from her concerning any events prior to May 7, 1915, she will not be able to give it to you.'

They looked at the little man, stupefied. He nodded cheerfully.

'It's a pity,' he said. 'A great pity, especially as I gather, Sir James, that the matter is important. But there it is, she can tell you nothing.'

'But why, man? Darn it all, why?'

The little man shifted his benevolent glance to the excited young American.

'Because Janet Vandemeyer is suffering from a complete loss of memory!'

'*What?*'

'Quite so. An interesting case, a *very* interesting case. Not so uncommon, really, as you would think. There are several very well known parallels. It's the first case of the kind that I've had under my own personal observation, and I must admit that I've found it of absorbing interest.' There was something rather ghoulish in the little man's satisfaction.

'And she remembers nothing,' said Sir James slowly.

'Nothing prior to May 7, 1915. After that date her memory is as good as yours or mine.'

'Then the first thing she remembers?'

'Is landing with the survivors. Everything before that is a blank. She did not know her own name, or where she had come from, or where she was. She couldn't even speak her own tongue.'

'But surely all this is most unusual?' put in Julius.

'No, my dear sir. Quite normal under the circumstances. Severe shock to the nervous system. Loss of memory proceeds nearly always on the same lines. I suggested a specialist, of course. There's a very good man in Paris – makes a study of these cases – but Mrs Vandemeyer opposed the idea of publicity that might result from such a course.'

'I can imagine she would,' said Sir James grimly.

'I fell in with her views. There *is* a certain notoriety given to these cases. And the girl was very young –

nineteen, I believe. It seemed a pity that her infirmity should be talked about – might damage her prospects. Besides, there is no special treatment to pursue in such cases. It is really a matter of waiting.'

'Waiting?'

'Yes, sooner or later, the memory will return – as suddenly as it went. But in all probability the girl will have entirely forgotten the intervening period, and will take up life where she left off – at the sinking of the *Lusitania*.'

'And when do you expect this to happen?'

The doctor shrugged his shoulders.

'Ah, that I cannot say. Sometimes it is a matter of months, sometimes it has been known to be as long as twenty years! Sometimes another shock does the trick. One restores what the other took away.'

'Another shock, eh?' said Julius thoughtfully.

'Exactly. There was a case in Colorado –' The little man's voice trailed on, voluble, mildly enthusiastic.

Julius did not seem to be listening. He had relapsed into his own thoughts and was frowning. Suddenly he came out of his brown study, and hit the table such a resounding bang with his fist that everyone jumped, the doctor most of all.

'I've got it! I guess, doc, I'd like your medical opinion on the plan I'm about to outline. Say Jane was to cross the herring pond again, and the same thing was to happen. The submarine, the sinking ship, everyone to take to the boats – and so on. Wouldn't that do the trick? Wouldn't it give a mighty big bump to her subconscious self, or whatever the jargon is, and start it functioning again right away?'

'A very interesting speculation, Mr Hersheimmer. In my own opinion, it would be successful. It is unfortunate that there is no chance of the conditions repeating themselves as you suggest.'

'Not by nature, perhaps, doc. But I'm talking about art.'

'Art?'

'Why, yes. What's the difficulty? Hire the liner –'

'A liner!' murmured Dr Hall faintly.

'Hire some passengers, hire a submarine – that's the only difficulty, I guess. Governments are apt to be a bit hidebound over their engines of war. They won't sell to the first comer. Still, I guess that can be got over. Ever heard of the word 'graft,' sir? Well, graft gets there every time! I reckon that we shan't really need to fire a torpedo. If everyone hustles round and screams loud enough that the ship is sinking, it ought to be enough for an innocent young girl like Jane. By the time she's got a life-belt on her, and is being hustled into a boat, with a well-drilled lot of artistes doing the hysterical stunt on deck, why – she ought to be right back again where she was in May, 1915. How's that for the bare outline?'

Dr Hall looked at Julius. Everything that he was for the moment incapable of saying was eloquent in that look.

'No,' said Julius, in answer to it, 'I'm not crazy. The thing's perfectly possible. It's done every day in the States for the movies. Haven't you seen trains in collision on the screen? What's the difference between buying up a train and buying up a liner? Get the properties and you can go right ahead!'

Dr Hall found his voice.

'But the expense, my dear sir.' His voice rose. 'The expense! It will be *colossal*!'

'Money doesn't worry me any,' explained Julius simply.

Dr Hall turned an appealing face to Sir James, who smiled slightly.

'Mr Hersheimmer is very well off – very well off indeed.'

The doctor's glance came back to Julius with a new and subtle quality in it. This was no longer an eccentric young fellow with a habit of falling off trees. The doctor's eyes held the deference accorded to a really rich man.

'Very remarkable plan. Very remarkable,' he murmured. 'The movies – of course! Your American word for the cinema. Very interesting. I fear we are perhaps a little behind the times over here in our methods.

And you really mean to carry out this remarkable plan of yours.'

'You bet your bottom dollar I do.'

The doctor believed him – which was a tribute to his nationality. If an Englishman had suggested such a thing, he would have had grave doubts as to his sanity.

'I cannot guarantee a cure,' he pointed out. 'Perhaps I ought to make that quite clear.'

'Sure, that's all right,' said Julius. 'You just trot out Jane, and leave the rest to me.'

'Jane?'

'Miss Janet Vandemeyer, then. Can we get on the long distance to your place right away, and ask them to send her up; or shall I run down and fetch her in my car?'

The doctor stared.

'I beg your pardon, Mr Hersheimmer. I thought you understood.'

'Understood what?'

'That Miss Vandemeyer is no longer under my care.'

Chapter 15

Tuppence Receives a Proposal

Julius sprang up.

'What?'

'I thought you were aware of that.'

'When did she leave?'

'Let me see. Today is Monday, is it not? It must have been last Wednesday – why, surely – yes, it was the same evening that you – er – fell out of my tree.'

'That evening? Before, or after?'

'Let me see – oh yes, afterwards. A very urgent message arrived from Mrs Vandemeyer. The young lady and the nurse who was in charge of her left by the night train.'

Julius sank back again into his chair.

'Nurse Edith – left with a patient – I remember,' he muttered. 'My God, to have been so near!'

Dr Hall looked bewildered.

'I don't understand. Is the young lady not with her aunt, after all?'

Tuppence shook her head. She was about to speak when a warning glance from Sir James made her hold her tongue. The lawyer rose.

'I'm much obliged to you, Hall. We're very grateful for all you've told us. I'm afraid we're now in the position of having to track Miss Vandemeyer anew. What about the nurse who accompanied her; I suppose you don't know where she is?'

The doctor shook his head.

'We've not heard from her, as it happens. I understood she was to remain with Miss Vandemeyer for a while. But what can have happened? Surely the girl has not been kidnapped.'

'That remains to be seen,' said Sir James gravely.

The other hesitated.

'You do not think I ought to go to the police?'

'No, no. In all probability the young lady is with other relations.'

The doctor was not completely satisfied, but he saw that Sir James was determined to say no more, and realized that to try to extract more information from the famous K.C. would be mere waste of labour. Accordingly, he wished them goodbye, and they left the hotel. For a few minutes they stood by the car talking.

'How maddening,' cried Tuppence. 'To think that Julius must have been actually under the same roof with her for a few hours.'

'I was a darned idiot,' muttered Julius gloomily.

'You couldn't know,' Tuppence consoled him. 'Could he?' She appealed to Sir James.

'I should advise you not to worry,' said the latter kindly. 'No use crying over spilt milk, you know.'

'The great thing is what to do next,' added Tuppence the practical.

Sir James shrugged his shoulders.

'You might advertise for the nurse who accompanied the girl. That is the only course I can suggest, and I must confess I do not hope for much result. Otherwise there is nothing to be done.'

'Nothing?' said Tuppence blankly. 'And – Tommy?'

'We must hope for the best,' said Sir James. 'Oh yes, we must go on hoping.'

But over her downcast head his eyes met Julius's, and almost imperceptibly he shook his head. Julius understood. The lawyer considered the case hopeless. The young American's face grew grave. Sir James took Tuppence's hand.

'You must let me know if anything further comes to light. Letters will always be forwarded.'

Tuppence stared at him blankly.

'You are going away?'

'I told you. Don't you remember? To Scotland.'

'Yes, but I thought –' The girl hesitated.

Sir James shrugged his shoulders.

'My dear young lady, I can do nothing more, I fear. Our clues have all ended in thin air. You can take my word for it that there is nothing more to be done. If anything should arise, I shall be glad to advise you in any way I can.'

His words gave Tuppence an extraordinary desolate feeling.

'I suppose you're right,' she said. 'Anyway, thank you very much for trying to help us. Goodbye.'

Julius was bending over the car. A momentary pity came into Sir James's keen eyes, as he gazed into the girl's downcast face.

'Don't be too disconsolate, Miss Tuppence,' he said in a low voice. 'Remember, holiday-time isn't always all play-time. One sometimes manages to put in some work as well.'

Something in his tone made Tuppence glance up sharply. He shook his head with a smile.

'No, I shan't say any more. Great mistake to say too much. Remember that. Never tell all you know – not even to the person you know best. Understand? Goodbye.'

He strode away. Tuppence stared after him. She was beginning to understand Sir James's methods. Once before he had thrown her a hint in the same careless fashion. Was this a hint? What exactly lay behind those last brief words? Did he mean that, after all, he had not abandoned the case: that secretly, he would be working on it still while –

Her meditations were interrupted by Julius, who adjured her to 'get right in'.

'You're looking kind of thoughtful,' he remarked as they started off. 'Did the old guy say anything more?'

Tuppence opened her mouth impulsively, and then shut it again. Sir James's words sounded in her ears: 'Never tell all you know – not even to the person you know best.' And like a flash there came into her mind another memory. Julius before the safe in the flat, her own question and the pause before his reply, 'Nothing.' Was there really nothing? Or had he found something he wished to keep to himself? If he could make a reservation, so could she.

'Nothing particular,' she replied.

She felt rather than saw Julius throw a sideways glance at her.

'Say, shall we go for a spin in the park?'

'If you like.'

For a while they ran on under the trees in silence. It was a beautiful day. The keen rush through the air brought a new exhilaration to Tuppence.

'Say, Miss Tuppence, do you think I'm ever going to find Jane?'

Julius spoke in a discouraged voice. The mood was so alien to him that Tuppence turned and stared at him in surprise. He nodded.

'That's so. I'm getting down and out over the business. Sir James today hadn't got any hope at all, I could see that, I don't like him – we don't gee together somehow – but he's pretty cute, and I guess he wouldn't quit if there was any chance of success – now, would he?'

Tuppence felt rather uncomfortable, but clinging to her belief that Julius also had withheld something from her, she remained firm.

'He suggested advertising for the nurse,' she reminded him.

'Yes, with a "forlorn hope" flavour to his voice! No – I'm about fed up. I've half a mind to go back to the States right away.'

'Oh no!' cried Tuppence. 'We've got to find Tommy.'

'I sure forgot Beresford,' said Julius contritely. 'That's so. We must find him. But after – well, I've been day-dreaming ever since I started on this trip – and these dreams are rotten poor business. I'm quit of them. Say, Miss Tuppence, there's something I'd like to ask you.'

'Yes.'

'You and Beresford. What about it?'

'I don't understand you,' replied Tuppence with dignity, adding rather inconsequently: 'And, anyway, you're wrong!'

'Not got a sort of kindly feeling for one another?'

'Certainly not,' said Tuppence with warmth. 'Tommy and I are friends – nothing more.'

'I guess every pair of lovers has said that some time or another,' observed Julius.

'Nonsense!' snapped Tuppence. 'Do I look the sort of girl that's always falling in love with every man she meets?'

'You do not. You look the sort of girl that's mighty often getting fallen in love with!'

'Oh!' said Tuppence, rather taken aback. 'That's a compliment, I suppose?'

'Sure. Now let's get down to this. Supposing we never find Beresford and – and –'

'All right – say it! I can face facts. Supposing he's – dead! Well?'

'And all this business fiddles out. What are you going to do?'

'I don't know,' said Tuppence forlornly.

'You'll be darned lonesome, you poor kid.'

'I shall be all right,' snapped Tuppence with her usual resentment of any kind of pity.

'What about marriage?' inquired Julius. 'Got any views on the subject?'

'I intend to marry, of course,' replied Tuppence. 'That is, if' – she paused, knew a momentary longing to draw back, and then stuck to her guns bravely – 'I can find some one rich enough to make it worth my while. That's frank, isn't it? I dare say you despise me for it.'

'I never despise business instinct,' said Julius. 'What particular figure have you in mind?'

'Figure?' asked Tuppence, puzzled. 'Do you mean tall or short?'

'No. Sum – income.'

'Oh, I – haven't quite worked that out.'

'What about me?'

'*You?*'

'Sure thing.'

'Oh, I couldn't!'

'Why not?'

'I tell you I couldn't.'

'Again, why not?'

'It would seem so unfair.'

'I don't see anything unfair about it. I call your bluff, that's all. I admire you immensely, Miss Tuppence, more than any girl I've ever met. You're so darned plucky. I'd just love to give you a real, rattling good time. Say the word, and we'll run round right away to some high-class jeweller, and fix up the ring business.'

'I can't,' gasped Tuppence.

'Because of Beresford?'

'No, no, *no*!'

'Well then?'

Tuppence merely continued to shake her head violently.

'You can't reasonably expect more dollars than I've got.'

'Oh, it isn't that,' gasped Tuppence with an almost hysterical laugh. 'But thanking you very much, and all that, I think I'd better say no.'

'I'd be obliged if you'd do me the favour to think it over until tomorrow.'

'It's no use.'

'Still, I guess we'll leave it like that.'

'Very well,' said Tuppence meekly.

Neither of them spoke again until they reached the Ritz.

Tuppence went upstairs to her room. She felt morally battered to the ground after her conflict with Julius's vigorous personality. Sitting down in front of the glass, she stared at her own reflection for some minutes.

'Fool,' murmured Tuppence at length, making a grimace. 'Little fool. Everything you want – everything you've ever hoped for, and you go and bleat out "no" like an idiotic little sheep. It's your one chance. Why don't you take it? Grab it? Snatch at it? What more do you want?'

As if in answer to her own question, her eyes fell on a small snapshot of Tommy that stood on her dressing-table in a shabby frame. For a moment she struggled for self-control, and then abandoning all pretence, she held it to her lips and burst into a fit of sobbing.

'Oh, Tommy, Tommy,' she cried, 'I do love you so – and I may never see you again . . .'

At the end of five minutes Tuppence sat up, blew her nose, and pushed back her hair.

'That's that,' she observed sternly. 'Let's look facts in the face. I seem to have fallen in love – with an idiot of a boy who probably doesn't care two straws about me.' Here she paused. 'Anyway,' she resumed, as though arguing with an unseen opponent, 'I don't *know* that he does. He'd never have dared to say so. I've always jumped on sentiment – and here I am being more sentimental than anybody. What idiots girls are! I've always thought so. I suppose I shall sleep with his photograph under my pillow, and dream about him all night. It's dreadful to feel you've been false to your principles.'

Tuppence shook her head sadly, as she reviewed her back-sliding.

'I don't know what to say to Julius, I'm sure. Oh, what a fool I feel! I'll have to say *something* – he's so American and thorough, he'll insist upon having a reason. I wonder if he did find anything in that safe –'

Tuppence's meditations went off on another track. She reviewed the events of last night carefully and persistently. Somehow, they seemed bound up with Sir James's enigmatical words . . .

Suddenly she gave a great start – the colour faded out of her face. Her eyes, fascinated, gazed in front of her, the pupils dilated.

'Impossible,' she murmured. 'Impossible! I must be going mad even to think of such a thing . . .'

Monstrous – yet it explained everything . . .

After a moment's reflection she sat down and wrote a note, weighing each word as she did so. Finally she nodded her head as though satisfied, and slipped it into an envelope which she addressed to Julius. She went down the passage to his sitting-room and knocked at the door. As she had expected, the room was empty. She left the note on the table.

A small page-boy was waiting outside her own door when she returned to it.

'Telegram for you, miss.'

Tuppence took it from the salver, and tore it open carelessly. Then she gave a cry. The telegram was from Tommy!

Chapter 16

Further Adventures of Tommy

From a darkness punctuated with throbbing stabs of fire, Tommy dragged his senses slowly back to life. When he at last opened his eyes, he was conscious of nothing but an excruciating pain through his temples. He was vaguely aware of unfamiliar surroundings. Where was he? What had happened? He blinked feebly. This was not his bedroom at the Ritz. And what the devil was the matter with his head?

'Damn!' said Tommy, and tried to sit up. He had remembered. He was in that sinister house in Soho. He uttered a groan and fell back. Through his almost-closed eyelids he reconnoitred carefully.

'He is coming to,' remarked a voice very near Tommy's ear. He recognized it at once for that of the bearded and efficient German, and lay artistically inert. He felt that it would be a pity to come round too soon; and until the pain in his head became a little less acute, he felt quite incapable of collecting his wits.

Painfully he tried to puzzle out what had happened. Obviously somebody must have crept up behind him as he listened and struck him down with a blow on the head. They knew him now for a spy, and would in all probability give him short shrift. Undoubtedly he was in a tight place. Nobody knew where he was, therefore he need expect no outside assistance, and must depend solely on his own wits.

'Well, here goes,' murmured Tommy to himself, and repeated his former remark.

'Damn!' he observed, and this time succeeded in sitting up.

In a minute the German stepped forward and placed a glass to his lips, with the brief command 'Drink.' Tommy obeyed. The potency of the draught made him choke, but it cleared his brain in a marvellous manner.

He was lying on a couch in the room in which the meeting had been held. On one side of him was the German, on the other the villainous-faced doorkeeper who had let him in. The others were grouped together at a little distance away. But Tommy missed one face. The man known as Number One was no longer of the company.

'Feel better?' asked the German, as he removed the empty glass.

'Yes, thanks,' returned Tommy cheerfully.

'Ah, my young friend, it is lucky for you your skull is so thick. The good Conrad struck hard.' He indicated the evil-faced doorkeeper by a nod.

The man grinned.

Tommy twisted his head round with an effort.

'Oh,' he said, 'so you're Conrad, are you? It strikes me the thickness of my skull was lucky for you too. When I look at you I feel it's almost a pity I've enabled you to cheat the hangman.'

The man snarled, and the bearded man said quietly:

'He would have run no risk of that.'

'Just as you like,' replied Tommy. 'I know it's the fashion to run down the police. I rather believe in them myself.'

His manner was nonchalant to the last degree. Tommy Beresford was one of those young Englishmen not distinguished by any special intellectual ability, but who are emphatically at their best in what is known as a 'tight place'. Their natural diffidence and caution falls from them then like a glove. Tommy realized perfectly that in his own wits lay the only chance of escape, and behind his casual manner he was racking his brains furiously.

The cold accents of the German took up the conversation:

'Have you anything to say before you are put to death as a spy?'

'Simply lots of things,' replied Tommy with the same urbanity as before.

'Do you deny that you were listening at that door?'

'I do not. I must really apologize – but your conversation was so interesting that it overcame my scruples.'

'How did you get in?'

'Dear old Conrad here.' Tommy smiled deprecatingly at him. 'I hesitate to suggest pensioning off a faithful servant, but you really ought to have a better watchdog.'

Conrad snarled impotently, and said sullenly, as the man with the beard swung round upon him:

'He gave the word. How was I to know?'

'Yes,' Tommy chimed in. 'How was he to know? Don't blame the poor fellow. His hasty action has given me the pleasure of seeing you all face to face.'

He fancied that his words caused some discomposure among the group, but the watchful German stilled it with a wave of his hand.

'Dead men tell no tales,' he said evenly.

'Ah,' said Tommy, 'but I'm not dead yet!'

'You soon will be, my young friend,' said the German.

An assenting murmur came from the others.

Tommy's heart beat faster, but his casual pleasantness did not waver.

'I think not,' he said firmly. 'I should have a great objection to dying.'

He had got them puzzled, he saw that by the look on his captor's face.

'Can you give us any reason why we should not put you to death?' asked the German.

'Several,' replied Tommy. 'Look here, you've been asking me a lot of questions. Let me ask you one for a change. Why didn't you kill me off at once before I regained consciousness?'

The German hesitated, and Tommy seized his advantage.

'Because you didn't know how much I knew – and where I obtained that knowledge. If you kill me now, you never will know.'

But here the emotions of Boris became too much for him. He stepped forward waving his arms.

'You hell-hound of a spy,' he screamed. 'We will give you short shrift. Kill him! Kill him!'

There was a roar of applause.

'You hear?' said the German, his eyes on Tommy. 'What have you got to say to that?'

'Say?' Tommy shrugged his shoulders. 'Pack of fools. Let them ask themselves a few questions. How did I get into this place? Remember what dear old Conrad said – *with your own password*, wasn't it? How did I get hold of that? You don't suppose I came up those steps haphazard and said the first thing that came into my head?'

Tommy was pleased with the concluding words of this speech. His only regret was that Tuppence was not present to appreciate its full flavour.

'That is true,' said the working man suddenly. 'Comrades, we have been betrayed!'

An ugly murmur arose. Tommy smiled at them encouragingly.

'That's better. How can you hope to make a success of any job if you don't use your brains?'

'You will tell us who has betrayed us,' said the German. 'But that shall not save you – oh, no! You shall tell us all that you know. Boris, here, knows pretty ways of making people speak!'

'Bah!' said Tommy scornfully, fighting down a singularly unpleasant feeling in the pit of his stomach. 'You will neither torture me nor kill me.'

'And why not?' asked Boris.

'Because you'd kill the goose that lays the golden eggs,' replied Tommy quietly.

There was a momentary pause. It seemed as though Tommy's persistent assurance was at last conquering. They were no longer completely sure of themselves. The man in the shabby clothes stared at Tommy searchingly.

'He's bluffing you, Boris,' he said quietly.

Tommy hated him. Had the man seen through him?

The German, with an effort, turned roughly to Tommy.

'What do you mean?'

'What do you think I mean?' parried Tommy, searching desperately in his own mind.

Suddenly Boris stepped forward, and shook his fist in Tommy's face.

'Speak, you swine of an Englishman – speak!'

'Don't get so excited, my good fellow,' said Tommy calmly. 'That's the worst of you foreigners. You can't keep calm. Now, I ask you, do I look as though I thought there were the least chance of your killing me?'

He looked confidently round, and was glad they could not hear the persistent beating of his heart which gave the lie to his words.

'No,' admitted Boris at last sullenly, 'you do not.'

'Thank God, he's not a mind reader,' thought Tommy. Aloud he pursued his advantage:

'And why am I so confident? Because I know something that puts me in a position to propose a bargain.'

'A bargain?' The bearded man took him up sharply.

'Yes – a bargain. My life and liberty against –' He paused.

'Against what?'

The group pressed forward. You could have heard a pin drop.

Slowly Tommy spoke.

'The papers that Danvers brought over from America in the *Lusitania*.'

The effect of his words was electrical. Everyone was on his feet. The German waved them back. He leaned over Tommy, his face purple with excitement.

'*Himmel*! You have got them, then?'

With magnificent calm Tommy shook his head.

'You know where they are?' persisted the German.

Again Tommy shook his head. 'Not in the least.'

'Then – then –' angry and baffled, the words failed him.

Tommy looked round. He saw anger and bewilderment on every face, but his calm assurance had done its work – no one doubted but that something lay behind his words.

'I don't know where the papers are – but I believe that I can find them. I have a theory –'

'Pah!'

Tommy raised his hand, and silenced the clamours of disgust.

'I call it a theory – but I'm pretty sure of my facts – facts that are known to no one but myself. In any case what do you lose? If I can produce the papers – you give me my life and liberty in exchange. Is it a bargain?'

'And if we refuse?' said the German quietly.

Tommy lay back on the couch.

'The 29th,' he said thoughtfully, 'is less than a fortnight ahead –'

For a moment the German hesitated. Then he made a sign to Conrad.

'Take him into the other room.'

For five minutes Tommy sat on the bed in the dingy room next door. His heart was beating violently. He had risked all on this throw. How would they decide? And all the while that this agonized questioning went on within him, he talked flippantly to Conrad, enraging the cross-grained doorkeeper to the point of homicidal mania.

At last the door opened, and the German called imperiously to Conrad to return.

'Let's hope the judge hasn't put his black cap on,' remarked Tommy frivolously. 'That's right, Conrad, march me in. The prisoner is at the bar, gentlemen.'

The German was seated once more behind the table. He motioned to Tommy to sit down opposite to him.

'We accept,' he said harshly, 'on terms. The papers must be delivered to us before you go free.'

'Idiot!' said Tommy amiably. 'How do you think I can look for them if you keep me tied by the leg here?'

'What do you expect, then?'

'I must have liberty to go about the business in my own way.'

The German laughed.

'Do you think we are little children to let you walk out of here leaving us a pretty story full of promises?'

'No,' said Tommy thoughtfully. 'Though infinitely simpler for me, I did not really think you would agree to that plan. Very well, we must arrange a compromise. How would it be if you attached little Conrad here to my person. He's a faithful fellow, and very ready with the fist.'

'We prefer,' said the German coldly, 'that you should remain here. One of our number will carry out your instructions minutely. If the operations are complicated, he will return to you with a report and you can instruct him further.'

'You're trying my hands,' complained Tommy. 'It's a very delicate affair, and the other fellow will muff it up as likely as not, and then where shall I be? I don't believe one of you has got an ounce of tact.'

The German rapped the table.

'Those are our terms. Otherwise, death!'

Tommy leaned back wearily.

'I like your style. Curt, but attractive. So be it, then. But one thing is essential, I must see the girl.'

'What girl?'

'Jane Finn, of course.'

The other looked at him curiously for some minutes,

then he said slowly, and as though choosing his words with care:

'Do you not know that she can tell you nothing?'

Tommy's heart beat a little faster. Would he succeed in coming face to face with the girl he was seeking?

'I shall not ask her to tell me anything,' he said quietly. 'Not in so many words, that is.'

'Then why see her?'

Tommy paused.

'To watch her face when I ask her one question,' he replied at last.

Again there was a look in the German's eyes that Tommy did not quite understand.

'She will not be able to answer your question.'

'That does not matter. I shall have seen her face when I ask it.'

'And you think that will tell you anything?' He gave a short disagreeable laugh. More than ever, Tommy felt that there was a factor somewhere that he did not understand. The German looked at him searchingly. 'I wonder whether, after all, you know as much as we think?' he said softly.

Tommy felt his ascendancy less sure than a moment before. His hold had slipped a little. But he was puzzled. What had he said wrong? He spoke out on the impulse of the moment.

'There may be things that you know which I do not.

I have not pretended to be aware of all the details of your show. But equally I've got something up my sleeve that *you* don't know about. And that's where I mean to score. Danvers was a damned clever fellow –' He broke off as if he had said too much.

But the German's face had lightened a little.

'Danvers,' he murmured. I see –' He paused a minute, then waved to Conrad. 'Take him away. Upstairs – you know.'

'Wait a minute,' said Tommy. 'What about the girl?'

'That may perhaps be arranged.'

'It must be.'

'We will see about it. Only one person can decide that.'

'Who?' asked Tommy. But he knew the answer.

'Mr Brown –'

'Shall I see him?'

'Perhaps.'

'Come,' said Conrad harshly.

Tommy rose obediently. Outside the door his gaoler motioned to him to mount the stairs. He himself followed close behind. On the floor above Conrad opened a door and Tommy passed into a small room. Conrad lit a hissing gas burner and went out. Tommy heard the sound of the key being turned in the lock.

He set to work to examine his prison. It was a smaller room than the one downstairs, and there was something peculiarly airless about the atmosphere of it. Then he realized that there was no window. He walked round it. The walls were filthily dirty, as everywhere else. Four pictures hung crookedly on the wall representing scenes from 'Faust,' Marguerite with her box of jewels, the church scene, Siebel and his flowers, and Faust and Mephistopheles. The latter brought Tommy's mind back to Mr Brown again. In this sealed and closed chamber, with its close-fitting heavy door, he felt cut off from the world, and the sinister power of the arch-criminal seemed more real. Shout as he would, no one could ever hear him. The place was a living tomb . . .

With an effort Tommy pulled himself together. He sank on to the bed and gave himself up to reflection. His head ached badly; also, he was hungry. The silence of the place was dispiriting.

'Anyway,' said Tommy, trying to cheer himself, 'I shall see the chief – the mysterious Mr Brown, and with a bit of luck in bluffing I shall see the mysterious Jane Finn also. After that –'

After that Tommy was forced to admit the prospect looked dreary.

Chapter 17
Annette

The troubles of the future, however, soon faded before the troubles of the present. And of these, the most immediate and pressing was that of hunger. Tommy had a healthy and vigorous appetite. The steak and chips partaken of for lunch seemed now to belong to another decade. He regretfully recognized the fact that he would not make a success of a hunger strike.

He prowled aimlessly about his prison. Once or twice he discarded dignity, and pounded on the door. But nobody answered the summons.

'Hang it all!' said Tommy indignantly. 'They can't mean to starve me to death.' A new-born fear passed through his mind that this might, perhaps, be one of those 'pretty ways' of making a prisoner speak, which had been attributed to Boris. But on reflection he dismissed the idea.

'It's that sour-faced brute Conrad,' he decided. 'That's

a fellow I shall enjoy getting even with one of these days. This is just a bit of spite on his part. I'm certain of it.'

Further meditations induced in him the feeling that it would be extremely pleasant to bring something down with a whack on Conrad's egg-shaped head. Tommy stroked his own head tenderly, and gave himself up to the pleasures of imagination. Finally a bright idea flashed across his brain. Why not convert imagination into reality! Conrad was undoubtedly the tenant of the house. The others, with the possible exception of the bearded German, merely used it as a rendezvous. Therefore, why not wait in ambush for Conrad behind the door, and when he entered bring down a chair, or one of the decrepit pictures, smartly on to his head. One would, of course, be careful not to hit too hard. And then – and then, simply walk out! If he met anyone on the way down, well – Tommy brightened at the thought of an encounter with his fists. Such an affair was infinitely more in his line than the verbal encounter of this afternoon. Intoxicated by his plan, Tommy gently unhooked the picture of the Devil and Faust, and settled himself in position. His hopes were high. The plan seemed to him simple but excellent.

Time went on, but Conrad did not appear. Night and day were the same in this prison room, but Tommy's wrist-watch, which enjoyed a certain degree of accuracy, informed him that it was nine o'clock in the evening. Tommy reflected gloomily that if supper did not arrive soon it would be a question of waiting for breakfast. At ten o'clock hope deserted him, and he flung himself on the bed to seek consolation in sleep. In five minutes his woes were forgotten.

The sound of the key turning in the lock awoke him from his slumbers. Not belonging to the type of hero who is famous for awaking in full possession of his faculties, Tommy merely blinked at the ceiling and wondered vaguely where he was. Then he remembered, and looked at his watch. It was eight o'clock.

'It's either early morning tea or breakfast,' deduced the young man, 'and pray God it's the latter!'

The door swung open. Too late, Tommy remembered his scheme of obliterating the unprepossessing Conrad. A moment later he was glad that he had, for it was not Conrad who entered, but a girl. She carried a tray which she set down on the table.

In the feeble light of the gas burner Tommy blinked at her. He decided at once that she was one of the most beautiful girls he had ever seen. Her hair was a full rich brown, with sudden glints of gold in it as though there were imprisoned sunbeams struggling in its depths. There was a wild-rose quality about her face. Her eyes, set wide apart, were hazel, a golden hazel that again recalled a memory of sunbeams.

A delirious thought shot through Tommy's mind.

'Are you Jane Finn?' he asked breathlessly.

The girl shook her head wonderingly.

'My name is Annette, monsieur.'

She spoke in a soft, broken English.

'Oh!' said Tommy, rather taken aback. '*Française*?' he hazarded.

'Oui, monsieur. Monsieur parle français?'

'Not for any length of time,' said Tommy. 'What's that? Breakfast?'

The girl nodded. Tommy dropped off the bed and came and inspected the contents of the tray. It consisted of a loaf, some margarine, and a jug of coffee.

'The living is not equal to the Ritz,' he observed with a sigh. 'But for what we are at last about to receive the Lord has made me truly thankful. Amen.'

He drew up a chair, and the girl turned away to the door.

'Wait a sec,' cried Tommy. 'There are lots of things I want to ask you, Annette. What are you doing in this house? Don't tell me you're Conrad's niece, or daughter, or anything, because I can't believe it.'

'I do the *service*, monsieur. I am not related to anybody.'

'I see,' said Tommy. 'You know what I asked you just now. Have you ever heard that name?'

'I have heard people speak of Jane Finn, I think.'

'You don't know where she is?'

Annette shook her head.

'She's not in this house, for instance?'

'Oh no, monsieur. I must go now – they will be waiting for me.'

She hurried out. They key turned in the lock.

'I wonder who "they" are,' mused Tommy, as he continued to make inroads on the loaf. 'With a bit of luck, that girl might help me to get out of here. She doesn't look like one of the gang.'

At one o'clock Annette reappeared with another tray, but this time Conrad accompanied her.

'Good morning,' said Tommy amiably. 'You have *not* used Pear's soap, I see.'

Conrad growled threateningly.

'No light repartee, have you, old bean? There, there, we can't always have brains as well as beauty. What have we for lunch? Stew? How did I know? Elementary, my dear Watson – the smell of onions is unmistakable.'

'Talk away,' grunted the man. 'It's little enough time you'll have to talk in, maybe.'

The remark was unpleasant in its suggestion, but Tommy ignored it. He sat down at the table.

'Retire, varlet,' he said, with a wave of his hand. 'Prate not to thy betters.'

That evening Tommy sat on the bed, and cogitated deeply. Would Conrad again accompany the girl? If he did not, should he risk trying to make an ally of her? He decided that he must leave no stone unturned. His position was desperate.

At eight o'clock the familiar sound of the key turning made him spring to his feet. The girl was alone.

'Shut the door,' he commanded. 'I want to speak to you.'

She obeyed.

'Look here, Annette, I want you to help me get out of this.'

She shook her head.

'Impossible. There are three of them on the floor below.'

'Oh!' Tommy was secretly grateful for the information. 'But you would help me if you could?'

'No, monsieur.'

'Why not?'

The girl hesitated.

'I think – they are my own people. You have spied upon them. They are quite right to keep you here.'

'They're a bad lot, Annette. If you'll help me, I'll take you away from the lot of them. And you'd probably get a good whack of money.'

But the girl merely shook her head.

'I dare not, monsieur. I am afraid of them.'

She turned away.

'Wouldn't you do anything to help another girl?'

cried Tommy. 'She's about your age too. Won't you save her from their clutches?'

'You mean Jane Finn?'

'Yes.'

'It is her you came here to look for? Yes?'

'That's it.'

The girl looked at him, then passed her hand across her forehead.

'Jane Finn. Always I hear that name. It is familiar.'

Tommy came forward eagerly.

'You must know *something* about her?'

But the girl turned away abruptly.

'I know nothing – only the name.' She walked towards the door. Suddenly she uttered a cry. Tommy stared. She had caught sight of the picture he had laid against the wall the night before. For a moment he caught a look of terror in her eyes. As inexplicably it changed to relief. Then abruptly, she went out of the room. Tommy could make nothing of it. Did she fancy that he had meant to attack her with it? Surely not. He rehung the picture on the wall thoughtfully.

Three more days went by in dreary inaction. Tommy felt the strain telling on his nerves. He saw no one but Conrad and Annette, and the girl had become dumb. She spoke only in monosyllables. A kind of dark suspicion smouldered in her eyes. Tommy felt that if this solitary confinement went on much longer he would go mad. He gathered from Conrad that they were waiting for orders from 'Mr Brown'. Perhaps, thought Tommy, he was abroad or away, and they were obliged to wait for his return.

But the evening of the third day brought a rude awakening.

It was barely seven o'clock when he heard the tramp of footsteps outside in the passage. In another minute the door was flung open. Conrad entered. With him was the evil-looking Number Fourteen. Tommy's heart sank at the sight of them.

'Evenin', gov'nor,' said the man with a leer. 'Got those ropes, mate?'

The silent Conrad produced a length of fine cord. The next minute Number Fourteen's hands, horribly dexterous, were winding the cord round his limbs, while Conrad held him down.

'What the devil –?' began Tommy.

But the slow, speechless grin of the silent Conrad froze the words on his lips.

Number Fourteen proceeded deftly with his task. In another minute Tommy was a mere helpless bundle. Then at last Conrad spoke:

'Thought you'd bluffed us, did you? With what you knew, and what you didn't know. Bargained with us! And all the time it was bluff! Bluff! You know less than a kitten. But your number's up all right, you b— swine.'

Tommy lay silent. There was nothing to say. He had failed. Somehow or other the omnipotent Mr Brown had seen through his pretensions. Suddenly a thought occurred to him.

'A very good speech, Conrad,' he said approvingly. 'But wherefore the bonds and fetters? Why not let this kind gentleman here cut my throat without delay?'

'Garn,' said Number Fourteen unexpectedly. 'Think we're as green as to do you in here, and have the police nosing round? Not 'alf! We've ordered the carriage for your lordship tomorrow mornin', but in the meantime we're not taking any chances, see!'

'Nothing,' said Tommy, 'could be plainer than your words – unless it was your face.'

'Stow it,' said Number Fourteen.

'With pleasure,' replied Tommy. 'You're making a sad mistake – but yours will be the loss.'

'You don't kid us that way again,' said Number Fourteen. 'Talking as though you were still at the blooming Ritz, aren't you?'

Tommy made no reply. He was engaged in wondering how Mr Brown had discovered his identity. He decided that Tuppence, in the throes of anxiety, had gone to the police, and that his disappearance having been made public the gang had not been slow to put two and two together.

The two men departed and the door slammed.

Tommy was left to his meditations. They were not pleasant ones. Already his limbs felt cramped and stiff. He was utterly helpless, and he could see no hope anywhere.

About an hour had passed when he heard the key softly turned, and the door opened. It was Annette. Tommy's heart beat a little faster. He had forgotten the girl. Was it possible that she had come to his help?

Suddenly he heard Conrad's voice:

'Come out of it, Annette. He doesn't want any supper tonight.'

'*Oui, oui, je sais bien*. But I must take the other tray. We need the things on it.'

'Well, hurry up,' growled Conrad.

Without looking at Tommy the girl went over to the table, and picked up the tray. She raised a hand and turned out the light.

'Curse you,' – Conrad had come to the door – 'why did you do that?'

'I always turn it out. You should have told me. Shall I relight it, Monsieur Conrad?'

'No, come on out of it.'

'*Le beau petit monsieur*,' cried Annette, pausing by the bed in the darkness. 'You have tied him up well, *hein*? He is liked a trussed chicken!' The frank amusement in her tone jarred on the boy but at that moment to his amazement, he felt her hand running lightly over his bonds, and something small and cold was pressed into the palm of his hand.

'Come on, Annette.'

'*Mais me voilà.*'

The door shut. Tommy heard Conrad say:

'Lock it and give me the key.'

The footsteps died away. Tommy lay petrified with amazement. The object Annette had thrust into his hand was a small penknife, the blade open. From the way she had studiously avoided looking at him, and her action with the light, he came to the conclusion that the room was overlooked. There must be a peep-hole somewhere in the walls. Remembering how guarded she had always been in her manner, he saw that he had probably been under observation all the time. Had he said anything to give himself away? Hardly. He had revealed a wish to escape and a desire to find Jane Finn, but nothing that could have given a clue to his own identity. True, his question to Annette had proved that he was personally unacquainted with Jane Finn, but he had never pretended otherwise. The question now was, did Annette really know more? Were her denials intended primarily for the listeners? On that point he could come to no conclusion.

But there was a more vital question that drove out all others. Could he, bound as he was, manage to cut his bonds? He essayed cautiously to rub the open blade up and down on the cord that bound his two wrists together. It was an awkward business and drew a smothered 'Ow' of pain from him as the knife cut into his wrist. But slowly and doggedly he went on sawing to and fro. He cut the flesh badly, but at last he felt the cord slacken. With his hands free, the rest was easy. Five minutes later he stood upright with some difficulty owing to the cramp in his limbs. His first care was to bind up his bleeding wrist. Then he sat on the edge of the bed to think. Conrad had taken the key of the door, so he could expect little more assistance from Annette. The only outlet from the room was the door, consequently he would perforce have to wait until the two men returned to fetch him. But when they did . . . Tommy smiled! Moving with infinite caution in the dark room, he found and unhooked the famous picture. He felt an economical pleasure that his first plan would not be wasted. There was now nothing to do but to wait. He waited.

The night passed slowly. Tommy lived through an eternity of hours, but at last he heard footsteps. He stood upright, drew a deep breath, and clutched the picture firmly.

The door opened. A faint light streamed in from outside. Conrad went straight towards the gas to light it. Tommy deeply regretted that it was he who had entered first. It would have been pleasant to get even with

Conrad. Number Fourteen followed. As he stepped across the threshold, Tommy brought the picture down with terrific force on his head. Number Fourteen went down amidst a stupendous crash of broken glass. In a minute Tommy had slipped out and pulled to the door. The key was in the lock. He turned it and withdrew it just as Conrad hurled himself against the door from the inside with a volley of curses.

For a moment Tommy hesitated. There was the sound of someone stirring on the floor below. Then the German's voice came up the stairs.

'*Gott im Himmel*! Conrad, what is it?'

Tommy felt a small hand thrust into his. Beside him stood Annette. She pointed up a rickety ladder that apparently led to some attics.

'Quick – up here!' She dragged him after her up the ladder. In another moment they were standing in a dusty garret littered with lumber. Tommy looked round.

'This won't do. It's a regular trap. There's no way out.'

'Hush! Wait.' The girl put her finger to her lips. She crept to the top of the ladder and listened.

The banging and beating on the door was terrific. The German and another were trying to force the door in. Annette explained in a whisper:

'They will think you are still inside. They cannot

hear what Conrad says. The door is too thick.'

'I thought you could hear what went on in the room?'

'There is a peep-hole into the next room. It was clever of you to guess. But they will not think of that – they are only anxious to get in.'

'Yes – but look here –'

'Leave it to me.' She bent down. To his amazement, Tommy saw that she was fastening the end of a long piece of string to the handle of a big cracked jug. She arranged it carefully, then turned to Tommy.

'Have you the key of the door?'

'Yes.'

'Give it to me.'

He handed it to her.

'I am going down. Do you think you can go half-way, and then swing yourself down *behind* the ladder, so that they will not see you?'

Tommy nodded.

'There's a big cupboard in the shadow of the landing. Stand behind it. Take the end of this string in your hand. When I've let the others out – *pull*!'

Before he had time to ask her anything more, she had flitted lightly down the ladder and was in the midst of the group with a loud cry:

'*Mon Dieu! Mon Dieu! Qu'est-ce qu'il y a*?'

The German turned on her with an oath.

'Get out of this. Go to your room!'

Very cautiously Tommy swung himself down the back of the ladder. So long as they did not turn round, all was well. He crouched behind the cupboard. They were still between him and the stairs.

'Ah!' Annette appeared to stumble over something. She stooped. '*Mon Dieu, voilà la clef*!'

The German snatched it from her. He unlocked the door. Conrad stumbled out, swearing.

'Where is he? Have you got him?'

'We have seen no one,' said the German sharply. His face paled. 'Who do you mean?'

Conrad gave vent to another oath.

'He's got away.'

'Impossible. He would have passed us.'

At that moment, with an ecstatic smile Tommy pulled the string. A crash of crockery came from the attic above. In a trice the men were pushing each other up the rickety ladder and had disappeared into the darkness above.

Quick as a flash Tommy leapt from his hiding-place and dashed down the stairs, pulling the girl with him. There was no one in the hall. He fumbled over the bolts and chain. At last they yielded, the door swung open. He turned. Annette had disappeared.

Tommy stood spell-bound. Had she run upstairs again? What madness possessed her! He fumed with impatience, but he stood his ground. He would not go without her.

And suddenly there was an outcry overhead, an exclamation from the German, and then Annette's voice, clear and high:

'*Ma foi*, he has escaped! And quickly! Who would have thought it?'

Tommy still stood rooted to the ground. Was that a command to him to go? He fancied it was.

And then, louder still, the words floated down to him:

'This is a terrible house. I want to go back to Marguerite. To Marguerite. *To Marguerite*!'

Tommy had run back to the stairs. She wanted him to go and leave her? But why? At all costs he must try to get her away with him. Then his heart sank. Conrad was leaping down the stairs uttering a savage cry at the sight of him. After him came the others.

Tommy stopped Conrad's rush with a straight blow with his fist. It caught the other on the point of the jaw and he fell like a log. The second man tripped over his body and fell. From higher up the staircase there was a flash, and a bullet grazed Tommy's ear. He realized that it would be good for his health to get out of this house as soon as possible. As regards Annette he could do nothing. He had got even with Conrad, which was one satisfaction. The blow had been a good one.

He leapt for the door, slamming it behind him. The square was deserted. In front of the house was a baker's van. Evidently he was to have been taken out of London in that, and his body found many miles from the house in Soho. The driver jumped to the pavement and tried to bar Tommy's way. Again Tommy's fist shot out, and the driver sprawled on the pavement.

Tommy took to his heels and ran – none too soon. The front door opened and a hail of bullets followed him. Fortunately none of them hit him. He turned the corner of the square.

'There's one thing,' he thought to himself, 'they can't go on shooting. They'll have the police after them if they do. I wonder they dared to there.'

He heard the footsteps of his pursuers behind him, and redoubled his own pace. Once he got out of these by-ways he would be safe. There would be a policeman about somewhere – not that he really wanted to invoke the aid of the police if he could possibly do without it. It meant explanation, and general awkwardness. In another moment he had reason to bless his luck. He stumbled over a prostrate figure, which started up with a yell of alarm and dashed off down the street. Tommy drew back into a doorway. In a minute he had the pleasure of seeing his two pursuers, of whom the German was one, industriously tracking down the red herring!

Tommy sat down quietly on the doorstep and allowed a few moments to elapse while he recovered his breath. Then he strolled gently in the opposite direction. He glanced at his watch. It was a little after half-past five. It was rapidly growing light. At the next corner he passed a policeman. The policeman cast a suspicious eye on him. Tommy felt slightly offended. Then, passing his hand over his face, he laughed. He had not shaved or washed for three days! What a guy he must look.

He betook himself without more ado to a Turkish Bath establishment which he knew to be open all night. He emerged into the busy daylight feeling himself once more, and able to make plans.

First of all, he must have a square meal. He had eaten nothing since midday yesterday. He turned into an A.B.C. shop and ordered eggs and bacon and coffee. Whilst he ate, he read a morning paper propped up in front of him. Suddenly he stiffened. There was a long article on Kramenin, who was described as the 'man behind Bolshevism' in Russia, and who had just arrived in London – some thought as an unofficial envoy. His career was sketched lightly, and it was firmly asserted that he, and not the figurehead leaders, had been the author of the Russian Revolution.

In the centre of the page was his portrait.

'So that's who Number One is,' said Tommy with

his mouth full of eggs and bacon. 'Not a doubt about it. I must push on.'

He paid for his breakfast, and betook himself to Whitehall. There he sent up his name, and the message that it was urgent. A few minutes later he was in the presence of the man who did not here go by the name of 'Mr Carter'. There was a frown on his face.

'Look here, you've no business to come asking for me in this way. I thought that was distinctly understood?'

'It was, sir. But I judged it important to lose no time.'

And as briefly and succinctly as possible he detailed the experiences of the last few days.

Half-way through, Mr Carter interrupted him to give a few cryptic orders through the telephone. All traces of displeasure had now left his face. He nodded energetically when Tommy had finished.

'Quite right. Every moment's of value. Fear we shall be too late anyway. They wouldn't wait. Would clear out at once. Still, they may have left something behind them that will be a clue. You say you've recognized Number One to be Kramenin? That's important. We want something against him badly to prevent the Cabinet falling on his neck too freely. What about the others? You say two faces were familiar to you? One's a Labour man, you think? Just look through these photos, and see if you can spot him.'

A minute later, Tommy held one up. Mr Carter exhibited some surprise.

'Ah, Westway! Shouldn't have thought it. Poses as being moderate. As for the other fellow, I think I can give a good guess.' He handed another photograph to Tommy, and smiled at the other's exclamation. 'I'm right, then. Who is he? Irishman. Prominent Unionist M.P. All a blind, of course. We've suspected it – but couldn't get any proof. Yes, you've done very well, young man. The 29th, you say, is the date. That gives us very little time – very little time indeed.'

'But –' Tommy hesitated.

Mr Carter read his thoughts.

'We can deal with the General Strike menace, I think. It's a toss-up – but we've got a sporting chance! But if that draft treaty turns up – we're done. England will be plunged in anarchy. Ah, what's that? The car? Come on, Beresford, we'll go and have a look at this house of yours.'

Two constables were on duty in front of the house in Soho. An inspector reported to Mr Carter in a low voice. The latter turned to Tommy.

'The birds have flown – as we thought. We might as well go over it.'

Going over the deserted house seemed to Tommy to partake of the character of a dream. Everything was just as it had been. The prison room with the crooked pictures, the broken jug in the attic, the meeting room with its long table. But nowhere was there a trace of papers. Everything of that kind had either been destroyed or taken away. And there was no sign of Annette.

'What you tell me about the girl puzzled me,' said Mr Carter. 'You believe that she deliberately went back?'

'It would seem so, sir. She ran upstairs while I was getting the door open.'

'H'm, she must belong to the gang, then; but, being a woman, didn't feel like standing by to see a personable young man killed. But evidently she's in with them, or she wouldn't have gone back.'

'I can't believe she's really one of them, sir. She – seemed so different –'

'Good-looking, I suppose?' said Mr Carter with a smile that made Tommy flush to the roots of his hair.

He admitted Annette's beauty rather shame-facedly.

'By the way,' observed Mr Carter, 'have you shown yourself to Miss Tuppence yet? She's been bombarding me with letters about you.'

'Tuppence? I was afraid she might get a bit rattled. Did she go to the police?'

Mr Carter shook his head.

'Then I wonder how they twigged me.'

Mr Carter looked inquiringly at him, and Tommy explained. The other nodded thoughtfully.

'True, that's rather a curious point. Unless the mention of the Ritz was an accidental remark?'

'It might have been, sir. But they must have found out about me suddenly in some way.'

'Well,' said Mr Carter, looking round him, 'there's nothing more to be done here. What about some lunch with me?'

'Thanks awfully, sir. But I think I'd better get back and rout out Tuppence.'

'Of course. Give her my kind regards and tell her not to believe you're killed too readily next time.'

Tommy grinned.

'I take a lot of killing, sir.'

'So I perceive,' said Mr Carter dryly. 'Well, goodbye. Remember you're a marked man now, and take reasonable care of yourself.'

'Thank you, sir.'

Hailing a taxi briskly Tommy stepped in, and was swiftly borne to the Ritz, dwelling the while on the pleasurable anticipation of startling Tuppence.

'Wonder what she's been up to. Dogging "Rita" most likely. By the way, I suppose that's who Annette meant by Marguerite. I didn't get it at the time.' The thought saddened him a little, for it seemed to prove that Mrs Vandemeyer and the girl were on intimate terms.

The taxi drew up at the Ritz. Tommy burst into its

sacred portals eagerly, but his enthusiasm received a check. He was informed that Miss Cowley had gone out a quarter of an hour ago.

Chapter 18
The Telegram

Baffled for the moment, Tommy strolled into the restaurant, and ordered a meal of surpassing excellence. His four days' imprisonment had taught him anew to value good food.

He was in the middle of conveying a particularly choice morsel of *sole à la Jeannette* to his mouth, when he caught sight of Julius entering the room. Tommy waved a menu cheerfully, and succeeded in attracting the other's attention. At the sight of Tommy, Julius's eyes seemed as though they would pop out of his head. He strode across, and pump-handled Tommy's hand with what seemed to the latter quite unnecessary vigour.

'Holy snakes!' he ejaculated. 'Is it really you?'

'Of course it is. Why shouldn't it be?'

'Why shouldn't it be? Say, man, don't you know you've been given up for dead? I guess we'd have had a solemn requiem for you in another few days.'

'Who thought I was dead?' demanded Tommy.

'Tuppence.'

'She remembered the proverb about the good dying young, I suppose. There must be a certain amount of original sin in me to have survived. Where is Tuppence, by the way?'

'Isn't she here?'

'No, the fellows at the office said she'd just gone out.'

'Gone shopping, I guess. I dropped her here in the car about an hour ago. But, say, can't you shed that British calm of yours, and get down to it? What on God's earth have you been doing all this time?'

'If you're feeding here,' replied Tommy, 'order now. It's going to be a long story.'

Julius drew up a chair to the opposite side of the table, summoned a hovering waiter, and dictated his wishes. Then he turned to Tommy.

'Fire ahead. I guess you've had some few adventures.'

'One or two,' replied Tommy modestly, and plunged into his recital.

Julius listened spell-bound. Half the dishes that were placed before him he forgot to eat. At the end he heaved a long sigh.

'Bully for you. Reads like a dime novel!'

'And now for the home front,' said Tommy, stretching out his hand for a peach.

'W – ell,' drawled Julius, 'I don't mind admitting we've had some adventures too.'

He, in his turn, assumed the rôle of narrator. Beginning with his unsuccessful reconnoitring at Bournemouth, he passed on to his return to London, the buying of the car, the growing anxieties of Tuppence, the call upon Sir James, and the sensational occurrences of the previous night.

'But who killed her?' asked Tommy. 'I don't quite understand.'

'The doctor kidded himself she took it herself,' replied Julius dryly.

'And Sir James? What did he think?'

'Being a legal luminary, he is likewise a human oyster,' replied Julius. 'I should say he "reserved judgment."' He went on to detail the events of the morning.

'Lost her memory, eh?' said Tommy with interest. 'By Jove, that explains why they looked at me so queerly when I spoke of questioning her. Bit of a slip on my part, that! But it wasn't the sort of thing a fellow would be likely to guess.'

'They didn't give you any sort of hint as to where Jane was?'

Tommy shook his head regretfully.

'Not a word. I'm a bit of an ass, as you know. I ought to have got more out of them somehow.'

'I guess you're lucky to be here at all. That bluff of yours was the goods all right. How you ever came to think of it all so pat beats me to a frazzle!'

'I was in such a funk I had to think of something,' said Tommy simply.

There was a moment's pause, and then Tommy reverted to Mrs Vandemeyer's death.

'There's no doubt it was chloral?'

'I believe not. At least they call it heart failure induced by an overdose, or some such claptrap. It's all right. We don't want to be worried with an inquest. But I guess Tuppence and I and even the highbrow Sir James have all got the same idea.'

'Mr Brown?' hazarded Tommy.

'Sure thing.'

Tommy nodded.

'All the same,' he said thoughtfully, 'Mr Brown hasn't got wings. I don't see how he got in and out.'

'How about some high-class thought transference stunt? Some magnetic influence that irresistibly impelled Mrs Vandemeyer to commit suicide?'

Tommy looked at him with respect.

'Good, Julius. Distinctly good. Especially the phraseology. But it leaves me cold. I yearn for a real Mr Brown of flesh and blood. I think the gifted young detectives must get to work, study the entrances and exits, and tap the bumps on their foreheads until the solution of the mystery dawns on them. Let's go round to the scene of the crime. I wish we could get hold of Tuppence. The Ritz would enjoy the spectacle of the glad reunion.'

Inquiry at the office revealed the fact that Tuppence had not yet returned.

'All the same, I guess I'll have a look round upstairs,' said Julius. 'She might be in my sitting-room.' He disappeared.

Suddenly a diminutive boy spoke at Tommy's elbow:

'The young lady – she's gone away by train, I think, sir,' he murmured shyly.

'What?' Tommy wheeled round upon him.

The small boy became pinker than before.

'The taxi, sir. I heard her tell the driver Charing Cross and to look sharp.'

Tommy stared at him, his eyes opening wide in surprise. Emboldened, the small boy proceeded. 'So I thought, having asked for an A.B.C. and a Bradshaw.'

Tommy interrupted him:

'When did she ask for an A.B.C. and a Bradshaw?'

'When I took her the telegram, sir.'

'A telegram?'

'Yes, sir.'

'When was that?'

'About half-past twelve, sir.'

'Tell me exactly what happened.'

The small boy drew a long breath.

'I took up a telegram to No. 891 – the lady was there. She opened it and gave a gasp, and then she said, very jolly like: "Bring me up a Bradshaw, and an A.B.C., and look sharp, Henry." My name isn't Henry, but –'

'Never mind your name,' said Tommy impatiently. 'Go on.'

'Yes, sir. I brought them, and she told me to wait, and looked up something. And then she looks up at the clock, and "Hurry up," she says. "Tell them to get me a taxi," and she begins a-shoving on of her hat in front of the glass, and she was down in two ticks, almost as quick as I was, and I seed her going down the steps and into the taxi, and I heard her call out what I told you.'

The small boy stopped and replenished his lungs. Tommy continued to stare at him. At that moment Julius rejoined him. He held an open letter in his hand.

'I say, Hersheimmer,' – Tommy turned to him – 'Tuppence has gone off sleuthing on her own.'

'Shucks!'

'Yes, she has. She went off in a taxi to Charing Cross in the deuce of a hurry after getting a telegram.' His eye fell on the letter in Julius's hand. 'Oh; she left a note for you. That's all right. Where's she off to?'

Almost unconsciously, he held out his hand for the

letter, but Julius folded it up and placed it in his pocket. He seemed a trifle embarrassed.

'I guess this is nothing to do with it. It's about something else – something I asked her that she was to let me know about.'

'Oh!' Tommy looked puzzled, and seemed waiting for more.

'See here,' said Julius suddenly, 'I'd better put you wise. I asked Miss Tuppence to marry me this morning.'

'Oh!' said Tommy mechanically. He felt dazed. Julius's words were totally unexpected. For the moment they benumbed his brain.

'I'd like to tell you,' continued Julius, 'that before I suggested anything of the kind to Miss Tuppence, I made it clear that I didn't want to butt in in any way between her and you –'

Tommy roused himself.

'That's all right,' he said quickly. 'Tuppence and I have been pals for years. Nothing more.' He lit a cigarette with a hand that shook ever so little. 'That's quite all right. Tuppence always said that she was looking out for –'

He stopped abruptly, his face crimsoning, but Julius was in no way discomposed.

'Oh, I guess it'll be the dollars that'll do the trick. Miss Tuppence put me wise to that right away. There's no humbug about her. We ought to gee along together very well.'

Tommy looked at him curiously for a minute, as though he were about to speak, then changed his mind and said nothing. Tuppence and Julius! Well, why not? Had she not lamented the fact that she knew no rich men? Had she not openly avowed her intention of marrying for money if she ever had the chance? Her meeting with the young American millionaire had given her the chance – and it was unlikely she would be slow to avail herself of it. She was out for money. She had always said so. Why blame her because she had been true to her creed?

Nevertheless, Tommy did blame her. He was filled with a passionate and utterly illogical resentment. It was all very well to *say* things like that – but a *real* girl would never marry for money. Tuppence was utterly cold-blooded and selfish, and he would be delighted if he never saw her again! And it was a rotten world!

Julius's voice broke in on these meditations.

'Yes, we ought to gee along together very well. I've heard that a girl always refuses you once – a sort of convention.'

Tommy caught his arm.

'Refuses? Did you say *refuses*?'

'Sure thing. Didn't I tell you that? She just rapped out a "no" without any kind of reason to it. The eternal feminine, the Huns call it, I've heard. But she'll come round right enough. Likely enough, I hustled her some –'

But Tommy interrupted regardless of decorum.

'What did she say in that note?' he demanded fiercely.

The obliging Julius handed it to him.

'There's no earthly clue in it as to where she's gone,' he assured Tommy. 'But you might as well see for yourself if you don't believe me.'

The note, in Tuppence's well-known schoolboy writing, ran as follows:

Dear Julius,

It's always better to have things in black and white. I don't feel I can be bothered to think of marriage until Tommy is found. Let's leave it till then.

Yours affectionately,

Tuppence.

Tommy handed it back, his eyes shining. His feelings had undergone a sharp reaction. He now felt that Tuppence was all that was noble and disinterested. Had she not refused Julius without hesitation? True, the note betokened signs of weakening, but he could excuse that. It read almost like a bribe to Julius to spur him on in his efforts to find Tommy, but he supposed she had not really meant it that way. Darling Tuppence, there was not a girl in the world to touch her! When he saw her – His thoughts were brought up with a sudden jerk.

'As you say,' he remarked, pulling himself together, 'there's not a hint here as to what she's up to. Hi – Henry!'

The small boy came obediently. Tommy produced five shillings.

'One thing more. Do you remember what the young lady did with the telegram?'

Henry gasped and spoke.

'She crumpled it up into a ball and threw it into the grate, and made a sort of noise like "Whoop!" sir.'

'Very graphic, Henry,' said Tommy. 'Here's your five shillings. Come on, Julius. We must find that telegram.'

They hurried upstairs. Tuppence had left the key in her door. The room was as she had left it. In the fireplace was a crumpled ball of orange and white. Tommy disentangled it and smoothed out the telegram.

Come at once, Moat House, Ebury, Yorkshire, great developments – Tommy.

They looked at each other in stupefaction. Julius spoke first:

'*You* didn't send it?'

'Of course not. What does it mean?'

'I guess it means the worst,' said Julius quietly. 'They've got her.'

'*What*?'

'Sure thing! They signed your name, and she fell into the trap like a lamb.'

'My God! What shall we do?'

'Get busy, and go after her! Right now! There's no time to waste. It's almighty luck that she didn't take the wire with her. If she had we'd probably never have traced her. But we've got to hustle. Where's that Bradshaw?'

The energy of Julius was infectious. Left to himself, Tommy would probably have sat down to think things out for a good half-hour before he decided on a plan of action. But with Julius Hersheimmer about, hustling was inevitable.

After a few muttered imprecations he handed the Bradshaw to Tommy as being more conversant with its mysteries. Tommy abandoned it in favour of an A.B.C.

'Here we are. Ebury, Yorks. From King's Cross. Or St Pancras. (Boy must have made a mistake. It was King's Cross, not *Charing* Cross) 12.50, that's the train she went by; 2.10, that's gone; 3.20 is the next – and a damned slow train, too.'

'What about the car?'

Tommy shook his head.

'Send it up if you like, but we'd better stick to the train. The great thing is to keep calm.'

Julius groaned.

'That's so. But it gets my goat to think of that innocent young girl in danger!'

Tommy nodded abstractedly. He was thinking. In a moment or two, he said:

'I say, Julius, what do they want her for, anyway?'

'Eh? I don't get you?'

'What I mean is that I don't think it's their game to do her any harm,' explained Tommy, puckering his brow with the strain of his mental processes. 'She's a hostage, that's what she is. She's in no immediate danger, because if we tumble on to anything, she'd be damned useful to them. As long as they've got her, they've got the whip hand of us. See?'

'Sure thing,' said Julius thoughtfully. 'That's so.'

'Besides,' added Tommy, as an afterthought, 'I've great faith in Tuppence.'

The journey was wearisome, with many stops, and crowded carriages. They had to change twice, once at Doncaster, once at a small junction. Ebury was a deserted station with a solitary porter, to whom Tommy addressed himself:

'Can you tell me the way to the Moat House?'

'The Moat House? It's a tidy step from here. The big house near the sea, you mean?'

Tommy assented brazenly. After listening to the porter's meticulous but perplexing directions, they prepared to leave the station. It was beginning to rain, and they turned up the collars of their coats as they trudged through the slush of the road. Suddenly Tommy halted.

'Wait a moment.' He ran back to the station and tackled the porter anew.

'Look here, do you remember a young lady who arrived by an earlier train, the 12.10 from London? She'd probably ask you the way to the Moat House.'

He described Tuppence as well as he could, but the porter shook his head. Several people had arrived by the train in question. He could not call to mind one young lady in particular. But he was quite certain that no one had asked him the way to the Moat House.

Tommy rejoined Julius, and explained. Depression was settling down on him like a leaden weight. He felt convinced that their quest was going to be unsuccessful. The enemy had over three hours' start. Three hours was more than enough for Mr Brown. He would not ignore the possibility of the telegram having been found.

The way seemed endless. Once they took the wrong turning and went nearly half a mile out of their direction. It was past seven o'clock when a small boy told them that 't' Moat House' was just past the next corner.

A rusty iron gate swinging dismally on its hinges! An over-grown drive thick with leaves. There was something about the place that struck a chill to both their hearts. They went up the deserted drive. The leaves deadened their footsteps. The daylight was almost gone. It was like walking in a world of ghosts. Overhead the branches flapped and creaked with a mournful note. Occasionally a sodden leaf drifted silently down, startling them with its cold touch on their cheeks.

A turn of the drive brought them in sight of the house. That, too, seemed empty and deserted. The shutters were closed, the steps up to the door overgrown with moss. Was it indeed to this desolate spot that Tuppence had been decoyed? It seemed hard to believe that a human footstep had passed this way for months.

Julius jerked the rusty bell handle. A jangling peal rang discordantly, echoing through the emptiness within. No one came. They rang again and again – but there was no sign of life. Then they walked completely round the house. Everywhere silence, and shuttered windows. If they could believe the evidence of their eyes the place was empty.

'Nothing doing,' said Julius.

They retraced their steps slowly to the gate.

'There must be a village handy,' continued the young American. 'We'd better make inquiries there. They'll know something about the place, and whether there's been anyone there lately.'

'Yes, that's not a bad idea.'

Proceeding up the road they soon came to a little hamlet. On the outskirts of it, they met a workman swinging his bag of tools, and Tommy stopped him with a question.

'The Moat House? It's empty. Been empty for years. Mrs Sweeney's got the key if you want to go over it – next to the post office.'

Tommy thanked him. They soon found the post office, which was also a sweet and general fancy shop, and knocked at the door of the cottage next to it. A clean, wholesome-looking woman opened it. She readily produced the key of the Moat House.

'Though I doubt if it's the kind of place to suit you, sir. In a terrible state of repair. Ceilings leaking and all. 'Twould need a lot of money spent on it.'

'Thanks,' said Tommy cheerily. 'I dare say it'll be a wash-out, but houses are scarce nowadays.'

'That they are,' declared the woman heartily. 'My daughter and son-in-law have been looking for a decent cottage for I don't know how long. It's all the war. Upset things terribly, it has. But excuse me, sir, it'll be too dark for you to see much of the house. Hadn't you better wait until tomorrow?'

'That's all right. We'll have a look round this evening, anyway. We'd have been here before only we lost our way. What's the best place to stay at for the night round here?'

Mrs Sweeney looked doubtful.

'There's the Yorkshire Arms, but it's not much of a place for gentlemen like you.'

'Oh, it will do very well. Thanks. By the way, you've not had a young lady here asking for this key today?'

The woman shook her head.

'No one's been over the place for a long time.'

'Thanks very much.'

They retraced their steps to the Moat House. As the front door swung back on its hinges, protesting loudly, Julius struck a match and examined the floor carefully. Then he shook his head.

'I'd swear no one's passed this way. Look at the dust. Thick. Not a sign of a footmark.'

They wandered round the deserted house. Everywhere the same tale. Thick layers of dust apparently undisturbed.

'This gets me,' said Julius. 'I don't believe Tuppence was ever in this house.'

'She must have been.'

Julius shook his head without replying.

'We'll go over it again tomorrow,' said Tommy. 'Perhaps we'll see more in the daylight.'

On the morrow they took up the search once more, and were reluctantly forced to the conclusion that the house had not been invaded for some considerable time.

They might have left the village altogether but for a fortunate discovery of Tommy's. As they were retracing their steps to the gate, he gave a sudden cry, and stooping, picked something up from among the leaves, and held it out to Julius. It was a small gold brooch.

'That's Tuppence's!'

'Are you sure?'

'Absolutely. I've often seen her wear it.'

Julius drew a deep breath.

'I guess that settles it. She came as far as here, anyway. We'll make that pub our headquarters, and raise hell round here until we find her. Somebody *must* have seen her.'

Forthwith the campaign began. Tommy and Julius worked separately and together, but the result was the same. Nobody answering to Tuppence's description had been seen in the vicinity. They were baffled – but not discouraged. Finally they altered their tactics. Tuppence had certainly not remained long in the neighbourhood of the Moat House. That pointed to her having been overcome and carried away in a car. They renewed inquiries. Had anyone seen a car standing somewhere near the Moat House that day? Again they met with no success.

Julius wired to town for his own car, and they scoured the neighbourhood daily with unflagging zeal. A grey limousine on which they had set high hopes was traced to Harrogate, and turned out to be the property of a highly respectable maiden lady!

Each day saw them set out on a new quest. Julius was like a hound on the leash. He followed up the slenderest clue. Every car that had passed through the village on the fateful day was tracked down. He forced his way into country properties and submitted the owners of the cars to searching cross-examination. His apologies were as thorough as his methods, and seldom failed in disarming the indignation of his victims; but, as day succeeded day, they were no nearer to discovering Tuppence's whereabouts. So well had the abduction been planned that the girl seemed literally to have vanished into thin air.

And another preoccupation was weighing on Tommy's mind.

'Do you know how long we've been here?' he asked one morning as they sat facing each other at breakfast. 'A week! We're no nearer to finding Tuppence, *and next Sunday is the 29th*!'

'Shucks!' said Julius thoughtfully. 'I'd almost forgotten about the 29th. I've been thinking of nothing but Tuppence.'

'So have I. At least, I hadn't forgotten about the 29th, but it didn't seem to matter a damn in comparison to finding Tuppence. But today's the 23rd, and time's getting short. If we're ever going to get hold of her at all, we must do it before the 29th – her life won't be worth an hour's purchase afterwards. The hostage game will be played out by then. I'm beginning to feel that we've made a big mistake in the way we've set about this. We've wasted time and we're no forrader.'

'I'm with you there. We've been a couple of mutts, who've bitten off a bigger bit than they can chew. I'm going to quit fooling right away!'

'What do you mean?'

'I'll tell you. I'm going to do what we ought to have done a week ago. I'm going right back to London to put the case in the hands of your British police. We fancied ourselves as sleuths. Sleuths! It was a piece of damn-fool foolishness! I'm through! I've had enough of it. Scotland Yard for me!'

'You're right,' said Tommy slowly. 'I wish to God we'd gone there right away.'

'Better late than never. We've been like a couple of babes playing "Here we go round the Mulberry Bush." Now I'm going right along to Scotland Yard to ask them to take me by the hand and show me the way I should go. I guess the professional always scores over the amateur in the end. Are you coming along with me?'

Tommy shook his head.

'What's the good? One of us is enough. I might as well stay here and nose round a bit longer. Something *might* turn up. One never knows.'

'Sure thing. Well, so long. I'll be back in a couple of shakes with a few inspectors along. I shall tell them to pick out their brightest and best.'

But the course of events was not to follow the plan Julius had laid down. Later in the day Tommy received a wire:

Join me Manchester Midland Hotel. Important news – JULIUS.

At 7.30 that night Tommy alighted from a slow cross-country train. Julius was on the platform.

'Thought you'd come by this train if you weren't out when my wire arrived.'

Tommy grasped him by the arm.

'What is it? Is Tuppence found?'

Julius shook his head.

'No. But I found this waiting in London. Just arrived.'

He handed the telegraph form to the other. Tommy's eyes opened as he read:

Jane Finn found. Come Manchester Midland Hotel immediately – PEEL EDGERTON.

Julius took the form back and folded it up.

'Queer,' he said thoughtfully. 'I thought that lawyer chap had quit!'

Chapter 19
Jane Finn

'My train got in half an hour ago,' explained Julius, as he led the way out of the station. 'I reckoned you'd come by this before I left London, and wired accordingly to Sir James. He's booked rooms for us, and will be round to dine at eight.'

'What made you think he'd ceased to take any interest in the case?' asked Tommy curiously.

'What he said,' replied Julius dryly. 'The old bird's as close as an oyster! Like all the darned lot of them, he wasn't going to commit himself till he was sure he could deliver the goods.'

'I wonder,' said Tommy thoughtfully.

Julius turned on him.

'You wonder what?'

'Whether that was his real reason.'

'Sure. You bet your life it was.'

Tommy shook his head unconvinced.

Sir James arrived punctually at eight o'clock, and Julius introduced Tommy. Sir James shook hands with him warmly.

'I am delighted to make your acquaintance, Mr Beresford. I have heard so much about you from Miss Tuppence' – he smiled involuntarily – 'that it really seems as though I already know you quite well.'

'Thank you, sir,' said Tommy with his cheerful grin. He scanned the great lawyer eagerly. Like Tuppence, he felt the magnetism of the other's personality. He was reminded of Mr Carter. The two men, totally unlike so far as physical resemblance went, produced a similar effect. Beneath the weary manner of the one and the professional reserve of the other, lay the same quality of mind, keen-edged like a rapier.

In the meantime he was conscious of Sir James's close scrutiny. When the lawyer dropped his eyes the young man had the feeling that the other had read him through and through like an open book. He could not but wonder what the final judgment was, but there was little chance of learning that. Sir James took in everything, but gave out only what he chose. A proof of that occurred almost at once.

Immediately the first greetings were over Julius broke out into a flood of eager questions. How had Sir James managed to track the girl? Why had he not let them know that he was still working on the case? And so on.

Sir James stroked his chin and smiled. At last he said:

'Just so, just so. Well, she's found. And that's the great thing, isn't it? Eh! Come now, that's the great thing?'

'Sure it is. But just how did you strike her trail? Miss Tuppence and I thought you'd quit for good and all.'

'Ah!' The lawyer shot a lightning glance at him, then resumed operations on his chin. 'You thought that, did you? Did you really? H'm, dear me.'

'But I guess I can take it we were wrong,' pursued Julius.

'Well, I don't know that I should go so far as to say that. But it's certainly fortunate for all parties that we've managed to find the young lady.'

'But where is she?' demanded Julius, his thoughts flying off on another tack. 'I thought you'd be sure to bring her along?'

'That would hardly be possible,' said Sir James gravely.

'Why?'

'Because the young lady was knocked down in a street accident, and has sustained slight injuries to the head. She was taken to the infirmary, and on recovering consciousness gave her name as Jane Finn. When – ah! – I heard that, I arranged for her to be removed to the house of a doctor – a friend of mine, and wired at once for you. She relapsed into unconsciousness and has not spoken since.'

'She's not seriously hurt?'

'Oh, a bruise and a cut or two; really, from a medical point of view, absurdly slight injuries to have produced such a condition. Her state is probably to be attributed to the mental shock consequent on recovering her memory.'

'It's come back?' cried Julius excitedly.

Sir James tapped the table rather impatiently.

'Undoubtedly, Mr Hersheimmer, since she was able to give her real name. I thought you had appreciated that point.'

'And you just happened to be on the spot,' said Tommy. 'Seems quite like a fairy tale?'

But Sir James was far too wary to be drawn.

'Coincidences are curious things,' he said dryly.

Nevertheless, Tommy was now certain of what he had before only suspected. Sir James's presence in Manchester was not accidental. Far from abandoning the case, as Julius supposed, he had by some means of his own successfully run the missing girl to earth. The only thing that puzzled Tommy was the reason for all this secrecy? He concluded that it was a foible of the legal mind.

Julius was speaking.

'After dinner,' he announced, 'I shall go right away and see Jane.'

'That will be impossible, I fear,' said Sir James. 'It is very unlikely they would allow her to see visitors at this time of night. I should suggest tomorrow morning about ten o'clock.'

Julius flushed. There was something in Sir James which always stirred him to antagonism. It was a conflict of two masterful personalities.

'All the same, I reckon I'll go round there tonight and see if I can't ginger them up to break through their silly rules.'

'It will be quite useless, Mr Hersheimmer.'

The words came out like the crack of a pistol, and Tommy looked up with a start. Julius was nervous and excited. The hand with which he raised his glass to his lips shook slightly, but his eyes held Sir James's defiantly. For a moment the hostility between the two seemed likely to burst into flame, but in the end Julius lowered his eyes, defeated.

'For the moment, I reckon you're the boss.'

'Thank you,' said the other. 'We will say ten o'clock then?' With consummate ease of manner he turned to Tommy. 'I must confess, Mr Beresford, that it was something of a surprise to me to see you here this evening. The last I heard of you was that your friends were in grave anxiety on your behalf. Nothing had been heard of you for some days, and Miss Tuppence was inclined to think you had got into difficulties.'

'I had, sir!' Tommy grinned reminiscently. 'I was never in a tighter place in my life.'

Helped out by questions from Sir James, he gave an abbreviated account of his adventures. The lawyer looked at him with renewed interest as he brought the tale to a close.

'You got yourself out of a tight place very well,' he said gravely. 'I congratulate you. You displayed a great deal of ingenuity and carried your part through well.'

Tommy blushed, his face assuming a prawn-like hue at the praise.

'I couldn't have got away but for the girl, sir.'

'No.' Sir James smiled a little. 'It was lucky for you she happened to – er – take a fancy to you.' Tommy appeared about to protest, but Sir James went on. 'There's no doubt about her being one of the gang, I suppose?'

'I'm afraid not, sir. I thought perhaps they were keeping her there by force, but the way she acted didn't fit in with that. You see, she went back to them when she could have got away.'

Sir James nodded thoughtfully.

'What did she say? Something about wanting to be taken to Marguerite?'

'Yes, sir. I suppose she meant Mrs Vandemeyer.

'She always signed herself Rita Vandemeyer. All her friends spoke of her as Rita. Still, I suppose the girl must have been in the habit of calling her by her full name. And, at the moment she was crying out to her, Mrs Vandemeyer was either dead or dying! Curious! There are one or two points that strike me as being obscure – their sudden change of attitude towards yourself, for instance. By the way, the house was raided, of course?'

'Yes, sir, but they'd cleared out.'

'Naturally,' said Sir James dryly.

'And not a clue left behind.'

'I wonder –' The lawyer tapped the table thoughtfully.

Something in his voice made Tommy look up. Would this man's eyes have seen something where theirs had been blind? He spoke impulsively:

'I wish you'd been there, sir, to go over the house!'

'I wish I had,' said Sir James quietly. He sat for a moment in silence. Then he looked up. 'And since then? What have you been doing?'

For a moment, Tommy stared at him. Then it dawned on him that of course the lawyer did not know.

'I forgot that you didn't know about Tuppence,' he said slowly. The sickening anxiety, forgotten for a while in the excitement of knowing Jane Finn found at last, swept over him again.

The lawyer laid down his knife and fork sharply.

'Has anything happened to Miss Tuppence?' His voice was keen-edged.

'She's disappeared,' said Julius.

'When?'

'A week ago.'

'How?'

Sir James's questions fairly shot out. Between them Tommy and Julius gave the history of the last week and their futile search.

Sir James went at once to the root of the matter.

'A wire signed with your name? They knew enough of you both for that. They weren't sure of how much you had learnt in that house. Their kidnapping of Miss Tuppence is the counter-move to your escape. If necessary they could seal your lips with what might happen to her.'

Tommy nodded.

'That's just what I thought, sir.'

Sir James looked at him keenly. '*You* had worked that out, had you? Not bad – not at all bad. The curious thing is that they certainly did not know anything about you when they first held you prisoner. You are sure that you did not in any way disclose your identity?'

Tommy shook his head.

'That's so,' said Julius with a nod. 'Therefore I reckon

someone put them wise – and not earlier than Sunday afternoon.'

'Yes, but who?'

'That almighty omniscient Mr Brown, of course!'

There was a faint note of derision in the American's voice which made Sir James look up sharply.

'You don't believe in Mr Brown, Mr Hersheimmer?'

'No, sir, I do not,' returned the young American with emphasis. 'Not as such, that is to say. I reckon it out that he's a figurehead – just a bogy name to frighten the children with. The real head of this business is that Russian chap Kramenin. I guess he's quite capable of running revolutions in three countries at once if he chose! The man Whittington is probably the head of the English branch.'

'I disagree with you,' said Sir James shortly. 'Mr Brown exists.' He turned to Tommy. 'Did you happen to notice where that wire was handed in?'

'No, sir, I'm afraid I didn't.'

'H'm. Got it with you?'

'It's upstairs, sir, in my kit.'

'I'd like to have a look at it sometime. No hurry. You've wasted a week,' – Tommy hung his head – 'a day or so more is immaterial. We'll deal with Miss Jane Finn first. Afterwards, we'll set to work to rescue Miss Tuppence from bondage. I don't think she's in any immediate danger. That is, so long as they don't know that we've got Jane Finn, and that her memory has returned. We must keep that dark at all costs. You understand?'

The other two assented, and, after making arrangements for meeting on the morrow, the great lawyer took his leave.

At ten o'clock, the two young men were at the appointed spot. Sir James had joined them on the doorstep. He alone appeared unexcited. He introduced them to the doctor.

'Mr Hersheimmer – Mr Beresford – Dr Roylance. How's the patient?'

'Going on well. Evidently no idea of the flight of time. Asked this morning how many had been saved from the *Lusitania*. Was it in the papers yet? That, of course, was only what was to be expected. She seems to have something on her mind, though.'

'I think we can relieve her anxiety. May we go up?'

'Certainly.'

Tommy's heart beat sensibly faster as they followed the doctor upstairs. Jane Finn at last! The long-sought, the mysterious, the elusive Jane Finn! How wildly improbable success had seemed! And here in this house, her memory almost miraculously restored, lay the girl who held the future of England in her hands. A half groan broke from Tommy's lips. If only Tuppence could have been at his side to share in the triumphant conclusion of their joint venture! Then he put the thought of Tuppence resolutely aside. His confidence in Sir James was growing. There was a man who would unerringly ferret out Tuppence's whereabouts. In the meantime, Jane Finn! And suddenly a dread clutched at his heart. It seemed too easy . . . Suppose they should find her dead . . . stricken down by the hand of Mr Brown?

In another minute he was laughing at these melodramatic fancies. The doctor held open the door of a room and they passed in. On the white bed, bandages round her head, lay the girl. Somehow the whole scene seemed unreal. It was so exactly what one expected that it gave the effect of being beautifully staged.

The girl looked from one to the other of them with large wondering eyes. Sir James spoke first.

'Miss Finn,' he said, 'this is your cousin, Mr Julius P. Hersheimmer.'

A faint flush flitted over the girl's face, as Julius stepped forward and took her hand.

'How do, Cousin Jane?' he said lightly.

But Tommy caught the tremor in his voice.

'Are you really Uncle Hiram's son?' she asked wonderingly.

Her voice, with the slight warmth of the Western accent, had an almost thrilling quality. It seemed vaguely familiar to Tommy, but he thrust the impression aside as impossible.

'Sure thing.'

'We used to read about Uncle Hiram in the newspapers,' continued the girl, in her soft tones. 'But I never thought I'd meet you one day. Mother figured it out that Uncle Hiram would never get over being mad with her.'

'The old man was like that,' admitted Julius. 'But I guess the new generation's sort of different. Got no use for the family feud business. First thing I thought about, soon as the war was over, was to come along and hunt you up.'

A shadow passed over the girl's face.

'They've been telling me things – dreadful things – that my memory went, and that there are years I shall never know about – years lost out of my life.'

'You didn't realize that yourself?'

The girl's eyes opened wide.

'Why, no. It seems to me as though it were no time since we were being hustled into those boats. I can see it all now!' She closed her eyes with a shudder.

Julius looked across at Sir James, who nodded.

'Don't worry any. It isn't worth it. Now, see here, Jane, there's something we want to know about. There was a man aboard that boat with some mighty important papers on him, and the big guns in this country have got a notion that he passed on the goods to you. Is that so?'

The girl hesitated, her glance shifting to the other two. Julius understood.

'Mr Beresford is commissioned by the British Government to get those papers back. Sir James Peel Edgerton is an English Member of Parliament, and might be a big gun in the Cabinet if he liked. It's owing to him that we've ferreted you out at last. So you can go right ahead and tell us the whole story. Did Danvers give you the papers?'

'Yes. He said they'd have a better chance with me, because they would have the women and children first.'

'Just as we thought,' said Sir James.

'He said they were very important – that they might make all the difference to the Allies. But, if it's all so long ago, and the war's over, what does it matter now?'

'I guess history repeats itself, Jane. First there was a great hue and cry over those papers, then it all died down, and now the whole caboodle's started all over again – for rather different reasons. Then you can hand them over to us right away?'

'But I can't.'

'What?'

'I haven't got them.'

'You – haven't – got them?' Julius punctuated the words with little pauses

'No – I hid them.'

'You *hid* them?'

'Yes. I got uneasy. People seemed to be watching me. It scared me – badly.' She put her hand to her head. 'It's almost the last thing I remember before waking up in the hospital . . .'

'Go on,' said Sir James, in his quiet penetrating tones. 'What do you remember?'

She turned to him obediently.

'It was at Holyhead. I came that way – I don't remember why . . .'

'That doesn't matter. Go on.'

'In the confusion on the quay I slipped away. Nobody saw me. I took a car. Told the man to drive me out of the town. I watched when we got on the open road. No other car was following us. I saw a path at the side of the road. I told the man to wait.'

She paused, then went on. 'The path led to the cliff, and down to the sea between big yellow gorse bushes – they were like golden flames. I looked round. There wasn't a soul in sight. But just level with my head there was a hole in the rock. It was quite small – I could only just get my hand in, but it went a long way back. I took the oilskin packet from round my neck and shoved it right in as far as I could. Then I tore off a bit of gorse – My! but it did prick – and plugged the hole with it so that you'd never guess there was a crevice of any kind there. Then I marked the place carefully in my own mind, so that I'd find it again. There was a queer boulder in the path just there – for all the world like a dog sitting up begging. Then I went back to the road. The car was waiting, and I drove back. I just caught the train. I was a bit ashamed of myself for fancying things maybe, but, by and by, I saw the man opposite me wink at a woman who was sitting next to me, and I felt scared again, and was glad the papers were safe. I went out in the corridor to get a little air. I thought I'd slip into another carriage. But the woman called me back, said I'd dropped something, and when I stooped to look, something seemed to hit me – here.' She placed her hand to the back of her head. 'I don't remember anything more until I woke up in the hospital.'

There was a pause.

'Thank you, Miss Finn.' It was Sir James who spoke. 'I hope we have not tired you?'

'Oh, that's all right. My head aches a little, but otherwise I feel fine.'

Julius stepped forward and took her hand again.

'So long, Cousin Jane. I'm going to get busy after those papers, but I'll be back in two shakes of a dog's tail, and I'll tote you up to London and give you the time of your young life before we go back to the States! I mean it – so hurry up and get well.'

Chapter 20

Too Late

In the street they held an informal council of war. Sir James had drawn a watch from his pocket.

'The boat train to Holyhead stops at Chester at 12.14. If you start at once I think you can catch the connexion.'

Tommy looked up, puzzled.

'Is there any need to hurry, sir? Today is only the 24th.'

'I guess it's always well to get up early in the morning,' said Julius, before the lawyer had time to reply. 'We'll make tracks for the depot right away.'

A little frown had settled on Sir James's brow.

'I wish I could come with you. I am due to speak at a meeting at two o'clock. It is unfortunate.'

The reluctance in his tone was very evident. It was clear, on the other hand, that Julius was easily disposed to put up with the loss of the other's company.

'I guess there's nothing complicated about this deal,' he remarked. 'Just a game of hide-and-seek, that's all.'

'I hope so,' said Sir James.

'Sure thing. What else could it be?'

'You are still young, Mr Hersheimmer. At my age you will probably have learnt one lesson: "Never underestimate your adversary."'

The gravity of his tone impressed Tommy, but had little effect upon Julius.

'You think Mr Brown might come along and take a hand! If he does, I'm ready for him.' He slapped his pocket. 'I carry a gun. Little Willie here travels round with me everywhere.' He produced a murderous-looking automatic, and tapped it affectionately before returning it to its home. 'But he won't be needed on this trip. There's nobody to put Mr Brown wise.'

The lawyer shrugged his shoulders.

'There was nobody to put Mr Brown wise to the fact that Mrs Vandemeyer meant to betray him. Nevertheless, *Mrs Vandemeyer died without speaking.*'

Julius was silenced for once, and Sir James added on a lighter note:

'I only want to put you on your guard. Goodbye, and good luck. Take no unnecessary risks once the papers are in your hands. If there is any reason to believe that you have been shadowed, destroy them at once. Good luck to you. The game is in your hands now.' He shook hands with them both.

Ten minutes later the two men were seated in a first-class carriage *en route* for Chester.

For a long time neither of them spoke. When at length Julius broke the silence, it was with a totally unexpected remark.

'Say,' he observed thoughtfully, 'did you ever make a darn fool of yourself over a girl's face?'

Tommy, after a moment's astonishment, searched his mind.

'Can't say I have,' he replied at last. 'Not that I can recollect, anyhow. Why?'

'Because for the last two months I've been making a sentimental idiot of myself over Jane! First moment I clapped eyes on her photograph my heart did all the usual stunts you read about in novels. I guess I'm ashamed to admit it, but I came over here determined to find her and fix it all up, and take her back as Mrs Julius P. Hersheimmer!'

'Oh!' said Tommy, amazed.

Julius uncrossed his legs brusquely and continued:

'Just shows what an almighty fool a man can make of himself! One look at the girl in the flesh, and I was cured!'

Feeling more tongue-tied than ever, Tommy ejaculated 'Oh!' again.

'No disparagement to Jane, mind you,' continued the

other. 'She's a real nice girl, and some fellow will fall in love with her right away.'

'I thought her a very good-looking girl,' said Tommy, finding his tongue.

'Sure she is. But she's not like her photo one bit. At least I suppose she is in a way – must be – because I recognized her right off. If I'd seen her in a crowd I'd have said "There's a girl whose face I know" right away without hesitation. But there was something about that photo' – Julius shook his head, and heaved a sigh – 'I guess romance is a mighty queer thing!'

'It must be,' said Tommy coldly, 'if you can come over here in love with one girl, and propose to another within a fortnight.'

Julius had the grace to look discomposed.

'Well, you see, I'd got sort of tired feeling that I'd never find Jane – and that it was all plumb foolishness anyway. And then – oh well, the French, for instance, are much more sensible in the way they look at things. They keep romance and marriage apart –'

Tommy flushed.

'Well, I'm damned! If that's –'

Julius hastened to interrupt.

'Say now, don't be hasty. I don't mean what you mean. I take it Americans have a higher opinion of morality than you have even. What I meant was that the French set about marriage in a business-like way – find two people who are suited to one another, look after the money affairs, and see the whole thing practically, and in a business-like spirit.'

'If you ask me,' said Tommy, 'we're all too damned business-like nowadays. We're always saying, "Will it pay?" The men are bad enough, and the girls are worse!'

'Cool down, son. Don't get so heated.'

'I feel heated,' said Tommy.

Julius looked at him and judged it wise to say no more.

However, Tommy had plenty of time to cool down before they reached Holyhead, and the cheerful grin had returned to his countenance as they alighted at their destination.

After consultation and with the aid of a road map, they were fairly well agreed as to direction, so were able to hire a taxi without more ado and drive out on the road leading to Treaddur Bay. They instructed the man to go slowly, and watched narrowly so as not to miss the path. They came to it not long after leaving the town, and Tommy stopped the car promptly, asked in a casual tone whether the path led down to the sea, and hearing it did paid off the man in handsome style.

A moment later the taxi was slowly chugging back to Holyhead. Tommy and Julius watched it out of sight, and then turned to the narrow path.

'It's the right one, I suppose?' asked Tommy doubtfully. 'There must be simply heaps along here.'

'Sure it is. Look at the gorse. Remember what Jane said?'

Tommy looked at the swelling hedges of golden blossom which bordered the path on either side, and was convinced.

They went down in single file, Julius leading. Twice Tommy turned his head uneasily. Julius looked back.

'What is it?'

'I don't know. I've got the wind up somehow. Keep fancying there's someone following us.'

'Can't be,' said Julius positively. 'We'd see him.'

Tommy had to admit that this was true. Nevertheless, his sense of uneasiness deepened. In spite of himself he believed in the omniscience of the enemy.

'I rather wish that fellow would come along,' said Julius. He patted his pocket. 'Little William here is just aching for exercise!'

'Do you always carry it – him – with you?' inquired Tommy with burning curiosity.

'Most always. I guess you never know what might turn up.'

Tommy kept a respectful silence. He was impressed by Little William. It seemed to remove the menace of Mr Brown farther away.

The path was now running along the side of the

cliff, parallel to the sea. Suddenly Julius came to such an abrupt halt that Tommy cannoned into him.

'What's up?' he inquired.

'Look there. If that doesn't beat the band!'

Tommy looked. Standing out and half obstructing the path was a huge boulder which certainly bore a fanciful resemblance to a 'begging' terrier.

'Well,' said Tommy, refusing to share Julius's emotion, 'it's what we expected to see, isn't it?'

Julius looked at him sadly and shook his head.

'British phlegm! Sure we expected it – but it kind of rattles me, all the same, to see it sitting there just where we expected to find it!'

Tommy, whose calm was, perhaps, more assumed than natural, moved his feet impatiently.

'Push on. What about the hole?'

They scanned the cliff-side narrowly. Tommy heard himself saying idiotically:

'The gorse won't be there after all these years.'

And Julius replied solemnly:

'I guess you're right.'

Tommy suddenly pointed with a shaking hand.

'What about that crevice there?'

Julius replied in an awestricken voice:

'That's it – for sure.'

They looked at each other.

'When I was in France,' said Tommy reminiscently,

'whenever my batman failed to call me, he always said that he had come over queer. I never believed it. But whether he felt it or not, there *is* such a sensation. I've got it now! Badly!'

He looked at the rock with a kind of agonized passion.

'Damn it!' he cried. 'It's impossible! Five years! Think of it! Birds'-nesting boys, picnic parties, thousands of people passing! It can't be there! It's a hundred to one against its being there! It's against all reason!'

Indeed, he felt it to be impossible – more, perhaps, because he could not believe in his own success where so many others had failed. The thing was too easy, therefore it could not be. The hole would be empty.

Julius looked at him with a widening smile.

'I guess you're rattled now all right,' he drawled with some enjoyment. 'Well, here goes!' He thrust his hand into the crevice, and made a slight grimace. 'It's a tight fit. Jane's hand must be a few sizes smaller than mine. I don't feel anything – no – say, what's this? Gee whiz!' And with a flourish he waved aloft a small discoloured packet. 'It's the goods all right. Sewn up in oilskin. Hold it while I get my penknife.'

The unbelievable had happened. Tommy held the precious packet tenderly between his hands. They had succeeded!

'It's queer,' he murmured idly, 'you'd think the

stitches would have rotted. They look just as good as new.'

They cut them carefully and ripped away the oilskin. Inside was a small folded sheet of paper. With trembling fingers they unfolded it. The sheet was blank! They stared at each other, puzzled.

'A dummy!' hazarded Julius. 'Was Danvers just a decoy?'

Tommy shook his head. That solution did not satisfy him. Suddenly his face cleared.

'I've got it! *Sympathetic ink!*'

'You think so?'

'Worth trying anyhow. Heat usually does the trick. Get some sticks. We'll make a fire.'

In a few minutes the little fire of twigs and leaves was blazing merrily. Tommy held the sheet of paper near the glow. The paper curled a little with the heat. Nothing more.

Suddenly Julius grasped his arm, and pointed to where characters were appearing in a faint brown colour.

'Gee whiz! You've got it! Say, that idea of yours was great. It never occurred to me.'

Tommy held the paper in position some minutes longer until he judged the heat had done its work. Then he withdrew it. A moment later he uttered a cry.

Across the sheet in neat brown printing ran the words:

WITH THE COMPLIMENTS OF MR BROWN.

Chapter 21

Tommy Makes a Discovery

For a moment or two they stood staring at each other stupidly, dazed with the shock. Somehow, inexplicably, Mr Brown had forestalled them. Tommy accepted defeat quietly. Not so Julius.

'How in tarnation did he get ahead of us? That's what beats me!' he ended up.

Tommy shook his head, and said dully:

'It accounts for the stitches being new. We might have guessed . . .'

'Never mind the darned stitches. How did he get ahead of us? We hustled all we knew. It's downright impossible for anyone to get here quicker than we did. And, anyway, how did he know? Do you reckon there was a dictaphone in Jane's room? I guess there must have been.'

But Tommy's common sense pointed out objections.

'No one could have known beforehand that she was

going to be in that house – much less that particular room.'

'That's so,' admitted Julius. 'Then one of the nurses was a crook and listened at the door. How's that?'

'I don't see that it matters anyway,' said Tommy wearily. 'He may have found out some months ago, and removed the papers, then – No, by Jove, that won't wash! They'd have been published at once.'

'Sure thing they would! No, someone's got ahead of us today by an hour or so. But how they did it gets my goat.'

'I wish that chap Peel Edgerton had been with us,' said Tommy thoughtfully.

'Why?' Julius stared. 'The mischief was done when we came.'

'Yes –' Tommy hesitated. He could not explain his own feeling – the illogical idea that the K.C.'s presence would somehow have averted the catastrophe. He reverted to his former point of view. 'It's no good arguing about how it was done. The game's up. We've failed. There's only one thing for me to do.'

'What's that?'

'Get back to London as soon as possible. Mr Carter must be warned. It's only a matter of hours now before the blow falls. But, at any rate, he ought to know the worst.'

The duty was an unpleasant one, but Tommy had

no intention of shirking it. He must report his failure to Mr Carter. After that his work was done. He took the midnight mail to London. Julius elected to stay the night at Holyhead.

Half an hour after arrival, haggard and pale, Tommy stood before his chief.

'I've come to report, sir. I've failed – failed badly.'

Mr Carter eyed him sharply.

'You mean that the treaty –'

'Is in the hands of Mr Brown, sir.'

'Ah!' said Mr Carter quietly. The expression on his face did not change, but Tommy caught the flicker of despair in his eyes. It convinced him as nothing else had done that the outlook was hopeless.

'Well,' said Mr Carter after a minute or two, 'we mustn't sag at the knees, I suppose. I'm glad to know definitely. We must do what we can.'

Through Tommy's mind flashed the assurance: 'It's hopeless, and he knows it's hopeless!'

The other looked up at him.

'Don't take it to heart, lad,' he said kindly. 'You did your best. You were up against one of the biggest brains of the century. And you came very near success. Remember that.'

'Thank you, sir. It's awfully decent of you.'

'I blame myself. I have been blaming myself ever since I heard this other news.'

Something in his tone attracted Tommy's attention. A new fear gripped at his heart.

'Is there – something more, sir?'

'I'm afraid so,' said Mr Carter gravely. He stretched out his hand to a sheet on the table.

'Tuppence –?' faltered Tommy.

'Read for yourself.'

The typewritten words danced before his eyes. The description of a green toque, a coat with a handkerchief in the pocket marked P.L.C. He looked an agonized question at Mr Carter. The latter replied to it:

'Washed up on the Yorkshire coast – near Ebury. I'm afraid – it looks very much like foul play.'

'My God!' gasped Tommy. '*Tuppence!* Those devils – I'll never rest till I've got even with them! I'll hunt them down! I'll –'

The pity on Mr Carter's face stopped him.

'I know what you feel like, my poor boy. But it's no good. You'll waste your strength uselessly. It may sound harsh, but my advice to you is: Cut your losses. Time's merciful. You'll forget.'

'Forget Tuppence? Never!'

Mr Carter shook his head.

'So you think now. Well, it won't bear thinking of – that brave little girl! I'm sorry about the whole business – confoundedly sorry.'

Tommy came to himself with a start.

'I'm taking up your time, sir,' he said with an effort. 'There's no need for you to blame yourself. I dare say we were a couple of young fools to take on such a job. You warned us all right. But I wish to God *I*'d been the one to get it in the neck. Goodbye, sir.'

Back at the Ritz, Tommy packed up his few belongings mechanically, his thoughts far away. He was still bewildered by the introduction of tragedy into his cheerful commonplace existence. What fun they had had together, he and Tuppence! And now – oh, he couldn't believe it – it couldn't be true! *Tuppence – dead!* Little Tuppence, brimming over with life! It was a dream, a horrible dream. Nothing more.

They brought him a note, a few kind words of sympathy from Peel Edgerton, who had read the news in the paper. (There had been a large headline: EX-V.A.D. FEARED DROWNED.) The letter ended with the offer of a post on a ranch in Argentine, where Sir James had considerable interests.

'Kind old beggar,' muttered Tommy, as he flung it aside.

The door opened, and Julius burst in with his usual violence. He held an open newspaper in his hand.

'Say, what's all this? They seem to have got some fool idea about Tuppence.'

'It's true,' said Tommy quietly.

'You mean they've done her in?'

Tommy nodded.

'I suppose when they got the treaty she – wasn't any good to them any longer, and they were afraid to let her go.'

'Well, I'm darned!' said Julius. 'Little Tuppence. She sure was the pluckiest little girl –'

But suddenly something seemed to crack in Tommy's brain. He rose to his feet.

'Oh, get out! You don't really care, damn you! You asked her to marry you in your rotten cold-blooded way, but I *loved* her. I'd have given the soul out of my body to save her from harm. I'd have stood by without a word and let her marry you, because you could have given her the sort of time she ought to have had, and I was only a poor devil without a penny to bless himself with. But it wouldn't have been because I didn't care!'

'See here,' began Julius temperately.

'Oh, go to the devil! I can't stand your coming here and talking about "little Tuppence". Go and look after your cousin. Tuppence is my girl! I've always loved her, from the time we played together as kids. We grew up and it was just the same. I shall never forget when I was in hospital, and she came in in that ridiculous cap and apron! It was like a miracle to see the girl I loved turn up in a nurse's kit –'

But Julius interrupted him.

'A nurse's kit! Gee whiz! I must be going to Coney Hatch! I could swear I've seen Jane in a nurse's cap too. And that's plumb impossible! No, by gum, I've got it! It was her I saw talking to Whittington at that nursing home in Bournemouth. She wasn't a patient there! She was a nurse!'

'I dare say,' said Tommy angrily, 'she's probably been in with them from the start. I shouldn't wonder if she stole those papers from Danvers to begin with.'

'I'm darned if she did!' shouted Julius. 'She's my cousin, and as patriotic a girl as ever stepped.'

'I don't care a damn who she is, but get out of here!' retorted Tommy also at the top of his voice.

The young men were on the point of coming to blows. But suddenly, with an almost magical abruptness, Julius's anger abated.

'All right, son,' he said quietly, 'I'm going. I don't blame you any for what you've been saying. It's mighty lucky you did say it. I've been the most almighty blithering darned idiot that it's possible to imagine. Calm down,' – Tommy had made an impatient gesture – 'I'm going right away now – going to the London and North Western Railway depot, if you want to know.'

'I don't care a damn where you're going,' growled Tommy.

As the door closed behind Julius, he returned to his suitcase.

'That's the lot,' he murmured, and rang the bell.

'Take my luggage down.'

'Yes, sir. Going away, sir?'

'I'm going to the devil,' said Tommy, regardless of the menial's feelings.

That functionary, however, merely replied respectfully:

'Yes, sir. Shall I call a taxi?'

Tommy nodded.

Where was he going? He hadn't the faintest idea. Beyond a fixed determination to get even with Mr Brown he had no plans. He had re-read Sir James's letter, and shook his head. Tuppence must be avenged. Still, it was kind of the old fellow.

'Better answer it, I suppose.' He went across to the writing-table. With the usual perversity of bedroom stationery, there were innumerable envelopes and no paper. He rang. No one came. Tommy fumed at the delay. Then he remembered that there was a good supply in Julius's sitting-room. The American had announced his immediate departure. There would be no fear of running up against him. Besides, he wouldn't mind if he did. He was beginning to be rather ashamed of the things he had said. Old Julius had taken them jolly well. He'd apologize if he found him there.

But the room was deserted. Tommy walked across to the writing-table, and opened the middle drawer. A photograph, carelessly thrust in face upwards, caught his eye. For a moment he stood rooted to the ground. Then he took it out, shut the drawer, walked slowly over to an arm-chair, and sat down still staring at the photograph in his hand.

What on earth was a photograph of the French girl Annette doing in Julius Hersheimmer's writing-table?

Chapter 22

In Downing Street

The Prime Minister tapped the desk in front of him with nervous fingers. His face was worn and harassed. He took up his conversation with Mr Carter at the point it had broken off.

'I don't understand,' he said. 'Do you really mean that things are not so desperate after all?'

'So this lad seems to think.'

'Let's have a look at his letter again.'

Mr Carter handed it over. It was written in a sprawling boyish hand.

Dear Mr Carter,

Something's turned up that has given me a jar. Of course I may be simply making an awful ass of myself, but I don't think so. If my conclusions are right, that girl at Manchester was just a plant. The whole thing was prearranged, sham packet and all, with the object of making us think the game was up – therefore I fancy that we must have been pretty hot on the scent.

I think I know who the real Jane Finn is, and I've even got an idea where the papers are. That last's only a guess, of course, but I've a sort of feeling it'll turn out right. Anyhow, I enclose it in a sealed envelope for what it's worth. I'm going to ask you not to open it until the very last moment, midnight on the 28th, in fact. You'll understand why in a minute. You see, I've figured it out that those things of Tuppence's are a plant too, and she's no more drowned than I am. The way I reason is this: as a last chance they'll let Jane Finn escape in the hope that she's been shamming this memory stunt, and that once she thinks she's free she'll go right away to the cache. Of course it's an awful risk for them to take, because she knows all about them – but they're pretty desperate to get hold of that treaty. But if they know that the papers have been recovered by us, *neither of those two girls' lives will be worth an hour's purchase. I must try and get hold of Tuppence before Jane escapes.*

I want a repeat of that telegram that was sent to Tuppence at the Ritz. Sir James Peel Edgerton said you would be able to manage that for me. He's frightfully clever.

One last thing – please have that house in Soho watched day and night.

Yours, etc.,

Thomas Beresford.

The Prime Minister looked up.

'The enclosure?'

Mr Carter smiled dryly.

'In the vaults of the Bank. I am taking no chances.'

'You don't think' – the Prime Minister hesitated a minute – 'that it would be better to open it now? Surely we ought to secure the document, that is, provided the young man's guess turns out to be correct, at once. We can keep the fact of having done so quite secret.'

'Can we? I'm not so sure. There are spies all round us. Once it's known I wouldn't give that' – he snapped his fingers – 'for the life of those two girls. No, the boy trusted me, and I shan't let him down.'

'Well, well, we must leave it at that, then. What's he like, this lad?'

'Outwardly, he's an ordinary clean-limbed, rather block-headed young Englishman. Slow in his mental processes. On the other hand, it's quite impossible to lead him astray through his imagination. He hasn't got any – so he's difficult to deceive. He worries things out slowly, and once he's got hold of anything he doesn't let go. The little lady's quite different. More intuition and less common sense. They make a pretty pair working together. Pace and stamina.'

'He seems confident,' mused the Prime Minister.

'Yes, and that's what gives me hope. He's the kind of diffident youth who would have to be *very* sure before he ventured an opinion at all.'

A half smile came to the other's lips.

'And it is this – boy who will defeat the master criminal of our time?'

'This – boy, as you say! But I sometimes fancy I see a shadow behind.'

'You mean?'

'Peel Edgerton.'

'Peel Edgerton?' said the Prime Minister in astonishment.

'Yes. I see his hand in *this*.' He struck the open letter. 'He's there – working in the dark, silently, unobtrusively. I've always felt that if anyone was to run Mr Brown to earth, Peel Edgerton would be the man. I tell you he's on the case now, but doesn't want it known. By the way, I got rather an odd request from him the other day.'

'Yes?'

'He sent me a cutting from some American paper. It referred to a man's body found near the docks in New York about three weeks ago. He asked me to collect any information on the subject I could.'

'Well?'

Carter shrugged his shoulders.

'I couldn't get much. Young fellow about thirty-five – poorly dressed – face very badly disfigured. He was never identified.'

'And you fancy that the two matters are connected in some way?'

'Somehow I do. I may be wrong, of course.'

There was a pause, then Mr Carter continued:

'I asked him to come round here. Not that we'll get anything out of him he doesn't want to tell. His legal instincts are too strong. But there's no doubt he can throw light on one or two obscure points in young Beresford's letter. Ah, here he is!'

The two men rose to greet the newcomer. A half whimsical thought flashed across the Premier's mind. 'My successor, perhaps!'

'We've had a letter from young Beresford,' said Mr Carter, coming to the point at once. 'You've seen him, I suppose?'

'You suppose wrong,' said the lawyer.

'Oh!' Mr Carter was a little nonplussed.

Sir James smiled, and stroked his chin.

'He rang me up,' he volunteered.

'Would you have any objection to telling us exactly what passed between you?'

'Not at all. He thanked me for a certain letter which I had written to him – as a matter of fact, I had offered him a job. Then he reminded me of something I had said to him at Manchester respecting that bogus telegram which lured Miss Cowley away. I asked him if anything untoward had occurred. He said it had – that in a drawer in Mr Hersheimmer's room he had discovered a photograph.' The lawyer paused, then continued: 'I asked him if the photograph bore the name and address of a Californian photographer. He replied: "You're on to it, sir. It had." Then he went on to tell me something I *didn't* know. The original of that photograph was the French girl, Annette, who saved his life.'

'What?'

'Exactly. I asked the young man with some curiosity what he had done with the photograph. He replied that he had put it back where he found it.' The lawyer paused again. 'That was good, you know – distinctly good. He can use his brains, that young fellow. I congratulated him. The discovery was a providential one. Of course, from the moment that the girl in Manchester was proved to be a plant everything was altered. Young Beresford saw that for himself without my having to tell it him. But he felt he couldn't trust his judgment on the subject of Miss Cowley. Did I think she was alive? I told him, duly weighing the evidence, that there was a very decided chance in favour of it. That brought us back to the telegram.'

'Yes?'

'I advised him to apply to you for a copy of the original wire. It had occurred to me as probable that, after Miss Cowley flung it on the floor, certain words might have been erased and altered with the express intention of setting searchers on a false trail.'

Carter nodded. He took a sheet from his pocket, and read aloud:

Come at once, Astley Priors, Gatehouse, Kent. Great developments – Tommy.

'Very simple,' said Sir James, 'and very ingenious. Just a few words to alter, and the thing was done. And the one important clue they overlooked.'

'What was that?'

'The page-boy's statement that Miss Cowley drove to Charing Cross. They were so sure of themselves that they took it for granted he had made a mistake.'

'Then young Beresford is now?'

'At Gatehouse, Kent, unless I am much mistaken.'

Mr Carter looked at him curiously.

'I rather wonder you're not there too, Peel Edgerton?'

'Ah, I'm busy on a case.'

'I thought you were on your holiday?'

'Oh, I've not been briefed. Perhaps it would be more correct to say I'm preparing a case. Any more facts about that American chap for me?'

'I'm afraid not. Is it important to find out who he was?'

'Oh, I know who he was,' said Sir James easily. 'I can't prove it yet – but I know.'

The other two asked no questions. They had an instinct that it would be mere waste of breath.

'But what I don't understand,' said the Prime Minister suddenly, 'is how that photograph came to be in Mr Hersheimmer's drawer?'

'Perhaps it never left it,' suggested the lawyer gently.

'But the bogus inspector? Inspector Brown?'

'Ah!' said Sir James thoughtfully. He rose to his feet, 'I mustn't keep you. Go on with the affairs of the nation. I must get back to – my case.'

Two days later Julius Hersheimmer returned from Manchester. A note from Tommy lay on his table:

Dear Hersheimmer,

Sorry I lost my temper. In case I don't see you again, goodbye. I've been offered a job in the Argentine, and might as well take it.

Yours,

Tommy Beresford.

A peculiar smile lingered for a moment on Julius's face. He threw the letter into the waste-paper basket.

'The darned fool!' he murmured.

Chapter 23

A Race Against Time

After ringing up Sir James, Tommy's next procedure was to make a call at South Audley Mansions. He found Albert discharging his professional duties, and introduced himself without more ado as a friend of Tuppence's. Albert unbent immediately.

'Things has been very quiet here lately,' he said wistfully. 'Hope the young lady's keeping well, sir?'

'That's just the point, Albert. She's disappeared.'

'You don't mean as the crooks have got her?'

'They have.'

'In the Underworld?'

'No, dash it all, in this world!'

'It's a h'expression, sir,' explained Albert. 'At the pictures the crooks always have a restoorant in the Underworld. But do you think as they've done her in, sir?'

'I hope not. By the way, have you by any chance

an aunt, a cousin, grandmother, or any other suitable female relation who might be represented as being likely to kick the bucket?'

A delighted grin spread slowly over Albert's countenance.

'I'm on, sir. My poor aunt what lives in the country has been mortal bad for a long time, and she's asking for me with her dying breath.'

Tommy nodded approval.

'Can you report this in the proper quarter and meet me at Charing Cross in an hour's time?'

'I'll be there, sir. You can count on me.'

As Tommy had judged, the faithful Albert proved an invaluable ally. The two took up their quarters at the inn in Gatehouse. To Albert fell the task of collecting information. There was no difficulty about it.

Astley Priors was the property of a Dr Adams. The doctor no longer practised, had retired, the landlord believed, but he took a few private patients – here the good fellow tapped his forehead knowingly – 'Balmy ones! You understand!' The doctor was a popular figure in the village, subscribed freely to all the local sports – 'a very pleasant affable gentleman.' Been there long? Oh, a matter of ten years or so – might be longer. Scientific gentleman, he was. Professors and people often came down from town to see him. Anyway, it was a gay house, always visitors.

In the face of all this volubility, Tommy felt doubts. Was it possible that this genial, well-known figure could be in reality a dangerous criminal? His life seemed so open and above-board. No hint of sinister doings. Suppose it was all a gigantic mistake? Tommy felt a cold chill at the thought.

Then he remembered the private patients – 'balmy ones.' He inquired carefully if there was a young lady amongst them, describing Tuppence. But nothing much seemed to be known about the patients – they were seldom seen outside the grounds. A guarded description of Annette also failed to provoke recognition.

Astley Priors was a pleasant red-brick edifice, surrounded by well-wooded grounds which effectually shielded the house from observation from the road.

On the first evening Tommy, accompanied by Albert, explored the grounds. Owing to Albert's insistence they dragged themselves along painfully on their stomachs, thereby producing a great deal more noise than if they had stood upright. In any case, these precautions were totally unnecessary. The grounds, like those of any other private house after nightfall, seemed untenanted. Tommy had imagined a possible fierce watchdog. Albert's fancy ran to a puma, or a tame cobra. But they reached a shrubbery near the house quite unmolested.

The blinds of the dining-room window were up. There was a large company assembled round the table. The port was passing from hand to hand. It seemed a normal, pleasant company. Through the open window scraps of conversation floated out disjointedly on the night air. It was a heated discussion on county cricket!

Again Tommy felt that cold chill of uncertainty. It seemed impossible to believe that these people were other than they seemed. Had he been fooled once more? The fair-bearded, spectacled gentleman who sat at the head of the table looked singularly honest and normal.

Tommy slept badly that night. The following morning the indefatigable Albert, having cemented an alliance with the greengrocer's boy, took the latter's place and ingratiated himself with the cook at Malthouse. He returned with the information that she was undoubtedly 'one of the crooks,' but Tommy mistrusted the vividness of his imagination. Questioned, he could adduce nothing in support of his statement except his own opinion that she wasn't the usual kind. You could see that at a glance.

The substitution being repeated (much to the pecuniary advantage of the real greengrocer's boy) on the following day, Albert brought back the first piece of hopeful news. There *was* a French young lady staying in the house. Tommy put his doubts aside. Here was confirmation of his theory. But time pressed. Today was the 27th. The 29th was the much-talked-of 'Labour Day,' about which all sorts of rumours were running riot. Newspapers were getting agitated. Sensational hints of a Labour *coup d'état* were freely reported. The Government said nothing. It knew and was prepared. There were rumours of dissension among the Labour leaders. They were not of one mind. The more far-seeing among them realized that what they proposed might well be a death-blow to the England that at heart they loved. They shrank from the starvation and misery a general strike would entail, and were willing to meet the Government half-way. But behind them were subtle, insistent forces at work, urging the memories of old wrongs, deprecating the weakness of half-and-half measures, fomenting misunderstandings.

Tommy felt that, thanks to Mr Carter, he understood the position fairly accurately. With the fatal document in the hands of Mr Brown, public opinion would swing to the side of the Labour extremists and revolutionists. Failing that, the battle was an even chance. The Government with a loyal army and police force behind them might win – but at a cost of great suffering. But Tommy nourished another and a preposterous dream. With Mr Brown unmasked and captured he believed, rightly or wrongly, that the whole organization would crumble ignominiously and instantaneously.

The strange permeating influence of the unseen chief held it together. Without him, Tommy believed an instant panic would set in; and, the honest men left to themselves, an eleventh-hour reconciliation would be possible.

'This is a one-man show,' said Tommy to himself. 'The thing to do is to get hold of the man.'

It was partly in furtherance of this ambitious design that he had requested Mr Carter not to open the sealed envelope. The draft treaty was Tommy's bait. Every now and then he was aghast at his own presumption. How dared he think that he had discovered what so many wiser and cleverer men had overlooked? Nevertheless, he stuck tenaciously to his idea.

That evening he and Albert once more penetrated the grounds of Astley Priors. Tommy's ambition was somehow or other to gain admission to the house itself. As they approached cautiously, Tommy gave a sudden gasp.

On the second-floor window someone standing between the window and the light in the room threw a silhouette on the blind. It was one Tommy would have recognized anywhere! Tuppence was in that house!

He clutched Albert by the shoulder.

'Stay here! When I begin to sing, watch that window.'

He retreated hastily to a position on the main drive,

and began in a deep roar, coupled with an unsteady gait, the following ditty:

I am a soldier
A jolly British soldier;
You can see that I'm a soldier by my feet . . .

It had been a favourite on the gramophone in Tuppence's hospital days. He did not doubt but that she would recognize it and draw her own conclusions. Tommy had not a note of music in his voice, but his lungs were excellent. The noise he produced was terrific.

Presently an unimpeachable butler, accompanied by an equally unimpeachable footman, issued from the front door. The butler remonstrated with him. Tommy continued to sing, addressing the butler affectionately as 'dear old whiskers'. The footman took him by one arm, the butler by the other. They ran him down the drive, and neatly out of the gate. The butler threatened him with the police if he intruded again. It was beautifully done – soberly and with perfect decorum. Anyone would have sworn that the butler was a real butler, the footman a real footman – only, as it happened, the butler was Whittington!

Tommy retired to the inn and waited for Albert's return. At last that worthy made his appearance.

'Well?' cried Tommy eagerly.

'It's all right. While they was a-running of you out the window opened, and something was chucked out.' He handed a scrap of paper to Tommy. 'It was wrapped round a letter-weight.'

On the paper were scrawled three words: 'Tomorrow – same time.'

'Good egg!' cried Tommy. 'We're getting going.'

'I wrote a message on a piece of paper, wrapped it round a stone, and chucked it through the window,' continued Albert breathlessly.

Tommy groaned.

'Your zeal will be the undoing of us, Albert. What did you say?'

'Said we was a-staying at the inn. If she could get away, to come there and croak like a frog.'

'She'll know that's you,' said Tommy with a sigh of relief. 'Your imagination runs away with you, you know, Albert. Why, you wouldn't recognize a frog croaking if you heard it.'

Albert looked rather crestfallen.

'Cheer up,' said Tommy. 'No harm done. That butler's an old friend of mine – I bet he knew who I was, though he didn't let on. It's not their game to show suspicion. That's why we've found it fairly plain sailing. They don't want to discourage me altogether. On the other hand, they don't want to make it too easy. I'm a pawn in their game, Albert, that's what I am. You see, if the spider lets the fly walk out too easily, the fly might suspect it was a put-up job. Hence the usefulness of that promising youth, Mr T. Beresford, who's blundered in just at the right moment for them. But later, Mr T. Beresford had better look out!'

Tommy retired for the night in a state of some elation. He had elaborated a careful plan for the following evening. He felt sure that the inhabitants of Astley Priors would not interfere with him up to a certain point. It was after that that Tommy proposed to give them a surprise.

About twelve o'clock, however, his calm was rudely shaken. He was told that someone was demanding him in the bar. The applicant proved to be a rude-looking carter well coated with mud.

'Well, my good fellow, what is it?' asked Tommy.

'Might this be for you, sir?' The carter held out a very dirty folded note, on the outside of which was written: 'Take this to the gentleman at the inn near Astley Priors. He will give you ten shillings.'

The handwriting was Tuppence's. Tommy appreciated her quick-wittedness in realizing that he might be staying at the inn under an assumed name. He snatched at it.

'That's all right.'

The man withheld it.

'What about my ten shillings?'

Tommy hastily produced a ten-shilling note, and the man relinquished his find. Tommy unfastened it.

Dear Tommy,

I knew it was you last night. Don't go this evening. They'll be lying in wait for you. They're taking us away this morning. I heard something about Wales – Holyhead, I think. I'll drop this on the road if I get a chance. Annette told me how you'd escaped. Buck up.

Yours,

Twopence.

Tommy raised a shout for Albert before he had even finished perusing this characteristic epistle.

'Pack my bag! We're off!'

'Yes, sir.' The boots of Albert could be heard racing upstairs.

Holyhead? Did that mean that, after all – Tommy was puzzled. He read on slowly.

The boots of Albert continued to be active on the floor above.

Suddenly a second shout came from below.

'Albert! I'm a damned fool! Unpack that bag!'

'Yes, sir.'

Tommy smoothed out the note thoughtfully.

'Yes, a damned fool,' he said softly. 'But so's someone else! And at last I know who it is!'

Chapter 24

Julius Takes a Hand

In his suite at Claridge's, Kramenin reclined on a couch and dictated to his secretary in sibilant Russian.

Presently the telephone at the secretary's elbow purred, and he took up the receiver, spoke for a minute or two, then turned to his employer.

'Someone below is asking for you.'

'Who is it?'

'He gives the name of Mr Julius P. Hersheimmer.'

'Hersheimmer,' repeated Kramenin thoughtfully. 'I have heard that name before.'

'His father was one of the steel kings of America,' explained the secretary, whose business it was to know everything. 'This young man must be a millionaire several times over.'

The other's eyes narrowed appreciatively.

'You had better go down and see him, Ivan. Find out what he wants.'

The secretary obeyed, closing the door noiselessly behind him. In a few minutes he returned.

'He declines to state his business – says it is entirely private and personal, and that he must see you.'

'A millionaire several times over,' murmured Kramenin. 'Bring him up, my dear Ivan.'

The secretary left the room once more, and returned escorting Julius.

'Monsieur Kramenin?' said the latter abruptly.

The Russian, studying him attentively with his pale venomous eyes, bowed.

'Pleased to meet you,' said the American. 'I've got some very important business I'd like to talk over with you, if I can see you alone.' He looked pointedly at the other.

'My secretary, Monsieur Grieber, from whom I have no secrets.'

'That may be so – but I have,' said Julius dryly. 'So I'd be obliged if you'd tell him to scoot.'

'Ivan,' said the Russian softly, 'perhaps you would not mind retiring into the next room –'

'The next room won't do,' interrupted Julius. 'I know these ducal suites – and I want this one plumb empty except for you and me. Send him round to a store to buy a penn'orth of peanuts.'

Though not particularly enjoying the American's free and easy manner of speech, Kramenin was devoured by curiosity.

'Will your business take long to state?'

'Might be an all night job if you caught on.'

'Very good. Ivan, I shall not require you again this evening. Go to the theatre – take a night off.'

'Thank you, your excellency.'

The secretary bowed and departed.

Julius stood at the door watching his retreat. Finally, with a satisfied sigh, he closed it, and came back to his position in the centre of the room.

'Now, Mr Hersheimmer, perhaps you will be so kind as to come to the point?'

'I guess that won't take a minute,' drawled Julius. Then, with an abrupt change of manner: 'Hands up – or I shoot!'

For a moment Kramenin stared blindly into the big automatic, then, with almost comical haste, he flung up his hands above his head. In that instant Julius had taken his measure. The man he had to deal with was an abject physical coward – the rest would be easy.

'This is an outrage,' cried the Russian in a high hysterical voice. 'An outrage! Do you mean to kill me?'

'Not if you keep your voice down. Don't go edging sideways towards that bell. That's better.'

'What do you want? Do nothing rashly. Remember my life is of the utmost value to my country. I may have been maligned –'

'I reckon,' said Julius, 'that the man who let daylight into you would be doing humanity a good turn. But you needn't worry any. I'm not proposing to kill you this trip – that is, if you're reasonable.'

The Russian qualied before the stern menace in the other's eyes. He passed his tongue over his dry lips.

'What do you want? Money?'

'No. I want Jane Finn.'

'Jane Finn? I – never heard of her!'

'You're a darned liar! You know perfectly who I mean.'

'I tell you I've never heard of the girl.'

'And I tell you,' retorted Julius, 'that Little Willie here is just hopping mad to go off!'

The Russian wilted visibly.

'You wouldn't dare –'

'Oh, yes I would, son!'

Kramenin must have recognized something in the voice that carried conviction, for he said sullenly:

'Well? Granted I do know who you mean – what of it?'

'You will tell me now – right here – where she is to be found.'

Kramenin shook his head.

'I daren't.'

'Why not?'

'I daren't. You ask an impossibility.'

'Afraid, eh? Of whom? Mr Brown? Ah, that tickles you up! There is such a person, then? I doubted it. And the mere mention of him scares you stiff!'

'I have seen him,' said the Russian slowly. 'Spoken to him face to face. I did not know it until afterwards. He was one of the crowd. I should not know him again. Who is he really? I do not know. But I know this – he is a man to fear.'

'He'll never know,' said Julius.

'He knows everything – and his vengeance is swift. Even I – Kramenin! – would not be exempt!'

'Then you won't do as I ask you?'

'You ask an impossibility.'

'Sure that's a pity for you,' said Julius cheerfully. 'But the world in general will benefit.' He raised the revolver.

'Stop,' shrieked the Russian. 'You cannot mean to shoot me?'

'Of course I do. I've always heard you Revolutionists held life cheap, but it seems there's a difference when it's your own life in question. I gave you just one chance of saving your dirty skin, and that you wouldn't take!'

'They would kill me!'

'Well,' said Julius pleasantly, 'it's up to you. But I'll just say this. Little Willie here is a dead cert, and if I was you I'd take a sporting chance with Mr Brown!'

'You will hang if you shoot me,' muttered the Russian irresolutely.

'No, stranger, that's where you're wrong. You forget the dollars. A big crowd of solicitors will get busy, and they'll get some high-brow doctors on the job, and the end of it all will be that they'll say my brain was unhinged. I shall spend a few months in a quiet sanatorium, my mental health will improve, the doctors will declare me sane again, and all will end happily for little Julius. I guess I can bear a few months' retirement in order to rid the world of you, but don't you kid yourself I'll hang for it!'

The Russian believed him. Corrupt himself, he believed implicitly in the power of money. He had read of American murder trials running much on the lines indicated by Julius. He had bought and sold justice himself. This virile young American with the significant drawling voice, had the whip hand of him.

'I'm going to count five,' continued Julius, 'and I guess, if you let me get past four, you needn't worry any about Mr Brown. Maybe he'll send some flowers to the funeral, but *you* won't smell them! Are you ready? I'll begin. One – two – three – four –'

The Russian interrupted with a shriek:

'Do not shoot. I will do all you wish.'

Julius lowered the revolver.

'I thought you'd hear sense. Where is the girl?'

'At Gatehouse, in Kent. Astley Priors, the place is called.'

'Is she a prisoner there?'

'She's not allowed to leave the house – though it's safe enough really. The little fool has lost her memory, curse her!'

'That's been annoying for you and your friends, I reckon. What about the other girl, the one you decoyed away over a week ago?'

'She's there too,' said the Russian sullenly.

'That's good,' said Julius. 'Isn't it all panning out beautifully? And a lovely night for the run!'

'What run?' demanded Kramenin, with a stare.

'Down to Gatehouse, sure. I hope you're fond of motoring?'

'What do you mean? I refuse to go.'

'Now don't get mad. You must see I'm not such a kid as to leave you here. You'd ring up your friends on that telephone first thing! Ah!' He observed the fall on the other's face. 'You see, you'd got it all fixed. No, sir, you're coming along with me. This your bedroom next door here? Walk right in. Little Willie and I will come behind. Put on a thick coat, that's right. Fur lined? And you a Socialist! Now we're ready. We walk downstairs and out through the hall to where my car's waiting. And don't you forget I've got you covered every inch of the way. I can shoot just as well through my coat pocket. One word or a glance even, at one of those liveried menials, and there'll sure be a strange face in the Sulphur and Brimstone Works!'

Together they descended the stairs, and passed out to the waiting car. The Russian was shaking with rage. The hotel servants surrounded them. A cry hovered on his lips, but at the last minute his nerve failed him. The American was a man of his word.

When they reached the car, Julius breathed a sigh of relief, the danger-zone was passed. Fear had successfully hypnotized the man by his side.

'Get in,' he ordered. Then as he caught the other's side-long glance, 'No, the chauffeur won't help you any. Naval man. Was on a submarine in Russia when the Revolution broke out. A brother of his was murdered by your people. George!'

'Yes, sir?' The chauffeur turned his head.

'This gentleman is a Russian Bolshevik. We don't want to shoot him, but it may be necessary. You understand?'

'Perfectly, sir.'

'I want to go to Gatehouse in Kent. Know the road at all?'

'Yes, sir, it will be about an hour and a half's run.'

'Make it an hour. I'm in a hurry.'

'I'll do my best, sir.' The car shot forward through the traffic.

Julius ensconced himself comfortably by the side of his victim. He kept his hand in the pocket of his coat, but his manner was urbane to the last degree.

'There was a man I shot once in Arizona –' he began cheerfully.

At the end of the hour's run the unfortunate Kramenin was more dead than alive. In succession to the anecdote of the Arizona man, there had been a tough from 'Frisco, and an episode in the Rockies. Julius's narrative style, if not strictly accurate, was picturesque!

Slowing down, the chauffeur called over his shoulder that they were just coming into Gatehouse. Julius bade the Russian direct them. His plan was to drive straight up to the house. There Kramenin was to ask for the two girls. Julius explained to him that Little Willie would not be tolerant of failure. Kramenin, by this time, was as putty in the other's hand. The terrific pace they had come had still further unmanned him. He had given himself up for dead at every corner.

The car swept up the drive, and stopped before the porch. The chauffeur looked round for orders.

'Turn the car first, George. Then ring the bell, and get back to your place. Keep the engine going, and be ready to scoot like hell when I give the word.'

'Very good, sir.'

The front door was opened by the butler. Kramenin felt the muzzle of the revolver pressed against his ribs.

'Now,' hissed Julius. 'And be careful.'

The Russian beckoned. His lips were white, and his voice was not very steady:

'It is I – Kramenin! Bring down the girl at once! There is no time to lose!'

Whittington had come down the steps. He uttered an exclamation of astonishment at seeing the other.

'You! What's up? Surely you know the plan –'

Kramenin interrupted him, using the words that have created many unnecessary panics:

'We have been betrayed! Plans must be abandoned. We must save our own skins. The girl! And at once! It's our only chance.'

Whittington hesitated, but for hardly a moment.

'You have orders – from *him?*'

'Naturally! Should I be here otherwise? Hurry! There is no time to be lost. The other little fool had better come too.'

Whittington turned and ran back into the house. The agonizing minutes went by. Then – two figures hastily huddled in cloaks appeared on the steps and were hustled into the car. The smaller of the two was inclined to resist and Whittington shoved her in unceremoniously. Julius leaned forward, and in doing so the light from the open door lit up his face. Another man on the steps behind Whittington gave a startled exclamation. Concealment was at an end.

'Get a move on, George,' shouted Julius.

The chauffeur slipped in his clutch, and with a bound the car started.

The man on the steps uttered an oath. His hand went to his pocket. There was a flash and a report. The bullet just missed the taller girl by an inch.

'Get down, Jane,' cried Julius. 'Flat on the bottom of the car.' He thrust her sharply forward, then standing up, he took careful aim and fired.

'Have you hit him?' cried Tuppence eagerly.

'Sure,' replied Julius. 'He isn't killed, though. Skunks like that take a lot of killing. Are you all right, Tuppence?'

'Of course I am. Where's Tommy? And who's this?' She indicated the shivering Kramenin.

'Tommy's making tracks for the Argentine. I guess he thought you'd turned up your toes. Steady through the gate, George! That's right. It'll take 'em at least five minutes to get busy after us. They'll use the telephone, I guess, so look out for snares ahead – and don't take the direct route. Who's this, did you say, Tuppence? Let me present Monsieur Kramenin. I persuaded him to come on the trip for his health.'

The Russian remained mute, still livid with terror.

'But what made them let us go?' demanded Tuppence suspiciously.

'I reckon Monsieur Kramenin here asked them so

prettily they just couldn't refuse!'

This was too much for the Russian. He burst out vehemently:

'Curse you – curse you! They know now that I betrayed them. My life won't be safe for an hour in this country.'

'That's so,' assented Julius. 'I'd advise you to make tracks for Russia right away.'

'Let me go, then,' cried the other. 'I have done what you asked. Why do you still keep me with you?'

'Not for the pleasure of your company. I guess you can get right off now if you want to. I thought you'd rather I tooled you back to London.'

'You may never reach London,' snarled the other. 'Let me go here and now.'

'Sure thing. Pull up, George. The gentleman's not making the return trip. If I ever come to Russia, Monsieur Kramenin, I shall expect a rousing welcome and –'

But before Julius had finished his speech, and before the car had finally halted, the Russian had swung himself out and disappeared into the night.

'Just a mite impatient to leave us,' commented Julius, as the car gathered way again. 'And no idea of saying goodbye politely to the ladies. Say, Jane, you can get up on the seat now.'

For the first time the girl spoke.

'How did you "persuade" him?' she asked.

Julius tapped his revolver.

'Little Willie here takes the credit!'

'Splendid!' cried the girl. The colour surged into her face, her eyes looked admiringly at Julius.

'Annette and I didn't know what was going to happen to us,' said Tuppence. 'Old Whittington hurried us off. We thought it was lambs to the slaughter.'

'Annette,' said Julius. 'Is that what you call her?'

His mind seemed to be trying to adjust itself to a new idea.

'It's her name,' said Tuppence, opening her eyes very wide.

'Shucks!' retorted Julius. 'She may think it's her name, because her memory's gone, poor kid. But it's the one real and original Jane Finn we've got here.'

'What –?' cried Tuppence.

But she was interrupted. With an angry spurt, a bullet embedded itself in the upholstery of the car just behind her head.

'Down with you,' cried Julius. 'It's an ambush. These guys have got busy pretty quickly. Push her a bit, George.'

The car fairly leapt forward. Three more shots rang out, but went happily wide. Julius, upright, leant over the back of the car.

'Nothing to shoot at,' he announced gloomily. 'But

I guess there'll be another little picnic soon. Ah!'

He raised his hand to his cheek.

'You are hurt?' said Annette quickly.

'Only a scratch.'

The girl sprang to her feet.

'Let me out! Let me out, I say! Stop the car. It is me they're after. I'm the one they want. You shall not lose your lives because of me. Let me go.' She was fumbling with the fastenings of the door.

Julius took her by both arms, and looked at her. She had spoken with no trace of foreign accent.

'Sit down, kid,' he said gently. 'I guess there's nothing wrong with your memory. Been fooling them all the time, eh?'

The girl looked at him, nodded, and then suddenly burst into tears. Julius patted her on the shoulder.

'There, there – just you sit tight. We're not going to let you quit.'

Through her sobs the girl said indistinctly:

'You're from home. I can tell by your voice. It makes me home-sick.'

'Sure I'm from home. I'm your cousin – Julius Hersheimmer. I came over to Europe on purpose to find you – and a pretty dance you've led me.'

The car slackened speed. George spoke over his shoulder:

'Cross-roads here, sir. I'm not sure of the way.'

The car slowed down till it hardly moved. As it did so a figure climbed suddenly over the back, and plunged head first into the midst of them.

'Sorry,' said Tommy, extricating himself.

A mass of confused exclamations greeted him. He replied to them severally:

'Was in the bushes by the drive. Hung on behind. Couldn't let you know before at the pace you were going. It was all I could do to hang on. Now then, you girls, get out!'

'Get out?'

'Yes. There's a station just up that road. Train due in three minutes. You'll catch it if you hurry.'

'What the devil are you driving at?' demanded Julius. 'Do you think you can fool them by leaving the car?'

'You and I aren't going to leave the car. Only the girls.'

'You're crazed, Beresford. Stark staring mad! You can't let those girls go off alone. It'll be the end of it if you do.'

Tommy turned to Tuppence.

'Get out at once, Tuppence. Take her with you, and do just as I say. No one will do you any harm. You're safe. Take the train to London. Go straight to Sir James Peel Edgerton. Mr Carter lives out of town, but you'll be safe with him.'

'Darn you!' cried Julius. 'You're mad. Jane, you stay where you are.'

With a sudden swift movement, Tommy snatched the revolver from Julius's hand, and levelled it at him.

'Now will you believe I'm in earnest? Get out, both of you, and do as I say – or I'll shoot!'

Tuppence sprang out, dragging the unwilling Jane after her.

'Come on, it's all right. If Tommy's sure – he's sure. Be quick. We'll miss the train.'

They started running.

Julius's pent-up rage burst forth.

'What the hell –'

Tommy interrupted him.

'Dry up! I want a few words with you, Mr Julius Hersheimmer.'

Chapter 25

Jane's Story

Her arm through Jane's, dragging her along, Tuppence reached the station. Her quick ears caught the sound of the approaching train.

'Hurry up,' she panted, 'or we'll miss it.'

They arrived on the platform just as the train came to a standstill. Tuppence opened the door of an empty first-class compartment, and the two girls sank down breathless on the padded seats.

A man looked in, then passed on to the next carriage. Jane started nervously. Her eyes dilated with terror. She looked questioningly at Tuppence.

'Is he one of them, do you think?' she breathed.

Tuppence shook her head.

'No, no. It's all right.' She took Jane's hand in hers. 'Tommy wouldn't have told us to do this unless he was sure we'd be all right.'

'But he doesn't know them as I do!' The girl shivered.

'You can't understand. Five years! Five long years! Sometimes I thought I should go mad.'

'Never mind. It's all over.'

'Is it?'

The train was moving now, speeding through the night at a gradually increasing rate. Suddenly Jane Finn started up.

'What was that? I thought I saw a face – looking in through the window.'

'No, there's nothing. See.' Tuppence went to the window, and lifting the strap let the pane down.

'You're sure?'

'Quite sure.'

The other seemed to feel some excuse was necessary:

'I guess I'm acting like a frightened rabbit, but I can't help it. If they caught me now they'd –' Her eyes opened wide and staring.

'*Don't*!' implored Tuppence. 'Lie back, and *don't think*. You can be quite sure that Tommy wouldn't have said it was safe if it wasn't.'

'My cousin didn't think so. He didn't want us to do this.'

'No,' said Tuppence, rather embarrassed.

'What are you thinking of?' said Jane sharply.

'Why?'

'Your voice was so – queer!'

'I *was* thinking of something,' confessed Tuppence.

'But I don't want to tell you – not now. I may be wrong, but I don't think so. It's just an idea that came into my head a long time ago. Tommy's got it too – I'm almost sure he has. But don't *you* worry – there'll be time enough for that later. And it mayn't be so at all! Do what I tell you – lie back and don't think of anything.'

'I'll try.' The long lashes drooped over the hazel eyes.

Tuppence, for her part, sat bolt upright – much in the attitude of a watchful terrier on guard. In spite of herself she was nervous. Her eyes flashed continually from one window to the other. She noted the exact position of the communication cord. What it was that she feared, she would have been hard put to it to say. But in her own mind she was far from feeling the confidence displayed in her words. Not that she disbelieved in Tommy, but occasionally she was shaken with doubts as to whether anyone so simple and honest as he was could ever be a match for the fiendish subtlety of the arch-criminal.

If they once reached Sir James Peel Edgerton in safety, all would be well. But would they reach him? Would not the silent forces of Mr Brown already be assembling against them? Even that last picture of Tommy, revolver in hand, failed to comfort her. By now he might be overpowered, borne down by sheer force of numbers . . . Tuppence mapped out her plan of campaign.

As the train at length drew slowly into Charing Cross, Jane Finn sat up with a start.

'Have we arrived? I never thought we should!'

'Oh, I thought we'd get to London all right. If there's going to be any fun, now is when it will begin. Quick, get out. We'll nip into a taxi.'

In another minute they were passing the barrier, had paid the necessary fares, and were stepping into a taxi.

'King's Cross,' directed Tuppence. Then she gave a jump. A man looked in at the window, just as they started. She was almost certain it was the same man who had got into the carriage next to them. She had a horrible feeling of being slowly hemmed in on every side.

'You see,' she explained to Jane, 'if they think we're going to Sir James, this will put them off the scent. Now they'll imagine we're going to Mr Carter. His country place is north of London somewhere.'

Crossing Holborn there was a block, and the taxi was held up. This was what Tuppence had been waiting for.

'Quick,' she whispered. 'Open the right-hand door!'

The two girls stepped out into the traffic. Two minutes later they were seated in another taxi and were retracing their steps, this time direct to Carlton House Terrace.

'There,' said Tuppence, with great satisfaction, 'this ought to do them. I can't help thinking that I'm really rather clever! How that other taxi man will swear! But I took his number, and I'll send him a postal order tomorrow, so that he won't lose by it if he happens to be genuine. What's this thing swerving – Oh!'

There was a grinding noise and a bump. Another taxi had collided with them.

In a flash Tuppence was out on the pavement. A policeman was approaching. Before he arrived Tuppence had handed the driver five shillings, and she and Jane had merged themselves in the crowd.

'It's only a step or two now,' said Tuppence breathlessly. The accident had taken place in Trafalgar Square.

'Do you think the collision was an accident, or done deliberately?'

'I don't know. It might have been either.'

Hand-in-hand, the two girls hurried along.

'It may be my fancy,' said Tuppence suddenly, 'but I feel as though there was someone behind us.'

'Hurry!' murmured the other. 'Oh, hurry!'

They were now at the corner of Carlton House Terrace, and their spirits lightened. Suddenly a large and apparently intoxicated man barred their way.

'Good evening, ladies,' he hiccupped. 'Whither away so fast?'

'Let us pass, please,' said Tuppence imperiously.

'Just a word with your pretty friend here.' He stretched out an unsteady hand, and clutched Jane by the shoulder. Tuppence heard other footsteps behind. She did not pause to ascertain whether they were friends or foes. Lowering her head, she repeated a manœuvre of childish days, and butted their aggressor full in the capacious middle. The success of these unsportsmanlike tactics was immediate. The man sat down abruptly on the pavement. Tuppence and Jane took to their heels. The house they sought was some way down. Other footsteps echoed behind them. Their breath was coming in choking gasps as they reached Sir James's door. Tuppence seized the bell and Jane the knocker.

The man who had stopped them reached the foot of the steps. For a moment he hesitated, and as he did so the door opened. They fell into the hall together. Sir James came forward from the library door.

'Hullo! What's this?'

He stepped forward and put his arm round Jane as she swayed uncertainly. He half carried her into the library, and laid her on the leather couch. From a tantalus on the table he poured out a few drops of brandy, and forced her to drink them. With a sigh she sat up, her eyes still wild and frightened.

'It's all right. Don't be afraid, my child. You're quite safe.'

Her breath came more normally, and the colour was returning to her cheeks. Sir James looked at Tuppence quizzically.

'So you're not dead, Miss Tuppence, any more than that Tommy boy of yours was!'

'The Young Adventures take a lot of killing,' boasted Tuppence.

'So it seems,' said Sir James dryly. 'Am I right in thinking that the joint venture has ended in success, and that this' – he turned to the girl on the couch – 'is Miss Jane Finn?'

Jane sat up.

'Yes,' she said quietly, 'I am Jane Finn. I have a lot to tell you.'

'When you are stronger –'

'No – now!' Her voice rose a little. 'I shall feel safer when I have told everything.'

'As you please,' said the lawyer.

He sat down in one of the big arm-chairs facing the couch. In a low voice Jane began her story.

'I came over on the *Lusitania* to take up a post in Paris. I was fearfully keen about the war, and just dying to help somehow or other. I had been studying French, and my teacher said they were wanting help in a hospital in Paris, so I wrote and offered my services, and they were accepted. I hadn't got any folk of my own, so it made it easy to arrange things.

'When the *Lusitania* was torpedoed, a man came up to me. I'd noticed him more than once – and I'd figured it out in my own mind that he was afraid of somebody or something. He asked me if I was a patriotic American, and told me he was carrying papers which were just life or death to the Allies. He asked me to take charge of them. I was to watch for an advertisement in *The Times*. If it didn't appear, I was to take them to the American Ambassador.

'Most of what followed seems like a nightmare still. I see it in my dreams sometimes . . . I'll hurry over that part. Mr Danvers had told me to watch out. He might have been shadowed from New York, but he didn't think so. At first I had no suspicions, but on the boat to Holyhead I began to get uneasy. There was one woman who had been very keen to look after me, and chum up with me generally – a Mrs Vandemeyer. At first I'd been only grateful to her for being so kind to me; but all the time I felt there was something about her I didn't like, and on the Irish boat I saw her talking to some queer-looking men, and from the way they looked I saw that they were talking about me. I remembered that she'd been quite near me on the *Lusitania* when Mr Danvers gave me the packet, and before that she'd tried to talk to him once or twice. I began to get scared, but I didn't quite see what to do.

'I had a wild idea of stopping at Holyhead, and not going on to London that day, but I soon saw that would be plumb foolishness. The only thing was to act as though I'd noticed nothing, and hope for the best. I couldn't see how they could get me if I was on my guard. One thing I'd done already as a precaution – ripped open the oilskin packet and substituted blank paper, and then sewn it up again. So, if anyone did manage to rob me of it, it wouldn't matter.

'What to do with the real thing worried me no end. Finally I opened it out flat – there were only two sheets – and laid it between two of the advertisement pages of a magazine. I stuck the two pages together round the edge with some gum off an envelope. I carried the magazine carelessly stuffed into the pocket of my ulster.

'At Holyhead I tried to get into a carriage with people that looked all right, but in a queer way there seemed always to be a crowd round me shoving and pushing me just the way I didn't want to go. There was something uncanny and frightening about it. In the end I found myself in a carriage with Mrs Vandemeyer after all. I went out into the corridor, but all the other carriages were full, so I had to go back and sit down. I consoled myself with the thought that there were other people in the carriage – there was quite a nice-looking man and his wife sitting just opposite. So I felt almost happy about it until just outside London. I had leaned back and closed my eyes. I guess they thought I was asleep, but my eyes weren't quite shut, and suddenly I saw the nice-looking man get something out of his bag and hand it to Mrs Vandemeyer, and as he did so he *winked* . . .

'I can't tell you how that wink sort of froze me through and through. My only thought was to get out in the corridor as quick as ever I could. I got up, trying to look natural and easy. Perhaps they saw something – I don't know – but suddenly Mrs Vandemeyer said "Now," and flung something over my nose and mouth as I tried to scream. At the same moment I felt a terrific blow on the back of my head . . .'

She shuddered. Sir James murmured something sympathetically. In a minute she resumed:

'I don't know how long it was before I came back to consciousness. I felt very ill and sick. I was lying on a dirty bed. There was a screen round it, but I could hear two people talking in the room. Mrs Vandemeyer was one of them. I tried to listen, but at first I couldn't take much in. When at last I did begin to grasp what was going on – I was just terrified! I wonder I didn't scream right out there and then.

'They hadn't found the papers. They'd got the oilskin packet with the blanks, and they were just mad! They didn't know whether *I*'d changed the papers, or whether Danvers had been carrying a dummy message, while the real one was sent another way. They spoke of' – she closed her eyes – 'torturing me to find out!'

'I'd never known what fear – really sickening fear – was before! Once they came to look at me. I shut my eyes and pretended to be still unconscious, but I was afraid they'd hear the beating of my heart. However, they went away again. I began thinking madly. What could I do? I knew I wouldn't be able to stand up against torture very long.

'Suddenly something put the thought of loss of memory into my head. The subject had always interested me, and I'd read an awful lot about it. I had the whole thing at my finger-tips. If only I could succeed in carrying the bluff through, it might save me. I said a prayer, and drew a long breath. Then I opened my eyes and started babbling in *French*!

'Mrs Vandemeyer came round the screen at once. Her face was so wicked I nearly died, but I smiled up at her doubtfully, and asked her in French where I was.

'It puzzled her, I could see. She called the man she had been talking to. He stood by the screen with his face in shadow. He spoke to me in French. His voice was very ordinary and quiet but somehow, I don't know why, he scared me, but I went on playing my part. I asked again where I was, and then went on that there was something I *must* remember – *must* remember –

only for the moment it was all gone. I worked myself up to be more and more distressed. He asked me my name. I said I didn't know – that I couldn't remember anything at all.

'Suddenly he caught my wrist, and began twisting it. The pain was awful. I screamed. He went on. I screamed and screamed, but I managed to shriek out things in French. I don't know how long I could have gone on, but luckily I fainted. The last thing I heard was his voice saying: "That's not bluff! Anyway, a kid of her age wouldn't know enough.' I guess he forgot American girls are older for their age than English ones, and take more interest in scientific subjects.

'When I came to, Mrs Vandemeyer was sweet as honey to me. She'd had her orders, I guess. She spoke to me in French – told me I'd had a shock and been very ill. I should be better soon. I pretended to be rather dazed – murmured something about the "doctor" having hurt my wrist. She looked relieved when I said that.

'By and by she went out of the room altogether. I was suspicious still, and lay quite quiet for some time. In the end, however, I got up and walked round the room, examining it. I thought that even if anyone *was* watching me from somewhere, it would seem natural enough under the circumstances. It was a squalid, dirty place. There were no windows, which seemed queer. I guessed the door would be locked, but I didn't try it.

There were some battered old pictures on the walls, representing scenes from *Faust*.'

Jane's two listeners gave a simultaneous 'Ah!' The girl nodded.

'Yes – it was the place in Soho where Mr Beresford was imprisoned. Of course at the time I didn't even know if I was in London. One thing was worrying me dreadfully, but my heart gave a great throb of relief when I saw my ulster lying carelessly over the back of a chair. *And the magazine was still rolled up in the pocket!*

'If only I could be certain that I was not being overlooked! I looked carefully round the walls. There didn't seem to be a peep-hole of any kind – nevertheless I felt kind of sure there must be. All of a sudden I sat down on the edge of the table, and put my face in my hands, sobbing out a "Mon Dieu! Mon Dieu!" I've got very sharp ears. I distinctly heard the rustle of a dress, and slight creak. That was enough for me. I was being watched!

'I lay down on the bed again, and by and by Mrs Vandemeyer brought me some supper. She was still sweet as they make them. I guess she'd been told to win my confidence. Presently she produced the oilskin packet, and asked me if I recognized it, watching me like a lynx all the time.

'I took it and turned it over in a puzzled sort of

way. Then I shook my head. I said that I felt I *ought* to remember something about it, that it was just as though it was all coming back, and then, before I could get hold of it, it went again. Then she told me that I was her niece, and that I was to call her "Aunt Rita." I did obediently, and she told me not to worry – my memory would soon come back.

'That was an awful night. I'd made my plan whilst I was waiting for her. The papers were safe so far, but I couldn't take the risk of leaving them there any longer. They might throw that magazine away any minute. I lay awake waiting until I judged it must be about two o'clock in the morning. Then I got up as softly as I could, and felt in the dark along the left-hand wall. Very gently, I unhooked one of the pictures from its nail – Marguerite with her casket of jewels. I crept over to my coat and took out the magazine, and an odd envelope or two that I had shoved in. Then I went to the washstand, and damped the brown paper at the back of the picture all round. Presently I was able to pull it away. I had already torn out the two stuck-together pages from the magazine, and now I slipped them with their precious enclosure between the picture and its brown paper backing. A little gum from the envelopes helped me to stick the latter up again. No one would dream the picture had ever been tampered with. I rehung it on the wall, put the magazine back in my coat pocket, and crept back to bed. I was pleased with my hiding-place. They'd never think of pulling to pieces one of their own pictures. I hoped that they'd come to the conclusion that Danvers had been carrying a dummy all along, and that, in the end, they'd let me go.

'As a matter of fact, I guess that's what they did think at first and, in a way, it was dangerous for me. I learnt afterwards that they nearly did away with me then and there – there was never much chance of their "letting me go" – but the first man, who was the boss, preferred to keep me alive on the chance of my having hidden them, and being able to tell where if I recovered my memory. They watched me constantly for weeks. Sometimes they'd ask me questions by the hour – I guess there was nothing they didn't know about the third degree! – but somehow I managed to hold my own. The strain of it was awful, though . . .

'They took me back to Ireland, and over every step of the journey again, in case I'd hidden it somewhere *en route.* Mrs Vandemeyer and another woman never left me for a moment. They spoke of me as a young relative of Mrs Vandemeyer's whose mind was affected by the shock of the *Lusitania.* There was no one I could appeal to for help without giving myself away to *them,* and if I risked it and failed – and Mrs Vandemeyer looked so rich, and so beautifully dressed, that I felt convinced they'd take her word against mine, and think it was part of my mental trouble to think myself "persecuted" – I felt that the horrors in store for me would be too awful once they knew I'd been only shamming.'

Sir James nodded comprehendingly.

'Mrs Vandemeyer was a woman of great personality. With that and her social position she would have had little difficulty in imposing her point of view in preference to yours. Your sensational accusations against her would not easily have found credence.'

'That's what I thought. It ended in my being sent to a sanatorium at Bournemouth. I couldn't make up my mind at first whether it was a sham affair or genuine. A hospital nurse had charge of me. I was a special patient. She seemed so nice and normal that at last I determined to confide in her. A merciful providence just saved me in time from falling into the trap. My door happened to be ajar, and I heard her talking to someone in the passage. *She was one of them!* They still fancied it might be a bluff on my part, and she was put in charge of me to make sure! After that, my nerve went completely. I dared trust nobody.

'I think I almost hypnotized myself. After a while, I almost forgot that I was really Jane Finn. I was so bent on playing the part of Janet Vandemeyer that my nerves began to play tricks. I became really ill – for months I sank into a sort of stupor. I felt sure I should die soon, and that nothing really mattered. A sane person shut up in a lunatic asylum often ends by becoming insane, they say. I guess I was like that. Playing my part had become second nature to me. I wasn't even unhappy in the end – just apathetic. Nothing seemed to matter. And the years went on.

'And then suddenly things seemed to change. Mrs Vandemeyer came down from London. She and the doctor asked me questions, experimented with various treatments. There was some talk of sending me to a specialist in Paris. In the end, they did not dare risk it. I overheard something that seemed to show that other people – friends – were looking for me. I learnt later that the nurse who had looked after me went to Paris, and consulted a specialist, representing herself to be me. He put her through some searching tests, and exposed her loss of memory to be fraudulent; but she had taken a note of his methods and reproduced them on me. I dare say I couldn't have deceived the specialist for a minute – a man who has made a lifelong study of a thing is unique – but I managed once again to hold my own with them. The fact that I'd not thought of myself as Jane Finn for so long made it easier.

'One night I was whisked off to London at a moment's notice. They took me back to the house in Soho. Once I got away from the sanatorium I felt different – as though something in me that had been buried for a long time was waking up again.

'They sent me in to wait on Mr Beresford. (Of course I didn't know his name then.) I was suspicious – I thought it was another trap. But he looked so honest, I could hardly believe it. However I was careful in all I said, for I knew we could be overheard. There's a small hole, high up in the wall.

'But on the Sunday afternoon a message was brought to the house. They were all very disturbed. Without their knowing, I listened. Word had come that he was to be killed. I needn't tell the next part, because you know it. I thought I'd have time to rush up and get the papers from their hiding-place, but I was caught. So I screamed out that he was escaping, and I said I wanted to go back to Marguerite. I shouted the name three times very loud. I knew the others would think I meant Mrs Vandemeyer, but I hoped it might make Mr Beresford think of the picture. He'd unhooked one the first day – that's what made me hesitate to trust him.'

She paused.

'Then the papers,' said Sir James slowly, 'are still at the back of the picture in that room.'

'Yes.' The girl had sunk back on the sofa exhausted with the strain of the long story.

Sir James rose to his feet. He looked at his watch.

'Come,' he said, 'we must go at once.'

'Tonight? queried Tuppence, surprised.

'Tomorrow may be too late,' said Sir James gravely. 'Besides, by going tonight we have the chance of capturing that great man and super-criminal – Mr Brown!'

There was dead silence, and Sir James continued:

'You have been followed here – not a doubt of it. When we leave the house we shall be followed again, but not molested *for it is Mr Brown's plan that we are to lead him.* But the Soho house is under police supervision night and day. There are several men watching it. When we enter that house, Mr Brown will not draw back – he will risk all, on the chance of obtaining the spark to fire his mine. And he fancies the risk not great – since he will enter in the guise of a friend!'

Tuppence flushed, then opened her mouth impulsively.

'But there's something you don't know – that we haven't told you.' Her eyes dwelt on Jane in perplexity.

'What is that?' asked the other sharply. 'No hesitations, Miss Tuppence. We need to be sure of our going.'

But Tuppence, for once, seemed tongue-tied.

'It's so difficult – you see, if I'm wrong – oh, it would be dreadful.' She made a grimace at the unconscious Jane. 'Never forgive me,' she observed cryptically.

'You want me to help you out, eh?'

'Yes, please. *You* know who Mr Brown is, don't you?'

'Yes,' said Sir James gravely. 'At last I do.'

'At last?' queried Tuppence doubtfully. 'Oh, but I thought –' She paused.

'You thought correctly, Miss Tuppence. I have been morally certain of his identity for some time – ever since the night of Mrs Vandemeyer's mysterious death.'

'Ah!' breathed Tuppence.

'For there we are up against the logic of facts. There are only two solutions. Either the chloral was administered by her own hand, which theory I reject utterly, or else –'

'Yes?'

'Or else it was administered in the brandy you gave her. Only three people touched that brandy – you, Miss Tuppence, I myself, and one other – Mr Julius Hersheimmer!'

Jane Finn stirred and sat up, regarding the speaker with wide astonished eyes.

'At first, the thing seemed utterly impossible. Mr Hersheimmer, as the son of a prominent millionaire, was a well-known figure in America. It seemed utterly impossible that he and Mr Brown could be one and the same. But you cannot escape from the logic of facts. Since the thing was so – it must be accepted. Remember

Mrs Vandemeyer's sudden and inexplicable agitation. Another proof, if proof was needed.

'I took an early opportunity of giving you a hint. From some words of Mr Hersheimmer's at Manchester, I gathered that you had understood and acted on that hint. Then I set to work to prove the impossible possible. Mr Beresford rang me up and told me, what I had already suspected, that the photograph of Miss Jane Finn had never really been out of Mr Hersheimmer's possession –'

But the girl interrupted. Springing to her feet, she cried out angrily:

'What do you mean? What are you trying to suggest? That Mr Brown is *Julius*? Julius – my own cousin!'

'No, Miss Finn,' said Sir James unexpectedly. 'Not your cousin. The man who calls himself Julius Hersheimmer is no relation to you whatsoever.'

Chapter 26

Mr Brown

Sir James's words came like a bombshell. Both girls looked equally puzzled. The lawyer went across to his desk, and returned with a small newspaper cutting, which he handed to Jane. Tuppence read it over her shoulder. Mr Carter would have recognized it. It referred to the mysterious man found dead in New York.

'As I was saying to Miss Tuppence,' resumed the lawyer, 'I set to work to prove the impossible possible. The great stumbling-block was the undeniable fact that Julius Hersheimmer was not an assumed name. When I came across this paragraph my problem was solved. Julius Hersheimmer set out to discover what had become of his cousin. He went out West, where he obtained news of her and her photograph to aid him in his search. On the eve of his departure from New York he was set upon and murdered. His body was dressed in shabby clothes, and the face disfigured to prevent identification. Mr Brown took his place. He sailed immediately for England. None of the real Hersheimmer's friends or intimates saw him before he sailed – though indeed it would hardly have mattered if they had, the impersonation was so perfect. Since then he had been hand in glove with those sworn to hunt him down. Every secret of theirs had been known to him. Only once did he come near disaster. Mrs Vandemeyer knew his secret. It was no part of his plan that that huge bribe should ever be offered to her. But for Miss Tuppence's fortunate change of plan, she would have been far away from the flat when we arrived there. Exposure stared him in the face. He took a desperate step, trusting in his assumed character to avert suspicion. He nearly succeeded – but not quite.'

'I can't believe it,' murmured Jane. 'He seemed so splendid.'

'The real Julius Hersheimmer *was* a splendid fellow! And Mr Brown is a consummate actor. But ask Miss Tuppence if she also has not had her suspicions.'

Jane turned mutely to Tuppence. The latter nodded.

'I didn't want to say it, Jane – I knew it would hurt you. And, after all, I couldn't be sure. I still don't understand why, if he's Mr Brown, he rescued us.'

'Was it Julius Hersheimmer who helped you to escape?'

Tuppence recounted to Sir James the exciting events of the evening, ending up: 'But I can't see *why*!'

'Can't you? I can. So can young Beresford, by his actions. As a last hope Jane Finn was to be allowed to escape – and the escape must be managed so that she harbours no suspicions of its being a put-up job. They're not averse to young Beresford's being in the neighbourhood, and, if necessary, communicating with you. They'll take care to get him out of the way at the right minute. Then Julius Hersheimmer dashes up and rescues you in true melodramatic style. Bullets fly – but don't hit anybody. What would have happened next? You would have driven straight to the house in Soho and secured the document which Miss Finn would probably have entrusted to her cousin's keeping. Or, if he conducted the search, he would have pretended to find the hiding-place already rifled. He would have had a dozen ways of dealing with the situation, but the result would have been the same. And I rather fancy some accident would have happened to both of you. You see, you know rather an inconvenient amount. That's a rough outline. I admit I was caught napping; but somebody else wasn't.'

'Tommy,' said Tuppence softly.

'Yes. Evidently when the right moment came to get

rid of him – he was too sharp for them. All the same, I'm not too easy in my mind about him.'

'Why?'

'Because Julius Hersheimmer is Mr Brown,' said Sir James dryly. 'And it takes more than one man and a revolver to hold up Mr Brown . . .'

Tuppence paled a little.

'What can we do?'

'Nothing until we've been to the house in Soho. If Beresford has still got the upper hand, there's nothing to fear. If otherwise, our enemy will come to find us, and he will not find us unprepared!' From a drawer in the desk, he took a Service revolver, and placed it in his coat pocket.

'Now we're ready. I know better than even to suggest going without you, Miss Tuppence –'

'I should think so indeed!'

'But I do suggest that Miss Finn should remain here. She will be perfectly safe, and I am afraid she is absolutely worn out with all she has been through.'

But to Tuppence's surprise Jane shook her head.

'No. I guess I'm going too. Those papers were my trust. I must go through with this business to the end. I'm heaps better now anyway.'

Sir James's car was ordered round. During the short drive Tuppence's heart beat tumultuously. In spite of momentary qualms of uneasiness respecting Tommy, she could not but feel exultation. They were going to win!

The car drew up at the corner of the square and they got out. Sir James went up to a plain-clothes man who was on duty with several others, and spoke to him. Then he rejoined the girls.

'No one has gone into the house so far. It is being watched at the back as well, so they are quite sure of that. Anyone who attempts to enter after we have done so will be arrested immediately. Shall we go in?'

A policeman produced a key. They all knew Sir James well. They had also had orders respecting Tuppence. Only the third member of the party was unknown to them. The three entered the house, pulling the door to behind them. Slowly they mounted the rickety stairs. At the top was the ragged curtain hiding the recess where Tommy had hidden that day. Tuppence had heard the story from Jane in her character of 'Annette'. She looked at the tattered velvet with interest. Even now she could almost swear it moved – as though *someone* was behind it. So strong was the illusion that she almost fancied she could make out the outline of a form . . . Supposing Mr Brown – Julius – was there waiting . . .

Impossible of course! Yet she almost went back to put the curtain aside and make sure . . .

Now they were entering the prison room. No place for anyone to hide here, thought Tuppence, with a sigh of relief, then chided herself indignantly. She must not give way to this foolish fancying – this curious insistent feeling that *Mr Brown was in the house* . . . Hark! what was that? A stealthy footstep on the stairs? There *was* someone in the house! Absurd! She was becoming hysterical.

Jane had gone straight to the picture of Marguerite. She unhooked it with a steady hand. The dust lay thick upon it, and festoons of cobwebs lay between it and the wall. Sir James handed her a pocket-knife, and she stripped away the brown paper from the back . . . The advertisement page of a magazine fell out. Jane picked it up. Holding apart the frayed inner edges she extracted two thin sheets covered with writing!

No dummy this time! The real thing!

'We've got it,' said Tuppence. 'At last . . .'

The moment was almost breathless in its emotion. Forgotten the faint creakings, the imagined noises of a minute ago. None of them had eyes for anything but what Jane held in her hand.

Sir James took it, and scrutinized it attentively.

'Yes,' he said quietly, 'this is the ill-fated draft treaty!'

'We've succeeded,' said Tuppence. There was awe and an almost wondering unbelief in her voice.

Sir James echoed her words as he folded the paper carefully and put it away in his pocket-book, then he looked curiously round the dingy room.

'It was here that your young friend was confined for so long, was it not?' he said. 'A truly sinister room. You notice the absence of windows, and the thickness of the close-fitting door. Whatever took place here would never be heard by the outside world.'

Tuppence shivered. His words woke a vague alarm in her. What if there *was* someone concealed in the house? Someone who might bar that door on them, and leave them to die like rats in a trap? Then she realized the absurdity of her thought. The house was surrounded by police who, if they failed to reappear, would not hesitate to break in and make a thorough search. She smiled at her own foolishness – then looked up with a start to find Sir James watching her. He gave her an emphatic little nod.

'Quite right, Miss Tuppence. You scent danger. So do I. So does Miss Finn.'

'Yes,' admitted Jane. 'It's absurd – but I can't help it.'

Sir James nodded again.

'You feel – as we all feel – *the presence of Mr Brown*. Yes' – as Tuppence made a movement – 'not a doubt of it – *Mr Brown is here . . .*'

'In this house?'

'In this room . . . You don't understand? *I am Mr Brown . . .*'

Stupefied, unbelieving, they stared at him. The very

lines of his face had changed. It was a different man who stood before them. He smiled a slow cruel smile.

'Neither of you will leave this room alive! You said just now we had succeeded. *I* have succeeded! The draft treaty is mine.' His smile grew wider as he looked at Tuppence. 'Shall I tell you how it will be? Sooner or later the police will break in, and they will find three victims of Mr Brown – three, not two, you understand, but fortunately the third will not be dead, only wounded, and will be able to describe the attack with a wealth of detail! The treaty? It is in the hands of Mr Brown. So no one will think of searching the pockets of Sir James Peel Edgerton!'

He turned to Jane.

'You outwitted me. I make my acknowledgments. But you will not do it again.'

There was a faint sound behind him, but intoxicated with success he did not turn his head.

He slipped his hand into his pocket.

'Checkmate to the Young Adventurers,' he said, and slowly raised the big automatic.

But, even as he did so, he felt himself seized from behind in a grip of iron. The revolver was wrenched from his hand, and the voice of Julius Hersheimmer said drawlingly:

'I guess you're caught red-handed with the goods upon you.'

The blood rushed to the K.C.'s face, but his self-control was marvellous, as he looked from one to the other of his two captors. He looked longest at Tommy.

'You,' he said beneath his breath. '*You!* I might have known.'

Seeing that he was disposed to offer no resistance, their grip slackened. Quick as a flash his left hand, the hand which bore the big signet ring, was raised to his lips . . .

'"*Ave Cæsar! te morituri salutant*,"' he said, still looking at Tommy.

Then his face changed, and with a long convulsive shudder he fell forward in a crumpled heap, whilst an odour of bitter almonds filled the air.

Chapter 27

A Supper Party at the Savoy

The supper party given by Mr Julius Hersheimmer to a few friends on the evening of the 30th will long be remembered in catering circles. It took place in a private room, and Mr Hersheimmer's orders were brief and forcible. He gave carte blanche – and when a millionaire gives carte blanche he usually gets it!

Every delicacy out of season was duly provided. Waiters carried bottles of ancient and royal vintage with loving care. The floral decorations defied the seasons, and fruits of the earth as far apart as May and November found themselves miraculously side by side. The list of guests was small and select. The American Ambassador, Mr Carter, who had taken the liberty, he said, of bringing an old friend, Sir William Beresford, with him, Archdeacon Cowley, Dr Hall, those two youthful adventurers, Miss Prudence Cowley and Mr Thomas Beresford, and last, but not least, as guest of honour, Miss Jane Finn.

Julius had spared no pains to make Jane's appearance a success. A mysterious knock had brought Tuppence to the door of the apartment she was sharing with the American girl. It was Julius. In his hand he held a cheque.

'Say, Tuppence,' he began, 'will you do me a good turn? Take this, and get Jane regularly togged up for this evening. You're all coming to supper with me at the Savoy. See? Spare no expense. You get me?'

'Sure thing,' mimicked Tuppence. 'We shall enjoy ourselves! It will be a pleasure dressing Jane. She's the loveliest thing I've ever seen.'

'That's so,' agreed Mr Hersheimmer fervently.

His fervour brought a momentary twinkle to Tuppence's eye.

'By the way, Julius,' she remarked demurely, 'I – haven't given you my answer yet.'

'Answer?' said Julius. His face paled.

'You know – when you asked me to – marry you,' faltered Tuppence, her eyes downcast in the true manner of the early Victorian heroine, 'and wouldn't take no for an answer. I've thought it well over –'

'Yes?' said Julius. The perspiration stood on his forehead.

Tuppence relented suddenly.

'You great idiot!' she said. 'What on earth induced you to do it? I could see at the time you didn't care a twopenny dip for me!'

'Not at all. I had – and still have – the highest sentiments of esteem and respect – and admiration for you –'

'H'm!' said Tuppence. 'Those are the kind of sentiments that very soon go to the wall when the other sentiment comes along! Don't they, old thing?'

'I don't know what you mean,' said Julius stiffly, but a large and burning blush overspread his countenance.

'Shucks!' retorted Tuppence. She laughed and closed the door, reopening it to add with dignity: 'Morally, I shall always consider I have been jilted!'

'What was it?' asked Jane as Tuppence rejoined her.

'Julius.'

'What did he want?'

'Really, I think, he wanted to see you, but I wasn't going to let him. Not until tonight, when you're going to burst upon everyone like King Solomon in his glory! Come on! *We're going to shop!*'

To most people the 29th, the much-heralded 'Labour Day,' had passed much as any other day. Speeches were made in the Park and Trafalgar Square. Straggling processions, singing *The Red Flag*, wandered through the streets in a more or less aimless manner. Newspapers which had hinted at a general strike, and the inauguration of a reign of terror, were forced to hide their diminished heads. The bolder and more astute among them sought to prove that peace had been effected by following their counsels. In the Sunday papers a brief notice of the sudden death of Sir James Peel Edgerton, the famous K.C., had appeared. Monday's paper dealt appreciatively with the dead man's career. The exact manner of his sudden death was never made public.

Tommy had been right in his forecast of the situation. It had been a one-man show. Deprived of their chief, the organization fell to pieces. Kramenin had made a precipitate return to Russia, leaving England early on Sunday morning. The gang had fled from Astley Priors in a panic, leaving behind, in their haste, various damaging documents which compromised them hopelessly. With these proofs of conspiracy in their hands, aided further by a small brown diary, taken from the pocket of the dead man which had contained a full and damning résumé of the whole plot, the Government had called an eleventh-hour conference. The Labour leaders were forced to recognize that they had been used as a cat's paw. Certain concessions were made by the Government, and were eagerly accepted. It was to be Peace, not War!

But the Cabinet knew by how narrow a margin they had escaped utter disaster. And burnt in on Mr Carter's brain was the strange scene which had taken place in the house in Soho the night before.

He had entered the squalid room to find that great

man, the friend of a lifetime, dead – betrayed out of his own mouth. From the dead man's pocket-book he had retrieved the ill-omened draft treaty, and then and there, in the presence of the other three, it had been reduced to ashes . . . England was saved!

And now, on the evening of the 30th, in a private room at the Savoy, Mr Julius P. Hersheimmer was receiving his guests.

Mr Carter was the first to arrive. With him was a choleric-looking old gentleman, at sight of whom Tommy flushed up to the roots of his hair. He came forward.

'Ha!' said the old gentleman surveying him apoplectically. 'So you're my nephew, are you? Not much to look at – but you've done good work, it seems. Your mother must have brought you up well after all. Shall we let bygones be bygones, eh? You're my heir, you know; and in future I propose to make you an allowance – and you can look upon Chalmers Park as your home.'

'Thank you, sir, it's awfully decent of you.'

'Where's this young lady I've been hearing such a lot about?'

Tommy introduced Tuppence.

'Ha!' said Sir William, eyeing her. 'Girls aren't what they used to be in my young days.'

'Yes, they are,' said Tuppence. 'Their clothes are different, perhaps, but they themselves are just the same.'

'Well, perhaps you're right. Minxes then – minxes now!'

'That's it,' said Tuppence. 'I'm a frightful minx myself.'

'I believe you,' said the old gentleman, chuckling, and pinched her ear in high good-humour. Most young women were terrified of the 'old bear,' as they termed him. Tuppence's pertness delighted the old misogynist.

Then came the timid archdeacon, a little bewildered by the company in which he found himself, glad that his daughter was considered to have distinguished herself, but unable to help glancing at her from time to time with nervous apprehension. But Tuppence behaved admirably. She forbore to cross her legs, set a guard upon her tongue, and steadfastly refused to smoke.

Dr Hall came next, and he was followed by the American Ambassador.

'We might as well sit down,' said Julius, when he had introduced all his guests to each other. 'Tuppence, will you –'

He indicated the place of honour with a wave of his hand.

But Tuppence shook her head.

'No – that's Jane's place! When one thinks of how she's held out all these years, she ought to be made the queen of the feast tonight.'

Julius flung her a grateful glance, and Jane came

forward shyly to the allotted seat. Beautiful as she had seemed before, it was as nothing to the loveliness that now went fully adorned. Tuppence had performed her part faithfully. The model gown supplied by a famous dressmaker had been entitled 'A tiger lily'. It was all golds and reds and browns, and out of it rose the pure column of the girl's white throat, and the bronze masses of hair that crowned her lovely head. There was admiration in every eye, as she took her seat.

Soon the supper party was in full swing, and with one accord Tommy was called upon for a full and complete explanation.

'You've been too darned close about the whole business,' Julius accused him. 'You let on to me that you were off to the Argentine – though I guess you had your reasons for that. The idea of both you and Tuppence casting me for the part of Mr Brown just tickles me to death!'

'The idea was not original to them,' said Mr Carter gravely. 'It was suggested, and the poison very carefully instilled, by a past-master in the art. The paragraph in the New York paper suggested the plan to him, and by means of it he wove a web that nearly enmeshed you fatally.'

'I never liked him,' said Julius. 'I felt from the first that there was something wrong about him, and I always suspected that it was he who silenced Mrs Vandemeyer so appositely. But it wasn't till I heard that the order for Tommy's execution came right on the heels of our interview with him that Sunday that I began to tumble to the fact that he was the big bug himself.'

'I never suspected it at all,' lamented Tuppence. 'I've always thought I was so much cleverer than Tommy – but he's undoubtedly scored over me handsomely.'

Julius agreed.

'Tommy's been the goods this trip! And, instead of sitting there as dumb as a fish, let him banish his blushes, and tell us all about it.'

'Hear! hear!'

'There's nothing to tell,' said Tommy, acutely uncomfortable. 'I was an awful mug – right up to the time I found that photograph of Annette, and realized that she was Jane Finn. Then I remembered how persistently she had shouted out that word "Marguerite" – and I thought of the pictures, and – well, that's that. Then of course I went over the whole thing to see where I'd made an ass of myself.'

'Go on,' said Mr Carter, as Tommy showed signs of taking refuge in silence once more.

'That business about Mrs Vandemeyer had worried me when Julius told me about it. On the face of it, it seemed that he or Sir James must have done the trick. But I didn't know which. Finding that photograph in the drawer, after that story of how it had been got from him by Inspector Brown, made me suspect Julius. Then I remembered that it was Sir James who had discovered the false Jane Finn. In the end, I couldn't make up my mind – and just decided to take no chances either way. I left a note for Julius, in case he was Mr Brown, saying I was off to the Argentine, and I dropped Sir James's letter with the offer of the job by the desk so that he would see it was a genuine stunt. Then I wrote my letter to Mr Carter and rang up Sir James. Taking him into my confidence would be the best thing either way, so I told him everything except where I believed the papers to be hidden. The way he helped me to get on the track of Tuppence and Annette almost disarmed me, but not quite. I kept my mind open between the two of them. And then I got a bogus note from Tuppence – and then I knew!'

'But how?'

Tommy took the note in question from his pocket and passed it round the table.

'It's her handwriting all right, but I knew it wasn't from her because of the signature. She'd never spell her name "Twopence," but anyone who'd never seen it written might quite easily do so. Julius *had* seen it – he showed me a note of hers to him once – but *Sir James hadn't*! After that everything was plain sailing. I sent off Albert post-haste to Mr Carter. I pretended to go away, but doubled back again. When Julius came bursting up in his car, I felt it wasn't part of Mr Brown's plan – and that there would probably be trouble. Unless Sir James was actually caught in the act, so to speak, I knew Mr Carter would never believe it of him on my bare word –'

'I didn't,' interposed Mr Carter ruefully.

'That's why I sent the girls off to Sir James. I was sure they'd fetch up at the house in Soho sooner or later. I threatened Julius with the revolver, because I wanted Tuppence to repeat that to Sir James, so that he wouldn't worry about us. The moment the girls were out of sight I told Julius to drive like hell for London, and as we went along I told him the whole story. We got to the Soho house in plenty of time and met Mr Carter outside. After arranging things with him we went in and hid behind the curtain in the recess. The policemen had orders to say, if they were asked, that no one had gone into the house. That's all.'

And Tommy came to an abrupt halt.

There was silence for a moment.

'By the way,' said Julius suddenly, 'you're all wrong about that photograph of Jane. It *was* taken from me, but I found it again.'

'Where?' cried Tuppence.

'In that little safe on the wall in Mrs Vandermeyer's bedroom.'

'I knew you found something,' said Tuppence

reproachfully. 'To tell you the truth, that's what started me off suspecting you. Why didn't you say?'

'I guess I was a mite suspicious too. It had been got away from me once, and I determined I wouldn't let on I'd got it until a photographer had made a dozen copies of it!'

'We all kept back something or other,' said Tuppence thoughtfully. 'I suppose secret service work makes you like that!'

In the pause that ensued, Mr Carter took from his pocket a small shabby brown book.

'Beresford has just said that I would not have believed Sir James Peel Edgerton to be guilty unless, so to speak, he was caught in the act. That is so. Indeed, not until I read the entries in this little book could I bring myself fully to credit the amazing truth. This book will pass into the possession of Scotland Yard, but it will never be publicly exhibited. Sir James's long association with the law would make it undesirable. But to you, who know the truth, I propose to read certain passages which will throw some light on the extraordinary mentality of this great man.'

He opened the book, and turned the thin pages.

'. . . It is madness to keep this book. I know that. It is documentary evidence against me. But I have never shrunk from taking risks. And I feel an urgent need for self-expression . . . The book will only be taken from my dead body . . .

'. . . From an early age I realized that I had exceptional abilities. Only a fool underestimates his capabilities. My brain power was greatly above the average. I know that I was born to succeed. My appearance was the only thing against me. I was quiet and insignificant – utterly nondescript . . .

'. . . When I was a boy I heard a famous murder trial. I was deeply impressed by the power and eloquence of the counsel for the defence. For the first time I entertained the idea of taking my talents to that particular market . . . Then I studied the criminal in the dock . . . The man was a fool – he had been incredibly, unbelievably stupid. Even the eloquence of his counsel was hardly likely to save him . . . I felt an immeasurable contempt for him . . . Then it occurred to me that the criminal standard was a low one. It was the wastrels, the failures, the general riff-raff of civilization who drifted into crime . . . Strange that men of brains had never realized its extraordinary opportunities . . . I played with the idea . . . What a magnificent field – what unlimited possibilities! It made my brain reel . . .

'. . . I read standard works on crime and criminals. They all confirmed my opinion. Degeneracy, disease – never the deliberate embracing of a career by a far-seeing man. Then I considered. Supposing my utmost ambitions were realized – that I was called to the bar, and rose to the height of my profession? That I entered politics – say, even, that I became Prime Minister of England? What then? Was that power? Hampered at every turn by my colleagues, fettered by the democratic system of which I should be the mere figurehead! No – the power I dreamed of was absolute! An autocrat! A dictator! And such power could only be obtained by working outside the law. To play on the weaknesses of human nature, then on the weaknesses of nations – to get together and control a vast organization, and finally to overthrow the existing order, and rule! The thought intoxicated me . . .

'. . . I saw that I must lead two lives. A man like myself is bound to attract notice. I must have a successful career which would mask my true activities . . . Also I must cultivate a personality. I modelled myself upon famous K.C.'s. I reproduced their mannerisms, their magnetism. If I had chosen to be an actor, I should have been the greatest actor living! No disguises – no grease paint – no false beards! Personality! I put it on like a glove! When I shed it, I was myself, quiet, unobtrusive, a man like every other man. I called myself Mr Brown. There are hundreds of men called Brown – there are hundreds of men looking just like me . . .

'. . . I succeeded in my false career. I was bound to

succeed. I shall succeed in the other. A man like me cannot fail . . .

'. . . I have been reading a life of Napoleon. He and I have much in common . . .

'. . . I make a practice of defending criminals. A man should look after his own people . . .

'. . . Once or twice I have felt afraid. The first time was in Italy. There was a dinner given. Professor D—, the great alienist, was present. The talk fell on insanity. He said, "A great many men are mad, and no one knows it. They do not know it themselves." I do not understand why he looked at me when he said that. His glance was strange . . . I did not like it . . .

'. . . The war has disturbed me . . . I thought it would further my plans. The Germans are so efficient. Their spy system, too, was excellent. The streets are full of these boys in khaki. All empty-headed young fools . . . Yet I do not know . . . They won the war . . . It disturbs me . . .

'. . . My plans are going well . . . A girl butted in – I do not think she really knew anything . . . But we must give up the Esthonia . . . No risks now . . .

'. . . All goes well. The loss of memory is vexing. It cannot be a fake. No girl could deceive ME! . . .

'. . . The 29th . . . That is very soon . . .' Mr Carter paused.

'I will not read the details of the *coup* that was planned. But there are just two small entries that refer to the three of you. In the light of what happened they are interesting.

'. . . By inducing the girl to come to me of her own accord, I have succeeded in disarming her. But she has intuitive flashes that might be dangerous . . . She must be got out of the way . . . I can do nothing with the American. He suspects and dislikes me. But he cannot know. I fancy my armour is impregnable . . . Sometimes I fear I have underestimated the other boy. He is not clever, but it is hard to blind his eyes to facts . . .'

Mr Carter shut the book.

'A great man,' he said. 'Genius, or insanity, who can say?'

There was silence.

Then Mr Carter rose to his feet.

'I will give you a toast. The Joint Venture which has so amply justified itself by success!'

It was drunk with acclamation.

'There's something more we want to hear,' continued Mr Carter. He looked at the American Ambassador. 'I speak for you also, I know. We'll ask Miss Jane Finn to tell us the story that only Miss Tuppence has heard so far – but before we do so we'll drink her health. The health of one of the bravest of America's daughters, to whom is due the thanks and gratitude of two great countries!'

Chapter 28

And After

'That was a mighty good toast, Jane,' said Mr Hersheimmer, as he and his cousin were being driven back in the Rolls-Royce to the Ritz.

'The one to the joint venture?'

'No – the one to you. There isn't another girl in the world who could have carried it through as you did. You were just wonderful!'

Jane shook her head.

'I don't feel wonderful. At heart I'm just tired and lonesome – and longing for my own country.'

'That brings me to something I wanted to say. I heard the Ambassador telling you his wife hoped you would come to them at the Embassy right away. That's good enough, but I've got another plan. Jane – I want you to marry me! Don't get scared and say no at once. You can't love me right away, of course, that's impossible. But I've loved you from the very moment I set eyes on your photo – and now I've seen you I'm simply crazy about you! If you'll only marry me, I won't worry you any – you shall take your own time. Maybe you'll never come to love me, and if that's the case I'll manage to set you free. But I want the right to look after you, and take care of you.'

'That's what I want,' said the girl wistfully. 'Someone who'll be good to me. Oh, you don't know how lonesome I feel!'

'Sure thing I do. Then I guess that's all fixed up, and I'll see the archbishop about a special licence tomorrow morning.'

'Oh, Julius!'

'Well, I don't want to hustle you any, Jane, but there's no sense in waiting about. Don't be scared – I shan't expect you to love me all at once.'

But a small hand was slipped into his.

'I love you now, Julius,' said Jane Finn. 'I loved you that first moment in the car when the bullet grazed your cheek . . .'

Five minutes later Jane murmured softly:

'I don't know London very well, Julius, but is it such a very long way from the Savoy to the Ritz?'

'It depends how you go,' explained Julius unblushingly. 'We're going by way of Regent's Park!'

'Oh, Julius – what will the chauffeur think?'

'At the wages I pay him, he knows better than to do

any independent thinking. Why, Jane, the only reason I had the supper at the Savoy was so that I could drive you home. I didn't see how I was ever going to get hold of you alone. You and Tuppence have been sticking together like Siamese twins. I guess another day of it would have driven me and Beresford stark staring mad!'

'Oh. Is he –?'

'Of course he is. Head over ears.'

'I thought so,' said Jane thoughtfully.

'Why?'

'From all the things Tuppence didn't say!'

'There you have me beat,' said Mr Hersheimmer.

But Jane only laughed.

In the meantime, the Young Adventurers were sitting bolt upright, very stiff and ill at ease, in a taxi which, with a singular lack of originality, was also returning to the Ritz via Regent's Park.

A terrible constraint seemed to have settled down between them. Without quite knowing what had happened, everything seemed changed. They were tongue-tied – paralysed. All the old *cameraderie* was gone.

Tuppence could think of nothing to say.

Tommy was equally afflicted.

They sat very straight and forbore to look at each other.

At last Tuppence made a desperate effort.

'Rather fun, wasn't it?'

'Rather.'

Another silence.

'I like Julius,' essayed Tuppence again.

Tommy was suddenly galvanized into life.

'You're not going to marry him, do you hear?' he said dictatorially. 'I forbid it.'

'Oh!' said Tuppence meekly.

'Absolutely, you understand.'

'He doesn't want to marry me – he really only asked me out of kindness.'

'That's not very likely,' scoffed Tommy.

'It's quite true. He's head over ears in love with Jane. I expect he's proposing to her now.'

'She'll do for him very nicely,' said Tommy condescendingly.

'Don't you think she's the most lovely creature you've ever seen?'

'Oh, I dare say.'

'But I suppose you prefer sterling worth,' said Tuppence demurely.

'I – oh, dash it all, Tuppence, you know!'

'I like your uncle, Tommy,' said Tuppence, hastily creating a diversion. 'By the way, what are you going to do, accept Mr Carter's offer of a Government job, or accept Julius's invitation and take a richly remunerated post in America on his ranch?'

'I shall stick to the old ship, I think, though it's awfully good of Hersheimmer. But I feel you'd be more at home in London.'

'I don't see where I come in.'

'I do,' said Tommy positively.

Tuppence stole a glance at him sideways.

'There's the money, too,' she observed thoughtfully.

'What money?'

'We're going to get a cheque each. Mr Carter told me so.'

'Did you ask how much?' inquired Tommy sarcastically.

'Yes,' said Tuppence triumphantly. 'But I shan't tell you.'

'Tuppence, you are the limit!'

'It has been fun, hasn't it, Tommy? I do hope we shall have lots more adventures.'

'You're insatiable, Tuppence. I've had quite enough adventures for the present.'

'Well, shopping is almost as good,' said Tuppence dreamily. 'Thinking of buying old furniture, and bright carpets, and futurist silk curtains, and a polished dining-table, and a divan with lots of cushions –'

'Hold hard,' said Tommy. 'What's all this for?'

'Possibly a house – but I think a flat.'

'Whose flat?'

'You think I mind saying it, but I don't in the least! *Ours*, so there!'

'You darling!' cried Tommy, his arms tightly round her. 'I was determined to make you say it. I owe you something for the relentless way you've squashed me whenever I've tried to be sentimental.'

Tuppence raised her face to his. The taxi proceeded on its course round the north side of Regent's Park.

'You haven't really proposed now,' pointed out Tuppence. 'Not what our grandmothers would call a proposal. But after listening to a rotten one like Julius's, I'm inclined to let you off.'

'You won't be able to get out of marrying me, so don't you think it.'

'What fun it will be,' responded Tuppence. 'Marriage is called all sorts of things, a haven, a refuge, and a crowning glory, and a state of bondage, and lots more. But do you know what I think it is?'

'What?'

'A sport!'

'And a damned good sport too,' said Tommy.